MW01129082

JULES VERNE
COLLECTION VOL. 3
Captain's Nemo Trilogy

TWENTY THOUSAND LEAGUES UNDER THE SEA (SUBMARINE TOUR OF THE WORLD)

IN SEARCH OF THE CASTAWAYS (OR CAPTAIN GRANT'S CHILDREN)

THE MYSTERIOUS ISLAND

Translation by Stephen W. White

CONTENTS

BOOK ONE. TWENTY THOUSAND LEAGUES UNDER THE SEA 1

PART ONE 1

CHAPTER I. A SHIFTING REEF 1

CHAPTER II. PRO AND CON 5

CHAPTER III. I FORM MY RESOLUTION 8

CHAPTER IV. NED LAND 10

CHAPTER V. AT A VENTURE 14

CHAPTER VI. AT FULL STEAM 17

CHAPTER VII. AN UNKNOWN SPECIES OF WHALE 22

CHAPTER VIII. MOBILIS IN MOBILI 26

CHAPTER IX. NED LAND'S TEMPERS 30

CHAPTER X. THE MAN OF THE SEAS 32

CHAPTER XI. ALL BY ELECTRICITY 41

CHAPTER XII. SOME FIGURES 44

CHAPTER XIII. THE BLACK RIVER 48

CHAPTER XIV. A NOTE OF INVITATION 52

CHAPTER XV. A WALK ON THE BOTTOM OF THE SEA 56

CHAPTER XVI. A SUBMARINE FOREST 59

CHAPTER XVII. FOUR THOUSAND LEAGUES UNDER THE PACIFIC 63

CHAPTER XVIII. VANIKORO 66

CHAPTER XIX. TORRES STRAITS 71

CHAPTER XX. A FEW DAYS ON LAND 75

CHAPTER XXI. CAPTAIN NEMO'S THUNDERBOLT 81

CHAPTER XXII. "AEGRI SOMNIA" 87

CHAPTER XXIII. THE CORAL KINGDOM 92

PART TWO 96

CHAPTER I. THE INDIAN OCEAN.. 96

CHAPTER II. A NOVEL PROPOSAL OF CAPTAIN NEMO'S 101

CHAPTER III. A PEARL OF TEN MILLIONS 104

CHAPTER IV. THE RED SEA 110

CHAPTER V. THE ARABIAN TUNNEL 116

CHAPTER VI. THE GRECIAN ARCHIPELAGO 121

CHAPTER VII. THE MEDITERRANEAN IN FORTY-EIGHT HOURS............................ 127

CHAPTER VIII. VIGO BAY 129

CHAPTER IX. A VANISHED CONTINENT 135

CHAPTER X. THE SUBMARINE COAL-MINES 140

CHAPTER XI. THE SARGASSO SEA 145

CHAPTER XII. CACHALOTS AND WHALES 148

CHAPTER XIII. THE ICEBERG 154

CHAPTER XIV. THE SOUTH POLE 159

CHAPTER XV. ACCIDENT OR INCIDENT? 165

CHAPTER XVI. WANT OF AIR 169

CHAPTER XVII. FROM CAPE HORN TO THE AMAZON 175

CHAPTER XVIII. THE POULPS... 179

CHAPTER XIX. THE GULF STREAM 184

CHAPTER XX. FROM LATITUDE 47° 24' TO LONGITUDE 17° 28' 189

CHAPTER XXI. A HECATOMB 192

CHAPTER XXII. THE LAST WORDS OF CAPTAIN NEMO 197

CHAPTER XXIII. CONCLUSION 201

BOOK TWO. IN SEARCH OF THE CASTAWAYS.. 203

CHAPTER I. THE SHARK... 203

CHAPTER II. THE THREE DOCUMENTS. 207

CHAPTER III. THE CAPTAIN'S CHILDREN.. 212

CHAPTER IV. LADY GLENARVAN'S PROPOSAL. 216

CHAPTER V. THE DEPARTURE OF THE DUNCAN. 220

CHAPTER VI. AN UNEXPECTED PASSENGER. 224

CHAPTER VII. JACQUES PAGANEL IS UNDECEIVED. 229

CHAPTER VIII. THE GEOGRAPHER'S RESOLUTION. 233

CHAPTER IX. THROUGH THE STRAIT OF MAGELLAN... 236

CHAPTER X. THE COURSE DECIDED. 239
CHAPTER XI. TRAVELING IN CHILI. 244
CHAPTER XII. ELEVEN THOUSAND FEET ALOFT. 248
CHAPTER XIII. A SUDDEN DESCENT. 251
CHAPTER XIV. PROVIDENTIALLY RESCUED. 257
CHAPTER XV. THALCAVE. 261
CHAPTER XVI. NEWS OF THE LOST CAPTAIN. 266
CHAPTER XVII. A SERIOUS NECESSITY. 271
CHAPTER XVIII. IN SEARCH OF WATER. 274
CHAPTER XIX. THE RED WOLVES. 279
CHAPTER XX. STRANGE SIGNS. 286
CHAPTER XXI. A FALSE TRAIL. 289
CHAPTER XXII. THE FLOOD. 294
CHAPTER XXIII. A SINGULAR ABODE. 300
CHAPTER XXIV. PAGANEL'S DISCLOSURE. 306
CHAPTER XXV. BETWEEN FIRE AND WATER. 311
CHAPTER XXVI. THE RETURN ON BOARD. 316
CHAPTER XXVII. A NEW DESTINATION. 321
CHAPTER XXVIII. TRISTAN D'ACUNHA AND THE ISLE OF AMSTERDAM. 325
CHAPTER XXIX. THE STORM ON THE INDIAN OCEAN. 328
CHAPTER XXX. A HOSPITABLE COLONIST. 333
CHAPTER XXXI. THE QUARTERMASTER OF THE BRITANNIA. 338
CHAPTER XXXII. PREPARATIONS FOR THE JOURNEY. 344
CHAPTER XXXIII. AN ACCIDENT. 348
CHAPTER XXXIV. AUSTRALIAN EXPLORERS. 352
CHAPTER XXXV. CRIME OR CALAMITY? 354
CHAPTER XXXVI. FRESH FACES. 358
CHAPTER XXXVII. A WARNING. 360
CHAPTER XXXVIII. WEALTH IN THE WILDERNESS. 367
CHAPTER XXXIX. SUSPICIOUS OCCURRENCES. 373
CHAPTER XL. A STARTLING DISCOVERY 378
CHAPTER XLI. THE PLOT UNVEILED. 385
CHAPTER XLII. FOUR DAYS OF ANGUISH. 391
CHAPTER XLIII. HELPLESS AND HOPELESS. 397
CHAPTER XLIV. A ROUGH CAPTAIN. 402
CHAPTER XLV. THE WRECK OF THE MACQUARIE. 407
CHAPTER XLVI. VAIN EFFORTS. 414
CHAPTER XLVII. A DREADED COUNTRY. 419
CHAPTER XLVIII. INTRODUCTION TO THE CANNIBALS. 426
CHAPTER XLIX. A MOMENTOUS INTERVIEW. 431
CHAPTER L. THE CHIEF'S FUNERAL. 435
CHAPTER LI. STRANGELY LIBERATED. 440
CHAPTER LII. THE SACRED MOUNTAIN. 445
CHAPTER LIII. A BOLD STRATAGEM. 453
CHAPTER LIV. FROM PERIL TO SAFETY. 458
CHAPTER LV. WHY THE DUNCAN WENT TO NEW ZEALAND. 461
CHAPTER LVI. AYRTON'S OBSTINACY. 465
CHAPTER LVII. A DISCOURAGING CONFESSION. 469
CHAPTER LVIII. A CRY IN THE NIGHT. 475
CHAPTER LIX. CAPTAIN GRANT'S STORY. 481
CHAPTER LX. PAGANEL'S LAST ENTANGLEMENT. 487
BOOK THREE. THE MYSTERIOUS ISLAND... 489
PART I. SHIPWRECKED IN THE AIR 489
CHAPTER I. THE HURRICANE OF 1865 489
CHAPTER II. AN EPISODE OF THE REBELLION 493
CHAPTER III. FIVE O'CLOCK IN THE AFTERNOON - THE LOST ONE.........................499
CHAPTER IV. THE LITHODOMES 503
CHAPTER V. ARRANGING THE CHIMNEYS 508
CHAPTER VI. THE CASTAWAYS' INVENTORY 513
CHAPTER VII. NEB HAS NOT YET RETURNED 517

CHAPTER VIII. IS CYPRUS SMITH ALIVE? 523
CHAPTER IX. CYRUS IS HERE 528
CHAPTER X. THE ENGINEER'S INVENTION..535
CHAPTER XI. AT THE SUMMIT OF THE CONE 539
CHAPTER XII. REGULATION OF WATCHES 545
CHAPTER XIII. TOP'S CONTRIBUTION 550
CHAPTER XIV. THE MEASURE OF THE GRANITE WALL..556
CHAPTER XV. WINTER SETS IN...561
CHAPTER XVI. THE QUESTION OF A DWELLING DISCUSSED AGAIN 566
CHAPTER XVII. A VISIT TO THE LAKE 571
CHAPTER XVIII. PENCROFF DOUBTS NO MORE 576
CHAPTER XIX. SMITH'S PLAN...581
CHAPTER XX. THE RAINY SEASON 586
CHAPTER XXI. SEVERAL DEGREES BELOW ZERO 590
CHAPTER XXII. THE TRAPS 595
PART II. THE ABANDONED **603**
CHAPTER XXIII. CONCERNING THE LEADEN PELLET..603
CHAPTER XXIV. TRIAL OF THE CANOE 608
CHAPTER XXV. THE DEPARTURE 614
CHAPTER XXVI. GOING TOWARD THE COAST...619
CHAPTER XXVII. PROPOSAL TO RETURN BY THE SOUTH COAST 623
CHAPTER XXVIII. PENCROFF'S HALLOOS 629
CHAPTER XXIX. PROJECTS TO BE CARRIED OUT..636
CHAPTER XXX. CLOTHING—SEAL-SKIN BOOTS..641
CHAPTER XXXI. BAD WEATHER...646
CHAPTER XXXII. SHIP BUILDING...652
CHAPTER XXXIII. WINTER—FULLING CLOTH 657
CHAPTER XXXIV. RIGGING THE LAUNCH..662
CHAPTER XXXV. DEPARTURE DECIDED UPON 669
CHAPTER XXXVI. THE INVENTORY 674
CHAPTER XXXVII. THE RETURN-DISCUSSION 680
CHAPTER XXXVIII. A MYSTERY TO BE SOLVED 684
CHAPTER XXXIX. ALWAYS APART 691
CHAPTER XL. A TALK—SMITH AND SPILETT...698
CHAPTER XLI. THOUGHTS OF HOME 704
CHAPTER XLII. NIGHT AT SEA—SHARK GULF 710
PART III. THE SECRET OF THE ISLAND..**715**
CHAPTER XLIII. LOST OR SAVED? 715
CHAPTER XLIV. DISCUSSIONS 720
CHAPTER XLV. THE MIST RISES 725
CHAPTER XLVI. THE COLONISTS ON THE BEACH..730
CHAPTER XLVII. THE ENGINEER'S THEORY 736
CHAPTER XLVIII. THE PROJECTED EXPEDITION...740
CHAPTER XLIX. THE REPORTER AND PENCROFF 745
CHAPTER L. THE CONVICTS IN THE NEIGHBORHOOD...750
CHAPTER LI. NO NEWS OF NEB...752
CHAPTER LII. HERBERT CARRIED TO GRANITE HOUSE..756
CHAPTER LIII. AN INEXPLICABLE MYSTERY 759
CHAPTER LIV. EXPLORATION OF REPTILE END 763
CHAPTER LV. AYRTON'S RECITAL..768
CHAPTER LVI. AFTER THREE YEARS...774
CHAPTER LVII. THE AWAKENING OF THE VOLCANO...777
CHAPTER LVIII. CAPTAIN NEMO 785
CHAPTER LIX. THE LAST HOURS OF CAPTAIN NEMO 791
CHAPTER LX. THE REFLECTIONS OF THE COLONISTS 796
CHAPTER LXI. SMITH'S RECITAL...803
CHAPTER LXII. AN ISOLATED ROCK IN THE PACIFIC 810

THE VOYAGES EXTRAORDINAIRES

This is the name of the sequence of fifty-four novels written Jules Verne, originally published between 1863 and 1905.

Verne's editor Pierre-Jules Hetzel, said that the goal of these novels was "to outline all the geographical, geological, physical, and astronomical knowledge amassed by modern science and to recount, in an entertaining and picturesque format ... the history of the universe."

In Verne's own words, his intention was "to complete, before my working days are done, a series which shall conclude in story form my whole survey of the world's surface and the heavens; there are still left corners of the world to which my thoughts have not yet penetrated. As you know, I have dealt with the moon, but a great deal remains to be done, and if health and strength permit me, I hope to finish the task."

Verne's meticulous attention to detail and scientific trivia, coupled with his sense of wonder and exploration, are the backbone of the Voyages. Part of the reason for the broad appeal of his work was the sense that the reader could acquire knowledge of geology, biology, astronomy, paleontology, oceanography, etc., as well as to travel to the exotic locations and cultures of the world through the adventures of Verne's protagonists.

Some of the best known and most popular novels in history are part of this series, including Five Weeks in a Balloon (1863); Journey to the Center of the Earth (1864); Twenty Thousand Leagues under the Sea (1869–70); From the Earth to the Moon (1865); Around the World in Eighty Days (1873), etc.

The list is very long in this amazing collection now at your disposal, written by one of the most brilliant and inspired minds in the world.

A man who, if he really couldn't see the future, then, was the most gifted forecaster in history... For writing in the 1860's Paris, that a century later, a rocket will depart from Cape Canaveral, Florida, to reach the moon (from the almost exact coordinates of the actual launch)... that was... that was Jules Verne at his best!

Wizard of Science, Seer of the Future, Explore of Humanity, Extremely Entertaining Writer...

Welcome to the world and the voyages extraordinaires of Master Jules Verne!

This is the list of Verne's works available from the Timeless Wisdom Collection:

1. Five Weeks in a Balloon, 1863
2. The Adventures of Captain Hatteras, 1866
3. Journey to the Center of the Earth, 1864,
4. From the Earth to the Moon, 1865
5. Les Enfants du capitaine Grant (In Search of the Castaways, 1867–8)
6. (Twenty Thousand Leagues under the Sea, 1869–70)
7. Autour de la lune (Around The Moon, 1870)
8. Une ville flottante (A Floating City, 1871)
9. The Adventures of Three Englishmen and Three Russians in South Africa, 1872)
10. Le Pays des fourrures (The Fur Country, 1873)
11. Le Tour du monde en quatre-vingts jours (Around the World in Eighty Days)
12. L'Île mystérieuse (The Mysterious Island, 1874–5)

13. Le Chancellor (The Survivors of the Chancellor, 1875)
14. Michel Strogoff (Michael Strogoff, 1876)
15. Hector Servadac (Off on a Comet, 1877)
16. Les Indes noires (The Child of the Cavern, 1877)
17. Un capitaine de quinze ans (Dick Sand, A Captain at Fifteen, 1878)
18. Les Cinq Cents Millions de la Bégum (The Begum's Millions, 1879)
19. Tribulations of a Chinaman in China, 1879
20. La Maison à vapeur (The Steam House, 1880)
21. La Jangada (Eight Hundred Leagues on the Amazon, 1881)
22. L'École des Robinsons (Godfrey Morgan, 1882)
23. Le Rayon vert (The Green Ray, 1882)
24. Kéraban-le-têtu (Kéraban the Inflexible, 1883)
25. L'Étoile du sud (The Vanished Diamond, 1884)
26. L'Archipel en feu (The Archipelago on Fire, 1884)
27. Mathias Sandorf (Mathias Sandorf, 1885)
28. Un billet de loterie (The Lottery Ticket, 1886)
29. Robur-le-Conquérant (Robur the Conqueror, 1886)
30. Nord contre Sud (North Against South, 1887)
31. Le Chemin de France (The Flight to France, 1887)
32. Deux Ans de vacances (Two Years' Vacation, 1888)
33. Famille-sans-nom (Family Without a Name, 1889)
34. Sans dessus dessous (The Purchase of the North Pole, 1889)
35. César Cascabel (César Cascabel, 1890)
36. Mistress Branican (Mistress Branican, 1891)
37. Le Château des Carpathes (Carpathian Castle, 1892)
38. Claudius Bombarnac (Claudius Bombarnac, 1892)
39. P'tit-Bonhomme (Foundling Mick, 1893)
40. Mirifiques Aventures de Maître Antifer (Captain Antifer, 1894)
41. L'Île à hélice (Propeller Island, 1895)
42. Face au drapeau (Facing the Flag, 1896)
43. Clovis Dardentor (Clovis Dardentor, 1896)
44. Le Sphinx des glaces (An Antarctic Mystery, 1897)
45. Le Superbe Orénoque (The Mighty Orinoco, 1898)
46. Le Testament d'un excentrique (The Will of an Eccentric, 1899)
47. Seconde Patrie (The Castaways of the Flag, 1900)
48. Le Village aérien (The Village in the Treetops, 1901)
49. Les Histoires de Jean-Marie Cabidoulin (The Sea Serpent, 1901)
50. Les Frères Kip (The Kip Brothers, 1902)
51. Bourses de voyage (Traveling Scholarships, 1903)
52. Un drame en Livonie (A Drama in Livonia, 1904)
53. Maître du monde (Master of the World, 1904)
54. L'Invasion de la mer (Invasion of the Sea, 1905)

BOOK ONE.
TWENTY THOUSAND LEAGUES UNDER THE SEA
(SUBMARINE TOUR OF THE WORLD)

Jules Verne's Voyages extraordinaires Book #6

PART ONE

CHAPTER I. A SHIFTING REEF

The year 1866 was marked by a bizarre incident, an unexplained and unexplainable phenomenon, which doubtless no one has yet forgotten. Not to mention rumours which agitated the maritime population and excited the public mind in the interior of the continents, the people of the sea were particularly moved.

Merchants, ship-owners, captains of vessels, skippers, and masters both of Europe and America, naval officers of all countries, and the Governments of several States on the two continents, were deeply concerned about the matter.

For some time past vessels had been met at sea by "an enormous thing," a long object, spindle-shaped, occasionally phosphorescent, and infinitely larger and faster than a whale.

The facts relating to this apparition (entered in various log-books) agreed with great exactitude as to the shape of the object or being in question, the untiring speed of its movements, its surprising power of locomotion, and the peculiar life with which it seemed endowed.

If it was a whale, it surpassed in size all those hitherto classified in science.

Neither Cuvier, Lacépède, M. Duméril, nor M. de Quatrefages[1] would have accepted that such a monster existed—unless they had seen it, seen it with their own eyes of savants.

Taking into consideration the average of the observations made at different occasions —rejecting the timid estimate of those who assigned to this object a length of two hundred feet, and leaving aside the exaggerated opinions which set it down as a mile in width and three in length—we might fairly conclude that this mysterious being surpassed greatly all dimensions admitted to that day by the ichthyologists, if it existed at all.

---

[1] Famous French Naturalists and Zoologists of the XVIII and XIX centuries.

But it did exist, the fact in itself was no longer deniable; and, with that tendency which disposes the human mind in favour of the marvellous, we can understand the excitement produced in the entire world by this supernatural apparition.

As to classing it in the reign of fables, the idea was out of the question.

In fact, on the 20th of July, 1866, the steamer Governor Higginson, of the Calcutta and Burnach Steam Navigation Company, had met this moving mass five miles off the east coast of Australia.

Captain Baker thought at first that he was in the presence of an unknown reef; he even prepared to determine its exact position when two columns of water, projected by the mysterious object, shot with a hissing noise a hundred and fifty feet up into the air. Now, unless the reef had been submitted to the intermittent eruption of a geyser, the Governor Higginson had to do neither more nor less than with an aquatic mammal, unknown till then, which threw up from its blow-holes columns of water mixed with air and vapour.

Similar facts were observed on the 23rd of July in the same year, in the Pacific Ocean, by the *Cristobal Colon (*Christopher Columbus)*, of the West India and Pacific Steam Navigation Company.

But this extraordinary creature could transport itself from one place to another with surprising velocity; as, in an interval of three days, the Governor Higginson and the Columbus had observed it at two different points of the chart, separated by a distance of more than seven hundred nautical leagues.

Fifteen days later, two thousand miles farther off, the Helvetia, of the Compagnie-Nationale, and the Shannon, of the Royal Mail Steamship Company, sailing to windward in that portion of the Atlantic lying between the United States and Europe, respectively signalled the monster to each other in 42° 15' N. lat. and 60° 35' W. long. In these simultaneous observations they thought themselves justified in estimating the minimum length of the mammal at more than three hundred and fifty English feet, as the Shannon and Helvetia were of smaller dimensions than it, though they measured one hundred meters (300 *feet*) from stem to stern.

Now the largest whales, those which frequent those parts of the sea round the Aleutian, Kulammak, and Umgullich islands, have never exceeded the length of fifty-six meters (168 *feet*), if they attain that.

These reports arrived in quick succession; new observations made on board the transatlantic Pereire; a collision between the Etna, of the Inman line, and the monster; a report prepared by the officers of the French frigate Normandie; a serious survey by the staff of Commodore Fitz-James on board the Lord Clyde, deeply stirred up public opinion.

In *easy going* countries, they took the phenomenon in fun; but in serious and practical countries -England, America, Germany-, there was deep concern.

In every major city the monster became *à la mode*. They sang of it in the cafes, ridiculed it in the papers, and represented it on the stage.

The press had a good occasion for *"the ducks to lay eggs of any color."* There appeared in the papers caricatures of every gigantic and imaginary creature, from the white whale, the terrible "Moby Dick" of sub-arctic regions, to the immense kraken, whose tentacles could entangle a ship of five hundred tons and hurry it into the abyss of the ocean. Even the oral legends of ancient times were revived; the opinions of Aristotle and Pliny, who admitted the existence of these monsters; the Norwegian stories of Bishop Pontoppidan; the stories of Paul Heggede, and finally the reports of Mr. Harrington, whose good faith cannot be suspected when he claims to have seen, being aboard the Castilian in 1857, this huge snake that had never previously frequented but the seas of the ancient *Constitutional*.

Then burst forth the unending controversy between believers and unbelievers in the savant societies and the scientific journals. "The question of the monster" inflamed all minds. Scientific Journalists quarrelling with Journalist "of the spirit", spilled seas of ink during this memorable campaign, some even spilled two or three drops of blood; for from the sea-serpent they came to personalities in the most offensive way.

For six months, the war continued with diverse battles.

To the editorials of the Geographical Institute of Brazil, of the Royal Academy of Sciences at Berlin, of the British Association, the Smithsonian Institution in Washington; to the discussions of *The Indian Archipelago*, Abbe Moigno's *Cosmos*, and Petermann's *Mittheilungen;* to the scientific chronicles of major newspapers in France and abroad, the small press retaliated with inexhaustible verve.

Their spiritual writers parodied a word of Linnaeus, quoted by the monster´s opponents, contending that "nature does not make fools," and they adjured their contemporaries not to call nature a liar, and to admit the existence of Krakens, sea serpents, "Moby Dick" and other rantings by delirious sailors.

Finally, in an article from a dreaded satirical newspaper, the most beloved of its editors, stitching on the whole, pushed the monster, and like Hippolytus, gave him a last coup, and finished it, among a burst of universal laughter.

The spirit had defeated science.

During the first months of the year 1867 the question seemed buried, and it did not seem that it could revive, when new facts were brought before the public. It was then no longer a scientific problem to be solved, but a real danger seriously to be avoided. The question took quite another shape. The monster became a small island, a rock, a reef, but a reef of indefinite and shifting proportions.

On the 5th of March, 1867, the Moravian, of the Montreal Ocean Company, finding herself during the night in 27° 30' lat. and 72° 15' long., struck on her starboard quarter a rock, marked in no chart for that part of the sea. Under the combined efforts of the wind and its four hundred horse power, it was going at the rate of thirteen knots. Had it not been for the superior strength of the hull of the Moravian, she would have been broken by the shock and gone down with the 237 passengers she was bringing from Canada.

The accident happened about five o'clock in the morning, as the day was breaking. The officers of the quarter-deck hurried to the after-part of the vessel. They examined the sea with the most scrupulous attention. They saw nothing but a strong eddy about three cables' length distant, as if the surface had been violently agitated.

The bearings of the place were taken exactly, and the Moravian continued its route without apparent damage. Had it struck on a submerged rock, or on an enormous wreck? They could not tell; but, on examination of the ship's bottom when undergoing repairs, it was found that part of her keel was broken.

This fact, so grave in itself, might perhaps have been forgotten like many others if, three weeks after, it had not been re-enacted under similar circumstances. But, thanks to the nationality of the ship, victim of this new incident, and thanks to the reputation of the company to which the vessel belonged, the event had immense reverberation.

The 13th of April, 1867, the sea being beautiful, the breeze favourable, the Scotia, of the Cunard Company's line, found herself in 15° 12' long. and 45° 37' lat. She was going at the speed of thirteen knots and a half.

At seventeen minutes past four in the afternoon, whilst the passengers were assembled at lunch in the great saloon, a slight shock was felt on the hull of the Scotia, on her quarter, a little aft of the port-paddle.

The Scotia had not struck, but she had been struck, and seemingly by something rather sharp and penetrating than blunt. The shock had been so slight that no one had been alarmed, had it not been for the shouts of the carpenter's watch, who rushed on to the bridge, exclaiming, "We are sinking! we are sinking!" At first the passengers were much frightened, but Captain Anderson hastened to reassure them. The danger could not be imminent. The Scotia, divided into seven compartments by strong partitions, could brave with impunity any leak. Captain Anderson went down immediately into the hold. He found that the sea was pouring into the fifth compartment; and the rapidity of the influx proved that the force of the water was considerable. Fortunately this compartment did not hold the boilers, or the fires would have been immediately extinguished. Captain Anderson ordered the engines to be stopped at once, and one of the men went down to ascertain the extent of the injury. Some minutes afterwards they discovered the existence of a large hole, two yards in diameter, in the ship's bottom. Such a leak could not be stopped; and the Scotia, her paddles half submerged, was obliged to continue her course. She was then three hundred miles from Cape Clear, and, after three days' delay, which caused great uneasiness in Liverpool, she entered the basin of the company.

The engineers visited the Scotia, which was put in dry dock. They could scarcely believe it possible; at two yards and a half below water-mark was a regular rent, in the form of an isosceles triangle. The broken place in the iron plates was so perfectly defined that it could not have been more neatly done by a punch. It was clear, then, that the instrument producing the perforation was not of a common stamp and, after having been driven with prodigious strength, and piercing an iron plate 1 3/8 inches thick, had withdrawn itself by a backward motion.

Such was the last fact, which resulted in exciting once more the torrent of public opinion. From this moment all unlucky casualties which could not be otherwise accounted for were put down to the monster.

Upon this imaginary creature rested the responsibility of all these shipwrecks, which unfortunately were considerable; for of three thousand ships whose loss was annually recorded at Lloyd's, the number of sailing and steam-ships supposed to be totally lost, from the absence of all news, amounted to not less than two hundred!

Now, it was the "monster" who, justly or unjustly, was accused of their disappearance, and, thanks to it, communication between the different continents became more and more dangerous. The public demanded sharply that the seas should at any price be relieved from this formidable cetacean.

CHAPTER II. PRO AND CON

At the period when these events took place, I had just returned from a scientific research in the disagreeable territory of Nebraska, in the United States. In virtue of my office as Assistant Professor in the Museum of Natural History in Paris, the French Government had attached me to that expedition. After six months in Nebraska, I arrived in New York towards the end of March, laden with a precious collection. My departure for France was fixed for the first days in May. Meanwhile I was occupying myself in classifying my mineralogical, botanical, and zoological riches, when the accident happened to the Scotia.

I was perfectly up in the subject which was the question of the day. How could I be otherwise? I had read and reread all the American and European papers without being any nearer a conclusion. This mystery puzzled me. Under the impossibility of forming an opinion, I jumped from one extreme to the other. That there really was something could not be doubted, and the incredulous were invited to put their finger on the wound of the Scotia.

On my arrival at New York the question was at its height. The theory of the floating island, and the unapproachable sandbank, supported by minds little competent to form a judgment, was abandoned. And, indeed, unless this shoal had a machine in its stomach, how could it change its position with such astonishing rapidity?

From the same cause, the idea of a floating hull of an enormous wreck was given up.

There remained, then, only two possible solutions of the question, which created two distinct parties: on one side, those who were for a monster of colossal strength; on the other, those who were for a submarine vessel of enormous motive power.

But this last theory, plausible as it was, could not stand against inquiries made in both worlds. That a private gentleman should have such a machine at his command was not likely. Where, when, and how was it built? and how could its construction have been kept secret? Certainly a Government might possess such a destructive machine. And in these disastrous times, when the ingenuity of man has multiplied the power of weapons of war, it was possible that, without the knowledge of others, a State might try to work such a formidable engine.

But the idea of a war machine fell before the declaration of Governments. As public interest was in question, and transatlantic communications suffered, their veracity could not be doubted. But how admit that the construction of this submarine boat had escaped the public eye? For a private gentleman to keep the secret under such circumstances would be very difficult, and for a State whose every act is persistently watched by powerful rivals, certainly impossible.

Upon my arrival in New York several persons did me the honour of consulting me on the phenomenon in question. I had published in France a work in quarto, in two volumes, entitled Mysteries of the Great Submarine Grounds. This book, highly approved of in the learned world, gained for me a special reputation in this rather obscure branch of Natural History. My advice was asked. As long as I could deny the reality of the fact, I confined myself to a decided negative. But soon, finding myself driven into a corner, I was obliged to explain myself point by point. I discussed the question in all its forms, politically and scientifically; and I give here an extract from a carefully-studied article which I published in the number of the 30th of April. It ran as follows:

"After examining one by one the different theories, rejecting all other suggestions, it becomes necessary to admit the existence of a marine animal of enormous power.

"The great depths of the ocean are entirely unknown to us. Soundings cannot reach them. What passes in those remote depths—what beings live, or can live, twelve or fifteen miles beneath the surface of the waters—what is the organisation of these animals, we can scarcely conjecture. However, the solution of the problem submitted to me may modify the form of the dilemma. Either we do know all the varieties of beings which people our planet, or we do not. If we do NOT know them all—if Nature has still secrets in the deeps for us, nothing is more conformable to reason than to admit the existence of fishes, or cetaceans of other kinds, or even of new species, of an organisation formed to inhabit the strata inaccessible to soundings, and which an accident of some sort has brought at long intervals to the upper level of the ocean.

"If, on the contrary, we DO know all living kinds, we must necessarily seek for the animal in question amongst those marine beings already classed; and, in that case, I should be disposed to admit the existence of a gigantic narwhal.

"The common narwhal, or unicorn of the sea, often attains a length of sixty feet. Increase its size fivefold or tenfold, give it strength proportionate to its size, lengthen its destructive weapons, and you obtain the animal required. It

6

will have the proportions determined by the officers of the Shannon, the instrument required by the perforation of the Scotia, and the power necessary to pierce the hull of the steamer.

"Indeed, the narwhal is armed with a sort of ivory sword, a halberd, according to the expression of certain naturalists. The principal tusk has the hardness of steel. Some of these tusks have been found buried in the bodies of whales, which the unicorn always attacks with success. Others have been drawn out, not without trouble, from the bottoms of ships, which they had pierced through and through, as a gimlet pierces a barrel. The Museum of the Faculty of Medicine of Paris possesses one of these defensive weapons, two yards and a quarter in length, and fifteen inches in diameter at the base.

"Very well! suppose this weapon to be six times stronger and the animal ten times more powerful; launch it at the rate of twenty miles an hour, and you obtain a shock capable of producing the catastrophe required. Until further information, therefore, I shall maintain it to be a sea-unicorn of colossal dimensions, armed not with a halberd, but with a real spur, as the armoured frigates, or the `rams' of war, whose massiveness and motive power it would possess at the same time. Thus may this puzzling phenomenon be explained, unless there be something over and above all that one has ever conjectured, seen, perceived, or experienced; which is just within the bounds of possibility."

These last words were cowardly on my part; but, up to a certain point, I wished to shelter my dignity as professor, and not give too much cause for laughter to the Americans, who laugh well when they do laugh. I reserved for myself a way of escape. In effect, however, I admitted the existence of the "monster." My article was warmly discussed, which procured it a high reputation. It rallied round it a certain number of partisans. The solution it proposed gave, at least, full liberty to the imagination. The human mind delights in grand conceptions of supernatural beings. And the sea is precisely their best vehicle, the only medium through which these giants (against which terrestrial animals, such as elephants or rhinoceroses, are as nothing) can be produced or developed.

The industrial and commercial papers treated the question chiefly from this point of view. The Shipping and Mercantile Gazette, the Lloyd's List, the Packet-Boat, and the Maritime and Colonial Review, all papers devoted to insurance companies which threatened to raise their rates of premium, were unanimous on this point. Public opinion had been pronounced. The United States were the first in the field; and in New York they made preparations for an expedition destined to pursue this narwhal. A frigate of great speed, the Abraham Lincoln, was put in commission as soon as possible. The arsenals were opened to Commander Farragut, who hastened the arming of his frigate; but, as it always happens, the moment it was decided to pursue the monster, the monster did not appear. For two months no one heard it spoken of. No ship met with it. It seemed as if this unicorn knew of the plots weaving around it. It had been so much talked of, even through the Atlantic cable, that jesters pretended that this slender fly had stopped a telegram on its passage and was making the most of it.

So when the frigate had been armed for a long campaign, and provided with formidable fishing apparatus, no one could tell what course to pursue. Impatience grew apace, when, on the 2nd of July, they learned that a steamer of the line of San Francisco, from California to Shanghai, had seen the animal three weeks before in the North Pacific Ocean. The excitement caused by this news was extreme. The ship was revictualled and well stocked with coal.

Three hours before the Abraham Lincoln left Brooklyn pier, I received a letter worded as follows:

To M. ARONNAX, Professor in the Museum of Paris, Fifth Avenue Hotel, New York.

SIR,—If you will consent to join the Abraham Lincoln in this expedition, the Government of the United States will with pleasure see France represented in the enterprise. Commander Farragut has a cabin at your disposal.

Very cordially yours, J.B. HOBSON, Secretary of Marine.

CHAPTER III. I FORM MY RESOLUTION

Three seconds before the arrival of J. B. Hobson's letter I no more thought of pursuing the unicorn than of attempting the passage of the North Sea. Three seconds after reading the letter of the honourable Secretary of Marine, I felt that my true vocation, the sole end of my life, was to chase this disturbing monster and purge it from the world.

But I had just returned from a fatiguing journey, weary and longing for repose. I aspired to nothing more than again seeing my country, my friends, my little lodging by the Jardin des Plantes, my dear and precious collections— but nothing could keep me back! I forgot all—fatigue, friends and collections— and accepted without hesitation the offer of the American Government.

"Besides," thought I, "all roads lead back to Europe; and the unicorn may be amiable enough to hurry me towards the coast of France. This worthy animal may allow itself to be caught in the seas of Europe (for my particular benefit), and I will not bring back less than half a yard of his ivory halberd to the Museum of Natural History." But in the meanwhile I must seek this narwhal in the North Pacific Ocean, which, to return to France, was taking the road to the antipodes.

"Conseil," I called in an impatient voice.

Conseil was my servant, a true, devoted Flemish boy, who had accompanied me in all my travels. I liked him, and he returned the liking well. He was quiet by nature, regular from principle, zealous from habit, evincing little disturbance at the different surprises of life, very quick with his hands, and apt at any service required of him; and, despite his name, never giving advice—even when asked for it.

Conseil had followed me for the last ten years wherever science led. Never once did he complain of the length or fatigue of a journey, never make an objection to pack his portmanteau for whatever country it might be, or however far away, whether China or Congo. Besides all this, he had good health, which defied all sickness, and solid muscles, but no nerves; good morals are understood. This boy was thirty years old, and his age to that of his master as fifteen to twenty. May I be excused for saying that I was forty years old?

But Conseil had one fault: he was ceremonious to a degree, and would never speak to me but in the third person, which was sometimes provoking.

"Conseil," said I again, beginning with feverish hands to make preparations for my departure.

Certainly I was sure of this devoted boy. As a rule, I never asked him if it were convenient for him or not to follow me in my travels; but this time the expedition in question might be prolonged, and the enterprise might be hazardous in pursuit of an animal capable of sinking a frigate as easily as a nutshell. Here there was matter for reflection even to the most impassive man in the world. What would Conseil say?

"Conseil," I called a third time.

Conseil appeared.

"Did you call, sir?" said he, entering.

"Yes, my boy; make preparations for me and yourself too. We leave in two hours."

"As you please, sir," replied Conseil, quietly.

"Not an instant to lose; lock in my trunk all travelling utensils, coats, shirts, and stockings—without counting, as many as you can, and make haste."

"And your collections, sir?" observed Conseil.

"They will keep them at the hotel."

"We are not returning to Paris, then?" said Conseil.

"Oh! certainly," I answered, evasively, "by making a curve."

"Will the curve please you, sir?"

"Oh! it will be nothing; not quite so direct a road, that is all. We take our passage in the Abraham, Lincoln."

"As you think proper, sir," coolly replied Conseil.

"You see, my friend, it has to do with the monster—the famous narwhal. We are going to purge it from the seas. A glorious mission, but a dangerous one! We cannot tell where we may go; these animals can be very capricious. But we will go whether or no; we have got a captain who is pretty wide-awake."

Our luggage was transported to the deck of the frigate immediately. I hastened on board and asked for Commander Farragut. One of the sailors conducted me to the poop, where I found myself in the presence of a good-looking officer, who held out his hand to me.

"Monsieur Pierre Aronnax?" said he.

"Himself," replied I. "Commander Farragut?"

"You are welcome, Professor; your cabin is ready for you."

I bowed, and desired to be conducted to the cabin destined for me.

The Abraham Lincoln had been well chosen and equipped for her new destination. She was a frigate of great speed, fitted with high-pressure engines which admitted a pressure of seven atmospheres. Under this the Abraham Lincoln attained the mean speed of nearly eighteen knots and a third an hour— a considerable speed, but, nevertheless, insufficient to grapple with this gigantic cetacean.

The interior arrangements of the frigate corresponded to its nautical qualities. I was well satisfied with my cabin, which was in the after part, opening upon the gunroom.

"We shall be well off here," said I to Conseil.

"As well, by your honour's leave, as a hermit-crab in the shell of a whelk," said Conseil.

I left Conseil to stow our trunks conveniently away, and remounted the poop in order to survey the preparations for departure.

At that moment Commander Farragut was ordering the last moorings to be cast loose which held the Abraham Lincoln to the pier of Brooklyn. So in a quarter of an hour, perhaps less, the frigate would have sailed without me. I should have missed this extraordinary, supernatural, and incredible expedition, the recital of which may well meet with some suspicion.

But Commander Farragut would not lose a day nor an hour in scouring the seas in which the animal had been sighted. He sent for the engineer.

"Is the steam full on?" asked he.

"Yes, sir," replied the engineer.

"Go ahead," cried Commander Farragut.

CHAPTER IV. NED LAND

Captain Farragut was a good seaman, worthy of the frigate he commanded. His vessel and he were one. He was the soul of it. On the question of the monster there was no doubt in his mind, and he would not allow the existence of the animal to be disputed on board. He believed in it, as certain good women believe in the leviathan—by faith, not by reason. The monster did exist, and he had sworn to rid the seas of it. Either Captain Farragut would kill the narwhal, or the narwhal would kill the captain. There was no third course.

The officers on board shared the opinion of their chief. They were ever chatting, discussing, and calculating the various chances of a meeting, watching narrowly the vast surface of the ocean. More than one took up his quarters voluntarily in the cross-trees, who would have cursed such a berth under any other circumstances. As long as the sun described its daily course, the rigging was crowded with sailors, whose feet were burnt to such an extent by the heat of the deck as to render it unbearable; still the Abraham Lincoln had not yet breasted the suspected waters of the Pacific. As to the ship's company, they desired nothing better than to meet the unicorn, to harpoon it, hoist it on board, and despatch it. They watched the sea with eager attention.

Besides, Captain Farragut had spoken of a certain sum of two thousand dollars, set apart for whoever should first sight the monster, were he cabin-boy, common seaman, or officer.

I leave you to judge how eyes were used on board the Abraham Lincoln.

For my own part I was not behind the others, and, left to no one my share of daily observations. The frigate might have been called the Argus, for a hundred reasons. Only one amongst us, Conseil, seemed to protest by his indifference against the question which so interested us all, and seemed to be out of keeping with the general enthusiasm on board.

I have said that Captain Farragut had carefully provided his ship with every apparatus for catching the gigantic cetacean. No whaler had ever been better armed. We possessed every known engine, from the harpoon thrown by the hand to the barbed arrows of the blunderbuss, and the explosive balls of the duck-gun. On the forecastle lay the perfection of a breech-loading gun, very thick at the breech, and very narrow in the bore, the model of which had been in the Exhibition of 1867. This precious weapon of American origin could throw with ease a conical projectile of nine pounds to a mean distance of ten miles.

Thus the Abraham Lincoln wanted for no means of destruction; and, what was better still she had on board Ned Land, the prince of harpooners.

Ned Land was a Canadian, with an uncommon quickness of hand, and who knew no equal in his dangerous occupation. Skill, coolness, audacity, and cunning he possessed in a superior degree, and it must be a cunning whale to escape the stroke of his harpoon.

Ned Land was about forty years of age; he was a tall man (more than six feet high), strongly built, grave and taciturn, occasionally violent, and very passionate when contradicted. His person attracted attention, but above all the boldness of his look, which gave a singular expression to his face.

Who calls himself Canadian calls himself French; and, little communicative as Ned Land was, I must admit that he took a certain liking for me. My nationality drew him to me, no doubt. It was an opportunity for him to talk, and for me to hear, that old language of Rabelais, which is still in use in some Canadian provinces. The harpooner's family was originally from Quebec, and was already a tribe of hardy fishermen when this town belonged to France.

Little by little, Ned Land acquired a taste for chatting, and I loved to hear the recital of his adventures in the polar seas. He related his fishing, and his combats, with natural poetry of expression; his recital took the form of an epic poem, and I seemed to be listening to a Canadian Homer singing the Iliad of the regions of the North.

I am portraying this hardy companion as I really knew him. We are old friends now, united in that unchangeable friendship which is born and cemented amidst extreme dangers. Ah, brave Ned! I ask no more than to live a hundred years longer, that I may have more time to dwell the longer on your memory.

Now, what was Ned Land's opinion upon the question of the marine monster? I must admit that he did not believe in the unicorn, and was the only one on board who did not share that universal conviction. He even avoided the subject, which I one day thought it my duty to press upon him. One magnificent evening, the 30th July (that is to say, three weeks after our departure), the frigate was abreast of Cape Blanc, thirty miles to leeward of the coast of Patagonia. We had crossed the tropic of Capricorn, and the Straits of Magellan opened less than seven hundred miles to the south. Before eight days were over the Abraham Lincoln would be ploughing the waters of the Pacific.

Seated on the poop, Ned Land and I were chatting of one thing and another as we looked at this mysterious sea, whose great depths had up to this time been inaccessible to the eye of man. I naturally led up the conversation to the giant unicorn, and examined the various chances of success or failure of the expedition. But, seeing that Ned Land let me speak without saying too much himself, I pressed him more closely.

"Well, Ned," said I, "is it possible that you are not convinced of the existence of this cetacean that we are following? Have you any particular reason for being so incredulous?"

The harpooner looked at me fixedly for some moments before answering, struck his broad forehead with his hand (a habit of his), as if to collect himself, and said at last, "Perhaps I have, Mr. Aronnax."

"But, Ned, you, a whaler by profession, familiarised with all the great marine mammalia—YOU ought to be the last to doubt under such circumstances!"

"That is just what deceives you, Professor," replied Ned. "As a whaler I have followed many a cetacean, harpooned a great number, and killed several; but, however strong or well-armed they may have been, neither their tails nor their weapons would have been able even to scratch the iron plates of a steamer."

"But, Ned, they tell of ships which the teeth of the narwhal have pierced through and through."

"Wooden ships—that is possible," replied the Canadian, "but I have never seen it done; and, until further proof, I deny that whales, cetaceans, or sea-unicorns could ever produce the effect you describe."

"Well, Ned, I repeat it with a conviction resting on the logic of facts. I believe in the existence of a mammal power fully organised, belonging to the branch of vertebrata, like the whales, the cachalots, or the dolphins, and furnished with a horn of defence of great penetrating power."

"Hum!" said the harpooner, shaking his head with the air of a man who would not be convinced.

"Notice one thing, my worthy Canadian," I resumed. "If such an animal is in existence, if it inhabits the depths of the ocean, if it frequents the strata lying miles below the surface of the water, it must necessarily possess an organisation the strength of which would defy all comparison."

"And why this powerful organisation?" demanded Ned.

"Because it requires incalculable strength to keep one's self in these strata and resist their pressure. Listen to me. Let us admit that the pressure of the atmosphere is represented by the weight of a column of water thirty-two feet high. In reality the column of water would be shorter, as we are speaking of sea water, the density of which is greater than that of fresh water. Very well, when you dive, Ned, as many times 32 feet of water as there are above you, so many times does your body bear a pressure equal to that of the atmosphere, that is to say, 15 lb. for each square inch of its surface. It follows, then, that at 320 feet this pressure equals that of 10 atmospheres, of 100 atmospheres at 3,200 feet, and of 1,000 atmospheres at 32,000 feet, that is, about 6 miles; which is equivalent to saying that if you could attain this depth in the ocean, each square three-eighths of an inch of the surface of your body would bear a pressure of 5,600 lb. Ah! my brave Ned, do you know how many square inches you carry on the surface of your body?"

"I have no idea, Mr. Aronnax."

"About 6,500; and as in reality the atmospheric pressure is about 15 lb. to the square inch, your 6,500 square inches bear at this moment a pressure of 97,500 lb."

"Without my perceiving it?"

"Without your perceiving it. And if you are not crushed by such a pressure, it is because the air penetrates the interior of your body with equal pressure. Hence perfect equilibrium between the interior and exterior pressure, which thus neutralise each other, and which allows you to bear it without inconvenience. But in the water it is another thing."

"Yes, I understand," replied Ned, becoming more attentive; "because the water surrounds me, but does not penetrate."

"Precisely, Ned: so that at 32 feet beneath the surface of the sea you would undergo a pressure of 97,500 lb.; at 320 feet, ten times that pressure; at 3,200 feet, a hundred times that pressure; lastly, at 32,000 feet, a thousand times that pressure would be 97,500,000 lb.—that is to say, that you would be flattened as if you had been drawn from the plates of a hydraulic machine!"

"The devil!" exclaimed Ned.

"Very well, my worthy harpooner, if some vertebrate, several hundred yards long, and large in proportion, can maintain itself in such depths—of those whose surface is represented by millions of square inches, that is by tens of millions of pounds, we must estimate the pressure they undergo. Consider, then, what must be the resistance of their bony structure, and the strength of their organisation to withstand such pressure!"

"Why!" exclaimed Ned Land, "they must be made of iron plates eight inches thick, like the armoured frigates."

"As you say, Ned. And think what destruction such a mass would cause, if hurled with the speed of an express train against the hull of a vessel."

"Yes—certainly—perhaps," replied the Canadian, shaken by these figures, but not yet willing to give in.

"Well, have I convinced you?"

"You have convinced me of one thing, sir, which is that, if such animals do exist at the bottom of the seas, they must necessarily be as strong as you say."

"But if they do not exist, mine obstinate harpooner, how explain the accident to the Scotia?"

CHAPTER V. AT A VENTURE

The voyage of the Abraham Lincoln was for a long time marked by no special incident. But one circumstance happened which showed the wonderful dexterity of Ned Land, and proved what confidence we might place in him.

The 30th of June, the frigate spoke some American whalers, from whom we learned that they knew nothing about the narwhal. But one of them, the captain of the Monroe, knowing that Ned Land had shipped on board the Abraham Lincoln, begged for his help in chasing a whale they had in sight. Commander Farragut, desirous of seeing Ned Land at work, gave him permission to go on board the Monroe. And fate served our Canadian so well that, instead of one whale, he harpooned two with a double blow, striking one straight to the heart, and catching the other after some minutes' pursuit. Decidedly, if the monster ever had to do with Ned Land's harpoon, I would not bet in its favour.

The frigate skirted the south-east coast of America with great rapidity. The 3rd of July we were at the opening of the Straits of Magellan, level with Cape Vierges. But Commander Farragut would not take a tortuous passage, but doubled Cape Horn.

The ship's crew agreed with him. And certainly it was possible that they might meet the narwhal in this narrow pass. Many of the sailors affirmed that the monster could not pass there, "that he was too big for that!"

The 6th of July, about three o'clock in the afternoon, the Abraham Lincoln, at fifteen miles to the south, doubled the solitary island, this lost rock at the extremity of the American continent, to which some Dutch sailors gave the name of their native town, Cape Horn. The course was taken towards the north-west, and the next day the screw of the frigate was at last beating the waters of the Pacific.

"Keep your eyes open!" called out the sailors.

And they were opened widely. Both eyes and glasses, a little dazzled, it is true, by the prospect of two thousand dollars, had not an instant's repose.

I myself, for whom money had no charms, was not the least attentive on board. Giving but few minutes to my meals, but a few hours to sleep, indifferent to either rain or sunshine, I did not leave the poop of the vessel. Now leaning on the netting of the forecastle, now on the taffrail, I devoured with eagerness the soft foam which whitened the sea as far as the eye could reach; and how often have I shared the emotion of the majority of the crew, when some capricious whale raised its black back above the waves! The poop of the vessel was crowded on a moment. The cabins poured forth a torrent of sailors and officers, each with heaving breast and troubled eye watching the course of the cetacean. I looked and looked till I was nearly blind, whilst Conseil kept repeating in a calm voice:

"If, sir, you would not squint so much, you would see better!"

But vain excitement! The Abraham Lincoln checked its speed and made for the animal signalled, a simple whale, or common cachalot, which soon disappeared amidst a storm of abuse.

But the weather was good. The voyage was being accomplished under the most favourable auspices. It was then the bad season in Australia, the July of that zone corresponding to our January in Europe, but the sea was beautiful and easily scanned round a vast circumference.

The 20th of July, the tropic of Capricorn was cut by 105d of longitude, and the 27th of the same month we crossed the Equator on the 110th meridian. This passed, the frigate took a more decided westerly direction, and scoured the central waters of the Pacific. Commander Farragut thought, and with reason, that it was better to remain in deep water, and keep clear of continents or islands, which the beast itself seemed to shun (perhaps because there was not enough water for him! suggested the greater part of the crew). The frigate passed at some distance from the Marquesas and the Sandwich Islands, crossed the tropic of Cancer, and made for the China Seas. We were on the theatre of the last diversions of the monster: and, to say truth, we no longer LIVED on board. The entire ship's crew were undergoing a nervous excitement, of which I can give no idea: they could not eat, they could not sleep—twenty times a day, a misconception or an optical illusion of some sailor seated on the taffrail, would cause dreadful perspirations, and these emotions, twenty times repeated, kept us in a state of excitement so violent that a reaction was unavoidable.

And truly, reaction soon showed itself. For three months, during which a day seemed an age, the Abraham Lincoln furrowed all the waters of the Northern Pacific, running at whales, making sharp deviations from her course, veering suddenly from one tack to another, stopping suddenly, putting on steam, and backing ever and anon at the risk of deranging her machinery, and not one point of the Japanese or American coast was left unexplored.

The warmest partisans of the enterprise now became its most ardent detractors. Reaction mounted from the crew to the captain himself, and certainly, had it not been for the resolute determination on the part of Captain Farragut, the frigate would have headed due southward. This useless search could not last much longer. The Abraham Lincoln had nothing to reproach herself with, she had done her best to succeed. Never had an American ship's crew shown more zeal or patience; its failure could not be placed to their charge—there remained nothing but to return.

This was represented to the commander. The sailors could not hide their discontent, and the service suffered. I will not say there was a mutiny on board, but after a reasonable period of obstinacy, Captain Farragut (as Columbus did) asked for three days' patience. If in three days the monster did not appear, the man at the helm should give three turns of the wheel, and the Abraham Lincoln would make for the European seas.

This promise was made on the 2nd of November. It had the effect of rallying the ship's crew. The ocean was watched with renewed attention. Each one wished for a last glance in which to sum up his remembrance. Glasses were used with feverish activity. It was a grand defiance given to the giant narwhal, and he could scarcely fail to answer the summons and "appear."

Two days passed, the steam was at half pressure; a thousand schemes were tried to attract the attention and stimulate the apathy of the animal in case it should be met in those parts. Large quantities of bacon were trailed in the wake of the ship, to the great satisfaction (I must say) of the sharks. Small craft radiated in all directions round the Abraham Lincoln as she lay to, and did not leave a spot of the sea unexplored. But the night of the 4th of November arrived without the unveiling of this submarine mystery.

The next day, the 5th of November, at twelve, the delay would (morally speaking) expire; after that time, Commander Farragut, faithful to his promise, was to turn the course to the south-east and abandon for ever the northern regions of the Pacific.

The frigate was then in 31° 15' N. lat. and 136° 42' E. long. The coast of Japan still remained less than two hundred miles to leeward. Night was approaching. They had just struck eight bells; large clouds veiled the face of the moon, then in its first quarter. The sea undulated peaceably under the stern of the vessel.

At that moment I was leaning forward on the starboard netting. Conseil, standing near me, was looking straight before him. The crew, perched in the ratlines, examined the horizon which contracted and darkened by degrees. Officers with their night glasses scoured the growing darkness: sometimes the ocean sparkled under the rays of the moon, which darted between two clouds, then all trace of light was lost in the darkness.

In looking at Conseil, I could see he was undergoing a little of the general influence. At least I thought so. Perhaps for the first time his nerves vibrated to a sentiment of curiosity.

"Come, Conseil," said I, "this is the last chance of pocketing the two thousand dollars."

"May I be permitted to say, sir," replied Conseil, "that I never reckoned on getting the prize; and, had the government of the Union offered a hundred thousand dollars, it would have been none the poorer."

"You are right, Conseil. It is a foolish affair after all, and one upon which we entered too lightly. What time lost, what useless emotions! We should have been back in France six months ago."

"In your little room, sir," replied Conseil, "and in your museum, sir; and I should have already classed all your fossils, sir. And the Babiroussa would have been installed in its cage in the Jardin des Plantes, and have drawn all the curious people of the capital!"

"As you say, Conseil. I fancy we shall run a fair chance of being laughed at for our pains."

"That's tolerably certain," replied Conseil, quietly; "I think they will make fun of you, sir. And, must I say it——?"

"Go on, my good friend."

"Well, sir, you will only get your deserts."

"Indeed!"

"When one has the honour of being a *savant* as you are, sir, one should not expose one's self to——"

Conseil had not time to finish his compliment. In the midst of general silence a voice had just been heard. It was the voice of Ned Land shouting:

"Look out there! The very thing we are looking for—on our weather beam!"

CHAPTER VI. AT FULL STEAM

At this cry the whole ship's crew hurried towards the harpooner—commander, officers, masters, sailors, cabin boys; even the engineers left their engines, and the stokers their furnaces.

The order to stop her had been given, and the frigate now simply went on by her own momentum. The darkness was then profound, and, however good the Canadian's eyes were, I asked myself how he had managed to see, and what he had been able to see. My heart beat as if it would break. But Ned Land was not mistaken, and we all perceived the object he pointed to. At two cables' length from the Abraham Lincoln, on the starboard quarter, the sea seemed to be illuminated all over. It was not a mere phosphoric phenomenon. The monster emerged some fathoms from the water, and then threw out that very intense but mysterious light mentioned in the report of several captains. This magnificent irradiation must have been produced by an agent of great SHINING power. The luminous part traced on the sea an immense oval, much elongated, the centre of which condensed a burning heat, whose overpowering brilliancy died out by successive gradations.

"It is only a massing of phosphoric particles," cried one of the officers.

"No, sir, certainly not," I replied. "That brightness is of an essentially electrical nature. Besides, see, see! it moves; it is moving forwards, backwards; it is darting towards us!"

A general cry arose from the frigate.

"Silence!" said the captain. "Up with the helm, reverse the engines."

The steam was shut off, and the Abraham Lincoln, beating to port, described a semicircle.

"Right the helm, go ahead," cried the captain.

These orders were executed, and the frigate moved rapidly from the burning light.

I was mistaken. She tried to sheer off, but the supernatural animal approached with a velocity double her own.

We gasped for breath. Stupefaction more than fear made us dumb and motionless. The animal gained on us, sporting with the waves. It made the round of the frigate, which was then making fourteen knots, and enveloped it with its electric rings like luminous dust.

Then it moved away two or three miles, leaving a phosphorescent track, like those volumes of steam that the express trains leave behind. All at once from the dark line of the horizon whither it retired to gain its momentum, the monster rushed suddenly towards the Abraham Lincoln with alarming rapidity, stopped suddenly about twenty feet from the hull, and died out—not diving under the water, for its brilliancy did not abate—but suddenly, and as if the source of this brilliant emanation was exhausted. Then it reappeared on the other side of the vessel, as if it had turned and slid under the hull. Any moment a collision might have occurred which would have been fatal to us. However, I was astonished at the manoeuvres of the frigate. She fled and did not attack.

On the captain's face, generally so impassive, was an expression of unaccountable astonishment.

"Mr. Aronnax," he said, "I do not know with what formidable being I have to deal, and I will not imprudently risk my frigate in the midst of this darkness. Besides, how attack this unknown thing, how defend one's self from it? Wait for daylight, and the scene will change."

"You have no further doubt, captain, of the nature of the animal?"

"No, sir; it is evidently a gigantic narwhal, and an electric one."

"Perhaps," added I, "one can only approach it with a torpedo."

"Undoubtedly," replied the captain, "if it possesses such dreadful power, it is the most terrible animal that ever was created. That is why, sir, I must be on my guard."

The crew were on their feet all night. No one thought of sleep. The Abraham Lincoln, not being able to struggle with such velocity, had moderated its pace, and sailed at half speed. For its part, the narwhal, imitating the frigate, let the waves rock it at will, and seemed decided not to leave the scene of the struggle. Towards midnight, however, it disappeared, or, to use a more appropriate term, it "died out" like a large glow-worm. Had it fled? One could only fear, not hope it. But at seven minutes to one o'clock in the morning a deafening whistling was heard, like that produced by a body of water rushing with great violence.

The captain, Ned Land, and I were then on the poop, eagerly peering through the profound darkness.

"Ned Land," asked the commander, "you have often heard the roaring of whales?"

"Often, sir; but never such whales the sight of which brought me in two thousand dollars. If I can only approach within four harpoons' length of it!"

"But to approach it," said the commander, "I ought to put a whaler at your disposal?"

"Certainly, sir."

"That will be trifling with the lives of my men."

"And mine too," simply said the harpooner.

Towards two o'clock in the morning, the burning light reappeared, not less intense, about five miles to windward of the Abraham Lincoln. Notwithstanding the distance, and the noise of the wind and sea, one heard distinctly the loud strokes of the animal's tail, and even its panting breath. It seemed that, at the moment that the enormous narwhal had come to take breath at the surface of the water, the air was engulfed in its lungs, like the steam in the vast cylinders of a machine of two thousand horse-power.

"Hum!" thought I, "a whale with the strength of a cavalry regiment would be a pretty whale!"

We were on the qui vive till daylight, and prepared for the combat. The fishing implements were laid along the hammock nettings. The second lieutenant loaded the blunder busses, which could throw harpoons to the distance of a mile, and long duck-guns, with explosive bullets, which inflicted mortal wounds even to the most terrible animals. Ned Land contented himself with sharpening his harpoon—a terrible weapon in his hands.

At six o'clock day began to break; and, with the first glimmer of light, the electric light of the narwhal disappeared. At seven o'clock the day was sufficiently advanced, but a very thick sea fog obscured our view, and the best spy glasses could not pierce it. That caused disappointment and anger.

I climbed the mizzen-mast. Some officers were already perched on the mast-heads. At eight o'clock the fog lay heavily on the waves, and its thick scrolls rose little by little. The horizon grew wider and clearer at the same time. Suddenly, just as on the day before, Ned Land's voice was heard:

"The thing itself on the port quarter!" cried the harpooner.

Every eye was turned towards the point indicated. There, a mile and a half from the frigate, a long blackish body emerged a yard above the waves. Its tail, violently agitated, produced a considerable eddy. Never did a tail beat the sea with such violence. An immense track, of dazzling whiteness, marked the passage of the animal, and described a long curve.

The frigate approached the cetacean. I examined it thoroughly.

The reports of the Shannon and of the Helvetia had rather exaggerated its size, and I estimated its length at only two hundred and fifty feet. As to its dimensions, I could only conjecture them to be admirably proportioned. While I watched this phenomenon, two jets of steam and water were ejected from its vents, and rose to the height of 120 feet; thus I ascertained its way of breathing. I concluded definitely that it belonged to the vertebrate branch, class mammalia.

The crew waited impatiently for their chief's orders. The latter, after having observed the animal attentively, called the engineer. The engineer ran to him.

"Sir," said the commander, "you have steam up?"

"Yes, sir," answered the engineer.

"Well, make up your fires and put on all steam."

Three hurrahs greeted this order. The time for the struggle had arrived. Some moments after, the two funnels of the frigate vomited torrents of black smoke, and the bridge quaked under the trembling of the boilers.

The Abraham Lincoln, propelled by her wonderful screw, went straight at the animal. The latter allowed it to come within half a cable's length; then, as if disdaining to dive, it took a little turn, and stopped a short distance off.

This pursuit lasted nearly three-quarters of an hour, without the frigate gaining two yards on the cetacean. It was quite evident that at that rate we should never come up with it.

"Well, Mr. Land," asked the captain, "do you advise me to put the boats out to sea?"

"No, sir," replied Ned Land; "because we shall not take that beast easily."

"What shall we do then?"

"Put on more steam if you can, sir. With your leave, I mean to post myself under the bowsprit, and, if we get within harpooning distance, I shall throw my harpoon."

"Go, Ned," said the captain. "Engineer, put on more pressure."

Ned Land went to his post. The fires were increased, the screw revolved forty-three times a minute, and the steam poured out of the valves. We heaved the log, and calculated that the Abraham Lincoln was going at the rate of 18 1/2 miles an hour.

But the accursed animal swam at the same speed.

For a whole hour the frigate kept up this pace, without gaining six feet. It was humiliating for one of the swiftest sailers in the American navy. A stubborn anger seized the crew; the sailors abused the monster, who, as before, disdained to answer them; the captain no longer contented himself with twisting his beard—he gnawed it.

The engineer was called again.

"You have turned full steam on?"

"Yes, sir," replied the engineer.

The speed of the Abraham Lincoln increased. Its masts trembled down to their stepping holes, and the clouds of smoke could hardly find way out of the narrow funnels.

They heaved the log a second time.

"Well?" asked the captain of the man at the wheel.

"Nineteen miles and three-tenths, sir."

"Clap on more steam."

The engineer obeyed. The manometer showed ten degrees. But the cetacean grew warm itself, no doubt; for without straining itself, it made 19 3/10 miles.

What a pursuit! No, I cannot describe the emotion that vibrated through me. Ned Land kept his post, harpoon in hand. Several times the animal let us gain upon it.—"We shall catch it! we shall catch it!" cried the Canadian. But just as he was going to strike, the cetacean stole away with a rapidity that could not be estimated at less than thirty miles an hour, and even during our maximum of speed, it bullied the frigate, going round and round it. A cry of fury broke from everyone!

At noon we were no further advanced than at eight o'clock in the morning.

The captain then decided to take more direct means.

"Ah!" said he, "that animal goes quicker than the Abraham Lincoln. Very well! we will see whether it will escape these conical bullets. Send your men to the forecastle, sir."

The forecastle gun was immediately loaded and slewed round. But the shot passed some feet above the cetacean, which was half a mile off.

"Another, more to the right," cried the commander, "and five dollars to whoever will hit that infernal beast."

An old gunner with a grey beard—that I can see now—with steady eye and grave face, went up to the gun and took a long aim. A loud report was heard, with which were mingled the cheers of the crew.

The bullet did its work; it hit the animal, and, sliding off the rounded surface, was lost in two miles depth of sea.

The chase began again, and the captain, leaning towards me, said:

"I will pursue that beast till my frigate bursts up."

"Yes," answered I; "and you will be quite right to do it."

I wished the beast would exhaust itself, and not be insensible to fatigue like a steam engine. But it was of no use. Hours passed, without its showing any signs of exhaustion.

However, it must be said in praise of the Abraham Lincoln that she struggled on indefatigably. I cannot reckon the distance she made under three hundred miles during this unlucky day, November the 6th. But night came on, and overshadowed the rough ocean.

Now I thought our expedition was at an end, and that we should never again see the extraordinary animal. I was mistaken. At ten minutes to eleven in the evening, the electric light reappeared three miles to windward of the frigate, as pure, as intense as during the preceding night.

The narwhal seemed motionless; perhaps, tired with its day's work, it slept, letting itself float with the undulation of the waves. Now was a chance of which the captain resolved to take advantage.

He gave his orders. The Abraham Lincoln kept up half steam, and advanced cautiously so as not to awake its adversary. It is no rare thing to meet in the middle of the ocean whales so sound asleep that they can be successfully attacked, and Ned Land had harpooned more than one during its sleep. The Canadian went to take his place again under the bowsprit.

The frigate approached noiselessly, stopped at two cables' lengths from the animal, and following its track. No one breathed; a deep silence reigned on the bridge. We were not a hundred feet from the burning focus, the light of which increased and dazzled our eyes.

At this moment, leaning on the forecastle bulwark, I saw below me Ned Land grappling the martingale in one hand, brandishing his terrible harpoon in the other, scarcely twenty feet from the motionless animal. Suddenly his arm straightened, and the harpoon was thrown; I heard the sonorous stroke of the weapon, which seemed to have struck a hard body. The electric light went out suddenly, and two enormous waterspouts broke over the bridge of the frigate, rushing like a torrent from stem to stern, overthrowing men, and breaking the lashings of the spars. A fearful shock followed, and, thrown over the rail without having time to stop myself, I fell into the sea.

CHAPTER VII. AN UNKNOWN SPECIES OF WHALE

This unexpected fall so stunned me that I have no clear recollection of my sensations at the time. I was at first drawn down to a depth of about twenty feet. I am a good swimmer (though without pretending to rival Byron or Edgar Poe, who were masters of the art), and in that plunge I did not lose my presence of mind. Two vigorous strokes brought me to the surface of the water. My first care was to look for the frigate. Had the crew seen me disappear? Had the Abraham Lincoln veered round? Would the captain put out a boat? Might I hope to be saved?

The darkness was intense. I caught a glimpse of a black mass disappearing in the east, its beacon lights dying out in the distance. It was the frigate! I was lost.

"Help, help!" I shouted, swimming towards the Abraham Lincoln in desperation.

My clothes encumbered me; they seemed glued to my body, and paralysed my movements.

I was sinking! I was suffocating!

"Help!"

This was my last cry. My mouth filled with water; I struggled against being drawn down the abyss. Suddenly my clothes were seized by a strong hand, and I felt myself quickly drawn up to the surface of the sea; and I heard, yes, I heard these words pronounced in my ear:

"If master would be so good as to lean on my shoulder, master would swim with much greater ease."

I seized with one hand my faithful Conseil's arm.

"Is it you?" said I, "you?"

"Myself," answered Conseil; "and waiting master's orders."

"That shock threw you as well as me into the sea?"

"No; but, being in my master's service, I followed him."

The worthy fellow thought that was but natural.

"And the frigate?" I asked.

"The frigate?" replied Conseil, turning on his back; "I think that master had better not count too much on her."

"You think so?"

"I say that, at the time I threw myself into the sea, I heard the men at the wheel say, `The screw and the rudder are broken.'

"Broken?"

"Yes, broken by the monster's teeth. It is the only injury the Abraham Lincoln has sustained. But it is a bad look-out for us—she no longer answers her helm."

"Then we are lost!"

"Perhaps so," calmly answered Conseil. "However, we have still several hours before us, and one can do a good deal in some hours."

Conseil's imperturbable coolness set me up again. I swam more vigorously; but, cramped by my clothes, which stuck to me like a leaden weight, I felt great difficulty in bearing up. Conseil saw this.

"Will master let me make a slit?" said he; and, slipping an open knife under my clothes, he ripped them up from top to bottom very rapidly. Then he cleverly slipped them off me, while I swam for both of us. Then I did the same for Conseil, and we continued to swim near to each other.

Nevertheless, our situation was no less terrible. Perhaps our disappearance had not been noticed; and, if it had been, the frigate could not tack, being without its helm. Conseil argued on this supposition, and laid his plans accordingly. This quiet boy was perfectly self-possessed. We then decided that, as our only chance of safety was being picked up by the Abraham Lincoln's boats, we ought to manage so as to wait for them as long as possible. I resolved then to husband our strength, so that both should not be exhausted at the same time; and this is how we managed: while one of us lay on our back, quite still, with arms crossed, and legs stretched out, the other would swim and push the other on in front. This towing business did not last more than ten minutes each; and relieving each other thus, we could swim on for some hours, perhaps till day-break. Poor chance! but hope is so firmly rooted in the heart of man! Moreover, there were two of us. Indeed I declare (though it may seem improbable) if I sought to destroy all hope—if I wished to despair, I could not.

The collision of the frigate with the cetacean had occurred about eleven o'clock in the evening before. I reckoned then we should have eight hours to swim before sunrise, an operation quite practicable if we relieved each other. The sea, very calm, was in our favour. Sometimes I tried to pierce the intense darkness that was only dispelled by the phosphorescence caused by our movements. I watched the luminous waves that broke over my hand, whose mirror-like surface was spotted with silvery rings. One might have said that we were in a bath of quicksilver.

Near one o'clock in the morning, I was seized with dreadful fatigue. My limbs stiffened under the strain of violent cramp. Conseil was obliged to keep me up, and our preservation devolved on him alone. I heard the poor boy pant; his breathing became short and hurried. I found that he could not keep up much longer.

"Leave me! leave me!" I said to him.

"Leave my master? Never!" replied he. "I would drown first."

Just then the moon appeared through the fringes of a thick cloud that the wind was driving to the east. The surface of the sea glittered with its rays. This kindly light reanimated us. My head got better again. I looked at all points of the horizon. I saw the frigate! She was five miles from us, and looked like a dark mass, hardly discernible. But no boats!

I would have cried out. But what good would it have been at such a distance! My swollen lips could utter no sounds. Conseil could articulate some words, and I heard him repeat at intervals, "Help! help!"

Our movements were suspended for an instant; we listened. It might be only a singing in the ear, but it seemed to me as if a cry answered the cry from Conseil.

"Did you hear?" I murmured.

"Yes! Yes!"

And Conseil gave one more despairing cry.

This time there was no mistake! A human voice responded to ours! Was it the voice of another unfortunate creature, abandoned in the middle of the ocean, some other victim of the shock sustained by the vessel? Or rather was it a boat from the frigate, that was hailing us in the darkness?

Conseil made a last effort, and, leaning on my shoulder, while I struck out in a desperate effort, he raised himself half out of the water, then fell back exhausted.

"What did you see?"

"I saw——" murmured he; "I saw—but do not talk—reserve all your strength!"

What had he seen? Then, I know not why, the thought of the monster came into my head for the first time! But that voice! The time is past for Jonahs to take refuge in whales' bellies! However, Conseil was towing me again. He raised his head sometimes, looked before us, and uttered a cry of recognition, which was responded to by a voice that came nearer and nearer. I scarcely heard it. My strength was exhausted; my fingers stiffened; my hand afforded me support no longer; my mouth, convulsively opening, filled with salt water. Cold crept over me. I raised my head for the last time, then I sank.

At this moment a hard body struck me. I clung to it: then I felt that I was being drawn up, that I was brought to the surface of the water, that my chest collapsed—I fainted.

It is certain that I soon came to, thanks to the vigorous rubbings that I received. I half opened my eyes.

"Conseil!" I murmured.

"Does master call me?" asked Conseil.

Just then, by the waning light of the moon which was sinking down to the horizon, I saw a face which was not Conseil's and which I immediately recognised.

"Ned!" I cried.

"The same, sir, who is seeking his prize!" replied the Canadian.

"Were you thrown into the sea by the shock to the frigate?"

"Yes, Professor; but more fortunate than you, I was able to find a footing almost directly upon a floating island."

"An island?"

"Or, more correctly speaking, on our gigantic narwhal."

"Explain yourself, Ned!"

"Only I soon found out why my harpoon had not entered its skin and was blunted."

"Why, Ned, why?"

"Because, Professor, that beast is made of sheet iron."

The Canadian's last words produced a sudden revolution in my brain. I wriggled myself quickly to the top of the being, or object, half out of the water, which served us for a refuge. I kicked it. It was evidently a hard, impenetrable body, and not the soft substance that forms the bodies of the great marine mammalia. But this hard body might be a bony covering, like that of the antediluvian animals; and I should be free to class this monster among amphibious reptiles, such as tortoises or alligators.

Well, no! the blackish back that supported me was smooth, polished, without scales. The blow produced a metallic sound; and, incredible though it may be, it seemed, I might say, as if it was made of riveted plates.

There was no doubt about it! This monster, this natural phenomenon that had puzzled the learned world, and over thrown and misled the imagination of seamen of both hemispheres, it must be owned was a still more astonishing phenomenon, inasmuch as it was a simply human construction.

We had no time to lose, however. We were lying upon the back of a sort of submarine boat, which appeared (as far as I could judge) like a huge fish of steel. Ned Land's mind was made up on this point. Conseil and I could only agree with him.

Just then a bubbling began at the back of this strange thing (which was evidently propelled by a screw), and it began to move. We had only just time to seize hold of the upper part, which rose about seven feet out of the water, and happily its speed was not great.

"As long as it sails horizontally," muttered Ned Land, "I do not mind; but, if it takes a fancy to dive, I would not give two straws for my life."

The Canadian might have said still less. It became really necessary to communicate with the beings, whatever they were, shut up inside the machine. I searched all over the outside for an aperture, a panel, or a manhole, to use a technical expression; but the lines of the iron rivets, solidly driven into the joints of the iron plates, were clear and uniform. Besides, the moon disappeared then, and left us in total darkness.

At last this long night passed. My indistinct remembrance prevents my describing all the impressions it made. I can only recall one circumstance. During some lulls of the wind and sea, I fancied I heard several times vague sounds, a sort of fugitive harmony produced by words of command. What was, then, the mystery of this submarine craft, of which the whole world vainly sought an explanation? What kind of beings existed in this strange boat? What mechanical agent caused its prodigious speed?

Daybreak appeared. The morning mists surrounded us, but they soon cleared off. I was about to examine the hull, which formed on deck a kind of horizontal platform, when I felt it gradually sinking.

"Oh! confound it!" cried Ned Land, kicking the resounding plate. "Open, you inhospitable rascals!"

Happily the sinking movement ceased. Suddenly a noise, like iron works violently pushed aside, came from the interior of the boat. One iron plate was moved, a man appeared, uttered an odd cry, and disappeared immediately.

Some moments after, eight strong men, with masked faces, appeared noiselessly, and drew us down into their formidable machine.

CHAPTER VIII. MOBILIS IN MOBILI

This forcible abduction, so roughly carried out, was accomplished with the rapidity of lightning. I shivered all over. Whom had we to deal with? No doubt some new sort of pirates, who explored the sea in their own way. Hardly had the narrow panel closed upon me, when I was enveloped in darkness. My eyes, dazzled with the outer light, could distinguish nothing. I felt my naked feet cling to the rungs of an iron ladder. Ned Land and Conseil, firmly seized, followed me. At the bottom of the ladder, a door opened, and shut after us immediately with a bang.

We were alone. Where, I could not say, hardly imagine. All was black, and such a dense black that, after some minutes, my eyes had not been able to discern even the faintest glimmer.

Meanwhile, Ned Land, furious at these proceedings, gave free vent to his indignation.

"Confound it!" cried he, "here are people who come up to the Scotch for hospitality. They only just miss being cannibals. I should not be surprised at it, but I declare that they shall not eat me without my protesting."

"Calm yourself, friend Ned, calm yourself," replied Conseil, quietly. "Do not cry out before you are hurt. We are not quite done for yet."

"Not quite," sharply replied the Canadian, "but pretty near, at all events. Things look black. Happily, my bowie knife I have still, and I can always see well enough to use it. The first of these pirates who lays a hand on me——"

"Do not excite yourself, Ned," I said to the harpooner, "and do not compromise us by useless violence. Who knows that they will not listen to us? Let us rather try to find out where we are."

I groped about. In five steps I came to an iron wall, made of plates bolted together. Then turning back I struck against a wooden table, near which were ranged several stools. The boards of this prison were concealed under a thick mat, which deadened the noise of the feet. The bare walls revealed no trace of window or door. Conseil, going round the reverse way, met me, and we went back to the middle of the cabin, which measured about twenty feet by ten. As to its height, Ned Land, in spite of his own great height, could not measure it.

Half an hour had already passed without our situation being bettered, when the dense darkness suddenly gave way to extreme light. Our prison was suddenly lighted, that is to say, it became filled with a luminous matter, so strong that I could not bear it at first. In its whiteness and intensity I recognised that electric light which played round the submarine boat like a magnificent phenomenon of phosphorescence. After shutting my eyes involuntarily, I opened them, and saw that this luminous agent came from a half globe, unpolished, placed in the roof of the cabin.

"At last one can see," cried Ned Land, who, knife in hand, stood on the defensive.

"Yes," said I; "but we are still in the dark about ourselves."

"Let master have patience," said the imperturbable Conseil.

The sudden lighting of the cabin enabled me to examine it minutely. It only contained a table and five stools. The invisible door might be hermetically sealed. No noise was heard. All seemed dead in the interior of this boat. Did it move, did it float on the surface of the ocean, or did it dive into its depths? I could not guess.

A noise of bolts was now heard, the door opened, and two men appeared.

One was short, very muscular, broad-shouldered, with robust limbs, strong head, an abundance of black hair, thick moustache, a quick penetrating look, and the vivacity which characterises the population of Southern France.

The second stranger merits a more detailed description. I made out his prevailing qualities directly: self-confidence—because his head was well set on his shoulders, and his black eyes looked around with cold assurance; calmness—for his skin, rather pale, showed his coolness of blood; energy— evinced by the rapid contraction of his lofty brows; and courage—because his deep breathing denoted great power of lungs.

Whether this person was thirty-five or fifty years of age, I could not say. He was tall, had a large forehead, straight nose, a clearly cut mouth, beautiful teeth, with fine taper hands, indicative of a highly nervous temperament. This man was certainly the most admirable specimen I had ever met. One particular feature was his eyes, rather far from each other, and which could take in nearly a quarter of the horizon at once.

This faculty—(I verified it later)—gave him a range of vision far superior to Ned Land's. When this stranger fixed upon an object, his eyebrows met, his large eyelids closed around so as to contract the range of his vision, and he looked as if he magnified the objects lessened by distance, as if he pierced those sheets of water so opaque to our eyes, and as if he read the very depths of the seas.

The two strangers, with caps made from the fur of the sea otter, and shod with sea boots of seal's skin, were dressed in clothes of a particular texture, which allowed free movement of the limbs. The taller of the two, evidently the chief on board, examined us with great attention, without saying a word; then, turning to his companion, talked with him in an unknown tongue. It was a sonorous, harmonious, and flexible dialect, the vowels seeming to admit of very varied accentuation.

The other replied by a shake of the head, and added two or three perfectly incomprehensible words. Then he seemed to question me by a look.

I replied in good French that I did not know his language; but he seemed not to understand me, and my situation became more embarrassing.

"If master were to tell our story," said Conseil, "perhaps these gentlemen may understand some words."

I began to tell our adventures, articulating each syllable clearly, and without omitting one single detail. I announced our names and rank, introducing in person Professor Aronnax, his servant Conseil, and master Ned Land, the harpooner.

The man with the soft calm eyes listened to me quietly, even politely, and with extreme attention; but nothing in his countenance indicated that he had understood my story. When I finished, he said not a word.

There remained one resource, to speak English. Perhaps they would know this almost universal language. I knew it—as well as the German language— well enough to read it fluently, but not to speak it correctly. But, anyhow, we must make ourselves understood.

"Go on in your turn," I said to the harpooner; "speak your best Anglo-Saxon, and try to do better than I."

Ned did not beg off, and recommenced our story.

To his great disgust, the harpooner did not seem to have made himself more intelligible than I had. Our visitors did not stir. They evidently understood neither the language of England nor of France.

Very much embarrassed, after having vainly exhausted our speaking resources, I knew not what part to take, when Conseil said:

"If master will permit me, I will relate it in German."

But in spite of the elegant terms and good accent of the narrator, the German language had no success. At last, nonplussed, I tried to remember my first lessons, and to narrate our adventures in Latin, but with no better success. This last attempt being of no avail, the two strangers exchanged some words in their unknown language, and retired.

The door shut.

"It is an infamous shame," cried Ned Land, who broke out for the twentieth time. "We speak to those rogues in French, English, German, and Latin, and not one of them has the politeness to answer!"

"Calm yourself," I said to the impetuous Ned; "anger will do no good."

"But do you see, Professor," replied our irascible companion, "that we shall absolutely die of hunger in this iron cage?"

"Bah!" said Conseil, philosophically; "we can hold out some time yet."

"My friends," I said, "we must not despair. We have been worse off than this. Do me the favour to wait a little before forming an opinion upon the commander and crew of this boat."

"My opinion is formed," replied Ned Land, sharply. "They are rascals."

"Good! and from what country?"

"From the land of rogues!"

"My brave Ned, that country is not clearly indicated on the map of the world; but I admit that the nationality of the two strangers is hard to determine. Neither English, French, nor German, that is quite certain. However, I am inclined to think that the commander and his companion were born in low latitudes. There is southern blood in them. But I cannot decide by their appearance whether they are Spaniards, Turks, Arabians, or Indians. As to their language, it is quite incomprehensible."

"There is the disadvantage of not knowing all languages," said Conseil, "or the disadvantage of not having one universal language."

As he said these words, the door opened. A steward entered. He brought us clothes, coats and trousers, made of a stuff I did not know. I hastened to dress myself, and my companions followed my example. During that time, the steward—dumb, perhaps deaf—had arranged the table, and laid three plates.

"This is something like!" said Conseil.

"Bah!" said the angry harpooner, "what do you suppose they eat here? Tortoise liver, filleted shark, and beef steaks from seadogs."

"We shall see," said Conseil.

The dishes, of bell metal, were placed on the table, and we took our places. Undoubtedly we had to do with civilised people, and, had it not been for the electric light which flooded us, I could have fancied I was in the dining-room of the Adelphi Hotel at Liverpool, or at the Grand Hotel in Paris. I must say, however, that there was neither bread nor wine. The water was fresh and clear, but it was water and did not suit Ned Land's taste. Amongst the dishes which were brought to us, I recognised several fish delicately dressed; but of some, although excellent, I could give no opinion, neither could I tell to what kingdom they belonged, whether animal or vegetable. As to the dinner-service, it was elegant, and in perfect taste. Each utensil—spoon, fork, knife, plate—had a letter engraved on it, with a motto above it, of which this is an exact facsimile:

MOBILIS IN MOBILI N

The letter N was no doubt the initial of the name of the enigmatical person who commanded at the bottom of the seas.

Ned and Conseil did not reflect much. They devoured the food, and I did likewise. I was, besides, reassured as to our fate; and it seemed evident that our hosts would not let us die of want.

However, everything has an end, everything passes away, even the hunger of people who have not eaten for fifteen hours. Our appetites satisfied, we felt overcome with sleep.

"Faith! I shall sleep well," said Conseil.

"So shall I," replied Ned Land.

My two companions stretched themselves on the cabin carpet, and were soon sound asleep. For my own part, too many thoughts crowded my brain, too many insoluble questions pressed upon me, too many fancies kept my eyes half open. Where were we? What strange power carried us on? I felt—or rather fancied I felt—the machine sinking down to the lowest beds of the sea. Dreadful nightmares beset me; I saw in these mysterious asylums a world of unknown animals, amongst which this submarine boat seemed to be of the same kind, living, moving, and formidable as they. Then my brain grew calmer, my imagination wandered into vague unconsciousness, and I soon fell into a deep sleep.

CHAPTER IX. NED LAND'S TEMPERS

How long we slept I do not know; but our sleep must have lasted long, for it rested us completely from our fatigues. I woke first. My companions had not moved, and were still stretched in their corner.

Hardly roused from my somewhat hard couch, I felt my brain freed, my mind clear. I then began an attentive examination of our cell. Nothing was changed inside. The prison was still a prison—the prisoners, prisoners. However, the steward, during our sleep, had cleared the table. I breathed with difficulty. The heavy air seemed to oppress my lungs. Although the cell was large, we had evidently consumed a great part of the oxygen that it contained. Indeed, each man consumes, in one hour, the oxygen contained in more than 176 pints of air, and this air, charged (as then) with a nearly equal quantity of carbonic acid, becomes unbreathable.

It became necessary to renew the atmosphere of our prison, and no doubt the whole in the submarine boat. That gave rise to a question in my mind. How would the commander of this floating dwelling-place proceed? Would he obtain air by chemical means, in getting by heat the oxygen contained in chlorate of potash, and in absorbing carbonic acid by caustic potash? Or—a more convenient, economical, and consequently more probable alternative—would he be satisfied to rise and take breath at the surface of the water, like a whale, and so renew for twenty-four hours the atmospheric provision?

In fact, I was already obliged to increase my respirations to eke out of this cell the little oxygen it contained, when suddenly I was refreshed by a current of pure air, and perfumed with saline emanations. It was an invigorating sea breeze, charged with iodine. I opened my mouth wide, and my lungs saturated themselves with fresh particles.

At the same time I felt the boat rolling. The iron-plated monster had evidently just risen to the surface of the ocean to breathe, after the fashion of whales. I found out from that the mode of ventilating the boat.

When I had inhaled this air freely, I sought the conduit pipe, which conveyed to us the beneficial whiff, and I was not long in finding it. Above the door was a ventilator, through which volumes of fresh air renewed the impoverished atmosphere of the cell.

I was making my observations, when Ned and Conseil awoke almost at the same time, under the influence of this reviving air. They rubbed their eyes, stretched themselves, and were on their feet in an instant.

"Did master sleep well?" asked Conseil, with his usual politeness.

"Very well, my brave boy. And you, Mr. Land?"

"Soundly, Professor. But, I don't know if I am right or not, there seems to be a sea breeze!"

A seaman could not be mistaken, and I told the Canadian all that had passed during his sleep.

"Good!" said he. "That accounts for those roarings we heard, when the supposed narwhal sighted the Abraham Lincoln."

"Quite so, Master Land; it was taking breath."

"Only, Mr. Aronnax, I have no idea what o'clock it is, unless it is dinner-time."

"Dinner-time! my good fellow? Say rather breakfast-time, for we certainly have begun another day."

"So," said Conseil, "we have slept twenty-four hours?"

"That is my opinion."

"I will not contradict you," replied Ned Land. "But, dinner or breakfast, the steward will be welcome, whichever he brings."

"Master Land, we must conform to the rules on board, and I suppose our appetites are in advance of the dinner hour."

"That is just like you, friend Conseil," said Ned, impatiently. "You are never out of temper, always calm; you would return thanks before grace, and die of hunger rather than complain!"

Time was getting on, and we were fearfully hungry; and this time the steward did not appear. It was rather too long to leave us, if they really had good intentions towards us. Ned Land, tormented by the cravings of hunger, got still more angry; and, notwithstanding his promise, I dreaded an explosion when he found himself with one of the crew.

For two hours more Ned Land's temper increased; he cried, he shouted, but in vain. The walls were deaf. There was no sound to be heard in the boat; all was still as death. It did not move, for I should have felt the trembling motion of the hull under the influence of the screw. Plunged in the depths of the waters, it belonged no longer to earth: this silence was dreadful.

I felt terrified, Conseil was calm, Ned Land roared.

Just then a noise was heard outside. Steps sounded on the metal flags. The locks were turned, the door opened, and the steward appeared.

Before I could rush forward to stop him, the Canadian had thrown him down, and held him by the throat. The steward was choking under the grip of his powerful hand.

Conseil was already trying to unclasp the harpooner's hand from his half-suffocated victim, and I was going to fly to the rescue, when suddenly I was nailed to the spot by hearing these words in French:

"Be quiet, Master Land; and you, Professor, will you be so good as to listen to me?"

CHAPTER X. THE MAN OF THE SEAS

It was the commander of the vessel who thus spoke.

At these words, Ned Land rose suddenly. The steward, nearly strangled, tottered out on a sign from his master. But such was the power of the commander on board, that not a gesture betrayed the resentment which this man must have felt towards the Canadian. Conseil interested in spite of himself, I stupefied, awaited in silence the result of this scene.

The commander, leaning against the corner of a table with his arms folded, scanned us with profound attention. Did he hesitate to speak? Did he regret the words which he had just spoken in French? One might almost think so.

After some moments of silence, which not one of us dreamed of breaking, "Gentlemen," said he, in a calm and penetrating voice, "I speak French, English, German, and Latin equally well. I could, therefore, have answered you at our first interview, but I wished to know you first, then to reflect. The story told by each one, entirely agreeing in the main points, convinced me of your identity. I know now that chance has brought before me M. Pierre Aronnax, Professor of Natural History at the Museum of Paris, entrusted with a scientific mission abroad, Conseil, his servant, and Ned Land, of Canadian origin, harpooner on board the frigate Abraham Lincoln of the navy of the United States of America."

I bowed assent. It was not a question that the commander put to me. Therefore there was no answer to be made. This man expressed himself with perfect ease, without any accent. His sentences were well turned, his words clear, and his fluency of speech remarkable. Yet, I did not recognise in him a fellow-countryman.

He continued the conversation in these terms:

"You have doubtless thought, sir, that I have delayed long in paying you this second visit. The reason is that, your identity recognised, I wished to weigh maturely what part to act towards you. I have hesitated much. Most annoying circumstances have brought you into the presence of a man who has broken all the ties of humanity. You have come to trouble my existence."

"Unintentionally!" said I.

"Unintentionally?" replied the stranger, raising his voice a little. "Was it unintentionally that the Abraham Lincoln pursued me all over the seas? Was it unintentionally that you took passage in this frigate? Was it unintentionally that your cannon-balls rebounded off the plating of my vessel? Was it unintentionally that Mr. Ned Land struck me with his harpoon?"

I detected a restrained irritation in these words. But to these recriminations I had a very natural answer to make, and I made it.

"Sir," said I, "no doubt you are ignorant of the discussions which have taken place concerning you in America and Europe. You do not know that divers accidents, caused by collisions with your submarine machine, have excited public feeling in the two continents. I omit the theories without number by which it was sought to explain that of which you alone possess the secret. But you must understand that, in pursuing you over the high seas of the Pacific, the Abraham Lincoln believed itself to be chasing some powerful sea-monster, of which it was necessary to rid the ocean at any price."

A half-smile curled the lips of the commander: then, in a calmer tone:

"M. Aronnax," he replied, "dare you affirm that your frigate would not as soon have pursued and cannonaded a submarine boat as a monster?"

This question embarrassed me, for certainly Captain Farragut might not have hesitated. He might have thought it his duty to destroy a contrivance of this kind, as he would a gigantic narwhal.

"You understand then, sir," continued the stranger, "that I have the right to treat you as enemies?"

I answered nothing, purposely. For what good would it be to discuss such a proposition, when force could destroy the best arguments?

"I have hesitated some time," continued the commander; "nothing obliged me to show you hospitality. If I chose to separate myself from you, I should have no interest in seeing you again; I could place you upon the deck of this vessel which has served you as a refuge, I could sink beneath the waters, and forget that you had ever existed. Would not that be my right?"

"It might be the right of a savage," I answered, "but not that of a civilised man."

"Professor," replied the commander, quickly, "I am not what you call a civilised man! I have done with society entirely, for reasons which I alone have the right of appreciating. I do not, therefore, obey its laws, and I desire you never to allude to them before me again!"

This was said plainly. A flash of anger and disdain kindled in the eyes of the Unknown, and I had a glimpse of a terrible past in the life of this man. Not only had he put himself beyond the pale of human laws, but he had made himself independent of them, free in the strictest acceptation of the word, quite beyond their reach! Who then would dare to pursue him at the bottom of the sea, when, on its surface, he defied all attempts made against him?

What vessel could resist the shock of his submarine monitor? What cuirass, however thick, could withstand the blows of his spur? No man could demand from him an account of his actions; God, if he believed in one—his conscience, if he had one—were the sole judges to whom he was answerable.

These reflections crossed my mind rapidly, whilst the stranger personage was silent, absorbed, and as if wrapped up in himself. I regarded him with fear mingled with interest, as, doubtless, OEdiphus regarded the Sphinx.

After rather a long silence, the commander resumed the conversation.

"I have hesitated," said he, "but I have thought that my interest might be reconciled with that pity to which every human being has a right. You will remain on board my vessel, since fate has cast you there. You will be free; and, in exchange for this liberty, I shall only impose one single condition. Your word of honour to submit to it will suffice."

"Speak, sir," I answered. "I suppose this condition is one which a man of honour may accept?"

"Yes, sir; it is this: It is possible that certain events, unforeseen, may oblige me to consign you to your cabins for some hours or some days, as the case may be. As I desire never to use violence, I expect from you, more than all the others, a passive obedience. In thus acting, I take all the responsibility: I acquit you entirely, for I make it an impossibility for you to see what ought not to be seen. Do you accept this condition?"

Then things took place on board which, to say the least, were singular, and which ought not to be seen by people who were not placed beyond the pale of social laws. Amongst the surprises which the future was preparing for me, this might not be the least.

"We accept," I answered; "only I will ask your permission, sir, to address one question to you—one only."

"Speak, sir."

"You said that we should be free on board."

"Entirely."

"I ask you, then, what you mean by this liberty?"

"Just the liberty to go, to come, to see, to observe even all that passes here save under rare circumstances—the liberty, in short, which we enjoy ourselves, my companions and I."

It was evident that we did not understand one another.

"Pardon me, sir," I resumed, "but this liberty is only what every prisoner has of pacing his prison. It cannot suffice us."

"It must suffice you, however."

"What! we must renounce for ever seeing our country, our friends, our relations again?"

"Yes, sir. But to renounce that unendurable worldly yoke which men believe to be liberty is not perhaps so painful as you think."

"Well," exclaimed Ned Land, "never will I give my word of honour not to try to escape."

"I did not ask you for your word of honour, Master Land," answered the commander, coldly.

"Sir," I replied, beginning to get angry in spite of my self, "you abuse your situation towards us; it is cruelty."

"No, sir, it is clemency. You are my prisoners of war. I keep you, when I could, by a word, plunge you into the depths of the ocean. You attacked me. You came to surprise a secret which no man in the world must penetrate—the secret of my whole existence. And you think that I am going to send you back to that world which must know me no more? Never! In retaining you, it is not you whom I guard—it is myself."

These words indicated a resolution taken on the part of the commander, against which no arguments would prevail.

"So, sir," I rejoined, "you give us simply the choice between life and death?"

"Simply."

"My friends," said I, "to a question thus put, there is nothing to answer. But no word of honour binds us to the master of this vessel."

"None, sir," answered the Unknown.

Then, in a gentler tone, he continued:

"Now, permit me to finish what I have to say to you. I know you, M. Aronnax. You and your companions will not, perhaps, have so much to complain of in the chance which has bound you to my fate. You will find amongst the books which are my favourite study the work which you have published on `the depths of the sea.' I have often read it. You have carried out your work as far as terrestrial science permitted you. But you do not know all—you have not seen all. Let me tell you then, Professor, that you will not regret the time passed on board my vessel. You are going to visit the land of marvels."

These words of the commander had a great effect upon me. I cannot deny it. My weak point was touched; and I forgot, for a moment, that the contemplation of these sublime subjects was not worth the loss of liberty. Besides, I trusted to the future to decide this grave question. So I contented myself with saying:

"By what name ought I to address you?"

"Sir," replied the commander, "I am nothing to you but Captain Nemo; and you and your companions are nothing to me but the passengers of the Nautilus."

Captain Nemo called. A steward appeared. The captain gave him his orders in that strange language which I did not understand. Then, turning towards the Canadian and Conseil:

"A repast awaits you in your cabin," said he. "Be so good as to follow this man.

"And now, M. Aronnax, our breakfast is ready. Permit me to lead the way."

"I am at your service, Captain."

I followed Captain Nemo; and as soon as I had passed through the door, I found myself in a kind of passage lighted by electricity, similar to the waist of a ship. After we had proceeded a dozen yards, a second door opened before me.

I then entered a dining-room, decorated and furnished in severe taste. High oaken sideboards, inlaid with ebony, stood at the two extremities of the room, and upon their shelves glittered china, porcelain, and glass of inestimable value. The plate on the table sparkled in the rays which the luminous ceiling shed around, while the light was tempered and softened by exquisite paintings.

In the centre of the room was a table richly laid out. Captain Nemo indicated the place I was to occupy.

The breakfast consisted of a certain number of dishes, the contents of which were furnished by the sea alone; and I was ignorant of the nature and mode of preparation of some of them. I acknowledged that they were good, but they had a peculiar flavour, which I easily became accustomed to. These different aliments appeared to me to be rich in phosphorus, and I thought they must have a marine origin.

Captain Nemo looked at me. I asked him no questions, but he guessed my thoughts, and answered of his own accord the questions which I was burning to address to him.

"The greater part of these dishes are unknown to you," he said to me. "However, you may partake of them without fear. They are wholesome and nourishing. For a long time I have renounced the food of the earth, and I am never ill now. My crew, who are healthy, are fed on the same food."

"So," said I, "all these eatables are the produce of the sea?"

"Yes, Professor, the sea supplies all my wants. Sometimes I cast my nets in tow, and I draw them in ready to break. Sometimes I hunt in the midst of this element, which appears to be inaccessible to man, and quarry the game which dwells in my submarine forests. My flocks, like those of Neptune's old shepherds, graze fearlessly in the immense prairies of the ocean. I have a vast property there, which I cultivate myself, and which is always sown by the hand of the Creator of all things."

"I can understand perfectly, sir, that your nets furnish excellent fish for your table; I can understand also that you hunt aquatic game in your submarine forests; but I cannot understand at all how a particle of meat, no matter how small, can figure in your bill of fare."

"This, which you believe to be meat, Professor, is nothing else than fillet of turtle. Here are also some dolphins' livers, which you take to be ragout of pork. My cook is a clever fellow, who excels in dressing these various products of the ocean. Taste all these dishes. Here is a preserve of sea-cucumber, which a Malay would declare to be unrivalled in the world; here is a cream, of which the milk has been furnished by the cetacea, and the sugar by the great fucus of the North Sea; and, lastly, permit me to offer you some preserve of anemones, which is equal to that of the most delicious fruits."

I tasted, more from curiosity than as a connoisseur, whilst Captain Nemo enchanted me with his extraordinary stories.

"You like the sea, Captain?"

"Yes; I love it! The sea is everything. It covers seven tenths of the terrestrial globe. Its breath is pure and healthy. It is an immense desert, where man is never lonely, for he feels life stirring on all sides. The sea is only the embodiment of a supernatural and wonderful existence. It is nothing but love and emotion; it is the `Living Infinite,' as one of your poets has said. In fact, Professor, Nature manifests herself in it by her three kingdoms—mineral, vegetable, and animal. The sea is the vast reservoir of Nature. The globe began with sea, so to speak; and who knows if it will not end with it? In it is supreme tranquillity. The sea does not belong to despots. Upon its surface men can still exercise unjust laws, fight, tear one another to pieces, and be carried away with terrestrial horrors. But at thirty feet below its level, their reign ceases, their influence is quenched, and their power disappears. Ah! sir, live—live in the bosom of the waters! There only is independence! There I recognise no masters! There I am free!"

Captain Nemo suddenly became silent in the midst of this enthusiasm, by which he was quite carried away. For a few moments he paced up and down, much agitated. Then he became more calm, regained his accustomed coldness of expression, and turning towards me:

"Now, Professor," said he, "if you wish to go over the Nautilus, I am at your service."

Captain Nemo rose. I followed him. A double door, contrived at the back of the dining-room, opened, and I entered a room equal in dimensions to that which I had just quitted.

It was a library. High pieces of furniture, of black violet ebony inlaid with brass, supported upon their wide shelves a great number of books uniformly bound. They followed the shape of the room, terminating at the lower part in huge divans, covered with brown leather, which were curved, to afford the greatest comfort. Light movable desks, made to slide in and out at will, allowed one to rest one's book while reading. In the centre stood an immense table, covered with pamphlets, amongst which were some newspapers, already of old date. The electric light flooded everything; it was shed from four unpolished globes half sunk in the volutes of the ceiling. I looked with real admiration at this room, so ingeniously fitted up, and I could scarcely believe my eyes.

"Captain Nemo," said I to my host, who had just thrown himself on one of the divans, "this is a library which would do honour to more than one of the continental palaces, and I am absolutely astounded when I consider that it can follow you to the bottom of the seas."

"Where could one find greater solitude or silence, Professor?" replied Captain Nemo. "Did your study in the Museum afford you such perfect quiet?"

"No, sir; and I must confess that it is a very poor one after yours. You must have six or seven thousand volumes here."

"Twelve thousand, M. Aronnax. These are the only ties which bind me to the earth. But I had done with the world on the day when my Nautilus plunged for the first time beneath the waters. That day I bought my last volumes, my last pamphlets, my last papers, and from that time I wish to think that men no longer think or write. These books, Professor, are at your service besides, and you can make use of them freely."

I thanked Captain Nemo, and went up to the shelves of the library. Works on science, morals, and literature abounded in every language; but I did not see one single work on political economy; that subject appeared to be strictly proscribed. Strange to say, all these books were irregularly arranged, in whatever language they were written; and this medley proved that the Captain of the Nautilus must have read indiscriminately the books which he took up by chance.

"Sir," said I to the Captain, "I thank you for having placed this library at my disposal. It contains treasures of science, and I shall profit by them."

"This room is not only a library," said Captain Nemo, "it is also a smoking-room."

"A smoking-room!" I cried. "Then one may smoke on board?"

"Certainly."

"Then, sir, I am forced to believe that you have kept up a communication with Havannah."

"Not any," answered the Captain. "Accept this cigar, M. Aronnax; and, though it does not come from Havannah, you will be pleased with it, if you are a connoisseur."

I took the cigar which was offered me; its shape recalled the London ones, but it seemed to be made of leaves of gold. I lighted it at a little brazier, which was supported upon an elegant bronze stem, and drew the first whiffs with the delight of a lover of smoking who has not smoked for two days.

"It is excellent, but it is not tobacco."

"No!" answered the Captain, "this tobacco comes neither from Havannah nor from the East. It is a kind of sea-weed, rich in nicotine, with which the sea provides me, but somewhat sparingly."

At that moment Captain Nemo opened a door which stood opposite to that by which I had entered the library, and I passed into an immense drawing-room splendidly lighted.

It was a vast, four-sided room, thirty feet long, eighteen wide, and fifteen high. A luminous ceiling, decorated with light arabesques, shed a soft clear light over all the marvels accumulated in this museum. For it was in fact a museum, in which an intelligent and prodigal hand had gathered all the treasures of nature and art, with the artistic confusion which distinguishes a painter's studio.

Thirty first-rate pictures, uniformly framed, separated by bright drapery, ornamented the walls, which were hung with tapestry of severe design. I saw works of great value, the greater part of which I had admired in the special collections of Europe, and in the exhibitions of paintings. The several schools of the old masters were represented by a Madonna of Raphael, a Virgin of Leonardo da Vinci, a nymph of Corregio, a woman of Titan, an Adoration of Veronese, an Assumption of Murillo, a portrait of Holbein, a monk of Velasquez, a martyr of Ribera, a fair of Rubens, two Flemish landscapes of Teniers, three little "genre" pictures of Gerard Dow, Metsu, and Paul Potter, two specimens of Gericault and Prudhon, and some sea-pieces of Backhuysen and Vernet. Amongst the works of modern painters were pictures with the signatures of Delacroix, Ingres, Decamps, Troyon, Meissonier, Daubigny, etc.; and some admirable statues in marble and bronze, after the finest antique models, stood upon pedestals in the corners of this magnificent museum. Amazement, as the Captain of the Nautilus had predicted, had already begun to take possession of me.

"Professor," said this strange man, "you must excuse the unceremonious way in which I receive you, and the disorder of this room."

"Sir," I answered, "without seeking to know who you are, I recognise in you an artist."

"An amateur, nothing more, sir. Formerly I loved to collect these beautiful works created by the hand of man. I sought them greedily, and ferreted them out indefatigably, and I have been able to bring together some objects of great value. These are my last souvenirs of that world which is dead to me. In my eyes, your modern artists are already old; they have two or three thousand years of existence; I confound them in my own mind. Masters have no age."

"And these musicians?" said I, pointing out some works of Weber, Rossini, Mozart, Beethoven, Haydn, Meyerbeer, Herold, Wagner, Auber, Gounod, and a number of others, scattered over a large model piano-organ which occupied one of the panels of the drawing-room.

"These musicians," replied Captain Nemo, "are the contemporaries of Orpheus; for in the memory of the dead all chronological differences are effaced; and I am dead, Professor; as much dead as those of your friends who are sleeping six feet under the earth!"

Captain Nemo was silent, and seemed lost in a profound reverie. I contemplated him with deep interest, analysing in silence the strange expression of his countenance. Leaning on his elbow against an angle of a costly mosaic table, he no longer saw me,—he had forgotten my presence.

I did not disturb this reverie, and continued my observation of the curiosities which enriched this drawing-room.

Under elegant glass cases, fixed by copper rivets, were classed and labelled the most precious productions of the sea which had ever been presented to the eye of a naturalist. My delight as a professor may be conceived.

The division containing the zoophytes presented the most curious specimens of the two groups of polypi and echinodermes. In the first group, the tubipores, were gorgones arranged like a fan, soft sponges of Syria, ises of the Moluccas, pennatules, an admirable virgularia of the Norwegian seas, variegated unbellulairae, alcyonariae, a whole series of madrepores, which my master Milne Edwards has so cleverly classified, amongst which I remarked some wonderful flabellinae oculinae of the Island of Bourbon, the "Neptune's car" of the Antilles, superb varieties of corals—in short, every species of those curious polypi of which entire islands are formed, which will one day become continents. Of the echinodermes, remarkable for their coating of spines, asteri, sea-stars, pantacrinae, comatules, asterophons, echini, holothuri, etc., represented individually a complete collection of this group.

A somewhat nervous conchyliologist would certainly have fainted before other more numerous cases, in which were classified the specimens of molluscs. It was a collection of inestimable value, which time fails me to describe minutely. Amongst these specimens I will quote from memory only the elegant royal hammer-fish of the Indian Ocean, whose regular white spots stood out brightly on a red and brown ground, an imperial spondyle, bright-coloured, bristling with spines, a rare specimen in the European museums—(I estimated its value at not less than L1000); a common hammer-fish of the seas of New Holland, which is only procured with difficulty; exotic buccardia of Senegal; fragile white bivalve shells, which a breath might shatter like a soap-bubble; several varieties of the aspirgillum of Java, a kind of calcareous tube, edged with leafy folds, and much debated by amateurs; a whole series of trochi, some a greenish-yellow, found in the American seas, others a reddish-brown, natives of Australian waters; others from the Gulf of Mexico, remarkable for their imbricated shell; stellari found in the Southern Seas; and last, the rarest of all, the magnificent spur of New Zealand; and every description of delicate and fragile shells to which science has given appropriate names.

Apart, in separate compartments, were spread out chaplets of pearls of the greatest beauty, which reflected the electric light in little sparks of fire; pink pearls, torn from the pinna-marina of the Red Sea; green pearls of the haliotyde iris; yellow, blue and black pearls, the curious productions of the divers molluscs of every ocean, and certain mussels of the water-courses of the North; lastly, several specimens of inestimable value which had been gathered from the rarest pintadines. Some of these pearls were larger than a pigeon's egg, and were worth as much, and more than that which the traveller Tavernier sold to the Shah of Persia for three millions, and surpassed the one in the possession of the Imaum of Muscat, which I had believed to be unrivalled in the world.

Therefore, to estimate the value of this collection was simply impossible. Captain Nemo must have expended millions in the acquirement of these various specimens, and I was thinking what source he could have drawn from, to have been able thus to gratify his fancy for collecting, when I was interrupted by these words: "You are examining my shells, Professor? Unquestionably they must be interesting to a naturalist; but for me they have a far greater charm, for I have collected them all with my own hand, and there is not a sea on the face of the globe which has escaped my researches."

"I can understand, Captain, the delight of wandering about in the midst of such riches. You are one of those who have collected their treasures themselves. No museum in Europe possesses such a collection of the produce of the ocean. But if I exhaust all my admiration upon it, I shall have none left for the vessel which carries it. I do not wish to pry into your secrets: but I must confess that this Nautilus, with the motive power which is confined in it, the contrivances which enable it to be worked, the powerful agent which propels it, all excite my curiosity to the highest pitch. I see suspended on the walls of this room instruments of whose use I am ignorant."

"You will find these same instruments in my own room, Professor, where I shall have much pleasure in explaining their use to you. But first come and inspect the cabin which is set apart for your own use. You must see how you will be accommodated on board the Nautilus."

I followed Captain Nemo who, by one of the doors opening from each panel of the drawing-room, regained the waist. He conducted me towards the bow, and there I found, not a cabin, but an elegant room, with a bed, dressing-table, and several other pieces of excellent furniture.

I could only thank my host.

"Your room adjoins mine," said he, opening a door, "and mine opens into the drawing-room that we have just quitted."

I entered the Captain's room: it had a severe, almost a monkish aspect. A small iron bedstead, a table, some articles for the toilet; the whole lighted by a skylight. No comforts, the strictest necessaries only.

Captain Nemo pointed to a seat.

"Be so good as to sit down," he said. I seated myself, and he began thus:

CHAPTER XI. ALL BY ELECTRICITY

"Sir," said Captain Nemo, showing me the instruments hanging on the walls of his room, "here are the contrivances required for the navigation of the Nautilus. Here, as in the drawing-room, I have them always under my eyes, and they indicate my position and exact direction in the middle of the ocean. Some are known to you, such as the thermometer, which gives the internal temperature of the Nautilus; the barometer, which indicates the weight of the air and foretells the changes of the weather; the hygrometer, which marks the dryness of the atmosphere; the storm-glass, the contents of which, by decomposing, announce the approach of tempests; the compass, which guides my course; the sextant, which shows the latitude by the altitude of the sun; chronometers, by which I calculate the longitude; and glasses for day and night, which I use to examine the points of the horizon, when the Nautilus rises to the surface of the waves."

"These are the usual nautical instruments," I replied, "and I know the use of them. But these others, no doubt, answer to the particular requirements of the Nautilus. This dial with movable needle is a manometer, is it not?"

"It is actually a manometer. But by communication with the water, whose external pressure it indicates, it gives our depth at the same time."

"And these other instruments, the use of which I cannot guess?"

"Here, Professor, I ought to give you some explanations. Will you be kind enough to listen to me?"

He was silent for a few moments, then he said:

"There is a powerful agent, obedient, rapid, easy, which conforms to every use, and reigns supreme on board my vessel. Everything is done by means of it. It lights, warms it, and is the soul of my mechanical apparatus. This agent is electricity."

"Electricity?" I cried in surprise.

"Yes, sir."

"Nevertheless, Captain, you possess an extreme rapidity of movement, which does not agree well with the power of electricity. Until now, its dynamic force has remained under restraint, and has only been able to produce a small amount of power."

"Professor," said Captain Nemo, "my electricity is not everybody's. You know what sea-water is composed of. In a thousand grammes are found 96 1/2 per cent. of water, and about 2 2/3 per cent. of chloride of sodium; then, in a smaller quantity, chlorides of magnesium and of potassium, bromide of magnesium, sulphate of magnesia, sulphate and carbonate of lime. You see, then, that chloride of sodium forms a large part of it. So it is this sodium that I extract from the sea-water, and of which I compose my ingredients. I owe all to the ocean; it produces electricity, and electricity gives heat, light, motion, and, in a word, life to the Nautilus."

"But not the air you breathe?"

"Oh! I could manufacture the air necessary for my consumption, but it is useless, because I go up to the surface of the water when I please. However, if electricity does not furnish me with air to breathe, it works at least the powerful pumps that are stored in spacious reservoirs, and which enable me to prolong at need, and as long as I will, my stay in the depths of the sea. It gives a uniform and unintermittent light, which the sun does not. Now look at this clock; it is electrical, and goes with a regularity that defies the best chronometers. I have divided it into twenty-four hours, like the Italian clocks, because for me there is neither night nor day, sun nor moon, but only that factitious light that I take with me to the bottom of the sea. Look! just now, it is ten o'clock in the morning."

"Exactly."

"Another application of electricity. This dial hanging in front of us indicates the speed of the Nautilus. An electric thread puts it in communication with the screw, and the needle indicates the real speed. Look! now we are spinning along with a uniform speed of fifteen miles an hour."

"It is marvelous! And I see, Captain, you were right to make use of this agent that takes the place of wind, water, and steam."

"We have not finished, M. Aronnax," said Captain Nemo, rising. "If you will allow me, we will examine the stern of the Nautilus."

Really, I knew already the anterior part of this submarine boat, of which this is the exact division, starting from the ship's head: the dining-room, five yards long, separated from the library by a water-tight partition; the library, five yards long; the large drawing-room, ten yards long, separated from the Captain's room by a second water-tight partition; the said room, five yards in length; mine, two and a half yards; and, lastly a reservoir of air, seven and a half yards, that extended to the bows. Total length thirty five yards, or one hundred and five feet. The partitions had doors that were shut hermetically by means of india-rubber instruments, and they ensured the safety of the Nautilus in case of a leak.

I followed Captain Nemo through the waist, and arrived at the centre of the boat. There was a sort of well that opened between two partitions. An iron ladder, fastened with an iron hook to the partition, led to the upper end. I asked the Captain what the ladder was used for.

"It leads to the small boat," he said.

"What! have you a boat?" I exclaimed, in surprise.

"Of course; an excellent vessel, light and insubmersible, that serves either as a fishing or as a pleasure boat."

"But then, when you wish to embark, you are obliged to come to the surface of the water?"

"Not at all. This boat is attached to the upper part of the hull of the Nautilus, and occupies a cavity made for it. It is decked, quite water-tight, and held together by solid bolts. This ladder leads to a man-hole made in the hull of the Nautilus, that corresponds with a similar hole made in the side of the boat. By this double opening I get into the small vessel. They shut the one belonging to the Nautilus; I shut the other by means of screw pressure. I undo the bolts, and the little boat goes up to the surface of the sea with prodigious rapidity. I then open the panel of the bridge, carefully shut till then; I mast it, hoist my sail, take my oars, and I'm off."

"But how do you get back on board?"

"I do not come back, M. Aronnax; the Nautilus comes to me."

"By your orders?"

"By my orders. An electric thread connects us. I telegraph to it, and that is enough."

"Really," I said, astonished at these marvels, "nothing can be more simple."

After having passed by the cage of the staircase that led to the platform, I saw a cabin six feet long, in which Conseil and Ned Land, enchanted with their repast, were devouring it with avidity. Then a door opened into a kitchen nine feet long, situated between the large store-rooms. There electricity, better than gas itself, did all the cooking. The streams under the furnaces gave out to the sponges of platina a heat which was regularly kept up and distributed. They also heated a distilling apparatus, which, by evaporation, furnished excellent drinkable water. Near this kitchen was a bathroom comfortably furnished, with hot and cold water taps.

Next to the kitchen was the berth-room of the vessel, sixteen feet long. But the door was shut, and I could not see the management of it, which might have given me an idea of the number of men employed on board the Nautilus.

At the bottom was a fourth partition that separated this office from the engine-room. A door opened, and I found myself in the compartment where Captain Nemo—certainly an engineer of a very high order—had arranged his locomotive machinery. This engine-room, clearly lighted, did not measure less than sixty-five feet in length. It was divided into two parts; the first contained the materials for producing electricity, and the second the machinery that connected it with the screw. I examined it with great interest, in order to understand the machinery of the Nautilus.

"You see," said the Captain, "I use Bunsen's contrivances, not Ruhmkorff's. Those would not have been powerful enough. Bunsen's are fewer in number, but strong and large, which experience proves to be the best. The electricity produced passes forward, where it works, by electro-magnets of great size, on a system of levers and cog-wheels that transmit the movement to the axle of the screw. This one, the diameter of which is nineteen feet, and the thread twenty-three feet, performs about 120 revolutions in a second."

"And you get then?"

"A speed of fifty miles an hour."

"I have seen the Nautilus manoeuvre before the Abraham Lincoln, and I have my own ideas as to its speed. But this is not enough. We must see where we go. We must be able to direct it to the right, to the left, above, below. How do you get to the great depths, where you find an increasing resistance, which is rated by hundreds of atmospheres? How do you return to the surface of the ocean? And how do you maintain yourselves in the requisite medium? Am I asking too much?"

"Not at all, Professor," replied the Captain, with some hesitation; "since you may never leave this submarine boat. Come into the saloon, it is our usual study, and there you will learn all you want to know about the Nautilus."

CHAPTER XII. SOME FIGURES

A moment after we were seated on a divan in the saloon smoking. The Captain showed me a sketch that gave the plan, section, and elevation of the Nautilus. Then he began his description in these words:

"Here, M. Aronnax, are the several dimensions of the boat you are in. It is an elongated cylinder with conical ends. It is very like a cigar in shape, a shape already adopted in London in several constructions of the same sort. The length of this cylinder, from stem to stern, is exactly 232 feet, and its maximum breadth is twenty-six feet. It is not built quite like your long-voyage steamers, but its lines are sufficiently long, and its curves prolonged enough, to allow the water to slide off easily, and oppose no obstacle to its passage. These two dimensions enable you to obtain by a simple calculation the surface and cubic contents of the Nautilus. Its area measures 6,032 feet; and its contents about 1,500 cubic yards; that is to say, when completely immersed it displaces 50,000 feet of water, or weighs 1,500 tons.

"When I made the plans for this submarine vessel, I meant that nine-tenths should be submerged: consequently it ought only to displace nine-tenths of its bulk, that is to say, only to weigh that number of tons. I ought not, therefore, to have exceeded that weight, constructing it on the aforesaid dimensions.

"The Nautilus is composed of two hulls, one inside, the other outside, joined by T-shaped irons, which render it very strong. Indeed, owing to this cellular arrangement it resists like a block, as if it were solid. Its sides cannot yield; it coheres spontaneously, and not by the closeness of its rivets; and its perfect union of the materials enables it to defy the roughest seas.

"These two hulls are composed of steel plates, whose density is from .7 to .8 that of water. The first is not less than two inches and a half thick and weighs 394 tons. The second envelope, the keel, twenty inches high and ten thick, weighs only sixty-two tons. The engine, the ballast, the several accessories and apparatus appendages, the partitions and bulkheads, weigh 961.62 tons. Do you follow all this?"

"I do."

"Then, when the Nautilus is afloat under these circumstances, one-tenth is out of the water. Now, if I have made reservoirs of a size equal to this tenth, or capable of holding 150 tons, and if I fill them with water, the boat, weighing then 1,507 tons, will be completely immersed. That would happen, Professor. These reservoirs are in the lower part of the Nautilus. I turn on taps and they fill, and the vessel sinks that had just been level with the surface."

"Well, Captain, but now we come to the real difficulty. I can understand your rising to the surface; but, diving below the surface, does not your submarine contrivance encounter a pressure, and consequently undergo an upward thrust of one atmosphere for every thirty feet of water, just about fifteen pounds per square inch?"

"Just so, sir."

"Then, unless you quite fill the Nautilus, I do not see how you can draw it down to those depths."

"Professor, you must not confound statics with dynamics or you will be exposed to grave errors. There is very little labour spent in attaining the lower regions of the ocean, for all bodies have a tendency to sink. When I wanted to find out the necessary increase of weight required to sink the Nautilus, I had only to calculate the reduction of volume that sea-water acquires according to the depth."

"That is evident."

"Now, if water is not absolutely incompressible, it is at least capable of very slight compression. Indeed, after the most recent calculations this reduction is only .000436 of an atmosphere for each thirty feet of depth. If we want to sink

3,000 feet, I should keep account of the reduction of bulk under a pressure equal to that of a column of water of a thousand feet. The calculation is easily verified. Now, I have supplementary reservoirs capable of holding a hundred tons. Therefore I can sink to a considerable depth. When I wish to rise to the level of the sea, I only let off the water, and empty all the reservoirs if I want the Nautilus to emerge from the tenth part of her total capacity."

I had nothing to object to these reasonings.

"I admit your calculations, Captain," I replied; "I should be wrong to dispute them since daily experience confirms them; but I foresee a real difficulty in the way."

"What, sir?"

"When you are about 1,000 feet deep, the walls of the Nautilus bear a pressure of 100 atmospheres. If, then, just now you were to empty the supplementary reservoirs, to lighten the vessel, and to go up to the surface, the pumps must overcome the pressure of 100 atmospheres, which is 1,500 lbs. per square inch. From that a power——"

"That electricity alone can give," said the Captain, hastily. "I repeat, sir, that the dynamic power of my engines is almost infinite. The pumps of the Nautilus have an enormous power, as you must have observed when their jets of water burst like a torrent upon the Abraham Lincoln. Besides, I use subsidiary reservoirs only to attain a mean depth of 750 to 1,000 fathoms, and that with a view of managing my machines. Also, when I have a mind to visit the depths of the ocean five or six mlles below the surface, I make use of slower but not less infallible means."

"What are they, Captain?"

"That involves my telling you how the Nautilus is worked."

"I am impatient to learn."

"To steer this boat to starboard or port, to turn, in a word, following a horizontal plan, I use an ordinary rudder fixed on the back of the stern-post, and with one wheel and some tackle to steer by. But I can also make the Nautilus rise and sink, and sink and rise, by a vertical movement by means of two inclined planes fastened to its sides, opposite the centre of flotation, planes that move in every direction, and that are worked by powerful levers from the interior. If the planes are kept parallel with the boat, it moves horizontally. If slanted, the Nautilus, according to this inclination, and under the influence of the screw, either sinks diagonally or rises diagonally as it suits me. And even if I wish to rise more quickly to the surface, I ship the screw, and the pressure of the water causes the Nautilus to rise vertically like a balloon filled with hydrogen."

"Bravo, Captain! But how can the steersman follow the route in the middle of the waters?"

"The steersman is placed in a glazed box, that is raised about the hull of the Nautilus, and furnished with lenses."

"Are these lenses capable of resisting such pressure?"

"Perfectly. Glass, which breaks at a blow, is, nevertheless, capable of offering considerable resistance. During some experiments of fishing by electric light in 1864 in the Northern Seas, we saw plates less than a third of an inch thick resist a pressure of sixteen atmospheres. Now, the glass that I use is not less than thirty times thicker."

"Granted. But, after all, in order to see, the light must exceed the darkness, and in the midst of the darkness in the water, how can you see?"

"Behind the steersman's cage is placed a powerful electric reflector, the rays from which light up the sea for half a mile in front."

"Ah! bravo, bravo, Captain! Now I can account for this phosphorescence in the supposed narwhal that puzzled us so. I now ask you if the boarding of the Nautilus and of the Scotia, that has made such a noise, has been the result of a chance rencontre?"

"Quite accidental, sir. I was sailing only one fathom below the surface of the water when the shock came. It had no bad result."

"None, sir. But now, about your rencontre with the Abraham Lincoln?"

"Professor, I am sorry for one of the best vessels in the American navy; but they attacked me, and I was bound to defend myself. I contented myself, however, with putting the frigate hors de combat; she will not have any difficulty in getting repaired at the next port."

"Ah, Commander! your Nautilus is certainly a marvellous boat."

"Yes, Professor; and I love it as if it were part of myself. If danger threatens one of your vessels on the ocean, the first impression is the feeling of an abyss above and below. On the Nautilus men's hearts never fail them. No defects to be afraid of, for the double shell is as firm as iron; no rigging to attend to; no sails for the wind to carry away; no boilers to burst; no fire to fear, for the vessel is made of iron, not of wood; no coal to run short, for electricity is the only mechanical agent; no collision to fear, for it alone swims in deep water; no tempest to brave, for when it dives below the water it reaches absolute tranquillity. There, sir! that is the perfection of vessels! And if it is true that the engineer has more confidence in the vessel than the builder, and the builder than the captain himself, you understand the trust I repose in my Nautilus; for I am at once captain, builder, and engineer."

"But how could you construct this wonderful Nautilus in secret?"

"Each separate portion, M. Aronnax, was brought from different parts of the globe."

"But these parts had to be put together and arranged?"

"Professor, I had set up my workshops upon a desert island in the ocean. There my workmen, that is to say, the brave men that I instructed and educated, and myself have put together our Nautilus. Then, when the work was finished, fire destroyed all trace of our proceedings on this island, that I could have jumped over if I had liked."

"Then the cost of this vessel is great?"

"M. Aronnax, an iron vessel costs L145 per ton. Now the Nautilus weighed 1,500. It came therefore to L67,500, and L80,000 more for fitting it up, and about L200,000, with the works of art and the collections it contains."

"One last question, Captain Nemo."

"Ask it, Professor."

"You are rich?"

"Immensely rich, sir; and I could, without missing it, pay the national debt of France."

I stared at the singular person who spoke thus. Was he playing upon my credulity? The future would decide that.

CHAPTER XIII. THE BLACK RIVER

The portion of the terrestrial globe which is covered by water is estimated at upwards of eighty millions of acres. This fluid mass comprises two billions two hundred and fifty millions of cubic miles, forming a spherical body of a diameter of sixty leagues, the weight of which would be three quintillions of tons. To comprehend the meaning of these figures, it is necessary to observe that a quintillion is to a billion as a billion is to unity; in other words, there are as many billions in a quintillion as there are units in a billion. This mass of fluid is equal to about the quantity of water which would be discharged by all the rivers of the earth in forty thousand years.

During the geological epochs the ocean originally prevailed everywhere. Then by degrees, in the silurian period, the tops of the mountains began to appear, the islands emerged, then disappeared in partial deluges, reappeared, became settled, formed continents, till at length the earth became geographically arranged, as we see in the present day. The solid had wrested from the liquid thirty-seven million six hundred and fifty-seven square miles, equal to twelve billions nine hundred and sixty millions of acres.

The shape of continents allows us to divide the waters into five great portions: the Arctic or Frozen Ocean, the Antarctic, or Frozen Ocean, the Indian, the Atlantic, and the Pacific Oceans.

The Pacific Ocean extends from north to south between the two Polar Circles, and from east to west between Asia and America, over an extent of 145 degrees of longitude. It is the quietest of seas; its currents are broad and slow, it has medium tides, and abundant rain. Such was the ocean that my fate destined me first to travel over under these strange conditions.

"Sir," said Captain Nemo, "we will, if you please, take our bearings and fix the starting-point of this voyage. It is a quarter to twelve; I will go up again to the surface."

The Captain pressed an electric clock three times. The pumps began to drive the water from the tanks; the needle of the manometer marked by a different pressure the ascent of the Nautilus, then it stopped.

"We have arrived," said the Captain.

I went to the central staircase which opened on to the platform, clambered up the iron steps, and found myself on the upper part of the Nautilus.

The platform was only three feet out of water. The front and back of the Nautilus was of that spindle-shape which caused it justly to be compared to a cigar. I noticed that its iron plates, slightly overlaying each other, resembled the shell which clothes the bodies of our large terrestrial reptiles. It explained to me how natural it was, in spite of all glasses, that this boat should have been taken for a marine animal.

Toward the middle of the platform the longboat, half buried in the hull of the vessel, formed a slight excrescence. Fore and aft rose two cages of medium height with inclined sides, and partly closed by thick lenticular glasses; one destined for the steersman who directed the Nautilus, the other containing a brilliant lantern to give light on the road.

The sea was beautiful, the sky pure. Scarcely could the long vehicle feel the broad undulations of the ocean. A light breeze from the east rippled the surface of the waters. The horizon, free from fog, made observation easy. Nothing was in sight. Not a quicksand, not an island. A vast desert.

Captain Nemo, by the help of his sextant, took the altitude of the sun, which ought also to give the latitude. He waited for some moments till its disc touched the horizon. Whilst taking observations not a muscle moved, the instrument could not have been more motionless in a hand of marble.

"Twelve o'clock, sir," said he. "When you like——"

I cast a last look upon the sea, slightly yellowed by the Japanese coast, and descended to the saloon.

"And now, sir, I leave you to your studies," added the Captain; "our course is E.N.E., our depth is twenty-six fathoms. Here are maps on a large scale by which you may follow it. The saloon is at your disposal, and, with your permission, I will retire." Captain Nemo bowed, and I remained alone, lost in thoughts all bearing on the commander of the Nautilus.

For a whole hour was I deep in these reflections, seeking to pierce this mystery so interesting to me. Then my eyes fell upon the vast planisphere spread upon the table, and I placed my finger on the very spot where the given latitude and longitude crossed.

The sea has its large rivers like the continents. They are special currents known by their temperature and their colour. The most remarkable of these is known by the name of the Gulf Stream. Science has decided on the globe the direction of five principal currents: one in the North Atlantic, a second in the South, a third in the North Pacific, a fourth in the South, and a fifth in the Southern Indian Ocean. It is even probable that a sixth current existed at one time or another in the Northern Indian Ocean, when the Caspian and Aral Seas formed but one vast sheet of water.

At this point indicated on the planisphere one of these currents was rolling, the Kuro-Scivo of the Japanese, the Black River, which, leaving the Gulf of Bengal, where it is warmed by the perpendicular rays of a tropical sun, crosses the Straits of Malacca along the coast of Asia, turns into the North Pacific to the Aleutian Islands, carrying with it trunks of camphor-trees and other indigenous productions, and edging the waves of the ocean with the pure indigo of its warm water. It was this current that the Nautilus was to follow. I followed it with my eye; saw it lose itself in the vastness of the Pacific, and felt myself drawn with it, when Ned Land and Conseil appeared at the door of the saloon.

My two brave companions remained petrified at the sight of the wonders spread before them.

"Where are we, where are we?" exclaimed the Canadian. "In the museum at Quebec?"

"My friends," I answered, making a sign for them to enter, "you are not in Canada, but on board the Nautilus, fifty yards below the level of the sea."

"But, M. Aronnax," said Ned Land, "can you tell me how many men there are on board? Ten, twenty, fifty, a hundred?"

"I cannot answer you, Mr. Land; it is better to abandon for a time all idea of seizing the Nautilus or escaping from it. This ship is a masterpiece of modern industry, and I should be sorry not to have seen it. Many people would accept the situation forced upon us, if only to move amongst such wonders. So be quiet and let us try and see what passes around us."

"See!" exclaimed the harpooner, "but we can see nothing in this iron prison! We are walking—we are sailing—blindly."

Ned Land had scarcely pronounced these words when all was suddenly darkness. The luminous ceiling was gone, and so rapidly that my eyes received a painful impression.

We remained mute, not stirring, and not knowing what surprise awaited us, whether agreeable or disagreeable. A sliding noise was heard: one would have said that panels were working at the sides of the Nautilus.

"It is the end of the end!" said Ned Land.

Suddenly light broke at each side of the saloon, through two oblong openings. The liquid mass appeared vividly lit up by the electric gleam. Two crystal plates separated us from the sea. At first I trembled at the thought that this frail partition might break, but strong bands of copper bound them, giving an almost infinite power of resistance.

The sea was distinctly visible for a mile all round the Nautilus. What a spectacle! What pen can describe it? Who could paint the effects of the light through those transparent sheets of water, and the softness of the successive gradations from the lower to the superior strata of the ocean?

We know the transparency of the sea and that its clearness is far beyond that of rock-water. The mineral and organic substances which it holds in suspension heightens its transparency. In certain parts of the ocean at the Antilles, under seventy-five fathoms of water, can be seen with surprising clearness a bed of sand. The penetrating power of the solar rays does not seem to cease for a depth of one hundred and fifty fathoms. But in this middle fluid travelled over by the Nautilus, the electric brightness was produced even in the bosom of the waves. It was no longer luminous water, but liquid light.

On each side a window opened into this unexplored abyss. The obscurity of the saloon showed to advantage the brightness outside, and we looked out as if this pure crystal had been the glass of an immense aquarium.

"You wished to see, friend Ned; well, you see now."

"Curious! curious!" muttered the Canadian, who, forgetting his ill-temper, seemed to submit to some irresistible attraction; "and one would come further than this to admire such a sight!"

"Ah!" thought I to myself, "I understand the life of this man; he has made a world apart for himself, in which he treasures all his greatest wonders."

For two whole hours an aquatic army escorted the Nautilus. During their games, their bounds, while rivalling each other in beauty, brightness, and velocity, I distinguished the green labre; the banded mullet, marked by a double line of black; the round-tailed goby, of a white colour, with violet spots on the back; the Japanese scombrus, a beautiful mackerel of these seas, with a blue body and silvery head; the brilliant azurors, whose name alone defies description; some banded spares, with variegated fins of blue and yellow; the woodcocks of the seas, some specimens of which attain a yard in length; Japanese salamanders, spider lampreys, serpents six feet long, with eyes small and lively, and a huge mouth bristling with teeth; with many other species.

Our imagination was kept at its height, interjections followed quickly on each other. Ned named the fish, and Conseil classed them. I was in ecstasies with the vivacity of their movements and the beauty of their forms. Never had it been given to me to surprise these animals, alive and at liberty, in their natural element. I will not mention all the varieties which passed before my dazzled eyes, all the collection of the seas of China and Japan. These fish, more numerous than the birds of the air, came, attracted, no doubt, by the brilliant focus of the electric light.

Suddenly there was daylight in the saloon, the iron panels closed again, and the enchanting vision disappeared. But for a long time I dreamt on, till my eyes fell on the instruments hanging on the partition. The compass still showed the course to be E.N.E., the manometer indicated a pressure of five atmospheres, equivalent to a depth of twenty five fathoms, and the electric log gave a speed of fifteen miles an hour. I expected Captain Nemo, but he did not appear. The clock marked the hour of five.

Ned Land and Conseil returned to their cabin, and I retired to my chamber. My dinner was ready. It was composed of turtle soup made of the most delicate hawks bills, of a surmullet served with puff paste (the liver of which, prepared by itself, was most delicious), and fillets of the emperor-holocanthus, the savour of which seemed to me superior even to salmon.

I passed the evening reading, writing, and thinking. Then sleep overpowered me, and I stretched myself on my couch of zostera, and slept profoundly, whilst the Nautilus was gliding rapidly through the current of the Black River.

CHAPTER XIV. A NOTE OF INVITATION

The next day was the 9th of November. I awoke after a long sleep of twelve hours. Conseil came, according to custom, to know "how I passed the night," and to offer his services. He had left his friend the Canadian sleeping like a man who had never done anything else all his life. I let the worthy fellow chatter as he pleased, without caring to answer him. I was preoccupied by the absence of the Captain during our sitting of the day before, and hoping to see him to-day.

As soon as I was dressed I went into the saloon. It was deserted. I plunged into the study of the shell treasures hidden behind the glasses.

The whole day passed without my being honoured by a visit from Captain Nemo. The panels of the saloon did not open. Perhaps they did not wish us to tire of these beautiful things.

The course of the Nautilus was E.N.E., her speed twelve knots, the depth below the surface between twenty-five and thirty fathoms.

The next day, 10th of November, the same desertion, the same solitude. I did not see one of the ship's crew: Ned and Conseil spent the greater part of the day with me. They were astonished at the puzzling absence of the Captain. Was this singular man ill?—had he altered his intentions with regard to us?

After all, as Conseil said, we enjoyed perfect liberty, we were delicately and abundantly fed. Our host kept to his terms of the treaty. We could not complain, and, indeed, the singularity of our fate reserved such wonderful compensation for us that we had no right to accuse it as yet.

That day I commenced the journal of these adventures which has enabled me to relate them with more scrupulous exactitude and minute detail.

11th November, early in the morning. The fresh air spreading over the interior of the Nautilus told me that we had come to the surface of the ocean to renew our supply of oxygen. I directed my steps to the central staircase, and mounted the platform.

It was six o'clock, the weather was cloudy, the sea grey, but calm. Scarcely a billow. Captain Nemo, whom I hoped to meet, would he be there? I saw no one but the steersman imprisoned in his glass cage. Seated upon the projection formed by the hull of the pinnace, I inhaled the salt breeze with delight.

By degrees the fog disappeared under the action of the sun's rays, the radiant orb rose from behind the eastern horizon. The sea flamed under its glance like a train of gunpowder. The clouds scattered in the heights were coloured with lively tints of beautiful shades, and numerous "mare's tails," which betokened wind for that day. But what was wind to this Nautilus, which tempests could not frighten!

I was admiring this joyous rising of the sun, so gay, and so life-giving, when I heard steps approaching the platform. I was prepared to salute Captain Nemo, but it was his second (whom I had already seen on the Captain's first visit) who appeared. He advanced on the platform, not seeming to see me. With his powerful glass to his eye, he scanned every point of the horizon with great attention. This examination over, he approached the panel and pronounced a sentence in exactly these terms. I have remembered it, for every morning it was repeated under exactly the same conditions. It was thus worded:

"Nautron respoc lorni virch."

What it meant I could not say.

These words pronounced, the second descended. I thought that the Nautilus was about to return to its submarine navigation. I regained the panel and returned to my chamber.

Five days sped thus, without any change in our situation. Every morning I mounted the platform. The same phrase was pronounced by the same individual. But Captain Nemo did not appear.

I had made up my mind that I should never see him again, when, on the 16th November, on returning to my room with Ned and Conseil, I found upon my table a note addressed to me. I opened it impatiently. It was written in a bold, clear hand, the characters rather pointed, recalling the German type. The note was worded as follows:

TO PROFESSOR ARONNAX, On board the Nautilus. 16th of November, 1867.

Captain Nemo invites Professor Aronnax to a hunting-party, which will take place to-morrow morning in the forests of the Island of Crespo. He hopes that nothing will prevent the Professor from being present, and he will with pleasure see him joined by his companions.

CAPTAIN NEMO, Commander of the Nautilus.

"A hunt!" exclaimed Ned.

"And in the forests of the Island of Crespo!" added Conseil.

"Oh! then the gentleman is going on terra firma?" replied Ned Land.

"That seems to me to be clearly indicated," said I, reading the letter once more.

"Well, we must accept," said the Canadian. "But once more on dry ground, we shall know what to do. Indeed, I shall not be sorry to eat a piece of fresh venison."

Without seeking to reconcile what was contradictory between Captain Nemo's manifest aversion to islands and continents, and his invitation to hunt in a forest, I contented myself with replying:

"Let us first see where the Island of Crespo is."

I consulted the planisphere, and in 32° 40' N. lat. and 157° 50' W. long., I found a small island, recognised in 1801 by Captain Crespo, and marked in the ancient Spanish maps as Rocca de la Plata, the meaning of which is The Silver Rock. We were then about eighteen hundred miles from our starting-point, and the course of the Nautilus, a little changed, was bringing it back towards the southeast.

I showed this little rock, lost in the midst of the North Pacific, to my companions.

"If Captain Nemo does sometimes go on dry ground," said I, "he at least chooses desert islands."

Ned Land shrugged his shoulders without speaking, and Conseil and he left me.

After supper, which was served by the steward, mute and impassive, I went to bed, not without some anxiety.

The next morning, the 17th of November, on awakening, I felt that the Nautilus was perfectly still. I dressed quickly and entered the saloon.

Captain Nemo was there, waiting for me. He rose, bowed, and asked me if it was convenient for me to accompany him. As he made no allusion to his absence during the last eight days, I did not mention it, and simply answered that my companions and myself were ready to follow him.

We entered the dining-room, where breakfast was served.

"M. Aronnax," said the Captain, "pray, share my breakfast without ceremony; we will chat as we eat. For, though I promised you a walk in the forest, I did not undertake to find hotels there. So breakfast as a man who will most likely not have his dinner till very late."

I did honour to the repast. It was composed of several kinds of fish, and slices of sea-cucumber, and different sorts of seaweed. Our drink consisted of pure water, to which the Captain added some drops of a fermented liquor, extracted by the Kamschatcha method from a seaweed known under the name of Rhodomenia palmata. Captain Nemo ate at first without saying a word. Then he began:

"Sir, when I proposed to you to hunt in my submarine forest of Crespo, you evidently thought me mad. Sir, you should never judge lightly of any man."

"But Captain, believe me——"

"Be kind enough to listen, and you will then see whether you have any cause to accuse me of folly and contradiction."

"I listen."

"You know as well as I do, Professor, that man can live under water, providing he carries with him a sufficient supply of breathable air. In submarine works, the workman, clad in an impervious dress, with his head in a metal helmet, receives air from above by means of forcing pumps and regulators."

"That is a diving apparatus," said I.

"Just so, but under these conditions the man is not at liberty; he is attached to the pump which sends him air through an india-rubber tube, and if we were obliged to be thus held to the Nautilus, we could not go far."

"And the means of getting free?" I asked.

"It is to use the Rouquayrol apparatus, invented by two of your own countrymen, which I have brought to perfection for my own use, and which will allow you to risk yourself under these new physiological conditions without any organ whatever suffering. It consists of a reservoir of thick iron plates, in which

I store the air under a pressure of fifty atmospheres. This reservoir is fixed on the back by means of braces, like a soldier's knapsack. Its upper part forms a box in which the air is kept by means of a bellows, and therefore cannot escape unless at its normal tension. In the Rouquayrol apparatus such as we use, two india rubber pipes leave this box and join a sort of tent which holds the nose and mouth; one is to introduce fresh air, the other to let out the foul, and the tongue closes one or the other according to the wants of the respirator. But I, in encountering great pressures at the bottom of the sea, was obliged to shut my head, like that of a diver in a ball of copper; and it is to this ball of copper that the two pipes, the inspirator and the expirator, open."

"Perfectly, Captain Nemo; but the air that you carry with you must soon be used; when it only contains fifteen per cent. of oxygen it is no longer fit to breathe."

"Right! But I told you, M. Aronnax, that the pumps of the Nautilus allow me to store the air under considerable pressure, and on those conditions the reservoir of the apparatus can furnish breathable air for nine or ten hours."

"I have no further objections to make," I answered. "I will only ask you one thing, Captain—how can you light your road at the bottom of the sea?"

"With the Ruhmkorff apparatus, M. Aronnax; one is carried on the back, the other is fastened to the waist. It is composed of a Bunsen pile, which I do not work with bichromate of potash, but with sodium. A wire is introduced which collects the electricity produced, and directs it towards a particularly made lantern. In this lantern is a spiral glass which contains a small quantity of carbonic gas. When the apparatus is at work this gas becomes luminous, giving out a white and continuous light. Thus provided, I can breathe and I can see."

"Captain Nemo, to all my objections you make such crushing answers that I dare no longer doubt. But, if I am forced to admit the Rouquayrol and Ruhmkorff apparatus, I must be allowed some reservations with regard to the gun I am to carry."

"But it is not a gun for powder," answered the Captain.

"Then it is an air-gun."

"Doubtless! How would you have me manufacture gun powder on board, without either saltpetre, sulphur, or charcoal?"

"Besides," I added, "to fire under water in a medium eight hundred and fifty-five times denser than the air, we must conquer very considerable resistance."

"That would be no difficulty. There exist guns, according to Fulton, perfected in England by Philip Coles and Burley, in France by Furcy, and in Italy by Landi, which are furnished with a peculiar system of closing, which can fire under these conditions. But I repeat, having no powder, I use air under great pressure, which the pumps of the Nautilus furnish abundantly."

"But this air must be rapidly used?"

"Well, have I not my Rouquayrol reservoir, which can furnish it at need? A tap is all that is required. Besides M. Aronnax, you must see yourself that, during our submarine hunt, we can spend but little air and but few balls."

"But it seems to me that in this twilight, and in the midst of this fluid, which is very dense compared with the atmosphere, shots could not go far, nor easily prove mortal."

"Sir, on the contrary, with this gun every blow is mortal; and, however lightly the animal is touched, it falls as if struck by a thunderbolt."

"Why?"

"Because the balls sent by this gun are not ordinary balls, but little cases of glass. These glass cases are covered with a case of steel, and weighted with a pellet of lead; they are real Leyden bottles, into which the electricity is forced to a very high tension. With the slightest shock they are discharged, and the animal, however strong it may be, falls dead. I must tell you that these cases are size number four, and that the charge for an ordinary gun would be ten."

"I will argue no longer," I replied, rising from the table. "I have nothing left me but to take my gun. At all events, I will go where you go."

Captain Nemo then led me aft; and in passing before Ned's and Conseil's cabin, I called my two companions, who followed promptly. We then came to a cell near the machinery-room, in which we put on our walking-dress.

CHAPTER XV. A WALK ON THE BOTTOM OF THE SEA

This cell was, to speak correctly, the arsenal and wardrobe of the Nautilus. A dozen diving apparatuses hung from the partition waiting our use.

Ned Land, on seeing them, showed evident repugnance to dress himself in one.

"But, my worthy Ned, the forests of the Island of Crespo are nothing but submarine forests."

"Good!" said the disappointed harpooner, who saw his dreams of fresh meat fade away. "And you, M. Aronnax, are you going to dress yourself in those clothes?"

"There is no alternative, Master Ned."

"As you please, sir," replied the harpooner, shrugging his shoulders; "but, as for me, unless I am forced, I will never get into one."

"No one will force you, Master Ned," said Captain Nemo.

"Is Conseil going to risk it?" asked Ned.

"I follow my master wherever he goes," replied Conseil.

At the Captain's call two of the ship's crew came to help us dress in these heavy and impervious clothes, made of india-rubber without seam, and constructed expressly to resist considerable pressure. One would have thought it a suit of armour, both supple and resisting. This suit formed trousers and waistcoat. The trousers were finished off with thick boots, weighted with heavy leaden soles. The texture of the waistcoat was held together by bands of copper, which crossed the chest, protecting it from the great pressure of the water, and leaving the lungs free to act; the sleeves ended in gloves, which in no way restrained the movement of the hands. There was a vast difference noticeable between these consummate apparatuses and the old cork breastplates, jackets, and other contrivances in vogue during the eighteenth century.

Captain Nemo and one of his companions (a sort of Hercules, who must have possessed great strength), Conseil and myself were soon enveloped in the dresses. There remained nothing more to be done but to enclose our heads in the metal box. But, before proceeding to this operation, I asked the Captain's permission to examine the guns.

One of the Nautilus men gave me a simple gun, the butt end of which, made of steel, hollow in the centre, was rather large. It served as a reservoir for compressed air, which a valve, worked by a spring, allowed to escape into a metal tube. A box of projectiles in a groove in the thickness of the butt end contained about twenty of these electric balls, which, by means of a spring, were forced into the barrel of the gun. As soon as one shot was fired, another was ready.

"Captain Nemo," said I, "this arm is perfect, and easily handled: I only ask to be allowed to try it. But how shall we gain the bottom of the sea?"

"At this moment, Professor, the Nautilus is stranded in five fathoms, and we have nothing to do but to start."

"But how shall we get off?"

"You shall see."

Captain Nemo thrust his head into the helmet, Conseil and I did the same, not without hearing an ironical "Good sport!" from the Canadian. The upper part of our dress terminated in a copper collar upon which was screwed the metal helmet. Three holes, protected by thick glass, allowed us to see in all directions, by simply turning our head in the interior of the head-dress. As soon as it was in position, the Rouquayrol apparatus on our backs began to act; and, for my part, I could breathe with ease.

With the Ruhmkorff lamp hanging from my belt, and the gun in my hand, I was ready to set out. But to speak the truth, imprisoned in these heavy garments, and glued to the deck by my leaden soles, it was impossible for me to take a step.

But this state of things was provided for. I felt myself being pushed into a little room contiguous to the wardrobe room. My companions followed, towed along in the same way. I heard a water-tight door, furnished with stopper plates, close upon us, and we were wrapped in profound darkness.

After some minutes, a loud hissing was heard. I felt the cold mount from my feet to my chest. Evidently from some part of the vessel they had, by means of a tap, given entrance to the water, which was invading us, and with which the room was soon filled. A second door cut in the side of the Nautilus then opened. We saw a faint light. In another instant our feet trod the bottom of the sea.

And now, how can I retrace the impression left upon me by that walk under the waters? Words are impotent to relate such wonders! Captain Nemo walked in front, his companion followed some steps behind. Conseil and I remained near each other, as if an exchange of words had been possible through our metallic cases. I no longer felt the weight of my clothing, or of my shoes, of my reservoir of air, or my thick helmet, in the midst of which my head rattled like an almond in its shell.

The light, which lit the soil thirty feet below the surface of the ocean, astonished me by its power. The solar rays shone through the watery mass easily, and dissipated all colour, and I clearly distinguished objects at a distance of a hundred and fifty yards. Beyond that the tints darkened into fine gradations of ultramarine, and faded into vague obscurity. Truly this water which surrounded me was but another air denser than the terrestrial atmosphere, but almost as transparent. Above me was the calm surface of the sea. We were walking on fine, even sand, not wrinkled, as on a flat shore, which retains the impression of the billows. This dazzling carpet, really a reflector, repelled the rays of the sun with wonderful intensity, which accounted for the vibration which penetrated every atom of liquid. Shall I be believed when I say that, at the depth of thirty feet, I could see as if I was in broad daylight?

For a quarter of an hour I trod on this sand, sown with the impalpable dust of shells. The hull of the Nautilus, resembling a long shoal, disappeared by degrees; but its lantern, when darkness should overtake us in the waters, would help to guide us on board by its distinct rays.

Soon forms of objects outlined in the distance were discernible. I recognised magnificent rocks, hung with a tapestry of zoophytes of the most beautiful kind, and I was at first struck by the peculiar effect of this medium.

It was then ten in the morning; the rays of the sun struck the surface of the waves at rather an oblique angle, and at the touch of their light, decomposed by refraction as through a prism, flowers, rocks, plants, shells, and polypi were shaded at the edges by the seven solar colours. It was marvellous, a feast for the eyes, this complication of coloured tints, a perfect kaleidoscope of green, yellow, orange, violet, indigo, and blue; in one word, the whole palette of an enthusiastic colourist! Why could I not communicate to Conseil the lively sensations which were mounting to my brain, and rival him in expressions of admiration? For aught I knew, Captain Nemo and his companion might be able to exchange thoughts by means of signs previously agreed upon. So, for want of better, I talked to myself; I declaimed in the copper box which covered my head, thereby expending more air in vain words than was perhaps wise.

Various kinds of isis, clusters of pure tuft-coral, prickly fungi, and anemones formed a brilliant garden of flowers, decked with their collarettes of blue tentacles, sea-stars studding the sandy bottom. It was a real grief to me to crush under my feet the brilliant specimens of molluscs which strewed the ground by thousands, of hammerheads, donaciae (veritable bounding shells), of staircases, and red helmet-shells, angel-wings, and many others produced by this inexhaustible ocean. But we were bound to walk, so we went on, whilst above our heads waved medusae whose umbrellas of opal or rose-pink, escalloped with a band of blue, sheltered us from the rays of the sun and fiery pelagiae, which, in the darkness, would have strewn our path with phosphorescent light.

All these wonders I saw in the space of a quarter of a mile, scarcely stopping, and following Captain Nemo, who beckoned me on by signs. Soon the nature of the soil changed; to the sandy plain succeeded an extent of slimy mud which the Americans call "ooze," composed of equal parts of silicious and calcareous shells. We then travelled over a plain of seaweed of wild and luxuriant vegetation. This sward was of close texture, and soft to the feet, and rivalled the softest carpet woven by the hand of man. But whilst verdure was spread at our feet, it did not abandon our heads. A light network of marine plants, of that inexhaustible family of seaweeds of which more than two thousand kinds are known, grew on the surface of the water.

I noticed that the green plants kept nearer the top of the sea, whilst the red were at a greater depth, leaving to the black or brown the care of forming gardens and parterres in the remote beds of the ocean.

We had quitted the Nautilus about an hour and a half. It was near noon; I knew by the perpendicularity of the sun's rays, which were no longer refracted. The magical colours disappeared by degrees, and the shades of emerald and sapphire were effaced. We walked with a regular step, which rang upon the ground with astonishing intensity; the slightest noise was transmitted with a quickness to which the ear is unaccustomed on the earth; indeed, water is a better conductor of sound than air, in the ratio of four to one. At this period the earth sloped downwards; the light took a uniform tint. We were at a depth of a hundred and five yards and twenty inches, undergoing a pressure of six atmospheres.

At this depth I could still see the rays of the sun, though feebly; to their intense brilliancy had succeeded a reddish twilight, the lowest state between day and night; but we could still see well enough; it was not necessary to resort to the Ruhmkorff apparatus as yet. At this moment Captain Nemo stopped; he waited till I joined him, and then pointed to an obscure mass, looming in the shadow, at a short distance.

"It is the forest of the Island of Crespo," thought I; and I was not mistaken.

CHAPTER XVI. A SUBMARINE FOREST

We had at last arrived on the borders of this forest, doubtless one of the finest of Captain Nemo's immense domains. He looked upon it as his own, and considered he had the same right over it that the first men had in the first days of the world. And, indeed, who would have disputed with him the possession of this submarine property? What other hardier pioneer would come, hatchet in hand, to cut down the dark copses?

This forest was composed of large tree-plants; and the moment we penetrated under its vast arcades, I was struck by the singular position of their branches—a position I had not yet observed.

Not an herb which carpeted the ground, not a branch which clothed the trees, was either broken or bent, nor did they extend horizontally; all stretched up to the surface of the ocean. Not a filament, not a ribbon, however thin they might be, but kept as straight as a rod of iron. The fuci and llianas grew in rigid perpendicular lines, due to the density of the element which had produced them. Motionless yet, when bent to one side by the hand, they directly resumed their former position. Truly it was the region of perpendicularity!

I soon accustomed myself to this fantastic position, as well as to the comparative darkness which surrounded us. The soil of the forest seemed covered with sharp blocks, difficult to avoid. The submarine flora struck me as being very perfect, and richer even than it would have been in the arctic or tropical zones, where these productions are not so plentiful. But for some minutes I involuntarily confounded the genera, taking animals for plants; and who would not have been mistaken? The fauna and the flora are too closely allied in this submarine world.

These plants are self-propagated, and the principle of their existence is in the water, which upholds and nourishes them. The greater number, instead of leaves, shoot forth blades of capricious shapes, comprised within a scale of colours pink, carmine, green, olive, fawn, and brown.

"Curious anomaly, fantastic element!" said an ingenious naturalist, "in which the animal kingdom blossoms, and the vegetable does not!"

In about an hour Captain Nemo gave the signal to halt; I, for my part, was not sorry, and we stretched ourselves under an arbour of alariae, the long thin blades of which stood up like arrows.

This short rest seemed delicious to me; there was nothing wanting but the charm of conversation; but, impossible to speak, impossible to answer, I only put my great copper head to Conseil's. I saw the worthy fellow's eyes glistening with delight, and, to show his satisfaction, he shook himself in his breastplate of air, in the most comical way in the world.

After four hours of this walking, I was surprised not to find myself dreadfully hungry. How to account for this state of the stomach I could not tell. But instead I felt an insurmountable desire to sleep, which happens to all divers. And my eyes soon closed behind the thick glasses, and I fell into a heavy slumber, which the movement alone had prevented before. Captain Nemo and his robust companion, stretched in the clear crystal, set us the example.

How long I remained buried in this drowsiness I cannot judge, but, when I woke, the sun seemed sinking towards the horizon. Captain Nemo had already risen, and I was beginning to stretch my limbs, when an unexpected apparition brought me briskly to my feet.

A few steps off, a monstrous sea-spider, about thirty-eight inches high, was watching me with squinting eyes, ready to spring upon me. Though my diver's dress was thick enough to defend me from the bite of this animal, I could not help shuddering with horror. Conseil and the sailor of the Nautilus awoke at this moment. Captain Nemo pointed out the hideous crustacean, which a blow from the butt end of the gun knocked over, and I saw the horrible claws of the monster writhe in terrible convulsions. This incident reminded me that other animals more to be feared might haunt these obscure depths, against whose attacks my diving-dress would not protect me. I had never thought of it before, but I now resolved to be upon my guard. Indeed, I thought that this halt would mark the termination of our walk; but I was mistaken, for, instead of returning to the Nautilus, Captain Nemo continued his bold excursion. The ground was still on the incline, its declivity seemed to be getting greater, and to be leading us to greater depths. It must have been about three o'clock when we reached a narrow valley, between high perpendicular walls, situated about seventy-five fathoms deep. Thanks to the perfection of our apparatus, we were forty-five fathoms below the limit which nature seems to have imposed on man as to his submarine excursions.

I say seventy-five fathoms, though I had no instrument by which to judge the distance. But I knew that even in the clearest waters the solar rays could not penetrate further. And accordingly the darkness deepened. At ten paces not an object was visible. I was groping my way, when I suddenly saw a brilliant white light. Captain Nemo had just put his electric apparatus into use; his companion did the same, and Conseil and I followed their example. By turning a screw I established a communication between the wire and the spiral glass, and the sea, lit by our four lanterns, was illuminated for a circle of thirty-six yards.

As we walked I thought the light of our Ruhmkorff apparatus could not fail to draw some inhabitant from its dark couch. But if they did approach us, they at least kept at a respectful distance from the hunters. Several times I saw Captain Nemo stop, put his gun to his shoulder, and after some moments drop it and walk on. At last, after about four hours, this marvellous excursion came to an end. A wall of superb rocks, in an imposing mass, rose before us, a heap of gigantic blocks, an enormous, steep granite shore, forming dark grottos, but which presented no practicable slope; it was the prop of the Island of Crespo. It was the earth! Captain Nemo stopped suddenly. A gesture of his brought us all to a halt; and, however desirous I might be to scale the wall, I was obliged to stop. Here ended Captain Nemo's domains. And he would not go beyond them. Further on was a portion of the globe he might not trample upon.

The return began. Captain Nemo had returned to the head of his little band, directing their course without hesitation. I thought we were not following the same road to return to the Nautilus. The new road was very steep, and consequently very painful. We approached the surface of the sea rapidly. But this return to the upper strata was not so sudden as to cause relief from the pressure too rapidly, which might have produced serious disorder in our organisation, and brought on internal lesions, so fatal to divers. Very soon light reappeared and grew, and, the sun being low on the horizon, the refraction edged the different objects with a spectral ring. At ten yards and a half deep, we walked amidst a shoal of little fishes of all kinds, more numerous than the birds of the air, and also more agile; but no aquatic game worthy of a shot had as yet met our gaze, when at that moment I saw the Captain shoulder his gun quickly, and follow a moving object into the shrubs. He fired; I heard a slight hissing, and a creature fell stunned at some distance from us. It was a magnificent sea-otter, an enhydrus, the only exclusively marine quadruped. This otter was five feet long, and must have been very valuable. Its skin, chestnut-brown above and silvery underneath, would have made one of those beautiful furs so sought after in the Russian and Chinese markets: the fineness and the lustre of its coat would certainly fetch L80. I admired this curious mammal, with its rounded head ornamented with short ears, its round eyes, and white whiskers like those of a cat, with webbed feet and nails, and tufted tail. This precious animal, hunted and tracked by fishermen, has now become very rare, and taken refuge chiefly in the northern parts of the Pacific, or probably its race would soon become extinct.

Captain Nemo's companion took the beast, threw it over his shoulder, and we continued our journey. For one hour a plain of sand lay stretched before us. Sometimes it rose to within two yards and some inches of the surface of the water. I then saw our image clearly reflected, drawn inversely, and above us appeared an identical group reflecting our movements and our actions; in a word, like us in every point, except that they walked with their heads downward and their feet in the air.

Another effect I noticed, which was the passage of thick clouds which formed and vanished rapidly; but on reflection I understood that these seeming clouds were due to the varying thickness of the reeds at the bottom, and I could even see the fleecy foam which their broken tops multiplied on the water, and the shadows of large birds passing above our heads, whose rapid flight I could discern on the surface of the sea.

On this occasion I was witness to one of the finest gun shots which ever made the nerves of a hunter thrill. A large bird of great breadth of wing, clearly visible, approached, hovering over us. Captain Nemo's companion shouldered his gun and fired, when it was only a few yards above the waves. The creature fell stunned, and the force of its fall brought it within the reach of dexterous hunter's grasp. It was an albatross of the finest kind.

Our march had not been interrupted by this incident. For two hours we followed these sandy plains, then fields of algae very disagreeable to cross. Candidly, I could do no more when I saw a glimmer of light, which, for a half mile, broke the darkness of the waters. It was the lantern of the Nautilus. Before twenty minutes were over we should be on board, and I should be able to breathe with ease, for it seemed that my reservoir supplied air very deficient in oxygen. But I did not reckon on an accidental meeting which delayed our arrival for some time.

I had remained some steps behind, when I presently saw Captain Nemo coming hurriedly towards me. With his strong hand he bent me to the ground, his companion doing the same to Conseil. At first I knew not what to think of this sudden attack, but I was soon reassured by seeing the Captain lie down beside me, and remain immovable.

I was stretched on the ground, just under the shelter of a bush of algae, when, raising my head, I saw some enormous mass, casting phosphorescent gleams, pass blusteringly by.

My blood froze in my veins as I recognised two formidable sharks which threatened us. It was a couple of tintoreas, terrible creatures, with enormous tails and a dull glassy stare, the phosphorescent matter ejected from holes pierced around the muzzle. Monstrous brutes! which would crush a whole man in their iron jaws. I did not know whether Conseil stopped to classify them; for my part, I noticed their silver bellies, and their huge mouths bristling with teeth, from a very unscientific point of view, and more as a possible victim than as a naturalist.

Happily the voracious creatures do not see well. They passed without seeing us, brushing us with their brownish fins, and we escaped by a miracle from a danger certainly greater than meeting a tiger full-face in the forest. Half an hour after, guided by the electric light we reached the Nautilus. The outside door had been left open, and Captain Nemo closed it as soon as we had entered the first cell. He then pressed a knob. I heard the pumps working in the midst of the vessel, I felt the water sinking from around me, and in a few moments the cell was entirely empty. The inside door then opened, and we entered the vestry.

There our diving-dress was taken off, not without some trouble, and, fairly worn out from want of food and sleep, I returned to my room, in great wonder at this surprising excursion at the bottom of the sea.

CHAPTER XVII. FOUR THOUSAND LEAGUES UNDER THE PACIFIC

The next morning, the 18th of November, I had quite recovered from my fatigues of the day before, and I went up on to the platform, just as the second lieutenant was uttering his daily phrase.

I was admiring the magnificent aspect of the ocean when Captain Nemo appeared. He did not seem to be aware of my presence, and began a series of astronomical observations. Then, when he had finished, he went and leant on the cage of the watch-light, and gazed abstractedly on the ocean. In the meantime, a number of the sailors of the Nautilus, all strong and healthy men, had come up onto the platform. They came to draw up the nets that had been laid all night. These sailors were evidently of different nations, although the European type was visible in all of them. I recognised some unmistakable Irishmen, Frenchmen, some Sclaves, and a Greek, or a Candiote. They were civil, and only used that odd language among themselves, the origin of which I could not guess, neither could I question them.

The nets were hauled in. They were a large kind of "chaluts," like those on the Normandy coasts, great pockets that the waves and a chain fixed in the smaller meshes kept open. These pockets, drawn by iron poles, swept through the water, and gathered in everything in their way. That day they brought up curious specimens from those productive coasts.

I reckoned that the haul had brought in more than nine hundredweight of fish. It was a fine haul, but not to be wondered at. Indeed, the nets are let down for several hours, and enclose in their meshes an infinite variety. We had no lack of excellent food, and the rapidity of the Nautilus and the attraction of the electric light could always renew our supply. These several productions of the sea were immediately lowered through the panel to the steward's room, some to be eaten fresh, and others pickled.

The fishing ended, the provision of air renewed, I thought that the Nautilus was about to continue its submarine excursion, and was preparing to return to my room, when, without further preamble, the Captain turned to me, saying:

"Professor, is not this ocean gifted with real life? It has its tempers and its gentle moods. Yesterday it slept as we did, and now it has woke after a quiet night. Look!" he continued, "it wakes under the caresses of the sun. It is going to renew its diurnal existence. It is an interesting study to watch the play of its organisation. It has a pulse, arteries, spasms; and I agree with the learned Maury, who discovered in it a circulation as real as the circulation of blood in animals.

"Yes, the ocean has indeed circulation, and to promote it, the Creator has caused things to multiply in it—caloric, salt, and animalculae."

When Captain Nemo spoke thus, he seemed altogether changed, and aroused an extraordinary emotion in me.

"Also," he added, "true existence is there; and I can imagine the foundations of nautical towns, clusters of submarine houses, which, like the Nautilus, would ascend every morning to breathe at the surface of the water, free towns, independent cities. Yet who knows whether some despot——"

Captain Nemo finished his sentence with a violent gesture. Then, addressing me as if to chase away some sorrowful thought: "M. Aronnax," he asked, "do you know the depth of the ocean?"

"I only know, Captain, what the principal soundings have taught us."

"Could you tell me them, so that I can suit them to my purpose?"

"These are some," I replied, "that I remember. If I am not mistaken, a depth of 8,000 yards has been found in the North Atlantic, and 2,500 yards in the Mediterranean. The most remarkable soundings have been made in the South Atlantic, near the thirty-fifth parallel, and they gave 12,000 yards, 14,000 yards, and 15,000 yards. To sum up all, it is reckoned that if the bottom of the sea were levelled, its mean depth would be about one and three-quarter leagues."

"Well, Professor," replied the Captain, "we shall show you better than that I hope. As to the mean depth of this part of the Pacific, I tell you it is only 4,000 yards."

Having said this, Captain Nemo went towards the panel, and disappeared down the ladder. I followed him, and went into the large drawing-room. The screw was immediately put in motion, and the log gave twenty miles an hour.

During the days and weeks that passed, Captain Nemo was very sparing of his visits. I seldom saw him. The lieutenant pricked the ship's course regularly on the chart, so I could always tell exactly the route of the Nautilus.

Nearly every day, for some time, the panels of the drawing-room were opened, and we were never tired of penetrating the mysteries of the submarine world.

The general direction of the Nautilus was south-east, and it kept between 100 and 150 yards of depth. One day, however, I do not know why, being drawn diagonally by means of the inclined planes, it touched the bed of the sea. The thermometer indicated a temperature of 4.25 (cent.): a temperature that at this depth seemed common to all latitudes.

At three o'clock in the morning of the 26th of November the Nautilus crossed the tropic of Cancer at 172° long. On 27th instant it sighted the Sandwich Islands, where Cook died, February 14, 1779. We had then gone 4,860 leagues from our starting-point. In the morning, when I went on the platform, I saw two miles to windward, Hawaii, the largest of the seven islands that form the group. I saw clearly the cultivated ranges, and the several mountain-chains that run parallel with the side, and the volcanoes that overtop Mouna-Rea, which rise 5,000 yards above the level of the sea. Besides other things the nets brought up, were several flabellariae and graceful polypi, that are peculiar to that part of the ocean. The direction of the Nautilus was still to the south-east. It crossed the equator December 1, in 142° long.; and on the 4th of the same month, after crossing rapidly and without anything in particular occurring, we sighted the Marquesas group. I saw, three miles off, Martin's peak in Nouka-Hiva, the largest of the group that belongs to France. I only saw the woody mountains against the horizon, because Captain Nemo did not wish to bring the ship to the wind. There the nets brought up beautiful specimens of fish: some with azure fins and tails like gold, the flesh of which is unrivalled; some nearly destitute of scales, but of exquisite flavour; others, with bony jaws, and yellow-tinged gills, as good as bonitos; all fish that would be of use to us. After leaving these charming islands protected by the French flag, from the 4th to the 11th of December the Nautilus sailed over about 2,000 miles.

During the daytime of the 11th of December I was busy reading in the large drawing-room. Ned Land and Conseil watched the luminous water through the half-open panels. The Nautilus was immovable. While its reservoirs were filled, it kept at a depth of 1,000 yards, a region rarely visited in the ocean, and in which large fish were seldom seen.

I was then reading a charming book by Jean Mace, The Slaves of the Stomach, and I was learning some valuable lessons from it, when Conseil interrupted me.

"Will master come here a moment?" he said, in a curious voice.

"What is the matter, Conseil?"

"I want master to look."

I rose, went, and leaned on my elbows before the panes and watched.

In a full electric light, an enormous black mass, quite immovable, was suspended in the midst of the waters. I watched it attentively, seeking to find out the nature of this gigantic cetacean. But a sudden thought crossed my mind. "A vessel!" I said, half aloud.

"Yes," replied the Canadian, "a disabled ship that has sunk perpendicularly."

Ned Land was right; we were close to a vessel of which the tattered shrouds still hung from their chains. The keel seemed to be in good order, and it had been wrecked at most some few hours. Three stumps of masts, broken off about two feet above the bridge, showed that the vessel had had to sacrifice its masts. But, lying on its side, it had filled, and it was heeling over to port. This skeleton of what it had once been was a sad spectacle as it lay lost under the waves, but sadder still was the sight of the bridge, where some corpses, bound with ropes, were still lying. I counted five—four men, one of whom was standing at the helm, and a woman standing by the poop, holding an infant in her arms. She was quite young. I could distinguish her features, which the water had not decomposed, by the brilliant light from the Nautilus. In one despairing effort, she had raised her infant above her head—poor little thing!—whose arms encircled its mother's neck. The attitude of the four sailors was frightful, distorted as they were by their convulsive movements, whilst making a last effort to free themselves from the cords that bound them to the vessel. The steersman alone, calm, with a grave, clear face, his grey hair glued to his forehead, and his hand clutching the wheel of the helm, seemed even then to be guiding the three broken masts through the depths of the ocean.

What a scene! We were dumb; our hearts beat fast before this shipwreck, taken as it were from life and photographed in its last moments. And I saw already, coming towards it with hungry eyes, enormous sharks, attracted by the human flesh.

However, the Nautilus, turning, went round the submerged vessel, and in one instant I read on the stern—"The Florida, Sunderland."

CHAPTER XVIII. VANIKORO

This terrible spectacle was the forerunner of the series of maritime catastrophes that the Nautilus was destined to meet with in its route. As long as it went through more frequented waters, we often saw the hulls of shipwrecked vessels that were rotting in the depths, and deeper down cannons, bullets, anchors, chains, and a thousand other iron materials eaten up by rust. However, on the 11th of December we sighted the Pomotou Islands, the old "dangerous group" of Bougainville, that extend over a space of 500 leagues at E.S.E. to W.N.W., from the Island Ducie to that of Lazareff. This group covers an area of 370 square leagues, and it is formed of sixty groups of islands, among which the Gambier group is remarkable, over which France exercises sway. These are coral islands, slowly raised, but continuous, created by the daily work of polypi. Then this new island will be joined later on to the neighboring groups, and a fifth continent will stretch from New Zealand and New Caledonia, and from thence to the Marquesas.

One day, when I was suggesting this theory to Captain Nemo, he replied coldly:

"The earth does not want new continents, but new men."

Chance had conducted the Nautilus towards the Island of Clermont-Tonnere, one of the most curious of the group, that was discovered in 1822 by Captain Bell of the Minerva. I could study now the madreporal system, to which are due the islands in this ocean.

Madrepores (which must not be mistaken for corals) have a tissue lined with a calcareous crust, and the modifications of its structure have induced M. Milne Edwards, my worthy master, to class them into five sections. The animalcule that the marine polypus secretes live by millions at the bottom of their cells. Their calcareous deposits become rocks, reefs, and large and small islands. Here they form a ring, surrounding a little inland lake, that communicates with the sea by means of gaps. There they make barriers of reefs like those on the coasts of New Caledonia and the various Pomoton islands. In other places, like those at Reunion and at Maurice, they raise fringed reefs, high, straight walls, near which the depth of the ocean is considerable.

Some cable-lengths off the shores of the Island of Clermont I admired the gigantic work accomplished by these microscopical workers. These walls are specially the work of those madrepores known as milleporas, porites, madrepores, and astraeas. These polypi are found particularly in the rough beds of the sea, near the surface; and consequently it is from the upper part that they begin their operations, in which they bury themselves by degrees with the debris of the secretions that support them. Such is, at least, Darwin's theory, who thus explains the formation of the *atolls*, a superior theory (to my mind) to that given of the foundation of the madreporical works, summits of mountains or volcanoes, that are submerged some feet below the level of the sea.

I could observe closely these curious walls, for perpendicularly they were more than 300 yards deep, and our electric sheets lighted up this calcareous matter brilliantly. Replying to a question Conseil asked me as to the time these colossal barriers took to be raised, I astonished him much by telling him that learned men reckoned it about the eighth of an inch in a hundred years.

Towards evening Clermont-Tonnerre was lost in the distance, and the route of the Nautilus was sensibly changed. After having crossed the tropic of Capricorn in 135° longitude, it sailed W.N.W., making again for the tropical zone. Although the summer sun was very strong, we did not suffer from heat, for at fifteen or twenty fathoms below the surface, the temperature did not rise above from ten to twelve degrees.

On 15th of December, we left to the east the bewitching group of the Societies and the graceful Tahiti, queen of the Pacific. I saw in the morning, some miles to the windward, the elevated summits of the island. These waters furnished our table with excellent fish, mackerel, bonitos, and some varieties of a sea-serpent.

On the 25th of December the Nautilus sailed into the midst of the New Hebrides, discovered by Quiros in 1606, and that Bougainville explored in 1768, and to which Cook gave its present name in 1773. This group is composed principally of nine large islands, that form a band of 120 leagues N.N.S. to S.S.W., between 15° and 2° S. lat., and 164 deg. and 168° long. We passed tolerably near to the Island of Aurou, that at noon looked like a mass of green woods, surmounted by a peak of great height.

That day being Christmas Day, Ned Land seemed to regret sorely the non-celebration of "Christmas," the family fete of which Protestants are so fond. I had not seen Captain Nemo for a week, when, on the morning of the 27th, he came into the large drawing-room, always seeming as if he had seen you five minutes before. I was busily tracing the route of the Nautilus on the planisphere. The Captain came up to me, put his finger on one spot on the chart, and said this single word.

"Vanikoro."

The effect was magical! It was the name of the islands on which La Perouse had been lost! I rose suddenly.

"The Nautilus has brought us to Vanikoro?" I asked.

"Yes, Professor," said the Captain.

"And I can visit the celebrated islands where the Boussole and the Astrolabe struck?"

"If you like, Professor."

"When shall we be there?"

"We are there now."

Followed by Captain Nemo, I went up on to the platform, and greedily scanned the horizon.

To the N.E. two volcanic islands emerged of unequal size, surrounded by a coral reef that measured forty miles in circumference. We were close to Vanikoro, really the one to which Dumont d'Urville gave the name of Isle de la Recherche, and exactly facing the little harbour of Vanou, situated in 16° 4' S. lat., and 164° 32' E. long. The earth seemed covered with verdure from the shore to the summits in the interior, that were crowned by Mount Kapogo, 476 feet high. The Nautilus, having passed the outer belt of rocks by a narrow strait, found itself among breakers where the sea was from thirty to forty fathoms deep. Under the verdant shade of some mangroves I perceived some savages, who appeared greatly surprised at our approach. In the long black body, moving between wind and water, did they not see some formidable cetacean that they regarded with suspicion?

Just then Captain Nemo asked me what I knew about the wreck of La Perouse.

"Only what everyone knows, Captain," I replied.

"And could you tell me what everyone knows about it?" he inquired, ironically.

"Easily."

I related to him all that the last works of Dumont d'Urville had made known—works from which the following is a brief account.

La Perouse, and his second, Captain de Langle, were sent by Louis XVI, in 1785, on a voyage of circumnavigation. They embarked in the corvettes Boussole and the Astrolabe, neither of which were again heard of. In 1791, the French Government, justly uneasy as to the fate of these two sloops, manned two large merchantmen, the Recherche and the Esperance, which left Brest the 28th of September under the command of Bruni d'Entrecasteaux.

Two months after, they learned from Bowen, commander of the Albemarle, that the debris of shipwrecked vessels had been seen on the coasts of New Georgia. But D'Entrecasteaux, ignoring this communication—rather uncertain, besides—directed his course towards the Admiralty Islands, mentioned in a report of Captain Hunter's as being the place where La Perouse was wrecked.

They sought in vain. The Esperance and the Recherche passed before Vanikoro without stopping there, and, in fact, this voyage was most disastrous, as it cost D'Entrecasteaux his life, and those of two of his lieutenants, besides several of his crew.

Captain Dillon, a shrewd old Pacific sailor, was the first to find unmistakable traces of the wrecks. On the 15th of May, 1824, his vessel, the St. Patrick, passed close to Tikopia, one of the New Hebrides. There a Lascar came alongside in a canoe, sold him the handle of a sword in silver that bore the print of characters engraved on the hilt. The Lascar pretended that six years before, during a stay at Vanikoro, he had seen two Europeans that belonged to some vessels that had run aground on the reefs some years ago.

Dillon guessed that he meant La Perouse, whose disappearance had troubled the whole world. He tried to get on to Vanikoro, where, according to the Lascar, he would find numerous debris of the wreck, but winds and tides prevented him.

Dillon returned to Calcutta. There he interested the Asiatic Society and the Indian Company in his discovery. A vessel, to which was given the name of the Recherche, was put at his disposal, and he set out, 23rd January, 1827, accompanied by a French agent.

The Recherche, after touching at several points in the Pacific, cast anchor before Vanikoro, 7th July, 1827, in that same harbour of Vanou where the Nautilus was at this time.

There it collected numerous relics of the wreck—iron utensils, anchors, pulley-strops, swivel-guns, an 18 lb. shot, fragments of astronomical instruments, a piece of crown work, and a bronze clock, bearing this inscription—"Bazin m'a fait," the mark of the foundry of the arsenal at Brest about 1785. There could be no further doubt.

Dillon, having made all inquiries, stayed in the unlucky place till October. Then he quitted Vanikoro, and directed his course towards New Zealand; put into Calcutta, 7th April, 1828, and returned to France, where he was warmly welcomed by Charles X.

But at the same time, without knowing Dillon's movements, Dumont d'Urville had already set out to find the scene of the wreck. And they had learned from a whaler that some medals and a cross of St. Louis had been found in the hands of some savages of Louisiade and New Caledonia. Dumont d'Urville, commander of the Astrolabe, had then sailed, and two months after Dillon had left Vanikoro he put into Hobart Town. There he learned the results of Dillon's inquiries, and found that a certain James Hobbs, second lieutenant of the Union of Calcutta, after landing on an island situated 8° 18' S. lat., and 156° 30' E. long., had seen some iron bars and red stuffs used by the natives of these parts. Dumont d'Urville, much perplexed, and not knowing how to credit the reports of low-class journals, decided to follow Dillon's track.

On the 10th of February, 1828, the Astrolabe appeared off Tikopia, and took as guide and interpreter a deserter found on the island; made his way to Vanikoro, sighted it on the 12th inst., lay among the reefs until the 14th, and not until the 20th did he cast anchor within the barrier in the harbour of Vanou.

On the 23rd, several officers went round the island and brought back some unimportant trifles. The natives, adopting a system of denials and evasions, refused to take them to the unlucky place. This ambiguous conduct led them to believe that the natives had ill-treated the castaways, and indeed they seemed to fear that Dumont d'Urville had come to avenge La Perouse and his unfortunate crew.

However, on the 26th, appeased by some presents, and understanding that they had no reprisals to fear, they led M. Jacquireot to the scene of the wreck.

There, in three or four fathoms of water, between the reefs of Pacou and Vanou, lay anchors, cannons, pigs of lead and iron, embedded in the limy concretions. The large boat and the whaler belonging to the Astrolabe were sent to this place, and, not without some difficulty, their crews hauled up an anchor weighing 1,800 lbs., a brass gun, some pigs of iron, and two copper swivel-guns.

Dumont d'Urville, questioning the natives, learned too that La Perouse, after losing both his vessels on the reefs of this island, had constructed a smaller boat, only to be lost a second time. Where, no one knew.

But the French Government, fearing that Dumont d'Urville was not acquainted with Dillon's movements, had sent the sloop Bayonnaise, commanded by Legoarant de Tromelin, to Vanikoro, which had been stationed on the west coast of America. The Bayonnaise cast her anchor before Vanikoro some months after the departure of the Astrolabe, but found no new document; but stated that the savages had respected the monument to La Perouse. That is the substance of what I told Captain Nemo.

"So," he said, "no one knows now where the third vessel perished that was constructed by the castaways on the island of Vanikoro?"

"No one knows."

Captain Nemo said nothing, but signed to me to follow him into the large saloon. The Nautilus sank several yards below the waves, and the panels were opened.

I hastened to the aperture, and under the crustations of coral, covered with fungi, syphonules, alcyons, madrepores, through myriads of charming fish—girelles, glyphisidri, pompherides, diacopes, and holocentres—I recognised certain debris that the drags had not been able to tear up—iron stirrups, anchors, cannons, bullets, capstan fittings, the stem of a ship, all objects clearly proving the wreck of some vessel, and now carpeted with living flowers. While I was looking on this desolate scene, Captain Nemo said, in a sad voice:

"Commander La Perouse set out 7th December, 1785, with his vessels La Boussole and the Astrolabe. He first cast anchor at Botany Bay, visited the Friendly Isles, New Caledonia, then directed his course towards Santa Cruz, and put into Namouka, one of the Hapai group. Then his vessels struck on the unknown reefs of Vanikoro. The Boussole, which went first, ran aground on the southerly coast. The Astrolabe went to its help, and ran aground too. The first vessel was destroyed almost immediately. The second, stranded under the wind, resisted some days. The natives made the castaways welcome. They installed themselves in the island, and constructed a smaller boat with the debris of the two large ones. Some sailors stayed willingly at Vanikoro; the others, weak and ill, set out with La Perouse. They directed their course towards the Solomon Islands, and there perished, with everything, on the westerly coast of the chief island of the group, between Capes Deception and Satisfaction."

"How do you know that?"

"By this, that I found on the spot where was the last wreck."

Captain Nemo showed me a tin-plate box, stamped with the French arms, and corroded by the salt water. He opened it, and I saw a bundle of papers, yellow but still readable.

They were the instructions of the naval minister to Commander La Perouse, annotated in the margin in Louis XVI's handwriting.

"Ah! it is a fine death for a sailor!" said Captain Nemo, at last. "A coral tomb makes a quiet grave; and I trust that I and my comrades will find no other."

CHAPTER XIX. TORRES STRAITS

During the night of the 27th or 28th of December, the Nautilus left the shores of Vanikoro with great speed. Her course was south-westerly, and in three days she had gone over the 750 leagues that separated it from La Perouse's group and the south-east point of Papua.

Early on the 1st of January, 1863, Conseil joined me on the platform.

"Master, will you permit me to wish you a happy New Year?"

"What! Conseil; exactly as if I was at Paris in my study at the Jardin des Plantes? Well, I accept your good wishes, and thank you for them. Only, I will ask you what you mean by a `Happy New Year' under our circumstances? Do you mean the year that will bring us to the end of our imprisonment, or the year that sees us continue this strange voyage?"

"Really, I do not know how to answer, master. We are sure to see curious things, and for the last two months we have not had time for dullness. The last marvel is always the most astonishing; and, if we continue this progression, I do not know how it will end. It is my opinion that we shall never again see the like. I think then, with no offence to master, that a happy year would be one in which we could see everything."

On 2nd January we had made 11,340 miles, or 5,250 French leagues, since our starting-point in the Japan Seas. Before the ship's head stretched the dangerous shores of the coral sea, on the north-east coast of Australia. Our boat lay along some miles from the redoubtable bank on which Cook's vessel was lost, 10th June, 1770. The boat in which Cook was struck on a rock, and, if it did not sink, it was owing to a piece of coral that was broken by the shock, and fixed itself in the broken keel.

I had wished to visit the reef, 360 leagues long, against which the sea, always rough, broke with great violence, with a noise like thunder. But just then the inclined planes drew the Nautilus down to a great depth, and I could see nothing of the high coral walls. I had to content myself with the different specimens of fish brought up by the nets. I remarked, among others, some germons, a species of mackerel as large as a tunny, with bluish sides, and striped with transverse bands, that disappear with the animal's life.

These fish followed us in shoals, and furnished us with very delicate food. We took also a large number of gilt-heads, about one and a half inches long, tasting like dorys; and flying pyrapeds like submarine swallows, which, in dark nights, light alternately the air and water with their phosphorescent light. Among the molluscs and zoophytes, I found in the meshes of the net several species of alcyonarians, echini, hammers, spurs, dials, cerites, and hyalleae. The flora was represented by beautiful floating seaweeds, laminariae, and macrocystes, impregnated with the mucilage that transudes through their pores; and among which I gathered an admirable Nemastoma Geliniarois, that was classed among the natural curiosities of the museum.

Two days after crossing the coral sea, 4th January, we sighted the Papuan coasts. On this occasion, Captain Nemo informed me that his intention was to get into the Indian Ocean by the Strait of Torres. His communication ended there.

The Torres Straits are nearly thirty-four leagues wide; but they are obstructed by an innumerable quantity of islands, islets, breakers, and rocks, that make its navigation almost impracticable; so that Captain Nemo took all needful precautions to cross them. The Nautilus, floating betwixt wind and water, went at a moderate pace. Her screw, like a cetacean's tail, beat the waves slowly.

Profiting by this, I and my two companions went up on to the deserted platform. Before us was the steersman's cage, and I expected that Captain

Nemo was there directing the course of the Nautilus. I had before me the excellent charts of the Straits of Torres, and I consulted them attentively. Round the Nautilus the sea dashed furiously. The course of the waves, that went from south-east to north-west at the rate of two and a half miles, broke on the coral that showed itself here and there.

"This is a bad sea!" remarked Ned Land.

"Detestable indeed, and one that does not suit a boat like the Nautilus."

"The Captain must be very sure of his route, for I see there pieces of coral that would do for its keel if it only touched them slightly."

Indeed the situation was dangerous, but the Nautilus seemed to slide like magic off these rocks. It did not follow the routes of the Astrolabe and the Zelee exactly, for they proved fatal to Dumont d'Urville. It bore more northwards, coasted the Islands of Murray, and came back to the south-west towards Cumberland Passage. I thought it was going to pass it by, when, going back to north-west, it went through a large quantity of islands and islets little known, towards the Island Sound and Canal Mauvais.

I wondered if Captain Nemo, foolishly imprudent, would steer his vessel into that pass where Dumont d'Urville's two corvettes touched; when, swerving again, and cutting straight through to the west, he steered for the Island of Gilboa.

It was then three in the afternoon. The tide began to recede, being quite full. The Nautilus approached the island, that I still saw, with its remarkable border of screw-pines. He stood off it at about two miles distant. Suddenly a shock overthrew me. The Nautilus just touched a rock, and stayed immovable, laying lightly to port side.

When I rose, I perceived Captain Nemo and his lieutenant on the platform. They were examining the situation of the vessel, and exchanging words in their incomprehensible dialect.

She was situated thus: Two miles, on the starboard side, appeared Gilboa, stretching from north to west like an immense arm. Towards the south and east some coral showed itself, left by the ebb. We had run aground, and in one of those seas where the tides are middling—a sorry matter for the floating of the Nautilus. However, the vessel had not suffered, for her keel was solidly joined. But, if she could neither glide off nor move, she ran the risk of being for ever fastened to these rocks, and then Captain Nemo's submarine vessel would be done for.

I was reflecting thus, when the Captain, cool and calm, always master of himself, approached me. "An accident?" I asked.

"No; an incident."

"But an incident that will oblige you perhaps to become an inhabitant of this land from which you flee?"

Captain Nemo looked at me curiously, and made a negative gesture, as much as to say that nothing would force him to set foot on terra firma again. Then he said:

"Besides, M. Aronnax, the Nautilus is not lost; it will carry you yet into the midst of the marvels of the ocean. Our voyage is only begun, and I do not wish to be deprived so soon of the honour of your company."

"However, Captain Nemo," I replied, without noticing the ironical turn of his phrase, "the Nautilus ran aground in open sea. Now the tides are not strong in the Pacific; and, if you cannot lighten the Nautilus, I do not see how it will be reinflated."

"The tides are not strong in the Pacific: you are right there, Professor; but in Torres Straits one finds still a difference of a yard and a half between the level of high and low seas. To-day is 4th January, and in five days the moon will be full. Now, I shall be very much astonished if that satellite does not raise these masses of water sufficiently, and render me a service that I should be indebted to her for."

Having said this, Captain Nemo, followed by his lieutenant, redescended to the interior of the Nautilus. As to the vessel, it moved not, and was immovable, as if the coralline polypi had already walled it up with their in destructible cement.

"Well, sir?" said Ned Land, who came up to me after the departure of the Captain.

"Well, friend Ned, we will wait patiently for the tide on the 9th instant; for it appears that the moon will have the goodness to put it off again."

"Really?"

"Really."

"And this Captain is not going to cast anchor at all since the tide will suffice?" said Conseil, simply.

The Canadian looked at Conseil, then shrugged his shoulders.

"Sir, you may believe me when I tell you that this piece of iron will navigate neither on nor under the sea again; it is only fit to be sold for its weight. I think, therefore, that the time has come to part company with Captain Nemo."

"Friend Ned, I do not despair of this stout Nautilus, as you do; and in four days we shall know what to hold to on the Pacific tides. Besides, flight might be possible if we were in sight of the English or Provencal coast; but on the Papuan shores, it is another thing; and it will be time enough to come to that extremity if the Nautilus does not recover itself again, which I look upon as a grave event."

"But do they know, at least, how to act circumspectly? There is an island; on that island there are trees; under those trees, terrestrial animals, bearers of cutlets and roast beef, to which I would willingly give a trial."

"In this, friend Ned is right," said Conseil, "and I agree with him. Could not master obtain permission from his friend Captain Nemo to put us on land, if only so as not to lose the habit of treading on the solid parts of our planet?"

"I can ask him, but he will refuse."

"Will master risk it?" asked Conseil, "and we shall know how to rely upon the Captain's amiability."

To my great surprise, Captain Nemo gave me the permission I asked for, and he gave it very agreeably, without even exacting from me a promise to return to the vessel; but flight across New Guinea might be very perilous, and I should not have counselled Ned Land to attempt it. Better to be a prisoner on board the Nautilus than to fall into the hands of the natives.

At eight o'clock, armed with guns and hatchets, we got off the Nautilus. The sea was pretty calm; a slight breeze blew on land. Conseil and I rowing, we sped along quickly, and Ned steered in the straight passage that the breakers left between them. The boat was well handled, and moved rapidly.

Ned Land could not restrain his joy. He was like a prisoner that had escaped from prison, and knew not that it was necessary to re-enter it.

"Meat! We are going to eat some meat; and what meat!" he replied. "Real game! no, bread, indeed."

"I do not say that fish is not good; we must not abuse it; but a piece of fresh venison, grilled on live coals, will agreeably vary our ordinary course."

"Glutton!" said Conseil, "he makes my mouth water."

"It remains to be seen," I said, "if these forests are full of game, and if the game is not such as will hunt the hunter himself."

"Well said, M. Aronnax," replied the Canadian, whose teeth seemed sharpened like the edge of a hatchet; "but I will eat tiger—loin of tiger—if there is no other quadruped on this island."

"Friend Ned is uneasy about it," said Conseil.

"Whatever it may be," continued Ned Land, "every animal with four paws without feathers, or with two paws without feathers, will be saluted by my first shot."

"Very well! Master Land's imprudences are beginning."

"Never fear, M. Aronnax," replied the Canadian; "I do not want twenty-five minutes to offer you a dish, of my sort."

At half-past eight the Nautilus boat ran softly aground on a heavy sand, after having happily passed the coral reef that surrounds the Island of Gilboa.

CHAPTER XX. A FEW DAYS ON LAND

I was much impressed on touching land. Ned Land tried the soil with his feet, as if to take possession of it. However, it was only two months before that we had become, according to Captain Nemo, "passengers on board the Nautilus," but, in reality, prisoners of its commander.

In a few minutes we were within musket-shot of the coast. The whole horizon was hidden behind a beautiful curtain of forests. Enormous trees, the trunks of which attained a height of 200 feet, were tied to each other by garlands of bindweed, real natural hammocks, which a light breeze rocked. They were mimosas, figs, hibisci, and palm trees, mingled together in profusion; and under the shelter of their verdant vault grew orchids, leguminous plants, and ferns.

But, without noticing all these beautiful specimens of Papuan flora, the Canadian abandoned the agreeable for the useful. He discovered a coco-tree, beat down some of the fruit, broke them, and we drunk the milk and ate the nut with a satisfaction that protested against the ordinary food on the Nautilus.

"Excellent!" said Ned Land.

"Exquisite!" replied Conseil.

"And I do not think," said the Canadian, "that he would object to our introducing a cargo of coco-nuts on board."

"I do not think he would, but he would not taste them."

"So much the worse for him," said Conseil.

"And so much the better for us," replied Ned Land. "There will be more for us."

"One word only, Master Land," I said to the harpooner, who was beginning to ravage another coco-nut tree. "Coco-nuts are good things, but before filling the canoe with them it would be wise to reconnoitre and see if the island does not produce some substance not less useful. Fresh vegetables would be welcome on board the Nautilus."

"Master is right," replied Conseil; "and I propose to reserve three places in our vessel, one for fruits, the other for vegetables, and the third for the venison, of which I have not yet seen the smallest specimen."

"Conseil, we must not despair," said the Canadian.

"Let us continue," I returned, "and lie in wait. Although the island seems uninhabited, it might still contain some individuals that would be less hard than we on the nature of game."

"Ho! ho!" said Ned Land, moving his jaws significantly.

"Well, Ned!" said Conseil.

"My word!" returned the Canadian, "I begin to understand the charms of anthropophagy."

"Ned! Ned! what are you saying? You, a man-eater? I should not feel safe with you, especially as I share your cabin. I might perhaps wake one day to find myself half devoured."

"Friend Conseil, I like you much, but not enough to eat you unnecessarily."

"I would not trust you," replied Conseil. "But enough. We must absolutely bring down some game to satisfy this cannibal, or else one of these fine mornings, master will find only pieces of his servant to serve him."

While we were talking thus, we were penetrating the sombre arches of the forest, and for two hours we surveyed it in all directions.

Chance rewarded our search for eatable vegetables, and one of the most useful products of the tropical zones furnished us with precious food that we missed on board. I would speak of the bread-fruit tree, very abundant in the island of Gilboa; and I remarked chiefly the variety destitute of seeds, which bears in Malaya the name of "rima."

Ned Land knew these fruits well. He had already eaten many during his numerous voyages, and he knew how to prepare the eatable substance. Moreover, the sight of them excited him, and he could contain himself no longer.

"Master," he said, "I shall die if I do not taste a little of this bread-fruit pie."

"Taste it, friend Ned—taste it as you want. We are here to make experiments—make them."

"It won't take long," said the Canadian.

And, provided with a lentil, he lighted a fire of dead wood that crackled joyously. During this time, Conseil and I chose the best fruits of the bread-fruit. Some had not then attained a sufficient degree of maturity; and their thick skin covered a white but rather fibrous pulp. Others, the greater number yellow and gelatinous, waited only to be picked.

These fruits enclosed no kernel. Conseil brought a dozen to Ned Land, who placed them on a coal fire, after having cut them in thick slices, and while doing this repeating:

"You will see, master, how good this bread is. More so when one has been deprived of it so long. It is not even bread," added he, "but a delicate pastry. You have eaten none, master?"

"No, Ned."

"Very well, prepare yourself for a juicy thing. If you do not come for more, I am no longer the king of harpooners."

After some minutes, the part of the fruits that was exposed to the fire was completely roasted. The interior looked like a white pasty, a sort of soft crumb, the flavour of which was like that of an artichoke.

It must be confessed this bread was excellent, and I ate of it with great relish.

"What time is it now?" asked the Canadian.

"Two o'clock at least," replied Conseil.

"How time flies on firm ground!" sighed Ned Land.

"Let us be off," replied Conseil.

We returned through the forest, and completed our collection by a raid upon the cabbage-palms, that we gathered from the tops of the trees, little beans that I recognised as the "abrou" of the Malays, and yams of a superior quality.

We were loaded when we reached the boat. But Ned Land did not find his provisions sufficient. Fate, however, favoured us. Just as we were pushing off, he perceived several trees, from twenty-five to thirty feet high, a species of palm-tree.

At last, at five o'clock in the evening, loaded with our riches, we quitted the shore, and half an hour after we hailed the Nautilus. No one appeared on our arrival. The enormous iron-plated cylinder seemed deserted. The provisions embarked, I descended to my chamber, and after supper slept soundly.

The next day, 6th January, nothing new on board. Not a sound inside, not a sign of life. The boat rested along the edge, in the same place in which we had left it. We resolved to return to the island. Ned Land hoped to be more fortunate than on the day before with regard to the hunt, and wished to visit another part of the forest.

At dawn we set off. The boat, carried on by the waves that flowed to shore, reached the island in a few minutes.

We landed, and, thinking that it was better to give in to the Canadian, we followed Ned Land, whose long limbs threatened to distance us. He wound up the coast towards the west: then, fording some torrents, he gained the high plain that was bordered with admirable forests. Some kingfishers were rambling along the water-courses, but they would not let themselves be approached. Their circumspection proved to me that these birds knew what to expect from bipeds of our species, and I concluded that, if the island was not inhabited, at least human beings occasionally frequented it.

After crossing a rather large prairie, we arrived at the skirts of a little wood that was enlivened by the songs and flight of a large number of birds.

"There are only birds," said Conseil.

"But they are eatable," replied the harpooner.

"I do not agree with you, friend Ned, for I see only parrots there."

"Friend Conseil," said Ned, gravely, "the parrot is like pheasant to those who have nothing else."

"And," I added, "this bird, suitably prepared, is worth knife and fork."

Indeed, under the thick foliage of this wood, a world of parrots were flying from branch to branch, only needing a careful education to speak the human language. For the moment, they were chattering with parrots of all colours, and grave cockatoos, who seemed to meditate upon some philosophical problem, whilst brilliant red lories passed like a piece of bunting carried away by the breeze, papuans, with the finest azure colours, and in all a variety of winged things most charming to behold, but few eatable.

However, a bird peculiar to these lands, and which has never passed the limits of the Arrow and Papuan islands, was wanting in this collection. But fortune reserved it for me before long.

After passing through a moderately thick copse, we found a plain obstructed with bushes. I saw then those magnificent birds, the disposition of whose long feathers obliges them to fly against the wind. Their undulating flight, graceful aerial curves, and the shading of their colours, attracted and charmed one's looks. I had no trouble in recognising them.

"Birds of paradise!" I exclaimed.

The Malays, who carry on a great trade in these birds with the Chinese, have several means that we could not employ for taking them. Sometimes they put snares on the top of high trees that the birds of paradise prefer to frequent. Sometimes they catch them with a viscous birdlime that paralyses their movements. They even go so far as to poison the fountains that the birds generally drink from. But we were obliged to fire at them during flight, which gave us few chances to bring them down; and, indeed, we vainly exhausted one half our ammunition.

About eleven o'clock in the morning, the first range of mountains that form the centre of the island was traversed, and we had killed nothing. Hunger drove us on. The hunters had relied on the products of the chase, and they were wrong. Happily Conseil, to his great surprise, made a double shot and secured breakfast. He brought down a white pigeon and a wood-pigeon, which, cleverly plucked and suspended from a skewer, was roasted before a red fire of dead wood. While these interesting birds were cooking, Ned prepared the fruit of the bread-tree. Then the wood-pigeons were devoured to the bones, and declared excellent. The nutmeg, with which they are in the habit of stuffing their crops, flavours their flesh and renders it delicious eating.

"Now, Ned, what do you miss now?"

"Some four-footed game, M. Aronnax. All these pigeons are only side-dishes and trifles; and until I have killed an animal with cutlets I shall not be content."

"Nor I, Ned, if I do not catch a bird of paradise."

"Let us continue hunting," replied Conseil. "Let us go towards the sea. We have arrived at the first declivities of the mountains, and I think we had better regain the region of forests."

That was sensible advice, and was followed out. After walking for one hour we had attained a forest of sago-trees. Some inoffensive serpents glided away from us. The birds of paradise fled at our approach, and truly I despaired of getting near one when Conseil, who was walking in front, suddenly bent down, uttered a triumphal cry, and came back to me bringing a magnificent specimen.

"Ah! bravo, Conseil!"

"Master is very good."

"No, my boy; you have made an excellent stroke. Take one of these living birds, and carry it in your hand."

"If master will examine it, he will see that I have not deserved great merit."

"Why, Conseil?"

"Because this bird is as drunk as a quail."

"Drunk!"

"Yes, sir; drunk with the nutmegs that it devoured under the nutmeg-tree, under which I found it. See, friend Ned, see the monstrous effects of intemperance!"

"By Jove!" exclaimed the Canadian, "because I have drunk gin for two months, you must needs reproach me!"

However, I examined the curious bird. Conseil was right. The bird, drunk with the juice, was quite powerless. It could not fly; it could hardly walk.

This bird belonged to the most beautiful of the eight species that are found in Papua and in the neighbouring islands. It was the "large emerald bird, the most rare kind." It measured three feet in length. Its head was comparatively small, its eyes placed near the opening of the beak, and also small. But the shades of colour were beautiful, having a yellow beak, brown feet and claws, nut-coloured wings with purple tips, pale yellow at the back of the neck and head, and emerald colour at the throat, chestnut on the breast and belly. Two horned, downy nets rose from below the tail, that prolonged the long light feathers of admirable fineness, and they completed the whole of this marvellous bird, that the natives have poetically named the "bird of the sun."

But if my wishes were satisfied by the possession of the bird of paradise, the Canadian's were not yet. Happily, about two o'clock, Ned Land brought down a magnificent hog; from the brood of those the natives call "bari-outang." The animal came in time for us to procure real quadruped meat, and he was well received. Ned Land was very proud of his shot. The hog, hit by the electric ball, fell stone dead. The Canadian skinned and cleaned it properly, after having taken half a dozen cutlets, destined to furnish us with a grilled repast in the evening. Then the hunt was resumed, which was still more marked by Ned and Conseil's exploits.

Indeed, the two friends, beating the bushes, roused a herd of kangaroos that fled and bounded along on their elastic paws. But these animals did not take to flight so rapidly but what the electric capsule could stop their course.

"Ah, Professor!" cried Ned Land, who was carried away by the delights of the chase, "what excellent game, and stewed, too! What a supply for the Nautilus! Two! three! five down! And to think that we shall eat that flesh, and that the idiots on board shall not have a crumb!"

I think that, in the excess of his joy, the Canadian, if he had not talked so much, would have killed them all. But he contented himself with a single dozen of these interesting marsupians. These animals were small. They were a species of those "kangaroo rabbits" that live habitually in the hollows of trees, and whose speed is extreme; but they are moderately fat, and furnish, at least, estimable food. We were very satisfied with the results of the hunt. Happy Ned proposed to return to this enchanting island the next day, for he wished to depopulate it of all the eatable quadrupeds. But he had reckoned without his host. At six o'clock in the evening we had regained the shore; our boat was moored to the usual place. The Nautilus, like a long rock, emerged from the waves two miles from the beach. Ned Land, without waiting, occupied himself about the important dinner business. He understood all about cooking well. The "bari-outang," grilled on the coals, soon scented the air with a delicious odour.

Indeed, the dinner was excellent. Two wood-pigeons completed this extraordinary menu. The sago pasty, the artocarpus bread, some mangoes, half a dozen pineapples, and the liquor fermented from some coco-nuts, overjoyed us. I even think that my worthy companions' ideas had not all the plainness desirable.

"Suppose we do not return to the Nautilus this evening?" said Conseil.

"Suppose we never return?" added Ned Land.

Just then a stone fell at our feet and cut short the harpooner's proposition.

CHAPTER XXI. CAPTAIN NEMO'S THUNDERBOLT

We looked at the edge of the forest without rising, my hand stopping in the action of putting it to my mouth, Ned Land's completing its office.

"Stones do not fall from the sky," remarked Conseil, "or they would merit the name aerolites."

A second stone, carefully aimed, that made a savoury pigeon's leg fall from Conseil's hand, gave still more weight to his observation. We all three arose, shouldered our guns, and were ready to reply to any attack.

"Are they apes?" cried Ned Land.

"Very nearly—they are savages."

"To the boat!" I said, hurrying to the sea.

It was indeed necessary to beat a retreat, for about twenty natives armed with bows and slings appeared on the skirts of a copse that masked the horizon to the right, hardly a hundred steps from us.

Our boat was moored about sixty feet from us. The savages approached us, not running, but making hostile demonstrations. Stones and arrows fell thickly.

Ned Land had not wished to leave his provisions; and, in spite of his imminent danger, his pig on one side and kangaroos on the other, he went tolerably fast. In two minutes we were on the shore. To load the boat with provisions and arms, to push it out to sea, and ship the oars, was the work of an instant. We had not gone two cable-lengths, when a hundred savages, howling and gesticulating, entered the water up to their waists. I watched to see if their apparition would attract some men from the Nautilus on to the platform. But no. The enormous machine, lying off, was absolutely deserted.

Twenty minutes later we were on board. The panels were open. After making the boat fast, we entered into the interior of the Nautilus.

I descended to the drawing-room, from whence I heard some chords. Captain Nemo was there, bending over his organ, and plunged in a musical ecstasy.

"Captain!"

He did not hear me.

"Captain!" I said, touching his hand.

He shuddered, and, turning round, said, "Ah! it is you, Professor? Well, have you had a good hunt, have you botanised successfully?"

"Yes Captain; but we have unfortunately brought a troop of bipeds, whose vicinity troubles me."

"What bipeds?"

"Savages."

"Savages!" he echoed, ironically. "So you are astonished, Professor, at having set foot on a strange land and finding savages? Savages! where are there not any? Besides, are they worse than others, these whom you call savages?"

"But Captain——"

"How many have you counted?"

"A hundred at least."

"M. Aronnax," replied Captain Nemo, placing his fingers on the organ stops, "when all the natives of Papua are assembled on this shore, the Nautilus will have nothing to fear from their attacks."

The Captain's fingers were then running over the keys of the instrument, and I remarked that he touched only the black keys, which gave his melodies an essentially Scotch character. Soon he had forgotten my presence, and had plunged into a reverie that I did not disturb. I went up again on to the platform: night had already fallen; for, in this low latitude, the sun sets rapidly and without twilight. I could only see the island indistinctly; but the numerous fires, lighted on the beach, showed that the natives did not think of leaving it. I was alone for several hours, sometimes thinking of the natives—but without any dread of them, for the imperturbable confidence of the Captain was catching—sometimes forgetting them to admire the splendours of the night in the tropics. My remembrances went to France in the train of those zodiacal stars that would shine in some hours' time. The moon shone in the midst of the constellations of the zenith.

The night slipped away without any mischance, the islanders frightened no doubt at the sight of a monster aground in the bay. The panels were open, and would have offered an easy access to the interior of the Nautilus.

At six o'clock in the morning of the 8th January I went up on to the platform. The dawn was breaking. The island soon showed itself through the dissipating fogs, first the shore, then the summits.

The natives were there, more numerous than on the day before—five or six hundred perhaps—some of them, profiting by the low water, had come on to the coral, at less than two cable-lengths from the Nautilus. I distinguished them easily; they were true Papuans, with athletic figures, men of good race, large high foreheads, large, but not broad and flat, and white teeth. Their woolly hair, with a reddish tinge, showed off on their black shining bodies like those of the Nubians. From the lobes of their ears, cut and distended, hung chaplets of bones. Most of these savages were naked. Amongst them, I remarked some women, dressed from the hips to knees in quite a crinoline of herbs, that sustained a vegetable waistband. Some chiefs had ornamented their necks with a crescent and collars of glass beads, red and white; nearly all were armed with bows, arrows, and shields and carried on their shoulders a sort of net containing those round stones which they cast from their slings with great skill. One of these chiefs, rather near to the Nautilus, examined it attentively. He was, perhaps, a "mado" of high rank, for he was draped in a mat of banana-leaves, notched round the edges, and set off with brilliant colours.

I could easily have knocked down this native, who was within a short length; but I thought that it was better to wait for real hostile demonstrations. Between Europeans and savages, it is proper for the Europeans to parry sharply, not to attack.

During low water the natives roamed about near the Nautilus, but were not troublesome; I heard them frequently repeat the word "Assai," and by their gestures I understood that they invited me to go on land, an invitation that I declined.

So that, on that day, the boat did not push off, to the great displeasure of Master Land, who could not complete his provisions.

This adroit Canadian employed his time in preparing the viands and meat that he had brought off the island. As for the savages, they returned to the shore about eleven o'clock in the morning, as soon as the coral tops began to disappear under the rising tide; but I saw their numbers had increased considerably on the shore. Probably they came from the neighbouring islands, or very likely from Papua. However, I had not seen a single native canoe. Having nothing better to do, I thought of dragging these beautiful limpid waters, under which I saw a profusion of shells, zoophytes, and marine plants. Moreover, it was the last day that the Nautilus would pass in these parts, if it float in open sea the next day, according to Captain Nemo's promise.

I therefore called Conseil, who brought me a little light drag, very like those for the oyster fishery. Now to work! For two hours we fished unceasingly, but without bringing up any rarities. The drag was filled with midas-ears, harps, melames, and particularly the most beautiful hammers I have ever seen. We also brought up some sea-slugs, pearl-oysters, and a dozen little turtles that were reserved for the pantry on board.

But just when I expected it least, I put my hand on a wonder, I might say a natural deformity, very rarely met with. Conseil was just dragging, and his net came up filled with divers ordinary shells, when, all at once, he saw me plunge my arm quickly into the net, to draw out a shell, and heard me utter a cry.

"What is the matter, sir?" he asked in surprise. "Has master been bitten?"

"No, my boy; but I would willingly have given a finger for my discovery."

"What discovery?"

"This shell," I said, holding up the object of my triumph.

"It is simply an olive porphyry, genus olive, order of the pectinibranchidae, class of gasteropods, sub-class mollusca."

"Yes, Conseil; but, instead of being rolled from right to left, this olive turns from left to right."

"Is it possible?"

"Yes, my boy; it is a left shell."

Shells are all right-handed, with rare exceptions; and, when by chance their spiral is left, amateurs are ready to pay their weight in gold.

Conseil and I were absorbed in the contemplation of our treasure, and I was promising myself to enrich the museum with it, when a stone unfortunately thrown by a native struck against, and broke, the precious object in Conseil's hand. I uttered a cry of despair! Conseil took up his gun, and aimed at a savage who was poising his sling at ten yards from him. I would have stopped him, but his blow took effect and broke the bracelet of amulets which encircled the arm of the savage.

"Conseil!" cried I. "Conseil!"

"Well, sir! do you not see that the cannibal has commenced the attack?"

"A shell is not worth the life of a man," said I.

"Ah! the scoundrel!" cried Conseil; "I would rather he had broken my shoulder!"

Conseil was in earnest, but I was not of his opinion. However, the situation had changed some minutes before, and we had not perceived. A score of canoes surrounded the Nautilus. These canoes, scooped out of the trunk of a tree, long, narrow, well adapted for speed, were balanced by means of a long bamboo pole, which floated on the water. They were managed by skilful, half-naked paddlers, and I watched their advance with some uneasiness. It was evident that these Papuans had already had dealings with the Europeans and knew their ships. But this long iron cylinder anchored in the bay, without masts or chimneys, what could they think of it? Nothing good, for at first they kept at a respectful distance. However, seeing it motionless, by degrees they took courage, and sought to familiarise themselves with it. Now this familiarity was precisely what it was necessary to avoid. Our arms, which were noiseless, could only produce a moderate effect on the savages, who have little respect for aught but blustering things. The thunderbolt without the reverberations of thunder would frighten man but little, though the danger lies in the lightning, not in the noise.

At this moment the canoes approached the Nautilus, and a shower of arrows alighted on her.

I went down to the saloon, but found no one there. I ventured to knock at the door that opened into the Captain's room. "Come in," was the answer.

I entered, and found Captain Nemo deep in algebraical calculations of x and other quantities.

"I am disturbing you," said I, for courtesy's sake.

"That is true, M. Aronnax," replied the Captain; "but I think you have serious reasons for wishing to see me?"

"Very grave ones; the natives are surrounding us in their canoes, and in a few minutes we shall certainly be attacked by many hundreds of savages."

"Ah!" said Captain Nemo quietly, "they are come with their canoes?"

"Yes, sir."

"Well, sir, we must close the hatches."

"Exactly, and I came to say to you——"

"Nothing can be more simple," said Captain Nemo. And, pressing an electric button, he transmitted an order to the ship's crew.

"It is all done, sir," said he, after some moments. "The pinnace is ready, and the hatches are closed. You do not fear, I imagine, that these gentlemen could stave in walls on which the balls of your frigate have had no effect?"

"No, Captain; but a danger still exists."

"What is that, sir?"

"It is that to-morrow, at about this hour, we must open the hatches to renew the air of the Nautilus. Now, if, at this moment, the Papuans should occupy the platform, I do not see how you could prevent them from entering."

"Then, sir, you suppose that they will board us?"

"I am certain of it."

"Well, sir, let them come. I see no reason for hindering them. After all, these Papuans are poor creatures, and I am unwilling that my visit to the island should cost the life of a single one of these wretches."

Upon that I was going away; But Captain Nemo detained me, and asked me to sit down by him. He questioned me with interest about our excursions on shore, and our hunting; and seemed not to understand the craving for meat that possessed the Canadian. Then the conversation turned on various subjects, and, without being more communicative, Captain Nemo showed himself more amiable.

Amongst other things, we happened to speak of the situation of the Nautilus, run aground in exactly the same spot in this strait where Dumont d'Urville was nearly lost. Apropos of this:

"This D'Urville was one of your great sailors," said the Captain to me, "one of your most intelligent navigators. He is the Captain Cook of you Frenchmen. Unfortunate man of science, after having braved the icebergs of the South Pole, the coral reefs of Oceania, the cannibals of the Pacific, to perish miserably in a railway train! If this energetic man could have reflected during the last moments of his life, what must have been uppermost in his last thoughts, do you suppose?"

So speaking, Captain Nemo seemed moved, and his emotion gave me a better opinion of him. Then, chart in hand, we reviewed the travels of the French navigator, his voyages of circumnavigation, his double detention at the South Pole, which led to the discovery of Adelaide and Louis Philippe, and fixing the hydrographical bearings of the principal islands of Oceania.

"That which your D'Urville has done on the surface of the seas," said Captain Nemo, "that have I done under them, and more easily, more completely than he. The Astrolabe and the Zelee, incessantly tossed about by the hurricane, could not be worth the Nautilus, quiet repository of labour that she is, truly motionless in the midst of the waters.

"To-morrow," added the Captain, rising, "to-morrow, at twenty minutes to three p.m., the Nautilus shall float, and leave the Strait of Torres uninjured."

Having curtly pronounced these words, Captain Nemo bowed slightly. This was to dismiss me, and I went back to my room.

There I found Conseil, who wished to know the result of my interview with the Captain.

"My boy," said I, "when I feigned to believe that his Nautilus was threatened by the natives of Papua, the Captain answered me very sarcastically. I have but one thing to say to you: Have confidence in him, and go to sleep in peace."

"Have you no need of my services, sir?"

"No, my friend. What is Ned Land doing?"

"If you will excuse me, sir," answered Conseil, "friend Ned is busy making a kangaroo-pie which will be a marvel."

I remained alone and went to bed, but slept indifferently. I heard the noise of the savages, who stamped on the platform, uttering deafening cries. The night passed thus, without disturbing the ordinary repose of the crew. The presence of these cannibals affected them no more than the soldiers of a masked battery care for the ants that crawl over its front.

At six in the morning I rose. The hatches had not been opened. The inner air was not renewed, but the reservoirs, filled ready for any emergency, were now resorted to, and discharged several cubic feet of oxygen into the exhausted atmosphere of the Nautilus.

I worked in my room till noon, without having seen Captain Nemo, even for an instant. On board no preparations for departure were visible.

I waited still some time, then went into the large saloon. The clock marked half-past two. In ten minutes it would be high-tide: and, if Captain Nemo had not made a rash promise, the Nautilus would be immediately detached. If not, many months would pass ere she could leave her bed of coral.

However, some warning vibrations began to be felt in the vessel. I heard the keel grating against the rough calcareous bottom of the coral reef.

At five-and-twenty minutes to three, Captain Nemo appeared in the saloon.

"We are going to start," said he.

"Ah!" replied I.

"I have given the order to open the hatches."

"And the Papuans?"

"The Papuans?" answered Captain Nemo, slightly shrugging his shoulders.

"Will they not come inside the Nautilus?"

"How?"

"Only by leaping over the hatches you have opened."

"M. Aronnax," quietly answered Captain Nemo, "they will not enter the hatches of the Nautilus in that way, even if they were open."

I looked at the Captain.

"You do not understand?" said he.

"Hardly."

"Well, come and you will see."

I directed my steps towards the central staircase. There Ned Land and Conseil were slyly watching some of the ship's crew, who were opening the hatches, while cries of rage and fearful vociferations resounded outside.

The port lids were pulled down outside. Twenty horrible faces appeared. But the first native who placed his hand on the stair-rail, struck from behind by some invisible force, I know not what, fled, uttering the most fearful cries and making the wildest contortions.

Ten of his companions followed him. They met with the same fate.

Conseil was in ecstasy. Ned Land, carried away by his violent instincts, rushed on to the staircase. But the moment he seized the rail with both hands, he, in his turn, was overthrown.

"I am struck by a thunderbolt," cried he, with an oath.

This explained all. It was no rail; but a metallic cable charged with electricity from the deck communicating with the platform. Whoever touched it felt a powerful shock—and this shock would have been mortal if Captain Nemo had discharged into the conductor the whole force of the current. It might truly be said that between his assailants and himself he had stretched a network of electricity which none could pass with impunity.

Meanwhile, the exasperated Papuans had beaten a retreat paralysed with terror. As for us, half laughing, we consoled and rubbed the unfortunate Ned Land, who swore like one possessed.

But at this moment the Nautilus, raised by the last waves of the tide, quitted her coral bed exactly at the fortieth minute fixed by the Captain. Her screw swept the waters slowly and majestically. Her speed increased gradually, and, sailing on the surface of the ocean, she quitted safe and sound the dangerous passes of the Straits of Torres.

CHAPTER XXII. "AEGRI SOMNIA"

The following day 10th January, the Nautilus continued her course between two seas, but with such remarkable speed that I could not estimate it at less than thirty-five miles an hour. The rapidity of her screw was such that I could neither follow nor count its revolutions. When I reflected that this marvellous electric agent, after having afforded motion, heat, and light to the Nautilus, still protected her from outward attack, and transformed her into an ark of safety which no profane hand might touch without being thunderstricken, my admiration was unbounded, and from the structure it extended to the engineer who had called it into existence.

Our course was directed to the west, and on the 11th of January we doubled Cape Wessel, situation in 135° long. and 10° S. lat., which forms the east point of the Gulf of Carpentaria. The reefs were still numerous, but more equalised, and marked on the chart with extreme precision. The Nautilus easily avoided the breakers of Money to port and the Victoria reefs to starboard, placed at 130° long. and on the 10th parallel, which we strictly followed.

On the 13th of January, Captain Nemo arrived in the Sea of Timor, and recognised the island of that name in 122° long.

From this point the direction of the Nautilus inclined towards the south-west. Her head was set for the Indian Ocean. Where would the fancy of Captain Nemo carry us next? Would he return to the coast of Asia or would he approach again the shores of Europe? Improbable conjectures both, to a man who fled from inhabited continents. Then would he descend to the south? Was he going to double the Cape of Good Hope, then Cape Horn, and finally go as far as the Antarctic pole? Would he come back at last to the Pacific, where his Nautilus could sail free and independently? Time would show.

After having skirted the sands of Cartier, of Hibernia, Seringapatam, and Scott, last efforts of the solid against the liquid element, on the 14th of January we lost sight of land altogether. The speed of the Nautilus was considerably abated, and with irregular course she sometimes swam in the bosom of the waters, sometimes floated on their surface.

During this period of the voyage, Captain Nemo made some interesting experiments on the varied temperature of the sea, in different beds. Under ordinary conditions these observations are made by means of rather complicated instruments, and with somewhat doubtful results, by means of thermometrical sounding-leads, the glasses often breaking under the pressure of the water, or an apparatus grounded on the variations of the resistance of metals to the electric currents. Results so obtained could not be correctly calculated. On the contrary, Captain Nemo went himself to test the temperature in the depths of the sea, and his thermometer, placed in communication with the different sheets of water, gave him the required degree immediately and accurately.

It was thus that, either by overloading her reservoirs or by descending obliquely by means of her inclined planes, the Nautilus successively attained the depth of three, four, five, seven, nine, and ten thousand yards, and the definite result of this experience was that the sea preserved an average temperature of four degrees and a half at a depth of five thousand fathoms under all latitudes.

On the 16th of January, the Nautilus seemed becalmed only a few yards beneath the surface of the waves. Her electric apparatus remained inactive and her motionless screw left her to drift at the mercy of the currents. I supposed that the crew was occupied with interior repairs, rendered necessary by the violence of the mechanical movements of the machine.

My companions and I then witnessed a curious spectacle. The hatches of the saloon were open, and, as the beacon light of the Nautilus was not in action, a dim obscurity reigned in the midst of the waters. I observed the state of the sea, under these conditions, and the largest fish appeared to me no more than scarcely defined shadows, when the Nautilus found herself suddenly transported into full light. I thought at first that the beacon had been lighted, and was casting its electric radiance into the liquid mass. I was mistaken, and after a rapid survey perceived my error.

The Nautilus floated in the midst of a phosphorescent bed which, in this obscurity, became quite dazzling. It was produced by myriads of luminous animalculae, whose brilliancy was increased as they glided over the metallic hull of the vessel. I was surprised by lightning in the midst of these luminous sheets, as though they had been rivulets of lead melted in an ardent furnace or metallic masses brought to a white heat, so that, by force of contrast, certain portions of light appeared to cast a shade in the midst of the general ignition, from which all shade seemed banished. No; this was not the calm irradiation of our ordinary lightning. There was unusual life and vigour: this was truly living light!

In reality, it was an infinite agglomeration of coloured infusoria, of veritable globules of jelly, provided with a threadlike tentacle, and of which as many as twenty-five thousand have been counted in less than two cubic half-inches of water.

During several hours the Nautilus floated in these brilliant waves, and our admiration increased as we watched the marine monsters disporting themselves like salamanders. I saw there in the midst of this fire that burns not the swift and elegant porpoise (the indefatigable clown of the ocean), and some swordfish ten feet long, those prophetic heralds of the hurricane whose formidable sword would now and then strike the glass of the saloon. Then appeared the smaller fish, the balista, the leaping mackerel, wolf-thorn-tails, and a hundred others which striped the luminous atmosphere as they swam. This dazzling spectacle was enchanting! Perhaps some atmospheric condition increased the intensity of this phenomenon. Perhaps some storm agitated the surface of the waves. But at this depth of some yards, the Nautilus was unmoved by its fury and reposed peacefully in still water.

So we progressed, incessantly charmed by some new marvel. The days passed rapidly away, and I took no account of them. Ned, according to habit, tried to vary the diet on board. Like snails, we were fixed to our shells, and I declare it is easy to lead a snail's life.

Thus this life seemed easy and natural, and we thought no longer of the life we led on land; but something happened to recall us to the strangeness of our situation.

On the 18th of January, the Nautilus was in 105° long. and 15° S. lat. The weather was threatening, the sea rough and rolling. There was a strong east wind. The barometer, which had been going down for some days, foreboded a coming storm. I went up on to the platform just as the second lieutenant was taking the measure of the horary angles, and waited, according to habit till the daily phrase was said. But on this day it was exchanged for another phrase not less incomprehensible. Almost directly, I saw Captain Nemo appear with a glass, looking towards the horizon.

For some minutes he was immovable, without taking his eye off the point of observation. Then he lowered his glass and exchanged a few words with his lieutenant. The latter seemed to be a victim to some emotion that he tried in vain to repress. Captain Nemo, having more command over himself, was cool.

He seemed, too, to be making some objections to which the lieutenant replied by formal assurances. At least I concluded so by the difference of their tones and gestures. For myself, I had looked carefully in the direction indicated without seeing anything. The sky and water were lost in the clear line of the horizon.

However, Captain Nemo walked from one end of the platform to the other, without looking at me, perhaps without seeing me. His step was firm, but less regular than usual. He stopped sometimes, crossed his arms, and observed the sea. What could he be looking for on that immense expanse?

The Nautilus was then some hundreds of miles from the nearest coast.

The lieutenant had taken up the glass and examined the horizon steadfastly, going and coming, stamping his foot and showing more nervous agitation than his superior officer. Besides, this mystery must necessarily be solved, and before long; for, upon an order from Captain Nemo, the engine, increasing its propelling power, made the screw turn more rapidly.

Just then the lieutenant drew the Captain's attention again. The latter stopped walking and directed his glass towards the place indicated. He looked long. I felt very much puzzled, and descended to the drawing-room, and took out an excellent telescope that I generally used. Then, leaning on the cage of the watch-light that jutted out from the front of the platform, set myself to look over all the line of the sky and sea.

But my eye was no sooner applied to the glass than it was quickly snatched out of my hands.

I turned round. Captain Nemo was before me, but I did not know him. His face was transfigured. His eyes flashed sullenly; his teeth were set; his stiff body, clenched fists, and head shrunk between his shoulders, betrayed the violent agitation that pervaded his whole frame. He did not move. My glass, fallen from his hands, had rolled at his feet.

Had I unwittingly provoked this fit of anger? Did this incomprehensible person imagine that I had discovered some forbidden secret? No; I was not the object of this hatred, for he was not looking at me; his eye was steadily fixed upon the impenetrable point of the horizon. At last Captain Nemo recovered himself. His agitation subsided. He addressed some words in a foreign language to his lieutenant, then turned to me. "M. Aronnax," he said, in rather an imperious tone, "I require you to keep one of the conditions that bind you to me."

"What is it, Captain?"

"You must be confined, with your companions, until I think fit to release you."

"You are the master," I replied, looking steadily at him. "But may I ask you one question?"

"None, sir."

There was no resisting this imperious command, it would have been useless. I went down to the cabin occupied by Ned Land and Conseil, and told them the Captain's determination. You may judge how this communication was received by the Canadian.

But there was not time for altercation. Four of the crew waited at the door, and conducted us to that cell where we had passed our first night on board the Nautilus.

Ned Land would have remonstrated, but the door was shut upon him.

"Will master tell me what this means?" asked Conseil.

I told my companions what had passed. They were as much astonished as I, and equally at a loss how to account for it.

Meanwhile, I was absorbed in my own reflections, and could think of nothing but the strange fear depicted in the Captain's countenance. I was utterly at a loss to account for it, when my cogitations were disturbed by these words from Ned Land:

"Hallo! breakfast is ready."

And indeed the table was laid. Evidently Captain Nemo had given this order at the same time that he had hastened the speed of the Nautilus.

"Will master permit me to make a recommendation?" asked Conseil.

"Yes, my boy."

"Well, it is that master breakfasts. It is prudent, for we do not know what may happen."

"You are right, Conseil."

"Unfortunately," said Ned Land, "they have only given us the ship's fare."

"Friend Ned," asked Conseil, "what would you have said if the breakfast had been entirely forgotten?"

This argument cut short the harpooner's recriminations.

We sat down to table. The meal was eaten in silence.

Just then the luminous globe that lighted the cell went out, and left us in total darkness. Ned Land was soon asleep, and what astonished me was that Conseil went off into a heavy slumber. I was thinking what could have caused his irresistible drowsiness, when I felt my brain becoming stupefied. In spite of my efforts to keep my eyes open, they would close. A painful suspicion seized me. Evidently soporific substances had been mixed with the food we had just taken. Imprisonment was not enough to conceal Captain Nemo's projects from us, sleep was more necessary. I then heard the panels shut. The undulations of the sea, which caused a slight rolling motion, ceased. Had the Nautilus quitted the surface of the ocean? Had it gone back to the motionless bed of water? I tried to resist sleep. It was impossible. My breathing grew weak. I felt a mortal cold freeze my stiffened and half-paralysed limbs. My eye lids, like leaden caps, fell over my eyes. I could not raise them; a morbid sleep, full of hallucinations, bereft me of my being. Then the visions disappeared, and left me in complete insensibility.

CHAPTER XXIII. THE CORAL KINGDOM

The next day I woke with my head singularly clear. To my great surprise, I was in my own room. My companions, no doubt, had been reinstated in their cabin, without having perceived it any more than I. Of what had passed during the night they were as ignorant as I was, and to penetrate this mystery I only reckoned upon the chances of the future.

I then thought of quitting my room. Was I free again or a prisoner? Quite free. I opened the door, went to the half-deck, went up the central stairs. The panels, shut the evening before, were open. I went on to the platform.

Ned Land and Conseil waited there for me. I questioned them; they knew nothing. Lost in a heavy sleep in which they had been totally unconscious, they had been astonished at finding themselves in their cabin.

As for the Nautilus, it seemed quiet and mysterious as ever. It floated on the surface of the waves at a moderate pace. Nothing seemed changed on board.

The second lieutenant then came on to the platform, and gave the usual order below.

As for Captain Nemo, he did not appear.

Of the people on board, I only saw the impassive steward, who served me with his usual dumb regularity.

About two o'clock, I was in the drawing-room, busied in arranging my notes, when the Captain opened the door and appeared. I bowed. He made a slight inclination in return, without speaking. I resumed my work, hoping that he would perhaps give me some explanation of the events of the preceding night. He made none. I looked at him. He seemed fatigued; his heavy eyes had not been refreshed by sleep; his face looked very sorrowful. He walked to and fro, sat down and got up again, took a chance book, put it down, consulted his instruments without taking his habitual notes, and seemed restless and uneasy. At last, he came up to me, and said:

"Are you a doctor, M. Aronnax?"

I so little expected such a question that I stared some time at him without answering.

"Are you a doctor?" he repeated. "Several of your colleagues have studied medicine."

"Well," said I, "I am a doctor and resident surgeon to the hospital. I practised several years before entering the museum."

"Very well, sir."

My answer had evidently satisfied the Captain. But, not knowing what he would say next, I waited for other questions, reserving my answers according to circumstances.

"M. Aronnax, will you consent to prescribe for one of my men?" he asked.

"Is he ill?"

"Yes."

"I am ready to follow you."

"Come, then."

I own my heart beat, I do not know why. I saw certain connection between the illness of one of the crew and the events of the day before; and this mystery interested me at least as much as the sick man.

Captain Nemo conducted me to the poop of the Nautilus, and took me into a cabin situated near the sailors' quarters.

There, on a bed, lay a man about forty years of age, with a resolute expression of countenance, a true type of an Anglo-Saxon.

I leant over him. He was not only ill, he was wounded. His head, swathed in bandages covered with blood, lay on a pillow. I undid the bandages, and the wounded man looked at me with his large eyes and gave no sign of pain as I did it. It was a horrible wound. The skull, shattered by some deadly weapon, left the brain exposed, which was much injured. Clots of blood had formed in the bruised and broken mass, in colour like the dregs of wine.

There was both contusion and suffusion of the brain. His breathing was slow, and some spasmodic movements of the muscles agitated his face. I felt his pulse. It was intermittent. The extremities of the body were growing cold already, and I saw death must inevitably ensue. After dressing the unfortunate man's wounds, I readjusted the bandages on his head, and turned to Captain Nemo.

"What caused this wound?" I asked.

"What does it signify?" he replied, evasively. "A shock has broken one of the levers of the engine, which struck myself. But your opinion as to his state?"

I hesitated before giving it.

"You may speak," said the Captain. "This man does not understand French."

I gave a last look at the wounded man.

"He will be dead in two hours."

"Can nothing save him?"

"Nothing."

Captain Nemo's hand contracted, and some tears glistened in his eyes, which I thought incapable of shedding any.

For some moments I still watched the dying man, whose life ebbed slowly. His pallor increased under the electric light that was shed over his death-bed. I looked at his intelligent forehead, furrowed with premature wrinkles, produced probably by misfortune and sorrow. I tried to learn the secret of his life from the last words that escaped his lips.

"You can go now, M. Aronnax," said the Captain.

I left him in the dying man's cabin, and returned to my room much affected by this scene. During the whole day, I was haunted by uncomfortable suspicions, and at night I slept badly, and between my broken dreams I fancied

I heard distant sighs like the notes of a funeral psalm. Were they the prayers of the dead, murmured in that language that I could not understand?

The next morning I went on to the bridge. Captain Nemo was there before me. As soon as he perceived me he came to me.

"Professor, will it be convenient to you to make a submarine excursion to-day?"

"With my companions?" I asked.

"If they like."

"We obey your orders, Captain."

"Will you be so good then as to put on your cork jackets?"

It was not a question of dead or dying. I rejoined Ned Land and Conseil, and told them of Captain Nemo's proposition. Conseil hastened to accept it, and this time the Canadian seemed quite willing to follow our example.

It was eight o'clock in the morning. At half-past eight we were equipped for this new excursion, and provided with two contrivances for light and breathing. The double door was open; and, accompanied by Captain Nemo, who was followed by a dozen of the crew, we set foot, at a depth of about thirty feet, on the solid bottom on which the Nautilus rested.

A slight declivity ended in an uneven bottom, at fifteen fathoms depth. This bottom differed entirely from the one I had visited on my first excursion under the waters of the Pacific Ocean. Here, there was no fine sand, no submarine prairies, no sea-forest. I immediately recognised that marvellous region in which, on that day, the Captain did the honours to us. It was the coral kingdom.

The light produced a thousand charming varieties, playing in the midst of the branches that were so vividly coloured. I seemed to see the membraneous and cylindrical tubes tremble beneath the undulation of the waters. I was tempted to gather their fresh petals, ornamented with delicate tentacles, some just blown, the others budding, while a small fish, swimming swiftly, touched them slightly, like flights of birds. But if my hand approached these living flowers, these animated, sensitive plants, the whole colony took alarm. The white petals re-entered their red cases, the flowers faded as I looked, and the bush changed into a block of stony knobs.

Chance had thrown me just by the most precious specimens of the zoophyte. This coral was more valuable than that found in the Mediterranean, on the coasts of France, Italy and Barbary. Its tints justified the poetical names of "Flower of Blood," and "Froth of Blood," that trade has given to its most beautiful productions. Coral is sold for L20 per ounce; and in this place the watery beds would make the fortunes of a company of coral-divers. This precious matter, often confused with other polypi, formed then the inextricable plots called "macciota," and on which I noticed several beautiful specimens of pink coral.

But soon the bushes contract, and the arborisations increase. Real petrified thickets, long joints of fantastic architecture, were disclosed before us. Captain Nemo placed himself under a dark gallery, where by a slight declivity we reached a depth of a hundred yards. The light from our lamps produced sometimes magical effects, following the rough outlines of the natural arches and pendants disposed like lustres, that were tipped with points of fire.

At last, after walking two hours, we had attained a depth of about three hundred yards, that is to say, the extreme limit on which coral begins to form. But there was no isolated bush, nor modest brushwood, at the bottom of lofty trees. It was an immense forest of large mineral vegetations, enormous petrified trees, united by garlands of elegant sea-bindweed, all adorned with clouds and reflections. We passed freely under their high branches, lost in the shade of the waves.

Captain Nemo had stopped. I and my companions halted, and, turning round, I saw his men were forming a semi-circle round their chief. Watching attentively, I observed that four of them carried on their shoulders an object of an oblong shape.

We occupied, in this place, the centre of a vast glade surrounded by the lofty foliage of the submarine forest. Our lamps threw over this place a sort of clear twilight that singularly elongated the shadows on the ground. At the end of the glade the darkness increased, and was only relieved by little sparks reflected by the points of coral.

Ned Land and Conseil were near me. We watched, and I thought I was going to witness a strange scene. On observing the ground, I saw that it was raised in certain places by slight excrescences encrusted with limy deposits, and disposed with a regularity that betrayed the hand of man.

In the midst of the glade, on a pedestal of rocks roughly piled up, stood a cross of coral that extended its long arms that one might have thought were made of petrified blood. Upon a sign from Captain Nemo one of the men advanced; and at some feet from the cross he began to dig a hole with a pickaxe that he took from his belt. I understood all! This glade was a cemetery, this hole a tomb, this oblong object the body of the man who had died in the night! The Captain and his men had come to bury their companion in this general resting-place, at the bottom of this inaccessible ocean!

The grave was being dug slowly; the fish fled on all sides while their retreat was being thus disturbed; I heard the strokes of the pickaxe, which sparkled when it hit upon some flint lost at the bottom of the waters. The hole was soon large and deep enough to receive the body. Then the bearers approached; the body, enveloped in a tissue of white linen, was lowered into the damp grave. Captain Nemo, with his arms crossed on his breast, and all the friends of him who had loved them, knelt in prayer.

The grave was then filled in with the rubbish taken from the ground, which formed a slight mound. When this was done, Captain Nemo and his men rose; then, approaching the grave, they knelt again, and all extended their hands in sign of a last adieu. Then the funeral procession returned to the Nautilus, passing under the arches of the forest, in the midst of thickets, along the coral bushes, and still on the ascent. At last the light of the ship appeared, and its luminous track guided us to the Nautilus. At one o'clock we had returned.

As soon as I had changed my clothes I went up on to the platform, and, a prey to conflicting emotions, I sat down near the binnacle. Captain Nemo joined me. I rose and said to him:

"So, as I said he would, this man died in the night?"

"Yes, M. Aronnax."

"And he rests now, near his companions, in the coral cemetery?"

"Yes, forgotten by all else, but not by us. We dug the grave, and the polypi undertake to seal our dead for eternity." And, burying his face quickly in his hands, he tried in vain to suppress a sob. Then he added: "Our peaceful cemetery is there, some hundred feet below the surface of the waves."

"Your dead sleep quietly, at least, Captain, out of the reach of sharks."

"Yes, sir, of sharks and men," gravely replied the Captain.

PART TWO

CHAPTER I. THE INDIAN OCEAN

We now come to the second part of our journey under the sea. The first ended with the moving scene in the coral cemetery which left such a deep impression on my mind. Thus, in the midst of this great sea, Captain Nemo's life was passing, even to his grave, which he had prepared in one of its deepest abysses. There, not one of the ocean's monsters could trouble the last sleep of the crew of the Nautilus, of those friends riveted to each other in death as in life. "Nor any man, either," had added the Captain. Still the same fierce, implacable defiance towards human society!

I could no longer content myself with the theory which satisfied Conseil.

That worthy fellow persisted in seeing in the Commander of the Nautilus one of those unknown *savants* who return mankind contempt for indifference. For him, he was a misunderstood genius who, tired of earth's deceptions, had taken refuge in this inaccessible medium, where he might follow his instincts freely. To my mind, this explains but one side of Captain Nemo's character. Indeed, the mystery of that last night during which we had been chained in prison, the sleep, and the precaution so violently taken by the Captain of snatching from my eyes the glass I had raised to sweep the horizon, the mortal wound of the man, due to an unaccountable shock of the Nautilus, all put me on a new track. No; Captain Nemo was not satisfied with shunning man. His formidable apparatus not only suited his instinct of freedom, but perhaps also the design of some terrible retaliation.

At this moment nothing is clear to me; I catch but a glimpse of light amidst all the darkness, and I must confine myself to writing as events shall dictate.

That day, the 24th of January, 1868, at noon, the second officer came to take the altitude of the sun. I mounted the platform, lit a cigar, and watched the operation. It seemed to me that the man did not understand French; for several times I made remarks in a loud voice, which must have drawn from him some involuntary sign of attention, if he had understood them; but he remained undisturbed and dumb.

As he was taking observations with the sextant, one of the sailors of the Nautilus (the strong man who had accompanied us on our first submarine excursion to the Island of Crespo) came to clean the glasses of the lantern. I examined the fittings of the apparatus, the strength of which was increased a hundredfold by lenticular rings, placed similar to those in a lighthouse, and which projected their brilliance in a horizontal plane. The electric lamp was combined in such a way as to give its most powerful light. Indeed, it was produced in vacuo, which insured both its steadiness and its intensity. This vacuum economised the graphite points between which the luminous arc was developed—an important point of economy for Captain Nemo, who could not easily have replaced them; and under these conditions their waste was imperceptible. When the Nautilus was ready to continue its submarine journey, I went down to the saloon. The panel was closed, and the course marked direct west.

We were furrowing the waters of the Indian Ocean, a vast liquid plain, with a surface of 1,200,000,000 of acres, and whose waters are so clear and transparent that any one leaning over them would turn giddy. The Nautilus usually floated between fifty and a hundred fathoms deep. We went on so for some days. To anyone but myself, who had a great love for the sea, the hours would have seemed long and monotonous; but the daily walks on the platform, when I steeped myself in the reviving air of the ocean, the sight of the rich waters through the windows of the saloon, the books in the library, the compiling of my memoirs, took up all my time, and left me not a moment of ennui or weariness.

For some days we saw a great number of aquatic birds, sea-mews or gulls. Some were cleverly killed and, prepared in a certain way, made very acceptable water-game. Amongst large-winged birds, carried a long distance from all lands and resting upon the waves from the fatigue of their flight, I saw some magnificent albatrosses, uttering discordant cries like the braying of an ass, and birds belonging to the family of the long-wings.

As to the fish, they always provoked our admiration when we surprised the secrets of their aquatic life through the open panels. I saw many kinds which I never before had a chance of observing.

I shall notice chiefly ostracions peculiar to the Red Sea, the Indian Ocean, and that part which washes the coast of tropical America. These fishes, like the tortoise, the armadillo, the sea-hedgehog, and the Crustacea, are protected by a breastplate which is neither chalky nor stony, but real bone. In some it takes the form of a solid triangle, in others of a solid quadrangle. Amongst the triangular I saw some an inch and a half in length, with wholesome flesh and a delicious flavour; they are brown at the tail, and yellow at the fins, and I recommend their introduction into fresh water, to which a certain number of sea-fish easily accustom themselves. I would also mention quadrangular ostracions, having on the back four large tubercles; some dotted over with white spots on the lower part of the body, and which may be tamed like birds; trigons provided with spikes formed by the lengthening of their bony shell, and which, from their strange gruntings, are called "seapigs"; also dromedaries with large humps in the shape of a cone, whose flesh is very tough and leathery.

I now borrow from the daily notes of Master Conseil. "Certain fish of the genus petrodon peculiar to those seas, with red backs and white chests, which are distinguished by three rows of longitudinal filaments; and some electrical, seven inches long, decked in the liveliest colours. Then, as specimens of other kinds, some ovoides, resembling an egg of a dark brown colour, marked with white bands, and without tails; diodons, real sea-porcupines, furnished with spikes, and capable of swelling in such a way as to look like cushions bristling with darts; hippocampi, common to every ocean; some pegasi with lengthened snouts, which their pectoral fins, being much elongated and formed in the shape of wings, allow, if not to fly, at least to shoot into the air; pigeon spatulae, with tails covered with many rings of shell; macrognathi with long jaws, an excellent fish, nine inches long, and bright with most agreeable colours; pale-coloured calliomores, with rugged heads; and plenty of chaetpdons, with long and tubular muzzles, which kill insects by shooting them, as from an air-gun, with a single drop of water. These we may call the flycatchers of the seas.

"In the eighty-ninth genus of fishes, classed by Lacepede, belonging to the second lower class of bony, characterised by opercules and bronchial membranes, I remarked the scorpaena, the head of which is furnished with spikes, and which has but one dorsal fin; these creatures are covered, or not, with little shells, according to the sub-class to which they belong. The second sub-class gives us specimens of didactyles fourteen or fifteen inches in length, with yellow rays, and heads of a most fantastic appearance. As to the first sub-class, it gives several specimens of that singular looking fish appropriately called a 'seafrog,' with large head, sometimes pierced with holes, sometimes swollen with protuberances, bristling with spikes, and covered with tubercles; it has irregular and hideous horns; its body and tail are covered with callosities; its sting makes a dangerous wound; it is both repugnant and horrible to look at."

From the 21st to the 23rd of January the Nautilus went at the rate of two hundred and fifty leagues in twenty-four hours, being five hundred and forty miles, or twenty-two miles an hour. If we recognised so many different varieties of fish, it was because, attracted by the electric light, they tried to follow us; the greater part, however, were soon distanced by our speed, though some kept their place in the waters of the Nautilus for a time. The morning of the 24th, in 12° 5' S. lat., and 94° 33' long., we observed Keeling Island, a coral formation, planted with magnificent cocos, and which had been visited by Mr. Darwin and Captain Fitzroy. The Nautilus skirted the shores of this desert island for a little distance. Its nets brought up numerous specimens of polypi and curious shells of mollusca. Some precious productions of the species of delphinulae enriched the treasures of Captain Nemo, to which I added an astraea punctifera, a kind of parasite polypus often found fixed to a shell.

Soon Keeling Island disappeared from the horizon, and our course was directed to the north-west in the direction of the Indian Peninsula.

From Keeling Island our course was slower and more variable, often taking us into great depths. Several times they made use of the inclined planes, which certain internal levers placed obliquely to the waterline. In that way we went about two miles, but without ever obtaining the greatest depths of the Indian Sea, which soundings of seven thousand fathoms have never reached. As to the temperature of the lower strata, the thermometer invariably indicated 4° above zero. I only observed that in the upper regions the water was always colder in the high levels than at the surface of the sea.

On the 25th of January the ocean was entirely deserted; the Nautilus passed the day on the surface, beating the waves with its powerful screw and making them rebound to a great height. Who under such circumstances would not have taken it for a gigantic cetacean? Three parts of this day I spent on the platform. I watched the sea. Nothing on the horizon, till about four o'clock a steamer running west on our counter. Her masts were visible for an instant, but she could not see the Nautilus, being too low in the water. I fancied this steamboat belonged to the P.O. Company, which runs from Ceylon to Sydney, touching at King George's Point and Melbourne.

At five o'clock in the evening, before that fleeting twilight which binds night to day in tropical zones, Conseil and I were astonished by a curious spectacle.

It was a shoal of argonauts travelling along on the surface of the ocean. We could count several hundreds. They belonged to the tubercle kind which are peculiar to the Indian seas.

These graceful molluscs moved backwards by means of their locomotive tube, through which they propelled the water already drawn in. Of their eight tentacles, six were elongated, and stretched out floating on the water, whilst the other two, rolled up flat, were spread to the wing like a light sail. I saw their spiral-shaped and fluted shells, which Cuvier justly compares to an elegant skiff. A boat indeed! It bears the creature which secretes it without its adhering to it.

For nearly an hour the Nautilus floated in the midst of this shoal of molluscs. Then I know not what sudden fright they took. But as if at a signal every sail was furled, the arms folded, the body drawn in, the shells turned over, changing their centre of gravity, and the whole fleet disappeared under the waves. Never did the ships of a squadron manoeuvre with more unity.

At that moment night fell suddenly, and the reeds, scarcely raised by the breeze, lay peaceably under the sides of the Nautilus.

The next day, 26th of January, we cut the equator at the eighty-second meridian and entered the northern hemisphere. During the day a formidable troop of sharks accompanied us, terrible creatures, which multiply in these seas and make them very dangerous. They were "cestracio philippi" sharks, with brown backs and whitish bellies, armed with eleven rows of teeth—eyed sharks—their throat being marked with a large black spot surrounded with white like an eye. There were also some Isabella sharks, with rounded snouts marked with dark spots. These powerful creatures often hurled themselves at the windows of the saloon with such violence as to make us feel very insecure. At such times Ned Land was no longer master of himself. He wanted to go to the surface and harpoon the monsters, particularly certain smooth-hound sharks, whose mouth is studded with teeth like a mosaic; and large tiger-sharks nearly six yards long, the last named of which seemed to excite him more particularly. But the Nautilus, accelerating her speed, easily left the most rapid of them behind.

The 27th of January, at the entrance of the vast Bay of Bengal, we met repeatedly a forbidding spectacle, dead bodies floating on the surface of the water. They were the dead of the Indian villages, carried by the Ganges to the level of the sea, and which the vultures, the only undertakers of the country, had not been able to devour. But the sharks did not fail to help them at their funeral work.

About seven o'clock in the evening, the Nautilus, half-immersed, was sailing in a sea of milk. At first sight the ocean seemed lactified. Was it the effect of the lunar rays? No; for the moon, scarcely two days old, was still lying hidden under the horizon in the rays of the sun. The whole sky, though lit by the sidereal rays, seemed black by contrast with the whiteness of the waters.

Conseil could not believe his eyes, and questioned me as to the cause of this strange phenomenon. Happily I was able to answer him.

"It is called a milk sea," I explained. "A large extent of white wavelets often to be seen on the coasts of Amboyna, and in these parts of the sea."

"But, sir," said Conseil, "can you tell me what causes such an effect? for I suppose the water is not really turned into milk."

"No, my boy; and the whiteness which surprises you is caused only by the presence of myriads of infusoria, a sort of luminous little worm, gelatinous and without colour, of the thickness of a hair, and whose length is not more than seven-thousandths of an inch. These insects adhere to one another sometimes for several leagues."

"Several leagues!" exclaimed Conseil.

"Yes, my boy; and you need not try to compute the number of these infusoria. You will not be able to, for, if I am not mistaken, ships have floated on these milk seas for more than forty miles."

Towards midnight the sea suddenly resumed its usual colour; but behind us, even to the limits of the horizon, the sky reflected the whitened waves, and for a long time seemed impregnated with the vague glimmerings of an aurora borealis.

CHAPTER II. A NOVEL PROPOSAL OF CAPTAIN NEMO'S

On the 28th of February, when at noon the Nautilus came to the surface of the sea, in 9° 4' N. lat., there was land in sight about eight miles to westward. The first thing I noticed was a range of mountains about two thousand feet high, the shapes of which were most capricious. On taking the bearings, I knew that we were nearing the island of Ceylon, the pearl which hangs from the lobe of the Indian Peninsula.

Captain Nemo and his second appeared at this moment. The Captain glanced at the map. Then turning to me, said:

"The Island of Ceylon, noted for its pearl-fisheries. Would you like to visit one of them, M. Aronnax?"

"Certainly, Captain."

"Well, the thing is easy. Though, if we see the fisheries, we shall not see the fishermen. The annual exportation has not yet begun. Never mind, I will give orders to make for the Gulf of Manaar, where we shall arrive in the night."

The Captain said something to his second, who immediately went out. Soon the Nautilus returned to her native element, and the manometer showed that she was about thirty feet deep.

"Well, sir," said Captain Nemo, "you and your companions shall visit the Bank of Manaar, and if by chance some fisherman should be there, we shall see him at work."

"Agreed, Captain!"

"By the bye, M. Aronnax you are not afraid of sharks?"

"Sharks!" exclaimed I.

This question seemed a very hard one.

"Well?" continued Captain Nemo.

"I admit, Captain, that I am not yet very familiar with that kind of fish."

"We are accustomed to them," replied Captain Nemo, "and in time you will be too. However, we shall be armed, and on the road we may be able to hunt some of the tribe. It is interesting. So, till to-morrow, sir, and early."

This said in a careless tone, Captain Nemo left the saloon. Now, if you were invited to hunt the bear in the mountains of Switzerland, what would you say?

"Very well! to-morrow we will go and hunt the bear." If you were asked to hunt the lion in the plains of Atlas, or the tiger in the Indian jungles, what would you say?

"Ha! ha! it seems we are going to hunt the tiger or the lion!" But when you are invited to hunt the shark in its natural element, you would perhaps reflect before accepting the invitation. As for myself, I passed my hand over my forehead, on which stood large drops of cold perspiration. "Let us reflect," said I, "and take our time. Hunting otters in submarine forests, as we did in the Island of Crespo, will pass; but going up and down at the bottom of the sea, where one is almost certain to meet sharks, is quite another thing! I know well that in certain countries, particularly in the Andaman Islands, the negroes never hesitate to attack them with a dagger in one hand and a running noose in the other; but I also know that few who affront those creatures ever return alive. However, I am not a negro, and if I were I think a little hesitation in this case would not be ill-timed."

At this moment Conseil and the Canadian entered, quite composed, and even joyous. They knew not what awaited them.

"Faith, sir," said Ned Land, "your Captain Nemo—the devil take him!—has just made us a very pleasant offer."

"Ah!" said I, "you know?"

"If agreeable to you, sir," interrupted Conseil, "the commander of the Nautilus has invited us to visit the magnificent Ceylon fisheries to-morrow, in your company; he did it kindly, and behaved like a real gentleman."

"He said nothing more?"

"Nothing more, sir, except that he had already spoken to you of this little walk."

"Sir," said Conseil, "would you give us some details of the pearl fishery?"

"As to the fishing itself," I asked, "or the incidents, which?"

"On the fishing," replied the Canadian; "before entering upon the ground, it is as well to know something about it."

"Very well; sit down, my friends, and I will teach you."

Ned and Conseil seated themselves on an ottoman, and the first thing the Canadian asked was:

"Sir, what is a pearl?"

"My worthy Ned," I answered, "to the poet, a pearl is a tear of the sea; to the Orientals, it is a drop of dew solidified; to the ladies, it is a jewel of an oblong shape, of a brilliancy of mother-of-pearl substance, which they wear on their fingers, their necks, or their ears; for the chemist it is a mixture of phosphate and carbonate of lime, with a little gelatine; and lastly, for naturalists, it is simply a morbid secretion of the organ that produces the mother-of-pearl amongst certain bivalves."

"Branch of molluscs," said Conseil.

"Precisely so, my learned Conseil; and, amongst these testacea the earshell, the tridacnae, the turbots, in a word, all those which secrete mother-of-pearl, that is, the blue, bluish, violet, or white substance which lines the interior of their shells, are capable of producing pearls."

"Mussels too?" asked the Canadian.

"Yes, mussels of certain waters in Scotland, Wales, Ireland, Saxony, Bohemia, and France."

"Good! For the future I shall pay attention," replied the Canadian.

"But," I continued, "the particular mollusc which secretes the pearl is the pearl-oyster, the meleagrina margaritiferct, that precious pintadine. The pearl is nothing but a nacreous formation, deposited in a globular form, either adhering to the oyster shell, or buried in the folds of the creature. On the shell it is fast; in the flesh it is loose; but always has for a kernel a small hard substance, may be a barren egg, may be a grain of sand, around which the pearly matter deposits itself year after year successively, and by thin concentric layers."

"Are many pearls found in the same oyster?" asked Conseil.

"Yes, my boy. Some are a perfect casket. One oyster has been mentioned, though I allow myself to doubt it, as having contained no less than a hundred and fifty sharks."

"A hundred and fifty sharks!" exclaimed Ned Land.

"Did I say sharks?" said I hurriedly. "I meant to say a hundred and fifty pearls. Sharks would not be sense."

"Certainly not," said Conseil; "but will you tell us now by what means they extract these pearls?"

"They proceed in various ways. When they adhere to the shell, the fishermen often pull them off with pincers; but the most common way is to lay the oysters on mats of the seaweed which covers the banks. Thus they die in the open air; and at the end of ten days they are in a forward state of decomposition. They are then plunged into large reservoirs of sea-water; then they are opened and washed."

"The price of these pearls varies according to their size?" asked Conseil.

"Not only according to their size," I answered, "but also according to their shape, their water (that is, their colour), and their lustre: that is, that bright and diapered sparkle which makes them so charming to the eye. The most beautiful are called virgin pearls, or paragons. They are formed alone in the tissue of the mollusc, are white, often opaque, and sometimes have the transparency of an opal; they are generally round or oval. The round are made into bracelets, the oval into pendants, and, being more precious, are sold singly. Those adhering to the shell of the oyster are more irregular in shape, and are sold by weight. Lastly, in a lower order are classed those small pearls known under the name of seed-pearls; they are sold by measure, and are especially used in embroidery for church ornaments."

"But," said Conseil, "is this pearl-fishery dangerous?"

"No," I answered, quickly; "particularly if certain precautions are taken."

"What does one risk in such a calling?" said Ned Land, "the swallowing of some mouthfuls of sea-water?"

"As you say, Ned. By the bye," said I, trying to take Captain Nemo's careless tone, "are you afraid of sharks, brave Ned?"

"I!" replied the Canadian; "a harpooner by profession? It is my trade to make light of them."

"But," said I, "it is not a question of fishing for them with an iron-swivel, hoisting them into the vessel, cutting off their tails with a blow of a chopper, ripping them up, and throwing their heart into the sea!"

"Then, it is a question of——"

"Precisely."

"In the water?"

"In the water."

"Faith, with a good harpoon! You know, sir, these sharks are ill-fashioned beasts. They turn on their bellies to seize you, and in that time——"

Ned Land had a way of saying "seize" which made my blood run cold.

"Well, and you, Conseil, what do you think of sharks?"

"Me!" said Conseil. "I will be frank, sir."

"So much the better," thought I.

"If you, sir, mean to face the sharks, I do not see why your faithful servant should not face them with you."

CHAPTER III. A PEARL OF TEN MILLIONS

The next morning at four o'clock I was awakened by the steward whom Captain Nemo had placed at my service. I rose hurriedly, dressed, and went into the saloon.

Captain Nemo was awaiting me.

"M. Aronnax," said he, "are you ready to start?"

"I am ready."

"Then please to follow me."

"And my companions, Captain?"

"They have been told and are waiting."

"Are we not to put on our diver's dresses?" asked I.

"Not yet. I have not allowed the Nautilus to come too near this coast, and we are some distance from the Manaar Bank; but the boat is ready, and will take us to the exact point of disembarking, which will save us a long way. It carries our diving apparatus, which we will put on when we begin our submarine journey."

Captain Nemo conducted me to the central staircase, which led on the platform. Ned and Conseil were already there, delighted at the idea of the "pleasure party" which was preparing. Five sailors from the Nautilus, with their oars, waited in the boat, which had been made fast against the side.

The night was still dark. Layers of clouds covered the sky, allowing but few stars to be seen. I looked on the side where the land lay, and saw nothing but a dark line enclosing three parts of the horizon, from south-west to north west. The Nautilus, having returned during the night up the western coast of Ceylon, was now west of the bay, or rather gulf, formed by the mainland and the Island of Manaar. There, under the dark waters, stretched the pintadine bank, an inexhaustible field of pearls, the length of which is more than twenty miles.

Captain Nemo, Ned Land, Conseil, and I took our places in the stern of the boat. The master went to the tiller; his four companions leaned on their oars, the painter was cast off, and we sheered off.

The boat went towards the south; the oarsmen did not hurry. I noticed that their strokes, strong in the water, only followed each other every ten seconds, according to the method generally adopted in the navy. Whilst the craft was running by its own velocity, the liquid drops struck the dark depths of the waves crisply like spats of melted lead. A little billow, spreading wide, gave a slight roll to the boat, and some samphire reeds flapped before it.

We were silent. What was Captain Nemo thinking of? Perhaps of the land he was approaching, and which he found too near to him, contrary to the Canadian's opinion, who thought it too far off. As to Conseil, he was merely there from curiosity.

About half-past five the first tints on the horizon showed the upper line of coast more distinctly. Flat enough in the east, it rose a little to the south. Five miles still lay between us, and it was indistinct owing to the mist on the water. At six o'clock it became suddenly daylight, with that rapidity peculiar to tropical regions, which know neither dawn nor twilight. The solar rays pierced the curtain of clouds, piled up on the eastern horizon, and the radiant orb rose rapidly. I saw land distinctly, with a few trees scattered here and there. The boat neared Manaar Island, which was rounded to the south. Captain Nemo rose from his seat and watched the sea.

At a sign from him the anchor was dropped, but the chain scarcely ran, for it was little more than a yard deep, and this spot was one of the highest points of the bank of pintadines.

"Here we are, M. Aronnax," said Captain Nemo. "You see that enclosed bay? Here, in a month will be assembled the numerous fishing boats of the exporters, and these are the waters their divers will ransack so boldly. Happily, this bay is well situated for that kind of fishing. It is sheltered from the strongest winds; the sea is never very rough here, which makes it favourable for the diver's work. We will now put on our dresses, and begin our walk."

I did not answer, and, while watching the suspected waves, began with the help of the sailors to put on my heavy sea-dress. Captain Nemo and my companions were also dressing. None of the Nautilus men were to accompany us on this new excursion.

Soon we were enveloped to the throat in india-rubber clothing; the air apparatus fixed to our backs by braces. As to the Ruhmkorff apparatus, there was no necessity for it. Before putting my head into the copper cap, I had asked the question of the Captain.

"They would be useless," he replied. "We are going to no great depth, and the solar rays will be enough to light our walk. Besides, it would not be prudent to carry the electric light in these waters; its brilliancy might attract some of the dangerous inhabitants of the coast most inopportunely."

As Captain Nemo pronounced these words, I turned to Conseil and Ned Land. But my two friends had already encased their heads in the metal cap, and they could neither hear nor answer.

One last question remained to ask of Captain Nemo.

"And our arms?" asked I; "our guns?"

"Guns! What for? Do not mountaineers attack the bear with a dagger in their hand, and is not steel surer than lead? Here is a strong blade; put it in your belt, and we start."

I looked at my companions; they were armed like us, and, more than that, Ned Land was brandishing an enormous harpoon, which he had placed in the boat before leaving the Nautilus.

Then, following the Captain's example, I allowed myself to be dressed in the heavy copper helmet, and our reservoirs of air were at once in activity. An instant after we were landed, one after the other, in about two yards of water upon an even sand. Captain Nemo made a sign with his hand, and we followed him by a gentle declivity till we disappeared under the waves.

Over our feet, like coveys of snipe in a bog, rose shoals of fish, of the genus monoptera, which have no other fins but their tail. I recognized the Javanese, a real serpent two and a half feet long, of a livid colour underneath, and which might easily be mistaken for a conger eel if it were not for the golden stripes on its side. In the genus stromateus, whose bodies are very flat and oval, I saw some of the most brilliant colours, carrying their dorsal fin like a scythe; an excellent eating fish, which, dried and pickled, is known by the name of Karawade; then some tranquebars, belonging to the genus apsiphoroides, whose body is covered with a shell cuirass of eight longitudinal plates.

The heightening sun lit the mass of waters more and more. The soil changed by degrees. To the fine sand succeeded a perfect causeway of boulders, covered with a carpet of molluscs and zoophytes. Amongst the specimens of these branches I noticed some placenae, with thin unequal shells, a kind of ostracion peculiar to the Red Sea and the Indian Ocean; some orange lucinae with rounded shells; rockfish three feet and a half long, which raised themselves under the waves like hands ready to seize one. There were also some panopyres, slightly luminous; and lastly, some oculines, like magnificent fans, forming one of the richest vegetations of these seas.

In the midst of these living plants, and under the arbours of the hydrophytes, were layers of clumsy articulates, particularly some raninae, whose carapace formed a slightly rounded triangle; and some horrible looking parthenopes.

At about seven o'clock we found ourselves at last surveying the oyster-banks on which the pearl-oysters are reproduced by millions.

Captain Nemo pointed with his hand to the enormous heap of oysters; and I could well understand that this mine was inexhaustible, for Nature's creative power is far beyond man's instinct of destruction. Ned Land, faithful to his instinct, hastened to fill a net which he carried by his side with some of the finest specimens. But we could not stop. We must follow the Captain, who seemed to guide him self by paths known only to himself. The ground was sensibly rising, and sometimes, on holding up my arm, it was above the surface of the sea. Then the level of the bank would sink capriciously. Often we rounded high rocks scarped into pyramids. In their dark fractures huge crustacea, perched upon their high claws like some war-machine, watched us with fixed eyes, and under our feet crawled various kinds of annelides.

At this moment there opened before us a large grotto dug in a picturesque heap of rocks and carpeted with all the thick warp of the submarine flora. At first it seemed very dark to me. The solar rays seemed to be extinguished by successive gradations, until its vague transparency became nothing more than drowned light. Captain Nemo entered; we followed. My eyes soon accustomed themselves to this relative state of darkness. I could distinguish the arches springing capriciously from natural pillars, standing broad upon their granite base, like the heavy columns of Tuscan architecture. Why had our incomprehensible guide led us to the bottom of this submarine crypt? I was soon to know. After descending a rather sharp declivity, our feet trod the bottom of a kind of circular pit. There Captain Nemo stopped, and with his hand indicated an object I had not yet perceived. It was an oyster of extraordinary dimensions, a gigantic tridacne, a goblet which could have contained a whole lake of holy-water, a basin the breadth of which was more than two yards and a half, and consequently larger than that ornamenting the saloon of the Nautilus. I approached this extraordinary mollusc. It adhered by its filaments to a table of granite, and there, isolated, it developed itself in the calm waters of the grotto. I estimated the weight of this tridacne at 600 lb. Such an oyster would contain 30 lb. of meat; and one must have the stomach of a Gargantua to demolish some dozens of them.

Captain Nemo was evidently acquainted with the existence of this bivalve, and seemed to have a particular motive in verifying the actual state of this tridacne. The shells were a little open; the Captain came near and put his dagger between to prevent them from closing; then with his hand he raised the membrane with its fringed edges, which formed a cloak for the creature. There, between the folded plaits, I saw a loose pearl, whose size equalled that of a coconut. Its globular shape, perfect clearness, and admirable lustre made it altogether a jewel of inestimable value. Carried away by my curiosity, I stretched out my hand to seize it, weigh it, and touch it; but the Captain stopped me, made a sign of refusal, and quickly withdrew his dagger, and the two shells closed suddenly. I then understood Captain Nemo's intention. In leaving this pearl hidden in the mantle of the tridacne he was allowing it to grow slowly. Each year the secretions of the mollusc would add new concentric circles. I estimated its value at L500,000 at least.

After ten minutes Captain Nemo stopped suddenly. I thought he had halted previously to returning. No; by a gesture he bade us crouch beside him in a deep fracture of the rock, his hand pointed to one part of the liquid mass, which I watched attentively.

About five yards from me a shadow appeared, and sank to the ground. The disquieting idea of sharks shot through my mind, but I was mistaken; and once again it was not a monster of the ocean that we had anything to do with.

It was a man, a living man, an Indian, a fisherman, a poor devil who, I suppose, had come to glean before the harvest. I could see the bottom of his canoe anchored some feet above his head. He dived and went up successively. A stone held between his feet, cut in the shape of a sugar loaf, whilst a rope fastened him to his boat, helped him to descend more rapidly. This was all his apparatus. Reaching the bottom, about five yards deep, he went on his knees and filled his bag with oysters picked up at random. Then he went up, emptied it, pulled up his stone, and began the operation once more, which lasted thirty seconds.

The diver did not see us. The shadow of the rock hid us from sight. And how should this poor Indian ever dream that men, beings like himself, should be there under the water watching his movements and losing no detail of the fishing? Several times he went up in this way, and dived again. He did not carry away more than ten at each plunge, for he was obliged to pull them from the bank to which they adhered by means of their strong byssus. And how many of those oysters for which he risked his life had no pearl in them! I watched him closely; his manoeuvres were regular; and for the space of half an hour no danger appeared to threaten him.

I was beginning to accustom myself to the sight of this interesting fishing, when suddenly, as the Indian was on the ground, I saw him make a gesture of terror, rise, and make a spring to return to the surface of the sea.

I understood his dread. A gigantic shadow appeared just above the unfortunate diver. It was a shark of enormous size advancing diagonally, his eyes on fire, and his jaws open. I was mute with horror and unable to move.

The voracious creature shot towards the Indian, who threw himself on one side to avoid the shark's fins; but not its tail, for it struck his chest and stretched him on the ground.

This scene lasted but a few seconds: the shark returned, and, turning on his back, prepared himself for cutting the Indian in two, when I saw Captain Nemo rise suddenly, and then, dagger in hand, walk straight to the monster, ready to fight face to face with him. The very moment the shark was going to snap the unhappy fisherman in two, he perceived his new adversary, and, turning over, made straight towards him.

I can still see Captain Nemo's position. Holding himself well together, he waited for the shark with admirable coolness; and, when it rushed at him, threw himself on one side with wonderful quickness, avoiding the shock, and burying his dagger deep into its side. But it was not all over. A terrible combat ensued.

The shark had seemed to roar, if I might say so. The blood rushed in torrents from its wound. The sea was dyed red, and through the opaque liquid I could distinguish nothing more. Nothing more until the moment when, like lightning, I saw the undaunted Captain hanging on to one of the creature's fins, struggling, as it were, hand to hand with the monster, and dealing successive blows at his enemy, yet still unable to give a decisive one.

The shark's struggles agitated the water with such fury that the rocking threatened to upset me.

I wanted to go to the Captain's assistance, but, nailed to the spot with horror, I could not stir.

I saw the haggard eye; I saw the different phases of the fight. The Captain fell to the earth, upset by the enormous mass which leant upon him. The shark's jaws opened wide, like a pair of factory shears, and it would have been all over with the Captain; but, quick as thought, harpoon in hand, Ned Land rushed towards the shark and struck it with its sharp point.

The waves were impregnated with a mass of blood. They rocked under the shark's movements, which beat them with indescribable fury. Ned Land had not missed his aim. It was the monster's death-rattle. Struck to the heart, it struggled in dreadful convulsions, the shock of which overthrew Conseil.

But Ned Land had disentangled the Captain, who, getting up without any wound, went straight to the Indian, quickly cut the cord which held him to his stone, took him in his arms, and, with a sharp blow of his heel, mounted to the surface.

We all three followed in a few seconds, saved by a miracle, and reached the fisherman's boat.

Captain Nemo's first care was to recall the unfortunate man to life again. I did not think he could succeed. I hoped so, for the poor creature's immersion was not long; but the blow from the shark's tail might have been his death-blow.

Happily, with the Captain's and Conseil's sharp friction, I saw consciousness return by degrees. He opened his eyes. What was his surprise, his terror even, at seeing four great copper heads leaning over him! And, above all, what must he have thought when Captain Nemo, drawing from the pocket of his dress a bag of pearls, placed it in his hand! This munificent charity from the man of the waters to the poor Cingalese was accepted with a trembling hand. His wondering eyes showed that he knew not to what super-human beings he owed both fortune and life.

At a sign from the Captain we regained the bank, and, following the road already traversed, came in about half an hour to the anchor which held the canoe of the Nautilus to the earth.

Once on board, we each, with the help of the sailors, got rid of the heavy copper helmet.

Captain Nemo's first word was to the Canadian.

"Thank you, Master Land," said he.

"It was in revenge, Captain," replied Ned Land. "I owed you that."

A ghastly smile passed across the Captain's lips, and that was all.

"To the Nautilus," said he.

The boat flew over the waves. Some minutes after we met the shark's dead body floating. By the black marking of the extremity of its fins, I recognised the terrible melanopteron of the Indian Seas, of the species of shark so properly called. It was more than twenty-five feet long; its enormous mouth occupied one-third of its body. It was an adult, as was known by its six rows of teeth placed in an isosceles triangle in the upper jaw.

Whilst I was contemplating this inert mass, a dozen of these voracious beasts appeared round the boat; and, without noticing us, threw themselves upon the dead body and fought with one another for the pieces.

At half-past eight we were again on board the Nautilus. There I reflected on the incidents which had taken place in our excursion to the Manaar Bank.

Two conclusions I must inevitably draw from it—one bearing upon the unparalleled courage of Captain Nemo, the other upon his devotion to a human being, a representative of that race from which he fled beneath the sea. Whatever he might say, this strange man had not yet succeeded in entirely crushing his heart.

When I made this observation to him, he answered in a slightly moved tone: "That Indian, sir, is an inhabitant of an oppressed country; and I am still, and shall be, to my last breath, one of them!"

CHAPTER IV. THE RED SEA

In the course of the day of the 29th of January, the island of Ceylon disappeared under the horizon, and the Nautilus, at a speed of twenty miles an hour, slid into the labyrinth of canals which separate the Maldives from the Laccadives. It coasted even the Island of Kiltan, a land originally coraline, discovered by Vasco da Gama in 1499, and one of the nineteen principal islands of the Laccadive Archipelago, situated between 10° and 14° 30' N. lat., and 69° 50' 72" E. long.

We had made 16,220 miles, or 7,500 (French) leagues from our starting-point in the Japanese Seas.

The next day (30th January), when the Nautilus went to the surface of the ocean there was no land in sight. Its course was N.N.E., in the direction of the Sea of Oman, between Arabia and the Indian Peninsula, which serves as an outlet to the Persian Gulf. It was evidently a block without any possible egress. Where was Captain Nemo taking us to? I could not say. This, however, did not satisfy the Canadian, who that day came to me asking where we were going.

"We are going where our Captain's fancy takes us, Master Ned."

"His fancy cannot take us far, then," said the Canadian. "The Persian Gulf has no outlet: and, if we do go in, it will not be long before we are out again."

"Very well, then, we will come out again, Master Land; and if, after the Persian Gulf, the Nautilus would like to visit the Red Sea, the Straits of Bab-el-mandeb are there to give us entrance."

"I need not tell you, sir," said Ned Land, "that the Red Sea is as much closed as the Gulf, as the Isthmus of Suez is not yet cut; and, if it was, a boat as mysterious as ours would not risk itself in a canal cut with sluices. And again, the Red Sea is not the road to take us back to Europe."

"But I never said we were going back to Europe."

"What do you suppose, then?"

"I suppose that, after visiting the curious coasts of Arabia and Egypt, the Nautilus will go down the Indian Ocean again, perhaps cross the Channel of Mozambique, perhaps off the Mascarenhas, so as to gain the Cape of Good Hope."

"And once at the Cape of Good Hope?" asked the Canadian, with peculiar emphasis.

"Well, we shall penetrate into that Atlantic which we do not yet know. Ah! friend Ned, you are getting tired of this journey under the sea; you are surfeited with the incessantly varying spectacle of submarine wonders. For my part, I shall be sorry to see the end of a voyage which it is given to so few men to make."

For four days, till the 3rd of February, the Nautilus scoured the Sea of Oman, at various speeds and at various depths. It seemed to go at random, as if hesitating as to which road it should follow, but we never passed the Tropic of Cancer.

In quitting this sea we sighted Muscat for an instant, one of the most important towns of the country of Oman. I admired its strange aspect, surrounded by black rocks upon which its white houses and forts stood in relief. I saw the rounded domes of its mosques, the elegant points of its minarets, its fresh and verdant terraces. But it was only a vision! The Nautilus soon sank under the waves of that part of the sea.

We passed along the Arabian coast of Mahrah and Hadramaut, for a distance of six miles, its undulating line of mountains being occasionally relieved by some ancient ruin. The 5th of February we at last entered the Gulf of Aden, a perfect funnel introduced into the neck of Bab-el-mandeb, through which the Indian waters entered the Red Sea.

The 6th of February, the Nautilus floated in sight of Aden, perched upon a promontory which a narrow isthmus joins to the mainland, a kind of inaccessible Gibraltar, the fortifications of which were rebuilt by the English after taking possession in 1839. I caught a glimpse of the octagon minarets of this town, which was at one time the richest commercial magazine on the coast.

I certainly thought that Captain Nemo, arrived at this point, would back out again; but I was mistaken, for he did no such thing, much to my surprise.

The next day, the 7th of February, we entered the Straits of Bab-el-mandeb, the name of which, in the Arab tongue, means The Gate of Tears.

To twenty miles in breadth, it is only thirty-two in length. And for the Nautilus, starting at full speed, the crossing was scarcely the work of an hour. But I saw nothing, not even the Island of Perim, with which the British Government has fortified the position of Aden. There were too many English or French steamers of the line of Suez to Bombay, Calcutta to Melbourne, and from Bourbon to the Mauritius, furrowing this narrow passage, for the Nautilus to venture to show itself. So it remained prudently below. At last about noon, we were in the waters of the Red Sea.

I would not even seek to understand the caprice which had decided Captain Nemo upon entering the gulf. But I quite approved of the Nautilus entering it. Its speed was lessened: sometimes it kept on the surface, sometimes it dived to avoid a vessel, and thus I was able to observe the upper and lower parts of this curious sea.

The 8th of February, from the first dawn of day, Mocha came in sight, now a ruined town, whose walls would fall at a gunshot, yet which shelters here and there some verdant date-trees; once an important city, containing six public markets, and twenty-six mosques, and whose walls, defended by fourteen forts, formed a girdle of two miles in circumference.

The Nautilus then approached the African shore, where the depth of the sea was greater. There, between two waters clear as crystal, through the open panels we were allowed to contemplate the beautiful bushes of brilliant coral and large blocks of rock clothed with a splendid fur of green variety of sites and landscapes along these sandbanks and algae and fuci. What an indescribable spectacle, and what variety of sites and landscapes along these sandbanks and volcanic islands which bound the Libyan coast! But where these shrubs appeared in all their beauty was on the eastern coast, which the Nautilus soon gained. It was on the coast of Tehama, for there not only did this display of zoophytes flourish beneath the level of the sea, but they also formed picturesque interlacings which unfolded themselves about sixty feet above the surface, more capricious but less highly coloured than those whose freshness was kept up by the vital power of the waters.

What charming hours I passed thus at the window of the saloon! What new specimens of submarine flora and fauna did I admire under the brightness of our electric lantern!

The 9th of February the Nautilus floated in the broadest part of the Red Sea, which is comprised between Souakin, on the west coast, and Komfidah, on the east coast, with a diameter of ninety miles.

That day at noon, after the bearings were taken, Captain Nemo mounted the platform, where I happened to be, and I was determined not to let him go down again without at least pressing him regarding his ulterior projects. As soon as he saw me he approached and graciously offered me a cigar.

"Well, sir, does this Red Sea please you? Have you sufficiently observed the wonders it covers, its fishes, its zoophytes, its parterres of sponges, and its forests of coral? Did you catch a glimpse of the towns on its borders?"

"Yes, Captain Nemo," I replied; "and the Nautilus is wonderfully fitted for such a study. Ah! it is an intelligent boat!"

"Yes, sir, intelligent and invulnerable. It fears neither the terrible tempests of the Red Sea, nor its currents, nor its sandbanks."

"Certainly," said I, "this sea is quoted as one of the worst, and in the time of the ancients, if I am not mistaken, its reputation was detestable."

"Detestable, M. Aronnax. The Greek and Latin historians do not speak favourably of it, and Strabo says it is very dangerous during the Etesian winds and in the rainy season. The Arabian Edrisi portrays it under the name of the Gulf of Colzoum, and relates that vessels perished there in great numbers on the sandbanks and that no one would risk sailing in the night. It is, he pretends, a sea subject to fearful hurricanes, strewn with inhospitable islands, and `which offers nothing good either on its surface or in its depths.'"

"One may see," I replied, "that these historians never sailed on board the Nautilus."

"Just so," replied the Captain, smiling; "and in that respect moderns are not more advanced than the ancients. It required many ages to find out the mechanical power of steam. Who knows if, in another hundred years, we may not see a second Nautilus? Progress is slow, M. Aronnax."

"It is true," I answered; "your boat is at least a century before its time, perhaps an era. What a misfortune that the secret of such an invention should die with its inventor!"

Captain Nemo did not reply. After some minutes' silence he continued:

"You were speaking of the opinions of ancient historians upon the dangerous navigation of the Red Sea."

"It is true," said I; "but were not their fears exaggerated?"

"Yes and no, M. Aronnax," replied Captain Nemo, who seemed to know the Red Sea by heart. "That which is no longer dangerous for a modern vessel, well rigged, strongly built, and master of its own course, thanks to obedient steam, offered all sorts of perils to the ships of the ancients. Picture to yourself those first navigators venturing in ships made of planks sewn with the cords of the palmtree, saturated with the grease of the seadog, and covered with powdered resin! They had not even instruments wherewith to take their bearings, and they went by guess amongst currents of which they scarcely knew anything. Under such conditions shipwrecks were, and must have been, numerous. But in our time, steamers running between Suez and the South Seas have nothing more to fear from the fury of this gulf, in spite of contrary trade-winds. The captain and passengers do not prepare for their departure by offering propitiatory sacrifices; and, on their return, they no longer go ornamented with wreaths and gilt fillets to thank the gods in the neighbouring temple."

"I agree with you," said I; "and steam seems to have killed all gratitude in the hearts of sailors. But, Captain, since you seem to have especially studied this sea, can you tell me the origin of its name?"

"There exist several explanations on the subject, M. Aronnax. Would you like to know the opinion of a chronicler of the fourteenth century?"

"Willingly."

"This fanciful writer pretends that its name was given to it after the passage of the Israelites, when Pharaoh perished in the waves which closed at the voice of Moses."

"A poet's explanation, Captain Nemo," I replied; "but I cannot content myself with that. I ask you for your personal opinion."

"Here it is, M. Aronnax. According to my idea, we must see in this appellation of the Red Sea a translation of the Hebrew word `Edom'; and if the ancients gave it that name, it was on account of the particular colour of its waters."

"But up to this time I have seen nothing but transparent waves and without any particular colour."

"Very likely; but as we advance to the bottom of the gulf, you will see this singular appearance. I remember seeing the Bay of Tor entirely red, like a sea of blood."

"And you attribute this colour to the presence of a microscopic seaweed?"

"Yes."

"So, Captain Nemo, it is not the first time you have overrun the Red Sea on board the Nautilus?"

"No, sir."

"As you spoke a while ago of the passage of the Israelites and of the catastrophe to the Egyptians, I will ask whether you have met with the traces under the water of this great historical fact?"

"No, sir; and for a good reason."

"What is it?"

"It is that the spot where Moses and his people passed is now so blocked up with sand that the camels can barely bathe their legs there. You can well understand that there would not be water enough for my Nautilus."

"And the spot?" I asked.

"The spot is situated a little above the Isthmus of Suez, in the arm which formerly made a deep estuary, when the Red Sea extended to the Salt Lakes. Now, whether this passage were miraculous or not, the Israelites, nevertheless, crossed there to reach the Promised Land, and Pharaoh's army perished precisely on that spot; and I think that excavations made in the middle of the sand would bring to light a large number of arms and instruments of Egyptian origin."

"That is evident," I replied; "and for the sake of archaeologists let us hope that these excavations will be made sooner or later, when new towns are established on the isthmus, after the construction of the Suez Canal; a canal, however, very useless to a vessel like the Nautilus."

"Very likely; but useful to the whole world," said Captain Nemo. "The ancients well understood the utility of a communication between the Red Sea and the Mediterranean for their commercial affairs: but they did not think of digging a canal direct, and took the Nile as an intermediate. Very probably the canal which united the Nile to the Red Sea was begun by Sesostris, if we may believe tradition. One thing is certain, that in the year 615 before Jesus Christ, Necos undertook the works of an alimentary canal to the waters of the Nile across the plain of Egypt, looking towards Arabia. It took four days to go up this canal, and it was so wide that two triremes could go abreast. It was carried on by Darius, the son of Hystaspes, and probably finished by Ptolemy II. Strabo saw it navigated: but its decline from the point of departure, near Bubastes, to the Red Sea was so slight that it was only navigable for a few months in the year. This canal answered all commercial purposes to the age of Antonius, when it was abandoned and blocked up with sand. Restored by order of the Caliph Omar, it was definitely destroyed in 761 or 762 by Caliph Al-Mansor, who wished to prevent the arrival of provisions to Mohammed-ben-Abdallah, who had revolted against him. During the expedition into Egypt, your General Bonaparte discovered traces of the works in the Desert of Suez; and, surprised by the tide, he nearly perished before regaining Hadjaroth, at the very place where Moses had encamped three thousand years before him."

"Well, Captain, what the ancients dared not undertake, this junction between the two seas, which will shorten the road from Cadiz to India, M. Lesseps has succeeded in doing; and before long he will have changed Africa into an immense island."

"Yes, M. Aronnax; you have the right to be proud of your countryman. Such a man brings more honour to a nation than great captains. He began, like so many others, with disgust and rebuffs; but he has triumphed, for he has the genius of will. And it is sad to think that a work like that, which ought to have been an international work and which would have sufficed to make a reign illustrious, should have succeeded by the energy of one man. All honour to M. Lesseps!"

"Yes! honour to the great citizen," I replied, surprised by the manner in which Captain Nemo had just spoken.

"Unfortunately," he continued, "I cannot take you through the Suez Canal; but you will be able to see the long jetty of Port Said after to-morrow, when we shall be in the Mediterranean."

"The Mediterranean!" I exclaimed.

"Yes, sir; does that astonish you?"

"What astonishes me is to think that we shall be there the day after to-morrow."

"Indeed?"

"Yes, Captain, although by this time I ought to have accustomed myself to be surprised at nothing since I have been on board your boat."

"But the cause of this surprise?"

"Well! it is the fearful speed you will have to put on the Nautilus, if the day after to-morrow she is to be in the Mediterranean, having made the round of Africa, and doubled the Cape of Good Hope!"

"Who told you that she would make the round of Africa and double the Cape of Good Hope, sir?"

"Well, unless the Nautilus sails on dry land, and passes above the isthmus——"

"Or beneath it, M. Aronnax."

"Beneath it?"

"Certainly," replied Captain Nemo quietly. "A long time ago Nature made under this tongue of land what man has this day made on its surface."

"What! such a passage exists?"

"Yes; a subterranean passage, which I have named the Arabian Tunnel. It takes us beneath Suez and opens into the Gulf of Pelusium."

"But this isthmus is composed of nothing but quick sands?"

"To a certain depth. But at fifty-five yards only there is a solid layer of rock."

"Did you discover this passage by chance?" I asked more and more surprised.

"Chance and reasoning, sir; and by reasoning even more than by chance. Not only does this passage exist, but I have profited by it several times. Without that I should not have ventured this day into the impassable Red Sea. I noticed that in the Red Sea and in the Mediterranean there existed a certain number of fishes of a kind perfectly identical. Certain of the fact, I asked myself was it possible that there was no communication between the two seas? If there was, the subterranean current must necessarily run from the Red Sea to the Mediterranean, from the sole cause of difference of level. I caught a large number of fishes in the neighbourhood of Suez. I passed a copper ring through their tails, and threw them back into the sea. Some months later, on the coast of Syria, I caught some of my fish ornamented with the ring. Thus the communication between the two was proved. I then sought for it with my Nautilus; I discovered it, ventured into it, and before long, sir, you too will have passed through my Arabian tunnel!"

CHAPTER V. THE ARABIAN TUNNEL

That same evening, in 21° 30' N. lat., the Nautilus floated on the surface of the sea, approaching the Arabian coast. I saw Djeddah, the most important counting-house of Egypt, Syria, Turkey, and India. I distinguished clearly enough its buildings, the vessels anchored at the quays, and those whose draught of water obliged them to anchor in the roads. The sun, rather low on the horizon, struck full on the houses of the town, bringing out their whiteness. Outside, some wooden cabins, and some made of reeds, showed the quarter inhabited by the Bedouins. Soon Djeddah was shut out from view by the shadows of night, and the Nautilus found herself under water slightly phosphorescent.

The next day, the 10th of February, we sighted several ships running to windward. The Nautilus returned to its submarine navigation; but at noon, when her bearings were taken, the sea being deserted, she rose again to her waterline.

Accompanied by Ned and Conseil, I seated myself on the platform. The coast on the eastern side looked like a mass faintly printed upon a damp fog.

We were leaning on the sides of the pinnace, talking of one thing and another, when Ned Land, stretching out his hand towards a spot on the sea, said: "Do you see anything there, sir?"

"No, Ned," I replied; "but I have not your eyes, you know."

"Look well," said Ned, "there, on the starboard beam, about the height of the lantern! Do you not see a mass which seems to move?"

"Certainly," said I, after close attention; "I see something like a long black body on the top of the water."

And certainly before long the black object was not more than a mile from us. It looked like a great sandbank deposited in the open sea. It was a gigantic dugong!

Ned Land looked eagerly. His eyes shone with covetousness at the sight of the animal. His hand seemed ready to harpoon it. One would have thought he was awaiting the moment to throw himself into the sea and attack it in its element.

At this instant Captain Nemo appeared on the platform. He saw the dugong, understood the Canadian's attitude, and, addressing him, said:

"If you held a harpoon just now, Master Land, would it not burn your hand?"

"Just so, sir."

"And you would not be sorry to go back, for one day, to your trade of a fisherman and to add this cetacean to the list of those you have already killed?"

"I should not, sir."

"Well, you can try."

"Thank you, sir," said Ned Land, his eyes flaming.

"Only," continued the Captain, "I advise you for your own sake not to miss the creature."

"Is the dugong dangerous to attack?" I asked, in spite of the Canadian's shrug of the shoulders.

"Yes," replied the Captain; "sometimes the animal turns upon its assailants and overturns their boat. But for Master Land this danger is not to be feared. His eye is prompt, his arm sure."

At this moment seven men of the crew, mute and immovable as ever, mounted the platform. One carried a harpoon and a line similar to those employed in catching whales. The pinnace was lifted from the bridge, pulled from its socket, and let down into the sea. Six oarsmen took their seats, and the coxswain went to the tiller. Ned, Conseil, and I went to the back of the boat.

"You are not coming, Captain?" I asked.

"No, sir; but I wish you good sport."

The boat put off, and, lifted by the six rowers, drew rapidly towards the dugong, which floated about two miles from the Nautilus.

Arrived some cables-length from the cetacean, the speed slackened, and the oars dipped noiselessly into the quiet waters. Ned Land, harpoon in hand, stood in the fore part of the boat. The harpoon used for striking the whale is generally attached to a very long cord which runs out rapidly as the wounded creature draws it after him. But here the cord was not more than ten fathoms long, and the extremity was attached to a small barrel which, by floating, was to show the course the dugong took under the water.

I stood and carefully watched the Canadian's adversary. This dugong, which also bears the name of the halicore, closely resembles the manatee; its oblong body terminated in a lengthened tail, and its lateral fins in perfect fingers. Its difference from the manatee consisted in its upper jaw, which was armed with two long and pointed teeth which formed on each side diverging tusks.

This dugong which Ned Land was preparing to attack was of colossal dimensions; it was more than seven yards long. It did not move, and seemed to be sleeping on the waves, which circumstance made it easier to capture.

The boat approached within six yards of the animal. The oars rested on the rowlocks. I half rose. Ned Land, his body thrown a little back, brandished the harpoon in his experienced hand.

Suddenly a hissing noise was heard, and the dugong disappeared. The harpoon, although thrown with great force; had apparently only struck the water.

"Curse it!" exclaimed the Canadian furiously; "I have missed it!"

"No," said I; "the creature is wounded—look at the blood; but your weapon has not stuck in his body."

"My harpoon! my harpoon!" cried Ned Land.

The sailors rowed on, and the coxswain made for the floating barrel. The harpoon regained, we followed in pursuit of the animal.

The latter came now and then to the surface to breathe. Its wound had not weakened it, for it shot onwards with great rapidity.

The boat, rowed by strong arms, flew on its track. Several times it approached within some few yards, and the Canadian was ready to strike, but the dugong made off with a sudden plunge, and it was impossible to reach it.

Imagine the passion which excited impatient Ned Land! He hurled at the unfortunate creature the most energetic expletives in the English tongue. For my part, I was only vexed to see the dugong escape all our attacks.

We pursued it without relaxation for an hour, and I began to think it would prove difficult to capture, when the animal, possessed with the perverse idea of vengeance of which he had cause to repent, turned upon the pinnace and assailed us in its turn.

This manoeuvre did not escape the Canadian.

"Look out!" he cried.

The coxswain said some words in his outlandish tongue, doubtless warning the men to keep on their guard.

The dugong came within twenty feet of the boat, stopped, sniffed the air briskly with its large nostrils (not pierced at the extremity, but in the upper part of its muzzle). Then, taking a spring, he threw himself upon us.

The pinnace could not avoid the shock, and half upset, shipped at least two tons of water, which had to be emptied; but, thanks to the coxswain, we caught it sideways, not full front, so we were not quite overturned. While Ned Land, clinging to the bows, belaboured the gigantic animal with blows from his harpoon, the creature's teeth were buried in the gunwale, and it lifted the whole thing out of the water, as a lion does a roebuck. We were upset over one another, and I know not how the adventure would have ended, if the Canadian, still enraged with the beast, had not struck it to the heart.

I heard its teeth grind on the iron plate, and the dugong disappeared, carrying the harpoon with him. But the barrel soon returned to the surface, and shortly after the body of the animal, turned on its back. The boat came up with it, took it in tow, and made straight for the Nautilus.

It required tackle of enormous strength to hoist the dugong on to the platform. It weighed 10,000 lb.

The next day, 11th February, the larder of the Nautilus was enriched by some more delicate game. A flight of sea-swallows rested on the Nautilus. It was a species of the Sterna nilotica, peculiar to Egypt; its beak is black, head grey and pointed, the eye surrounded by white spots, the back, wings, and tail of a greyish colour, the belly and throat white, and claws red. They also took some dozen of Nile ducks, a wild bird of high flavour, its throat and upper part of the head white with black spots.

About five o'clock in the evening we sighted to the north the Cape of Ras-Mohammed. This cape forms the extremity of Arabia Petraea, comprised between the Gulf of Suez and the Gulf of Acabah.

The Nautilus penetrated into the Straits of Jubal, which leads to the Gulf of Suez. I distinctly saw a high mountain, towering between the two gulfs of Ras-Mohammed. It was Mount Horeb, that Sinai at the top of which Moses saw God face to face.

At six o'clock the Nautilus, sometimes floating, sometimes immersed, passed some distance from Tor, situated at the end of the bay, the waters of which seemed tinted with red, an observation already made by Captain Nemo. Then night fell in the midst of a heavy silence, sometimes broken by the cries of the pelican and other night-birds, and the noise of the waves breaking upon the shore, chafing against the rocks, or the panting of some far-off steamer beating the waters of the Gulf with its noisy paddles.

From eight to nine o'clock the Nautilus remained some fathoms under the water. According to my calculation we must have been very near Suez. Through the panel of the saloon I saw the bottom of the rocks brilliantly lit up by our electric lamp. We seemed to be leaving the Straits behind us more and more.

At a quarter-past nine, the vessel having returned to the surface, I mounted the platform. Most impatient to pass through Captain Nemo's tunnel, I could not stay in one place, so came to breathe the fresh night air.

Soon in the shadow I saw a pale light, half discoloured by the fog, shining about a mile from us.

"A floating lighthouse!" said someone near me.

I turned, and saw the Captain.

"It is the floating light of Suez," he continued. "It will not be long before we gain the entrance of the tunnel."

"The entrance cannot be easy?"

"No, sir; for that reason I am accustomed to go into the steersman's cage and myself direct our course. And now, if you will go down, M. Aronnax, the Nautilus is going under the waves, and will not return to the surface until we have passed through the Arabian Tunnel."

Captain Nemo led me towards the central staircase; half way down he opened a door, traversed the upper deck, and landed in the pilot's cage, which it may be remembered rose at the extremity of the platform. It was a cabin measuring six feet square, very much like that occupied by the pilot on the steamboats of the Mississippi or Hudson. In the midst worked a wheel, placed vertically, and caught to the tiller-rope, which ran to the back of the Nautilus. Four light-ports with lenticular glasses, let in a groove in the partition of the cabin, allowed the man at the wheel to see in all directions.

This cabin was dark; but soon my eyes accustomed themselves to the obscurity, and I perceived the pilot, a strong man, with his hands resting on the spokes of the wheel. Outside, the sea appeared vividly lit up by the lantern, which shed its rays from the back of the cabin to the other extremity of the platform.

"Now," said Captain Nemo, "let us try to make our passage."

Electric wires connected the pilot's cage with the machinery room, and from there the Captain could communicate simultaneously to his Nautilus the direction and the speed. He pressed a metal knob, and at once the speed of the screw diminished.

I looked in silence at the high straight wall we were running by at this moment, the immovable base of a massive sandy coast. We followed it thus for an hour only some few yards off.

Captain Nemo did not take his eye from the knob, suspended by its two concentric circles in the cabin. At a simple gesture, the pilot modified the course of the Nautilus every instant.

I had placed myself at the port-scuttle, and saw some magnificent substructures of coral, zoophytes, seaweed, and fucus, agitating their enormous claws, which stretched out from the fissures of the rock.

At a quarter-past ten, the Captain himself took the helm. A large gallery, black and deep, opened before us. The Nautilus went boldly into it. A strange roaring was heard round its sides. It was the waters of the Red Sea, which the incline of the tunnel precipitated violently towards the Mediterranean. The Nautilus went with the torrent, rapid as an arrow, in spite of the efforts of the machinery, which, in order to offer more effective resistance, beat the waves with reversed screw.

On the walls of the narrow passage I could see nothing but brilliant rays, straight lines, furrows of fire, traced by the great speed, under the brilliant electric light. My heart beat fast.

At thirty-five minutes past ten, Captain Nemo quitted the helm, and, turning to me, said:

"The Mediterranean!"

In less than twenty minutes, the Nautilus, carried along by the torrent, had passed through the Isthmus of Suez.

CHAPTER VI. THE GRECIAN ARCHIPELAGO

The next day, the 12th of February, at the dawn of day, the Nautilus rose to the surface. I hastened on to the platform. Three miles to the south the dim outline of Pelusium was to be seen. A torrent had carried us from one sea to another. About seven o'clock Ned and Conseil joined me.

"Well, Sir Naturalist," said the Canadian, in a slightly jovial tone, "and the Mediterranean?"

"We are floating on its surface, friend Ned."

"What!" said Conseil, "this very night."

"Yes, this very night; in a few minutes we have passed this impassable isthmus."

"I do not believe it," replied the Canadian.

"Then you are wrong, Master Land," I continued; "this low coast which rounds off to the south is the Egyptian coast. And you who have such good eyes, Ned, you can see the jetty of Port Said stretching into the sea."

The Canadian looked attentively.

"Certainly you are right, sir, and your Captain is a first-rate man. We are in the Mediterranean. Good! Now, if you please, let us talk of our own little affair, but so that no one hears us."

I saw what the Canadian wanted, and, in any case, I thought it better to let him talk, as he wished it; so we all three went and sat down near the lantern, where we were less exposed to the spray of the blades.

"Now, Ned, we listen; what have you to tell us?"

"What I have to tell you is very simple. We are in Europe; and before Captain Nemo's caprices drag us once more to the bottom of the Polar Seas, or lead us into Oceania, I ask to leave the Nautilus."

I wished in no way to shackle the liberty of my companions, but I certainly felt no desire to leave Captain Nemo.

Thanks to him, and thanks to his apparatus, I was each day nearer the completion of my submarine studies; and I was rewriting my book of submarine depths in its very element. Should I ever again have such an opportunity of observing the wonders of the ocean? No, certainly not! And I could not bring myself to the idea of abandoning the Nautilus before the cycle of investigation was accomplished.

"Friend Ned, answer me frankly, are you tired of being on board? Are you sorry that destiny has thrown us into Captain Nemo's hands?"

The Canadian remained some moments without answering. Then, crossing his arms, he said:

"Frankly, I do not regret this journey under the seas. I shall be glad to have made it; but, now that it is made, let us have done with it. That is my idea."

"It will come to an end, Ned."

"Where and when?"

"Where I do not know—when I cannot say; or, rather, I suppose it will end when these seas have nothing more to teach us."

"Then what do you hope for?" demanded the Canadian.

"That circumstances may occur as well six months hence as now by which we may and ought to profit."

"Oh!" said Ned Land, "and where shall we be in six months, if you please, Sir Naturalist?"

"Perhaps in China; you know the Nautilus is a rapid traveller. It goes through water as swallows through the air, or as an express on the land. It does not fear frequented seas; who can say that it may not beat the coasts of France, England, or America, on which flight may be attempted as advantageously as here."

"M. Aronnax," replied the Canadian, "your arguments are rotten at the foundation. You speak in the future, `We shall be there! we shall be here!' I speak in the present, `We are here, and we must profit by it.'"

Ned Land's logic pressed me hard, and I felt myself beaten on that ground. I knew not what argument would now tell in my favour.

"Sir," continued Ned, "let us suppose an impossibility: if Captain Nemo should this day offer you your liberty; would you accept it?"

"I do not know," I answered.

"And if," he added, "the offer made you this day was never to be renewed, would you accept it?"

"Friend Ned, this is my answer. Your reasoning is against me. We must not rely on Captain Nemo's good-will. Common prudence forbids him to set us at liberty. On the other side, prudence bids us profit by the first opportunity to leave the Nautilus."

"Well, M. Aronnax, that is wisely said."

"Only one observation—just one. The occasion must be serious, and our first attempt must succeed; if it fails, we shall never find another, and Captain Nemo will never forgive us."

"All that is true," replied the Canadian. "But your observation applies equally to all attempts at flight, whether in two years' time, or in two days'. But the question is still this: If a favourable opportunity presents itself, it must be seized."

"Agreed! And now, Ned, will you tell me what you mean by a favourable opportunity?"

"It will be that which, on a dark night, will bring the Nautilus a short distance from some European coast."

"And you will try and save yourself by swimming?"

"Yes, if we were near enough to the bank, and if the vessel was floating at the time. Not if the bank was far away, and the boat was under the water."

"And in that case?"

"In that case, I should seek to make myself master of the pinnace. I know how it is worked. We must get inside, and the bolts once drawn, we shall come to the surface of the water, without even the pilot, who is in the bows, perceiving our flight."

"Well, Ned, watch for the opportunity; but do not forget that a hitch will ruin us."

"I will not forget, sir."

"And now, Ned, would you like to know what I think of your project?"

"Certainly, M. Aronnax."

"Well, I think—I do not say I hope—I think that this favourable opportunity will never present itself."

"Why not?"

"Because Captain Nemo cannot hide from himself that we have not given up all hope of regaining our liberty, and he will be on his guard, above all, in the seas and in the sight of European coasts."

"We shall see," replied Ned Land, shaking his head determinedly.

"And now, Ned Land," I added, "let us stop here. Not another word on the subject. The day that you are ready, come and let us know, and we will follow you. I rely entirely upon you."

Thus ended a conversation which, at no very distant time, led to such grave results. I must say here that facts seemed to confirm my foresight, to the Canadian's great despair. Did Captain Nemo distrust us in these frequented seas? or did he only wish to hide himself from the numerous vessels, of all nations, which ploughed the Mediterranean? I could not tell; but we were oftener between waters and far from the coast. Or, if the Nautilus did emerge, nothing was to be seen but the pilot's cage; and sometimes it went to great depths, for, between the Grecian Archipelago and Asia Minor we could not touch the bottom by more than a thousand fathoms.

Thus I only knew we were near the Island of Carpathos, one of the Sporades, by Captain Nemo reciting these lines from Virgil:

"Est Carpathio Neptuni gurgite vates,

Caeruleus Proteus,"

as he pointed to a spot on the planisphere.

It was indeed the ancient abode of Proteus, the old shepherd of Neptune's flocks, now the Island of Scarpanto, situated between Rhodes and Crete. I saw nothing but the granite base through the glass panels of the saloon.

The next day, the 14th of February, I resolved to employ some hours in studying the fishes of the Archipelago; but for some reason or other the panels remained hermetically sealed. Upon taking the course of the Nautilus, I found that we were going towards Candia, the ancient Isle of Crete. At the time I embarked on the Abraham Lincoln, the whole of this island had risen in insurrection against the despotism of the Turks. But how the insurgents had fared since that time I was absolutely ignorant, and it was not Captain Nemo, deprived of all land communications, who could tell me.

I made no allusion to this event when that night I found myself alone with him in the saloon. Besides, he seemed to be taciturn and preoccupied. Then, contrary to his custom, he ordered both panels to be opened, and, going from one to the other, observed the mass of waters attentively. To what end I could not guess; so, on my side, I employed my time in studying the fish passing before my eyes.

In the midst of the waters a man appeared, a diver, carrying at his belt a leathern purse. It was not a body abandoned to the waves; it was a living man, swimming with a strong hand, disappearing occasionally to take breath at the surface.

I turned towards Captain Nemo, and in an agitated voice exclaimed:

"A man shipwrecked! He must be saved at any price!"

The Captain did not answer me, but came and leaned against the panel.

The man had approached, and, with his face flattened against the glass, was looking at us.

To my great amazement, Captain Nemo signed to him. The diver answered with his hand, mounted immediately to the surface of the water, and did not appear again.

"Do not be uncomfortable," said Captain Nemo. "It is Nicholas of Cape Matapan, surnamed Pesca. He is well known in all the Cyclades. A bold diver! water is his element, and he lives more in it than on land, going continually from one island to another, even as far as Crete."

"You know him, Captain?"

"Why not, M. Aronnax?"

Saying which, Captain Nemo went towards a piece of furniture standing near the left panel of the saloon. Near this piece of furniture, I saw a chest bound with iron, on the cover of which was a copper plate, bearing the cypher of the Nautilus with its device.

At that moment, the Captain, without noticing my presence, opened the piece of furniture, a sort of strong box, which held a great many ingots.

They were ingots of gold. From whence came this precious metal, which represented an enormous sum? Where did the Captain gather this gold from? and what was he going to do with it?

I did not say one word. I looked. Captain Nemo took the ingots one by one, and arranged them methodically in the chest, which he filled entirely. I estimated the contents at more than 4,000 lb. weight of gold, that is to say, nearly L200,000.

The chest was securely fastened, and the Captain wrote an address on the lid, in characters which must have belonged to Modern Greece.

This done, Captain Nemo pressed a knob, the wire of which communicated with the quarters of the crew. Four men appeared, and, not without some trouble, pushed the chest out of the saloon. Then I heard them hoisting it up the iron staircase by means of pulleys.

At that moment, Captain Nemo turned to me.

"And you were saying, sir?" said he.

"I was saying nothing, Captain."

"Then, sir, if you will allow me, I will wish you good night."

Whereupon he turned and left the saloon.

I returned to my room much troubled, as one may believe. I vainly tried to sleep—I sought the connecting link between the apparition of the diver and the chest filled with gold. Soon, I felt by certain movements of pitching and tossing that the Nautilus was leaving the depths and returning to the surface.

Then I heard steps upon the platform; and I knew they were unfastening the pinnace and launching it upon the waves. For one instant it struck the side of the Nautilus, then all noise ceased.

Two hours after, the same noise, the same going and coming was renewed; the boat was hoisted on board, replaced in its socket, and the Nautilus again plunged under the waves.

So these millions had been transported to their address. To what point of the continent? Who was Captain Nemo's correspondent?

The next day I related to Conseil and the Canadian the events of the night, which had excited my curiosity to the highest degree. My companions were not less surprised than myself.

"But where does he take his millions to?" asked Ned Land.

To that there was no possible answer. I returned to the saloon after having breakfast and set to work. Till five o'clock in the evening I employed myself in arranging my notes. At that moment—(ought I to attribute it to some peculiar idiosyncrasy)—I felt so great a heat that I was obliged to take off my coat. It was strange, for we were under low latitudes; and even then the Nautilus, submerged as it was, ought to experience no change of temperature. I looked at the manometer; it showed a depth of sixty feet, to which atmospheric heat could never attain.

I continued my work, but the temperature rose to such a pitch as to be intolerable.

"Could there be fire on board?" I asked myself.

I was leaving the saloon, when Captain Nemo entered; he approached the thermometer, consulted it, and, turning to me, said:

"Forty-two degrees."

"I have noticed it, Captain," I replied; "and if it gets much hotter we cannot bear it."

"Oh, sir, it will not get better if we do not wish it."

"You can reduce it as you please, then?"

"No; but I can go farther from the stove which produces it."

"It is outward, then!"

"Certainly; we are floating in a current of boiling water."

"Is it possible!" I exclaimed.

"Look."

The panels opened, and I saw the sea entirely white all round. A sulphurous smoke was curling amid the waves, which boiled like water in a copper. I placed my hand on one of the panes of glass, but the heat was so great that I quickly took it off again.

"Where are we?" I asked.

"Near the Island of Santorin, sir," replied the Captain. "I wished to give you a sight of the curious spectacle of a submarine eruption."

"I thought," said I, "that the formation of these new islands was ended."

"Nothing is ever ended in the volcanic parts of the sea," replied Captain Nemo; "and the globe is always being worked by subterranean fires. Already, in the nineteenth year of our era, according to Cassiodorus and Pliny, a new island, Theia (the divine), appeared in the very place where these islets have recently been formed. Then they sank under the waves, to rise again in the year 69, when they again subsided. Since that time to our days the Plutonian work has been suspended. But on the 3rd of February, 1866, a new island, which they named George Island, emerged from the midst of the sulphurous vapour near Nea Kamenni, and settled again the 6th of the same month. Seven days after, the 13th of February, the Island of Aphroessa appeared, leaving between Nea Kamenni and itself a canal ten yards broad. I was in these seas when the phenomenon occurred, and I was able therefore to observe all the different phases. The Island of Aphroessa, of round form, measured 300 feet in diameter, and 30 feet in height. It was composed of black and vitreous lava, mixed with fragments of felspar. And lastly, on the 10th of March, a smaller island, called Reka, showed itself near Nea Kamenni, and since then these three have joined together, forming but one and the same island."

"And the canal in which we are at this moment?" I asked.

"Here it is," replied Captain Nemo, showing me a map of the Archipelago. "You see, I have marked the new islands."

I returned to the glass. The Nautilus was no longer moving, the heat was becoming unbearable. The sea, which till now had been white, was red, owing to the presence of salts of iron. In spite of the ship's being hermetically sealed,

126

an insupportable smell of sulphur filled the saloon, and the brilliancy of the electricity was entirely extinguished by bright scarlet flames. I was in a bath, I was choking, I was broiled.

"We can remain no longer in this boiling water," said I to the Captain.

"It would not be prudent," replied the impassive Captain Nemo.

An order was given; the Nautilus tacked about and left the furnace it could not brave with impunity. A quarter of an hour after we were breathing fresh air on the surface. The thought then struck me that, if Ned Land had chosen this part of the sea for our flight, we should never have come alive out of this sea of fire. The next day, the 16th of February, we left the basin which, between Rhodes and Alexandria, is reckoned about 1,500 fathoms in depth, and the Nautilus, passing some distance from Cerigo, quitted the Grecian Archipelago after having doubled Cape Matapan.

CHAPTER VII. THE MEDITERRANEAN IN FORTY-EIGHT HOURS

The Mediterranean, the blue sea par excellence, "the great sea" of the Hebrews, "the sea" of the Greeks, the "mare nostrum" of the Romans, bordered by orange-trees, aloes, cacti, and sea-pines; embalmed with the perfume of the myrtle, surrounded by rude mountains, saturated with pure and transparent air, but incessantly worked by underground fires; a perfect battlefield in which Neptune and Pluto still dispute the empire of the world!

It is upon these banks, and on these waters, says Michelet, that man is renewed in one of the most powerful climates of the globe. But, beautiful as it was, I could only take a rapid glance at the basin whose superficial area is two million of square yards. Even Captain Nemo's knowledge was lost to me, for this puzzling person did not appear once during our passage at full speed. I estimated the course which the Nautilus took under the waves of the sea at about six hundred leagues, and it was accomplished in forty-eight hours. Starting on the morning of the 16th of February from the shores of Greece, we had crossed the Straits of Gibraltar by sunrise on the 18th.

It was plain to me that this Mediterranean, enclosed in the midst of those countries which he wished to avoid, was distasteful to Captain Nemo. Those waves and those breezes brought back too many remembrances, if not too many regrets. Here he had no longer that independence and that liberty of gait which he had when in the open seas, and his Nautilus felt itself cramped between the close shores of Africa and Europe.

Our speed was now twenty-five miles an hour. It may be well understood that Ned Land, to his great disgust, was obliged to renounce his intended flight. He could not launch the pinnace, going at the rate of twelve or thirteen yards every second. To quit the Nautilus under such conditions would be as bad as jumping from a train going at full speed—an imprudent thing, to say the least of it. Besides, our vessel only mounted to the surface of the waves at night to renew its stock of air; it was steered entirely by the compass and the log.

I saw no more of the interior of this Mediterranean than a traveller by express train perceives of the landscape which flies before his eyes; that is to say, the distant horizon, and not the nearer objects which pass like a flash of lightning.

We were then passing between Sicily and the coast of Tunis. In the narrow space between Cape Bon and the Straits of Messina the bottom of the sea rose almost suddenly. There was a perfect bank, on which there was not more than nine fathoms of water, whilst on either side the depth was ninety fathoms.

The Nautilus had to manoeuvre very carefully so as not to strike against this submarine barrier.

I showed Conseil, on the map of the Mediterranean, the spot occupied by this reef.

"But if you please, sir," observed Conseil, "it is like a real isthmus joining Europe to Africa."

"Yes, my boy, it forms a perfect bar to the Straits of Lybia, and the soundings of Smith have proved that in former times the continents between Cape Boco and Cape Furina were joined."

"I can well believe it," said Conseil.

"I will add," I continued, "that a similar barrier exists between Gibraltar and Ceuta, which in geological times formed the entire Mediterranean."

"What if some volcanic burst should one day raise these two barriers above the waves?"

"It is not probable, Conseil."

"Well, but allow me to finish, please, sir; if this phenomenon should take place, it will be troublesome for M. Lesseps, who has taken so much pains to pierce the isthmus."

"I agree with you; but I repeat, Conseil, this phenomenon will never happen. The violence of subterranean force is ever diminishing. Volcanoes, so plentiful in the first days of the world, are being extinguished by degrees; the internal heat is weakened, the temperature of the lower strata of the globe is lowered by a perceptible quantity every century to the detriment of our globe, for its heat is its life."

"But the sun?"

"The sun is not sufficient, Conseil. Can it give heat to a dead body?"

"Not that I know of."

"Well, my friend, this earth will one day be that cold corpse; it will become uninhabitable and uninhabited like the moon, which has long since lost all its vital heat."

"In how many centuries?"

"In some hundreds of thousands of years, my boy."

"Then," said Conseil, "we shall have time to finish our journey—that is, if Ned Land does not interfere with it."

And Conseil, reassured, returned to the study of the bank, which the Nautilus was skirting at a moderate speed.

During the night of the 16th and 17th February we had entered the second Mediterranean basin, the greatest depth of which was 1,450 fathoms. The Nautilus, by the action of its crew, slid down the inclined planes and buried itself in the lowest depths of the sea.

On the 18th of February, about three o'clock in the morning, we were at the entrance of the Straits of Gibraltar. There once existed two currents: an upper one, long since recognised, which conveys the waters of the ocean into the basin of the Mediterranean; and a lower counter-current, which reasoning has now shown to exist. Indeed, the volume of water in the Mediterranean, incessantly added to by the waves of the Atlantic and by rivers falling into it, would each year raise the level of this sea, for its evaporation is not sufficient to restore the equilibrium. As it is not so, we must necessarily admit the existence of an under-current, which empties into the basin of the Atlantic through the Straits of Gibraltar the surplus waters of the Mediterranean. A fact indeed; and it was this counter-current by which the Nautilus profited. It advanced rapidly by the narrow pass. For one instant I caught a glimpse of the beautiful ruins of the temple of Hercules, buried in the ground, according to Pliny, and with the low island which supports it; and a few minutes later we were floating on the Atlantic.

CHAPTER VIII. VIGO BAY

The Atlantic! a vast sheet of water whose superficial area covers twenty-five millions of square miles, the length of which is nine thousand miles, with a mean breadth of two thousand seven hundred—an ocean whose parallel winding shores embrace an immense circumference, watered by the largest rivers of the world, the St. Lawrence, the Mississippi, the Amazon, the Plata, the Orinoco, the Niger, the Senegal, the Elbe, the Loire, and the Rhine, which carry water from the most civilised, as well as from the most savage, countries! Magnificent field of water, incessantly ploughed by vessels of every nation, sheltered by the flags of every nation, and which terminates in those two terrible points so dreaded by mariners, Cape Horn and the Cape of Tempests.

The Nautilus was piercing the water with its sharp spur, after having accomplished nearly ten thousand leagues in three months and a half, a distance greater than the great circle of the earth. Where were we going now, and what was reserved for the future? The Nautilus, leaving the Straits of Gibraltar, had gone far out. It returned to the surface of the waves, and our daily walks on the platform were restored to us.

I mounted at once, accompanied by Ned Land and Conseil. At a distance of about twelve miles, Cape St. Vincent was dimly to be seen, forming the south-western point of the Spanish peninsula. A strong southerly gale was blowing. The sea was swollen and billowy; it made the Nautilus rock violently. It was almost impossible to keep one's foot on the platform, which the heavy rolls of the sea beat over every instant. So we descended after inhaling some mouthfuls of fresh air.

I returned to my room, Conseil to his cabin; but the Canadian, with a preoccupied air, followed me. Our rapid passage across the Mediterranean had not allowed him to put his project into execution, and he could not help showing his disappointment. When the door of my room was shut, he sat down and looked at me silently.

"Friend Ned," said I, "I understand you; but you cannot reproach yourself. To have attempted to leave the Nautilus under the circumstances would have been folly."

Ned Land did not answer; his compressed lips and frowning brow showed with him the violent possession this fixed idea had taken of his mind.

"Let us see," I continued; "we need not despair yet. We are going up the coast of Portugal again; France and England are not far off, where we can easily find refuge. Now if the Nautilus, on leaving the Straits of Gibraltar, had gone to the south, if it had carried us towards regions where there were no continents, I should share your uneasiness. But we know now that Captain Nemo does not fly from civilised seas, and in some days I think you can act with security."

Ned Land still looked at me fixedly; at length his fixed lips parted, and he said, "It is for to-night."

I drew myself up suddenly. I was, I admit, little prepared for this communication. I wanted to answer the Canadian, but words would not come.

"We agreed to wait for an opportunity," continued Ned Land, "and the opportunity has arrived. This night we shall be but a few miles from the Spanish coast. It is cloudy. The wind blows freely. I have your word, M. Aronnax, and I rely upon you."

As I was silent, the Canadian approached me.

"To-night, at nine o'clock," said he. "I have warned Conseil. At that moment Captain Nemo will be shut up in his room, probably in bed. Neither the engineers nor the ship's crew can see us. Conseil and I will gain the central staircase, and you, M. Aronnax, will remain in the library, two steps from us, waiting my signal. The oars, the mast, and the sail are in the canoe. I have even succeeded in getting some provisions. I have procured an English wrench, to unfasten the bolts which attach it to the shell of the Nautilus. So all is ready, till to-night."

"The sea is bad."

"That I allow," replied the Canadian; "but we must risk that. Liberty is worth paying for; besides, the boat is strong, and a few miles with a fair wind to carry us is no great thing. Who knows but by to-morrow we may be a hundred leagues away? Let circumstances only favour us, and by ten or eleven o'clock we shall have landed on some spot of terra firma, alive or dead. But adieu now till to-night."

With these words the Canadian withdrew, leaving me almost dumb. I had imagined that, the chance gone, I should have time to reflect and discuss the matter. My obstinate companion had given me no time; and, after all, what could I have said to him? Ned Land was perfectly right. There was almost the opportunity to profit by. Could I retract my word, and take upon myself the responsibility of compromising the future of my companions? To-morrow Captain Nemo might take us far from all land.

At that moment a rather loud hissing noise told me that the reservoirs were filling, and that the Nautilus was sinking under the waves of the Atlantic.

A sad day I passed, between the desire of regaining my liberty of action and of abandoning the wonderful Nautilus, and leaving my submarine studies incomplete.

What dreadful hours I passed thus! Sometimes seeing myself and companions safely landed, sometimes wishing, in spite of my reason, that some unforeseen circumstance, would prevent the realisation of Ned Land's project.

Twice I went to the saloon. I wished to consult the compass. I wished to see if the direction the Nautilus was taking was bringing us nearer or taking us farther from the coast. But no; the Nautilus kept in Portuguese waters.

I must therefore take my part and prepare for flight. My luggage was not heavy; my notes, nothing more.

As to Captain Nemo, I asked myself what he would think of our escape; what trouble, what wrong it might cause him and what he might do in case of its discovery or failure. Certainly I had no cause to complain of him; on the contrary, never was hospitality freer than his. In leaving him I could not be taxed with ingratitude. No oath bound us to him. It was on the strength of circumstances he relied, and not upon our word, to fix us for ever.

I had not seen the Captain since our visit to the Island of Santorin. Would chance bring me to his presence before our departure? I wished it, and I feared it at the same time. I listened if I could hear him walking the room contiguous to mine. No sound reached my ear. I felt an unbearable uneasiness. This day of waiting seemed eternal. Hours struck too slowly to keep pace with my impatience.

My dinner was served in my room as usual. I ate but little; I was too preoccupied. I left the table at seven o'clock. A hundred and twenty minutes (I counted them) still separated me from the moment in which I was to join Ned Land. My agitation redoubled. My pulse beat violently. I could not remain quiet. I went and came, hoping to calm my troubled spirit by constant movement. The idea of failure in our bold enterprise was the least painful of my anxieties; but the thought of seeing our project discovered before leaving the Nautilus, of being brought before Captain Nemo, irritated, or (what was worse) saddened, at my desertion, made my heart beat.

I wanted to see the saloon for the last time. I descended the stairs and arrived in the museum, where I had passed so many useful and agreeable hours. I looked at all its riches, all its treasures, like a man on the eve of an eternal exile, who was leaving never to return.

These wonders of Nature, these masterpieces of art, amongst which for so many days my life had been concentrated, I was going to abandon them for ever! I should like to have taken a last look through the windows of the saloon into the waters of the Atlantic: but the panels were hermetically closed, and a cloak of steel separated me from that ocean which I had not yet explored.

In passing through the saloon, I came near the door let into the angle which opened into the Captain's room. To my great surprise, this door was ajar. I drew back involuntarily. If Captain Nemo should be in his room, he could see me. But, hearing no sound, I drew nearer. The room was deserted. I pushed open the door and took some steps forward. Still the same monklike severity of aspect.

Suddenly the clock struck eight. The first beat of the hammer on the bell awoke me from my dreams. I trembled as if an invisible eye had plunged into my most secret thoughts, and I hurried from the room.

There my eye fell upon the compass. Our course was still north. The log indicated moderate speed, the manometer a depth of about sixty feet.

I returned to my room, clothed myself warmly—sea boots, an otterskin cap, a great coat of byssus, lined with sealskin; I was ready, I was waiting. The vibration of the screw alone broke the deep silence which reigned on board. I listened attentively. Would no loud voice suddenly inform me that Ned Land had been surprised in his projected flight. A mortal dread hung over me, and I vainly tried to regain my accustomed coolness.

At a few minutes to nine, I put my ear to the Captain's door. No noise. I left my room and returned to the saloon, which was half in obscurity, but deserted.

I opened the door communicating with the library. The same insufficient light, the same solitude. I placed myself near the door leading to the central staircase, and there waited for Ned Land's signal.

At that moment the trembling of the screw sensibly diminished, then it stopped entirely. The silence was now only disturbed by the beatings of my own heart. Suddenly a slight shock was felt; and I knew that the Nautilus had stopped at the bottom of the ocean. My uneasiness increased. The Canadian's signal did not come. I felt inclined to join Ned Land and beg of him to put off his attempt. I felt that we were not sailing under our usual conditions.

At this moment the door of the large saloon opened, and Captain Nemo appeared. He saw me, and without further preamble began in an amiable tone of voice:

"Ah, sir! I have been looking for you. Do you know the history of Spain?"

Now, one might know the history of one's own country by heart; but in the condition I was at the time, with troubled mind and head quite lost, I could not have said a word of it.

"Well," continued Captain Nemo, "you heard my question! Do you know the history of Spain?"

"Very slightly," I answered.

"Well, here are learned men having to learn," said the Captain. "Come, sit down, and I will tell you a curious episode in this history. Sir, listen well," said he; "this history will interest you on one side, for it will answer a question which doubtless you have not been able to solve."

"I listen, Captain," said I, not knowing what my interlocutor was driving at, and asking myself if this incident was bearing on our projected flight.

"Sir, if you have no objection, we will go back to 1702. You cannot be ignorant that your king, Louis XIV, thinking that the gesture of a potentate was sufficient to bring the Pyrenees under his yoke, had imposed the Duke of Anjou, his grandson, on the Spaniards. This prince reigned more or less badly under the name of Philip V, and had a strong party against him abroad. Indeed, the preceding year, the royal houses of Holland, Austria, and England had concluded a treaty of alliance at the Hague, with the intention of plucking the crown of Spain from the head of Philip V, and placing it on that of an archduke to whom they prematurely gave the title of Charles III.

"Spain must resist this coalition; but she was almost entirely unprovided with either soldiers or sailors. However, money would not fail them, provided that their galleons, laden with gold and silver from America, once entered their ports. And about the end of 1702 they expected a rich convoy which France was escorting with a fleet of twenty-three vessels, commanded by Admiral Chateau-Renaud, for the ships of the coalition were already beating the Atlantic. This convoy was to go to Cadiz, but the Admiral, hearing that an English fleet was cruising in those waters, resolved to make for a French port.

"The Spanish commanders of the convoy objected to this decision. They wanted to be taken to a Spanish port, and, if not to Cadiz, into Vigo Bay, situated on the northwest coast of Spain, and which was not blocked.

"Admiral Chateau-Renaud had the rashness to obey this injunction, and the galleons entered Vigo Bay.

"Unfortunately, it formed an open road which could not be defended in any way. They must therefore hasten to unload the galleons before the arrival of the combined fleet; and time would not have failed them had not a miserable question of rivalry suddenly arisen.

"You are following the chain of events?" asked Captain Nemo.

"Perfectly," said I, not knowing the end proposed by this historical lesson.

"I will continue. This is what passed. The merchants of Cadiz had a privilege by which they had the right of receiving all merchandise coming from the West Indies. Now, to disembark these ingots at the port of Vigo was depriving them of their rights. They complained at Madrid, and obtained the consent of the weak-minded Philip that the convoy, without discharging its cargo, should remain sequestered in the roads of Vigo until the enemy had disappeared.

"But whilst coming to this decision, on the 22nd of October, 1702, the English vessels arrived in Vigo Bay, when Admiral Chateau-Renaud, in spite of inferior forces, fought bravely. But, seeing that the treasure must fall into the enemy's hands, he burnt and scuttled every galleon, which went to the bottom with their immense riches."

Captain Nemo stopped. I admit I could not see yet why this history should interest me.

"Well?" I asked.

"Well, M. Aronnax," replied Captain Nemo, "we are in that Vigo Bay; and it rests with yourself whether you will penetrate its mysteries."

The Captain rose, telling me to follow him. I had had time to recover. I obeyed. The saloon was dark, but through the transparent glass the waves were sparkling. I looked.

For half a mile around the Nautilus, the waters seemed bathed in electric light. The sandy bottom was clean and bright. Some of the ship's crew in their diving-dresses were clearing away half-rotten barrels and empty cases from the midst of the blackened wrecks. From these cases and from these barrels escaped ingots of gold and silver, cascades of piastres and jewels. The sand was heaped up with them. Laden with their precious booty, the men returned to the Nautilus, disposed of their burden, and went back to this inexhaustible fishery of gold and silver.

I understood now. This was the scene of the battle of the 22nd of October, 1702. Here on this very spot the galleons laden for the Spanish Government had sunk. Here Captain Nemo came, according to his wants, to pack up those millions with which he burdened the Nautilus. It was for him and him alone America had given up her precious metals. He was heir direct, without anyone to share, in those treasures torn from the Incas and from the conquered of Ferdinand Cortez.

"Did you know, sir," he asked, smiling, "that the sea contained such riches?"

"I knew," I answered, "that they value money held in suspension in these waters at two millions."

"Doubtless; but to extract this money the expense would be greater than the profit. Here, on the contrary, I have but to pick up what man has lost—and not only in Vigo Bay, but in a thousand other ports where shipwrecks have happened, and which are marked on my submarine map. Can you understand now the source of the millions I am worth?"

"I understand, Captain. But allow me to tell you that in exploring Vigo Bay you have only been beforehand with a rival society."

"And which?"

"A society which has received from the Spanish Government the privilege of seeking those buried galleons. The shareholders are led on by the allurement of an enormous bounty, for they value these rich shipwrecks at five hundred millions."

"Five hundred millions they were," answered Captain Nemo, "but they are so no longer."

"Just so," said I; "and a warning to those shareholders would be an act of charity. But who knows if it would be well received? What gamblers usually regret above all is less the loss of their money than of their foolish hopes. After all, I pity them less than the thousands of unfortunates to whom so much riches well-distributed would have been profitable, whilst for them they will be for ever barren."

I had no sooner expressed this regret than I felt that it must have wounded Captain Nemo.

"Barren!" he exclaimed, with animation. "Do you think then, sir, that these riches are lost because I gather them? Is it for myself alone, according to your idea, that I take the trouble to collect these treasures? Who told you that I did not make a good use of it? Do you think I am ignorant that there are suffering beings and oppressed races on this earth, miserable creatures to console, victims to avenge? Do you not understand?"

Captain Nemo stopped at these last words, regretting perhaps that he had spoken so much. But I had guessed that, whatever the motive which had forced him to seek independence under the sea, it had left him still a man, that his heart still beat for the sufferings of humanity, and that his immense charity was for oppressed races as well as individuals. And I then understood for whom those millions were destined which were forwarded by Captain Nemo when the Nautilus was cruising in the waters of Crete.

CHAPTER IX. A VANISHED CONTINENT

The next morning, the 19th of February, I saw the Canadian enter my room. I expected this visit. He looked very disappointed.

"Well, sir?" said he.

"Well, Ned, fortune was against us yesterday."

"Yes; that Captain must needs stop exactly at the hour we intended leaving his vessel."

"Yes, Ned, he had business at his bankers."

"His bankers!"

"Or rather his banking-house; by that I mean the ocean, where his riches are safer than in the chests of the State."

I then related to the Canadian the incidents of the preceding night, hoping to bring him back to the idea of not abandoning the Captain; but my recital had no other result than an energetically expressed regret from Ned that he had not been able to take a walk on the battlefield of Vigo on his own account.

"However," said he, "all is not ended. It is only a blow of the harpoon lost. Another time we must succeed; and to-night, if necessary——"

"In what direction is the Nautilus going?" I asked.

"I do not know," replied Ned.

"Well, at noon we shall see the point."

The Canadian returned to Conseil. As soon as I was dressed, I went into the saloon. The compass was not reassuring. The course of the Nautilus was S.S.W. We were turning our backs on Europe.

I waited with some impatience till the ship's place was pricked on the chart. At about half-past eleven the reservoirs were emptied, and our vessel rose to the surface of the ocean. I rushed towards the platform. Ned Land had preceded me. No more land in sight. Nothing but an immense sea. Some sails on the horizon, doubtless those going to San Roque in search of favourable winds for doubling the Cape of Good Hope. The weather was cloudy. A gale of wind was preparing. Ned raved, and tried to pierce the cloudy horizon. He still hoped that behind all that fog stretched the land he so longed for.

At noon the sun showed itself for an instant. The second profited by this brightness to take its height. Then, the sea becoming more billowy, we descended, and the panel closed.

An hour after, upon consulting the chart, I saw the position of the Nautilus was marked at 16° 17' long., and 33° 22' lat., at 150 leagues from the nearest coast. There was no means of flight, and I leave you to imagine the rage of the Canadian when I informed him of our situation.

For myself, I was not particularly sorry. I felt lightened of the load which had oppressed me, and was able to return with some degree of calmness to my accustomed work.

That night, about eleven o'clock, I received a most unexpected visit from Captain Nemo. He asked me very graciously if I felt fatigued from my watch of the preceding night. I answered in the negative.

"Then, M. Aronnax, I propose a curious excursion."

"Propose, Captain?"

"You have hitherto only visited the submarine depths by daylight, under the brightness of the sun. Would it suit you to see them in the darkness of the night?"

"Most willingly."

"I warn you, the way will be tiring. We shall have far to walk, and must climb a mountain. The roads are not well kept."

"What you say, Captain, only heightens my curiosity; I am ready to follow you."

"Come then, sir, we will put on our diving-dresses."

Arrived at the robing-room, I saw that neither of my companions nor any of the ship's crew were to follow us on this excursion. Captain Nemo had not even proposed my taking with me either Ned or Conseil.

In a few moments we had put on our diving-dresses; they placed on our backs the reservoirs, abundantly filled with air, but no electric lamps were prepared. I called the Captain's attention to the fact.

"They will be useless," he replied.

I thought I had not heard aright, but I could not repeat my observation, for the Captain's head had already disappeared in its metal case. I finished harnessing myself. I felt them put an iron-pointed stick into my hand, and some minutes later, after going through the usual form, we set foot on the bottom of the Atlantic at a depth of 150 fathoms. Midnight was near. The waters were profoundly dark, but Captain Nemo pointed out in the distance a reddish spot, a sort of large light shining brilliantly about two miles from the Nautilus. What this fire might be, what could feed it, why and how it lit up the liquid mass, I could not say. In any case, it did light our way, vaguely, it is true, but I soon accustomed myself to the peculiar darkness, and I understood, under such circumstances, the uselessness of the Ruhmkorff apparatus.

As we advanced, I heard a kind of pattering above my head. The noise redoubling, sometimes producing a continual shower, I soon understood the cause. It was rain falling violently, and crisping the surface of the waves. Instinctively the thought flashed across my mind that I should be wet through! By the water! in the midst of the water! I could not help laughing at the odd idea. But, indeed, in the thick diving-dress, the liquid element is no longer felt, and one only seems to be in an atmosphere somewhat denser than the terrestrial atmosphere. Nothing more.

After half an hour's walk the soil became stony. Medusae, microscopic crustacea, and pennatules lit it slightly with their phosphorescent gleam. I caught a glimpse of pieces of stone covered with millions of zoophytes and masses of sea weed. My feet often slipped upon this sticky carpet of sea weed, and without my iron-tipped stick I should have fallen more than once. In turning round, I could still see the whitish lantern of the Nautilus beginning to pale in the distance.

But the rosy light which guided us increased and lit up the horizon. The presence of this fire under water puzzled me in the highest degree. Was I going towards a natural phenomenon as yet unknown to the *savants* of the earth? Or even (for this thought crossed my brain) had the hand of man aught to do with this conflagration? Had he fanned this flame? Was I to meet in these depths companions and friends of Captain Nemo whom he was going to visit, and who, like him, led this strange existence? Should I find down there a whole colony of exiles who, weary of the miseries of this earth, had sought and found independence in the deep ocean? All these foolish and unreasonable ideas pursued me. And in this condition of mind, over-excited by the succession of wonders continually passing before my eyes, I should not have been surprised to meet at the bottom of the sea one of those submarine towns of which Captain Nemo dreamed.

Our road grew lighter and lighter. The white glimmer came in rays from the summit of a mountain about 800 feet high. But what I saw was simply a reflection, developed by the clearness of the waters. The source of this inexplicable light was a fire on the opposite side of the mountain.

In the midst of this stony maze furrowing the bottom of the Atlantic, Captain Nemo advanced without hesitation. He knew this dreary road.

Doubtless he had often travelled over it, and could not lose himself. I followed him with unshaken confidence. He seemed to me like a genie of the sea; and, as he walked before me, I could not help admiring his stature, which was outlined in black on the luminous horizon.

It was one in the morning when we arrived at the first slopes of the mountain; but to gain access to them we must venture through the difficult paths of a vast copse.

Yes; a copse of dead trees, without leaves, without sap, trees petrified by the action of the water and here and there overtopped by gigantic pines. It was like a coal-pit still standing, holding by the roots to the broken soil, and whose branches, like fine black paper cuttings, showed distinctly on the watery ceiling. Picture to yourself a forest in the Hartz hanging on to the sides of the mountain, but a forest swallowed up. The paths were encumbered with seaweed and fucus, between which grovelled a whole world of crustacea. I went along, climbing the rocks, striding over extended trunks, breaking the sea bind-weed which hung from one tree to the other; and frightening the fishes, which flew from branch to branch. Pressing onward, I felt no fatigue. I followed my guide, who was never tired. What a spectacle! How can I express it? how paint the aspect of those woods and rocks in this medium—their under parts dark and wild, the upper coloured with red tints, by that light which the reflecting powers of the waters doubled? We climbed rocks which fell directly after with gigantic bounds and the low growling of an avalanche. To right and left ran long, dark galleries, where sight was lost. Here opened vast glades which the hand of man seemed to have worked; and I sometimes asked myself if some inhabitant of these submarine regions would not suddenly appear to me.

But Captain Nemo was still mounting. I could not stay behind. I followed boldly. My stick gave me good help. A false step would have been dangerous on the narrow passes sloping down to the sides of the gulfs; but I walked with firm step, without feeling any giddiness. Now I jumped a crevice, the depth of which would have made me hesitate had it been among the glaciers on the land; now I ventured on the unsteady trunk of a tree thrown across from one abyss to the other, without looking under my feet, having only eyes to admire the wild sites of this region.

There, monumental rocks, leaning on their regularly-cut bases, seemed to defy all laws of equilibrium. From between their stony knees trees sprang, like a jet under heavy pressure, and upheld others which upheld them. Natural towers, large scarps, cut perpendicularly, like a "curtain," inclined at an angle which the laws of gravitation could never have tolerated in terrestrial regions.

Two hours after quitting the Nautilus we had crossed the line of trees, and a hundred feet above our heads rose the top of the mountain, which cast a shadow on the brilliant irradiation of the opposite slope. Some petrified shrubs ran fantastically here and there. Fishes got up under our feet like birds in the long grass. The massive rocks were rent with impenetrable fractures, deep grottos, and unfathomable holes, at the bottom of which formidable creatures might be heard moving. My blood curdled when I saw enormous antennae blocking my road, or some frightful claw closing with a noise in the shadow of some cavity. Millions of luminous spots shone brightly in the midst of the darkness. They were the eyes of giant crustacea crouched in their holes; giant lobsters setting themselves up like halberdiers, and moving their claws with the clicking sound of pincers; titanic crabs, pointed like a gun on its carriage; and frightful-looking poulps, interweaving their tentacles like a living nest of serpents.

We had now arrived on the first platform, where other surprises awaited me. Before us lay some picturesque ruins, which betrayed the hand of man and not that of the Creator. There were vast heaps of stone, amongst which might be traced the vague and shadowy forms of castles and temples, clothed with a world of blossoming zoophytes, and over which, instead of ivy, sea-weed and fucus threw a thick vegetable mantle. But what was this portion of the globe which had been swallowed by cataclysms? Who had placed those rocks and stones like cromlechs of prehistoric times? Where was I? Whither had Captain Nemo's fancy hurried me?

I would fain have asked him; not being able to, I stopped him—I seized his arm. But, shaking his head, and pointing to the highest point of the mountain, he seemed to say:

"Come, come along; come higher!"

I followed, and in a few minutes I had climbed to the top, which for a circle of ten yards commanded the whole mass of rock.

I looked down the side we had just climbed. The mountain did not rise more than seven or eight hundred feet above the level of the plain; but on the opposite side it commanded from twice that height the depths of this part of the Atlantic. My eyes ranged far over a large space lit by a violent fulguration. In fact, the mountain was a volcano.

At fifty feet above the peak, in the midst of a rain of stones and scoriae, a large crater was vomiting forth torrents of lava which fell in a cascade of fire into the bosom of the liquid mass. Thus situated, this volcano lit the lower plain like an immense torch, even to the extreme limits of the horizon. I said that the submarine crater threw up lava, but no flames. Flames require the oxygen of the air to feed upon and cannot be developed under water; but streams of lava, having in themselves the principles of their incandescence, can attain a white heat, fight vigorously against the liquid element, and turn it to vapour by contact.

Rapid currents bearing all these gases in diffusion and torrents of lava slid to the bottom of the mountain like an eruption of Vesuvius on another Terra del Greco.

There indeed under my eyes, ruined, destroyed, lay a town—its roofs open to the sky, its temples fallen, its arches dislocated, its columns lying on the ground, from which one would still recognise the massive character of Tuscan architecture. Further on, some remains of a gigantic aqueduct; here the high base of an Acropolis, with the floating outline of a Parthenon; there traces of a quay, as if an ancient port had formerly abutted on the borders of the ocean, and disappeared with its merchant vessels and its war-galleys. Farther on again, long lines of sunken walls and broad, deserted streets—a perfect Pompeii escaped beneath the waters. Such was the sight that Captain Nemo brought before my eyes!

Where was I? Where was I? I must know at any cost. I tried to speak, but Captain Nemo stopped me by a gesture, and, picking up a piece of chalk-stone, advanced to a rock of black basalt, and traced the one word:

ATLANTIS

What a light shot through my mind! Atlantis! the Atlantis of Plato, that continent denied by Origen and Humbolt, who placed its disappearance amongst the legendary tales. I had it there now before my eyes, bearing upon it the unexceptional testimony of its catastrophe. The region thus engulfed was beyond Europe, Asia, and Lybia, beyond the columns of Hercules, where those powerful people, the Atlantides, lived, against whom the first wars of ancient Greeks were waged.

Thus, led by the strangest destiny, I was treading under foot the mountains of this continent, touching with my hand those ruins a thousand generations old and contemporary with the geological epochs. I was walking on the very spot where the contemporaries of the first man had walked.

Whilst I was trying to fix in my mind every detail of this grand landscape, Captain Nemo remained motionless, as if petrified in mute ecstasy, leaning on a mossy stone. Was he dreaming of those generations long since disappeared? Was he asking them the secret of human destiny? Was it here this strange man came to steep himself in historical recollections, and live again this ancient life—he who wanted no modern one? What would I not have given to know his thoughts, to share them, to understand them! We remained for an hour at this place, contemplating the vast plains under the brightness of the lava, which was some times wonderfully intense. Rapid tremblings ran along the mountain caused by internal bubblings, deep noise, distinctly transmitted through the liquid medium were echoed with majestic grandeur. At this moment the moon appeared through the mass of waters and threw her pale rays on the buried continent. It was but a gleam, but what an indescribable effect! The Captain rose, cast one last look on the immense plain, and then bade me follow him.

We descended the mountain rapidly, and, the mineral forest once passed, I saw the lantern of the Nautilus shining like a star. The Captain walked straight to it, and we got on board as the first rays of light whitened the surface of the ocean.

CHAPTER X. THE SUBMARINE COAL-MINES

The next day, the 20th of February, I awoke very late: the fatigues of the previous night had prolonged my sleep until eleven o'clock. I dressed quickly, and hastened to find the course the Nautilus was taking. The instruments showed it to be still toward the south, with a speed of twenty miles an hour and a depth of fifty fathoms.

The species of fishes here did not differ much from those already noticed. There were rays of giant size, five yards long, and endowed with great muscular strength, which enabled them to shoot above the waves; sharks of many kinds; amongst others, one fifteen feet long, with triangular sharp teeth, and whose transparency rendered it almost invisible in the water.

Amongst bony fish Conseil noticed some about three yards long, armed at the upper jaw with a piercing sword; other bright-coloured creatures, known in the time of Aristotle by the name of the sea-dragon, which are dangerous to capture on account of the spikes on their back.

About four o'clock, the soil, generally composed of a thick mud mixed with petrified wood, changed by degrees, and it became more stony, and seemed strewn with conglomerate and pieces of basalt, with a sprinkling of lava. I thought that a mountainous region was succeeding the long plains; and accordingly, after a few evolutions of the Nautilus, I saw the southerly horizon blocked by a high wall which seemed to close all exit. Its summit evidently passed the level of the ocean. It must be a continent, or at least an island—one of the Canaries, or of the Cape Verde Islands. The bearings not being yet taken, perhaps designedly, I was ignorant of our exact position. In any case, such a wall seemed to me to mark the limits of that Atlantis, of which we had in reality passed over only the smallest part.

Much longer should I have remained at the window admiring the beauties of sea and sky, but the panels closed. At this moment the Nautilus arrived at the side of this high, perpendicular wall. What it would do, I could not guess. I returned to my room; it no longer moved. I laid myself down with the full intention of waking after a few hours' sleep; but it was eight o'clock the next day when I entered the saloon. I looked at the manometer. It told me that the Nautilus was floating on the surface of the ocean. Besides, I heard steps on the platform. I went to the panel. It was open; but, instead of broad daylight, as I expected, I was surrounded by profound darkness. Where were we? Was I mistaken? Was it still night? No; not a star was shining and night has not that utter darkness.

I knew not what to think, when a voice near me said:

"Is that you, Professor?"

"Ah! Captain," I answered, "where are we?"

"Underground, sir."

"Underground!" I exclaimed. "And the Nautilus floating still?"

"It always floats."

"But I do not understand."

"Wait a few minutes, our lantern will be lit, and, if you like light places, you will be satisfied."

I stood on the platform and waited. The darkness was so complete that I could not even see Captain Nemo; but, looking to the zenith, exactly above my head, I seemed to catch an undecided gleam, a kind of twilight filling a circular hole. At this instant the lantern was lit, and its vividness dispelled the faint light. I closed my dazzled eyes for an instant, and then looked again. The Nautilus was stationary, floating near a mountain which formed a sort of quay. The lake, then, supporting it was a lake imprisoned by a circle of walls, measuring two miles in diameter and six in circumference. Its level (the manometer showed) could only be the same as the outside level, for there must necessarily be a communication between the lake and the sea. The high partitions, leaning forward on their base, grew into a vaulted roof bearing the shape of an immense funnel turned upside down, the height being about five or six hundred yards. At the summit was a circular orifice, by which I had caught the slight gleam of light, evidently daylight.

"Where are we?" I asked.

"In the very heart of an extinct volcano, the interior of which has been invaded by the sea, after some great convulsion of the earth. Whilst you were sleeping, Professor, the Nautilus penetrated to this lagoon by a natural canal, which opens about ten yards beneath the surface of the ocean. This is its harbour of refuge, a sure, commodious, and mysterious one, sheltered from all gales. Show me, if you can, on the coasts of any of your continents or islands, a road which can give such perfect refuge from all storms."

"Certainly," I replied, "you are in safety here, Captain Nemo. Who could reach you in the heart of a volcano? But did I not see an opening at its summit?"

"Yes; its crater, formerly filled with lava, vapour, and flames, and which now gives entrance to the life-giving air we breathe."

"But what is this volcanic mountain?"

"It belongs to one of the numerous islands with which this sea is strewn— to vessels a simple sandbank—to us an immense cavern. Chance led me to discover it, and chance served me well."

"But of what use is this refuge, Captain? The Nautilus wants no port."

"No, sir; but it wants electricity to make it move, and the wherewithal to make the electricity—sodium to feed the elements, coal from which to get the sodium, and a coal-mine to supply the coal. And exactly on this spot the sea covers entire forests embedded during the geological periods, now mineralised and transformed into coal; for me they are an inexhaustible mine."

"Your men follow the trade of miners here, then, Captain?"

"Exactly so. These mines extend under the waves like the mines of Newcastle. Here, in their diving-dresses, pick axe and shovel in hand, my men extract the coal, which I do not even ask from the mines of the earth. When I burn this combustible for the manufacture of sodium, the smoke, escaping from the crater of the mountain, gives it the appearance of a still-active volcano."

"And we shall see your companions at work?"

"No; not this time at least; for I am in a hurry to continue our submarine tour of the earth. So I shall content myself with drawing from the reserve of sodium I already possess. The time for loading is one day only, and we continue our voyage. So, if you wish to go over the cavern and make the round of the lagoon, you must take advantage of to-day, M. Aronnax."

I thanked the Captain and went to look for my companions, who had not yet left their cabin. I invited them to follow me without saying where we were. They mounted the platform. Conseil, who was astonished at nothing, seemed to look upon it as quite natural that he should wake under a mountain, after having fallen asleep under the waves. But Ned Land thought of nothing but finding whether the cavern had any exit. After breakfast, about ten o'clock, we went down on to the mountain.

"Here we are, once more on land," said Conseil.

"I do not call this land," said the Canadian. "And besides, we are not on it, but beneath it."

Between the walls of the mountains and the waters of the lake lay a sandy shore which, at its greatest breadth, measured five hundred feet. On this soil one might easily make the tour of the lake. But the base of the high partitions was stony ground, with volcanic locks and enormous pumice-stones lying in picturesque heaps. All these detached masses, covered with enamel, polished by the action of the subterraneous fires, shone resplendent by the light of our electric lantern. The mica dust from the shore, rising under our feet, flew like a cloud of sparks. The bottom now rose sensibly, and we soon arrived at long circuitous slopes, or inclined planes, which took us higher by degrees; but we were obliged to walk carefully among these conglomerates, bound by no cement, the feet slipping on the glassy crystal, felspar, and quartz.

The volcanic nature of this enormous excavation was confirmed on all sides, and I pointed it out to my companions.

"Picture to yourselves," said I, "what this crater must have been when filled with boiling lava, and when the level of the incandescent liquid rose to the orifice of the mountain, as though melted on the top of a hot plate."

"I can picture it perfectly," said Conseil. "But, sir, will you tell me why the Great Architect has suspended operations, and how it is that the furnace is replaced by the quiet waters of the lake?"

"Most probably, Conseil, because some convulsion beneath the ocean produced that very opening which has served as a passage for the Nautilus. Then the waters of the Atlantic rushed into the interior of the mountain. There must have been a terrible struggle between the two elements, a struggle which ended in the victory of Neptune. But many ages have run out since then, and the submerged volcano is now a peaceable grotto."

"Very well," replied Ned Land; "I accept the explanation, sir; but, in our own interests, I regret that the opening of which you speak was not made above the level of the sea."

"But, friend Ned," said Conseil, "if the passage had not been under the sea, the Nautilus could not have gone through it."

We continued ascending. The steps became more and more perpendicular and narrow. Deep excavations, which we were obliged to cross, cut them here and there; sloping masses had to be turned. We slid upon our knees and crawled along. But Conseil's dexterity and the Canadian's strength surmounted all obstacles. At a height of about 31 feet the nature of the ground changed without becoming more practicable. To the conglomerate and trachyte succeeded black basalt, the first dispread in layers full of bubbles, the latter forming regular prisms, placed like a colonnade supporting the spring of the immense vault, an admirable specimen of natural architecture. Between the blocks of basalt wound long streams of lava, long since grown cold, encrusted with bituminous rays; and in some places there were spread large carpets of sulphur. A more powerful light shone through the upper crater, shedding a vague glimmer over these volcanic depressions for ever buried in the bosom of this extinguished mountain. But our upward march was soon stopped at a height of about two hundred and fifty feet by impassable obstacles. There was a complete vaulted arch overhanging us, and our ascent was changed to a circular walk. At the last change vegetable life began to struggle with the mineral. Some shrubs, and even some trees, grew from the fractures of the walls. I recognised some euphorbias, with the caustic sugar coming from them; heliotropes, quite incapable of justifying their name, sadly drooped their clusters of flowers, both their colour and perfume half gone. Here and there some chrysanthemums grew timidly at the foot of an aloe with long, sickly-looking leaves. But between the streams of lava, I saw some little violets still slightly perfumed, and I admit that I smelt them with delight. Perfume is the soul of the flower, and sea-flowers have no soul.

We had arrived at the foot of some sturdy dragon-trees, which had pushed aside the rocks with their strong roots, when Ned Land exclaimed:

"Ah! sir, a hive! a hive!"

"A hive!" I replied, with a gesture of incredulity.

"Yes, a hive," repeated the Canadian, "and bees humming round it."

I approached, and was bound to believe my own eyes. There at a hole bored in one of the dragon-trees were some thousands of these ingenious insects, so common in all the Canaries, and whose produce is so much esteemed. Naturally enough, the Canadian wished to gather the honey, and I could not well oppose his wish. A quantity of dry leaves, mixed with sulphur, he lit with a spark from his flint, and he began to smoke out the bees. The humming ceased by degrees, and the hive eventually yielded several pounds of the sweetest honey, with which Ned Land filled his haversack.

"When I have mixed this honey with the paste of the bread-fruit," said he, "I shall be able to offer you a succulent cake."

[Transcriber's Note: 'bread-fruit' has been substituted for 'artocarpus' in this ed.]

"'Pon my word," said Conseil, "it will be gingerbread."

"Never mind the gingerbread," said I; "let us continue our interesting walk."

At every turn of the path we were following, the lake appeared in all its length and breadth. The lantern lit up the whole of its peaceable surface, which knew neither ripple nor wave. The Nautilus remained perfectly immovable. On the platform, and on the mountain, the ship's crew were working like black shadows clearly carved against the luminous atmosphere. We were now going round the highest crest of the first layers of rock which upheld the roof. I then saw that bees were not the only representatives of the animal kingdom in the interior of this volcano. Birds of prey hovered here and there in the shadows, or fled from their nests on the top of the rocks. There were sparrow hawks, with white breasts, and kestrels, and down the slopes scampered, with their long legs, several fine fat bustards. I leave anyone to imagine the covetousness of the Canadian at the sight of this savoury game, and whether he did not regret having no gun. But he did his best to replace the lead by stones, and, after several fruitless attempts, he succeeded in wounding a magnificent bird. To say that he risked his life twenty times before reaching it is but the truth; but he managed so well that the creature joined the honey-cakes in his bag. We were now obliged to descend toward the shore, the crest becoming impracticable. Above us the crater seemed to gape like the mouth of a well. From this place the sky could be clearly seen, and clouds, dissipated by the west wind, leaving behind them, even on the summit of the mountain, their misty remnants— certain proof that they were only moderately high, for the volcano did not rise more than eight hundred feet above the level of the ocean. Half an hour after the Canadian's last exploit we had regained the inner shore. Here the flora was represented by large carpets of marine crystal, a little umbelliferous plant very good to pickle, which also bears the name of pierce-stone and sea-fennel. Conseil gathered some bundles of it. As to the fauna, it might be counted by thousands of crustacea of all sorts, lobsters, crabs, spider-crabs, chameleon shrimps, and a large number of shells, rockfish, and limpets. Three-quarters of an hour later we had finished our circuitous walk and were on board. The crew had just finished loading the sodium, and the Nautilus could have left that instant. But Captain Nemo gave no order. Did he wish to wait until night, and leave the submarine passage secretly? Perhaps so. Whatever it might be, the next day, the Nautilus, having left its port, steered clear of all land at a few yards beneath the waves of the Atlantic.

CHAPTER XI. THE SARGASSO SEA

That day the Nautilus crossed a singular part of the Atlantic Ocean. No one can be ignorant of the existence of a current of warm water known by the name of the Gulf Stream. After leaving the Gulf of Florida, we went in the direction of Spitzbergen. But before entering the Gulf of Mexico, about 45° of N. lat., this current divides into two arms, the principal one going towards the coast of Ireland and Norway, whilst the second bends to the south about the height of the Azores; then, touching the African shore, and describing a lengthened oval, returns to the Antilles. This second arm—it is rather a collar than an arm— surrounds with its circles of warm water that portion of the cold, quiet, immovable ocean called the Sargasso Sea, a perfect lake in the open Atlantic: it takes no less than three years for the great current to pass round it. Such was the region the Nautilus was now visiting, a perfect meadow, a close carpet of seaweed, fucus, and tropical berries, so thick and so compact that the stem of a vessel could hardly tear its way through it. And Captain Nemo, not wishing to entangle his screw in this herbaceous mass, kept some yards beneath the surface of the waves. The name Sargasso comes from the Spanish word "sargazzo" which signifies kelp. This kelp, or berry-plant, is the principal formation of this immense bank. And this is the reason why these plants unite in the peaceful basin of the Atlantic. The only explanation which can be given, he says, seems to me to result from the experience known to all the world. Place in a vase some fragments of cork or other floating body, and give to the water in the vase a circular movement, the scattered fragments will unite in a group in the centre of the liquid surface, that is to say, in the part least agitated. In the phenomenon we are considering, the Atlantic is the vase, the Gulf Stream the circular current, and the Sargasso Sea the central point at which the floating bodies unite.

I share Maury's opinion, and I was able to study the phenomenon in the very midst, where vessels rarely penetrate. Above us floated products of all kinds, heaped up among these brownish plants; trunks of trees torn from the Andes or the Rocky Mountains, and floated by the Amazon or the Mississippi; numerous wrecks, remains of keels, or ships' bottoms, side-planks stove in, and so weighted with shells and barnacles that they could not again rise to the surface. And time will one day justify Maury's other opinion, that these substances thus accumulated for ages will become petrified by the action of the water and will then form inexhaustible coal-mines—a precious reserve prepared by far-seeing Nature for the moment when men shall have exhausted the mines of continents.

In the midst of this inextricable mass of plants and sea weed, I noticed some charming pink halcyons and actiniae, with their long tentacles trailing after them, and medusae, green, red, and blue.

All the day of the 22nd of February we passed in the Sargasso Sea, where such fish as are partial to marine plants find abundant nourishment. The next, the ocean had returned to its accustomed aspect. From this time for nineteen days, from the 23rd of February to the 12th of March, the Nautilus kept in the middle of the Atlantic, carrying us at a constant speed of a hundred leagues in twenty-four hours. Captain Nemo evidently intended accomplishing his submarine programme, and I imagined that he intended, after doubling Cape Horn, to return to the Australian seas of the Pacific. Ned Land had cause for fear. In these large seas, void of islands, we could not attempt to leave the boat. Nor had we any means of opposing Captain Nemo's will. Our only course was to submit; but what we could neither gain by force nor cunning, I liked to think might be obtained by persuasion. This voyage ended, would he not consent to restore our liberty, under an oath never to reveal his existence?—an oath of honour which we should have religiously kept. But we must consider that delicate question with the Captain. But was I free to claim this liberty? Had he not himself said from the beginning, in the firmest manner, that the secret of his life exacted from him our lasting imprisonment on board the Nautilus? And would not my four months' silence appear to him a tacit acceptance of our situation? And would not a return to the subject result in raising suspicions which might be hurtful to our projects, if at some future time a favourable opportunity offered to return to them?

During the nineteen days mentioned above, no incident of any kind happened to signalise our voyage. I saw little of the Captain; he was at work. In the library I often found his books left open, especially those on natural history. My work on submarine depths, conned over by him, was covered with marginal notes, often contradicting my theories and systems; but the Captain contented himself with thus purging my work; it was very rare for him to discuss it with me. Sometimes I heard the melancholy tones of his organ; but only at night, in the midst of the deepest obscurity, when the Nautilus slept upon the deserted ocean. During this part of our voyage we sailed whole days on the surface of the waves. The sea seemed abandoned. A few sailing-vessels, on the road to India, were making for the Cape of Good Hope. One day we were followed by the boats of a whaler, who, no doubt, took us for some enormous whale of great price; but Captain Nemo did not wish the worthy fellows to lose their time and trouble, so ended the chase by plunging under the water. Our navigation continued until the 13th of March; that day the Nautilus was employed in taking soundings, which greatly interested me. We had then made about 13,000 leagues since our departure from the high seas of the Pacific. The bearings gave us 45° 37' S. lat., and 37° 53' W. long. It was the same water in which Captain Denham of the Herald sounded 7,000 fathoms without finding the bottom. There, too, Lieutenant Parker, of the American frigate Congress, could not touch the bottom with 15,140 fathoms. Captain Nemo intended seeking the bottom of the ocean by a diagonal sufficiently lengthened by means of lateral planes placed at an angle of 45° with the water-line of the Nautilus. Then the screw set to work at its maximum speed, its four blades beating the waves with in describable force. Under this powerful pressure, the hull of the Nautilus quivered like a sonorous chord and sank regularly under the water.

At 7,000 fathoms I saw some blackish tops rising from the midst of the waters; but these summits might belong to high mountains like the Himalayas or Mont Blanc, even higher; and the depth of the abyss remained incalculable. The Nautilus descended still lower, in spite of the great pressure. I felt the steel plates tremble at the fastenings of the bolts; its bars bent, its partitions groaned; the windows of the saloon seemed to curve under the pressure of the waters. And this firm structure would doubtless have yielded, if, as its Captain had said, it had not been capable of resistance like a solid block. We had attained a depth of 16,000 yards (four leagues), and the sides of the Nautilus then bore a pressure of 1,600 atmospheres, that is to say, 3,200 lb. to each square two-fifths of an inch of its surface.

"What a situation to be in!" I exclaimed. "To overrun these deep regions where man has never trod! Look, Captain, look at these magnificent rocks, these uninhabited grottoes, these lowest receptacles of the globe, where life is no longer possible! What unknown sights are here! Why should we be unable to preserve a remembrance of them?"

"Would you like to carry away more than the remembrance?" said Captain Nemo.

"What do you mean by those words?"

"I mean to say that nothing is easier than to make a photographic view of this submarine region."

I had not time to express my surprise at this new proposition, when, at Captain Nemo's call, an objective was brought into the saloon. Through the widely-opened panel, the liquid mass was bright with electricity, which was distributed with such uniformity that not a shadow, not a gradation, was to be seen in our manufactured light. The Nautilus remained motionless, the force of its screw subdued by the inclination of its planes: the instrument was propped on the bottom of the oceanic site, and in a few seconds we had obtained a perfect negative.

But, the operation being over, Captain Nemo said, "Let us go up; we must not abuse our position, nor expose the Nautilus too long to such great pressure."

"Go up again!" I exclaimed.

"Hold well on."

I had not time to understand why the Captain cautioned me thus, when I was thrown forward on to the carpet. At a signal from the Captain, its screw was shipped, and its blades raised vertically; the Nautilus shot into the air like a balloon, rising with stunning rapidity, and cutting the mass of waters with a sonorous agitation. Nothing was visible; and in four minutes it had shot through the four leagues which separated it from the ocean, and, after emerging like a flying-fish, fell, making the waves rebound to an enormous height.

CHAPTER XII. CACHALOTS AND WHALES

During the nights of the 13th and 14th of March, the Nautilus returned to its southerly course. I fancied that, when on a level with Cape Horn, he would turn the helm westward, in order to beat the Pacific seas, and so complete the tour of the world. He did nothing of the kind, but continued on his way to the southern regions. Where was he going to? To the pole? It was madness! I began to think that the Captain's temerity justified Ned Land's fears. For some time past the Canadian had not spoken to me of his projects of flight; he was less communicative, almost silent. I could see that this lengthened imprisonment was weighing upon him, and I felt that rage was burning within him. When he met the Captain, his eyes lit up with suppressed anger; and I feared that his natural violence would lead him into some extreme. That day, the 14th of March, Conseil and he came to me in my room. I inquired the cause of their visit.

"A simple question to ask you, sir," replied the Canadian.

"Speak, Ned."

"How many men are there on board the Nautilus, do you think?"

"I cannot tell, my friend."

"I should say that its working does not require a large crew."

"Certainly, under existing conditions, ten men, at the most, ought to be enough."

"Well, why should there be any more?"

"Why?" I replied, looking fixedly at Ned Land, whose meaning was easy to guess. "Because," I added, "if my surmises are correct, and if I have well understood the Captain's existence, the Nautilus is not only a vessel: it is also a place of refuge for those who, like its commander, have broken every tie upon earth."

"Perhaps so," said Conseil; "but, in any case, the Nautilus can only contain a certain number of men. Could not you, sir, estimate their maximum?"

"How, Conseil?"

"By calculation; given the size of the vessel, which you know, sir, and consequently the quantity of air it contains, knowing also how much each man expends at a breath, and comparing these results with the fact that the Nautilus is obliged to go to the surface every twenty-four hours."

Conseil had not finished the sentence before I saw what he was driving at.

"I understand," said I; "but that calculation, though simple enough, can give but a very uncertain result."

"Never mind," said Ned Land urgently.

"Here it is, then," said I. "In one hour each man consumes the oxygen contained in twenty gallons of air; and in twenty-four, that contained in 480 gallons. We must, therefore find how many times 480 gallons of air the Nautilus contains."

"Just so," said Conseil.

"Or," I continued, "the size of the Nautilus being 1,500 tons; and one ton holding 200 gallons, it contains 300,000 gallons of air, which, divided by 480, gives a quotient of 625. Which means to say, strictly speaking, that the air contained in the Nautilus would suffice for 625 men for twenty-four hours."

"Six hundred and twenty-five!" repeated Ned.

"But remember that all of us, passengers, sailors, and officers included, would not form a tenth part of that number."

"Still too many for three men," murmured Conseil.

The Canadian shook his head, passed his hand across his forehead, and left the room without answering.

"Will you allow me to make one observation, sir?" said Conseil. "Poor Ned is longing for everything that he can not have. His past life is always present to him; everything that we are forbidden he regrets. His head is full of old recollections. And we must understand him. What has he to do here? Nothing;

he is not learned like you, sir; and has not the same taste for the beauties of the sea that we have. He would risk everything to be able to go once more into a tavern in his own country."

Certainly the monotony on board must seem intolerable to the Canadian, accustomed as he was to a life of liberty and activity. Events were rare which could rouse him to any show of spirit; but that day an event did happen which recalled the bright days of the harpooner. About eleven in the morning, being on the surface of the ocean, the Nautilus fell in with a troop of whales—an encounter which did not astonish me, knowing that these creatures, hunted to death, had taken refuge in high latitudes.

We were seated on the platform, with a quiet sea. The month of October in those latitudes gave us some lovely autumnal days. It was the Canadian—he could not be mistaken—who signalled a whale on the eastern horizon. Looking attentively, one might see its black back rise and fall with the waves five miles from the Nautilus.

"Ah!" exclaimed Ned Land, "if I was on board a whaler, now such a meeting would give me pleasure. It is one of large size. See with what strength its blow-holes throw up columns of air an steam! Confound it, why am I bound to these steel plates?"

"What, Ned," said I, "you have not forgotten your old ideas of fishing?"

"Can a whale-fisher ever forget his old trade, sir? Can he ever tire of the emotions caused by such a chase?"

"You have never fished in these seas, Ned?"

"Never, sir; in the northern only, and as much in Behring as in Davis Straits."

"Then the southern whale is still unknown to you. It is the Greenland whale you have hunted up to this time, and that would not risk passing through the warm waters of the equator. Whales are localised, according to their kinds, in certain seas which they never leave. And if one of these creatures went from Behring to Davis Straits, it must be simply because there is a passage from one sea to the other, either on the American or the Asiatic side."

"In that case, as I have never fished in these seas, I do not know the kind of whale frequenting them!"

"I have told you, Ned."

"A greater reason for making their acquaintance," said Conseil.

"Look! look!" exclaimed the Canadian, "they approach: they aggravate me; they know that I cannot get at them!"

Ned stamped his feet. His hand trembled, as he grasped an imaginary harpoon.

"Are these cetaceans as large as those of the northern seas?" asked he.

"Very nearly, Ned."

"Because I have seen large whales, sir, whales measuring a hundred feet. I have even been told that those of Hullamoch and Umgallick, of the Aleutian Islands, are sometimes a hundred and fifty feet long."

"That seems to me exaggeration. These creatures are only balaeaopterons, provided with dorsal fins; and, like the cachalots, are generally much smaller than the Greenland whale."

"Ah!" exclaimed the Canadian, whose eyes had never left the ocean, "they are coming nearer; they are in the same water as the Nautilus."

Then, returning to the conversation, he said:

"You spoke of the cachalot as a small creature. I have heard of gigantic ones. They are intelligent cetacea. It is said of some that they cover themselves with seaweed and fucus, and then are taken for islands. People encamp upon them, and settle there; lights a fire——"

"And build houses," said Conseil.

"Yes, joker," said Ned Land. "And one fine day the creature plunges, carrying with it all the inhabitants to the bottom of the sea."

"Something like the travels of Sinbad the Sailor," I replied, laughing.

"Ah!" suddenly exclaimed Ned Land, "it is not one whale; there are ten— there are twenty—it is a whole troop! And I not able to do anything! hands and feet tied!"

"But, friend Ned," said Conseil, "why do you not ask Captain Nemo's permission to chase them?"

Conseil had not finished his sentence when Ned Land had lowered himself through the panel to seek the Captain. A few minutes afterwards the two appeared together on the platform.

Captain Nemo watched the troop of cetacea playing on the waters about a mile from the Nautilus.

"They are southern whales," said he; "there goes the fortune of a whole fleet of whalers."

"Well, sir," asked the Canadian, "can I not chase them, if only to remind me of my old trade of harpooner?"

"And to what purpose?" replied Captain Nemo; "only to destroy! We have nothing to do with the whale-oil on board."

"But, sir," continued the Canadian, "in the Red Sea you allowed us to follow the dugong."

"Then it was to procure fresh meat for my crew. Here it would be killing for killing's sake. I know that is a privilege reserved for man, but I do not approve of such murderous pastime. In destroying the southern whale (like the Greenland whale, an inoffensive creature), your traders do a culpable action, Master Land. They have already depopulated the whole of Baffin's Bay, and are annihilating a class of useful animals. Leave the unfortunate cetacea alone. They have plenty of natural enemies—cachalots, swordfish, and sawfish— without you troubling them."

The Captain was right. The barbarous and inconsiderate greed of these fishermen will one day cause the disappearance of the last whale in the ocean. Ned Land whistled "Yankee-doodle" between his teeth, thrust his hands into his pockets, and turned his back upon us. But Captain Nemo watched the troop of cetacea, and, addressing me, said:

"I was right in saying that whales had natural enemies enough, without counting man. These will have plenty to do before long. Do you see, M. Aronnax, about eight miles to leeward, those blackish moving points?"

"Yes, Captain," I replied.

"Those are cachalots—terrible animals, which I have met in troops of two or three hundred. As to those, they are cruel, mischievous creatures; they would be right in exterminating them."

The Canadian turned quickly at the last words.

"Well, Captain," said he, "it is still time, in the interest of the whales."

"It is useless to expose one's self, Professor. The Nautilus will disperse them. It is armed with a steel spur as good as Master Land's harpoon, I imagine."

The Canadian did not put himself out enough to shrug his shoulders. Attack cetacea with blows of a spur! Who had ever heard of such a thing?

"Wait, M. Aronnax," said Captain Nemo. "We will show you something you have never yet seen. We have no pity for these ferocious creatures. They are nothing but mouth and teeth."

Mouth and teeth! No one could better describe the macrocephalous cachalot, which is sometimes more than seventy-five feet long. Its enormous head occupies one-third of its entire body. Better armed than the whale, whose upper jaw is furnished only with whalebone, it is supplied with twenty-five large tusks, about eight inches long, cylindrical and conical at the top, each weighing two pounds. It is in the upper part of this enormous head, in great cavities divided by cartilages, that is to be found from six to eight hundred pounds of that precious oil called spermaceti. The cachalot is a disagreeable creature, more tadpole than fish, according to Fredol's description. It is badly formed, the whole of its left side being (if we may say it), a "failure," and being only able to see with its right eye. But the formidable troop was nearing us. They had seen the whales and were preparing to attack them. One could judge beforehand that the cachalots would be victorious, not only because they were better built for attack than their inoffensive adversaries, but also because they could remain longer under water without coming to the surface. There was only just time to go to the help of the whales. The Nautilus went under water. Conseil, Ned Land, and I took our places before the window in the saloon, and Captain Nemo joined the pilot in his cage to work his apparatus as an engine of destruction. Soon I felt the beatings of the screw quicken, and our speed increased. The battle between the cachalots and the whales had already begun when the Nautilus arrived. They did not at first show any fear at the sight of this new monster joining in the conflict. But they soon had to guard against its blows. What a battle! The Nautilus was nothing but a formidable harpoon, brandished by the hand of its Captain. It hurled itself against the fleshy mass, passing through from one part to the other, leaving behind it two quivering halves of the animal. It could not feel the formidable blows from their tails upon its sides, nor the shock which it produced itself, much more. One cachalot killed, it ran at the next, tacked on the spot that it might not miss its prey, going forwards and backwards, answering to its helm, plunging when the cetacean dived into the deep waters, coming up with it when it returned to the surface, striking it front or sideways, cutting or tearing in all directions and at any pace, piercing it with its terrible spur. What carnage! What a noise on the surface of the waves! What sharp hissing, and what snorting peculiar to these enraged animals! In the midst of these waters, generally so peaceful, their tails made perfect billows. For one hour this wholesale massacre continued, from which the cachalots could not escape. Several times ten or twelve united tried to crush the Nautilus by their weight. From the window we could see their enormous mouths, studded with tusks, and their formidable eyes. Ned Land could not contain himself; he threatened and swore at them. We could feel them clinging to our vessel like dogs worrying a wild boar in a copse. But the Nautilus, working its screw, carried them here and there, or to the upper levels of the ocean, without caring for their enormous weight, nor the powerful strain on the vessel. At length the mass of cachalots broke up, the waves became quiet, and I felt that we were rising to the surface. The panel opened, and we hurried on to the platform. The sea was covered with mutilated bodies. A formidable explosion could not have divided and torn this fleshy mass with more violence. We were floating amid gigantic bodies, bluish on the back and white underneath, covered with enormous protuberances. Some terrified cachalots were flying towards the horizon. The waves were dyed red for several miles, and the Nautilus floated in a sea of blood: Captain Nemo joined us.

"Well, Master Land?" said he.

"Well, sir," replied the Canadian, whose enthusiasm had somewhat calmed; "it is a terrible spectacle, certainly. But I am not a butcher. I am a hunter, and I call this a butchery."

"It is a massacre of mischievous creatures," replied the Captain; "and the Nautilus is not a butcher's knife."

"I like my harpoon better," said the Canadian.

"Every one to his own," answered the Captain, looking fixedly at Ned Land.

I feared he would commit some act of violence, which would end in sad consequences. But his anger was turned by the sight of a whale which the Nautilus had just come up with. The creature had not quite escaped from the cachalot's teeth. I recognised the southern whale by its flat head, which is entirely black. Anatomically, it is distinguished from the white whale and the North Cape whale by the seven cervical vertebrae, and it has two more ribs than its congeners. The unfortunate cetacean was lying on its side, riddled with holes from the bites, and quite dead. From its mutilated fin still hung a young whale which it could not save from the massacre. Its open mouth let the water flow in and out, murmuring like the waves breaking on the shore. Captain Nemo steered close to the corpse of the creature. Two of his men mounted its side, and I saw, not without surprise, that they were drawing from its breasts all the milk which they contained, that is to say, about two or three tons. The Captain offered me a cup of the milk, which was still warm. I could not help showing my repugnance to the drink; but he assured me that it was excellent, and not to be distinguished from cow's milk. I tasted it, and was of his opinion. It was a useful reserve to us, for in the shape of salt butter or cheese it would form an agreeable variety from our ordinary food. From that day I noticed with uneasiness that Ned Land's ill-will towards Captain Nemo increased, and I resolved to watch the Canadian's gestures closely.

CHAPTER XIII. THE ICEBERG

The Nautilus was steadily pursuing its southerly course, following the fiftieth meridian with considerable speed. Did he wish to reach the pole? I did not think so, for every attempt to reach that point had hitherto failed. Again, the season was far advanced, for in the Antarctic regions the 13th of March corresponds with the 13th of September of northern regions, which begin at the equinoctial season. On the 14th of March I saw floating ice in latitude 55°, merely pale bits of debris from twenty to twenty-five feet long, forming banks over which the sea curled. The Nautilus remained on the surface of the ocean. Ned Land, who had fished in the Arctic Seas, was familiar with its icebergs; but Conseil and I admired them for the first time. In the atmosphere towards the southern horizon stretched a white dazzling band. English whalers have given it the name of "ice blink." However thick the clouds may be, it is always visible, and announces the presence of an ice pack or bank. Accordingly, larger blocks soon appeared, whose brilliancy changed with the caprices of the fog. Some of these masses showed green veins, as if long undulating lines had been traced with sulphate of copper; others resembled enormous amethysts with the light shining through them. Some reflected the light of day upon a thousand crystal facets. Others shaded with vivid calcareous reflections resembled a perfect town of marble. The more we neared the south the more these floating islands increased both in number and importance.

At 60° lat. every pass had disappeared. But, seeking carefully, Captain Nemo soon found a narrow opening, through which he boldly slipped, knowing, however, that it would close behind him. Thus, guided by this clever hand, the Nautilus passed through all the ice with a precision which quite charmed Conseil; icebergs or mountains, ice-fields or smooth plains, seeming to have no limits, drift-ice or floating ice-packs, plains broken up, called palchs when they are circular, and streams when they are made up of long strips. The temperature was very low; the thermometer exposed to the air marked 2 deg. or 3° below zero, but we were warmly clad with fur, at the expense of the sea-bear and seal. The interior of the Nautilus, warmed regularly by its electric apparatus, defied the most intense cold. Besides, it would only have been necessary to go some yards beneath the waves to find a more bearable temperature. Two months earlier we should have had perpetual daylight in these latitudes; but already we had had three or four hours of night, and by and by there would be six months of darkness in these circumpolar regions. On the 15th of March we were in the latitude of New Shetland and South Orkney. The Captain told me that formerly numerous tribes of seals inhabited them; but that English and American whalers, in their rage for destruction, massacred both old and young; thus, where there was once life and animation, they had left silence and death.

About eight o'clock on the morning of the 16th of March the Nautilus, following the fifty-fifth meridian, cut the Antarctic polar circle. Ice surrounded us on all sides, and closed the horizon. But Captain Nemo went from one opening to another, still going higher. I cannot express my astonishment at the beauties of these new regions. The ice took most surprising forms. Here the grouping formed an oriental town, with innumerable mosques and minarets; there a fallen city thrown to the earth, as it were, by some convulsion of nature. The whole aspect was constantly changed by the oblique rays of the sun, or lost in the greyish fog amidst hurricanes of snow. Detonations and falls were heard on all sides, great overthrows of icebergs, which altered the whole landscape like a diorama. Often seeing no exit, I thought we were definitely prisoners; but, instinct guiding him at the slightest indication, Captain Nemo would discover a new pass. He was never mistaken when he saw the thin threads of bluish water trickling along the ice-fields; and I had no doubt that he had already ventured into the midst of these Antarctic seas before. On the 16th of March, however, the ice-fields absolutely blocked our road. It was not the iceberg itself, as yet, but vast fields cemented by the cold. But this obstacle could not stop Captain Nemo: he hurled himself against it with frightful violence. The Nautilus entered the brittle mass like a wedge, and split it with frightful crackings. It was the battering ram of the ancients hurled by infinite strength. The ice, thrown high in the air, fell like hail around us. By its own power of impulsion our apparatus made a canal for itself; some times carried away by its own impetus, it lodged on the ice-field, crushing it with its weight, and sometimes buried beneath it, dividing it by a simple pitching movement, producing large rents in it. Violent gales assailed us at this time, accompanied by thick fogs, through which, from one end of the platform to the other, we could see nothing. The wind blew sharply from all parts of the compass, and the snow lay in such hard heaps that we had to break it with blows of a pickaxe. The temperature was always at 5 deg. below zero; every outward part of the Nautilus was covered with ice. A rigged vessel would have been entangled in the blocked up gorges. A vessel without sails, with electricity for its motive power, and wanting no coal, could alone brave such high latitudes. At length, on the 18th of March, after many useless assaults, the Nautilus was positively blocked. It was no longer either streams, packs, or ice-fields, but an interminable and immovable barrier, formed by mountains soldered together.

"An iceberg!" said the Canadian to me.

I knew that to Ned Land, as well as to all other navigators who had preceded us, this was an inevitable obstacle. The sun appearing for an instant at noon,

Captain Nemo took an observation as near as possible, which gave our situation at 51° 30' long. and 67° 39' of S. lat. We had advanced one degree more in this Antarctic region. Of the liquid surface of the sea there was no longer a glimpse. Under the spur of the Nautilus lay stretched a vast plain, entangled with confused blocks. Here and there sharp points and slender needles rising to a height of 200 feet; further on a steep shore, hewn as it were with an axe and clothed with greyish tints; huge mirrors, reflecting a few rays of sunshine, half drowned in the fog. And over this desolate face of nature a stern silence reigned, scarcely broken by the flapping of the wings of petrels and puffins. Everything was frozen—even the noise. The Nautilus was then obliged to stop in its adventurous course amid these fields of ice. In spite of our efforts, in spite of the powerful means employed to break up the ice, the Nautilus remained immovable. Generally, when we can proceed no further, we have return still open to us; but here return was as impossible as advance, for every pass had closed behind us; and for the few moments when we were stationary, we were likely to be entirely blocked, which did indeed happen about two o'clock in the afternoon, the fresh ice forming around its sides with astonishing rapidity. I was obliged to admit that Captain Nemo was more than imprudent. I was on the platform at that moment. The Captain had been observing our situation for some time past, when he said to me:

"Well, sir, what do you think of this?"

"I think that we are caught, Captain."

"So, M. Aronnax, you really think that the Nautilus cannot disengage itself?"

"With difficulty, Captain; for the season is already too far advanced for you to reckon on the breaking of the ice."

"Ah! sir," said Captain Nemo, in an ironical tone, "you will always be the same. You see nothing but difficulties and obstacles. I affirm that not only can the Nautilus disengage itself, but also that it can go further still."

"Further to the South?" I asked, looking at the Captain.

"Yes, sir; it shall go to the pole."

"To the pole!" I exclaimed, unable to repress a gesture of incredulity.

"Yes," replied the Captain, coldly, "to the Antarctic pole—to that unknown point from whence springs every meridian of the globe. You know whether I can do as I please with the Nautilus!"

Yes, I knew that. I knew that this man was bold, even to rashness. But to conquer those obstacles which bristled round the South Pole, rendering it more inaccessible than the North, which had not yet been reached by the boldest navigators—was it not a mad enterprise, one which only a maniac would have conceived? It then came into my head to ask Captain Nemo if he had ever discovered that pole which had never yet been trodden by a human creature?

"No, sir," he replied; "but we will discover it together. Where others have failed, I will not fail. I have never yet led my Nautilus so far into southern seas; but, I repeat, it shall go further yet."

"I can well believe you, Captain," said I, in a slightly ironical tone. "I believe you! Let us go ahead! There are no obstacles for us! Let us smash this iceberg! Let us blow it up; and, if it resists, let us give the Nautilus wings to fly over it!"

"Over it, sir!" said Captain Nemo, quietly; "no, not over it, but under it!"

"Under it!" I exclaimed, a sudden idea of the Captain's projects flashing upon my mind. I understood; the wonderful qualities of the Nautilus were going to serve us in this superhuman enterprise.

"I see we are beginning to understand one another, sir," said the Captain, half smiling. "You begin to see the possibility—I should say the success—of this attempt. That which is impossible for an ordinary vessel is easy to the Nautilus. If a continent lies before the pole, it must stop before the continent; but if, on the contrary, the pole is washed by open sea, it will go even to the pole."

"Certainly," said I, carried away by the Captain's reasoning; "if the surface of the sea is solidified by the ice, the lower depths are free by the Providential law which has placed the maximum of density of the waters of the ocean one degree higher than freezing-point; and, if I am not mistaken, the portion of this iceberg which is above the water is as one to four to that which is below."

"Very nearly, sir; for one foot of iceberg above the sea there are three below it. If these ice mountains are not more than 300 feet above the surface, they are not more than 900 beneath. And what are 900 feet to the Nautilus?"

"Nothing, sir."

"It could even seek at greater depths that uniform temperature of sea-water, and there brave with impunity the thirty or forty degrees of surface cold."

"Just so, sir—just so," I replied, getting animated.

"The only difficulty," continued Captain Nemo, "is that of remaining several days without renewing our provision of air."

"Is that all? The Nautilus has vast reservoirs; we can fill them, and they will supply us with all the oxygen we want."

"Well thought of, M. Aronnax," replied the Captain, smiling. "But, not wishing you to accuse me of rashness, I will first give you all my objections."

"Have you any more to make?"

"Only one. It is possible, if the sea exists at the South Pole, that it may be covered; and, consequently, we shall be unable to come to the surface."

"Good, sir! but do you forget that the Nautilus is armed with a powerful spur, and could we not send it diagonally against these fields of ice, which would open at the shocks."

"Ah! sir, you are full of ideas to-day."

"Besides, Captain," I added, enthusiastically, "why should we not find the sea open at the South Pole as well as at the North? The frozen poles of the earth do not coincide, either in the southern or in the northern regions; and, until it is proved to the contrary, we may suppose either a continent or an ocean free from ice at these two points of the globe."

"I think so too, M. Aronnax," replied Captain Nemo. "I only wish you to observe that, after having made so many objections to my project, you are now crushing me with arguments in its favour!"

The preparations for this audacious attempt now began. The powerful pumps of the Nautilus were working air into the reservoirs and storing it at high pressure. About four o'clock, Captain Nemo announced the closing of the panels on the platform. I threw one last look at the massive iceberg which we were going to cross. The weather was clear, the atmosphere pure enough, the cold very great, being 12° below zero; but, the wind having gone down, this temperature was not so unbearable. About ten men mounted the sides of the Nautilus, armed with pickaxes to break the ice around the vessel, which was soon free. The operation was quickly performed, for the fresh ice was still very thin. We all went below. The usual reservoirs were filled with the newly-liberated water, and the Nautilus soon descended. I had taken my place with Conseil in the saloon; through the open window we could see the lower beds of the Southern Ocean. The thermometer went up, the needle of the compass deviated on the dial. At about 900 feet, as Captain Nemo had foreseen, we were floating beneath the undulating bottom of the iceberg. But the Nautilus went lower still—it went to the depth of four hundred fathoms. The temperature of the water at the surface showed twelve degrees, it was now only ten; we had gained two. I need not say the temperature of the Nautilus was raised by its heating apparatus to a much higher degree; every manoeuvre was accomplished with wonderful precision.

"We shall pass it, if you please, sir," said Conseil.

"I believe we shall," I said, in a tone of firm conviction.

In this open sea, the Nautilus had taken its course direct to the pole, without leaving the fifty-second meridian. From 67° 30' to 90 deg., twenty-two degrees and a half of latitude remained to travel; that is, about five hundred leagues. The Nautilus kept up a mean speed of twenty-six miles an hour—the speed of an express train. If that was kept up, in forty hours we should reach the pole.

For a part of the night the novelty of the situation kept us at the window. The sea was lit with the electric lantern; but it was deserted; fishes did not sojourn in these imprisoned waters; they only found there a passage to take them from the Antarctic Ocean to the open polar sea. Our pace was rapid; we could feel it by the quivering of the long steel body. About two in the morning I took some hours' repose, and Conseil did the same. In crossing the waist I did not meet Captain Nemo: I supposed him to be in the pilot's cage. The next morning, the 19th of March, I took my post once more in the saloon. The electric log told me that the speed of the Nautilus had been slackened. It was then going towards the surface; but prudently emptying its reservoirs very slowly. My heart beat fast. Were we going to emerge and regain the open polar atmosphere? No! A shock told me that the Nautilus had struck the bottom of the iceberg, still very thick, judging from the deadened sound. We had in deed "struck," to use a sea expression, but in an inverse sense, and at a thousand feet deep. This would give three thousand feet of ice above us; one thousand being above the water-mark. The iceberg was then higher than at its borders—not a very reassuring fact. Several times that day the Nautilus tried again, and every time it struck the wall which lay like a ceiling above it. Sometimes it met with but 900 yards, only 200 of which rose above the surface. It was twice the height it was when the Nautilus had gone under the waves. I carefully noted the different depths, and thus obtained a submarine profile of the chain as it was developed under the water. That night no change had taken place in our situation. Still ice between four and five hundred yards in depth! It was evidently diminishing, but, still, what a thickness between us and the surface of the ocean! It was then eight. According to the daily custom on board the Nautilus, its air should have been renewed four hours ago; but I did not suffer much, although Captain Nemo had not yet made any demand upon his reserve of oxygen. My sleep was painful that night; hope and fear besieged me by turns: I rose several times. The groping of the Nautilus continued. About three in the morning, I noticed that the lower surface of the iceberg was only about fifty feet deep. One hundred and fifty feet now separated us from the surface of the waters. The iceberg was by degrees becoming an ice-field, the mountain a plain. My eyes never left the manometer. We were still rising diagonally to the surface, which sparkled under the electric rays. The iceberg was stretching both above and beneath into lengthening slopes; mile after mile it was getting thinner. At length, at six in the morning of that memorable day, the 19th of March, the door of the saloon opened, and Captain Nemo appeared.

"The sea is open!!" was all he said.

CHAPTER XIV. THE SOUTH POLE

I rushed on to the platform. Yes! the open sea, with but a few scattered pieces of ice and moving icebergs—a long stretch of sea; a world of birds in the air, and myriads of fishes under those waters, which varied from intense blue to olive green, according to the bottom. The thermometer marked 3° C. above zero. It was comparatively spring, shut up as we were behind this iceberg, whose lengthened mass was dimly seen on our northern horizon.

"Are we at the pole?" I asked the Captain, with a beating heart.

"I do not know," he replied. "At noon I will take our bearings."

"But will the sun show himself through this fog?" said I, looking at the leaden sky.

"However little it shows, it will be enough," replied the Captain.

About ten miles south a solitary island rose to a height of one hundred and four yards. We made for it, but carefully, for the sea might be strewn with banks. One hour afterwards we had reached it, two hours later we had made the round of it. It measured four or five miles in circumference. A narrow canal separated it from a considerable stretch of land, perhaps a continent, for we could not see its limits. The existence of this land seemed to give some colour to Maury's theory. The ingenious American has remarked that, between the South Pole and the sixtieth parallel, the sea is covered with floating ice of enormous size, which is never met with in the North Atlantic. From this fact he has drawn the conclusion that the Antarctic Circle encloses considerable continents, as icebergs cannot form in open sea, but only on the coasts. According to these calculations, the mass of ice surrounding the southern pole forms a vast cap, the circumference of which must be, at least, 2,500 miles. But the Nautilus, for fear of running aground, had stopped about three cable-lengths from a strand over which reared a superb heap of rocks. The boat was launched; the Captain, two of his men, bearing instruments, Conseil, and myself were in it. It was ten in the morning. I had not seen Ned Land. Doubtless the Canadian did not wish to admit the presence of the South Pole. A few strokes of the oar brought us to the sand, where we ran ashore. Conseil was going to jump on to the land, when I held him back.

"Sir," said I to Captain Nemo, "to you belongs the honour of first setting foot on this land."

"Yes, sir," said the Captain, "and if I do not hesitate to tread this South Pole, it is because, up to this time, no human being has left a trace there."

Saying this, he jumped lightly on to the sand. His heart beat with emotion. He climbed a rock, sloping to a little promontory, and there, with his arms crossed, mute and motionless, and with an eager look, he seemed to take possession of these southern regions. After five minutes passed in this ecstasy, he turned to us.

"When you like, sir."

I landed, followed by Conseil, leaving the two men in the boat. For a long way the soil was composed of a reddish sandy stone, something like crushed brick, scoriae, streams of lava, and pumice-stones. One could not mistake its volcanic origin. In some parts, slight curls of smoke emitted a sulphurous smell, proving that the internal fires had lost nothing of their expansive powers, though, having climbed a high acclivity, I could see no volcano for a radius of several miles. We know that in those Antarctic countries, James Ross found two craters, the Erebus and Terror, in full activity, on the 167th meridian, latitude 77° 32'. The vegetation of this desolate continent seemed to me much restricted. Some lichens lay upon the black rocks; some microscopic plants, rudimentary diatomas, a kind of cells placed between two quartz shells; long purple and scarlet weed, supported on little swimming bladders, which the breaking of the waves brought to the shore. These constituted the meagre flora of this region. The shore was strewn with molluscs, little mussels, and limpets. I also saw myriads of northern clios, one-and-a-quarter inches long, of which a whale would swallow a whole world at a mouthful; and some perfect sea-butterflies, animating the waters on the skirts of the shore.

There appeared on the high bottoms some coral shrubs, of the kind which, according to James Ross, live in the Antarctic seas to the depth of more than 1,000 yards. Then there were little kingfishers and starfish studding the soil. But where life abounded most was in the air. There thousands of birds fluttered and flew of all kinds, deafening us with their cries; others crowded the rock, looking at us as we passed by without fear, and pressing familiarly close by our feet. There were penguins, so agile in the water, heavy and awkward as they are on the ground; they were uttering harsh cries, a large assembly, sober in gesture, but extravagant in clamour. Albatrosses passed in the air, the expanse of their wings being at least four yards and a half, and justly called the vultures of the ocean; some gigantic petrels, and some damiers, a kind of small duck, the underpart of whose body is black and white; then there were a whole series of petrels, some whitish, with brown-bordered wings, others blue, peculiar to the Antarctic seas, and so oily, as I told Conseil, that the inhabitants of the Ferroe Islands had nothing to do before lighting them but to put a wick in.

"A little more," said Conseil, "and they would be perfect lamps! After that, we cannot expect Nature to have previously furnished them with wicks!"

About half a mile farther on the soil was riddled with ruffs' nests, a sort of laying-ground, out of which many birds were issuing. Captain Nemo had some hundreds hunted. They uttered a cry like the braying of an ass, were about the size of a goose, slate-colour on the body, white beneath, with a yellow line round their throats; they allowed themselves to be killed with a stone, never trying to escape. But the fog did not lift, and at eleven the sun had not yet shown itself. Its absence made me uneasy. Without it no observations were possible. How, then, could we decide whether we had reached the pole? When I rejoined Captain Nemo, I found him leaning on a piece of rock, silently watching the sky. He seemed impatient and vexed. But what was to be done? This rash and powerful man could not command the sun as he did the sea. Noon arrived without the orb of day showing itself for an instant. We could not even tell its position behind the curtain of fog; and soon the fog turned to snow.

"Till to-morrow," said the Captain, quietly, and we returned to the Nautilus amid these atmospheric disturbances.

The tempest of snow continued till the next day. It was impossible to remain on the platform. From the saloon, where I was taking notes of incidents happening during this excursion to the polar continent, I could hear the cries of petrels and albatrosses sporting in the midst of this violent storm. The Nautilus did not remain motionless, but skirted the coast, advancing ten miles more to the south in the half-light left by the sun as it skirted the edge of the horizon. The next day, the 20th of March, the snow had ceased. The cold was a little greater, the thermometer showing 2° below zero. The fog was rising, and I hoped that that day our observations might be taken. Captain Nemo not having yet appeared, the boat took Conseil and myself to land. The soil was still of the same volcanic nature; everywhere were traces of lava, scoriae, and basalt; but the crater which had vomited them I could not see. Here, as lower down, this continent was alive with myriads of birds. But their rule was now divided with large troops of sea-mammals, looking at us with their soft eyes. There were several kinds of seals, some stretched on the earth, some on flakes of ice, many going in and out of the sea. They did not flee at our approach, never having had anything to do with man; and I reckoned that there were provisions there for hundreds of vessels.

"Sir," said Conseil, "will you tell me the names of these creatures?"

"They are seals and morses."

It was now eight in the morning. Four hours remained to us before the sun could be observed with advantage. I directed our steps towards a vast bay cut in the steep granite shore. There, I can aver that earth and ice were lost to sight by the numbers of sea-mammals covering them, and I involuntarily sought for old Proteus, the mythological shepherd who watched these immense flocks of Neptune. There were more seals than anything else, forming distinct groups, male and female, the father watching over his family, the mother suckling her little ones, some already strong enough to go a few steps. When they wished to change their place, they took little jumps, made by the contraction of their bodies, and helped awkwardly enough by their imperfect fin, which, as with the lamantin, their cousins, forms a perfect forearm. I should say that, in the water, which is their element—the spine of these creatures is flexible; with smooth and close skin and webbed feet—they swim admirably. In resting on the earth they take the most graceful attitudes. Thus the ancients, observing their soft and expressive looks, which cannot be surpassed by the most beautiful look a woman can give, their clear voluptuous eyes, their charming positions, and the poetry of their manners, metamorphosed them, the male into a triton and the female into a mermaid. I made Conseil notice the considerable development of the lobes of the brain in these interesting cetaceans. No mammal, except man, has such a quantity of brain matter; they are also capable of receiving a certain amount of education, are easily domesticated, and I think, with other naturalists, that if properly taught they would be of great service as fishing-dogs. The greater part of them slept on the rocks or on the sand. Amongst these seals, properly so called, which have no external ears (in which they differ from the otter, whose ears are prominent), I noticed several varieties of seals about three yards long, with a white coat, bulldog heads, armed with teeth in both jaws, four incisors at the top and four at the bottom, and two large canine teeth in the shape of a fleur-de-lis. Amongst them glided sea-elephants, a kind of seal, with short, flexible trunks. The giants of this species measured twenty feet round and ten yards and a half in length; but they did not move as we approached.

"These creatures are not dangerous?" asked Conseil.

"No; not unless you attack them. When they have to defend their young their rage is terrible, and it is not uncommon for them to break the fishing-boats to pieces."

"They are quite right," said Conseil.

"I do not say they are not."

Two miles farther on we were stopped by the promontory which shelters the bay from the southerly winds. Beyond it we heard loud bellowings such as a troop of ruminants would produce.

"Good!" said Conseil; "a concert of bulls!"

"No; a concert of morses."

"They are fighting!"

"They are either fighting or playing."

We now began to climb the blackish rocks, amid unforeseen stumbles, and over stones which the ice made slippery. More than once I rolled over at the expense of my loins. Conseil, more prudent or more steady, did not stumble, and helped me up, saying:

"If, sir, you would have the kindness to take wider steps, you would preserve your equilibrium better."

Arrived at the upper ridge of the promontory, I saw a vast white plain covered with morses. They were playing amongst themselves, and what we heard were bellowings of pleasure, not of anger.

As I passed these curious animals I could examine them leisurely, for they did not move. Their skins were thick and rugged, of a yellowish tint, approaching to red; their hair was short and scant. Some of them were four yards and a quarter long. Quieter and less timid than their cousins of the north, they did not, like them, place sentinels round the outskirts of their encampment. After examining this city of morses, I began to think of returning. It was eleven o'clock, and, if Captain Nemo found the conditions favourable for observations, I wished to be present at the operation. We followed a narrow pathway running along the summit of the steep shore. At half-past eleven we had reached the place where we landed. The boat had run aground, bringing the Captain. I saw him standing on a block of basalt, his instruments near him, his eyes fixed on the northern horizon, near which the sun was then describing a lengthened curve. I took my place beside him, and waited without speaking. Noon arrived, and, as before, the sun did not appear. It was a fatality. Observations were still wanting. If not accomplished to-morrow, we must give up all idea of taking any. We were indeed exactly at the 20th of March. To-morrow, the 21st, would be the equinox; the sun would disappear behind the horizon for six months, and with its disappearance the long polar night would begin. Since the September equinox it had emerged from the northern horizon, rising by lengthened spirals up to the 21st of December. At this period, the summer solstice of the northern regions, it had begun to descend; and to-morrow was to shed its last rays upon them. I communicated my fears and observations to Captain Nemo.

"You are right, M. Aronnax," said he; "if to-morrow I cannot take the altitude of the sun, I shall not be able to do it for six months. But precisely because chance has led me into these seas on the 21st of March, my bearings will be easy to take, if at twelve we can see the sun."

"Why, Captain?"

"Because then the orb of day described such lengthened curves that it is difficult to measure exactly its height above the horizon, and grave errors may be made with instruments."

"What will you do then?"

"I shall only use my chronometer," replied Captain Nemo. "If to-morrow, the 21st of March, the disc of the sun, allowing for refraction, is exactly cut by the northern horizon, it will show that I am at the South Pole."

"Just so," said I. "But this statement is not mathematically correct, because the equinox does not necessarily begin at noon."

"Very likely, sir; but the error will not be a hundred yards and we do not want more. Till to-morrow, then!"

Captain Nemo returned on board. Conseil and I remained to survey the shore, observing and studying until five o'clock. Then I went to bed, not, however, without invoking, like the Indian, the favour of the radiant orb. The next day, the 21st of March, at five in the morning, I mounted the platform. I found Captain Nemo there.

"The weather is lightening a little," said he. "I have some hope. After breakfast we will go on shore and choose a post for observation."

That point settled, I sought Ned Land. I wanted to take him with me. But the obstinate Canadian refused, and I saw that his taciturnity and his bad humour grew day by day. After all, I was not sorry for his obstinacy under the circumstances. Indeed, there were too many seals on shore, and we ought not to lay such temptation in this unreflecting fisherman's way. Breakfast over, we went on shore. The Nautilus had gone some miles further up in the night. It was a whole league from the coast, above which reared a sharp peak about five hundred yards high. The boat took with me Captain Nemo, two men of the crew, and the instruments, which consisted of a chronometer, a telescope, and a barometer. While crossing, I saw numerous whales belonging to the three kinds peculiar to the southern seas; the whale, or the English "right whale," which has no dorsal fin; the "humpback," with reeved chest and large, whitish fins, which, in spite of its name, do not form wings; and the fin-back, of a yellowish brown, the liveliest of all the cetacea. This powerful creature is heard a long way off when he throws to a great height columns of air and vapour, which look like whirlwinds of smoke. These different mammals were disporting themselves in troops in the quiet waters; and I could see that this basin of the Antarctic Pole serves as a place of refuge to the cetacea too closely tracked by the hunters. I also noticed large medusae floating between the reeds.

At nine we landed; the sky was brightening, the clouds were flying to the south, and the fog seemed to be leaving the cold surface of the waters. Captain Nemo went towards the peak, which he doubtless meant to be his observatory. It was a painful ascent over the sharp lava and the pumice-stones, in an atmosphere often impregnated with a sulphurous smell from the smoking cracks. For a man unaccustomed to walk on land, the Captain climbed the steep slopes with an agility I never saw equalled and which a hunter would have envied. We were two hours getting to the summit of this peak, which was half porphyry and half basalt. From thence we looked upon a vast sea which, towards the north, distinctly traced its boundary line upon the sky. At our feet lay fields of dazzling whiteness. Over our heads a pale azure, free from fog. To the north the disc of the sun seemed like a ball of fire, already horned by the cutting of the horizon. From the bosom of the water rose sheaves of liquid jets by hundreds. In the distance lay the Nautilus like a cetacean asleep on the water. Behind us, to the south and east, an immense country and a chaotic heap of rocks and ice, the limits of which were not visible. On arriving at the summit Captain Nemo carefully took the mean height of the barometer, for he would have to consider that in taking his observations. At a quarter to twelve the sun, then seen only by refraction, looked like a golden disc shedding its last rays upon this deserted continent and seas which never man had yet ploughed. Captain Nemo, furnished with a lenticular glass which, by means of a mirror, corrected the refraction, watched the orb sinking below the horizon by degrees, following a lengthened diagonal. I held the chronometer. My heart beat fast. If the disappearance of the half-disc of the sun coincided with twelve o'clock on the chronometer, we were at the pole itself.

"Twelve!" I exclaimed.

"The South Pole!" replied Captain Nemo, in a grave voice, handing me the glass, which showed the orb cut in exactly equal parts by the horizon.

I looked at the last rays crowning the peak, and the shadows mounting by degrees up its slopes. At that moment Captain Nemo, resting with his hand on my shoulder, said:

"I, Captain Nemo, on this 21st day of March, 1868, have reached the South Pole on the ninetieth degree; and I take possession of this part of the globe, equal to one-sixth of the known continents."

"In whose name, Captain?"

"In my own, sir!"

Saying which, Captain Nemo unfurled a black banner, bearing an "N" in gold quartered on its bunting. Then, turning towards the orb of day, whose last rays lapped the horizon of the sea, he exclaimed:

"Adieu, sun! Disappear, thou radiant orb! rest beneath this open sea, and let a night of six months spread its shadows over my new domains!"

CHAPTER XV. ACCIDENT OR INCIDENT?

The next day, the 22nd of March, at six in the morning, preparations for departure were begun. The last gleams of twilight were melting into night. The cold was great, the constellations shone with wonderful intensity. In the zenith glittered that wondrous Southern Cross—the polar bear of Antarctic regions. The thermometer showed 120 below zero, and when the wind freshened it was most biting. Flakes of ice increased on the open water. The sea seemed everywhere alike. Numerous blackish patches spread on the surface, showing the formation of fresh ice. Evidently the southern basin, frozen during the six winter months, was absolutely inaccessible. What became of the whales in that time? Doubtless they went beneath the icebergs, seeking more practicable seas. As to the seals and morses, accustomed to live in a hard climate, they remained on these icy shores. These creatures have the instinct to break holes in the ice-field and to keep them open. To these holes they come for breath; when the birds, driven away by the cold, have emigrated to the north, these sea mammals remain sole masters of the polar continent. But the reservoirs were filling with water, and the Nautilus was slowly descending. At 1,000 feet deep it stopped;

its screw beat the waves, and it advanced straight towards the north at a speed of fifteen miles an hour. Towards night it was already floating under the immense body of the iceberg. At three in the morning I was awakened by a violent shock. I sat up in my bed and listened in the darkness, when I was thrown into the middle of the room. The Nautilus, after having struck, had rebounded violently. I groped along the partition, and by the staircase to the saloon, which was lit by the luminous ceiling. The furniture was upset. Fortunately the windows were firmly set, and had held fast. The pictures on the starboard side, from being no longer vertical, were clinging to the paper, whilst those of the port side were hanging at least a foot from the wall. The Nautilus was lying on its starboard side perfectly motionless. I heard footsteps, and a confusion of voices; but Captain Nemo did not appear. As I was leaving the saloon, Ned Land and Conseil entered.

"What is the matter?" said I, at once.

"I came to ask you, sir," replied Conseil.

"Confound it!" exclaimed the Canadian, "I know well enough! The Nautilus has struck; and, judging by the way she lies, I do not think she will right herself as she did the first time in Torres Straits."

"But," I asked, "has she at least come to the surface of the sea?"

"We do not know," said Conseil.

"It is easy to decide," I answered. I consulted the manometer. To my great surprise, it showed a depth of more than 180 fathoms. "What does that mean?" I exclaimed.

"We must ask Captain Nemo," said Conseil.

"But where shall we find him?" said Ned Land.

"Follow me," said I, to my companions.

We left the saloon. There was no one in the library. At the centre staircase, by the berths of the ship's crew, there was no one. I thought that Captain Nemo must be in the pilot's cage. It was best to wait. We all returned to the saloon. For twenty minutes we remained thus, trying to hear the slightest noise which might be made on board the Nautilus, when Captain Nemo entered. He seemed not to see us; his face, generally so impassive, showed signs of uneasiness. He watched the compass silently, then the manometer; and, going to the planisphere, placed his finger on a spot representing the southern seas. I would not interrupt him; but, some minutes later, when he turned towards me, I said, using one of his own expressions in the Torres Straits:

"An incident, Captain?"

"No, sir; an accident this time."

"Serious?"

"Perhaps."

"Is the danger immediate?"

"No."

"The Nautilus has stranded?"

"Yes."

"And this has happened—how?"

"From a caprice of nature, not from the ignorance of man. Not a mistake has been made in the working. But we cannot prevent equilibrium from producing its effects. We may brave human laws, but we cannot resist natural ones."

Captain Nemo had chosen a strange moment for uttering this philosophical reflection. On the whole, his answer helped me little.

"May I ask, sir, the cause of this accident?"

"An enormous block of ice, a whole mountain, has turned over," he replied. "When icebergs are undermined at their base by warmer water or reiterated shocks their centre of gravity rises, and the whole thing turns over. This is what has happened; one of these blocks, as it fell, struck the Nautilus, then, gliding under its hull, raised it with irresistible force, bringing it into beds which are not so thick, where it is lying on its side."

"But can we not get the Nautilus off by emptying its reservoirs, that it might regain its equilibrium?"

"That, sir, is being done at this moment. You can hear the pump working. Look at the needle of the manometer; it shows that the Nautilus is rising, but the block of ice is floating with it; and, until some obstacle stops its ascending motion, our position cannot be altered."

Indeed, the Nautilus still held the same position to starboard; doubtless it would right itself when the block stopped. But at this moment who knows if we may not be frightfully crushed between the two glassy surfaces? I reflected on all the consequences of our position. Captain Nemo never took his eyes off the manometer. Since the fall of the iceberg, the Nautilus had risen about a hundred and fifty feet, but it still made the same angle with the perpendicular. Suddenly a slight movement was felt in the hold. Evidently it was righting a little. Things hanging in the saloon were sensibly returning to their normal position. The partitions were nearing the upright. No one spoke. With beating hearts we watched and felt the straightening. The boards became horizontal under our feet. Ten minutes passed.

"At last we have righted!" I exclaimed.

"Yes," said Captain Nemo, going to the door of the saloon.

"But are we floating?" I asked.

"Certainly," he replied; "since the reservoirs are not empty; and, when empty, the Nautilus must rise to the surface of the sea."

We were in open sea; but at a distance of about ten yards, on either side of the Nautilus, rose a dazzling wall of ice. Above and beneath the same wall. Above, because the lower surface of the iceberg stretched over us like an immense ceiling. Beneath, because the overturned block, having slid by degrees, had found a resting-place on the lateral walls, which kept it in that position. The Nautilus was really imprisoned in a perfect tunnel of ice more than twenty yards in breadth, filled with quiet water. It was easy to get out of it by going either forward or backward, and then make a free passage under the iceberg, some hundreds of yards deeper. The luminous ceiling had been extinguished, but the saloon was still resplendent with intense light. It was the powerful reflection from the glass partition sent violently back to the sheets of the lantern. I cannot describe the effect of the voltaic rays upon the great blocks so capriciously cut; upon every angle, every ridge, every facet was thrown a different light, according to the nature of the veins running through the ice; a dazzling mine of gems, particularly of sapphires, their blue rays crossing with the green of the emerald. Here and there were opal shades of wonderful softness, running through bright spots like diamonds of fire, the brilliancy of which the eye could not bear. The power of the lantern seemed increased a hundredfold, like a lamp through the lenticular plates of a first-class lighthouse.

"How beautiful! how beautiful!" cried Conseil.

"Yes," I said, "it is a wonderful sight. Is it not, Ned?"

"Yes, confound it! Yes," answered Ned Land, "it is superb! I am mad at being obliged to admit it. No one has ever seen anything like it; but the sight may cost us dear. And, if I must say all, I think we are seeing here things which God never intended man to see."

Ned was right, it was too beautiful. Suddenly a cry from Conseil made me turn.

"What is it?" I asked.

"Shut your eyes, sir! Do not look, sir!" Saying which, Conseil clapped his hands over his eyes.

"But what is the matter, my boy?"

"I am dazzled, blinded."

My eyes turned involuntarily towards the glass, but I could not stand the fire which seemed to devour them. I understood what had happened. The Nautilus had put on full speed. All the quiet lustre of the ice-walls was at once changed into flashes of lightning. The fire from these myriads of diamonds was blinding. It required some time to calm our troubled looks. At last the hands were taken down.

"Faith, I should never have believed it," said Conseil.

It was then five in the morning; and at that moment a shock was felt at the bows of the Nautilus. I knew that its spur had struck a block of ice. It must have been a false manoeuvre, for this submarine tunnel, obstructed by blocks, was not very easy navigation. I thought that Captain Nemo, by changing his course, would either turn these obstacles or else follow the windings of the tunnel. In any case, the road before us could not be entirely blocked. But, contrary to my expectations, the Nautilus took a decided retrograde motion.

"We are going backwards?" said Conseil.

"Yes," I replied. "This end of the tunnel can have no egress."

"And then?"

"Then," said I, "the working is easy. We must go back again, and go out at the southern opening. That is all."

In speaking thus, I wished to appear more confident than I really was. But the retrograde motion of the Nautilus was increasing; and, reversing the screw, it carried us at great speed.

"It will be a hindrance," said Ned.

"What does it matter, some hours more or less, provided we get out at last?"

"Yes," repeated Ned Land, "provided we do get out at last!"

For a short time I walked from the saloon to the library. My companions were silent. I soon threw myself on an ottoman, and took a book, which my eyes overran mechanically. A quarter of an hour after, Conseil, approaching me, said, "Is what you are reading very interesting, sir?"

"Very interesting!" I replied.

"I should think so, sir. It is your own book you are reading."

"My book?"

And indeed I was holding in my hand the work on the Great Submarine Depths. I did not even dream of it. I closed the book and returned to my walk. Ned and Conseil rose to go.

"Stay here, my friends," said I, detaining them. "Let us remain together until we are out of this block."

"As you please, sir," Conseil replied.

Some hours passed. I often looked at the instruments hanging from the partition. The manometer showed that the Nautilus kept at a constant depth of more than three hundred yards; the compass still pointed to south; the log indicated a speed of twenty miles an hour, which, in such a cramped space, was very great. But Captain Nemo knew that he could not hasten too much, and that minutes were worth ages to us. At twenty-five minutes past eight a second shock took place, this time from behind. I turned pale. My companions were close by my side. I seized Conseil's hand. Our looks expressed our feelings better than words. At this moment the Captain entered the saloon. I went up to him.

"Our course is barred southward?" I asked.

"Yes, sir. The iceberg has shifted and closed every outlet."

"We are blocked up then?"

"Yes."

CHAPTER XVI. WANT OF AIR

Thus around the Nautilus, above and below, was an impenetrable wall of ice. We were prisoners to the iceberg. I watched the Captain. His countenance had resumed its habitual imperturbability.

"Gentlemen," he said calmly, "there are two ways of dying in the circumstances in which we are placed." (This puzzling person had the air of a mathematical professor lecturing to his pupils.) "The first is to be crushed; the second is to die of suffocation. I do not speak of the possibility of dying of hunger, for the supply of provisions in the Nautilus will certainly last longer than we shall. Let us, then, calculate our chances."

"As to suffocation, Captain," I replied, "that is not to be feared, because our reservoirs are full."

"Just so; but they will only yield two days' supply of air. Now, for thirty-six hours we have been hidden under the water, and already the heavy atmosphere of the Nautilus requires renewal. In forty-eight hours our reserve will be exhausted."

"Well, Captain, can we be delivered before forty-eight hours?"

"We will attempt it, at least, by piercing the wall that surrounds us."

"On which side?"

"Sound will tell us. I am going to run the Nautilus aground on the lower bank, and my men will attack the iceberg on the side that is least thick."

Captain Nemo went out. Soon I discovered by a hissing noise that the water was entering the reservoirs. The Nautilus sank slowly, and rested on the ice at a depth of 350 yards, the depth at which the lower bank was immersed.

"My friends," I said, "our situation is serious, but I rely on your courage and energy."

"Sir," replied the Canadian, "I am ready to do anything for the general safety."

"Good! Ned," and I held out my hand to the Canadian.

"I will add," he continued, "that, being as handy with the pickaxe as with the harpoon, if I can be useful to the Captain, he can command my services."

"He will not refuse your help. Come, Ned!"

I led him to the room where the crew of the Nautilus were putting on their cork-jackets. I told the Captain of Ned's proposal, which he accepted. The Canadian put on his sea-costume, and was ready as soon as his companions. When Ned was dressed, I re-entered the drawing-room, where the panes of glass were open, and, posted near Conseil, I examined the ambient beds that supported the Nautilus. Some instants after, we saw a dozen of the crew set foot on the bank of ice, and among them Ned Land, easily known by his stature. Captain Nemo was with them. Before proceeding to dig the walls, he took the soundings, to be sure of working in the right direction. Long sounding lines were sunk in the side walls, but after fifteen yards they were again stopped by the thick wall. It was useless to attack it on the ceiling-like surface, since the iceberg itself measured more than 400 yards in height. Captain Nemo then sounded the lower surface. There ten yards of wall separated us from the water, so great was the thickness of the ice-field. It was necessary, therefore, to cut from it a piece equal in extent to the waterline of the Nautilus. There were about 6,000 cubic yards to detach, so as to dig a hole by which we could descend to the ice-field. The work had begun immediately and carried on with indefatigable energy. Instead of digging round the Nautilus which would have involved greater difficulty, Captain Nemo had an immense trench made at eight yards from the port-quarter. Then the men set to work simultaneously with their screws on several points of its circumference. Presently the pickaxe attacked this compact matter vigorously, and large blocks were detached from the mass. By a curious effect of specific gravity, these blocks, lighter than water, fled, so to speak, to the vault of the tunnel, that increased in thickness at the top in proportion as it diminished at the base. But that mattered little, so long as the lower part grew thinner. After two hours' hard work, Ned Land came in exhausted. He and his comrades were replaced by new workers, whom Conseil and I joined. The second lieutenant of the Nautilus superintended us. The water seemed singularly cold, but I soon got warm handling the pickaxe. My movements were free enough, although they were made under a pressure of thirty atmospheres. When I re-entered, after working two hours, to take some food and rest, I found a perceptible difference between the pure fluid with which the Rouquayrol engine supplied me and the atmosphere of the Nautilus, already charged with carbonic acid. The air had not been renewed for forty-eight hours, and its vivifying qualities were considerably enfeebled. However, after a lapse of twelve hours, we had only raised a block of ice one yard thick, on the marked surface, which was about 600 cubic yards! Reckoning that it took twelve hours to accomplish this much it would take five nights and four days to bring this enterprise to a satisfactory conclusion. Five nights and four days! And we have only air enough for two days in the reservoirs! "Without taking into account," said Ned, "that, even if we get out of this infernal prison, we shall also be imprisoned under the iceberg, shut out from all possible communication with the atmosphere." True enough! Who could then foresee the minimum of time necessary for our deliverance? We might be suffocated before the Nautilus could regain the surface of the waves? Was it destined to perish in this ice-tomb, with all those it enclosed? The situation was terrible. But everyone had looked the danger in the face, and each was determined to do his duty to the last.

As I expected, during the night a new block a yard square was carried away, and still further sank the immense hollow. But in the morning when, dressed in my cork-jacket, I traversed the slushy mass at a temperature of six or seven degrees below zero, I remarked that the side walls were gradually closing in. The beds of water farthest from the trench, that were not warmed by the men's work, showed a tendency to solidification. In presence of this new and imminent danger, what would become of our chances of safety, and how hinder the solidification of this liquid medium, that would burst the partitions of the Nautilus like glass?

I did not tell my companions of this new danger. What was the good of damping the energy they displayed in the painful work of escape? But when I went on board again, I told Captain Nemo of this grave complication.

"I know it," he said, in that calm tone which could counteract the most terrible apprehensions. "It is one danger more; but I see no way of escaping it; the only chance of safety is to go quicker than solidification. We must be beforehand with it, that is all."

On this day for several hours I used my pickaxe vigorously. The work kept me up. Besides, to work was to quit the Nautilus, and breathe directly the pure air drawn from the reservoirs, and supplied by our apparatus, and to quit the impoverished and vitiated atmosphere. Towards evening the trench was dug one yard deeper. When I returned on board, I was nearly suffocated by the carbonic acid with which the air was filled—ah! if we had only the chemical means to drive away this deleterious gas. We had plenty of oxygen; all this water contained a considerable quantity, and by dissolving it with our powerful piles, it would restore the vivifying fluid. I had thought well over it; but of what good was that, since the carbonic acid produced by our respiration had invaded every part of the vessel? To absorb it, it was necessary to fill some jars with caustic potash, and to shake them incessantly. Now this substance was wanting on board, and nothing could replace it. On that evening, Captain Nemo ought to open the taps of his reservoirs, and let some pure air into the interior of the Nautilus; without this precaution we could not get rid of the sense of suffocation. The next day, March 26th, I resumed my miner's work in beginning the fifth yard. The side walls and the lower surface of the iceberg thickened visibly. It was evident that they would meet before the Nautilus was able to disengage itself. Despair seized me for an instant; my pickaxe nearly fell from my hands. What was the good of digging if I must be suffocated, crushed by the water that was turning into stone?—a punishment that the ferocity of the savages even would not have invented! Just then Captain Nemo passed near me. I touched his hand and showed him the walls of our prison. The wall to port had advanced to at least four yards from the hull of the Nautilus. The Captain understood me, and signed me to follow him. We went on board. I took off my cork-jacket and accompanied him into the drawing-room.

"M. Aronnax, we must attempt some desperate means, or we shall be sealed up in this solidified water as in cement."

"Yes; but what is to be done?"

"Ah! if my Nautilus were strong enough to bear this pressure without being crushed!"

"Well?" I asked, not catching the Captain's idea.

"Do you not understand," he replied, "that this congelation of water will help us? Do you not see that by its solidification, it would burst through this field of ice that imprisons us, as, when it freezes, it bursts the hardest stones? Do you not perceive that it would be an agent of safety instead of destruction?"

"Yes, Captain, perhaps. But, whatever resistance to crushing the Nautilus possesses, it could not support this terrible pressure, and would be flattened like an iron plate."

"I know it, sir. Therefore we must not reckon on the aid of nature, but on our own exertions. We must stop this solidification. Not only will the side walls be pressed together; but there is not ten feet of water before or behind the Nautilus. The congelation gains on us on all sides."

"How long will the air in the reservoirs last for us to breathe on board?"

The Captain looked in my face. "After to-morrow they will be empty!"

A cold sweat came over me. However, ought I to have been astonished at the answer? On March 22, the Nautilus was in the open polar seas. We were at 26°. For five days we had lived on the reserve on board. And what was left of the respirable air must be kept for the workers. Even now, as I write, my recollection is still so vivid that an involuntary terror seizes me and my lungs seem to be without air. Meanwhile, Captain Nemo reflected silently, and evidently an idea had struck him; but he seemed to reject it. At last, these words escaped his lips:

"Boiling water!" he muttered.

"Boiling water?" I cried.

"Yes, sir. We are enclosed in a space that is relatively confined. Would not jets of boiling water, constantly injected by the pumps, raise the temperature in this part and stay the congelation?"

"Let us try it," I said resolutely.

"Let us try it, Professor."

The thermometer then stood at 7° outside. Captain Nemo took me to the galleys, where the vast distillatory machines stood that furnished the drinkable water by evaporation. They filled these with water, and all the electric heat from the piles was thrown through the worms bathed in the liquid. In a few minutes this water reached 100°. It was directed towards the pumps, while fresh water replaced it in proportion. The heat developed by the troughs was such that cold water, drawn up from the sea after only having gone through the machines, came boiling into the body of the pump. The injection was begun, and three hours after the thermometer marked 6° below zero outside. One degree was gained. Two hours later the thermometer only marked 4°.

"We shall succeed," I said to the Captain, after having anxiously watched the result of the operation.

"I think," he answered, "that we shall not be crushed. We have no more suffocation to fear."

During the night the temperature of the water rose to 1° below zero. The injections could not carry it to a higher point. But, as the congelation of the sea-water produces at least 2°, I was at least reassured against the dangers of solidification.

The next day, March 27th, six yards of ice had been cleared, twelve feet only remaining to be cleared away. There was yet forty-eight hours' work. The air could not be renewed in the interior of the Nautilus. And this day would make it worse. An intolerable weight oppressed me. Towards three o'clock in the evening this feeling rose to a violent degree. Yawns dislocated my jaws. My lungs panted as they inhaled this burning fluid, which became rarefied more and more. A moral torpor took hold of me. I was powerless, almost unconscious. My brave Conseil, though exhibiting the same symptoms and suffering in the same manner, never left me. He took my hand and encouraged me, and I heard him murmur, "Oh! if I could only not breathe, so as to leave more air for my master!"

Tears came into my eyes on hearing him speak thus. If our situation to all was intolerable in the interior, with what haste and gladness would we put on our cork-jackets to work in our turn! Pickaxes sounded on the frozen ice-beds. Our arms ached, the skin was torn off our hands. But what were these fatigues, what did the wounds matter? Vital air came to the lungs! We breathed! we breathed!

All this time no one prolonged his voluntary task beyond the prescribed time. His task accomplished, each one handed in turn to his panting companions the apparatus that supplied him with life. Captain Nemo set the example, and submitted first to this severe discipline. When the time came, he gave up his apparatus to another and returned to the vitiated air on board, calm, unflinching, unmurmuring.

On that day the ordinary work was accomplished with unusual vigour. Only two yards remained to be raised from the surface. Two yards only separated us from the open sea. But the reservoirs were nearly emptied of air. The little that remained ought to be kept for the workers; not a particle for the Nautilus. When I went back on board, I was half suffocated. What a night! I know not how to describe it. The next day my breathing was oppressed. Dizziness accompanied the pain in my head and made me like a drunken man. My companions showed the same symptoms. Some of the crew had rattling in the throat.

On that day, the sixth of our imprisonment, Captain Nemo, finding the pickaxes work too slowly, resolved to crush the ice-bed that still separated us from the liquid sheet. This man's coolness and energy never forsook him. He subdued his physical pains by moral force.

By his orders the vessel was lightened, that is to say, raised from the ice-bed by a change of specific gravity. When it floated they towed it so as to bring it above the immense trench made on the level of the water-line. Then, filling his reservoirs of water, he descended and shut himself up in the hole.

Just then all the crew came on board, and the double door of communication was shut. The Nautilus then rested on the bed of ice, which was not one yard thick, and which the sounding leads had perforated in a thousand places. The taps of the reservoirs were then opened, and a hundred cubic yards of water was let in, increasing the weight of the Nautilus to 1,800 tons. We waited, we listened, forgetting our sufferings in hope. Our safety depended on this last chance. Notwithstanding the buzzing in my head, I soon heard the humming sound under the hull of the Nautilus. The ice cracked with a singular noise, like tearing paper, and the Nautilus sank.

"We are off!" murmured Conseil in my ear.

I could not answer him. I seized his hand, and pressed it convulsively. All at once, carried away by its frightful overcharge, the Nautilus sank like a bullet under the waters, that is to say, it fell as if it was in a vacuum. Then all the electric force was put on the pumps, that soon began to let the water out of the reservoirs. After some minutes, our fall was stopped. Soon, too, the manometer indicated an ascending movement. The screw, going at full speed, made the iron hull tremble to its very bolts and drew us towards the north. But if this floating under the iceberg is to last another day before we reach the open sea, I shall be dead first.

Half stretched upon a divan in the library, I was suffocating. My face was purple, my lips blue, my faculties suspended. I neither saw nor heard. All notion of time had gone from my mind. My muscles could not contract. I do not know how many hours passed thus, but I was conscious of the agony that was coming over me. I felt as if I was going to die. Suddenly I came to. Some breaths of air penetrated my lungs. Had we risen to the surface of the waves? Were we free of the iceberg? No! Ned and Conseil, my two brave friends, were sacrificing themselves to save me. Some particles of air still remained at the bottom of one apparatus. Instead of using it, they had kept it for me, and, while they were being suffocated, they gave me life, drop by drop. I wanted to push back the thing; they held my hands, and for some moments I breathed freely. I looked at the clock; it was eleven in the morning. It ought to be the 28th of March. The Nautilus went at a frightful pace, forty miles an hour. It literally tore through the water. Where was Captain Nemo? Had he succumbed? Were his companions dead with him? At the moment the manometer indicated that we were not more than twenty feet from the surface. A mere plate of ice separated us from the atmosphere. Could we not break it? Perhaps. In any case the Nautilus was going to attempt it. I felt that it was in an oblique position, lowering the stern, and raising the bows. The introduction of water had been the means of disturbing its equilibrium. Then, impelled by its powerful screw, it attacked the ice-field from beneath like a formidable battering-ram. It broke it by backing and then rushing forward against the field, which gradually gave way; and at last, dashing suddenly against it, shot forwards on the ice-field, that crushed beneath its weight. The panel was opened—one might say torn off—and the pure air came in in abundance to all parts of the Nautilus.

CHAPTER XVII. FROM CAPE HORN TO THE AMAZON

How I got on to the platform, I have no idea; perhaps the Canadian had carried me there. But I breathed, I inhaled the vivifying sea-air. My two companions were getting drunk with the fresh particles. The other unhappy men had been so long without food, that they could not with impunity indulge in the simplest aliments that were given them. We, on the contrary, had no end to restrain ourselves; we could draw this air freely into our lungs, and it was the breeze, the breeze alone, that filled us with this keen enjoyment.

"Ah!" said Conseil, "how delightful this oxygen is! Master need not fear to breathe it. There is enough for everybody."

Ned Land did not speak, but he opened his jaws wide enough to frighten a shark. Our strength soon returned, and, when I looked round me, I saw we were alone on the platform. The foreign seamen in the Nautilus were contented with the air that circulated in the interior; none of them had come to drink in the open air.

The first words I spoke were words of gratitude and thankfulness to my two companions. Ned and Conseil had prolonged my life during the last hours of this long agony. All my gratitude could not repay such devotion.

"My friends," said I, "we are bound one to the other for ever, and I am under infinite obligations to you."

"Which I shall take advantage of," exclaimed the Canadian.

"What do you mean?" said Conseil.

"I mean that I shall take you with me when I leave this infernal Nautilus."

"Well," said Conseil, "after all this, are we going right?"

"Yes," I replied, "for we are going the way of the sun, and here the sun is in the north."

"No doubt," said Ned Land; "but it remains to be seen whether he will bring the ship into the Pacific or the Atlantic Ocean, that is, into frequented or deserted seas."

I could not answer that question, and I feared that Captain Nemo would rather take us to the vast ocean that touches the coasts of Asia and America at the same time. He would thus complete the tour round the submarine world, and return to those waters in which the Nautilus could sail freely. We ought, before long, to settle this important point. The Nautilus went at a rapid pace. The polar circle was soon passed, and the course shaped for Cape Horn. We were off the American point, March 31st, at seven o'clock in the evening. Then all our past sufferings were forgotten. The remembrance of that imprisonment in the ice was effaced from our minds. We only thought of the future. Captain Nemo did not appear again either in the drawing-room or on the platform. The point shown each day on the planisphere, and, marked by the lieutenant, showed me the exact direction of the Nautilus. Now, on that evening, it was evident, to, my great satisfaction, that we were going back to the North by the Atlantic. The next day, April 1st, when the Nautilus ascended to the surface some minutes before noon, we sighted land to the west. It was Terra del Fuego, which the first navigators named thus from seeing the quantity of smoke that rose from the natives' huts. The coast seemed low to me, but in the distance rose high mountains. I even thought I had a glimpse of Mount Sarmiento, that rises 2,070 yards above the level of the sea, with a very pointed summit, which, according as it is misty or clear, is a sign of fine or of wet weather. At this moment the peak was clearly defined against the sky. The Nautilus, diving again under the water, approached the coast, which was only some few miles off. From the glass windows in the drawing-room, I saw long seaweeds and gigantic fuci and varech, of which the open polar sea contains so many specimens, with their sharp polished filaments; they measured about 300 yards in length—real cables, thicker than one's thumb; and, having great tenacity, they are often used as ropes for vessels. Another weed known as velp, with leaves four feet long, buried in the coral concretions, hung at the bottom. It served as nest and food for myriads of crustacea and molluscs, crabs, and cuttlefish. There seals and otters had splendid repasts, eating the flesh of fish with sea-vegetables, according to the English fashion. Over this fertile and luxuriant ground the Nautilus passed with great rapidity. Towards evening it approached the Falkland group, the rough summits of which I recognised the following day. The depth of the sea was moderate. On the shores our nets brought in beautiful specimens of sea weed, and particularly a certain fucus, the roots of which were filled with the best mussels in the world. Geese and ducks fell by dozens on the platform, and soon took their places in the pantry on board.

When the last heights of the Falklands had disappeared from the horizon, the Nautilus sank to between twenty and twenty-five yards, and followed the American coast. Captain Nemo did not show himself. Until the 3rd of April we did not quit the shores of Patagonia, sometimes under the ocean, sometimes at the surface. The Nautilus passed beyond the large estuary formed by the Uraguay. Its direction was northwards, and followed the long windings of the coast of South America. We had then made 1,600 miles since our embarkation in the seas of Japan. About eleven o'clock in the morning the Tropic of Capricorn was crossed on the thirty-seventh meridian, and we passed Cape Frio standing out to sea. Captain Nemo, to Ned Land's great displeasure, did not like the neighbourhood of the inhabited coasts of Brazil, for we went at a giddy speed. Not a fish, not a bird of the swiftest kind could follow us, and the natural curiosities of these seas escaped all observation.

This speed was kept up for several days, and in the evening of the 9th of April we sighted the most westerly point of South America that forms Cape San Roque. But then the Nautilus swerved again, and sought the lowest depth of a submarine valley which is between this Cape and Sierra Leone on the African coast. This valley bifurcates to the parallel of the Antilles, and terminates at the mouth by the enormous depression of 9,000 yards. In this place, the geological basin of the ocean forms, as far as the Lesser Antilles, a cliff to three and a half miles perpendicular in height, and, at the parallel of the Cape Verde Islands, an other wall not less considerable, that encloses thus all the sunk continent of the Atlantic. The bottom of this immense valley is dotted with some mountains, that give to these submarine places a picturesque aspect. I speak, moreover, from the manuscript charts that were in the library of the Nautilus—charts evidently due to Captain Nemo's hand, and made after his personal observations. For two days the desert and deep waters were visited by means of the inclined planes. The Nautilus was furnished with long diagonal broadsides which carried it to all elevations. But on the 11th of April it rose suddenly, and land appeared at the mouth of the Amazon River, a vast estuary, the embouchure of which is so considerable that it freshens the sea-water for the distance of several leagues.

The equator was crossed. Twenty miles to the west were the Guianas, a French territory, on which we could have found an easy refuge; but a stiff breeze was blowing, and the furious waves would not have allowed a single boat to face them. Ned Land understood that, no doubt, for he spoke not a word about it. For my part, I made no allusion to his schemes of flight, for I would not urge him to make an attempt that must inevitably fail. I made the time pass pleasantly by interesting studies. During the days of April 11th and 12th, the Nautilus did not leave the surface of the sea, and the net brought in a marvellous haul of Zoophytes, fish and reptiles. Some zoophytes had been fished up by the chain of the nets; they were for the most part beautiful phyctallines, belonging to the actinidian family, and among other species the phyctalis protexta, peculiar to that part of the ocean, with a little cylindrical trunk, ornamented With vertical lines, speckled with red dots, crowning a marvellous blossoming of tentacles. As to the molluscs, they consisted of some I had already observed—turritellas, olive porphyras, with regular lines intercrossed, with red spots standing out plainly against the flesh; odd pteroceras, like petrified scorpions; translucid hyaleas, argonauts, cuttle-fish (excellent eating), and certain species of calmars that naturalists of antiquity have classed amongst the flying-fish, and that serve principally for bait for cod-fishing. I had now an opportunity of studying several species of fish on these shores. Amongst the cartilaginous ones, petromyzons-pricka, a sort of eel, fifteen inches long, with a greenish head, violet fins, grey-blue back, brown belly, silvered and sown with bright spots, the pupil of the eye encircled with gold—a curious animal, that the current of the Amazon had drawn to the sea, for they inhabit fresh waters—tuberculated streaks, with pointed snouts, and a long loose tail, armed with a long jagged sting; little sharks, a yard long, grey and whitish skin, and several rows of teeth, bent back, that are generally known by the name of pantouffles; vespertilios, a kind of red isosceles triangle, half a yard long, to which pectorals are attached by fleshy prolongations that make them look like bats, but that their horny appendage, situated near the nostrils, has given them the name of sea-unicorns; lastly, some species of balistae, the curassavian, whose spots were of a brilliant gold colour, and the capriscus of clear violet, and with varying shades like a pigeon's throat.

I end here this catalogue, which is somewhat dry perhaps, but very exact, with a series of bony fish that I observed in passing belonging to the apteronotes, and whose snout is white as snow, the body of a beautiful black, marked with a very long loose fleshy strip; odontognathes, armed with spikes; sardines nine inches long, glittering with a bright silver light; a species of mackerel provided with two anal fins; centronotes of a blackish tint, that are fished for with torches, long fish, two yards in length, with fat flesh, white and firm, which, when they arc fresh, taste like eel, and when dry, like smoked salmon; labres, half red, covered with scales only at the bottom of the dorsal and anal fins; chrysoptera, on which gold and silver blend their brightness with that of the ruby and topaz; golden-tailed spares, the flesh of which is extremely delicate, and whose phosphorescent properties betray them in the midst of the waters; orange-coloured spares with long tongues; maigres, with gold caudal fins, dark thorn-tails, anableps of Surinam, etc.

Notwithstanding this "et cetera," I must not omit to mention fish that Conseil will long remember, and with good reason. One of our nets had hauled up a sort of very flat ray fish, which, with the tail cut off, formed a perfect disc, and weighed twenty ounces. It was white underneath, red above, with large round spots of dark blue encircled with black, very glossy skin, terminating in a bilobed fin. Laid out on the platform, it struggled, tried to turn itself by convulsive movements, and made so many efforts, that one last turn had nearly sent it into the sea. But Conseil, not wishing to let the fish go, rushed to it, and, before I could prevent him, had seized it with both hands. In a moment he was overthrown, his legs in the air, and half his body paralysed, crying—

"Oh! master, master! help me!"

It was the first time the poor boy had spoken to me so familiarly. The Canadian and I took him up, and rubbed his contracted arms till he became sensible. The unfortunate Conseil had attacked a cramp-fish of the most dangerous kind, the cumana. This odd animal, in a medium conductor like water, strikes fish at several yards' distance, so great is the power of its electric organ, the two principal surfaces of which do not measure less than twenty-seven square feet. The next day, April 12th, the Nautilus approached the Dutch coast, near the mouth of the Maroni. There several groups of sea-cows herded together; they were manatees, that, like the dugong and the stellera, belong to the skenian order. These beautiful animals, peaceable and inoffensive, from eighteen to twenty-one feet in length, weigh at least sixteen hundredweight. I told Ned Land and Conseil that provident nature had assigned an important role to these mammalia. Indeed, they, like the seals, are designed to graze on the submarine prairies, and thus destroy the accumulation of weed that obstructs the tropical rivers.

"And do you know," I added, "what has been the result since men have almost entirely annihilated this useful race? That the putrefied weeds have poisoned the air, and the poisoned air causes the yellow fever, that desolates these beautiful countries. Enormous vegetations are multiplied under the torrid seas, and the evil is irresistibly developed from the mouth of the Rio de la Plata to Florida. If we are to believe Toussenel, this plague is nothing to what it would be if the seas were cleaned of whales and seals. Then, infested with poulps, medusae, and cuttle-fish, they would become immense centres of infection, since their waves would not possess 'these vast stomachs that God had charged to infest the surface of the seas.'"

CHAPTER XVIII. THE POULPS

For several days the Nautilus kept off from the American coast. Evidently it did not wish to risk the tides of the Gulf of Mexico or of the sea of the Antilles. April 16th, we sighted Martinique and Guadaloupe from a distance of about thirty miles. I saw their tall peaks for an instant. The Canadian, who counted on carrying out his projects in the Gulf, by either landing or hailing one of the numerous boats that coast from one island to another, was quite disheartened. Flight would have been quite practicable, if Ned Land had been able to take possession of the boat without the Captain's knowledge. But in the open sea it could not be thought of. The Canadian, Conseil, and I had a long conversation on this subject. For six months we had been prisoners on board the Nautilus. We had travelled 17,000 leagues; and, as Ned Land said, there was no reason why it should come to an end. We could hope nothing from the Captain of the

Nautilus, but only from ourselves. Besides, for some time past he had become graver, more retired, less sociable. He seemed to shun me. I met him rarely. Formerly he was pleased to explain the submarine marvels to me; now he left me to my studies, and came no more to the saloon. What change had come over him? For what cause? For my part, I did not wish to bury with me my curious and novel studies. I had now the power to write the true book of the sea; and this book, sooner or later, I wished to see daylight. The land nearest us was the archipelago of the Bahamas. There rose high submarine cliffs covered with large weeds. It was about eleven o'clock when Ned Land drew my attention to a formidable pricking, like the sting of an ant, which was produced by means of large seaweeds.

"Well," I said, "these are proper caverns for poulps, and I should not be astonished to see some of these monsters."

"What!" said Conseil; "cuttlefish, real cuttlefish of the cephalopod class?"

"No," I said, "poulps of huge dimensions."

"I will never believe that such animals exist," said Ned.

"Well," said Conseil, with the most serious air in the world, "I remember perfectly to have seen a large vessel drawn under the waves by an octopus's arm."

"You saw that?" said the Canadian.

"Yes, Ned."

"With your own eyes?"

"With my own eyes."

"Where, pray, might that be?"

"At St. Malo," answered Conseil.

"In the port?" said Ned, ironically.

"No; in a church," replied Conseil.

"In a church!" cried the Canadian.

"Yes; friend Ned. In a picture representing the poulp in question."

"Good!" said Ned Land, bursting out laughing.

"He is quite right," I said. "I have heard of this picture; but the subject represented is taken from a legend, and you know what to think of legends in the matter of natural history. Besides, when it is a question of monsters, the imagination is apt to run wild. Not only is it supposed that these poulps can draw down vessels, but a certain Olaus Magnus speaks of an octopus a mile long that is more like an island than an animal. It is also said that the Bishop of Nidros was building an altar on an immense rock. Mass finished, the rock began to walk, and returned to the sea. The rock was a poulp. Another Bishop, Pontoppidan, speaks also of a poulp on which a regiment of cavalry could manoeuvre. Lastly, the ancient naturalists speak of monsters whose mouths were like gulfs, and which were too large to pass through the Straits of Gibraltar."

"But how much is true of these stories?" asked Conseil.

"Nothing, my friends; at least of that which passes the limit of truth to get to fable or legend. Nevertheless, there must be some ground for the imagination of the story-tellers. One cannot deny that poulps and cuttlefish exist of a large species, inferior, however, to the cetaceans. Aristotle has stated the dimensions of a cuttlefish as five cubits, or nine feet two inches. Our fishermen frequently see some that are more than four feet long. Some skeletons of poulps are preserved in the museums of Trieste and Montpelier, that measure two yards in length. Besides, according to the calculations of some naturalists, one of these animals only six feet long would have tentacles twenty-seven feet long. That would suffice to make a formidable monster."

"Do they fish for them in these days?" asked Ned.

"If they do not fish for them, sailors see them at least. One of my friends, Captain Paul Bos of Havre, has often affirmed that he met one of these monsters of colossal dimensions in the Indian seas. But the most astonishing fact, and which does not permit of the denial of the existence of these gigantic animals, happened some years ago, in 1861."

"What is the fact?" asked Ned Land.

"This is it. In 1861, to the north-east of Teneriffe, very nearly in the same latitude we are in now, the crew of the despatch-boat Alector perceived a monstrous cuttlefish swimming in the waters. Captain Bouguer went near to the animal, and attacked it with harpoon and guns, without much success, for balls and harpoons glided over the soft flesh. After several fruitless attempts the crew tried to pass a slip-knot round the body of the mollusc. The noose slipped as far as the tail fins and there stopped. They tried then to haul it on board, but its weight was so considerable that the tightness of the cord separated the tail from the body, and, deprived of this ornament, he disappeared under the water."

"Indeed! is that a fact?"

"An indisputable fact, my good Ned. They proposed to name this poulp `Bouguer's cuttlefish.'"

"What length was it?" asked the Canadian.

"Did it not measure about six yards?" said Conseil, who, posted at the window, was examining again the irregular windings of the cliff.

"Precisely," I replied.

"Its head," rejoined Conseil, "was it not crowned with eight tentacles, that beat the water like a nest of serpents?"

"Precisely."

"Had not its eyes, placed at the back of its head, considerable development?"

"Yes, Conseil."

"And was not its mouth like a parrot's beak?"

"Exactly, Conseil."

"Very well! no offence to master," he replied, quietly; "if this is not Bouguer's cuttlefish, it is, at least, one of its brothers."

I looked at Conseil. Ned Land hurried to the window.

"What a horrible beast!" he cried.

I looked in my turn, and could not repress a gesture of disgust. Before my eyes was a horrible monster worthy to figure in the legends of the marvellous. It was an immense cuttlefish, being eight yards long. It swam crossways in the direction of the Nautilus with great speed, watching us with its enormous staring green eyes. Its eight arms, or rather feet, fixed to its head, that have given the name of cephalopod to these animals, were twice as long as its body, and were twisted like the furies' hair. One could see the 250 air holes on the inner side of the tentacles. The monster's mouth, a horned beak like a parrot's, opened and shut vertically. Its tongue, a horned substance, furnished with several rows of pointed teeth, came out quivering from this veritable pair of shears. What a freak of nature, a bird's beak on a mollusc! Its spindle-like body formed a fleshy mass that might weigh 4,000 to 5,000 lb.; the, varying colour changing with great rapidity, according to the irritation of the animal, passed successively from livid grey to reddish brown. What irritated this mollusc? No doubt the presence of the Nautilus, more formidable than itself, and on which its suckers or its jaws had no hold. Yet, what monsters these poulps are! what vitality the Creator has given them! what vigour in their movements! and they possess three hearts! Chance had brought us in presence of this cuttlefish, and I did not wish to lose the opportunity of carefully studying this specimen of cephalopods. I overcame the horror that inspired me, and, taking a pencil, began to draw it.

"Perhaps this is the same which the Alector saw," said Conseil.

"No," replied the Canadian; "for this is whole, and the other had lost its tail."

"That is no reason," I replied. "The arms and tails of these animals are re-formed by renewal; and in seven years the tail of Bouguer's cuttlefish has no doubt had time to grow."

By this time other poulps appeared at the port light. I counted seven. They formed a procession after the Nautilus, and I heard their beaks gnashing against the iron hull. I continued my work. These monsters kept in the water with such precision that they seemed immovable. Suddenly the Nautilus stopped. A shock made it tremble in every plate.

"Have we struck anything?" I asked.

"In any case," replied the Canadian, "we shall be free, for we are floating."

The Nautilus was floating, no doubt, but it did not move. A minute passed. Captain Nemo, followed by his lieutenant, entered the drawing-room. I had not seen him for some time. He seemed dull. Without noticing or speaking to us, he went to the panel, looked at the poulps, and said something to his lieutenant. The latter went out. Soon the panels were shut. The ceiling was lighted. I went towards the Captain.

"A curious collection of poulps?" I said.

"Yes, indeed, Mr. Naturalist," he replied; "and we are going to fight them, man to beast."

I looked at him. I thought I had not heard aright.

"Man to beast?" I repeated.

"Yes, sir. The screw is stopped. I think that the horny jaws of one of the cuttlefish is entangled in the blades. That is what prevents our moving."

"What are you going to do?"

"Rise to the surface, and slaughter this vermin."

"A difficult enterprise."

"Yes, indeed. The electric bullets are powerless against the soft flesh, where they do not find resistance enough to go off. But we shall attack them with the hatchet."

"And the harpoon, sir," said the Canadian, "if you do not refuse my help."

"I will accept it, Master Land."

"We will follow you," I said, and, following Captain Nemo, we went towards the central staircase.

There, about ten men with boarding-hatchets were ready for the attack. Conseil and I took two hatchets; Ned Land seized a harpoon. The Nautilus had then risen to the surface. One of the sailors, posted on the top ladderstep, unscrewed the bolts of the panels. But hardly were the screws loosed, when the panel rose with great violence, evidently drawn by the suckers of a poulp's arm. Immediately one of these arms slid like a serpent down the opening and twenty others were above. With one blow of the axe, Captain Nemo cut this formidable tentacle, that slid wriggling down the ladder. Just as we were pressing one on the other to reach the platform, two other arms, lashing the air, came down on the seaman placed before Captain Nemo, and lifted him up with irresistible power. Captain Nemo uttered a cry, and rushed out. We hurried after him.

What a scene! The unhappy man, seized by the tentacle and fixed to the suckers, was balanced in the air at the caprice of this enormous trunk. He rattled in his throat, he was stifled, he cried, "Help! help!" These words, spoken in French, startled me! I had a fellow-countryman on board, perhaps several! That heart-rending cry! I shall hear it all my life. The unfortunate man was lost. Who could rescue him from that powerful pressure? However, Captain Nemo had rushed to the poulp, and with one blow of the axe had cut through one arm. His lieutenant struggled furiously against other monsters that crept on the flanks of the Nautilus. The crew fought with their axes. The Canadian, Conseil, and I buried our weapons in the fleshy masses; a strong smell of musk penetrated the atmosphere. It was horrible!

For one instant, I thought the unhappy man, entangled with the poulp, would be torn from its powerful suction. Seven of the eight arms had been cut off. One only wriggled in the air, brandishing the victim like a feather. But just as Captain Nemo and his lieutenant threw themselves on it, the animal ejected a stream of black liquid. We were blinded with it. When the cloud dispersed, the cuttlefish had disappeared, and my unfortunate countryman with it. Ten or twelve poulps now invaded the platform and sides of the Nautilus. We rolled pell-mell into the midst of this nest of serpents, that wriggled on the platform in the waves of blood and ink. It seemed as though these slimy tentacles sprang up like the hydra's heads. Ned Land's harpoon, at each stroke, was plunged into the staring eyes of the cuttle fish. But my bold companion was suddenly overturned by the tentacles of a monster he had not been able to avoid.

Ah! how my heart beat with emotion and horror! The formidable beak of a cuttlefish was open over Ned Land. The unhappy man would be cut in two. I rushed to his succour. But Captain Nemo was before me; his axe disappeared between the two enormous jaws, and, miraculously saved, the Canadian, rising, plunged his harpoon deep into the triple heart of the poulp.

"I owed myself this revenge!" said the Captain to the Canadian.

Ned bowed without replying. The combat had lasted a quarter of an hour. The monsters, vanquished and mutilated, left us at last, and disappeared under the waves. Captain Nemo, covered with blood, nearly exhausted, gazed upon the sea that had swallowed up one of his companions, and great tears gathered in his eyes.

CHAPTER XIX. THE GULF STREAM

This terrible scene of the 20th of April none of us can ever forget. I have written it under the influence of violent emotion. Since then I have revised the recital; I have read it to Conseil and to the Canadian. They found it exact as to facts, but insufficient as to effect. To paint such pictures, one must have the pen of the most illustrious of our poets, the author of The Toilers of the Deep.

I have said that Captain Nemo wept while watching the waves; his grief was great. It was the second companion he had lost since our arrival on board, and what a death! That friend, crushed, stifled, bruised by the dreadful arms of a poulp, pounded by his iron jaws, would not rest with his comrades in the peaceful coral cemetery! In the midst of the struggle, it was the despairing cry uttered by the unfortunate man that had torn my heart. The poor Frenchman, forgetting his conventional language, had taken to his own mother tongue, to utter a last appeal! Amongst the crew of the Nautilus, associated with the body and soul of the Captain, recoiling like him from all contact with men, I had a fellow-countryman. Did he alone represent France in this mysterious association, evidently composed of individuals of divers nationalities? It was one of these insoluble problems that rose up unceasingly before my mind!

Captain Nemo entered his room, and I saw him no more for some time. But that he was sad and irresolute I could see by the vessel, of which he was the soul, and which received all his impressions. The Nautilus did not keep on in its settled course; it floated about like a corpse at the will of the waves. It went at random. He could not tear himself away from the scene of the last struggle, from this sea that had devoured one of his men. Ten days passed thus. It was not till the 1st of May that the Nautilus resumed its northerly course, after having sighted the Bahamas at the mouth of the Bahama Canal. We were then following the current from the largest river to the sea, that has its banks, its fish, and its proper temperatures. I mean the Gulf Stream. It is really a river, that flows freely to the middle of the Atlantic, and whose waters do not mix with the ocean waters. It is a salt river, salter than the surrounding sea. Its mean depth is 1,500 fathoms, its mean breadth ten miles. In certain places the current flows with the speed of two miles and a half an hour. The body of its waters is more considerable than that of all the rivers in the globe. It was on this ocean river that the Nautilus then sailed.

I must add that, during the night, the phosphorescent waters of the Gulf Stream rivalled the electric power of our watch-light, especially in the stormy weather that threatened us so frequently. May 8th, we were still crossing Cape Hatteras, at the height of the North Caroline. The width of the Gulf Stream there is seventy-five miles, and its depth 210 yards. The Nautilus still went at random; all supervision seemed abandoned. I thought that, under these circumstances, escape would be possible. Indeed, the inhabited shores offered anywhere an easy refuge. The sea was incessantly ploughed by the steamers that ply between New York or Boston and the Gulf of Mexico, and overrun day and night by the little schooners coasting about the several parts of the American coast. We could hope to be picked up. It was a favourable opportunity, notwithstanding the thirty miles that separated the Nautilus from the coasts of the Union. One unfortunate circumstance thwarted the Canadian's plans. The weather was very bad. We were nearing those shores where tempests are so frequent, that country of waterspouts and cyclones actually engendered by the current of the Gulf Stream. To tempt the sea in a frail boat was certain destruction. Ned Land owned this himself. He fretted, seized with nostalgia that flight only could cure.

"Master," he said that day to me, "this must come to an end. I must make a clean breast of it. This Nemo is leaving land and going up to the north. But I declare to you that I have had enough of the South Pole, and I will not follow him to the North."

"What is to be done, Ned, since flight is impracticable just now?"

"We must speak to the Captain," said he; "you said nothing when we were in your native seas. I will speak, now we are in mine. When I think that before long the Nautilus will be by Nova Scotia, and that there near New foundland is a large bay, and into that bay the St. Lawrence empties itself, and that the St. Lawrence is my river, the river by Quebec, my native town—when I think of this, I feel furious, it makes my hair stand on end. Sir, I would rather throw myself into the sea! I will not stay here! I am stifled!"

The Canadian was evidently losing all patience. His vigorous nature could not stand this prolonged imprisonment. His face altered daily; his temper became more surly. I knew what he must suffer, for I was seized with home-sickness myself. Nearly seven months had passed without our having had any news from land; Captain Nemo's isolation, his altered spirits, especially since the fight with the poulps, his taciturnity, all made me view things in a different light.

"Well, sir?" said Ned, seeing I did not reply.

"Well, Ned, do you wish me to ask Captain Nemo his intentions concerning us?"

"Yes, sir."

"Although he has already made them known?"

"Yes; I wish it settled finally. Speak for me, in my name only, if you like."

"But I so seldom meet him. He avoids me."

"That is all the more reason for you to go to see him."

I went to my room. From thence I meant to go to Captain Nemo's. It would not do to let this opportunity of meeting him slip. I knocked at the door. No answer. I knocked again, then turned the handle. The door opened, I went in. The Captain was there. Bending over his work-table, he had not heard me. Resolved not to go without having spoken, I approached him. He raised his head quickly, frowned, and said roughly, "You here! What do you want?"

"To speak to you, Captain."

"But I am busy, sir; I am working. I leave you at liberty to shut yourself up; cannot I be allowed the same?"

This reception was not encouraging; but I was determined to hear and answer everything.

"Sir," I said coldly, "I have to speak to you on a matter that admits of no delay."

"What is that, sir?" he replied, ironically. "Have you discovered something that has escaped me, or has the sea delivered up any new secrets?"

We were at cross-purposes. But, before I could reply, he showed me an open manuscript on his table, and said, in a more serious tone, "Here, M. Aronnax, is a manuscript written in several languages. It contains the sum of my studies of the sea; and, if it please God, it shall not perish with me. This manuscript, signed with my name, complete with the history of my life, will be shut up in a little floating case. The last survivor of all of us on board the Nautilus will throw this case into the sea, and it will go whither it is borne by the waves."

This man's name! his history written by himself! His mystery would then be revealed some day.

"Captain," I said, "I can but approve of the idea that makes you act thus. The result of your studies must not be lost. But the means you employ seem to me to be primitive. Who knows where the winds will carry this case, and in whose hands it will fall? Could you not use some other means? Could not you, or one of yours——"

"Never, sir!" he said, hastily interrupting me.

"But I and my companions are ready to keep this manuscript in store; and, if you will put us at liberty——"

"At liberty?" said the Captain, rising.

"Yes, sir; that is the subject on which I wish to question you. For seven months we have been here on board, and I ask you to-day, in the name of my companions and in my own, if your intention is to keep us here always?"

"M. Aronnax, I will answer you to-day as I did seven months ago: Whoever enters the Nautilus, must never quit it."

"You impose actual slavery upon us!"

"Give it what name you please."

"But everywhere the slave has the right to regain his liberty."

"Who denies you this right? Have I ever tried to chain you with an oath?"

He looked at me with his arms crossed.

"Sir," I said, "to return a second time to this subject will be neither to your nor to my taste; but, as we have entered upon it, let us go through with it. I repeat, it is not only myself whom it concerns. Study is to me a relief, a diversion, a passion that could make me forget everything. Like you, I am willing to live obscure, in the frail hope of bequeathing one day, to future time, the result of my labours. But it is otherwise with Ned Land. Every man, worthy of the name, deserves some consideration. Have you thought that love of liberty, hatred of slavery, can give rise to schemes of revenge in a nature like the Canadian's; that he could think, attempt, and try——"

I was silenced; Captain Nemo rose.

"Whatever Ned Land thinks of, attempts, or tries, what does it matter to me? I did not seek him! It is not for my pleasure that I keep him on board! As for you, M. Aronnax, you are one of those who can understand everything, even silence. I have nothing more to say to you. Let this first time you have come to treat of this subject be the last, for a second time I will not listen to you."

I retired. Our situation was critical. I related my conversation to my two companions.

"We know now," said Ned, "that we can expect nothing from this man. The Nautilus is nearing Long Island. We will escape, whatever the weather may be."

But the sky became more and more threatening. Symptoms of a hurricane became manifest. The atmosphere was becoming white and misty. On the horizon fine streaks of cirrhous clouds were succeeded by masses of cumuli. Other low clouds passed swiftly by. The swollen sea rose in huge billows. The birds disappeared with the exception of the petrels, those friends of the storm. The barometer fell sensibly, and indicated an extreme extension of the vapours. The mixture of the storm glass was decomposed under the influence of the electricity that pervaded the atmosphere. The tempest burst on the 18th of May, just as the Nautilus was floating off Long Island, some miles from the port of New York. I can describe this strife of the elements! for, instead of fleeing to the depths of the sea, Captain Nemo, by an unaccountable caprice, would brave it at the surface. The wind blew from the south-west at first. Captain Nemo, during the squalls, had taken his place on the platform. He had made himself fast, to prevent being washed overboard by the monstrous waves. I had hoisted myself up, and made myself fast also, dividing my admiration between the tempest and this extraordinary man who was coping with it. The raging sea was swept by huge cloud-drifts, which were actually saturated with the waves. The Nautilus, sometimes lying on its side, sometimes standing up like a mast, rolled and pitched terribly. About five o'clock a torrent of rain fell, that lulled neither sea nor wind. The hurri cane blew nearly forty leagues an hour. It is under these conditions that it overturns houses, breaks iron gates, displaces twenty-four pounders. However, the Nautilus, in the midst of the tempest, confirmed the words of a clever engineer, "There is no well-constructed hull that cannot defy the sea." This was not a resisting rock; it was a steel spindle, obedient and movable, without rigging or masts, that braved its fury with impunity. However, I watched these raging waves attentively. They measured fifteen feet in height, and 150 to 175 yards long, and their speed of propagation was thirty feet per second. Their bulk and power increased with the depth of the water. Such waves as these, at the Hebrides, have displaced a mass weighing 8,400 lb. They are they which, in the tempest of December 23rd, 1864, after destroying the town of Yeddo, in Japan, broke the same day on the shores of America. The intensity of the tempest increased with the night. The barometer, as in 1860 at Reunion during a cyclone, fell seven-tenths at the close of day. I saw a large vessel pass the horizon struggling painfully. She was trying to lie to under half steam, to keep up above the waves. It was probably one of the steamers of the line from New York to Liverpool, or Havre. It soon disappeared in the gloom. At ten o'clock in the evening the sky was on fire. The atmosphere was streaked with vivid lightning. I could not bear the brightness of it; while the captain, looking at it, seemed to envy the spirit of the tempest. A terrible noise filled the air, a complex noise, made up of the howls of the crushed waves, the roaring of the wind, and the claps of thunder. The wind veered suddenly to all points of the horizon; and the cyclone, rising in the east, returned after passing by the north, west, and south, in the inverse course pursued by the circular storm of the southern hemisphere. Ah, that Gulf Stream! It deserves its name of the King of Tempests. It is that which causes those formidable cyclones, by the difference of temperature between its air and its currents. A shower of fire had succeeded the rain. The drops of water were changed to sharp spikes. One would have thought that Captain Nemo was courting a death worthy of himself, a death by lightning. As the Nautilus, pitching dreadfully, raised its steel spur in the air, it seemed to act as a conductor, and I saw long sparks burst from it. Crushed and without strength I crawled to the panel, opened it, and descended to the saloon. The storm was then at its height. It was impossible to stand upright in the interior of the Nautilus. Captain Nemo came down about twelve. I heard the reservoirs filling by degrees, and the Nautilus sank slowly beneath the waves. Through the open windows in the saloon I saw large fish terrified, passing like phantoms in the water. Some were struck before my eyes. The Nautilus was still descending. I thought that at about eight fathoms deep we should find a calm. But no! the upper beds were too violently agitated for that. We had to seek repose at more than twenty-five fathoms in the bowels of the deep. But there, what quiet, what silence, what peace! Who could have told that such a hurricane had been let loose on the surface of that ocean?

CHAPTER XX. FROM LATITUDE 47° 24' TO LONGITUDE 17° 28'

In consequence of the storm, we had been thrown eastward once more. All hope of escape on the shores of New York or St. Lawrence had faded away; and poor Ned, in despair, had isolated himself like Captain Nemo. Conseil and I, however, never left each other. I said that the Nautilus had gone aside to the east. I should have said (to be more exact) the north-east. For some days, it wandered first on the surface, and then beneath it, amid those fogs so dreaded by sailors. What accidents are due to these thick fogs! What shocks upon these reefs when the wind drowns the breaking of the waves! What collisions between vessels, in spite of their warning lights, whistles, and alarm bells! And the bottoms of these seas look like a field of battle, where still lie all the conquered of the ocean; some old and already encrusted, others fresh and reflecting from their iron bands and copper plates the brilliancy of our lantern.

On the 15th of May we were at the extreme south of the Bank of Newfoundland. This bank consists of alluvia, or large heaps of organic matter, brought either from the Equator by the Gulf Stream, or from the North Pole by the counter-current of cold water which skirts the American coast. There also are heaped up those erratic blocks which are carried along by the broken ice; and close by, a vast charnel-house of molluscs, which perish here by millions. The depth of the sea is not great at Newfoundland—not more than some hundreds of fathoms; but towards the south is a depression of 1,500 fathoms. There the Gulf Stream widens. It loses some of its speed and some of its temperature, but it becomes a sea.

It was on the 17th of May, about 500 miles from Heart's Content, at a depth of more than 1,400 fathoms, that I saw the electric cable lying on the bottom. Conseil, to whom I had not mentioned it, thought at first that it was a gigantic sea-serpent. But I undeceived the worthy fellow, and by way of consolation related several particulars in the laying of this cable. The first one was laid in the years 1857 and 1858; but, after transmitting about 400 telegrams, would not act any longer. In 1863 the engineers constructed an other one, measuring 2,000 miles in length, and weighing 4,500 tons, which was embarked on the Great Eastern. This attempt also failed.

On the 25th of May the Nautilus, being at a depth of more than 1,918 fathoms, was on the precise spot where the rupture occurred which ruined the enterprise. It was within 638 miles of the coast of Ireland; and at half-past two in the afternoon they discovered that communication with Europe had ceased. The electricians on board resolved to cut the cable before fishing it up, and at eleven o'clock at night they had recovered the damaged part. They made another point and spliced it, and it was once more submerged. But some days after it broke again, and in the depths of the ocean could not be recaptured. The Americans, however, were not discouraged. Cyrus Field, the bold promoter of the enterprise, as he had sunk all his own fortune, set a new subscription on foot, which was at once answered, and another cable was constructed on better principles. The bundles of conducting wires were each enveloped in gutta-percha, and protected by a wadding of hemp, contained in a metallic covering. The Great Eastern sailed on the 13th of July, 1866. The operation worked well. But one incident occurred. Several times in unrolling the cable they observed that nails had recently been forced into it, evidently with the motive of destroying it. Captain Anderson, the officers, and engineers consulted together, and had it posted up that, if the offender was surprised on board, he would be thrown without further trial into the sea. From that time the criminal attempt was never repeated.

On the 23rd of July the Great Eastern was not more than 500 miles from Newfoundland, when they telegraphed from Ireland the news of the armistice concluded between Prussia and Austria after Sadowa. On the 27th, in the midst of heavy fogs, they reached the port of Heart's Content. The enterprise was successfully terminated; and for its first despatch, young America addressed old Europe in these words of wisdom, so rarely understood: "Glory to God in the highest, and on earth peace, goodwill towards men."

I did not expect to find the electric cable in its primitive state, such as it was on leaving the manufactory. The long serpent, covered with the remains of shells, bristling with foraminiferae, was encrusted with a strong coating which served as a protection against all boring molluscs. It lay quietly sheltered from the motions of the sea, and under a favourable pressure for the transmission of the electric spark which passes from Europe to America in .32 of a second. Doubtless this cable will last for a great length of time, for they find that the gutta-percha covering is improved by the sea-water. Besides, on this level, so well chosen, the cable is never so deeply submerged as to cause it to break. The Nautilus followed it to the lowest depth, which was more than 2,212 fathoms, and there it lay without any anchorage; and then we reached the spot where the accident had taken place in 1863. The bottom of the ocean then formed a valley about 100 miles broad, in which Mont Blanc might have been placed without its summit appearing above the waves. This valley is closed at the east by a perpendicular wall more than 2,000 yards high. We arrived there on the 28th of May, and the Nautilus was then not more than 120 miles from Ireland.

Was Captain Nemo going to land on the British Isles? No. To my great surprise he made for the south, once more coming back towards European seas. In rounding the Emerald Isle, for one instant I caught sight of Cape Clear, and the light which guides the thousands of vessels leaving Glasgow or Liverpool. An important question then arose in my mind. Did the Nautilus dare entangle itself in the Manche? Ned Land, who had re-appeared since we had been nearing land, did not cease to question me. How could I answer? Captain Nemo remained invisible. After having shown the Canadian a glimpse of American shores, was he going to show me the coast of France?

But the Nautilus was still going southward. On the 30th of May, it passed in sight of Land's End, between the extreme point of England and the Scilly Isles, which were left to starboard. If we wished to enter the Manche, he must go straight to the east. He did not do so.

During the whole of the 31st of May, the Nautilus described a series of circles on the water, which greatly interested me. It seemed to be seeking a spot it had some trouble in finding. At noon, Captain Nemo himself came to work the ship's log. He spoke no word to me, but seemed gloomier than ever. What could sadden him thus? Was it his proxim ity to European shores? Had he some recollections of his abandoned country? If not, what did he feel? Remorse or regret? For a long while this thought haunted my mind, and I had a kind of presentiment that before long chance would betray the captain's secrets.

The next day, the 1st of June, the Nautilus continued the same process. It was evidently seeking some particular spot in the ocean. Captain Nemo took the sun's altitude as he had done the day before. The sea was beautiful, the sky clear. About eight miles to the east, a large steam vessel could be discerned on the horizon. No flag fluttered from its mast, and I could not discover its nationality. Some minutes before the sun passed the meridian, Captain Nemo took his sextant, and watched with great attention. The perfect rest of the water greatly helped the operation. The Nautilus was motionless; it neither rolled nor pitched.

I was on the platform when the altitude was taken, and the Captain pronounced these words: "It is here."

He turned and went below. Had he seen the vessel which was changing its course and seemed to be nearing us? I could not tell. I returned to the saloon. The panels closed, I heard the hissing of the water in the reservoirs. The Nautilus began to sink, following a vertical line, for its screw communicated no motion to it. Some minutes later it stopped at a depth of more than 420 fathoms, resting on the ground. The luminous ceiling was darkened, then the panels were opened, and through the glass I saw the sea brilliantly illuminated by the rays of our lantern for at least half a mile round us.

I looked to the port side, and saw nothing but an immensity of quiet waters. But to starboard, on the bottom appeared a large protuberance, which at once attracted my attention. One would have thought it a ruin buried under a coating of white shells, much resembling a covering of snow. Upon examining the mass attentively, I could recognise the ever-thickening form of a vessel bare of its masts, which must have sunk. It certainly belonged to past times. This wreck, to be thus encrusted with the lime of the water, must already be able to count many years passed at the bottom of the ocean.

What was this vessel? Why did the Nautilus visit its tomb? Could it have been aught but a shipwreck which had drawn it under the water? I knew not what to think, when near me in a slow voice I heard Captain Nemo say:

"At one time this ship was called the Marseillais. It carried seventy-four guns, and was launched in 1762. In 1778, the 13th of August, commanded by La Poype-Ver trieux, it fought boldly against the Preston. In 1779, on the 4th of July, it was at the taking of Grenada, with the squadron of Admiral Estaing. In 1781, on the 5th of September, it took part in the battle of Comte de Grasse, in Chesapeake Bay. In 1794, the French Republic changed its name. On the 16th of April, in the same year, it joined the squadron of Villaret Joyeuse, at Brest, being entrusted with the escort of a cargo of corn coming from America, under the command of Admiral Van Stebel. On the 11th and 12th Prairal of the second year, this squadron fell in with an English vessel. Sir, to-day is the 13th Prairal, the first of June, 1868. It is now seventy-four years ago, day for day on this very spot, in latitude 47° 24', longitude 17° 28', that this vessel, after fighting heroically, losing its three masts, with the water in its hold, and the third of its crew disabled, preferred sinking with its 356 sailors to surrendering; and, nailing its colours to the poop, disappeared under the waves to the cry of `Long live the Republic!'"

"The Avenger!" I exclaimed.

"Yes, sir, the Avenger! A good name!" muttered Captain Nemo, crossing his arms.

CHAPTER XXI. A HECATOMB

The way of describing this unlooked-for scene, the history of the patriot ship, told at first so coldly, and the emotion with which this strange man pronounced the last words, the name of the Avenger, the significance of which could not escape me, all impressed itself deeply on my mind. My eyes did not leave the Captain, who, with his hand stretched out to sea, was watching with a glowing eye the glorious wreck. Perhaps I was never to know who he was, from whence he came, or where he was going to, but I saw the man move, and apart from the *savant*. It was no common misanthropy which had shut Captain Nemo and his companions within the Nautilus, but a hatred, either monstrous or sublime, which time could never weaken. Did this hatred still seek for vengeance? The future would soon teach me that. But the Nautilus was rising slowly to the surface of the sea, and the form of the Avenger disappeared by degrees from my sight. Soon a slight rolling told me that we were in the open air. At that moment a dull boom was heard. I looked at the Captain. He did not move.

"Captain?" said I.

He did not answer. I left him and mounted the platform. Conseil and the Canadian were already there.

"Where did that sound come from?" I asked.

"It was a gunshot," replied Ned Land.

I looked in the direction of the vessel I had already seen. It was nearing the Nautilus, and we could see that it was putting on steam. It was within six miles of us.

"What is that ship, Ned?"

"By its rigging, and the height of its lower masts," said the Canadian, "I bet she is a ship-of-war. May it reach us; and, if necessary, sink this cursed Nautilus."

"Friend Ned," replied Conseil, "what harm can it do to the Nautilus? Can it attack it beneath the waves? Can its cannonade us at the bottom of the sea?"

"Tell me, Ned," said I, "can you recognise what country she belongs to?"

The Canadian knitted his eyebrows, dropped his eyelids, and screwed up the corners of his eyes, and for a few moments fixed a piercing look upon the vessel.

"No, sir," he replied; "I cannot tell what nation she belongs to, for she shows no colours. But I can declare she is a man-of-war, for a long pennant flutters from her main mast."

For a quarter of an hour we watched the ship which was steaming towards us. I could not, however, believe that she could see the Nautilus from that distance; and still less that she could know what this submarine engine was. Soon the Canadian informed me that she was a large, armoured, two-decker ram. A thick black smoke was pouring from her two funnels. Her closely-furled sails were stopped to her yards. She hoisted no flag at her mizzen-peak. The distance prevented us from distinguishing the colours of her pennant, which floated like a thin ribbon. She advanced rapidly. If Captain Nemo allowed her to approach, there was a chance of salvation for us.

"Sir," said Ned Land, "if that vessel passes within a mile of us I shall throw myself into the sea, and I should advise you to do the same."

I did not reply to the Canadian's suggestion, but continued watching the ship. Whether English, French, American, or Russian, she would be sure to take us in if we could only reach her. Presently a white smoke burst from the fore part of the vessel; some seconds after, the water, agitated by the fall of a heavy body, splashed the stern of the Nautilus, and shortly afterwards a loud explosion struck my ear.

"What! they are firing at us!" I exclaimed.

"So please you, sir," said Ned, "they have recognised the unicorn, and they are firing at us."

"But," I exclaimed, "surely they can see that there are men in the case?"

"It is, perhaps, because of that," replied Ned Land, looking at me.

A whole flood of light burst upon my mind. Doubtless they knew now how to believe the stories of the pretended monster. No doubt, on board the Abraham Lincoln, when the Canadian struck it with the harpoon, Commander Farragut had recognised in the supposed narwhal a submarine vessel, more dangerous than a supernatural cetacean. Yes, it must have been so; and on every sea they were now seeking this engine of destruction. Terrible indeed! if, as we supposed, Captain Nemo employed the Nautilus in works of vengeance. On the night when we were imprisoned in that cell, in the midst of the Indian Ocean, had he not attacked some vessel? The man buried in the coral cemetery, had he not been a victim to the shock caused by the Nautilus? Yes, I repeat it, it must be so. One part of the mysterious existence of Captain Nemo had been unveiled; and, if his identity had not been recognised, at least, the nations united against him were no longer hunting a chimerical creature, but a man who had vowed a deadly hatred against them. All the formidable past rose before me. Instead of meeting friends on board the approaching ship, we could only expect pitiless enemies. But the shot rattled about us. Some of them struck the sea and ricochetted, losing themselves in the distance. But none touched the Nautilus. The vessel was not more than three miles from us. In spite of the serious cannonade, Captain Nemo did not appear on the platform; but, if one of the conical projectiles had struck the shell of the Nautilus, it would have been fatal. The Canadian then said, "Sir, we must do all we can to get out of this dilemma. Let us signal them. They will then, perhaps, understand that we are honest folks."

Ned Land took his handkerchief to wave in the air; but he had scarcely displayed it, when he was struck down by an iron hand, and fell, in spite of his great strength, upon the deck.

"Fool!" exclaimed the Captain, "do you wish to be pierced by the spur of the Nautilus before it is hurled at this vessel?"

Captain Nemo was terrible to hear; he was still more terrible to see. His face was deadly pale, with a spasm at his heart. For an instant it must have ceased to beat. His pupils were fearfully contracted. He did not speak, he roared, as, with his body thrown forward, he wrung the Canadian's shoulders. Then, leaving him, and turning to the ship of war, whose shot was still raining around him, he exclaimed, with a powerful voice, "Ah, ship of an accursed nation, you know who I am! I do not want your colours to know you by! Look! and I will show you mine!"

And on the fore part of the platform Captain Nemo unfurled a black flag, similar to the one he had placed at the South Pole. At that moment a shot struck the shell of the Nautilus obliquely, without piercing it; and, rebounding near the Captain, was lost in the sea. He shrugged his shoulders; and, addressing me, said shortly, "Go down, you and your companions, go down!"

"Sir," I cried, "are you going to attack this vessel?"

"Sir, I am going to sink it."

"You will not do that?"

"I shall do it," he replied coldly. "And I advise you not to judge me, sir. Fate has shown you what you ought not to have seen. The attack has begun; go down."

"What is this vessel?"

"You do not know? Very well! so much the better! Its nationality to you, at least, will be a secret. Go down!"

We could but obey. About fifteen of the sailors surrounded the Captain, looking with implacable hatred at the vessel nearing them. One could feel that the same desire of vengeance animated every soul. I went down at the moment another projectile struck the Nautilus, and I heard the Captain exclaim:

"Strike, mad vessel! Shower your useless shot! And then, you will not escape the spur of the Nautilus. But it is not here that you shall perish! I would not have your ruins mingle with those of the Avenger!"

I reached my room. The Captain and his second had remained on the platform. The screw was set in motion, and the Nautilus, moving with speed, was soon beyond the reach of the ship's guns. But the pursuit continued, and Captain Nemo contented himself with keeping his distance.

About four in the afternoon, being no longer able to contain my impatience, I went to the central staircase. The panel was open, and I ventured on to the platform. The Captain was still walking up and down with an agitated step. He was looking at the ship, which was five or six miles to leeward.

He was going round it like a wild beast, and, drawing it eastward, he allowed them to pursue. But he did not attack. Perhaps he still hesitated? I wished to mediate once more. But I had scarcely spoken, when Captain Nemo imposed silence, saying:

"I am the law, and I am the judge! I am the oppressed, and there is the oppressor! Through him I have lost all that I loved, cherished, and venerated—country, wife, children, father, and mother. I saw all perish! All that I hate is there! Say no more!"

I cast a last look at the man-of-war, which was putting on steam, and rejoined Ned and Conseil.

"We will fly!" I exclaimed.

"Good!" said Ned. "What is this vessel?"

"I do not know; but, whatever it is, it will be sunk before night. In any case, it is better to perish with it, than be made accomplices in a retaliation the justice of which we cannot judge."

"That is my opinion too," said Ned Land, coolly. "Let us wait for night."

Night arrived. Deep silence reigned on board. The compass showed that the Nautilus had not altered its course. It was on the surface, rolling slightly. My companions and I resolved to fly when the vessel should be near enough either to hear us or to see us; for the moon, which would be full in two or three days, shone brightly. Once on board the ship, if we could not prevent the blow which threatened it, we could, at least we would, do all that circumstances would allow. Several times I thought the Nautilus was preparing for attack; but Captain Nemo contented himself with allowing his adversary to approach, and then fled once more before it.

Part of the night passed without any incident. We watched the opportunity for action. We spoke little, for we were too much moved. Ned Land would have thrown himself into the sea, but I forced him to wait. According to my idea, the Nautilus would attack the ship at her waterline, and then it would not only be possible, but easy to fly.

At three in the morning, full of uneasiness, I mounted the platform. Captain Nemo had not left it. He was standing at the fore part near his flag, which a slight breeze displayed above his head. He did not take his eyes from the vessel. The intensity of his look seemed to attract, and fascinate, and draw it onward more surely than if he had been towing it. The moon was then passing the meridian. Jupiter was rising in the east. Amid this peaceful scene of nature, sky and ocean rivalled each other in tranquillity, the sea offering to the orbs of night the finest mirror they could ever have in which to reflect their image. As I thought of the deep calm of these elements, compared with all those passions brooding imperceptibly within the Nautilus, I shuddered.

The vessel was within two miles of us. It was ever nearing that phosphorescent light which showed the presence of the Nautilus. I could see its green and red lights, and its white lantern hanging from the large foremast. An indistinct vibration quivered through its rigging, showing that the furnaces were heated to the uttermost. Sheaves of sparks and red ashes flew from the funnels, shining in the atmosphere like stars.

I remained thus until six in the morning, without Captain Nemo noticing me. The ship stood about a mile and a half from us, and with the first dawn of day the firing began afresh. The moment could not be far off when, the Nautilus attacking its adversary, my companions and myself should for ever leave this man. I was preparing to go down to remind them, when the second mounted the platform, accompanied by several sailors. Captain Nemo either did not or would not see them. Some steps were taken which might be called the signal for action. They were very simple. The iron balustrade around the platform was lowered, and the lantern and pilot cages were pushed within the shell until they were flush with the deck. The long surface of the steel cigar no longer offered a single point to check its manoeuvres. I returned to the saloon. The Nautilus still floated; some streaks of light were filtering through the liquid beds. With the undulations of the waves the windows were brightened by the red streaks of the rising sun, and this dreadful day of the 2nd of June had dawned.

At five o'clock, the log showed that the speed of the Nautilus was slackening, and I knew that it was allowing them to draw nearer. Besides, the reports were heard more distinctly, and the projectiles, labouring through the ambient water, were extinguished with a strange hissing noise.

"My friends," said I, "the moment is come. One grasp of the hand, and may God protect us!"

Ned Land was resolute, Conseil calm, myself so nervous that I knew not how to contain myself. We all passed into the library; but the moment I pushed the door opening on to the central staircase, I heard the upper panel close sharply. The Canadian rushed on to the stairs, but I stopped him. A well-known hissing noise told me that the water was running into the reservoirs, and in a few minutes the Nautilus was some yards beneath the surface of the waves. I understood the manoeuvre. It was too late to act. The Nautilus did not wish to strike at the impenetrable cuirass, but below the water-line, where the metallic covering no longer protected it.

We were again imprisoned, unwilling witnesses of the dreadful drama that was preparing. We had scarcely time to reflect; taking refuge in my room, we looked at each other without speaking. A deep stupor had taken hold of my mind: thought seemed to stand still. I was in that painful state of expectation preceding a dreadful report. I waited, I listened, every sense was merged in that of hearing! The speed of the Nautilus was accelerated. It was preparing to rush. The whole ship trembled. Suddenly I screamed. I felt the shock, but comparatively light. I felt the penetrating power of the steel spur. I heard rattlings and scrapings. But the Nautilus, carried along by its propelling power, passed through the mass of the vessel like a needle through sailcloth!

I could stand it no longer. Mad, out of my mind, I rushed from my room into the saloon. Captain Nemo was there, mute, gloomy, implacable; he was looking through the port panel. A large mass cast a shadow on the water; and, that it might lose nothing of her agony, the Nautilus was going down into the abyss with her. Ten yards from me I saw the open shell, through which the water was rushing with the noise of thunder, then the double line of guns and the netting. The bridge was covered with black, agitated shadows.

The water was rising. The poor creatures were crowding the ratlines, clinging to the masts, struggling under the water. It was a human ant-heap overtaken by the sea. Paralysed, stiffened with anguish, my hair standing on end, with eyes wide open, panting, without breath, and without voice, I too was watching! An irresistible attraction glued me to the glass! Suddenly an explosion took place. The compressed air blew up her decks, as if the magazines had caught fire. Then the unfortunate vessel sank more rapidly. Her topmast, laden with victims, now appeared; then her spars, bending under the weight of men; and, last of all, the top of her mainmast. Then the dark mass disappeared, and with it the dead crew, drawn down by the strong eddy.

I turned to Captain Nemo. That terrible avenger, a perfect archangel of hatred, was still looking. When all was over, he turned to his room, opened the door, and entered. I followed him with my eyes. On the end wall beneath his heroes, I saw the portrait of a woman, still young, and two little children. Captain Nemo looked at them for some moments, stretched his arms towards them, and, kneeling down, burst into deep sobs.

CHAPTER XXII. THE LAST WORDS OF CAPTAIN NEMO

The panels had closed on this dreadful vision, but light had not returned to the saloon: all was silence and darkness within the Nautilus. At wonderful speed, a hundred feet beneath the water, it was leaving this desolate spot. Whither was it going? To the north or south? Where was the man flying to after such dreadful retaliation? I had returned to my room, where Ned and Conseil had remained silent enough. I felt an insurmountable horror for Captain Nemo. Whatever he had suffered at the hands of these men, he had no right to punish thus. He had made me, if not an accomplice, at least a witness of his vengeance. At eleven the electric light reappeared. I passed into the saloon. It was deserted. I consulted the different instruments. The Nautilus was flying northward at the rate of twenty-five miles an hour, now on the surface, and now thirty feet below it. On taking the bearings by the chart, I saw that we were passing the mouth of the Manche, and that our course was hurrying us towards the northern seas at a frightful speed. That night we had crossed two hundred leagues of the Atlantic. The shadows fell, and the sea was covered with darkness until the rising of the moon. I went to my room, but could not sleep. I was troubled with dreadful nightmare. The horrible scene of destruction was continually before my eyes. From that day, who could tell into what part of the North Atlantic basin the Nautilus would take us? Still with unaccountable speed. Still in the midst of these northern fogs. Would it touch at Spitzbergen, or on the shores of Nova Zembla? Should we explore those unknown seas, the White Sea, the Sea of Kara, the Gulf of Obi, the Archipelago of Liarrov, and the unknown coast of Asia? I could not say. I could no longer judge of the time that was passing. The clocks had been stopped on board. It seemed, as in polar countries, that night and day no longer followed their regular course. I felt myself being drawn into that strange region where the foundered imagination of Edgar Poe roamed at will. Like the fabulous Gordon Pym, at every moment I expected to see "that veiled human figure, of larger proportions than those of any inhabitant of the earth, thrown across the cataract which defends the approach to the pole." I estimated (though, perhaps, I may be mistaken)—I estimated this adventurous course of the Nautilus to have lasted fifteen or twenty days. And I know not how much longer it might have lasted, had it not been for the catastrophe which ended this voyage. Of Captain Nemo I saw nothing whatever now, nor of his second. Not a man of the crew was visible for an instant. The Nautilus was almost incessantly under water. When we came to the surface to renew the air, the panels opened and shut mechanically. There were no more marks on the planisphere. I knew not where we were. And the Canadian, too, his strength and patience at an end, appeared no more. Conseil could not draw a word from him; and, fearing that, in a dreadful fit of madness, he might kill himself, watched him with constant devotion. One morning (what date it was I could not say) I had fallen into a heavy sleep towards the early hours, a sleep both painful and unhealthy, when I suddenly awoke. Ned Land was leaning over me, saying, in a low voice, "We are going to fly." I sat up.

"When shall we go?" I asked.

"To-night. All inspection on board the Nautilus seems to have ceased. All appear to be stupefied. You will be ready, sir?"

"Yes; where are we?"

"In sight of land. I took the reckoning this morning in the fog—twenty miles to the east."

"What country is it?"

"I do not know; but, whatever it is, we will take refuge there."

"Yes, Ned, yes. We will fly to-night, even if the sea should swallow us up."

"The sea is bad, the wind violent, but twenty miles in that light boat of the Nautilus does not frighten me. Unknown to the crew, I have been able to procure food and some bottles of water."

"I will follow you."

"But," continued the Canadian, "if I am surprised, I will defend myself; I will force them to kill me."

"We will die together, friend Ned."

I had made up my mind to all. The Canadian left me. I reached the platform, on which I could with difficulty support myself against the shock of the waves. The sky was threatening; but, as land was in those thick brown shadows, we must fly. I returned to the saloon, fearing and yet hoping to see Captain Nemo, wishing and yet not wishing to see him. What could I have said to him? Could I hide the involuntary horror with which he inspired me? No. It was better that I should not meet him face to face; better to forget him. And yet—— How long seemed that day, the last that I should pass in the Nautilus. I remained alone. Ned Land and Conseil avoided speaking, for fear of betraying themselves. At six I dined, but I was not hungry; I forced myself to eat in spite of my disgust, that I might not weaken myself. At half-past six Ned Land came to my room, saying, "We shall not see each other again before our departure. At ten the moon will not be risen. We will profit by the darkness. Come to the boat; Conseil and I will wait for you."

The Canadian went out without giving me time to answer. Wishing to verify the course of the Nautilus, I went to the saloon. We were running N.N.E. at frightful speed, and more than fifty yards deep. I cast a last look on these wonders of nature, on the riches of art heaped up in this museum, upon the unrivalled collection destined to perish at the bottom of the sea, with him who had formed it. I wished to fix an indelible impression of it in my mind. I remained an hour thus, bathed in the light of that luminous ceiling, and passing in review those treasures shining under their glasses. Then I returned to my room.

I dressed myself in strong sea clothing. I collected my notes, placing them carefully about me. My heart beat loudly. I could not check its pulsations. Certainly my trouble and agitation would have betrayed me to Captain Nemo's eyes. What was he doing at this moment? I listened at the door of his room. I heard steps. Captain Nemo was there. He had not gone to rest. At every moment I expected to see him appear, and ask me why I wished to fly. I was constantly on the alert. My imagination magnified everything. The impression became at last so poignant that I asked myself if it would not be better to go to the Captain's room, see him face to face, and brave him with look and gesture.

It was the inspiration of a madman; fortunately I resisted the desire, and stretched myself on my bed to quiet my bodily agitation. My nerves were somewhat calmer, but in my excited brain I saw over again all my existence on board the Nautilus; every incident, either happy or unfortunate, which had happened since my disappearance from the Abraham Lincoln—the submarine hunt, the Torres Straits, the savages of Papua, the running ashore, the coral cemetery, the passage of Suez, the Island of Santorin, the Cretan diver, Vigo Bay, Atlantis, the iceberg, the South Pole, the imprisonment in the ice, the fight among the poulps, the storm in the Gulf Stream, the Avenger, and the horrible scene of the vessel sunk with all her crew. All these events passed before my eyes like scenes in a drama. Then Captain Nemo seemed to grow enormously, his features to assume superhuman proportions. He was no longer my equal, but a man of the waters, the genie of the sea.

It was then half-past nine. I held my head between my hands to keep it from bursting. I closed my eyes; I would not think any longer. There was another half-hour to wait, another half-hour of a nightmare, which might drive me mad.

At that moment I heard the distant strains of the organ, a sad harmony to an undefinable chant, the wail of a soul longing to break these earthly bonds. I listened with every sense, scarcely breathing; plunged, like Captain Nemo, in that musical ecstasy, which was drawing him in spirit to the end of life.

Then a sudden thought terrified me. Captain Nemo had left his room. He was in the saloon, which I must cross to fly. There I should meet him for the last time. He would see me, perhaps speak to me. A gesture of his might destroy me, a single word chain me on board.

But ten was about to strike. The moment had come for me to leave my room, and join my companions.

I must not hesitate, even if Captain Nemo himself should rise before me. I opened my door carefully; and even then, as it turned on its hinges, it seemed to me to make a dreadful noise. Perhaps it only existed in my own imagination.

I crept along the dark stairs of the Nautilus, stopping at each step to check the beating of my heart. I reached the door of the saloon, and opened it gently. It was plunged in profound darkness. The strains of the organ sounded faintly. Captain Nemo was there. He did not see me. In the full light I do not think he would have noticed me, so entirely was he absorbed in the ecstasy.

I crept along the carpet, avoiding the slightest sound which might betray my presence. I was at least five minutes reaching the door, at the opposite side, opening into the library.

I was going to open it, when a sigh from Captain Nemo nailed me to the spot. I knew that he was rising. I could even see him, for the light from the library came through to the saloon. He came towards me silently, with his arms crossed, gliding like a spectre rather than walking. His breast was swelling with sobs; and I heard him murmur these words (the last which ever struck my ear):

"Almighty God! enough! enough!"

Was it a confession of remorse which thus escaped from this man's conscience?

In desperation, I rushed through the library, mounted the central staircase, and, following the upper flight, reached the boat. I crept through the opening, which had already admitted my two companions.

"Let us go! let us go!" I exclaimed.

"Directly!" replied the Canadian.

The orifice in the plates of the Nautilus was first closed, and fastened down by means of a false key, with which Ned Land had provided himself; the opening in the boat was also closed. The Canadian began to loosen the bolts which still held us to the submarine boat.

Suddenly a noise was heard. Voices were answering each other loudly. What was the matter? Had they discovered our flight? I felt Ned Land slipping a dagger into my hand.

"Yes," I murmured, "we know how to die!"

The Canadian had stopped in his work. But one word many times repeated, a dreadful word, revealed the cause of the agitation spreading on board the Nautilus. It was not we the crew were looking after!

"The maelstrom! the maelstrom!" Could a more dreadful word in a more dreadful situation have sounded in our ears! We were then upon the dangerous coast of Norway. Was the Nautilus being drawn into this gulf at the moment our boat was going to leave its sides? We knew that at the tide the pent-up waters between the islands of Ferroe and Loffoden rush with irresistible violence, forming a whirlpool from which no vessel ever escapes. From every point of the horizon enormous waves were meeting, forming a gulf justly called the "Navel of the Ocean," whose power of attraction extends to a distance of twelve miles. There, not only vessels, but whales are sacrificed, as well as white bears from the northern regions.

It is thither that the Nautilus, voluntarily or involuntarily, had been run by the Captain.

It was describing a spiral, the circumference of which was lessening by degrees, and the boat, which was still fastened to its side, was carried along with giddy speed. I felt that sickly giddiness which arises from long-continued whirling round.

We were in dread. Our horror was at its height, circulation had stopped, all nervous influence was annihilated, and we were covered with cold sweat, like a sweat of agony! And what noise around our frail bark! What roarings repeated by the echo miles away! What an uproar was that of the waters broken on the sharp rocks at the bottom, where the hardest bodies are crushed, and trees worn away, "with all the fur rubbed off," according to the Norwegian phrase!

What a situation to be in! We rocked frightfully. The Nautilus defended itself like a human being. Its steel muscles cracked. Sometimes it seemed to stand upright, and we with it!

"We must hold on," said Ned, "and look after the bolts. We may still be saved if we stick to the Nautilus."

He had not finished the words, when we heard a crashing noise, the bolts gave way, and the boat, torn from its groove, was hurled like a stone from a sling into the midst of the whirlpool.

My head struck on a piece of iron, and with the violent shock I lost all consciousness.

CHAPTER XXIII. CONCLUSION

Thus ends the voyage under the seas. What passed during that night—how the boat escaped from the eddies of the maelstrom—how Ned Land, Conseil, and myself ever came out of the gulf, I cannot tell.

But when I returned to consciousness, I was lying in a fisherman's hut, on the Loffoden Isles. My two companions, safe and sound, were near me holding my hands. We embraced each other heartily.

At that moment we could not think of returning to France. The means of communication between the north of Norway and the south are rare. And I am therefore obliged to wait for the steamboat running monthly from Cape North.

And, among the worthy people who have so kindly received us, I revise my record of these adventures once more. Not a fact has been omitted, not a detail exaggerated. It is a faithful narrative of this incredible expedition in an element inaccessible to man, but to which Progress will one day open a road.

Shall I be believed? I do not know. And it matters little, after all. What I now affirm is, that I have a right to speak of these seas, under which, in less than ten months, I have crossed 20,000 leagues in that submarine tour of the world, which has revealed so many wonders.

But what has become of the Nautilus? Did it resist the pressure of the maelstrom? Does Captain Nemo still live? And does he still follow under the ocean those frightful retaliations? Or, did he stop after the last hecatomb?

Will the waves one day carry to him this manuscript containing the history of his life? Shall I ever know the name of this man? Will the missing vessel tell us by its nationality that of Captain Nemo?

I hope so. And I also hope that his powerful vessel has conquered the sea at its most terrible gulf, and that the Nautilus has survived where so many other vessels have been lost! If it be so—if Captain Nemo still inhabits the ocean, his adopted country, may hatred be appeased in that savage heart! May the contemplation of so many wonders extinguish for ever the spirit of vengeance! May the judge disappear, and the philosopher continue the peaceful exploration of the sea! If his destiny be strange, it is also sublime. Have I not understood it myself? Have I not lived ten months of this unnatural life? And to the question asked by Ecclesiastes three thousand years ago, "That which is far off and exceeding deep, who can find it out?" two men alone of all now living have the right to give an answer——

CAPTAIN NEMO AND MYSELF.

BOOK TWO.
IN SEARCH OF THE CASTAWAYS

Or Captain Grant's Children
(Jules Verne's Voyages extraordinaires Book #5)

CHAPTER I. THE SHARK.

On the 26th of July, 1864, under a strong wind from the northeast, a magnificent yacht was steaming at full speed through the waves of the North Channel. The flag of England fluttered at her yard-arm, while at the top of the mainmast floated a blue pennon, bearing the initials E. G., worked in gold and surmounted by a ducal coronet.

The yacht was called the Duncan, and belonged to Lord Glenarvan, one of the sixteen Scottish peers sitting in the House of Lords, and also a most distinguished member of the "Royal Thames Yacht Club," so celebrated throughout the United Kingdom.

Lord Edward Glenarvan was on board with his young wife, Lady Helena, and one of his cousins, Major MacNabb.

The Duncan, newly constructed, had just been making a trial voyage several miles beyond the Frith of Clyde, and was now on her return to Glasgow. Already Arran Island was appearing on the horizon, when the look-out signaled an enormous fish that was sporting in the wake of the yacht.

The captain, John Mangles, at once informed Lord Glenarvan of that encounter. He mounted on deck with Major MacNabb, and asked the captain what he thought of the animal.

"Indeed, your honor," replied John Mangles, "I think it is a shark of large proportions."

"A shark in these regions!" exclaimed Glenarvan.

"Without doubt," replied the captain. "This fish belongs to a species of sharks that are found in all seas and all latitudes. It is the 'balance-fish,' and, if I am not greatly mistaken, we are now dealing with one of these fellows here. If your honor consents, and it pleases Lady Helena to witness such a novel chase, we will soon see what we have to deal with."

"What do you think, MacNabb?" said Lord Glenarvan to the major; "are you of the opinion to try the adventure?"

"I am of whatever opinion pleases you," answered the major, calmly.

"Besides," continued Captain Mangles, "we cannot too soon exterminate these terrible beasts. Let us take advantage of the ocassion, and, if your honor pleases, it shall be an exciting spectacle as well as a good action."

"Do it, John," said Lord Glenarvan.

He then summoned Lady Helena, who joined him on deck, tempted by the exciting sport.

The sea was magnificent. You could easily follow along its surface the rapid motions of the fish, as it plunged and rose again with surprising agility. Captain Mangles gave his orders, and the sailors threw over the starboard ratling a stout rope, to which was fastened a hook baited with a thick piece of pork.

The shark, although still at a distance of fifty yards, scented the bait offered to his voracity. He rapidly approached the yacht. You could see his fins, gray at their extremity and black at their base, beat the waves with violence, while his "caudal appendage" kept him in a rigorously straight line. As he advanced, his great glaring eyes seemed inflamed with eagerness, and his yawning jaws, when he turned, disclosed a quadruple row of teeth. His head was large, and shaped like a double-headed hammer. Captain Mangles was right. It was a very large specimen of the most rapacious family of sharks,—the "balance fish" of the English and the "jew-fish" of the Provençals.

All on board of the Duncan followed the movements of the shark with lively attention. The animal was soon within reach of the hook; he turned upon his back, in order to seize it better, and the enormous bait disappeared down his vast gullet. At the same time he hooked himself, giving the line a violent shake, whereupon the sailors hoisted the huge creature by means of a pulley at the end of the yard-arm.

The shark struggled violently at feeling himself drawn from his natural element, but his violence was of no avail. A rope with a slip-noose confined his tail and paralyzed his movements. A few moments afterward he was hauled over the ratlings, and precipitated upon the deck of the yacht. One of the sailors at once approached him, not without caution, and with a vigorous blow of the hatchet cut off the formidable tail of the animal.

The chase was ended, and there was nothing more to fear from the monster. The vengeance of the sailors was satisfied, but not their curiosity. Indeed, it is customary on board of every vessel to carefully examine the stomachs of sharks.

The men, knowing the inordinate voracity of the creature, wait with some anxiety, and their wait is not always in vain.

Lady Glenarvan, not wishing to witness this repugnant "exploration," retired to the cabin.

The shark was still panting. He was ten feet long, and weighed more than six hundred pounds. These dimensions and weigth are nothing extraordinary; for if the balance-fish is not classed among the giants of this species, at least he belongs to the most formidable of their family.

The enormous fish was soon cut open by a blow of the hatchet, without further ceremony. The hook had penetrated to the stomach, which was absolutely empty. Evidently the animal had fasted a long time, and the disappointed seamen were about to cast the remains into the sea, when the attention of the boatswain was attracted by a bulky object firmly imbedded in the viscera.

"Ha! what is this?" he exclaimed.

"That," replied one of the sailors, "is a piece of rock that the creature has taken in for ballast."

"Good!" said another; "it is probably a bullet that this fellow has received in the stomach, and could not digest."

"Shut up, all of you!" cried Tom Austin, the first officer; "do you not see that the animal was a great drunkard? and to lose nothing, has drank not only the wine, but the bottle too!"

"What!" exclaimed Lord Glenarvan, "is it a bottle that this shark has in his stomach?"

"A real bottle!" replied the boatswain, "but you can easily see that it does not come from the wine-cellar."

"Well, Tom," said Glenarvan, "draw it out carefully. Bottles found at sea frequently contain precious documents."

"Do you think so...?" said Major MacNabb.

"I do; at least, that it may happen so."

"Oh! I do not contradict you," replied the major. "Perhaps there may be a secret in this."

"We shall see," said Glenarvan. "Well, Tom?"

"Here it is," said the mate, displaying the shapeless object that he had just drawn with difficulty from the interior of the shark.

"Good," said Glenarvan; "wash the dirty thing, and bring it into the cabin."

Tom obeyed; and the bottle found under such singular circumstances was placed on the cabin-table, around which Lord Glenarvan, Major MacNabb, and Captain John Mangles took their seats, together with Lady Helena; for a woman, they say, is always a little curious.

Everything causes excitement at sea. For a moment there was silence. Each gazed wonderingly at this strange waif. Did it contain the secret of a disaster, or only an insignificant message confided to the mercy of the waves by some idle navigator?

However, they must know what it was, and Glenarvan, without waiting longer, proceeded to examine the bottle. He took, moreover, all necessary precautions. You would have thought a coroner was pointing out the particulars of a suspicious quest. And Glenarvan was right, for the most insignificant mark in appearance may often put them on track to an important discovery.

Before examining it internally, the bottle was inspected externally. It had a slender neck, the mouth of which was protected by an iron wire considerably rusted. Its sides were very thick, and capable of supporting a pressure of several atmospheres, betraying evidently previous connection with champagne. With these bottles the wine-dressers of Aï and Epernay block carriage-wheels without their showing the slightest fracture. This one could, therefore, bear with impunity the hardships of a long voyage.

"A bottle of the Maison Cliquot," said the major simply.

And, as if he ought to know, his affirmation was accepted without contest.

"My dear major," said Lady Helena, "it matters little what this bottle is, if we don´t know whence it comes."

"We shall know, my dear," said Lord Edward, "and already we can affirm that it has come from far. See the petrified particles that cover it, these mineralized substances, so to speak, under the action of the sea-water. This waif had already taken a long voyage in the ocean, before being engulfed in the stomach of a shark."

"I cannot but be of your opinion," replied the major; "this fragile vase, protected by its strong envelope, must have made a long journey."

"But whence does it come?" inquired Lady Glenarvan.

"Wait, my dear Helena, wait. We must be patient with bottles. If I am not greatly mistaken, this one will itself answer all our questions."

And so saying, Glenarvan began to scrape off the hard particles that protected the neck. Soon the cork appeared, but very much damaged with the salt water.

"Annoying circumstance," said Glenarvan; "for if there is any paper in it, it will be in a bad condition."

"That's what I fear," replied the major.

"I will add," continued Glenarvan, "that this badly-corked bottle would soon have sunk; and it is fortunate that this shark swallowed it, and brought it on board of the Duncan."

"Certainly," interposed Captain Mangles; "it would have been better, however, had it been caught in the open sea on a well-known latitude and longitude. We could then, by studying the atmospheric and marine currents, have discovered the course traversed; but with a guide like one of these sharks who travels against wind and tide, we cannot know whence it comes."

"We shall soon see," answered Glenarvan. At the same time he drew out the cork with the greatest care, and a strong saline odor permeated the cabin.

"Well?" said Lady Helena, with a truly feminine impatience.

"Yes," said Glenarvan; "I was not mistaken! Here are papers!"

"Documents! documents!" cried Lady Helena.

"Only," replied Glenarvan, "they appear to be damaged by the water. It is impossible to remove them, for they adhere to the sides of the bottle."

"Let us break it," said MacNabb.

"I would rather keep it whole," replied Glenarvan.

"I should, too," said the major.

"Undoubtely," added Lady Helena; "however, the contents are more valuable than the container, and it is better to sacrifice one than the other."

"Let your lordship only break off the neck," said the captain, "and that will enable you to draw them out without injury."

"Do it, do it, my dear Edward!" cried Lady Glenarvan.

It was difficult to proceed in any other way, and, at all hazards, Glenarvan determined to break the neck of the precious bottle. It was necessary to use a hammer, for the stony covering had acquired the hardness of granite. The fragments soon strewed the table, and several pieces of paper were perceived adhering to each other. Glenarvan drew them out carefully, separating and examining them closely, while Lady Helena, the major, and the captain crowded around him.

CHAPTER II. THE THREE DOCUMENTS.

These pieces of paper, half destroyed by the sea-water, exhibited only a few words, the traces of handwriting almost entirely effaced. For several minutes Lord Glenarvan examined them attentively, turned them about in every way, and exposed them to the light of day, observing the least traces of writing spared by the sea. Then he looked at his friends, who were regarding him with anxious eyes.

"There are here," said he, "three distinct documents, probably three copies of the same missive, translated into three different languages: one English, another French, and the third German. The few words that remain leave no doubt on this point."

"But these words have at least a meaning?" said Lady Glenarvan.

"That is difficult to say, my dear Helena. The words traced on these papers are very imperfect."

"Perhaps they will complete each other," said the major.

"That may be," replied Captain Mangles. "It is not probable that the water has obliterated these lines in exactly the same places on each, and by comparing these remains of phrases we shall arrive at some intelligible meaning."

"We will do so," said Lord Glenarvan; "but let us proceed systematically. And, first, here is the English document."

It showed the following arrangement of lines and words:

"That does not mean much," said the major, with an air of disappointment.

"Whatever it may mean," replied the captain, "it is good English."

"There is no doubt of that," said his lordship. "The words *wreck, aland, this, and, lost,* are perfect. *Cap* evidently means *captain,* referring to the captain of a shipwrecked vessel."

"Let us add," said the captain, "the portions of the words *docu* and *ssistance,* the meaning of which is plain."

"Well, something is gained already!" added Lady Helena.

"Unfortunately," replied the major, "entire lines are wanting. How can we find the name of the lost vessel, or the place of shipwreck?"

"We shall find them," said Lord Edward.

"Very likely," answered the major, who was invariably of the opinion of every one else; "but how?"

"By comparing one document with another."

"Let us see!" cried Lady Helena.

The second piece of paper, more damaged than the former, exhibited only isolated words, arranged thus:

7 Juni   .   *Glas*

zwei   *atrosen*

graus

bringt ihnen

"This is written in German," said Captain Mangles, when he had cast his eyes upon it.

"And do you know that language?" asked Glenarvan.

"Perfectly, your lordship."

"Well, tell us what these few words mean."

The captain examined the document closely, and expressed himself as follows:

"First, the date of the event is determined. *7 Juni* means June 7th, and by comparing this figure with the figures '62,' furnished by the English document, we have the date complete,—June 7th, 1862."

"Very well!" exclaimed Lady Helena. "Go on."

"On the same line," continued the young captain, "I find the word *Glas,* which, united with the word *gow* of the first document, gives *Glasgow.* It is plainly a ship from the port of Glasgow."

"That was my opinion," said the major.

"The second line is missing entirely," continued Captain Mangles; "but on the third I meet with two important words *zwei,* which means *two,* and *atrosen,* or rather *matrosen,* which signifies *sailors* in German."

"There were a captain and two sailors, then?" said Lady Helena.

"Probably," replied her husband.

"I will confess, your lordship," said the captain, "that the next word, *graus*, puzzles me. I do not know how to translate it. Perhaps the third document will enable us to understand it. As to the two last words, they are easily explained. *Bringt ihnen* means *bring to them*, and if we compare these with the English word, which is likewise on the sixth line of the first document (I mean the word *assistance*), we shall have the phrase *bring them assistance*."

"Yes, bring them assistance," said Glenarvan. "But where are the unfortunates? We have not yet a single indication of the place, and the scene of the catastrophe is absolutely unknown."

"Let us hope that the French document will be more explicit," said Lady Helena.

"Let us look at it, then," replied Glenarvan; "and, as we all know this language, our examination will be more easy."

Here is an exact fac-simile of the third document:

"There are figures!" cried Lady Helena. "Look, gentlemen, look!"

"Let us proceed in order," said Lord Glenarvan, "and start at the beginning. Permit me to point out one by one these scattered and incomplete words. I see from the first letters *troi ats* (*trois-mats*), that it is a brig, the name of which, thanks to the English and French documents, is entirely preserved: *The Britannia*. Of the two following words, *gonie* and *austral*, only the last has an intelligible meaning."

"That is an important point," replied Captain Mangles; "the shipwreck took place in the southern hemisphere."

"That is indefinite," said the major.

"I will continue," resumed Glenarvan. "The word *abor* is the trace of the verb *aborder* (to land). These unfortunates have landed somewhere. But where? *Contin!* Is it on a continent? *Cruel!*"

"'Cruel!'" cried Mangles; "that explains the German word *graus, grausam, cruel!*"

"Go on, go on!" cried Glenarvan, whose interest was greatly excited as the meaning of these incomplete words was elucidated. "*Indi!* Is it India, then, where these sailors have been cast? What is the meaning of the word *ongit*? Ha, longitude! And here is the latitude, 37° 11'. In short, we have a definite indication."

"But the longitude is wanting," said MacNabb.

"We cannot have everything, my dear major," replied Glenarvan; "and an exact degree of latitude is something. This French document is decidedly the most complete of the three. Each of them was evidently a literal translation of the others, for they all convey the same information. We must, therefore, unite and translate them into one language, and seek their most probable meaning, the one that is most logical and explicit."

"Shall we make this translation in French, English, or German?" asked the major.

"In English," answered Glenarvan, "since that is our own language."

"Your lordship is right," said Captain Mangles, "besides, it was also theirs."

"It is agreed, then. I will write this document, uniting these parts of words and fragments of phrases, leaving the gaps that separate them, and filling up those the meaning of which is not ambiguous. Then we will compare them and form an opinion."

Glenarvan at once took a pen, and, in a few moments, presented to his friends a paper on which were written the following lines:

June 7, 1862	brig Britannia	Glasgow
wrecked	gonia	Southern
	ashore	two sailors
Captain Gr	rea	
contin	pr	cruel Indi
	thrown this document	of longitude
and 37° 11′ of latitude		Bring them assistance
	lost.	

At this moment a sailor informed the captain that the Duncan was entering the Frith of Clyde, and asked his orders.

"What are your lordship's wishes?" said the captain, addressing Lord Glenarvan.

"Reach Dumbarton as quickly as possible, captain. Then, while Lady Helena returns to Malcolm Castle, I will go to London and submit this document to the authorities."

The captain gave his orders in pursuance of this, and the mate executed them.

"Now, my friends," said Glenarvan, "we will continue our investigations. We are on the track of a great catastrophe. The lives of several men depend upon our sagacity. Let us use therefore all our ingenuity to divine the secret of this enigma."

"We are ready, my dear Edward," replied Lady Helena.

"First of all," continued Glenarvan, "we must consider three distinct points in this document. First, what is known; second, what can be conjectured; and third, what is unknown. What do we know? That on the 7th of June, 1862, a brig, the Britannia, of Glasgow, was wrecked; that two sailors and the captain threw this document into the sea in latitude 37° 11′, and in it ask for assistance."

"Exactly," replied the major.

"What can we conjecture?" resumed Glenarvan. "First, that the shipwreck took place in the South Seas; and now I call your attention to the word *gonia*. Does it not indicate the name of the country which they reached?"

"Patagonia!" cried Lady Helena.

"Probably."

"But is Patagonia crossed by the thirty-seventh parallel?" asked the major.

"That is easily seen," said the captain, taking out a map of South America. "It is so: Patagonia is bisected by the thirty-seventh parallel, which crosses Araucania, over the Pampas, north of Patagonia, and is lost in the Atlantic."

"Well, let us continue our conjectures. The two sailors and the captain *abor, land.* Where? *Contin,*—the *continent,* you understand; a continent, not an island. What becomes of them? We have fortunately two letters, *pr,* which inform us of their fate. These unfortunates, in short, are *captured* (pris) or *prisoners.* By whom? The *cruel Indians.* Are you convinced? Do not the words fit naturally into the vacant places? Does not the document grow clear to your eyes? Does not light break in upon your mind?"

Glenarvan spoke with conviction. His looks betokened an absolute confidence; and his enthusiasm was communicated to his hearers. Like him they cried, "It is plain! it is plain!"

A moment after Lord Edward resumed, in these terms:

"All these hypotheses, my friends, seem to me extremely plausible. In my opinion, the catastrophe took place on the shores of Patagonia. However, I will inquire at Glasgow what was the destination of the Britannia, and we shall know whether she could have been led to these regions."

"We do not need to go so far," replied the captain; "I have here the shipping news of the *Mercantile and Shipping Gazette,* which will give us definite information."

"Let us see! let us see!" said Lady Glenarvan.

Captain Mangles took a file of papers of the year 1862, and began to turn over the leaves rapidly. His search was soon ended; as he said, in a tone of satisfaction,—

"May 30, 1862, Callao, Peru, *Britannia,* Captain Grant, bound for Glasgow."

"Grant!" exclaimed Lord Glenarvan; "that hardy Scotchman who wished to found a new Scotland in the waters of the Pacific?"

"Yes," answered the captain, "the very same, who, in 1861, embarked in the Britannia at Glasgow, and of whom nothing has since been heard."

"Exactly! exactly!" said Glenarvan; "it is indeed he. The Britannia left Callao the 30th of May, and on the 7th of June, eight days after her departure, she was lost on the shores of Patagonia. This is the whole story elucidated from the remains of these words that seemed undecipherable. You see, my friends, that what we can conjecture is very important. As to what we do not know, this is reduced to one item, the missing degree of longitude."

"It is of no account," added Captain Mangles, "since the country is known; and with the latitude alone, I will undertake to go straight to the scene of the shipwreck."

"We know all, then?" said Lady Glenarvan.

"All, my dear Helena: and these blanks that the sea has made between the words of the document, I can as easily fill out as though I were writing at the dictation of Captain Grant."

Accordingly Lord Glenarvan took the pen again, and wrote, without hesitation, the following note:

"June 7, 1862.—The brig Britannia of Glasgow was wrecked on the shores of Patagonia, in the Southern Hemisphere. Directing their course to land, two sailors and Captain Grant attempted to reach the continent, where they will be prisoners of the cruel Indians. They have thrown this document into the sea, at longitude —, latitude 37° 11'. Bring them assistance or they are lost."

"Good! good! my dear Edward!" said Lady Glenarvan; "and if these unfortunates see their native country again, they will owe this happiness to you."

"And they shall see it again," replied Glenarvan. "This document is too explicit, too clear, too certain, for Englishmen to hesitate. What has been done for Sir John Franklin, and so many others, will also be done for the shipwrecked of the Britannia."

"But these unfortunates," answered Lady Helena, "have, without doubt, a family that mourns their loss. Perhaps this poor Captain Grant has a wife, children—"

"You are right, my dear lady; and I charge myself with informing them that all hope is not yet lost. And now, my friends, let us go on deck, for we must be approaching the harbor."

Indeed, the Duncan had forced on steam, and was now skirting the shores of Bute Island. Rothesay, with its charming little village nestling in its fertile valley, was left on the starboard, and the vessel entered the narrow inlets of the frith, passed Greenock, and, at six in the evening, was anchored at the foot of the basaltic rocks of Dumbarton, crowned by the celebrated castle.

Here a coach was waiting to take Lady Helena and Major MacNabb back to Malcolm Castle. Lord Glenarvan, after embracing his young wife, hurried to take the express train for Glasgow. But before going, he confided an important message to a more rapid agent, and a few moments after the electric telegraph conveyed to the *Times* and *Morning Chronicle* an advertisement in the following terms:

"For any information concerning the brig Britannia of Glasgow, Captain Grant, address Lord Glenarvan, Malcolm Castle, Luss, County of Dumbarton, Scotland."

CHAPTER III. THE CAPTAIN'S CHILDREN.

The castle of Malcolm, one of the most romantic in Scotland, is situated near the village of Luss, whose pretty valley it crowns. The limpid waters of Loch Lomond bathe the granite of its walls. From time immemorial it has belonged to the Glenarvan family, who have preserved in the country of Rob

Roy and Fergus MacGregor the hospitable customs of the ancient heroes of Walter Scott. At the epoch of the social revolution in Scotland, a great number of vassals were expelled, because they could not pay the great rents to the ancient chiefs of the clans. Some died of hunger, others became fishermen, others emigrated. There was general despair.

Among all these the Glenarvans alone believed that fidelity bound the high as well as the low, and they remained faithful to their tenants. Not one left the roof under which he was born; not one abandoned the soil where his ancestors reposed; all continued in the clan of their ancient lords. Thus at this epoch, in this age of disaffection and disunion, the Glenarvan family considered the Scots at Malcolm Castle as their own people. All were descended from the vassals of their kinsmen; were children of the counties of Stirling and Dumbarton, and honestly devoted, body and estate, to their master.

Lord Glenarvan possessed an immense fortune, which he employed in doing much good. His kindness exceeded even his generosity, for one was boundless, while the other was necessarily limited. The lord of Luss, the "laird" of Malcolm, represented his fellows in the House of Lords; but with true Scottish ideas, little pleasing to the southrons, he was disliked by many of them especially because he adhered to the traditions of his ancestors, and energetically opposed some dicta of modern political economy.

He was not, however, a backward man, either in wit or shrewdness; but while ready to enter every door of progress, he remained Scotch at heart, and it was for the glory of his native land that he contended with his racing yachts in the matches of the Royal Thames Yacht Club.

Lord Edward Glenarvan was thirty-two years old. His form was erect and his features sharp, but his look was mild, and his character thoroughly imbued with the poetry of the Highlands. He was known to be brave to excess, enterprising, chivalrous, a Fergus of the nineteenth century; but good above all, better than Saint Martin himself, for he would have given his very cloak to the poor people of the Highlands.

He had been married scarcely three months, having espoused Miss Helena Tuffnel, daughter of the great traveler, William Tuffnel, one of the numerous victims to the great passion for geographical discoveries.

Miss Helena did not belong to a noble family, but she was Scotch, which equaled all nobilities in the eyes of Lord Glenarvan. This charming young creature, high-minded and devoted, the lord of Luss had made the companion of his life. He found her one day living alone, an orphan, almost without fortune, in the house of her father at Kilpatrick. He saw that the poor girl would make a noble wife, and he married her.

Miss Tuffnel was twenty-two, a youthful blonde, with eyes as blue as the waters of the Scotch lakes on a beautiful morning in spring. Her love for her husband exceeded even her gratitude. She loved him as if she had been the rich heiress, and he the friendless orphan. As to their tenants and servants, they were ready to lay down their lives for her whom they called "our good lady of Luss."

Lord and Lady Glenarvan lived happily at Malcolm Castle, in the midst of the grand and wild scenery of the Highlands, rambling in the shady alleys of horse-chestnuts and sycamores, along the shores of the lake, where still resounded the war cries of ancient times, or in the depths of those uncultivated gorges in which the history of Scotland lies written in ruins from age to age. One day they would wander in the forests of beeches and larches, and in the midst of the masses of heather; another, they would scale the precipitous summits of Ben Lomond, or traverse on horseback the solitary glens, studying, comprehending, and admiring this poetic country, still called "the land of Rob Roy," and all those celebrated sites so grandly sung by Walter Scott.

In the sweet, still evening, when the "lantern of Mac Farlane" illumined the horizon, they would stroll along the "bartizans," an old circular balcony that formed a chain of battlements to Malcolm Castle, and there, pensive, oblivious, and as if alone in the world, seated on some detached rock, under the pale rays of the moon, while night gradually enveloped the rugged summits of the mountains, they would continue wrapt in that pure ecstasy and inward delight known only to loving hearts.

Thus passed the first months of their married life. But Lord Glenarvan did not forget that his wife was the daughter of a great traveler. He thought that Lady Helena must have in her heart all the aspirations of her father, and he was not mistaken. The Duncan was constructed, and was designed to convey Lord and Lady Glenarvan to the most beautiful countries of the world, along the waves of the Mediterranean, and to the isles of the Archipelago. Imagine the joy of Lady Helena when her husband placed the Duncan at her disposal! Indeed, can there be a greater happiness than to lead your love towards those charming "isles where Sappho sung," and behold the enchanting scenes of the Orient, with all their spirit-stirring memories?

Meantime Lord Glenarvan had started for London. The safety of the unfortunate shipwrecked men was at stake. Thus, in his temporary absence, Lady Helena showed herself more anxious than sad. The next day a dispatch from her husband made her hope for a speedy return; in the evening a letter hinted at its postponement. His proposal had to encounter some difficulties, and the following day a second letter came, in which Lord Glenarvan did not conceal his indignation against the authorities.

On that day Lady Helena began to be uneasy. At evening she was alone in her chamber, when the steward of the castle, Mr. Halbert, came to ask if she would see a young girl and boy who desired to speak with Lord Glenarvan.

"People of the country?" asked Lady Helena.

"No, madam," replied the steward, "for I do not know them. They have just arrived by the Balloch railway, and from Balloch to Luss they tell me they have made the journey on foot."

"Bid them come up, steward," said Lady Glenarvan.

The steward withdrew. Some moments afterward the young girl and boy were ushered into Lady Helena's chamber. They were brother and sister; you could not doubt it by their resemblance.

The sister was sixteen. Her pretty face showed weariness, her eyes must have shed many tears; her resigned, but courageous, countenance, and her humble, but neat, attire, all prepossessed one in her favor. She held by the hand a boy of twelve years, of determined look, who seemed to take his sister under his protection. Indeed, whoever had insulted the young girl would have had to settle with this little gentleman.

The sister stopped, a little surprised at seeing herself before Lady Helena; but the latter hastened to open the conversation.

"You wish to speak with me?" said she, with an encouraging look at the young girl.

"No," answered the boy, in a decided tone; "not with you, but with Lord Glenarvan himself."

"Excuse him, madam," said the sister, looking at her brother.

"Lord Glenarvan is not at the castle," replied Lady Helena; "but I am his wife, and if I can supply his place with you—"

"You are Lady Glenarvan?" said the young girl.

"Yes, miss."

"The wife of Lord Glenarvan, of Malcolm Castle, who published an advertisement in the *Times* in regard to the shipwreck of the Britannia?"

"Yes, yes!" answered Lady Helena, with alacrity. "And you?"

"I am Miss Grant, and this is my brother."

"Miss Grant! Miss Grant!" cried Lady Helena, drawing the young girl towards her, and taking her hands, while she also drew the boy towards her.

"Madam," replied the young girl, "what do you know of the shipwreck of my father? Is he living? Shall we ever see him again? Speak! oh, please tell me!"

"My dear child," said Lady Helena, "God forbid that I should answer you lightly on such a subject; I would not give you a vain hope—"

"Please, madam, speak! I am strong against grief, and can hear all."

"My dear child," answered Lady Helena, "the hope is very slight, but with the help of God who can do everything, it is possible that you will one day see your father again."

"Alas, alas!" exclaimed Miss Grant, who could not restrain her tears, while Robert covered the hands of Lady Glenarvan with kisses.

When the first paroxysm of this mournful joy was past, the young girl began to ask innumerable questions. Lady Helena related the story of the document, how that the Britannia had been lost on the shores of Patagonia; in what way, after the shipwreck, the captain and two sailors, the only survivors, must have reached the continent; and, at last, how they implored the assistance of the whole world in this document, written in three languages, and abandoned to the caprices of the ocean.

During this recital Robert Grant devoured Lady Helena with his eyes; his life seemed to hang on her lips. In his childish imagination he reviewed the terrible scenes of which his father must have been the victim. He saw him on the deck of the Britannia; he followed him to the bosom of the waves; he clung with him to the rocks of the shore; he dragged himself panting along the beach, out of reach of the waves.

Often during the course of this narration words escaped his lips.

"Oh, papa! my poor papa!" he cried, pressing close to his sister.

As for Miss Grant, she listened with clasped hands, and did not utter a word until the story was ended, when she said,—

"Oh, madam, the document! the document!"

"I no longer have it, my dear child," replied Lady Helena.

"You no longer have it?"

"No; for the very sake of your father, Lord Glenarvan had to take it to London; but I have told you all it contained, word for word, and how we succeeded in discovering the exact meaning. Among these remains of the almost effaced words the water had spared some characters. Unfortunately the record of the longitude had altogether been destroyed, but that was the only missing point. Thus you see, Miss Grant, the minutest details of this document are known to you as well as me."

"Yes, madam," replied the young girl; "but I would like to have seen my father's writing."

"Well, to-morrow, perhaps, Lord Glenarvan will return. My husband desired to submit this indisputable document to the authorities in London, to induce them to send a vessel immediately in search of Captain Grant."

"Is it possible, madam!" cried the young girl. "Did you do this for us?"

"Yes, my dear miss, and I expect Lord Glenarvan every moment."

"Madam," said the young girl, in a deep tone of gratitude, and with fervency, "may Heaven bless Lord Glenarvan and you!"

"Dear child," answered Lady Helena, "we deserve no thanks. Any other person in our place would have done the same. May the hopes that are kindled be realized! Till Lord Glenarvan's return you will remain at the castle."

"Madam," said the young girl, "I would not presume on the sympathy you show to us strangers—"

"Strangers! Dear child, neither your brother nor you are strangers in this house; and I desire that Lord Glenarvan on his arrival should inform the children of Captain Grant of what is to be attempted to save their father."

It was not possible to refuse an invitation made with so much cordiality. It was, therefore, decided that Miss Grant and her brother should await at Malcolm Castle the return of Lord Glenarvan.

CHAPTER IV. LADY GLENARVAN'S PROPOSAL.

During this conversation, Lady Helena had not spoken of the fears expressed in her husband's letters concerning the reception of his petition by the London officials; nor was a word said in regard to the probable captivity of

Captain Grant among the Indians of South America. Why afflict these poor children with their father's situation, and check the hopes they had just conceived? It would not change matters. Lady Helena was, therefore, silent on this point, and, after satisfying all Miss Grant's inquiries, she questioned her concerning her life, and situation in the world in which she seemed to be the sole protectress of her brother. It was a simple and touching story, which still more increased Lady Glenarvan's sympathy for the young girl.

Mary and Robert Grant were the only children of Captain Harry Grant, whose wife had died at the birth of Robert, and during his long voyages his children were left to the care of his good old cousin. Captain Grant was a hardy sailor, a man well acquainted with his profession, and a good negotiator, combining thus a twofold aptitude for his calling commercially. His home was at Dundee, in the county of Forfar, and he was moreover, by birth, a child of that "bonnie" place. His father, a minister of Saint Catherine's Church, had given him a thorough education, knowing that it would be sure to help all, even a sea-captain.

During his early voyages, first as mate, and afterwards in the capacity of skipper, Harry Grant prospered, and some years after the birth of his son Robert, he found himself the possessor of a considerable fortune.

Then a great idea entered his mind which made his name popular throughout Scotland. Like the Glenarvans and several other great families of the Highlands, he was opposed in heart, if not in deed, to the advance and prevalence of English thought and feeling. The interests of his country could not be in his eyes the same as those of the Anglo-Saxons, and, in order to give the former a peculiar and national development, he resolved to found a Scottish colony in some part of the Southern World. Did he dream of that independence in the future of which the United States had set the example, and which the Indies and Australia cannot fail one day to acquire? Very likely; but he allowed his secret hopes to be divined. It was, therefore, known that the Government refused to lend their aid in his project of colonization; nay, they even raised obstacles which in any other country would have overcome the project.

But Harry Grant would not be discouraged. He appealed to the patriotism of his countrymen, gave his fortune to serve the cause, built a vessel and furnished it with a fine crew, confided his children to the care of his old cousin, and set sail to explore the great islands of the Pacific.

It was the year 1861. Until May, 1862, they had received news of him, but since his departure from Callao, in the month of June, no one had heard anything of the Britannia, and the marine intelligencers became silent concerning the fate of the captain.

At this juncture of affairs the old cousin of Harry Grant died, and the two children were left alone in the world. Mary Grant was then fourteen. Her courageous soul did not flinch at the situation that was presented, but she devoted herself entirely to her brother, who was still a child. She must bring him up and instruct him. By dint of economy, prudence, and sagacity, laboring night and day, sacrificing all for him, denying herself everything, the sister succeeded in educating her brother and bravely fulfilled her sisterly duties.

The two children lived thus at Dundee, and valiantly overcame their sorrowful and lonely circumstances. Mary thought only of her brother, and dreamed of a happy future for him. As for herself, alas! the Britannia was lost forever, and her father dead! We must not, therefore, attempt to depict her emotion when the advertisement in the *Times* accidentally met her eye, and suddenly raised her from her despair.

It was no time to hesitate. Her resolution was immediately taken. Even if she should learn that her father's dead body had been found on a desert coast, or in the hull of a shipwrecked vessel, it was better than this continual doubt, this eternal torment of uncertainty. She told her brother all; and the same day the two children took the Perth Railroad, and at evening arrived at Malcolm Castle, where Mary, after so many harassing thoughts, began to hope.

Such was the sorrowful story that the young girl related to Lady Glenarvan, in an artless manner, without thinking that through all those long years of trial she had behaved herself like an heroic daughter. But Lady Helena thought of this, and several times, without hiding her tears, she clasped in her arms the two children of Captain Grant.

As for Robert, it seemed as if he heard this story for the first time: for he opened his eyes in astonishment, as he listened to his sister; comprehended what she had done, what she had suffered; and at last, encircling her with his arms, he exclaimed, unable longer to restrain the cry that came from the very depths of his heart,—

"Oh, mamma! my dear mamma!"

Night had now fully set in; and Lady Helena, remembering the fatigue of the two children, would not longer continue the conversation. Mary and Robert were conducted to their chambers, and fell asleep dreaming of a brighter future.

After they had retired, Lady Helena saw the major, and told him all the events of the day.

"That Mary Grant is a brave girl," said MacNabb, when he had heard his cousin's story.

"May Heaven grant my husband success in his enterprise!" replied Lady Helena; "for the situation of the two children would be terrible!"

"He will succeed," answered MacNabb, "or the hearts of the authorities must be harder than the stone of Portland."

In spite of the major's assurance, Lady Helena passed the night in the greatest anxiety, and could scarce gain an hour's repose.

The next morning Mary and her brother rose at daybreak, and were walking in the galleries and water terraces of the castle, when the sound of a coach was heard in the great court-yard. It was Lord Glenarvan returning to Malcolm Castle at the full speed of his horses. Almost immediately Lady Helena, accompanied by the major, appeared in the court-yard, and flew to meet her husband. But he seemed sad, disappointed, and angry. He clasped his wife in his arms, and was silent.

"Well, Edward!" she exclaimed.

"Well, my dear Helena," he replied, "those people have no hearts!"

"They refused?"

"Yes, they refused me a vessel: they spoke of the millions vainly spent in searching for Franklin; they declared the document was vague and unintelligible; they said that the shipwreck of these unfortunates had happened two years ago, and that there was little chance of finding them. They maintained too, that, if prisoners of the Indians, they must have been carried into the interior of the country; that they could not ransack all Patagonia to find three men,—three Scotchmen; the search would be vain and perilous, and would cost the lives of more men than it would save. In short, they gave all the absurd reasons of people who mean to refuse. They remembered the captain's projects, and I fear that the unfortunate man is forever lost!"

"My father, my poor father!" cried Mary Grant, throwing herself at the feet of Lord Glenarvan.

"Your father! What, Miss—?" said he, surprised at seeing a young girl at his feet.

"Yes, Edward, Miss Grant and her brother," replied Lady Helena; "the two children of Captain Grant, who have thus been condemned to remain orphans."

"Ah, miss!" answered Lord Glenarvan, "if I had known of your presence—"

He said no more. A painful silence, interrupted only by sobs, reigned in the court-yard. No one raised his voice, neither Lord Glenarvan, Lady Helena, the major, nor the servants of the castle, who were standing about even at this early hour. But by their attitude they all protested against the conduct of the officials.

After several moments the major resumed the conversation, and, addressing Lord Glenarvan, said,—"Then you have no more hope?"

"None."

"Well," cried young Robert, "I will go to these people, and—we shall see—"

He did not finish his threat, for his sister stopped him; but his clinched hands indicated his intentions.

"No, Robert," said she, "no; let us thank these kind people for what they have done for us. Let us always keep them in remembrance; but now we must take our departure."

"Mary!" cried Lady Helena.

"Miss, where would you go?" said Lord Glenarvan.

"I am going to throw myself at the feet of the Queen," replied the young girl, "and we shall see if she will be deaf to the prayers of two children imploring help for their father."

Lord Glenarvan shook his head; not that he doubted the clemency of Her Gracious Majesty, but he doubted whether Mary Grant would gain access to her; for but few suppliants reach the steps of a throne.

Lady Helena understood her husband's thoughts. She knew that the young girl might make a fruitless journey, and she pictured to herself these two children leading henceforth a cheerless existence. Then it was that she conceived a grand and noble idea.

"Mary Grant," she exclaimed, "wait, my child; listen to what I am about to say."

The young girl held her brother by the hand, and was preparing to go. She stopped.

Then Lady Helena, with tearful eye, but firm voice and animated features, advanced towards her husband.

"Edward," said she, "when Captain Grant wrote that letter, and cast it into the sea, he confided it to the care of God himself, who has brought it to us. Without doubt He designed to charge us with the safety of these unfortunates."

"What do you mean, Helena?" inquired Lord Glenarvan, whilst all waited in silence.

"I mean," replied Lady Helena, "that we ought to consider ourselves happy in beginning our married life with a good action. You, my dear Edward, to please me, have planned a pleasure voyage. But what pleasure can be more genuine or more beneficent than to save these unfortunates whom hope has almost abandoned?"

"Helena!" cried Lord Glenarvan.

"Yes, you understand me, Edward. The Duncan is a good, staunch vessel. It can brave the Southern seas; it can make the tour of the world,—and it will, if necessary! Let us start, Edward,—let us go in search of Captain Grant!"

At these courageous words Lord Glenarvan had extended his arms to his wife. He smiled. He pressed her to his heart, while Mary and Robert kissed her hands.

And during this touching scene the servants of the castle, affected and enthusiastic, uttered from their hearts this cry of gratitude,—

"Hurrah for the lady of Luss! Hurrah! three times hurrah, for Lord and Lady Glenarvan!"

CHAPTER V. THE DEPARTURE OF THE DUNCAN.

It has been already said that Lady Helena had a brave and generous soul. What she had just done was an undeniable proof of it, and Lord Glenarvan had good reason to trust in this noble woman, who was capable of comprehending and following him. The idea of sailing to the rescue of Captain Grant had already taken possession of him when he saw his petition rejected at London; but he could not have thought of separating from her. Yet, since she desired to go herself, all hesitation was at an end. The servants of the castle had received her proposal with cries of joy; the safety of their brother Scots was at stake, and Lord Glenarvan joined heartily in the hurrahs that greeted the lady of Luss.

The scheme once resolved upon, there was not an hour to lose. That very day Lord Glenarvan sent to Captain Mangles orders to bring the Duncan to Glasgow, and make every preparation for a voyage to the South Seas, which might become one of circumnavigation. Moreover, in her plans Lady Helena had not overestimated the qualities of the Duncan: of first-class construction with regard to strength and swiftness, she could without injury sustain a long voyage.

The Duncan was a steam yacht of one hundred and ten tons burden. She had two masts,—a foremast with fore-sail, main-sail, foretop and foretop-gallant sails; and a mainmast, carrying a main-sail and fore-staff. Her rigging was, therefore, sufficient, and she could profit by the wind like a simple clipper; but she relied especially upon her mechanical power. Her engine was of an effective force of one hundred and sixty horse power, and was constructed on a new plan. It possessed apparatus for overheating, which gave its steam a very great tension. It was a high-pressure engine, and produced motion by a double screw. The Duncan under full steam could acquire a speed equal to any vessel of that day. Indeed, during her trial trip in the Frith of Clyde, she had made, according to the log, seventeen knots an hour. She was, therefore, fully capable of circumnavigating the world; and her captain had only to occupy himself with the internal arrangement.

His first care was to increase his store-room, and take in the greatest possible quantity of coal, for it would be difficult to renew their supplies on the voyage. The same precaution was taken with the steward's room, and provisions for two years were stowed away. Money, of course, was not wanting, and a pivot-gun was furnished, which was fixed at the forecastle. You do not know what may happen, and it is always best to have the means of defense in your reach.

Captain Mangles, we must say, understood his business. Although he commanded only a pleasure yacht, he was ranked among the ablest of the Glasgow captains. He was thirty years of age, with rather rough features, indicating courage and kindness. When a child, the Glenarvan family had taken him under their care, and made him an excellent seaman. He had often given proofs of skill, energy, and coolness during his long voyages, and when Lord Glenarvan offered him the command of the Duncan, he accepted it with pride and pleasure, for he loved the lord of Malcolm Castle as a brother, and until then had vainly sought an opportunity to devote himself to his service.

The mate, Tom Austin, was an old sailor worthy of all confidence; and the crew of the Duncan was composed of twenty-five men, including the captain and mate. They all belonged to the county of Dumbarton, were all tried seamen, sons of the tenants of the family, and formed on shipboard a genuine clan of honest people, who of course were not without the national bagpipe. Lord Glenarvan had, in them, a band of faithful subjects, happy in their avocation, devoted, courageous, and skillful in the use of arms, as well as in the management of a ship, while they were ready to follow him on the most perilous expeditions. When they learned where they were going, they could not restrain their joyous emotion, and the echoes of the rocks of Dumbarton awoke to their cries of enthusiasm.

Captain Mangles, while occupied in lading and provisioning his craft, did not forget to prepare Lord and Lady Glenarvan's apartments for a long voyage. He likewise provided cabins for Captain Grant's children, for Lady Helena could not refuse Mary permission to accompany her on the expedition.

As for young Robert, he would have hidden in the hold sooner than not go; even if he had been compelled to serve as cabin-boy, like Lord Nelson and Sir John Franklin, he would have embarked on board the Duncan. To think of opposing such a little gentleman! It was not attempted. They were even obliged to take him other than as passenger, for as cabin-boy or sailor he *would serve*. The captain was accordingly commissioned to teach him the duties of a seaman.

"Good!" said Robert; "and let him not spare a few blows of the rope's end if I do not walk straight."

"Be easy, my boy," replied Glenarvan, without adding that the use of the "cat-o'-nine-tails" was prohibited, and moreover quite needless, on board the Duncan.

To complete the roll of the passengers, it will be sufficient to describe Major MacNabb. The major was a man of fifty, of calm, regular features, who did as he was bid; of an excellent and superior character, modest, taciturn, peaceable, and mild; always agreeing with anything or any one, disputing nothing, and neither contradicting himself nor exaggerating. He would mount with measured step the staircase to his bed-chamber, even were a cannon-ball behind him; and probably to his dying day would never find an opportunity to fly into a passion.

This man possessed, in a high degree, not only the common courage of the battle-field (that physical bravery due only to nervous strength), but, better still, moral courage, that is to say, firmness of soul. If he had a fault, it was that of being absolutely Scotch from head to foot, a pure-blooded Caledonian, an infatuated observer of the ancient customs of his country. Through his relationship to the Glenarvans he lived at Malcolm Castle; and as major and military man it was very natural that he should be found on board the Duncan.

Such, then, were the passengers of this yacht, summoned by unforeseen circumstances to accomplish one of the most surprising voyages of modern times. Since her arrival at the wharf at Glasgow, she had monopolized the public attention. A considerable number came every day to visit her. They were interested in her alone, and spoke only of her, to the great umbrage of the other captains of the port, among others Captain Burton, commanding the Scotia, a magnificent steamer, moored beside the Duncan, and bound for Calcutta. The Scotia, from her size, had a right to consider the Duncan as a mere fly-boat. Nevertheless, all the attraction centred in Lord Glenarvan's yacht, and increased from day to day.

The time of departure approached. Captain Mangles had shown himself skillful and expeditious. A month after her trial trip in the Frith of Clyde, the

Duncan, laden, provisioned, and equipped, was ready to put to sea. The 25th of August was appointed for the time of departure, which would enable the yacht to reach the southern latitudes by the beginning of spring. Lord Glenarvan, when his plan was matured, did not neglect to make investigations into the hardships and perils of the voyage; yet he did not hesitate on this account, but prepared to leave Malcolm Castle.

On the 24th of August, Lord and Lady Glenarvan, Major MacNabb, Mary and Robert Grant, Mr. Olbinett, the steward of the yacht, and his wife, who was in the service of Lady Glenarvan, left the castle, after taking an affectionate farewell of their family servants. Several hours afterward they found themselves on board. Many of the population of Glasgow welcomed with sympathetic admiration the young and courageous lady who renounced the pleasures of a life of luxury, and sailed to the rescue of the shipwrecked sailors.

The apartments of Lord Glenarvan and his wife occupied the entire stern of the vessel. They consisted of two bed-chambers, a parlor, and two dressing-rooms, adjoining which was an open square inclosed by six cabins, five of which were occupied by Mary and Robert Grant, Mr. and Mrs. Olbinett, and Major MacNabb. As for the cabins of the captain and the mate, they were situated in the forecastle, and opened on the deck. The crew were lodged between-decks very comfortably, for the yacht of course carried nothing but her coal, provisions, and armament.

The Duncan was to start on the night of the 24th, as the tide fell at three o'clock in the morning. But first those who were present were witness to a touching scene. At eight in the evening Lord Glenarvan and his companions, the entire crew, from the firemen to the captain, all who were to take part in this voyage of sacrifice, left the yacht, and betook themselves to Saint Mungo, the ancient cathedral of Glasgow. This antique church, an uninjured relic in the midst of the ruins caused by the Reformation, and so marvelously described by Walter Scott, received beneath its massive arches the owners and sailors of the Duncan.

A numerous throng accompanied them. There in the spacious aisle, filled with tombs of the great and good, the Rev. Mr. Morton implored the blessing of Heaven, and commended the expedition to the care of Providence. For a moment the voice of Mary Grant arose in the old church. The young girl was praying for her benefactors, and shedding before God the sweet tears of gratitude. The assembly retired under the influence of a deep emotion.

At eleven, every one was on board. The captain and the crew occupied themselves with the final preparations. At midnight the fires were kindled, and soon clouds of black smoke mingled with the vapors of the night; the sails of the Duncan had been carefully reefed in a canvas sheathing, which served to protect them from injury. The wind blew from the southeast, and did not favor the progress of the vessel; but at two o'clock the ship began to heave under the action of her boilers. The manometer indicated a pressure of four atmospheres, and the overheated steam whistled through the escape-valves. The sea was tranquil, and soon daylight enabled them to distinguish the passes of the Clyde between the buoys and beacons, whose lights were gradually extinguished as the morning dawned.

Captain Mangles informed Lord Glenarvan, who at once came on deck. Very soon the ebb-tide was felt. The Duncan gave a few shrill whistles, slackened her cables, and separated from the surrounding vessels. Her screw was set in motion, which propelled her into the channel of the river. The captain had taken no pilot. He was perfectly acquainted with the navigation of the Clyde, and no one could have commanded better. At a sign from him the yacht started. With his right hand he controlled the engine, and with his left the tiller, with silent but unerring skill.Soon the last workshops on the shore gave place to villas, built here and there upon the hills, and the sounds of the city died away in the distance. An hour afterwards, the Duncan passed the rocks of Dumbarton; two hours later she was in the Frith of Clyde; and at six o'clock in the morning she doubled Cantyre Point, emerged from the North Channel, and gained the open sea.

CHAPTER VI. AN UNEXPECTED PASSENGER.

During the first day's voyage the sea was quite rough, and the wind freshened towards evening. The Duncan rolled considerably, so that the ladies did not appear on deck, but very wisely remained in their cabins. The next day the wind changed a point, and the captain set the main-, fore-, and foretop-sails, thus causing less perception of the rolling and pitching motion.

Lady Helena and Mary Grant were able before daybreak to join Lord Glenarvan, the major, and the captain, on deck. The sunrise was magnificent. The orb of day, like a gilded metal disk, rose from the ocean, as from an immense and silvery basin. The ship glided in the midst of a splendid iridescence, and you would truly have thought that her sails expanded under the influence of the sun's rays, whilst even the crew of the yacht silently admired this reappearance of the orb of day.

"What a magnificent spectacle!" said Lady Helena, at last. "This is the beginning of a beautiful day. May the wind not prove contrary, but favor the progress of the Duncan!"

"No better weather could be desired, my dear Helena," replied Lord Glenarvan; "we have no reason to complain of the commencement of the voyage."

"Will it be a long one, my dear Edward?"

"That is for the captain to answer," said he. "Are we progressing well? Are you satisfied with your vessel, captain?"

"Very well indeed," was the answer. "She is a marvelous craft, and a sailor likes to feel her under his feet. Never were hull and engine more in unison. See how smooth her wake is, and how easily she rides the waves. We are moving at the rate of seventeen knots an hour. If this continues, we shall cross the line in ten days, and in five weeks shall double Cape Horn."

"You hear, Mary," said Lady Helena: "in five weeks!"

"Yes," replied the young girl, "I hear; and my heart beat quickly at the words of the captain."

"And how do you bear this voyage, Miss Mary?" inquired Lord Glenarvan.

"Very well, my lord; I do not experience very many discomforts. Besides, I shall soon be accustomed to it."

"And young Robert?"

"Oh, Robert!" replied Captain Mangles: "when he is not engaged with the engine he is perched at mast-head. I tell you he is a boy who mocks sea-sickness. Only look at him!"

At a gesture of the captain, all eyes were turned towards the mainmast, and every one could perceive Robert, suspended by the stays of the foretop-gallant sail, a hundred feet aloft. Mary could not restrain a motion of fear.

"Oh, be easy, miss!" said Captain Mangles. "I will answer for him, and promise you I will present, in a short time, a famous sailor to Captain Grant; for we shall find that worthy captain."

"May Heaven hear you, sir!" replied the young girl.

"My dear child," said Lord Glenarvan, "there is in all this something providential, which ought to give us hope. We are not merely going, we are led; we are not seeking blindly, we are guided. And then see all these brave people enrolled in the service of so good a cause. Not only shall we succeed in our enterprise, but it will be accomplished without difficulty. I have promised Lady Helena a pleasure voyage; and, if I am not mistaken, I shall keep my word."

"Edward," said Lady Glenarvan, "you are the best of men."

"Not so; but I have the best of crews, on the best of ships. Do you not wonder at our Duncan, Miss Mary?"

"On the contrary, my lord," answered the young girl, "I don't so much wonder as admire; for I am well acquainted with ships."

"Ah! indeed!"

"When a mere child, I played on my father's ships. He ought to have made a sailor of me. If it were necessary, perhaps I should not now be embarrassed in taking a reef or twisting a gasket."

"What is that you're saying, miss?" exclaimed the captain.

"If you talk so," continued Lord Glenarvan, "you will make a great friend of Captain John; for he thinks nothing in the world can equal the life of a sailor. He sees no other, even for a woman. Is it not so, John?"

"Undoubtedly, your lordship," replied the young captain; "and yet, I confess, Miss Grant is better in her place on deck, than taking a reef in the top-sail. But still I am very much flattered to hear her speak so."

"And especially when she admires the Duncan!" added Glenarvan.

"Right, my lord; for she deserves it."

"Upon my word," said Lady Helena, "since you are so proud of your yacht, you make me anxious to examine her to the very hold, and see how our brave sailors are quartered between-decks."

"Admirably," replied the captain; "they are quite at home there."

"Indeed they are, my dear Helena," said Lord Glenarvan. "This yacht is a part of our old Caledonia,—a detached portion of the county of Dumbarton, traveling by special favor, so that we have not left our country. The Duncan is Malcolm Castle, and the ocean is Loch Lomond."

"Well, then, my dear Edward, do the honors of the castle," said Lady Helena.

"I am at your disposal, madam," answered her husband; "but first let me inform Olbinett."

The steward of the yacht was an excellent manager, a Scotchman, who deserved to have been a Frenchman from his self-importance, and, moreover, fulfilled his duties with zeal and intelligence. He was at once ready for his master's commands.

"Olbinett, we are going to make a tour of the vessel before breakfast," said Glenarvan, as if a journey to Tarbet or Loch Katrine was in question. "I hope we shall find the table ready on our return."

Olbinett bowed gravely.

"Do you accompany us, major?" asked Lady Helena.

"If you order it," replied MacNabb.

"Oh!" said Lord Glenarvan, "the major is absorbed in the smoke of his cigar; we must not disturb him, for I assure you he is an inveterate smoker, Miss Mary; he smokes all the time, even in his sleep."

The major made a sign of assent, and the passengers descended between-decks.

MacNabb remained alone, talking to himself, according to his custom, but never contradicting himself. Enveloped in a dense cloud of smoke, he stood motionless, gazing back at the wake of the yacht. After a few moments of contemplation, he turned and found himself face to face with a new character. If *anything* could have surprised him, it must have been this meeting, for the passenger was absolutely unknown to him.

This man, tall, lank, and shriveled, might have been forty years old. He resembled a long, broad-headed nail, for his head was large and thick, his forehead high, his nose prominent, his mouth wide, and his chin blunt. As for his eyes, they were hidden behind enormous eye-glasses, and his look seemed to have that indecision peculiar to nyctalops. His countenance indicated an intelligent and lively person, while it had not the crabbed air of those stern people who from principle never laugh, and whose stupidity is hidden beneath a serious guise. The nonchalance and amiable freedom of this unknown nonentity clearly proved that he knew how to take men and things at their best advantage. Even without his speaking you felt that he was a talker; but he was abstracted, after the manner of those who do not see what they are looking at or hear what they are listening to. He wore a traveling cap, stout yellow buskins and leather gaiters, pantaloons of maroon velvet, and a jacket of the same material, whose innumerable pockets seemed stuffed with note-books, memoranda, scraps, portfolios, and a thousand articles as inconvenient as they were useless, not to speak of a telescope which he carried in a sling.

The curiosity of this unknown being was a singular contrast to the calmness of the major. He walked around MacNabb, and gazed at him questioningly, whilst the latter did not trouble himself whence the stranger came, whither he was going, or why he was on board the Duncan.

When this enigmatical character saw his approaches mocked by the indifference of the major, he seized his telescope, which at its full length measured four feet; and motionless, with legs straddled, like a sign-post on a highway, he pointed his instrument to the line where sky and water met. After a few moments of examination, he lowered it, and resting it on the deck, leaned upon it as upon a cane. But immediately the joints of the instrument closed, and the newly discovered passenger, whose point of support suddenly failed, was stretched at the foot of the mainmast.

Any one else in the major's place would at least have smiled, but he did not even wink. The unknown then assumed his rôle.

"Steward!" he cried, with an accent that betokened a foreigner.

He waited. No one appeared.

"Steward!" he repeated, in a louder tone.

Mr. Olbinett was passing just then on his way to the kitchen under the forecastle. What was his astonishment to hear himself thus addressed by this tall individual, who was utterly unknown to him!

"Where did this person come from?" said he to himself. "A friend of Lord Glenarvan? It is impossible."

However, he came on deck, and approached the stranger.

"Are you the steward of the vessel?" the latter asked him.

"Yes, sir," replied Olbinett; "but I have not the honor—"

"I am the passenger of cabin number six."

"Number six?" repeated the steward.

"Certainly; and your name is—?"

"Olbinett."

"Well, Olbinett, my friend," answered the stranger of cabin number six, "I must think of dinner, and acutely, too. For thirty-six hours I have eaten nothing, or, rather, have slept, which is pardonable in a man come all the way from Paris to Glasgow. What hour do you dine, if you please?"

"At nine o'clock," answered Olbinett, mechanically.

The stranger attempted to consult his watch; but this took some time, for he did not find it till he came to his ninth pocket.

"Well," said he, "it is not yet eight o'clock; therefore, Olbinett, a biscuit and a glass of sherry for the present; for I am fainting with hunger."

Olbinett listened without understanding. Moreover, the unknown kept talking, and passed from one subject to another with extreme volubility.

"Well," said he, "has not the captain risen yet? And the mate? What is he doing? Is he asleep, too? Fortunately, the weather is beautiful, the wind favorable, and the ship goes on quite by herself—"

Just as he said this, Captain Mangles appeared at the companion-way.

"Here is the captain," said Olbinett.

"Ah, I am delighted," cried the stranger, "delighted to make your acquaintance, Captain Burton!"

If any one was ever astounded, John Mangles certainly was, not less at hearing himself called "Captain Burton," than at seeing this stranger on board his vessel.

The latter continued, with more animation:

"Permit me to shake hands with you, and if I did not do so day before yesterday, it was that no one might be embarrassed at the moment of departure. But to-day, captain, I am truly happy to meet you."

Captain Mangles opened his eyes in measureless astonishment, looking first at Olbinett, and then at the new comer.

"Now," continued the latter, "the introduction is over, and we are old friends. Let us have a talk; and tell me, are you satisfied with the Scotia?"

"What do you mean by the Scotia?" asked the captain, at last.

"Why, the Scotia that carries us: a good ship, whose commander, the brave Captain Burton, I have heard praised no less for his physical than his moral qualities. Are you the father of the great African traveler of that name? If so, my compliments!"

"Sir," replied Captain Mangles, "not only am I not the father of the traveler Burton, but I am not even Captain Burton."

"Ah!" said the unknown, "it is the mate of the Scotia then, Mr. Burdness, whom I am addressing at this moment?"

"Mr. Burdness?" replied Captain Mangles, who began to suspect the truth. But was he talking to a fool, or a rogue? This was a question in his mind, and he was about to explain himself intelligibly, when Lord Glenarvan, his wife, and Miss Grant came on deck.

The stranger perceived them, and cried,—

"Ah! passengers! passengers! excellent! I hope, Mr. Burdness, you are going to introduce me—"

And advancing with perfect ease, without waiting for the captain,—

"Madam" said he to Miss Grant, "Miss" to Lady Helena, "Sir" he added, addressing Lord Glenarvan.

"Lord Glenarvan," said Captain Mangles.

"My lord," continued the unknown, "I beg your pardon for introducing myself, but at sea we must relax a little from etiquette. I hope we shall soon be acquainted, and that, in the society of these ladies, the passage of the Scotia will seem as short to us as agreeable."

Lady Helena and Miss Grant could not find a word to answer. They were completely bewildered by the presence of this intruder.

"Sir," said Glenarvan, at length, "whom have I the honor of addressing?"

"Jacques Eliacim François Marie Paganel, secretary of the Geographical Society of Paris; corresponding member of the societies of Berlin, Bombay, Darmstadt, Leipsic, London, St. Petersburg, Vienna, and New York; honorary member of the Royal Geographical and Ethnographical Institute of the East Indies, who, after passing twenty years of his life in studying geography, designs now to enter upon a roving life, and is directing his course to India to continue there the labors of the great travelers."

CHAPTER VII. JACQUES PAGANEL IS UNDECEIVED.

The secretary of the Geographical Society must have been an agreeable person, for all this was said with much modesty. Lord Glenarvan, moreover, knew perfectly whom he had met. The name and merit of Jacques Paganel were well known to him. His geographical labors, his reports on modern discoveries, published in the bulletins of the Society, his correspondence with the entire world, had made him one of the most distinguished scientific men of France. Thus Glenarvan extended his hand very cordially to his unexpected guest.

"And now that our introduction is over," added he, "will you permit me, Monsieur Paganel, to ask you a question?"

"Twenty, my lord," replied Jacques Paganel; "it will always be a pleasure to converse with you."

"You arrived on board this vessel the day before yesterday?"

"Yes, my lord, day before yesterday, at eight o'clock in the evening. I took a cab from the Caledonian Railway to the Scotia, in which I had engaged cabin number six at Paris. The night was dark. I saw no one on board. Feeling fatigued by thirty hours of travel, and knowing that a good way to avoid sea-sickness is to go to bed on embarking, and not stir from your bunk for the first days of the voyage, I retired immediately, and have conscientiously slept thirty-six hours, I assure you."

Jacques Paganel's hearers now knew the reason of his presence on board. The Frenchman, mistaking the vessel, had embarked while the crew of the Duncan were engaged in the ceremony at Saint Mungo. Everything was explained. But what would the geographer say, when he learned the name and destination of the vessel on which he had taken passage?

"So, Monsieur Paganel," said Glenarvan, "you have chosen Calcutta as your centre of action?"

"Yes, my lord. To see India is an idea that I have cherished all my life. It is my brightest dream, which shall be realized at last in the country of the elephants and the Thugs."

"Then you would not care to visit another country?"

"No, my lord; it would be even disagreeable, for I have letters from Lord Somerset to the governor-general of India, and a mission from the Geographical Society which I must fulfil."

"Ah! you have a mission?"

"Yes, a useful and curious voyage to undertake, the programme of which has been arranged by my scientific friend and colleague, M. Vivien de Saint Martin. It is to follow in the steps of the brothers Schlagintweit, and many other celebrated travelers. I hope to succeed where Missionary Krick unfortunately failed in 1846. In a word, I wish to discover the course of the Yaroo-tsang-bo-tsoo, which waters Thibet, and finally to settle whether this river does not join the Brahmapootra in the northeast part of Assam. A gold medal is promised to that traveler who shall succeed in supplying this much-needed information on Indian geography."

Paganel was grandiloquent. He spoke with a lofty animation, and was carried away in the rapid flight of imagination. It would have been as impossible to check him as to stay the Rhine at the Falls of Schaffhausen.

"Monsieur Jacques Paganel," said Lord Glenarvan, after a moment of silence, "that is certainly a fine voyage, and one for which science would be very grateful; but I will not further prolong your ignorance. For the present, you must give up the pleasure of seeing India."

"Give it up! And why?"

"Because you are turning your back upon the Indian peninsula."

"How? Captain Burton—"

"I am not Captain Burton," replied John Mangles.

"But the Scotia?"

"This vessel is not the Scotia."

Paganel's amazement cannot be depicted. He looked first at Lord Glenarvan, always serious; then at Lady Helena and Miss Grant, whose features expressed a sympathetic disappointment; and finally at Captain Mangles, who was smiling, and the imperturbable major. Then, raising his shoulders and drawing down his glasses from his forehead to his eyes, he exclaimed,—

"What a joke!"

But at that his eyes fell upon the steering wheel, on which were inscribed these two words, thus:

DUNCAN

GLASGOW.

"The Duncan! the Duncan!" he cried in a tone of real despair; and, leaping down the companion-way, he rushed to his cabin.

When the unfortunate geographer had disappeared, no one on board, except the major, could retain gravity, and the laugh was communicated even to the sailors. To mistake the railroad was not so bad; to take the train to Dumbarton, instead of Edinburgh, would do. But to mistake the vessel, and be sailing to Chili, when he wished to go to India, was the height of absent-mindedness.

"On the whole, I am not astonished at this on the part of Jacques Paganel," said Glenarvan; "he is noted for such blunders. He once published a celebrated map of America, in which he located Japan. However, he is a distinguished scholar, and one of the best geographers of France."

"But what are we going to do with the poor gentleman?" asked Lady Helena. "We cannot take him to Patagonia."

"Why not?" replied MacNabb gravely. "We are not responsible for his errors. Suppose he were in a railroad car, would it stop for him?"

"No; but he could get out at the first station," answered Lady Helena.

"Well," said Glenarvan, "he can do so now, if he pleases, at our first landing."

At this moment Paganel, woeful and humble, reappeared on deck, after convincing himself that his baggage was on board. He kept repeating those fatal words: "The Duncan! the Duncan!" He could find no others in his vocabulary. He went to and fro, examining the rigging of the yacht, and questioning the mute horizon of the open sea. At last he returned to Lord Glenarvan.

"And this Duncan is going—?" he asked.

"To America, Monsieur Paganel."

"And where especially?"

"To Concepcion."

"To Chili! to Chili!" cried the unfortunate geographer. "And my mission to India! But what will M. de Quatrefages say, the President of the Central Commission? How shall I represent myself at the sessions of the Society?"

"Come, monsieur," said Glenarvan, "do not despair. Everything can be arranged, and you will only have to submit to a delay of little consequence. The Yaroo-tsang-bo-tsoo will wait for you in the mountains of Thibet. We shall soon reach Madeira, and there you will find a vessel to take you back to Europe."

"I thank you, my lord, and must be resigned. But we can say this is an extraordinary adventure, which would not have happened but for me. And my cabin which is engaged on board the Scotia?"

"Oh, as for the Scotia, I advise you to give her up for the present."

"But," said Paganel after examining the vessel again, "the Duncan is a pleasure yacht."

"Yes, sir," replied Captain Mangles, "and belongs to his lordship, Lord Glenarvan—"

"Who begs you to make free use of his hospitality," said Glenarvan.

"A thousand thanks, my lord," replied Paganel; "I am truly sensible to your courtesy. But permit me to make a simple remark. India is a beautiful country. It offers marvelous surprises to travelers. These ladies have probably never visited it. Well, the man at the helm needs only to give a turn to the wheel, and the Duncan will go as easily to Calcutta as Concepcion. Now, since this is a pleasure voyage—"

The negative reception that met Paganel's proposal did not permit him to develop it. He paused.

"Monsieur Paganel," said Lady Helena at length, "if this were only a pleasure voyage, I would answer: 'Let us all go to India,' and Lord Glenarvan would not disapprove. But the Duncan is going to recover some shipwrecked sailors, abandoned on the coast of Patagonia; and she cannot change so humane a course."

In a few moments the Frenchman was acquainted with the situation of affairs, and learned, not without emotion, the providential discovery of the documents, the story of Captain Grant, and Lady Helena's generous proposal.

"Madam," said he, "permit me to admire your conduct in all this, and to admire it without reserve. May your yacht continue on her course; I would reproach myself for delaying her a single day."

"Will you then join in our search?" asked Lady Helena.

"It is impossible, madam; I must fulfil my mission. I shall disembark at your first landing."

"At Madeira then," said Captain Mangles.

"At Madeira let it be. I shall be only one hundred and eighty leagues from Lisbon, and will wait there for means of further conveyance."

"Well, Monsieur Paganel," said Glenarvan, "it shall be as you desire; and, for my part, I am happy that I can offer you for a few days the hospitalities of my vessel. May you not grow weary of our company."

"Oh, my lord," exclaimed the geographer, "I am still too happy in being so agreeably disappointed. However, it is a very ludicrous situation for a man who takes passage for India, and is sailing to America."

In spite of this mortifying reflection, Paganel made the best use of a delay that he could not avoid. He showed himself amiable, and even gay; he enchanted the ladies with his good humor, and before the end of the day he was the friend of every one. At his request the famous document was shown to him. He studied it carefully, long and minutely. No other interpretation appeared to him possible. Mary Grant and her brother inspired him with the liveliest interest. He gave them good hopes. His way of distinguishing the events, and the undeniable success that he predicted for the Duncan, elicited a smile from the young girl.

As to Lady Helena, when he learned that she was the daughter of William Tuffnel, there was an outburst of surprise and admiration. He had known her father. What a bold discoverer! How many letters they had exchanged when the latter was corresponding member of the Society! He it was who had introduced him to M. Malte-Brun. What a meeting! and how much pleasure to travel with the daughter of such a man! Finally, he asked Lady Helena's permission to kiss her, to which she consented, although it was perhaps a little "improper."

CHAPTER VIII. THE GEOGRAPHER'S RESOLUTION.

Meanwhile the yacht, favored by the currents, was advancing rapidly towards the equator. In a few days the island of Madeira came in view. Glenarvan, faithful to his promise, offered to land his new guest here.

"My dear lord," replied Paganel, "I will not be formal with you. Before my arrival on board, did you intend to stop at Madeira?"

"No," said Glenarvan.

"Well, permit me to profit by the consequences of my unlucky blunder. Madeira is an island too well known. Everything has been said and written about it; and it is, moreover, rapidly declining in point of civilization. If, then, it is all the same to you, let us land at the Canaries."

"Very well, at the Canaries," replied Glenarvan. "That will not take us out of our way."

"I know it, my dear lord. At the Canaries, you see, there are three groups to study, not to speak of the Peak of Teneriffe, which I have always desired to see. This is a fine opportunity. I will profit by it; and, while waiting for a vessel, will attempt the ascent of this celebrated mountain."

"As you please, my dear Paganel," replied Glenarvan, who could not help smiling, and with good reason.

The Canaries are only a short distance from Madeira, scarcely two hundred and fifty miles, a mere trifle for so good a vessel as the Duncan.

The same day, at two o'clock in the afternoon, Captain Mangles and Paganel were walking on the deck. The Frenchman pressed his companion with lively questions concerning Chili. All at once the captain interrupted him, and pointing towards the southern horizon, said,—

"Mr. Paganel!"

"My dear captain," replied the geographer.

"Please cast your eyes in that direction. Do you see nothing?"

"Nothing."

"You are not looking right. It is not on the horizon, but above, in the clouds."

"In the clouds? I look in vain."

"Stop, now, just on a line with the end of the bowsprit."

"I see nothing."

"You do not wish to see. However that may be, although we are forty miles distant, you understand, the Peak of Teneriffe is visible above the horizon."

Whether Paganel wished to see or not, he had to yield to the evidence some hours afterwards, or, at least, confess himself blind.

"You perceive it now?" said his companion.

"Yes, yes, perfectly!" replied Paganel. "And that," added he in a contemptuous tone, "is what you call the Peak of Teneriffe?"

"The same."

"It appears to be of very moderate height."

"Yet it is eleven thousand feet above the level of the sea."

"Not so high as Mont Blanc."

"Very possibly; but when you come to climb it, you will find it, perhaps, high enough."

"Oh! climb it, my dear captain? What is the use, I ask you, after Humboldt and Bonpland? What can I do after these great men?"

"Indeed," replied Captain Mangles, "there is nothing left but to wander about. It is a pity, for you would be very tired waiting for a vessel at Teneriffe. You cannot look for many distractions there."

"Except my own," said Paganel, laughing. "But, my dear captain, have not the Cape Verd Islands important landings?"

"Certainly. Nothing is easier than to land at Villa-Praïa."

"Not to speak of an advantage that is not to be despised," answered Paganel; "that the Cape Verd Islands are not far from Senegal, where I shall find fellow-countrymen."

"As you please, Mr. Paganel," replied Captain Mangles. "I am certain that geographical science will gain by your sojourn in these islands. We must land there to take in coal; you will, therefore, cause us no delay."

So saying, the captain gave the order to pass to the southeast of the Canaries. The celebrated peak was soon left on the larboard; and the Duncan, continuing her rapid course, cut the Tropic of Cancer the next morning at five o'clock. The weather there changed. The atmosphere had the moisture and oppressiveness of the rainy season, disagreeable to travelers, but beneficial to the inhabitants of the African islands, who have no trees, and consequently need water. The sea was boisterous, and prevented the passengers from remaining on deck; but the conversation in the cabin was not less animated.

The next day Paganel began to collect his baggage preparatory to his approaching departure. In a short time they entered the bay of Villa-Praïa, and anchored opposite the city in eight fathoms of water. The weather was stormy and the surf high, although the bay was sheltered from the winds. The rain fell in torrents so that they could scarcely see the city, which was on an elevated plain in the form of a terrace, resting on volcanic rocks three hundred feet in height. The appearance of the island through this rainy curtain was misty.

Shipping the coal was not accomplished without great difficulty, and the passengers saw themselves confined to the cabin, while sea and sky mingled their waters in an indescribable tumult. The weather was, therefore, the topic of conversation on board. Each one had his say except the major, who would have witnessed the deluge itself with perfect indifference. Paganel walked to and fro, shaking his head.

"It is an imperative fact," said he.

"It is certain," replied Glenarvan, "that the elements declare themselves against you."

"I will see about that."

"You cannot face such a storm," said Lady Helena.

"I, madam? Certainly. I fear only for my baggage and instruments. They will all be lost."

"Our landing is the only thing doubtful," resumed Glenarvan. "Once at Villa-Praïa, you will not have very uncomfortable quarters; rather uncleanly, to be sure, in the company of monkeys and swine, whose surroundings are not always agreeable; but a traveler does not regard that so critically. Besides, you can hope in seven or eight months to embark for Europe."

"Seven or eight months!" exclaimed Paganel.

"At least that. The Cape Verd Islands are very rarely frequented during the rainy season. But you can employ your time profitably. This archipelago is still little known. There is much to do, even now."

"But," replied Paganel in a pitiful tone, "what could I do after the investigations of the geologist Deville?"

"That is really a pity," said Lady Helena. "What will become of you, Monsieur Paganel?"

Paganel was silent for a few moments.

"You had decidedly better have landed at Madeira," rejoined Glenarvan, "although there is no wine there."

"My dear Glenarvan," continued Paganel at last, "where shall you land next?"

"At Concepcion."

"Alas! but that would bring me directly away from India!"

"No; for when you have passed Cape Horn you approach the Indies."

"I very much doubt it."

"Besides," continued Glenarvan with the greatest gravity, "as long as you are at the Indies, what difference does it make whether they are the East or the West?"

"'What difference does it make'?"

"The inhabitants of the Pampas of Patagonia are Indians as well as the natives of the Punjab."

"Eh! my lord," exclaimed Paganel, "that is a reason I should never have imagined!"

"And then, my dear Paganel, you know that you can gain the gold medal in any country whatever. There is something to do, to seek, to discover, everywhere, in the chains of the Cordilleras as well as the mountains of Thibet."

"But the course of the Yaroo-tsang-bo-tsoo?"

"Certainly. You can replace that by the Rio Colorado. This is a river very little known, and one of those which flow on the map too much according to the fancy of the geographer."

"I know it, my dear lord; there are errors of several degrees. I do not doubt that at my request the Society would have sent me to Patagonia as well as to India; but I did not think of it."

"The result of your continual abstraction."

"Well, Monsieur Paganel, shall you accompany us?" asked Lady Helena in her most persuasive tone.

"And my mission, madam?"

"I inform you that we shall pass through the Strait of Magellan," continued Glenarvan.

"My lord, you are a tempter."

"I add that we shall visit Port Famine."

"Port Famine!" cried the Frenchman, assailed on all sides; "that port so celebrated in geographical fasts!"

"Consider also, Monsieur Paganel," continued Lady Helena, "that in this enterprise you will have the right to associate the name of France with that of Scotland."

"Yes; doubtless."

"A geographer may be very serviceable to our expedition; and what is more noble than for science to enlist in the service of humanity?"

"That is well said, madam."

"Believe me, try chance, or rather Providence. Imitate us. It has sent us this document; we have started. It has cast you on board the Duncan; do not leave her."

"And do you, indeed, wish me, my good friends?" replied Paganel. "Well, you desire me to stay very much?"

"And you, Paganel, you are dying to stay," retorted Glenarvan.

"Truly," cried the geographer, "but I fear I am very indiscreet."

Thus far the Duncan had acquitted herself admirably: in every way her powers for steaming or sailing had been sufficiently tested, and her captain and passengers were alike satisfied with her performance and with one another.

CHAPTER IX. THROUGH THE STRAIT OF MAGELLAN.

The joy on board was general, when Paganel's resolution was known. Young Robert threw himself on his neck with very demonstrative delight. The worthy geographer almost fell backwards. "A rough little gentleman," said he; "I will teach him geography." As Captain Mangles had engaged to make him a sailor, Glenarvan a man of honor, the major a boy of coolness, Lady Helena a noble and generous being, and Mary Grant a pupil grateful towards such patrons, Robert was evidently to become one day an accomplished gentleman.

The Duncan soon finished shipping her coal, and then leaving these gloomy regions she gained the current from the southeast coast of Brazil, and, after crossing the equator with a fine breeze from the north, she entered the southern hemisphere. The passage was effected without difficulty, and every one had good hopes. On this voyage in search of Captain Grant, the probabilities increased every day. Their captain was one of the most confident on board; but his confidence proceeded especially from the desire that he cherished so strongly at heart, of seeing Miss Mary happy and consoled. He was particularly interested in this young girl; and this feeling he concealed so well, that, except Miss Grant and himself, no one on board the Duncan had perceived it.

As for the learned geographer, he was probably the happiest man in the southern hemisphere. He passed his time in studying the maps with which he covered the cabin-table; and then followed daily discussions with Mr. Olbinett, so that he could scarcely set the table.

But Paganel had all the passengers on his side except the major, who was very indifferent to geographical questions, especially at dinner-time. Having discovered a whole cargo of odd books in the mate's chests, and among them a number of Cervantes' works, the Frenchman resolved to learn Spanish, which nobody on board knew, and which would facilitate his search on the shores of Chili. Thanks to his love for philology, he did not despair of speaking this new tongue fluently on arriving at Concepcion. He therefore studied assiduously, and was heard incessantly muttering heterogeneous syllables. During his leisure hours he did not fail to give young Robert practical instruction, and taught him the history of the country they were rapidly approaching.

In the meantime the Duncan was proceeding at a remarkable rate. She cut the Tropic of Capricorn, and her prow was headed toward the strait of the celebrated geographer. Now and then the low shores of Patagonia were seen, but like an almost invisible line on the horizon. They sailed along the coast for more than ten miles, but Paganel's famous telescope gave him only a vague idea of these American shores.

The vessel soon found herself at the head of the strait, and entered without hesitation. This way is generally preferred by steam-vessels bound for the Pacific. Its exact length is three hundred and seventy-six miles. Ships of the greatest tonnage can always find deep water, even near its shores, an excellent bottom, and many springs of water. The rivers abound in fish, the forest in game, there are safe and easy landings at twenty places, and, in short, a thousand resources that are wanting in the Strait of Lemaire, and off the terrible rocks of Cape Horn, which are continually visited by storms and tempests.

During the first hours of the passage, till you reach Cape Gregory, the shores are low and sandy. The entire passage lasted scarcely thirty-six hours, and this moving panorama of the two shores well rewarded the pains the geographer took to admire it under the radiant beams of the southern sun. No inhabitant appeared on the shores of the continent; and only a few Fuegians wandered along the barren rocks of Terra del Fuego.

At one moment the Duncan rounded the peninsula of Brunswick between two magnificent sights. Just here the strait cuts between stupendous masses of granite. The base of the mountains was hidden in the heart of immense forests, while their summits, whitened with eternal snow, were lost in the clouds. Towards the southeast Mount Taru towered six thousand five hundred feet aloft. Night came, preceded by a long twilight, the light melting away insensibly by gentle degrees, while the sky was studded with brilliant stars.

In the midst of this partial obscurity, the yacht boldly continued on her course, without casting anchor in the safe bays with which the shores abound. Sometimes the tips of her yards would graze the branches of the beeches that hung over the waves. At others her propeller would beat the waters of the great rivers, starting geese, ducks, snipe, teal, and all the feathered tribes of the marshes. Soon deserted ruins appeared, and fallen monuments, to which the night lent a grand aspect; these were the mournful remains of an abandoned colony, whose name will be an eternal contradiction to the fertility of the coasts and the rich game of the forests. It was Port Famine, the place that the Spaniard Sarmiento colonized in 1581 with four hundred emigrants. Here he founded the city of San Felipe. But the extreme severity of the cold weakened the colony; famine devoured those whom the winter had spared, and in 1587 the explorer Cavendish found the last of these four hundred unfortunates dying of hunger amid the ruins of a city only six years in existence.

The vessel coasted along these deserted shores. At daybreak she sailed in the midst of the narrow passes, between beeches, ash-trees, and birches, from the bosom of which emerged ivy-clad domes, cupolas tapestried with the hardy holly, and lofty spires, among which the obelisk of Buckland rose to a great height. Far out in the sea sported droves of seals and whales of great size, judging by their spouting, which could be seen at a distance of four miles. At last they doubled Cape Froward, still bristling with the ices of winter. On the other side of the strait, on Terra del Fuego, rose Mount Sarmiento to the height of six thousand feet, an enormous mass of rock broken by bands of clouds which formed as it were an aerial archipelago in the sky.

Cape Froward is the real end of the American continent, for Cape Horn is only a lone rock in the sea. Passing this point the strait narrowed between Brunswick Peninsula, and Desolation Island. Then to fertile shores succeeded a line of wild barren coast, cut by a thousand inlets of this tortuous labyrinth.

The Duncan unerringly and unhesitatingly pursued its capricious windings, mingling her columns of smoke with the mists on the rocks. Without lessening her speed, she passed several Spanish factories established on these deserted shores. At Cape Tamar the strait widened. The yacht rounded the Narborough Islands, and approached the southern shores. At last, thirty-six hours after entering the strait, the rocks of Cape Pilares were discerned at the extreme point of Desolation Island. An immense open glittering sea extended before her prow, and Jacques Paganel, hailing it with an enthusiastic gesture, felt moved like Ferdinand Magellan himself, when the sails of the Trinidad swelled before the breezes of the Pacific.

CHAPTER X. THE COURSE DECIDED.

Eight days after doubling Cape Pilares the Duncan entered at full speed the Bay of Talcahuana, a magnificent estuary, twelve miles long and nine broad. The weather was beautiful. Not a cloud is seen in the sky of this country from November to March, and the wind from the south blows continually along these coasts, which are protected by the chain of the Andes.

Captain Mangles, according to Lord Glenarvan's orders, had kept close to the shore of the continent, examining the numerous wrecks that lined it. A waif, a broken spar, a piece of wood fashioned by the hand of man, might guide the Duncan to the scene of the shipwreck. But nothing was seen, and the yacht continued her course and anchored in the harbor of Talcahuana forty-two days after her departure from the waters of the Clyde.

Glenarvan at once lowered the boat, and, followed by Paganel, landed at the foot of the palisade. The learned geographer, profiting by the circumstance, would have made use of the language which he had studied so conscientiously; but, to his great astonishment, he could not make himself understood by the natives.

"The accent is what I need," said he.

"Let us go to the Custom-house," replied Glenarvan.

There they were informed by means of several English words, accompanied by expressive gestures, that the British consul resided at Concepcion. It was only an hour's journey. Glenarvan easily found two good horses, and, a short time after, Paganel and he entered the walls of this great city, which was built by the enterprising genius of Valdivia, the valiant companion of Pizarro.

How greatly it had declined from its ancient splendor! Often pillaged by the natives, burnt in 1819, desolate, ruined, its walls still blackened with the flames of devastation, eclipsed by Talcahuana, it now scarcely numbered eight thousand souls. Under the feet of its idle inhabitants the streets had grown into prairies. There was no commerce, no activity, no business. The mandolin resounded from every balcony, languishing songs issued from the lattices of the windows, and Concepcion, the ancient city of men, had become a village of women and children.

Glenarvan appeared little desirous of seeking the causes of this decline— though Jacques Paganel attacked him on this subject—and, without losing an instant, betook himself to the house of J. R. Bentock, Esq., consul of Her Britannic Majesty. This individual received him very courteously, and when he learned the story of Captain Grant undertook to search along the entire coast.

The question whether the Britannia had been wrecked on the shores of Chili or Araucania was decided in the negative. No report of such an event had come either to the consul, or his colleagues in other parts of the country.

But Glenarvan was not discouraged. He returned to Talcahuana, and, sparing neither fatigue, trouble, or money, he sent men to the coast, but their search was in vain. The most minute inquiries among the people of the vicinity were of no avail. They were forced to conclude that the Britannia had left no trace of her shipwreck.

Glenarvan then informed his companions of the failure of his endeavors. Mary Grant and her brother could not restrain their grief. It was now six days since the arrival of the Duncan at Talcahuana. The passengers were together in the cabin. Lady Helena was consoling, not by her words—for what could she say?—but by her caresses, the two children of the captain. Jacques Paganel had taken up the document again, and was regarding it with earnest attention, as if he would have drawn from it new secrets. For an hour he had examined it thus, when Glenarvan, addressing him, said,—

"Paganel, I appeal to your sagacity. Is the interpretation we have made of this document incorrect? Is the sense of these words illogical?"

Paganel did not answer. He was reflecting.

"Are we mistaken as to the supposed scene of the shipwreck?" continued Glenarvan. "Does not the name Patagonia suggest itself at once to the mind?"

Paganel was still silent.

"In short," said Glenarvan, "does not the word *Indian* justify us still more?"

"Perfectly," replied MacNabb.

"And therefore, is it not evident that these shipwrecked men, when they wrote these lines, expected to be prisoners of the Indians?"

"There you are wrong, my dear lord," said Paganel, at last; "and if your other conclusions are just, the last at least does not seem to me rational."

"What do you mean?" asked Lady Helena, while all eyes were turned towards the geographer.

"I mean," answered Paganel, emphasizing his words, "that Captain Grant is *now prisoner of the Indians*: and I will add that the document leaves no doubt on this point."

"Explain yourself, sir," said Miss Grant.

"Nothing is easier, my dear Mary. Instead of reading *they will be prisoners*, read *they are prisoners*, and all will be clear."

"But that is impossible," replied Glenarvan.

"Impossible? And why, my noble friend?" asked Paganel, smiling.

"Because the bottle must have been thrown when the vessel was breaking on the rocks. Hence the degrees of longitude and latitude apply to the very place of shipwreck."

"Nothing proves it," said Paganel, earnestly; "and I do not see why the shipwrecked sailors, after being carried by the Indians into the interior of the country, could not have sought to make known by means of this bottle the place of their captivity."

"Simply, my dear Paganel, because to throw a bottle into the sea it is necessary, at least, that the sea should be before you."

"Or, in the absence of the sea," added Paganel, "the rivers which flow into it."

An astonished silence followed this unexpected, yet reasonable, answer. By the flash that brightened the eyes of his hearers Paganel knew that each of them had conceived a new hope. Lady Helena was the first to resume the conversation.

"What an idea!" she exclaimed.

"What a *good* idea!" added the geographer, simply.

"Your advice then?" asked Glenarvan.

"My advice is to find the thirty-seventh parallel, just where it meets the American coast, and follow it, without deviating half a degree, to the point where it strikes the Atlantic. Perhaps we shall find on its course the survivors of the Britannia."

"A feeble chance," replied the major.

"However feeble it may be," continued Paganel, "we ought not to neglect it. If I am right that this bottle reached the sea by following the current of a river, we cannot fail to come upon the traces of the prisoners. Look, my friends, look at the map of this country, and I will convince you beyond a doubt."

So saying, Paganel spread out before them upon the table a large map of Chili and the Argentine Provinces. "Look," said he, "and follow me in this passage across the American continent. Let us pass over the narrow strip of Chili and the Cordilleras of the Andes, and descend into the midst of the Pampas. Are rivers, streams, water-courses, wanting in these regions? No. Here are the Rio Negro, the Rio Colorado, and their affluents, cut by the thirty-seventh parallel, all of which might have served to transport the document. There, perhaps, in the midst of a tribe, in the hands of settled Indians, on the shores of these unknown rivers, in the gorges of the sierras, those whom I have the right to call our friends are awaiting an interposition of Providence. Ought we, then, to disappoint their hopes? Do you not think we should follow across these countries an unswerving course? And if, contrary to all expectation, I am still mistaken, is it not our duty to trace this parallel to the very end, and, if necessary, make upon it the tour of the world?"

These words, spoken with a noble enthusiasm, excited a deep emotion among Paganel's hearers. All rose to shake hands with him.

"Yes, my father is there!" cried Robert Grant, devouring the map with his eyes.

"And wherever he is," replied Glenarvan, "we shall find him, my child. Nothing is more consistent than our friend Paganel's interpretation, and we must follow without hesitation the course he has indicated. Either Captain Grant is in the hands of countless Indians, or is prisoner in a feeble tribe. In the latter case, we will rescue him. In the former, after ascertaining his situation, we will join the Duncan on the eastern coast, sail to Buenos Ayres, and with a detachment, organized by the major, can overcome all the Indians of the Argentine Plains."

"Yes, yes, your lordship," answered Captain Mangles; "and I will add that this passage of the continent will be without peril."

"Without peril, or fatigue," continued Paganel. "How many have already accomplished it who had scarcely our means for success, and whose courage was not sustained by the grandeur of the undertaking!"

"Sir, sir," exclaimed Mary Grant, in a voice broken with emotion, "how can I thank a devotion that exposes you to so many dangers?"

"Dangers!" cried Paganel. "Who uttered the word *danger*?"

"Not I!" replied Robert Grant, with flashing eye and determined look.

"Danger!" repeated Paganel; "does such a thing exist? Moreover, what is the question? A journey of scarcely three hundred and fifty leagues, since we shall proceed in a straight line; a journey which will be accomplished in a favorable latitude and climate; in short, a journey whose duration will be only a month at most. It is a mere walk."

"Monsieur Paganel," asked Lady Helena at last, "do you think that, if the shipwrecked sailors have fallen into the power of the Indians, their lives have been spared?"

"Certainly I do, madam. The Indians are not cannibals; far from that, one of my countrymen whom I knew in the Society was three years prisoner among the Indians of the Pampas. He suffered, was ill-treated, but at last gained the victory in this trying ordeal. A European is a useful person in these countries. The Indians know his value, and esteem him very highly."

"Well then, there is no more hesitation," said Glenarvan; "we must start, and that, too, without delay. What course shall we take?"

"An easy and agreeable one," replied Paganel. "A few mountains to begin with; then a gentle descent on the eastern slope of the Andes; and at last a level, grassy, sandy plain, a real garden."

"Let us see the map," said the major.

"Here it is, my dear MacNabb. We shall begin at the end of the thirty-seventh parallel on the coast of Chili. After passing through the capital of Araucania, we shall strike the Cordilleras, and descending their steep declivities across the Rio Colorado, we shall reach the Pampas. Passing the frontiers of Buenos Ayres, we shall continue our search until we reach the shores of the Atlantic."

Thus speaking and developing the programme of the expedition, Paganel did not even take the trouble to look at the map spread before him. And he had no need to; educated in the schools of Frézier, Molina, Humboldt, and Miers, his unerring memory could neither be deceived nor baffled. After finishing his plan, he added:

"Therefore, my dear friends, the course is straight. In thirty days we shall accomplish it, and arrive before the Duncan on the eastern shore, since the westerly winds will delay her progress."

"The Duncan then," said Captain Mangles, "will cross the thirty-seventh parallel between Cape Corrientes and Cape St. Antonio?"

"Exactly."

"And whom would you constitute the members of such an expedition?" asked Glenarvan.

"The fewer the better. The only point is to ascertain the situation of Captain Grant, and not to engage in combat with the Indians. I think that Lord Glenarvan, as our chief, the major, who would yield his place to no one, your servant Jacques Paganel—"

"And I!" cried Robert Grant.

"Robert?" said Mary.

"And why not?" answered Paganel. "Travels develop youth. We four, then, and three sailors of the Duncan—"

"What," exclaimed Captain Mangles, "your lordship does not intercede for me?"

"My dear fellow," replied Glenarvan, "we shall leave the ladies on board, the dearest objects we have in the world. Who would watch over them, if not the devoted captain of the Duncan?"

"We cannot accompany you, then," said Lady Helena, whose eyes were dimmed by a mist of sadness.

"My dear wife," replied Glenarvan, "our journey will be performed with unusual rapidity, our separation will be short, and—"

"Yes, yes; I understand you," answered Lady Helena. "Go, then, and may you succeed in your enterprise."

"Besides, this is not a journey," added Paganel.

"What is it, then?" asked Lady Helena.

"A passage, nothing more. We shall pass, that is all, like honest men, over the country and do all the good possible. '*Transire benefaciendo*' is our motto."

With these words the discussion ended. The preparations were begun that very day, and it was resolved to keep the expedition secret, in order not to alarm the Indians. The 14th of October was fixed for the day of departure.

When they came to choose the sailors who were to go, they all offered their services, and Glenarvan was forced to make a choice. He preferred to have them draw lots, that he might not mortify such brave men. This was accordingly done; and the mate, Tom Austin, Wilson, a powerful fellow, and Mulready, were the fortunate ones.

Lord Glenarvan had displayed great energy in his preparations, for he wished to be ready at the day appointed; and he was. Captain Mangles likewise supplied his ship with coal, that he might put to sea at any moment. He wished to gain the Argentine shore before the travelers. Hence there was a real rivalry between Glenarvan and the captain, which was of advantage to both.

At last, on the 14th of October, at the time agreed upon, every one was ready. At the moment of departure the passengers of the yacht assembled in the cabin. The Duncan was on the point of starting, and already her propeller was agitating the quiet waters of Talcahuana Bay. Glenarvan, Paganel, MacNabb, Robert Grant, Tom Austin, Wilson and Mulready, armed with carbines and Colt's revolvers, were preparing to leave the vessel. Guides and mules were waiting for them on shore.

"It is time," said Lord Glenarvan at last.

"Go, then, my husband!" replied Lady Helena, restraining her emotion.

He pressed her to his breast, while Robert threw himself upon the neck of his sister.

"And now, dear companions," said Jacques Paganel, "one last clasp of the hand to last us till we reach the shores of the Atlantic."

It was not asking much, but these were clasps which would strengthen the hopes of the worthy geographer.

They then returned to the deck, and the seven travelers left the vessel. They soon reached the wharf, which the yacht approached within less than half a cable's length.

Lady Helena cried for the last time,—

"My friends, God help you!"

"And he will help us, madam," answered Jacques Paganel; "for, I assure you, we shall help ourselves."

"Forward!" shouted Captain Mangles to his engineer.

"*En route!*" returned Glenarvan; and at the same instant that the travelers, giving reins to their animals, followed the road along the shore, the Duncan started again at full speed on the highway of the ocean.

CHAPTER XI. TRAVELING IN CHILI.

The native troop engaged by Glenarvan consisted of three men and a boy. The leader of the muleteers was an Englishman who had lived in the country for twenty years. His occupation was to let mules to travelers, and guide them across the passes of the Andes. Then he consigned them to the care of a "laqueano" (Argentine guide), who was familiar with the road over the Pampas.

This Englishman had not so forgotten his native tongue, in the company of mules and Indians, that he could not converse with the travelers. Hence it was easy for Glenarvan to make known his wishes, and for the muleteer to execute his orders, of which circumstance the former availed himself, since Paganel had not yet succeeded in making himself understood.

This leader, or "catapaz," in the language of Chili, was assisted by two native peons and a boy of twelve. The peons had charge of the mules laden with the baggage of the party, and the boy led the madrina (little mare), which wore small bells, and went in advance of the other ten mules. The travelers were mounted on seven, and the catapaz on one, of these animals, while the two others carried the provisions and a few rolls of cloth designed to insure the good-will of the chiefs of the plains. The peons traveled on foot according to their custom. This journey in South America was, therefore, to be performed under the most favorable conditions of safety and speed.

Crossing the Andes is not an ordinary journey. It cannot be undertaken without employing those hardy mules, of which the most preferable belong to the Argentine Republic. These excellent animals have attained in that country a development superior to their pristine quality and strength. They are not very particular about their food, drink only once a day, and easily make ten leagues in eight hours.

There are no taverns on this route, from one ocean to the other. You eat dried meat, rice seasoned with allspice, and whatever game can be captured on the way. In the mountains the torrents, and in the plains the rivers, furnish water, generally flavored with a few drops of rum, of which each has a supply in an ox-horn called "chiffle." However, care must be taken not to indulge too much in alcoholic drinks, which are specially injurious in a region where the nervous system is peculiarly excited.

As for your bedding, it consists merely of the native saddle called "recado." This saddle is made of sheep-skins tanned on one side and covered with wool on the other, and is supported by broad girths elaborately embroidered. A traveler wrapped in one of these warm coverings can brave with impunity the dampness of the nights, and enjoy the soundest repose.

Glenarvan, who knew how to travel and conform to the customs of different countries, had adopted the Chilian costume for himself and his friends. Paganel and Robert, two children (a large and a small one), felt no pleasure in introducing their heads into the national poncho (a large blanket with a hole in the centre), and their legs into leathern stirrups. They would rather have seen their mules richly caparisoned, with the Arab bit in their mouths, a long bridle of braided leather for a whip, and their heads adorned with metal ornaments and the "alforjas" (double saddle-bags containing the provisions).

Paganel, always absent-minded, received three or four kicks from his excellent animal just as he was mounting. Once in the saddle, however, with his inseparable telescope in a sling and his feet confined in the stirrups, he confided himself to the sagacity of his beast, and had no reason to repent. As for young Robert, he showed from the first a remarkable capacity for becoming an excellent horseman.

They started. The day was magnificent, the sky was perfectly clear, and the atmosphere sufficiently refreshed by the sea-breezes in spite of the heat of the sun. The little party followed at a rapid pace the winding shores of the bay, and made good progress the first day across the reeds of old dried marshes. Little was said. The parting farewells had left a deep impression upon the minds of all. They could still see the smoke of the Duncan as she gradually disappeared on the horizon. All were silent, except Paganel; this studious geographer kept asking himself questions, and answering them, in his new language.

The catapaz was, moreover, quite a taciturn man, whose avocation had not made him loquacious. He scarcely spoke to his peons, for they understood their duty very well. Whenever a mule stopped, they urged him with a guttural cry. If this did not suffice, a good pebble thrown with sure aim overcame his obstinacy. If a girth gave way or a bridle was loosened, the peon, taking off his poncho, enveloped the head of the animal, which, when the injury was repaired, resumed its pace.

The custom of the muleteers is to set out at eight o'clock in the morning after breakfast, and travel thus till it is time to rest at four o'clock in the afternoon. Glenarvan, accordingly, conformed to this custom. Precisely when the signal to halt was given by the catapaz, the travelers arrived at the city of Arauco, situated at the southern extremity of the bay, without having left the foam-washed shore of the ocean. They would have had to proceed twenty miles farther to the west to reach the limits of the thirty-seventh parallel; but Glenarvan's agents had already traversed that part of the coast without meeting with any signs of shipwreck. A new exploration became, therefore, useless, and it was decided that the city of Arauco should be chosen as their point of departure. From this their course was to be directed towards the east in a rigorously straight line. The little party entered the city and took up their quarters in the open court of a tavern, whose accommodations were still in a rudimentary state.

While supper was preparing, Glenarvan, Paganel and the catapaz took a walk among the thatch-roofed houses. Except a church and the remains of a convent of Franciscans, Arauco presented nothing interesting. Glenarvan attempted to make some inquiries, but failed, while Paganel was in despair at not being able to make himself understood by the inhabitants. But, since they spoke Araucanian, his Spanish served him as little as Hebrew.

The next day, the madrina at the head, and the peons in the rear, the little troop resumed the line of the thirty-seventh parallel towards the east. They now crossed the fertile territory of Araucania, rich in vineyards and flocks. But gradually solitude ensued. Scarcely, from mile to mile, was there a hut of "rastreadores" (Indian horse-tamers). Now and then they came upon an abandoned relay-station, that only served as a shelter to some wanderer on the plains; and, by means of a ford, they crossed the Rio Tubal, the mountains visible in the distance.

At four o'clock in the afternoon, after a journey of thirty-five miles, they halted in the open country under a group of giant myrtles. The mules were unharnessed, and left to graze at will upon the rich herbage of the prairie. The saddle-bags furnished the usual meat and rice, the pelions spread on the ground served as covering, the saddles as pillows, and each one found on these improvised beds a ready repose, while the peons and the catapaz watched in turn.

As the weather continued pleasant, all the travelers, not excepting Robert, were still in good health; and, since the journey had begun under such favorable auspices, they thought it best to profit by it, and push on. The following day they advanced rapidly, crossed without accident Bell Rapids, and at evening encamped on the banks of the Rio Biobio. There were thirty-five miles more to travel before they were out of Chili.

The country had not changed. It was still rich in amaryllis, violets, date-trees, and golden-flowered cactuses. A few animals, among others the ocelot, inhabited the thickets. A heron, a solitary owl, thrushes and snipes wary of the talons of the hawk, were the only representatives of the feathered tribe.

Of the natives few were seen; only some "guassos" (degenerate children of the Indians and Spanish), galloping on horses which they lacerated with the gigantic spurs that adorned their naked feet, and passing like shadows. They met on the way no one who could inform them, and inquiries were therefore utterly impossible.

Glenarvan thought that Captain Grant, if prisoner of the Indians, must have been carried by them beyond the Andes. Their search could be successful only in the Pampas. They must be patient, and travel on swiftly and continuously.

They advanced in the same order as before, which Robert with difficulty kept, for his eagerness led him to press forward, to the great annoyance of his animal. Nothing but a command from Glenarvan would keep the young boy at his place in the line. The country now became more uneven; and several hillocks indicated that they were approaching the mountains.

Paganel still continued his study of Spanish.

"What a language it is!" exclaimed he; "so full and sonorous!"

"But you are making progress, of course?" replied Glenarvan.

"Certainly, my dear lord. Ah! if there were only no accent! But, alas! there is one!"

In studying this language, Paganel did not, however, neglect his geographical observations. In these, indeed, he was astonishingly clever, and could not have found his superior. When Glenarvan questioned the catapaz about some peculiarity of the country, his learned companion would always anticipate the answer of the guide, who then gazed at him with a look of amazement.

That same day they met a road which crossed the line that they had hitherto pursued. Lord Glenarvan naturally asked its name of their guide, and Paganel as naturally answered,—

"The road from Yumbel to Los Angelos."

Glenarvan looked at the catapaz.

"Exactly," replied he.

Then, addressing the geographer, he said,—

"You have traveled in this country?"

"Certainly," replied Paganel gravely.

"On a mule?"

"No; in an arm-chair."

The catapaz did not understand, for he shrugged his shoulders and returned to the head of the troop.

At five o'clock in the afternoon they stopped in a shallow gorge, a few miles above the little town of Loja; and that night the travelers encamped at the foot of the first slopes of the Andes.

CHAPTER XII. ELEVEN THOUSAND FEET ALOFT.

The route through Chili had as yet presented no serious obstacles; but now the dangers that attend a journey across the mountains suddenly increased, the struggle with the natural difficulties was about to begin in earnest.

An important question had to be decided before starting. By what pass could they cross the Andes with the least departure from the prescribed course? The catapaz was questioned on this subject.

"I know," he replied, "of but two passes that are practicable in this part of the Andes."

"Doubtless the pass of Arica," said Paganel, "which was discovered by Valdivia Mendoza."

"Exactly."

"And that of Villarica, situated to the south of Nevado."

"You are right."

"Well, my friend, these two passes have only one difficulty; they will carry us to the south, or the north, farther than we wish."

"Have you another pass to propose?" asked the major.

"Yes," replied Paganel; "the pass of Antuco."

"Well," said Glenarvan; "but do you know this pass, catapaz?"

"Yes, my lord, I have crossed it, and did not propose it because it is only a cattle-track for the Indian herdsmen of the eastern slopes."

"Never mind, my friend," continued Glenarvan; "where the herds of the Indians pass, we can also; and, since this will keep us in our course, let us start for the pass of Antuco."

The signal for departure was immediately given, and they entered the valley of Los Lejos between great masses of crystalized limestone, and ascended a very gradual slope. Towards noon they had to pass around the shores of a small lake, the picturesque reservoir of all the neighboring streams which flowed into it.

Above the lake extended vast "llanos," lofty plains, covered with grass, where the herds of the Indians grazed. Then they came upon a swamp which extended to the south and north, but which the instinct of the mules enabled them to avoid. Soon Fort Ballenare appeared on a rocky peak which it crowned with its dismantled walls. The ascent had already become abrupt and stony, and the pebbles, loosened by the hoofs of the mules, rolled under their feet in a rattling torrent.

The road now became difficult, and even perilous. The steepness increased, the walls on either side approached each other more and more, while the precipices yawned frightfully. The mules advanced cautiously in single file, with their noses to the ground, scenting the way.

Now and then, at a sudden turn, the madrina disappeared, and the little caravan was then guided by the distant tinkling of her bell. Sometimes, too, the capricious windings of the path would bend the column into two parallel lines, and the catapaz could talk to the peons, while a crevasse, scarcely two fathoms wide, but two hundred deep, formed an impassable abyss between them.

Under these conditions it was difficult to distinguish the course. The almost incessant action of subterranean and volcanic agency changes the road, and the landmarks are never the same. Therefore the catapaz hesitated, stopped, looked about him, examined the form of the rocks, and searched on the crumbling stones for the tracks of Indians.

Glenarvan followed in the steps of his guide. He perceived, he *felt*, his embarrassment, increasing with the difficulties of the way. He did not dare to question him, but thought that it was better to trust to the instinct of the muleteers and mules.

For an hour longer the catapaz wandered at a venture, but always seeking the more elevated parts of the mountain. At last he was forced to stop short. They were at the bottom of a narrow valley,—one of those ravines that the Indians call "quebradas." A perpendicular wall of porphyry barred their exit.

The catapaz, after searching vainly for a passage, dismounted, folded his arms, and waited. Glenarvan approached him.

"Have you lost your way?" he asked.

"No, my lord," replied the catapaz.

"But we are not at the pass of Antuco?"

"We are."

"Are you not mistaken?"

"I am not. Here are the remains of a fire made by the Indians, and the tracks left by their horses."

"Well, they passed this way?"

"Yes; but we cannot. The last earthquake has made it impracticable."

"For mules," replied the major; "but not for men."

"That is for you to decide," said the catapaz. "I have done what I could. My mules and I are ready to turn back, if you please, and search for the other passes of the Andes."

"But that will cause a delay."

"Of three days, at least."

Glenarvan listened in silence to the words of the catapaz, who had evidently acted in accordance with his engagement. His mules could go no farther; but when the proposal was made to retrace their steps, Glenarvan turned towards his companions, and said,—

"Do you wish to go on?"

"We will follow you," replied Tom Austin.

"And even precede you," added Paganel. "What is it, after all? To scale a chain of mountains whose opposite slopes afford an unusually easy descent.

This accomplished, we can find the Argentine laqueanos, who will guide us across the Pampas, and swift horses accustomed to travel over the plains. Forward, then, without hesitation."

"Forward!" cried his companions.

"You do not accompany us?" said Glenarvan to the catapaz.

"I am the muleteer," he replied.

"As you say."

"Never mind," said Paganel; "on the other side of this wall we shall find the pass of Antuco again, and I will lead you to the foot of the mountain as directly as the best guide of the Andes."

Glenarvan accordingly settled with the catapaz, and dismissed him, his peons, and his mules. The arms, the instruments, and the remaining provisions, were divided among the seven travelers. By common consent it was decided that the ascent should be undertaken immediately, and that, if necessary, they should travel part of the night. Around the precipice to the left wound a steep path that mules could not ascend. The difficulties were great; but, after two hours of fatigue and wandering, Glenarvan and his companions found themselves again in the pass of Antuco.

They were now in that part of the Andes properly so called, not far from the main ridge of the mountains; but of the path traced out, of the pass, nothing could be seen. All this region had just been thrown into confusion by the recent earthquakes.

They ascended all night, climbed almost inaccessible plateaus, and leaped over broad and deep crevasses. Their arms took the place of ropes, and their shoulders served as steps. The strength of Mulready and the skill of Wilson were often called into requisition. Many times, without their devotion and courage, the little party could not have advanced.

Glenarvan never lost sight of young Robert, whose youth and eagerness led him to acts of rashness, while Paganel pressed on with all the ardor of a Frenchman. As for the major, he only moved as much as was necessary, no more, no less, and mounted the path by an almost insensible motion. Did he perceive that he had been ascending for several hours? It is not certain. Perhaps he imagined he was descending.

At five o'clock in the morning the travelers had attained a height of seven thousand five hundred feet. They were now on the lower ridges, the last limit of arborescent vegetation. At this hour the aspect of these regions was entirely changed. Great blocks of glittering ice, of a bluish color in certain parts, rose on all sides, and reflected the first rays of the sun.

The ascent now became very perilous. They no longer advanced without carefully examining the ice. Wilson had taken the lead, and with his foot tested the surface of the glaciers. His companions followed exactly in his footsteps, and avoided uttering a word, for the least sound might have caused the fall of the snowy masses suspended eight hundred feet above their heads.

They had reached the region of shrubs, which, four hundred and fifty feet higher, gave place to grass and cactuses. At eleven thousand feet all traces of vegetation disappeared. The travelers had stopped only once to recruit their strength by a hasty repast, and with superhuman courage they resumed the ascent in the face of the ever-increasing dangers.

The strength of the little troop, however, in spite of their courage, was almost gone. Glenarvan, seeing the exhaustion of his companions, regretted having engaged in the undertaking. Young Robert struggled against fatigue, but could go no farther.

Glenarvan stopped.

"We must take a rest," said he, for he clearly saw that no one else would make this proposal.

"Take a rest?" replied Paganel; "how? where? we have no shelter."

"It is indispensable, if only for Robert."

"No, my lord," replied the courageous child; "I can still walk—do not stop."

"We will carry you, my boy," said Paganel, "but we must, at all hazards, reach the eastern slope. There, perhaps, we shall find some hut in which we can take refuge. I ask for two hours more of travel."

"Do you all agree?" asked Glenarvan.

"Yes," replied his companions.

"I will take charge of the brave boy," added the equally brave Mulready.

They resumed their march towards the east. Two hours more of terrible exertion followed. They kept ascending, in order to reach the highest summit of this part of the mountain.

Whatever were the desires of these courageous men, the moment now came when the most valiant failed, and dizziness, that terrible malady of the mountains, exhausted not only their physical strength but their moral courage. It is impossible to struggle with impunity against fatigues of this kind. Soon falls became frequent, and those who fell could only advance by dragging themselves on their knees.

Exhaustion was about to put an end to this too prolonged ascent; and Glenarvan was considering with terror the extent of the snow, the cold which in this fatal region was so much to be dreaded, the shadows that were deepening on the solitary peaks, and the absence of a shelter for the night, when the major stopped him, and, in a calm tone, said,—

"A hut!"

CHAPTER XIII. A SUDDEN DESCENT.

Any one but MacNabb would have passed by, around, or even over this hut a hundred times without suspecting its existence. A projection on the surface of the snow scarcely distinguished it from the surrounding rocks. It was necessary to uncover it; after half an hour of persistent labor, Wilson and

Mulready had cleared away the entrance to the "casucha," and the little party stepped in.

This casucha, constructed by the Indians, was made of adobes, a kind of bricks dried in the sun. Ten persons could easily find room inside, and, if its walls had not been sufficiently water-tight in the rainy season, at this time, at least, they were some protection against the severity of the cold. There was, besides, a sort of fireplace with a flue of bricks very poorly laid, which enabled them to kindle a fire, and thus withstand the external temperature.

"Here is a shelter, at least," said Glenarvan, "even if it is not comfortable. Providence has led us hither, and we cannot do better than accept this fortune."

"Why," replied Paganel, "it is a palace. It only wants sentries and courtiers. We shall get along admirably here."

"Especially when a good fire is blazing on the hearth," said Tom Austin; "for, if we are hungry, we are none the less cold it seems to me; and, for my part, a good fagot would delight me more than a slice of venison."

"Well, Tom," said Paganel, "we will try to find something combustible."

"Something combustible on the top of the Andes?" said Mulready, shaking his head doubtfully.

"Since a chimney has been made in this hut," replied the major, "there is probably something here to burn."

"Our friend is right," added Glenarvan. "Prepare everything for supper; and I will play the part of wood-cutter."

"I will accompany you with Wilson," said Paganel.

"If you need me—," said Robert, rising.

"No, rest yourself, my brave boy," replied Glenarvan. "You will be a man when others are only children."

Glenarvan, Paganel, and Wilson went out of the hut. It was six o'clock in the evening. The cold was keen and cutting, in spite of the calmness of the air. The azure of the sky was already fading, and the sun shedding his last rays on the lofty peaks of the mountains.

Reaching a hillock of porphyry, they scanned the horizon in every direction. They had now gained the summit of the Andes, which commanded an extended prospect. To the east the sides of the mountains declined by gentle gradations, down which they could see the peons sliding several hundred feet below. In the distance extended long lines of scattered rocks and stones that had been crowded back by glacial avalanches. The valley of the Colorado was already growing dim in the increasing twilight; the elevations of land, the crags and the peaks, illumined by the rays of the sun, gradually faded, and darkness covered the whole eastern slope of the Andes.

Towards the north undulated a succession of ridges that mingled together insensibly. To the south, however, the view was magnificent; and, as night descended, the grandeur was inimitable. Looking down into the wild valley of Torbido, you saw Mount Antuco, whose yawning crater was two miles distant. The volcano, like some enormous monster, belched forth glowing smoke mingled with torrents of bright flame. The circle of the mountains that inclosed it seemed to be on fire. Showers of incandescent stones, clouds of reddish vapors, and streams of lava, united in glittering columns. A loud rumbling that increased every moment, and was followed by a dazzling flash, filled this vast circuit with its sharp reverberations, while the sun, his light gradually fading, disappeared as a star is extinguished in the shadows of the horizon.

Paganel and Glenarvan would have remained a long time to contemplate this magnificent struggle of the fires of earth with those of heaven, and the improvised wood-cutters were becoming admirers of nature; but Wilson, less enthusiastic, reminded them of their situation. Wood was wanting, it is true, but fortunately a scanty and dry moss clothed the rocks. An ample supply was taken, as well as of a plant whose roots were quite combustible. This precious fuel was brought to the hut, and piled in the fire-place; but it was difficult to kindle the fire, and especially to keep it burning.

When the viands were prepared, each one drank several mouthfuls of hot coffee with delight. As for the dried meat, it appeared a little unsatisfactory, which provoked on the part of Paganel a remark as useless as it was true.

"Indeed," said he, "I must confess a llama-steak would not be bad just now."

"What!" cried the major, "are you not content with our supper, Paganel?"

"Enchanted, my good major; but I acknowledge a plate of venison would be welcome."

"You are a sybarite," said MacNabb.

"I accept the title, major; but you yourself, whatever you may say, would not be displeased with a beefsteak."

"Probably not."

"And if you were asked to take your post at the cannon, you would go without a word."

"Certainly: and, although it pleases you—"

His companions had not heard any more, when distant and prolonged howls were heard. They were not the cries of scattered animals, but those of a herd approaching with rapidity. Would Providence, after furnishing them with shelter, give them their supper? Such was the thought of the geographer. But Glenarvan humbled his joy somewhat by observing that the animals of the Andes were never met with in so elevated a region.

"Whence comes the noise, then?" asked Tom Austin. "Hear how it approaches!"

"An avalanche!" said Mulready.

"Impossible! these are real howls!" replied Paganel.

"Let us see," cried Glenarvan.

"Let us see like hunters," answered the major, as he took his rifle.

All rushed out of the hut. Night had come. It was dark, but the sky was studded with stars. The moon had not yet shown her disk. The peaks on the north and east were lost in the darkness, and the eye only perceived the grotesque outlines of a few towering rocks.

The howls—those of terrified animals—were redoubled. They came from the dark side of the mountain. What was going on?

Suddenly there came a furious avalanche, but one of living creatures, mad with terror. The whole plateau seemed to tremble. There were hundreds, perhaps thousands, of these animals. Were they wild beasts of the Pampas, or only llamas? The whole party had only time to throw themselves to the earth, while this living whirlwind passed a few feet above them.

At this moment the report of a fire-arm was heard. The major had shot at a venture. He thought that a large animal fell a few paces from him, while the whole herd, carried along by their resistless motion, disappeared down the slopes illumined by the volcano.

"Ah, I have them!" cried a voice, that of Paganel.

"What have you?" asked Glenarvan.

"My glasses, to be sure!"

"You are not wounded?"

"No, a little kick,—but by what?"

"By this," replied the major, dragging after him the animal he had shot.

Each one hastened to gain the hut; and by the light of the fire MacNabb's prize was examined. It was a pretty animal, resembling a little camel without a hump. It had a small head, flat body, long legs and claws, fine coffee-colored hair, and its breast was spotted with white.

Scarcely had Paganel looked at it when he exclaimed,—

"It is a guanaco!"

"What is that?" asked Glenarvan.

"An animal that eats itself."

"And is it good?"

"Delicious! a dish for the gods! I knew well that you would like fresh meat for supper. And what meat this is! But who will dress the animal?"

"I will," said Wilson.

"Well, I will engage to broil it," replied Paganel.

"You are a cook, then, Monsieur Paganel?" said Robert.

"Certainly, my boy. A Frenchman is always a cook."

In a little while Paganel placed large slices of meat on the coals, and, in a short time, served up to his companions this appetizing viand. No one hesitated, but each attacked it ravenously. To the great amazement of the geographer, a general grimace accompanied by a "pwah!" followed the first mouthful.

"It is horrible!" said one.

"It is not eatable!" replied another.

The poor geographer, whatever was the difficulty, was forced to agree that this steak was not acceptable even to starving men. They therefore began to launch jokes at him, and deride his "dish for the gods," while he himself sought a reason for this unaccountable result.

"I have it!" he cried. "I have it!"

"Is the meat too old?" asked MacNabb, calmly.

"No, my intolerant major; but it has traveled too much. How could I forget that?"

"What do you mean?" asked Tom Austin.

"I mean that the animal is not good unless killed when at rest. I can affirm from the taste that it has come from a distance, and, consequently, the whole herd."

"You are certain of this?" said Glenarvan.

"Absolutely so."

"But what event could have terrified these animals so, and driven them at a time when they ought to be peacefully sleeping in their lairs."

"As to that, my dear Glenarvan," said Paganel, "it is impossible for me to say. If you believe me, let us search no farther. For my part I am dying for want of sleep. Let us retire, major!"

"Very well, Paganel."

Thereupon each wrapped himself in his poncho, the fuel was replenished for the night, and soon all but Glenarvan were buried in profound repose.

He alone did not sleep. A secret uneasiness held him in a state of wakeful fatigue. He could not help thinking of that herd, flying in one common direction, of their inexplicable terror. They could not have been pursued by wild beasts: at that height there were scarcely any, and yet fewer hunters. What fright had driven them over the abysses of Antuco, and what was the cause of it? He thought of their strange situation, and felt a presentiment of coming danger.

However, under the influence of a partial drowsiness, his ideas gradually modified, and fear gave place to hope. He saw himself in anticipation, on the morrow, on the plain at the foot of the Andes. There his actual search was to begin; and success was not, perhaps, far distant. He thought of Captain Grant and his two sailors, delivered from a cruel slavery.

These images passed rapidly before his mind, every instant interrupted by a flash of fire, a spark, a flame, illumining the faces of his sleeping companions, and casting a flickering shadow over the walls of the hut. Then his presentiments returned with more vividness, while he listened vaguely to the external sounds so difficult to explain on these solitary summits.

At one moment he thought he heard distant rumblings, dull and threatening like the rollings of thunder. These sounds could be caused only by a tempest, raging on the sides of the mountain. He wished to convince himself, and left the hut.

The moon had risen, and the sky was clear and calm. Not a cloud was to be seen either above or below, only now and then the moving shadows of the flames of the volcano. At the zenith twinkled thousands of stars, while the rumblings still continued. They seemed to approach, and run along the chain of the mountains.

Glenarvan returned more uneasy than before, seeking to divine what relation there was between these subterranean noises and the flight of the guanacos. He looked at his watch; it was two o'clock.

However, having no certain knowledge of immediate danger, he did not wake his companions, whom fatigue held in a deep repose, but fell himself into a heavy sleep that lasted several hours.

All at once a violent crash startled him to his feet. It was a deafening roar, like the irregular noise of innumerable artillery wagons rolling over a hollow pavement. Glenarvan suddenly felt the earth tremble beneath his feet. He saw the hut sway and start open.

"Look out!" he cried.

His companions, awakened and thrown into confusion, were hurried down a rapid descent. The day was breaking, and the scene was terrible. The form of the mountains suddenly changed, their tops were truncated, the tottering peaks disappeared, as if a pitfall had opened at their base. A mass, several miles in extent, became detached entire, and slid towards the plain.

"An earthquake!" cried Paganel.

He was not mistaken. It was one of those phenomena frequent on the mountain frontier of Chili. This portion of the globe is disturbed by subterranean fires, and the volcanoes of this chain afford only insufficient outlets for the confined vapors.

In the meantime the plateau, to which seven stunned and terrified men clung by the tufts of moss, glided with the rapidity of an express. Not a cry was possible, not a movement of escape. They could not hear each other. The internal rumblings, the din of the avalanche, the crash of the blocks of granite, and the whirlwinds of snow, rendered all communication with each other impossible.

At one time the mass would slide without jolts or jars; at another, seized with a pitching and rolling motion like the deck of a vessel shaken by the billows, it would run along the edge of the abysses into which the fragments of the mountain fell, uproot the trees of centuries, and level with the precision of an enormous scythe all the inequalities of the eastern slope.

How long this indescribable scene lasted, no one could tell; in what abyss all were to be engulfed, no one was able to foresee. Whether they were all there alive, or whether one of them was lying at the bottom of a crevasse, no one could say. Stunned by the swiftness of the descent, chilled by the keenness of the cold, blinded by the whirlwinds of snow, they panted, exhausted and almost inanimate, and only clung to the rocks by the supreme instinct of preservation.

All at once a shock of unusual violence arrested their gliding vehicle. They were thrown forward and rolled upon the last declivities of the mountains. The plateau had stopped short.

For a few moments no one stirred. At last one rose, deafened by the shock, but yet firm. It was the major. He shook off the snow that blinded him, and looked around. His companions were not very far from one another. He counted them. All but one lay on the ground. The missing one was Robert Grant.

CHAPTER XIV. PROVIDENTIALLY RESCUED.

The eastern side of the Andes consists of long slopes, declining gradually to the plain upon which a portion of the mass had suddenly stopped. In this new country, garnished with rich pastures and adorned with magnificent vegetation, an incalculable number of apple-trees, planted at the time of the conquest, glowed with their golden fruit and formed true forests. It seemed as if a part of beautiful Normandy had been cast into these monotonous regions, and under any other circumstances the eye of a traveler would have been struck with this sudden transition from desert to oasis, from snowy peak to verdant prairie, from winter to summer.

The earth had regained an absolute immobility, and the earthquake had ceased. But without doubt the subterranean forces were still exerting their devastating action at a distance, for the chain of the Andes is always agitated or trembling in some part. This time, however, the commotion had been of extreme violence. The outline of the mountains was entirely changed; a new view of summits, crests, and peaks was defined against the azure of the sky; and the guide of the Pampas would have sought in vain for his accustomed landmarks.

A wonderfully beautiful day was breaking. The rays of the sun, issuing from their watery bed in the Atlantic, glittered over the Argentine plains and were already silvering the waves of the other ocean. It was eight o'clock in the morning.

Glenarvan and his companions, revived by the aid of the major, gradually recovered consciousness. Indeed, they had only undergone a severe giddiness. The mountain was descended, and they would have applauded a means of locomotion which had been entirely at nature's expense, if one of the feeblest, Robert Grant, had not been missing. Every one loved the courageous boy: Paganel was particularly attached to him; the major, too, in spite of his coldness; but especially Glenarvan.

When the latter learned of Robert's disappearance, he was desperate. He pictured to himself the poor child engulfed in some abyss, and calling vainly for him whom he considered his second father.

"My friends," said he, scarcely restraining his tears, "we must search for him, we must find him! We cannot abandon him thus! Every valley, every precipice, every abyss must be explored to the very bottom! You shall tie a rope around me and let me down! I will do it, you hear me, I will! May Heaven grant that Robert is still living! Without him, how could we dare find his father? What right have we to save Captain Grant, if his rescue costs the life of his child?"

His companions listened without speaking. They felt that he was seeking in their looks some ray of hope, and they lowered their eyes.

"Well," continued Glenarvan, "you understand me; you are silent! You have no more hope!"

A few moments of silence ensued, when MacNabb inquired:

"Who of you, my friends, remembers when Robert disappeared?"

To this question no answer was given.

"At least," continued the major, "you can tell with whom the boy was during the descent."

"With me," replied Wilson.

"Well, at what moment did you last see him with you? Recall the circumstances. Speak."

"This is all that I remember. Robert Grant was at my side, his hand grasping a tuft of moss, less than two minutes before the shock that caused our descent."

"Less than two minutes? Remember, Wilson, the minutes may have seemed long to you. Are you not mistaken?"

"I think not—yes, it is so, less than two minutes."

"Well," said MacNabb; "and was Robert on your right, or on your left?"

"On my left. I remember that his poncho flapped in my face."

"And where were you situated in reference to us?"

"On the left also."

"Then Robert could have disappeared only on this side," said the major, turning towards the mountain, and pointing to the right. "And also considering the time that has elapsed since his disappearance, the child must have fallen at a high part of the mountain. There we must search, and, by taking different ways, we shall find him."

Not a word more was said. The six men, scaling the declivities of the mountain, stationed themselves at different heights along the ridge, and began their search. They kept always to the right of their line of descent, sounding the smallest fissures, descending to the bottom of precipices half filled with fragments of the mass; and more than one came forth with his garments in shreds, his feet and hands lacerated, at the peril of his life.

All this portion of the Andes, except a few inaccessible plateaus, was carefully explored for many hours without one of these brave men thinking of rest. But it was a vain search. The child had not only found death in the mountains, but also a tomb, the stone of which, made of some enormous rock, was forever closed over him.

Towards noon Glenarvan and his companions, bruised and exhausted, found themselves again in the valley. The former was a prey to the most violent grief. He scarcely spoke, and from his lips issued only these words, broken by sighs,—"I will not go; I will not go!"

Each understood this determination, and respected it.

"We will wait," said Paganel to the major and Tom Austin. "Let us take some rest, and recruit our strength. We shall need it, whether to begin our search or continue our journey."

"Yes," replied MacNabb, "let us remain, since Edward wishes it. He hopes: but what does he hope?"

"God knows!" said Tom Austin.

"Poor Robert!" replied Paganel, wiping his eyes.

Trees thronged the valley in great numbers. The major chose a group of lofty carob-trees, under which was established a temporary encampment. A few blankets, the arms, a little dried meat, and some rice, was all that remained to the travelers. A stream, which flowed not far off, furnished water, still muddy from the effects of the avalanche. Mulready kindled a fire on the grass, and soon presented to his master a warm and comforting repast. But Glenarvan refused it, and remained stretched on his poncho in profound prostration.

Thus the day passed. Night came, clear and calm as the preceding. While his companions lay motionless, although wakeful, Glenarvan reascended the mountain. He listened closely, still hoping that a last cry might reach him. He ventured alone and afar, pressing his ear to the ground, listening, restraining the beatings of his heart, and calling in a voice of despair.

The whole night long he wandered on the mountain. Sometimes Paganel, sometimes the major, followed him, ready to help him on the slippery summits, or on the edge of the chasms, where his rashness led him. But his last efforts were fruitless; and to the cry of "Robert! Robert!" a thousand times repeated, echo alone replied.

Day dawned, and it was necessary to go in search of Glenarvan on the mountain, and bring him in spite of his reluctance back to the encampment. His despair was terrible. Who would now dare to speak to him of departure, and propose leaving this fatal valley? But the provisions were failing. They would soon meet the Argentine guides and horses to take them across the Pampas. To retrace their steps was more difficult than to advance. Besides, the Atlantic was the place appointed to meet the Duncan. All these reasons did not permit a longer delay, and it was for the interest of all that the hour for departure should be no longer deferred.

MacNabb attempted to draw Glenarvan from his grief. For a long time he spoke without his friend appearing to hear him. Glenarvan shook his head. At length, words escaped his lips.

"Go?" said he.

"Yes, go."

"One hour more!"

"Well, one hour more," replied the worthy major.

When it had passed, Glenarvan asked for another. You would have thought a condemned man was praying for his life. Thus it continued till about noon, when MacNabb, by the advice of all, would no longer hesitate, and told

Glenarvan that they must go, the lives of his companions depended upon a prompt decision.

"Yes, yes," replied Glenarvan, "we will go, we will go!"

But as he spoke his eyes were turned away from MacNabb. His gaze was fixed upon a black speck in the air. Suddenly his hand rose, and remained immovable, as if petrified.

"There! there!" cried he. "See! see!"

All eyes were raised towards the sky, in the direction so imperatively indicated. At that moment the black speck visibly increased. It was a bird hovering at a measureless height.

"A condor," said Paganel.

"Yes, a condor," replied Glenarvan. "Who knows? He is coming, he is descending! Let us wait."

What did Glenarvan hope? Was his reason wandering? He had said, "Who knows?" Paganel was not mistaken. The condor became more distinct every moment.

This magnificent bird, long revered by the Incas, is the king of the southern Andes. In these regions he attains an extraordinary development. His strength is prodigious; and he often precipitates oxen to the bottom of the abysses. He attacks sheep, goats, and calves wandering on the plain, and carries them in his talons to a great height. Sometimes he hovers at an elevation beyond the limit of human vision, and there this king of the air surveys, with a piercing look, the regions below, and distinguishes the faintest objects with a power of sight that is the astonishment of naturalists.

What had the condor seen? A corpse,—that of Robert Grant? "Who knows?" repeated Glenarvan, without losing sight of him. The enormous bird approached, now hovering, now falling with the swiftness of inert bodies. He soon described circles of larger extent, and could be perfectly distinguished. He measured fifteen feet across his wings, which supported him in the air almost without motion, for it is the peculiarity of these great birds to sail with a majestic calmness unlike all others of the winged tribes.

The major and Wilson had seized their rifles, but Glenarvan stopped them with a gesture. The condor was approaching in the circles of his flight a sort of inaccessible plateau a quarter of a mile distant. He was turning with a vertical rapidity, opening and closing his formidable claws, and shaking his cartilaginous neck.

"There! there!" cried Glenarvan.

Then suddenly a thought flashed through his mind.

"If Robert is still living!" exclaimed he, with a cry of terror, "this bird! Fire, my friends, fire!"

But he was too late. The condor had disappeared behind the lofty boulders. A second passed that seemed an eternity. Then the enormous bird reappeared, heavily laden, and rising slowly.

A cry of horror was uttered. In the claws of the condor an inanimate body was seen suspended and dangling. It was Robert Grant. The bird had raised him by his garments, and was now hovering in mid-air at least one hundred and fifty feet above the encampment. He had perceived the travelers, and was violently striving to escape with his heavy prey.

"May Robert's body be dashed upon these rocks," cried Glenarvan, "rather than serve—"

He did not finish, but, seizing Wilson's rifle, attempted to take aim at the condor. But his arm trembled; he could not sight the piece. His eyes were dimmed.

"Let me try," said the major.

With clear eye, steady hand, and motionless body, he aimed at the bird, that was already three hundred feet above him. But he had not pressed the trigger, when a report resounded in the valley. A light smoke curled up between two rocks, and the condor, shot in the head, fell, slowly turning, sustained by his broad outspread wings. He had not released his prey, and at last reached the ground, ten paces from the banks of the stream.

"Quick! quick!" said Glenarvan; and without seeking whence this providential shot had come, he rushed towards the condor. His companions closely followed him.

When they arrived the bird was dead, and the body of Robert was hidden under its great wings. Glenarvan threw himself upon the child, released him from the talons of the condor, stretched him on the grass, and pressed his ear to his breast.

Never did a wilder cry of joy issue from human lips than when Glenarvan rose, exclaiming:

"He lives! he lives!"

In an instant Robert was stripped of his garments, and his face bathed with fresh water. He made a movement, opened his eyes, looked around, and uttered a few words:

"You, my lord—my father!—"

Glenarvan could not speak. Emotion stifled him, and, kneeling, he wept beside this child so miraculously saved.

CHAPTER XV. THALCAVE.

After the great danger that he had just escaped, Robert incurred another, no less great,—that of being overwhelmed with caresses. However feeble he was still, not one of these good people could refrain from pressing him to his heart. But it must be confessed that these well-meant embraces are not fatal, for the boy did not die.

When his rescue was certain, thought reverted to his rescuer, and the major very naturally thought of looking around him. Fifty paces from the stream, a man of lofty stature was standing, motionless, on one of the first ledges of the mountain. A long gun lay at his feet. This individual, who had so suddenly appeared, had broad shoulders, and long hair tied with leathern thongs. His height exceeded six feet, and his bronzed face was red between his eyes and mouth, black below his eyelids, and white on his forehead. After the manner of the Patagonians of the frontiers, the native wore a splendid cloak, decorated with red arabesques, made of the skin of a guanaco, its silky fur turned outward, and sewed with ostrich-tendons. Under his cloak a tippet of fox-skin encircled his neck and terminated in a point in front. At his girdle hung a little bag containing the colors with which he painted his face. His leggings were of ox-hide, and fastened to the ankle with straps regularly crossed.

The figure of this Patagonian was fine, and his face denoted real intelligence in spite of the colors that adorned (!) it. He waited in an attitude full of dignity, and, seeing him so motionless and stern on his pedestal of rocks, you would have taken him for a statue.

The major, as soon as he perceived him, pointed him out to Glenarvan, who hastened towards him. The Patagonian took two steps forward; Glenarvan took his hand, and pressed it. There was in the latter's look, in his physiognomy, such a feeling, such an expression of gratitude, that the native could not mistake it. He inclined his head gently, and uttered a few words that neither the major nor his friend could understand.

The Patagonian, after regarding the strangers attentively, now changed the language; but whatever it was, this new idiom was no better understood than the first. However, certain expressions which he used struck Glenarvan. They seemed to belong to the Spanish language, of which he knew several common words.

"Spanish?" said he.

The Patagonian nodded.

"Well," said the major, "this is our friend Paganel's business. It is fortunate that he thought of learning Spanish."

Paganel was called. He came at once and with all the grace of a Frenchman saluted the Patagonian, to which the latter paid no attention. The geographer was informed of the state of affairs, and was only too glad to use his diligently-acquired knowledge.

"Exactly," said he. And opening his mouth widely in order to articulate better, he said, in his best Spanish,—

"You—are—a—brave—man."

The native listened, but did not answer.

"He does not understand," said the geographer.

"Perhaps you do not pronounce well," replied the major.

"Very true! Curse the pronunciation!"

And again Paganel began, but with no better success.

"I will change the expression," said he. And pronouncing with magisterial slowness, he uttered these words,—

"A—Patagonian,—doubtless?"

The native remained mute as before.

"Answer!" added Paganel.

The Patagonian did not reply.

"Do—you—understand?" cried Paganel, violently enough to damage his organs of speech.

It was evident that the Indian did not understand, for he answered, but in Spanish,—

"I do not understand."

It was Paganel's turn now to be astonished, and he hastily put on his glasses, like one irritated.

"May I be hanged," said he, "if I understand a word of this infernal jargon! It is certainly Araucanian."

"No," replied Glenarvan; "this man answered in Spanish."

And, turning to the Patagonian, he repeated,—

"Spanish?"

"Yes," replied the native.

Paganel's surprise became amazement. The major and Glenarvan looked at him quizzingly.

"Ah, my learned friend!" said the major, while a half smile played about his lips, "you have committed one of those blunders peculiar to you."

"What!" cried the geographer, starting.

"Yes, it is plain that this Patagonian speaks Spanish."

"He?"

"Yes. By mistake you have learnt another language, while thinking that you studied—"

MacNabb did not finish. A loud "Oh!" from the geographer, accompanied by shrugs of the shoulders, cut him short.

"Major, you are going a little too far," said Paganel in a very dry tone.

"To be sure, since you do not understand."

"I do not understand because this native speaks so badly!" answered the geographer, who began to be impatient.

"That is to say, he speaks badly, because you do not understand," returned the major, calmly.

"MacNabb," said Glenarvan, "that is not a probable supposition. However abstracted our friend Paganel may be, we cannot suppose that his blunder was to learn one language for another."

"Now, my dear Edward, or rather you, my good Paganel, explain to me what the difficulty is."

"I will not explain," replied Paganel, "I insist. Here is the book in which I practice daily the difficulties of the Spanish language! Examine it, major, and you will see whether I impose upon you."

So saying, Paganel groped in his numerous pockets. After searching a few moments, he drew forth a volume in a very bad state, and presented it with an air of assurance. The major took the book, and looked at it.

"Well, what work is this?" he asked.

"The Lusiad," replied Paganel; "an admirable poem which—"

"The Lusiad!" cried Glenarvan.

"Yes, my friend, the Lusiad of the immortal Camoëns, nothing more or less."

"Camoëns!" repeated Glenarvan; "but, unfortunate friend, Camoëns was a Portuguese! It is Portuguese that you have been studying for six weeks."

"Camoëns! Lusiad! Portuguese!"

Paganel could say no more. His eyes wandered, while a peal of Homeric laughter rang in his ears.

The Patagonian did not wink; he waited patiently for the explanation of this event, which was totally incomprehensible to him.

"Insensate! fool!" cried Paganel, at last. "What! is it so? Is it not a mere joke? Have I done this? It is the confusion of languages, as at Babel. My friends! my friends! to start for India and arrive at Chili! to learn Spanish and speak Portuguese! this is too much, and, if it continues, I shall some day throw myself out of the window instead of my cigar."

To hear Paganel take his blunder thus, to see his comical actions, it was impossible to keep serious. Besides, he set the example himself.

"Laugh, my friends," said he, "laugh with a will! you cannot laugh as much as I do at myself."

And he uttered the most formidable peal of laughter that ever issued from the mouth of a geographer.

"But we are none the less without an interpreter," said the major.

"Oh, do not be troubled," replied Paganel. "The Portuguese and Spanish resemble each other so much that I made a mistake. However, this very resemblance will soon enable me to rectify my error, and in a short time I will thank this worthy Patagonian in the language he speaks so well."

Paganel was right, for he could soon exchange a few words with the native. He even learned that his name was Thalcave, a word which signifies in Araucanian "the thunderer." This surname was doubtless given to him for his skill in the use of fire-arms.

But Glenarvan was particularly rejoiced to discover that the Patagonian was a guide, and, moreover, a guide of the Pampas. There was, therefore, something so providential in this meeting that the success of the enterprise seemed already an accomplished fact, and no one any longer doubted the rescue of Captain Grant.

In the meantime the travelers and the Patagonian had returned to Robert. The latter stretched his arms towards the native, who, without a word, placed his hand upon his head. He examined the child and felt his wounded limbs.

Then, smiling, he went and gathered on the banks of the stream a few handfuls of wild celery, with which he rubbed the boy's body. Under this treatment, performed with an extreme gentleness, the child felt his strength revive, and it was plain that a few hours would suffice to restore him.

It was therefore decided that that day and the following night should be passed at the encampment. Besides, two important questions remained to be settled—food, and means of conveyance. Provisions and mules were both wanting. Fortunately Thalcave solved the difficulty. This guide, who was accustomed to conduct travelers along the Patagonian frontiers, and was one of the most intelligent baqueanos of the country, engaged to furnish Glenarvan all that his little party needed. He offered to take him to a "tolderia" (encampment) of Indians, about four miles distant, where they would find everything necessary for the expedition. This proposal was made partly by gestures, partly by Spanish words which Paganel succeeded in understanding. It was accepted, and Glenarvan and his learned friend, taking leave of their companions, reascended the stream under the guidance of the Patagonian.

They proceeded at a good pace for an hour and a half, taking long strides to keep up to the giant Thalcave. All the region was charming, and of a rich fertility. The grassy pastures succeeded each other, and could easily have fed thousands of cattle. Large ponds, united by a winding chain of streams, gave these plains a verdant moisture. Black-headed swans sported on the mirror-like surface, and disputed the empire of the waters with numberless ostriches that gamboled over the plains, while the brilliant feathered tribes were in wonderful variety. Jacques Paganel proceeded from admiration to ecstasy. Exclamations of delight continually escaped his lips, to the astonishment of the Patagonian, who thought it very natural that there should be birds in the air, swans on the lakes, and grass on the prairies. The geographer had no reason to regret his walk, or complain of its length. He scarcely believed himself started, or that the encampment would soon come in sight.

This tolderia was at the bottom of a narrow valley among the mountains. Here in huts of branches lived thirty wandering natives, grazing large herds of milch cows, sheep, cattle and horses. Thus they roamed from one pasture to another, always finding a repast ready for their four-footed companions.

Thalcave took upon himself the negotiation, which was not long. In return for seven small Argentine horses, all saddled, a hundred pounds of dried meat, a few measures of rice, and some leathern bottles for water, the Indians received twenty ounces of gold, the value of which they perfectly understood. Glenarvan would have bought another horse for the Patagonian, but he intimated that it was unnecessary.

The bargain concluded, Glenarvan took leave of his new "providers," as Paganel expressed it, and returned to the encampment. His arrival was welcomed by cries of joy at sight of the provisions and horses. Every one ate with avidity. Robert partook of some nourishment; he had almost entirely regained his strength, and the remainder of the day was passed in perfect rest.

Various subjects were alluded to: the absent dear ones, the Duncan, Captain Mangles, his brave crew, and Harry Grant who was, perhaps, not far distant.

As for Paganel, he did not leave the Indian. He became Thalcave's shadow, and could not remain quiet in the presence of a real Patagonian, in comparison with whom he would have passed for a dwarf. He overwhelmed the grave Indian with Spanish phrases, to which the latter quietly listened. The geographer studied this time without a book, and was often heard repeating words aloud. "If I do not get the accent," said he to the major, "you must not be angry with me. Who would have thought that one day a Patagonian would teach me Spanish!"

CHAPTER XVI. NEWS OF THE LOST CAPTAIN.

At eight o'clock the next morning Thalcave gave the signal for departure. The slope was gradual, and the travelers had only to descend a gentle declivity to the sea.

When the Patagonian declined the horse that Glenarvan offered him, the latter thought that he preferred to go on foot, according to the custom of certain guides; and indeed, his long legs ought to have made walking easy. But he was mistaken.

At the moment of departure Thalcave whistled in a peculiar manner. Immediately a magnificent Argentine horse, of superb form, issued from a small wood near by, and approached at the call of his master. The animal was perfectly beautiful. His brown color indicated a sound, spirited and courageous beast. He had a small and elegantly poised head, widely opening nostrils, a fiery eye, large hams, swelling withers, broad breast, long pasterns, in short, all the qualities that constitute strength and suppleness. The major, like a perfect horseman, admired unreservedly this specimen of the horses of the plains. This beautiful creature was called Thaouka, which means "bird" in the Patagonian language, and he justly merited this appellation.

When Thalcave was in the saddle, the horse pranced with spirited grace, and the Patagonian, a skillful rider, was magnificent to behold. His outfit comprised two weapons of the chase, the "bolas" and the lasso. The bolas consists of three balls tied together by a leathern string, which are fastened to the front of the saddle. The Indians frequently throw them the distance of a hundred paces at the animal or enemy that they are pursuing, and with such precision that they twist about their legs and bring them to the ground. It is, therefore, in their hands a formidable instrument, and they handle it with surprising dexterity. The lasso, on the contrary, does not leave the hand that wields it. It consists simply of a leathern thong thirty feet in length, terminating in a slip-noose which works upon an iron ring. The right hand throws the slip-noose, while the left hand holds the remainder of the lasso, the end of which is firmly tied to the saddle. A long carbine in a sling completed the Patagonian's armament.

Thalcave, without observing the admiration caused by his natural grace, ease and courage, took the lead, and the party advanced, now at a gallop, and now at a walk, for their horses seemed entirely unaccustomed to trotting. Robert mounted with much boldness, and speedily convinced Glenarvan of his ability to keep his seat.

On issuing from the gorges of the Andes, they encountered a great number of sand-ridges, called "medanos," real waves incessantly agitated by the wind, when the roots of the herbage did not confine them to the earth. This sand is of an extreme fineness; and, at the least breath, they saw it float away in light clouds, or form regular sand-columns which rose to a considerable height. This spectacle caused pleasure as well as annoyance to the eyes. Pleasure, for nothing was more curious than these columns, wandering over the plain, struggling, mingling, sinking and rising in inexpressible confusion; and annoyance, since an impalpable dust emanated from these innumerable medanos and penetrated the eyelids, however tightly they were closed.

This phenomenon continued during a great part of the day. Nevertheless, they advanced rapidly, and towards six o'clock the Andes, forty miles distant, presented a darkish aspect already fading in the mists of the evening.

The travelers were a little fatigued with their journey, and, therefore, saw with pleasure the approach of the hour for retiring. They encamped on the shores of a turbulent stream, enclosed by lofty red cliffs. Toward noon of the next day, the sun's rays became very oppressive, and at evening a line of clouds on the horizon indicated a change in the weather. The Patagonian could not be deceived, and pointed out to the geographer the western portion of the sky.

"Good, I know," said Paganel, and addressing his companions: "A change in the weather is about to take place. We shall have a 'pampero.'"

He explained that this pampero is frequent on the Argentine Plains. It is a very dry wind from the southwest. Thalcave was not mistaken, and during the night, which was quite uncomfortable for people sheltered with a simple poncho, the wind blew with great violence. The horses lay down on the ground, and the men near them in a close group. Glenarvan feared they would be delayed if the storm continued; but Paganel reassured him after consulting his barometer.

"Ordinarily," said he, "this wind creates tempests, which last for three days; but when the barometer rises as it does now, you are free from these furious hurricanes in a few hours. Be assured, then, my dear friend; at break of day the sky will have resumed its usual clearness."

"You talk like a book, Paganel," replied Glenarvan.

"And I am one," replied Paganel, "which you are free to consult as much as you please."

He was not mistaken. At one o'clock in the morning the wind suddenly subsided, and every one was able to enjoy an invigorating sleep. The next morning they rose bright and fresh, especially Paganel, who displayed great cheerfulness and animation.

During this passage across the continent, Lord Glenarvan watched with scrupulous attention for the approach of the natives. He wished to question them concerning Captain Grant, by the aid of the Patagonian, with whom Paganel had begun to converse considerably. But they followed a path little frequented by the Indians, for the trails over the Pampas, which lead from the Argentine Republic to the Andes, are situated too far to the north. If by chance a wandering horseman appeared in the distance, he fled rapidly away, little caring to come in contact with strangers.

However, although Glenarvan, in the interest of his search, regretted the absence of the Indians, an incident took place which singularly justified the interpretation of the document.

Several times the course pursued by the expedition crossed paths on the Pampas, among others quite an important road—that from Carmen to Mendoza—distinguishable by the bones of such animals as mules, horses, sheep and oxen, whose remains were scattered by the birds of prey, and lay bleaching in the sun. There were thousands of them, and, without doubt, more than one human skeleton had added its bones to those of these humbler animals.

Hitherto Thalcave had made no remark concerning the line so rigorously followed. He understood, however, that if they kept no definite course over the Pampas, they would not come to cities or villages. Every morning they advanced towards the rising sun, without deviating from the straight line, and every evening the setting sun was behind them. In his capacity of guide, Thalcave must, therefore, have been astonished to see that not only he did not guide them, but that they guided him. Nevertheless, if he was astonished, with the reserve natural to the Indians he made no remark. But to-day arriving at the above-mentioned road, he stopped his horse, and turned towards Paganel.

"Road to Carmen," said he.

"Yes, my good Patagonian," replied the geographer, in his purest Spanish; "road to Carmen and Mendoza."

"We do not take it?" resumed Thalcave.

"No," answered Paganel.

"And we are going—?"

"Always to the east."

"That is going nowhere."

"Who knows?"

Thalcave was silent, and gazed at the geographer with profound surprise. He did not admit, however, that Paganel was joking the least in the world. An Indian, with his natural seriousness, never imagines that you are not speaking in earnest.

"You are not going to Carmen then?" he added, after an instant of silence.

"No," replied Paganel.

"Nor to Mendoza?"

"No."

At this moment Glenarvan, rejoining Paganel, asked what Thalcave said, and why he had stopped.

When he had told him, Glenarvan said,—

"Could you not explain to him the object of our expedition, and why we must always proceed toward the east?"

"That would be very difficult," answered Paganel, "for an Indian understands nothing of geography."

"But," said the major seriously, "is it the history, or the historian, that he cannot understand?"

"Ah, MacNabb," said Paganel, "you still doubt my Spanish!"

"Try, my worthy friend."

"Very well."

Paganel turned to the Patagonian, and began a discourse, frequently interrupted for want of words and from the difficulty of explaining to a half-ignorant savage details which were rather incomprehensible to him.

The geographer was just then a curious sight. He gesticulated, articulated, and exerted himself in a hundred ways, while great drops of sweat rolled down his face. When his tongue could no longer move, his arm came to his aid. He dismounted, and traced on the sand a geographical map, with lines of latitude and longitude, the two oceans, and the road to Carmen. Never was professor in such embarrassment. Thalcave watched these manœuvres without showing whether he comprehended or not.

The lesson in geography lasted more than half an hour. At last Paganel ceased, wiped his face, which was wet with perspiration, and looked at the Patagonian.

"Did he understand?" inquired Glenarvan.

"We shall see," replied Paganel; "but, if he did not, I give it up."

Thalcave did not stir. He no longer spoke. His eyes were fixed upon the figures traced on the sand, which the wind was gradually effacing.

"Well?" asked Paganel.

Thalcave did not appear to hear him. Paganel already saw an ironical smile forming upon the lips of the major, and, wishing to save his reputation, had begun with renewed energy his geographical demonstrations, when the Patagonian stopped him with a gesture.

"You are searching for a prisoner?" he said.

"Yes," replied Paganel.

"And exactly on the line from the setting to the rising sun?" said Thalcave, indicating by a comparison, in the Indian manner, the course from west to east.

"Yes, yes, that is it!"

"And it is your God," said the Patagonian, "who has confided to the waves of the vast ocean the secrets of the prisoner?"

"God himself."

"May his will be accomplished then!" replied Thalcave, with a certain solemnity. "We will go to the east, and, if necessary, even to the sun."

Paganel, in his exultation over his pupil, immediately translated to his companions the replies of the Indian.

Glenarvan requested Paganel to ask the Patagonian if he had heard of any strangers falling into the hands of the Indians, which was accordingly done.

"Perhaps," replied the Patagonian.

As soon as this word was translated, Thalcave was surrounded by the seven travelers, who gazed at him with questioning looks. Paganel, excited and scarcely finding his words, resumed these interesting interrogatories, while his eyes, fixed upon the grave Indian, strove to anticipate his reply before it issued from his lips. Every word the Patagonian said he repeated in English, so that his companions heard the Indian speak, as it were, in their own language.

"And this prisoner?" inquired Paganel.

"He was a stranger," replied Thalcave slowly; "a European."

"You have seen him?"

"No, but he is mentioned in the accounts of the Indians. He was a brave man."

"You understand, my friends," said Paganel; "a courageous man!"

"My father!" cried Robert Grant.

Then, addressing Paganel:

"How do you say 'It is my father,' in Spanish?" he asked.

"*Es mio padre*," answered the geographer.

Immediately Robert, taking Thalcave's hands, said in a sweet voice,—

"*Es mio padre!*"

"*Suo padre!*" replied the Patagonian, whose look brightened.

He took the boy in his arms, lifted him from his horse, and gazed at him with the most curious sympathy. His intelligent countenance became suffused with a peaceful emotion.

But Paganel had not finished his inquiries. Where was this prisoner? What was he doing? When had Thalcave heard of him? All these questions thronged his mind at once. He did not have to wait long for answers, but learnt that the European was a slave of one of the Indian tribes that scour the plains.

"But where was he last?" asked Paganel.

"With the cazique Calfoucoura," answered Thalcave.

"On the line we have been following?"

"Yes."

"And who is this cazique?"

"The chief of the Poyuches Indians; a man with two tongues and two hearts."

"That is to say, false in word and in deed," said Paganel, after translating to his companions this beautiful metaphor of the Indian language. "And can we rescue our friend?" he added.

"Perhaps so, if your friend is still in the hands of the Indians."

"And when did you hear of him?"

"A long time ago, and, since then, the sun has brought back two summers to the sky."

Glenarvan's joy could not be described. This answer coincided exactly with the date of the document. But one question remained to be asked.

"You speak of a prisoner," said Paganel; "but were there not three?"

"I do not know," replied Thalcave.

"And you know nothing of their actual situation?"

"Nothing."

This last word ended the conversation. It was possible that the three prisoners had been separated a long time. But the substance of the Patagonian's information was that the Indians spoke of a European who had fallen into their power. The date of his captivity, the place where he must have been, everything, even to the Patagonian phrase used to express his courage, related evidently to Captain Harry Grant.

Their progress was now somewhat slow and difficult; their next object being to reach and cross the river Colorado, to which at length their horses brought them. Here Paganel's first care was to bathe "geographically" in its waters, which are colored by a reddish clay. He was surprised to find the depth so great as it really was, this being the result of the snow having melted rapidly under the first heat of summer. The width likewise of this stream was so considerable that it was almost impossible for their horses to swim across; but they happily discovered a sort of weir-bridge, of wattles looped and fastened together, which the Indians were in the habit of using; and by its aid the little troop was enabled to pass over to the left bank, where they rested for the night.

CHAPTER XVII. A SERIOUS NECESSITY.

They set out at daybreak. The horses advanced at a brisk pace among the tufts of "paja-brava," a kind of grass that serves the Indians as a shelter during the storms. At certain distances, but less and less frequent, pools of shallow water contributed to the growth of willows and a certain plant which is found in the neighborhood of fresh water. Here the horses drank their fill, to fortify themselves for the journey. Thalcave, who rode in advance, beat the bushes, and thus frightened away the "cholinas" (vipers), while the agile Thaouka bounded over all obstacles, and aided his master in clearing a passage for the horses that followed.

Early in the afternoon, the first traces of animals were encountered—the bones of an innumerable drove of cattle, in whitened heaps. These fragments did not extend in a winding line, such as animals exhausted and falling one by one would leave behind them. Thus no one, not even Paganel, knew how to explain this chain of skeletons in a space comparatively circumscribed. He therefore questioned Thalcave, who was not at a loss for a reply.

"What is this?" they asked, after Paganel had inquired of the Indian.

"The fire of heaven," replied the geographer.

"What! the lightning could not have produced such a disaster," said Tom Austin, "and stretched five hundred head of cattle on the earth!"

But Thalcave reaffirmed it, and he was not mistaken; for the storms of the Pampas are noted for their violence.

At evening they stopped at an abandoned rancho, made of interlaced branches plastered with mud and covered with thatch. This structure stood within an inclosure of half-rotten stakes which, however, sufficed to protect the horses during the night against the attacks of the foxes. Not that they had anything to fear personally from these animals, but the malicious beasts gnawed the halters, so that the horses could escape.

A few paces from the rancho, a hole was dug which served as a kitchen and contained half-cooled embers. Within, there was a bench, a bed of ox-hide, a saucepan, a spit, and a pot for boiling maté. The maté is a drink very much in use in South America. It is the Indian's tea, consisting of a decoction of leaves dried in the fire, and is imbibed through a straw. At Paganel's request, Thalcave prepared several cups of this beverage, which very agreeably accompanied the ordinary eatables, and was declared excellent.

The next day they resumed their journey towards the east. About noon a change took place in the appearance of the Pampas, which could not escape eyes wearied with its monotony. The grass became more and more scanty, and gave place to sickly burdocks and gigantic thistles; while stunted nettles and other thorny shrubs grew here and there. Heretofore, a certain moisture, preserved by the clay of the prairie, freshened the meadows; the vegetation was thick and luxuriant. But now a patchy growth, bare in many places, exposed the earth, and indicated the poverty of the soil. These signs of increasing dryness could not be mistaken, and Thalcave called attention to them.

"I am not sorry at this change," said Tom Austin; "to see always grass, nothing but grass, becomes tiresome before long."

"But where there is grass there is water," replied the major.

"Oh, we are not in want," said Wilson, "and shall find some river on our course."

However, when Wilson said that the supply of water would not fail he had not calculated for the unquenchable thirst that consumed his companions all that day; and, when he added that they would meet with some stream in their journey he had anticipated too much. Indeed, not only were rivers wanting, but even the artificial wells dug by the Indians were empty. On seeing these indications of dryness increase from mile to mile, Paganel asked Thalcave where he expected to find water.

"At Lake Salinas," replied the Indian.

"And when shall we arrive there?"

"To-morrow evening."

The natives ordinarily, when they travel on the Pampas, dig wells, and find water a few feet below the surface; but the travelers, destitute of the necessary implements, could not employ this expedient. It was therefore necessary to obtain a supply in some other way, for, if they did not absolutely suffer from the tormenting desire for drink, no one could entirely allay his thirst.

At evening they halted, after a journey of thirty miles. Every one relied upon a good night to recruit himself after the fatigues of the day; but they were greatly annoyed by a very persistent swarm of mosquitoes, which disappeared, however, after the wind changed.

If the major preserved his calmness in the midst of the petty annoyances of life, Paganel, on the contrary, could not treat the matter so indifferently. He fought the mosquitoes, and sadly regretted the absence of his acid-water, which would have soothed the pain of their bites. Although the major endeavored to console him, he awoke in a very bad humor.

However, he was very easily persuaded to set out at daybreak, for it was important to arrive at Lake Salinas the same day. The horses were very much exhausted: they were dying of thirst; and, although their riders had denied themselves on their account, still their share of water had been very limited. The dryness was to-day even greater, and the heat no less intolerable, with the dusty wind, the simoom of the Pampas.

During the day the monotony of the journey was interrupted. Mulready, who rode in advance, turned back, signaling the approach of a party of Indians. This meeting elicited different opinions. Glenarvan thought of the information that these natives might furnish concerning the shipwrecked seamen of the Britannia. Thalcave, for his part, scarcely enjoyed meeting in his journey the wandering Indians of the plains. He considered them plunderers and robbers, and only sought to avoid them. According to his orders, the little party collected together, and made ready their fire-arms. It was necessary to be prepared for any emergency.

The Indian detachment was soon perceived. It consisted of only ten men, which fact reassured the Patagonian. They approached within a hundred paces, so that they could be easily distinguished. Their high foreheads, prominent rather than receding, their tall forms, and their olive color, showed them to be magnificent types of the Indian race. They were clad in the skins of guanacos, and carried various weapons of war and the chase, while their dexterity in horsemanship was remarkable.

Having halted, they appeared to hold a conference, crying and gesticulating. Glenarvan advanced toward them; but he had not proceeded two yards, when the detachment wheeled about and disappeared with incredible swiftness. The tired horses of the travelers could never have overtaken them.

"The cowards!" cried Paganel.

"They fly too fast for honest men," said MacNabb.

"What are these Indians?" inquired Paganel of Thalcave.

"Gauchos!" replied the Patagonian.

"Gauchos!" repeated Paganel, turning toward his companions, "Gauchos! We had no need, then, to take such precautions. There was nothing to fear!"

"Why?" asked the major.

"Because the Gauchos are inoffensive peasants."

"Do you think so, Paganel?"

"Certainly. They took us for robbers, and fled."

Glenarvan was quite disappointed in not speaking with them, as he expected to obtain additional tidings of the lost sailors; but it was necessary to push on, if they would reach their destination that evening.

At eight o'clock Thalcave, who had gone a little in advance, announced that the lake so long desired was in sight. A quarter of an hour afterward the little party descended the high banks. But here a serious disappointment awaited them,—the lake was dry!

CHAPTER XVIII. IN SEARCH OF WATER.

Lake Salinas terminates the cluster of lagoons that adjoin the Ventana and Guamini mountains. Numerous expeditions are made to this place to obtain supplies of salt, with which these waters are strongly impregnated. But now the water had evaporated under the heat of the sun, and the lake was only a vast glittering basin.

When Thalcave announced the presence of a drinkable liquid at Lake Salinas, he meant the streams of fresh water that flow from it in many places. But at this time its affluents were as dry as itself. The burning sun had absorbed everything. Hence, the consternation was general when the thirsty party arrived at the parched shores of Lake Salinas.

It was necessary to take counsel. The little water in the leathern bottles was half spoiled, and could not quench their thirst, which began to make itself acutely felt. Hunger and fatigue gave place to this imperative want. A "roukah," a kind of upright tent, of leather, which stood in a hollow, and had been abandoned by the natives, served as a refuge for the travelers, while their horses, stretched on the muddy shores of the lake, ate the saline plants and dry reeds, although reluctantly.

When each had sat down in the roukah, Paganel asked Thalcave's advice as to what was best to be done. A rapid conversation, of which Glenarvan caught a few words, ensued between the geographer and the Indian. Thalcave spoke calmly, while Paganel gesticulated for both. This consultation lasted a few minutes, and then the Patagonian folded his arms.

"What did he say?" inquired Glenarvan. "I thought I understood him to advise us to separate."

"Yes, into two parties," replied Paganel. "Those of us whose horses are so overcome with fatigue and thirst that they can scarcely move will continue the journey as well as possible. Those who are better mounted, on the contrary, will ride in advance, and reconnoitre the Guamini River, which empties into Lake

San Lucas. If there is sufficient water there, they will wait for their companions on the banks of the stream; if not, they will return to save the rest a useless journey."

"And then?" asked Tom Austin.

"Then we must go southward to the first branches of the Ventana mountains, where the rivers are numerous."

"The plan is good," replied Glenarvan, "and we will follow it without delay. My horse has not suffered so much yet from want of water, and I offer to accompany Thalcave."

"Oh, my lord, take me!" cried Robert, as if a pleasure excursion were in question.

"But can you keep up with us, my child?"

"Yes, I have a good beast that asks nothing better than to go in advance. Will you, my lord? I beseech you!"

"Come then, my boy," said Glenarvan, delighted not to be separated from Robert. "And we three," he added, "will be very stupid if we do not discover some clear and fresh stream."

"And I?" said Paganel.

"Oh, you, my dear Paganel!" replied the major, "you will remain with the reserve detachment. You know the course, the Guamini River, and the Pampas, too well to abandon us. Neither Wilson, Mulready, nor myself are capable of rejoining Thalcave at his rendezvous, unless we advance confidently under the guidance of the brave Jacques Paganel."

"I resign," said the geographer, very much flattered to obtain a higher command.

"But no distractions!" added the major. "Do not lead us where we have nothing to do, and bring us back to the shores of the Pacific!"

"You would deserve it, my intolerable major," said Paganel, smiling. "But tell me, my dear Glenarvan, how will you understand Thalcave's language?"

"I suppose," answered Glenarvan, "that the Patagonian and I will not need to talk. Besides, with the few Spanish words that I know, I shall succeed well enough on an emergency in giving him my opinion and understanding his."

"Go then, my worthy friend," replied Paganel.

"Let us eat first," said Glenarvan, "and sleep till the hour of departure."

They ate supper without drink, which was rather unrefreshing, and then fell asleep. Paganel dreamed of torrents, cascades, streams, rivers, ponds, brooks, nay even full bottles, in short, of everything which generally contains water. It was a real nightmare.

The next morning at six o'clock the horses were saddled. They gave them the last drink of water left, which they took with more dislike than pleasure, for it was very nauseating. The three horsemen then mounted.

"*Au revoir!*" said the major, Austin, Wilson, and Mulready.

Soon the Patagonian, Glenarvan, and Robert (not without a certain throbbing of the heart) lost sight of the detachment confided to the sagacity of the geographer.

Thalcave was right in first proceeding towards the Guamini, since this stream lay on the prescribed course, and was the nearest. The three horses galloped briskly forward. These excellent beasts perceived, doubtless, by instinct, whither their masters were guiding them. Thaouka, especially, showed a spirit that neither fatigue nor thirst could overcome. The other horses followed, at a slower pace, but incited by his example.

The Patagonian frequently turned his head to look at Robert Grant, and, seeing the young boy firm and erect, in an easy and graceful position, testified his satisfaction by a word of encouragement.

"Bravo, Robert!" said Glenarvan. "Thalcave seems to congratulate you. He praises you, my boy!"

"And why, my lord?"

"Because of the way you ride."

"Oh, I merely keep firm; that is all," replied Robert, who blushed with pleasure at hearing himself complimented.

"That is the main point, Robert," said Glenarvan; "but you are too modest, and I am sure you cannot fail to become an accomplished equestrian."

"Well," said Robert, "but what will papa say, who wishes to make a sailor of me?"

"The one does not interfere with the other. If all horsemen do not make good sailors, all sailors may certainly make good horsemen. To ride on the yards, you must learn to keep yourself firm. As for knowing how to manage your horse, that comes more easily."

"Poor father!" exclaimed Robert; "how he will thank you when you have found him!" And, so saying, he took his lordship's hand and pressed it to his lips.

"You love him well, Robert?"

"Yes, my lord; he was so kind to sister and me. He thought only of us, and every voyage brought us a memento of the countries he visited, and, what was better, tender caresses and kind words, on his return. Ah! you will love him too, when you know him! Mary resembles him. He has a sweet voice like her. It is singular for a sailor, is it not?"

"Yes, very singular, Robert," said Glenarvan.

"I see him still," replied the boy, as if speaking to himself. "Good and brave papa! He rocked me to sleep on his knees, when I was little, and kept humming an old Scottish song which is sung around the lakes of our country. I sometimes recall the air, but indistinctly. How we loved him, my lord! Well, I think one must be very young to love his father well."

"And old to reverence him, my child," replied Glenarvan, quite moved by the words that came from this young heart.

During this conversation, their horses had relaxed their pace and fallen behind the other; but Thalcave called them, and they resumed their former gait. It was soon evident, however, that, with the exception of Thaouka, the horses could not long maintain this speed. At noon it was necessary to give them an hour's rest.

Glenarvan grew uneasy. The signs of dryness did not diminish, and the want of water might result in disastrous consequences. Thalcave said nothing, but probably thought that if the Guamini was dry it would then be time to despair, if indeed an Indian's heart has ever experienced such an emotion.

They therefore kept on, and by use of whip and spur the horses were induced to continue their journey, but they could not quicken their pace. Thalcave might easily have gone ahead, for in a few hours Thaouka could have carried him to the banks of the stream. He doubtless thought of it, but probably did not like to leave his two companions alone in the midst of this desert, and, that he might not outstrip them, he forced Thaouka to lessen his speed. It was not, however, without much resistance, prancing and neighing, that Thalcave's horse consented to keep pace with the others. It was not so much the strength as the voice of his master which restrained him; the Indian actually talked to his horse; and the animal, if he did not answer, at least comprehended him. The Patagonian must have used excellent arguments, for, after "discussing" some time, Thaouka yielded, and obeyed his master's commands.

But, if Thaouka understood Thalcave, Thalcave had none the less understood Thaouka. The intelligent animal, through his superior instincts, had perceived a moisture in the air. He inhaled it eagerly, and kept moving his tongue, as if it were steeped in a grateful liquid. The Patagonian could not be deceived; water was not far distant.

He therefore encouraged his companions by explaining the impatience of his horse, which the others were not long in understanding. They made a final effort, and galloped after the Indian.

About three o'clock a bright line appeared in a hollow of the plain. It trembled under the rays of the sun. "Water!" cried Glenarvan.

"Water, yes, water!" cried Robert.

They had no more need to urge their horses. The poor beasts, feeling their strength renewed, rushed forward with an irresistible eagerness. In a few moments they had reached the Guamini River, and, saddled as they were, plunged to their breasts into the cooling stream. Their masters imitated their example, without reluctance, and took an afternoon bath which was as healthful as it was pleasant.

"Ah, how good it is!" said Robert, as he quenched his thirst in the middle of the river.

"Be moderate, my boy," said Glenarvan, who did not set a good example.

Nothing was heard but the sound of rapid drinking. As for Thalcave, he drank quietly, without hurrying, long and deeply, till they might perhaps fear that the stream would be drained.

"Well," said Glenarvan, "our friends will not be disappointed in their expectations. They are sure, on arriving at the Guamini, to find an abundance of clear water, if Thalcave leaves any!"

"But could we not go to meet them?" asked Robert. "We could spare them several hours of anxiety."

"Doubtless, my boy; but how carry the water? Wilson has charge of the water-bottles. No, it is better to wait, as we agreed. Calculating the necessary time, and the slow pace of the horses, our friends will be here at night. Let us, then, prepare them a safe shelter and a good repast."

Thalcave had not waited for Glenarvan's orders to search for a place to encamp. He had very fortunately found on the banks of the river a "ramada," a kind of inclosure designed for a cattle-fold and shut in on three sides. The situation was excellent for the purpose, so long as one did not fear to sleep in the open air; and that was the least anxiety of Thalcave's companions. Thus they did not seek a better retreat, but stretched themselves on the ground in the sun to dry their water-soaked garments.

"Well, since here is shelter," said Glenarvan, "let us think of supper. Our friends must be satisfied with the couriers whom they have sent forward; and, if I am not greatly mistaken, they will have no reason to complain. I think an hour's hunting will not be time lost. Are you ready, Robert?"

"Yes, my lord," replied he, with gun in hand.

Glenarvan had conceived this idea because the banks of the Guamini seemed to be the haunt of the game of the surrounding plains. "Tinamous," a kind of partridge, plovers called "teru-teru," yellow rails, and water-fowl of magnificent green were seen rising in flocks. As for quadrupeds, they did not make their appearance; but Thalcave, pointing to the tall grass and thick coppice, explained that they were hidden there. The hunters had only to take a few steps to find themselves in one of the best game-coverts in the world.

They began to hunt, therefore, and, disdaining the feathered tribe, their first attempts were made upon the large game of the Pampas. Soon hares and guanacos, like those that had attacked them so violently on the Andes, started up before them by hundreds; but these very timid animals fled with such swiftness that it was impossible to come within gun-shot. The hunters, therefore, attacked other game that was less fleet. A dozen partridges and rails were brought down, and Glenarvan shot a peccary, which was very good eating.

In less than half an hour they had obtained without difficulty all the game they needed. Robert captured a curious animal called an armadillo, which was covered with a sort of helmet of movable bony pieces and measured a foot and a half in length. It was very fat, and would be an excellent dish, as the Patagonian said; while Robert was proud of his success.

As for Thalcave, he showed his companions a "nandou" hunt. This bird, peculiar to the Pampas, is a kind of ostrich, whose swiftness is marvelous.

The Indian did not try to decoy so nimble an animal, but urged his horse to a gallop, straight towards the bird, so as to overtake it at once, for, if the first attack should fail, the nandou would soon fatigue both horse and rider with its giddy backward and forward movements.

Thalcave, arriving at a proper distance, launched his "bolas" with a strong hand, and so skillfully that they twisted about the legs of the ostrich and paralyzed its efforts. In a few moments it lay on the ground. The Indian soon captured his prize and contributed it to the common repast. The string of partridges, Thalcave's ostrich, Glenarvan's peccary, and Robert's armadillo were brought back to camp. The ostrich and the peccary were immediately stripped of their skin and cut into small slices. As for the armadillo, it is a dainty animal which carries its roasting dish with it, and it was, accordingly, placed in its own bony covering on the glowing embers.

The three hunters were satisfied with the partridges for supper, and kept the rounds of beef for their friends. This repast was washed down with clear water, which was then considered superior to all the wines in the world.

The horses were not forgotten. A great quantity of dry fodder, piled in the ramada, served them for food and bedding. When everything was ready, Glenarvan, Robert, and the Indian wrapped themselves in their ponchos, and stretched their limbs on a bundle of alfafares, the usual bed of the hunters of the Pampas.

CHAPTER XIX. THE RED WOLVES.

Night came,—the night of the new moon, only the uncertain light of the stars illumined the plain. On the horizon the zodiacal light faded away in a dark mist. The waters of the Guamini flowed without a murmur, while birds, quadrupeds, and reptiles reposed after the fatigues of the day. The silence of the desert reigned on the vast expanse of the Pampas.

Glenarvan, Robert, and Thalcave had yielded to the common law, and, stretched on their thick beds of grass, they enjoyed a refreshing sleep. The horses, overcome with fatigue, had lain down on the ground: Thaouka alone, like a true blooded horse, slept standing, spirited in repose as in action, and ready to start at the least sign from his master. Perfect tranquillity reigned within the inclosure, and the embers of the night-fire, as they gradually died out, cast their last rays over the silent obscurity.

About ten o'clock, after a short sleep, the Indian awoke. His eyes became fixed beneath his lowered eyebrows, and his head was turned in a listening attitude towards the plain. He seemed endeavoring to detect some scarcely perceptible sound. A vague uneasiness was soon expressed on his face, usually so calm. Had he perceived the approach of prowling Indians, or the coming of jaguars, water-tigers, and other formidable beasts which are numerous in the neighborhood of rivers? This last possibility doubtless appeared plausible to him, for he cast a rapid glance over the combustible materials piled in the inclosure, and his anxiety increased. In fact, all this dry bedding would quickly be consumed, and could not long intimidate the audacious animals.

According to this conjecture, Thalcave had only to await the progress of events, which he did, half reclining, his head resting on his hands, his elbows on his knees, his eyes motionless, in the attitude of a man whom a sudden anxiety has awakened from sleep.

An hour passed. Any other person but Thalcave, reassured by the outward silence, would have lain down again. But where a stranger would have suspected nothing, the highly-trained senses and natural instinct of the Indian foresaw the coming danger.

While he was listening and watching, Thaouka gave a low neigh. His nose was stretched towards the entrance to the ramada. The Patagonian suddenly started.

"Thaouka has scented some enemy," said he.

He arose and scanned the plain attentively. Silence still reigned, but not tranquillity. Thalcave discerned shadows moving noiselessly among the tufts of grass. Here and there glittered luminous points, which spread on all sides, now fading away, and now gleaming forth again. You would have thought fantastic elves were dancing on the surface of an immense lagoon. A stranger would doubtless have taken these flitting sparks for glow-worms, which shine, when night comes, in many parts of the Pampas. But Thalcave was not deceived; he knew with what enemies he had to deal. He loaded his carbine, and took a position near the first stakes of the inclosure.

He did not wait long. A strange cry, a mingling of barks and howls, resounded over the plain. The report of the carbine answered it, and was followed by a hundred frightful yelps. Glenarvan and Robert suddenly awoke.

"What is the matter?" asked Robert.

"Indians?" said Glenarvan.

"No," replied Thalcave, "aguaras."

Robert looked at Glenarvan.

"Aguaras?" said he.

"Yes," replied Glenarvan, "the red wolves of the Pampas."

Both seized their weapons, and joined the Indian. The latter pointed to the plain, from which arose a series of formidable howls. Robert involuntarily took a step backward.

"You are not afraid of the wolves, my boy?" said Glenarvan.

"No, my lord," replied Robert, in a firm tone. "With you I fear nothing."

"So much the better. These aguaras are not very formidable beasts; and were it not for their numbers I should not even think of them."

"What does it matter?" replied Robert. "We are well armed. Let them come."

"And they shall be well received."

Speaking thus, Glenarvan endeavored to reassure the lad; but he did not think without a secret terror of that dense horde of exasperated beasts. Perhaps there were hundreds of them; and these three, however well armed, could not advantageously contend against so many and such antagonists.

By the howls that resounded over the Pampas, and by the multitude of shadows that flitted about the plain, Glenarvan could not be mistaken as to the number. These animals had scented a sure prey, horse-flesh or human flesh, and not one among them would return to his lair without having his portion. The situation was, therefore, very alarming.

Meanwhile the circle of wolves grew gradually narrower. The horses, awakened, gave signs of the liveliest terror. Thaouka alone pawed the ground, seeking to break his halter, and ready to rush out. His master succeeded in calming him only by whistling continually.

Glenarvan and Robert had stationed themselves so as to defend the entrance of the ramada, and with their loaded rifles were about to fire at the first ranks of wolves, when Thalcave turned aside their weapons already poised for a shot.

"What does Thalcave wish?" asked Robert.

"He prohibits us from firing," answered Glenarvan.

"Why?"

"Perhaps he does not consider it the proper time."

This was not, however, the motive which actuated the Indian, but a graver reason, which Glenarvan understood when Thalcave, raising his powder-flask and inverting it, showed that it was almost empty.

"Well?" said Robert.

"We must economize our ammunition. Our hunt to-day has cost us dear, and we are deficient in powder and shot. We have not twenty charges left."

The boy answered nothing.

"You are not afraid, Robert?"

"No, my lord."

"Very well, my boy."

At this moment another report resounded. Thalcave had brought down a too bold enemy. The wolves that were advancing in close ranks recoiled, and gathered together again a hundred paces from the inclosure.

Glenarvan, at a sign from the Indian, took his place at once, while the latter, collecting the bedding, grass, and all combustible materials, piled them at the entrance of the ramada and threw on a burning ember. Soon a curtain of flame was defined against the dark background of the sky, and through the openings the plain appeared illumined by great moving reflections. Glenarvan could therefore judge of the great number of animals against which they had to defend themselves. Never had so many wolves been seen together before, nor so excited by rapacity. The fiery barrier that Thalcave had just opposed to them had redoubled their fury. Some, however, advanced to the very fire, crowded by the rear ranks, and burned their paws. From time to time a shot was necessary to check the howling horde, and at the end of an hour fifteen bodies lay on the prairie.

The besieged were now in a situation relatively less dangerous. So long as their supplies lasted, so long as the barrier of fire stood at the entrance to the ramada, invasion was not to be feared. But what was to be done if all these methods of repelling the wolves should fail at the same time?

Glenarvan gazed at Robert, and felt his heart beat quick with excitement. He forgot himself, and thought only of this poor child, who displayed a courage beyond his years. Robert was pale, but his hand did not leave his weapon, and he awaited with firm bearing the assault of the enraged wolves.

Meantime, Glenarvan, after coolly considering the situation, resolved to do something decisive.

"In one hour," said he, "we shall have no more powder, shot, or fire. We must not wait till then to make a sally."

He turned towards Thalcave, and, recalling a few words of Spanish, began a conversation with the Indian, frequently interrupted by the cracks of the rifle.

It was not without difficulty that these two men succeeded in understanding each other. Glenarvan, fortunately, knew the habits of the red wolf. Without this knowledge he could not have interpreted the words and gestures of the Patagonian.

Nevertheless, a quarter of an hour passed before he could give to Robert the meaning of Thalcave's answer. He had questioned the Indian concerning their situation.

"And what did he answer?" inquired Robert.

"He said that, cost what it may, we must hold out till daybreak. The aguara goes out only at night, and when morning comes he returns to his lair. He is the wolf of darkness, a cowardly beast that fears the daylight."

"Well, let us defend ourselves till day."

"Yes, my boy, and with our knives if we can no longer use our guns."

Already Thalcave had set the example, and when a wolf approached the fire, the long knife of the Patagonian was thrust through the flames and drawn back again red with blood.

However, the means of defense were failing. About two o'clock in the morning, Thalcave threw into the fire the last armful of fuel, and the besieged had only five charges left.

Glenarvan cast about him a sorrowful glance. He thought of the child who was there, of his companions, of all whom he loved. Robert said nothing; perhaps the danger did not appear imminent to his hopeful spirit. But Glenarvan pictured to himself that terrible event, now apparently inevitable, the being devoured alive! He was not master of his emotion; he drew the child to his breast, he clasped him to his heart, he pressed his lips to his forehead, while tears flowed from his eyes.

Robert gazed at him with a smile. "I am not afraid," said he.

"No, my boy, no," replied Glenarvan; "and you are right. In two hours, day will appear, and we shall be saved! Well done, Thalcave, my brave Patagonian!"

cried he, as the Indian killed with the butt of his gun two enormous beasts that were attempting to cross the glowing barrier.

But at this moment the dying light of the fire showed him the aguaras advancing in a dense body to assail the ramada. The dénouement of the bloody drama was approaching. The fire gradually subsided, for want of fuel; the flames sank; the plain, before illumined, now relapsed into shadow, and in the shadow reappeared the terrible eyes of the red wolves. A few moments more, and the whole drove would rush into the inclosure.

Thalcave discharged his carbine for the last time, stretched out one more of their enemies, and, as his ammunition was exhausted, folded his arms. His head sank upon his breast; he appeared to be questioning himself. Was he searching for some bold, novel, or rash scheme for repelling this furious herd? Glenarvan did not venture to ask him.

At this moment a change took place in the action of the wolves. They seemed to be retreating, and their howls, so deafening before, suddenly ceased. An ominous silence reigned over the plain.

"They are going," said Robert.

"Perhaps," replied Glenarvan, who was listening with intentness.

But Thalcave shook his head. He knew well that the animals would not abandon a certain prey until at daybreak they returned to their holes and dens.

However, the tactics of their enemies had evidently changed, they no longer endeavored to force the entrance of the ramada; but their new manœuvres were already causing a still more imminent danger.

The wolves, abandoning their design of penetrating the inclosure by this entrance, which was defended by weapon and fire, went to the back of the ramada and sought to assail it in the rear. Their claws were soon heard rattling against the half-decayed wood. Already their powerful paws and bloody mouths had forced their way between the shattered stakes. The horses, bewildered and panic-stricken, broke their halters and dashed into the inclosure. Glenarvan seized Robert in his arms, to defend him to the last extremity; and he would have attempted a rash flight, and rushed out of the ramada, had not his eyes fallen upon the Indian.

Thalcave, turning like a deer, had suddenly approached his horse, which was neighing with impatience, and was beginning to saddle him carefully, forgetting neither strap nor buckle. He seemed no longer to care for the howls, that were now redoubled. Glenarvan gazed at him with a dark foreboding.

"He is leaving us!" cried he, seeing Thalcave gather up his reins as though he were about to mount.

"He? never!" said Robert.

In truth the Indian was about to make a venture, not to leave his friends, but to save them by sacrificing himself. Thaouka was ready. He champed his bit; he pranced; his eyes, full of a fiery spirit, shot forth lightning flashes; he understood his master.

Just as the Indian was seizing the mane of his horse, Glenarvan caught him by the arm with a convulsive grasp.

"You are going?" said he, pointing to the plain, which was now deserted.

"Yes," replied the Indian, who comprehended the gesture of his companion; and, with vehement gesticulations which were however perfectly intelligible, he added a few words in Spanish, which signified: "Thaouka—good horse—swift—will draw the wolves after him."

"Ha! Thalcave!" cried Glenarvan.

"Quick, quick!" continued the Indian; while Glenarvan said to Robert, in a voice broken by emotion,—

"Robert, my lad, you hear! He will sacrifice himself for us; he will rush out over the plain, and turn aside the fury of the wolves upon himself."

"Friend Thalcave," replied Robert, looking imploringly at the Patagonian, "friend Thalcave, do not leave us!"

"No," said Glenarvan, "he will not leave us."

And, turning to the Indian, he added, pointing to the terrified horses crowding against the stakes,—

"Let us go together."

"No," said the Indian, who was not mistaken as to the meaning of these words. "Bad beasts—frightened—Thaouka—good horse."

"Very well," said Glenarvan. "Thalcave shall not leave, Robert. He shows me what I have to do. It is my duty to go, and his to remain with you."

Then, seizing Thaouka's bridle, he added,—

"I will go."

"No," replied the Patagonian, calmly.

"I tell you," cried Glenarvan, taking the bridle from the hands of the Indian, "I will go. Save this boy! I trust him to you, Thalcave!"

Glenarvan, in his excitement, mingled English and Spanish together. But what matters the language? In such a terrible situation, signs tell all, and men quickly understand each other.

However, Thalcave resisted, and the discussion was prolonged. The danger was increasing every moment. Already the broken stakes were yielding to the teeth and claws of the wolves. But neither Glenarvan nor Thalcave appeared willing to yield. The Indian had drawn Glenarvan towards the entrance of the inclosure. He pointed to the plain, now free from wolves. In his animated language, he explained that not a moment was to be lost; that the danger, if this plan failed, would be greater for those who remained; in short, that he alone knew Thaouka well enough to employ his marvelous agility and speed for the common safety. Glenarvan blindly persisted in his resolve to sacrifice himself, when suddenly he was pushed violently back. Thaouka pranced, reared on his hind legs, and all at once, with a spring, cleared the barrier of fire and the rampart of bodies, while a boyish voice cried,—

"God save you, my lord!"

Glenarvan and Thalcave had scarcely time to perceive Robert, who, clinging to the horse's mane, disappeared in the darkness.

"Robert, unfortunate!" cried Glenarvan.

But these words the Indian himself could not hear. Frightful howls resounded. The wolves, starting on the track of the horse, fled into the darkness with a terrible speed.

Thalcave and Glenarvan rushed out of the ramada. Already the plain had resumed its tranquillity, and they could scarcely distinguish a moving line which undulated afar in the shadows of the night.

Glenarvan sank upon the ground, overcome, in despair, clasping his hands. He gazed at Thalcave, who smiled with his accustomed calmness.

"Thaouka—good horse—brave child—he will be saved!" he repeated, nodding his head.

"But if he falls?" said Glenarvan.

"He will not fall!"

In spite of Thalcave's confidence, his companion passed the night in terrible anguish. He was no longer even mindful of the danger still to be feared from the wolves. He would have gone in search of Robert, but the Indian restrained him, and explained that their horses could not overtake the boy, that Thaouka must have distanced his enemies, and could not be found in the darkness. They must wait for day to start in search of Robert.

At four o'clock in the morning day began to break. The mists of the horizon were soon tinged with pale rays. A sparkling dew covered the plain, and the tall grass began to wave under the first breezes of the dawn.

The moment of departure had arrived.

"Forward!" said the Indian.

Glenarvan did not reply, but sprang upon Robert's horse, and the two were soon galloping towards the west in the direction from which their companions were to come.

For an hour they traveled thus with great speed, gazing around for Robert, and dreading at each step to behold his mangled body. Glenarvan tortured the flanks of his horse with his spurs. Suddenly shots were heard, and reports at regular intervals, like signals for recognition.

"It is they!" cried Glenarvan.

Thalcave and he urged their horses to a more rapid pace, and a few moments afterwards they joined the party led by Paganel.

To Glenarvan's joy, Robert was there, alive, borne by the noble Thaouka, who neighed with pleasure at seeing his master.

"Ah, my boy! my boy!" cried Glenarvan, with unspeakable tenderness; and Robert and he, dismounting, rushed into each other's arms.

Then it was the Indian's turn to clasp to his breast the courageous son of Captain Grant.

"He lives! he lives!" exclaimed Glenarvan.

"Yes," replied Robert, "thanks to Thaouka."

The Indian had not waited for these words of gratitude to embrace his horse, but at that very moment he spoke to him and embraced him, as if human blood flowed in the veins of the noble animal. Then, turning towards Paganel, he pointed to young Robert.

"A brave boy!" said he.

Glenarvan, however, asked, even while he admired the lad,—

"Why, my son, did you not let Thalcave or me try this last chance of saving you?"

"My lord," replied he, in accents of the liveliest gratitude, "was it not my duty to sacrifice myself, when Thalcave has saved my life, and you are going to save my father?"

CHAPTER XX. STRANGE SIGNS.

After their first outbursts of joy at meeting were over, Paganel, Austin, Wilson, and Mulready—all who had remained behind, except the major—were conscious of one thing, namely, that they were suffering from thirst. Fortunately, the Guamini flowed at no great distance. They accordingly continued their journey, and at seven o'clock in the morning the little party arrived at the ramada. On seeing its entrance strewn with the bodies of the wolves, it was easy to understand the violence of the attack and the vigor of the defense. The travelers, after fully quenching their thirst, devoted their attention to breakfast in the inclosure. The ostrich-steaks were declared excellent, and the armadillo, roasted in its own covering, was a delicious dish.

"To eat reasonably of this," said Paganel, "would be ingratitude towards Providence. We really must eat immoderately."

And he did so accordingly,—but was not sick, thanks to the clear water of the Guamini, which appeared to possess superior digestive properties.

At ten o'clock Glenarvan gave the signal for departure. The water-bottles were filled, and they set out. The horses, being greatly revived, evinced much spirit, and maintained an easy and almost continuous canter. The next morning they crossed the boundary which separates the Argentine Plains from the Pampas. Here Thalcave hoped to meet the chiefs in whose hands he doubted not that he should find Harry Grant and rescue him and his two companions from slavery.

Since they had left the Guamini, the travelers noticed, with great satisfaction, a considerable change in the temperature, thanks to the cold winds of Patagonia, which cause continual currents of air. Neither man nor beast had any reason to complain, after suffering so much from dryness and heat. They therefore pushed on with courage and confidence. But, whatever might have been said, the country seemed to be entirely uninhabited, or, to use a more exact word, "disinhabited."

Frequently they skirted the shores of fresh-water lagoons, on whose banks, in the shelter of the bushes, tiny wrens skipped and melodious larks warbled, in company with the brilliant-plumaged tanagers. These pretty birds gayly fluttered about, heedless of the haughty starlings that strutted on the banks like soldiers with their epaulettes and red breasts. In the thorny coppices the nests of the annubis swung like hammocks, and on the shores of the lagoons magnificent flamingoes, marching in regular file, spread their fiery-colored wings to the wind. Their nests were seen, by thousands together, like a small village, in the shape of truncated cones a foot high. The birds were not startled at the approach of the travelers, which was contrary to Paganel's calculations.

"I have been curious for a long time," said he to the major, "to see a flamingo fly."

"Well," said MacNabb.

"Now, since I have an opportunity, I shall profit by it."

"Do so, Paganel."

"Come with me, major, and you too, Robert; I need witnesses."

And Paganel, leaving his companions to go on, proceeded towards the flock of flamingoes, followed by Robert and the major. Arriving within range, Paganel fired a blank charge (for he would not needlessly destroy even a bird), and all the flamingoes flew away, while the geographer gazed at them attentively through his glasses.

"Well," said he to the major, when the flock had disappeared, "did you see them fly?"

"Certainly," replied MacNabb; "you could not do otherwise, unless you were blind. But let us hasten on, for we have fallen a mile behind."

When he had joined his companions, Paganel found Glenarvan in excited conversation with the Indian, whom he did not appear to understand. Thalcave had frequently stopped to examine the horizon, and each time his countenance expressed a lively astonishment. Glenarvan, not seeing his ordinary interpreter present, had attempted, but in vain, to question the Patagonian. So, as soon as he perceived the geographer at a distance, he cried,—

"Come, friend Paganel, Thalcave and I can scarcely succeed in understanding each other."

Paganel conversed a few moments with the Indian, and, turning to Glenarvan, said,—

"Thalcave is astonished at a circumstance that is really strange."

"What?"

"At meeting neither Indians, nor any traces of them, on these plains, which are usually furrowed with their trails, whether they are driving home the cattle stolen from the ranchos, or going to the Andes to sell their zorillo carpets and whips of braided leather."

"And to what does Thalcave attribute this abandonment?"

"He cannot tell; he is astonished. That is all."

"But what Indians did he expect to find in this part of the Pampas?"

"The very ones who have had foreign prisoners; those natives who are commanded by the caziques Calfoucoura, Catriel, and Yanchetruz."

"Who are these caziques?"

"Chiefs of tribes that were very powerful thirty years ago, before they were driven beyond the sierras. Since that time they have been subdued as much as an Indian can be, and now scour the Pampas as well as the province of Buenos Ayres. I am therefore astonished, like Thalcave, at not encountering traces of them in a country where they generally pursue the calling of plunderers."

"Well, then," inquired Glenarvan, "what course ought we to take?"

"I will see," replied Paganel.

After a few moments' conversation with Thalcave, he said,—

"This is his advice, which seems to me very wise. We must continue our journey to the east as far as Fort Independence; and there, if we have no news of Captain Grant, we shall at least know what has become of the Indians of the plain."

"Is Fort Independence far?"

"No; it is situated at Tandil, sixty miles distant."

"And when shall we arrive there?"

"On the evening of the day after to-morrow."

Glenarvan was quite disconcerted at finding no Indians on the Pampas, a circumstance which was little expected. There are ordinarily too many of them. Some special cause must therefore have removed them. But a serious question was to be considered. If Captain Grant was a prisoner of one of these tribes, had he been carried to the north or to the south? This problem harassed Glenarvan. It was advisable at all hazards to keep track of the captain. In short, it was better to follow Thalcave's advice and reach the village of Tandil, where at least they could obtain information.

About four o'clock in the afternoon they approached a hill that might have passed for a mountain in so level a country. It was Tapalquem Sierra, and at its foot the travelers encamped for the night.

The passage of this mountain was accomplished the next day with the greatest ease. They followed the sandy undulations of a gradually sloping terrace, which certainly did not present difficulties to people who had scaled the Andes, and the horses scarcely relaxed their rapid pace. At noon they reached the abandoned Fort Tapalquem, the first of the chain of forts built on the southern frontier against the plundering natives. But not a shadow of an Indian did they encounter, to the increasing surprise of Thalcave; although, towards the middle of the day, three rovers of the plain, well armed and mounted, gazed for a moment at the little party, but prevented their approach, galloping away with incredible rapidity. Glenarvan was furious.

"Gauchos," said the Patagonian.

"Ah! Gauchos," replied MacNabb. "Well, Paganel, what do you think of these creatures?"

"I think they look like famous bandits," answered Paganel.

"And hence of course are, my dear geographer?"

"Of course, my dear major." Paganel's avowal was followed by a general laugh, which did not disconcert him at all.

According to Thalcave's orders, they advanced in close ranks, and at evening encamped in a spacious abandoned rancho, where the chief Catriel generally assembled his bands of natives. From an examination of the ground and the absence of fresh tracks, the Patagonian knew that it had not been occupied for a long time.

The next morning Glenarvan and his companions found themselves again on the plain. The first estancias (vast establishments for raising cattle), which border upon the Tandil, were descried; but Thalcave resolved not to stop, but to keep straight on to Fort Independence, where he wished to obtain information, especially concerning the singular condition of this abandoned country.

The trees, so rare since leaving the Andes, now reappeared. The greater part of these have been planted since the arrival of the Europeans on the American continent. They generally surround "corrals," vast cattle-inclosures protected with stakes. Here thousands of cattle, sheep, cows, and horses, branded with the mark of the owner, graze and fatten, while large numbers of huge dogs keep watch. The soil is admirably adapted to raising cattle, and yields an excellent fodder.

The people lead the life of the shepherds of the Bible. Their flocks are perhaps even more numerous than those which fed on the plains of Mesopotamia; but the family element is wanting, and the owners of the great folds of the Pampas have little to recommend themselves or their manner of life. Paganel explained all these particulars to his companions, and even succeeded in interesting the major.

Thalcave, meanwhile, hastened their progress, as he wished to arrive that evening at Fort Independence. The horses, urged on by their masters, and following the example of Thaouka, dashed through the tall grass. They passed several farms, fortified and defended by deep ditches. The principal house was provided with an elevated terrace, from which the inmates could fire upon the plunderers of the plain. Glenarvan might perhaps have obtained here the information that he sought; but it was wisest to go to the village of Tandil. They did not stop, therefore, and soon the feet of the horses struck the grassy sward of the first mountain slopes. An hour afterward the village appeared at the bottom of a narrow gorge crowned by the embattled walls of Fort Independence.

CHAPTER XXI. A FALSE TRAIL.

Paganel, after giving his companions a brief account of the village of Tandil, added that they could not fail to obtain information there; moreover, the fort was always garrisoned by a detachment of national troops. Glenarvan, accordingly, put the horses into the stable of a "fonda;" and Paganel, the major,

Robert, and he, under the guidance of Thalcave, proceeded towards Fort Independence.

After ascending the ridges of the mountains for a short time, they arrived at the postern, rather carelessly guarded by a native sentinel. They passed without difficulty, and inferred either great negligence or extreme security. A few soldiers were exercising on the parade-ground of the fort, the oldest of whom was not more than twenty and the youngest scarcely ten. In fact, they were a dozen young children and boys who were drilling very nicely. Their uniform consisted of a striped shirt confined at the waist by a leathern girdle. The mildness of the climate justified this light costume. Each of these young soldiers carried a gun and a sword, which were too long and heavy for the little fellows. All had a certain family resemblance, and the corporal who commanded resembled them too: they were twelve brothers, who were parading under the orders of the thirteenth.

Paganel was not astonished. He remembered his Argentine statistics, and knew that in this country the average number of children in a family exceeds nine. But what surprised him exceedingly was to see these little soldiers practicing the French tactics, and to hear the orders of the corporal given in his own native language.

"This is singular," said he.

But Glenarvan had not come to see boys drill, still less to occupy himself with their nationality or relationship. He did not, therefore, give Paganel time to express further astonishment, but besought him to ask for the commander of the fortress. Paganel did so, and one of the soldiers proceeded towards a small building which served as the barracks.

A few moments after, the commander appeared in person. He was a man of fifty, robust, with a military air, thick whiskers, prominent cheek-bones, gray hair, and commanding look, so far as one could judge through the clouds of smoke that issued from his short pipe.

Thalcave, addressing him, introduced Lord Glenarvan and his companions. While he spoke, the commander kept scrutinizing Paganel with quite embarrassing persistence. The geographer did not know what the trooper meant, and was about to ask him, when the latter unceremoniously seized his hand, and said, in a joyous tone, in his own language,—

"A Frenchman?"

"Yes, a Frenchman," replied Paganel.

"Ah, I am delighted! Welcome, welcome! I am almost a Frenchman," cried the commander, shaking the geographer's arm with rather painful violence.

"One of your friends?" asked the major of Paganel.

"Yes," replied he, with national pride; "we have friends in all parts of the world!"

He then entered into conversation with the commander. Glenarvan would gladly have put in a word in regard to his affairs, but the soldier was telling his story, and was not in the mood to be interrupted. This honest man had left

France a long time before; and the native language was no longer perfectly familiar to him: he had forgotten, if not words, at least the manner of combining them. As his visitors soon learned, he had been a sergeant in the French army. Since the foundation of the fort he had not left it, and commanded it by appointment from the Argentine government. He was by parentage a Basque, and his name was Manuel Ipharaguerre. A year after his arrival in the country, Sergeant Manuel was naturalized, joined the Argentine army, and married an honest Indian woman, who had twins,—boys, to be sure, for the sergeant's worthy consort would never present him with daughters. Manuel did not think of any other calling than that of the soldier, and hoped, in time, with the help of God, to offer to the republic a whole battalion of young soldiers.

"You have seen them?" said he. "Charming fellows! Good soldiers! José! Juan! Miguel! Pepe! Pepe is only seven years old, and is already biting his cartridge!"

Pepe, hearing himself complimented, joined his two little feet, and presented arms with perfect precision.

"He will do!" added the sergeant. "He will be a major—or brigadier-general one day!"

This story lasted a quarter of an hour, to Thalcave's great astonishment. The Indian could not understand how so many words could come from a single throat. No one interrupted the commander; and even a French sergeant had to conclude at last, though not without forcing his guests to accompany him to his dwelling. Here they were introduced to Madame Ipharaguerre, who appeared to be "a good-looking person," if this expression may be employed in regard to an Indian.

When he had exhausted himself, the sergeant asked his guests to what he owed the honor of their visit. And now it was their turn to explain.

Paganel, opening the conversation in French, told him of their journey across the Pampas, and ended by asking why the Indians had abandoned the country.

"War!" replied the sergeant.

"War?"

"Yes, civil war."

"Civil war?" rejoined Paganel.

"Yes, war between Paraguay and Buenos Ayres," answered the sergeant.

"Well?"

"Why, all the Indians of the north are in the rear of General Flores, and those of the plains are plundering."

"But the caziques?"

"The caziques with them."

This answer was reported to Thalcave, who shook his head. Indeed, he either did not know, or had forgotten, that a civil war, which was afterwards to involve Brazil, was decimating two-thirds of the republic. The Indians had everything to gain in these internal struggles, and could not neglect such fine opportunities for plunder. The sergeant, therefore, was not mistaken in attributing this desertion of the Pampas to the civil war that was being waged in the northern part of the Argentine Provinces.

But this event disconcerted Glenarvan's hopes. If Captain Grant was a prisoner of the caziques, he must have been carried by them to the northern frontiers. Yet how and where to find him? Must they attempt a perilous and almost useless search to the northern limits of the Pampas? It was a serious matter, which was to be earnestly considered.

However, one important question was still to be asked of the sergeant, and the major thought of this, while his companions were looking at each other in silence.

"Have you heard of any Europeans being retained as prisoners by the caziques of the Pampas?"

Manuel reflected for a few moments, like a man who recalls events to recollection. "Yes," said he, at length.

"Ah!" cried Glenarvan, conceiving a new hope.

Paganel, MacNabb, Robert, and he now surrounded the sergeant.

"Speak, speak!" cried they, gazing at him with eagerness even in their looks.

"Several years ago," replied Manuel, "yes,—that is it,—European prisoners—but have never seen them."

"Several years ago?" said Glenarvan. "You are mistaken. The date of the shipwreck is definite. The Britannia was lost in June, 1862, less than two years ago."

"Oh, more than that, my lord!"

"Impossible!" cried Paganel.

"Not at all. It was when Pepe was born. There were two men."

"No, three!" said Glenarvan.

"Two," replied the sergeant, in a positive tone.

"Two?" exclaimed Glenarvan, very much chagrined. "Two Englishmen?"

"No," continued the sergeant. "Who speaks of Englishmen? It was a Frenchman and an Italian."

"An Italian who was massacred by the Indians?" cried Paganel.

"Yes, and I learned afterwards—Frenchman saved."

"Saved!" exclaimed Robert, whose very life seemed to hang on the sergeant's lips.

"Yes, saved from the hands of the Indians," replied Manuel.

Each looked to the geographer, who beat his brow in despair.

"Ah! I understand," said he, at last. "All is clear, all is explained."

"But what is to be done?" asked Glenarvan, with as much anxiety as impatience.

"My friends," answered Paganel, taking Robert's hands, "we must submit to a severe misfortune. We have followed a false trail! The captive in question is not the captain, but one of my countrymen (whose companion, Marco Vazello, was actually assassinated by the Indians), a Frenchman who often accompanied these cruel savages to the banks of the Colorado, and who, after fortunately escaping from their hands, returned to France. While thinking that we were on the track of Captain Grant, we have fallen upon that of young Guinnard."

A profound silence followed this declaration. The mistake was palpable. The sergeant's story, the nationality of the prisoner, the murder of his companion, and his escape from the hands of the Indians, all accorded with the evident facts. Glenarvan gazed at Thalcave with a bewildered air. The Indian then resumed the conversation.

"Have you never heard of three English captives?" he asked the sergeant.

"Never," replied Manuel. "It would have been known at Tandil. I should have heard of it. No, it cannot be."

Glenarvan, after this formal response, had nothing more to do at Fort Independence. He and his friends, therefore, departed, not without thanking the sergeant and shaking hands with him.

Glenarvan was in despair at this complete overthrow of his hopes. Robert walked beside him in silence, with tearful eyes, while his protector could not find a single word to console him. Paganel gesticulated and talked to himself. The major did not open his lips. As for Thalcave, his Indian pride seemed humbled at having gone astray on a false trail. No one, however, thought of reproaching him for so excusable an error.

They returned to the encampment, saddened indeed. Still, not one of the courageous and devoted men regretted so many hardships uselessly endured, so many dangers vainly incurred. But each saw all hope of success annihilated in an instant. Could they find Captain Grant between Tandil and the sea? No. If any prisoner had fallen into the hands of the Indians on the Atlantic coast, Sergeant Manuel would certainly have been informed.

An event of such a nature could not have escaped the natives who trade from Tandil to Carmen. Among the traders of the Argentine Plains everything is known and reported. There was therefore but one course now to take,—to join, without delay, the Duncan at Cape Medano, the appointed rendezvous.

In the meantime, Paganel had asked Glenarvan for the document, by relying on which their search had resulted so unfortunately. He read it again with unconcealed vexation, seeking to discover a new interpretation. "This document is, at all events, clear," said Glenarvan. "It explains in the most definite manner the shipwreck of the captain and the place of his captivity."

"No," replied the geographer, stamping with his foot, "a hundred times no! Since Captain Grant is not on the Pampas, he is not in America. This document ought to tell where he is; and it shall, my friends, or I am no longer Jacques Paganel."

CHAPTER XXII. THE FLOOD.

Fort Independence is one hundred and fifty miles from the shores of the Atlantic. But for unforeseen and unexpected delays, Glenarvan could have rejoined the Duncan in four days. He could not, however, reconcile himself to the idea of returning on board without Captain Grant, and failing so completely in his search; and did not therefore, as usual, give the orders for departure. But the major assumed the task of saddling the horses, renewing the provisions, and making his arrangements for the journey. Thanks to his activity, the little party, at eight o'clock in the morning, was on its way down the grassy slopes of the Tandil Sierra.

Glenarvan, with Robert at his side, galloped on in silence. His lordship's bold and resolute character did not permit him to accept this disappointment calmly. His heart beat violently, and his brain was on fire. Paganel, tormented by the mystery of the document, arranged the words in every way, as if to draw from them a new meaning. Thalcave silently resigned himself to Thaouka's sagacity. The major, always confident, performed his duties like a man upon whom discouragement can have no effect. Tom Austin and his two sailors shared their master's annoyance. Once, when a timid hare crossed the path in front of them, the superstitious Scotchmen gazed at one another.

"A bad omen," said Wilson.

"Yes, in the Highlands," replied Mulready.

"What is bad in the Highlands is no better here," added Wilson, sententiously.

About noon the travelers had descended the mountains and gained the undulating plains that extend to the sea; the boundless prairie spread its broad carpet of verdure before them.

More than once during the journey the attention and interest of all, but especially of Paganel, were arrested by the curious illusion of the mirage, by which was presented in the sky, at the limits of the horizon, a semblance of the estancias, the poplars and willows near them, and other objects; the images being so much like the reality that it required a strong effort to realize their deceptive character.

The weather hitherto had been fine, but now the sky assumed a less pleasing aspect. Masses of vapor, generated by the high temperature of the preceding days, condensed into thick clouds and threatened to dissolve in showers of rain. Moreover, the proximity of the Atlantic, and the west wind, which here reigns supreme, rendered the climate of this region peculiarly moist. However, for that day at least the heavy clouds did not break; and at evening the horses, after traveling forty miles, halted on the edge of a deep "cañada," an immense natural ditch filled with water. A shelter was wanting, but the ponchos served for tents as well as clothing, and peaceful slumbers enwrapped all.

The next day, as they progressed farther, the presence of subterranean streams betrayed itself more noticeably, and moisture was seen in every depression of the ground. Soon they came to large ponds, some already deep and others just forming. So long as there were only lagoons, the horses could easily extricate themselves; but with these treacherous swamps it was more difficult. Tall grass obstructed them, and it was necessary to incur the danger before it could be understood. These quagmires had been already fatal to more than one human being.

Robert, who had ridden half a mile in advance, returned at a gallop, crying,—

"Monsieur Paganel! Monsieur Paganel! A forest of horns!"

"What!" replied the geographer, "have you found a forest of horns?"

"Yes, yes; or at least a field."

"A field! you are dreaming, my boy," said Paganel, shrugging his shoulders.

"I am not dreaming," retorted Robert; "you shall see for yourself. This is a strange country! People sow horns, and they spring up like corn! I should like very well to have some of the seed."

"But he speaks seriously," said the major.

"Yes, major, you shall see."

Robert was not mistaken, and soon they found themselves before a vast field of horns, regularly planted.

"Well?" said Robert.

"This is something singular," replied Paganel, turning towards the Indian with a questioning look.

"The horns come from the ground," explained Thalcave; "and the cattle are under it."

"What!" cried Paganel, "is there a whole drove in this mire?"

"Yes," answered the Patagonian.

In fact, a vast herd had perished in this bog, which had given way beneath them. Hundreds of cattle had thus met their death, side by side, by suffocation in this vast quagmire. This circumstance, which sometimes takes place on the plains, could not be ignored by the Indian, and it was a warning which it was proper to heed. They passed around this immense hecatomb, which would have satisfied the most exacting gods of antiquity; and an hour after the field of horns was far behind.

Thalcave now began to observe with an anxious air the state of things around him. He frequently stopped, and rose in his stirrups. His tall form enabled him to survey a wide range; but, perceiving nothing that could enlighten him, he resumed his undeviating course. A mile farther, he stopped again, and, turning from the beaten track, proceeded a short distance, first to the north, then to the south, and then resumed his place at the head of the party, without saying either what he hoped or what he feared.

These manœuvres, many times repeated, puzzled Paganel and annoyed Glenarvan. The geographer was accordingly requested to interrogate the Indian, which he did at once. Thalcave replied that he was astonished to see the plain so soaked with moisture. Never within his recollection, since he had performed the office of guide, had his feet trodden a soil so saturated. Even in the season of the great rains the Argentine plain was always easily passed.

"But to what do you attribute this increasing moisture?" asked Paganel.

"I know not," replied the Indian; "and what if I did?"

"Do the mountain streams, when swollen with the rains, ever overflow their banks?"

"Sometimes."

"And now, perhaps?"

"Perhaps," said Thalcave.

Paganel was forced to be contented with this answer, and communicated to Glenarvan the result of the conversation.

"And what does Thalcave advise?" inquired Glenarvan.

"What is to be done?" asked Paganel of the Patagonian.

"Advance quickly," replied the Indian.

This advice was easier to give than to follow. The horses were quickly fatigued with treading a soil that sank beneath them deeper and deeper as they progressed, so that this part of the plain might have been compared to an immense basin in which the invading waters would rapidly accumulate. It was advisable, therefore, to cross without delay these sloping terraces that an inundation would have instantly transformed into a lake.

They hastened their pace, though there was no great depth to the water which spread out in a sheet beneath the horses' feet. About two o'clock the flood-gates of the heavens opened, and tropical torrents of rain descended. Never was a finer opportunity presented for showing oneself a philosopher. There was no chance of escaping this deluge, and it was better for the travelers to receive it stoically. Their ponchos were soon dripping, and their hats wet them still more, like roofs whose gutters have overflowed. The fringes of the saddle-cloths seemed so many liquid streams; and the horsemen, bespattered by their animals, whose hoofs splashed in the water at every step, rode in a double shower, which came from the ground as well as the sky.

It was in this wretchedly cold and exhausted state that they arrived, towards evening, at a very miserable rancho. Only people who were not fastidious could have given it the name of a shelter, only travelers in distress would consent to occupy it. But Glenarvan and his companions had no choice. They therefore cowered down in the abandoned hut which would not have satisfied even a poor Indian of the plains. A sorry fire of grass, which gave out more smoke than heat, was kindled with difficulty. The torrents of rain made havoc without, and large drops oozed through the mouldy thatch. The fire was extinguished twenty times, and twenty times did Wilson and Mulready struggle against the invading water.

The supper was very meagre and comfortless, and every one's appetite failed. The major alone did justice to the water-soaked repast, and did not lose a mouthful: he was superior to misfortune. As for Paganel, like a Frenchman, he tried to joke; but now he failed.

"My jokes are wet," said he: "they miss fire."

However, as it was more agreeable—if possible, under the circumstances—to sleep, each one sought in slumber a temporary forgetfulness of his fatigues.

The night was stormy. The sides of the rancho cracked as if they would break, while the frail structure bent beneath the gusts of wind and threatened to give way at every shock. The unfortunate horses neighed in terror without, exposed to the inclemency of the tempest; and their masters did not suffer less in their miserable shelter. However, sleep drowned all their troubles at last. Robert first closed his eyes, reclining his head on Lord Glenarvan's shoulder; and soon all the inmates of the rancho slept under the protection of God.

They woke the next morning at the call of Thaouka, who, always ready, neighed without, and struck the wall of the hut vigorously with his hoof, as though to give the signal for departure. They owed him too much not to obey him, and they accordingly resumed their journey.

The rain had ceased, but the hard earth held what had fallen. On the impenetrable clay, pools, marshes, and ponds overflowed and formed immense "bañados" of treacherous depth. Paganel, on consulting his map, judged rightly that the Grande and Nivarota Rivers, into which the waters of the plain usually flow, must have mingled together in one broad stream.

An extremely rapid advance, therefore, became necessary. The common safety was at stake. If the inundation increased, where could they find a refuge? The vast circle of the horizon did not offer a single point, and on this level plain the progress of the water must be rapid. The horses were urged to their utmost speed. Thaouka took the lead, and might have borne the name of sea-horse, for he pranced as if he had been in his native element.

Suddenly, about six o'clock in the evening, he manifested signs of extreme agitation. He turned frequently towards the vast expanse to the south; his neighs were prolonged, his nostrils keenly snuffed the air, and he reared violently. Thalcave, whom his antics could not unseat, managed his steed without difficulty. The froth from the horse's mouth was mingled with blood under the action of the firmly-closed bit, and yet the spirited animal could not be calm. If free, his master felt but too well that he would have fled away at full speed towards the north.

"What is the matter with Thaouka?" asked Paganel. "Has he been bitten by those voracious blood-suckers of the Argentine waters?"

"No," replied the Indian.

"Is he terrified, then, at some danger?"

"Yes, he has scented danger."

"What?"

"I do not know."

Although the eye did not yet reveal the peril that Thaouka divined, the ear could already detect it. A low murmur, like the sound of a rising tide, was heard as from the limit of the horizon. The wind blew in damp gusts laden with spray; the birds, as if fleeing from some unknown phenomenon, shot swiftly through the air; and the horses, wading to their knees, felt the first impulse of the current. Soon a mingled roar, like bellowing, neighing, and bleating, resounded half a mile to the south, and immense herds appeared, tumbling, rising, and rushing, a confused mass of terrified beasts, and fled by with frightful rapidity. It was scarcely possible to distinguish them in the midst of the clouds of spray dashed up by their flight. "Quick! quick!" cried Thalcave, in a piercing voice.

"What is it?" said Paganel.

"The flood! the flood!" replied Thalcave, spurring his horse towards the north.

"The inundation!" cried Paganel; and his companions, with him at their head, fled away in the track of Thaouka.

It was time. Five miles to the south a high and broad wall of water was rushing over the plain, which was fast becoming an ocean. The tall grass disappeared as before the scythe, and the tufts of mimosas, torn up by the current, separated and formed floating islands. The mass of waters spread itself in broad waves of irresistible power. The dikes of the great rivers had evidently given way, and perhaps the waters of the Colorado and Rio Negro were now mingling in a common stream.

The wall of water descried by Thalcave advanced with the speed of a race-horse. The travelers fled before it like a cloud driven by the storm. Their eyes sought in vain a place of refuge. Sky and water mingled together on the horizon. The horses, excited by the danger, dashed along in a mad gallop, so that their riders could scarcely keep their seats. Glenarvan frequently glanced behind him. "The water is overtaking us," he thought.

"Quick! quick!" cried Thalcave.

The unfortunate beasts were urged to a swifter pace. From their flanks, lacerated with the spur, flowed bright red streams, which marked their course on the water by long, crimson lines. They stumbled in the hollows of the ground; they were entangled in the hidden grass; they fell and rose again continually. The depth of the water sensibly increased. Long surges announced the on-rush of the mass of water that tossed its foaming crests less than two miles distant.

For a quarter of an hour this final struggle against the most terrible of elements was prolonged. The fugitives could keep no account of the distance they had traversed; but, judging by the rapidity of their flight, it must have been considerable.

Meantime the horses, immersed to their breasts, could no longer advance without extreme difficulty. Glenarvan, Paganel, Austin, all believed themselves lost, victims of the horrible death of unfortunates abandoned at sea. Their animals began to lose their footing; six feet of water was sufficient to drown them.

We must forbear to picture the acute anguish of these eight men overtaken by a rising inundation. They felt their powerlessness to struggle against these convulsions of nature, superior to human strength. Their safety was no longer in their own hands.

Five minutes after, the horses were swimming, while the current alone carried them along with irresistible force and furious swiftness. All safety seemed impossible, when the voice of the major was heard. "A tree!" said he.

"A tree!" cried Glenarvan.

"Yes, yonder!" replied Thalcave, and he pointed northward to a kind of gigantic walnut-tree, which rose solitary from the midst of the waters.

His companions had no need to be urged. This tree that was opportunely presented to them they must reach at all hazards. The horses probably could not accomplish the distance; but the men, at least, could be saved,—the current would carry them.

At that moment Tom Austin's horse gave a stifled neigh and disappeared. His rider, extricating himself from the stirrups, began to swim vigorously.

"Cling to my saddle!" cried Glenarvan to him.

"Thanks, my lord," replied he, "my arms are strong."

"Your horse, Robert?" continued Glenarvan, turning towards the boy.

"All right, my lord, all right! He swims like a fish."

"Attention!" cried the major, in a loud voice.

This word was scarcely pronounced, when the enormous wall of water reached them. A huge wave, forty feet high, overwhelmed the fugitives with a terrible roar. Men and beasts, everything, disappeared in a whirlpool of foam. A ponderous liquid mass engulfed them in its furious tide. When the deluge had passed, the men regained the surface, and rapidly counted their numbers; but the horses, except Thaouka, had disappeared forever.

"Courage! courage!" cried Glenarvan, who supported Paganel with one arm and swam with the other.

"All right! all right!" replied the worthy geographer; "indeed I am not sorry–"

What was he not sorry for? No one ever knew; for the poor man was forced to swallow the end of his sentence in half a pint of muddy water.

The major calmly advanced, taking a regular stroke of which the most skillful swimmer would not have been ashamed. The sailors worked their way along like porpoises in their native element. As for Robert, he clung to Thaouka's mane, and was thus drawn along. The horse proudly cut the waters, and kept himself instinctively on a line with the tree, towards which the current bore him, and which was now not far distant.

In a few moments the entire party reached it. It was fortunate; for, if this refuge had failed, all chance of safety would have vanished, and they must have perished in the waves. The water was up to the top of the trunk where the main branches grew, so that it was easy to grasp them.

Thalcave, leaving his horse, and lifting Robert, seized the first limb, and soon his powerful arms had lodged the exhausted swimmers in a place of safety. But Thaouka, carried away by the current, was rapidly disappearing. He turned his intelligent head towards his master, and, shaking his long mane, neighed for him beseechingly.

"Do you abandon him?" said Paganel.

"I?" cried the Indian, and, plunging into the tempestuous waters, he reappeared some distance from the tree. A few moments after, his arm rested upon the neck of Thaouka, and horse and horseman swam away together towards the misty horizon of the north.

CHAPTER XXIII. A SINGULAR ABODE.

The tree upon which Glenarvan and his companions had just found refuge resembled a walnut-tree. It had the same shining foliage and rounded form. It was the "ombu," which is met with only on the Argentine Plains. It had an enormous, twisted trunk, and was confined to the earth not only by its great roots, but also by strong shoots which held it most tenaciously. It had thus resisted the force of the inundation.

This ombu measured one hundred feet in height, and might have covered with its shade a circumference of three hundred and sixty feet. All the upper part rested on three great branches, which forked from the top of the trunk, that was six feet in diameter. Two of these branches were nearly perpendicular, and supported the immense canopy of foliage, whose crossed, twisted, and interlaced limbs, as if woven by the hand of a basket-maker, formed an impenetrable shelter. The third branch, on the contrary, extended almost horizontally over the roaring waters; its leaves were bathed in them, while it seemed a promontory to this island of verdure surrounded by an ocean. There was abundant space, also, in the interior of this gigantic tree. The foliage, which was not very dense at its outer circumference, left large openings like sky-lights, and made it well ventilated and cool. At sight of these branches rising in innumerable ramifications towards the clouds, while the parasitic convolvuli bound them to each other, and the rays of the sun shone through the interstices of the leaves, you would really have thought that the trunk of this ombu bore upon itself alone an entire forest.

On the arrival of the fugitives, a feathered population flew away to the top branches, protesting by their cries against so flagrant a usurpation of their dwelling. These birds, that had themselves sought refuge upon this solitary ombu, were seen by hundreds,—blackbirds, starlings, and many other richly-feathered varieties; and when they flew away it seemed as if a gust of wind had stripped the tree of its leaves.

Such was the asylum offered to Glenarvan's little party. Robert and the nimble Wilson were scarcely perched in the tree, before they hastened to climb to the topmost branches. Their heads protruded above the dome of verdure. From this lofty position the view embraced a wide range. The ocean created by the inundation surrounded them on all sides, and their eyes could discern no limit. No other tree emerged from the watery surface; the ombu, alone in the midst of the unconfined waters, groaned at every shock. At a distance, borne along by the impetuous current, floated uprooted trunks, twisted branches, thatch torn from some demolished rancho, beams swept by the waters from the roofs of cattle-folds, bodies of drowned animals, bloody skins, and, on a swaying tree, a whole family of growling jaguars that clung with their claws to this fragile raft. Still farther off, a black speck almost invisible attracted Wilson's attention. It was Thalcave and his faithful Thaouka, disappearing in the distance.

"Thalcave, friend Thalcave!" cried Robert, stretching out his hands towards the courageous Patagonian.

"He will be saved, Mr. Robert," said Wilson; "but let us join Lord Glenarvan."

A moment after, Robert and the sailor descended the three stories of branches and found themselves among their companions. Glenarvan, Paganel, the major, Austin, and Mulready were seated astraddle, or dangling in the branches, according to their own inclinations. Wilson gave an account of their visit to the top of the tree. All shared his opinion in regard to Thalcave. The only question was, whether Thalcave would save Thaouka, or Thaouka Thalcave.

The present situation of these refugees was undeniably insecure. The tree would not probably give way to the force of the current, but the rising waters might reach the top branches, for the depression of the soil made this part of the plain a deep reservoir. Glenarvan's first care, therefore, was to establish, by means of notches, points of comparison which enabled him to note the different heights of the water. The flood was now stationary, and it appeared to have reached its greatest elevation. This was encouraging.

"And now what shall we do?" asked Glenarvan.

"Build our nest, of course," replied Paganel.

"Build our nest!" cried Robert.

"Certainly, my boy, and live the life of birds, since we cannot live the life of fishes."

"Very well," said Glenarvan; "but who will give us our beakful?"

"I," replied the major.

All eyes were turned towards MacNabb, who was comfortably seated in a natural arm-chair formed of two pliant branches, and with one hand was holding out the wet though well-filled saddle-bags.

"Ah, MacNabb," cried Glenarvan, "this is just like you! You think of everything, even under circumstances where it is allowable to forget."

"As soon as it was decided not to be drowned, I concluded not to die of hunger."

"I should not have thought of this," said Paganel, innocently; "but I am so absent-minded!"

"And what do the saddle-bags contain?" inquired Tom Austin.

"Provisions for seven men for two days," replied MacNabb.

"Well," said Glenarvan, "I hope that the inundation will be considerably lower twenty-four hours hence."

"Or that we shall find some means of gaining *terra firma*," added Paganel.

"Our first business, then, is to breakfast," said Glenarvan.

"After drying ourselves," observed the major.

"And fire?" said Wilson.

"Why, we must make one," replied Paganel.

"Where?"

"At the top of the trunk, of course."

"With what?"

"With dead wood that we shall cut in the tree."

"But how kindle it?" said Glenarvan. "Our tinder is like a wet sponge."

"We will manage that," answered Paganel; "a little dry moss, a ray of sunlight, the lens of my telescope, and you will see by what a fire I will dry myself. Who will go for wood in the forest?"

"I!" cried Robert, and, followed by his friend Wilson, he disappeared like a cat in the depths of the foliage.

During their absence Paganel found dry moss in sufficient quantity; he availed himself of a ray of sunlight, which was easy, for the orb of day now shone with a vivid brightness, and then, with the aid of his lens, he kindled without difficulty the combustible materials which were laid on a bed of leaves in the fork of the branches. It was a natural fireplace, with no danger of conflagration.

Wilson and Robert soon returned with an armful of dead wood, which was cast on the fire. Paganel, to cause a draught, placed himself above the fireplace, his long legs crossed in the Arab fashion; then, moving his body rapidly up and down, he produced, by means of his poncho, a strong current of air. The wood kindled, and a bright, roaring flame soon rose from this improvised oven. Each dried himself in his own way, while the ponchos, hung on the branches, swung to and fro in the breeze.

They now breakfasted, sparingly however, for they had to allow for the following day. The immense basin might not perhaps be empty so soon as Glenarvan hoped, and, moreover, the provisions were limited. The tree bore no fruit; but fortunately it afforded a remarkable supply of fresh eggs, thanks to the numerous nests that loaded the branches, not to speak of their feathered occupants. These resources were by no means to be despised. The question now was, therefore, in case of a prolonged stay, how to secure comfortable quarters.

"Since the kitchen and dining-room are on the ground floor," said Paganel, "we will sleep in the first story. The house is large, the rent reasonable, and we must take our ease. I perceive that above there are natural cradles, in which, when we have once laid ourselves, we shall sleep as well as in the best beds in the world. We have nothing to fear; moreover, we will keep watch, and there are enough of us to repulse all the wild animals."

"Only we have no arms," said Tom Austin.

"I have my revolvers," said Glenarvan.

"And I mine," replied Robert.

"What use," continued Tom Austin, "if Mr. Paganel does not find the means of manufacturing powder?"

"It is not necessary," replied MacNabb, showing a full flask.

"Where did you get that, major?" inquired Paganel.

"Of Thalcave. He thought it might be useful to us, and gave it to me before going back to Thaouka."

"Brave and generous Indian!" cried Glenarvan.

"Yes," added Tom Austin, "if all the Patagonians are fashioned after this model, I pay my respects to Patagonia."

"I desire that the horse be not forgotten," said Paganel. "He forms part of the Patagonian, and, if I am not greatly mistaken, we shall see them again."

"How far are we from the Atlantic?" inquired the major.

"Not more than forty miles," answered Paganel. "And now, my friends, since each is free to act, I ask permission to leave you. I am going to choose an observatory above, and, with the aid of my telescope, will keep you acquainted with what goes on here."

The geographer was allowed to go. He very adroitly swung himself from branch to branch, and disappeared behind the thick curtain of foliage. His companions at once occupied themselves with making the sleeping-room and preparing their beds, which was neither a difficult nor a lengthy task. As there were no bedclothes to fix nor furniture to arrange, each soon resumed his place by the fire.

They then conversed, but not about their present condition, which they must patiently endure. They returned to the inexhaustible subject of Captain Grant's recovery. If the waters subsided, in three days the travelers would be again on board the Duncan. But the captain and his two sailors, those unfortunate castaways, would not be with them; and it even seemed after this failure, after this vain search in South America, as if all hope of finding them were irrevocably lost. Whither direct a new search? What, too, would be the grief of Lady Helena and Mary Grant on learning that the future had no hope in store for them!

"Poor sister!" exclaimed Robert; "all is over for us!"

Glenarvan, for the first time, had no consoling answer to make. What hope could he give the child? Had he not followed with rigorous exactitude the directions of the document?

"At all events," said he, "this thirty-seventh degree of latitude is no vain indication. Have we not supposed, interpreted, and ascertained that it relates to the shipwreck or the captivity of Captain Grant? Have we not read it with our own eyes?"

"All that is true, my lord," replied Tom Austin; "nevertheless our search has not succeeded."

"It is discouraging as well as annoying," said Glenarvan.

"Annoying if you will," replied MacNabb, in a calm tone, "but not discouraging. Precisely because we thus have a definite item, we must thoroughly exhaust all its instructions."

"What do you mean?" inquired Glenarvan. "What do you think ought to be done?"

"A very simple and reasonable thing, my dear Edward. Let us turn our faces towards the east, when we are on board the Duncan, and follow the thirty-seventh parallel even around to our starting-point, if necessary."

"Do you think, my dear major, that I have not thought of this?" replied Glenarvan. "Indeed I have, a hundred times. But what chance have we of succeeding? Is not leaving the American continent departing from the place indicated by Captain Grant himself, from Patagonia, so clearly named in the document?"

"Do you wish to begin your search in the Pampas again," replied the major, "when you are sure that the shipwreck of the Britannia did not take place on the Pacific or Atlantic coast?"

Glenarvan did not answer.

"And however feeble the chance of finding Captain Grant by following this latitude may be, still ought we not to attempt it?"

"I do not deny it," replied Glenarvan.

"And you, my friends," added the major, addressing the sailors, "are you not of my opinion?"

"Entirely," answered Tom Austin, while Wilson and Mulready nodded assent.

"Listen to me, my friends," continued Glenarvan, after a few moments of reflection, "and you too, Robert, for this is a serious question. I shall do everything possible to find Captain Grant, as I have undertaken to do, and shall devote my entire life, if necessary, to this object. All Scotland would join me to save this noble man who sacrificed himself for her. I too think, however slight may be the chance, that we ought to make the tour of the world on the thirty-seventh parallel; and I shall do so. But this is not the point to be settled: there is a much more important one, and it is this: Ought we once and for all to abandon our search on the American continent?"

This question, so directly asked, was unanswered. No one dared to declare his opinion.

"Well?" resumed Glenarvan, addressing the major more especially.

"My dear Edward," replied MacNabb, "it would involve too great a responsibility to answer you now. The case requires consideration. But first of all I desire to know what countries the thirty-seventh parallel crosses."

"That is Paganel's business," replied Glenarvan.

"Let us ask him, then," said the major.

The geographer was no longer to be seen, as he was hidden by the thick foliage. It was necessary to call him.

"Paganel! Paganel!" cried Glenarvan.

"Present!" answered a voice which seemed to come to them from the sky.

"Where are you?"

"In my tower."

"What are you doing?"

"Surveying the wide horizon."

"Can you come down a moment?"

"Do you need me?"

"Yes."

"What for?"

"To know what countries the thirty-seventh parallel crosses."

"Nothing easier," replied Paganel; "I need not even disturb myself to tell you."

"Very well, then."

"Leaving America, the thirty-seventh parallel crosses the Atlantic."

"Good."

"It strikes Tristan d'Acunha Island."

"Well?"

"It passes two degrees to the south of the Cape of Good Hope."

"And then?"

"It runs across the Indian Ocean."

"And then?"

"It grazes St. Paul's Island of the Amsterdam group."

"Go on."

"It cuts Australia across the province of Victoria."

"Proceed."

"Leaving Australia—"

This last sentence was not finished. Did the geographer hesitate? Did he know no more? No; but a startling cry was heard in the top of the tree. Glenarvan and his friends grew pale as they gazed at each other. Had a new calamity happened? Had the unfortunate Paganel fallen? Already Wilson and Mulready were hastening to his assistance, when a long body appeared. Paganel dangled from branch to branch. His hands could grasp nothing. Was he alive, or dead? They did not know; but he was about to fall into the roaring waters, when the major, with a strong hand, arrested his progress.

"Very much obliged, MacNabb!" cried Paganel.

"Why, what is the matter with you?" said the major.

"What has got into you? Is this another of your eternal distractions?"

"Yes, yes," replied Paganel, in a voice choked with emotion (and leaves). "Yes, a distraction,—phenomenal this time."

"What is it?"

"We have been mistaken! We are still mistaken!"

"Explain yourself."

"Glenarvan, major, Robert, my friends," cried Paganel, "all you who hear me, we are seeking Captain Grant where he is not."

"What do you say?" cried Glenarvan.

"Not only where he is not," added Paganel, "but even where he has never been."

CHAPTER XXIV. PAGANEL'S DISCLOSURE.

A profound astonishment greeted these unexpected words. What did the geographer mean? Had he lost his senses? He spoke, however, with such conviction that all eyes were turned towards Glenarvan. This declaration of Paganel was a direct answer to the question the former had asked. But Glenarvan confined himself to a negative gesture, indicating disbelief in the geographer, who, as soon as he was master of his emotion, resumed.

"Yes," said he, in a tone of conviction, "yes, we have gone astray in our search, and have read in the document what is not written there."

"Explain yourself, Paganel," said the major; "and more calmly."

"That is very simple, major. Like you, I was in error; like you, I struck upon a false interpretation. When, but a moment ago, at the top of this tree, in answer to the question, at the word 'Australia' an idea flashed through my mind, and all was clear."

"What!" cried Glenarvan, "do you pretend that Captain Grant—"

"I pretend," replied Paganel, "that the word *Austral* in the document is not complete, as we have hitherto supposed, but the root of the word *Australia*."

"This is something singular," said the major.

"Singular!" replied Glenarvan, shrugging his shoulders; "it is simply impossible!"

"Impossible," continued Paganel, "is a word that we do not allow in France."

"What!" added Glenarvan, in a tone of the greatest incredulity, "do you pretend, with that document in your possession, that the shipwreck of the Britannia took place on the shores of Australia?"

"I am sure of it!" replied Paganel.

"By my faith, Paganel," said Glenarvan, "this is a pretension that astonishes me greatly, coming from the secretary of a geographical society."

"Why?" inquired Paganel, touched in his sensitive point.

"Because, if you admit the word Australia, you admit at the same time that there are Indians in that country, a fact which has not yet been proved."

Paganel was by no means surprised at this argument. He seemingly expected it, and began to smile.

"My dear Glenarvan," said he, "do not be too hasty in your triumph. I am going to defeat you completely, as no Englishman has ever been defeated."

"I ask nothing better. Defeat me, Paganel."

"Listen, then. You say that the Indians mentioned in the document belong exclusively to Patagonia. The incomplete word *indi* does not mean Indians, but natives (*indigènes*). Now do you admit that there are natives in Australia?"

It must be confessed that Glenarvan now gazed fixedly at Paganel.

"Bravo, Paganel!" said the major.

"Do you admit my interpretation, my dear lord?"

"Yes," replied Glenarvan, "if you can prove to me that the imperfect word *gonie* does not relate to the country of the Patagonians."

"No," cried Paganel, "it certainly does not mean Patagonia. Read anything you will but that."

"But what?"

"*Cosmogonie! théogonie! agonie!*"

"*Agonie!*" cried the major.

"That is indifferent to me," replied Paganel; "the word has no importance. I shall not even search for what it may signify. The principal point is that *Austral* means Australia, and we must have been blindly following a false trail, not to have discovered before so evident a meaning. If I had found the document, if my judgment had not been set aside by your interpretation, I should never have understood it otherwise."

This time cheers, congratulations, and compliments greeted Paganel's words. Austin, the sailors, the major, and Robert especially, were delighted to revive their hopes, and applauded the worthy geographer. Glenarvan, who had gradually been undeceived, was, as he said, almost ready to surrender.

"One last remark, my dear Paganel, and I have only to bow before your sagacity."

"Speak!"

"How do you arrange these newly-interpreted words, and in what way do you read the document?"

"Nothing is easier. Here is the document," said Paganel, producing the precious paper that he had studied so conscientiously for several days. A profound silence ensued, while the geographer, collecting his thoughts, took his time to answer. His finger followed the incomplete lines on the document, while, in a confident tone, he expressed himself in the following terms:

"'June 7th, 1862, the brig Britannia, of Glasgow, foundered after'—let us put, if you wish, 'two days, three days,' or, 'a long struggle,'—it matters little, it is quite unimportant,—'on the coast of Australia. Directing their course to shore, two sailors and Captain Grant endeavored to land,' or 'did land on the continent, where they will be,' or 'are prisoners of cruel natives. They cast this document,' and so forth. Is it clear?"

"It is clear," replied Glenarvan, "if the word *continent* can be applied to Australia, which is only an island."

"Be assured, my dear Glenarvan, the best geographers are agreed in naming this island the Australian continent."

"Then I have but one thing to say, my friends," cried Glenarvan. "To Australia, and may Heaven assist us!"

"To Australia!" repeated his companions, with one accord.

"Do you know, Paganel," added Glenarvan, "that your presence on board the Duncan is a providential circumstance?"

"Well," replied Paganel, "let us suppose that I am an envoy of Providence, and say no more about it."

Thus ended this conversation, that in the future led to such great results. It completely changed the moral condition of the travelers. They had caught again the thread of the labyrinth in which they had thought themselves forever lost. A new hope arose on the ruins of their fallen projects. They could fearlessly leave behind them this American continent, and already all their thoughts flew away to the Australian land. On reaching the Duncan, they would not bring despair on board, and Lady Helena and Mary Grant would not have to lament the irrevocable loss of the captain. Thus they forgot the dangers of their situation in their new-found joy, and their only regret was that they could not start at once.

It was now four o'clock in the afternoon, and they resolved to take supper at six. Paganel wished to celebrate this joyful day by a splendid banquet. As the bill of fare was very limited, he proposed to Robert that they should go hunting "in the neighboring forest," at which idea the boy clapped his hands. They took Thalcave's powder-flask, cleaned the revolvers, loaded them with fine shot, and started.

"Do not go far," said the major, gravely, to the two huntsmen.

After their departure Glenarvan and MacNabb went to consult the notches on the tree, while Wilson and Mulready revived the smouldering embers.

Arriving at the surface of this immense lake, they saw no sign of abatement. The waters seemed to have attained their highest elevation; but the violence with which they rolled from south to north proved that the equilibrium of the Argentine rivers was not yet established. Before the liquid mass could lower, it must first become calm, like the sea when flood-tide ends and ebb begins. They could not, therefore, expect a subsidence of the waters so long as they flowed towards the north with such swiftness.

While Glenarvan and the major were making these observations, reports resounded in the tree, accompanied by cries of joy almost as noisy. The clear treble of Robert contrasted sharply with the deep bass of Paganel, and the strife was which should be the most boyish. The hunt promised well, and gave hopes of culinary wonders.

When the major and Glenarvan returned to the fire, they had to congratulate Wilson upon an excellent idea. The honest sailor had devoted himself to fishing with wonderful success, with the aid of a pin and a piece of string. Several dozen of little fish, delicate as smelts, called "mojarras," wriggled in a fold of his poncho, and seemed likely to make an exquisite dish.

At this moment the hunters descended from the top of the tree. Paganel carefully carried some black swallows' eggs and a string of sparrows, which he meant afterwards to serve up as larks. Robert had adroitly brought down several pairs of "hilgueros,"—little green-and-yellow birds, which are excellent eating, and very much in demand in the Montevideo market. The geographer, who knew many ways of preparing eggs, had to confine himself this time to cooking them in the hot ashes. However, the repast was as varied as it was delicate. The dried meat, the hard eggs, the broiled mojarras, and the roast sparrows and hilgueros, formed a repast which was long remembered.

The conversation was very animated. Paganel was greatly complimented in his twofold capacity of hunter and cook, and accepted these encomiums with the modesty that belongs to true merit. Then he gave himself up to singular observations on the magnificent tree that sheltered them with its foliage, and whose extent, as he declared, was immense.

"Robert and I," said he jokingly, "imagined ourselves in the open forest during the hunt. One moment I thought we should be lost. I could not find my way. The sun was declining towards the horizon. I sought in vain to retrace my steps. Hunger made itself felt acutely. Already the gloomy coppices were resounding with the growls of ferocious beasts,—but no, there are no ferocious beasts, and I am sorry."

"What!" cried Glenarvan, "you are sorry there are no ferocious beasts?"

"Certainly."

"But, when you have everything to fear from their ferocity—"

"Ferocity does not exist,—scientifically speaking," replied the geographer.

"Ha! this time, Paganel," said the major, "you will not make me admit the utility of ferocious beasts. What are they good for?"

"Major," cried Paganel, "they are good to form classifications, orders, families, genera, sub-genera, species—"

"Very fine!" said MacNabb. "I should not have thought of that! If I had been one of Noah's companions at the time of the deluge, I should certainly have prevented that imprudent patriarch from putting into the ark pairs of tigers, lions, bears, panthers, and other animals as destructive as they were useless."

"Should you have done so?" inquired Paganel.

"I should."

"Well, you would have been wrong in a zoological point of view."

"But not in a human one."

"This is shocking," continued Paganel; "for my part, I should have preserved all the animals before the deluge of which we are so unfortunately deprived."

"I tell you," replied MacNabb, "that Noah was right in abandoning them to their fate, admitting that they lived in his time."

"I tell you that Noah was wrong," retorted Paganel, "and deserves the malediction of scholars to the end of time."

The listeners to this argument could not help laughing at seeing the two friends dispute about what Noah ought to have done or left undone. The major, who had never argued with any one in his life, contrary to all his principles, was every day at war with Paganel, who must have particularly excited him.

Glenarvan, according to his custom, interrupted the debate, and said,—

"However much it is to be regretted, in a scientific or human point of view, that we are deprived of ferocious animals, we must be resigned to-day to their absence. Paganel could not hope to encounter any in this aerial forest."

"No," replied the geographer, "although we beat the bush. It is a pity, for it would have been a glorious hunt. A ferocious man-eater like the jaguar! With one blow of his paw he can twist the neck of a horse. When he has tasted human flesh, however, he returns to it ravenously. What he likes best is the Indian, then the negro, then the mulatto, and then the white man."

"However that may be, my good Paganel," said Glenarvan, "so long as there are no Indians, mulattoes, or negroes among us, I rejoice in the absence of your dear jaguars. Our situation is not, of course, so agreeable—"

"What!" cried Paganel, "you complain of your lot?"

"Certainly," replied Glenarvan. "Are you at your ease in these uncomfortable and uncushioned branches?"

"I have never been more so, even in my own study. We lead the life of birds; we sing and flutter about. I almost think that men were destined to live in the trees."

"They only want wings," said the major.

"They will make them some day."

"In the meantime," replied Glenarvan, "permit me, my dear friend, to prefer the sand of a park, the floor of a house, or the deck of a vessel to this aerial abode."

"Glenarvan," said Paganel, "we must take things as they come. If favorable, so much the better; if unfavorable, we must not mind it. I see you long for the comforts of Malcolm Castle."

"No, but—"

"I am certain that Robert is perfectly happy," interrupted Paganel, to secure one advocate, at least, of his theories.

"Yes, Monsieur Paganel!" cried the boy, in a joyful tone.

"It is natural at his age," replied Glenarvan.

"And at mine," added the geographer. "The less ease we have, the fewer wants; the fewer wants, the happier we are."

"Well," said the major, "here is Paganel going to make an attack upon riches and gilded splendor."

"No, my dear major," continued Paganel; "but, if you wish, I will tell you, in this connection, a little Arab story that occurs to me."

"Yes, yes, Monsieur Paganel," cried Robert.

"And what will your story prove?" asked the major.

"What all stories prove, my brave companion."

"Not much, then," replied MacNabb. "But go on, Scheherezade, and tell one of those stories that you relate so well."

"There was once upon a time," said Paganel, "a son of the great Haroun-al-Raschid who was not happy. He accordingly consulted an old dervish, who told him that happiness was a very difficult thing to find in this world. 'However,' added he, 'I know an infallible way to procure you happiness.' 'What is it?' inquired the young prince. 'It is,' replied the dervish, 'to put on the shirt of a happy man.' Thereupon the prince embraced the old man, and set out in search of his talisman. He visited all the capitals of the earth; he tried the shirts of kings, emperors, princes, and nobles; but it was a useless task, he was no happier. Then he put on the shirts of artists, warriors, and merchants, but with no more success. He had thus traveled far, without finding happiness. At last, desperate from having tried so many shirts, he was returning very sadly one beautiful day to the palace of his father, when he spied in the field an honest laborer, who was joyously singing as he ploughed. 'Here is, at all events, a man who possesses happiness,' said he to himself, 'or happiness does not exist on earth.' He approached him. 'Good man,' said he, 'are you happy?' 'Yes,' replied the other. 'You wish for nothing?' 'No.' 'You would not change your lot for that of a king?' 'Never!' 'Well, sell me your shirt!' 'My shirt! I have none!'"

CHAPTER XXV. BETWEEN FIRE AND WATER.

Jacques Paganel's story had a very great success. He was greatly applauded, but each retained his own opinion, and the geographer obtained the result common to most discussions,—of convincing nobody. However, they were agreed on this point, that it was necessary to have courage for every fortune, and be contented with a tree when one has neither palace nor cottage.

During the course of this confabulation evening had come on. Only a good sleep could thoroughly refresh, after this eventful day. The inmates of the tree felt themselves not only fatigued by the sudden changes of the inundation, but especially overcome by the heat, which had been excessive. Their feathered companions had already set the example; the hilgueros, those nightingales of the Pampas, had ceased their melodious warblings, and all the birds had disappeared in the recesses of the foliage. The best plan was to imitate them.

But before "retiring to their nest," as Paganel said, Glenarvan, Robert, and he climbed to the observatory, to examine for the last time the watery expanse. It was about nine o'clock. The sun had just set in the sparkling mists of the horizon, and all the western part of the firmament was bathed in a warm vapor. The constellations, usually so dazzling, seemed veiled in a soft haze. Still they could be distinguished, and Paganel pointed out to Robert, for Glenarvan's benefit, that zone where the stars are most brilliant.

While the geographer was discoursing thus, the whole eastern horizon assumed a stormy aspect. A dense and dark band, clearly defined, gradually rose, dimming the light of the stars. This cloud of threatening appearance soon invaded almost the entire vault of the sky. Its motive power must have been inherent in itself, for there was not a breath of wind. Not a leaf stirred on the tree, not a ripple curled the surface of the waters. Even the air seemed to fail, as if some huge pneumatic machine had rarefied it. A strong electric current was perceptible in the atmosphere, and every creature felt it course along the nerves. Glenarvan, Paganel, and Robert were sensibly affected by these electric currents.

"We shall have a storm," said Paganel.

"You are not afraid of thunder?" asked Glenarvan of the boy.

"Oh, no, my lord," replied Robert.

"Well, so much the better; for the storm is now not far distant."

"And it will be violent," continued Paganel, "so far as I can judge from the state of the sky."

"It is not the storm that troubles me," said Glenarvan, "but the torrents of rain with which it will be accompanied. We shall be drenched to the skin again. Whatever you may say, Paganel, a nest cannot suffice a man, as you will soon learn to your cost."

"Oh, yes, it can, with philosophy," briskly replied the geographer.

"Philosophy does not prevent you from getting wet."

"No, but it warms you."

"Well, then," said Glenarvan, "let us join our friends and persuade them to envelop us with their philosophy and their ponchos as closely as possible, and especially to lay in a stock of patience, for we shall need it."

So saying, he gave another look at the threatening sky. The mass of clouds now covered it entirely. A faint line of light towards the horizon was scarcely discernible in the dimness. The sombre appearance of the water had increased, and between the dark mass below and the clouds above there was scarcely a separation. At the same time all perception seemed dulled; and a leaden torpor rested upon both eyes and ears, while the silence was profound.

"Let us go down," said Glenarvan; "the lightning will soon be here."

His two companions and himself slid down the smooth branches, and were somewhat surprised to find themselves in a remarkable kind of twilight, which was produced by myriads of luminous objects that crossed each other and buzzed on the surface of the water.

"Phosphorescences?" said Glenarvan.

"No," replied Paganel, "but phosphorescent insects, real glow-worms,— living diamonds, and not expensive, of which the ladies of Buenos Ayres make magnificent ornaments for themselves."

"What!" cried Robert, "are these things, that fly like sparks, insects?"

"Yes, my boy."

Robert caught one of the brilliant creatures. Paganel was right. It was a kind of large beetle, an inch in length, to which the Indians give the name of "tuco-tuco." This curious insect threw out flashes at two points situated in front of its sheath, and its light would have enabled one to read in the darkness. Paganel, on bringing it close to his watch, saw that it was ten o'clock.

Glenarvan now joined the major and the three sailors, and gave them instructions for the night. A terrible storm was to be expected. After the first rollings of the thunder, the wind would doubtless break forth and the tree be violently shaken. It was, therefore, advisable for every one to tie himself firmly to the bed of branches that had been appropriated to him. If they could not avoid the torrents of the sky, they must at least guard against those of the earth, and not fall into the rapid current that broke against the trunk of the tree. They wished each other good night without much hope of passing one, and then each, getting into his aerial resting-place, wrapped himself in his poncho and waited for sleep.

But the approach of a mighty tempest brings to the hearts of most sentient beings a vague anxiety of which the bravest cannot divest themselves. The occupants of the tree, agitated and fearful, could not close their eyes, and the first thunder-clap found them all awake. It took place about eleven o'clock, resembling a distant rumbling. Glenarvan climbed to the end of the branch, and peered out from the foliage. The dark firmament was fitfully illumined by vivid and brilliant flashes, which the waters brightly reflected, and which disclosed great rifts in the clouds. Glenarvan, after surveying the zenith and the horizon, returned to his couch.

"What do you think, Glenarvan?" asked Paganel.

"I think that the storm is beginning, and, if it continues, it will be terrible."

"So much the better," replied the enthusiastic Paganel. "I like a fine spectacle, especially when I cannot avoid it. Only one thing would make me anxious, if anxiety served to avert danger," added he, "and that is, that the culminating point of this plain is the ombu upon which we are perched. A lightning-conductor would be very useful here, for this very tree among all those of the Pampas is the one that particularly attracts the lightning. And then, as you are aware, my friends, meteorologists advise us not to take refuge under trees during a storm."

"Well," said the major, "that is timely advice."

"It must be confessed, Paganel," replied Glenarvan, "that you choose a good time to tell us these encouraging things!"

"Bah!" replied Paganel; "all times are good to receive information. Ah, it is beginning!"

Violent thunder-claps interrupted this conversation, and their intensity increased till they reached the most deafening peals. They soon became sonorous, and made the atmosphere vibrate in rapid oscillations. The firmament was on fire, and during this commotion it was impossible to distinguish from what electric spark emanated the indefinitely-prolonged rumblings that reverberated throughout the abysses of the sky.

The incessant flashes assumed various forms. Some, darting perpendicularly towards the earth, were repeated five or six times in the same place; others, separating into a thousand different branches, spread in zigzag lines and produced on the dark vault of the heavens astonishing jets of arborescent flame. Soon the sky, from east to north, was crossed by a phosphorescent band of intense brilliancy. This illumination gradually overspread the entire horizon, lighting up the clouds like a bonfire, and was reflected in the mirror-like waters, forming what seemed to be an immense circle of fire, of which the tree occupied the centre.

Glenarvan and his companions watched this terrific spectacle in silence. Sheets of dazzling light glided towards them, and blinding flashes followed in rapid succession, now showing the calm countenance of the major, then the speculative face of Paganel or the energetic features of Glenarvan, and again the frightened look of Robert or the unconcerned expression of the sailors. The rain, however, did not fall as yet, nor had the wind risen. But soon the flood-gates of the heavens opened, and the rain came down in torrents, the drops, as they struck the surface of the water, rebounding in thousands of sparks illuminated by the incessant lightning.

Did this rain predict the end of the storm? Were Glenarvan and his companions to be released with a few thorough drenchings? At the height of this struggle of the elements, suddenly there appeared at the end of the branch which extended horizontally, a flaming globe, of the size of a fist, and surrounded by a black smoke. This ball, after revolving a few moments, burst like a bombshell, and with a noise that was distinguishable in the midst of the general tumult. A sulphurous vapor filled the atmosphere. There was a moment of silence, and then Tom Austin was heard crying,—

"The tree is on fire!"

He was right. In a moment the flame, as if it had been communicated to an immense piece of fireworks, spread along the west side of the tree. The dead limbs, the nests of dry grass, and finally the live wood itself, furnished material for the devouring element.

The wind now rose and fanned the flames into fury. Glenarvan and his friends, speechless with terror, and venturing upon limbs that bent beneath their weight, hastily took refuge in the other, the eastern part of the tree.

Meantime the boughs shriveled, crackled, and twisted in the fire like burning serpents. The glowing fragments fell into the rushing waters and floated away in the current, sending forth flashes of ruddy light. The flames at one moment would rise to a fearful height, to be lost in the aerial conflagration, and the next, beaten back by the furious hurricane, would envelop the tree like a robe of molten gold.

Glenarvan, Robert, the major, Paganel, and the sailors, were terrified. A thick smoke was stifling them; an intolerable heat was scorching them. The fire was extending to the lower part of the tree on their side; nothing could stop or extinguish it; and they felt themselves irrevocably doomed to the torture of those victims who are confined within the burning sides of a sacrificial fire-basket.

At last their situation was no longer tenable, and of two deaths they were forced to choose the least cruel.

"To the water!" cried Glenarvan.

Wilson, whom the flames had reached, had already plunged into the current, when they heard him cry, in tones of the greatest terror,—

"Help! help!"

Austin rushed towards him and assisted him to regain the trunk.

"What is the matter?"

"Caymans! caymans!" replied Wilson. And, in truth, the foot of the tree was seen to be surrounded by the most formidable monsters. Their scales glittered in broad plates of light, sharply defined by the conflagration. Their flat tails, their pointed heads, their protruding eyes, their jaws, extending back of their ears, all these characteristic signs were unmistakable. Paganel recognized the voracious alligators peculiar to America, and called caymans in Spanish countries. There were a dozen of them, beating the water with their powerful tails, and attacking the tree with their terrible teeth.

At this sight the unfortunate travelers felt themselves lost indeed. A horrible death was in store for them,—to perish either by the flames or by the teeth of the alligators. There are circumstances in which man is powerless to struggle, and where a raging element can only be repulsed by another equally strong. Glenarvan, with a wild look, gazed at the fire and water leagued against him, not knowing what aid to implore of Heaven.

The storm had now begun to abate; but it had developed in the air a great quantity of vapor, which the electric phenomena were about to set in violent commotion. To the south an enormous water-spout was gradually forming,—an inverted cone of mist, uniting the raging waters below to the stormy clouds above. It advanced revolving with frightful rapidity, collected at its centre a liquid column, and by a powerful attraction, caused by its gyratory motion, drew towards it all the surrounding currents of air.

In a few moments the gigantic water-spout struck the ombu and enveloped it in its watery folds. The tree was shaken to its very base, so that Glenarvan might have thought that the alligators had attacked it with their powerful jaws and were uprooting it from the ground. His companions and he, clinging to one another, felt the mighty tree give way and fall, and saw its flaming branches plunge into the tumultuous waters with a frightful hiss. It was the work of a second. The water-spout had passed, to exert elsewhere its destructive violence, and pumping the waters of the plain as if it would exhaust them.

The tree now, loosened from its moorings, floated onward under the combined impulses of wind and current. The alligators had fled, except one which crawled along the upturned roots and advanced with open jaws; but Mulready, seizing a large brand, struck the creature so powerful a blow that he broke its back. The vanquished animal sank in the eddies of the torrent, still lashing his formidable tail with terrible violence.

Glenarvan and his companions, delivered from these voracious creatures, took refuge on the branches to leeward of the fire, while the tree, wrapped by the blast of the hurricane in glowing sheets of flame, floated on like a burning ship in the darkness of the night.

CHAPTER XXVI. THE RETURN ON BOARD.

For two hours the tree floated on the immense lake without reaching *terra firma*. The flames had gradually died out, and thus the principal danger of this terrible voyage had vanished. The current, still keeping its original direction, flowed from southwest to northeast; the darkness, though illumined now and then by flashes, had become profound, and Paganel sought in vain for his bearings. But the storm was abating, the large drops of rain gave place to light spray that was scattered by the wind, while the huge distended clouds were crossed by light bands.

The tree advanced rapidly on the impetuous torrent, gliding with surprising swiftness, as if some powerful propelling means were inclosed within its trunk. There was as yet no certainty that they would not float on thus for many days. About three o'clock in the morning, however, the major observed that the roots now and then struck the bottom. Tom Austin, by means of a long branch, carefully sounded, and declared that the water was growing shallow. Twenty minutes later, a shock was felt, and the progress of the tree was checked.

"Land! land!" cried Paganel, in ringing tones.

The ends of the charred branches had struck against a hillock on the ground, and never were navigators more delighted to land. Already Robert and Wilson, having reached a firm plateau, were uttering shouts of joy, when a well-known whistle was heard. The sound of a horse's hoofs was heard upon the plain, and the tall form of the Indian emerged from the darkness.

"Thalcave!" cried Robert.

"Thalcave!" repeated his companions, as with one voice.

"Friends!" said the Patagonian, who had waited for them there, knowing that the current would carry them as it had carried him.

At the same moment he raised Robert in his arms and clasped him to his breast. Glenarvan, the major, and the sailors, delighted to see their faithful guide again, shook his hands with the most earnest cordiality. The Patagonian then conducted them to an abandoned estancia. Here a good fire was burning, which revived them, and on the coals were roasting succulent slices of venison, to which they did ample justice. And when their refreshed minds began to reflect, they could scarcely believe that they had escaped so many perils,—the fire, the water, and the formidable alligators.

Thalcave, in a few words, told his story to Paganel, and ascribed to his intrepid horse all the honor of having saved him. Paganel then endeavored to explain to him the new interpretation of the document, and the hopes it led them to entertain. Did the Indian understand the geographer's ingenious suppositions? It was very doubtful; but he saw his friends happy and very confident, and he desired nothing more.

It may be easily believed that these courageous travelers, after their day of rest on the tree, needed no urging to resume their journey. At eight o'clock in the morning they were ready to start. They were too far south to procure means of transport, and were therefore obliged to travel on foot. The distance, however, was only forty miles, and Thaouka would not refuse to carry from time to time a tired pedestrian. In thirty-six hours they would reach the shores of the Atlantic.

As soon as refreshed the guide and his companions left behind them the immense basin, still covered with the waters, and proceeded across elevated plains, on which, here and there, were seen groves planted by Europeans, meadows, and occasionally native trees. Thus the day passed.

The next morning, fifteen miles before reaching the ocean, its proximity was perceptible. They hastened on in order to reach Lake Salado, on the shores of the Atlantic, the same day. They were beginning to feel fatigued, when they perceived sand-hills that hid the foaming waves, and soon the prolonged murmur of the rising tide struck upon their ears.

"The ocean!" cried Paganel.

"Yes, the ocean!" replied Thalcave.

And these wanderers, whose strength had seemed almost about to fail, climbed the mounds with wonderful agility. But the darkness was profound, and their eyes wandered in vain over the gloomy expanse. They looked for the Duncan, but could not discern her.

"She is there, at all events," said Glenarvan, "waiting for us."

"We shall see her to-morrow," replied MacNabb.

Tom Austin shouted seaward, but received no answer. The wind was very strong, and the sea tempestuous. The clouds were driving from the west, and the foaming crests of the waves broke over the beach in masses of spray. If the Duncan was at the appointed rendezvous, the lookout man could neither hear nor be heard. The coast afforded no shelter. There was no bay, no harbor, no cove; not even a creek. The beach consisted of long sand-banks that were lost in the sea, and the vicinity of which is more dangerous than that of the rocks in the face of wind and tide. These banks, in fact, increase the waves; the sea is peculiarly boisterous around them, and ships are sure to be lost if they strike on these bars in heavy storms.

It was therefore very natural that the Duncan, considering this coast dangerous, and knowing it to be without a port of shelter, kept at a distance. Captain Mangles must have kept to the windward as far as possible. This was Tom Austin's opinion, and he declared that the Duncan was not less than five miles at sea.

The major, accordingly, persuaded his impatient relative to be resigned, as there was no way of dissipating the thick darkness. And why weary their eyes in scanning the gloomy horizon? He established a kind of encampment in the shelter of the sand-hills; the remains of the provisions furnished them a final repast; and then each, following the major's example, hollowed out a comfortable bed in the sand, and, covering himself up to his chin, was soon wrapped in profound repose.

Glenarvan watched alone. The wind continued strong, and the ocean still showed the effects of the recent storm. The tumultuous waves broke at the foot of the sand-banks with the noise of thunder. Glenarvan could not convince himself that the Duncan was so near him; but as for supposing that she had not arrived at her appointed rendezvous, it was impossible, for such a ship there were no delays. The storm had certainly been violent and its fury terrible on the vast expanse of the ocean, but the yacht was a good vessel and her captain an able seaman; she must, therefore, be at her destination.

These reflections, however, did not pacify Glenarvan. When heart and reason are at variance, the latter is the weaker power. The lord of Malcolm Castle seemed to see in the darkness all those whom he loved, his dear Helena, Mary Grant, and the crew of the Duncan. He wandered along the barren coast which the waves covered with phosphorescent bubbles. He looked, he listened, and even thought that he saw a fitful light on the sea.

"I am not mistaken," he soliloquized; "I saw a ship's light, the Duncan's. Ah! why cannot my eyes pierce the darkness?"

Then an idea occurred to him. Paganel called himself a nyctalops; he could see in the night.

The geographer was sleeping like a mole in his bed, when a strong hand dragged him from his sandy couch.

"Who is that?" cried he.

"I."

"Who?"

"Glenarvan. Come, I need your eyes."

"My eyes?" replied Paganel, rubbing them vigorously.

"Yes, your eyes, to distinguish the Duncan in this darkness. Come."

"And why my eyes?" said Paganel to himself, delighted, nevertheless, to be of service to Glenarvan.

He rose, shaking his torpid limbs in the manner of one awakened from sleep, and followed his friend along the shore. Glenarvan requested him to survey the dark horizon to seaward. For several moments Paganel conscientiously devoted himself to this task.

"Well, do you perceive nothing?" asked Glenarvan.

"Nothing. Not even a cat could see two paces before her."

"Look for a red or a green light, on the starboard or the larboard side."

"I see neither a red nor a green light. All is darkness," replied Paganel, whose eyes were thereupon involuntarily closed.

For half an hour he mechanically followed his impatient friend in absolute silence, with his head bowed upon his breast, sometimes raising it suddenly. He tottered along with uncertain steps, like those of a drunken man. At last Glenarvan, seeing that the geographer was in a state of somnambulism, took him by the arm, and, without waking him, led him back to his sand-hole, and comfortably deposited him therein.

At break of day they were all started to their feet by the cry,—

"The Duncan! the Duncan!"

"Hurrah! hurrah!" replied Glenarvan's companions, rushing to the shore.

The Duncan was indeed in sight. Five miles distant, the yacht was sailing under low pressure, her main-sails carefully reefed, while her smoke mingled with the mists of the morning. The sea was high, and a vessel of her tonnage could not approach the shore without danger.

Glenarvan, provided with Paganel's telescope, watched the movements of the Duncan. Captain Mangles could not have perceived them, for he did not approach, but continued to coast along with only a reefed top-sail.

At this moment Thalcave, having loaded his carbine heavily, fired it in the direction of the yacht. They gazed and listened. Three times the Indian's gun resounded, waking the echoes of the shore.

At last a white smoke issued from the side of the yacht.

"They see us!" cried Glenarvan. "It is the Duncan's cannon."

A few moments after, a heavy report rang out on the air, and the Duncan, shifting her sail and putting on steam, was seen to be approaching the shore. By the aid of the glass they saw a boat leave the ship's side.

"Lady Helena cannot come," said Tom Austin: "the sea is too rough."

"Nor Captain Mangles," replied MacNabb: "he cannot leave his vessel."

"My sister! my sister!" cried Robert, stretching his arms towards the yacht, which rolled heavily.

"I hope I shall soon get on board!" exclaimed Glenarvan.

"Patience, Edward! You will be there in two hours," replied MacNabb.

Glenarvan now joined Thalcave, who, standing with folded arms alongside of Thaouka, was calmly gazing at the waves.

Glenarvan took his hand, and, pointing to the yacht, said,—

"Come!"

The Indian shook his head.

"Come, my friend!" continued Glenarvan.

"No," replied Thalcave, gently. "Here is Thaouka, and there are the Pampas!" he added, indicating with a sweep of his hand the vast expanse of the plains.

It was clear that the Indian would never leave the prairies, where the bones of his fathers whitened. Glenarvan knew the strong attachment of these children of the desert to their native country. He therefore shook Thalcave's hand, and did not insist; not even when the Indian, smiling in his peculiar way, refused the price of his services, saying,—

"It was done out of friendship."

His lordship, however, desired to give the brave Indian something which might at least serve as a souvenir of his European friends. But what had he left? His arms, his horses, everything had been lost in the inundation. His friends were no richer than himself. For some moments he was at a loss how to repay the disinterested generosity of the brave guide; but at last a happy idea occurred to him. He drew from his pocket-book a costly medallion inclosing an admirable portrait, one of Lawrence's master-pieces, and presented it to Thalcave.

"My wife," said Glenarvan.

Thalcave gazed with wonder at the portrait, and pronounced these simple words,—

"Good and beautiful!"

Then Robert, Paganel, the major, Tom Austin, and the two sailors bade an affectionate adieu to the noble Patagonian, who clasped each one in succession to his broad breast. All were sincerely sorry at parting with so courageous and devoted a friend. Paganel forced him to accept a map of South America and the two oceans, which the Indian had frequently examined with interest. It was the geographer's most precious possession. As for Robert, he had nothing to give but caresses, which he freely lavished upon his deliverer and upon Thaouka.

At that instant the Duncan's boat approached, and, gliding into the narrow channel between the sand-banks, grounded on the beach.

"My wife?" asked Glenarvan.

"My sister?" cried Robert.

"Lady Helena and Miss Grant await you on board," replied the cockswain. "But we have not a moment to lose, my lord, for the tide is beginning to ebb."

The last acknowledgments were given, and Thalcave accompanied his friends to the boat. Just as Robert was about to embark, the Indian took him in his arms and gazed at him tenderly.

"Now go," said he; "you are a man!"

"Adieu, my friend, adieu!" cried Glenarvan.

"Shall we ever see each other again?" asked Paganel.

"Who knows?" replied Thalcave, raising his arms towards heaven.

They pushed off, and the boat was rapidly borne from the shore by the ebbing tide. For a long time the motionless outline of the Indian was seen through the foam of the waves. Then his tall form grew indistinct, and soon became invisible. An hour afterwards they reached the Duncan. Robert was the first to spring upon the deck, where he threw himself upon his sister's neck, while the crew of the yacht filled the air with their joyous shouts.

Thus had our travelers accomplished the journey across South America on a rigorously straight line. Neither mountains nor rivers had turned them aside from their course; and, although they were not forced to struggle against the evil designs of men, the relentless fury of the elements had often tested their generous intrepidity to its utmost powers of endurance.

CHAPTER XXVII. A NEW DESTINATION.

The first moments were consecrated to the happiness of meeting. Lord Glenarvan did not wish the joy in the hearts of his friends to be chilled by tidings of their want of success. His first words, therefore, were,—

"Courage, my friends, courage! Captain Grant is not with us, but we are sure to find him."

It needed only such an assurance to restore hope to the passengers of the Duncan. Lady Helena and Mary Grant, while the boat was approaching the ship, had experienced all the anguish of suspense. From the deck they endeavored to count those who were returning. At one time the young girl would despair; at another she would think she saw her father. Her heart beat quickly; she could not speak; she could scarcely stand. Lady Helena supported her, while Captain Mangles stood beside her in silence. His keen eyes, accustomed to distinguish distant objects, could not discern the captain.

"He is there! he is coming! my father!" murmured the young girl.

But as the boat gradually drew near, the illusion vanished. Not only Lady Helena and the captain, but Mary Grant, had now lost all hope. It was, therefore, time for Glenarvan to utter his assuring words.

After the first embraces, all were informed of the principal incidents of the journey; and, first of all, Glenarvan made known the new interpretation of the document, due to the sagacity of Jacques Paganel. He also praised Robert, of whom his sister had a right to be proud. His courage, his devotion, and the dangers that he had overcome, were conspicuously set forth by his noble friend, so that the boy would not have known where to hide himself, if his sister's arms had not afforded him a sure refuge.

"You need not blush, Robert," said Captain Mangles; "you have behaved like the worthy son of Captain Grant."

He stretched out his arms towards Mary's brother, and pressed his lips to the boy's cheeks, which were still wet with tears.

They then spoke of the generous Thalcave. Lady Helena regretted that she could not have shaken hands with the brave Indian. MacNabb, after the first outbursts of enthusiasm, repaired to his cabin to shave himself. As for Paganel, he flitted hither and thither, like a bee, extracting the honey of compliments and smiles. He wished to embrace all on board the Duncan, and, beginning with Lady Helena and Mary Grant, ended with Mr. Olbinett, the steward, who could not better recognize such politeness than by announcing breakfast.

"Breakfast!" cried Paganel.

"Yes, Mr. Paganel," replied Olbinett.

"A real breakfast, on a real table, with table-cloth and napkins?"

"Certainly."

"And shall we not eat hard eggs, or ostrich steaks?"

"Oh, Mr. Paganel!" replied the worthy steward, greatly embarrassed.

"I did not mean to offend you, my friend," said the geographer; "but for a month our food has been of that sort, and we have dined, not at a table, but stretched on the ground, except when we were astride of the trees. This breakfast that you have just announced seemed to me, therefore, like a dream, a fiction, a chimera."

"Well, we will test its reality, Monsieur Paganel," replied Lady Helena, who could not help laughing.

"Accept my arm," said the gallant geographer.

"Has your lordship any orders to give?" inquired Captain Mangles.

"After breakfast, my dear fellow," replied Glenarvan, "we will discuss in council the programme of the new expedition."

The passengers and the young captain then descended to the cabin. Orders were given to the engineer to keep up steam, that they might start at the first signal. The major and the travelers, after a rapid toilette, seated themselves at the table. Ample justice was done to Mr. Olbinett's repast, which was declared excellent and even superior to the splendid banquets of the Pampas. Paganel called twice for every dish, "through absent-mindedness," as he said. This unfortunate word led Lady Helena to inquire if the amiable Frenchman had occasionally shown his habitual failing. The major and Lord Glenarvan looked at each other with a smile. As for Paganel, he laughed heartily, and promised "upon his honor" not to commit a single blunder during the entire voyage. He then in a very comical way told the story of his mistake in the study of Spanish.

"After all," he added, in conclusion, "misfortunes are sometimes beneficial, and I do not regret my error."

"And why, my worthy friend?" asked the major.

"Because I not only know Spanish, but Portuguese also. I speak two languages instead of one."

"By my faith, I should not have thought of that," replied MacNabb. "My compliments, Paganel, my sincere compliments!"

Paganel was applauded, but did not lose a single mouthful. He did not, however, notice one peculiarity observed by Glenarvan, and that was the young captain's attentions to his neighbor, Mary Grant. A slight sign from Lady Helena to her husband told him how matters stood. He gazed at the two young people with affectionate sympathy, and finally addressed the captain, but upon a different subject.

"How did you succeed with your voyage, captain?" he inquired.

"Excellently," replied the captain; "only I must inform your lordship that we did not return by way of the Strait of Magellan."

"What!" cried Paganel, "you doubled Cape Horn, and I was not there!"

"Hang yourself!" said the major.

"Selfish fellow! you give me this advice in order that you may share my rope!" retorted the geographer.

"Well, my dear Paganel," added Glenarvan, "unless we are endowed with ubiquity, we cannot be everywhere. Since you crossed the Pampas, you could not at the same time double Cape Horn."

"Nevertheless, I am sorry," replied the geographer.

Captain Mangles now told the story of his voyage, and was congratulated by Glenarvan, who, addressing Mary Grant, said,—

"My dear young lady, I see that Captain John pays his homage to your noble qualities, and I am happy to find that you are not displeased with his ship."

"Oh, how could I be?" replied Mary, gazing at Lady Helena, and perhaps also at the young captain.

"My sister loves you, Mr. Captain," cried Robert, "and I do too."

"And I return your love, my dear boy," replied Captain Mangles, a little confused by Robert's words, which also brought a slight blush to the face of the young girl.

Then, changing the conversation to a less embarrassing subject, the captain added,—

"Since I have related the Duncan's voyage, will not your lordship give us a few particulars of your travels, and the exploits of our young hero?"

No recital could have been more agreeable to Lady Helena and Miss Grant, and Glenarvan hastened to satisfy their curiosity. He told, word for word, all about their journey from ocean to ocean. The passage of the Andes, the earthquake, Robert's disappearance, his capture by the condor, Thalcave's fortunate shot, the adventure with the wolves, the boy's devotion, the meeting with Sergeant Manuel, the inundation, their refuge in the tree, the lightning, the fire, the alligators, the water-spout, the night on the shores of the Atlantic, all these incidents, cheerful or serious, excited alternately the joy and terror of his hearers. Many a circumstance was related that brought Robert the caresses of his sister and Lady Helena. Never was boy more highly praised, or by more enthusiastic friends.

"Now, my friends," remarked Lord Glenarvan, when he had finished his recital, "let us think of the present. Let us return to the subject of Captain Grant."

When breakfast was over, the party repaired to Lady Helena's state-room, and, taking seats around a table loaded with maps and charts, resumed the conversation. Glenarvan explained that the shipwreck had not taken place on the shores either of the Pacific or the Atlantic, and that, consequently, the document had been wrongly interpreted so far as Patagonia was concerned; that Paganel, by a sudden inspiration, had discovered the mistake and proved that they had been following a false trail. The geographer was accordingly asked to explain the French document, which he did to the satisfaction of every one. When he had finished his demonstration, Glenarvan announced that the Duncan would immediately set sail for Australia.

The major, however, before the order was given, asked permission to make a single remark.

"Speak, major," said Glenarvan.

"My object," said MacNabb, "is not to invalidate the arguments of my friend Paganel, still less to refute them. I consider them rational, sagacious, and worthy of our whole attention. But I desire to submit them to a final examination, that their validity may be incontestable."

No one knew what the prudent MacNabb meant, and his hearers listened with some anxiety.

"Go on, major," said Paganel: "I am ready to answer all your questions."

"Nothing can be simpler," said the major. "Five months ago, in the Frith of Clyde, when we studied the three documents, their interpretation seemed clear to us. No place but the western coast of Patagonia could, we thought, have been the scene of the shipwreck. We had not even the shadow of a doubt on the subject."

"Very true," added Glenarvan.

"Afterwards," resumed the major, "when Paganel, in a moment of providential absent-mindedness, embarked on board our vessel, the documents were submitted to him, and he unhesitatingly sanctioned our search upon the American coast."

"You are right," observed the geographer.

"And, nevertheless, we are mistaken," said the major.

"Yes, we are mistaken," repeated Paganel; "but to be mistaken is only to be human, while it is the part of a madman to persist in his error."

"Wait, Paganel," continued the major; "do not get excited. I do not mean that our search ought to be prolonged in America."

"What do you ask, then?" inquired Glenarvan.

"Simply the acknowledgment that Australia now seems to be the scene of the Britannia's shipwreck as much as South America did before."

"Granted," replied Paganel.

"Who knows, then," resumed the major, "whether, after Australia, another country may not offer us the same probabilities, and whether, when this new search proves vain, it may not seem evident that we ought to have searched elsewhere?"

Glenarvan and Paganel glanced at each other. The major's remarks were strictly correct.

"I desire, therefore," added MacNabb, "that a final test be made before we start for Australia. Here are the documents and maps. Let us examine successively all points that the thirty-seventh parallel crosses, and see if there is not some other country to which the document has as precise a reference."

"Nothing is easier," replied Paganel.

The map was placed before Lady Helena, and all showed themselves ready to follow Paganel's demonstration. After carefully examining the documents, it was unanimously agreed that Paganel's interpretation was the correct one.

"I leave you, therefore, my friends," said he, in conclusion, "to decide whether all the probabilities are not in favor of the Australian continent."

"Evidently," replied the passengers and the captain with unanimity.

"Captain," said Glenarvan, "have you sufficient provisions and coal?"

"Yes, my lord, I procured ample supplies at Talcahuana, and, besides, we can lay in a fresh stock of fuel at Cape Town."

"One more remark," said the major.

"A thousand, if you please!"

"Whatever may be the guarantees for success in Australia, will it not be well to call for a day or two, in passing, at the islets of Tristan d'Acunha and Amsterdam? They are situated so near our strict line of search, that it is worth our while to ascertain if there be on them any trace of the shipwreck of the Britannia."

"The unbeliever!" said Paganel.

"I do not want to have to return to them, monsieur, if Australia does not after all realize our newly-conceived expectations."

"The precaution is not a bad one," said Glenarvan.

"And I do not wish to dissuade you; quite the contrary," replied the geographer.

"Well, then, we will adopt it, and start forthwith," said Lord Glenarvan.

"Immediately, my lord," replied the captain, as he went on deck, while Robert and Mary Grant uttered the liveliest expressions of gratitude; and the Duncan, leaving the American coast and heading to the east, was soon swiftly ploughing the waves of the Atlantic.

CHAPTER XXVIII. TRISTAN D'ACUNHA AND THE ISLE OF AMSTERDAM.

The Duncan now had before her a broad stretch of ocean but little traversed by navigators. Between the shores of South America and the little speck in the ocean known by the name of Tristan d'Acunha, there was no probability of her meeting with any strange sail; and under some circumstances, or in some company, the days might have been monotonous and the hours might have hung wearily. But so ardent was the desire for success, and so accomplished, yet varied, were the characters of those who composed the little assembly, that the voyage on the South Atlantic, though devoid of striking incident, was by no means wanting in interest. Much of the time was spent on deck, where the ladies' cabins were now located, Mary Grant especially training her hand, head, and heart in feeling, thought, and action. The geographer set to work on a composition entitled "Travels of a Geographer on the Argentine Pampas;" but many a blank page did he leave. Tho Scottish peer (when tired of examining for the thousandth time all that belonged to his yacht) could look at the books and documents which he had brought with him, intending to peruse them carefully. And as to the major he was never in company and never out of company; his cigar insured, nothing else was wanted.

Ever and anon many miles of the ocean would be covered by masses of sea-weed; these different species of algæ would afford subject for research; specimens must be preserved, authorities must be consulted, and as one result at least all would become wiser. Then a discussion would ensue on some geographical problem, and maps that were not attainable were of course appealed to by each disputant, though the subject in question was often of very trivial moment. It was in the midst of a debate of this kind, during the evening, that a sailor cried out,—

"Land ahead!"

"In what direction?" asked Paganel.

"To windward," replied the sailor.

The landsmen's eyes were strained, but to no purpose. The geographer's telescope was brought into requisition, but with no avail. "I do not see the land," said its owner.

"Look into the clouds," said the captain.

"Ah!" replied Paganel, struck with the idea, and shortly with the reality also; for there was the barren mountain-top of Tristan d'Acunha.

"Then," said he, "if I remember aright, we are eighty miles from it. Is not that the distance from which this mountain is visible?"

"Exactly so," replied the captain.

A few hours brought them much nearer to the group of high and steep rocks, and at sunrise they saw the conical peak of Tristan, seemingly separated from all the rest of the rocky group, and reflecting the glory of the blue heavens and of the rising orb on the placid sea at its base.

There are three islets in this group,—Tristan d'Acunha, Inaccessible, and Rossignol; but it was only at the first of these that the Duncan called. Inquiry was made of the authorities (for these islets are governed by a British official from the Cape of Good Hope) if there were any tidings of the Britannia. But nothing was known of such a ship; they were told of the shipwrecks which had occurred, but there was nothing that afforded a clue to that which they sought. They spent some hours in examination of the fauna and flora, which were not very extensive. They saw and were seen by the sparse population that subsist here, and in the afternoon of the same day the yacht left the islands and islanders so rarely visited.

Whilst the passengers had been thus engaged, Lord Glenarvan had allowed his crew to employ their time advantageously to themselves in capturing some of the seals which are so plentiful in these latitudes. A few hours of their united toil resulted in the death of a large number of seals who were "caught napping," and in the stowing away, for the profit of the crew when they should reach the Australian market, several barrels of the oil obtained from their carcases.

Still onward on the same parallel lay the course of the Duncan, towards the Isles of Amsterdam and St. Paul; and the same subjects of conversation, study, and speculation engaged them all, until, one morning, they espied the first mentioned island, far ahead; and as they drew nearer, a peak rose clearly before their vision which strongly reminded them of the Peak of Teneriffe they had beheld a few months before.

The Isle of Amsterdam or St. Peter, and the Isle of St. Paul, have been visited by very few, and but little is known of them. The latter is uninhabited; but our friends found a few voluntary exiles on the former island, who, by means of seal-fishing, eke out a scanty existence in this out-of-the-way spot. Here again inquiry was made, but in vain, for any information of the Britannia, her voyage, or her shipwreck.Neither on the Isle of Amsterdam nor on that of St. Paul, which the whalers and seal-fishers sometimes visit, had there been any trace of the catastrophe.

Desolate as these lonely islands appeared to our travelers, they still were not devoid of objects of interest. They were meagre enough in vegetation and in animal life; but there were warm springs which well repaid a visit. Captain Mangles found the temperature of their waters to be 166° Fahrenheit; and, inasmuch as this was sufficient to cook fish, Paganel decided that it was not necessary for him to bathe here "geographically."

When they resumed their course, though many miles were before them, there was a growing sense of anticipation; they were not to pause again until the "Australian continent" was reached; and more and more did the conversation and discussions tend towards this continent as their subject. On one occasion so certain was Paganel as to the ease with which they would be able to pursue their search, when they arrived, that he asserted that more than fifty geographers had already made the course clear for them.

"What! fifty, do you say?" asked the major, with an air of doubt.

"Yes, MacNabb, decidedly," said the geographer, piqued at the hesitancy to believe him.

"Impossible!" replied the major.

"Not at all; and if you doubt my veracity, I will cite their names."

"Ah!" said the major, quietly, "you clever people stick at nothing."

"Major," said Paganel, "will you wager your rifle against my telescope that I cannot name at least fifty Australian explorers?"

"Of course, Paganel, if you like," replied MacNabb, seeing that he could not now recede from his position without incurring the ridicule of the company.

"Well, then," said Paganel to Lady Helena and Miss Grant, "come and be umpires, and Master Robert shall count for us." And forthwith the learned geographer opened his budget, and poured forth the history of the discovery of

Australia, with the names of its discoverers and the dates of their explorations, as fluently as though his sole calling in life was to be professor of Australian history. Rapidly he mentioned the first twenty who found or traversed the Austral shores; as rapidly did the names of the second score flow from his lips; and after the prescribed fifty had been enumerated, he kept on as though his list were inexhaustible.

"Enough, enough, Monsieur Paganel!" said Lady Helena. "You have shown that there is nothing, great or small, about Australia, of which you are ignorant."

"Nay, madam," said the geographer, with a bow.

Then, with a peculiar expression, he smiled as he said to the major, "We will talk about the rifle at another time."

CHAPTER XXIX. THE STORM ON THE INDIAN OCEAN.

Two days after this conversation, Captain Mangles took an observation, and the passengers saw, to their great satisfaction, upon consulting the map, that they were in the vicinity of Cape Bernouilli, which they might expect to reach in four days. The west wind had hitherto favored the progress of the yacht, but for several days it had shown a tendency to fail, and now there was a perfect calm. The sails flapped idly against the masts, and had it not been for her powerful screw, the Duncan would have been becalmed on the ocean.

This state of things might be prolonged indefinitely. At evening Glenarvan consulted the captain on the subject. The latter, whose supply of coal was rapidly diminishing, appeared much disturbed at the subsidence of the wind. He had covered his ship with canvas, and set his studding- and main-sails, that he might take advantage of the least breeze; but, in nautical language, there was not enough wind "to fill a hat."

"At all events," said Glenarvan, "we need not complain. It is better to be without wind than to have a contrary one."

"Your lordship is right," replied Captain Mangles; "but I dread some sudden change in the weather. We are now in the neighborhood of the trade-winds, which, from October to April, blow from the northeast, and our progress will, therefore, be very much retarded."

"But what can we do, captain? If this misfortune occurs, we must submit to it. It will only be a delay, after all."

"Probably, if a storm does not come upon us too."

"Do you fear bad weather?" asked Glenarvan, looking at the sky, which, however, was cloudless.

"Yes," replied the captain. "I tell your lordship, but would conceal my apprehensions from Lady Helena and Miss Grant."

"You act wisely. What do you apprehend?"

"There are signs of a great storm. Do not trust the appearance of the sky, my lord; nothing is more deceptive. For two days the barometer has fallen to an alarming degree. This is a warning that I cannot disregard. I particularly fear the storms of the South Seas, for I have been already exposed to them."

"John," replied Glenarvan, "the Duncan is a stout vessel, and her captain a skillful seaman. Let the storm come; we will take care of ourselves."

Captain Mangles, while giving expression to his fears, was by no means forgetful of his duty as a sailor. The steady fall of the barometer caused him to take every measure of precaution. The sky, as yet, gave no indication of the approaching tempest; but the warnings of his infallible instrument were not to be disregarded.

The young captain accordingly remained on deck all night. About eleven o'clock the sky grew threatening towards the south. All hands were immediately called on deck, to take in the sails. At midnight the wind freshened. The creaking of the masts, the rattling of the rigging, and the groaning of bulkheads informed the passengers of the state of affairs. Paganel, Glenarvan, the major, and Robert came on deck to render assistance if it should be needed. Over the sky, that they had left clear and studded with stars, now rolled thick clouds broken by light bands and spotted like the skin of a leopard.

"Has the storm broken upon us?" asked Glenarvan.

"Not yet, but it will presently," replied the captain.

At that moment he gave the order to reef the top-sail. The sailors sprang into the windward rattlings, and with difficulty accomplished their task. Captain Mangles wished to keep on as much sail as possible, to support the yacht and moderate her rolling. After these precautions had been taken, he told the mate and the boatswain to prepare for the assault of the tempest, which could not be long in breaking forth. Still, like an officer at the storming of a breach, he did not leave the point of observation, but from the upper deck endeavored to draw from the stormy sky its secrets.

It was now one o'clock in the morning. Lady Helena and Miss Grant, aroused by the unusual bustle, ventured to come on deck. The wind was sharply whistling through the cordage, which, like the strings of a musical instrument, resounded as if some mighty bow had caused their rapid vibrations; the pulleys clashed against each other; the ropes creaked with a sharp sound in their rough sockets; the sails cracked like cannon, and vast waves rolled up to assail the yacht, as it lightly danced on their foaming crests.

When the captain perceived the ladies, he approached and besought them to return to the cabin. Several waves had already been shipped, and the deck might be swept at any moment. The din of the elements was now so piercing that Lady Helena could scarcely hear the young captain.

"Is there any danger?" she managed to ask him during a momentary lull in the storm.

"No, madam," replied he; "but neither you nor Miss Mary can remain on deck."

The ladies did not oppose an order that seemed more like an entreaty, and returned to the cabin just as a wave, rolling over the stern, shook the compass-lights in their sockets. The violence of the wind redoubled; the masts bent under the pressure of sail, and the yacht seemed to rise on the billows.

"Brail up the main-sail!" cried the captain; "haul in the top-sails and jibs!"

The sailors sprang to their places; the halyards were loosened, the brails drawn down, the jibs taken in with a noise that rose above the storm, and the Duncan, whose smoke-stack belched forth torrents of black smoke, rolled heavily in the sea.

Glenarvan, the major, Paganel, and Robert gazed with admiration and terror at this struggle with the waves. They clung tightly to the rigging, unable to exchange a word, and watched the flocks of stormy petrels, those melancholy birds of the storm, as they sported in the raging winds.

At that moment a piercing sound was heard above the roar of the hurricane. The steam was rapidly escaping, not through the escape-valve, but through the pipes of the boiler. The alarm-whistle sounded with unusual shrillness; the yacht gave a terrible lurch, and Wilson, who was at the helm, was overthrown by an unexpected blow of the wheel. The vessel was in the trough of the sea, and no longer manageable.

"What is the matter?" cried Captain Mangles, rushing to the stern.

"The ship is careening!" replied Austin.

"Is the rudder unhinged?"

"To the engine! to the engine!" cried the engineer.

The captain rushed down the ladder. A cloud of steam filled the engine-room; the pistons were motionless in their cylinders, and the cranks gave no movement to the shaft. The engineer, seeing that all efforts were useless, and fearing for his boilers, had let out the steam through the escape-valve.

"What has happened?" asked the captain.

"The screw is either bent or entangled," replied the engineer; "it will not work."

"Is it impossible to free it?"

"Impossible, at present."

To attempt to repair the accident at that moment was out of the question. The screw would not move, and the steam, being no longer effective, had escaped through the valves. The captain was, therefore, forced to rely on his sails, and seek the aid of the wind, which had been hitherto his most dangerous enemy.

He came on deck, and, briefly informing Glenarvan of the situation, begged him to return to the cabin with the others; but the latter wished to remain.

"No, my lord," replied Captain Mangles, in a firm tone: "I must be alone here with my crew. Go! The ship may be in danger, and the waves would drench you unmercifully."

"But we may be of use—"

"Go, go, my lord; you must! There are times when I am master on board. Retire, as I wish!"

For John Mangles to express himself so authoritatively, the situation must have been critical. Glenarvan understood that it was his duty to obey. He therefore left the deck, followed by his three companions, and joined the ladies in the cabin, who were anxiously awaiting the result of this struggle with the elements.

"My brave John is an energetic man," remarked Glenarvan as he entered.

Meantime Captain Mangles lost no time in extricating the ship from her perilous situation. He resolved to keep towards the Cape, that he might deviate as little as possible from his prescribed course. It was, therefore, necessary to brace the sails obliquely to the wind. The top-sail was reefed, a kind of fore-sail rigged on the main-stay, and the helm crowded hard aport. The yacht, which was a stanch and fleet vessel, started like a spirited horse that feels the spur, and proudly breasted the angry billows.

The rest of the night was passed in this situation. They hoped that the tempest would abate by break of day. Vain hope! At eight o'clock in the morning it was still blowing hard, and the wind soon became a hurricane.

The captain said nothing, but he trembled for his vessel and those whom she carried. The Duncan now and then gave a fearful lurch; her stanchions cracked, and sometimes the yards of the mainmast struck the crests of the waves. At one moment the crew thought the yacht would not rise again. Already the sailors, hatchet in hand, were rushing to cut away the fore-shrouds, when they were violently torn from their fastenings by the blast. The ship righted herself, but, without support on the waves, she was tossed about so terribly that the masts threatened to break at their very foundations. She could not long endure such rolling; she was growing weak, and soon her shattered sides and opening seams must give way for the water.

Captain Mangles had but one resource,—to rig a storm-jib. He succeeded after several hours' labor, but it was not until three o'clock in the afternoon that the jib was hauled to the main-stay and set to the wind. With this piece of canvas the Duncan flew before the wind with inconceivable rapidity. It was necessary to keep up the greatest possible speed, for upon this alone depended her safety. Sometimes, outstripping the waves, she cut them with her slender prow and plunged beneath them, like an enormous sea-monster, while the water swept her deck from stem to stern. At other times her swiftness barely equaled that of the surges, her rudder lost all power, and she gave terrific lurches that threatened to capsize her. Then, impelled by the hurricane, the billows outran her; they leaped over the taffrail, and the whole deck was swept with tremendous violence.

The situation was indeed alarming. The captain would not leave his post for an instant. He was tortured by fears that his impassive face would not betray, and persistently sought to penetrate with his gaze the gathering gloom. And he had good cause for fear. The Duncan, driven out of her course, was running towards the Australian coast with a swiftness that nothing could arrest. He felt, too, as if by instinct, that a strong current was drawing him along. At every moment he feared the shock of a reef upon which the yacht would be dashed into a thousand pieces, and he calculated that the shore was not more than a dozen miles to leeward.

Finally he went in search of Lord Glenarvan, consulted with him in private, explained their actual situation, viewed it with the coolness of a sailor who is ready for any emergency, and ended by saying that he should be obliged perhaps to run the Duncan ashore.

"To save those she carries, if possible, my lord," he added.

"Very well, captain," replied Glenarvan.

"And Lady Helena and Miss Grant?"

"I will inform them only at the last moment, when all hope is gone of keeping at sea. You will tell me."

"I will, my lord."

Glenarvan returned to the ladies, who, without knowing all the danger, felt it to be imminent. They displayed, however, a noble courage, equal at least to that of their companions. Paganel gave himself up to the most unreasonable theories concerning the direction of atmospheric currents, while the major awaited the end with the indifference of a Mussulman.

About eleven o'clock the hurricane seemed to moderate a little, the heavy mists were gradually dissipated, and through the openings the captain could see a low land at least six miles to leeward. He steered directly for it. Huge waves rolled to a prodigious height, and he knew that they must have a firm point of support to reach such an elevation.

"There are sand-bars here," said he to Tom Austin.

"That is my opinion," replied the mate.

"We are in the hands of God," continued the captain. "If He does not himself guide the Duncan over the bar, we are lost."

"It is high tide now, captain; perhaps we may do it."

"But see the fury of those waves! What ship could resist them? God help us, my friend!"

Meantime the Duncan dashed towards the shore with terrible swiftness. Soon she was only two miles from the sand-bars. The mists still continued to conceal the land. Nevertheless Captain Mangles thought he perceived, beyond this foaming barrier, a tranquil haven, where the Duncan would be in comparative safety. But how to reach it?

He called the passengers on deck, for he did not wish, when the hour of shipwreck had come, that they should be confined in the cabin. Glenarvan and his companions gazed at the awful sea. Mary Grant grew pale.

"John," said Glenarvan in a low tone to the young captain, "I will try to save my wife, or will perish with her. Do you take charge of Miss Grant."

"Yes, your lordship," was the prompt reply.

The Duncan was now only a few cable-lengths from the sand-bars. As it was high tide, there would doubtless have been sufficient water to enable the yacht to cross these dangerous shoals; but the enormous waves upon which she rose and fell would infallibly have wrecked her. Was there then any means of allaying these billows, of calming this tumultuous sea?

A sudden idea occurred to the captain.

"The oil!" cried he; "pour on oil, men, pour on oil!"

These words were quickly understood by all the crew. They were about to employ a method that sometimes succeeds. The fury of the sea can often be appeased by covering it with a sheet of oil, which floats on the surface and destroys the shock of the waters. The effect is instantaneous, but transient. As soon as a ship has crossed this treacherous sea, it redoubles its fury; and woe to those who would venture to follow.

The barrels containing the supply of seal-oil were hoisted into the forecastle by the crew, to whom the danger gave new strength. Here they were stove in with a blow of the hatchet, and suspended over the starboard rattlings.

"Hold on!" cried the captain, waiting for the favorable moment.

In a few seconds the yacht reached the entrance to the pass, which was barred by a terrible line of foam.

"Let go!" cried the young captain.

The barrels were inverted, and from their sides streamed floods of oil. Immediately the unctuous liquid leveled the foaming surface of the sea, and the Duncan sailed on calm waters, and was soon in a quiet harbor beyond the terrible sand-bars; and then the ocean, released from its fetters, bounded after its escaped prey with indescribable fury.

CHAPTER XXX. A HOSPITABLE COLONIST.

The captain's first care was to secure anchorage. He moored the vessel in five fathoms of water. The bottom was good, a hard gravel, affording an excellent hold. There was no danger of drifting, or of stranding at low tide. The Duncan, after so many hours of peril, was now in a sort of creek sheltered by a high promontory from the fury of the wind.

Lord Glenarvan shook the hand of the young captain, saying,—

"Thanks, John!"

And Captain Mangles felt himself fully rewarded by these simple words. Glenarvan kept to himself the secret of his anguish, and neither Lady Helena, Mary Grant, nor Robert suspected the magnitude of the perils they had just escaped.

One important point remained to be settled. On what part of the coast had the Duncan been cast by the storm? How could she regain her prescribed course? How far were they from Cape Bernouilli? Such were the first questions addressed to the captain, who at once took his bearings and noted his observations on the map. The Duncan had not deviated very far from her route.

She was at Cape Catastrophe, on the southern coast of Australia, not three hundred miles from Cape Bernouilli.

But could the Duncan's injuries be repaired? This was the question to decide. The captain wished to know the extent of the damage. It was discovered, by diving, that a flange of the screw was bent and came in contact with the stern-post. Hence it was impossible for the screw to rotate. This injury was considered serious enough to necessitate going into dry-dock, which of course could not be done in their present locality.

Glenarvan and the captain, after mature reflection, resolved that the Duncan should follow the western shore, seeking traces of the Britannia, should stop at Cape Bernouilli, where further information could be obtained, and then continue southward to Melbourne, where her injuries could be repaired; and, as soon as this was done, that she should cruise along the eastern shores to finish the search.

This arrangement was approved, and Captain Mangles resolved to take advantage of the first favorable wind. He did not have to wait long. Towards evening the hurricane had entirely subsided, and a moderate breeze was blowing from the southwest. Preparations were made for getting under way; new sails were set, and at four o'clock in the morning the sailors heaved at the capstan, the anchor was weighed, and the Duncan, with all sails set, cruised close to windward along the coast.

They arrived at Cape Bernouilli without finding the least trace of the lost vessel. But this failure proved nothing. Indeed, during the two years since the shipwreck, the sea might have scattered or destroyed the fragments of the brig. Besides, the natives, who scent shipwrecks as a vulture does a corpse, might have carried away every vestige of it. Harry Grant and his two companions, therefore, without doubt, had been taken prisoners the moment the waves cast them ashore, and been carried into the interior of the country.

But here one of Paganel's ingenious suppositions failed. So long as they were in the Argentine territory, the geographer could rightly maintain that the latitude of the document referred to the place of captivity,—not to the scene of the shipwreck. Indeed, the great rivers of the Pampas and their numerous affluents could easily bear the document to the sea. In this part of Australia, on the contrary, few streams cross the thirty-seventh parallel, and the principal Australian rivers—the Murray, the Yara, the Torrens, and the Darling—either flow into each other, or empty into the ocean by mouths where navigation is active. What probability was there, then, that a fragile bottle could have descended these continually navigated waters, and reached the Indian Ocean? This consideration could not escape such sagacious minds. Paganel's supposition, plausible in Patagonia, was illogical in Australia. The geographer perceived this in a discussion on the subject with the major. It was clear that the latitude applied only to the place of shipwreck, and that consequently the bottle had been cast into the sea where the Britannia was wrecked,—on the western coast of Australia.

However, as Glenarvan justly observed, this interpretation did not preclude the possibility of Captain Grant's captivity, who, moreover, had intimated as much by the words "where they will be prisoners of the cruel Indians." But there was no more reason for seeking the prisoners on the thirty-seventh parallel than on any other.

This conclusion, after much discussion, was finally accepted, and it was decided that, if no traces of the Britannia were found at Cape Bernouilli, Lord Glenarvan should return to Europe, relinquishing all hope of finding the object of their search.

This resolution occasioned profound grief to the children of the lost captain. As the boats containing the whole of the party were rowed ashore, they felt that the fate of their father would soon be probably decided; irrevocably, we may say, for Paganel, in a former discussion, had clearly demonstrated that the shipwrecked seamen would have reached their country long ago, if their vessel had stranded on the other, the eastern coast.

"Hope! hope! never cease to hope!" said Lady Helena to the young girl seated beside her, as they approached the shore. "The hand of God will never fail us."

"Yes, Miss Mary," said the captain; "when men have exhausted human resources, then Heaven interposes, and, by some unforeseen event, opens to them new ways."

"God grant it, captain!" replied Mary.

The shore was now only a cable's length distant. The cape terminated in gentle declivities extending far out into the sea. The boat entered a small creek, between banks of coral in process of formation, which in time would form a chain of reefs along the southern coast of the island.

The passengers of the Duncan disembarked on a perfectly barren shore. Steep cliffs formed a lofty sea-wall, and it would have been difficult to scale this natural rampart without ladders or cramping-irons. Fortunately, the captain discovered a breach half a mile southward, caused by a partial crumbling of the cliffs. Probably the sea, during violent equinoctial storms, had beaten against this fragile barrier, and thus caused the fall of the upper portions of the mass.

Glenarvan and his companions entered this opening, and reached the summit of the cliffs by a very steep ascent. Robert climbed an abrupt declivity with the agility of a cat, and arrived first at the top, to the great chagrin of Paganel, who was quite mortified at seeing himself outstripped by a mere lad of twelve. However, he distanced the peaceable major; but that worthy was utterly indifferent to his defeat.

The little party surveyed the plain that stretched out beneath them. It was a vast, uncultivated tract, covered with bushes and brushwood, and was compared by Glenarvan to the glens of the Scottish lowlands, and by Paganel to the barren lands of Brittany. But though the country along the coast was evidently uninhabited, the presence of man, not the savage, but the civilized worker, was betokened by several substantial structures in the distance.

"A mill!" cried Robert.

True enough, at no great distance apparently, the sails of a mill were seen.

"It is indeed a mill," replied Paganel. "Here is a beacon as modest as it is useful, the sight of which delights my eyes."

"It is almost a belfry," said Lady Helena.

"Yes, madam; and while one makes bread for the body, the other announces bread for the soul. In this respect they resemble each other."

"Let us go to the mill," replied Glenarvan.

They accordingly started. After half an hour's walk the soil assumed a new aspect. The transition from barren plains to cultivated fields was sudden. Instead of brushwood, quick-set hedges surrounded an inclosure freshly ploughed. Some cattle, and half a dozen horses, grazed in pastures encircled by acacias. Then fields of corn were reached, several acres of land bristling with the yellow ears, haycocks like great bee-hives, vineyards with blooming inclosures, a beautiful garden, where the useful and the ornamental mingled; in short, a fair and comfortable locality, which the merry mill crowned with its pointed gable and caressed with the moving shadow of its sails.

At this moment a man of about fifty, of prepossessing countenance, issued from the principal house, at the barking of three great dogs that announced the coming of the strangers. Five stout and handsome boys, his sons, accompanied by their mother, a tall, robust woman, followed him. This man, surrounded by his healthful family, in the midst of these new erections, in this almost virgin country, presented the perfect type of the colonist, who, endeavoring to better his lot, seeks his fortune and happiness beyond the seas.

Glenarvan and his friends had not yet introduced themselves, they had not had time to declare either their names or their rank, when these cordial words saluted them:—

"Strangers, welcome to the house of Patrick O'Moore."

"You are an Irishman?" said Glenarvan, taking the hand that the colonist offered him.

"I was," replied Mr. O'Moore. "Now I am an Australian. But come in, whoever you are, gentlemen; this house is at your service."

The invitation so hospitably given was accepted without ceremony. Lady Helena and Mary Grant, conducted by Mrs. O'Moore, entered the house, while the colonist's sons relieved the visitors of their fire-arms.

A large, cool, airy room occupied the ground-floor of the house, which was built of stout beams arranged horizontally. Several wooden benches, built into the walls, and painted in gay colors, ten stools, two oaken trunks, in which white china and jugs of polished pewter were arranged, and a long table, at which twenty people could be comfortably seated, constituted the furniture, worthy of the house and its hardy inhabitants.

Dinner was soon served. Dishes of soup smoked between roast beef and legs of mutton, flanked by large plates of olives, grapes, and oranges. The host and hostess had such an engaging air, and the fare was so tempting, so ample, and so abundantly furnished, that it would have been unbecoming not to accept this rural bounty. The domestics of the farm, the equals of their master, had already come to partake of the repast; and the host reserved the place of honor for the strangers.

"I expected you," said he, quietly, to Lord Glenarvan.

"You did?" replied the latter, very much surprised.

"I always expect those who are coming," replied the Irishman.

Then, in a grave voice, while his household stood respectfully, he invoked a Divine blessing. Lady Helena was much affected by his perfect simplicity of manner, and a look from her husband told her that he likewise was touched by it.

Ample justice was done to the repast. The conversation was general. The colonist told his story. It was like that of most deserving and voluntary emigrants. Many go far to seek their fortunes, and find only sorrow and disaster; they accuse fate, forgetting to blame their ignorance, laziness, and vices. The man who is sober and persevering, economical and honest, is almost sure to succeed.

This had been the case with Mr. O'Moore. He had left Dundalk, where he was poor, and, emigrating with his family to Australia, had landed at Adelaide. At first he engaged in mining, but soon relinquished this for the less hazardous pursuits of the farmer, in which he had been successful beyond his highest anticipations. His agricultural knowledge was a great aid to him. He economized, and bought new lands with the profits of the first. His family flourished, as well as his farm. The Irish peasant had become a landed proprietor, and, although his establishment was only two years old, he owned at that moment five hundred acres of well-cultivated land and five hundred head of cattle, was his own master, and as independent as one can be even in the freest country in the world.

His guests congratulated him sincerely when his story was finished. He doubtless expected a similar confidence, but did not urge it. Glenarvan had an immediate interest in speaking of the Duncan, of his own presence at Cape Bernouilli, and of the search that they had pursued so perseveringly. But, like a man who considers the main object in view, he first questioned his host concerning the shipwreck of the Britannia.

The Irishman's answer was not cheering. He had never heard of the ship. No vessel had for some time been lost on the coast; and, as the shipwreck had occurred only two years before, he could affirm with absolute certainty that the sailors had not been cast on that part of the western shore.

"And now, my lord," added he, "may I be allowed to ask why you have inquired of me concerning this shipwreck?"

Glenarvan then told the story of the document, the voyage of the Duncan, and the attempts made to find Captain Grant. He confessed that his dearest hopes had been destroyed by Mr. O'Moore's discouraging information, and that he now despaired of ever finding the shipwrecked seamen of the Britannia.

These words produced a gloomy impression upon his hearers. Robert and Mary listened to them with tearful eyes. Paganel could not find a word of consolation or hope. Captain Mangles suffered a grief that he could not subdue. Despair was seizing upon the souls of the noble people whom the Duncan had vainly brought to these distant shores, when all at once a voice was heard:—

"My lord, praise and thank God! If Captain Grant is living, he is in Australia."

CHAPTER XXXI. THE QUARTERMASTER OF THE BRITANNIA.

The astonishment that these words produced cannot be described. Glenarvan sprang to his feet, and, pushing back his chair, cried,—

"Who says that?"

"I!" replied one of O'Moore's workmen, seated at the end of the table.

"You, Ayrton?" said the colonist, no less astonished than Glenarvan.

"I," repeated Ayrton, in an excited but firm tone; "I, a Scotchman like yourself, my lord, one of the shipwrecked sailors of the Britannia!"

Mary Grant, half fainting with emotion, and overcome with happiness, sank into the arms of Lady Helena; while Captain Mangles, Robert, and Paganel went towards the man whom their host had called Ayrton.

He was a somewhat rough-looking, broad-shouldered man, of about forty-five, of more than medium height, and with piercing eyes sunk deeply beneath his projecting brows. His strength must have been unusual, even considering his stature, for he was all bone and sinew. His countenance, full of intelligence and energy, although the features were stern, prepossessed one in his favor. The sympathy that he elicited was still more increased by the traces of recent hardships imprinted upon his face. It was evident that he had suffered much, although he seemed a man able to brave, endure, and conquer suffering.

The travelers felt all this at first sight. Ayrton's appearance had interested them; and Glenarvan, acting as spokesman for all, pressed him with inquiries. This strange meeting had evidently produced a bewildering effect, and the first questions were, to some extent, without order.

"You are one of the sailors of the Britannia?" asked Glenarvan.

"Yes, my lord; Captain Grant's quartermaster," replied Ayrton.

"Saved with him from the shipwreck?"

"No, my lord. At that terrible moment I was washed overboard and cast ashore."

"You are not one of the sailors, then, of whom the document makes mention?"

"No; I did not know of the existence of such a document. The captain must have thrown it overboard after I was gone."

"But the captain, the captain?"

"I suppose he was lost, drowned, with the rest of the crew. I thought I was the sole survivor."

"But you said that Captain Grant was living!"

"No. I said, 'if the captain is living'—"

"'He is in Australia,' you added."

"He can be nowhere else."

"You do not know, then, where he is?"

"No, my lord. I repeat that I thought he was buried in the waves or dashed upon the rocks. You say that perhaps he is still living."

"What do you know, then?" asked Glenarvan.

"Simply this, that if Captain Grant is living he is in Australia."

"Where did the shipwreck take place?" inquired the major.

This should have been the first question; but, in the excitement of the moment, Glenarvan, anxious to know where Captain Grant was, had not inquired where the Britannia was lost. From this point the conversation assumed a more definite form, and soon the details of the complicated story appeared clear and exact to the minds of Ayrton's hearers.

To the major's question Ayrton replied,—

"When I was washed from the forecastle, as I was hauling down the jib, the Britannia was driving towards the coast of Australia, which was not two cable-lengths distant. The shipwreck, therefore, took place at that point."

"In latitude thirty-seven?" asked Captain Mangles.

"Thirty-seven," replied Ayrton.

"On the west coast?"

"No. On the east coast."

"And when?"

"On the night of June 27th, 1862."

"The same! the very same!" cried Glenarvan.

"You see, then, my lord," added Ayrton, "that I was right in saying that, if Captain Grant still lives, you must seek him in Australia."

"And we will seek, find, and save him, my friend!" cried Paganel. "Ah, precious document!" added he, with perfect simplicity: "it must be confessed that you have fallen into the hands of very sagacious people."

No one noticed these flattering words of Paganel. Glenarvan, Lady Helena, Mary, and Robert had crowded around Ayrton, and eagerly clasped his hands. It seemed as if the presence of this man was a guarantee of the safety of Harry Grant. Since the sailor had escaped the dangers of shipwreck, why should not the captain be safe and sound? Ayrton repeated his declaration that if Captain Grant were living he must be in Australia. He answered with remarkable intelligence and clearness the many questions that were propounded to him. Miss Mary, while he spoke, held one of his hands in her own. This sailor had been a companion of her father, one of the shipwrecked survivors of the Britannia. He had lived with Harry Grant, had sailed the seas with him, had braved the same dangers! She could not withdraw her eyes from that weather-beaten face, and she wept with happiness.

Hitherto no one had thought of doubting the veracity of the quartermaster. Only the major, and perhaps Captain Mangles, questioned whether Ayrton's story merited *entire* confidence. This unexpected meeting might be suspicious. To be sure, Ayrton had mentioned facts and dates that agreed, and striking particulars. But details, however exact they may be, do not constitute a certainty; and generally, as we know, falsehood endeavors to strengthen itself by its preciseness. MacNabb, therefore, reserved his opinion.

As for Captain Mangles, his doubts did not stand long before the assertions of the sailor, and he considered him a real companion of Captain Grant when he heard him speak to the young girl of her father. Ayrton knew Mary and Robert perfectly. He had seen them at Glasgow on the departure of the Britannia. He remembered that they had been present at the farewell dinner given on board to the friends of the captain. Sheriff MacIntyre was one of the guests. Robert—scarcely ten years old—had been confided to the care of Dick Turner, the boatswain, but had escaped from him and climbed to the top-sail yard-arm.

"It is true! it is true!" cried Robert.

The quartermaster remembered, too, a thousand little circumstances to which he did not seem to attach so much importance as did Captain Mangles. When he stopped, Mary said, in her sweet voice,—

"Mr. Ayrton, please tell us more about our father."

Ayrton acceded to the young girl's request. Glenarvan was reluctant to interrupt him, and yet many more important questions thronged his mind. But Lady Helena, pointing out to him Mary's joyful excitement, checked his inquiries.

The quartermaster now told the story of the Britannia and her voyage across the Pacific. During the period of a year Harry Grant landed at the principal ports of Oceanica, opposing unjustifiable captures, and often a victim to the hostility of unjust traders. He found, however, an important point on the western coast of Papua. Here the establishment of a Scottish colony appeared to him feasible, and its prosperity assured. After examining Papua, the Britannia sailed to Callao for provisions, and left that port on the 30th of May, 1862, to return to Europe by the way of the Indian Ocean and the Cape. Three weeks after her departure, a terrible tempest disabled her. It became necessary to cut away the masts. A leak was discovered in the hold, which they did not succeed in stopping. The crew were soon overtasked and exhausted. The pumps could not be worked. For eight days the vessel was at the mercy of the storm. There were six feet of water in her hold, and she gradually foundered. The boats had been washed overboard, and the crew had given themselves up for lost, when on the night of June 22nd, as Paganel had rightly interpreted, they descried the eastern coast of Australia. The vessel soon stranded. A violent shock was felt. At this moment Ayrton, borne by a wave, was cast into the midst of the breakers, and lost all consciousness. When he came to himself, he was in the hands of the natives, who carried him into the interior of the country. Since then he had heard nothing more of the Britannia, and naturally supposed that she had been wrecked, with all on board, on the dangerous reefs of Twofold Bay.

This was Ayrton's story, which elicited more than once exclamations of sympathy. The major could not justly doubt its correctness; and after this recital the quartermaster's own experiences possessed a more real interest. Indeed, thanks to the document, they no longer doubted that Captain Grant had survived the shipwreck with two of his sailors. From the fate of the one they could fairly conjecture that of the other.

Ayrton was invited to tell of his own adventures, which was soon and simply done. The shipwrecked sailor, prisoner of a native tribe, was carried into the interior regions watered by the Darling. Here he led a very wretched existence, because the tribe itself was miserable; but he was not maltreated. For two long years he endured a painful slavery. However, the hope of regaining his liberty sustained his courage. He watched for the least opportunity of escaping, although his flight would plunge him into the midst of innumerable perils. One night in October he eluded the vigilance of the natives, and took refuge in the depths of extensive forests. For a month, living on roots, edible ferns, and the gum of the mimosa, often overcome by despair, he wandered in those vast solitudes, with the sun as his guide by day and the stars by night. In this way he crossed marshes, rivers, mountains, in short, all that uninhabited portion of country that few travelers have explored. At last, exhausted and almost dead, he reached the hospitable dwelling of Mr. O'Moore, where his labor insured him a comfortable livelihood.

"And if Ayrton is pleased with me," said the Irish colonist, when the story was finished, "I cannot but be pleased with him. He is an honest and intelligent man, a good worker, and, if he chooses, this house shall long be at his service."

Ayrton thanked Mr. O'Moore, and waited for further questions. He probably thought, however, that the legitimate curiosity of his hearers ought to be satisfied. What could he say that had not been repeated a hundred times already? Glenarvan was, therefore, about to open the conversation on a new topic, to profit by the information received from Ayrton, when the major, addressing him, said:

"You were quartermaster of the Britannia?"

"Yes," replied Ayrton.

But perceiving that a certain feeling of distrust, a doubt, however slight, had suggested this inquiry, he added,—

"I saved my contract from the wreck."

He immediately left the room in search of this authoritative document. During his absence, which lasted but a few moments, Mr. O'Moore said:

"My lord, I will answer for it that Ayrton is an honest man. During the two months that he has been in my employ, I have had no fault to find with him. I knew the story of his shipwreck and captivity. He is a true man, and worthy of your entire confidence."

Glenarvan was about to answer that he had never doubted Ayrton's honesty, when the latter returned and presented his contract. It was a paper signed by the owners of the Britannia and Captain Grant, whose writing Mary recognized immediately. It stated that "Tom Ayrton, able seaman, was engaged as quartermaster on board the brig Britannia of Glasgow." There was, therefore, no possible doubt of Ayrton's identity, for it would have been difficult to suppose that this contract could be in his hands and not belong to him.

"Now," said Glenarvan, "I appeal to you all for advice as to what is best to be done. Your advice, Ayrton, would be particularly valuable, and I should be much obliged if you would give it to us."

The sailor reflected a few moments, and then replied:

"I thank you, my lord, for the confidence you place in me, and hope to show myself worthy of it. I have some knowledge of the country, and of the customs of the natives; and, if I can be of use to you—"

"Certainly," replied Glenarvan.

"I think, like you," continued Ayrton, "that Captain Grant and his two sailors were saved from the shipwreck; but, since they have not reached the English possessions, since they have not reappeared, I doubt not that their fate was the same as my own, and that they are prisoners of the natives."

"You repeat, Mr. Ayrton, the arguments that I have already substantiated," said Paganel. "The shipwrecked seamen are evidently prisoners of the natives, as they feared. But ought we to suppose that, like you, they have been carried to the north?"

"It is quite likely, sir," replied Ayrton. "The hostile tribes would hardly remain in the neighborhood of the English provinces."

"This fact will complicate our search," said Glenarvan, quite disconcerted. "How shall we find the traces of the prisoners in the interior of so vast a continent?"

A prolonged silence followed this remark. Lady Helena frequently cast a questioning glance at her companions, but without eliciting a responsive sign. Paganel himself was silent, contrary to his custom. His usual ingenuity now failed him. Captain Mangles paced the room with long strides, as if he had been on the deck of his vessel, involved in some difficulty.

"And you, Mr. Ayrton," said Lady Helena, at length, to the quartermaster, "what would you do?"

"Madam," replied he, promptly, "I should re-embark on board the Duncan, and go straight to the place of the shipwreck. There I should act according to circumstances, or indications that chance might furnish."

"Very good," said Glenarvan; "but we must wait till the Duncan is repaired."

"Ah! you have suffered injuries?" inquired Ayrton.

"Yes," replies the captain.

"Serious?"

"No; but they necessitate repairs which cannot be made on board. One of the flanges of the screw is bent, and this work can be done only at Melbourne."

"Can you not sail?" asked the quartermaster.

"Yes; but, if the wind is contrary, it would take considerable time to reach Twofold Bay, and at any rate we should have to return to Melbourne."

"Well, let the yacht go to Melbourne," said Paganel, "and we will go without her to Twofold Bay."

"But how?"

"By crossing Australia, as we crossed South America."

"But the Duncan?" added Ayrton, with singular persistency.

"The Duncan will join us, or we will join her, according to circumstances. If Captain Grant is found during our journey, we will return together to Melbourne. If, on the contrary, we continue our search to the coast, the Duncan shall join us there. Who has any objections to make to this plan? Have you, major?"

"No," replied MacNabb, "if it is practicable."

"So practicable," said Paganel, "that I propose that Lady Helena and Miss Grant accompany us."

"Do you speak seriously, Paganel?" asked Glenarvan.

"Quite seriously, my lord. It is a journey of three hundred and fifty miles. At the rate of twelve miles a day it would last scarcely a month,—long enough to give time for repairing the Duncan."

"But the ferocious animals?" said Glenarvan, wishing to state all possible objections.

"There are none in Australia."

"But the savages?"

"There are none in the course we shall take."

"Well, then, the convicts?"

"There are no convicts in the southern provinces of Australia, but only in the eastern colonies."

"Mr. Paganel is perfectly right," said O'Moore; "they have all left the southern provinces. Since I have lived on this farm, I have not heard of one."

"And, for my part, I never met one," added Ayrton.

"You see, my friends," continued Paganel, "that there are few savages, no wild beasts, and no convicts. There are not many countries of Europe of which we could say as much. Well, is it agreed?"

"What do you think, Helena?" asked Glenarvan.

"What we all think," replied she, turning towards her companions. "Forward!"

343

CHAPTER XXXII. PREPARATIONS FOR THE JOURNEY.

It was not Glenarvan's habit to lose time in adopting and executing a plan. As soon as Paganel's proposal was accepted, he at once resolved that the preparations for the journey should be completed as soon as possible.

And what was to be the result of this search? The existence of Harry Grant seemed to have become undeniable, which increased the probabilities of success. No one expected to find the captain exactly on the line of the thirty-seventh parallel; but perhaps they would come upon traces of him, and, at all events, their course would bring them straight to the scene of the shipwreck, which was the principal point.

Moreover, if Ayrton would consent to join the travelers, to guide them through the forests, and to the eastern coast, there was another chance of success. Glenarvan felt the importance of this arrangement, and was therefore particularly desirous of obtaining the services of Captain Grant's companion. He inquired of his host whether he was willing for him to propose to Ayrton to accompany them. Mr. O'Moore consented, though not without regret at losing so good an assistant.

"Well, Ayrton, will you aid us in our search for the sailors of the Britannia?"

The quartermaster did not answer immediately; he seemed to hesitate for a few moments, but finally, after reflecting, said:

"Yes, my lord, I will follow you; and, if I do not set you upon the track of Captain Grant, I will at least guide you to the place where his vessel was wrecked."

"Thanks," replied Glenarvan.

"One question, my lord."

"Ask it."

"Where will you join the Duncan?"

"At Melbourne, if we do not cross Australia; on the eastern coast, if our search is continued so far."

"But the captain of the Duncan?"

"He will await my orders at Melbourne."

"Very well, my lord," said Ayrton; "rely on me."

"I will," replied Glenarvan.

The quartermaster was heartily thanked by the travelers. Captain Grant's children lavished upon him their most grateful caresses. All were delighted at his decision, except the colonist, who would lose in him an intelligent and faithful assistant. But he understood the importance that Glenarvan attached to this new addition to his force, and was resigned. He had, moreover, engaged to furnish them with the means of conveyance for the journey, and, this business being settled, the party returned on board.

Everything was now changed; all hesitation had vanished. These courageous searchers were no longer to wander on blindly. Harry Grant, they believed, had found a refuge on the continent, and each heart was full of the satisfaction that certainty brings when it takes the place of doubt. In two months, perhaps, the Duncan would land the lost captain on the shores of Scotland.

When Captain Mangles seconded the proposal that they should attempt to cross Australia with the ladies, he supposed that this time he would accompany the expedition. He therefore consulted Glenarvan on the subject, and brought forward various arguments in his own favor, such as his desire to take part in the search for his countryman, and his usefulness in the undertaking.

"One question, John," said Glenarvan. "You have absolute confidence in your mate?"

"Absolute," replied he. "Tom Austin is a good sailor. He will take the Duncan to Melbourne, repair her thoroughly, and bring her back at the appointed time. He is a man devoted to duty and discipline, and will never take the responsibility of changing or delaying the execution of an order. You can rely upon him as fully as on myself."

"Very well, captain," replied Glenarvan; "you shall accompany us; for," added he, smiling, "you certainly ought to be present when we find Mary Grant's father."

"Ah, my lord!" murmured Captain Mangles, with something like a blush upon his swarthy cheeks.

The next day the captain, accompanied by the carpenter and by the sailors loaded with provisions, returned to the farm of Mr. O'Moore, who was to assist him in the preparations. All the family were waiting for him, ready to work under his orders. Ayrton was there, and freely gave them the benefit of his experience. He and his employer were agreed on this point, that the ladies ought to make the journey in an ox-cart, and the gentlemen on horseback. The colonist could procure them the animals and vehicle.

The vehicle was a cart twenty feet long and covered with an awning, the whole resting upon four wheels, without spokes, felloes, or tires. The front wheels were a long way from the hind ones, and were joined together by a rude contrivance that made it impossible to turn short. To the body of the cart was attached a pole thirty-five feet long, to which three pairs of oxen were coupled. The animals, thus arranged, drew by means of a yoke across their necks, to which the bow was fastened with an iron pin. It required great skill to manage this long, narrow, tottering vehicle, and guide the oxen by means of the whip. But Ayrton had served his apprenticeship at O'Moore's farm, and his employer guaranteed his dexterity. Upon him, therefore, devolved the duty of driving.

The cart, being without springs, was not very easy; but our travelers were obliged to conform to circumstances as much as they could. As no change was possible in its rude construction, Captain Mangles arranged the interior in the most comfortable manner. He divided it into two compartments by a wooden partition. The rear one was designed for the provisions, the baggage, and Mr.

Olbinett's portable kitchen, while the forward one was reserved exclusively for the ladies. The carpenter converted it into a convenient chamber, covered it with a thick carpet, and furnished it with a dressing-table and two berths for Lady Helena and Mary Grant. Thick leathern curtains secured privacy, when necessary, and were a protection against the chilliness of the night. In rainy weather the men could find shelter under the awning; but a tent was to serve this purpose at the time of encampment. Captain Mangles succeeded in crowding into this narrow space all that two ladies could need, and Lady Helena and Mary Grant did not greatly miss the comfortable cabins of the Duncan.

As for the men, seven strong horses were apportioned to Lord Glenarvan, Paganel, Robert Grant, Major MacNabb, Captain Mangles, and the two sailors, Wilson and Mulready, who accompanied this new expeditionary party. The horses and oxen grazed near at hand, and could be easily collected at the moment of departure.

Having made his arrangements, and given his orders to the carpenter, Captain Mangles returned on board with the colonist's family, who wished to pay Lord Glenarvan a visit. Ayrton thought proper to join them, and about four o'clock the captain crossed the gangway of the Duncan.

Of course, Glenarvan invited his visitors to dinner, and they willingly accepted his return hospitality. Mr. O'Moore was amazed. The furniture of the cabins, the tapestry, the upholstery, and the fancy-work of maple and ebony excited his admiration. Ayrton, on the contrary, gave only a secondary attention to these costly luxuries. He first examined the yacht from a sailor's point of view. He explored the hold; he went down into the engine-room; he looked at the engine, inquired its effective power and consumption; he visited the coal-house, the pantry, and the powder-magazine, and took particular interest in the gun-room and the mounted cannon in the forecastle. Glenarvan now had to deal with a man who was a critical judge, as he could see by Ayrton's keen inquiries. At last the quartermaster finished his exploration by inspecting the masts and rigging; and, after a few moments of general review, said:

"You have a fine vessel, my lord."

"A good one, too," replied Glenarvan.

"How many tons' burden is she?"

"Two hundred and ten."

"Shall I be greatly mistaken," added Ayrton, "if I say that the Duncan can easily make fifteen knots an hour at full speed?"

"Say seventeen," interposed the captain, "and you will be nearer right."

"Seventeen!" cried the quartermaster: "why, then, no man-of-war, not even the best, could overtake her."

"Not one," said the captain. "The Duncan is a real racing yacht, and is not to be beaten in any way."

"Not even in sailing?" asked Ayrton.

"Not even in sailing."

"Well, my lord, and you, captain, accept the compliments of a sailor who knows what a vessel is worth."

"Thanks, Ayrton," replied Glenarvan; "and now remain on board, and it will be your own fault if the ship is not all you can desire."

"I will think of it, my lord," said the quartermaster, modestly.

Mr. Olbinett now approached, and informed Lord Glenarvan that dinner was ready; and they all adjourned to the saloon.

"That Ayrton is an intelligent man," said Paganel to the major.

"Too intelligent!" growled MacNabb, who, without any apparent reason, disliked the looks and manners of the quartermaster.

During dinner, Ayrton gave some interesting information concerning Australia, with which he was perfectly familiar. He inquired the number of sailors that Glenarvan intended to take with him in his expedition. When he learned that only two, Wilson and Mulready, were to accompany them, he seemed astonished. He advised Glenarvan to form his party of the best seamen of the Duncan. He even insisted upon this point, which must have removed all suspicion from the mind of the major.

"But," said Glenarvan, "is there any danger in our journey across Australia?"

"None," replied Ayrton.

"Well, then, let us leave on board as many as possible. There must be men to navigate the Duncan and take charge of her. It is especially important that she should arrive promptly at the place of meeting, which we will appoint hereafter. Let us not, therefore, lessen the crew."

Ayrton seemed to appreciate this reason, and no longer insisted.

At evening the party separated. Ayrton and O'Moore's family returned to their home. The horses and cart were to be ready the next day, and the travelers were to start at eight o'clock in the morning.

Lady Helena and Mary Grant now made their last preparations, which were short and less minute than those of Jacques Paganel. The geographer passed half the night in unscrewing, cleaning, and screwing on again the lenses of his telescope. He was still asleep the next morning, when the major awoke him early with a loud summons.

The baggage had already been conveyed to the farm through the care of Captain Mangles. A boat was waiting for the travelers, and they were not long in embarking. The young captain gave his last orders to Tom Austin, and instructed him above all to await the commands of Lord Glenarvan at Melbourne, and execute them scrupulously whatever they might be. The trusty sailor replied that they might rely on him. In the name of the crew he offered to his lordship their best wishes for the success of the expedition. The boat put off, and a thunder of applause rent the air. In a few moments the party reached the shore, and in no great length of time arrived at O'Moore's farm.

Everything was ready. Lady Helena was delighted with her quarters. The immense cart, with its rude wheels and massive timbers, especially pleased her.

The six oxen yoked in pairs seemed to indicate primeval simplicity, and were a novel sight. Ayrton, whip in hand, awaited the orders of his new chief.

"I declare!" said Paganel, "this is an admirable vehicle, worth all the mail-coaches in the world. I know of no better way of traversing the earth than in this style, like mountebanks. A house that moves when you please and stops wherever you please is all you can desire."

"Monsieur Paganel," replied Lady Helena, "I hope to have the pleasure of receiving you in my parlor."

"Madam," replied the geographer, "you do me great honor! Have you chosen a day?"

"I shall be at home every day for my friends," replied Lady Helena, smiling, "and you are—"

"The most devoted of all," added Paganel, gallantly.

This exchange of compliments was interrupted by the arrival of seven horses, all harnessed, driven by one of O'Moore's sons. Lord Glenarvan paid for these new acquisitions, and added many thanks, which the honest colonist seemed to value as highly as the gold and notes which he received.

The signal for departure was now given. Lady Helena and Miss Grant seated themselves in their compartment, Ayrton and Olbinett took their places respectively in front and in the rear part of the cart, while Glenarvan, the major, Paganel, Robert, Captain Mangles, and the two sailors, all armed with carbines and revolvers, mounted their horses. A "God bless you" was Mr. O'Moore's parting salute, which was echoed in chorus by his family. Ayrton uttered a peculiar cry, and started his long team. The cart moved, the timbers cracked, the axles creaked, and the farm of the honest hospitable Irishman soon disappeared from view at the turn of the road.

CHAPTER XXXIII. AN ACCIDENT.

Our travelers made tolerably good progress by their new mode of conveyance. The heat was great, but endurable, and the road was quite easy for the horses. They were still in the province of South Australia, and in this part at least the scenery was not of the most interesting character. A succession of small hills, with very dusty tracks, small shrubs, and scant herbage, had to be traversed for several miles; and when these had been passed they reached the "Mosquito Plains," whose very name describes them, and serves to tell of the tortures that our friends had to encounter. Both the bipeds and the quadrupeds suffered terribly from the infliction of these flying pests, whom to avoid was impossible; but there was some consolation for the former in the spirits of hartshorn, carried in the medicine-chest, which alleviated the pain caused by the sting of those whom Paganel was continually consigning to a place and person whom they would not visit.

But shortly a more pleasant neighborhood was reached. Hedges of acacias, then a newly cut and better made roadway, then European imported trees—oaks, olives, and lemons,—then a well-kept fence,—all these signs told of their approach to Red-gum Station, the home and settlement of an emigrant engaged in the cattle-breeding which is the source of so much Australian wealth. It was in itself an establishment of small importance; but to its owners it was a home, and to its visitors, on this occasion, it was a hotel, as the "station" generally is to the traveler.

Glenarvan's party invariably found beneath the roof of these solitary settlers a well-spread and hospitable table; and in the Australian farmer they always met an obliging host.

After a night spent at this resting-place the party advanced through a grove, and at evening encamped on the shores of a brackish and muddy lake. Mr. Olbinett prepared supper with his usual promptness, and the travelers—some in the cart and others under the tent—were not long in falling asleep, in spite of the dismal howlings of the dingos,—the jackals of Australia.

The next morning Glenarvan and his companions were greeted with a magnificent sight. As far as the eye could reach, the landscape seemed to be one flowery meadow in spring-like luxuriance. The delicate blue of the slender-leaved flax-plant mingled with the flaming scarlet of the acanthus, and the ground was clothed with a rich carpet of green and crimson. After a rapid journey of about ten miles, the cart wound through tall groups of acacias, mimosas, and white gum-trees. The vegetable kingdom on these plains did not show itself ungrateful towards the orb of day, and repaid in perfume and color what it received in sunshine.

As for the animal kingdom, it was no less lavish of its products. Several cassowaries bounded over the plain with unapproachable swiftness. The major was skillful enough to shoot a very rare bird,—a "jabiru," or giant crane. This creature was five feet high; and its broad, black, sharp conical beak measured eighteen inches in length. The violet and purple colors of its head contrasted strongly with the lustrous green of its neck, the dazzling white of its breast, and the vivid red of its long legs.

This bird was greatly admired, and the major would have won the honors of the day, if young Robert had not encountered a few miles farther on, and bravely vanquished, an unsightly beast, half hedgehog, half ant-eater, a chaotic-looking animal, like those of pre-historic periods. A long, glutinous, extensible tongue hung out of its mouth, and fished up the ants that constituted its principal food. Of course, Paganel wished to carry away the hideous creature, and proposed to put it in the baggage-room; but Mr. Olbinett opposed this with such indignation that the geographer gave up his idea of preserving this curious specimen.

Hitherto few colonists or squatters had been seen. The country seemed deserted. There was not even the trace of a native; for the savage tribes wander farther to the north, over the immense wastes watered by the Darling and the Murray. But now a singular sight was presented to Glenarvan's party. They were fortunate enough to see one of those vast herds of cattle which bold speculators bring from the eastern mountains to the provinces of Victoria and South Australia.

About four o'clock in the afternoon, Captain Mangles descried, three miles in advance, an enormous column of dust that spread along the horizon. What occasioned this? It would have been very difficult to say. Paganel was inclined to regard it as some phenomenon, for which his lively imagination already sought a natural cause. But Ayrton dissipated all his conjectures by declaring that this cloud of dust proceeded from a drove of cattle.

The quartermaster was not mistaken. The thick cloud approached, from the midst of which issued a chorus of bleatings, neighings, and bellowings, while the human voice mingled in cries and whistles with this pastoral symphony. A man emerged from the noisy multitude; it was the commander-in-chief of this four-footed army. Glenarvan advanced to meet him, and friendly relations were established without ceremony. The leader, or, to give him his real title, the "stock-keeper," was proprietor of a part of the herd. His name was Sam Machell, and he was on his way from the eastern provinces to Portland Bay. His cattle comprised one thousand oxen, eleven thousand sheep, and seventy-five horses. All these animals, bought when lean on the plains of the Blue Mountains, were to be fattened in the healthy pastures of South Australia, where they would be sold for a large price.

Sam Machell briefly told his story, while the drove continued its course through the clumps of mimosas. Lady Helena, Mary Grant, and the horsemen dismounted, and, seated in the shade of a huge gum-tree, listened to the stock-keeper's narrative.

He had set out seven months before, and had made about ten miles a day, at which rate his journey would last three months longer. To aid him in this laborious task, he had with him twenty dogs and thirty men. Five of the men were blacks, who are very skillful in recovering stray animals. Six carts followed the drove; and the drivers, provided with stock-whips, the handles of which were eighteen inches and the lashes nine feet in length, moved among the ranks and maintained order, while the canine light dragoons hovered about on the wings.

The travelers were amazed at the discipline of this novel army. The different classes advanced separately, for wild oxen and sheep do not associate well; the first will never graze where the second have passed. Hence it was necessary to place the oxen at the head; and these accordingly, divided into two battalions, took the lead. Five regiments of sheep, commanded by five drivers, followed, and the platoon of horses formed the rear-guard.

The stock-keeper observed to his hearers that the leaders of the army were neither dogs nor men, but oxen, whose superiority was recognized by their mates. They advanced in the front rank with perfect gravity, choosing the best course by instinct, and thoroughly convinced of their right to be treated with consideration.

Thus the discipline was maintained, for the drove obeyed them without resistance. If it pleased them to stop, the others were obliged to yield, and it was useless to attempt to resume the line of march if the leaders did not give the signal.

Such was Sam Machell's account, during which a great part of the herd had advanced in good order. It was now time for him to join his army, and choose the best pastures. He therefore took leave of Lord Glenarvan, mounted a fine native horse that one of his men was holding for him, and a few moments after had disappeared in a cloud of dust, while the cart, resuming its interrupted journey, stopped at nightfall at the foot of Mount Talbot.

The next day they reached the shores of the Wimerra, which is half a mile wide, and flows in a limpid stream between tall rows of gum-trees and acacias. Magnificent myrtles raised aloft their long, drooping branches, adorned with crimson flowers, while thousands of goldfinches, chaffinches, and golden-winged pigeons, not to speak of chattering parrots, fluttered about in the foliage. Below, on the surface of the stream, sported a pair of black swans, shy and unapproachable.

Meantime the cart had stopped on a carpet of turf whose fringes hung over the swiftly flowing waters. There was neither raft nor bridge, but they must cross at all hazard. Ayrton busied himself in searching for a practicable ford. A quarter of a mile up-stream, the river seemed to him less deep, and from this point he resolved to reach the other bank. Various soundings gave a depth of only three feet. The cart could, therefore, pass over this shallow without running much risk.

"Is there no other way of crossing the river?" asked Glenarvan of the quartermaster.

"No, my lord," replied Ayrton; "but this passage does not seem to me dangerous. We can extricate ourselves from any difficulty."

"Shall Lady Helena and Miss Grant leave the cart?"

"Not at all. My oxen are sure-footed, and I will engage to keep them in the right track."

"Well, Ayrton," said Glenarvan, "I trust to you."

The horsemen surrounded the heavy vehicle, and the party boldly entered the river. Usually, when these fordings are attempted, the carts are encircled by a ring of empty barrels, which support them on the water. But here this buoyant girdle was wanting, and it was, therefore, necessary to confide to the sagacity of the oxen, guided by the cautious Ayrton. The major and the two sailors dashed through the rapid current some distance ahead, while Glenarvan and Captain Mangles, one on each side of the cart, stood ready to assist the ladies, and Paganel and Robert brought up the rear.

Everything went well till they reached the middle of the river, but here the depth increased, and the water rose above the felloes. The oxen, if thrown out of their course, might lose their footing and overturn the unsteady vehicle. Ayrton exerted himself to the utmost. He leaped into the water, and, seizing the oxen by the horns, succeeded in keeping them in the right track.

At this moment an accident, impossible to foresee, took place. A crack was heard; the cart inclined at an alarming angle; the water reached the feet of the ladies, and the whole vehicle threatened to give way. It was an anxious moment.

Fortunately a vigorous blow upon the yoke brought the cart nearer the shore. The river grew shallower, and soon men and beasts were in safety on the opposite bank. Only the front wheels of the cart were damaged, and Glenarvan's horse had lost the shoes of his fore-feet.

This mishap required immediate repair. The travelers gazed at each other in some degree of perplexity, when Ayrton proposed to go to Black Point Station, twenty miles to the north, and bring a farrier.

"Very well, Ayrton," said Glenarvan. "How much time do you need to make the journey and return to the encampment?"

"Fifteen hours," replied Ayrton.

"Go, then; and, while waiting for your return, we will encamp on the banks of the Wimerra."

A few moments after, the quartermaster, mounted on Wilson's horse, disappeared behind the thick curtain of mimosas.

CHAPTER XXXIV. AUSTRALIAN EXPLORERS.

After the departure of Ayrton, and during this compulsory halt, promenades and conversations became the order of the day. There was an abundance of agreeable surroundings to talk about, and nature seemed dressed in one of her most attractive garbs. Birds, novel and varied in their plumage, with flowers such as they had never before gazed on, were the constant theme of the travelers' remark; and when, in addition, they had in Mr. Olbinett one who knew how to spread before them and make the best of all the culinary novelties that were within reach, a very substantial foundation was possible for the "feast of reason and the flow of soul" which followed, and for which, as usual, they were to no small extent indebted to their learned historico-geographical professor, whose stock of information was as varied as it was pleasant.

After dinner the traveling party had, as if in anticipation, seated themselves at the foot of a magnificent banksia; the young moon was rising high into the heavens, lengthening the twilight, and prolonging it into the evening hour; whilst the smoke of the major's cigar was seen curling upwards, losing itself in the foliage of the tree.

"Monsieur Paganel," said Lady Helena, "you have never given us the history that you promised when you supplied us with that long list of names."

The gentleman addressed did not require any lengthened entreaties on this subject, but, with an attentive auditory, and in the grandest of all lecture-rooms, he rehearsed to them the two great dramas of Australian travel, which have made the names of Burke and Stuart immortal in the history of that continent.

He told them that it was on the 20th of August, 1860, that Robert O'Hara Burke set out, under the auspices of the Royal Society of Melbourne, to cross the continent from south to north, and so to reach the Indian Ocean. Eleven others—including a botanist, an astronomer, and an army officer—accompanied him, with horses and other beasts of burden. But the expedition did not long continue so numerous or so well provided; in consequence of misunderstandings, several returned, and Burke pressed on with but few followers and fewer aids. Again, on the 20th of November, he still further diminished his numbers by leaving behind at an encampment several of his companions, that he and three others might press on towards the north with as little incumbrance as possible. After a very painful journey across a stony desert, they arrived at the extreme point reached by Stuart in 1845; and from this point, after determining as accurately as possible their latitude and longitude, they again started northward and seaward.

By the 7th of January they had gone so far as to reach the southern limit of the tropical heat; and now under a scorching sun, deceived by the mirage, often without water, and then hailing a storm as a source of refreshment, now and then meeting with the aborigines, who could in no wise help them, they had indeed a hard road to travel, though having neither rivers, lakes, nor mountains to bar their path.

At length, however, there were various signs that they were approaching the sea; by-and-by they reached the bank of a river which flows into the Gulf of Carpentaria; and finally Burke and Wills, after terrible hardships, arrived at the point where the sea-water flowed up to and inundated the marshes, though the sea-shore itself they did not reach. With naught but barrenness in sight on either hand, their great desire was to get back and rejoin their companions; but peril after peril awaited them, many of which their note-book has preserved an account of, but many more will be forever unrecorded. The three survivors (for one of the party had succumbed to the hardships) now strained every effort to reach the encampment, where they hoped to find their companions and a store of provisions. On the 21st of April they gained the goal, but the prize was missing; only seven hours before, after five months of waiting in vain, their companions had taken their departure. Of course nothing remained but to follow them with their feeble strength and scanty means of subsistence; but calamities still dogged their footsteps, and at last the leader, Burke, lay down exhausted, saying to his companion, King, "I have not many hours to live; here are my watch and my notes; when I am dead, place a pistol in my right hand, and leave me without burial." His forebodings were realized, and the next morning he died. King, in despair, went in search of some Australian tribe, for now Wills had begun to sink, and he shortly afterwards died also. At length the sole survivor was rescued by an expedition sent out in search of Burke; and thus the sad tale was told of this Australian tragedy.

The narrative concerning Stuart was a less melancholy one, though the trials endured on his expedition were likewise great. Aided by the parliament of South Australia, he likewise proceeded northward, in the year 1862, about seven degrees to the west of the line taken by Burke. He found his route to be a more accessible and easy one than the other, and was rewarded for his toil when, on the 24th of July, he beheld the waters of the Indian Ocean, and proudly unfurled the Australian flag from the topmost branch of the highest tree he could find. His return to the inhabited regions was successfully accomplished, and his entry into Adelaide, on the 17th of December, was an ovation indeed. But his health was shattered, and, after receiving the gold medal of the Royal Geographical Society, and returning to his native Scotland, he died on the 5th of June, 1866.

The histories of these Australian travels were lengthy, as told by Paganel. When he had finished, hope and despair seemed to fight for the mastery in the breasts of his listeners; but they did not fight long, for peaceful slumbers soon enwrapped the company, except those whose turn it was to watch over their fellow-travelers.

CHAPTER XXXV. CRIME OR CALAMITY?

It was not without a certain feeling of apprehension that the major had seen Ayrton leave the Wimerra to procure a farrier at Black Point Station. However, he did not breathe a word of his personal suspicions, but contented himself with exploring the surroundings of the river, whose tranquillity was undisturbed. As for Glenarvan, his only fear was to see Ayrton return alone. In the absence of skilled labor, the cart could not resume its journey, which would be interrupted for several days perhaps; and his longings for success and eagerness to attain his end admitted of no delay.

Fortunately, Ayrton had lost neither his time nor his trouble. The next morning he reappeared at break of day. A man accompanied him, by profession a farrier. He was a tall, stout fellow, but of a low and brutish appearance, which did not prepossess one in his favor. However, this was of little importance, if he knew his business. At all events his breath was not wasted in idle words.

"Is he an efficient workman?" inquired Captain Mangles of the quartermaster.

"I know no more than you, captain," replied Ayrton. "We shall see."

The farrier began his work. He was a man who understood his trade, as one could see by the way in which he repaired the wheels of the cart. He labored skillfully and with uncommon energy.

During the operation, the major noticed that the farrier's wrists were considerably eroded, and that they were each encircled by a blackish ring of extravasated blood. These were the marks of recent wounds, which the sleeves of a miserable woolen shirt but partially concealed. MacNabb questioned the man about these erosions, which must have been very painful. He, however, made no reply, but stolidly kept on at his work.

Two hours after, the injuries of the cart were repaired. As for Glenarvan's horse, he was quickly shod. The farrier had taken care to bring shoes all prepared. There was a peculiarity about them, however, which did not escape the major. It was a trefoil rudely carved on the outer rim. He pointed it out to Ayrton.

"It is the Black Point mark," replied the quartermaster, "which enables them to follow the tracks of the horses that stray from the station, and not confound them with others."

The farrier, having done all that was required of him, now claimed his wages, and departed without having spoken four words.

Half an hour later, the travelers were on the move. Beyond the curtain of mimosas extended a broad, uncovered space, which justly deserved its name of "open plain." Fragments of quartz and ferruginous rocks lay among the bushes, tall grass, and hedgerows that protected numerous flocks. Several miles farther on, the wheels of the cart sank deeply in the marshy lowlands, through which ran winding creeks, half hidden beneath a canopy of gigantic rushes. The journey, notwithstanding, was neither difficult nor tedious.

Lady Helena invited the horsemen to call upon her in turn, for her parlor was very small. Each was thus relieved from the fatigue of horseback riding, and enjoyed the society of this amiable lady, who, assisted by Miss Mary, performed with perfect grace the honors of her movable mansion. Captain Mangles was not forgotten in these invitations, and his rather sober conversation was not at all displeasing.

At eleven o'clock they arrived at Carlsbrook, quite an important municipality. Ayrton thought it best to pass by the city without entering. Glenarvan was of the same opinion; but Paganel, always eager for something new, desired to visit the place. Accordingly, the geographer, taking Robert with him as usual, started on his explorations, while the cart slowly continued its journey. Their inspection of the town was very rapid, and shortly afterwards they had joined their companions.

While they were passing through this region, the travelers requested Paganel to give them some account of its progress, and the geographer, in compliance with their wishes, had just begun a lecture upon the civilization of the country, when he was interrupted by a shrill whistle. The party were not a mile from the railroad.

A locomotive, coming from the south, and going slowly, had stopped just where the road they were following crossed the iron track. At this point the railway passes over the Lutton on an iron bridge, and thither Ayrton directed his cart, preceded by the horsemen. The travelers were attracted, moreover, by a lively feeling of curiosity, for a considerable crowd was already rushing towards the bridge. The inhabitants of the neighboring stations, leaving their houses, and the shepherds their flocks, lined the sides of the track. Frequent cries were heard. Some serious event must have taken place to cause such excitement,—a great accident, perhaps.

Glenarvan, followed by his companions, urged on his horse, and in a few moments arrived at Camden Bridge. Here the cause of this agitation was at once manifest. A terrible accident had occurred, not a collision, but a running off the track and a fall into the river, which was filled with the fragments of cars and locomotives. Either the bridge had given way, or the engine had run off the track; for five coaches out of six had been precipitated into the bed of the

Lutton. The last car, miraculously preserved by the breaking of its coupling, stood on the very verge of the abyss. Below was to be seen nothing but a terrible heap of blackened and bent axle-trees, broken cars, twisted rails, and charred timbers. The boiler, which had burst at the shock, had thrown its iron plates to an enormous distance. From this mass of unsightly objects issued flames and spiral wreaths of steam, mingled with black smoke. Large spots of blood, scattered limbs, and trunks of burnt bodies appeared here and there; and no one dared to estimate the number of victims buried beneath the ruins.

Glenarvan, Paganel, the major, and Captain Mangles mingled with the crowd, and listened to the conjectures that passed from one to another. Each sought to explain the catastrophe, while laboring to save what was left.

"The bridge has broken," said one.

"Broken?" replied others. "That cannot be, for it is still uninjured. They forgot to close it for the passage of the train, that is all."

It was a draw-bridge, which had been constructed for the convenience of the shipping. Had the man on guard, through unpardonable negligence, forgotten to close it, and thus precipitated the train, at full speed, into the bed of the Lutton? This supposition seemed plausible, for one half of the bridge lay beneath the fragments of the cars, while the other still hung intact in its chains. Doubt was no longer possible; surely carelessness must have caused the calamity.

The accident had happened to the night express, which left Melbourne at forty-five minutes past eleven. It must have been a quarter-past three in the morning when the train reached Camden Bridge, where this terrible destruction of life and property took place. The travelers and employés of the last car at once busied themselves in seeking assistance; but the telegraph-wires, whose poles lay on the ground, were no longer available. It took the authorities of Castlemaine three hours to reach the scene of the disaster; and it was, therefore, six o'clock in the morning before a corps of workers was organized under the direction of the surveyor-general of the district, and a detachment of policemen, commanded by an officer. The squatters had come to their aid, and exerted themselves to extinguish the fire, which consumed the heap of ruins with unconquerable fierceness. Several unrecognizable bodies lay on the edge of the embankment, but it was impossible to rescue a living being from this furnace. The fire had rapidly accomplished the work of destruction. Of the travelers in the train, whose number was not known, only ten survived, those in the last car. The railroad company had just sent an extra locomotive to convey them to Castlemaine.

Meantime, Lord Glenarvan, having made the acquaintance of the surveyor-general, was conversing with him and the police-officer. The latter was a tall, thin man, of imperturbable coolness, who, if he had any feeling, betrayed no sign of it on his impassible features. He was like a mathematician engaged upon a problem; he was seeking to elucidate the mystery of the disaster. To Glenarvan's first words, "This is a great calamity!" he replied, calmly, "It is more than that."

"More than that!" cried Glenarvan; "and what can be more than that?"

"It is a crime!" replied the officer, coolly.

Glenarvan turned to Mr. Mitchell, the surveyor-general, with a questioning look.

"That is correct," said the latter; "our examination has convinced us that the catastrophe is the result of a crime. The last baggage-wagon was robbed. The surviving travelers were attacked by a party of five or six malefactors. The bridge was opened intentionally; and, taking into account this fact with the disappearance of the guard, I cannot but come to the conclusion that the miserable man was the accomplice of the criminals."

The police-officer, at these words, slowly shook his head.

"You are not of my opinion?" inquired Mr. Mitchell.

"Not as regards the complicity of the guard."

"At any rate, this assumed complicity," continued the surveyor-general, "enables us to attribute the crime to the natives who wander about the country. Without the guard's assistance these natives could not have opened the draw-bridge, for they do not understand its working."

"Exactly," replied the officer.

"Now, it is known," added Mr. Mitchell, "from the testimony of a boatman, whose boat passed Camden Bridge at forty minutes past ten in the evening, that the bridge was closed according to regulation, after his passage."

"Quite right."

"Therefore the complicity of the guard seems to me to be proved incontestably."

The officer again made a gesture of dissent.

"Then you do not attribute the crime to the natives?" inquired Glenarvan.

"I do not."

"To whom, then?"

At this moment a loud uproar was heard half a mile up the river. A crowd had formed, which rapidly increased, and was now approaching the station. In the midst of the multitude two men were bearing a corpse. It was that of the guard, already cold. A poniard-thrust had pierced him to the heart. The assassins had dragged the body some distance from Camden Bridge, doubtless intending by this means to mislead the police in their first investigations. This discovery clearly justified the doubts of the officer. The natives had no hand in the crime.

"Those who struck the blow," said he, "are persons already familiar with the use of these little instruments."

As he spoke he displayed a pair of "darbies," a kind of manacles consisting of a double ring of iron, furnished with a padlock.

"Before long," added he, "I shall have the pleasure of presenting them with these bracelets as a new year's gift."

"Then you suspect—?"

"People who have 'traveled free on Her Majesty's vessels.'"

"What! convicts?" cried Paganel, who recognized the phrase employed in the Australian colonies.

"I thought," observed Glenarvan, "that those who have been transported had no right to stay in the province of Victoria."

"Ah, well," replied the officer, "if they have not the right, they take it! Sometimes they escape; and, if I am not greatly mistaken, these fellows have come direct from Perth. Well, they shall return again, you may be sure."

Mr. Mitchell nodded approvingly at the words of the officer. At this moment the cart arrived at the railroad crossing. Glenarvan, wishing to spare the ladies the spectacle at Camden Bridge, took leave of the surveyor-general, and made a sign to his companions to follow him.

"There is no occasion," said he, "for us to interrupt our journey."

On reaching the cart, Glenarvan simply told Lady Helena that a railroad accident had taken place, without mentioning the part that the convicts had played in the catastrophe. He reserved this matter that he might question Ayrton in private. The little party then crossed the track, not far above the bridge, and resumed their route towards the east.

CHAPTER XXXVI. FRESH FACES.

They had not proceeded far before they reached a native cemetery, pleasantly situated and with abundance of shady trees. Here for a time they halted, and, whilst Robert and Paganel were exploring, Lord and Lady Glenarvan almost stumbled over a queer object. It was human, indigenous, and sleeping; but at first this was all that they could decide, until, as the eyes opened and the sleeper roused to active life, they saw before them a boy of eight years, with a notice pinned to the back of his jacket which read as follows: "TOLINÉ, to be conducted to Echuca, care of Jeff Smith, Railway Porter. Prepaid."

Here, it would seem, was another waif that Providence had cast in their path. They questioned him, and his answers were pertinent and clear. He had been educated in the Wesleyan Methodist day-school at Melbourne, and was now going for a time to visit his parents, who were living with the rest of their tribe in Lachlan. He had been in the train to which the accident had happened, and had, with childlike confidence, troubled less about his fate than did those of older years. Going to a little distance, and laying himself on the grass, he had soon fallen into the slumber from which our travelers had aroused him.

Paganel and the others had now gathered round, and Toliné had to answer many a question. He came out of his examination very creditably; the reverence with which he spoke of the Creator and of the Bible produced a very favorable impression on the Scottish heads of the expedition, whilst the fact that he had taken "the first prize in geography" was sufficient introduction to Monsieur Paganel, who forthwith tested his knowledge, greatly to his own satisfaction, and considerably to the credit of his young pupil. The curiosity of his discoverers having been fully satisfied, Toliné was made welcome, and partook with the others of the general repast. Many were the plans and purposes concerning him, and much wonder was expressed as to how they could speed him on his way; but in the morning it was discovered that he had solved the problem for himself, and a bouquet of fresh leaves and flowers, laid by the side of Lady Helena's seat, was the only memento that Toliné had left.

The party were now approaching the district which, in the years 1851 and 1852, was so much talked of throughout the civilized world, and attracted from all parts so many reckless adventurers and fortune-hunters. The line of the thirty-seventh parallel, on which they were traveling, led them through the diggings and municipality of Mount Alexander, which was one of the most successful spots for the digger at the commencement of the gold fever, in consequence of the comparatively level nature of the ground and the general richness of the soil, so different from some other localities where only once in a while wassome enormous nugget to be found. As they drew near to the streets of this hastily-built town, Ayrton and Mulready, who were in charge of the cart, were sent forward, whilst the others walked through the place to inspect what there might be of interest, as well as to ascertain what might be learned concerning the object of their expedition.

Thus, in this strange gathering of all nationalities and creeds and professions, the regular inhabitants beheld a still more extraordinary sight than that every day afforded them: folks who to the refinement which education and civilization give added both the earnestness of the worker and the freshness and vigor of the pleasure-seeking tourist. In the streets, in connection with the strange sign-boards and announcements, the novel erections and purposes to which some of them were adapted, Paganel had a history and commentary for every one.

Still more did he expatiate upon the thousand-and-one topics of interest when they visited the bank building, which here is the centre of more than one agency connected with this great gold-bearing district. Here was the mineralogical museum, in which might be seen specimens illustrative of all the various ways in which the gold has been found, whether in combination with clay or other minerals, or—as it is sometimes, to the great joy of the finder, discovered—*pur et simple*. Here also were models, diagrams, and even the tools themselves, to illustrate the different methods by which the object of search was dug out, or washed, or crushed, or tested. Here also was an almost unequaled collection of precious stones, gems of all sorts, making the gallery in which they were placed a real Golconda for its wealth and attractions.

Besides all this, here was the centre of the varied agencies by which the reports were brought in from the companies established for mining purposes, and also from each isolated worker, of the space purchased, the number of feet or yards dug, the ore extracted, the comparative richness or poverty of the soil here, there, and elsewhere, which in their summarized and aggregate form have greatly helped to a correct knowledge of the comparative and absolute gold-bearing value of various spots. Then, in addition to the usual operations of a banking establishment, it was here that the ore was stored, from hence that it was sent, under government escort and with government guarantee, subject to a fixed, though moderate, charge, so that the transport to Melbourne, which at first was a dangerous and expensive "middle passage," was now as easily and inexpensively accomplished as is the transmission of freight from London to Paris.

Over the whole of this establishment they were conducted by the most courteous and obliging of officials, and the services thus rendered charmed the Frenchman, who was none the less loquacious, and was in truth able even to enlighten his guides.

But his joy culminated when, after some time spent in the hotel, the party left the town, and passed through the "diggings," properly so called. It was difficult to persuade Paganel and Robert—who kept together—to come on, in order that they might not leave Ayrton and Mulready too long in suspense. Now the Frenchman would see just the key that he needed to understand a point not before clear to him; anon you might see him as in the illustration, when he had picked up a pebble and was sure that it was in itself so interesting as a mineralogical specimen that he must treasure it up for the Bank of France, so that his own land might have at least one part of Australia. All this was done with such a mingling of childish good-nature and scientific and national pride that it was useless to do anything but laugh, and an irrepressible smile came over even the major's features. At length, however, by drawing him into a lecture, they succeeded in persuading him to follow them; and, as they left the diggings, he told them the history of the prophecies, the discovery, and the spread of knowledge as to the rich auriferous deposits of this part of Australia. He could give them facts and incidents and dates as to the ingress into Melbourne, and the exodus therefrom to the diggings, in the year 1852; he told them how the energy and the love of order which characterize the English-speaking peoples had reduced to system, method, subordination, the chaotic surgings and restlessness which marked the first weeks and months of this new era; and he detailed, as though he had studied the subject to the entire neglect of other matters, the working of the system,—how the land was registered, what was the sum paid in the aggregate, how the taxes were collected, wherein the system had been found faulty. All this occupied much time, and, before he had finished, the cart was in sight, in which Lady Helena and Miss Grant reseated themselves, and for the remainder of the day and the succeeding night their progress was in the accustomed order.

CHAPTER XXXVII. A WARNING.

At sunrise the travelers left the gold regions and crossed the frontiers of the county of Talbot. Their line of travel now struck the dusty roads of the county of Dalhousie. Half the journey was accomplished. In fifteen days more of travel equally rapid the little party would reach the shores of Twofold Bay. Moreover, every one was in good health. Paganel's assertions as to the salubrity of this climate were verified. There was little or no moisture, and the heat was quite endurable. Neither men nor animals complained.

Only one change had been made in the line of march since leaving Camden Bridge. The criminal disaster on the railway, when made known to Ayrton, had induced him to take precautions hitherto needless. The horsemen were not to lose sight of the cart. During the hours of encampment one of them was always on guard. Morning and evening the priming of the fire-arms was renewed. It was certain that a band of malefactors were scouring the country; and, although nothing gave cause for immediate suspicion, still it was necessary to be ready for any emergency.

In truth they had reason to act thus. An imprudence, or negligence even, might cost them dear. Glenarvan, moreover, was not alone in giving heed to this state of affairs. In the isolated towns and stations the inhabitants and squatters took precautions against any attack or surprise. The houses were closed at nightfall. The dogs were let loose within the palisades, and barked at the slightest alarm. There was not a shepherd, collecting his numerous flocks on horseback for the evening return, who did not carry a carbine suspended from the pommel of his saddle. The news of the crime committed at Camden Bridge was the reason for this excessive caution, and many a colonist who had formerly slept with open doors and windows now carefully locked his house at twilight.

After awhile, the cart entered a grove of giant trees, the finest they had hitherto seen. There was a cry of admiration at sight of the eucalyptuses, two hundred feet high, whose spongy bark was five inches in thickness. The trunks measured twenty feet in circumference, and were furrowed by streams of odorous sap. Not a branch, not a twig, not a wanton shoot, not even a knot, disfigured their perfect symmetry. They could not have issued smoother from the hand of the turner. They were like so many columns exactly mated, and could be counted by hundreds, spreading at a vast height into capitals of finely-shaped branches adorned with vertical leaves, from which hung solitary flowers, whose calices were like inverted urns.

Under this evergreen canopy the air circulated freely. A continual ventilation absorbed the moisture of the earth, and horses, herds of cattle, and carts could easily pass between these trees, which were widely separated and arranged in straight rows. It was neither a wood with thickets crowded and obstructed by brambles, nor a virgin forest barricaded with fallen trunks and entangled with inextricable parasites, where only axe and fire can clear a way for the pioneers. A carpet of herbage below, and a sheet of verdure above; long vistas of noble pillars; little shade or coolness; a peculiar light, like the rays that sift through a delicate tissue; shadows sharply defined upon the ground: all this constituted a strange sight. The forests of Oceanica are entirely different from those of the New World, and the eucalyptus—the "tara" of the aborigines—is the most perfect tree of the Australian flora.

The shade is not dense, nor the darkness profound, beneath these domes of verdure, owing to a strange peculiarity in the arrangement of the leaves of the eucalyptus. Not one presents its face to the sun, but only its sharp edge. The eye sees nothing but profiles in this singular foliage. Thus the rays of the sun glide to the earth as if they had passed between the slats of a window-blind.

Every one observed this and seemed surprised. Why this particular arrangement? This question was naturally addressed to Paganel, who replied like a man who is never at fault.

"What astonishes me," said he, "is not the freak of nature, for she knows what she does; but botanists do not always know what they say. Nature was not mistaken in giving to these trees this singular foliage; but men are wrong in calling them eucalyptuses."

"What does the word mean?" asked Mary Grant.

"It comes from the Greek words εὖ καλύπτω;, signifying *I cover well*. But you all see that the eucalyptus covers badly."

"Just so, my dear Paganel," replied Glenarvan; "and now tell us why the leaves grow thus."

"In this country, where the air is dry," said Paganel, "where rains are rare and the soil is parched, the trees need neither wind nor sun. Hence these narrow leaves seek to defend themselves against the elements and preserve themselves from too great an evaporation. They therefore present their edges, and not their faces, to the action of the solar rays. There is nothing more intelligent than a leaf."

"Nor more selfish," remarked the major. "They thought only of themselves, and not at all of travelers."

The entire party was inclined to be of MacNabb's opinion, except Paganel, who, as he wiped his face, congratulated himself upon traveling beneath these shadowless trees. However, this arrangement of foliage was to be regretted; for the journey through these forests is frequently very long and painful, since nothing protects the traveler from the heat of the sun.

All day long our travelers pursued their way under these interminable arches. They met neither quadruped nor human being. A few cockatoos inhabited the tops of the trees; but at that height they could scarcely be distinguished, and their chattering was an almost inaudible murmur. Sometimes a flock of parrots would shoot across a distant vista, illumining it with a rapid flash of variegated light. But generally a deep silence reigned in this vast temple of verdure, and the measured tread of the horses, a few words exchanged now and then in desultory conversation, the creaking of the cart-wheels, and from time to time a cry from Ayrton as he urged on his sluggish team, were the only sounds that disturbed this vast solitude.

At evening they encamped at the foot of some trees that bore the marks of a recent fire. They formed tall chimneys, as it were, for the flames had hollowed them out internally throughout their entire length. Having only this shell of bark remaining, they no longer suffered severely from this treatment.

However, this lamentable habit of the squatters and natives will finally destroy these magnificent trees, and they will disappear like the cedars of

Lebanon, so many centuries old, consumed by the careless fires of wandering encampments.

Olbinett, according to Paganel's advice, kindled a fire in one of these tubular trunks. He obtained a draught at once, and the smoke soon disappeared in the dark mass of foliage. The necessary precautions were taken for the night, and Ayrton, Mulready, Wilson, and Captain Mangles watched by turns till sunrise.

During all the next day the interminable forest presented its long, monotonous avenues, till it seemed as if it would never end. Towards evening, however, the rows of trees became thinner; and a few miles farther on, upon a small plain, appeared a collection of regularly built houses.

"Seymour!" cried Paganel. "This is the last place we shall meet with before leaving the province of Victoria."

"Is it an important town?" inquired Lady Helena.

"Madam," replied he, "it is a simple parish that would like to become a municipality."

"Shall we find a comfortable hotel?" asked Glenarvan.

"I hope so," answered the geographer.

"Well, then, let us go into the town; for the ladies will not be sorry, I imagine, to rest here one night."

"My dear Edward," replied Lady Helena, "Mary and I accept; but on the condition that it shall cause no trouble or delay."

"None at all," said Lord Glenarvan. "Moreover, our oxen are fatigued. To-morrow we will start at break of day."

It was now nine o'clock. The moon was approaching the horizon, and her rays were dimmed by the gathering mist. The darkness was increasing. The whole party, accordingly, entered the broad street of Seymour under the guidance of Paganel, who always seemed to be perfectly acquainted with what he had never seen. But his instinct directed him, and he went straight to Campbell's North British Hotel. Horses and oxen were taken to the stable, the cart was put under the shed, and the travelers were conducted to quite comfortable apartments.

At ten o'clock the guests took their seats at a table, over which Olbinett had cast his experienced eye. Paganel had just explored the town, in company with Robert, and now related his nocturnal impressions in a very laconic style. He had seen absolutely nothing.

However, a man less absent-minded would have observed a certain excitement in the streets of Seymour. Groups were formed here and there, which gradually increased. People talked at the doors of the houses, and questioned each other with an air of anxiety. Various daily papers were read aloud, commented upon, and discussed. These signs, one might suppose, could not have escaped the most careless observer; Paganel, however, had suspected nothing.

The major, on the contrary, without even leaving the hotel, had ascertained the fears that were agitating the little community. Ten minutes' conversation with the loquacious landlord had informed him; but he did not utter a word. Not until supper was over, and Lady Helena, Mary, and Robert had retired to their chambers, did the major say to his companions:

"They have traced the authors of the crime committed at Camden Bridge."

"Have they been arrested?" asked Ayrton, quickly.

"No," replied MacNabb, without seeming to notice the eagerness of the quartermaster.

"So much the worse," added Ayrton.

"Well," inquired Glenarvan, "to whom do they attribute the crime?"

"Read," said the major, handing to Glenarvan a copy of the *Australian and New Zealand Gazette*, "and you will see that the police-officer was not mistaken."

Glenarvan read aloud the following passage:

"Sydney, Jan. 2, 1865.—It will be remembered that on the night of December 29 an accident took place at Camden Bridge, five miles from Castlemaine Station, on the Melbourne and Sandhurst Railway, by which the night express was precipitated at full speed into the Lutton River. Numerous thefts committed after the accident, and the corpse of the guard found half a mile above, prove that it was the result of a crime; and, in accordance with the verdict at the inquest, this crime is to be attributed to a band of convicts who escaped, six months ago, from the Perth penitentiary, in Western Australia, as they were about to be transferred to Norfolk Island. These convicts are twenty-nine in number, and are commanded by a certain Ben Joyce, a dangerous criminal, who arrived in Australia several months ago in some way, and upon whom justice has not yet succeeded in laying hands. The inhabitants of the cities, and the colonists and squatters of the stations, are warned to be on their guard, and requested to send to the undersigned any information which may assist his investigations.

"J. P. MITCHELL, Surveyor-General."

When Glenarvan had finished reading this article, MacNabb turned to the geographer and said:

"You see, Paganel, that there may yet be convicts in Australia."

"Runaways there may be, of course," replied Paganel, "but not those who have been transported and regularly received. These people have no right to be here."

"Well, at any rate they are here," continued Glenarvan; "but I do not suppose that their presence need cause us to change our plans or delay our journey. What do you think, captain?"

Captain Mangles did not answer immediately. He hesitated between the grief that the abandonment of the search would cause the two children, and the fear of compromising the safety of the party.

"If Lady Glenarvan and Miss Grant were not with us," said he, "I should care very little for this band of wretches."

Glenarvan understood him, and added:

"Of course it is not advisable to give up our undertaking; but perhaps it would be prudent for the sake of the ladies to join the Duncan at Melbourne, and continue our search for Captain Grant towards the east. What do you think, MacNabb?"

"Before replying," said the major, "I should like to hear Ayrton's opinion."

The quartermaster, thus addressed, looked at Glenarvan.

"I think," said he, "that, as we are two hundred miles from Melbourne, the danger, if there is any, is as great on the southern as on the eastern road. Both are little frequented, and one is as good as the other. Moreover, I do not think that thirty malefactors can intimidate eight well-armed and resolute men. Therefore, in the absence of better advice, I should go on."

"Well said," replied Paganel. "By continuing our course we shall cross Captain Grant's track, while by returning to the south we should go directly away from it. I agree with you, therefore, and shall give myself no uneasiness about the runaway convicts."

Thus the determination to make no change in the programme was unanimously approved of.

"One more remark, my lord," said Ayrton, as they were about to separate.

"Speak."

"Would it not be advisable to send an order to the Duncan to sail to the coast?"

"Why?" asked Captain Mangles. "It will be time enough to send the order when we arrive at Twofold Bay. If any unforeseen event should compel us to return to Melbourne, we might be sorry not to find the Duncan there. Moreover, her injuries cannot yet have been repaired. I think, therefore, that it would be better to wait."

"Well," replied Ayrton, without further remark.

The next day the little party, armed and ready for any emergency, left Seymour, and half an hour after re-entered the forest of eucalyptuses, which appeared again towards the east. Glenarvan would have preferred to travel in the open country, for a plain is less favorable to sudden attacks and ambuscades than a thick wood. But they had no alternative; and the cart kept on all day between the tall, monotonous trees, and at evening encamped on the borders of the district of Murray.

They were now setting foot on one of the least frequented portions of the Australian continent, a vast uninhabited region stretching away to the Australian Alps. At some future day its forests will be leveled, and the home of the colonist will stand where now all is desolation; but at present it is a desert. In this region is situated the so-styled "reserve for the blacks." On these remote plains various spots have been set apart, where the aboriginal race can enjoy to the full the privilege of gradually becoming extinct. Though the white man is at perfect liberty to invade this "reserved" territory, yet the black may call it his own.

Paganel, who was in his element wherever statistics or history was concerned, went into full details respecting the native races. He gave a long account of the cruelties to which these unfortunate beings had been subjected at the hands of the early colonists, and showed how little had been done by the interference of the government. As a striking instance of the manner in which the aborigines melt away before the advance of civilization, he cited the case of Tasmania, which at the beginning of this century had five thousand native inhabitants, but in 1863 had only seven.

"Fifty years ago," said he, "we should have met in our course many a tribe of natives; whereas thus far we have not seen even one. A century hence, the black race will have utterly disappeared from this continent."

At that moment Robert, halting in front of a group of eucalyptuses, cried out:

"A monkey! there is a monkey!"

The cart was instantly stopped, and, looking in the direction indicated by the boy, our travellers saw a huge black form moving with astonishing agility from branch to branch, until it was lost from view in the depths of the grove.

"What sort of a monkey is that?" asked MacNabb.

"That monkey," answered Paganel, "is a full-blooded Australian."

Just then were heard sounds of voices at some little distance; the oxen were put in motion, and after proceeding a few hundred paces the party came suddenly upon an encampment of aborigines, consisting of some ten or twelve tents, made of strips of bark arranged in the manner of tiles, and giving shelter to their wretched inhabitants on only one side. Of these miserable beings there were about thirty, men, women, and children, dressed in ragged kangaroo-skins. Their first movement was one of flight; but a few words from Ayrton restored confidence, and they slowly approached the party of Europeans.

The major jocularly insisted that Robert was correct in saying that he had seen a monkey; but Lady Helena declined to accept his views, and, getting out of the cart, made friendly advances to these degraded beings, who seemed to look upon her as a divinity. Reassured by her gentle manner, they surrounded the travelers, and began to cast wishful glances at the provisions which the cart contained. Glenarvan, at the request of his wife, distributed a quantity of food among the hungry group.

After this had been dispatched, our friends were favored by their new acquaintances with a sham fight, which lasted about ten minutes, the women urging on the combatants and pretending to mutilate those who fell in the fray. Suddenly the excited crowd dropped their arms, and a profound silence succeeded to the din of war. A flight of cockatoos had made its appearance in the neighboring trees; and the opportunity to display their proficiency in the use of the boomerang was at once improved by the Australians. The skill manifested in the construction and use of this instrument served Lady Helena as a strong argument against the monkey theory, though the major pretended that he was not yet convinced.

Lord Glenarvan was now about to give the order to advance, when a native came running up with the news that he had discovered half a dozen cassowaries. The chase that followed, with the ingenious disguise assumed by the hunter, and the marvelous fidelity with which he imitated the movements and cries of the bird, was witnessed with interest by the travelers. Lady Helena adduced the skill displayed as a still further argument against the major's theory; but the obstinate MacNabb declined to recede from his position, citing to his antagonist the statement of the negroes concerning the orang-outangs,— that they are negroes like themselves, only that they are too cunning to talk, for fear of being made to work.

CHAPTER XXXVIII. WEALTH IN THE WILDERNESS.

After a peaceful night, the travelers, at seven o'clock in the morning, resumed their journey eastward over the plains. Twice they crossed the tracks of squatters, leading towards the north; and then the different hoof-prints would have been confounded if Glenarvan's horse had not left upon the dust the Black Point mark, distinguishable by its three trefoils.

Sometimes the plain was furrowed with winding creeks, bordered by box-wood, which took their source on the slopes of the Buffalo Range, a chain of mountains whose picturesque outlines stretched along the horizon, and which the party resolved to reach that evening. Ayrton urged on his oxen, and, after a journey of thirty-five miles, they reached the place. The tent was pitched beneath a great tree. Night had come, and supper was quickly dispatched; all thought more of sleeping than of eating, after the fatigues of the day.

Paganel, to whom fell the first watch, did not lie down, but, rifle on shoulder, guarded the encampment, walking to and fro that he might the better resist sleep. In spite of the absence of the moon, the night was almost bright with the splendor of the southern constellations; and the geographer amused himself in reading the great book of the firmament, which is always open. The silence of sleeping nature was broken only by the sound of the horses' chains as they rattled against their feet. Paganel was becoming fully absorbed in his astronomical meditations, and occupying himself more with the things of heaven than those of earth, when a distant sound startled him from his reverie.

He listened attentively, and, to his great astonishment, thought he distinguished the tones of a piano. A few boldly-struck chords wafted to his ears their harmonious vibrations. He could not be mistaken.

"A piano in the desert!" said he to himself. "It cannot be!"

It was indeed very surprising, and Paganel began to think that some strange Australian bird was imitating the sound of the instrument.

But at that moment a voice, harmoniously pitched, was heard. The pianist was accompanied by a vocalist. The geographer listened incredulously, but in a few moments was forced to recognize the sublime air that struck upon his ear. It was "*Il mio tesoro tanto*" from Don Juan.

"Parbleu!" thought the geographer, "however strange the Australian birds may be, or even though the parrots were the most musical in the world, they could not sing Mozart."

He listened to the end of this grand inspiration of the master. The effect of this sweet melody, in the stillness of the starlit night, was indescribable. He remained a long time under the influences of its enchantment. At last the voice ceased, and all was silent.

When Wilson came to relieve the geographer, he found him wrapt in a profound reverie. Paganel said nothing to the sailor, but, reserving his account of the incident for Glenarvan the next day, he crept into the tent.

In the morning the whole party were awakened by unexpected bayings. Glenarvan at once arose. Two magnificent pointers were gamboling along the edge of a small wood; but at the approach of the travelers they disappeared among the trees, barking loudly.

"There must be a station in this desert," said Glenarvan, "and hunters, since those are hunting-dogs."

Paganel was just about to relate his experiences of the past night, when two men appeared, in hunting costume, mounted on fine horses. They naturally stopped at sight of the little party, encamped in gypsy-like fashion, and seemed to be wondering what the presence of armed men in this place meant, when they perceived the ladies, who were alighting from the cart.

They immediately dismounted, and advanced towards them, hat in hand. Glenarvan went to meet them, and introduced himself and party, giving the name and rank of each member. The young men bowed, and one of them, the elder, said:

"My lord, will your ladies, your companions, and yourself do us the honor to accompany us to our house?"

"May I ask, gentlemen, whom I have the honor of addressing?" inquired Glenarvan.

"Michael and Alexander Patterson, proprietors of Hottam Station. You are already on the grounds of the establishment, and have but a quarter of a mile to go."

"Gentlemen," replied Glenarvan, "I should be unwilling to slight a hospitality so graciously offered—"

"My lord," interrupted Michael Patterson, "by accepting you will confer a favor upon two poor colonists, who will be only too happy to extend to you the honors of the desert."

Glenarvan bowed in token of assent.

"Sir," said Paganel, addressing Michael Patterson, "should I be too inquisitive were I to ask if it was you who sang that divine air of Mozart last night?"

"It was I, sir," replied the gentleman; "and my brother accompanied me."

"Well, sir," continued Paganel, extending his hand, "accept the sincere compliments of a Frenchman, who is an ardent admirer of Mozart's music."

The young man modestly returned the geographer's greeting, and then pointed towards the right to the road they were to take. The horses had been confided to the care of Ayrton and the sailors, and the travelers at once betook themselves on foot to Hottam Station, under the guidance of the two young men.

It was a magnificent establishment, characterized by the perfect order of an English park. Immense meadows, inclosed by fences, extended as far as the eye could reach. Here grazed thousands of oxen and sheep. Numerous shepherds and still more numerous dogs tended this vast herd, while with the bellowing and bleating mingled the baying of mastiffs and the sharp crack of stock-whips.

To the east the prospect was broken by a border of gum-trees, beyond which rose the imposing peak of Mount Hottam, seven thousand five hundred feet high. Long avenues of tall trees stretched in all directions, while here and there stood dense clumps of grass-trees, shrubby plants about ten feet high, resembling the dwarf palm, with a thick foliage of long narrow leaves. The air was laden with the perfume of laurels, whose clusters of white flowers in full bloom exhaled the most delicate fragrance.

With the charming groups of native trees were mingled those transplanted from European climes. The peach, the pear, the apple, the fig, the orange, and even the oak were hailed with delight by the travelers, who, if they were not astonished at walking in the shade of the trees of their country, wondered, at least, at the sight of the birds that fluttered among the branches, the satin-birds with their silky plumage, and the canaries, clad in golden and black velvet.

Here, for the first time, they saw the menure, or lyre-bird, whose tail has the form of the graceful instrument of Orpheus. As the bird fled away among the arborescent ferns, its tail striking the branches, they almost expected to hear those harmonious chords that helped Amphion to rebuild the walls of Thebes.

Lord Glenarvan was not satisfied with merely admiring the fairy wonders of this oasis of the Australian desert. He listened with profound interest to the young men's story. In England, in the heart of civilization, a new-comer would have first informed his host whence he came and whither he was going; but here, by a nice shade of distinction, Michael and Sandy Patterson thought they should make themselves known to the travelers to whom they offered their hospitalities, and briefly told their story.

It was like that of all intelligent and active young Englishmen, who do not believe that the possession of riches absolves from the responsibility to labor for the welfare of others. Michael and Alexander Patterson were the sons of a London banker. When they were twenty years old, their father had said: "Here is money, my sons. Go to some distant land, found there a useful establishment, and acquire in labor the knowledge of life. If you succeed, so much the better; if you fail, it matters little. We shall not regret the money that will have enabled you to become men." They obeyed; they chose the province of Victoria as the place to sow the paternal bank-notes, and had no reason to repent. At the end of three years their establishment had attained its present prosperity.

They had just finished the brief account of their career, when the dwelling came in sight at the end of a fine avenue of trees. It was a charming house of wood and brick, surrounded by clusters of plants, and had the elegant form of a Swiss cottage, while a veranda, from which hung Chinese lanterns, encircled it like a Roman impluvium. The windows were shaded by brilliant-colored awnings, which at a distance looked almost like masses of flowers. Nothing could be prettier, cozier, or pleasanter to the sight. On the lawn and among the shrubbery round about stood bronze candelabra, supporting elegant lamps with glass globes, which at nightfall illumined the whole garden with a beauteous light.

No farm-hands, stables, or outhouses were to be seen,—nothing that indicated scenes of toil. The dwellings of the workmen—a regular village, consisting of some twenty cottages—were a quarter of a mile distant, in the heart of a little valley. Telegraph-wires secured immediate communication between the village and the house of the proprietors, which, far from all tumult, was in truth "a thing of beauty."

The avenue was soon passed. A little iron bridge, of great elegance, crossing a murmuring stream, gave access to the private grounds. A courteous attendant advanced to meet the travelers; the doors of the house were opened, and the guests of Hottam Station entered the sumptuous dwelling.

All the luxuries of refined and civilized life seemed to be present. Into the vestibule, which was adorned with decorative subjects, illustrating the turf or the chase, opened a spacious parlor, lighted with five windows. A piano, covered with classic and modern music; easels, upon which were half-finished paintings; marble statues, mounted on tasteful pedestals; on the walls, a few pictures by Flemish masters; rich carpets, soft to the feet as grassy meadows; panels of tapestry, descriptive of pleasing mythological episodes; an antique chandelier, costly chinaware, delicate vases, and a great variety of articles of *virtù*, indicated a high appreciation of beauty and comfort. Everything that could please, everything that could relieve the tedium of a voluntary exile, everything that could remind one of a luxurious European home, was to be found in this fairy abode. It would have been easy to imagine oneself in some princely castle of England, France, or Germany.

The five windows admitted, through delicate curtains, a light tempered and softened by the shadows of the veranda. Lady Helena looked out, and was astonished. The house, upon this side, commanded the view of a broad valley, which extended to the eastern mountains. The alternation of meadow and woodland, broken here and there by vast clearings, the graceful sweep of the hill-sides, and the outlines of the entire landscape, formed a picture beyond the power of description. This vast panorama, intersected by broad bands of light and shade, changed every hour with the progress of the sun.

In the mean time, in accordance with the hosts' orders, breakfast had been prepared by the steward of the station, and in less than a quarter of an hour the travelers were seated at a bountiful table. The quality of the viands and the wines was unexceptionable; but what was especially gratifying, in the midst of these refinements of wealth, was the evident pleasure experienced by the young settlers in dispensing to strangers, beneath their own roof, this magnificent hospitality.

The young gentlemen were soon made acquainted with the object of the expedition, and took a lively interest in Glenarvan's search, giving also great encouragement to the captain's children.

"Harry Grant," said Michael, "has evidently fallen into the hands of the natives, since he has not appeared in the settlements on the coast. He knew his position exactly, as the document proves, and, as he has not reached any English colony, he must have been made prisoner by the natives as soon as he landed."

"That is precisely what happened to his quartermaster, Ayrton," replied Captain Mangles.

"But, gentlemen," inquired Lady Helena, "have you never heard of the shipwreck of the Britannia?"

"Never, madam," said Michael.

"And what treatment do you think Captain Grant would experience as a prisoner among the Australians?"

"The Australians are not cruel, madam," replied the young settler: "Miss Grant may reassure herself on this point. There are many instances of their kindness; and some Europeans have lived a long time among them, without having any reason to complain of brutality." These words corroborated the information previously given by Paganel and Ayrton.

When the ladies had left the table, the conversation turned upon convicts. The settlers had heard of the accident at Camden Bridge, but the band of runaways gave no uneasiness, they would not dare to attack a station that was guarded by more than a hundred men. They were confident, too, that they would not venture into the deserted regions of the Murray, nor into the colonies of New South Wales, where the roads are well protected.

Glenarvan could not decline the invitation of his amiable hosts to spend the entire day at Hottam Station. The delay thus occasioned could be turned to good account: the horses and oxen would be greatly benefited by their rest in the comfortable stables of the establishment. It was, therefore, decided to remain, and the two young men submitted to their guests a programme for the day's sports, which was adopted with alacrity.

At noon, seven fine hunters pawed the ground at the gate of the house. For the ladies was provided an elegant coach, and the long reins enabled their driver to show his skill in manœuvring the "four-in-hand." The horsemen, accompanied by outriders, and well armed, galloped beside the carriage, while the pack of hounds bayed joyously in the coppices.

For four hours the cavalcade traversed the paths and avenues of these spacious grounds. As for game, an army of bushmen could not have started up a greater number of animals. Young Robert, who kept close to the major's side, accomplished wonders. The intrepid boy, in spite of his sister's injunctions, was always ahead, and the first to fire. But Captain Mangles had promised to watch over him, a fact which tended not a little to allay Miss Grant's apprehension for her brother's safety.

Of all the sports of the day the most interesting was unquestionably a kangaroo hunt. About four o'clock the dogs started a troop of these curious animals. The little ones took refuge in their mothers' pouches, and the whole drove rushed away in single file. Nothing can be more astonishing than the enormous bounds of the kangaroo, whose hind legs are twice as long as its fore ones, and bend like a spring. At the head of the drove was a male five feet high,—"an old man," in the language of the bushmen.

For four or five miles the chase was briskly continued. The kangaroos did not slacken their pace; and the dogs, who feared, with good reason, the powerful blows of their formidable paws, did not venture to approach them. But at last the drove stopped in exhaustion, and "the old man" braced himself against the trunk of a tree, ready to fight for his life. One of the pointers, carried on by the impetus of his course, rolled within reach of him. A moment after, the unfortunate dog was tossed into the air, and fell back lifeless. The entire pack, deterred by the fate of their comrade, kept at a respectful distance. It became necessary to dispatch the kangaroo with the rifle, and nothing but bullets could bring down the gigantic quadruped.

At this juncture Robert narrowly escaped being the victim of his rashness. In order to make sure of his aim, he approached so near the kangaroo that the animal made a spring at him. Robert fell. A cry of alarm resounded. Mary Grant, speechless with apprehension, stretched her hands towards her brother. No one dared to fire, for fear of hitting the boy.

Suddenly Captain Mangles, with his hunting-knife open, rushed upon the kangaroo, at the risk of his life, and stabbed it to the heart. The beast fell dead, and Robert rose unharmed. An instant after, he was in the arms of his sister.

"Thanks, Captain Mangles! thanks!" said Mary, extending her hand to the young captain.

"I promised to take care of him," replied the captain, as he took the trembling hand of the young girl.

This adventure ended the hunt. The troop of kangaroos had scattered after the death of their leader, whose carcass was brought to the house.

It was now six o'clock, and dinner was in readiness for the hunters; comprising, among other dishes, a soup of kangaroo's tail, prepared in the native style.

After a dessert of ices and sherbet, the party repaired to the parlor, where the evening was devoted to music. Lady Helena, who was a good pianiste, presided at the instrument, while Michael and Alexander Patterson sang with great taste selections from the latest compositions of the modern musical masters.

At eleven o'clock tea was served in true English style. Paganel having desired to taste the Australian tea, a liquid, black as ink, was brought to him. It consisted of a quart of water, in which half a pound of tea had been boiled four hours. Paganel, with a wry face, pronounced it excellent. At midnight the guests were conducted to cool and comfortable chambers, where they renewed in dreams the pleasures of the day.

The next morning, at sunrise, they took leave of the two young settlers, with many thanks, and with warmly-expressed hopes to see them at Malcolm Castle at no very distant day. The cart then started, and in a few minutes, as the road wound around the foot of Mount Hottam, the hospitable habitation disappeared, like a passing vision, from the eyes of the travelers. For five miles farther they traversed the grounds of the station, and not till nine o'clock did the little party pass the last palisade and enter upon the almost unknown districts of the country before them.

CHAPTER XXXIX. SUSPICIOUS OCCURRENCES.

A mighty barrier crossed the road on the southeast. It was the chain of the Australian Alps, which extend in capricious windings fifteen hundred miles, and are capped with clouds four thousand feet aloft.

The sky was dull and lowering, and the rays of the sun struggled through dense masses of mist. The temperature was, therefore, endurable; but the journey was difficult on account of the irregularity of the surface. The unevenness of the plain constantly increased, and here and there rose mounds, covered with young green gum-trees. Farther on, these excrescences formed the first slopes of the great Alps. The ascent was very laborious, as was shown by the efforts of the oxen, whose yokes cracked under the tension of the heavy vehicle. The animals panted heavily, and the muscles of their hams were strained almost to breaking. The axles threatened to give way under the sudden jolts that Ayrton, with all his skill, could not prevent. The ladies, however, lost none of their accustomed cheerfulness.

Captain Mangles and the two sailors rode a few hundred paces in advance, to choose practicable passes. It was a difficult and often a perilous task. Several times Wilson was forced to make a way with his hatchet through the midst of dense thickets. Their course deviated in many windings, which impassable obstacles, lofty blocks of granite, deep ravines, and treacherous swamps compelled them to make. At evening they encamped at the foot of the Alps, on the banks of a small stream that flowed along the edge of a plain covered with tall shrubbery, whose bright-red foliage enlivened the banks.

"We shall have difficulty in passing here," said Glenarvan, as he gazed at the chain of mountains, whose outlines were already growing dim in the twilight. "Alps! that is a name suggestive of arduous climbing."

"You will change your opinion, my dear Glenarvan," replied Paganel. "You must not think you are in Switzerland."

"Then these Australian Alps—?" asked Lady Helena.

"Are miniature mountains," continued Paganel. "You will cross them without noticing it."

The next day, in spite of the assurances of the confident geographer, the little party found great difficulty in crossing the mountains. They were forced to advance at a venture, and descend into deep and narrow gorges that, for aught they knew, might end in a wall of rock. Ayrton would doubtless have been eventually nonplused had they not, after an hour's climbing, caught sight of a tavern on one of the paths of the mountain.

"Well!" said Paganel, as they reached the hostelry, "the proprietor of this inn cannot make a great fortune in such a place. Of what use can he be?"

"To give us the information we need for our journey," replied Glenarvan. "Let us go in."

Glenarvan, followed by Ayrton, entered the tavern. The landlord of "Bush Inn" was a coarse man, of forbidding appearance, who had to consider himself as the principal customer for the gin, brandy, and whisky of his tavern, and scarcely ever saw any one but squatters or herdsmen.

He replied in an ill-humored way to the questions that were addressed him; but his answers sufficed to determine Ayrton upon his course. Glenarvan, however, remunerated the tavern-keeper for the little trouble they had given him, and was about to leave the inn, when a placard, affixed to the wall, attracted his attention. It was a notice of the colonial police, detailing the escape of the convicts from Perth, and setting a price upon the head of Ben Joyce—a hundred pounds sterling to any one who should deliver him up.

"Indeed," said Glenarvan, "that is a rascal worth hanging."

"And especially worth taking," replied Ayrton. "A hundred pounds! What a sum! He is not worth it."

"As for the inn-keeper," added Glenarvan, as he left the room, "I scarcely put faith in him, despite his placard."

"Nor I either," said Ayrton.

Glenarvan and the quartermaster rejoined the party, and they all proceeded to where a narrow pass wound across the chain. Here they began the ascent.

But it was an arduous task. More than once the ladies and their companions had to dismount, and it was often necessary to push the wheels of the heavy vehicle at some steep ascent, or to hold it back along the edge of some dangerous precipice. The oxen, as they could not work to advantage at sudden turns, had frequently to be unyoked, and the cart blocked to prevent it from sliding back. Ayrton was repeatedly forced to bring the already exhausted horses to his assistance.

Whether this exertion was too prolonged, or whether from some other cause, one of the horses gave out during the ascent. He fell suddenly, without an instant's warning. It was Mulready's horse; and when the sailor attempted to help him up, he found that he was dead. Ayrton examined the animal carefully, but did not seem to understand the cause of this sudden death.

"The beast must have burst a blood-vessel," said Glenarvan.

"Evidently," replied Ayrton.

"Take my horse, Mulready," added Glenarvan; "I will join Lady Helena in the cart."

Mulready obeyed, and the little party continued their fatiguing ascent, abandoning the body to the crows.

The next day they began the descent, which was much more rapid. During its course a violent hail-storm burst on them, and they were forced to seek a shelter beneath the rocks. Not hailstones, but pieces of ice as large as one's hand, were precipitated from the angry clouds. A sling could not have hurled them with greater force, and several sharp blows warned Paganel and Robert to be on their guard. The cart was pierced through in many places: indeed, few roofs could have resisted the fall of these cutting missiles, some of which froze to the trunks of the trees. It was necessary to wait for the end of this avalanche, for fear of being stoned to death, and it was an hour before the party regained the steep path, still slippery with icy incrustations. At evening the cart, considerably shattered, but still firm on its wooden wheels, descended the last slopes of the Alps, between tall solitary pines, and reached the plains of Gippsland.

All were impatient to gain their destination, the Pacific Ocean, where the Britannia had been wrecked. There only could traces of the shipwrecked seamen be found, and not in these desert regions. Ayrton urged Lord Glenarvan to send an order to the Duncan to repair to the coast, that he might have at his disposal all the aid possible in his search. In his opinion they ought to take advantage of the Lucknow road, which would lead them to Melbourne. Afterwards this might be difficult, for highways leading directly to the capital would be absolutely wanting.

This advice of the quartermaster seemed reasonable. Paganel seconded it. He thought, too, that the yacht would be very useful under the present circumstances, and added that they could no longer communicate with Melbourne after passing the Lucknow road.

Glenarvan was undecided, and perhaps would have sent the order that Ayrton so particularly desired, if the major had not opposed this plan with great energy. He explained that Ayrton's presence was necessary to the expedition; that on approaching the coast the country would be unknown; that, if chance set them on the track of Captain Grant, the quartermaster would be more capable than any one else of following it; in short, that he alone could point out the place where the Britannia was lost.

MacNabb, therefore, advocated their continuing on the journey without change. Captain Mangles was of the same opinion. The young captain observed that his lordship's orders could more easily reach the Duncan if sent from

Twofold Bay, than by dispatching a messenger two hundred miles over a wild country.

The major carried his point, and it was therefore decided that they should proceed to Twofold Bay. MacNabb noticed that Ayrton seemed quite disappointed, but he said nothing, and, according to his custom, kept his thoughts to himself.

Early in the afternoon they passed through a curious forest of ferns. These arborescent plants, in full bloom, measured thirty feet in height. Horses and horsemen could easily pass beneath their drooping branches, and sometimes the rowel of a spur would ring, as it struck against their solid stalks. The coolness of the grove was very grateful to the wearied travelers. Paganel, always demonstrative, gave vent to exclamations of delight that startled flocks of parrots and cockatoos.

All at once his companions saw the geographer reel in the saddle, and fall to the ground like a log. Was it giddiness, or sunstroke, caused by the heat?

They hastened to him.

"Paganel! Paganel! what is the matter?" cried Lord Glenarvan.

"The matter is, my dear friend," replied Paganel, extricating himself from the stirrups, "that I no longer have a horse."

"What! your horse—?"

"Is dead, stricken like Mulready's."

At once Glenarvan, Captain Mangles, and Wilson examined the animal. Paganel was right. His horse had been suddenly stricken dead.

"This is singular," said the captain.

"Very singular indeed," muttered the major.

Glenarvan could not restrain a feeling of uneasiness at this strange occurrence. It was impossible for them to retrace their steps in this desert; while, if an epidemic were to seize all the horses, it would be very difficult to continue the journey.

Before the end of the day his fears seemed to be justified. A third horse, Wilson's, fell dead, and, what was worse, one of the oxen was also stricken. Their means of conveyance now consisted of only three oxen and four horses.

The situation had grown serious. The mounted horsemen could, of course, take turns in traveling on foot. But, if it should be necessary to leave the cart behind, what would become of the ladies? Could they accomplish the one hundred and twenty miles that still separated them from Twofold Bay?

Captain Mangles and Glenarvan anxiously examined the remaining horses: perhaps preventives might be found against new calamities. No sign of disease, however, could be detected. The animals were in perfect health, and bravely endured the hardships of the journey. Glenarvan, therefore, was inclined to think that this mysterious epidemic would have no more victims. This was Ayrton's opinion too, who declared that he could not at all understand the cause of the frightful mortality.

They started again, and the cart served to convey the pedestrians, who rode in it by turns. At evening, after a journey of only ten miles, the signal to halt was given, the encampment arranged, and the night was passed comfortably beneath a large group of arborescent ferns, among whose branches fluttered enormous bats.

The next day they made an excellent beginning, and accomplished fifteen miles. Everything led them to hope that they would encamp that evening on the banks of the Snowy River. Evening came, and a fog, clearly defined against the horizon, marked the course of the long-looked-for stream. A forest of tall trees was seen at a bend in the road, behind a moderate elevation. Ayrton guided his oxen towards the tall trunks dimly discerned in the shadow, and was just passing the boundary of the wood, when the cart sank into the earth to the hubs.

"What is the matter?" asked Glenarvan, when he perceived that the cart had come to a stop.

"We are fast in the mud," replied Ayrton.

He urged his oxen with voice and whip, but they were up to their knees in the mire, and could not stir.

"Let us encamp here," said Captain Mangles.

"That is the best plan," answered Ayrton. "To-morrow, at daybreak, we can see to extricate ourselves."

"Very well: be it so," replied Glenarvan.

Night had set in rapidly, after a short twilight, but the heat had not departed with the sun. The air was heavy with stifling mists. Flashes of lightning, the dazzling forerunners of a coming storm, every now and then illumined the horizon.

The beds were prepared, and the sunken cart was made as comfortable as possible. The sombre arch of the great trees sheltered the tent of the travelers. Provided no rain fell, they would have no reason to complain.

Ayrton succeeded with difficulty in extricating his three oxen from the mud, in which they had by this time sunk to their flanks. The quartermaster picketed them with the four horses, and would allow no one to give them their fodder. This service he performed himself with great exactness, and that evening Glenarvan observed that his care was redoubled, for which he thanked him, as the preservation of the team was of paramount importance.

Meantime, the travelers partook of a hasty supper. Fatigue and heat had driven away hunger, and they needed rest more than nourishment. Lady Helena and Miss Grant, wishing their companions good-night, retired to their accustomed bedroom. As for the men, some crawled under the tent, while others stretched themselves on the thick grass at the foot of the trees.

Gradually each sank into a heavy sleep. The darkness increased beneath the curtain of dense clouds that covered the sky. Not a breath of air was felt. The silence of the night was only interrupted by the occasional howlings of wild animals.

About eleven o'clock, after an uneasy slumber, the major awoke. His half-closed eyes were attracted by a dim light that flickered beneath the great trees. One would have thought it was a whitish sheet glittering like the surface of a lake. MacNabb imagined, at first, that the flames of a conflagration were spreading over the ground.

He rose and walked towards the wood. His surprise was great when he found himself in the presence of a purely natural phenomenon. Before him extended an immense field of mushrooms, which emitted phosphorescent flashes.

The major, who was not selfish, was about to waken Paganel, that the geographer might witness the spectacle with his own eyes, when an unexpected sight stopped him.

The phosphorescent light illumined the wood for the space of half a mile, and MacNabb thought he saw shadows rapidly moving along the edge of the clearing. Did his eyes deceive him? Was he the sport of an illusion?

He crouched down, and, after a long and attentive observation, distinctly perceived several men, who seemed by their movements to be searching the ground for something. What could these men want? He must know, and, without an instant's hesitation or awakening his companions, he crawled along on all-fours, carefully concealing himself in the tall grass.

CHAPTER XL. A STARTLING DISCOVERY.

It was a terrible night. At two o'clock in the morning the rain began to fall in torrents, which continued to pour from the stormy clouds till daylight. The tent was an insufficient shelter. Glenarvan and his companions took refuge in the cart, where they passed the time in conversing upon various subjects. The major, however, whose short absence no one had noticed, contented himself with listening in silence. The fury of the tempest gave them considerable uneasiness, since it might cause an inundation, by which the cart, fast in the mire, would be overwhelmed.

More than once Mulready, Ayrton, and Captain Mangles went to ascertain the height of the rushing waters, and returned drenched from head to foot.

At length day appeared. The rain ceased, but the rays of the sun failed to penetrate the thick veil of clouds. Large pools of muddy, yellowish water covered the ground. A warm vapor issued from the water-soaked earth and saturated the atmosphere with a sickly moisture.

Glenarvan, first of all, turned his attention to the cart. In his eyes, this was their main support. It was imbedded fast in the midst of a deep hollow of sticky clay. The fore wheels were almost entirely out of sight, and the hind ones were buried up to the hubs. It would be a very difficult matter to pull out the heavy vehicle, and would undoubtedly require the united strength of men, oxen, and horses.

"We must make haste," said Captain Mangles. "If this clay dries, the work will be more difficult."

Glenarvan, the two sailors, the captain, and Ayrton then entered the wood, where the animals had passed the night.

It was a tall forest of gloomy gum-trees. Nothing met the eye but dead trunks, widely separated, which had been destitute of their bark for centuries. Not a bird built its nest on these lofty skeletons; not a leaf trembled on the dry branches, that rattled together like a bundle of dry bones. Glenarvan, as he walked on, gazed at the leaden sky, against which the branches of the gum-trees were sharply defined. To Ayrton's great astonishment, there was no trace of the horses and oxen in the place where he had left them. The fettered animals, however, could not have gone far.

They searched for them in the wood, but failed to find them. Ayrton then returned to the banks of the river, which was bordered by magnificent mimosas. He uttered a cry well known to his oxen, but there was no answer. The quartermaster seemed very anxious, and his companions glanced at each other in dismay.

An hour passed in a vain search, and Glenarvan was returning to the cart, which was at least a mile off, when a neigh fell upon his ear, followed almost immediately by a bellow.

"Here they are!" cried Captain Mangles, forcing his way between the tall tufts of the gastrolobium, which were high enough to conceal a whole herd.

Glenarvan, Mulready, and Ayrton rushed after him, and soon shared his astonishment. Two oxen and three horses lay upon the ground, stricken like the others. Their bodies were already cold, and a flock of hungry crows, croaking in the mimosas, waited for their unexpected prey.

Glenarvan and his friends gazed at each other, and Wilson did not suppress an oath that rose to his lips.

"What is the matter, Wilson?" said Lord Glenarvan, scarcely able to control himself. "We can do nothing. Ayrton, bring the ox and horse that are left. They must extricate us from the difficulty."

"If the cart were once out of the mud," replied Captain Mangles, "these two animals, by short journeys, could draw it to the coast. We must, therefore, at all events, release the clumsy vehicle."

"We will try, John," said Glenarvan. "Let us return to camp, for there must be anxiety at our long absence."

Ayrton took charge of the ox, and Mulready of the horse, and the party returned along the winding banks of the river. Half an hour after, Paganel, MacNabb, Lady Helena, and Miss Grant were told the state of affairs.

"By my faith," the major could not help exclaiming, "it is a pity, Ayrton, that you did not shoe all our animals on crossing the Wimerra."

"Why so, sir?" asked Ayrton.

"Because of all our horses only the one you put into the hands of the farrier has escaped the common fate."

"That is true," said Captain Mangles; "and it is a singular coincidence!"

"A coincidence, and nothing more," replied the quartermaster, gazing fixedly at the major.

MacNabb compressed his lips, as if he would repress the words ready to burst from them. Glenarvan, the captain, and Lady Helena seemed to expect that he would finish his sentence; but he remained silent, and walked towards the cart, which Ayrton was now examining.

"What did he mean?" inquired Glenarvan of Captain Mangles.

"I do not know," replied the young captain. "However, the major is not the man to speak without cause."

"No," said Lady Helena; "Major MacNabb must have suspicions of Ayrton."

"What suspicions?" asked Glenarvan. "Does he suppose him capable of killing our horses and oxen? For what purpose, pray? Are not Ayrton's interests identical with ours?"

"You are right, my dear Edward," said Lady Helena. "Besides, the quartermaster has given us, ever since the beginning of the journey, indubitable proofs of his devotion to our comfort."

"True," replied Captain Mangles. "But, then, what does the major's remark mean? I must have an understanding."

"Perhaps he thinks he is in league with these convicts?" remarked Paganel, imprudently.

"What convicts?" inquired Miss Grant.

"Monsieur Paganel is mistaken," said Captain Mangles quickly: "he knows that there are no convicts in the province of Victoria."

"Yes, yes, that is so," eagerly replied Paganel, who would fain have retracted his words. "What could I have been thinking of? Convicts? Who ever heard of convicts in Australia? Moreover, as soon as they land, they make very honest people. The climate, you know, Miss Mary, the moral effect of the climate—"

In his desire to correct his blunder, the poor geographer became hopelessly involved. Lady Helena looked at him, wondering what had deprived him of his usual coolness; but, not wishing to embarrass him further, she retired with Mary to the tent, where Mr. Olbinett was engaged in preparing breakfast.

"I deserve to be transported myself," said Paganel piteously.

"I think so," replied Glenarvan.

Ayrton and the two sailors were still trying to extricate the cart. The ox and the horse, yoked side by side, were pulling with all their strength; the traces were stretched almost to breaking, and the bows threatened to give way to the strain. Wilson and Mulready pushed at the wheels, while the quartermaster, with voice and whip, urged on the ill-matched team. But the heavy vehicle did not stir. The clay, now dry, held it as if it had been cemented.

Captain Mangles wetted the clay to make it yield, but to no purpose: the cart was immovable. Unless the vehicle was taken to pieces, they must give up the idea of getting it out of the quagmire. As tools were wanting, of course they could not undertake such a task. Ayrton, however, who seemed determined to overcome the difficulty at any cost, was about to renew his exertions, when Lord Glenarvan stopped him.

"Enough, Ayrton! enough!" said he. "We must be careful of the ox and horse that remain. If we are to continue our journey on foot, one can carry the two ladies and the other the provisions. They may do us good service yet."

"Very well, my lord," replied the quartermaster, unyoking his exhausted animals.

"Now, my friends," added Glenarvan, "let us return to camp, deliberate, consider our situation, know what our chances are, and come to a resolution."

A few minutes after, the travelers were indemnifying themselves for their sleeplessness the past night by a good breakfast, and the discussion of their affairs began.

The first question was to determine the exact position of the encampment. Paganel was charged with this duty, and fulfilled it with his customary precision.

"How far are we from Twofold Bay?" asked Glenarvan.

"Seventy-five miles," replied Paganel.

"And Melbourne is—?"

"Two hundred miles distant, at least."

"Very well. Our position being determined," continued Glenarvan, "what is it best to do?"

The answer was unanimous,—make for the coast without delay. Lady Helena and Mary Grant engaged to travel fifteen miles a day. The courageous women did not shrink from traversing the entire distance on foot, if necessary.

"But are we certain to find at the bay the resources that we need?" asked Glenarvan.

"Without doubt," replied Paganel. "Eden is not a new municipality; and its harbor must have frequent communication with Melbourne. I even believe that thirty-five miles from here, at the parish of Delegete, we can obtain provisions and the means of conveyance."

"And the Duncan?" asked Ayrton. "Do you not think it advisable to order her to the bay?"

"What say you, captain?" said Glenarvan.

"I do not think that there is any necessity for such a proceeding," replied the young captain, after reflection. "There will be plenty of time to send your orders to Tom Austin and summon him to the coast."

"That is quite true," added Paganel.

"Besides," continued Captain Mangles, "in four or five days we shall be at Eden."

"Four or five days!" interposed Ayrton, shaking his head; "say fifteen or twenty, captain, if you do not wish to regret your error hereafter."

"Fifteen or twenty days to make seventy-five miles!" exclaimed Glenarvan.

"At least, my lord. You will have to cross the most difficult portion of Victoria,—plains covered with underbrush, without any cleared roads, where it has been impossible to establish stations. You will have to travel with the hatchet or the torch in your hand; and, believe me, you will not advance rapidly."

Ayrton's tone was that of a man who is thoroughly acquainted with his subject. Paganel, towards whom questioning glances were turned, nodded approvingly at the words of the quartermaster.

"I acknowledge the difficulties," said Captain Mangles, at length. "Well, in fifteen days, my lord, you can send your orders to the Duncan."

"I may add," resumed Ayrton, "that the principal obstacles do not proceed from the roughness of the journey. We must cross the Snowy, and, very probably, have to wait for the subsidence of the waters."

"Wait!" cried the captain. "Can we not find a ford?"

"I think not," replied Ayrton. "This morning I searched in vain for a practicable one. It is unusual to find a river so much swollen at this season; it is a fatality against which I am powerless."

"This Snowy River is broad, then?" remarked Lady Glenarvan.

"Broad and deep, madam," answered Ayrton; "a mile in breadth, with a strong current. A good swimmer could not cross it without danger."

"Well, then, let us build a boat!" cried Robert, who was never at fault for a plan. "We can cut down a tree, hollow it out, embark, and the thing is done."

"Good for the son of Captain Grant!" replied Paganel.

"The boy is right," continued Captain Mangles. "We shall be forced to this. I therefore think it useless to waste our time in further discussions."

"What do you think, Ayrton?" asked Glenarvan.

"I think, my lord, that if no assistance comes, in a month we shall still be detained on the banks of the Snowy."

"But have you a better plan?" inquired Captain Mangles, somewhat impatiently.

"Yes; let the Duncan leave Melbourne, and sail to the eastern coast."

"How can her presence in the bay assist us to arrive there?"

Ayrton meditated for a few moments, and then said, evasively:

"I do not wish to obtrude my opinion. What I do is for the interest of all, and I am disposed to start as soon as your lordship gives the signal for departure."

Then he folded his arms.

"That is no answer, Ayrton," continued Glenarvan. "Tell us your plan, and we will discuss it. What do you propose?"

In a calm and confident tone the quartermaster thereupon expressed himself as follows:

"I propose that we do not venture beyond the Snowy in our present destitute condition. We must wait for assistance in this very place, and this assistance can come only from the Duncan. Let us encamp here where provisions are not wanting, while one of us carries to Tom Austin the order to repair to Twofold Bay."

This unexpected proposal was received with a murmur of astonishment, and Captain Mangles took no pains to conceal his aversion.

"In the mean time," continued Ayrton, "either the waters of the Snowy will have subsided, which will enable us to find a practicable ford, or we shall have to resort to a boat, and shall have time to construct it. This, my lord, is the plan which I submit to your approval."

"Very well, Ayrton," replied Glenarvan; "your idea deserves to be seriously considered. Its greatest objection is the delay it will cause; but it spares us severe hardships, and perhaps real dangers. What do you think, friends?"

"Let us hear your advice, major," said Lady Helena. "During the whole discussion you have contented yourself with listening simply."

"Since you ask my opinion," answered the major, "I will give it to you very frankly. Ayrton seems to me to have spoken like a wise and prudent man, and I advocate his proposition."

This answer was rather unexpected; for hitherto MacNabb had always opposed Ayrton's ideas on this subject. Ayrton, too, was surprised, and cast a quick glance at the major. Paganel, Lady Helena, and the sailors had been favorably disposed to the quartermaster's project, and no longer hesitated after MacNabb's declaration. Glenarvan, therefore, announced that Ayrton's plan was adopted.

"And now, captain," added he, "do you not think that prudence dictates this course, and that we should encamp on the banks of the river while waiting for the means of conveyance?"

"Yes," replied Captain Mangles, "if the messenger succeeds in crossing the Snowy, which we cannot cross ourselves."

All looked at the quartermaster, who smiled with the air of a man who knows perfectly well what he is about to do.

"The messenger will not cross the river," said he.

"Ah!" cried Captain Mangles.

"He will strike the Lucknow road, which will take him direct to Melbourne."

"Two hundred miles on foot!" exclaimed the captain.

"On horseback," continued Ayrton. "There is one good horse left. It will be a journey of but four days. Add two days for the Duncan to reach the bay, twenty-four hours for the return to the encampment, and in a week the messenger will be back again with the crew."

The major again nodded approvingly at these words, to the great astonishment of Captain Mangles. But the quartermaster's proposition had gained all the votes, and the only question was how to execute this apparently well-conceived plan.

"Now, my friends," said Glenarvan, "it remains only to choose our messenger. He will have a difficult and dangerous mission; that is certain. Who is willing to devote himself for his companions, and carry our instructions to Melbourne?"

Wilson, Mulready, Captain Mangles, Paganel, and Robert offered themselves immediately. The captain particularly insisted that this mission should be confided to him; but Ayrton, who had not yet finished, resumed the conversation, and said:

"If it please your lordship, I will go. I am acquainted with the country, and have often crossed more difficult regions. I can extricate myself where another would fail. I therefore claim, for the common welfare, the right to go to Melbourne. One word will place me on a good footing with your mate, and in six days I engage to bring the Duncan to Twofold Bay."

"Well said!" replied Glenarvan. "You are a brave and intelligent man, Ayrton, and will succeed."

The quartermaster was evidently more capable than any one else of fulfilling this difficult mission. Captain Mangles raised one final objection, that Ayrton's presence was necessary to enable them to find traces of the Brittania or Captain Grant; but the major observed that they should remain encamped on the banks of the Snowy till the messenger's return, that it was not proposed to resume the search without him, and that consequently his absence could be in no way prejudicial to their interests.

"Well then, Ayrton, start," said Glenarvan. "Make haste, and return to the encampment by way of Eden."

A gleam of satisfaction seemed to light up the eyes of the quartermaster. He turned his head to one side, though not so quickly but that Captain Mangles had intercepted his glance, and instinctively felt his suspicions increased.

The quartermaster made his preparations for departure, aided by the two sailors, one of whom attended to his horse, and the other to his provisions. Meantime Glenarvan wrote the letter designed for Tom Austin.

He ordered the mate of the Duncan to repair without delay to Twofold Bay, and recommended the quartermaster to him as a man in whom he could place entire confidence. As soon as he arrived at the bay, he was to send a detachment of sailors under the command of Ayrton.

He had just reached this part of his letter, when the major, who had been looking over his shoulder, asked him, in a singular tone, how he wrote the word Ayrton.

"As it is pronounced," replied Glenarvan.

"That is a mistake," said the major coolly. "It is pronounced Ayrton, but it is written 'Ben Joyce'!"

CHAPTER XLI. THE PLOT UNVEILED.

The sound of the name of Ben Joyce fell upon the party like a thunderbolt. Ayrton suddenly sprang to his feet. In his hand was a revolver. A report was heard; and Glenarvan fell, struck by a bullet.

Before Captain Mangles and the sailors recovered from the surprise into which this unexpected turn of affairs had thrown them, the audacious convict had escaped, and joined his band, scattered along the edge of the wood of gum-trees.

The tent did not offer a sufficient shelter against the bullets, and it was clearly necessary to beat a retreat. Glenarvan, who was but slightly injured, had risen.

"To the cart! to the cart!" cried Captain Mangles, as he hurried on Lady Helena and Mary Grant, who were soon in safety behind its stout sides.

The captain, the major, Paganel, and the sailors then seized their rifles, and stood ready to repel the convicts. Glenarvan and Robert had joined the ladies, while Olbinett hastened to the common defence.

These events had transpired with the rapidity of lightning. Captain Mangles attentively watched the edge of the wood; but the reports suddenly ceased on the arrival of Ben Joyce, and a profound silence succeeded the noisy fusillade. A few wreaths of white smoke were still curling up between the branches of the gum-trees, but the tall tufts of gastrolobium were motionless and all signs of attack had disappeared.

The major and Captain Mangles extended their examinations as far as the great trees. The place was abandoned. Numerous footprints were seen, and a few half-burnt cartridges smoked on the ground. The major, like a prudent man, extinguished them, for a spark was enough to kindle a formidable conflagration in this forest of dry trees.

"The convicts have disappeared," said Captain Mangles.

"Yes," replied the major; "and this disappearance alarms me. I should prefer to meet them face to face. It is better to encounter a tiger in the open plain than a serpent in the grass. Let us search these bushes around the cart."

The major and captain scoured the surrounding country. But from the edge of the wood to the banks of the Snowy they did not meet with a single convict. Ben Joyce's band seemed to have flown away, like a flock of mischievous birds. This disappearance was too strange to inspire a perfect security. They therefore resolved to keep on the watch. The cart, which was a really immovable fortress, became the centre of the encampment, and two men kept guard, relieving each other every hour.

Lady Helena and Mary Grant's first care had been to dress Glenarvan's wound. At the very moment that her husband fell, from Ben Joyce's bullet, in her terror she had rushed towards him. Then, controlling her emotion, this courageous woman had assisted Glenarvan to the cart. Here the shoulder of the wounded man was laid bare, and the major perceived that the ball had lacerated the flesh, causing no other injury. Neither bones nor large muscles seemed affected. The wound bled considerably, but Glenarvan, by moving the fingers of his hand and fore-arm, encouraged his friends to expect a favorable result. When his wound was dressed, he no longer desired any attention, and explanations followed. The travelers, except Wilson and Mulready, who were keeping guard outside, had taken seats as well as possible in the cart, and the major was requested to speak.

Before beginning his story, he informed Lady Helena of the escape of a band of convicts from Perth, their appearance in the province of Victoria, and their complicity in the railway disaster. He gave her the number of the *Australian and New Zealand Gazette* purchased at Seymour, and added that the police had set a price on the head of Ben Joyce, a formidable bandit, whom eighteen months of crime had given a wide-spread notoriety.

But how had MacNabb recognized this Ben Joyce in the quartermaster Ayrton? Here was the mystery that all wished to solve; and the major explained.

Since the day of his meeting with Ayrton he had suspected him. Two or three almost insignificant circumstances, a glance exchanged between the quartermaster and the farrier at Wimerra River, Ayrton's hesitation to pass through the towns and villages, his strong wish to order the Duncan to the coast, the strange death of the animals confided to his care, and, finally, a want of frankness in his actions,—all these facts, gradually noticed, had roused the major's suspicions.

However, he could form no direct accusation until the events that had transpired the preceding night. Gliding between the tall clumps of shrubbery, as was related in the previous chapter, he approached near the suspicious shadows that had attracted his attention half a mile from the encampment. The phosphorescent plants cast their pale rays through the darkness. Three men were examining some tracks on the ground, and among them he recognized the farrier of Black Point Station.

"Here they are," said one.

"Yes," replied another, "here is the trefoil of the hoofs again."

"It has been like this since leaving the Wimerra."

"All the horses are dead."

"The poison is not far away."

"There is enough here to settle an entire troop of cavalry. This gastrolobium is a useful plant."

"Then they were silent," added MacNabb, "and departed. I wanted to know more: I followed them. The conversation soon began again. 'A cunning man, this Ben Joyce,' said the farrier; 'a famous quartermaster, with his invented shipwreck. If his plan succeeds, it will be a stroke of fortune. Devilish Ayrton! Call him Ben Joyce, for he has well earned his name.' These rascals then left the wood of gum-trees. I knew what I wished, and returned to the encampment with the certainty that all the convicts in Australia are not reformed, in spite of Paganel's arguments."

"Then," said Glenarvan, whose face was pale with anger, "Ayrton has brought us here to rob and assassinate us?"

"Yes," replied the major.

"And, since leaving the Wimerra, his band has followed and watched us, waiting for a favorable opportunity?"

"Yes."

"But this wretch is not, then, a sailor of the Britannia? He has stolen his name and contract?"

All eyes were turned towards MacNabb, who must have considered this matter.

"These," replied he, in his calm voice, "are the proofs that can be derived from this obscure state of affairs. In my opinion this man's real name is Ayrton. Ben Joyce is his fighting title. It is certain that he knows Harry Grant, and has been quartermaster on board the Britannia. These facts, proved already by the precise details given by Ayrton, are still further corroborated by the conversation of the convicts that I have related. Let us not, therefore, be led astray by vain conjectures, but only be certain that Ayrton is Ben Joyce, a sailor of the Britannia, now chief of a band of convicts."

The major's explanation was accepted as conclusive.

"Now," replied Glenarvan, "will you tell me how and why Harry Grant's quartermaster is in Australia?"

"How, I do not know," said MacNabb; "and the police declare they know no more than I on the subject. Why, it is also impossible for me to say. Here is a mystery that the future will explain."

"The police do not even know the identity of Ayrton and Ben Joyce," said Captain Mangles.

"You are right, John," replied the major; "and such information would be likely to facilitate their search."

"This unfortunate, then," remarked Lady Helena, "intruded into O'Moore's farm with a criminal intention?"

"There is no doubt of it," continued MacNabb. "He was meditating some hostile attack upon the Irishman, when a better opportunity was offered. Chance threw us in his way. He heard Glenarvan's story of the shipwreck, and, like a bold man, he promptly decided to take part in the expedition. At the Wimerra he communicated with one of his friends, the farrier of Black Point, and thus left distinguishable traces of our course. His band followed us. A poisonous plant enabled him to gradually kill our oxen and horses. Then, at the proper moment, he entangled us in the marshes of the Snowy, and surrendered us to the convicts he commanded."

Everything possible had been said concerning Ben Joyce. His past had just been reviewed by the major, and the wretch appeared as he was,—a bold and formidable criminal. His intentions had been clearly proved, and required, on the part of Glenarvan, extreme vigilance. Fortunately, there was less to fear from the detected bandit than the secret traitor.

But one serious fact appeared from this explanation. No one had yet thought of it; only Mary Grant, disregarding the past, looked forward to the future. Captain Mangles first saw her pale and disconsolate. He understood what was passing in her mind.

"Miss Mary!" cried he, "you are weeping!"

"What is the matter, my child?" asked Lady Helena.

"My father, madam, my father!" replied the young girl.

She could not continue. But a sudden revelation dawned on the mind of each. They comprehended Mary's grief, why the tears flowed from her eyes, why the name of her father rose to her lips.

The discovery of Ayrton's treachery destroyed all hope. The convict, to entice Glenarvan on, had invented a shipwreck. In their conversation, overheard by MacNabb, his accomplices had clearly confessed it. The Britannia had never been wrecked on the reefs of Twofold Bay! Harry Grant had never set foot on the Australian continent!

For the second time an erroneous interpretation of the document had set the searchers of the Britannia on a false trail. All, in the face of this situation and the grief of the two children, preserved a mournful silence. Who then could have found words of hope? Robert wept in his sister's arms. Paganel murmured, in a voice of despair,—

"Ah, unlucky document! You can boast of having sorely puzzled the brains of a dozen brave people!"

And the worthy geographer was fairly furious against himself, and frantically beat his forehead.

In the mean time Glenarvan had joined Mulready and Wilson, who were on guard without. A deep silence reigned on the plain lying between the wood and the river. Heavy clouds covered the vault of the sky. In this deadened and torpid atmosphere the least sound would have been clearly transmitted; but nothing was heard. Ben Joyce and his band must have fled to a considerable distance; for flocks of birds that sported on the low branches of the trees, several kangaroos peacefully browsing on the young shoots, and a pair of cassowaries, whose unsuspecting heads were thrust between the tall bushes, proved that the presence of man did not disturb these peaceful solitudes.

"You have not seen nor heard anything for an hour?" inquired Glenarvan of the two sailors.

"Nothing, my lord," replied Wilson. "The convicts must be several miles away."

"They cannot have been in sufficient force to attack us," added Mulready. "This Ben Joyce probably intended to recruit some bandits, like himself, among the bushrangers that wander at the foot of the Alps."

"Very likely, Mulready," replied Glenarvan. "These rascals are cowards. They know we are well armed, and are perhaps waiting for darkness to commence their attack. We must redouble our vigilance at nightfall. If we could only leave this marshy plain and pursue our journey towards the coast! But the swollen waters of the river bar our progress. I would pay its weight in gold for a raft that would transport us to the other side!"

"Why," said Wilson, "does not your lordship give us the order to construct this raft? There is plenty of wood."

"No, Wilson," answered Glenarvan; "this Snowy is not a river, it is an impassable torrent."

At this moment Captain Mangles, the major, and Paganel joined Glenarvan. They had been to examine the Snowy. The waters, swollen by the recent rains, had risen a foot above low-water mark, and formed an impetuous current. It was impossible to venture upon this roaring deluge, these rushing floods, broken into a thousand eddies by the depressions of the river-bed. Captain Mangles declared that the passage was impracticable.

"But," added he, "we ought not to remain here without making any attempt. What we wished to do before Ayrton's treason is still more necessary now."

"What do you say, captain?" asked Glenarvan.

"I say that assistance is needed; and since we cannot go to Twofold Bay, we must go to Melbourne. One horse is left. Let your lordship give him to me, and I will go."

"But it is a perilous venture, John," said Glenarvan. "Aside from the dangers of this journey of two hundred miles across an unknown country, all the roads may be guarded by Ben Joyce's accomplices."

"I know it, my lord; but I know, too, that our situation cannot be prolonged. Ayrton only asked eight days' absence to bring back the crew of the Duncan. But I will return in six days to the banks of the Snowy. What are your lordship's orders?"

"Before Glenarvan speaks," said Paganel, "I must make a remark. It is well that one of us should go to Melbourne, but not that these dangers should be incurred by Captain Mangles. He is the captain of the Duncan, and must not, therefore, expose himself. Allow me to go in his place."

"Well said," replied the major; "but why should it be you, Paganel?"

"Are we not here?" cried Wilson and Mulready.

"And do you believe," continued MacNabb, "that I am afraid to make a journey of two hundred miles on horseback?"

"My friends," said Glenarvan, "if one of us is to go to Melbourne, let fate decide. Paganel, write our names—"

"Not yours at least, my lord," insisted Captain Mangles.

"And why?" asked Glenarvan.

"Separate you from Lady Helena, when your wound is not yet healed?"

"Glenarvan," interposed Paganel, "you cannot leave the encampment."

"No," resumed the major; "your place is here. Edward, you must not go."

"There are dangers to incur," replied Glenarvan; "and I will not leave my part to others. Write, Paganel; let my name be mingled with those of my companions, and Heaven grant that it may be the first drawn."

All yielded to this wish; and Glenarvan's name was added to the others. They then proceeded to draw, and the lot fell upon Mulready. The brave sailor uttered a cry of joy.

"My lord, I am ready to go," said he.

Glenarvan clasped his hand, and then turned towards the cart, leaving the major and Captain Mangles to guard the encampment. Lady Helena was at once informed of the decision taken to send a messenger to Melbourne, and of the result of the drawing by lot. She spoke words to Mulready that went to the heart of that noble sailor. They knew that he was brave, intelligent, hardy, and persevering. The lot could not have fallen better.

It was decided that Mulready should depart at eight o'clock, after the short twilight. Wilson charged himself with getting the horse ready. He took the precaution to change the tell-tale shoe that he wore on his left foot, and to replace it by one belonging to the horses that had died in the night. The convicts could not now track Mulready, or follow him, unless mounted.

While Wilson was occupied with these arrangements, Glenarvan was preparing the letter designed for Tom Austin; but his wounded arm disabled him, and he asked Paganel to write for him. The geographer, who seemed absorbed in one idea, was oblivious to what was passing around him. It must be confessed that Paganel, in all this succession of sad misfortunes, thought only of his false interpretation of the document. He turned the words about in every way to draw from them a new meaning, and remained wrapt in these meditations. Thus he did not hear Glenarvan's request, and the latter was forced to repeat it.

"Very well," replied Paganel; "I am ready."

So saying, he mechanically produced his note-book. He tore out a blank page, and then, with his pencil in his hand, made ready to write. Glenarvan began to dictate the following instructions: "Order for Tom Austin to put to sea, and bring the Duncan—"

Paganel had just finished this last word when his eyes fell upon the number of the *Australian and New Zealand Gazette* that lay upon the ground. The paper, being folded, only allowed him to see the two last syllables of its title. His pencil stopped, and he seemed to completely forget Glenarvan and his letter.

"Well, Paganel?" said Glenarvan.

"Ah!" continued the geographer, uttering a cry.

"What is the matter?" asked the major.

"Nothing! nothing!" replied Paganel. Then, in a lower tone, he repeated: "Aland! aland! aland!"

He had risen; he had seized the paper. He shook it, seeking to repress words ready to escape his lips. Lady Helena, Mary, Robert, and Glenarvan gazed at him without understanding this inexplicable agitation. Paganel was like a man whom a sudden frenzy has seized. But this state of nervous excitation did not last. He gradually grew calm. The joy that gleamed in his eyes died away, and, resuming his place, he said, in a quiet tone:

"When you wish, my lord, I am at your disposal."

Glenarvan continued the dictation of his letter, which was distinctly worded as follows: "Order for Tom Austin to put to sea, and bring the Duncan to the eastern coast of Australia."

"Australia?" cried Paganel. "Ah, yes, Australia!"

The letter was now finished, and presented to Glenarvan for his signature, who, although affected by his recent wound, acquitted himself as well as possible of this formality. The note was then folded and sealed, while Paganel, with a hand that still trembled from excitement, wrote the following address:

"Tom Austin, Mate of the Yacht Duncan, Melbourne."

Thereupon he left the cart, gesticulating, and repeating these incomprehensible words: "Aland! aland! Zealand!"

CHAPTER XLII. FOUR DAYS OF ANGUISH.

The rest of the day passed without any other incident. Everything was ready for the departure of Mulready, who was happy to give his master this proof of his devotion.

Paganel had regained his coolness and accustomed manners. His look still indicated an uneasy state of mind, but he appeared decided to keep his secret. He had doubtless strong reasons for acting thus, for the major overheard him repeating these words, like a man who is struggling with himself:

"No, no! they would not believe me! And, besides what use is it? It is too late!"

This resolution taken, he occupied himself with giving Mulready the necessary directions for reaching Melbourne, and, with the map before him, marked out his course. All the trails of the prairie converged towards the Lucknow road, which, after extending straight southward to the coast, suddenly turned in the direction towards Melbourne. It was simply necessary to follow this, and not attempt to cross the unknown country. Mulready could not, therefore, go astray. As for dangers, they lay only a few miles beyond the encampment, where Ben Joyce and his band were probably lying in wait. This point once passed, Mulready was sure he could easily distance the convicts and accomplish his important mission.

At six o'clock supper was eaten in common. A heavy rain was falling. The tent no longer afforded sufficient shelter, and each had taken refuge in the cart, which was a safe retreat. The sticky clay held it in its place as firm as a fort on its foundations. The fire-arms consisted of seven rifles and seven revolvers, and thus enabled them to sustain a long siege, for neither ammunition nor provisions were wanting. In six days the Duncan would anchor in Twofold Bay. Twenty-four hours after, her crew would reach the opposite bank of the river; and, if the passage was not then practicable, at least the convicts would be compelled to retreat before superior forces. But, first of all, it was necessary that Mulready should succeed in his enterprise.

At eight o'clock the darkness became intense. It was the time to start. The horse was brought out. His feet had been muffled; as an additional precaution, and made no sound. The animal seemed fatigued, but upon his surefootedness and endurance depended the safety of all. The major advised the sailor to spare his beast as soon as he was out of reach of the convicts. It was better to lose half a day and reach his destination safely. Captain Mangles gave him a revolver, which he had loaded with the greatest care. Mulready mounted.

"Here is the letter which you are to take to Tom Austin," said Glenarvan. "Let him not lose an hour, but start for Twofold Bay; and, if he does not find us there, if we have not crossed the river, let him come to us without delay. Now go, my brave sailor, and may God guide you!"

Glenarvan, Lady Helena, Mary Grant, all clasped Mulready's hand. This departure on a dark and stormy night, over a road beset with dangers, across the unknown stretches of a desert, would have appalled a heart less courageous than that of the sailor.

"Adieu, my lord," said he, in a calm voice, and soon disappeared by a path along the edge of the wood.

At that moment the tempest redoubled its violence. The lofty branches of the trees shook dismally in the darkness. You could hear the fall of the dry twigs on the drenched earth. More than one giant tree, whose sap was gone, but which had stood till then, fell during this terrible hurricane. The wind roared amid the cracking of the trees and mingled its mournful sounds with the rushing of the river. The heavy clouds that chased across the sky poured forth masses of mist, while a dismal darkness increased still more the horrors of the night.

The travelers, after Mulready's departure, ensconced themselves in the cart. Lady Helena, Mary Grant, Glenarvan, and Paganel occupied the front compartment, which had been made water-tight. In the rear part Olbinett, Wilson, and Robert had found a sufficient shelter, while the major and Captain Mangles were on guard without. This precaution was necessary, for an attack by the convicts was easy and possible.

These two faithful guardians, therefore, took turns and philosophically received the blasts that blew sharply in their faces. They strove to pierce with their eyes the shades so favorable for an ambuscade, for the ear could detect nothing amid the din of the storm, the roaring of the wind, the rattling of the branches, the fall of trees, and the rushing of the impetuous waters.

In the mean time there were several lulls in the fury of the tempest, the wind ceasing as if to take breath. The river only moaned adown the motionless reeds and the black curtain of the gum-trees, and the silence seemed more profound during these momentary rests. The major and Captain Mangles now listened attentively. During one of these intervals a sharp whistle reached their ears.

The captain hastened to the major. "Did you hear anything?" asked he.

"Yes," replied MacNabb. "Was it a man or an animal?"

"A man," said the captain.

They both listened again. The mysterious whistle was suddenly repeated, and something like a report followed it, but almost inaudibly, for the storm just then broke forth with renewed violence. They could not hear themselves talk, and took their stations to leeward of the cart.

At this moment the leathern curtains were raised, and Glenarvan joined his two companions. He likewise had heard the suspicious whistle, and the report.

"From what direction?" he asked.

"Yonder," said the captain, pointing to the dark line, towards which Mulready had gone.

"How far?"

"The wind carried it," was the reply. "It must be three miles distant at least."

"Let us go!" said Glenarvan, throwing his rifle over his shoulder.

"No," interposed the major; "it is a decoy to entice us away from the cart."

"But if Mulready has fallen beneath the shots of these wretches!" continued Glenarvan, seizing MacNabb's hand.

"We shall know to-morrow," replied the latter, firmly determined to prevent Glenarvan from committing a useless imprudence.

"You cannot leave the encampment, my lord," said Captain Mangles; "I will go alone."

"No!" cried MacNabb, with energy. "Will you have us, then, perish singly, diminish our numbers, and be left to the mercy of these criminals? If Mulready has been their victim, it is a calamity that we must not repeat a second time. He has gone according to lot. If the lot had chosen me, I should have gone like him, but should neither have asked nor expected any assistance."

In restraining Glenarvan and Captain Mangles the major was right from every point of view. To attempt to reach the sailor, to go on such a dark night to meet the convicts, ambuscaded in some coppice, was useless madness. Glenarvan's little party did not number enough men to sacrifice any more.

However, Glenarvan seemed unwilling to yield to these reasons. His hand played nervously with his rifle. He walked to and fro around the cart; he listened to the least sound; he strove to pierce the dismal obscurity. The thought that one of his friends was mortally wounded, helplessly abandoned, calling in vain upon those for whose sake he had sacrificed himself, tortured him. MacNabb feared that he should not succeed in restraining him, that Glenarvan, carried away by his feelings, would cast himself into the power of Ben Joyce.

"Edward," said he, "be calm; listen to a friend; think of Lady Helena, Mary Grant, all who remain! Besides, where will you go? Where find Mulready? He was attacked two miles distant at least. On what road? What path take?"

At this very moment, as if in answer to the major, a cry of distress was heard.

"Listen!" said Glenarvan.

The cry came from the very direction whence the report had sounded, but less than a quarter of a mile distant. Glenarvan, pushing back MacNabb, was advancing along the path, when, not far from the cart, these words were uttered:

"Help! help!"

It was a plaintive and despairing voice. Captain Mangles and the major rushed towards it. In a few moments they perceived, on the edge of the coppice, a human form that was dragging itself along and groaning piteously. It was Mulready, wounded and half dead. When his companions raised him, they felt their hands dabbling in blood. The rain now increased, and the wind howled through the branches of the dead trees. In the midst of these terrific gusts, Glenarvan, the major, and the captain bore the body of Mulready.

On arriving at the cart, Paganel, Robert, Wilson, and Olbinett came out, and Lady Helena gave up her room to the poor sailor. The major took off Mulready's vest, wet with blood and rain. He discovered the wound. It was a poniard stab, which the unfortunate had received in his right side.

MacNabb dressed it skillfully. Whether the weapon had reached the vital parts, he could not say. A stream of bright-red blood spurted forth, while the paleness and the swoon of the wounded man proved that he had been seriously injured. The major accordingly placed upon the opening of the wound, after first washing it with fresh water, a thick wad of tinder, and then a few layers of lint, confined by a bandage, and thus succeeded in stopping the hemorrhage. The patient was then laid on his side, his head and breast raised, and Lady Helena gave him a refreshing draught.

At the end of a quarter of an hour, the wounded man, who had been motionless till then, made a movement. His eyes half opened, his lips murmured disconnected words, and the major, putting down his ear, heard him say:

"My lord—the letter—Ben Joyce—"

The major repeated these words, and glanced at his companions. What did Mulready mean? Ben Joyce had attacked the sailor, but why? Was it not simply for the purpose of preventing him from reaching the Duncan? This letter— Glenarvan examined the sailor's pockets. The letter addressed to Tom Austin was gone.

The night passed in anxiety and anguish. They feared every moment that the wounded man would die. A burning fever consumed him. Lady Helena and Mary Grant, as though his sisters, did not leave him; never was patient better nursed, or by more tender hands.

Day appeared. The rain had ceased. Heavy clouds still rolled along the vault of the sky, and the earth was strewn with the fragments of branches. The clay, soaked by floods of water, had yielded; and the sides of the cart became unsteady, but sank no deeper.

Captain Mangles, Paganel, and Glenarvan took a tour of exploration around the camp. They traversed the path still marked with blood, but found no trace of Ben Joyce or his band. They went to the place where the attack had been made. Here two corpses lay on the ground, shot by Mulready. One was the farrier of Black Point. His face, which had mortified, was a horrible sight.

Glenarvan did not pursue his investigations farther, prudence forbidding. He therefore returned to the cart, much alarmed by the seriousness of the situation.

"We cannot think of sending another messenger to Melbourne," said he.

"But we must," replied Captain Mangles; "and I will make the attempt, since my sailor has failed."

"No, John. You have not even a horse to carry you these two hundred miles."

Indeed, Mulready's horse, the only one that remained, had not reappeared. Had he fallen beneath the shots of the murderers? Was he running wild over the desert? Had the convicts captured him?

"Whatever happens," continued Glenarvan, "we will separate no more. Let us wait eight or fifteen days, till the waters of the river resume their natural level. We will then reach Twofold Bay by short journeys, and from there send to the Duncan by a surer way the order to sail for the coast."

"This is the only feasible plan," replied Paganel.

"Well, then, my friends," resumed Glenarvan, "no more separation! A man risks too much to venture alone across this desert, infested with bandits. And now may God save our poor sailor and protect ourselves!"

Glenarvan was right in both resolves, first to forbid any single attempt to cross the plains, and next to wait patiently on the banks of the river for a practicable passage. Scarcely thirty-five miles separated them from Delegete, the first frontier town of New South Wales, where they would find means of reaching Twofold Bay. From this point he could telegraph his orders to the Duncan.

These measures were wise, but they had been adopted rather tardily. If they had not sent Mulready with the letter, what misfortunes would have been avoided, not to speak of the attack upon the sailor!

On arriving at the camp, Glenarvan found his companions less anxious; they seemed to have regained hope.

"He is better!" cried Robert, running to meet him.

"Mulready?"

"Yes, Edward," replied Lady Helena. "A reaction has taken place. The major is more encouraged. Our sailor will live."

"Where is MacNabb?" asked Glenarvan.

"With him. Mulready wished to speak with him. We must not disturb them."

Indeed, within an hour the wounded man had rallied from his swoon, and the fever had diminished. But the sailor's first care, on recovering memory and speech was to ask for Lord Glenarvan, or, in his absence, the major MacNabb, seeing him so feeble, would have forbidden all conversation; but Mulready insisted with such energy that he was forced to yield. The interview had already lasted some time, and they were only waiting for the major's report.

Soon the curtains of the cart moved, and he appeared. He joined his friends at the foot of a gum-tree. His face, usually so calm, betokened a serious anxiety. When his eyes encountered Lady Helena and the young girl, they expressed a deep sadness. Glenarvan questioned him, and learned what the sailor had related.

On leaving the encampment, Mulready had followed one of the paths indicated by Paganel. He hastened, as much at least as the darkness of the night permitted him. According to his estimate, he had traveled a distance of about two miles, when several men—five, he thought—sprang to his horse's head. The animal reared. Mulready seized his revolver and fired. He thought that two of his assailants fell. By the flash of the report, he recognized Ben Joyce, but that was all. He had not time to fully discharge his weapon. A violent blow was struck upon his right side, which brought him to the ground. However, he had not yet lost consciousness. The assassins believed him dead. He felt them search him. Then a conversation ensued. "I have the letter," said one of them. "Give it to me," replied Ben Joyce; "and now the Duncan is ours!"

At this point in the story Glenarvan could not restrain a cry.

MacNabb continued:

"'Now, you others,' said Ben Joyce, 'catch the horse. In two days I shall be on board the Duncan, and in six at Twofold Bay. There is the place of meeting. The lord's party will be still fast in the marshes of the Snowy. Cross the river at Kemple Pier bridge, go to the coast, and wait for me. I will find means to bring you on board. With the crew once at sea, and a vessel like the Duncan, we shall be masters of the Indian Ocean.' 'Hurrah for Ben Joyce!' cried the convicts. Mulready's horse was then led up, and Ben Joyce disappeared at a gallop on the Lucknow road, while the band proceeded southeastward to the Snowy River. Mulready, although severely wounded, had strength to drag himself within two hundred paces of the encampment, where we picked him up almost dead. This," added MacNabb, "is Mulready's sad story. You understand now why the courageous sailor wished so much to speak."

This revelation terrified all.

"Pirates! pirates!" cried Glenarvan. "My crew massacred, my Duncan in the hands of these bandits!"

"Yes, for Ben Joyce will surprise the vessel," replied the major, "and then—"

"Well, we must reach the coast before these wretches," said Paganel.

"But how cross the Snowy?" asked Wilson.

"Like them," answered Glenarvan. "They will cross Kemple Pier bridge, and we will do the same."

"But what will become of Mulready?" inquired Lady Helena.

"We will take turns in carrying him. Shall I give up my defenceless crew to Ben Joyce's band?"

The plan of crossing Kemple Pier bridge was practicable, but perilous. The convicts might locate themselves at this point to defend it. It would be at least thirty against seven! But there are moments when we do not think of these things, when we must advance at all hazards.

"My lord," said Captain Mangles, at length, "before risking our last chance, before venturing towards the bridge, it is prudent to reconnoitre it first. I will undertake this."

"I will accompany you, captain," replied Paganel.

This proposal was accepted, and the captain and Paganel prepared to start immediately. They were to follow along the bank of the river till they came to the place indicated by Ben Joyce, and keep out of sight of the convicts, who were probably lying in wait. These two courageous men accordingly, well furnished with arms and provisions, set out, and soon disappeared among the tall rushes of the river.

All day the little party waited for them. At evening they had not yet returned, and great fears were entertained. At last, about eleven o'clock, Wilson announced their approach. They arrived, worn out with the fatigues of a six-mile journey.

"The bridge? Is it there?" asked Glenarvan, rushing to meet them.

"Yes, a bridge of rushes," said Captain Mangles. "The convicts passed, it is true, but—"

"But what?" cried Glenarvan, who foresaw a new calamity.

"They burned it after their passage," replied Paganel.

CHAPTER XLIII. HELPLESS AND HOPELESS.

It was not the time to despair, but to act. If Kemple Pier bridge was destroyed, they must cross the Snowy at all events, and reach Twofold Bay before Ben Joyce's band. They lost no time, therefore, in vain words; but the next day Captain Mangles and Glenarvan went to examine the river, preparatory to a passage.

The tumultuous waters, swollen by the rains, had not subsided. They whirled along with indescribable fury. It was certain death to brave this torrent. Glenarvan, with folded arms and lowered head, stood motionless.

"Do you wish me to try to swim to the opposite bank?" asked Captain Mangles.

"No, John," replied Glenarvan, seizing the bold young man by the hand; "let us wait."

They both returned to the encampment. The day was passed in the most lively anxiety. Ten times did Glenarvan return to the river. He sought to contrive some bold plan of crossing it, but in vain. It would not have been more impassable if a torrent of lava had flowed between its banks.

During these long hours of delay, Lady Helena, with the major's assistance, bestowed upon Mulready the most skillful care. The sailor felt that he was returning to life. MacNabb ventured to affirm that no vital organ had been injured, the loss of blood sufficiently explained the patient's weakness. Thus, as soon as his wound was healed and the hemorrhage stopped, only time and rest were needed for his complete restoration. Lady Helena had insisted upon his occupying her end of the cart. Mulready felt greatly honored. His greatest anxiety was in the thought that his condition might delay Glenarvan, and he forced them to promise that they would leave him at the camp in charge of Wilson, as soon as the river became fordable.

Unfortunately, this was not possible, either that day or the next. At seeing himself thus detained, Glenarvan despaired. Lady Helena and the major tried in vain to pacify and exhort him to patience. Patience! when, at that moment perhaps, Ben Joyce was going on board the yacht, when the Duncan was weighing anchor and steaming towards that fatal coast, to which every hour brought her nearer!

Captain Mangles felt at heart all Glenarvan's anguish, and, as he wished to overcome the difficulty at all hazards, he constructed a canoe in the Australian fashion, with large pieces of the bark of the gum-trees. These slabs, which were very light, were held together by wooden cross-bars, and formed a very frail craft.

The captain and the sailor tried the canoe. All that skill, strength, or courage could do they did. But scarcely were they in the current, when they capsized and narrowly escaped with their lives. The boat was drawn into the eddies and disappeared. Captain Mangles and Wilson had not advanced ten yards into the river, which was swollen by the rains and melting snows till it was now a mile in breadth.

Two days were wasted in this way. The major and Glenarvan went five miles up stream without finding a practicable ford. Everywhere was the same impetuosity, the same tumultuous rush of water; all the southern slopes of the mountains had poured their liquid torrents into this single stream. They were forced, therefore, to give up any hope of saving the Duncan. Five days had passed since Ben Joyce's departure, the yacht was probably that very moment at the coast, in the hands of the convicts.

However, this state of things could not last long. Indeed, on the morning of the third day, Paganel perceived that the waters were beginning to subside. He reported to Glenarvan the result of his observations.

"What does it matter now?" replied Glenarvan; "it is too late!"

"That is no reason for prolonging our stay at the encampment," replied the major.

"Certainly not," said Captain Mangles; "to-morrow, perhaps, it will be possible to cross."

"But will that save my unfortunate crew?" cried Glenarvan.

"Listen to me, my lord," continued Captain Mangles. "I know Tom Austin. He was to execute your orders, and start as soon as his departure was possible. Who knows whether the Duncan was ready, or her injuries repaired, on the arrival of Ben Joyce at Melbourne? Supposing the yacht could not put to sea, and suffered one or two days of delay?"

"You are right, John," replied Glenarvan. "We must reach Twofold Bay. We are only thirty-five miles from Delegete."

"Yes," said Paganel, "and in that town we shall find rapid means of conveyance. Who knows whether we shall not arrive in time to prevent this calamity?"

"Let us start!" cried Glenarvan.

Captain Mangles and Wilson at once occupied themselves in constructing a raft of large dimensions. Experience had proved that pieces of bark could not resist the violence of the torrent. The captain cut down several gum-trees, of which he made a rude but substantial raft. It was a tedious task, and that day ended before the work was completed; but the next day it was finished.

The waters had now considerably subsided. The torrent had become a river again, with a rapid current. However, with proper management, the captain hoped to reach the opposite bank.

At noon they put on board as much provisions as each could carry for two days' travel. The rest was abandoned with the cart and the tent. Mulready was well enough to be moved; he was recovering rapidly.

Each took his place on the raft, which was moored to the bank. Captain Mangles had arranged on the starboard side, and confided to Wilson, a kind of oar to sustain the raft against the current, and prevent its drifting. As for himself, he stood at the stern, and steered by means of a clumsy rudder. Lady Helena and Mary Grant occupied the centre of the raft near Mulready. Glenarvan, the major, Paganel, and Robert surrounded them, ready to lend assistance.

"Are we ready, Wilson?" asked Captain Mangles.

"Yes, captain," replied the sailor, seizing his oar with a firm hand.

"Attention, and bear up against the current."

Captain Mangles unmoored the raft, and with one push launched it into the current of the river. All went well for some time, and Wilson resisted the leeway. But soon the craft was drawn into the eddies, and turned round and round, so that neither oar nor rudder could keep it in a straight course. In spite of their efforts, they were soon placed in a position where it was impossible to use the oars.

They were forced to be passive; there was no means of preventing this gyratory motion. They were whirled about with a giddy rapidity, and sent out of their course. The captain, with pale face and set teeth, stood and gazed at the eddying water.

However, the raft was entangled in the midst of the river, half a mile below where they started. The current here was very strong, and, as it broke the eddies, it lessened the whirling motion. The captain and Wilson resumed their oars, and succeeded in propelling the craft in an oblique direction. In this way they approached nearer the left bank, and were only a few yards distant, when Wilson's oar broke. The raft, no longer sustained against the current, was carried down stream. The captain endeavored to prevent it, at the risk of breaking his rudder, and Wilson with bleeding hands assisted him.

At last they succeeded, and the raft, after a voyage of more than half an hour, ran upon the steeply-sloping bank. The shock was violent; the timbers were thrown apart, the ropes broken, and the foaming water came through. The travelers had only time to cling to the bushes that hung over the stream. They extricated Mulready and the two ladies, who were half drenched. In short, everybody was saved; but the greater part of the provisions and arms, except the major's rifle, were swept away with the fragments of the raft.

The river was crossed, but the little party were without resources, thirty-five miles from Delegete, in the midst of these untrodden deserts. They resolved to start without delay. Mulready saw that he would cause trouble, and desired to remain behind, even alone, and wait for aid from Delegete. But Glenarvan refused. He could not reach the town before three days. If the Duncan had left Melbourne several days before, what mattered a delay of a few hours?

"No, my friend," said he; "I will not abandon any one. We will make a litter, and take turns in carrying you."

The litter was made of branches covered with leaves, and upon this Mulready was placed. Glenarvan wished to be the first to bear the sailor, and, seizing one end of the litter and Wilson the other, they started.

What a sad sight! and how disastrously this journey, so well begun, had ended! They were no longer going in search of Captain Grant. This continent— where he was not, nor had ever been—threatened to be fatal to those who were seeking traces of him, and perhaps new discouragements still awaited them.

The first day passed silently and painfully. Every ten minutes they took turns in carrying the litter. All the sailor's companions uncomplainingly imposed upon themselves this duty, which was made still more arduous by the great heat.

At evening, after accomplishing only five miles, they encamped under a group of gum-trees. The rest of the provisions that had escaped the shipwreck furnished the evening meal. They must hereafter rely on the major's rifle; but he found no opportunity to fire a single shot. Fortunately, Robert found a nest of bustards, containing a dozen large eggs, which Olbinett cooked in the hot ashes. In addition to these embarrassments, their way became very difficult. The sandy plains were bristling with thorny plants that tore their garments and lacerated their limbs. The courageous ladies, however, did not complain, but valiantly advanced, setting the example, and encouraging each other by a word or a look.

On the third day Mulready traveled part of the way on foot. His wound had entirely healed. The town of Delegete was only ten miles distant, and at evening they encamped on the very frontiers of New South Wales.

A fine and penetrating rain had been falling for several hours, and all shelter would have failed, if Captain Mangles had not fortunately discovered a ruined and abandoned sawyer's hut. They were obliged to content themselves with this miserable hovel of branches and thatch. Wilson attempted to kindle a fire to prepare the food, and accordingly collected some dead wood that strewed the ground. But when he attempted to light the fuel he did not succeed; the great quantity of aluminous material that it contained prevented combustion. It was, therefore, necessary to dispense with fire and food, and sleep in wet garments, while the birds, hidden in the lofty branches, seemed to mock these unfortunate travelers.

However, Glenarvan and his friends were approaching the end of their sufferings; and it was time. The two ladies exerted themselves heroically, but their strength was failing every hour. They dragged themselves along, they no longer walked.

The next day they started at daybreak, and at eleven o'clock Delegete came in sight, fifty miles from Twofold Bay. Here means of conveyance were quickly obtained. Feeling himself so near the coast, hope returned to Glenarvan's heart; perhaps there had been some slight delay, and he would arrive before the Duncan! In twenty-four hours he would reach the bay!

At noon, after a comforting repast, all the travelers took their seats in a mail-coach, and left Delegete at the full speed of five strong horses. The postilions, stimulated by the promise of a large reward, drove them along at a rapid rate, over a well-kept road. No time was lost inchanging horses, and it seemed as if Glenarvan had inspired all with his own intense eagerness.

All day and all night they traveled with the same swiftness, and at sunrise the next morning a low murmur announced the proximity of the Indian Ocean. It was necessary, however, to pass around the bay to gain that part of the coast where Tom Austin was to meet the travelers.

When the sea appeared, all eyes quickly surveyed the wide expanse. Was the Duncan there, by a miracle of Providence, as she had been discerned before by some of them on the Argentine coast? Nothing was seen; sky and water mingled in an unbroken horizon; not a sail brightened the vast extent of ocean.

One hope still remained. Perhaps Tom Austin had thought it best to cast anchor in Twofold Bay, as the sea was rough and a vessel could not be moored in safety near such shores.

"To Eden!" said Glenarvan.

The mail-coach at once took the road to the right, which ran along the edge of the bay, and proceeded towards the little town of Eden, only five miles distant. The postilions stopped not far from the light that guarded the entrance to the harbor. Several ships were anchored in the roadstead, but none displayed the flag of Malcolm Castle.

Glenarvan, Captain Mangles, and Paganel alighted immediately, and hastened to the custom-house. Here they questioned the employees, and consulted the latest arrivals. No vessel had entered the bay for a week.

"She may not have started!" cried Glenarvan, who would not despair. "Perhaps we have arrived before her!"

Captain Mangles shook his head. He knew Tom Austin; his mate would never have delayed so long to execute an order.

"I will know what this means," said Glenarvan. "Certainty is better than doubt."

Fifteen minutes later a telegram was sent to the ship-brokers of Melbourne, and the travelers repaired to the Victoria Hotel. Not long after an answer was delivered to Lord Glenarvan. It read as follows:

"Lord Glenarvan, Eden, Twofold Bay.

"Duncan started on the 18th instant for some unknown destination."

The dispatch fell from Glenarvan's hands. There was no more doubt! The honest Scotch yacht, in Ben Joyce's hands, had become a pirate-vessel!

Thus ended their search in Australia, begun under such favorable auspices. The traces of Captain Grant and his shipwrecked sailors seemed irrecoverably lost. This failure had cost the lives of an entire crew. Lord Glenarvan was crushed by the blow, and this courageous searcher, whom the leagued elements had failed to deter, was now baffled by the malice of men.

CHAPTER XLIV. A ROUGH CAPTAIN.

If ever the searchers for Captain Grant had reason to despair of seeing him again, was it not when every hope forsook them at once? To what part of the world should they venture a new expedition? how explore unknown countries? The Duncan was no longer in their possession, and they could not be immediately reconciled to their misfortune. The undertaking of these generous Scots had, therefore, failed. Failure! sad word, that finds no echo in a valiant soul; and yet, amid all the changes of destiny, Glenarvan was forced to acknowledge his powerlessness to pursue this work of mercy.

Mary Grant, in this situation, no longer had the courage to utter the name of her father. She suppressed her own anguish by thinking of the unfortunate crew. Controlling herself in the presence of her friend, it was she who consoled Lady Helena, from whom she had received so many consolations. The young girl was the first to speak of their return to Scotland. At seeing her so courageous and resigned, Captain Mangles admired her, and would have spoken a final word in favor of Captain Grant, if Mary had not stopped him with a look and then said:

"No, Mr. John; let us think of those who have sacrificed themselves. Lord Glenarvan must return to England."

"You are right, Miss Mary," replied he; "he must. The English authorities must also be informed of the fate of the Duncan. But do not give up all hope. The search that we have begun I would continue alone, rather than abandon. I will find Captain Grant, or succumb to the task!"

This was a solemn compact which John Mangles thus made. Mary accepted it, and gave her hand to the young captain, as if to ratify this treaty. On the part of the latter it was a devotion of his entire life; on the part of the former, an unchanging gratitude.

The time of their departure was now definitely decided. They resolved to proceed to Melbourne without delay. The next day Captain Mangles went to inquire about vessels that were upon the point of sailing. He expected to find frequent communication between Eden and Melbourne, but he was disappointed. The vessels were few; two or three anchored in Twofold Bay composed the entire fleet of the place. There were none for Melbourne, Sydney, or Point-de-Galle.

In this state of affairs, what was to be done? Wait for a ship? They might be delayed a long time, for Twofold Bay is little frequented. After some deliberation, Glenarvan was about to decide upon reaching Sydney by the coast, when Paganel made a proposal that was unexpected to every one.

The geographer had just returned from Twofold Bay. He knew that there were no means of transportation to Sydney or Melbourne; but, of the three vessels anchored in the roadstead, one was preparing to start for Auckland, the capital of Ika-na-Maoui, the northern island of New Zealand. Thither Paganel proposed to go by the bark in question, and from Auckland it would be easy to return to England by the steamers of the English company.

This proposition was taken into serious consideration, although Paganel did not enter into those extended arguments of which he was usually so lavish. He confined himself to stating the fact, and added that the voyage would not last more than five or six days.

Captain Mangles advocated Paganel's plan. He thought it should be adopted, since they could not wait for the uncertain arrival of other vessels. But, before deciding, he judged it advisable to visit the ship in question. Accordingly, he, with Glenarvan, the major, Paganel, and Robert, took a boat, and pulled out to where it was anchored.

It was a brig of two hundred and fifty tons, called the Macquarie, which traded between the different ports of Australia and New Zealand. The captain, or rather the "master," received his visitors very gruffly. They saw that they had to deal with an uneducated man, whose manners were not different from those of the five sailors of his crew. A coarse red face, big hands, a flat nose, a blinded eye, lips blackened by his pipe, and a specially brutish appearance, made Will Halley a very forbidding character. But they had no choice, and for a voyage of a few days there was no need to be very particular.

"What do you want?" asked Will Halley, as the strangers reached the deck of his vessel.

"The captain," replied Mangles.

"I am he," said Halley. "What then?"

"The Macquarie is loading for Auckland?"

"Yes. What of it?"

"What does she carry?"

"Anything that is bought or sold."

"When does she sail?"

"To-morrow, at the noon tide."

"Would she take passengers?"

"That depends upon the passengers, and whether they would be satisfied with the ship's mess."

"They would take their own provisions."

"Well, how many are there?"

"Nine,—two of them ladies."

"I have no cabins."

"We will arrange a place for their exclusive use."

"What then?"

"Do you accept?" asked Captain Mangles, who was not embarrassed by this curtness.

"I must see," replied the master of the Macquarie. He took a turn or two, striking the deck with his heavy, hobnailed boots; then, turning to Captain Mangles, said: "What do you pay?"

"What do you ask?" was the reply.

"Fifty pounds."

Glenarvan nodded assent.

"Very well! Fifty pounds."

"But the passage in cash!" added Halley.

"In cash."

"Food separate?"

"Separate."

"Agreed. Well?" said Will Halley, holding out his hand.

"What?"

"The advance-money."

"Here is half the fare,—twenty-five pounds," said Captain Mangles, counting out the sum, which the master pocketed without saying "thank you."

"Be on board to-morrow," said he. "Whether you are here or not, I shall weigh anchor."

"We will be here."

Thereupon Glenarvan, the major, Robert, Paganel, and Captain Mangles left the vessel, without Will Halley's having so much as touched the brim of his hat.

"What a stupid fellow!" was their first remark.

"Well, I like him," replied Paganel. "He is a real sea-wolf."

"A real bear!" remarked the major.

"And I imagine," added Captain Mangles, "that this bear has at some time traded in human flesh."

"What matter," replied Glenarvan, "so long as he commands the Macquarie, which goes to New Zealand? We shall see very little of him on the voyage."

Lady Helena and Mary Grant were very much pleased to know that they were to start the next day. Glenarvan observed, however, that the Macquarie could not equal the Duncan for comfort; but, after so many hardships, they were not likely to be overcome by trifles. Mr. Olbinett was requested to take charge of the provisions. The poor man, since the loss of the Duncan, had often lamented the unhappy fate of his wife, who had remained on board, and would be, consequently, the victim of the convicts' brutality. However, he fulfilled his duties as steward with his accustomed zeal, and their food might yet consist of dishes that were never seen on the ship's table.

In the mean time the major discounted at a money-changer's some drafts that Glenarvan had on the Union Bank of Melbourne. As for Paganel, he procured an excellent map of New Zealand.

Mulready was now quite well. He scarcely felt his wound, which had so nearly proved fatal. A few hours at sea would complete his recovery.

Wilson went on board first, charged with arranging the passengers' quarters. Under his vigorous use of the brush and broom the aspect of things was greatly changed. Will Halley shrugged his shoulders, but allowed the sailor to do as he pleased. As for Glenarvan and his friends, he scarcely noticed them; he did not even know their names, nor did he care to. This increase of cargo was worth fifty pounds to him, but he valued it less than the two hundred tons of tanned leather with which his hold was crowded,—the skins first, and the passengers next. He was a real trader; and by his nautical ability he passed for a good navigator of these seas, rendered so very dangerous by the coral reefs.

During the afternoon, Glenarvan wished to visit once more the supposed place of the shipwreck. Ayrton had certainly been the quartermaster of the Britannia, and the vessel might really have been lost on that part of the coast. And there, at all events, the Duncan had fallen into the hands of the convicts. Had there been a fight? Perhaps they would find on the beach traces of a struggle. If the crew had perished in the waves, would not the bodies have been cast ashore?

Glenarvan, accompanied by his faithful captain, undertook this examination. The landlord of Victoria Hotel furnished them with two horses, and they set out. But it was a sad journey. They rode in silence. The same thoughts, the same anxieties, tortured the mind of each. They gazed at the rocks worn by the sea. They had no need to question or answer; no sign of the Duncan could be found,—the whole coast was bare. Captain Mangles, however, found on the margin of the shore evident signs of an encampment, the remains of fires recently kindled beneath the few trees. Had a wandering tribe of natives passed there within a few days? No, for an object struck Glenarvan's eye, which proved incontestably that the convicts had visited that part of the coast.

It was a gray and yellow jacket, worn and patched, left at the foot of a tree. It bore a number and badge of the Perth penitentiary. The convict was no longer there, but his cast-off garment betrayed him.

"You see, John," said Glenarvan, "the convicts have been here! And our poor comrades of the Duncan—"

"Yes," replied the captain, in a low voice, "they have certainly been landed, and have perished!"

"The wretches!" cried Glenarvan. "If they ever fall into my hands, I will avenge my crew!"

Grief and exposure had hardened Glenarvan's features. For several moments he gazed at the vast expanse of water, seeking perhaps to discern some ship in the dim distance. Then his eyes relaxed their fierceness, he regained his composure, and, without adding a word or making a sign, took the road to Eden.

Only one duty remained to be fulfilled,—to inform the constable of the events that had just transpired, which was done the same evening. The magistrate, Thomas Banks, could scarcely conceal his satisfaction at making out the official record. He was simply delighted at the departure of Ben Joyce and his band. The whole village shared his joy. The convicts had left Australia because of a new crime; but, at all events, they had gone. This important news was immediately telegraphed to the authorities of Melbourne and Sydney.

Having accomplished his object, Glenarvan returned to the Victoria Hotel. The travelers passed this last evening in Australia in sadness. Their thoughts wandered over this country, so fertile in misfortunes. They recalled the hopes they had reasonably conceived at Cape Bernouilli, now so cruelly disappointed at Twofold Bay.

Paganel was a prey to a feverish agitation. Captain Mangles, who had watched him since the incident at Snowy River, many times pressed him with questions which Paganel did not answer. But that evening, as he went with him to his chamber, the captain asked him why he was so nervous.

"My friend," replied Paganel evasively, "I am no more nervous than usual."

"Mr. Paganel, you have a secret that troubles you."

"Well, as you will," cried the geographer; "it is stronger than I."

"What is stronger than you?"

"My joy on the one hand, and my despair on the other."

"You are joyful and despairing at the same time?"

"Yes; joyful and despairing at visiting New Zealand."

"Have you any news?" asked Captain Mangles. "Have you discovered the lost trail?"

"No, friend. *People never return from New Zealand!* But yet—well, you know human nature. As long as we breathe we can hope; and my motto is 'dum spiro, spero,' which is the best in the world."

406

CHAPTER XLV. THE WRECK OF THE MACQUARIE.

The next day the travelers were installed on board the Macquarie. Will Halley had not offered the ladies his cabin, which was not to be regretted, as the lair was only fit for the brute.

At noon they made ready to take the flood-tide. The anchor was weighed. A moderate breeze blew from the southwest. The sails were gradually set, but the five men worked slowly. At last, incited by the oaths of the skipper, they accomplished their task. But in spite of her spread of canvas the brig scarcely advanced. Yet, however poorly she sailed, in five or six days they hoped to reach the harbor of Auckland. At seven o'clock in the evening they lost sight of the shores of Australia, and the lighthouse at Eden. The sea was rough, and the vessel labored heavily in the trough of the waves. The passengers found their situation very uncomfortable; but, as they could not remain on deck, they were forced to submit to confinement.

That evening conversation very naturally turned upon the land to which they were now sailing, its discovery and colonization; and just as naturally all turned to Paganel as to a bookcase, for some information thereon. It was very readily accessible, although evidently to the geographer's mind there was something of a painful character connected with the name, the impression, and the very thoughts of New Zealand and its Maori inhabitants.

"Monsieur Paganel," said Lady Helena, "have your friends, the English, been the only ones to search out this island?"

"By no means, madam," was the prompt reply. "On the contrary, they have come second, nay, third, in the race; only," and he looked half roguishly and half maliciously, "*they stayed when they came.*"

And then he told them of its first discovery by Abel Tasman, the Dutch navigator, in 1642; that, when first he landed, there seemed to be amicable feelings expressed by the islanders toward himself, a number of them coming back to his ship, and being apparently well pleased to cultivate intercourse. But on the next day, as he sent his boat to find good anchorage nearer to the shore, seven canoes of the islanders attacked it most violently and suddenly, causing it to capsize, and so vigorously assailing its occupants with their pikes that it was with difficulty any of them were able to swim back to their ship, leaving those of their companions who were not drowned to be butchered by the natives.

Of course he did not forget to mention that a French navigator, Surville by name, was the next to visit the shores, and that his visit likewise was the cause of bloodshed and misery. But he gave them a more lengthy and extended narrative of Captain Cook's voyages, which were the most important in their results as well as the most interesting and tragic in many of their incidents. It was on the 6th of October, 1769, that this navigator first landed on the shores which he visited twice afterwards, and each time added greatly to the stock of previous knowledge concerning these islands, their productions, and their inhabitants. By him it was first ascertained that cannibalism was practiced by some, if not all, of the tribes at that time; and it was very evident, from the manner of Paganel's narration, that hereabout lay the extremely sensitive point of the worthy geographer's fears and forebodings. However, he was not deterred from rehearsing how one and another not merely visited, but began to settle, on the island, so that in the treaty of 1814 it was formally recognized as belonging to Great Britain, and twenty years after was important enough to have a separate official and governmental establishment.

Paganel also told, at great length, the tales of many of the sad incidents which from time to time have marked even the commercial intercourse between the European and the Maori; as, for instance, the sad tale of conflict and bloodshed connected with the death of Captain Marion, a French navigator, in 1772. He had landed near the spot where Surville had ill-treated some of the natives and traitorously seized a son of the chief, Takouri, who yet appeared to welcome this next French visitant, though remembering none the less the terrible duty of vengeance which is felt by the Maori to be so binding.

For a long time the cloak of friendship was worn by the natives, the more thoroughly to lull the suspicions of the whites, and to entice a larger number on shore; in which endeavor they succeeded only too well. The French ships being greatly out of repair, Marion was induced to fell timber at some distance in the interior, and to establish in this occupation a great number of his men, going frequently to them, and remaining with them and the apparently friendly chiefs.

On one of these occasions the Maoris fulfilled their revengeful project with a terrible satisfaction to themselves. Only one man, of all those in the interior, managed to escape, the commander himself falling a prey to their vengeance. They then endeavored to kill the second in command, who, with several others, was nearer to the shore. These, of course, at once started for their boats; breathless, they reached them, hotly pursued to the water's edge by the insatiate savages. Then, safe themselves, the French marksmen picked off the chief, and the previous exultation of the aborigines was, even in the hour of their triumph, turned to lamentation, coupled with wonder at the terrible power of the white man's fire-barrel.

All this and much more did the geographer narrate; but it must be confessed that he neither spoke, nor did they listen, with the complacency evinced in his previous tales. Besides, their surroundings were at the time uncomfortable, and the first prognostications of a speedy passage were not likely to be verified.

Unfortunately, this painful voyage was prolonged. Six days after her departure, the Macquarie had not descried the shores of Auckland. The wind was fair, however, and still blew from the southwest; but nevertheless the brig did not make much headway. The sea was rough, the rigging creaked, the ribs cracked, and the vessel rode the waves with difficulty.

Fortunately, Will Halley, like a man who was in no hurry, did not crowd on sail, or his masts would inevitably have snapped. Captain Mangles hoped, therefore, that this clumsy craft would reach its destination in safety; still, he was pained to see his companions on board in such miserable quarters.

But neither Lady Helena nor Mary Grant complained, although the continual rain kept them confined, and the want of air and rolling of the ship seriously incommoded them. Their friends sought to divert them, and Paganel strove to while the time with his stories, but did not succeed so well as previously.

Of all the passengers, the one most to be pitied was Lord Glenarvan. They rarely saw him below; he could not keep still. His nervous and excitable nature would not submit to an imprisonment between four wooden walls. Day and night, heedless of the torrents of rain and the dashing spray of the sea, he remained on deck, sometimes bending over the rail, sometimes pacing up and down with feverish agitation. His eyes gazed continually into space, and, during the brief lulls, his glass persistently surveyed the horizon. He seemed to question the mute waves; the mist that veiled the sky, the masses of vapor, he would have penetrated with a glance; he could not be resigned, and his countenance betokened an acute grief. The power and hopefulness of this man, hitherto so energetic and courageous, had suddenly failed.

Captain Mangles seldom left him, but at his side endured the severity of the storm. That day, Glenarvan, wherever there was an opening in the mist, scanned the horizon with the utmost persistency. The young captain approached him.

"Is your lordship looking for land?" he asked.

Glenarvan shook his head.

"It will yet be some time before we leave the brig. We ought to have sighted Auckland light thirty-six hours ago."

Glenarvan did not answer. He still gazed, and for a moment his glass was pointed towards the horizon to windward of the vessel.

"The land is not on that side," said Captain Mangles. "Your lordship should look towards the starboard."

"Why, John?" replied Glenarvan. "It is not the land that I am seeking."

"What is it, my lord?"

"My yacht, my Duncan! She must be here, in these regions, plowing these seas, in that dreadful employment of a pirate. She is here, I tell you, John, on this course between Australia and New Zealand! I have a presentiment that we shall meet her!"

"God preserve us from such a meeting, my lord!"

"Why, John?"

"Your lordship forgets our situation. What could we do on this brig, if the Duncan should give us chase? We could not escape."

"Escape, John?"

"Yes, my lord. We should try in vain. We should be captured, at the mercy of the wretches. Ben Joyce has shown that he does not hesitate at a crime. I should sell my life dearly. We would defend ourselves to the last extremity. Well! But, then, think of Lady Helena and Mary Grant!"

"Poor women!" murmured Glenarvan. "John, my heart is broken, and sometimes I feel as if despair had invaded it. It seems to me as if new calamities awaited us, as if Heaven had decreed against us! I am afraid!"

"You, my lord?"

"Not for myself, John, but for those whom I love, and whom you love also."

"Take courage, my lord," replied the young captain. "We need no longer fear. The Macquarie is a poor sailer, but still she sails. Will Halley is a brutish creature; but I am here, and if the approach to the land seems to me dangerous I shall take the ship to sea again. Therefore from this quarter there is little or no danger. But as for meeting the Duncan, God preserve us, and enable us to escape!"

Captain Mangles was right. To encounter the Duncan would be fatal to the Macquarie, and this misfortune was to be feared in these retired seas, where pirates could roam without danger. However, that day, at least, the Duncan did not appear, and the sixth night since their departure from Twofold Bay arrived without Captain Mangles's fears being realized.

But that night was destined to be one of terror. Darkness set in almost instantaneously towards evening; the sky was very threatening. Even Will Halley, whose sense of danger was superior to the brutishness of intoxication, was startled by these warning signs. He left his cabin, rubbing his eyes and shaking his great red head. Then he drew a long breath, and examined the masts. The wind was fresh, and was blowing strong towards the New Zealand coast.Captain Halley summoned his men, with many oaths, and ordered them to reef the top-sails. Captain Mangles approved in silence. He had given up remonstrating with this coarse seaman; but neither he nor Glenarvan left the deck.

Two hours passed. The sea grew more tempestuous, and the vessel received such severe shocks that it seemed as if her keel were grating on the sand. There was no unusual roughness, but yet this clumsy craft labored heavily, and the deck was deluged by the huge waves. The boat that hung in the larboard davits was swept overboard by a rising billow.

Captain Mangles could not help being anxious. Any other vessel would have mocked these surges; but with this heavy hulk they might well fear foundering, for the deck was flooded with every plunge, and the masses of water, not finding sufficient outlet by the scuppers, might submerge the ship. It would have been wise, as a preparation for any emergency, to cut away the waistcloth to facilitate the egress of the water; but Will Halley refused to take this precaution.

However, a greater danger threatened the Macquarie, and probably there was no longer time to prevent it. About half-past eleven Captain Mangles and Wilson, who were standing on the leeward side, were startled by an unusual sound. Their nautical instincts were roused, and the captain seized the sailor's hand. "The surf!" said he.

"Yes," replied Wilson. "The sea is breaking on the reefs."

"Not more than two cable-lengths distant."

"Not more! The shore is here!"

Captain Mangles leaned over the railing, gazed at the dark waves, and cried: "The sounding-lead, Wilson!"

The skipper, who was in the forecastle, did not seem to suspect his situation. Wilson grasped the sounding-line, which lay coiled in its pail, and rushed into the port-shrouds. He cast the lead; the rope slipped between his fingers; at the third knot it stopped.

"Three fathoms!" cried Wilson.

"We are on the breakers!" shouted the sober captain to the stupefied one.

Whether the former saw Halley shrug his shoulders or not is of little consequence. At all events, he rushed towards the wheel and crowded the helm hard alee, while Wilson, letting go the line, hauled upon the top-sail yard-arms to luff the ship. The sailor who was steering, and had been forcibly pushed aside, did not at all understand this sudden attack.

"To the port-yards! let loose the sails!" cried the young captain, managing so as to escape the reefs.

For half a minute, the starboard side of the brig grazed the rocks, and, in spite of the darkness, John perceived a roaring line of breakers that foamed a few yards from the ship.

At this moment Will Halley, becoming conscious of the imminent danger, lost his presence of mind. His sailors, who were scarcely sober, could not comprehend his orders. Moreover, his incoherent words and contradictory commands showed that this stupid drunkard's coolness had failed. He was surprised by the nearness of the land, which was only eight miles off, when he thought it thirty or forty. The currents had taken him unawares, and thrown him out of his ordinary course.

However, Captain Mangles's prompt management had rescued the brig from her peril; but he did not know his position. Perhaps he was inclosed by a chain of reefs. The wind blew fresh from the east, and at every pitch they might strike bottom.

The roar of the surf was soon redoubled, and it was necessary to luff still more. John crowded the helm down and braced farther to leeward. The breakers multiplied beneath the prow of the ship, and they were obliged to tack so as to put to sea. Would this manœuvre succeed with such an unsteady vessel, and under such reduced sail? It was uncertain, but as their only chance they must venture it.

"Hard alee!" cried Captain Mangles to Wilson.

The Macquarie began to approach the new line of reefs. Soon the water foamed above the submerged rocks. It was a moment of torturing suspense. The spray glittered on the crests of the waves. You would have thought a phosphorescent glow had suddenly illumined the water. Wilson and Mulready forced down the wheel with their whole weight.

Suddenly a shock was felt. The vessel had struck upon a rock. The bob-stays broke, and nearly overthrew the mainmast. Could they come about without any other injury? No; for all at once there was a calm, and the ship veered to windward again, and her movements suddenly ceased. A lofty wave seized and bore her forward towards the reefs, while she rolled heavily. The mainmast went by the board with all its rigging, the brig heaved twice and was motionless, leaning over to starboard. The pump-lights were shattered in pieces, and the passengers rushed to the deck; but the waves were sweeping it from one end to the other, and they could not remain without danger. Captain Mangles, knowing that the ship was firmly imbedded in the sand, besought them for their own sakes to go below again.

"The truth, John?" asked Glenarvan, faintly.

"The truth, my lord, is that we shall not founder. As for being destroyed by the sea, that is another question; but we have time to take counsel."

"Is it midnight?"

"Yes, my lord, and we must wait for daylight."

"Can we not put to sea in the boat?"

"In this storm and darkness it is impossible. And, moreover, where should we strike land?"

"Well, John, let us remain here till morning."

Meantime Will Halley was running about the deck like a madman. His sailors, who had recovered from their stupor, stove in a brandy-barrel and began to drink. Mangles foresaw that their drunkenness would lead to terrible scenes. The captain could not be relied upon to restrain them; the miserable man tore his hair and wrung his hands; he thought only of his cargo, which was not insured.

"I am ruined! I am lost!" cried he, running to and fro.

Captain Mangles scarcely thought of consoling him. He armed his companions, and all stood ready to repel the sailors, who were filling themselves with brandy, and cursing frightfully.

"The first of these wretches who approaches," said the major calmly, "I will shoot like a dog."

The sailors doubtless saw that the passengers were determined to keep them at bay, for, after a few attempts at plunder, they disappeared. Captain Mangles paid no more attention to these drunken men, but waited impatiently for day.

The ship was now absolutely immovable. The sea grew gradually calm, and the wind subsided. The hull could, therefore, hold out a few hours longer. At sunrise they would examine the shore. If it seemed easy to land, the yawl, now the only boat on board, would serve to transport the crew and passengers. It would require three trips, at least, to accomplish this, for there was room for only four persons. As for the gig, it had been swept overboard, during the storm, as before mentioned.

While reflecting on the dangers of his situation, the young captain, leaning against the binnacle, listened to the roar of the surf. He strove to pierce the dense darkness, and estimate how far he was from that desired yet dreaded coast. Breakers are frequently heard several leagues at sea. Could the frail cutter weather so long a voyage in her present shattered state?

While he was thinking thus, and longing for a little light in the gloomy sky, the ladies, relying upon his words, were reposing in their berths. The steadiness of the brig secured them several hours of rest. Glenarvan and the others, no longer hearing the cries of the drunken crew, refreshed themselves also by a hasty sleep, and, early in the morning, deep silence reigned on board this vessel, which had sunk to rest, as it were, upon her bed of sand.

About four o'clock the first light appeared in the east. The clouds were delicately tinged by the pale rays of the dawn. Captain Mangles came on deck. Along the horizon extended a curtain of mist. A few vague outlines floated in the vapors of the morning. A gentle swell still agitated the sea, and the outer waves were lost in the dense, motionless fog.

He waited. The light gradually brightened, and the horizon glowed with crimson hues. The misty curtain gradually enveloped the vast vault of the firmament. Black rocks emerged from the water. Then, a line was defined along a border of foam, and a luminous point kindled like a lighthouse at the summit of a peak against the still invisible disk of the rising sun.

"Land!" cried Captain Mangles.

His companions, awakened by his voice, rushed on deck, and gazed in silence at the coast that was seen on the horizon. Whether hospitable or fatal, it was to be their place of refuge.

"Where is that Halley?" asked Glenarvan.

"I do not know, my lord," replied Captain Mangles.

"And his sailors?"

"Disappeared, like himself."

"And like himself, doubtless, drunk," added MacNabb.

"Let us search for them," said Glenarvan; "we cannot abandon them on this vessel."

Mulready and Wilson went down to the bunks in the forecastle. The place was empty. They then visited between-decks, and the hold, but found neither Halley nor his sailors.

"What! nobody?" said Glenarvan.

"Have they fallen into the sea?" asked Paganel.

"Anything is possible," replied Captain Mangles, who cared little for their disappearance.

Then, turning towards the stern, he said: "To the boat!"

Wilson and Mulready followed, to assist in lowering it.

The yawl was gone!

CHAPTER XLVI. VAIN EFFORTS.

Will Halley and his crew, taking advantage of the night and the passengers' sleep, had fled with the only boat left. They could not doubt it. This captain, who was in duty bound to be the last on board, had been the first to leave.

"The rascals have fled," said Captain Mangles. "Well, so much the better, my lord. We are spared so many disagreeable scenes."

"I agree with you," replied Glenarvan. "Besides, there is a better captain on board, yourself, and courageous seamen, your companions. Command us; we are ready to obey you."

All endorsed Glenarvan's words, and, ranged along the deck, they stood ready for the young captain's orders.

"What is to be done?" asked Glenarvan.

John cast a glance over the ocean, looked at the shattered masts of the brig, and, after a few moments' reflection, said:

"We have two ways, my lord, of extricating ourselves from this situation: either to raise the vessel and put her to sea, or reach the coast on a raft, which can be easily constructed."

"If the vessel can be raised, let us raise it," replied Glenarvan. "That is the best plan, is it not?"

"Yes, my lord; for, once ashore, what would become of us without means of transport?"

"Let us avoid the coast," added Paganel. "We must beware of New Zealand."

"All the more so, as we have gone considerably astray," continued Captain Mangles. "Halley's carelessness has carried us to the south, that is evident. At noon I will take an observation; and if, as I presume, we are below Auckland, I will try to sail the Macquarie up along the coast."

"But the injuries of the brig?" inquired Lady Helena.

"I do not think they are serious, madam," replied Captain Mangles. "I shall rig a jury-mast at the bows; and we shall sail slowly, it is true, but still we shall go where we wish. If, unfortunately, the hull is stove in, or if the ship cannot be extricated, we must gain the coast, and travel by land to Auckland."

"Let us examine the state of the vessel, then," said the major. "This is of the first importance."

Glenarvan, the captain, and Mulready opened the main scuttle, and went down into the hold. About two hundred tons of tanned hides were there, very badly stowed away; but they could draw them aside without much difficulty, by means of the main-stay tackling, and they at once threw overboard part of this ballast so as to lighten the ship.

After three hours of hard labor, they could see the bottom timbers. Two seams in the larboard planking had sprung open as far up as the channel wales. As the Macquarie lay over on her starboard beams, her opposite side was raised, and the defective seams were out of water. Wilson hastened, therefore, to tighten the joints with oakum, over which he carefully nailed a copper plate.

On sounding they found less than two feet of water in the hold, which the pumps could easily exhaust, and thus relieve the ship. After his examination of the hull, the captain perceived that it had been little injured in stranding. It was probable that a part of the false keel would remain in the sand, but they could pass over it.

Wilson, after inspecting the interior of the brig, dived, in order to determine her position on the reef. The Macquarie was turned towards the northwest, and lay on a very shelving, slimy sand-bar. The lower end of her prow and two-thirds of her keel were deeply imbedded in the sand. The rest, as far as the stern, floated where the water was five fathoms deep. The rudder was not, therefore, confined, but worked freely. The captain considered it useless to lighten her, as he hoped they would be ready to make use of her at the earliest opportunity. The tides of the Pacific are not very strong, but he relied upon their influence to float the brig, which had stranded an hour before high water. The only point was to extricate her, which would be a long and painful task.

"To work!" cried the captain.

His improvised sailors were ready. He ordered them to reef the sails. The major, Robert, and Paganel, under Wilson's direction, climbed the maintop. The top-sail, swelled by the wind, would have prevented the extrication of the ship, and it was necessary to reef it, which was done as well as possible. At last, after much labor, severe to unaccustomed hands, the maintop-gallant was taken down. Young Robert, nimble as a cat, and bold as a cabin-boy, had rendered important services in this difficult operation.

It was now advisable to cast one anchor, perhaps two, at the stern of the vessel in the line of the keel. The effect of this would be to haul the Macquarie around into deep water. There is no difficulty in doing this when you have a boat, but here all the boats were gone, and something else must be supplied.

Glenarvan was familiar enough with the sea to understand the necessity of these arrangements. One anchor was to be cast to prevent the ship from stranding at low water.

"But what shall we do without a boat?" asked he of the captain.

"We will use the remains of the mizen-mast and the empty casks," was the reply. "It will be a difficult, but not impossible task, for the Macquarie's anchors are small. Once cast however, if they do not drag, I shall be encouraged."

"Very well, let us lose no time."

To accomplish their object, all were summoned on deck; each took part in the work. The rigging that still confined the mizen-mast was cut away, so that the maintop could be easily withdrawn. Out of this platform Captain Mangles designed to make a raft. He supported it by means of empty casks, and rendered it capable of carrying the anchors. A rudder was fastened to it, which enabled them to steer the concern.

This labor was half accomplished when the sun neared the meridian. The captain left Glenarvan to follow out his instructions, and turned his attention to determining his position, which was very important. Fortunately, he had found in Will Halley's cabin a Nautical Almanac and a sextant, with which he was able to take an observation. By consulting the map Paganel had bought at Eden, he saw that they had been wrecked at the mouth of Aotea Bay, above Cahua Point, on the shores of the province of Auckland. As the city was on the thirty-seventh parallel, the Macquarie had been carried a considerable distance out of her course. It was, therefore, necessary to sail northward to reach the capital of New Zealand.

"A journey of not more than twenty-five miles," said Glenarvan. "It is nothing."

"What is nothing at sea will be long and difficult on land," replied Paganel.

"Well, then," said Captain Mangles, "let us do all in our power to float the Macquarie."

This question being settled, their labors were resumed. It was high water, but they could not take advantage of it, since the anchors were not yet moored. Yet the captain watched the ship with some anxiety. Would she float with the tide? This point would soon be decided.

They waited. Several cracks were heard, caused either by a rising or starting of the keel. Great reliance had been placed upon the tide, but the brig did not stir.

The work was continued, and the raft was soon ready. The small anchor was put on board, and the captain and Wilson embarked, after mooring a small cable at the stern. The ebb-tide made them drift, and they therefore anchored, half a cable's length distant, in ten fathoms of water. The bottom afforded a firm hold.

The great anchor now remained. They lowered it with difficulty, transported it on the raft, and soon it was moored behind the other; the captain and his men returning to the vessel, and waiting for high water, which would be early in the morning. It was now six o'clock in the evening. The young captain complimented his sailors, and told Paganel that, with the aid of courage and good discipline, he might one day become quartermaster.

Meantime, Mr. Olbinett, after assisting in different operations, had returned to the kitchen, and prepared a very comforting and seasonable repast. The crew were tempted by a keen appetite, which was abundantly satisfied, and each felt himself invigorated for fresh exertions.

After dinner, Captain Mangles took a final precaution to insure the success of his experiment. He threw overboard a great part of the merchandise to lighten the brig; but the remainder of the ballast, the heavy spars, the spare yards, and a few tons of pig-iron, were carried to the stern, to aid by their weight in liberating the keel. Wilson and Mulready likewise rolled to the same place a number of casks filled with water. Midnight arrived before these labors were completed.

But at this hour the breeze subsided, and only a few capricious ripples stirred the surface of the water. Looking towards the horizon, the captain observed that the wind was changing from southwest to northwest. A sailor could not be mistaken in the peculiar arrangement and color of the clouds. He accordingly informed Glenarvan of these indications, and proposed to defer their work till the next day.

"And these are my reasons," said he. "First, we are very much fatigued, and all our strength is necessary to free the vessel. Then, when this is accomplished, how can we sail among the dangerous breakers, and in such profound darkness? Moreover, another reason induces me to wait. The wind promises to aid us, and I desire to profit by it, and am in hopes that it will drift the old hull out when the tide raises her. To-morrow, if I am not mistaken, the breeze will blow from the northwest. We will set the main-sails, and they will help to raise the brig."

These reasons were decisive. Glenarvan and Paganel, the most impatient on board, yielded, and the work was suspended.

The night passed favorably, and day appeared. Their captain's predictions were realized. The wind blew from the northwest, and continued to freshen. The crew were summoned. It was nine o'clock. Four hours were still to elapse before it would be high water, and that time was not lost. The laborers renewed their efforts with very good success.

Meantime the tide rose. The surface of the sea was agitated into ripples, and the points of the rocks gradually disappeared, like marine animals returning to their native element. The time for the final attempt approached. A feverish impatience thrilled all minds. No one spoke. Each gazed at the captain, and awaited his orders. He was leaning over the stern-railing, watching the water, and casting an uneasy glance towards the cables.

At last the tide reached its height. The experiment must now be made without delay. The main-sails were set, and the mast was bent with the force of the wind.

"To the windlass!" cried the captain.

Glenarvan, Mulready, and Robert on one side, and Paganel, the major, and Olbinett on the other, bore down upon the handles that moved the machine. At the same time the captain and Wilson added their efforts to those of their companions.

"Down! down!" cried the young captain; "all together!"

The cables were stretched taut under the powerful action of the windlass. The anchors held fast, and did not drag. But they must be quick, for high tide lasts only a few moments, and the water would not be long in lowering.

They redoubled their efforts. The wind blew violently, and forced the sails against the mast. A few tremors were felt in the hull, and the brig seemed on the point of rising. Perhaps a little more power would suffice to draw her from the sand.

"Helena! Mary!" cried Glenarvan.

The two ladies came and joined their efforts to those of their companions. A final crack was heard, but that was all! The experiment had failed. The tide was already beginning to ebb, and it was evident that, even with the aid of wind and tide, this insufficient crew could not float their ship.

As their first plan had failed, it was necessary to have recourse to the second without delay. It was plain that they could not raise the Macquarie, and that the only way was to abandon her. To wait on board for the uncertain arrival of assistance would have been folly and madness.

The captain therefore proposed to construct a raft strong enough to convey the passengers and a sufficient quantity of provisions to the New Zealand coast. It was not a time for discussion, but for action. The work was accordingly begun, and considerably advanced when night interrupted them.

In the evening, after supper, while Lady Helena and Mary Grant were reposing in their berths, Paganel and his friends conversed seriously as they paced the deck. The geographer had asked Captain Mangles whether the raft could not follow the coast as far as Auckland, instead of landing the passengers at once. The captain replied that it would be impossible with such a rude craft.

"And could we have done with the boat what we cannot do with the raft?"

"Yes, candidly speaking, we could," was the reply; "but with the necessity of sailing by day and anchoring by night."

"Then these wretches, who have abandoned us—"

"Oh," said Captain Mangles, "they were drunk, and in the profound darkness I fear they have paid for their cowardly desertion with their lives."

"So much the worse for them," continued Paganel; "and for us, too, as this boat would have been useful."

"What do you mean, Paganel?" said Glenarvan. "The raft will take us ashore."

"That is precisely what I would avoid," replied the geographer.

"What! can a journey of not more than twenty miles terrify us, after what has been done on the Pampas and in Australia?"

"My friends," resumed Paganel, "I do not doubt your courage, nor that of our fair companions. Twenty miles is nothing in any other country except New Zealand. Here, however, anything is better than venturing upon these treacherous shores."

"Anything is better than exposing yourself to certain death on a wrecked vessel," returned Captain Mangles.

"What have we to fear in New Zealand?" asked Glenarvan.

"The savages!" replied Paganel.

"The savages?" said Glenarvan. "Can we not avoid them by following the coast? Besides, an attack from a few wretches cannot intimidate ten well-armed and determined Europeans."

"It is not a question of wretches," rejoined Paganel. "The New Zealanders form terrible tribes that struggle against the English government, fight with invaders, frequently conquer them, and always eat them."

"Cannibals! cannibals!" cried Robert; and then he murmured, as though afraid to give full utterance to the words, "My sister! Lady Helena!"

"Never fear, my boy!" said Glenarvan; "our friend Paganel exaggerates."

"I do not exaggerate," replied Paganel. "With these New Zealanders war is what the sports of the chase are to civilized nations; and the game they hunt for they feast upon."

"Paganel," said the major, "this may be all very true, but have you forgotten the introduction of Christianity? has it not destroyed these anthropophagous habits?"

"No, it has not," was the prompt reply. "The records are yet fresh of ministers who have gone out to proclaim Christianity and have fallen victims to the murderous and cannibal instincts of those to whom they preached. Not long since, in the year 1864, one of these clergymen was seized by the chiefs, was hung to the tree, was tantalized and tortured to his last moments; and then, whilst some tore his body to pieces, others devoured the various members. No, the Maoris are still cannibals, and will remain so for some time to come."

But Paganel was on this point a pessimist, contrary to his usual characteristic.

CHAPTER XLVII. A DREADED COUNTRY.

What Paganel had stated was indisputable. The cruelty of the New Zealanders could not be doubted. There was, therefore, danger in landing. But if the danger had been a hundred times greater, it must have been faced. Captain Mangles felt the necessity of leaving this vessel, which would soon break up. Between two perils, one certain, the other only probable, there was no possible hesitation.

As for the chance of being picked up by some passing ship, they could not reasonably rely upon it, for the Macquarie was out of the course usually taken in going to New Zealand. The shipwreck had happened on the desert shores of Ika-Na-Maoui.

"When shall we start?" asked Glenarvan.

"To-morrow morning at ten o'clock," replied Captain Mangles. "The tide will begin to rise then, and will carry us ashore."

Early the next day the raft was finished. The captain had given his entire attention to its construction. They needed a steady and manageable craft, and one capable of resisting the waves for a voyage of nine miles. The masts of the brig could alone furnish the necessary materials.

The raft was at length completed. It could doubtless sustain the shock of the surges; but could it be steered, and the coast be reached, if the wind should veer? This was a question only to be decided by trial.

At nine o'clock the loading began. The provisions were first put on board in sufficient quantities to last until the arrival at Auckland, for there could be no reliance upon the products of this dreaded country. Olbinett furnished some preserved meats, the remains of the Macquarie's supplies. There was very little, however; and they were forced to depend upon the coarse fare of the mess, which consisted of very inferior ship-biscuits and two barrels of salt fish, greatly to the steward's regret.

These stores were inclosed in sealed cans and then secured to the foot of the mast. The arms and ammunition were put in a safe and dry place. Fortunately, the travelers were well supplied with rifles and revolvers.

A small anchor was taken on board, in case they should reach the shore at low tide and be forced to anchor in the offing. Flood-tide soon began, the breeze blew gently from the northwest, and a slight swell agitated the surface of the sea.

"Are we ready?" asked Captain Mangles.

"All is ready, captain," replied Wilson.

"Aboard, then!"

Lady Helena and Mary Grant descended the ship's side by a clumsy rope-ladder, and took their seats at the foot of the mast near the cases of provisions, their companions around them. Wilson took the helm, the captain stationed himself at the sail-tackling, and Mulready cut the cable that confined the raft to the brig. The sail was spread, and they began to move towards the shore under the combined influence of wind and tide.

The coast was only nine miles distant,—not a difficult voyage for a well-manned boat; but with the raft it was necessary to advance slowly. If the wind held out, they might perhaps reach land with this tide; but if there should be a calm, the ebb would carry them back, or they would be compelled to anchor and wait for the next tide.

However, Captain Mangles hoped to succeed. The wind freshened. As it had been flood now for some hours, they must either reach land soon, or anchor.

Fortune favored them. Gradually the black points of the rocks and the yellow sand of the bars disappeared beneath the waves; but great attention and extreme skill became necessary, in this dangerous neighborhood, to guide their unwieldy craft.

They were still five miles from shore. A clear sky enabled them to distinguish the principal features of the country. To the northeast rose a lofty mountain, whose outline was defined against the horizon in a very singular resemblance to the grinning profile of a monkey.

Paganel soon observed that all the sand-bars had disappeared.

"Except one," replied Lady Helena.

"Where?" asked Paganel.

"There," said Lady Helena, pointing to a black speck a mile ahead.

"That is true," answered Paganel. "Let us try to determine its position, that we may not run upon it when the tide covers it."

"It is exactly at the northern projection of the mountain," said Captain Mangles. "Wilson, bear away towards the offing."

"Yes, captain," replied the sailor, bearing with all his weight upon the steering oar.

They approached nearer; but, strange to say, the black point still rose above the water. The captain gazed at it attentively, and, to see better, employed Paganel's telescope.

"It is not a rock," said he, after a moment's examination; "it is a floating object, that rises and falls with the swell."

"Is it not a piece of the Macquarie's mast?" asked Lady Helena.

"No," replied Glenarvan; "no fragment could have drifted so far from the ship."

"Wait!" cried Captain Mangles. "I recognize it. It is the boat."

"The brig's boat?" said Glenarvan.

"Yes, my lord, the brig's boat, bottom upwards."

"The unfortunate sailors!" exclaimed Lady Helena, "they have perished!"

"Yes, madam," continued the captain; "and they might have foreseen it; for in the midst of these breakers, on a stormy sea, and in such profound darkness, they fled to certain death."

"May Heaven have pity on them!" murmured Mary Grant.

For a few moments the passengers were silent. They gazed at this frail bark towards which they drew nearer and nearer. It had evidently capsized a considerable distance from land, and of those who embarked in it probably not one had survived.

"But this boat may be useful," said Glenarvan.

"Certainly," replied Captain Mangles. "Come about, Wilson."

The direction of the raft was changed, but the wind subsided gradually, and it cost them much time to reach the boat. Mulready, standing at the bow, warded off the shock, and the yawl was drawn alongside.

"Empty?" asked Captain Mangles.

"Yes, captain," replied the sailor, "the boat is empty, and her seams have started open. She is of no use to us."

"Can we not save any part?" asked MacNabb.

"No," answered the captain. "She is only fit to burn."

"I am sorry," said Paganel, "for the yawl might have taken us to Auckland."

"We must be resigned, Mr. Paganel," rejoined the captain. "Moreover, on such a rough sea, I prefer our raft to that frail conveyance. A slight shock would dash it in pieces! Therefore, my lord, we have nothing more to stay here for."

"As you wish, John," said Glenarvan.

"Forward, Wilson," continued the young captain, "straight for the coast!"

The tide would yet flow for about an hour, and in this time they could accomplish a considerable distance. But soon the breeze subsided almost entirely, and the raft was motionless. Soon it even began to drift towards the open sea under the influence of the ebb.

The captain did not hesitate a moment.

"Anchor!" cried he.

Mulready, who was in an instant ready to execute this order, let fall the anchor, and the raft drifted till the cable was taut. The sail was reefed, and arrangements were made for a long detention. Indeed, the tide would not turn till late in the evening; and, as they did not care to sail in the dark, they anchored for the night in sight of land.

Quite a heavy swell agitated the surface of the water, and seemed to set steadily towards the shore. Glenarvan, therefore, when he learned that the whole night would be passed on board, asked why they did not take advantage of this current to approach the coast.

"My lord," replied the young captain, "is deceived by an optical illusion. The apparent onward movement is only an oscillation of the water, nothing more. Throw a piece of wood into the water, and you will see that it will remain stationary, so long as the ebb is not felt. We must therefore have patience."

"And dinner," added the major.

Olbinett took out of a case of provisions some pieces of dried meat and a dozen biscuits, though reluctant to offer such meagre fare. It was accepted, however, with good grace, even by the ladies, whose appetites the fresh sea air greatly improved.

Night approached. Already the sun's disk, glowing with crimson, was disappearing beneath the horizon; and the waters glistened and sparkled like sheets of liquid silver under his last rays. Nothing could be seen but sky and water, except one sharply-defined object, the hull of the Macquarie, motionless on the reefs. The short twilight was rapidly followed by the darkness, and soon the land that bounded the horizon some miles away was lost in the gloom. In this perplexing situation these shipwrecked people lapsed into an uneasy and distressing drowsiness, and as the result at daybreak all were more exhausted than refreshed.

With the turn of the tide the wind rose. It was six o'clock in the morning, and time was precious. Preparations were made for getting under way, and the order was given to weigh anchor; but the flukes, by the strain of the cable, were so deeply imbedded in the sand that without the windlass even the tackling that Wilson arranged could not draw them out.

Half an hour passed in useless efforts. The captain, impatient to set sail, cut the cable, and thus took away all possibility of anchoring, in case the tide should not enable them to reach the shore. The sail was unfurled, and they drifted slowly towards the land that rose in grayish masses against the background of the sky, illumined by the rising sun. The reefs were skillfully avoided, but, with the unsteady breeze, they did not seem to draw nearer the shore.

At last, however, land was less than a mile distant, craggy with rocks and very precipitous. It was necessary to find a practicable landing. The wind now moderated and soon subsided entirely, the sail flapping idly against the mast.

The tide alone moved the raft; but they had to give up steering, and masses of sea-weed retarded their progress.

After awhile they gradually became stationary three cable-lengths from shore. But they had no anchor, and would they not be carried out to sea again by the ebb? With eager glance and anxious heart the captain looked towards the inaccessible shore.

Just at this moment a shock was felt. The raft stopped. They had stranded on a sand-bar, not far from the coast. Glenarvan, Robert, Wilson, and Mulready leaped into the water, and moored their bark firmly with cables on the adjoining reefs. The ladies were carried in their companions' arms, and reached the shore without wetting a single fold of their garments; and soon all, with arms and provisions, had set foot on the inhospitable shores of New Zealand.

Glenarvan, without losing an hour, would have followed the coast to Auckland; but since early morning the sky had been heavy with clouds, which, towards noon, descended in torrents of rain. Hence it was impossible to start on their journey, and advisable to seek a shelter.

Wilson discovered, fortunately, a cavern, hollowed out by the sea in the basaltic rocks of the shore, and here the travelers took refuge with their arms and provisions. There was an abundance of dry sea-weed, lately cast up by the waves. This formed a soft couch, of which they availed themselves. Several pieces of wood were piled up at the entrance and then kindled; and while the fire served to dry their garments conversation beguiled the hours, as they lay or stood at ease.

Paganel, as usual, upon being appealed to, could tell them of the rise, extension, and consolidation of the British power upon the island; he informed them of the beginnings—and, to his belief, of the causes—of the strife which for years decimated the aborigines, and was very injurious to the colonists who had emigrated; then, in reply to Robert's questions, he went on to speak of those who on a narrower theatre had emulated by their heroism and patience the deeds of the world's great travelers and scientific explorers. He told them of Witcombe and Charlton Howitt, men known in their own circles and in connection with their own branch of the New Zealand government. At still greater length he detailed the adventures of Jacob Louper, who was the companion of Witcombe, and had gone as his assistant to discover a practicable route over the mountains in the north of the province of Canterbury. In those mountain wilds, which even the islanders rarely traverse, these two Europeans suffered greatly, but still worse was their fate when they descended to the water-level and essayed to cross the Taramakau near its mouth. Jacob Louper at length found two old and almost useless canoes, and by attaching the one to the other they hoped to accomplish the passage safely. Before they had reached the middle of the rapid current, however, both the tubs capsized. Louper, with difficulty, managed to support himself on one of them, and by clinging to it was at length carried to the river's bank, which his companion also reached; but when after a period of insensibility Louper returned to consciousness and found the body of Witcombe, it was lifeless. Though terribly bruised and still bleeding from his wounds, Louper hollowed a grave for the remains, and then, after many more days of privation and danger, came to the huts of some of the Maoris, by whose assistance he at length reached the settled parts of the colony.

These facts and reminiscences, it must be confessed, were not of the most inspiriting character; but they were in the same key as most of Paganel's disquisitions and information concerning these islands, and they were before a late hour exchanged for peaceful though probably dreamy slumbers, by his hearers.

Early the next morning the signal for departure was given. The rain had ceased during the night, and the sky was covered with grayish clouds, which intercepted the rays of the sun, so that the temperature thus moderated enabled them to endure the fatigues of the journey.

By consulting the map, Paganel had calculated that they would have to travel eight days. But, instead of following the windings of the coast, he considered it best to proceed to the village of Ngarnavahia, at the junction of the Waikato and Waipa rivers. Here the overland mail-road passed, and it would thence be easy to reach Drury, and rest, after their hardships, in a comfortable hotel.

But before they left the shore their attention was drawn to the large number of seals, of a peculiar appearance and genus, which lay on the broad sands daily washed by the tidal water. These seals, with their rounded heads, their upturned look, their expressive eyes, presented an appearance, almost a physiognomy, that was mild and wellnigh tender, and served to recall to the traveler's memory the tales about the sirens of the olden and modern times, who served as the enchantresses to just such inhospitable shores as that seemed on which they had themselves been cast. These animals, which are very numerous on the coast of New Zealand, are hunted and killed for the sake of their oil and their skins, and Paganel was of course able to tell how much within the last few years they had been searched for by the traders and navigators on these seas.

Whilst speaking of these matters, Robert drew Paganel's attention to some curious amphibious creatures, resembling the seals, but larger, which were devouring with rapidity the large stones lying on the shore.

"Look," said he, "here are seals which feed on pebbles."

Paganel assured them that these sea-elephants were only weighting themselves preparatory to their descent into the water, and protested that if they would but wait for a time they might see them descend and subsequently return when they had unloaded themselves. The first part of this programme they saw accomplished; but, greatly to Paganel's grief, Glenarvan would not longer delay the party, and they soon began to see inland beauties and curiosities of another sort.

The district through which they had to walk this day and the next was one very thick with brush and under-wood, and there was no possibility of horse or vehicle passing or meeting them. They now regretted the absence of their

Australian cart, for the height and frequency of the large ferns in the neighborhood prevented their making any rapid progress on foot.

Here and there, however, Robert and Paganel would rejoice together over some choice bush or bird that they had met with. Notable among the latter was the New Zealand "kiwi," known to naturalists as the apteryx, and which is becoming very scarce, from the pursuit of its many enemies. Robert discovered in a nest on the ground a couple of these birds without tails or wings, but with four toes on the foot, and a long beak or bill like that of a woodcock, and small white feathers all over its body. Of this bird there was then an entire absence in the zoological collections of Europe, and Paganel indulged the hope that he might be able to be the proud contributor of such a valuable specimen to the "Jardin" of his own city. For the present, at least, the realization of his hopes had to be deferred; and at length, after some days of weariness and continued travel, the party reached the banks of the Waipa. The country was deserted. There was no sign of natives, no path that would indicate the presence of man in these regions. The waters of the river flowed between tall bushes, or glided over sandy shallows, while the range of vision extended to the hills that inclosed the valley on the east.

At four o'clock in the afternoon nine miles had been valiantly accomplished. According to the map, which Paganel continually consulted, the junction of the Waikato and Waipa could not be more than five miles distant. The road to Auckland passed this point, and there they would encamp for the night. As for the fifty miles that would still separate them from the capital, two or three days would be sufficient for this, and even eight hours, if they should meet the mail-coach.

"Then," said Glenarvan, "we shall be compelled to encamp again to-night."

"Yes," replied Paganel; "but, as I hope, for the last time."

"So much the better; for these are severe hardships for Lady Helena and Mary Grant."

"And they endure them heroically," added Captain Mangles. "But, if I am not mistaken, Mr. Paganel, you have spoken of a village situated at the junction of the two rivers."

"Yes," answered the geographer; "here it is on the map. It is Ngarnavahia, about two miles below the junction."

"Well, could we not lodge there for the night? Lady Helena and Miss Grant would not hesitate to go two miles farther, if they could find a tolerable hotel."

"A hotel!" cried Paganel. "A hotel in a Maori village! There is not even a tavern. This village is only a collection of native huts; and, far from seeking shelter there, my advice is to avoid it most carefully."

"Always your fears, Paganel!" said Glenarvan.

"My dear lord, distrust is better than confidence among the Maoris. I do not know upon what terms they are with the English. Now, timidity aside, such as ourselves would be fine prizes, and I dislike to try New Zealand hospitality. I therefore think it wise to avoid this village, and likewise any meeting with the natives. Once at Drury, it will be different, and there our courageous ladies can refresh themselves at their ease for the fatigues of their journey."

The geographer's opinion prevailed. Lady Helena preferred to pass the last night in the open air rather than to expose her companions. Neither she nor Mary Grant required a halt, and they therefore continued to follow the banks of the river.

Two hours after, the first shadows of evening began to descend the mountains. The sun before disappearing below the western horizon had glinted a few rays through a rift in the clouds. The eastern peaks were crimsoned with the last beams of day.

Glenarvan and his friends hastened their pace. They knew the shortness of the twilight in this latitude, and how quickly night sets in. It was important to reach the junction of the two rivers before it became dark. But a dense fog rose from the earth, and made it very difficult to distinguish the way.

Fortunately, hearing availed in place of sight. Soon a distinct murmur of the waters indicated the union of the two streams in a common bed, and not long after the little party arrived at the point where the Waipa mingles with the Waikato in resounding cascades.

"Here is the Waikato," cried Paganel, "and the road to Auckland runs along its right bank."

"We shall see to-morrow," replied the major. "Let us encamp here. It seems to me as if those deeper shadows yonder proceeded from a little thicket of trees that has grown here expressly to shelter us. Let us eat and sleep."

"Eat," said Paganel, "but of biscuits and dried meat, without kindling a fire. We have arrived here unseen; let us try to go away in the same manner. Fortunately, this fog will render us invisible."

The group of trees was reached, and each conformed to the geographer's rigorous regulations. The cold supper was noiselessly eaten, and soon a profound sleep overcame the weary travelers.

CHAPTER XLVIII. INTRODUCTION TO THE CANNIBALS.

The next morning at break of day a dense fog was spreading heavily over the river, but the rays of the sun were not long in piercing the mist, which rapidly disappeared under the influence of the radiant orb. The banks of the stream were released from their shroud, and the course of the Waikato appeared in all its morning beauty.

A narrow tongue of land bristling with shrubbery ran out to a point at the junction of the two rivers. The waters of the Waipa, which flowed more swiftly, drove back those of the Waikato for a quarter of a mile before they mingled; but the calm power of the one soon overcame the boisterous impetuosity of the other, and both glided peacefully together to the broad bosom of the Pacific.

As the mist rose, a boat might have been seen ascending the Waikato. It was a canoe seventy feet long and five broad. The lofty prow resembled that of

426

a Venetian gondola, and the whole had been fashioned out of the trunk of a pine. A bed of dry fern covered the bottom. Eight oars at the bow propelled it up the river, while a man at the stern guided it by means of a movable paddle.

This man was a native, of tall form, about forty-five years old, with broad breast and powerful limbs. His protruding and deeply furrowed brow, his fierce look and his sinister countenance, showed him to be a formidable individual.

He was a Maori chief of high rank, as could be seen by the delicate and compact tattooing that striped his face and body. Two black spirals, starting from the nostrils of his aquiline nose, circled his tawny eyes, met on his forehead, and were lost in his abundant hair. His mouth, with its shining teeth, and his chin, were hidden beneath a net-work of varied colors, while graceful lines wound down to his sinewy breast.

There was no doubt as to his rank. The sharp albatross bone, used by Maori tattooers, had furrowed his face five times, in close and deep lines. That he had reached his fifth promotion was evident from his haughty bearing. A large flaxen mat, ornamented with dog-skins, enveloped his person; while a girdle, bloody with his recent conflicts, encircled his waist. From his ears dangled ear-rings of green jade, and around his neck hung necklaces of "pounamous," sacred stones to which the New Zealanders attribute miraculous properties. At his side lay a gun of English manufacture, and a "patou-patou," a kind of double-edged hatchet.

Near him nine warriors, of lower rank, armed and of ferocious aspect, some still suffering from recent wounds, stood in perfect immobility, enveloped in their flaxen mantles. Three dogs of wild appearance were stretched at their feet. The eight rowers seemed to be servants or slaves of the chief. They worked vigorously, and the boat ascended the current of the Waikato with remarkable swiftness.

In the centre of this long canoe, with feet tied, but hands free, were ten European prisoners clinging closely to each other. They were Lord Glenarvan and his companions.

The evening before, the little party, led astray by the dense fog, had encamped in the midst of a numerous tribe of natives. About midnight, the travelers, surprised in their sleep, were made prisoners and carried on board the canoe. They had not yet been maltreated, but had tried in vain to resist. Their arms and ammunition were in the hands of the savages, and their own bullets would have quickly stretched them on the earth had they attempted to escape.

They were not long in learning, by the aid of a few English words which the natives used, that, being driven back by the British troops, they were returning, vanquished and weakened, to the regions of the upper Waikato. Their chief, after an obstinate resistance, in which he lost his principal warriors, was now on his way to rouse again the river tribes. He was called Kai-Koumou, a terrible name, which signified in the native language "he who eats the limbs of his enemy." He was brave and bold, but his cruelty equaled his bravery. No pity could be expected from him. His name was well known to the English soldiers, and a price had been set upon his head by the governor of New Zealand.

This terrible catastrophe had come upon Glenarvan just as he was about reaching the long-desired harbor of Auckland, whence he would have returned to his native country. Yet, looking at his calm and passionless countenance, you could not have divined the depth of his anguish, for in his present critical situation he did not betray the extent of his misfortunes. He felt that he ought to set an example of fortitude to his wife and his companions, as being the husband and chief. Moreover, he was ready to die first for the common safety, if circumstances should require it.

His companions were worthy of him; they shared his noble thoughts, and their calm and haughty appearance would scarcely have intimated that they were being carried away to captivity and suffering. By common consent, at Glenarvan's suggestion, they had resolved to feign a proud indifference in the presence of the savages. It was the only way of influencing those fierce natures.

Since leaving the encampment, the natives, taciturn like all savages, had scarcely spoken to each other. However, from a few words exchanged, Glenarvan perceived that they were acquainted with the English language. He therefore resolved to question the chief in regard to the fate that was in store for them. Addressing Kai-Koumou, he said, in a fearless tone:

"Where are you taking us, chief?"

Kai-Koumou gazed at him coldly without answering.

"Say, what do you expect to do with us?" continued Glenarvan.

The chief's eyes blazed with a sudden light, and in a stern voice he replied:

"To exchange you, if your friends will ransom you; to kill you, if they refuse."

Glenarvan asked no more, but hope returned to his heart. Doubtless, some chiefs of the Maori tribe had fallen into the hands of the English, and the natives would attempt to recover them by way of exchange; their situation, therefore, was not one for despair.

Meantime the canoe rapidly ascended the river. Paganel, whose changeable disposition carried him from one extreme to another, had regained his hopefulness. He believed that the Maoris were sparing them the fatigue of their journey to the English settlements, and that they were certain to arrive at their destination. He was, therefore, quite resigned to his lot, and traced on his map the course of the Waikato across the plains and valleys of the province. Lady Helena and Mary Grant, suppressing their terror, conversed in low tones with Glenarvan, and the most skillful physiognomist could not have detected on their faces the anxiety of their hearts.

The Waikato River is worshiped by the natives, as Paganel knew, and English and German naturalists have never ascended beyond its junction with the Waipa. Whither did Kai-Koumou intend to take his captives? The geographer could not have guessed if the word "Taupo," frequently repeated, had not attracted his attention. By consulting his map, he saw that this name was applied to a celebrated lake in the most mountainous part of the island, and that from it the Waikato flows.

Paganel, addressing Captain Mangles in French, so as not to be understood by the savages, asked him how fast the canoe was going. The captain thought about three miles an hour.

"Then," replied the geographer, "if we do not travel during the night, our voyage to the lake will last about four days."

"But whereabouts are the English garrisons?" asked Glenarvan.

"It is difficult to say," replied Paganel. "At all events, the war must have reached the province of Taranaki, and probably the troops are collected beyond the mountains, on the side of the lake where the habitations of the savages are concentrated."

"God grant it!" said Lady Helena.

Glenarvan cast a sorrowful glance at his young wife and Mary Grant, exposed to the mercy of these fierce natives, and captives in a wild country, far from all human assistance. But he saw that he was watched by Kai-Koumou, and, not wishing to show that one of the captives was his wife, he prudently kept his thoughts to himself, and gazed at the banks of the river with apparent indifference.

The sun was just sinking below the horizon as the canoe ran upon a bank of pumice-stones, which the Waikato carries with it from its source in the volcanic mountains. Several trees grew here, as if designed to shelter an encampment. Kai-Koumou landed his prisoners.

The men had their hands tied, the ladies were free. All were placed in the centre of the encampment, around which large fires formed an impassable barrier.

Before Kai-Koumou had informed his captives of his intention to exchange them, Glenarvan and Captain Mangles had discussed various methods of recovering their liberty. What they could not venture in the boat they hoped to attempt on land, at the hour for encamping, under cover of the night.

But since Glenarvan's conversation with the chief, it seemed wise to abandon this design. They must be patient. It was the most prudent plan. The exchange offered chances that neither an open attack nor a flight across these unknown regions could afford. Many circumstances might indeed arise that would delay, and even prevent, such a transaction; but still it was better to await the result. What, moreover, could ten defenceless men do against thirty well-armed savages? Besides, Glenarvan thought it likely that Kai-Koumou's tribe had lost some chief of high rank whom they were particularly anxious to recover; and he was not mistaken.

The next day the canoe ascended the river with increased swiftness. It stopped for a moment at the junction of a small river which wound across the plains on the right bank. Here another canoe, with ten natives on board, joined Kai-Koumou. The warriors merely exchanged salutations, and then continued their course. The new-comers had recently fought against the English troops, as could be seen by their tattered garments, their gory weapons, and the wounds that still bled beneath their rags. They were gloomy and taciturn, and, with the indifference common to all savage races, paid no attention to the captives.

Towards evening Kai-Koumou landed at the foot of the mountains, whose nearer ridges reached precipitously to the river-bank. Here twenty natives, who had disembarked from their canoes, were making preparations for the night. Fires blazed beneath the trees. A chief, equal in rank to Kai-Koumou, advanced with measured pace, and, rubbing his nose against that of the latter, saluted him cordially. The prisoners were stationed in the centre of the encampment, and guarded with extreme vigilance.

The next morning the ascent of the Waikato was resumed. Other boats came from various affluents of the river. Sixty warriors, evidently fugitives from the last insurrection, had now assembled, and were returning, more or less wounded in the fray, to the mountain districts. Sometimes a song arose from the canoes, as they advanced in single file. One native struck up the patriotic ode of the mysterious "Pihé," the national hymn that calls the Maoris to battle. The full and sonorous voice of the singer waked the echoes of the mountains; and after each stanza his comrades struck their breasts, and sang the warlike verses in chorus. Then they seized their oars again, and the canoes were headed up stream.

During the day a singular sight enlivened the voyage. About four o'clock the canoe, without lessening its speed, guided by the steady hand of the chief, dashed through a narrow gorge. Eddies broke violently against numerous small islands, which rendered navigation exceeding dangerous. Never could it be more hazardous to capsize, for the banks afforded no refuge, and whoever had set foot on the porous crust of the shore would probably have perished. At this point the river flowed between warm springs, oxide of iron colored the muddy ground a brilliant red, and not a yard of firm earth could be seen. The air was heavy with a penetrating sulphureous odor. The natives did not regard it, but the captives were seriously annoyed by the noxious vapors exhaled from the fissures of the soil and the bubbles that burst and discharged their gaseous contents. Yet, however disagreeable these emanations were, the eye could not but admire this magnificent spectacle.

The canoes soon after entered a dense cloud of white smoke, whose wreaths rose in gradually decreasing circles above the river. On the shores a hundred geysers, some shooting forth masses of vapor, and others overflowing in liquid columns, varied their effects, like the jets and cascades of a fountain. It seemed as though some engineer was directing at his pleasure the outflowings of these springs, as the waters and vapor, mingling in the air, formed rainbows in the sunbeams.

For two miles the canoes glided within this vapory atmosphere, enveloped in its warm waves that rolled along the surface of the water. Then the sulphureous smoke disappeared, and a pure swift current of fresh air refreshed the panting voyagers. The region of the springs was passed. Before the close of the day two more rapids were ascended, and at evening Kai-Koumou encamped a hundred miles above the junction of the two streams. The river now turned towards the east, and then again flowed southward into Lake Taupo.

The next morning Jacques Paganel consulted his map and discovered on the right bank Mount Taubara, which rises to the height of three thousand feet. At noon the whole fleet of boats entered Lake Taupo, and the natives hailed with frantic gestures a shred of cloth that waved in the wind from the roof of a hut. It was the national flag.

CHAPTER XLIX. A MOMENTOUS INTERVIEW.

Long before historic times, an abyss, twenty-five miles long and twenty wide, must at some period have been formed by a subsidence of subterranean caverns in the volcanic district forming the centre of the island. The waters of the surrounding country have rushed down and filled this enormous cavity, and the abyss has become a lake, whose depth no one has yet been able to measure.

Such is this strange Lake Taupo, elevated eleven hundred and fifty feet above the level of the sea, and surrounded by lofty mountains. On the west of the prisoners towered precipitous rocks of imposing form; on the north rose several distant ridges, crowned with small forests; on the east spread a broad plain furrowed by a trail and covered with pumice-stones that glittered beneath a net-work of bushes; and on the north, behind a stretch of woodland, volcanic peaks majestically encircled this vast extent of water, the fury of whose tempests equaled that of the ocean cyclones.

But Paganel was scarcely disposed to enlarge his account of these wonders, nor were his friends in a mood to listen. They gazed in silence towards the northeast shore of the lake, whither the canoe was bringing them.

The mission established at Pukawa, on the western shores, no longer existed. The missionary had been driven by the war far from the principal dwellings of the insurrectionists. The prisoners were helpless, abandoned to the mercy of the vengeful Maoris, and in that wild part of the island to which Christianity has never penetrated. Kai-Koumou, leaving the waters of the Waikato, passed through the little creek which served as an outlet to the river, doubled a sharp promontory, and landed on the eastern border of the lake, at the base of the first slopes of Mount Manga.

A quarter of a mile distant, on a buttress of the mountain, appeared a "pah," a Maori fortification, situated in an impregnable position. The prisoners were taken ashore, with their hands and feet free, and conducted thither by the warriors. After quite a long détour, Glenarvan and his companions reached the pah.

This fortress was defended by an outer rampart of strong palisades, fifteen feet high. A second line of stakes, and then a fence of osiers, pierced with loop-holes, inclosed the inner space, the court-yard of the pah, in which stood several Maori tents, and forty huts which were symmetrically arranged.

On their arrival, the captives were terribly impressed at sight of the heads that ornamented the stakes of the second inclosure. Lady Helena and Mary Grant turned away their eyes with more of disgust than terror. These heads had most of them belonged to hostile chiefs, fallen in battle, whose bodies had served as food for the conquerors. The geographer knew them to be such by their hollow and eyeless sockets!

In Kai-Koumou's pah only the heads of his enemies formed this frightful museum; and here, doubtless, more than one English skull had served to increase the size of the chief's collection.

His hut, among those belonging to warriors of lower rank, stood at the rear of the pah, in front of a large open terrace. This structure was built of stakes, interlaced with branches, and lined inside with flax matting.

Only one opening gave access to the dwelling. A thick curtain, made of a vegetable tissue, served as a door. The roof projected so as to form a water-shed. Several faces, carved at the ends of the rafters, adorned the hut, and the curtain was covered with various imitations of foliage, symbolical figures, monsters, and graceful sculpturing, a curious piece of work, fashioned by the scissors of the native decorators.

Inside of the habitation the floor was made of hard-trodden earth, and raised six inches above the ground. Several rush screens and some mattresses, covered with woven matting of long leaves and twigs, served as beds. In the middle of the room a hole in a stone formed the fireplace, and another in the roof answered for a chimney.

The smoke, when it became sufficiently thick, perforce escaped at this outlet, but it of course blackened the walls of the house.

On one side of the hut were storehouses, containing the chief's provisions, his harvest of flax, potatoes, and edible ferns, and the ovens where the various articles of food were cooked by contact with heated stones. Farther off, in small pens, pigs and goats were confined, and dogs ran about seeking their scanty sustenance. They were rather poorly kept, for animals that formed the Maori daily food.

Glenarvan and his companions had taken in the whole at a glance. They awaited beside an empty hut the good pleasure of the chief, exposed to the insults of a crowd of old women, who surrounded them like harpies, and threatened them with their fists, crying and howling. Several English words that passed their lips clearly indicated that they were demanding immediate vengeance.

In the midst of these cries and threats, Lady Helena affected a calmness that she could not feel in her heart. This courageous woman, in order that her husband's coolness might not forsake him, heroically controlled her emotions. Poor Mary Grant felt herself growing weak, and Captain Mangles supported her, ready to die in her defence. The others endured this torrent of invectives in various ways, either indifferent like the major, or increasingly annoyed like Paganel.

Glenarvan, wishing to relieve Lady Helena from the assaults of these shrews, boldly approached Kai-Koumou, and, pointing to the hideous throng, said:

"Drive them away!"

The Maori chief gazed steadily at his prisoner without replying. Then with a gesture he silenced the noisy horde. Glenarvan bowed in token of thanks, and slowly resumed his place among his friends.

Kai-Koumou, fearing an insurrection of the fanatics of his tribe, now led his captives to a sacred place, situated at the other end of the pah, on the edge of a precipice. This hut rested against a rock that rose a hundred feet above it and was a steep boundary to this side of the fortification. In this consecrated temple the priests, or "arikis," instruct the New Zealanders. The building was spacious and tightly closed, and contained the holy and chosen food of the god.

Here the prisoners, temporarily sheltered from the fury of the natives, stretched themselves on the flax mats. Lady Helena, her strength exhausted and her energy overcome, sank into her husband's arms. Glenarvan pressed her to his breast, and said:

"Courage, my dear Helena; Heaven will not forsake us!"

Robert was scarcely within the hut before he climbed on Wilson's shoulders, and succeeded in thrusting his head through an opening between the roof and the wall, where strings of pipes were hanging. From this point his view commanded the whole extent of the pah, as far as Kai-Koumou's hut.

"They have gathered around the chief," said he, in a low voice. "They are waving their arms, and howling. Kai-Koumou is going to speak."

The boy was silent for a few moments, then continued:

"Kai-Koumou is speaking. The savages grow calm; they listen."

"This chief," said the major, "has evidently a personal interest in protecting us. He wishes to exchange his prisoners for some chiefs of his tribe. But will his warriors consent?"

"Yes, they are listening to him," continued Robert. "They are dispersing; some return to their huts,—others leave the fortification."

"Is it really so?" cried the major.

"Yes, Mr. MacNabb," replied Robert. "Kai-Koumou remains alone with the warriors that were in the canoe. Ha! one of them is coming towards us!"

"Get down, Robert," said Glenarvan.

At this moment Lady Helena, who had risen, seized her husband's arm.

"Edward," said she, in a firm voice, "neither Mary Grant nor I shall fall alive into the hands of those savages!"

And, so saying, she presented to her husband a loaded revolver.

"A weapon!" exclaimed Glenarvan, whose eyes suddenly brightened.

"Yes. The Maoris do not search their female prisoners; but this weapon is for us, Edward, not for them."

"Glenarvan," said MacNabb quickly, "hide the revolver. It is not time yet."

The weapon was immediately concealed in his clothes. The mat that closed the entrance of the hut was raised. A native appeared. He made a sign to the captives to follow him. Glenarvan and his companions passed through the pah, and stopped before Kai-Koumou.

Around him were assembled the principal warriors of his tribe, among whom was seen the chief whose canoe had first joined Kai-Koumou on the river. He was a man of about forty, robust, and of fierce and cruel aspect. His name was Kara-Tété, which means in the native language "The Irascible." Kai-Koumou treated him with some respect, and from the delicacy of his tattooing it was evident that he occupied a high rank in his tribe. An observer, however, would have detected a rivalry between the two chiefs. The major, indeed, perceived that Kara-Tété's influence surpassed that of Kai-Koumou. They both ruled the powerful tribes of the Waikato with equal rank; and, during this interview, although Kai-Koumou smiled, his eyes betrayed a deep hostility.

He now questioned Glenarvan. "You are English?" said he.

"Yes," replied Glenarvan, without hesitation, for this nationality would probably facilitate an exchange.

"And your companions?" asked Kai-Koumou.

"My companions are also English. We are shipwrecked travelers, and, if you care to know, we have taken no part in the war."

"No matter," replied Kara-Tété, brutally. "Every Englishman is our enemy. Your people have invaded our island. They have stolen away our fields; they have burned our villages."

"They have done wrong," said Glenarvan, in a grave tone. "I say so because I think so, and not because I am in your power."

"Listen," continued Kai-Koumou. "Tohonga, the high-priest of Nouï-Atoua, has fallen into the hands of your brothers. He is prisoner of the Pakekas (Europeans). Our god commands us to ransom his life. I would have torn out your heart, I would have hung your companions' heads and yours forever to the stakes of this palisade. But Nouï-Atoua has spoken."

So saying, Kai-Koumou, who had hitherto controlled himself, trembled with rage, and his countenance was flushed with a fierce exultation. Then, after a few moments, he resumed, more coolly: "Do you think the English will give us our Tohonga in exchange for you?"

Glenarvan hesitated, and watched the Maori chief very attentively.

"I do not know," said he, after a moment's silence.

"Speak," continued Kai-Koumou. "Is your life worth that of our Tohonga?"

"No," answered Glenarvan. "I am neither a chief nor a priest among my people."

Paganel was astounded at this reply, and gazed at Glenarvan in profound wonder. Kai-Koumou seemed equally surprised.

"Then you doubt it?" said he.

"I do not know," repeated Glenarvan.

"Will not your people accept you in exchange for our Tohonga?"

"Not me alone," replied Glenarvan; "but perhaps all of us."

"Among the Maoris," said Kai-Koumou, "it is one for one."

"Offer these ladies first in exchange for your priest," answered Glenarvan, pointing to Lady Helena and Mary Grant. Lady Helena would have rushed towards her husband, but the major restrained her.

"These two ladies," continued Glenarvan, turning respectfully towards them, "hold a high rank in their country."

The warrior glanced coldly at his prisoner. A malicious smile passed over his face; but he almost instantly repressed it, and replied, in a voice which he could scarcely control:

"Do you hope, then, to deceive Kai-Koumou by false words, cursed European? Do you think that Kai-Koumou's eyes cannot read your heart?"

Then, pointing to Lady Helena, he said:

"That is your wife!"

"No, mine!" cried Kara-Tété.

Then, pushing back the prisoners, the chief laid his hand on Lady Helena's shoulder, who grew pale at the touch.

"Edward!" cried the unfortunate woman, in terror.

Glenarvan, without uttering a word, raised his arm. A report resounded. Kara-Tété fell dead.

At this sound a crowd of natives issued from the huts. The pah was filled in an instant. A hundred arms were raised against the captives. Glenarvan's revolver was snatched from his hand.

Kai-Koumou cast a strange look at Glenarvan, and then, guarding with one hand the person of him who had fired, he controlled with the other the throng that was rushing upon the Europeans.

At last his voice rose above the tumult. "Taboo! taboo!" cried he.

At this word the crowd fell back before Glenarvan and his companions, thus temporarily preserved by a supernatural power. A few moments after they were led back to the temple that served as their prison; but Robert Grant and Paganel were no longer with them.

CHAPTER L. THE CHIEF'S FUNERAL.

Kai-Koumou, according to a custom quite ordinary in New Zealand, joined the rank of priest to that of chief, and could, therefore, extend to persons or objects the superstitious protection of the taboo.

The taboo, which is common to the tribes of Polynesia, has the power to prohibit at once all connection with the object or person tabooed. According to the Maori religion, whoever should lay his sacrilegious hand on what is declared taboo would be punished with death by the offended god; and in case the divinity should delay to avenge his own insult, the priests would not fail to excite his anger.

As for the prisoners confined in the temple, the taboo had rescued them from the fury of the tribe. Some of the natives, the friends and partisans of Kai-Koumou, had stopped suddenly at the command of their chief, and had protected the captives.

Glenarvan, however, was not blind to the fate that was reserved for him. Only his death could atone for the murder of a chief. Among savage races death is always preceded by a protracted torture. He therefore expected to cruelly expiate the righteous indignation that had nerved his arm, but hoped that Kai-Koumou's rage would fall only on himself.

What a night he and his companions passed! Who could depict their anguish, or measure their sufferings? Neither poor Robert nor brave Paganel had reappeared. But how could they doubt their fate? Were they not the first victims of the natives' vengeance? All hope had vanished even from the heart of the major, who did not easily despair. John Mangles felt himself growing mad at sight of the sad dejection of Mary Grant, thus separated from her brother. Glenarvan thought of that terrible request of Lady Helena, who, rather than yield to torture or slavery, preferred to die by his hand. Could he summon this fearful courage? As for an escape, that was plainly impossible. Ten warriors, armed to the teeth, guarded the entrance of the temple.

Morning came at last. There had been no communication between the natives and the prisoners. The hut contained a considerable quantity of food, which the unfortunates scarcely touched. Hunger gave place to grief. The day passed without bringing a change or a hope. Doubtless the hour for the dead chief's funeral and their torture would be the same.

However, although Glenarvan concluded that Kai-Koumou must have abandoned all idea of exchange, the major on this point retained a gleam of hope.

"Who knows," said he, reminding Glenarvan of the effect produced upon the chief by the death of Kara-Tété,—"who knows but that Kai-Koumou in reality feels obliged to you?"

But, in spite of these observations, Glenarvan would no longer hope. The next day also passed away without the preparations for torture being made. The reason of the delay was this.

The Maoris believe that the soul, for three days after death, inhabits the body of the deceased, and therefore during this time the corpse remains unburied. This custom was rigorously observed, and for two days the pah was deserted. Captain Mangles frequently stood on Wilson's shoulders and surveyed the fortification. No native was seen; only the sentinels guarded in turn at the door of their prison.

But on the third day the huts were opened. The savages, men, women, and children, to the number of several hundreds, assembled in the pah, silent and calm. Kai-Koumou came out of his house, and, surrounded by the principal warriors of his tribe, took his place on a mound several feet high in the centre of the fortification. The crowd of natives formed a semicircle around him, and the whole assembly preserved absolute silence.

At a sign from the chief, a warrior advanced towards the temple.

"Remember!" said Lady Helena to her husband.

Glenarvan clasped his wife to his heart. At this moment Mary Grant approached John Mangles.

"Lord and Lady Glenarvan," said she, "I think that, if a wife can die by the hand of her husband to escape a degrading existence, a maiden can likewise die by the hand of her lover. John (for I may tell you at this critical moment), have I not long been your betrothed in the depths of your heart? May I rely upon you, dear John, as Lady Helena does upon Lord Glenarvan?"

"Mary!" cried the young captain, in terror. "Ah! dear Mary—"

He could not finish: the mat was raised, and the captives were dragged towards Kai-Koumou. The two women were resigned to their fate, while the men concealed their anguish beneath a calmness that showed superhuman self-control. They came before the chief, who did not delay sentence.

"You killed Kara-Tété!" said he to Glenarvan.

"I did."

"You shall die to-morrow at sunrise."

"Alone?" inquired Glenarvan, whose heart beat quickly.

"What! as if our Tohonga's life were not more precious than yours!" cried Kai-Koumou, whose eyes expressed a fierce regret.

At this moment a commotion took place among the natives. Glenarvan cast a rapid glance around him. The crowd opened, and a warrior, dripping with sweat and overcome with fatigue, appeared.

As soon as Kai-Koumou perceived him, he said in English, evidently that he might be understood by the captives:

"You come from the camp of the pale-faces?"

"Yes," replied the Maori.

"You saw the prisoner, our Tohonga?"

"I did."

"Is he living?"

"He is dead! The English have shot him."

The fate of Glenarvan and his companions was settled.

"You shall all die to-morrow at daybreak!" cried Kai-Koumou.

The unfortunates were therefore to suffer a common death. Lady Helena and Mary Grant raised towards heaven a look of thankfulness.

The captives were not taken back to the temple. They were to attend that day the funeral of the dead chief, and the bloody ceremonies connected therewith. A party of natives conducted them to the foot of an enormous koudi, where these guardians remained without losing sight of their prisoners. The rest of the tribe, absorbed in their official mourning, seemed to have forgotten them.

The customary three days had elapsed since the death of Kara-Tété. The soul of the deceased had therefore forever abandoned its mortal abode. The sacred rites began.

The body was carried to a small mound in the centre of the fortification, clothed in splendid costume, and enveloped in a magnificent flaxen mat. The head was adorned with plumes, and wore a crown of green leaves. The face, arms, and breast had been rubbed with oil, and therefore showed no mortification.

The parents and friends of the deceased came to the foot of the mound, and all at once, as if some director were beating time to a funeral dirge, a great concert of cries, groans, and sobs arose on the air. They mourned the dead in plaintive and modulated cadences. His relations struck their heads together; his kinswomen lacerated their faces with their nails, and showed themselves more lavish of blood than of tears. These unfortunate females conscientiously fulfilled their barbarous duty.

But these demonstrations were not enough to appease the soul of the deceased, whose wrath would doubtless have smitten the survivors of his tribe; and his warriors, as they could not recall him to life, wished that he should have no cause to regret in the other world the happiness of this.

Kara-Tété's wife was not to forsake her husband in the tomb. Moreover, the unfortunate woman would not have been allowed to survive him; it was the custom, in accordance with duty, and examples of such sacrifices are not wanting in New Zealand history. The woman appeared. She was still young. Her hair floated in disorder over her shoulders. Vague words, lamentations, and broken phrases, in which she celebrated the virtues of the dead, interrupted her groans; and, in a final paroxysm of grief, she stretched herself at the foot of the mound, beating the ground with her head.

At this moment Kai-Koumou approached her. Suddenly the unfortunate victim rose; but a violent blow with the "méré," a formidable club, wielded by the hand of the chief, struck her lifeless to the earth.

Frightful cries at once broke forth. A hundred arms threatened the captives, who trembled at the horrible sight. But no one stirred, for the funeral ceremonies were not ended.

Kara-Tété's wife had joined her husband in the other world. Both bodies lay side by side. But for the eternal life his faithful spouse could not alone suffice the deceased. Who would serve them in presence of Noüi-Atoua, if their slaves did not follow them?

Six unfortunates were brought before the corpse of their master and mistress. They were servants, whom the pitiless laws of war had reduced to slavery. During the life of the chief they had undergone the severest privations, suffered a thousand abuses, had been scantily fed, and compelled constantly to labor like beasts; and now, according to the Maori belief, they were to continue their existence of servitude for eternity.

They appeared to be resigned to their fate, and were not astonished at a sacrifice they had long anticipated. Their freedom from all bonds showed that they would meet death unresistingly. Moreover, this death was rapid, protracted sufferings were spared them. These were reserved for the captives who stood trembling not twenty paces distant. Six blows of the méré, given by six stalwart warriors, stretched the victims on the ground in a pool of blood. It was the signal for a terrible scene of cannibalism, which followed in all its horrible details.

Glenarvan and his companions, breathless with fright, strove to hide this awful scene from the eyes of the two unhappy ladies. They now understood what awaited them at sunrise the next day, and what cruel tortures would doubtless precede such a death. They were dumb with horror.

The funeral dance now began. Strong spirits, extracted from an indigenous plant, maddened the savages till they seemed no longer human. Would they not forget the taboo of the chief, and throw themselves in their final outbreaks upon the prisoners who trembled at their frenzy?

But Kai-Koumou had preserved his reason in the midst of the general intoxication. He allowed this bloody orgy an hour to reach its utmost intensity. The last act of the funeral was played with the usual rites.

The bodies of Kara-Tété and his wife were taken up, and their limbs bent and gathered against the stomach, according to the New Zealand custom. The place for the tomb had been chosen outside of the fortification, about two miles distant, on the summit of a small mountain, called Maunganamu, situated on the right shore of the lake.

Thither the bodies were to be carried. Two very rude palanquins, or rather litters, were brought to the foot of the mound. The corpses, folded together, in a sitting posture, and tied in their clothes by a girdle of withes, were placed on this primitive bier. Four warriors bore it between them, and the entire tribe, chanting the funeral hymn, followed them in procession to the place of burial.

The captives, who were always watched, saw them leave the inner inclosure of the pah, and then the songs and cries gradually died away. For about half an hour this funeral escort continued in sight, in the depths of the valley. Finally they perceived it again winding along the mountain paths. The distance gave a fantastic appearance to the undulating movements of the long, sinuous column.

The tribe stopped at the summit of the mountain, which was eight hundred feet high, at the place prepared for Kara-Tété's interment. A common Maori would have had only a hole and a heap of stones for a grave; but for a powerful and dreaded chief, destined doubtless for a speedy deification, a tomb worthy of his exploits was reserved.

The sepulchre had been surrounded by palisades, while stakes, ornamented with faces reddened with ochre, stood beside the grave where the bodies were to lie. The relatives had not forgotten that the "waidoua" (the spirit of the dead) feeds on substantial nourishment like the body during this perishable life. Food had therefore been deposited in the inclosure, together with the weapons and clothes of the deceased.

Nothing was wanting for the comfort of the tomb. Husband and wife were laid side by side, and then covered with earth and grass after a series of renewed lamentations. Then the procession silently descended the mountain, and now no one could ascend it under penalty of death, for it was tabooed.

CHAPTER LI. STRANGELY LIBERATED.

Just as the sun was disappearing behind Lake Taupo, the captives were led back to their prison. They were not to leave it again until the summit of the Wahiti mountains should kindle with the first beams of the day. One night remained to prepare for death. In spite of the faintness, in spite of the horror with which they were seized, they shared their repast in common.

"We shall need all the strength possible to face death," said Glenarvan. "We must show these barbarians how Europeans and Christians can die."

The meal being finished, Lady Helena repeated the evening prayer aloud, while all her companions, with uncovered heads, joined her. Having fulfilled this duty, and enjoyed this privilege, the prisoners embraced each other. Lady Helena and Mary Grant then retired to one corner of the hut, and stretched themselves upon a mat. Sleep, which soothes all woes, soon closed their eyes, and they slumbered in each other's arms, overcome by fatigue and long wakefulness.

Glenarvan, taking his friends aside, said:

"My dear companions, our lives and those of these poor ladies are in God's hands. If Heaven has decreed that we shall die to-morrow, we can, I am sure, die like brave people, like Christians, ready to appear fearlessly before the final Judge. God, who does read the secrets of the soul, knows that we are fulfilling a noble mission. If death awaits us instead of success, it is his will. However severe his decree may be, I shall not murmur against it. But this is not death alone; it is torture, disgrace; and here are two women—"

Glenarvan's voice, hitherto firm, now faltered. He paused to control his emotion. After a moment's silence, he said to the young captain:

"John, you have promised Mary Grant what I have promised Lady Helena. What have you resolved?"

"This promise," replied John Mangles, "I believe I have the right in the sight of God to fulfill."

"Yes, John; but we have no weapons."

"Here is one," answered John, displaying a poniard. "I snatched it from Kara-Tété's hands when he fell at your feet. My lord, he of us who survives the other shall fulfill this vow."

At these words a profound silence reigned in the hut. At last the major interrupted it by saying:

"My friends, reserve this extreme measure till the last moment. I am no advocate of what is irremediable."

"I do not speak for ourselves," replied Glenarvan. "We can brave death, whatever it may be. Ah, if we were alone! Twenty times already would I have urged you to make a sally and attack those wretches. But *they*—"

At this moment Captain Mangles raised the mat and counted twenty-five natives, who were watching at the door of their prison. A great fire had been kindled, which cast a dismal light over the irregular outlines of the pah. Some of these savages were stretched around the fire; and others, standing and motionless, were darkly defined against the bright curtain of flame.

It is said that, between the jailer who watches and the prisoner who wishes to escape, the chances are on the side of the latter. Indeed, the design of one is stronger than that of the other, for the first may forget that he is guarding, but the second cannot forget that he is guarded; the captive thinks oftener of escaping than his guardian thinks of preventing his escape. But here it was hate and vengeance that watched the prisoners, and not an indifferent jailer. They had not been bound, for bonds were useless where twenty-five men guarded the only outlet of the prison.

This hut was built against the rock that terminated the fortification, and was only accessible by a narrow passage that connected it with the front of the pah. The other two sides of the building were flanked by towering precipices, and stood on the verge of an abyss a hundred feet deep. A descent this way was therefore impossible. There was no chance of escaping in the rear, which was guarded by the enormous rock. The only exit was the door of the temple, and the Maoris defended the narrow passage that connected it with the pah. All escape was therefore out of the question; and Glenarvan, after examining the walls of his prison, was forced to acknowledge this disheartening fact.

Meantime, the hours of this night of anguish were passing away. Dense darkness had covered the mountain. Neither moon nor stars illumined the deep shades. A few gusts of wind swept along the side of the pah. The stakes of the hut groaned, the fire of the natives suddenly revived at this passing draught, and the flames cast rapid flashes into the temple, illumining for a moment the group of prisoners. These poor people were absorbed with their last thoughts; a deathly silence reigned in the hut.

It must have been about four o'clock in the morning, when the major's attention was attracted by a slight sound that seemed to come from behind the rear stakes, in the back wall that lay towards the rock. At first he was indifferent to the noise, but finding that it continued, he listened. At last, puzzled by its persistence, he put his ear close to the ground to hear better. It seemed as if some one was scraping and digging outside.

When he was certain of this fact, he passed quietly towards Glenarvan and the captain, and led them to the rear of the hut.

"Listen," said he, in a low voice, motioning to them to bend down.

The scrapings became more and more audible. They could hear the little stones grate under the pressure of a sharp instrument and fall down outside.

"Some creature in its burrow," said Captain Mangles.

Glenarvan, with bewildered gaze, stood astonished.

"Who knows," said he, "but that it is a man?"

"Man or animal," replied the major, "I will know what is going on."

Wilson and Olbinett joined their companions, and all began to dig in the wall, the captain with his poniard, the others with stones pulled out of the ground, or with their nails, while Mulready, stretched on the earth, watched the group of natives through the loop-hole of the mat. But they were motionless around the fire, and did not suspect what was transpiring twenty paces from them.

The soil was loose and crumbling, and lay upon a bed of clay, so that, in spite of the want of tools, the hole rapidly enlarged. It was soon evident that somebody, clinging to the sides of the pah, was making a passage in its outer wall. What could be the object? Did he know of the existence of the prisoners, or could a mere chance attempt at escape explain the work that seemed nearly completed?

The captives redoubled their efforts. Their lacerated fingers bled, but still they dug on. After half an hour's labor, the hole they were drilling had reached a depth of three feet. They could perceive by the sounds, which were now more distinct, that only a thin layer of earth prevented immediate communication.

A few moments more elapsed, when suddenly the major drew back his hand, which was cut by a sharp blade. He suppressed a cry that was about to escape him. Captain Mangles, holding out his poniard, avoided the knife that was moving out of the ground, but seized the hand that held it. It was the hand of a woman or a youth, a European hand. Not a word had been uttered on either side. There was plainly an object in keeping silent.

"Is it Robert?" murmured Glenarvan.

But, though only whispering this name, Mary Grant, awakened by the movement that was taking place in the hut, glided towards Glenarvan, and, seizing this hand all soiled with mud, covered it with kisses.

"It is you! it is you!" cried the young girl, who could not be mistaken, "you, my Robert!"

"Yes, little sister," replied Robert, "I am here to save you all! But silence!"

"Brave lad!" repeated Glenarvan.

"Keep watch of the savages outside," continued Robert.

Mulready, whose attention had been diverted for a moment by the appearance of the hand, resumed his post of observation.

"All is well," said he. "Only four warriors are watching now. The others have fallen asleep."

"Courage!" replied Wilson.

In an instant the hole was widened, and Robert passed from the arms of his sister into those of Lady Helena. Around his body was wound a rope of flax.

"My boy! my boy!" murmured Lady Helena; "these savages did not kill you?"

"No, madam," replied Robert. "Somehow, during the uproar, I succeeded in escaping their vigilance. I crossed the yard. For two days I kept hidden behind the bushes. At night I wandered about, longing to see you again. While the tribe were occupied with the funeral of the chief, I came and examined this side of the fortification, where the prison stands, and saw that I could reach you. I stole this knife and rope in a deserted hut. The tufts of grass and the bushes helped me to climb. By chance I found a kind of grotto hollowed out in the very rock against which this hut rests. I had only a few feet to dig in the soft earth, and here I am."

Twenty silent kisses were his only answer.

"Let us start," said he, in a decided tone.

"Is Paganel below?" inquired Glenarvan.

"Mr. Paganel?" repeated the boy, surprised apparently at the question.

"Yes; is he waiting for us?"

"No, my lord. What! is he not here?"

"He is not, Robert," replied Mary Grant.

"What! have you not seen him?" exclaimed Glenarvan. "Did you not meet each other in the confusion? Did you not escape together?"

"No, my lord," answered Robert, at a loss to understand the disappearance of his friend Paganel.

"Let us start," said the major; "there is not a moment to lose. Wherever Paganel may be, his situation cannot be worse than ours here. Let us go."

Indeed, the moments were precious. It was high time to start. The escape presented no great difficulties, but for the almost perpendicular wall of rock outside of the grotto, twenty feet high. The declivity then sloped quite gently to the base of the mountain, from which point the captives could quickly gain the lower valleys, while the Maoris, if they chanced to discover their flight, would be forced to make a very long détour, since they were not aware of the passage that had been dug in the mountain.

They now prepared to escape, and every precaution was taken to insure their success. The captives crawled one by one through the narrow passage, and found themselves in the grotto. Captain Mangles, before leaving the hut, concealed all traces of their work, and glided in his turn through the opening, which he closed with the mats. Their outlet was therefore entirely hidden.

The object now was to descend the perpendicular wall of rock, which would have been impossible if Robert had not brought the flax rope. It was unwound, fastened to a point of rock, and thrown over the declivity.

Before allowing his friends to trust their weight to these flaxen fibres, Captain Mangles tested them. They seemed to be quite strong, but it would not answer to venture rashly, for a fall might be fatal.

"This rope," said he, "can only bear the weight of two bodies, and we must therefore act accordingly. Let Lord and Lady Glenarvan slide down first. When they have reached the bottom, three shakes at the rope will be the signal to follow them."

"I will go first," replied Robert. "I have discovered at the base of the slope a sort of deep excavation, where those who descend first can wait for the others in safety."

"Go then, my boy," said Glenarvan, clasping the boy's hand.

Robert disappeared through the opening of the grotto. A moment after, three shakes of the rope informed them that he had accomplished his descent successfully.

Glenarvan and Lady Helena now ventured out of the grotto. The darkness below was still profound, but the gray light of dawn was already tinging the top of the mountain. The keen cold of the morning reanimated the young wife; she felt stronger, and commenced her perilous escape.

First her husband, and then she, slid down the rope to the point where the perpendicular wall met the summit of the slope. Then Glenarvan, going before his wife and assisting her, began to descend the declivity of the mountain backwards. He sought for tufts of grass and bushes that offered a point of support, and tried them before placing Lady Helena's feet upon them. Several birds, suddenly awakened, flew away with shrill cries, and the fugitives shuddered when a large stone rolled noisily to the base of the mountain.

They had accomplished half the distance when a voice was heard at the opening of the grotto.

"Stop!" whispered Captain Mangles.

Glenarvan, clinging with one hand to a tuft of grass and holding his wife with the other, waited, scarcely breathing.

Wilson had taken alarm. Hearing some noise outside, he had returned to the hut, and, raising the mat, watched the Maoris. At a sign from him the captain had stopped Glenarvan.

In truth, one of the warriors, startled by some unaccustomed sound, had risen and approached the prison. Standing two paces from the hut, he listened with lowered head. He remained in this attitude for a moment, that seemed an hour, with ear intent and eye on the alert. Then, shaking his head as a man who is mistaken, he returned to his companions, took an armful of dead wood and threw it on the half-extinct fire, whose flames revived. His face, brightly illumined by the blaze, betrayed no more anxiety, and, after gazing at the first glimmers of dawn that tinged the horizon, he stretched himself beside the fire to warm his cold limbs.

"All right!" said Wilson.

The captain made a sign to Glenarvan to continue his descent. The latter, accordingly, slid gently down the slope, and soon Lady Helena and he stood on the narrow path where Robert was waiting for them. The rope was shaken three times, and next Captain Mangles, followed by Mary Grant, took the same perilous course. They were successful, and joined Lord and Lady Glenarvan.

Five minutes later all the fugitives, after their fortunate escape from the hut, left this temporary retreat, and, avoiding the inhabited shores of the lake, made their way by narrow paths farther down the mountain. They advanced rapidly, seeking to avoid all points where they might be seen. They did not speak, but glided like shadows through the bushes. Where were they going? At random, it is true, but they were free.

About five o'clock day began to break. Purple tints colored the lofty banks of clouds. The mountain peaks emerged from the mists of the morning. The orb of day would not be long in appearing, and instead of being the signal for torture, was to betray the flight of the condemned.

Before this dreaded moment arrived it was important that the fugitives should be beyond the reach of the savages. But they could not advance quickly, for the paths were steep. Lady Helena scaled the declivities, supported and even carried by Glenarvan, while Mary Grant leaned upon the arm of her betrothed. Robert, happy and triumphant, whose heart was full of joy at his success, took the lead, followed by the two sailors.

For half an hour the fugitives wandered at a venture. Paganel was not there to guide them,—Paganel, the object of their fears, whose absence cast a dark shadow over their happiness. However, they proceeded towards the east as well as possible, in the face of a magnificent dawn. They had soon reached an elevation of five hundred feet above Lake Taupo, and the morning air at this altitude was keen and cold. Hills and mountains rose one above another in indistinct outlines; but Glenarvan only wished to conceal himself and his companions. Afterwards they would see about issuing from this winding labyrinth.

At last the sun appeared and flashed his first rays into the faces of the fugitives. Suddenly a terrible yelling, the concentrated union of a hundred voices, broke forth upon the air. It rose from the pah, whose exact position Glenarvan did not now know. Moreover, a thick curtain of mist stretched at their feet, and prevented them from distinguishing the valleys below.

But the fugitives could not doubt that their escape had been discovered. Could they elude the pursuit of the natives? Had they been perceived? Would their tracks betray them?

At this moment the lower strata of vapor rose, enveloping them for an instant in a moist cloud, and they discerned, three hundred feet below them, the frantic crowd of savages.

They saw, but were also seen. Renewed yells resounded, mingled with barks; and the whole tribe, after vainly endeavoring to climb the rock, rushed out of the inclosure and hastened by the shortest paths in pursuit of the prisoners, who fled in terror from their vengeance.

CHAPTER LII. THE SACRED MOUNTAIN.

The summit of the mountain was a hundred feet higher. It was important for the fugitives to reach it, that they might conceal themselves from the sight of the Maoris, on the opposite slope. They hoped that some practicable ridge would then enable them to gain the neighboring peaks. The ascent was, therefore, hastened, as the threatening cries came nearer and nearer. The pursuers had reached the foot of the mountain.

"Courage, courage, my friends!" cried Glenarvan, urging his companions with word and gesture.

In less than five minutes they reached the top of the mountain. Here they turned around to consider their situation, and take some route by which they might evade the Maoris.

From this height the prospect commanded Lake Taupo, which extended towards the west in its picturesque frame of hills. To the north rose the peaks of Pirongia; to the south the flaming crater of Tongariro. But towards the east the view was limited by a barrier of peaks and ridges.

Glenarvan cast an anxious glance around him. The mist had dissolved under the rays of the sun, and his eye could clearly distinguish the least depressions of the earth. No movement of the Maoris could escape his sight.

The natives were not five hundred feet distant, when they reached the plateau upon which the solitary peak rested. Glenarvan could not, for ever so short a time, delay longer. At all hazards they must fly, at the risk of being hemmed in on all sides.

"Let us go down," cried he, "before our only way of escape is blocked up."

But just as the ladies rose by a final effort, MacNabb stopped them, and said:

"It is useless, Glenarvan. Look!"

And all saw, indeed, that an inexplicable change had taken place in the movements of the Maoris. Their pursuit had been suddenly interrupted. Their ascent of the mountain had ceased, as if by an imperious interdict. The crowd of natives had checked their swiftness, and halted, like the waves of the sea before an impassable rock.

All the savages, thirsting for blood, were now ranged along the foot of the mountain, yelling, gesticulating, and brandishing guns and hatchets; but they did not advance a single foot. Their dogs, like themselves, as though chained to earth, howled with rage.

What was the difficulty? What invisible power restrained the natives? The fugitives gazed without comprehending, fearing that the charm that enchained Kai-Koumou's tribe would dissolve.

Suddenly Captain Mangles uttered a cry that caused his companions to turn. He pointed to a little fortress at the summit of the peak.

"The tomb of the chief Kara-Tété!" cried Robert.

"Are you in earnest?" asked Glenarvan.

"Yes, my lord, it is the tomb; I recognize it."

Robert was right. Fifty feet above, at the extreme point of the mountain, stood a small palisaded inclosure of freshly-painted stakes. Glenarvan, likewise, recognized the sepulchre of the Maori chief. In their wanderings they had come to the top of the Maunganamu, where Kara-Tété had been buried.

Followed by his companions, he climbed the sides of the peak, to the very foot of the tomb. A large opening, covered with mats, formed the entrance. Glenarvan was about to enter, when, all at once, he started back suddenly.

"A savage!" said he.

"A savage in this tomb?" inquired the major.

"Yes, MacNabb."

"What matter? Let us enter."

Glenarvan, the major, Robert, and Captain Mangles passed into the inclosure. A Maori was there, clad in a great flax mantle. The darkness of the sepulchre did not permit them to distinguish his features. He appeared very calm, and was eating his breakfast with the most perfect indifference.

Glenarvan was about to address him, when the native, anticipating him, said, in an amiable tone, and in excellent English:

"Be seated, my dear lord; breakfast is awaiting you."

It was Paganel. At his voice all rushed into the tomb, and gazed with wonder at the worthy geographer. Paganel was found! The common safety was represented in him. They were going to question him: they wished to know how and why he was on the top of the mountain; but Glenarvan checked this unseasonable curiosity.

"The savages!" said he.

"The savages," replied Paganel, shrugging his shoulders, "are individuals whom I supremely despise."

"But can they not—?"

"They! the imbeciles! Come and see them."

Each followed Paganel, who issued from the tomb. The Maoris were in the same place, surrounding the foot of the peak, and uttering terrible cries.

"Cry and howl till you are tired, miserable creatures!" said Paganel. "I defy you to climb this mountain!"

"And why?" asked Glenarvan.

"Because the chief is buried here; this tomb protects us, and the mountain is tabooed."

"Tabooed?"

"Yes, my friends; and that is why I took refuge here, as in one of those asylums of the Middle Ages, open to unfortunates."

Indeed, the mountain was tabooed, and by this consecration had become inaccessible by the superstitious savages.

The safety of the fugitives was not yet certain, but there was a salutary respite, of which they strove to take advantage. Glenarvan, a prey to unspeakable emotion, did not venture a word; while the major nodded his head with an air of genuine satisfaction.

"And now, my friends," said Paganel, "if these brutes expect us to test their patience they are mistaken. In two days we shall be beyond the reach of these rascals."

"We will escape!" said Glenarvan; "but how?"

"I do not know," replied Paganel, "but we will do so all the same."

All now wished to hear the geographer's adventures. Strangely enough, in the case of a man loquacious usually, it was necessary to draw, as it were, the words from his mouth. He, who was so fond of telling stories, replied only in an evasive way to the questions of his friends.

"Paganel has changed," thought MacNabb.

Indeed, the countenance of the geographer was no longer the same. He wrapped himself gloomily in his great flaxen mantle, and seemed to shun too inquisitive looks. However, when they were all seated around him at the foot of the tomb, he related his experiences.

After the death of Kara-Tété, Paganel had taken advantage, like Robert, of the confusion of the natives, and escaped from the pah. But less fortunate than young Grant, he had fallen upon an encampment of Maoris, who were commanded by a chief of fine form and intelligent appearance, who was evidently superior to all the warriors of his tribe. This chief spoke English accurately, and bade him welcome by rubbing his nose against that of the geographer. Paganel wondered whether he should consider himself a prisoner; but seeing that he could not take a step without being graciously accompanied by the chief, he soon knew how matters stood on this point.

The chief, whose name was "Hihy" (sunbeam), was not a bad man. The spectacles and telescope gave him a high opinion of Paganel, whom he attached carefully to his person, not only by his benefits, but by strong flaxen ropes, especially at night.

This novel situation lasted three long days. Was he well or badly treated? Both, as he stated without further explanation. In short, he was a prisoner, and, except for the prospect of immediate torture, his condition did not seem more enviable than that of his unfortunate friends.

Fortunately, last night he succeeded in biting asunder his ropes and escaping. He had witnessed at a distance the burial of the chief, knew that he had been interred on the summit of Maunganamu mountain, and that it was tabooed in consequence. He therefore resolved to take refuge there, not wishing to leave the place where his companions were held captives. He succeeded in his undertaking, arrived at Kara-Tété's tomb, and waited in hope that Providence would in some way deliver his friends.

Such was Paganel's story. Did he omit designedly any circumstance of his stay among the natives? More than once his embarrassment led them to suspect so. However that might be, he received unanimous congratulations; and as the past was now known, they returned to the present.

Their situation was still exceedingly critical. The natives, if they did not venture to climb the mountain, expected that hunger and thirst would force their prisoners to surrender. It was only a matter of time, and the savages had great patience. Glenarvan did not disregard the difficulties of his position, but waited for the favorable issue which Providence seemed to promise.

And first he wished to examine this improvised fortress; not to defend it, for an attack was not to be feared, but that he might find a way of escaping. The major and the captain, Robert, Paganel, and himself, took the exact bearings of the mountain. They observed the direction of the paths, their branches and declivities. A ridge a mile in length united the Maunganamu to the Wahiti range, and then declined to the plain. Its narrow and winding summit presented the only practicable route, in case escape should become possible. If the fugitives could pass this point unperceived, under cover of the night, perhaps they might succeed in reaching the deep valleys and outwitting the Maoris.

But this course offered more than one danger, as they would have to pass below within gun-shot. The bullets of the natives on the lower ramparts of the pah might intercept them, and form a barrier that no one could safely cross.

Glenarvan and his friends, as soon as they ventured on the dangerous part of the ridge, were saluted with a volley of shots; but only a few wads, borne by the wind, reached them. They were made of printed paper. Paganel picked them up out of curiosity, but it was difficult to decipher them.

"Why!" said he, "do you know, my friends, what these creatures use for wads in their guns?"

"No," replied Glenarvan.

"Leaves of the Bible! If this is the use they make of the sacred writings, I pity the missionaries. They will have difficulty in founding Maori libraries."

"And what passage of the Scriptures have these natives fired at us?" asked Glenarvan.

"A mighty promise of God," replied Captain Mangles, who had also read the paper. "It bids us hope in Him," added the young captain, with the unshaken conviction of his Scottish faith.

"Read, John," said Glenarvan.

He read this line, which had so strangely reached them:

"Because he hath set his love upon Me, therefore will I deliver him:" Psalm xci. I.

"My friends," said Glenarvan, "we must make known the words of hope to our brave and dear ladies. Here is something to reanimate their hearts."

Glenarvan and his companions ascended the steep paths of the peak, and proceeded towards the tomb, which they wished to examine. On the way they were astonished to feel, at short intervals, a certain trembling of the ground. It was not an irregular agitation, but that continued vibration which the sides of a boiler undergo when it is fully charged. Steam, in large quantities, generated by the action of subterranean fires, seemed to be working beneath the crust of the mountain.

This peculiarity could not astonish people who had passed between the warm springs of the Waikato. They knew that this region of Ika-Na-Maoui is volcanic. It is like a sieve, from the holes of which ever issue the vapors of subterranean laboratories.

Paganel, who had already observed this, called the attention of his friends to the circumstance. The Maunganamu is only one of those numerous cones that cover the central portion of the island. The least mechanical action could provoke the formation of a crater in the clayey soil.

"And yet," said Glenarvan, "we seem to be in no more danger here than beside the boiler of the Duncan. This crust is firm."

"Certainly," replied the major; "but a boiler, however strong it may be, will always burst at last after too long use."

"MacNabb," said Paganel, "I do not desire to remain on this peak. Let Heaven show me a way of escape, and I will leave it instantly."

Lady Helena, who perceived Lord Glenarvan, now approached.

"My dear Edward," said she, "you have considered our position! Are we to hope or fear?"

"Hope, my dear Helena," replied Glenarvan. "The natives will never come to the top of the mountain, and we shall have abundant time to form a plan of escape."

"Moreover, madam," said Captain Mangles, "God himself encourages us to hope."

So saying, he gave her the text of the Bible which had been sent to them. She and Mary Grant, whose confiding soul was always open to the ministrations of Heaven, saw, in the words of the Holy Book, an infallible pledge of safety.

"Now to the tomb!" cried Paganel, gayly. "This is our fortress, our castle, our dining-room, and our workshop. No one is to disarrange it. Ladies, permit me to do the honors of this charming dwelling."

All followed the good-natured Paganel. When the savages saw the fugitives desecrate anew this tabooed sepulchre, they fired numerous volleys, and uttered yells no less terrible. But fortunately their bullets could not reach as far as their cries, for they only came half-way, while their vociferations were lost in empty air.

Lady Helena, Mary Grant, and their companions, quite reassured at seeing that the superstition of the Maoris was still stronger than their rage, entered the tomb. It was a palisade of red painted stakes. Symbolical faces, a real tattooing on wood, described the nobleness and exploits of the deceased. Strings of pipes, shells, and carved stones extended from one stake to another. Inside, the earth was hidden beneath a carpet of green leaves. In the centre a slight protuberance marked the freshly-made grave. Here reposed the weapons of the chief, his guns loaded and primed, his lance, his splendid hatchet of green jade, with a supply of powder and balls sufficient for the hunts of the other world.

"Here is a whole arsenal," said Paganel, "of which we will make a better use than the deceased. It is a good idea of these savages to carry their weapons to heaven with them."

"But these are English guns!" said the major.

"Doubtless," replied Glenarvan; "it is a very foolish custom to make presents of fire-arms to the savages, who then use them against the invaders, and with reason. At all events, these guns will be useful to us."

"But still more useful," said Paganel, "will be the provisions and water intended for Kara-Tété."

The parents and friends of the dead had, indeed, faithfully fulfilled their duties. The amount of food testified their esteem for the virtues of the chief. There were provisions enough to last ten persons fifteen days, or rather the deceased for eternity. They consisted of ferns, sweet yams, and potatoes, which were introduced some time before by the Europeans. Tall vases of fresh water stood near, and a dozen baskets, artistically woven, contained numerous tablets of green gum.

The fugitives were, therefore, fortified for several days against hunger and thirst, and they needed no urging to take their first meal at the chief's expense. Glenarvan directed Mr. Olbinett's attention to the food necessary for his companions; but he, with his usual exactness, even in critical situations, thought the bill of fare rather scanty. Moreover, he did not know how to prepare the roots, and there was no fire.

But Paganel solved the difficulty, and advised him to simply bury his ferns and potatoes in the ground itself, for the heat of the upper strata was very great. Olbinett, however, narrowly escaped a serious scalding, for, just as he had dug a hole to put his roots in, a stream of watery vapor burst forth, and rose to the height of several feet. The steward started back in terror.

"Close the hole!" cried the major, who, with the aid of the two sailors, covered the orifice with fragments of pumice-stone, while Paganel murmured these words:

"Well! well! ha! ha! very natural!"

"You are not scalded?" inquired MacNabb of Olbinett.

"No, Mr. MacNabb," replied the steward; "but I scarcely expected—"

"So many blessings," added Paganel, in a mirthful tone. "Consider Kara-Tété's water and provisions, and the fire of the earth! This mountain is a paradise! I propose that we found a colony here, cultivate the soil, and settle for the rest of our days. We will be Robinson Crusoes of Maunganamu. Indeed, I look in vain for any deficiency on this comfortable peak."

"Nothing is wanting if the earth is firm," replied Captain Mangles.

"Well, it was not created yesterday," said Paganel. "It has long resisted the action of internal fires, and will easily hold out till our departure."

"Breakfast is ready," announced Mr. Olbinett, as gravely as if he had been performing his duties at Malcolm Castle.

The fugitives at once sat down near the palisade, and enjoyed the repast that Providence had so opportunely furnished to them in this critical situation. No one appeared particular about the choice of food, but there was a diversity of opinion concerning the edible ferns. Some found them sweet and pleasant, and others mucilaginous, insipid, and acrid. The sweet potatoes, cooked in the hot earth, were excellent.

Their hunger being satiated, Glenarvan proposed that they should, without delay, arrange a plan of escape.

"So soon!" said Paganel, in a truly piteous tone. "What! are you thinking already of leaving this delightful place?"

"I think, first of all," replied Glenarvan, "that we ought to attempt an escape before we are forced to it by hunger. We have strength enough yet, and must take advantage of it. To-night let us try to gain the eastern valleys, and cross the circle of natives under cover of the darkness."

"Exactly," answered Paganel; "if the Maoris will let us pass."

"And if they prevent us?" asked Captain Mangles.

"Then we will employ the great expedients," said Paganel.

"You have great expedients, then?" inquired the major.

"More than I know what to do with," rejoined Paganel, without further explanation.

They could now do nothing but wait for night to attempt crossing the line of savages, who had not left their position. Their ranks even seemed increased by stragglers from the tribe. Here and there freshly-kindled fires formed a flaming girdle around the base of the peak. When darkness had invaded the surrounding valleys, the Maunganamu seemed to rise from a vast conflagration, while its summit was lost in a dense shade. Six hundred feet below were heard the tumult and cries of the enemy's camp.

At nine o'clock it was very dark, and Glenarvan and Captain Mangles resolved to make an exploration before taking their companions on this perilous journey. They noiselessly descended the declivity some distance, and reached the narrow ridge that crossed the line of natives fifty feet above the encampment.

All went well so far. The Maoris, stretched beside their fires, did not seem to perceive the two fugitives, who advanced a few paces farther. But suddenly, to the left and right of the ridge, a double volley resounded.

"Back!" cried Glenarvan; "these bandits have eyes like a cat, and the guns of riflemen!"

Captain Mangles and he reascended at once the precipitous slopes of the mountain, and speedily assured their terrified friends of their safety. Glenarvan's hat had been pierced by two bullets. It was, therefore, dangerous to venture on the ridge between these two lines of marksmen.

"Wait till to-morrow," said Paganel; "and since we cannot deceive the vigilance of these natives, permit me to give them a dose in my own way."

The temperature was quite cold. Fortunately, Kara-Tété wore in the tomb his best night-robes, warm, flaxen coverings, in which each one wrapped himself without hesitation; and soon the fugitives, protected by the native superstition, slept peacefully in the shelter of the palisades, on the earth that seemed to quake with the internal commotion.

CHAPTER LIII. A BOLD STRATAGEM.

The rising sun awakened with his first rays the sleepers on the Maunganamu. The Maoris for some time had been moving to and fro at the foot of the peak without wandering from their post of observation. Furious cries saluted the appearance of the Europeans as they issued from the desecrated tomb.

Each cast a longing glance towards the surrounding mountains, the deep valleys, still veiled in mist, and the surface of Lake Taupo, gently rippling beneath the morning wind. Then all, eager to know Paganel's new project, gathered around him with questioning looks; while the geographer at once satisfied the restless curiosity of his companions.

"My friends," said he, "my project has this advantage, that if it does not produce the result that I expect, or even fails, our situation will not be impaired. But it ought to and will succeed."

"And this project?" asked the major.

"This is it," replied Paganel. "The superstition of the natives has made this mountain a place of refuge, and this superstition must help us to escape. If I succeed in convincing Kai-Koumou that we have become the victims of our sacrilege, that the wrath of Heaven has fallen upon us, in short, that we have met a terrible death, do you think that he will abandon the mountain and return to his village?"

"Probably," said Glenarvan.

"And with what horrible death do you threaten us?" inquired Lady Helena.

"The death of the sacrilegious, my friends," continued Paganel. "The avenging flames are under our feet. Let us open a way for them."

"What! you would make a volcano?" cried Captain Mangles.

"Yes, a factitious, an improvised one, whose fury we will control. There is quite a supply of vapors and subterranean fires that only ask for an outlet. Let us arrange an artificial eruption for our own advantage."

"The idea is good," said the major, "and well conceived, Paganel."

"You understand," resumed the geographer, "that we are to feign being consumed by the flames of Pluto, and shall disappear spiritually in the tomb of Kara-Tété."

"Where we shall remain three, four, or five days, if necessary, till the savages are convinced of our death, and abandon the siege."

"But if they think of making sure of our destruction," said Miss Grant, "and climb the mountain?"

"No, my dear Mary," replied Paganel, "they will not do that. The mountain is tabooed, and if it shall itself devour its profaners the taboo will be still more rigorous."

"This plan is really well conceived," remarked Glenarvan. "There is only one chance against it, and that is, that the savages may persist in remaining at the foot of the mountain till the provisions fail us. But this is scarcely probable, especially if we play our part skillfully."

"And when shall we make this last venture?" asked Lady Helena.

"This very evening," answered Paganel, "at the hour of the greatest darkness."

"Agreed," said MacNabb. "Paganel, you are a man of genius; and although from habit I am scarcely ever enthusiastic, I will answer for your success. Ha! these rascals! we shall perform a little miracle for them that will delay their conversion a good century. May the missionaries pardon us!"

Paganel's plan was therefore adopted, and really, with the superstitious notions of the Maoris, it might and ought to succeed. It only remained to execute it. The idea was good, but in practice difficult. Might not this volcano consume the audacious ones who should dig the crater? Could they control and direct this eruption when the vapors, flames, and lava should be let loose? Would it not engulf the entire peak in a flood of fire? They were tampering with those phenomena whose absolute control is reserved for forces higher than theirs.

Paganel had foreseen these difficulties, but he expected to act prudently, and not to venture to extremes. An illusion was enough to deceive the Maoris, without the awful reality of a large eruption.

How long that day seemed! Each one counted the interminable hours. Everything was prepared for flight. The provisions of the tomb had been divided, and made into convenient bundles. Several mats, and the fire-arms, which had been found in the tomb of the chief, formed light baggage. Of course these preparations were made within the palisaded inclosure and unknown to the savages.

At six o'clock the steward served a farewell feast. Where and when they should eat in the valleys no one could foretell.

Twilight came on. The sun disappeared behind a bank of dense clouds of threatening aspect. A few flashes illumined the horizon, and a distant peal of thunder rumbled along the vault of the sky. Paganel welcomed the storm that came to the aid of his design.

At eight o'clock the summit of the mountain was hidden by a foreboding darkness, while the sky looked terribly black, as if for a background to the flaming outbreak that Paganel was about to inaugurate. The Maoris could no longer see their prisoners. The time for action had come. Rapidity was necessary, and Glenarvan, Paganel, MacNabb, Robert, the steward, and the two sailors at once set to work vigorously.

The place for the crater was chosen thirty paces from Kara-Tété's tomb. It was important that this structure should be spared by the eruption, for otherwise the taboo would become ineffective. Paganel had observed an enormous block of stone, around which the vapors seemed to pour forth with considerable force. This rocky mass covered a small natural crater in the peak, and only by its weight prevented the escape of the subterranean flames. If they could succeed in overturning it, the smoke and lava would immediately issue through the unobstructed opening.

The fugitives made themselves levers out of the stakes of the tomb, and with these they vigorously attacked the ponderous mass. Under their united efforts the rock was not long in moving. They dug a sort of groove for it down the side of the mountain, that it might slide on an inclined plane.

As their action increased, the trembling of the earth became more violent. Hollow rumblings and hissings sounded under the thin crust. But the bold experimenters, like real Vulcans, governing the underground fires, worked on in silence. Several cracks and a few gusts of hot smoke warned them that their position was becoming dangerous. But a final effort detached the block, which glided down the slope of the mountain and disappeared.

The thin covering at once yielded. An incandescent column poured forth towards the sky with loud explosions, while streams of boiling water and lava rolled towards the encampment of the natives and the valleys below. The whole peak trembled, and you might almost have thought that it was disappearing in a general conflagration.

Glenarvan and his companions had scarcely time to escape the shock of the eruption. They fled to the inclosure of the tomb, but not without receiving a few scalding drops of the water, which bubbled and exhaled a strong sulphureous odor.

Then mud, lava, and volcanic fragments mingled in the scene of devastation. Torrents of flame furrowed the sides of the Maunganamu. The adjoining mountains glowed in the light of the eruption, and the deep valleys were illumined with a vivid brightness.

The savages were soon aroused, both by the noise and the heat of the lava that flowed in a scalding tide through the midst of their encampment. Those whom the fiery flood had not reached fled, and ascended the surrounding hills, turning and gazing back at this terrific phenomenon, with which their god, in his wrath, had overwhelmed the desecrators of the sacred mountain; while at certain moments they were heard howling their consecratory cry:

"Taboo! taboo! taboo!"

Meantime an enormous quantity of vapor, melted stones, and lava had escaped from the crater. It was no longer a simple geyser. All this volcanic effervescence had hitherto been confined beneath the crust of the peak, since the outlets of Tangariro sufficed for its expansion; but as a new opening had been made, it had rushed forth with extreme violence.

All night long, during the storm that raged above and below, the peak was shaken with a commotion that could not but alarm Glenarvan. The prisoners, concealed behind the palisade of the tomb, watched the fearful progress of the outbreak.

Morning came. The fury of the volcano had not moderated. Thick, yellowish vapors mingled with the flames, and torrents of lava poured in every direction. Glenarvan, with eye alert and beating heart, glanced between the interstices of the inclosure, and surveyed the camp of the Maoris.

The natives had fled to the neighboring plateaus, beyond the reach of the volcano. Several corpses, lying at the foot of the peak, had been charred by the fire. Farther on, towards the pah, the lava had consumed a number of huts, that were still smoking. The savages, in scattered groups, were gazing at the vapory summit of Maunganamu with religious awe.

Kai-Koumou came into the midst of his warriors, and Glenarvan recognized him. The chief advanced to the base of the peak, on the side spared by the eruption, but did not cross the first slopes. Here, with outstretched arms, like a sorcerer exorcising, he made a few grimaces, the meaning of which did not escape the prisoners. As Paganel had foreseen, Kai-Koumou was invoking upon the mountain a more rigorous taboo.

Soon after, the natives descended, in single file, the winding paths that led towards the pah.

"They are going!" cried Glenarvan. "They are abandoning their post! God be thanked! Our scheme has succeeded! My dear Helena, my brave companions, we are now dead and buried; but this evening we will revive, we will leave our tomb, and flee from these barbarous tribes!"

It would be difficult to describe the joy that reigned within the palisade. Hope had reanimated all hearts. These courageous travelers forgot their past trials, dreaded not the future, and only rejoiced in their present deliverance; although very little reflection would show how difficult was the task of reaching an European settlement from their present position. But if Kai-Koumou was outwitted, they believed themselves safe from all the savages of New Zealand.

A whole day must pass before the decisive attempt could be made, and they employed their time in arranging a plan of escape. Paganel had preserved his map of New Zealand, and could therefore search out the safest routes.

After some discussion, the fugitives resolved to proceed eastward towards the Bay of Plenty. This course would lead them through districts that were very rarely visited. The travelers, who were already accustomed to overcoming natural difficulties, only feared meeting the Maoris. They therefore determined to avoid them at all hazards, and gain the eastern coast, where the missionaries have founded several establishments. Moreover, this portion of the island had hitherto escaped the ravages of the war and the depredations of the natives. As for the distance that separated Lake Taupo from the Bay of Plenty, it could not be more than one hundred miles. Ten days would suffice for the journey. The missions once reached, they could rest there, and wait for some favorable opportunity of gaining Auckland, their destination.

These points being settled, they continued to watch the savages till evening. Not one of them remained at the foot of the mountain, and when darkness invaded the valleys of the lake, no fire betokened the presence of the Maoris at the base of the peak. The coast was clear.

At nine o'clock it was dark night, and Glenarvan gave the signal for departure. His companions and he, armed and equipped at Kara-Tété's expense, began to cautiously descend the slopes of the Maunganamu. Captain Mangles and Wilson led the way, with eyes and ears on the alert. They stopped at the least sound,—they examined the faintest light; each slid down the declivity, the better to elude detection.

Two hundred feet below the summit, Captain Mangles and his sailor reached the dangerous ridge that had been so obstinately guarded by the natives. If, unfortunately, the Maoris, more crafty than the fugitives, had feigned a retreat to entice them within reach, if they had not been deceived by the eruption, their presence would be discovered at this point. Glenarvan, in spite of his confidence and Paganel's pleasantries, could not help trembling. The safety of his friends was at stake during the few moments necessary to cross the ridge. He felt Lady Helena's heart beat as she clung to his arm.

But neither he nor Captain Mangles thought of retreating. The young captain, followed by the others, and favored by the dense obscurity, crawled along the narrow path, only stopping when some detached stone rolled to the base of the mountain. If the savages were still in ambush, these unusual sounds would provoke from each side a formidable volley.

However, in gliding like serpents along this inclined crest, the fugitives could not advance rapidly. When Captain Mangles had gained the lowest part, scarcely twenty-five feet separated him from the plain where the natives had encamped the night before. Here the ridge ascended quite steeply towards a coppice about a quarter of a mile distant.

The travelers crossed this place without accident, and began the ascent in silence. The thicket was invisible, but they knew where it was, and, provided no ambuscade was laid there, Glenarvan hoped to find a secure refuge. However, he remembered that they were now no longer protected by the taboo. The ascending ridge did not belong to the sacred mountain, but to a chain that ran along the eastern shores of Lake Taupo. Therefore not only the shots of the savages, but also a hand-to-hand conflict, were to be feared.

For a short time the little party slowly mounted towards the upper elevations. The captain could not yet discern the dark coppice, but it could not be more than two hundred feet distant.

Suddenly he stopped, and almost recoiled. He thought he heard some sound in the darkness. His hesitation arrested the advance of his companions.

He stood motionless long enough to alarm those who followed him. With what agonizing suspense they waited could not be described. Would they be forced to return to the summit of the mountain?

But, finding that the noise was not repeated, their leader continued his ascent along the narrow path. The coppice was soon dimly defined in the gloom. In a few moments it was reached, and the fugitives were crouching beneath the thick foliage of the trees.

CHAPTER LIV. FROM PERIL TO SAFETY.

Darkness favored the escape; and making the greatest possible progress, they left the fatal regions of Lake Taupo. Paganel assumed the guidance of the little party, and his marvelous instinct as a traveler was displayed anew during this perilous journey. He managed with surprising dexterity in the thick gloom, chose unhesitatingly the almost invisible paths, and kept constantly an undeviating course.

At nine o'clock in the morning they had accomplished a considerable distance, and could not reasonably require more of the courageous ladies. Besides, the place seemed suitable for an encampment. The fugitives had reached the ravine that separates the Kaimanawa and Wahiti ranges. The road on the right ran southward to Oberland. Paganel, with his map in his hand, made a turn to the northeast, and at ten o'clock the little party had reached a sort of steep buttress, formed by a spur of the mountain.

The provisions were taken from the sacks, and all did ample justice to them. Mary Grant and the major, who had not hitherto been very well satisfied with the edible ferns, made this time a hearty meal of them. They rested here till two o'clock in the afternoon, then the journey towards the east was resumed, and at evening the travelers encamped eight miles from the mountains. They needed no urging to sleep in the open air.

The next day very serious difficulties were encountered. They were forced to pass through a curious region of volcanic lakes and geysers that extends eastward from the Wahiti ranges. It was pleasing to the eye, but fatiguing to the limbs. Every quarter of a mile there were obstacles, turns, and windings, far too many for rapid progress; but what strange appearances and what infinite variety does nature give to her grand scenes!

Over this expanse of twenty square miles the overflow of subterranean forces was displayed in every form. Salt springs, of a singular transparency, teeming with myriads of insects, issued from the porous ground. They exhaled a penetrating odor, and deposited on the earth a white coating like dazzling snow. Their waters, though clear, were at the boiling-point, while other neighboring springs poured forth ice-cold streams. On every side water-spouts, with spiral rings of vapor, spirted from the ground like the jets of a fountain, some continuous, others intermittent, as if controlled by some capricious sprite. They rose like an amphitheatre, in natural terraces one above another, their vapors gradually mingling in wreaths of white smoke; and flowing down the semi-transparent steps of these gigantic staircases, they fed the lakes with their boiling cascades.

It will be needless to dilate upon the incidents of the journey, which were neither numerous nor important. Their way led through forests and over plains. The captain took his bearings by the sun and stars. The sky, which was quite clear, was sparing of heat and rain. Still, an increasing weariness delayed the travelers, already so cruelly tried, and they had to make great efforts to reach their destination.

However, they still conversed together, but no longer in common. The little party was divided into groups, not by any narrow prejudice or ill feeling, but to some extent from sadness. Often Glenarvan was alone, thinking, as he approached the coast, of the Duncan and her crew. He forgot the dangers that still threatened him, in his grief for his lost sailors and the terrible visions that continually haunted his mind.

They no longer spoke of Harry Grant. And why should they, since they could do nothing for him? If the captain's name was ever pronounced, it was in the conversations of his daughter and her betrothed. The young captain had not reminded her of what she had said to him on the last night of their captivity on the mountain. His magnanimity would not take advantage of words uttered in a moment of supreme despair.

When he did speak of Captain Grant, he began to lay plans for a further search. He declared to Mary that Lord Glenarvan would resume this undertaking, hitherto so unsuccessful.

He maintained that the authenticity of the document could not be doubted. Her father must, therefore, be somewhere; and though it were necessary to search the whole world, they were sure to find him. The young girl was cheered by these words; and both, bound by the same thoughts, now sympathized in the same hope. Lady Helena often took part in the conversation, and was very careful not to discourage the young people with any sad forebodings.

Glenarvan and his companions, after many vicissitudes, reached the foot of Mount Ikirangi, whose peak towered five thousand feet aloft. They had now traveled almost one hundred miles since leaving the Maunganamu, and the coast was still thirty miles distant. Captain Mangles had hoped to make the journey in ten days, but he was ignorant then of the difficulties of the way. There were still two good days of travel before they could gain the ocean, and renewed activity and extreme vigilance became necessary, for they were entering a region frequented by the natives. However, each conquered the fatigue, and the little party continued their course.

Between Mount Ikirangi, some distance on their right, and Mount Hardy, whose summit rose to the left, was a large plain, thickly overspread with twining plants and underbrush. Progress here was tedious and difficult in the extreme; for the pliant tendrils wound a score of folds about their bodies like serpents. Hunting was impossible; the provisions were nearly exhausted, and could not be renewed, and water failed, so that they could not allay their thirst, rendered doubly acute by their fatigue. The sufferings of Glenarvan and his friends were terrible, and for the first time their moral energy now almost forsook them.

At last, dragging themselves along, wearied to the utmost degree in body, almost despairing in mind, they reached Lottin Point, on the shores of the Pacific.

At this place several deserted huts were seen, the ruins of a village recently devastated by the war; around them were abandoned fields, and everywhere the traces of plunder and conflagration. But here fate had reserved a new and fearful test for the unfortunate travelers.

They were walking along the coast, when, at no great distance, a number of natives appeared, who rushed towards the little party, brandishing their weapons. Glenarvan, shut in by the sea, saw that escape was impossible, and, summoning all his strength, was about to make preparations for battle, when Captain Mangles cried:

"A canoe! a canoe!"

And truly, twenty paces distant, a canoe, with six oars, was lying on the beach. To rush to it, set it afloat, and fly from this dangerous place was the work of an instant; the whole party seemed to receive at once a fresh accession of bodily strength and mental vigor.

In ten minutes the boat was at a considerable distance. The sea was calm. The captain, however, not wishing to wander too far from the coast, was about to give the order to cruise along the shore, when he suddenly ceased rowing. He had observed three canoes starting from Lottin Point, with the evident intention of overtaking and capturing the unfortunate fugitives.

"To sea! to sea!" cried he; "better perish in the waves than be captured!"

The canoe, under the strokes of its four oarsmen, at once put to sea, and for some time kept its distance. But the strength of the weakened fugitives soon grew less, and their pursuers gradually gained upon them. The boats were now scarcely a mile apart. There was therefore no possibility of avoiding the attack of the natives, who, armed with their long guns, were already preparing to fire.

What was Glenarvan doing? Standing at the stern of the canoe, he looked around as if for some expected aid. What did he expect? What did he wish? Had he a presentiment?

All at once his face brightened, his hand was stretched towards an indistinct object.

"A ship!" cried he; "my friends, a ship! Row, row!"

Not one of the four oarsmen turned to see this unexpected vessel, for they must not lose a stroke. Only Paganel, rising, directed his telescope towards the place indicated.

"Yes," said he, "a ship, a steamer, under full headway, coming towards us! Courage, captain!"

The fugitives displayed new energy, and for several moments longer they kept their distance. The steamer grew more and more distinct. They could clearly discern her masts, and the thick clouds of black smoke that issued from her smoke-stack. Glenarvan, giving the helm to Robert, had seized the geographer's glass, and did not lose a single movement of the vessel.

But what were Captain Mangles and his companions to think when they saw the expression of his features change, his face grow pale, and the instrument fall from his hands. A single word explained this sudden emotion.

"The Duncan!" cried Glenarvan,—"the Duncan and the convicts!"

"The Duncan?" repeated the captain, dropping his oar and rising.

"Yes, death on all sides!" moaned Glenarvan, overcome by so many calamities. It was indeed the yacht—without a doubt,—the yacht, with her crew of bandits! The major could not repress a malediction. This was too much.

Meantime the canoe was floating at random. Whither should they guide it, whither flee? Was it possible to choose between the savages and the convicts?

Just then a shot came from the native boat, that had approached nearer. The bullet struck Wilson's oar; but his companions still propelled the canoe towards the Duncan. The yacht was advancing at full speed, and was only half a mile distant. Captain Mangles, beset on all sides, no longer knew how to act, or in what direction to escape. The two poor ladies were on their knees, praying in their despair.

The savages were now firing a continued volley, and the bullets rained around the canoe. Just then a sharp report sounded, and a ball from the yacht's cannon passed over the heads of the fugitives, who remained motionless between the fire of the Duncan and the natives.

Captain Mangles, frantic with despair, seized his hatchet. He was on the point of sinking their own canoe, with his unfortunate companions, when a cry from Robert stopped him.

"Tom Austin! Tom Austin!" said the child. "He is on board! I see him! He has recognized us! He is waving his hat!"

The hatchet was suspended in mid-air. A second ball whistled over their heads, and demolished the nearest of the three canoes, while a loud hurrah was heard on board the Duncan. The savages fled in terror towards the coast.

"Help, help, Tom!" cried Captain Mangles, in a piercing voice. And a few moments afterwards the ten fugitives, without knowing how, or scarcely comprehending this unexpected good fortune, were all in safety on board the Duncan.

CHAPTER LV. WHY THE DUNCAN WENT TO NEW ZEALAND.

The feelings of Glenarvan and his friends, when the songs of old Scotland resounded in their ears, it is impossible to describe. As soon as they set foot on deck the bagpiper struck up a well remembered air, while hearty hurrahs welcomed the owner's return on board. Glenarvan, John Mangles, Paganel, Robert, and even the major, wept and embraced each other. Their emotions rose from joy to ecstasy. The geographer was fairly wild, skipping about and watching with his inseparable telescope the canoes returning to shore.

But at sight of Glenarvan and his companions, with tattered garments, emaciated features, and the traces of extreme suffering, the crew ceased their lively demonstrations. These were spectres, not the bold and dashing travelers whom, three months before, hope had stimulated to a search for the shipwrecked captain. Chance alone had led them back to this vessel that they had ceased to regard as theirs, and in what a sad state of exhaustion and feebleness!

However, before thinking of fatigue, or the imperative calls of hunger and thirst, Glenarvan questioned Tom Austin concerning his presence in these waters. Why was the Duncan on the eastern coast of New Zealand? Why was she not in the hands of Ben Joyce? By what providential working had God restored her to the fugitives? These were the questions that were hurriedly addressed to Tom Austin. The old sailor did not know which to answer first. He therefore concluded to listen only to Lord Glenarvan, and reply to him.

"But the convicts?" inquired Glenarvan. "What have you done with the convicts?"

"The convicts!" replied Tom Austin, like a man who is at a loss to understand a question.

"Yes; the wretches who attacked the yacht."

"What yacht, my lord? The Duncan?"

"Of course. Did not Ben Joyce come on board?"

"I do not know Ben Joyce; I have never seen him."

"Never?" cried Glenarvan, amazed at the answers of the old sailor. "Then will you tell me why the Duncan is now on the shores of New Zealand?"

Although Glenarvan and his friends did not at all understand Austin's astonishment, what was their surprise when he replied, in a calm voice:

"The Duncan is here by your lordship's orders."

"By my orders?" cried Glenarvan.

"Yes, my lord. I only conformed to the instructions contained in your letter."

"My letter?" exclaimed Glenarvan.

The ten travelers at once surrounded Tom Austin, and gazed at him in eager curiosity. The letter written at the Snowy River had reached the Duncan.

"Well," continued Glenarvan, "let us have an explanation; for I almost think I am dreaming. You received a letter, Tom?"

"Yes; a letter from your lordship."

"At Melbourne?"

"At Melbourne; just as I had finished the repair of the ship."

"And this letter?"

"It was not written by you; but it was signed by you, my lord."

"Exactly; it was sent by a convict, Ben Joyce."

"No; by the sailor called Ayrton, quartermaster of the Britannia."

"Yes, Ayrton or Ben Joyce; it is the same person. Well, what did the letter say?"

"It ordered me to leave Melbourne without delay, and come to the eastern shores of—"

"Australia!" cried Glenarvan, with an impetuosity that disconcerted the old sailor.

"Australia?" repeated Tom, opening his eyes. "No, indeed; New Zealand!"

"Australia, Tom! Australia!" replied Glenarvan's companions, with one voice.

Austin was now bewildered. Glenarvan spoke with such assurance, that he feared he had made a mistake in reading the letter. Could he, faithful and accurate sailor that he was, have committed such a blunder? He began to feel troubled.

"Be easy, Tom," said Lady Helena. "Providence has decreed—"

"No, madam, pardon me," returned the sailor; "no, it is not possible! I am not mistaken. Ayrton also read the letter, and he, on the contrary, wished to go to Australia."

"Ayrton?" cried Glenarvan.

"The very one. He maintained that it was a mistake, and that you had appointed Twofold Bay as the place of meeting."

"Have you the letter, Tom?" asked the major, greatly puzzled.

"Yes, Mr. MacNabb," replied Austin. "I will soon bring it."

He accordingly repaired to his own cabin. While he was gone, they gazed at each other in silence, except the major, who, with his eye fixed upon Paganel, said, as he folded his arms:

"Indeed, I must confess, Paganel, that this is a little too much."

At this moment Austin returned. He held in his hand the letter written by Paganel, and signed by Glenarvan.

"Read it, my lord," said the old sailor.

Glenarvan took the letter, and read: "Order for Tom Austin to put to sea, and bring the Duncan to the eastern coast of New Zealand."

"New Zealand?" cried Paganel, starting.

He snatched the letter from Glenarvan's hands, rubbed his eyes, adjusted his spectacles to his nose, and read in his turn.

"New Zealand!" repeated he, in an indescribable tone, while the letter slipped from his fingers.

Just then he felt a hand fall upon his shoulder. He turned, and found himself face to face with the major.

"Well, my good Paganel," said MacNabb, in a grave tone, "it is fortunate that you did not send the Duncan to Cochin-China."

This sally finished the poor geographer. A fit of laughter seized the whole crew. Paganel, as if mad, ran to and fro, holding his head in his hands, and tearing his hair. However, when he had recovered from his frenzy, there was still another unavoidable question to answer.

"Now, Paganel," said Glenarvan, "be candid. I acknowledge that your absent-mindedness has been providential. To be sure, without you the Duncan would have fallen into the hands of the convicts; without you we should have been recaptured by the Maoris. But do tell me, what strange association of ideas, what unnatural aberration, induced you to write New Zealand instead of Australia?"

"Very well," said Paganel. "It was—"

But at that moment his eyes fell upon Robert and Mary Grant, and he stopped short, finally replying: "Never mind, my dear Glenarvan. I am a madman, a fool, an incorrigible being, and shall die a most famous blunderer!"

The affair was no longer discussed. The mystery of the Duncan's presence there was solved; and the travelers, so miraculously saved, thought only of revisiting their comfortable cabins and partaking of a good breakfast.

However, leaving Lady Helena, Mary Grant, the major, Paganel, and Robert to enter the saloon, Glenarvan and Captain Mangles retained Tom Austin with them. They wished to question him further.

"Now, Tom," said Glenarvan, "let me know: did not this order to sail for the coast of New Zealand seem strange to you?"

"Yes, my lord," replied Austin. "I was very much surprised; but, as I am not in the habit of discussing the orders I receive, I obeyed. Could I act otherwise? If any accident had happened from not following your instructions should I not have been to blame? Would you have done differently, captain?"

"No, Tom," answered Captain Mangles.

"But what did you think?" asked Glenarvan.

"I thought, my lord, that, in the cause of Captain Grant, it was necessary to go wherever you directed me; that by some combination of circumstances another vessel would take you to New Zealand, and that I was to wait for you on the eastern coast of the island. Moreover, on leaving Melbourne, I kept my destination secret, and the crew did not know it till we were out at sea and the shores of Australia had disappeared from sight. But then an incident occurred that perplexed me very much."

"What do you mean, Tom?" inquired Glenarvan.

"I mean," he replied, "that when the quartermaster, Ayrton, learned, the day after our departure, the Duncan's destination—"

"Ayrton!" cried Glenarvan. "Is he on board?"

"Yes, my lord."

"Ayrton here!" repeated Glenarvan, glancing at Captain Mangles.

"Wonderful indeed!" said the young captain.

In an instant, with the swiftness of lightning, Ayrton's conduct, his long-contrived treachery, Glenarvan's wound, the attack upon Mulready, their sufferings in the marshes of the Snowy, all the wretch's deeds, flashed upon the minds of the two men. And now, by a strange fatality, the convict was in their power.

"Where is he?" asked Glenarvan quickly.

"In a cabin in the forecastle," replied Tom Austin, "closely guarded."

"Why this confinement?"

"Because, when Ayrton saw that the yacht was sailing for New Zealand, he flew into a passion; because he attempted to force me to change the ship's course; because he threatened me; and, finally, because he urged my men to a mutiny. I saw that he was a dangerous person, and was compelled, therefore, to take precautions against him."

"And since that time?"

"Since that time he has been in his cabin, without offering to come out."

"Good!"

At this moment Glenarvan and Captain Mangles were summoned to the saloon. Breakfast, which they so much needed, was ready. They took seats at the table, but did not speak of Ayrton.

However, when the meal was ended, and the passengers had assembled on deck, Glenarvan informed them of the quartermaster's presence on board. At the same time he declared his intention of sending for him.

"Can I be released from attending this tribunal?" asked Lady Helena. "I confess to you, my dear Edward, that the sight of this unfortunate would be very painful to me."

"It is only to confront him, Helena," replied Glenarvan. "Remain, if you can. Ben Joyce should see himself face to face with all his intended victims."

Lady Helena yielded to this request, and Mary Grant and she took their places beside him, while around them stood the major, Paganel, Captain Mangles, Robert, Wilson, Mulready, and Olbinett, all who had suffered so severely by the convict's treason. The crew of the yacht, who did not yet understand the seriousness of these proceedings, maintained a profound silence.

"Call Ayrton!" said Glenarvan.

CHAPTER LVI. AYRTON'S OBSTINACY.

Ayrton soon made his appearance. He crossed the deck with a confident step, and ascended the poop-stairs. His eyes had a sullen look, his teeth were set, and his fists clinched convulsively. His bearing displayed neither exultation nor humility. As soon as he was in Lord Glenarvan's presence, he folded his arms, and calmly and silently waited to be questioned:

"Ayrton," said Glenarvan, "here we all are, as you see, on board the Duncan, that you would have surrendered to Ben Joyce's accomplices."

At these words the lips of the quartermaster slightly trembled. A quick blush colored his hard features,—not the sign of remorse, but the shame of defeat. He was prisoner on this yacht that he had meant to command as master, and his fate was soon to be decided.

However, he made no reply. Glenarvan waited patiently, but Ayrton still persisted in maintaining an obstinate silence.

"Speak, Ayrton; what have you to say?" continued Glenarvan.

The convict hesitated, and the lines of his forehead were strongly contracted. At last he said, in a calm voice:

"I have nothing to say, my lord. I was foolish enough to let myself be taken. Do what you please."

Having given his answer, the quartermaster turned his eyes toward the coast that extended along the west, and affected a profound indifference for all that was passing around him. You would have thought, to look at him, that he was a stranger to this serious affair.

But Glenarvan had resolved to be patient. A powerful motive urged him to ascertain certain circumstances of Ayrton's mysterious life, especially as regarded Harry Grant and the Britannia. He therefore resumed his inquiries, speaking with extreme mildness, and imposing the most perfect calmness upon the violent agitation of his heart.

"I hope, Ayrton," continued he, "that you will not refuse to answer certain questions that I desire to ask you. And, first, am I to call you Ayrton or Ben Joyce? Are you the quartermaster of the Britannia?"

Ayrton remained unmoved, watching the coast, deaf to every question. Glenarvan, whose eye flashed with some inward emotion, continued to question him.

"Will you tell me how you left the Britannia, and why you were in Australia?"

There was the same silence, the same obstinacy.

"Listen to me, Ayrton," resumed Glenarvan. "It is for your interest to speak. We may reward a frank confession, which is your only resort. For the last time, will you answer my questions?"

Ayrton turned his head towards Glenarvan, and looked him full in the face.

"My lord," said he, "I have nothing to answer. It is for justice to prove against me."

"The proofs will be easy," replied Glenarvan.

"Easy, my lord?" continued the quartermaster, in a sneering tone. "Your lordship seems to me very hasty. I declare that the best judge in Westminster Hall would be puzzled to establish my identity. Who can say why I came to Australia, since Captain Grant is no longer here to inform you? Who can prove that I am that Ben Joyce described by the police, since they have never laid hands upon me, and my companions are at liberty? Who, except you, can charge me, not to say with a crime, but even with a culpable action?"

Ayrton soon made his appearance. He crossed the deck with a confident step, and ascended the poop-stairs. Ayrton had grown animated while speaking, but soon relapsed into his former indifference. He doubtless imagined that this declaration would end the examination: but Glenarvan resumed, and said:

"Ayrton, I am not a judge charged with trying you. This is not my business. It is important that our respective positions should be clearly defined. I ask nothing that can implicate you, for that is the part of justice. But you know what search I am pursuing, and, with a word, you can put me on the track I have lost. Will you speak?"

Ayrton shook his head, like a man determined to keep silent.

"Will you tell me where Captain Grant is?" asked Glenarvan.

"No, my lord."

"Will you point out where the Britannia was wrecked?"

"Certainly not."

"Ayrton," said Glenarvan, in almost a suppliant tone, "will you, at least, if you know where Captain Grant is, tell his poor children, who are only waiting for a word from your lips?"

The quartermaster hesitated; his features quivered; but, in a low voice, he muttered: "I cannot, my lord."

Then, as if he reproached himself for a moment's weakness, he added, angrily: "No, I will not speak! Hang me if you will!"

"Hang, then!" cried Glenarvan, overcome by a sudden feeling of indignation.

But finally controlling himself, he said, in a grave voice:

"There are neither judges nor hangmen here. At the first landing-place you shall be put into the hands of the English authorities."

"Just what I desire," replied the quartermaster.

Thereupon he was taken back to the cabin that served as his prison, and two sailors were stationed at the door, with orders to watch all his movements. The witnesses of this scene retired indignant and in despair.

Since Glenarvan had failed to overcome Ayrton's obstinacy, what was to be done? Evidently to follow the plan formed at Eden, of returning to England, and resuming hereafter this unsuccessful enterprise, for all traces of the Britannia now seemed irrevocably lost. The document admitted of no new interpretation. There was no other country on the line of the thirty-seventh parallel, and the only way was to sail for home.

He consulted his friends, and more especially Captain Mangles, on the subject of return. The captain examined his store-rooms. The supply of coal would not last more than fifteen days. It was, therefore, necessary to replenish the fuel at the first port. He accordingly proposed to Glenarvan to sail for Talcahuana Bay, where the Duncan had already procured supplies before undertaking her voyage. This was a direct passage. Then the yacht, with ample provisions, could double Cape Horn, and reach Scotland by way of the Atlantic.

This plan being adopted, the engineer was ordered to force on steam. Half an hour afterwards the yacht was headed towards Talcahuana, and at six o'clock in the evening the mountains of New Zealand had disappeared beneath the mists of the horizon.

It was a sad return for these brave searchers, who had left the shores of Scotland with such hope and confidence. To the joyous cries that had saluted Glenarvan on his return succeeded profound dejection. Each confined himself to the solitude of his cabin, and rarely appeared on deck. All, even the loquacious Paganel, were mournful and silent. If Glenarvan spoke of beginning his search again, the geographer shook his head like a man who has no more hope, for he seemed convinced as to the fate of the shipwrecked sailors. Yet there was one man on board who could have informed them about this catastrophe, but whose silence was still prolonged. There was no doubt that the rascally Ayrton knew, if not the actual situation of the captain, at least the place of the shipwreck. Probably Harry Grant, if found, would be a witness against him; hence he persisted in his silence, and was greatly enraged, especially towards the sailors who would accuse him of an evil design.

Several times Glenarvan renewed his attempts with the quartermaster. Promises and threats were useless. Ayrton's obstinacy was carried so far, and was so inexplicable, that the major came to the belief that he knew nothing; which opinion was shared by the geographer and corroborated his own ideas in regard to Captain Grant.

But if Ayrton knew nothing, why did he not plead his ignorance? It could not turn against him, while his silence increased the difficulty of forming a new plan. Ought they to infer the presence of Harry Grant in Australia from meeting the quartermaster on that continent? At all events, they must induce Ayrton to explain on this subject.

Lady Helena, seeing her husband's failures, now suggested an attempt, in her turn, to persuade the quartermaster. Where a man had failed, perhaps a woman could succeed by her gentle entreaty. Glenarvan, knowing the tact of his young wife, gave his hearty approval. Ayrton was, accordingly, brought to Lady Helena's boudoir. Mary Grant was to be present at the interview, for the young girl's influence might also be great, and Lady Helena would not neglect any chance of success.

For an hour the two ladies were closeted with the quartermaster, but nothing resulted from this conference. What they said, the arguments they used to draw out the convict's secret, all the details of this examination, remained unknown. Moreover, when Ayrton left them they did not appear to have succeeded, and their faces betokened real despair.

He contented himself with shrugging his shoulders, which so increased the rage of the crew, that nothing less than the intervention of the captain and his lordship could restrain them.

When the quartermaster was taken back to his cabin, therefore, the sailors saluted his appearance with violent threats. But he contented himself with shrugging his shoulders, which so increased the rage of the crew, that nothing less than the intervention of the captain and his lordship could restrain them.

But Lady Helena did not consider herself defeated. She wished to struggle to the last with this heartless man, and the next day she went herself to Ayrton's cabin, to avoid the scene that his appearance on deck occasioned.

For two long hours this kind and gentle Scotch lady remained alone face to face with the chief of the convicts. Glenarvan, a prey to nervous agitation, lingered near the cabin, now determined to thoroughly exhaust the chances of success, and now upon the point of drawing his wife away from this painful and prolonged interview.

But this time, when Lady Helena reappeared, her features inspired confidence. Had she, then, brought this secret to light, and stirred the dormant feeling of pity in the heart of this poor creature?

MacNabb, who saw her first, could not repress a very natural feeling of incredulity. However, the rumor soon spread among the crew that the quartermaster had at length yielded to Lady Helena's entreaties. All the sailors assembled on deck more quickly than if Tom Austin's whistle had summoned them.

"Has he spoken?" asked Lord Glenarvan of his wife.

"No," replied Lady Helena; "but in compliance with my entreaties he desires to see you."

"Ah, dear Helena, you have succeeded!"

"I hope so, Edward."

"Have you made any promise that I am to sanction?"

"Only one: that you will use all your influence to moderate the fate in store for him."

"Certainly, my dear Helena. Let him come to me immediately."

Lady Helena retired to her cabin, accompanied by Mary Grant, and the quartermaster was taken to the saloon where Glenarvan awaited him.

CHAPTER LVII. A DISCOURAGING CONFESSION.

As soon as the quartermaster was in Lord Glenarvan's presence his custodians retired.

"You desired to speak to me, Ayrton?" said Glenarvan.

"Yes, my lord," replied he.

"To me alone?"

"Yes; but I think that if Major MacNabb and Mr. Paganel were present at the interview it would be better."

"For whom?"

"For me."

Ayrton spoke calmly. Glenarvan gazed at him steadily, and then sent word to MacNabb and Paganel, who at once obeyed his summons.

"We are ready for you," said Glenarvan, as soon as his two friends were seated at the cabin-table.

Ayrton reflected for a few moments, and then said:

"My lord, it is customary for witnesses to be present at every contract or negotiation between two parties. That is why I requested the presence of Mr. Paganel and Major MacNabb; for, properly speaking, this is a matter of business that I am going to propose to you."

Glenarvan, who was accustomed to Ayrton's manners, betrayed no surprise, although a matter of business between this man and himself seemed strange.

"What is this business?" said he.

"This is it," replied Ayrton. "You desire to know from me certain circumstances which may be useful to you. I desire to obtain from you certain advantages which will be valuable to me. Now, I will make an exchange, my lord. Do you agree or not?"

"What are these circumstances?" asked Paganel, quickly.

"No," corrected Glenarvan: "what are these advantages?"

Ayrton bowed, showing that he understood the distinction.

"These," said he, "are the advantages for which I petition. You still intend, my lord, to deliver me into the hands of the English authorities?"

"Yes, Ayrton; it is only justice."

"I do not deny it," replied the quartermaster. "You would not consent, then, to set me at liberty?"

Glenarvan hesitated before answering a question so plainly asked. Perhaps the fate of Harry Grant depended upon what he was about to say. However, the feeling of duty towards humanity prevailed, and he said:

"No, Ayrton, I cannot set you at liberty."

"I do not ask it," replied the quartermaster, proudly.

"What do you wish, then?"

"An intermediate fate, my lord, between that which you think awaits me and the liberty that you cannot grant me."

"And that is—?"

"To abandon me on one of the desert islands of the Pacific, with the principal necessaries of life. I will manage as I can, and repent, if I have time."

Glenarvan, who was little prepared for this proposal, glanced at his two friends, who remained silent. After a few moments of reflection, he replied:

"Ayrton, if I grant your request, will you tell me all that it is for my interest to know?"

"Yes, my lord; that is to say, all that I know concerning Captain Grant and the Britannia."

"The whole truth?"

"The whole."

"But who will warrant—?"

"Oh, I see what troubles you, my lord. You do not like to trust to me,—to the word of a malefactor! That is right. But what can you do? The situation is thus. You have only to accept or refuse."

"I will trust you, Ayrton," said Glenarvan, simply.

"And you will be right, my lord. Moreover, if I deceive you, you will always have the power to revenge yourself."

"How?"

"By recapturing me on this island, from which I shall not be able to escape."

Ayrton had a reply for everything. He met all difficulties, and produced unanswerable arguments against himself. As was seen, he strove to treat in his business with good faith. It was impossible for a person to surrender with more perfect confidence, and yet he found means to advance still further in this disinterested course.

"My lord and gentlemen," added he, "I desire that you should be convinced that I am honorable. I do not seek to deceive you, but am going to give you a new proof of my sincerity in this affair. I act frankly, because I rely upon your loyalty."

"Go on, Ayrton," replied Glenarvan.

"My lord, I have not yet your promise to agree to my proposition, and still I do not hesitate to tell you that I know little concerning Harry Grant."

"Little!" cried Glenarvan.

"Yes, my lord; the circumstances that I am able to communicate to you are relative to myself. They are personal experiences, and will scarcely tend to put you on the track you have lost."

A keen disappointment was manifest on the features of Glenarvan and the major. They had believed the quartermaster to possess an important secret, and yet he now confessed that his disclosures would be almost useless.

However that may be, this avowal of Ayrton, who surrendered himself without security, singularly affected his hearers, especially when he added, in conclusion:

"Thus you are forewarned, my lord, that the business will be less advantageous for you than for me."

"No matter," replied Glenarvan; "I accept your proposal, Ayrton. You have my word that you shall be landed at one of the islands of the Pacific."

"Very well, my lord," said he.

Was this strange man pleased with this decision? You might have doubted it, for his impassive countenance betrayed no emotion. He seemed as if acting for another more than for himself.

"I am ready to answer," continued he.

"We have no questions to ask you," rejoined Glenarvan. "Tell us what you know, Ayrton, and, in the first place, who you are."

"Gentlemen," replied he, "I am really Tom Ayrton, quartermaster of the Britannia. I left Glasgow in Captain Grant's ship on the 12th of March, 1861. For fourteen months we traversed together the Pacific, seeking some favorable place to found a Scottish colony. Harry Grant was a man capable of performing great deeds, but frequently serious disputes arose between us. His character did not harmonize with mine. I could not yield; but with Harry Grant, when his resolution is taken, all resistance is impossible. He is like iron towards himself and others. However, I dared to mutiny, and attempted to involve the crew and gain possession of the vessel. Whether I did right or wrong is of little importance. However it may be, Captain Grant did not hesitate to land me, April 8, 1862, on the west coast of Australia."

"Australia!" exclaimed the major, interrupting Ayrton's story. "Then you left the Britannia before her arrival at Callao, where the last news of her was dated?"

"Yes," replied the quartermaster; "for the Britannia never stopped at Callao while I was on board. If I spoke of Callao at O'Moore's farm, it was your story that gave me this information."

"Go on, Ayrton," said Glenarvan.

"I found myself, therefore, abandoned on an almost desert coast, but only twenty miles from the penitentiary of Perth, the capital of Western Australia. Wandering along the shore, I met a band of convicts who had just escaped. I joined them. You will spare me, my lord, the account of my life for two years and a half. It is enough to know that I became chief of the runaways, under the name of Ben Joyce. In the month of September, 1864, I made my appearance at the Irishman's farm, and was received as a servant under my true name of Ayrton. Here I waited till an opportunity should be offered to gain possession of a vessel. This was my great object. Two months later the Duncan arrived. During your visit at the farm you related, my lord, the whole story of Captain Grant. I then learned what I had not known, the Britannia's stoppage at Callao, the last news of her, dated June, 1862, two months after my abandonment, the finding of the document, the shipwreck of the vessel, and finally the important reasons you had for seeking Captain Grant in Australia. I did not hesitate, but resolved to appropriate the Duncan,—a marvelous ship, that would have distanced the best of the British navy. However, there were serious injuries to be repaired. I therefore let her start for Melbourne, and offered myself to you in my real character of quartermaster, volunteering to guide you to the scene of the shipwreck, which I falsely located on the eastern coast of Australia. Thus followed at a distance and sometimes preceded by my band of convicts, I conducted your party across the province of Victoria. My companions committed a useless crime at Camden Bridge, since the Duncan, once at Twofold Bay, could not have escaped me, and with it I should have been master of the ocean. I brought you thus unsuspectingly as far as the Snowy River. The horses and oxen fell dead one by one, poisoned by the gastrolobium. I entangled the cart in the marshes. At my suggestion—but you know the rest, my lord, and can be certain that, except for Mr. Paganel's absent-mindedness, I should now be commander on board the Duncan. Such is my story, gentlemen. My disclosures, unfortunately, cannot set you on the track of Captain Grant, and you see that in dealing with me you have made a bad bargain."

The quartermaster ceased, crossed his arms, according to his custom, and waited. Glenarvan and his friends were silent. They felt that this strange criminal had told the entire truth. The capture of the Duncan had only failed through a cause altogether beyond his control. His accomplices had reached Twofold Bay, as the convict's blouse, found by Glenarvan, proved. There, faithful to the orders of their chief, they had lain in wait for the yacht, and at last, tired of watching, they had doubtless resumed their occupation of plunder and burning in the fields of New South Wales.

The major was the first to resume the examination, in order to determine the dates relative to the Britannia.

"It was the 8th of April, 1862, then, that you were landed on the west coast of Australia?" he asked of the quartermaster.

"Exactly," replied Ayrton.

"And do you know what Captain Grant's plans were then?"

"Vaguely."

"Continue, Ayrton," said Glenarvan. "The least sign may set us on the track."

"What I can say is this, my lord. Captain Grant intended to visit New Zealand. But this part of his programme was not carried out while I was on board. The Britannia might, therefore, after leaving Callao, have gained the shores of New Zealand. This would agree with the date, June 27, 1862, given in the document as the time of the shipwreck."

"Evidently," remarked Paganel.

"But," added Glenarvan, "there is nothing in these half-obliterated portions of the document which can apply to New Zealand."

"That I cannot answer," said the quartermaster.

"Well, Ayrton," continued Glenarvan, "you have kept your word, and I will keep mine. We will decide on what island of the Pacific you shall be abandoned."

"Oh, it matters little to me," answered Ayrton.

"Return to your cabin now, and await our decision."

The quartermaster retired, under guard of the two sailors.

"This villain might have been a great man," observed the major.

"Yes," replied Glenarvan. "He has a strong and self-reliant character. Why must his abilities be devoted to crime?"

"But Harry Grant?"

"I fear that he is forever lost! Poor children! who could tell them where their father is?"

"I!" cried Paganel.

As we have remarked, the geographer, although so loquacious and excitable usually, had scarcely spoken during Ayrton's examination. He had listened in total silence. But this last word that he had uttered was worth more than all the others, and startled Glenarvan at once.

"You, Paganel!" he exclaimed; "do you know where Captain Grant is?"

"As well as can be known," answered the geographer.

"And how do you know?"

"By that everlasting document."

"Ah!" said the major, in a tone of the most thorough incredulity.

"Listen first, MacNabb, and shrug your shoulders afterwards. I did not speak before, because you would not have believed me. Besides, it was useless. But if I speak to-day, it is because Ayrton's opinion corroborates mine."

"Then New Zealand—?" asked Glenarvan.

"Hear and judge," replied Paganel. "I did not commit the blunder that saved us, without reason. Just as I was writing that letter at Glenarvan's dictation, the word Zealand was troubling my brain. You remember that we were in the cart. MacNabb had just told Lady Helena the story of the convicts, and had handed her the copy of the *Australian and New Zealand Gazette* that gave an account of the accident at Camden Bridge. As I was writing, the paper lay on the ground, folded so that only two syllables of its title could be seen, and these were *aland*. What a light broke in upon my mind! 'Aland' was one of the very words in the English document,—a word that we had hitherto translated *ashore*, but which was the termination of the proper name Zealand."

"Ha!" cried Glenarvan.

"Yes," continued Paganel, with profound conviction, "this interpretation had escaped me, and do you know why? Because my examinations were naturally confined more particularly to the French document, where this important word was wanting."

"Ho! ho!" laughed the major, "that is too much imagination, Paganel. You forget your previous conclusions rather easily."

"Well, major, I am ready to answer you."

"Then what becomes of your word *austral*?"

"It is what it was at first. It simply means the southern (*australes*) countries."

"Very well. But that word *indi*, that was first the root of Indians (*indiens*), and then of natives (*indigènes*)?"

"The third and last time, it shall be the first two syllables of the word *indigence* (destitution)."

"And *contin*!" cried MacNabb; "does it still signify *continent*?"

"No, since New Zealand is only an island."

"Then?" inquired Glenarvan.

"My dear lord," replied Paganel, "I will translate the document for you, according to my third interpretation, and you shall judge. I only make two suggestions. First, forget as far as possible the previous interpretations; and next, although certain passages will seem to you forced, and I may translate them wrongly, still, remember that they have no special importance. Moreover, the French document serves as the basis of my interpretation, and you must consider that it was written by an Englishman who could not have been perfectly familiar with the idioms of our language."

So saying, Paganel, slowly pronouncing each syllable, read the following:

"On the 27th of June, 1862, the brig Britannia, of Glasgow, foundered, after a long struggle (*agonie*), in the South (*australes*) Seas, on the coasts of New

Zealand. Two sailors and Captain Grant succeeded in landing (*abor*der). Here, continually (*continuellement*) a prey (*proie*) to a cruel (*cruelle*) destitution (*indigence*), they cast this document into the sea, at longitude — and latitude 37° 11'. Come to their assistance, or they are lost."

Paganel stopped. His interpretation was admissible. But, although it appeared as probable as the other, still it might be as false. Glenarvan and the major therefore no longer attempted to dispute it. However, since the traces of the Britannia had not been encountered on the coasts of Patagonia or Australia, the chances were in favor of New Zealand.

"Now, Paganel," said Glenarvan, "will you tell me why, for about two months, you kept this interpretation secret?"

"Because I did not wish to give you vain hopes. Besides, we were going to Auckland, which is on the very latitude of the document."

"But afterwards, when we were taken out of our course, why did you not speak?"

"Because, however just this interpretation may be, it cannot contribute to the captain's rescue."

"Why, Paganel?"

"Because, admitting that Captain Grant was wrecked on the coast of New Zealand, as long as he has not made his appearance for two years since the disaster, he must have fallen a victim to the sea or the savages."

"Then your opinion is—?" asked Glenarvan.

"That we might perhaps find some traces of the shipwreck, but that the seamen of the Britannia have perished."

"Keep all this silent, my friends," replied Glenarvan, "and leave me to choose the time for telling this sad news to the children of Captain Grant."

CHAPTER LVIII. A CRY IN THE NIGHT.

The crew soon learned that Ayrton's disclosures had not thrown light upon the situation of Captain Grant. The despair on board was profound, for they had relied on the quartermaster, who, however, knew nothing that could put the Duncan on the track of the Britannia. The yacht therefore continued on the same course, and the only question now was to choose the island on which to leave Ayrton.

Paganel and Captain Mangles consulted the maps on board. Exactly on the thirty-seventh parallel was an island, generally known by the name of Maria Theresa, a lone rock in the midst of the Pacific, three thousand five hundred miles from the American coast, and one thousand five hundred miles from New Zealand. No ship ever came within hail of this solitary isle; no tidings from the world ever reached it. Only the storm-birds rested here during their long flights, and many maps do not even indicate its position.

If anywhere absolute isolation was to be found on earth, it was here, afar from the ocean's traveled highways. Its situation was made known to Ayrton, who consented to live there; and the vessel was accordingly headed towards the island. Two days later the lookout hailed land on the horizon. It was Maria Theresa, low, long, and scarcely emerging from the waves, appearing like some enormous sea-monster. Thirty miles still lay between it and the yacht, whose prow cut the waves with such speed that soon the island grew distinct. The sun, now sinking towards the west, defined its outlines in glowing light. Several slight elevations were tinged with the last rays of the day.

At five o'clock Captain Mangles thought he distinguished a faint smoke rising towards the sky.

"Is that a volcano?" he inquired of Paganel, who, with his telescope, was examining the land.

"I do not know what to think," replied the geographer. "Maria Theresa is a point little known. However, I should not be surprised if its origin was due to some volcanic upheaval."

"But then," said Glenarvan, "if an eruption created it, may we not fear that the same agency will destroy it?"

"That is scarcely probable," answered Paganel. "Its existence has been known for several centuries; and this seems a guarantee for its continuance."

"Well," continued Glenarvan, "do you think, captain, that we can land before night?"

"No, certainly not. I ought not to endanger the Duncan in the darkness, on a coast that is not familiar to me. I will keep a short distance from land, and to-morrow at daybreak we will send a boat ashore."

At eight o'clock Maria Theresa, although only five miles to windward, appeared like a lengthened shadow, scarcely visible. An hour later, quite a bright light, like a fire, blazed in the darkness. It was motionless and stationary.

"That would seem to indicate a volcano," said Paganel, watching it attentively.

"However," replied Captain Mangles, "at this distance we ought to hear the commotion that always accompanies an eruption, and yet the wind brings no sound to our ears."

"Indeed," observed Paganel, "this volcano glows, but does not speak. You might say that it throws out intermittent flashes like a lighthouse."

"You are right," continued Captain Mangles; "and yet we are not on the illuminated side. Ha!" cried he, "another fire! On the shore this time! See! it moves, it changes its place!"

He was not mistaken. A new light had appeared, that sometimes seemed to go out, and then all at once flash forth again.

"Is the island inhabited?" asked Glenarvan.

"Evidently, by savages," replied Paganel.

"Then we cannot abandon the quartermaster here."

"No," said the major; "that would be giving even savages too dangerous a present."

"We will seek some other deserted island," resumed Glenarvan, who could not help smiling at MacNabb's delicacy. "I promised Ayrton his life, and I will keep my promise."

"At all events, let us beware," added Paganel. "The New Zealanders have the barbarous custom of misleading ships by moving fires. The natives of Maria Theresa may understand this deception."

"Bear away a point," cried the captain to the sailor at the helm. "To-morrow, at sunrise, we shall know what is to be done."

At eleven o'clock the passengers and the captain retired to their cabins. At the bow the first watch was pacing the deck, while at the stern the helmsman was alone at his post.

In the stillness Mary and Robert Grant came on deck. The two children, leaning upon the railing, gazed sadly at the phosphorescent sea and the luminous wake of the yacht. Mary thought of Robert's future; Robert thought of his sister's; both thought of their father. Was that beloved parent still living? Yet must they give him up? But no, what would life be without him? What would become of them without his protection? What would have become of them already, except for the magnanimity of Lord and Lady Glenarvan?

The boy, taught by misfortune, divined the thoughts that were agitating his sister. He took her hand in his.

"Mary," said he, "we must never despair. Remember the lessons our father taught us. 'Courage compensates for everything in this world,' he said. Let us have that indomitable courage that overcomes all obstacles. Hitherto you have labored for me, my sister, but now I shall labor for you."

"Dear Robert!" replied the young girl.

"I must tell you one thing," continued he. "You will not be sorry, Mary?"

"Why should I be sorry, my child?"

"And you will let me do as I wish?"

"What do you mean?" asked she, anxiously.

"My sister, I shall be a sailor—!"

"And leave me?" cried the young girl, clasping her brother's hand.

"Yes, sister, I shall be a sailor, like my father, and like Captain John. Mary, my dear Mary, he has not lost all hope! You will have, like me, confidence in his devotion. He has promised that he will make me a thorough and efficient sailor, and we shall seek our father together. Say that you are willing, sister. What our father would have done for us it is our duty, or mine at least, to do for him. My life has but one object, to which it is wholly devoted,—to search always for him who would never have abandoned either of us. Dear Mary, how good our father was!"

"And so noble, so generous!" added Mary. "Do you know, Robert, that he was already one of the glories of our country, and would have ranked among its great men if fate had not arrested his course?"

"How well I know it!" answered Robert.

Mary pressed her brother to her heart, and the child felt tears dropping upon his forehead.

"Mary! Mary!" cried he, "it is in vain for them to speak, or to keep silent. I hope still, and shall always do so. A man like our father does not die till he has accomplished his purpose!"

Mary Grant could not reply; sobs choked her utterance. A thousand emotions agitated her soul at the thought that new attempts would be made to find her father, and that the young captain's devotion was boundless.

"Does Mr. John still hope?" asked she.

"Yes," replied Robert. "He is a brother who will never forsake us. I shall be a sailor, shall I not, sister,—a sailor to seek my father with him? Are you willing?"

"Yes," said Mary. "But must we be separated?"

"You will not be alone, Mary, I know. John has told me so. Lady Helena will not permit you to leave her. You are a woman, and can and ought to accept her benefits. To refuse them would be ungrateful. But a man, as my father has told me a hundred times, ought to make his own fortune."

"But what will become of our house at Dundee, so full of associations?"

"We will keep it, my sister. All that has been well arranged by our friend John and Lord Glenarvan, who will keep you at Malcolm Castle like a daughter. He said so to John, who told me. You will be at home there, and wait till John and I bring back our father. Ah, what a joyful day that will be!" cried Robert, whose face was radiant with enthusiasm.

"My brother, my child!" exclaimed Mary, "how happy our father would be if he could hear you! How much you resemble him, dear Robert! When you are a man you will be quite like him!"

"God grant it, Mary!" said Robert, glowing with holy and filial pride.

"But how shall we pay our debt to Lord and Lady Glenarvan?" continued Mary.

"Oh, that will not be difficult," answered Robert, with his boyish impulsiveness. "We will tell them how much we love and respect them, and we will show it to them by our actions."

"That is all we can do!" added the young girl, covering her brother's face with kisses; "and all that they will like, too!"

Then, relapsing into reveries, the two children of the captain gazed silently into the shadowy obscurity of the night. However, in fancy they still conversed, questioned, and answered each other. The sea rocked the ship in silence, and the phosphorescent waters glistened in the darkness.

But now a strange, a seemingly supernatural event took place. The brother and sister, by one of those magnetic attractions that mysteriously draw the souls of friends together, experienced at the same instant the same curious hallucination.

478

From the midst of these alternately brightening and darkening waves, they thought they heard a voice issue, whose depth of sadness stirred every fibre of their hearts.

"Help! help!" cried the voice.

"Mary," said Robert, "did you hear?"

And, raising their heads above the bulwarks, they both gazed searchingly into the misty shadows of the night. Yet there was nothing but the darkness stretching blankly before them.

"Robert," said Mary, pale with emotion, "I thought—yes, I thought like you."

At this moment another cry reached them, and this time the illusion was such that these words broke simultaneously from both their hearts:

"My father! my father!"

This was too much for Mary Grant. Overcome by emotion, she sank senseless into her brother's arms.

"Help!" cried Robert. "My sister! my father! help!"

The man at the helm hastened to Miss Grant's assistance, and after him the sailors of the watch, Captain Mangles, Lady Helena, and Lord Glenarvan, who had been suddenly awakened.

"My sister is dying, and my father is yonder!" exclaimed Robert, pointing to the waves.

No one understood his words.

"Yes," repeated he, "my father is yonder! I heard his voice, and Mary did too!"

Just then Mary Grant recovered consciousness, and, looking wildly around, cried:

"My father, my father is yonder!"

The unfortunate girl arose, and, leaning over the bulwark, would have thrown herself into the sea.

"My lord! Madam!" repeated she, clasping her hands, "I tell you my father is there! I declare to you that I heard his voice issue from the waves like a despairing wail, like a last adieu!"

Then her feelings overcame the poor girl, and she became insensible. They carried her to her cabin, and Lady Helena followed, to minister to her wants, while Robert kept repeating:

"My father! my father is there! I am sure of it, my lord!"

The witnesses of this sorrowful scene perceived at last that the two children had been the sport of an hallucination. But how undeceive their senses, which had been so strongly impressed? Glenarvan, however, attempted it, and taking Robert by the hand, said:

"You heard your father's voice, my dear boy?"

"Yes, my lord. Yonder, in the midst of the waves, he cried, 'Help! help!'"

"And you recognized the voice?"

"Did I recognize it? Oh, yes, I assure you! My sister heard and recognized it, too. How could both of us be deceived? My lord, let us go to his rescue. A boat! a boat!"

Glenarvan saw plainly that he could not undeceive the poor child. Still, he made a last attempt, and called the helmsman.

"Hawkins," asked he, "you were at the wheel when Miss Grant was so singularly affected?"

"Yes, my lord," replied Hawkins.

"And you did not see or hear anything?"

"Nothing."

"You see how it is, Robert."

"If it had been *his* father," answered the lad, with irrepressible energy, "he would not say so. It was *my* father, my lord! my father, my father—!"

Robert's voice was choked by a sob. Pale and speechless, he, too, like his sister, lost consciousness. Glenarvan had him carried to his bed, and the child, overcome by emotion, sank into a profound slumber.

"Poor orphans!" said Captain Mangles; "God tries them in a terrible way!"

"Yes," replied Glenarvan, "excessive grief has produced upon both at the same moment a similar effect."

"Upon both!" murmured Paganel. "That is strange!"

Then, leaning forward, after making a sign to keep still, he listened attentively. The silence was profound everywhere. Paganel called in a loud voice, but there was no answer.

"It is strange!" repeated the geographer, returning to his cabin; "an intimate sympathy of thought and grief does not suffice to explain this mystery."

Early the next morning the passengers (and among them were Robert and Mary, for it was impossible to restrain them) were assembled on deck. All wished to examine this land, which had been scarcely distinguishable the night before. The principal points of the island were eagerly scanned. The yacht coasted along about a mile from the shore, and the unassisted eye could easily discern the larger objects.

Suddenly Robert uttered a cry. He maintained that he saw two men running and gesticulating, while a third was waving a flag.

"Yes: the flag of England!" cried Captain Mangles, when he had used his glass.

"It is true!" said Paganel, turning quickly towards Robert.

"My lord!" exclaimed the boy, trembling with excitement,—"my lord, if you do not wish me to swim to the island, you will lower a boat! Ah, my lord, if you please, I do wish to be the first to land!"

No one knew what to say. Were there three men, shipwrecked sailors, Englishmen, on that island? All recalled the events of the night before, and thought of the voice heard by Robert and Mary. Perhaps, after all, they were not mistaken. A voice might have reached them. But could this voice be that of their father? No, alas, no! And each, thinking of the terrible disappointment that was probably in store, trembled lest this new trial would exceed their strength. But how restrain them? Lord Glenarvan had not the courage.

"Lower the boat!" cried he.

In a moment this was done; the two children, Glenarvan, Captain Mangles, and Paganel stepped into it, and six earnest and skilled oarsmen sped away towards the shore.

At ten yards therefrom, Mary uttered again the heart-rending cry:

"My father!"

A man was standing on the beach between two others. His form was tall and stout, while his weather-beaten yet pleasant countenance betrayed a strong resemblance to the features of Mary and Robert Grant. It was, indeed, the man whom the children had so often described. Their hearts had not deceived them. It was their father, it was Captain Grant!

He heard his daughter's cry, he opened his arms, and supported her fainting form.

CHAPTER LIX. CAPTAIN GRANT'S STORY.

Joy does not kill, for the long lost father and his recovered children were soon rejoicing together and preparing to return to the yacht. But how can we depict that scene, so little looked for by any? Words are powerless.

As soon as he gained the deck, Harry Grant sank upon his knees. The pious Scotchman, on touching what was to him the soil of his country, wished, first of all, to thank God for his deliverance. Then, turning towards Lady Helena; Lord Glenarvan, and their companions, he thanked them in a voice broken by emotion. While on their way to the yacht, his children had briefly told him the story of the Duncan.

How great a debt of gratitude did he feel that he owed this noble woman and her companions! From Lord Glenarvan down to the lowest sailor, had not all struggled and suffered for him? Harry Grant expressed the feelings of thankfulness that overflowed his heart with so much simplicity and nobleness, and his manly countenance was illumined by so pure and sincere a sentiment, that all felt themselves repaid for the trials they had undergone. Even the imperturbable major's eye was wet with a tear that he could not repress. As for Paganel, he wept like a child who does not think of hiding his emotion.

Captain Grant could not cease gazing at his daughter. He found her beautiful and charming, and told her so again and again, appealing to Lady Helena as if to be assured that his fatherly love was not mistaken. Then, turning to his son, he cried rapturously:

"How he has grown! He is a man!"

He lavished upon these two beings, so dearly loved, the thousand expressions of love that had been unuttered during long years of absence. Robert introduced him successively to all his friends. All had alike proved their kindness and good wishes towards the two orphans. When Captain Mangles came to be introduced, he blushed like a young girl, and his voice trembled as he saluted Mary's father.

Lady Helena then told the story of the voyage, and made the captain proud of his son and daughter. He learned the exploits of the young hero, and how the boy had already repaid part of his obligation to Lord Glenarvan at the peril of his life. Captain Mangles' language to Mary and concerning her was so truly loving, that Harry Grant, who had been already informed on this point by Lady Helena, placed the hand of his daughter in that of the noble young captain, and, turning towards Lord and Lady Glenarvan, said:

"My lord and lady, join with me to bless our children!"

It was not long before Glenarvan related Ayrton's story to the captain, who confirmed the quartermaster's declaration in regard to his having been abandoned on the Australian coast.

"He is a shrewd and courageous man," added he; "but his passions have ruined him. May meditation and repentance lead him to better feelings!"

But before Ayrton was transferred to Tabor Island, Harry Grant wished to show his new friends the bounds of his habitation. He invited them to visit his house, and sit for once at his table. Glenarvan and his companions cordially accepted the invitation, and Robert and Mary were not a little desirous to see those haunts where their father had doubtless at times bewailed his fate. A boat was manned, and the whole party soon disembarked on the shores of the island.

A few hours sufficed to traverse Captain Grant's domain. It was in reality the summit of a submarine mountain, covered with basaltic rocks and volcanic fragments. When the shipwrecked seamen of the Britannia took refuge here, the hand of man began to control the development of nature's resources, and in two years and a half the captain and his companions had completely metamorphosed their island home.

The visitors at last reached the house, shaded by verdant gum-trees, while before its windows stretched the glorious sea, glittering in the rays of the sun. Harry Grant set his table in the shade, and all took seats around it. Some cold roast meat, some of the produce of the breadfruit-tree, several bowls of milk, two or three bunches of wild chicory, and pure, fresh water, formed the elements of the simple but healthful repast. Paganel was in ecstasies. It recalled his old idea of Robinson Crusoe.

"That rascal Ayrton will have no cause to complain," cried he in his enthusiasm. "The island is a paradise!"

"Yes," replied Harry Grant, "a paradise for three poor sailors whom Heaven sheltered here. But I regret that Maria Theresa is not a large and fertile island, with a river instead of a rivulet, and a harbor instead of a coast so exposed to the force of the waves."

"And why, captain?" asked Glenarvan.

"Because I would have laid here the foundation of that colony that I wish to present to Scotland."

"Ah!" said Glenarvan. "Then you have not abandoned the idea that has made you so popular in your native land?"

"No, my lord; and God has saved me, through your instrumentality, only to permit me to accomplish it. Our poor brothers of old Caledonia shall yet have another Scotland in the New World. Our dear country must possess in these seas a colony of her own, where she can find that independence and prosperity that are wanting in many European empires."

"That is well said, captain," replied Lady Helena. "It is a noble project, and worthy of a great heart. But this island—?"

"No, madam, it is a rock, only large enough to support a few colonists; while we need a vast territory, rich in all primitive treasures."

"Well, captain," cried Glenarvan, "the future is before us! Let us seek this land together!"

The hands of both men met in a warm clasp, as if to ratify this promise. All now wished to hear the story of the shipwrecked sailors of the Britannia during those two long years of solitude. Harry Grant accordingly hastened to satisfy the desires of his new friends, and began as follows: "It was on the night of the 26th of June, 1862, that the Britannia, disabled by a six days' tempest, was wrecked on the rock of Maria Theresa. The sea was so high that to save anything was impossible, and all the crew perished except my two sailors, Bob Learce and Joe Bell, and myself; and we succeeded in reaching the coast after many struggles. The land that we thus reached was only a desert island, two miles wide and five long, with a few trees in the interior, some meadow land, and a spring of fresh water that, fortunately, has never ceased to flow. Alone with my two sailors, in this quarter of the globe, I did not despair, but, placing my confidence in God, engaged in a resolute struggle. Bob and Joe, my companions and friends in misfortune, energetically aided my efforts. We began, like Robinson Crusoe, by collecting the fragments of the vessel, some tools, a little powder, several weapons, and a bag of precious seeds. The first weeks were very toilsome, but soon hunting and fishing furnished us subsistence, for wild goats swarmed in the interior of the island, and marine animals abounded on its coast. Gradually our daily routine was regularly organized. I determined our exact situation by my instruments, which I had saved from the shipwreck. We were out of the regular course of ships, and could not be rescued except by a providential interposition. Although thinking of those who were dear to me, and whom I never expected to see again, still I accepted this trial with fortitude, and my most earnest prayers were for my two children. Meantime we labored resolutely. Much of the land was sown with the seeds taken from the Britannia; and potatoes, chicory, sorrel, and other vegetables improved and varied our daily food. We caught several goats, which were easily kept, and had milk and butter. The breadfruit-tree, which grew in the dry creeks, furnished us with a sort of nourishing bread, and the wants of life no longer gave us any alarm. We built a house out of the fragments of the Britannia, covered it with sails, carefully tarred, and under this shelter the rainy season was comfortably passed. Here many plans were discussed, and many dreams enjoyed, the best of which has just been realized! At first I thought of braving the sea in a boat made of the wreck of the vessel; but a vast distance separated us from the nearest land. No boat could have endured so long a voyage. I therefore abandoned my design, and no longer expected deliverance, except through a Divine interposition. Ah, my poor children, how many times, on the rocks of the coast, have we waited for ships at sea! During the entire period of our exile only two or three sails appeared on the horizon, and these soon to disappear again. Two years and a half passed thus. We no longer hoped, but still did not wholly despair. At last, yesterday afternoon, I had mounted the highest summit of the island, when I perceived a faint smoke in the west, which grew clearer, and I soon distinctly discerned a vessel that seemed to be coming towards us. But would she not avoid this island, which offered no landing-place? Ah, what a day of anguish, and how my heart throbbed! My companions kindled a fire on one of the peaks. Night came, but the ship gave no signal for approach. Deliverance was there, and should we see it vanish? I hesitated no longer. The darkness increased. The vessel might double the island during the night. I threw myself into the sea, to swim to her. Hope increased my strength. I beat the waves with almost superhuman energy, and approached the yacht. Scarcely thirty yards separated me, when she tacked. Then I uttered those despairing cries which my two children alone heard, for they were no illusion. I returned to the shore, exhausted and overcome by fatigue and emotion. It was a terrible night, this last one on the island. We believed ourselves forever abandoned, when, at daybreak, I perceived the yacht slowly coasting along the shores. Your boat was then lowered,—we were saved, and, thanks to the Divine goodness of Heaven, my dear children were there to stretch out their arms to me!"

Harry Grant's story was finished amid a fresh shower of kisses and caresses from Robert and Mary. The captain learned now, for the first time, that he owed his deliverance to that hieroglyphic document that, eight days after his shipwreck, he had inclosed in a bottle and confided to the mercy of the waves.

But what did Jacques Paganel think during this recital? The worthy geographer revolved the words of the document a thousand ways in his brain. He reviewed his three interpretations, which were all false. How had this island been indicated in these damaged papers? He could no longer restrain himself, but, seizing Harry Grant's hand, cried: "Captain, will you tell me what your undecipherable document contained?"

At this request curiosity was general, for the long-sought clew to the mystery would now be given.

"Well, captain," said Paganel, "do you remember the exact words of the document?"

"Perfectly," replied Harry Grant; "and scarcely a day has passed but memory has recalled those words upon which our only hope hung."

"And what are they, captain?" inquired Glenarvan. "Tell us, for our curiosity is great."

"I am ready to satisfy you," continued Harry Grant; "but you know that, to increase the chances of success, I inclosed in the bottle three documents, written in three languages. Which one do you wish to hear?"

"They are not identical, then?" cried Paganel.

"Yes, almost to a word."

"Well, give us the French document," said Glenarvan. "This one was spared the most by the waves, and has served as the principal basis for our search."

"This is it, my lord, word for word," answered Harry Grant.

"'On the 27th June, 1862, the brig Britannia, of Glasgow, was lost 1500 leagues from Patagonia, in the southern hemisphere. Carried by the waves, two sailors and Captain Grant reached Tabor Island—'"

"Ha!" interrupted Paganel.

"'Here,'" resumed Harry Grant, "'continually a prey to a cruel destitution, they cast this document into the sea at longitude 153° and latitude 37° 11'. Come to their aid, or they are lost.'"

At the word "Tabor," Paganel had suddenly risen, and then, controlling himself no longer, he cried:

"How Tabor Island? It is Maria Theresa."

"Certainly, Mr. Paganel," replied Harry Grant; "Maria Theresa on the English and German, but Tabor on the French maps."

At this moment a vigorous blow descended upon Paganel's shoulder. Truth compels us to say that it was from the major, who now failed in his strict habits of propriety. "A fine geographer you are!" said MacNabb, in a tone of badinage. "But no matter, since we have succeeded."

"No matter?" cried Paganel; "I ought never to have forgotten that twofold appellation! It is an unpardonable mistake, unworthy of the secretary of a Geographical Society. I am disgraced!"

When the meal was finished, Harry Grant put everything in order in his house. He took nothing away, for he was willing that the guilty convict should inherit his possessions.

They returned to the vessel; and, as he expected to sail the same day, Glenarvan gave orders for the quartermaster's landing. Ayrton was brought on deck, and found himself in the presence of Harry Grant.

"It is I, Ayrton," said he.

"Yes, captain," replied Ayrton, without betraying any astonishment at Harry Grant's appearance. "Well, I am not sorry to see you again in good health."

"It seems, Ayrton, that I made a mistake in landing you on an inhabited coast."

"It seems so, captain."

"You will take my place on this desert island. May Heaven lead you to repentance!"

"May it be so," rejoined Ayrton, in a calm tone.

Then Glenarvan, addressing the quartermaster, said:

"Do you still adhere, Ayrton, to this determination to be abandoned?"

"Yes, my lord."

"Does Tabor Island suit you?"

"Perfectly."

"Now listen to my last words. You will be far removed from every land, and deprived of all communication with your fellow-men. Miracles are rare, and you will not probably remove from this island, where we leave you. You will be alone, under the eye of God, who reads the uttermost depths of all hearts; but you will not be lost, as was Captain Grant. However unworthy you may be of the remembrance of men, still they will remember you. I know where you are, and will never forget you."

"Thank you, my lord!" replied Ayrton, simply.

Such were the last words exchanged between Glenarvan and the quartermaster. The boat was ready, and Ayrton embarked. Captain Mangles had previously sent to the island several cases of preserved food, some clothes, tools, weapons, and a supply of powder and shot. The abandoned man could therefore employ his time to advantage. Nothing was wanting, not even books, foremost among which was a Bible.

The hour for separation had come. The crew and passengers stood on deck. More than one felt the heart strangely moved. Lady Helena and Mary Grant could not repress their emotion.

"Must it then be so?" inquired the young wife of her husband. "Must this unfortunate be abandoned?"

"He must, Helena," answered Glenarvan. "It is his punishment."

At this moment the boat, commanded by Captain Mangles, started. Ayrton raised his hat and gave a grave salute. Glenarvan and the crew returned this last farewell, as if to a man about to die, as he departed, in a profound silence.

On reaching the shore, Ayrton leaped upon the sand, and the boat returned. It was then four o'clock in the afternoon, and from the upper deck the passengers could see the quartermaster, with folded arms, standing motionless as a statue, on a rock, and gazing at the vessel.

"Shall we start, my lord?" asked Captain Mangles.

"Yes, John," replied Glenarvan, quickly, with more emotion than he wished to manifest.

"All right!" cried the captain to the engineer. The steam hissed, the screw beat the waves, and at eight o'clock the last summits of Tabor Island disappeared in the shadows of the night.

CHAPTER LX. PAGANEL'S LAST ENTANGLEMENT.

Eleven days after leaving Tabor Island the Duncan came in sight of the American coast, and anchored in Talcahuana Bay. Five months had elapsed since her departure from this port, during which time the travelers had made the circuit of the world on this thirty-seventh parallel. Their efforts had not been in vain, for they had found the shipwrecked survivors of the Britannia.

The Duncan, having taken in her necessary stores, skirted the coasts of Patagonia, doubled Cape Horn, and steamed across the Atlantic. The voyage was very uneventful. The yacht carried a full complement of happy people; there seemed to be no secrets on board.

A mystery, however, still perplexed MacNabb. Why did Paganel always keep hermetically incased in his clothes, and wear a comforter over his ears? The major longed to know the motive for this singular fancy. But in spite of his questions, hints, and suspicions, Paganel did not unbutton his coat.

At last, fifty-three days after leaving Talcahuana, Captain Mangles descried the lighthouse of Cape Clear. The vessel entered St. George's Channel, crossed the Irish Sea, and passed into the Frith of Clyde. At eleven o'clock they anchored at Dumbarton, and early in the afternoon the travelers reached Malcolm Castle, amidst the hurrahs of their tenantry and friends.

Thus it was that Harry Grant and his two companions were rescued, and that John Mangles married Mary Grant in the old cathedral of St. Mungo, where the Rev. Mr. Morton, who nine months before had prayed for the rescue of the father, now blessed the union of the daughter with one of his deliverers. It was arranged that Robert should be a sailor, like his father and brother-in-law, and that he should continue the contemplated project of the former, under the munificent patronage of Lord Glenarvan.

But was Jacques Paganel to die a bachelor? Certainly not; for, after his heroic exploits, the worthy geographer could not escape celebrity. His eccentricities (and his abilities) made him much talked of in Scotland. People seemed as though they could not show him enough attention.

Just at this time an amiable lady of thirty, none other than the major's cousin, a little eccentric herself, but still agreeable and charming, fell in love with the geographer's peculiarities. Paganel was far from being insensible to Miss Arabella's attractions, yet did not dare to declare his sentiments.

The major accordingly undertook the part of Cupid's messenger between these two congenial hearts, and even told Paganel that marriage was "the last blunder" that he could commit. But the geographer was very much embarrassed, and, strangely enough, could not summon courage to speak for himself.

"Does not Miss Arabella please you?" MacNabb would say to him.

"Oh, major, she is charming!" cried Paganel,—"a thousand times too charming for me; and, if I must tell you, would please me better if she were less so. I should like to find a defect."

"Be easy," answered the major; "she has more than one. The most perfect woman always has her share. Well, then, Paganel, are you decided?"

"I do not dare."

"But, my learned friend, why do you hesitate?"

"I am unworthy of her!" was the geographer's invariable reply.

At last, one day, driven desperate by the irrepressible major, Paganel confessed to him, under the pledge of secrecy, a peculiarity that would facilitate his identification, if the police should ever be on his track!

"Bah!" exclaimed the major.

"It is as I tell you," persisted Paganel.

"What matter, my worthy friend?"

"Is that your opinion?"

"On the contrary, you are only more remarkable. This adds to your personal advantages. It makes you the inimitable individual of whom Arabella has dreamed."

And the major, preserving an imperturbable gravity, left Paganel a prey to the most acute anxiety.

A short interview took place between MacNabb and the lady, and fifteen weeks after a marriage was celebrated with great pomp in the chapel of Malcolm Castle.

The geographer's secret would doubtless have remained forever buried in the abysses of the unknown if the major had not told it to Glenarvan, who did not conceal it from Lady Helena, who communicated it to Mrs. Mangles. In short, it reached the ear of Mrs. Olbinett, and spread.

Jacques Paganel, during his three days' captivity among the Maoris, had been tattooed from head to foot, and bore on his breast the picture of an heraldic kiwi with outstretched wings, in the act of biting at his heart.

This was the only adventure of his great voyage for which Paganel could never be consoled or pardon the New Zealanders. In spite of the representations of his friends, he dared not go back to France, for fear of exposing the whole Geographical Society in his person to the jests and railleries of the caricaturists.

The return of Captain Grant to Scotland was welcomed as a cause for national rejoicing, and he became the popular man of old Caledonia. His son Robert has become a sailor like himself, and, under the patronage of Lord Glenarvan, has undertaken the plan of founding a Scottish colony on the shores washed by the Pacific Ocean.

THE END.

BOOK THREE.
THE MYSTERIOUS ISLAND

Jules Verne's Voyages extraordinaires Book # 12

PART I. SHIPWRECKED IN THE AIR

CHAPTER I. THE HURRICANE OF 1865

—CRIES IN THE AIR—A BALLOON CAUGHT BY A WATERSPOUT—ONLY THE SEA IN SIGHT—FIVE PASSENGERS—WHAT TOOK PLACE IN THE BASKET—LAND AHEAD!—THE END.

"Are we going up again?"

"No. On the contrary; we are going down!"

"Worse than that, Mr. Smith, we are falling!"

"For God's sake throw over all the ballast!"

"The last sack is empty!"

"And the balloon rises again?"

"No!"

"I hear the splashing waves!"

"The sea is under us!"

"It is not five hundred feet off!"

Then a strong, clear voice shouted:—

"Overboard with all we have, and God help us!"

Such were the words which rang through the air above the vast wilderness of the Pacific, towards 4 o'clock in the afternoon of the 23d of March, 1865:—

Doubtless, no one has forgotten that terrible northeast gale which vented its fury during the equinox of that year. It was a hurricane lasting without intermission from the 18th to the 26th of March. Covering a space of 1,800 miles, drawn obliquely to the equator, between the 35° of north latitude and 40° south, it occasioned immense destruction both in America and Europe and Asia. Cities in ruins, forests uprooted, shores devastated by the mountains of water hurled upon them, hundreds of shipwrecks, large tracts of territory desolated by the waterspouts which destroyed everything in their path, thousands of persons crushed to the earth or engulfed in the sea; such were the witnesses to its fury left behind by this terrible hurricane. It surpassed in disaster those storms which ravaged Havana and Guadeloupe in 1810 and 1825.

While these catastrophes were taking place upon the land and the sea, a scene not less thrilling was enacting in the disordered heavens.

A balloon, caught in the whirl of a column of air, borne like a ball on the summit of a waterspout, spinning around as in some aerial whirlpool, rushed through space with a velocity of ninety miles an hour. Below the balloon, dimly visible through the dense vapor, mingled with spray, which spread over the ocean, swung a basket containing five persons.

From whence came this aerial traveller, the sport of the awful tempest? Evidently it could not have been launched during the storm, and the storm had been raging five days, its symptoms manifesting themselves on the 18th. It must, therefore, have come from a great distance, as it could not have traversed less than 2,000 miles in twenty-four hours. The passengers, indeed, had been unable to determine the course traversed, as they had nothing with which to calculate their position; and it was a necessary effect, that, though borne along in the midst of this tempest; they were unconscious of its violence. They were whirled and spun about and carried up and down without any sense of motion. Their vision could not penetrate the thick fog massed together under the balloon. Around them everything was obscure. The clouds were so dense that they could not tell the day from the night. No reflection of light, no sound from the habitations of men, no roaring of the ocean had penetrated that profound obscurity in which they were suspended during their passage through the upper air. Only on their rapid descent had they become conscious of the danger threatening them by the waves.

Meanwhile the balloon, disencumbered of the heavy articles, such as munitions, arms, and provisions, had risen to a height of 4,500 feet, and the passengers having discovered that the sea was beneath them, and realizing that the dangers above were less formidable than those below, did not hesitate to throw overboard everything, no matter how necessary, at the same time endeavoring to lose none of that fluid, the soul of the apparatus, which sustained them above the abyss.

The night passed in the midst of dangers that would have proved fatal to souls less courageous; and with the coming of day the hurricane showed signs of abatement. At dawn, the emptied clouds rose high into the heavens; and, in a few hours more, the whirlwind had spent its force. The wind, from a hurricane, had subsided into what sailors would call a "three reef breeze."

Toward eleven o'clock, the lower strata of the air had lightened visibly. The atmosphere exhaled that humidity which is noticeable after the passage of great meteors. It did not seem as if the storm had moved westward, but rather as if it was ended. Perhaps it had flowed off in electric sheets after the whirlwind had spent itself, as is the case with the typhoon in the Indian Ocean.

Now, however, it became evident that the balloon was again sinking slowly but surely. It seemed also as if it was gradually collapsing, and that its envelope was lengthening and passing from a spherical into an oval form. It held 50,000 cubic feet of gas, and therefore, whether soaring to a great height or moving along horizontally, it was able to maintain itself for a long time in the air. In this emergency the voyagers threw overboard the remaining articles which weighed down the balloon, the few provisions they had kept, and everything they had in their pockets, while one of the party hoisted himself into the ring to which was fastened the cords of the net, and endeavored to closely tie the lower end of the balloon. But it was evident that the gas was escaping, and that the voyagers could no longer keep the balloon afloat.

They were lost!

There was no land, not even an island, visible beneath them. The wide expanse of ocean offered no point of rest, nothing upon which they could cast anchor. It was a vast sea on which the waves were surging with incomparable violence. It was the limitless ocean, limitless even to them from their commanding height. It was a liquid plain, lashed and beaten by the hurricane, until it seemed like a circuit of tossing billows, covered with a net-work of foam. Not even a ship was in sight.

In order, therefore, to save themselves from being swallowed up by the waves it was necessary to arrest this downward movement, let it cost what it might. And it was evidently to the accomplishment of this that the party were directing their efforts. But in spite of all they could do the balloon continued to descend, though at the same time moving rapidly along with the wind toward the southwest.

It was a terrible situation, this, of these unfortunate men. No longer masters of the balloon, their efforts availed them nothing. The envelope collapsed more and more, and the gas continued to escape. Faster and faster they fell, until at 1 o'clock they were not more than 600 feet above the sea. The gas poured out of a rent in the silk. By lightening the basket of everything the party had been able to continue their suspension in the air for several hours, but now the inevitable catastrophe could only be delayed, and unless some land appeared before nightfall, voyagers, balloon, and basket must disappear beneath the waves.

It was evident that these men were strong and able to face death. Not a murmur escaped their lips. They were determined to struggle to the last second to retard their fall, and they tried their last expedient. The basket, constructed of willow osiers, could not float, and they had no means of supporting it on the surface of the water. It was 2 o'clock, and the balloon was only 400 feet above the waves.

Then a voice was heard—the voice of a man whose heart knew no fear— responded to by others not less strong:—"Everything is thrown out?"

"No, we yet have 10,000 francs in gold."

A heavy bag fell into the sea.

"Does the balloon rise?"

"A little, but it will soon fall again."

"Is there nothing else we can get rid of?"

"Not a thing."

"Yes there is; there's the basket!"

"Catch hold of the net then, and let it go."

The cords which attached the basket to the hoop were cut, and the balloon, as the former fell into the sea, rose again 2,000 feet. This was, indeed, the last means of lightening the apparatus. The five passengers had clambered into the net around the hoop, and, clinging to its meshes, looked into the abyss below.

Every one knows the statical sensibility of a balloon. It is only necessary to relieve it of the lightest object in order to have it rise. The apparatus floating in air acts like a mathematical balance. One can readily understand, then, that when disencumbered of every weight relatively great, its upward movement will be sudden and considerable. It was thus in the present instance. But after remaining poised for a moment at its height, the balloon began to descend. It was impossible to repair the rent, through which the gas was rushing, and the men having done everything they could do, must look to God for succor.

At 4 o'clock, when the balloon was only 500 feet above the sea, the loud barking of a dog, holding itself crouched beside its master in the meshes of the net, was heard.

"Top has seen something!" cried one, and immediately afterwards another shouted:—"Land! Land!"

The balloon, which the wind had continued to carry towards the southwest, had since dawn passed over a distance of several hundred miles, and a high land began to be distinguishable in that direction. But it was still thirty miles to leeward, and even supposing they did not drift, it would take a full hour to reach it. An hour! Before that time could pass, would not the balloon be emptied of what gas remained? This was the momentous question.

The party distinctly saw that solid point which they must reach at all hazards. They did not know whether it was an island or a continent, as they were uninformed as to what part of the world the tempest had hurried them. But they knew that this land, whether inhabited or desert, must be reached.

At 4 o'clock it was plain that the balloon could not sustain itself much longer. It grazed the surface of the sea, and the crests of the higher waves several times lapped the base of the net, making it heavier; and, like a bird with a shot in its wing, could only half sustain itself.

A half hour later, and the land was scarcely a mile distant. But the balloon, exhausted, flabby, hanging in wrinkles, with only a little gas remaining in its upper portion, unable to sustain the weight of those clinging to the net, was plunging them in the sea, which lashed them with its furious billows. Occasionally the envelope of the balloon would belly out, and the wind taking it would carry it along like a ship. Perhaps by this means it would reach the shore. But when only two cables' length away four voices joined in a terrible cry. The balloon, though seemingly unable to rise again, after having been struck by a tremendous wave, made a bound into the air, as if it had been suddenly lightened of some of its weight. It rose 1,500 feet, and encountering a sort of eddy in the air, instead of being carried directly to land, it was drawn along in a direction nearly parallel thereto. In a minute or two, however, it reapproached the shore in an oblique direction, and fell upon the sand above the reach of the breakers. The passengers, assisting each other, hastened to disengage themselves from the meshes of the net; and the balloon, relieved of their weight, was caught up by the wind, and, like a wounded bird recovering for an instant, disappeared into space.

The basket had contained five passengers and a dog, and but four had been thrown upon the shore. The fifth one, then, had been washed off by the great wave which had struck the net, and it was owing to this accident that the lightened balloon had been able to rise for the last time before falling upon the land. Scarcely had the four castaways felt the ground beneath their feet than all thinking of the one who was lost, cried:—"Perhaps he is trying to swim ashore. Save him! Let us save him!"

CHAPTER II. AN EPISODE OF THE REBELLION

THE ENGINEER CYRUS SMITH—GIDEON SPILETT—THE BLACK MAN NEB— THE SAILOR PENCROFF—THE YOUTH, HERBERT—AN UNEXPECTED PROPOSAL—RENDEZVOUS AT 10 O'CLOCK P.M.—DEPARTURE IN THE STORM.

They were neither professional aeronauts nor amateurs in aerial navigation whom the storm had thrown upon this coast. They were prisoners of war whose audacity had suggested this extraordinary manner of escape. A hundred times they would have perished, a hundred times their torn balloon would have precipitated them into the abyss, had not Providence preserved them for a strange destiny, and on the 20th of March, after having flown from Richmond, besieged by the troops of General Ulysses Grant, they found themselves 7,000 miles from the Virginia capital, the principal stronghold of the Secessionists during that terrible war. Their aerial voyage had lasted five days.

Let us see by what curious circumstances this escape of prisoners was effected,—an escape which resulted in the catastrophe which we have seen.

This same year, in the month of February, 1865, in one of those surprises by which General Grant, though in vain, endeavored to take Richmond, many of his officers were captured by the enemy and confined within the city. One of the most distinguished of those taken was a Federal staff officer named Cyrus Smith.

Cyrus Smith was a native of Massachusetts, an engineer by profession, and a scientist of the first order, to whom the Government had given, during the war, the direction of the railways, which played such a great strategic part during the war.

A true Yankee, thin, bony, lean, about forty-five years old, with streaks of grey appearing in his close cut hair and heavy moustache. He had one of those fine classical heads that seem as if made to be copied upon medals; bright eyes, a serious mouth, and the air of a practiced officer. He was one of these engineers who began of his own wish with the pick and shovel, as there are generals who have preferred to rise from the ranks. Thus, while possessing inventive genius, he had acquired manual dexterity, and his muscles showed remarkable firmness. He was as much a man of action as of study; he moved without effort, under the influence of a strong vitality and his sanguine temperament defied all misfortune. Highly educated, practical, "clear-headed," his temperament was superb, and always retaining his presence of mind he combined in the highest degree the three conditions whose union regulates the energy of man: activity of body, strength of will, and determination. His motto might have been that of William of Orange in the XVIIth century—"I can undertake without hope, and persevere through failure."

Cyrus Smith was also the personification of courage. He had been in every battle of the war. After having begun under General Grant, with the Illinois volunteers, he had fought at Paducah, at Belmont, at Pittsburg Landing, at the siege of Corinth, at Port Gibson, at the Black River, at Chattanooga, at the Wilderness, upon the Potomac, everywhere with bravery, a soldier worthy of the General who said "I never counted my dead." And a hundred times Cyrus Smith would have been among the number of those whom the terrible Grant did not count; but in these combats, though he never spared himself, fortune always favored him, until the time he was wounded and taken prisoner at the siege of Richmond.

At the same time with Cyrus Smith another important personage fell into the power of the Southerners. This was no other than the honorable Gideon Spilett, reporter to the New York Herald, who had been detailed to follow the fortunes of the war with the armies of the North.

Gideon Spilett was of the race of astonishing chroniclers, English or American, such as Stanley and the like, who shrink from nothing in their endeavor to obtain exact information and to transmit it to their journal in the quickest manner. The journals of the United States, such as the New York *Herald*, are true powers, and their delegates are persons of importance. Gideon Spilett belonged in the first rank of these representatives.

A man of great merit; energetic, prompt, and ready; full of ideas, having been all over the world; soldier and artist; vehement in council; resolute in action; thinking nothing of pain, fatigue, or danger when seeking information, first for himself and afterwards for his journal; a master of recondite information of the unpublished, the unknown, the impossible. He was one of those cool observers who write amid the cannon balls, "reporting" under the bullets, and to whom all perils are welcome.

He also had been in all the battles, in the front rank, revolver in one hand and notebook in the other, his pencil never trembling in the midst of a cannonade. He did not tire the wires by incessant telegraphing, like those who speak when they have nothing to say, but each of his messages was short, condensed, clear, and to the purpose. For the rest, he did not lack humor. It was he who, after the affair of Black river, wishing at any price to keep his place at the telegraph wicket in order to announce the result, kept telegraphing for two hours the first chapters of the Bible. It cost the New York *Herald* $2,000, but the New York *Herald* had the first news.

Gideon Spilett was tall. He was forty years old or more. Sandy-colored whiskers encircled his face. His eye was clear, lively, and quick moving. It was the eye of a man who was accustomed to take in everything at a glance. Strongly built, he was tempered by all climates as a bar of steel is tempered by cold water. For ten years Gideon Spilett had been connected with the New York *Herald*, which he had enriched with his notes and his drawings, as he wielded the pencil as well as the pen. When captured he was about making a description and a sketch of the battle. The last words written in his note-book were these:—"A Southerner is aiming at me and—." And Gideon Spilett was missed; so, following his invariable custom, he escaped unscratched.

Cyrus Smith and Gideon Spilett, who knew each other only by reputation, were both taken to Richmond. The engineer recovered rapidly from his wound, and it was during his convalescence he met the reporter. The two soon learned to appreciate each-other. Soon their one aim was to rejoin the army of Grant and fight again in the ranks for the preservation of the Union.

The two Americans had decided to avail themselves of any chance; but although free to go and come within the city, Richmond was so closely guarded that an escape might be deemed impossible.

During this time Cyrus Smith was rejoined by a devoted servant. This man was a black man, born upon the engineer's estate, of slave parents, whom Smith, an abolitionist by conviction, had long since freed. The black man, though free, had no desire to leave his master, for whom he would have given his life. He was a man of thirty years, vigorous, agile, adroit, intelligent, quick, and self-possessed, sometimes ingenuous always smiling, ready and honest. He was named Nebuchadnezzar, but he answered to the nickname of Neb.

When Neb learned that his master had been taken prisoner he left Massachusetts without waiting a moment, arrived before Richmond, and, by a ruse, after having risked his life twenty times, he was able to get within the besieged city. The pleasure of Cyrus Smith on seeing again his servant, and the joy of Neb in finding his master, cannot be expressed. But while he had been able to get into Richmond it was much more difficult to get out, as the watch kept upon the Federal prisoners was very strict. It would require an extraordinary opportunity in order to attempt an escape with any chance of success; and that occasion not only did not present itself, but it was difficult to make. Meanwhile, Grant continued his energetic operations. The victory of Petersburg had been vigorously contested. His forces, reunited to those of Butler, had not as yet obtained any result before Richmond, and nothing indicated an early release to the prisoners. The reporter, whose tiresome captivity gave him no item worthy of note, grew impatient. He had but one idea; to get out of Richmond at any risk. Many times, indeed, he tried the experiment, and was stopped by obstacles insurmountable.

Meanwhile, the siege continued, and as the prisoners were anxious to escape in order to join the army of Grant, so there were certain of the besieged no less desirous to be free to join the army of the Secessionists; and among these was a certain Jonathan Forster, who was a violent Southerner. In truth, the Confederates were no more able to get out of the city than the Federal prisoners, as the army of Grant invested it around. The Mayor of Richmond had not for some time been able to communicate with General Lee, and it was of the highest importance to make the latter aware of the situation of the city, in order to hasten the march of the rescuing army. This Jonathan Forster had conceived the idea of passing over the lines of the besiegers in a balloon, and arriving by this means in the Confederate camp.

The Mayor authorized the undertaking, a balloon was made and placed at the disposal of Forster and five of his companions. They were provided with arms as they might have to defend themselves in descending, and food in case their aerial voyage should be prolonged. The departure of the balloon had been fixed for the 18th of March. It was to start in the night, and with a moderate breeze from the northeast, the party expected to arrive at the quarters of General Lee in a few hours. But the wind from the northeast was not a mere breeze. On the morning of the 18th there was every symptom of a storm, and soon the tempest broke forth, making it necessary for Forster to defer his departure, as it was impossible to risk the balloon and those whom it would carry, to the fury of the elements.

The balloon, inflated in the great square of Richmond, was all ready, waiting for the first lull in the storm; and throughout the city there was great vexation at the settled bad weather. The night of the 19th and 20th passed, but in the morning the storm was only developed in intensity, and departure was impossible.

On this day Cyrus Smith was accosted in one of the streets of Richmond by a man whom he did not know. It was a sailor named Pencroff, aged from thirty-five to forty years, strongly built, much sun-burnt, his eyes bright and glittering, but with a good countenance.

This Pencroff was a Yankee who had sailed every sea, and who had experienced every kind of extraordinary adventure that a two-legged being without wings could encounter. It is needless to say that he was of an adventurous nature, ready to dare anything and to be astonished at nothing. Pencroff, in the early part of this year, had come to Richmond on business, having with him Herbert Brown, of New Jersey, a lad fifteen years old, the son of Pencroff's captain, and an orphan whom he loved as his own child. Not having left the city at the beginning of the siege, he found himself, to his great displeasure, blocked. He also had but one idea: to get out. He knew the reputation of the engineer, and he knew with what impatience that determined man chaffed at his restraint. He did not therefore hesitate to address him without ceremony.

"Mr. Smith, have you had enough of Richmond?"

The engineer looked fixedly at the man who spoke thus, and who added in a low voice:"Mr. Smith, do you want to escape?"

"How?" answered the engineer, quickly, and it was evidently an inconsiderate reply, for he had not yet examined the man who spoke.

"Mr. Smith, do you want to escape?"

""Who are you?" he demanded, in a cold voice.

Pencroff made himself known.

"Sufficient," replied Smith. "And by what means do you propose to escape?"

"By this idle balloon which is doing nothing, and seems to me all ready to take us!"—

The sailor had no need to finish his sentence. The engineer had understood all in a word. He seized Pencroff by the arm and hurried him to his house. There the sailor explained his project, which, in truth, was simple enough:—They risked only their lives in carrying it out. The storm was at its height, it is true; but a skilful and daring engineer like Smith would know well how to manage a balloon. He, himself, would not have hesitated to have started, had he known how—with Herbert, of course. He had seen many storms and he thought nothing of them.

Cyrus Smith listened to the sailor without saying a word, but with glistening eyes. This was the opportunity, and he was not the man to let it escape him. The project was very dangerous, but it could be accomplished. During the night, in spite of the guards, they might reach the balloon, creep into the basket, and then cut the lines which held it! Certainly they risked being shot, but on the other hand they might succeed, and but for this tempest—but without this tempest the balloon would have been gone and the long-sought opportunity would not have been present.

"I am not alone," said Smith at length.

"How many would you want to take?" demanded the sailor.

"Two; my friend Spilett, and my man Neb."

"That would be three," replied Pencroff; "and, with Herbert and myself, five. Well, the balloon can carry six?"

"Very well. We will go!" said the engineer.

This "we" pledged the reporter, who was not a man to retreat, and who, when the project was told him, approved of it heartily. What astonished him was, that so simple a plan had not already occurred to himself. As to Neb, he followed his master wherever his master wanted to go.

"To-night, then," said Pencroff.

"To-night, at ten o'clock," replied Smith; "and pray heaven that this storm does not abate before we get off."

Pencroff took leave of the engineer, and returned to his lodging, where he found young Herbert Brown. This brave boy knew the plans of the sailor, and he was not without a certain anxiety as to the result of the proposal to the engineer. We see, therefore, five persons determined to throw themselves into the vortex of the storm.

The storm did not abate. And neither Jonathan Forster nor his companion dreamed of confronting it in that frail basket. The journey would be terrible. The engineer feared but one thing; that the balloon, held to the ground and beaten down under the wind, would be torn into a thousand pieces. During many hours he wandered about the nearly deserted square, watching the apparatus. Pencroff, his hands in his pockets, yawning like a man who is unable to kill time, did the same; but in reality he also feared that the balloon would be torn to pieces, or break from its moorings and be carried off.

Evening arrived and the night closed in dark and threatening. Thick masses of fog passed like clouds low down over the earth. Rain mingled with snow fell. The weather was cold. A sort of mist enveloped Richmond. It seemed as if in the face of this terrible tempest a truce had been agreed upon between the besiegers and besieged, and the cannon were silent before the heavy detonations of the storm. The streets of the city were deserted; it had not even seemed necessary, in such weather, to guard the square in which swung the balloon. Everything favored the departure of the prisoners; but this voyage, in the midst of the excited elements!—

"Bad weather," said Pencroff, holding his hat, which the wind was trying to take off, firmly to his head, "but pshaw, it can't last, all the same."

At half-past 9, Cyrus Smith and his companions glided by different routes to the square, which the gas lights, extinguished by the wind, left in profound darkness. They could not see even the huge balloon, as it lay pressed over against the ground. Beside the bags of ballast which held the cords of the net, the basket was held down by a strong cable passed through a ring fastened in the pavement, and the ends brought back on board.

The five prisoners came together at the basket. They had not been discovered, and such was the darkness that they could not see each other. Without saying a word, four of them took their places in the basket, while Pencroff, under the direction of the engineer, unfastened successively the bundles of ballast. It took but a few moments, and then the sailor joined his companions. The only thing that then held the balloon was the loop of the cable, and Cyrus Smith had but to give the word for them to let it slip. At that moment, a dog leaped with a bound into the basket. It was Top, the dog of the engineer, who, having broken his chain, had followed his master. Cyrus Smith, fearing to add to the weight, wanted to send the poor brute back, but Pencroff said, "Pshaw, it is but one more!" and at the same time threw overboard two bags of sand. Then, slipping the cable, the balloon, shooting off in an oblique direction, disappeared, after having dashed its basket against two chimneys, which it demolished in its rush.

Then the storm burst upon them with frightful violence. The engineer did not dare to descend during the night, and when day dawned all sight of the earth was hidden by the mists. It was not until five days later that the breaking of the clouds enabled them to see the vast sea extending below them, lashed by the wind into a terrific fury.

We have seen how, of these five men, who started on the 20th of March, four were thrown, four days later, on a desert coast, more than 6,000 miles from this country. And the one who was missing, the one to whose rescue the four survivors had hurried was their leader, Cyrus Smith.

[April 5th, Richmond fell into the hands of Grant, the Rebellion was repressed, Lee retreated and the cause of the Union triumphed.]

CHAPTER III. FIVE O'CLOCK IN THE AFTERNOON - THE LOST ONE

—THE DESPAIR OF NEB—SEARCH TO THE NORTHWARD—THE ISLAND—A NIGHT OF ANGUISH—THE FOG OF THE MORNING—NEB SWIMMING—SIGHT OF THE LAND—FORDING THE CHANNEL.

The engineer, on the giving way of the net, had been swept away by a wave. His dog had disappeared at the same time. The faithful animal had of its own accord sprung to the rescue of its master.

"Forward!" cried the reporter, and all four, forgetting weakness and fatigue, began their search. Poor Neb wept with grief and despair at the thought of having lost all that he loved in the world.

Not more than two minutes had passed between the moment that Smith had disappeared, and the instant of his companions landing. They were, therefore, hopeful of being in time to rescue him.

"Hunt, hunt for him," cried Neb.

"Yes, Neb, and we will find him," replied Spilett.

"Alive?"

"Alive!"

"Can he swim?" demanded Pencroff.

"Oh, yes," responded Neb. "And, besides, Top is with him—"

The sailor, looking at the roaring sea, shook his head.

It was at a point northward from this shore, and about half a mile from the place where the castaways had landed, that the engineer had disappeared, and if he had come ashore at the nearest point it was at least that distance from where they now were.

It was nearly 6 o'clock. The fog had risen and made the night very dark. The castaways followed northward along the shore of that land upon which chance had thrown them. A land unknown, whose geographical situation they could not guess. They walked upon a sandy soil, mixed with stones, seemingly destitute of any kind of vegetation. The ground, very uneven, seemed in certain places to be riddled with small holes, making the march very painful. From these holes, great, heavy-flying birds rushed forth, and were lost in the darkness. Others, more active, rose in flocks, and fled away like the clouds. The sailor thought he recognized gulls and sea-mews, whose sharp cries were audible above the raging of the sea.

From time to time the castaways would stop and call, listening for an answering voice from the ocean. They thought, too, that if they were near the place where the engineer had been, washed ashore, and he had been unable to make any response, that, at least, the barking of the dog Top would have been heard. But no sound was distinguishable above the roaring of the waves and the thud of the surf. Then the little party would resume their march, searching all the windings of the shore.

After a walk of twenty minutes the four castaways were suddenly stopped by a foaming line of breakers. They found themselves upon the extremity of a sharp point upon which the sea broke with fury.

"This is a promontory," said the sailor, "and it will be necessary to turn back, keeping to the right in order to gain the main land."

"But if he is there!" cried Neb, pointing towards the ocean, whose enormous waves showed white through the gloom.

"Well, let us call again."

And all together, uniting their voices, uttered a vigorous cry, but without response. They waited for a lull, and tried once more. And again there was no answer.

Then the castaways turned back, following the opposite side of the promontory over ground equally sandy and rocky. However, Pencroff observed that the shore was bolder, that the land rose somewhat, and he thought that it might gradually slope up to the high hill which was dimly visible through the darkness. The birds were less numerous on this shore. The sea also seemed less surging and tempestuous, and it was noticeable that the agitation of the waves was subsiding. They hardly heard the sound of the surf, and doubtless, this side of the promontory formed a semi-circular bay, protected by its sharp point from the long roll of the sea.

But by following this direction they were walking towards the south, which was going away from that place where Smith would have landed. After a tramp of a mile and a half, the shore presented no other curve which would permit of a return towards the north. It was evident that this promontory, the point of which they had turned, must be joined to the mainland. The castaways, although much fatigued, pushed on courageously, hoping each moment to find a sudden turn which would take them in the desired direction. What, then, was their disappointment when, after having walked nearly two miles, they found themselves again arrested by the sea, upon a high promontory of slippery rocks.

"We are on an island," exclaimed Pencroff; "and we have measured it from end to end!"

The words of the sailor were true. The castaways had been thrown, not upon a continent, but upon an island not more than two miles long, and of inconsiderable breadth.

This desert isle, covered with stones, without vegetation, desolate refuge of sea-birds, did it belong to a more important archipelago? They could not tell. The party in the balloon, when from their basket they saw the land through the clouds, had not been able to determine its size. But Pencroff, with the eyes of a sailor accustomed to piercing the gloom, thought, at the moment, that he could distinguish in the west confused masses, resembling a high coast. But at this time they were unable, on account of the obscurity, to determine to what system, whether simple or complex, their isle belonged. They were unable to get off, as the sea surrounded them, and it was necessary to wait until the next day to search for the engineer; who, alas! had made no cry to signal his presence.

"The silence of Cyrus proves nothing," said the reporter. "He may have fainted, or be wounded, and unable to reply, but we will not despair."

The reporter then suggested the idea of lighting a fire upon the point of the island, which would serve as a signal for the engineer. But they searched in vain for wood or dry branches. Sand and stones were all they found.

One can understand the grief of Neb and his companions, who were strongly attached to their brave comrade. It was too evident that they could not help him now, and that they must wait till day. The engineer had escaped, and was already safe upon the land, or he was lost forever. The hours were long and dreadful, the cold was intense, and the castaways suffered keenly, but they did not realize it. They did not think of sleep. Thinking only of their chief, hoping, wishing to hope, they moved back and forth upon that arid island, constantly returning to the northern end, where they would be closest to the place of the catastrophe. They listened, they shouted, they tried to catch some call, and, as a lull would come, or the roar of the surf fall with the waves, their hallooes must have sounded far into the distance.

Once the cry of Neb was answered by an echo; and Herbert made Pencroff notice it, saying:—"That proves that there is land not far to the west."

The sailor nodded; he knew his eyes could not deceive him. He thought he had seen land, and it must be there. But this distant echo was the only answer to the cries of Neb, and the silence about the island remained unbroken. Meanwhile the sky was clearing slowly. Towards midnight, some stars shone out, and, had the engineer been there with his companions, he would have noticed that these stars did not belong to the northern hemisphere. The pole star was not visible in this new horizon, the constellations in the zenith were not such as they had been accustomed to see from North America, and the Southern Cross shone resplendent in the heavens.

The night passed; and towards 5 o'clock in the morning the middle heavens began to brighten, though the horizon remained obscure; until with the first rays of day, a fog rose from the sea, so dense that the eye could scarcely penetrate twenty paces into its depths, and separated into great, heavy-moving masses. This was unfortunate, as the castaways were unable to distinguish anything about them. While the gaze of Neb and the reporter was directed towards the sea, the sailor and Herbert searched for the land in the west; but they could see nothing.

"Never mind," said Pencroff, "if I do not see the land. I feel that it is there,— just as sure as that we are not in Richmond."

But the fog, which was nothing more than a morning mist, soon rose. A clear sun warmed the upper air, its heat penetrating to the surface of the island.

At half-past 6, three quarters of an hour after sunrise, the mist was nearly gone. Though still thick overhead, it dissolved, below, and soon all the island appeared, as from a cloud. Then the sea appeared, limitless towards the east, but bounded on the west by a high and abrupt coast.

Yes, the land was there! There, safety was at least provisionally assured. The island and the main land were separated by a channel half a mile wide, through which rushed a strong current. Into this current one of the party, without saying a word or consulting with his companions, precipitated himself. It was Neb. He was anxious to be upon that coast and to be pushing forward towards the north. No one could keep him back. Pencroff called to him in vain. The reporter prepared to follow, but the sailor ran to him, exclaiming:—

"Are you determined to cross this channel?"

"I am," replied Spilett.

"Well, then, listen to me a moment. Neb can rescue his master alone. If we throw ourselves into the channel we are in danger of being carried out to sea by this strong current. Now, if I am not mistaken it is caused by the ebb. You see the tide is going out. Have patience until low water and then we may ford it."

"You are right," answered the reporter; "we will keep together as much as possible."

Meantime, Neb was swimming vigorously in a diagonal direction, against the current; his black shoulders were seen rising with each stroke. He was drawn backward with swiftness, but he was gaining towards the other shore. It took him more than half an hour to cross the half mile which separated the isle from the mainland, and when he reached the other side it was at a place a long distance from the point opposite to that which he had left.

Neb, having landed at the base of a high rocky wall, clambered quickly up its side, and, running, disappeared behind a point projecting into the sea, about the same height as the northern end of the island.

Neb's companions had watched with anxiety his daring attempt, and, when he was out of sight, they fixed their eyes upon that land from which they were going to demand refuge. They ate some of the shellfish which they found upon the sands; it was a poor meal, but then it was better than nothing.

The opposite coast formed an immense bay, terminated to the south by a sharp point bare of all vegetation, and having a most forbidding aspect. This point at its junction with the shore was abutted by high granite rocks. Towards the north, on the contrary, the bay widened, with a shore more rounded, extending from the southwest to the northeast, and ending in a narrow cape. Between these two points, the distance must have been about eight miles. A half mile from the shore the island, like an enormous whale, lay upon the sea. Its width could not have been greater than a quarter of a mile.

Before the Island, the shore began with a sandy beach strewn with black rocks, at this moment beginning to appear above the receding tide. Beyond this rose, like a curtain, a perpendicular granite wall, at least 300 feet high and terminated by a ragged edge. This extended for about three miles, ending abruptly on the right in a smooth face, as if cut by the hand of man. To the left on the contrary, above the promontory, this kind of irregular cliff, composed of heaped-up rocks and glistening in the light, sank and gradually mingled with the rocks of the southern point.

Upon the upper level of the coast not a tree was visible. It was a table-land, as barren though not as extensive as that around Cape Town, or at the Cape of Good Hope. At least so it appeared from the islet. To the right, however, and back of the smooth face of rock, some verdure appeared. The confused massing of large trees was easily distinguishable extending far as the eye could reach. This verdure gladdened the sight tired by the rough face of granite. Finally, back of and above the plateau, distant towards the northwest about seven miles, shone a white summit, reflecting the sun's rays. It was the snowy cap of some lofty mountain.

It was not possible at present to say whether this land was an island or part of a continent; but the sight of the broken rocks heaped together on the left would have proved to a geologist their volcanic origin, as they were incontestably the result of igneous action.

Gideon Spilett, Pencroff, and Herbert looked earnestly upon this land where they were to live, perhaps for long years; upon which, if out of the track of ships, they might have to die.

"Well," demanded Herbert, "what do you think of it, Pencroff?"

"Well," replied the sailor, "there's good and bad in it, as with everything else. But we shall soon see; for look; what I told you. In three hours we can cross, and once over there, we will see what we can do towards finding Mr. Smith."

Pencroff was not wrong in his predictions. Three hours later, at low tide, the greater part of the sandy bed of the channel was bare. A narrow strip of water, easily crossed, was all that separated the island from the shore. And at 10 o'clock, Spilett and his two companions, stripped of their clothing, which they carried in packages on their heads, waded through the water, which was nowhere more than five feet deep. Herbert, where the water was too deep, swam like a fish, acquitting himself well; and all arrived without difficulty at the other shore. There, having dried themselves in the sun, they put on their clothes, which had not touched the water, and took counsel together.

CHAPTER IV. THE LITHODOMES

THE MOUTH OF THE RIVER—THE "CHIMNEYS"—CONTINUATION OF THE SEARCH—THE FOREST OF EVERGREENS—GETTING FIREWOOD—WAITING FOR THE TIDE—ON TOP OF THE CLIFF—THE TIMBER-FLOAT—THE RETURN TO THE COAST.

Presently the reporter told the sailor to wait just where he was until he should come back, and without losing a moment, he walked back along the coast in the direction which Neb had taken some hours before, and disappeared quickly around a turn in the shore.

Herbert wished to go with him.

"Stay, my boy," said the sailor. "We must pitch our camp for the night, and try to find something to eat more satisfying than shellfish. Our friends will need food when they come back."

"I am ready, Pencroff," said Herbert.

"Good," said the sailor. "Let us set to work methodically. We are tired, cold, and hungry: we need shelter, fire, and food. There is plenty of wood in the forest, and we can get eggs from the nests; but we must find a house."

"Well," said Herbert, "I will look for a cave in these rocks, and I shall certainly find some hole in which we can stow ourselves."

"Right," said Pencroff; "let us start at once."

They walked along the base of the rocky wall, on the strand left bare by the receding waves. But instead of going northwards, they turned to the south. Pencroff had noticed, some hundreds of feet below the place where they had been thrown ashore, a narrow inlet in the coast, which he thought might be the mouth of a river or of a brook. Now it was important to pitch the camp in the neighborhood of fresh water; in that part of the island, too, Smith might be found.

The rock rose 300 feet, smooth and massive. It was a sturdy wall of the hardest granite, never corroded by the waves, and even at its base there was no cleft which might serve as a temporary abode. About the summit hovered a host of aquatic birds, mainly of the web-footed tribe, with long, narrow, pointed beaks. Swift and noisy, they cared little for the unaccustomed presence of man. A shot into the midst of the flock would have brought down a dozen; but neither Pencroff nor Herbert had a gun. Besides, gulls and sea-mews are barely eatable, and their eggs have a very disagreeable flavor.

Meanwhile Herbert, who was now to the left, soon noticed some rocks thickly strewn with sea weed, which would evidently be submerged again in a few hours. On them lay hosts of bivalves, not to be disdained by hungry men. Herbert called to Pencroff, who came running to him.

"Ah, they are mussels," said the sailor. "Now we can spare the eggs."

"They are not mussels," said Herbert, examining the mollusks carefully, "they are lithodomes."

"Can we eat them?" said Pencroff.

"Certainly."

"Then let us eat some lithodomes."

The sailor could rely on Herbert, who was versed in Natural History and very fond of it. He owed his acquaintance with this study in great part to his father, who had entered him in the classes of the best professors in Boston, where the child's industry and intelligence had endeared him to all.

These lithodomes were oblong shell-fish, adhering in clusters to the rocks. They belonged to that species of boring mollusk which can perforate a hole in the hardest stone, and whose shell has the peculiarity of being rounded at both ends.

Pencroff and Herbert made a good meal of these lithodomes. which lay gaping in the sun. They tasted like oysters, with a peppery flavor which left no desire for condiments of any kind.

Their hunger was allayed for the moment, but their thirst was increased by the spicy flavor of the mollusks. The thing now was to find fresh water, which was not likely to fail them in a region so undulating. Pencroff and Herbert, after having taken the precaution to fill their pockets and handkerchiefs with lithodomes, regained the foot of the hill.

Two hundred feet further on they reached the inlet, through which, as Pencroff had surmised, a little river was flowing with full current Here the rocky wall seemed to have been torn asunder by some volcanic convulsion. At its base lay a little creek, running at an acute angle. The water in this place was 100 feet across, while the banks on either side were scarcely 20 feet broad. The river buried itself at once between the two walls of granite, which began to decline as one went up stream.

"Here is water," said Pencroff, "and over there is wood. Well, Herbert, now we only want the house."

The river water was clear. The sailor knew that as the tide was now low there would be no influx from the sea, and the water would be fresh. When this important point had been settled, Herbert looked for some cave which might give them shelter, but it was in vain. Everywhere the wall was smooth, flat, and perpendicular.

However, over at the mouth of the watercourse, and above high-water mark, the detritus had formed, not a grotto, but a pile of enormous rocks, such as are often met with in granitic countries, and which are called *Chimneys*.

Pencroff and Herbert went down between the rocks, into those sandy corridors, lighted only by the huge cracks between the masses of granite, some of which only kept their equilibrium by a miracle. But with the light the wind came in, and with the wind the piercing cold of the outer air. Still, the sailor thought that by stopping up some of these openings with a mixture of stones and sand, the Chimneys might be rendered habitable. Their plan resembled the typographical sign, &, and by cutting off the upper curve of the sign, through which the south and the west wind rushed in, they could succeed without doubt in utilizing its lower portion.

"This is just what we want," said Pencroff, and if we ever see Mr. Smith again, he will know how to take advantage of this labyrinth."

"We shall see him again, Pencroff," said Herbert, "and when he comes back he must find here a home that is tolerably comfortable. We can make this so if we can build a fireplace in the left corridor with an opening for the smoke."

"That we can do, my boy," answered the sailor, "and these Chimneys will just serve our purpose. But first we must get together some firing. Wood will be useful, too, in blocking up these great holes through which the wind whistles so shrilly."

Herbert and Pencroff left the Chimneys, and turning the angle, walked up the left bank of the river, whose current was strong enough to bring down a quantity of dead wood. The return tide, which had already begun, would certainly carry it in the ebb to a great distance. "Why not utilize this flux and reflux," thought the sailor, "in the carriage of heavy timber?"

After a quarter of an hour's walk, the two reached the elbow which the river made in turning to the left. From this point onward it flowed through a forest of magnificent trees, which had preserved their verdure in spite of the season; for they belonged to that great cone-bearing family indigenous everywhere, from the poles to the tropics. Especially conspicuous were the "deodara," so numerous in the Himalayas, with their pungent perfume. Among them were clusters of pines, with tall trunks and spreading parasols of green. The ground was strewn with fallen branches, so dry as to crackle under their feet.

"Good," said the sailor, "I may not know the name of these trees, but I know they belong to the genus firewood, and that's the main thing for us."

It was an easy matter to gather the firewood. They did not need even to strip the trees; plenty of dead branches lay at their feet. This dry wood would burn rapidly, and they would need a large supply. How could two men carry such a load to the Chimneys? Herbert asked the question.

"My boy," said the sailor, "there's a way to do everything. If we had a car or a boat it would be too easy."

"We have the river," suggested Herbert.

"Exactly," said Pencroff. "The river shall be our road and our carrier, too. Timber-floats were not invented for nothing."

"But our carrier is going in the wrong direction," said Herbert, "since the tide is coming up from the sea."

"We have only to wait for the turn of tide," answered the sailor. "Let us get our float ready."

They walked towards the river, each carrying a heavy load of wood tied up in fagots. On the bank, too, lay quantities of dead boughs, among grass which the foot of man had probably never pressed before. Pencroff began to get ready his float.

In an eddy caused by an angle of the shore, which broke the flow of the current, they set afloat the larger pieces of wood, bound together by liana stems so as to form a sort of raft. On this raft they piled the rest of the wood, which would have been a load for twenty men. In an hour their work was finished, and the float was moored to the bank to wait for the turn of the tide. Pencroff and Herbert resolved to spend the mean time in gaining a more extended view of the country from the higher plateau. Two hundred feet behind the angle of the river, the wall terminating in irregular masses of rocks, sloped away gently to the edge of the forest. The two easily climbed this natural staircase, soon attained the summit, and posted themselves at the angle overlooking the mouth of the river.

Their first look was at that ocean over which they had been so frightfully swept. They beheld with emotion the northern part of the coast, the scene of the catastrophe, and of Smith's disappearance. They hoped to see on the surface some wreck of the balloon to which a man might cling. But the sea was a watery desert. The coast, too, was desolate. Neither Neb nor the reporter could be seen.

"Something tells me," said Herbert, "that a person so energetic as Mr. Smith would not let himself be drowned like an ordinary man. He must have got to shore; don't you think so, Pencroff?"

The sailor shook his head sadly. He never thought to see Smith again; but he left Herbert a hope.

"No doubt," said he, "our engineer could save himself where any one else would perish."

Meanwhile he took a careful observation of the coast. Beneath his eyes stretched out the sandy beach, bounded, upon the right of the river-mouth, by lines of breakers. The rocks which still were visible above the water were like groups of amphibious monsters lying in the surf. Beyond them the sea sparkled in the rays of the sun. A narrow point terminated the southern horizon, and it was impossible to tell whether the land stretched further in that direction, or whether it trended southeast and southwest, so as to make an elongated peninsula. At the northern end of the bay, the outline of the coast was continued to a great distance. There the shore was low and flat, without rocks, but covered by great sandbanks, left by the receding tide.

When Pencroff and Herbert walked back towards the west, their looks fell on the snowcapped mountain, which rose six or seven miles away. Masses of tree-trunks, with patches of evergreens, extended from its first declivities to within two miles of the coast. Then from the edge of this forest to the coast stretched a plateau strewn at random with clumps of trees. On the left shore through the glades the waters of the little river, which seemed to have returned in its sinuous course to the mountains which gave it birth.

"Are we upon an island?" muttered the sailor.

"It is big enough, at all events," said the boy.

"An island's an island, no matter how big," said Pencroff.

But this important question could not yet be decided. The country itself, isle or continent, seemed fertile, picturesque, and diversified in its products. For that they must be grateful. They returned along the southern ridge of the granite plateau, outlined by a fringe of fantastic rocks, in whose cavities lived hundreds of birds. A whole flock of them soared aloft as Herbert jumped over the rocks.

"Ah!" cried he, "these are neither gulls nor sea-mews."

"What are they?" said Pencroff. "They look for all the world like pigeons."

"So they are," said Herbert, "but they are wild pigeons, or rock pigeons." I know them by the two black bands on the wing, the white rump, and the ash-blue feathers. The rock pigeon is good to eat, and its eggs ought to be delicious; and if they have left a few in their nests—"

"We will let them hatch in an omelet," said Pencroff, gaily.

"But what will you make your omelet in?" asked Herbert; "in your hat?"

"I am not quite conjurer enough for that," said the sailor. "We must fall back on eggs in the shell, and I will undertake to despatch the hardest."

Pencroff and the boy examined carefully the cavities of the granite, and succeeded in discovering eggs in some of them. Some dozens were collected in the sailor's handkerchief, and, high tide approaching, the two went down again to the water-course.

It was 1 o'clock when they arrived at the elbow of the river, and the tide was already on the turn. Pencroff had no intention of letting his timber float at random, nor did he wish to get on and steer it. But a sailor is never troubled in a matter of ropes or cordage, and Pencroff quickly twisted from the dry lianas a rope several fathoms long. This was fastened behind the raft, and the sailor held it in his hand, while Herbert kept the float in the current by pushing it off from the shore with a long pole.

This expedient proved an entire success. The enormous load of wood kept well in the current. The banks were sheer, and there was no fear lest the float should ground; before 2 o'clock they reached the mouth of the stream, a few feet from the Chimneys.

CHAPTER V. ARRANGING THE CHIMNEYS

THE IMPORTANT QUESTION OF FIRE—THE MATCH BOX—SEARCH OVER THE SHORE—RETURN OF THE REPORTER AND NEB—ONE MATCH—THE CRACKLING FIRE—THE FISH SUPPER—THE FIRST NIGHT ON LAND.

The first care of Pencroff, after the raft had been unloaded, was to make the Chimneys habitable, by stopping up those passages traversed by the draughts of air. Sand, stones, twisted branches, and mud, hermetically sealed the galleries of the & open to the southerly winds, and shut out its upper curve. One narrow, winding passage, opening on the side; was arranged to carry out the smoke and to quicken the draught of the fire. The Chimneys were thus divided into three or four chambers, if these dark dens, which would hardly have contained a beast, might be so called. But they were dry, and one could stand up in them, or at least in the principal one, which was in the centre. The floor was covered with sand, and, everything considered, they could establish themselves in this place while waiting for one better.

While working, Herbert and Pencroff chatted together.

"Perhaps," said the boy, "our companions will have found a better place than ours."

"It is possible." answered the sailor, "but, until we know, don't let us stop. Better have two strings to one's bow than none at all!"

"Oh," repeated Herbert, "if they can only find Mr. Smith, and bring him back with them, how thankful we will be!"

"Yes," murmured Pencroff. "He was a good man."

"Was!" said Herbert. "Do you think we shall not see him again?"

"Heaven forbid!" replied the sailor.

The work of division was rapidly accomplished, and Pencroff declared himself satisfied. "Now," said he, "our friends may return, and they will find a good enough shelter."

Nothing remained but to fix the fireplace and to prepare the meal, which, in truth, was a task easy and simple enough. Large flat stones were placed at the mouth of the first gallery to the left, where the smoke passage had been made; and this chimney was made so narrow that but little heat would escape up the flue, and the cavern would be comfortably warmed. The stock of wood was piled up in one of the chambers, and the sailor placed some logs and broken branches upon the stones. He was occupied in arranging them when Herbert asked him if he had some matches.

"Certainly," replied Pencroff, "and moreover, fortunately; for without matches or tinder we would indeed be in trouble."

"Could not we always make fire as the savages do," replied Herbert, "by rubbing two bits of dry wood together?"

"Just try it, my boy, some time, and see if you do anything more than put your arms out of joint."

"Nevertheless, it is often done in the islands of the Pacific."

"I don't say that it is not," replied Pencroff, "but the savages must have a way of their own, or use a certain kind of wood, as more than once I have wanted to get fire in that way and have never yet been able to. For my part, I prefer matches; and, by the way, where are mine?"

Pencroff, who was an habitual smoker, felt in his vest for the box, which he was never without, but, not finding it, he searched the pockets of his trowsers, and to his profound amazement, it was not there.

"This is an awkward business," said he, looking at Herbert. "My box must have fallen from my pocket, and I can't find it. But you, Herbert, have you nothing: no steel, not anything, with which we can make fire?"

"Not a thing, Pencroff."

The sailor, followed by the boy, walked out, rubbing his forehead.

On the sand, among the rocks, by the bank of the river, both of them searched with the utmost care, but without result. The box was of copper, and had it been there, they must have seen it.

"Pencroff," asked Herbert, "did not you throw it out of the basket?"

"I took good care not to," said the sailor. "But when one has been knocked around as we have been, so small a thing could easily have been lost; even my pipe is gone. The confounded box; where can it be?"

"Well, the tide is out; let us run to the place where we landed," said Herbert.

It was little likely that they would find this box, which the sea would have rolled among the pebbles at high water; nevertheless, it would do no harm to search. They, therefore, went quickly to the place where they had first landed, some 200 paces from the Chimneys. There, among the pebbles, in the hollows of the rocks, they made minute search, but in vain. If the box had fallen here it must have been carried out by the waves. As the tide went down, the sailor peered into every crevice, but without success. It was a serious loss, and, for the time, irreparable. Pencroff did not conceal his chagrin. He frowned, but did not speak, and Herbert tried to console him by saying, that, most probably, the matches would have been so wetted as to be useless.

"No, my boy," answered the sailor. "They were in a tightly closing metal box. But now, what are we to do?"

"We will certainly find means of procuring fire," said Herbert. "Mr. Smith or Mr. Spilett will not be as helpless as we are."

"Yes, but in the meantime we are without it," said Pencroff, "and our companions will find but a very sorry meal on their return."

"But," said Herbert, hopefully, "it is not possible that they will have neither tinder nor matches."

"I doubt it," answered the sailor, shaking his head. "In the first place, neither Neb nor Mr. Smith smoke, and then I'm afraid Mr. Spilett has more likely kept his notebook than his match-box."

Herbert did not answer. This loss was evidently serious. Nevertheless, the lad thought surely they could make a fire in some way or other, but Pencroff, more experienced, although a man not easily discouraged, knew differently. At any rate there was but one thing to do:—to wait until the return of Neb and the reporter. It was necessary to give up the repast of cooked eggs which they had wished to prepare, and a diet of raw flesh did not seem to be, either for themselves or for the others, an agreeable prospect.

Before returning to the Chimneys, the companions, in case they failed of a fire, gathered a fresh lot of lithodomes, and then silently took the road to their dwelling. Pencroff, his eyes fixed upon the ground, still searched in every direction for the lost box. They followed again up the left bank of the river, from its mouth to the angle where the raft had been built. They returned to the upper plateau, and went in every direction, searching in the tall grass on the edge of the forest, but in vain. It was 5 o'clock when they returned again to the Chimneys, and it is needless to say that the passages were searched in their darkest recesses before all hope was given up.

Towards 6 o'clock, just as the sun was disappearing behind the high land in the west, Herbert, who was walking back and forth upon the shore, announced the return of Neb and of Gideon Spilett. They came back alone, and the lad felt his heart sink. The sailor had not, then, been wrong in his presentiments; they had been unable to find the engineer.

The reporter, when he came up, seated himself upon a rock, without speaking. Fainting from fatigue, half dead with hunger, he was unable to utter a word. As to Neb, his reddened eyes showed how he had been weeping, and the fresh tears which he was unable to restrain, indicated, but too clearly, that he had lost all hope.

The reporter at length gave the history of their search. Neb and he had followed the coast for more than eight miles, and, consequently, far beyond the point where the balloon had made the plunge which was followed by the disappearance of the engineer and Top. The shore was deserted. Not a recently turned stone, not a trace upon the sand, not a footprint, was upon all that part of the shore. It was evident that nobody inhabited that portion of the island. The sea was as deserted as the land; and it was there, at some hundreds of feet from shore, that the engineer had found his grave.

At that moment Neb raised his head, and in a voice which showed how he still struggled against despair, exclaimed: "No, he is not dead. It is impossible. It might happen to you or me, but never to him. He is a man who can get out of anything!"

Then his strength failing him, he murmured, "But I am used up."

Herbert ran to him and cried:—"Neb, we will find him; God will give him back to us; but you, you must be famishing; do eat something."

And while speaking the lad offered the poor black man a handful of shell-fish—a meagre and insufficient nourishment enough.

But Neb, though he had eaten nothing for hours, refused them. Poor fellow! deprived of his master, he wished no longer to live.

As to Gideon Spilett, he devoured the mollusks, and then laid down upon the sand at the foot of a rock. He was exhausted, but calm. Herbert, approaching him, took his hand.

"Mr. Spilett," said he, "we have discovered a shelter where you will be more comfortable. The night is coming on; so come and rest there. To-morrow we will see—"

The reporter rose, and, guided by the lad, proceeded towards the Chimneys. As he did so, Pencroff came up to him, and in an off-hand way asked him if, by chance, he had a match with him. The reporter stopped, felt in his pockets, and finding none, said:—

"I had some, but I must have thrown them all away."

Then the sailor called Neb and asked him the same question, receiving a like answer.

"Curse it!" cried the sailor, unable to restrain the word.

The reporter heard it, and going to him said:—"Have you no matches?"

"Not one; and, of course, no fire."

"Ah," cried Neb, "if he was here, my master, he could soon make one."

The four castaways stood still and looked anxiously at each other. Herbert was the first to break the silence, by saying:—

"Mr. Spilett, you are a smoker, you always have matches about you; perhaps you have not searched thoroughly. Look again; a single match will be enough."

The reporter rummaged the pockets of his trowsers, his vest, and coat, and to the great joy of Pencroff, as well as to his own surprise, felt a little sliver of wood caught in the lining of his vest. He could feel it from the outside, but his fingers were unable to disengage it. If this should prove a match, and only one, it was extremely necessary not to rub off the phosphorus.

"Let me try," said the lad. And very adroitly, without breaking it, he drew out this little bit of wood, this precious trifle, which to these poor men was of such great importance. It was uninjured.

"One match!" cried Pencroff." "Why, it is as good as if we had a whole ship-load!"

He took it, and, followed by his companions, regained the Chimneys. This tiny bit of wood, which in civilised lands is wasted with indifference, as valueless, it was necessary here to use with the utmost care. The sailor, having assured himself that it was dry, said:—

"We must have some paper."

"Here is some," answered Spilett, who, after a little hesitation, had torn a leaf from his note-book.

Pencroff took the bit of paper and knelt down before the fire-place, where some handfuls of grass, leaves, and dry moss had been placed under the faggots in such a way that the air could freely circulate and make the dry wood readily ignite. Then Pencroff shaping the paper into a cone, as pipe-smokers do in the wind, placed it among the moss. Taking, then, a slightly rough stone and wiping it carefully, with beating heart and suspended breath, he gave the match a little rub. The first stroke produced no effect, as Pencroff fearing to break off the phosphorus had not rubbed hard enough.

"Ho, I won't be able to do it," said he; "my hand shakes—the match will miss—I can't do it—I don't want to try!" And, rising, he besought Herbert to undertake it.

Certainly, the boy had never in his life been so affected. His heart beat furiously. Prometheus, about to steal the fire from heaven, could not have been more excited.

Nevertheless he did not hesitate, but rubbed the stone with a quick stroke. A little sputtering was heard, and a light blue flame sprung out and produced a pungent smoke. Herbert gently turned the match, so as to feed the flame, and then slid it under the paper cone. In a few seconds the paper took fire, and then the moss kindled. An instant later, the dry wood crackled, and a joyous blaze, fanned by the breath of the sailor, shone out from the darkness.

"At length," cried Pencroff, rising, "I never was so excited in my life!"

It was evident that the fire did well in the fireplace of flat stones. The smoke readily ascended through its passage; the chimney drew, and an agreeable warmth quickly made itself felt. As to the fire, it would be necessary to take care that it should not go out, and always to keep some embers among the cinders. But it was only a matter of care and attention as the wood was plenty, and the supply could always be renewed in good time.

Pencroff began at once to utilize the fire by preparing something more nourishing than a dish of lithodomes. Two dozen eggs were brought by

Herbert, and the reporter, seated in a corner, watched these proceedings without speaking. A triple thought held possession of his mind. Did Cyrus still live? If alive, where was he? If he had survived his plunge, why was it he had found no means of making his existence known? As to Neb, he roamed the sand like one distracted.

Pencroff, who knew fifty-two ways of cooking eggs, had no choice at this time. He contented himself with placing them in the hot cinders and letting them cook slowly. In a few minutes the operation was finished, and the sailor invited the reporter to take part in the supper. This was the first meal of the castaways upon this unknown coast. The hard eggs were excellent, and as the egg contains all the elements necessary for man's nourishment, these poor men found them sufficient, and felt their strength reviving.

Unfortunately, one was absent from this repast. If the five prisoners who had escaped from Richmond had all been there, under those piled-up rocks, before that bright and crackling fire upon that dry sand, their happiness would have been complete. But the most ingenious, as well as the most learned—he who was undoubtedly their chief, Cyrus Smith—alas! was missing, and his body had not even obtained burial.

Thus passed the 25th of March. The night was come. Outside they heard the whistling of the wind, the monotonous thud of the surf, and the grinding of the pebbles on the beach.

The reporter had retired to a dark corner, after having briefly noted the events of the day—the first sight of this new land, the loss of the engineer, the exploration of the shore, the incidents of the matches, etc.; and, overcome by fatigue, he was enabled to find some rest in sleep.

Herbert fell asleep at once. The sailor, dozing, with one eye open, passed the night by the fire, on which he kept heaping fuel.

One only of the castaways did not rest in the Chimneys. It was the inconsolable, the despairing Neb, who, during the whole night, and in spite of his companions' efforts to make him take some rest, wandered upon the sands calling his master.

CHAPTER VI. THE CASTAWAYS' INVENTORY

NO EFFECTS —THE CHARRED LINEN—AN EXPEDITION INTO THE FOREST—THE FLORA OF THE WOODS—THE FLIGHT OF THE JACAMAR—TRACKS OF WILD BEASTS—THE COUROUCOUS—THE HEATH-COCK—LINE-FISHING EXTRAORDINARY.

The inventory of the castaways can be promptly taken. Thrown upon a desert coast, they had nothing but the clothes they wore in the balloon. We must add Spilett's watch and note-book, which he had kept by some inadvertence; but there were no firearms and no tools, not even a pocket knife. Everything had been thrown overboard to lighten the balloon. Every necessary of life was wanting!

Yet if Cyrus Smith had been with them, his practical science and inventive genius would have saved them from despair. But, alas! they could hope to see him no more. The castaways could rely on Providence only, and on their own right hands.

And, first, should they settle down on this strip of coast without an effort to discover whether it was island or continent, inhabited or desert? It was an urgent question, for all their measures would depend upon its solution. However, it seemed to Pencroff better to wait a few days before undertaking an exploration. They must try to procure more satisfying food than eggs and shellfish, and repair their strength, exhausted by fatigue and by the inclemency of the weather. The Chimneys would serve as a house for a while. Their fire was lit, and it would be easy to keep alive some embers. For the time being there were plenty of eggs and shell-fish. They might even be able to kill, with a stick or a stone, some of the numerous pigeons which fluttered among the rocks. They might find fruit-trees in the neighboring forest, and they had plenty of fresh water. It was decided then to wait a few days at the Chimneys, and to prepare for an expedition either along the coast or into the interior of the country.

This plan was especially agreeable to Neb, who was in no hurry to abandon that part of the coast which had been the scene of the catastrophe. He could not and would not believe that Smith was dead. Until the waves should have thrown up the engineer's body—until Neb should have seen with his eyes and handled with his hands his master's corpse, he believed him alive. It was an illusion which the sailor had not the heart to destroy; and there was no use in talking to Neb. He was like the dog who would not leave his master's tomb, and his grief was such that he would probably soon follow him.

Upon the morning of the 26th of March, at daybreak, Neb started along the coast northward to the spot where the sea had doubtless closed over the unfortunate engineer.

For breakfast that morning they had only eggs and lithodomes, seasoned with salt which Herbert had found in the cavities of the rocks. When the meal was over they divided forces. The reporter stayed behind to keep up the fire, and in the very improbable case of Neb's needing him to go to his assistance. Herbert and Pencroff went into the forest.

"We will go hunting, Herbert, "said the sailor. "We shall find ammunition on our way, and we will cut our guns in the forest."

But, before starting, Herbert suggested that as they had no tinder they must replace it by burnt linen. They were sorry to sacrifice a piece of handkerchief, but the need was urgent, and a piece of Pencroff's large check handkerchief was soon converted into a charred rag, and put away in the central chamber in a little cavity of the rock, sheltered from wind and dampness.

By this time it was 9 o'clock. The weather was threatening and the breeze blew from the southeast. Herbert and Pencroff, as they left the Chimneys, cast a glance at the smoke which curled upwards from amid the rocks; then they walked up the left bank of the river.

When they reached the forest, Pencroff broke from the first tree two thick branches which he made into cudgels, and whose points Herbert blunted against a rock. What would he not have given for a knife? Then the hunters walked on in the high grass along the bank of the river, which, after its turn to the southwest, gradually narrowed, running between high banks and over-arched by interlacing trees. Pencroff, not to lose his way, determined to follow the course of the stream, which would bring him back to his point of departure. But the bank offered many obstacles. Here, trees whose flexible branches bent over to the brink of the current; there, thorns and lianas which they had to break with their sticks. Herbert often glided between the broken stumps with the agility of a young cat and disappeared in the copse, but Pencroff called him back at once, begging him not to wander away.

Meanwhile, the sailor carefully observed the character and peculiarities of the region. On this left bank the surface was flat, rising insensibly towards the interior. Sometimes it was moist and swampy, indicating the existence of a subterranean network of little streams emptying themselves into the river. Sometimes, too, a brook ran across the copse, which they crossed without trouble. The opposite bank was more undulating, and the valley, through whose bottom flowed the river, was more clearly defined. The hill, covered with trees rising in terraces, intercepted the vision. Along this right bank they could hardly have walked, for the descent was steep, and the trees which bent over the water were only sustained by their roots. It is needless to say that both forest and shore seemed a virgin wilderness. They saw fresh traces of animals whose species was unknown to them. Some seemed to them the tracks of dangerous wild beasts, but nowhere was there the mark of an axe on a tree-trunk, or the ashes of a fire, or the imprint of a foot. They should no doubt have been glad that it was so, for on this land in the mid-Pacific, the presence of man was a thing more to be dreaded than desired.

They hardly spoke, so great were the difficulties of the route; after an hour's walk they had but just compassed a mile. Hitherto their hunting had been fruitless. Birds were singing and flying to and fro under the trees; but they showed an instinctive fear of their enemy man. Herbert descried among them, in a swampy part of the forest, a bird with narrow and elongated beak, in shape something like a kingfisher, from which it was distinguished by its harsh and lustrous plumage.

"That must be a jacamar," said Herbert, trying to get within range of the bird.

"It would be a good chance to taste jacamar," answered the sailor, "if that fellow would only let himself be roasted."

In a moment a stone, adroitly aimed by the boy, struck the bird on the wing; but the jacamar took to his legs and disappeared in a minute.

"What a muff I am," said Herbert. 'Not at all," said the sailor. "It was a good shot, a great many would have missed the bird. Don't be discouraged, we'll catch him again some day."

The wood opened as the hunters went on, and the trees grew to a vast height, but none had edible fruits. Pencroff sought in vain for some of those precious palm trees, which lend themselves so wonderfully to the needs of mankind, and which grow from 40° north latitude to 35° south. But this forest was composed only of conifers, such as the deodars, already recognized by Herbert; the Douglas pines, which grow on the northeast coast of America; and magnificent fir trees, 150 feet high. Among their branches was fluttering a flock of birds, with small bodies and long, glittering tails. Herbert picked up some of the feathers, which lay scattered on the ground, and looked at them carefully.

"These are 'couroucous,'" said he.

"I would rather have a guinea-hen, or a heath-cock," said Pencroff, "but still, if they are good to eat"—

"They are good to eat," said Herbert; "their meat is delicious. Besides, I think we can easily get at them with our sticks."

Slipping through the grass, they reached the foot of a tree whose lower branches were covered with the little birds, who were snapping at the flying insects. Their feathered claws clutched tight the twigs on which they were sitting. Then the hunters rose to their feet, and using their sticks like a scythe, they mowed down whole rows of the couroucous, of whom 105 were knocked over before the stupid birds thought of escape.

"Good," said Pencroff, "this is just the sort of game for hunters like us. We could catch them in our hands."

They skewered the couroucous on a switch like field-larks, and continued to explore. The object of the expedition was, of course, to bring back as much game as possible to the Chimneys. So far it had not been altogether attained. They looked about everywhere, and were enraged to see animals escaping through the high grass. If they had only had Top! But Top, most likely, had perished with his master.

About 3 o'clock they entered a wood full of juniper trees, at whose aromatic berries flocks of birds were pecking. Suddenly they heard a sound like the blast of a trumpet. It was the note of those gallinaceæ, called "tetras" in the United States. Soon they saw several pairs of them, with brownish-yellow plumage and brown tails. Pencroff determined to capture one of these birds, for they were as big as hens, and their meat as delicious as a pullet. But they would not let him come near them. At last, after several unsuccessful attempts, he said,

"Well, since we can't kill them on the wing, we must take them with a line."

"Like a carp," cried the wondering Herbert.

"Like a carp," answered the sailor, gravely.

Pencroff had found in the grass half-a-dozen tetras nests, with two or three eggs in each.

He was very careful not to touch these nests, whose owners would certainly return to them. Around these he purposed to draw his lines, not as a snare, but with hook and bait. He took Herbert to some distance from the nests, and there made ready his singular apparatus with the care of a true disciple of Isaac Walton. Herbert watched the work with a natural interest, but without much faith in its success. The lines were made of small lianas tied together, from fifteen to twenty feet long, and stout thorns with bent points, broken from a thicket of dwarf acacias, and fastened to the ends of the lianas, served as hooks, and the great red worms which crawled at their feet made excellent bait. This done, Pencroff, walking stealthily through the grass, placed one end of his hook-and-line close to the nests of the tetras. Then he stole back, took the other end in his hand, and hid himself with Herbert behind a large tree. Herbert, it must be said, was not sanguine of success.

A good half hour passed, but as the sailor had foreseen, several pairs of tetras returned to their nests. They hopped about, pecking the ground, and little suspecting the presence of the hunters, who had taken care to station themselves to leeward of the gallinaceæ. Herbert held his breath with excitement, while Pencroff, with dilated eyes, open month, and lips parted as if to taste a morsel of tetras, scarcely breathed. Meanwhile the gallinaceæ walked heedlessly among the hooks. Pencroff then gave little jerks, which moved the bait up and down as if the worms were still alive. How much more intense was his excitement than the fisherman's who cannot see the approach of his prey!

The jerks soon aroused the attention of the gallinaceæ, who began to peck at the bait. Three of the greediest swallowed hook and bait together. Suddenly, with a quick jerk, Pencroff pulled in his line, and the flapping of wings showed that the birds were taken.

"Hurrah!" cried he, springing upon the game, of which he was master in a moment. Herbert clapped his hands. It was the first time he had seen birds taken with a line; but the modest sailor said it was not his first attempt, and, moreover, that the merit of the invention was not his.

"And at any rate," said he, "in our present situation we must hope for many such contrivances."

The tetras were tied together by the feet, and Pencroff, happy that they were not returning empty handed, and perceiving that the day was ending, thought it best to return home.

Their route was indicated by the river, and following it downward, by 6 o'clock, tired out by their excursion, Herbert and Pencroff re-entered the Chimneys.

CHAPTER VII. NEB HAS NOT YET RETURNED

THE REFLECTIONS OF THE REPORTER—THE SUPPER—PROSPECT OF A BAD NIGHT—THE STORM IS FRIGHTFUL—THEY GO OUT INTO THE NIGHT—STRUGGLE WITH THE RAIN AND WIND.

Gideon Spilett stood motionless upon the shore, his arms crossed, gazing on the sea, whose horizon was darkened towards the east by a huge black cloud mounting rapidly into the zenith. The wind, already strong, was freshening, the heavens had an angry look, and the first symptoms of a heavy blow were manifesting themselves.

Herbert went into the Chimneys, and Pencroff walked towards the reporter, who was too absorbed to notice his approach.

"We will have a bad night, Mr. Spilett," said the sailor. "Wind and rain enough for Mother Cary's chickens."

The reporter turning, and perceiving Pencroff, asked this question:—

"How far off from the shore do you think was the basket when it was struck by the sea that carried away our companion?"

The sailor had not expected this question. He reflected an instant before answering:—

"Two cables' lengths or more."

"How much is a cable's length?" demanded Spilett.

"About 120 fathoms, or 600 feet."

"Then," said the reporter, "Cyrus Smith would have disappeared not more than 1,200 feet from the shore?"

"Not more than that."

"And his dog, too?"

"Yes."

"What astonishes me," said the reporter, "admitting that our companion and Top have perished, is the fact that neither the body of the dog nor of his master has been cast upon the shore."

"That is not astonishing with so heavy a sea," replied the sailor. "Moreover, it is quite possible that there are currents which have carried them farther up the coast."

"Then it is really your opinion that our companion has been drowned?" asked, once more, the reporter.

"That is my opinion."

"And my opinion, Pencroff," said Spilett, "with all respect for your experience, is, that in this absolute disappearance of both Cyrus and Top, living or dead, there is something inexplicable and incredible."

"I wish I could think as you do, sir," responded Pencroff, "but, unhappily, I cannot."

After thus speaking the sailor returned to the Chimneys. A good fire was burning in the fireplace. Herbert had just thrown on a fresh armful of wood, and its flames lit up the dark recesses of the corridor.

Pencroff began at once to busy himself about dinner. It seemed expedient to provide something substantial, as all stood in need of nourishment, so two tetras were quickly plucked, spitted upon a stick, and placed to roast before at blazing fire. The couroucous were reserved for the next day.

At 7 o'clock Neb was still absent, and Pencroff began to be alarmed about him. He feared that he might have met with some accident in this unknown land, or that the poor fellow had been drawn by despair to some rash act. Herbert, on the contrary, argued that Neb's absence was owing to some fresh discovery which had induced him to prolong his researches. And anything new must be to Cyrus Smith's advantage. Why had not Neb come back, if some hope was not detaining him? Perhaps he had found some sign or footprint which had put him upon the track. Perhaps, at this moment he was following the trail. Perhaps, already, he was beside his master.

Thus the lad spoke and reasoned, unchecked by his companions. The reporter nodded approval, but Pencroff thought it more probable that Neb, in his search, had pushed on so far that he had not been able to return.

Meantime, Herbert, excited by vague presentiments, manifested a desire to go to meet Neb. But Pencroff showed him that it would be useless in the darkness and storm to attempt to find traces of the black man, and, that the better course was, to wait. If, by morning, Neb had not returned, Pencroff would not hesitate joining the lad in a search for him.

Gideon Spilett concurred with the sailor in his opinion that they had better remain together, and Herbert, though tearfully, gave up the project. The reporter could not help embracing the generous lad.

The storm began. A furious gust of wind passed over the coast from the southeast. They beard the sea, which was out, roaring upon the reef. The whirlwind drove the rain in clouds along the shore. The sand, stirred up by the wind, mingled with the rain, and the air was filled with mineral as well as aqueous dust. Between the mouth of the river and the cliff's face, the wind whirled about as in a maelstrom, and, finding no other outlet than the narrow valley through which ran the stream, it rushed through this with irresistible violence.

Often, too, the smoke from the chimney, driven back down its narrow vent, filled the corridors, and rendered them uninhabitable. Therefore, when the tetras were cooked Pencroff let the fire smoulder, only preserving some clear embers among the ashes.

At 8 o'clock Neb had not returned; but they could not help admitting that now the tempest alone was sufficient to account for his non-appearance, and that, probably, he had sought refuge in some cavern, waiting the end of the storm, or, at least, daybreak. As to going to meet him under present circumstances, that was simply impossible.

The birds were all they had for supper, but the party found them excellent eating. Pencroff and Herbert, their appetite sharpened by their long walk, devoured them. Then each one retired to his corner, and Herbert, lying beside the sailor, extended before the fireplace, was soon asleep.

Outside, as the night advanced, the storm developed formidable proportions. It was a hurricane equal to that which had carried the prisoners from Richmond. Such tempests, pregnant with catastrophes, spreading terror over a vast area, their fury withstood by no obstacle, are frequent during the equinox. We can understand how a coast facing the east, and exposed to the full fury of the storm, was attacked with a violence perfectly indescribable.

Happily the heap of rocks forming the Chimneys was composed of solid, enormous blocks of granite, though some of them, imperfectly balanced, seemed to tremble upon their foundations. Pencroff, placing his hand against the walls, could feel their rapid vibrations; but he said to himself, with reason, that there was no real danger, and that the improvised retreat would not tumble about their ears. Nevertheless, he heard the sound of rocks, torn from the top of the plateau by the gusts, crashing upon the shore. And some, falling perpendicularly, struck the Chimneys and flew off into fragments. Twice the sailor rose, and went to the opening of the corridor, to look abroad. But there was no danger from these inconsiderable showers of stones, and he returned to his place before the fire, where the embers glowed among the ashes.

In spite of the fury and fracas of the tempest Herbert slept profoundly, and, at length, sleep took possession of Pencroff, whose sailor life had accustomed him to such demonstrations. Gideon Spilett, who was kept awake by anxiety, reproached himself for not having accompanied Neb. We have seen that he had not given up all hope, and the presentiments which had disturbed Herbert had affected him also. His thoughts were fixed upon Neb; why had not the black man returned? He tossed about on his sandy couch, unheeding the warfare of the elements. Then, overcome by fatigue, he would close his eyes for an instant, only to be awakened by some sudden thought.

Meantime the night advanced; and it was about 2 o'clock when Pencroff was suddenly aroused from a deep sleep by finding himself vigorously shaken.

"What's the matter?" he cried, rousing and collecting himself with the quickness peculiar to sailors.

The reporter was bending over him and saying:—

"Listen, Pencroff, listen!"

The sailor listened, but could hear no sounds other than those caused by the gusts.

"It is the wind," he said.

"No," answered Spilett, listening again, "I think I heard—"

"What?"

"The barking of a dog!"

"A dog!" cried Pencroff, springing to his feet.

"Yes—the barking—"

"Impossible!" answered the sailor. "How, in the roarings of the tempest—"

"Wait—listen," said the reporter.

Pencroff listened most attentively, and at length, during a lull, he thought he caught the sound of distant barking.

"Is it?" asked the reporter, squeezing the sailor's hand.

"Yes—yes!" said Pencroff.

"It is Top! It is Top!" cried Herbert, who had just wakened, and the three rushed to the entrance of the Chimneys.

They had great difficulty in getting out, as the wind drove against them with fury, but at last they succeeded, and then they were obliged to steady themselves against the rocks. They were unable to speak, but they looked about them. The darkness was absolute. Sea, sky, and earth, were one intense blackness. It seemed as if there was not one particle of light diffused in the atmosphere.

For some moments the reporter and his two companions stood in this place, beset by the gusts, drenched by the rain, blinded by the sand. Then again, in the hush of the storm, they heard, far away, the barking of a dog. This must be Top. But was he alone or accompanied? Probably alone, for if Neb had been with him, the black man would have hastened, at once, to the Chimneys.

The sailor pressed the reporter's hand in a manner signifying that he was to remain without, and then returning to the corridor, emerged a moment later with a lighted fagot, which he threw into the darkness, at the same time whistling shrilly. At this signal, which seemed to have been looked for, the answering barks came nearer, and soon a dog bounded into the corridor, followed by the three companions. An armful of wood was thrown upon the coals, brightly lighting up the passage.

"It is Top!" cried Herbert.

It was indeed Top, a magnificent Anglo-Norman, uniting in the cross of the two breeds those qualities—swiftness of foot and keenness of scent—indispensable in coursing dogs. But he was alone! Neither his master nor Neb accompanied him.

It seemed inexplicable how, through the darkness and storm, the dog's instinct had directed him to the Chimneys, a place he was unacquainted with. But still more unaccountable was the fact that he was neither fatigued nor exhausted nor soiled with mud or sand. Herbert had drawn him towards him, patting his head; and the dog rubbed his neck against the lad's hands.

"If the dog is found, the master will be found also," said the reporter.

"God grant it!" responded Herbert. "Come, let us set out. Top will guide us!"

Pencroff made no objection. He saw that the dog's cunning had disproved his conjectures.

"Let us set out at once," he said; and covering the fire so that it could be relighted on their return, and preceded by the dog, who seemed to invite their departure, the sailor, having gathered up the remnants of the supper, followed by the reporter and Herbert, rushed into the darkness.

The tempest, then in all its violence, was, perhaps, at its maximum intensity. The new moon had not sufficient light to pierce the clouds. It was difficult to follow a straight course. The better way, therefore, was to trust to the instinct of Top; which was done. The reporter and the lad walked behind the dog, and the sailor followed after. To speak was impossible. The rain, dispersed by the wind, was not heavy, but the strength of the storm was terrible.

Fortunately, as it came from the southeast, the wind was at the back of the party, and the sand, hurled from behind, did not prevent their march. Indeed, they were often blown along so rapidly as nearly to be overthrown. But they were sustained by a great hope. This time, at least, they were not wandering at random. They felt, no doubt, that Neb had found his master and had sent the faithful dog to them. But was the engineer living, or had Neb summoned his companions only to render the last services to the dead?

After having passed the smooth face of rock, which they carefully avoided, the party stopped to take breath. The angle of the cliff sheltered them from the wind, and they could breathe freely after this tramp, or rather race, of a quarter of an hour. They were now able to hear themselves speak, and the lad having pronounced the name of Smith, the dog seemed to say by his glad barking that his master was safe.

"Saved! He is saved! Isn't he, Top?" repeated the boy. And the dog barked his answer.

It was half-past 2 when the march was resumed. The sea began to rise, and this, which was a spring tide backed up by the wind, threatened to be very high. The tremendous breakers thundered against the reef, assailing it so violently as probably to pass completely over the islet, which was invisible. The coast was no longer sheltered by this long breakwater, but was exposed to the full fury of the open sea.

After the party were clear of the precipice the storm attacked them again with fury. Crouching, with backs still to the wind, they followed Top, who never hesitated in his course. Mounting towards the north, they had upon their right the endless line of breakers deafening them with its thunders, and upon their left a region buried in darkness. One thing was certain, that they were upon an open plain, as the wind rushed over them without rebounding as it had done from the granite cliffs.

By 4 o'clock they estimated the distance travelled as eight miles. The clouds had risen a little, and the wind was drier and colder. Insufficiently clad, the three companions suffered cruelly, but no murmur passed their lips. They were determined to follow Top wherever he wished to lead them.

Towards 5 o'clock the day began to break. At first, overhead, where some grey shadowings bordered the clouds, and presently, under a dark band a bright streak of light sharply defined the sea horizon. The crests of the billows shone with a yellow light and the foam revealed its whiteness. At the same time, on the left, the hilly parts of the shore were confusedly defined in grey outlines upon the blackness of the night. At 6 o'clock it was daylight. The clouds sped rapidly overhead. The sailor and his companions were some six miles from the Chimneys, following a very flat shore, bordered in the offing by a reef of rocks whose surface only was visible above the high tide. On the left the country sloped up into downs bristling with thistles, giving a forbidding aspect to the vast sandy region. The shore was low, and offered no other resistance to the ocean than an irregular chain of hillocks. Here and there was a tree, leaning its trunks and branches towards the west. Far behind, to the southwest, extended the borders of the forest.

At this moment Top gave unequivocal signs of excitement. He ran ahead, returned, and seemed to try to hurry them on. The dog had left the coast, and guided by his wonderful instinct, without any hesitation had gone among the downs. They followed him through a region absolutely devoid of life.

The border of the downs, itself large, was composed of hills and hillocks, unevenly scattered here and there. It was like a little Switzerland of sand, and nothing but a dog's astonishing instinct could find the way.

Five minutes after leaving the shore the reporter and his companions reached a sort of hollow, formed in the back of a high down, before which Top stopped with a loud bark. The three entered the cave.

Neb was there, kneeling beside a body extended upon a bed of grass—

It was the body of Cyrus Smith.

CHAPTER VIII. IS CYPRUS SMITH ALIVE?

NEB'S STORY—FOOTPRINTS —AN INSOLUBLE QUESTION—THE FIRST WORDS OF SMITH—COMPARING THE FOOTPRINTS—RETURN TO THE CHIMNEYS—PENCROFF DEJECTED.

Neb did not move. The sailor uttered one word.

"Living!" he cried.

The black man did not answer. Spilett and Pencroff turned pale. Herbert, clasping his hands, stood motionless. But it was evident that the poor black man, overcome by grief, had neither seen his companions nor heard the voice of the sailor.

The reporter knelt down beside the motionless body, and, having opened the clothing, pressed his ear to the chest of the engineer. A minute, which seemed an age, passed, daring which he tried to detect some movement of the heart.

Neb raised up a little, and looked on as if in a trance. Overcome by exhaustion, prostrated by grief, the poor fellow was hardly recognizable. He believed his master dead. Gideon Spilett, after a long and attentive examination, rose up. "He lives!" he said.

Pencroff, in his turn, knelt down beside Cyrus Smith; he also detected some heartbeats, and a slight breath issuing from the lips of the engineer. Herbert, at a word from the reporter, hurried in search of water. A hundred paces off he found a clear brook swollen by the late rains and filtered by the sand. But there was nothing, not even a shell, in which to carry the water; so the lad had to content himself with soaking his handkerchief in the stream, and hastened back with it to the cave.

Happily the handkerchief held sufficient for Spilett's purpose, which was simply to moisten the lips of the engineer. The drops of fresh water produced an instantaneous effect. A sigh escaped from the breast of Smith, and it seemed as if he attempted to speak.

"We shall save him," said the reporter. Neb took heart at these words. He removed the clothing from his master to see if his body was anywhere wounded. But neither on his head nor body nor limbs was there a bruise or even a scratch, an astonishing circumstance, since he must have been tossed about among the rocks; even his hands were uninjured, and it was difficult to explain how the engineer should exhibit no mark of the efforts which he must have made in getting over the reef.

But the explanation of this circumstance would come later, when Cyrus Smith could speak. At present, it was necessary to restore his consciousness, and it was probable that this result could be accomplished by friction. For this purpose they mode use of the sailor's pea-jacket. The engineer, warmed by this rude rubbing, moved his arms slightly, and his breathing began to be more regular. He was dying from exhaustion, and, doubtless, had not the reporter and his companions arrived, it would have been all over with Cyrus Smith.

"You thought he was dead?" asked the sailor.

"Yes, I thought so," answered Neb. "And if Top had not found you and brought you back, I would have buried my master and died beside him."

The engineer had had a narrow escape!

Then Neb told them what had happened. The day before, after having left the Chimneys at day-break, he had followed along the coast in a direction due north, until he reached that part of the beach which he had already visited. There, though, as he said, without hope of success, he searched the shore, the rocks, the sand for any marks that could guide him, examining most carefully that part which was above high-water mark, as below that point the ebb and flow of the tide would have effaced all traces. He did not hope to find his master living. It was the discovery of the body which he sought, that he might bury it with his own hands. He searched a long time, without success. It seemed as if nothing human had ever been upon that desolate shore. Of the millions of shell-fish lying out of reach of the tide, not a shell was broken. There was no sign of a landing having ever been made there. The black man then decided to continue some miles further up the coast. It was possible that the currents had carried the body to some distant point. For Neb knew that a corpse, floating a little distance from a low shore, was almost certain, sooner or later, to be thrown upon the strand, and he was desirous to look upon his master one last time.

"I followed the shore two miles further, looking at it at low and high water, hardly hoping to find anything, when yesterday evening, about 5 o'clock, I discovered footprints upon the sand."

"Footprints," cried Pencroff.

"Yes, sir," replied Neb.

"And did they begin at the water?" demanded the reporter.

"No," answered the black man, "above high-water mark; below that the tide had washed out the others."

"Go on, Neb," said Spilett.

"The sight of these footprints made me wild with joy. They wore very plain, and went towards the downs. I followed them for a quarter of an hour, running so as not to tread on them. Five minutes later, as it was growing dark, I heard a dog bark. It was Top. And he brought me here, to my master."

Neb finished his recital by telling of his grief at the discovery of the inanimate body. Ha had tried to discover some signs of life still remaining in it. But all his efforts were in vain. There was nothing, therefore, to do but to perform the last offices to him whom he had loved so well. Then he thought of his companions. They, too, would wish to look once more upon their comrade.

Top was there. Could he not rely upon the sagacity of that faithful animal? So having pronounced several times the name of the reporter, who, of all the engineer's companions, was best known by Top, and having at the same time motioned towards the south, the dog bounded off in the direction indicated.

We have seen how, guided by an almost supernatural instinct, the dog had arrived at the Chimneys.

Neb's companions listened to his story with the greatest attention. How the engineer had been able to reach this cave in the midst of the downs, more than a mile from the beach, was as inexplicable as was his escape from the waves and rocks without a scratch.

"So you, Neb," said the reporter, "did not bring your master to this place?"

"No, it was not I," answered Neb.

"He certainly could not have come alone," said Pencroff.

"But he must have done it, though it does not seem credible," said the reporter.

They must wait for the solution of the mystery until the engineer could speak. Fortunately the rubbing had re-established the circulation of the blood, and life was returning. Smith moved his arm again, then his head, and a second time some incoherent words escaped his lips.

Neb, leaning over him, spoke, but the engineer seemed not to hear, and his eyes remained closed. Life was revealing itself by movement, but consciousness had not yet returned. Pencroff had, unfortunately, forgotten to bring the burnt linen, which could have been ignited with a couple of flints, and without it they had no means of making a fire. The pockets of the engineer were empty of everything but his watch. It was therefore the unanimous opinion that Cyrus Smith must be carried to the Chimneys as soon as possible.

Meantime the attention lavished on the engineer restored him to consciousness sooner than could have been hoped. The moistening of his lips had revived him, and Pencroff conceived the idea of mixing some of the juice of the tetras with water. Herbert ran to the shore and brought back two large shells; and the sailor made a mixture which they introduced between the lips of the engineer, who swallowed it with avidity. His eyes opened. Neb and the reporter were leaning over him.

"My master! my master!" cried Neb.

The engineer heard him. He recognized Neb and his companions, and his hand gently pressed theirs.

Again he spoke some words—doubtless the same which he had before uttered, and which indicated that some thoughts were troubling him. This time the words were understood.

"Island or continent?" he murmured.

"What the devil do we care," cried Pencroff, unable to restrain the exclamation, "now that you are alive, sir. Island or continent? "We will find that out later."

The engineer made a motion in the affirmative, and then seemed to sleep.

Taking care not to disturb him, the reporter set to work to provide the most comfortable means of moving him.

Neb, Herbert, and Pencroff left the cave and went towards a high down on which were some gnarled trees. On the way the sailor kept repeating:—

"Island or continent! To think of that, at his last gasp! What a man!"

Having reached the top of the down, Pencroff and his companions tore off the main branches from a tree, a sort of sea pine, sickly and stunted. And with these branches they constructed a litter, which they covered with leaves and grass.

This work occupied some little time, and it was 10 o'clock when the three returned to Smith and Spilett.

The engineer had just wakened from the sleep, or rather stupor, in which they had found him. The color had come back to his lips, which had been as pale as death. He raised himself slightly, and looked about, as if questioning where he was.

"Can you listen to me without being tired, Cyrus?" asked the reporter.

"Yes," responded the engineer.

"I think," said the sailor, "that Mr. Smith can listen better after having taken some more of this tetra jelly,—it is really tetra, sir," he continued, as he gave him some of the mixture, to which he had this time added some of the meat of the bird.

Cyrus Smith swallowed these bits of tetra, and the remainder was eaten by his companions, who were suffering from hunger, and who found the repast light enough.

"Well," said the sailor, "there are victuals waiting for us at the Chimneys, for you must know, Mr. Smith, that to the south of here we have a house with rooms and beds and fire-place, and in the pantry dozens of birds which our Herbert calls couroucous. Your litter is ready, and whenever you feel strong enough we will carry you to our house."

"Thanks, my friend," replied the engineer, "in an hour or two we will go. And now, Spilett, continue."

The reporter related everything that had happened. Recounting the events unknown to Smith; the last plunge of the balloon, the landing upon this unknown shore, its deserted appearance, the discovery of the Chimneys, the search for the engineer, the devotion of Neb, and what they owed to Top's intelligence, etc.

"But," asked Smith, in a feeble voice, "you did not pick me up on the beach?"

"No," replied the reporter.

"And it was not you who brought me to this hollow?"

"No."

"How far is this place from the reef?"

"At least half a mile," replied Pencroff, "and if you are astonished, we are equally surprised to find you here."

"It is indeed singular," said the engineer, who was gradually reviving and taking interest in these details.

"But," asked the sailor, "cannot you remember anything that happened after you were washed away by that heavy sea?"

Cyrus Smith tried to think, but he remembered little. The wave had swept him from the net of the balloon, and at first he had sunk several fathoms. Coming up to the surface, he was conscious, in the half-light, of something struggling beside him. It was Top, who had sprung to his rescue. Looking up, he could see nothing of the balloon, which, lightened by his and the dog's weight, had sped away like an arrow. He found himself in the midst of the tumultuous sea, more than half a mile from shore. He swum vigorously against the waves, and Top sustained him by his garments; but a strong current seized him, carrying him to the north, and, after struggling for half an hour, he sank, dragging the dog with him into the abyss. From that moment to the instant of his finding himself in the arms of his friends, he remembered nothing.

"Nevertheless," said Pencroff, "you must have been cast upon the shore, and had strength enough to walk to this place, since Neb found your tracks."

"Yes, that must be so," answered the engineer, reflectively. "And you have not seen any traces of inhabitants upon the shore?"

"Not a sign," answered the reporter. "Moreover, if by chance some one had rescued you from the waves, why should he then have abandoned you?"

"You are right, my dear Spilett. Tell me, Neb," inquired the engineer, turning towards his servant, "it was not you—you could not have been in a trance—during which—. No, that's absurd. Do any of the footprints still remain?"

"Yes, master," replied Neb; "there are some at the entrance, back of this mound, in a place sheltered from the wind and rain, but the others have been obliterated by the storm."

"Pencroff," said Cyrus, "will you take my shoes and see if they fit those footprints exactly?"

The sailor did as he had been asked. He and Herbert, guided by Neb, went to where the marks were, and in their absence Smith said to the reporter:—

"That is a thing passing belief."

"Inexplicable, indeed," answered the other.

"But do not dwell upon it at present, my dear Spilett, we will talk of it hereafter."

At this moment the others returned. All doubt was set at rest. The shoes of the engineer fitted the tracks exactly. Therefore it must have been Smith himself who had walked over the sand.

"So," he said, "I was the one in a trance, and not Neb! I must have walked like a somnambulist, without consciousness, and Top's instinct brought me here after he rescued me from the waves. Here, Top. Come here, dog."

The splendid animal sprang, barking, to his master, and caresses were lavished upon him. It was agreed that there was no other way to account for the rescue than by giving Top the credit of it.

Towards noon, Pencroff having asked Smith if he felt strong enough to be carried, the latter, for answer, by an effort which showed his strength of will, rose to his feet. But if he had not leaned upon the sailor he would have fallen.

"Capital," said Pencroff. "Summon the engineer's carriage!"

The litter was brought. The cross-branches had been covered with moss and grass; and when Smith was laid upon it they walked towards the coast, Neb and the sailor carrying him.

Eight miles had to be travelled, and as they could move but slowly, and would probably have to make frequent rests, it would take six hours or more to reach the Chimneys. The wind was still strong, but, fortunately, it had ceased raining. From his couch, the engineer, leaning upon his arm, observed the coast, especially the part opposite the sea. He examined it without comment, but undoubtedly the aspect of the country, its contour, its forests and diverse products were noted in his mind. But after two hours, fatigue overcame him, and he slept upon the litter.

At half-past 5 the little party reached the precipice, and soon after, were before the Chimneys. Stopping here, the litter was placed upon the sand without disturbing the slumber of the engineer.

Pencroff saw, to his surprise, that the terrible storm of the day before had altered the aspect of the place. Rocks had been displaced. Great fragments were strewn over the sand, and a thick carpet of several kinds of seaweed covered all the shore. It was plain that the sea sweeping over the isle had reached to the base of the enormous granite curtain.

Before the entrance to the Chimneys the ground had been violently torn up by the action of the waves. Pencroff, seized with a sudden fear, rushed into the corridor. Returning, a moment after, he stood motionless looking at his comrades.

The fire had been extinguished; the drowned cinders were nothing but mud. The charred linen, which was to serve them for tinder, had gone. The sea had penetrated every recess of the corridor, and everything was overthrown, everything was destroyed within the Chimneys.

CHAPTER IX. CYRUS IS HERE

PENCROFF'S ATTEMPTS—RUBBING WOOD—ISLAND OR CONTINENT —THE PLANS OF THE ENGINEER—WHEREABOUTS IN THE PACIFIC—IN THE DEPTHS OF THE FOREST—THE PISTACHIO PINE—A PIG CHASE—A SMOKE OF GOOD OMEN.

In a few words the others were informed of what had happened. This accident, which portended serious results—at least Pencroff foresaw such— affected each one differently. Neb, overjoyed in having recovered his master, did not listen or did not wish to think of what Pencroff said. Herbert shared in a measure the apprehensions of the sailor. As to the reporter, he simply answered:— "Upon my word, Pencroff, I don't think it matters much!"

"But I tell you again; we have no fire!"

"Pshaw!"

"Nor any means of lighting one!"

"Absurd!"

"But, Mr. Spilett—"

"Is not Cyrus here?" asked the reporter; "Isn't he alive? He will know well enough how to make fire!"

"And with what?"

"With nothing!"

What could Pencroff answer? He had nothing to say, as, in his heart, he shared his companion's confidence in Cyrus Smith's ability. To them the engineer was a microcosm, a compound of all science and all knowledge. They were better off on a desert island with Cyrus than without him in the busiest city of the Union. With him they could want for nothing; with him they would have no fear. If they had been told that a volcanic eruption would overwhelm the land, sinking it into the depths of the Pacific, the imperturbable answer of these brave men would have been, "Have we not Cyrus!"

Meantime, the engineer had sunk into a lethargy, the result of the journey, and his help could not be asked for just then. The supper, therefore, would be very meagre. All the tetras had been eaten, there was no way to cook other birds, and, finally, the couroucou which had been reserved had disappeared. Something, therefore, must be done.

First of all, Cyrus Smith was carried into the main corridor. There they were able to make for him a couch of seaweeds, and, doubtless, the deep sleep in which he was plunged, would strengthen him more than an abundant nourishment.

With night the temperature, which the northwest wind had raised, again became very cold, and, as the sea had washed away the partitions which Pencroff had constructed, draughts of air made the place scarcely habitable. The engineer would therefore have been in a bad plight if his companions had not covered him with clothing which they took from themselves.

The supper this evening consisted of the inevitable lithodomes, an ample supply of which Herbert and Neb had gathered from the beach. To these the lad had added a quantity of edible seaweed which clung to the high rocks and were only washed by the highest tides. These seaweeds, belonging to the family of Fucaceæ, were a species of Sargassum, which, when dry, furnish a gelatinous substance full of nutritive matter, much used by the natives of the Asiatic coast. After having eaten a quantity of lithodomes the reporter and his companions sucked some of the seaweed, which they agreed was excellent.

"Nevertheless," said the sailor, "it is time for Mr. Smith to help us."

Meantime the cold became intense, and, unfortunately, they had no means of protecting themselves. The sailor, much worried, tried every possible means of procuring a fire. He had found some dry moss, and by striking two stones together he obtained sparks; but the moss was not sufficiently inflammable to catch fire, nor had the sparks the strength of those struck by a steel. The operation amounted to nothing. Then Pencroff, although he had no confidence in the result, tried rubbing two pieces of dry wood together, after the manner of the savages. It is true that the motion of the man, if it could have been turned into heat, according to the new theory, would have heated the boiler of a steamer. But it resulted in nothing except putting him in a glow, and making the wood hot. After half an hour's work Pencroff was in a perspiration, and he threw away the wood in disgust.

"When you can make me believe that savages make fire after that fashion," said he, "it will he hot in winter! I might as well try to light my arms by rubbing them together."

But the sailor was wrong to deny the feasibility of this method. The savages frequently do light wood in this way. But it requires particular kinds of wood, and, moreover, the "knack," and Pencroff had not this "knack."

Pencroff's ill humor did not last long. The bits of wood which he had thrown away had been picked up by Herbert, who exerted himself to rub them well. The strong sailor could not help laughing at the boy's weak efforts to accomplish what he had failed in. "Rub away, my boy; rub hard!" he cried.

"I am rubbing them," answered Herbert, laughing, "but only to take my turn at getting warm, instead of sitting here shivering; and pretty soon I will be as hot as you are, Pencroff!"

This was the case, and though it was necessary for this night to give up trying to make a fire, Spilett, stretching himself upon the sand in one of the passages, repeated for the twentieth time that Smith could not be baffled by such a trifle. The others followed his example, and Top slept at the feet of his master.

The next day, the 28th of March, when the engineer awoke, about 8 o'clock, he saw his companions beside him watching, and, as on the day before, his first words were, "Island or continent?"

It was his one thought.

"Well, Mr. Smith," answered Pencroff, "we don't know."

"You haven't found out yet?"

"But we will," affirmed Pencroff, "when you are able to guide us in this country."

"I believe that I am able to do that now," answered the engineer, who, without much effort, rose up and stood erect.

"That is good," exclaimed the sailor.

"I am dying of hunger," responded Smith. "Give me some food, my friend, and I will feel better. You've fire, haven't you?"

This question met with no immediate answer. But after some moments the sailor said:—

"No, sir, we have no fire; at least, not now."

And he related what had happened the day before. He amused the engineer by recounting the history of their solitary match, and their fruitless efforts to procure fire like the savages.

"We will think about it," answered the engineer, "and if we cannot find something like tinder—"

"Well," asked the sailor.

"Well, we will make matches!"

"Friction matches?"

"Friction matches!"

"It's no more difficult than that," cried the reporter, slapping the sailor on the shoulder.

The latter did not see that it would be easy, but he said nothing, and all went out of doors. The day was beautiful. A bright sun was rising above the sea horizon, its rays sparkling and glistening on the granite wall. After having cast a quick look about him, the engineer seated himself upon a rock. Herbert offered him some handfuls of mussels and seaweed, saying:— "It is all that we have, Mr. Smith."

"Thank you, my boy," answered he, "it is enough—for this morning, at least."

And he ate with appetite this scanty meal, washing it down with water brought from the river in a large shell.

His companions looked on without speaking. Then, after having satisfied himself, he crossed his arms and said:—

"Then, my friends, you do not yet know whether we have been thrown upon an island or a continent?"

"No sir," answered Herbert.

"We will find out to-morrow," said the engineer. "Until then there is nothing to do."

"There is one thing," suggested Pencroff.

"What is that?"

"Some fire," replied the sailor, who thought of nothing else.

"We will have it, Pencroff," said Smith. "But when you were carrying me here yesterday, did not I see a mountain rising in the west?"

"Yes," said Spilett, "quite a high one."

"All right," exclaimed the engineer. "Tomorrow we will climb to its summit and determine whether this is an island or a continent; until then I repeat there is nothing to do."

"But there is; we want fire!" cried the obstinate sailor again.

"Have a little patience, Pencroff, and we will have the fire," said Spilett.

The other looked at the reporter as much as to say, "If there was only you to make it we would never taste roast meat." But he kept silent.

Smith had not spoken. He seemed little concerned about this question of fire. For some moments he remained absorbed in his own thoughts. Then he spoke as follows:—

"My friends, our situation is, doubtless, deplorable, nevertheless it is very simple. Either we are upon a continent, and, in that case, at the expense of greater or less fatigue, we will reach some inhabited place, or else we are on an island. In the latter case, it is one of two things; if the island is inhabited, we will get out of our difficulty by the help of the inhabitants; if it is deserted, we will get out of it by ourselves."

"Nothing could be plainer than that," said Pencroff.

"But," asked Spilett, "whether it is a continent or an island, whereabouts do you think this storm has thrown us, Cyrus?"

"In truth, I cannot say," replied the engineer, "but the probability is that we are somewhere in the Pacific. When we left Richmond the wind was northeast, and its very violence proves that its direction did not vary much. Supposing it unchanged, we crossed North and South Carolina, Georgia, the Gulf of Mexico, and the narrow part of Mexico, and a portion of the Pacific Ocean. I do not estimate the distance traversed by the balloon at less than 6,000 or 7,000 miles, and even if the wind had varied a half a quarter it would have carried us either to the Marquesas Islands or to the Low Archipelago; or, if it was stronger than I suppose, as far as New Zealand. If this last hypothesis is correct, our return home will be easy. English or Maoris, we shall always find somebody with whom to speak. If, on the other hand, this coast belongs to some barren island in the Micronesian Archipelago, perhaps we can reconnoitre it from the summit of this mountain, and then we will consider how to establish ourselves here as if we were never going to leave it."

"Never?" cried the reporter. "Do you say never, my dear Cyrus?"

"It is better to put things in their worst light at first," answered the engineer; "and to reserve those which are better, as a surprise."

"Well said," replied Pencroff. "And we hope that this island, if it is an island, will not be situated just outside of the route of ships; for that would, indeed, be unlucky."

"We will know how to act after having first ascended the mountain," answered Smith.

"But will you be able, Mr. Smith, to make the climb tomorrow?" asked Herbert.

"I hope so," answered the engineer, "if Pencroff and you, my boy, show yourselves to be good and ready hunters."

"Mr. Smith," said the sailor, "since you are speaking of game, if when I come back I am as sure of getting it roasted as I am of bringing it—"

"Bring it, nevertheless," interrupted Smith.

It was now agreed that the engineer and the reporter should spend the day at the Chimneys, in order to examine the shore and the plateau, while Neb, Herbert, and the sailor were to return to the forest, renew the supply of wood, and lay hands on every bird and beast that should cross their path. So, at 6 o'clock, the party left, Herbert confident. Neb happy, and Pencroff muttering to himself:— "If, when I get back I find a fire in the house, it will have been the lightning that lit it!"

The three climbed the bank, and having reached the turn in the river, the sailor stopped and said to his companions:— "Shall we begin as hunters or wood-choppers?"

"Hunters," answered Herbert. "See Top, who is already at it."

"Let us hunt, then," replied the sailor, "and on our return here we will lay in our stock of wood."

This said, the party made three clubs for themselves, and followed Top, who was jumping about in the high grass. This time, the hunters, instead of following the course of the stream, struck at once into the depths of the forests. The trees were for the most part of the pine family. And in certain places, where they stood in small groups, they were of such a size as to indicate that this country was in a higher latitude than the engineer supposed. Some openings, bristling with stumps decayed by the weather, were covered with dead timber which formed an inexhaustible reserve of firewood. Then, the opening passed, the underwood became so thick as to be nearly impenetrable.

To guide oneself among these great trees without any beaten path was very difficult. So the sailor from time to time blazed the route by breaking branches in a manner easily recognizable. But perhaps they would have done better to have followed the water course, as in the first instance, as, after an hour's march, no game had been taken. Top, running under the low boughs, only flashed birds that were unapproachable. Even the couroucou were invisible, and it seemed likely that the sailor would be obliged to return to that swampy place where he had fished for tetras with such good luck.

"Well, Pencroff," said Neb sarcastically, "if this is all the game you promised to carry back to my master it won't take much fire to roast it!"

"Wait a bit, Neb," answered the sailor; "it won't be game that will be wanting on our return."

"Don't you believe in Mr. Smith?"

"Yes."

"But you don't believe be will make a fire?"

"I will believe that when the wood is blazing in the fire-place."

"It will blaze, then, for my master has said so!"

"Well, we'll see!"

Meanwhile the sun had not yet risen to its highest point above the horizon. The exploration went on and was signalized by Herbert's discovery of a tree bearing edible fruit. It was the pistachio pine, which bears an excellent nut, much liked in the temperate regions of America and Europe. These nuts were perfectly ripe, and Herbert showed them to his companions, who feasted on them.

"Well," said Pencroff, "seaweed for bread, raw mussels for meat, and nuts for dessert, that's the sort of dinner for men who haven't a match in their pocket!"

"It's not worth while complaining," replied Herbert.

"I don't complain, my boy. I simply repeat that the meat is a little too scant in this sort of meal."

"Top has seen something!" cried Neb, running toward a thicket into which the dog had disappeared barking. With the dog's barks were mingled singular gruntings. The sailor and Herbert had followed the black man. If it was game, this was not the time to discuss how to cook it, but rather how to secure it.

The hunters, on entering the brush, saw Top struggling with an animal which he held by the ear. This quadruped was a species of pig, about two feet and a half long, of a brownish black color, somewhat lighter under the belly, having harsh and somewhat scanty hair, and its toes at this time strongly grasping the soil seemed joined together by membranes.

Herbert thought that he recognized in this animal a cabiai, or water-hog, one of the largest specimens of the order of rodents. The water-hog did not fight the dog. Its great eyes, deep sank in thick layers of fat, rolled stupidly from side to side. And Neb, grasping his club firmly, was about to knock the beast down, when the latter tore loose from Top, leaving a piece of his ear in the dog's mouth, and uttering a vigorous grunt, rushed against and overset Herbert and disappeared in the wood.

"The beggar!" cried Pencroff, as they all three darted after the hog. But just as they had come up to it again, the water-hog disappeared under the surface of a large pond, overshadowed by tall, ancient pines.

The three companions stopped, motionless. Top had plunged into the water, but the cabiai, hidden at the bottom of the pond, did not appear.

"Wait,", said the boy, "he will have to come to the surface to breathe."

"Won't he drown?" asked Neb.

"No," answered Herbert, "since he is fin-toed and almost amphibious. But watch for him."

Top remained in the water, and Pencroff and his companions took stations upon the bank, to cut off the animal's retreat, while the dog swam to and fro looking for him.

Herbert was not mistaken. In a few minutes the animal came again to the surface. Top was upon him at once, keeping him from diving again, and a moment later, the cabiai, dragged to the shore, was struck down by a blow from Neb's club.

"Hurrah!" cried Pencroff with all his heart. "Nothing but a clear fire, and this gnawer shall be gnawed to the bone."

Pencroff lifted the carcase to his shoulder, and judging by the sun that it must be near 2 o'clock, he gave the signal to return.

Top's instinct was useful to the hunters, as, thanks to that intelligent animal, they were enabled to return upon their steps. In half an hour they had reached the bend of the river. There, as before, Pencroff quickly constructed a raft, although, lacking fire, this seemed to him a useless job, and, with the raft keeping the current, they returned towards the Chimneys. But the sailor had not gone fifty paces when he stopped and gave utterance anew to a tremendous hurrah, and extending his hand towards the angle of the cliff—

"Herbert! Neb! See!" he cried.

Smoke was escaping and curling above the rocks!

CHAPTER X. THE ENGINEER'S INVENTION

ISLAND OR CONTINENT?—DEPARTURE FOR THE MOUNTAIN—THE FOREST—VOLCANIC SOIL—THE TRAGOPANS—THE MOUFFLONS —THE FIRST PLATEAU—ENCAMPING FOR THE NIGHT—THE SUMMIT OF THE CONE

A few minutes afterwards, the three hunters were seated before a sparkling fire. Beside them sat Cyrus Smith and the reporter. Pencroff looked from one to the other without saying a word, his cabiai in his hand.

"Yes, my good fellow," said the reporter, "a fire, a real fire, that will roast your game to a turn."

"But who lighted it?" said the sailor.

"The sun."

The sailor could not believe his eyes, and was too stupefied to question the engineer.

"Had you a burning-glass, sir?" asked Herbert of Cyrus Smith.

"No, my boy," said he, "but I made one."

And he showed his extemporized lens. It was simply the two glasses, from his own watch and the reporter's, which he had taken out, filled with water, and stuck together at the edges with a little clay. Thus he had made a veritable burning-glass, and by concentrating the solar rays on some dry moss had set it on fire.

The sailor examined the lens; then he looked at the engineer without saying a word, but his face spoke for him. If Smith was not a magician to him, he was certainly more than a man. At last his speech returned, and he said:—

"Put that down, Mr. Spilett, put that down in your book!"

"I have it down," said the reporter.

Then, with the help of Neb, the sailor arranged the spit, and dressed the cabiai for roasting, like a sucking pig, before the sparkling fire, by whose warmth, and by the restoration of the partitions, the Chimneys had been rendered habitable.

The engineer and his companion had made good use of their day. Smith had almost entirely recovered his strength, which he had tested by climbing the plateau above. From thence his eye, accustomed to measure heights and distances, had attentively examined the cone whose summit he proposed to reach on the morrow. The mountain, situated about six miles to the northwest, seemed to him to reach about 3,500 feet above the level of the sea, so that an observer posted at its summit, could command a horizon of fifty miles at least.

He hoped, therefore, for an easy solution of the urgent question, "Island or continent?"

They had a pleasant supper, and the meat of the cabiai was proclaimed excellent; the sargassum and pistachio-nuts completed the repast. But the engineer said little; he was planning for the next day. Once or twice Pencroff talked of some project for the future, but Smith shook his head.

"To-morrow," he said, "we will know how we are situated, and we can act accordingly."

After supper, more armfuls of wood were thrown on the fire, and the party lay down to sleep. The morning found them fresh and eager for the expedition which was to settle their fate.

Everything was ready. Enough was left of the cabiai for twenty-four hours' provisions, and they hoped to replenish their stock on the way. They charred a little linen for tinder, as the watch glasses had been replaced, and flint abounded in this volcanic region.

At half-past 7 they left the Chimneys, each with a stout cudgel. By Pencroff's advice, they took the route of the previous day, which was the shortest way to the mountain. They turned the southern angle, and followed the left bank of the river, leaving it where it bent to the southwest. They took the beaten path under the evergreens, and soon reached the northern border of the forest. The soil, flat and swampy, then dry and sandy, rose by a gradual slope towards the interior. Among the trees appeared a few shy animals, which rapidly took flight before Top. The engineer called his dog back; later, perhaps, they might hunt, but now nothing could distract him from his great object. He observed neither the character of the ground nor its products; he was going straight for the top of the mountain.

At 10 o'clock they were clear of the forest, and they halted for a while to observe the country. The mountain was composed of two cones. The first was truncated about 2,500 feet up, and supported by fantastic spurs, branching out like the talons of an immense claw, laid upon the ground. Between these spurs were narrow valleys, thick set with trees, whose topmost foliage was level with the flat summit of the first cone. On the northeast side of the mountain, vegetation was more scanty, and the ground was seamed here and there, apparently with currents of lava.

On the first cone lay a second, slightly rounded towards the summit. It lay somewhat across the other, like a huge hat cocked over the ear. The surface seemed utterly bare, with reddish rocks often protruding. The object of the expedition was to reach the top of this cone, and their best way was along the edge of the spurs.

"We are in a volcanic country," said Cyrus Smith, as they began to climb, little by little, up the side of the spurs, whose winding summit would most readily bring them out upon the lower plateau. The ground was strewn with traces of igneous convulsion. Here and there lay blocks, debris of basalt, pumice-stone, and obsidian. In isolated clumps rose some few of those conifers, which, some hundreds of feet lower, in the narrow gorges, formed a gigantic thicket, impenetrable to the sun. As they climbed these lower slopes, Herbert called attention to the recent marks of huge paws and hoofs on the ground.

"These brutes will make a fight for their territory," said Pencroff.

"Oh well," said the reporter, who had hunted tigers in India and lions in Africa, "we shall contrive to get rid of them. In the meanwhile, we must be on our guard."

While talking they were gradually ascending. The way was lengthened by detours around the obstacles which could not be directly surmounted. Sometimes, too, deep crevasses yawned across the ascent, and compelled them to return upon their track for a long distance, before they could find an available pathway. At noon, when the little company halted to dine at the foot of a great clump of firs, at whose foot babbled a tiny brook, they were still half way from the first plateau, and could hardly reach it before nightfall. From this point the sea stretched broad beneath their feet; but on the right their vision was arrested by the sharp promontory of the southeast, which left them in doubt whether there was land beyond. On the left they could see directly north for several miles; but the northwest was concealed from them by the crest of a fantastic spur, which formed a massive abutment to the central cone. They could, therefore, make no approach as yet to the solving of the great question.

At 1 o'clock, the ascent was again begun. The easiest route slanted upwards towards the southwest, through the thick copse. There, under the trees, were flying about a number of gallinaceæ of the pheasant family. These were "tragopans," adorned with a sort of fleshy wattles hanging over their necks and with two little cylindrical horns behind their eyes. Of these birds, which were about the size of a hen, the female was invariably brown, while the male was resplendent in a coat of red, with little spots of white. With a well-aimed stone Spilett killed one of the tragopans, which the hungry Pencroff looked at with longing eyes.

Leaving the copse, the climbers, by mounting on each other's shoulders, ascended for a hundred feet up a very steep hill, and reached a terrace, almost bare of trees, whose soil was evidently volcanic. From hence, their course was a zigzag towards the east, for the declivity was so steep that they had to take every point of vantage. Neb and Herbert led the way, then came Smith and the reporter; Pencroff was last. The animals who lived among these heights, and whose traces were not wanting, must have the sure foot and the supple spine of a chamois or an izard. They saw some to whom Pencroff gave a name of his own—"Sheep," he cried.

They all had stopped fifty feet from half-a-dozen large animals, with thick horns curved backwards and flattened at the end, and with woolly fleece, hidden under long silky fawn-colored hair. They were not the common sheep, but a species widely distributed through the mountainous regions of the temperate zone. Their name, according to Herbert, was *Moufflon*.

"Have they legs and chops?" asked the sailor.

"Yes," replied Herbert.

"Then they're sheep," said Pencroff. The animals stood motionless and astonished at their first sight of man. Then, seized with sudden fear, they fled, leaping away among the rocks.

"Good-bye till next time," cried Pencroff to them, in a tone so comical that the others could not forbear laughing.

As the ascension continued, the traces of lava were more frequent, and little sulphur springs intercepted their route. At some points sulphur had been deposited in crystals, in the midst of the sand and whitish cinders of feldspar which generally precede the eruption of lava. As they neared the first plateau, formed by the truncation of the lower cone, the ascent became very difficult. By 4 o'clock the last belt of trees had been passed. Here and there stood a few dwarfed and distorted pines, which had survived the attacks of the furious winds. Fortunately for the engineer and his party, it was a pleasant, mild day; for a high wind, at that altitude of 3,000 feet, would have interfered with them sadly. The sky overhead was extremely bright and clear. A perfect calm reigned around them. The sun was hidden by the upper mountain, which cast its shadow, like a vast screen, westward to the edge of the sea. A thin haze began to appear in the east, colored with all the rays of the solar spectrum.

There were only 500 feet between the explorers and the plateau where they meant to encamp for the night, but these 500 were increased to 2,000 and more by the tortuous route. The ground, so to speak, gave way under their feet. The angle of ascent was often so obtuse that they slipped upon the smooth-worn lava. Little by little the evening set in, and it was almost night when the party, tired out by a seven hours' climb, arrived at the top of the first cone.

Now they must pitch their camp, and think of supper and sleep. The upper terrace of the mountain rose upon a base of rocks, amid which they could soon find a shelter. Firewood was not plenty, yet the moss and dry thistles, so abundant on the plateau, would serve their turn. The sailor built up a fireplace with huge stones, while Neb and Herbert went after the combustibles. They soon came back with a load of thistles; and with flint and steel, the charred linen for tinder, and Neb to blow the fire, a bright blaze was soon sparkling behind the rocks. It was for warmth only, for they kept the pheasant for the next day, and supped off the rest of the cabiai and a few dozen pistachio-nuts.

It was only half-past 6 when the meal was ended. Cyrus Smith resolved to explore, in, the semi-obscurity, the great circular pediment which upheld the topmost cone of the mountain. Before taking rest, he was anxious to know whether the base of the cone could be passed, in case its flanks should prove too steep for ascent. So, regardless of fatigue, he left Pencroff and Neb to make the sleeping arrangements, and Spilett to note down the incidents of the day, and taking Herbert with him, began to walk around the base of the plateau towards the north.

The night was beautiful and still; and not yet very dark. They walked together in silence. Sometimes the plateau was wide and easy, sometimes so encumbered with rubbish that the two could not walk abreast. Finally, after twenty minutes tramp, they were brought to a halt. From this point the slant of the two cones was equal. To walk around the mountain upon an acclivity whose angle was nearly seventy-five degrees was impossible.

But though they had to give up their flank movement, the chance of a direct ascent was suddenly offered to them. Before them opened an immense chasm in the solid rock. It was the mouth of the upper crater, the gullet, so to speak, through which, when the volcano was active, the eruption took place. Inside, hardened lava and scoriæ formed a sort of natural staircase with enormous steps, by which they might possibly reach the summit. Smith saw the opportunity at a glance, and followed by the boy, he walked unhesitatingly into the huge crevasse, in the midst of the gathering darkness.

There were yet 1,000 feet to climb. Could they scale the interior wall of the crater? They would try, at all events. Fortunately, the long and sinuous declivities described a winding staircase, and greatly helped their ascent. The crater was evidently exhausted. Not a puff of smoke, not a glimmer of fire, escaped; not a sound or motion in the dark abyss, reaching down, perhaps, to the centre of the globe. The air within retained no taint of sulphur. The volcano was not only quiet, but extinct.

Evidently the attempt was to succeed. Gradually, as the two mounted the inner walls, they saw the crater grow larger over their heads. The light from the outer sky visibly increased. At each step, so to speak, which they made, new stars entered the field of their vision: The magnificent constellations of the southern sky shone resplendent. In the zenith glittered the splendid Antares of the Scorpion, and not far off that Beta of the Centaur, which is believed to be the nearest star to our terrestrial globe. Then, as the crater opened, appeared Fomalhaut of the Fish, the Triangle, and at last, almost at the Antarctic pole, the glowing Southern Cross.

It was nearly 8 o'clock when they set foot on the summit of the cone. The darkness was by this time complete, and they could hardly see a couple of miles around them. Was the land an island, or the eastern extremity of a continent? They could not yet discover. Towards the west a band of cloud, clearly defined against the horizon, deepened the obscurity, and confounded sea with sky.

But at one point of the horizon suddenly appeared a vague light, which slowly sank as the clouds mounted to the zenith. It was the slender crescent of the moon, just about to disappear. But the line of the horizon was now cloudless, and as the moon touched it, the engineer could see her face mirrored for an instant on a liquid surface. He seized the boy's hand—

"An island!" said he, as the lunar crescent disappeared behind the waves.

CHAPTER XI. AT THE SUMMIT OF THE CONE

THE INTERIOR OF THE CRATER—SEA EVERYWHERE —NO LAND IN SIGHT—A BIRD'S EYE VIEW OF THE COAST—HYDROGRAPHY AND OROGRAPHY —IS THE ISLAND INHABITED?—A GEOGRAPHICAL BAPTISM— LINCOLN ISLAND.

A half hour later they walked back to the camp. The engineer contented himself with saying to his comrades that the country was an island, and that to-morrow they would consider what to do. Then each disposed himself to sleep, and in this basalt cave, 2,500 feet above sea-level, they passed a quiet night in profound repose. The next day, March 30, after a hurried breakfast on roast trajopan, they started out for the summit of the volcano. All desired to see the isle on which perhaps they were to spend their lives, and to ascertain how far it lay from other land, and how near the course of vessels bound for the archipelagoes of the Pacific.

It was about 7 o'clock in the morning when they left the camp. No one seemed dismayed by the situation. They had faith in themselves, no doubt; but the source of that faith was not the same with Smith as with his companions. They trusted in him, he in his ability to extort from the wilderness around them all the necessaries of life. As for Pencroff, he would not have despaired, since the rekindling of the fire by the engineer's lens, if he had found himself upon a barren rock, if only Smith was with him.

"Bah!" said he, "we got out of Richmond without the permission of the authorities, and it will be strange if we can't get away some time from a place where no one wants to keep us!"

They followed the route of the day before, flanking the cone till they reached the enormous crevasse. It was a superb day, and the southern side of the mountain was bathed in sunlight. The crater, as the engineer had supposed, was a huge shaft gradually opening to a height of 1,000 feet above the plateau. From the bottom of the crevasse large currents of lava meandered down the flanks of the mountain, indicating the path of the eruptive matter down to the lower valleys which furrowed the north of the island.

The interior of the crater, which had an inclination of thirty-five or forty degrees, was easily scaled. They saw on the way traces of ancient lava, which had probably gushed from the summit of the cone before the lateral opening had given it a new way of escape. As to the volcano chimney which communicated with the subterranean abyss, its depth could not be estimated by the eye, for it was lost in obscurity; but there seemed no doubt that the volcano was completely extinct. Before 8 o'clock, the party were standing at the summit of the crater, on a conical elevation of the northern side.

"The sea! the sea everywhere!" was the universal exclamation. There it lay, an immense sheet of water around them on every side. Perhaps Smith had hoped that daylight would reveal some neighboring coast or island. But nothing appeared to the horizon-line, a radius of more than fifty miles. Not a sail was in sight. Around the island stretched a desert infinity of ocean.

Silent and motionless, they surveyed every point of the horizon. They strained their eyes to the uttermost limit of the ocean. But even Pencroff, to whom Nature had given a pair of telescopes instead of eyes, and who could have detected land even in the faintest haze upon the sea-line, could see nothing. Then they looked down upon their island, and the silence was broken by Spilett:—"How large do you think this island is?"

It seemed small enough in the midst of the infinite ocean.

Smith thought awhile, noticed the circumference of the island, and allowed for the elevation.

"My friends," he said, "if I am not mistaken, the coast of the island is more than 100 miles around."

"Then its surface will be—"

"That is hard to estimate; the outline is so irregular."

If Smith was right, the island would be about the size of Malta or Zante in the Mediterranean; but it was more irregular than they, and at the same time had fewer capes, promontories, points, bays, and creeks. Its form was very striking. When Spilett drew it they declared it was like some fantastic sea beast, some monstrous pteropode, asleep on the surface of the Pacific.

The exact configuration of the island may thus be described:—The eastern coast, upon which the castaways had landed, was a decided curve, embracing a large bay, terminating at the southeast in a sharp promontory, which the shape of the land had hidden from Pencroff on his first exploration. On the northeast, two other capes shut in the bay, and between them lay a narrow gulf like the half-open jaws of some formidable dog-fish. From northeast to northwest the coast was round and flat, like the skull of a wild beast; then came a sort of indeterminate hump, whose centre was occupied by the volcanic mountain. From this point the coast ran directly north and south. For two-thirds of its length it was bordered by a narrow creek; then it finished in along cue, like the tail of a gigantic alligator. This cue formed a veritable peninsula, which extended more than thirty miles into the sea, reckoning from the southeastern cape before mentioned. These thirty miles, the southern coast of the island, described an open bay. The narrowest part of the island, between the Chimneys and the creek, on the west, was ten miles wide, but its greatest length, from the jaw in the northeast to the extremity of the southwestern peninsula, was not less than thirty miles.

The general aspect of the interior was as follows:—The southern part, from the shore to the mountain, was covered with woods; the northern part was arid and sandy. Between the volcano and the eastern coast the party were surprised to see a lake, surrounded by evergreens, whose existence they had not suspected. Viewed from such a height it seemed to be on the same level with the sea, but, on reflection, the engineer explained to his companions that it must be at least 300 feet higher, for the plateau on which it lay was as high as that of the coast.

"So, then, it is a fresh water lake?" asked Pencroff.

"Yes," said the engineer, "for it must be fed by the mountain streams."

"I can see a little river flowing into it," said Herbert, pointing to a narrow brook whose source was evidently in the spurs of the western cliff.

"True," said Smith, "and since this brook flows into the lake, there is probably some outlet towards the sea for the overflow. We will see about that when we go back."

This little winding stream and the river so familiar to them were all the watercourses they could see. Nevertheless, it was possible that under those masses of trees which covered two-thirds of the island, other streams flowed towards the sea. This seemed the more probable from the fertility of the country and its magnificent display of the flora of the temperate zone. In the northern section there was no indication of running water; perhaps there might be stagnant pools in the swampy part of the northeast, but that was all; in the main this region was composed of arid sand-hills and downs, contrasting strongly with the fertility of the larger portion.

The volcano did not occupy the centre of the island. It rose in the northwest, and seemed to indicate the dividing line of the two zones. On the southwest, south, and southeast, the beginnings of the spurs were lost in masses of verdure. To the north, on the contrary, these ramifications were plainly visible, subsiding gradually to the level of the sandy plain. On this side, too, when the volcano was active, the eruptions had taken place, and a great bed of lava extended as far as the narrow jaw which formed the northeastern gulf.

They remained for an hour at the summit of the mountain. The island lay stretched before them like a plan in relief, with its different tints, green for the forests, yellow for the sands, blue for the water. They understood the configuration of the entire island; only the bottoms of the shady valleys and the depths of the narrow gorges between the spurs of the volcano, concealed by the spreading foliage, escaped their searching eye.

There remained a question of great moment, whose answer would have a controlling influence upon the fortunes of the castaways. Was the island inhabited? It was the reporter who put this question, which seemed already to have been answered in the negative by the minute examination which they had just made of the different portions of the island. Nowhere could they perceive the handiwork of man; no late settlement on the beach, not even a lonely cabin or a fisherman's hut. No smoke, rising on the air, betrayed a human presence. It is true, the observers were thirty miles from the long peninsula which extended to the southwest, and upon which even Pencroff's eye could hardly have discovered a dwelling. Nor could they raise the curtain of foliage which covered three-fourths of the island to see whether some village lay sheltered there. But the natives of these little islands in the Pacific usually live on the coast, and the coast seemed absolutely desert. Until they should make a more complete exploration, they might assume that the island was uninhabited. But was it ever frequented by the inhabitants of neighboring islands? This question was difficult to answer. No land appeared within a radius of fifty miles. But fifty miles could easily be traversed by Malay canoes or by the larger pirogues of the Polynesians. Everything depended upon the situation of the island—on its isolation in the Pacific, or its proximity to the archipelagoes. Could Smith succeed, without his instruments, in determining its latitude and longitude? It would be difficult, and in the uncertainty, they must take precautions against an attack from savage neighbors.

The exploration of the island was finished, its configuration determined, a map of it drawn, its size calculated, and the distribution of its land and water ascertained. The forests and the plains had been roughly sketched upon the reporter's map. They had only now to descend the declivities of the mountain, and to examine into the animal, vegetable, and mineral resources of the country. But before giving the signal of departure, Cyrus Smith, in a calm, grave voice, addressed his companions.

"Look, my friends, upon this little corner of the earth, on which the hand of the Almighty has cast us. Here, perhaps, we may long dwell. Perhaps, too, unexpected help will arrive, should some ship chance to pass. I say *chance*, because this island is of slight importance, without even a harbor for ships. I fear it is situated out of the usual course of vessels, too far south for those which frequent the archipelagoes of the Pacific, too far north for those bound to Australia round Cape Horn. I will not disguise from you our situation."

"And you are right, my dear Cyrus," said the reporter, eagerly. "You are dealing with men. They trust you, and you can count on them. Can he not, my friends?"

"I will obey you in everything, Mr. Smith," said Herbert, taking the engineer's hand.

"May I lose my name," said the sailor, "if I shirk my part! If you choose, Mr. Smith, we will make a little America here. We will build cities, lay railroads, establish telegraphs, and some day, when the island is transformed and civilized, offer her to the United States. But one thing I should like to ask."

"What is that?" said the reporter.

"That we should not consider ourselves any longer as castaways, but as colonists."

Cyrus Smith could not help smiling, and the motion was adopted. Then Smith thanked his companions, and added that he counted upon their energy and upon the help of Heaven.

"Well, let's start for the Chimneys," said Pencroff.

"One minute, my friends," answered the engineer; "would it not be well to name the island, as well as the capes, promontories, and water-courses, which we see before us?"

"Good," said the reporter. "That will simplify for the future the instructions which we may have to give or to take."

"Yes," added the sailor, "it will be something gained to be able to say whence we are coming and where we are going. We shall seem to be somewhere."

"At the Chimneys, for instance," said Herbert.

"Exactly," said the sailor. "That name has been quite convenient already, and I was the author of it. Shall we keep that name for our first encampment, Mr. Smith?"

"Yes, Pencroff, since you baptized it so."

"Good! the others will be easy enough," resumed the sailor, who was now in the vein. "Let us give them names like those of the Swiss family Robinson, whose story Herbert has read me more than once:—'Providence Bay,' 'Cochalot Point,' 'Cape Disappointment.'"

"Or rather Mr. Smith's name, Mr. Spilett's, or Neb's," said Herbert.

"My name!" cried Neb, showing his white teeth.

"Why not?" replied Pencroff, "'Port Neb' would sound first-rate! And 'Cape Gideon'—"

"I would rather have names, taken from our country," said the reporter, "which will recall America to us."

"Yes," said Smith, "the principal features, the bays and seas should be so named. For instance, let us call the great bay to the east Union Bay, the southern indentation Washington Bay, the mountain on which we are standing Mount Franklin, the lake beneath our feet Lake Grant. These names will recall our country and the great citizens who have honored it; but for the smaller features, let us choose names which will suggest their especial configuration. These will remain in our memory and be more convenient at the same time. The shape of the island is so peculiar that we shall have no trouble in finding appropriate names. The streams, the creeks, and the forest regions yet to be discovered we will baptize as they come. What say you, my friends?"

The engineer's proposal was unanimously applauded. The inland bay unrolled like a map before their eyes, and they had only to name the features of its contour and relief. Spilett would put down the names over the proper places, and the geographical nomenclature of the island would be complete. First, they named the two bays and the mountain as the engineer had suggested.

"Now," said the reporter, "to that peninsula projecting from the southwest I propose to give the name of Serpentine Peninsula, and to call the twisted curve at the termination of it Reptile End, for it is just like a snake's tail."

"Motion carried," said the engineer.

"And the other extremity of the island," said Herbert, "the gulf so like an open pair of jaws, let us call it Shark Gulf."

"Good enough," said Pencroff, "and we may complete the figure by calling the two sides of the gulf Mandible Cape."

"But there are two capes," observed the reporter.

"Well, we will have them North Mandible and South Mandible."

"I've put them down," said Spilett.

"Now we must name the southwestern extremity of the island," said Pencroff.

"You mean the end of Union Bay?" asked. Herbert.

"Claw Cape," suggested Neb, who wished to have his turn as godfather. And he had chosen an excellent name; for this Cape was very like the powerful claw of the fantastic animal to which they had compared the island. Pencroff was enchanted with the turn things were taking, and their active imaginations soon supplied other names. The river which furnished them with fresh water, and near which the balloon had cast them on shore, they called the Mercy, in gratitude to Providence. The islet on which they first set foot, was Safety Island; the plateau at the top of the high granite wall above the Chimneys, from which the whole sweep of the bay was visible, Prospect Plateau; and, finally, that mass of impenetrable woods which covered Serpentine Peninsula, the Forests of the Far West.

The engineer had approximately determined, by the height and position of the sun, the situation of the island with reference to the cardinal points, and had put Union Bay and Prospect Plateau to the east; but on the morrow, by taking the exact time of the sun's rising and setting, and noting its situation at the time exactly intermediate, he expected to ascertain precisely the northern point of the island; for, on account of its situation on the Southern Hemisphere, the sun at the moment of its culmination would pass to the north, and not to the south, as it does in the Northern Hemisphere.

All was settled, and the colonists were about to descend the mountain, when Pencroff cried:—"Why, what idiots we are!"

"Why so?" said Spilett, who had gotten up and closed his note-book.

"We have forgotten to baptize our island!"

Herbert was about to propose to give it the name of the engineer, and his companions would have applauded the choice, when Cyrus Smith said quietly:—

"Let us give it the name of a great citizen, my friends, of the defender of American unity! Let us call it Lincoln Island!"

They greeted the proposal with three hurrahs.

CHAPTER XII. REGULATION OF WATCHES

PENCROFF IS SATISFIED—A SUSPICIOUS SMOKE—THE COURSE OF RED CREEK—THE FLORA OF THE ISLAND—ITS FAUNA—MOUNTAIN PHEASANTS—A KANGAROO CHASE—THE AGOUTI—LAKE GRANT—RETURN TO THE CHIMNEYS.

The colonists of Lincoln Island cast a last look about them and walked once around the verge of the crater. Half an hour afterwards they were again upon the lower plateau, at their encampment of the previous night. Pencroff thought it was breakfast time, and so came up the question of regulating the watches of Smith and Spilett. The reporter's chronometer was uninjured by the sea water, as he had been cast high up on the sand beyond the reach of the waves. It was an admirable time-piece, a veritable pocket chronometer, and Spilett had wound it up regularly every day. The engineer's watch, of course, had stopped while he lay upon the downs. He now wound it up, and set it at 9 o'clock, estimating the time approximately by the height of the sun. Spilett was about to do the same, when the engineer stopped him.

"Wait, my dear Spilett," said he. "You have the Richmond time, have you not?"

"Yes."

"Your watch, then, is regulated by the meridian of that city, which is very nearly that of Washington?"

"Certainly."

"Well, keep it so. Wind it up carefully, but do not touch the hands. This may be of use to us."

"What's the use of that?" thought the sailor.

They made such a hearty meal, that little was left of the meat and pistachio-nuts; but Pencroff did not trouble himself about that. Top, who had not been forgotten in the feast, would certainly find some new game in the thicket. Besides, the sailor had made up his mind to ask Smith to make some powder and one or two shot-guns, which, he thought, would be an easy matter.

As they were leaving the plateau, Smith proposed to his companions to take a new road back to the Chimneys. He wished to explore Lake Grant, which lay surrounded so beautifully with trees. They followed the crest of one of the spurs in which the creek which fed the lake probably had its source. The colonists employed in conversation only the proper names which they had just devised, and found that they could express themselves much more easily. Herbert and Pencroff, one of whom was young and the other something of a child, were delighted, and the sailor said as they walked along:— "Well, Herbert, this is jolly! We can't lose ourselves now, my boy, since, whether we follow Lake Grant or get to the Mercy through the woods of the Far West, we must come to Prospect Plateau, and so to Union Bay."

It had been agreed that, without marching in a squad, the colonists should not keep too far apart. Dangerous wild beasts surely inhabited the forest recesses, and they must be on their guard. Usually Pencroff, Herbert, and Neb walked in front, preceded by Top, who poked his nose into every corner. The reporter and engineer walked together, the former ready to note down every incident, the latter seldom speaking, and turning aside only to pick up sometimes one thing, sometimes another, vegetable or mineral, which he put in his pocket without saying a word.

"What, the mischief, is he picking up?" muttered Pencroff. "There's no use in looking; I see nothing worth the trouble of stooping for."

About 10 o'clock the little company descended the last declivities of Mount Franklin. A few bushes and trees were scattered over the ground. They were walking on a yellowish, calcined soil, forming a plain about a mile long, which extended to the border of the wood. Large fragments of that basalt which, according to Bischof's theory, has taken 350,000,000 years to cool, strewed the uneven surface of the plain. Yet there was no trace of lava, which had especially found an exit down the northern declivities. Smith thought they should soon reach the creek, which he expected to find flowing under the trees by the plain, when he saw Herbert running back, and Neb and the sailor hiding themselves behind the rocks.

"What's the matter, my boy?" said Spilett.

"Smoke," answered Herbert. "We saw smoke ascending from among the rocks, a hundred steps in front."

"Men in this region!" cried the reporter.

"We must not show ourselves till we know with whom we have to deal," answered Smith. "I have more fear than hope of the natives, if there are any such on the island. Where is Top?"

"Top is on ahead."

"And has not barked?"

"No."

"That is strange. Still, let us try to call him back."

In a few moments the three had rejoined their companions, and had hidden themselves, like Neb and Pencroff, behind the basalt rubbish. Thence they saw, very evidently, a yellowish smoke curling into the air. Top was recalled by a low whistle from his master, who motioned to his comrades to wait, and stole forward under cover of the rocks. In perfect stillness the party awaited the result, when a call from Smith summoned them forward. In a moment they were by his side, and were struck at once by the disagreeable smell which pervaded the atmosphere. This odor, unmistakable as it was, had been sufficient to reassure the engineer.

"Nature is responsible for that fire," he said, "or rather for that smoke. It is nothing but a sulphur spring, which will be good for our sore throats."

"Good!" said Pencroff; "what a pity I have not a cold!"

The colonists walked towards the smoke. There they beheld a spring of sulphate of soda, which flowed in currents among the rocks, and whose waters, absorbing the oxygen of the air, gave off a lively odor of sulpho-hydric acid. Smith dipped his hand into the spring and found it oily. He tasted it, and perceived a sweetish savor. Its temperature he estimated at 95° Fahrenheit; and when Herbert asked him on what he based his estimate:—

"Simply, my boy," said he, "because when I put my hand into this water, I have no sensation either of heat or of cold. Therefore, it is at the same temperature as the human body, that is, about 95°."

Then as the spring of sulphur could be put to no present use, the colonists walked towards the thick border of the forest, a few hundred paces distant. There, as they had thought, the brook rolled its bright limpid waters between high, reddish banks, whose color betrayed the presence of oxide of iron. On account of this color, they instantly named the water course Red Creek. It was nothing but a large mountain brook, deep and clear, here, flowing quietly over the lands, there, gurgling amid rocks, or falling in a cascade, but always flowing towards the lake. It was a mile and a half long; its breadth varied from thirty to forty feet. Its water was fresh, which argued that those of the lake would be found the same—a fortunate occurrence, in case they should find upon its banks a more comfortable dwelling than the Chimneys.

The trees which, a few hundred paces down stream overshadowed the banks of the creek, belonged principally to the species which abound in the temperate zone of Australia or of Tasmania, and belong to those conifers which clothed the portion of the island already explored, some miles around Prospect Plateau. It was now the beginning of April, a month which corresponds in that hemisphere to our October, yet their leaves had not begun to fall. They were, especially, casuarinæ and eucalypti, some of which, in the ensuing spring, would furnish a sweetish manna like that of the East. Clumps of Australian cedars rose in the glades, covered high with that sort of moss which the New-Hollanders call *tussocks*; but the cocoa-palm, so abundant in the archipelagoes of the Pacific, was conspicuous by its absence. Probably the latitude of the island was too low.

"What a pity!" said Herbert, "such a useful tree and such splendid nuts!"

There were flocks of birds on the thin boughs of the eucalypti and the casuarinæ, which gave fine play to their wings. Black, white, and grey cockatoos, parrots and parroquets of all colors, king-birds, birds of paradise, of brilliant green, with a crowd of red, and blue lories, glowing with every prismatic color, flew about with deafening clamors. All at once, a strange volley of discordant sounds seemed to come from the thicket. The colonists heard, one after another, the song of birds, the cries of four-footed beasts, and a sort of clucking sound strangely human. Neb and Herbert rushed towards the thicket, forgetting the most elementary rules of prudence. Happily, there was neither formidable wild beast nor savage native, but merely half-a-dozen of those mocking birds which they recognized as "mountain pheasants." A few skillfully aimed blows with a stick brought this parody to an end, and gave them excellent game for dinner that evening. Herbert also pointed out superb pigeons with bronze-colored wings, some with a magnificent crest, others clad in green, like their congeners at Port-Macquarie; but like the troops of crows and magpies which flew about, they were beyond reach. A load of small-shot would have killed hosts of them; but the colonists had nothing but stones and sticks, very insufficient weapons. They proved even more inadequate when a troop of quadrupeds leaped away through the underbrush with tremendous bounds thirty feet long, so that they almost seemed to spring from tree to tree, like squirrels.

"Kangaroos!" cried Herbert.

"Can you eat them?" said Pencroff.

"They make a delicious stew," said the reporter.

The words had hardly escaped his lips, when the sailor, with Neb and Herbert at his heels, rushed after the kangaroos. Smith tried in vain to recall them, but equally in vain did they pursue the game, whose elastic leaps left them far behind. After five minutes' chase, they gave it up, out of breath.

"You see, Mr. Smith," said Pencroff, "that guns are a necessity. Will it be possible to make them?"

"Perhaps," replied the engineer; "but we will begin by making bows and arrows, and you will soon use them as skilfully as the Australian hunters."

"Bows and arrows!" said Pencroff, with a contemptuous look. "They are for children!"

"Don't be so proud, my friend," said the reporter. "Bows and arrows were sufficient for many centuries for the warfare of mankind. Powder is an invention of yesterday, while war, unhappily, is as old as the race."

"That's true, Mr. Spilett," said the sailor. "I always speak before I think. Forgive me."

Meanwhile Herbert, with his Natural History always uppermost in his thoughts, returned to the subject of kangaroos.

"Those which escaped us," he said, "belong to the species most difficult to capture—very large, with long grey hair, but I am sure there are black and red kangaroos, rock-kangaroos, kangaroo-rats—"

"Herbert," said the sailor, "for me there is only one kind—the 'kangaroo-on-the-spit'—and that is just what we haven't got."

They could not help laughing at Professor Pencroff's new classification. He was much cast down at the prospect of dining on mountain-phesants; but chance was once more kind to him. Top, who felt his dinner at stake, rushed hither and thither, his instinct quickened by sharp appetite. In fact, he would have left very little of what he might catch or any one else, had not Neb watched him shrewdly. About 3 o'clock he disappeared into the rushes, from which came grunts and growls which indicated a deadly tustle. Neb rushed in, and found Top greedily devouring an animal, which in ten seconds more would have totally disappeared. But the dog had luckily fallen on a litter, and two more rodents—for to this species did the beasts belong—lay strangled on the ground. Neb reappeared in triumph with a rodent in each hand. They had yellow hair, with patches of green, and the rudiments of a tail. They were a sort of agouti, a little larger than their tropical congeners, true American hares, with long ears and five molar teeth on either side.

"Hurrah!" cried Pencroff, "the roast is here; now we can go back to the house."

The journey was resumed. Red Creek still rolled its limped waters under the arching boughs of casuarence, bankseas and gigantic gum trees. Superb liliaceæ rose, to a height of twenty feet, and other arborescent trees of species unknown to the young naturalist, bent over the brook, which murmered gently beneath its leafy cradle. It widened sensibly, nevertheless, and the mouth was evidently near. As the party emerged from a massive thicket of fine trees, the lake suddenly appeared before them.

They were now on its left bank, and a picturesque region opened to their view. The smooth sheet of water, about seven miles in circumference and 250 acres in extent, lay sleeping among the trees. Towards the east, across the intermittent screen of verdure, appeared a shining horizon of sea. To the north the curve of the lake was concave, contrasting with the sharp outline of its lower extremity. Numerous aquatic birds frequented the banks of this little Ontario, in which the "Thousand Isles" of its American original were represented by a rock emerging from its surface some hundreds of feet from the southern bank. There lived in harmony several couples of kingfishers, perched upon rocks, grave and motionless, watching for fish; then they would plunge into the water and dive with a shrill cry, reappearing with the prey in their beaks. Upon the banks of the lake and the island were constantly strutting wild ducks, pelicans, water-hens and red-beaks. The waters of the lake were fresh and limpid, somewhat dark, and from the concentric circles on its surface, were evidently full of fish.

"How beautiful this lake is!" said Spilett. "We could live on its banks."

"We will live there!" answered Smith.

The colonists, desiring to get back to the Chimneys by the shortest route, went down towards the angle formed at the south by the junction of the banks. They broke a path with much labor through the thickets and brush wood, hitherto untouched by the hand of man, and walked towards the seashore, so as to strike it to the north of Prospect Plateau. After a two miles' walk they came upon the thick turf of the plateau, and saw before them the infinite ocean.

To get back to the Chimneys they had to walk across the plateau for a mile to the elbow formed by the first bend of the Mercy. But the engineer was anxious to know how and where the overflow of the lake escaped. It was probable that a river existed somewhere pouring through a gorge in the granite. In fine, the lake was an immense receptacle gradually filled at the expense of the creek, and its overflow must somehow find a way down to the sea. Why should they not utilize this wasted store of water-power? So they walked up the plateau, following the banks of Lake Grant, but after a tramp of a mile, they could find no outlet.

It was now half-past 4, and dinner had yet to be prepared. The party returned upon its track, and reached the Chimneys by the left bank of the Mercy. Then the fire was lighted, and Neb and Pencroff, on whom devolved the cooking, skilfully broiled the agouti, to which the hungry explorers did great honor. When the meal was over, and just as they were settling themselves to sleep, Smith drew from his pocket little specimens of various kinds of minerals, and said quietly,

"My friends, this is iron ore, this pyrites, this clay, this limestone, this charcoal. Nature gives us these as her part in the common task. To-morrow we must do our share!"

CHAPTER XIII. TOP'S CONTRIBUTION

MAKING BOWS AND ARROWS—A BRICK-KILN—A POTTERY—DIFFERENT COOKING UTENSILS—THE FIRST BOILED MEAT—MUGWORT—THE SOUTHERN CROSS—AN IMPORTANT ASTRONOMICAL OBSERVATION.

"Now then, Mr. Smith, where shall we begin?" asked Pencroff the next morning.

"At the beginning," answered the engineer.

And this, indeed, was necessary, as the colonists did not even possess implements with which to make implements. Neither were they in that condition of nature which "having time," economizes effort; the necessities of life must be provided for at once, and, if profiting by experience they had nothing to invent, at least they had everything to make. Their iron and steel was in the ore, their pottery was in the clay, their linen and clothes were still to be provided.

It must be remembered, however, that these colonists were *men*, in the best sense of the word. The engineer Smith could not have been aided by comrades more intelligent, or more devoted and zealous. He had questioned them, and knew their ability.

The reporter, having learned everything so as to be able to speak of everything, would contribute largely from his knowledge and skill towards the settlement of the island. He would not shirk work; and, a thorough sportsman, he would follow as a business what he had formerly indulged in as a pastime. Herbert, a manly lad, already well versed in natural science, would contribute his share to the common cause. Neb was devotion personified. Adroit, intelligent, indefatigable, robust, of iron constitution, knowing something of the work in a smithy, his assistance would be considerable. As to Pencroff, he had sailed every sea, had been a carpenter in the Brooklyn yards, an assistant tailor on board ship, and, during his leaves of absence, a gardener, farmer, etc.; in short, like every sailor, he was a Jack-of-all-trades.

Indeed, it would have been hard to bring together five men, more able to struggle against fate, and more certain to triumph in the end.

"At the beginning," Smith had said. And this beginning was the construction of an apparatus which would serve to transform the natural substances. Everyone knows what an important part heat plays in these transformations. Therefore, as wood and coal were already provided it was only necessary to make an oven to utilize them.

"What good is an oven," asked Pencroff.

"To make the pottery that we want," replied Smith.

"And how will we make an oven?"

"With bricks."

"And how will we make the bricks?"

"With the clay. Come, friends. We will set up our factory at the place of production, so as to avoid carriage. Neb will bring the provisions, and we shall not lack fire to cook food."

"No," replied the reporter, "but suppose we lack food, since we have no hunting implements?"

"If we only had a knife!" cried the sailor,

"What, then?" asked Smith.

"Why, I would make a bow and arrows. And game would be plenty in the larder."

"A knife. Something that will cut," said the engineer, as if talking to himself.

Suddenly his face brightened:

"Come here, Top," he called.

The dog bounded to his master, and Smith having taken off the collar which the animal had around his neck, broke it into halves, saying:— "Here are two knives, Pencroff."

For all response, the sailor gave a couple of cheers. Top's collar was made from a thin piece of tempered steel. All that was therefore necessary was to rub it to an edge upon a sand-stone, and then to sharpen it upon one of finer grain. These kind of stones were readily procurable upon the beach, and in a couple of hours the implements of the colony consisted of two strong blades, which it was easy to fasten into solid handles. The overcoming of this first difficulty was greeted as a triumph and it was indeed a fortunate event.

On setting out, it was the intention of the engineer to return to the western bank of the lake, where he had noticed the clay, of which he had secured a specimen. Following the bank of the Mercy they crossed Prospect Plateau, and after a walk of about five miles, they arrived at a glade some 200 paces distant from Lake Grant.

On the way, Herbert had discovered a tree from which the South American Indians make bows. It was the "crejimba," of the palm family. From it they cut long straight branches, which they peeled and shaped into bows. For cords they took the fibres of the "hibiscus heterophyltus" (Indian hemp), a malvaceous plant, the fibres of which are as strong as the tendons of an animal. Pencroff, having thus provided bows, only needed arrows. Those were easily made from straight, stiff branches, free from knots, but it was not so easy to arm them with a substitute for iron. But Pencroff said that he had accomplished this much, and that chance would do the rest.

The party had reached the place discovered the day before. The ground was composed of that clay which is used in making bricks and tiles, and was therefore just the thing for their purpose. The labor was not difficult. It was only necessary to scour the clay with sand, mould the bricks, and then bake them before a wood fire.

Usually, bricks are pressed in moulds, but the engineer contented himself with making these by hand. All this day and the next was employed in this work. The clay, soaked in water, was kneaded by the hands and feet of the manipulators, and then divided into blocks of equal size. A skilled workman can make, without machinery, as many as 10,000 bricks in twelve hours; but in the two days the brickmakers of Lincoln Island had made but 3,000, which were piled one upon the other to await the time when they would be dry enough to bake, which would be in three or four days.

On the 2d of April, Smith occupied himself in determining the position of the island.

The day before he had noted the precise minute at which the sun had set, allowing for the refraction. On this morning, he ascertained with equal precision the time of its rising. The intervening time was twelve hours and twenty-four minutes. Therefore six hours and twelve minutes after rising the sun would pass the meridian, and the point in the sky which it would occupy at that instant would be north.

At the proper hour Smith marked this point, and by getting two trees in line obtained a meridian for his future operations.

During the two days preceding the baking they occupied themselves by laying in a supply of firewood. Branches were cut from the edge of the clearing, and all the dead wood under the trees was picked up. And now and then they hunted in the neighborhood, the more successfully, as Pencroff had some dozens of arrows with very sharp points. It was Top who had provided these points by bringing in a porcupine, poor game enough, but of an undeniable value, thanks to the quills with which it bristled. These quills were firmly fastened to the ends of the arrows, and their flight was guided by feathering them with the cockatoo's feathers. The reporter and Herbert soon became expert marksmen, and all kinds of game, such as cabiais, pigeons, agoutis, heath-cock, etc., abounded at the Chimneys. Most of these were killed in that part of the forest upon the left bank of the Mercy, which they had called Jacamar Wood, after the kingfisher which Pencroff and Herbert had pursued there during their first exploration.

The meat was eaten fresh, but they preserved the hams of the cabiai by smoking them before a fire of green wood, having made them aromatic with odorous leaves. Thus, they had nothing but roast after roast, and they would have been glad to have heard a pot singing upon the hearth; but first they must have the pot, and for this they must have the oven.

During these excursions, the hunters noticed the recent tracks of large animals, armed with strong claws, but they could not tell their species; and Smith cautioned them to be prudent, as, doubtless, there were dangerous beasts in the forest.

He was right. For one day Spilett and Herbert saw an animal resembling a jaguar. But, fortunately, the beast did not attack them, as they could hardly have killed it without being themselves wounded. But, Spilett promised, if he should ever obtain a proper weapon, such as one of the guns Pencroff begged for, that he would wage relentless war on all ferocious beasts and rid the island of their presence.

They did not do anything to the Chimneys, as the engineer hoped to discover, or to build, if need be, a more convenient habitation, but contented themselves by spreading fresh quantities of moss and dry leaves upon the sand in the corridors, and upon these primitive beds the tired workmen slept soundly. They also reckoned the days already passed on Lincoln Island, and began keeping a calendar. On the 5th of April, which was a Wednesday, they had been twelve days upon the island.

On the morning of the 6th, the engineer with his companions met at the place where the bricks were to be baked. Of course the operation was to be conducted in the open air, and not in an oven, or, rather, the pile of bricks would in itself form a bake-oven. Carefully-prepared faggots were laid upon the ground, surrounding the tiers of dry bricks, which formed a great cube, in which air-holes had been left. The work occupied the whole day, and it was not until evening that they lit the fire, which all night long they kept supplied with fuel.

The work lasted forty-eight hours, and succeeded perfectly. Then, as it was necessary to let the smoking mass cool, Neb and Pencroff, directed by Mr. Smith, brought, on a hurdle made of branches, numerous loads of limestone which they found scattered in abundance to the north of the lake. These stones, decomposed by heat, furnished a thick quick-lime, which increased in bulk by slacking, and was fully as pure as if it had been produced by the calcination of chalk or marble. Mixed with sand in order to diminish its shrinkage while drying, this lime made an excellent mortar.

By the 9th of April the engineer had at his disposal a quantity of lime, all prepared, and some thousands of bricks. They, therefore, began at once the construction of an oven, in which to bake their pottery. This was accomplished without much difficulty; and, five days later, the oven was supplied with coal from the open vein, which the engineer had discovered near the mouth of Red Creek, and the first smoke escaped from a chimney twenty feet high. The glade was transformed into a manufactory, and Pencroff was ready to believe that all the products of modern industry would be produced from this oven.

Meantime the colonists made a mixture of the clay with lime and quartz, forming pipe-clay, from which they moulded pots and mugs, plates and jars, tubs to hold water, and cooking vessels. Their form was rude and defective, but after they had been baked at a high temperature, the kitchen of the Chimneys found itself provided with utensils as precious as if they were composed of the finest kaolin.

We must add that Pencroff, desirous of knowing whether this material deserved its name of pipe-clay, made some large pipes, which he would have found perfect, but for the want of tobacco. And, indeed, this was a great privation to the sailor.

"But the tobacco will come like everything else," he would say in his hopeful moments.

The work lasted until the 15th of April, and the time was well spent. The colonists having become potters, made nothing but pottery. When it would suit the engineer to make them smiths they would be smiths. But as the morrow would be Sunday, and moreover Easter Sunday, all agreed to observe the day by rest. These Americans were religious men, scrupulous observers of the precepts of the Bible, and their situation could only develop their trust in the Author of all things.

On the evening of the 15th they returned permanently to the Chimneys, bringing the rest of the pottery back with them, and putting out the oven fire until there should be use for it again. This return was marked by the fortunate discovery by the engineer of a substance that would answer for tinder, which, we know, is the spongy, velvety pulp of a mushroom of the polypore family. Properly prepared it is extremely inflammable, especially when previously saturated with gunpowder, or nitrate or chlorate of potash. But until then they had found no polypores, nor any fungi that would answer instead. Now, the engineer, having found a certain plant belonging to the mugwort family, to which belong wormwood, mint, etc., broke off some tufts, and, handing them to the sailor, said:—

"Here, Pencroff, is something for you."

Pencroff examined the plant, with its long silky threads and leaves covered with a cotton-like down.

"What is it, Mr. Smith?" he asked. "Ah, I know! It's tobacco!"

"No," answered Smith; "it is Artemesia wormwood, known to science as Chinese mugwort, but to us it will be tinder."

This mugwort, properly dried, furnished a very inflammable substance, especially after the engineer had impregnated it with nitrate of potash, which is the same as saltpetre, a mineral very plenty on the island.

This evening the colonists, seated in the central chamber, supped with comfort. Neb had prepared some agouti soup, a spiced ham, and the boiled corms of the "caladium macrorhizum," an herbaceous plant of the arad family, which under the tropics takes a tree form. These corms, which are very nutritious, had an excellent flavor, something like that of Portland sago, and measurably supplied the place of bread, which the colonists were still without.

Supper finished, before going to sleep the party took a stroll upon the beach. It was 8 o'clock, and the night was magnificent. The moon, which had been full five days before, was about rising, and in the zenith, shining resplendent above the circumpolar constellations, rode the Southern Cross. For some moments the engineer gazed at it attentively. At its summit and base were two stars of the first magnitude, and on the left arm and the right, stars, respectively, of the second magnitude and the third. Then, after some reflection, he said:—

"Herbert, is not to-day the 15th of April?"

"Yes, sir," answered the lad.

"Then, if I am not mistaken, to-morrow will be one of the four days in the year when the mean and real time are the same; that is to say, my boy, that to-morrow, within some seconds of noon by the clocks, the sun will pass the meridian. If, therefore, the weather is clear, I think I will be able to obtain the longitude of the island within a few degrees."

"Without a sextant or instruments?" asked Spilett.

"Yes," replied the engineer. And since it is so clear, I will try to-night to find our latitude by calculating the height of the Cross, that is, of the Southern Pole, above the horizon. You see, my friends, before settling down, it will not do to be content with determining this land to be an island; we must find out its locality."

"Indeed, instead of building a house, it will be better to build a ship, if we are within a hundred miles of an inhabited land."

"That is why I am now going to try to get the latitude of the place, and to-morrow noon to calculate the longitude."

If the engineer had possessed a sextant, the work would have been easy, as this evening, by taking the height of the pole, and to-morrow by the sun's passage of the meridian, he would have the co-ordinates of the island. But, having no instruments he must devise something. So returning to the Chimneys, he made, by the light of the fire, two little flat sticks which he fastened together with a thorn, in a way that they could be opened and shut like compasses, and returned with them to the beach. But as the sea horizon was hidden from this point by Claw Cape, the engineer determined to make his observation from Prospect Plateau, leaving, until the next day, the computation of the height of the latter, which could easily be done by elementary geometry.

The colonists, therefore, went to the edge of the plateau which faced the southeast, overlooking the fantastic rocks bordering the shore. The place rose some fifty feet above the right bank of the Mercy, which descended, by a double slope, to the end of Claw Cape and to the southern boundary of the island. Nothing obstructed the vision, which extended over half the horizon from the Cape to Reptile Promontory. To the south, this horizon, lit by the first rays of the moon, was sharply defined against the sky. The Cross was at this time reversed, the star Alpha being nearest the pole. This constellation is not situated as near to the southern as the polar star is to the northern pole; Alpha is about 27° from it, but Smith knew this and could calculate accordingly. He took care also to observe it at the instant when it passed the meridian under the pole, thus simplifying the operation.

The engineer opened the arms of his compass so that one pointed to the horizon and the other to the star, and thus obtained the angle of distance which separated them. And in order to fix this distance immovably, he fastened these arms, respectively, by means of thorns, to a cross piece of wood. This done, it was only necessary to calculate the angle obtained, bringing the observation to the level of the sea so as to allow for the depression of the horizon caused by the height of the plateau. The measurement of this angle would thus give the height of Alpha, or the pole, above the horizon; or, since the latitude of a point on the globe is always equal to the height of the pole above the horizon at that point, the latitude of the island.

This calculation was postponed until the next day, and by 10 o'clock everybody slept profoundly.

CHAPTER XIV. THE MEASURE OF THE GRANITE WALL

AN APPLICATION OF THE THEOREM OF SIMILAR TRIANGLES—THE LATITUDE OF THE ISLAND—AN EXCURSION TO THE NORTH—AN OYSTER-BED—PLANS FOR THE FUTURE—THE SUN'S PASSAGE OF THE MERIDIAN—THE CO-ORDINATES OF LINCOLN ISLAND.

At daybreak the next day, Easter Sunday, the colonists left the Chimneys and went to wash their linen and clean their clothing. The engineer intended to make some soap as soon as he could obtain some soda or potash and grease or oil. The important question of renewing their wardrobes would be considered in due time. At present they were strong, and able to stand hard wear for at least six months longer. But everything depended on the situation of the island as regarded inhabited countries, and that would be determined this day, providing the weather permitted.

The sun rising above the horizon, ushered in one of those glorious days which seem like the farewell of summer. The first thing to be done was to measure the height of Prospect Plateau above the sea.

"Do you not need another pair of compasses?" asked Herbert, of the engineer.

"No, my boy," responded the latter, "this time we will try another and nearly as precise a method."

Pencroff, Neb, and the reporter were busy at other things; but Herbert, who desired to learn, followed the engineer, who proceeded along the beach to the base of the granite wall.

Smith was provided with a pole twelve feet long, carefully measured off from his own height, which he knew to a hair. Herbert carried a plumb-line made from a flexible fibre tied to a stone. Having reached a point 20 feet from the shore and 500 feet from the perpendicular granite wall, Smith sunk the pole two feet in the sand, and, steadying it carefully, proceeded to make it plumb with the horizon. Then, moving back to a spot where, stretched upon the sand, he could sight over the top of the pole to the edge of the cliff, bringing the two points in line, he carefully marked this place with a stone. Then addressing Herbert,

"Do you know the first principles of geometry?" said he.

"Slightly, sir," answered Herbert, not wishing to seem forward.

"Then you remember the relation of similar triangles?"

"Yes, sir," answered Herbert. "Their like sides are proportional."

"Right, my boy. And I have just constructed two similar right angled triangles:—the smaller has for its sides the perpendicular pole and the distances from its base and top to the stake; the second has the wall which we are about to measure, and the distances from its base and summit to the stake, which are only the prolongation of the base and hypothenuse of the first triangle.

"I understand," cried Herbert. "As the distance from the stake to the pole is proportional to the distance from the stake to the base of the wall, so the height of the wall is proportional to the height of the rod."

"Exactly," replied the engineer, "and after measuring the first two distances, as we know the height of the pole, we have only to calculate the proportion in order to find the height of the wall."

The measurements were made with the pole and resulted in determining the distances from the stake to the foot of the pole and the base of the wall to be 15 and 500 feet respectively. The engineer and Herbert then returned to the Chimneys, where the former, using a flat stone and a bit of shell to figure with, determined the height of the wall to be 333.33 feet.

Then taking the compasses, and carefully measuring the angle which he had obtained the night before, upon a circle which he had divided into 360 parts, the engineer found that this angle, allowing for the differences already explained, was 53°. Which, subtracted from 90°—the distance of the pole from the equator—gave 37° as the latitude of Lincoln Island. And making an allowance of 5° for the imperfections of the observations, Smith, concluded it to be situated between the 35th and the 40th parallel of south latitude.

But, in order to establish the co-ordinates of the island, the longitude also must be taken. And this the engineer determined to do when the sun passed the meridian at noon.

They therefore resolved to spend the morning in a walk, or rather an exploration of that part of the island situated to the north of Shark Gulf and the lake; and, if they should have time, to push on as far as the western side of South Mandible Cape. They would dine on the downs and not return until evening.

At half-past 8 the little party set out, following the edge of the channel. Opposite, upon Safety Islet, a number of birds of the sphemiscus family strutted gravely about. There were divers, easily recognizable, by their disagreeable cry, which resembled the braying of an ass. Pencroff, regarding them with gastronomic intent, was pleased to learn that their flesh, though dark colored, was good to eat. They could also see amphibious animals, which probably were seals, crawling over the sand. It was not possible to think of these as food, as their oily flesh is detestable; nevertheless Smith observed them carefully, and without disclosing his plans to the others, he announced that they would very soon, make a visit to the island. The shore followed by the colonists was strewn with mollusks, which would have delighted a malacologist. But, what was more important, Neb discovered, about four miles from the Chimneys, among the rocks, a bed of oysters, left bare by the tide.

"Neb hasn't lost his day," said Pencroff, who saw that the bed extended some distance.

"It is, indeed, a happy discovery," remarked the reporter. "And when we remember that each oyster produces fifty or sixty thousand eggs a year, the supply is evidently inexhaustable."

"But I don't think the oyster is very nourishing," said Herbert.

"No," answered Smith. "Oysters contain very little azote, and it would be necessary for a man living on them alone to eat at least fifteen or sixteen dozen every day."

"Well," said Pencroff, "we could swallow dozens and dozens of these and not exhaust the bed. Shall we have some for breakfast?"

And, without waiting for an answer, which he well knew would be affirmative, the sailor and Neb detached a quantity of these mollusks from the rocks, and placed them with the other provisions for breakfast, in a basket which Neb had made from the hibiscus fibres. Then they continued along the shore between the downs and the sea.

From time to time Smith looked at his watch, so as to be ready for the noon observation.

All this portion of the island, as far as South Mandible Cape, was desert, composed of nothing but sand and shells, mixed with the debris of lava. A few sea birds, such as the sea-gulls and albatross, frequented the shore, and some wild ducks excited the covetousness of Pencroff. He tried to shoot some, but unsuccessfully, as they seldom lit, and he could not hit them flying.

This made the sailor say to the engineer:—

"You see, Mr. Smith, how much we need guns!"

"Doubtless, Pencroff," answered the reporter, "but it rests with you. You find iron for the barrels, steel for the locks, saltpetre, charcoal and sulphur for the powder, mercury and nitric acid for the fulminate, and last of all, lead for the balls, and Mr. Smith will make us guns of the best quality."

"Oh, we could probably find all these substances on the island," said the engineer. "But it requires fine tools to make such a delicate instrument as a firearm. However, we will see after awhile."

"Why, why did we throw the arms and everything else, even our penknives, out of the balloon?" cried Pencroff.

"If we hadn't, the balloon would have thrown us into the sea," answered Herbert.

"So it would, my boy," answered the sailor; and then another idea occurring to him:—

"I wonder what Mr. Forster and his friend thought," he said, "the next day, when they found they balloon had escaped?"

"I don't care what they thought," said the reporter.

"It was my plan," cried Pencroff, with a satisfied air.

"And a good plan it was, Pencroff," interrupted the reporter, laughing, "to drop us here!"

"I had rather be here than in the hands of the Southerners!" exclaimed the sailor, "especially since Mr. Smith has been kind enough to rejoin us!"

"And I, too," cried the reporter. "After all, what do we lack here? Nothing."

"That means—everything," answered the sailor, laughing and shrugging his shoulders. "But some day we will get away from this place."

"Sooner, perhaps, than you think, my friends," said the engineer, "if Lincoln Island is not very far from an inhabited archipelego or a continent. And we will find that out within an hour. I have no map of the Pacific, but I have a distinct recollection of its southern portion. Yesterday's observation places the island in the latitude of New Zealand and Chili. But the distance between these two countries is at least 6,000 miles. We must therefore determine what point in this space the island occupies, and that I hope to get pretty soon from the longitude.

"Is not the Low Archipelago nearest us in latitude," asked Herbert.

"Yes," replied the engineer, "but it is more than 1,200 miles distant."

"And that way?" inquired Neb, who followed the conversation with great interest, pointing towards the south.

"Nothing!" answered Pencroff.

"Nothing, indeed," added the engineer.

"Well, Cyrus," demanded the reporter, "if we find Lincoln Island to be only 200 or 300 miles from New Zealand or Chili?"

"We will build a ship instead of a house, and Pencroff shall command it."

"All right, Mr. Smith," cried the sailor; "I am all ready to be captain, provided you build something seaworthy."

"We will, if it is necessary," answered Smith.

While these men, whom nothing could discourage, were talking, the hour for taking the observation approached. Herbert could not imagine how Mr. Smith would be able to ascertain the time of the sun's passage of the meridian of the island without a single instrument. It was 11 o'clock, and the party, halting about six miles from the Chimneys, not far from the place where they had found the engineer after his inexplicable escape, set about preparing breakfast. Herbert found fresh water in a neighboring brook, and brought some back in a vessel which Neb had with him.

Meantime, the engineer made ready for his astronomical observation. He chose a smooth dry place upon the sand, which the sea had left perfectly level. It was no more necessary, however, for it to be horizontal, than for the rod which he stuck in the sand to be perpendicular. Indeed, the engineer inclined the rod towards the south or away from the sun, as it must not be forgotten that the colonists of Lincoln Island, being in the Southern Hemisphere, saw the orb of day describe his diurnal arc above the northern horizon.

Then Herbert understood how by means of the shadow of the rod on the sand, the engineer would be able to ascertain the culmination of the sun, that is to say, its passage of the meridian of the island, or, in other words, the *time* of the place. For the moment that the shadow obtained its minimum length it would be noon, and all they had to do was to watch carefully the end of the shadow. By inclining the rod from the sun Smith had made the shadow longer, and therefore its changes could be the more readily noted.

When he thought it was time, the engineer knelt down upon the sand and began marking the decrease in the length of the shadow by means of little wooden pegs. His companions, bending over him, watched the operation with the utmost interest.

The reporter, chronometer in hand, stood ready to mark the minute when the shadow would be shortest. Now, as this 16th of April was a day when the true and mean time are the same, Spilett's watch would give the true time of Washington, and greatly simplify the calculation.

Meantime the shadow diminished little by little, and as soon as Smith perceived it begin to lengthen he exclaimed:—

"Now!"

"One minute past 5," answered the reporter.

Nothing then remained but the easy work of summing up the result. There was, as we have seen, five hours difference between the meridian of Washington and that of the island. Now, the sun passes around the earth at the rate of 15° an hour. Fifteen multiplied by five gives seventy-five. And as Washington is in 77° 3' 11" from the meridian of Greenwich, it follows that the island was in the neighborhood of longitude 152° west.

Smith announced this result to his companions, and, making the same allowance as before, he was able to affirm that the bearing of the island was between the 35° and 37° of south latitude, and between the 150° and 155° of west longitude.

The difference in this calculation, attributable to errors in observation, was placed, as we have seen, at 5° or 300 miles in each direction. But this error did not influence the conclusion that Lincoln Island was so far from any continent or archipelago that they could not attempt to accomplish the distance in a small boat. In fact, according to the engineer, they were at least 1,200 miles from Tahiti and from the Low Archipelago, fully 1,800 miles from New Zealand, and more than 4,500 miles from the coast of America.

And when Cyrus Smith searched his memory, he could not remember any island in the Pacific occupying the position of Lincoln Island.

CHAPTER XV. WINTER SETS IN

THE METALLUGRIC QUESTION—THE EXPLORATION OF SAFETY ISLAND— A SEAL HUNT—CAPTURE OF AN ECHIDNA—THE AI—THE CATALONIAN METHOD—MAKING IRON AND STEEL.

The first words of the sailor, on the morning of the 17th of April, were:—

"Well, what are we going to do to-day?"

"Whatever Mr. Smith chooses," answered the reporter.

The companions of the engineer, having been brickmakers and potters, were about to become metal-workers.

The previous day, after lunch, the party had explored as far as the extremity of Mandible Cape, some seven miles from the Chimneys. The extensive downs here came to an end and the soil appeared volcanic. There were no longer high walls, as at Prospect Plateau, but the narrow gulf between the two capes was enframed by a fantastic border of the mineral matter discharged from the volcano. Having reached this point, the colonists retraced their steps to the Chimneys, but they could not sleep until the question whether they should look forwards to leaving Lincoln Island had been definitely settled.

The 1,200 miles to the Low Archipelago was a long distance. And now, at the beginning of the stormy season, a small boat would certainly not be able to accomplish it. The building of a boat, even when the proper tools are provided, is a difficult task, and as the colonists had none of these, the first thing to do was to make hammers, hatchets, adzes, saws, augers, planes, etc., which would take some time. It was therefore decided to winter on Lincoln Island, and to search for a more comfortable dwelling than the Chimneys in which to live during the inclement weather.

The first thing was to utilize the iron ore which the engineer had discovered, by transforming it into iron and steel.

Iron ore is usually found in combination with oxygen or sulphur. And it was so in this instance, as of the two specimens brought back by Cyrus Smith one was magnetic iron, and the other pyrites or sulphuret of iron. Of these, it was the first kind, the magnetic ore, or oxide of iron, which must be reduced by coal, that is to say, freed from the oxygen, in order to obtain the pure metal. This reduction is performed by submitting the ore to a great heat, either by the Catalonian method, which has the advantage of producing the metal at one operation, or by means of blast furnaces which first smelt the ore, and then the iron, carrying off the 3 or 4 per cent of coal combined with it.

The engineer wanted to obtain iron in the shortest way possible. The ore he had found was in itself very pure and rich. Such ore is found in rich grey masses, yielding a black dust crystallized in regular octahedrons, highly magnetic, and in Europe the best quality of iron is made from it. Not far from this vein was the coal field previously explored by the colonists, so that every facility existed for the treatment of the ore.

"Then, sir, are we going to work the iron?" questioned Pencroff. "Yes, my friend," answered the engineer.

"But first we will do something I think you will enjoy—have a seal hunt on the island."

"A seal hunt!" cried the sailor, addressing Spilett "Do we need seals to make iron?"

"It seems so, since Cyrus has said it," replied the reporter. But as the engineer had already left the Chimneys, Pencroff prepared for the chase without gaining an explanation.

Soon the whole party were gathered upon the beach at a point where the channel could be forded at low water without wading deeper than the knees. This was Smith's first visit to the islet upon which his companions had been thrown by the balloon. On their landing, hundreds of penguins looked fearlessly at them, and the colonists armed with clubs could have killed numbers of these birds, but it would have been useless slaughter, and it would not do to frighten the seals which were lying on the sand some cable lengths away. They respected also certain innocent-looking sphemiscus, with flattened side appendages, mere apologies for wings, and covered with scale-like vestiges of feathers.

The colonists marched stealthily forward over ground riddled with holes which formed the nests of aquatic birds. Towards the end of the island, black objects, like moving rocks, appeared above the surface of the water, they were the seals the hunters wished to capture.

It was necessary to allow them to land, as, owing to their shape, these animals, although capital swimmers and difficult to seize in the sea, can move but slowly on the shore. Pencroff, who knew their habits, counselled waiting until the seals were sunning themselves asleep on the sand. Then the party could manage so as to cut off their retreat and despatch them with a blow on the muzzle. The hunters therefore hid themselves behind the rocks and waited quietly.

In about an hour half a dozen seals crawled on to the sand, and Pencroff and Herbert went off round the point of the island so as to cut off their retreat, while the three others, hidden by the rocks, crept forward to the place of encounter.

Suddenly the tall form of the sailor was seen. He gave a shout, and the engineer and his companions hurriedly threw themselves between the seals and the sea. They succeeded in beating two of the animals to death, but the others escaped.

"Here are your seals, Mr. Smith," cried the sailor, coming forward.

"And now we will make bellows," replied the engineer.

"Bellows!" exclaimed the sailor. "These seals are in luck."

It was, in effect, a huge pair of bellows, necessary in the reduction of the ore, which the engineer expected to make from the skins of the seals. They were medium-sized, about six feet long, and had heads resembling those of dogs. As it was useless to burden themselves with the whole carcass, Neb and Pencroff resolved to skin them on the spot, while Smith and the reporter made the exploration of the island.

The sailor and the black man acquitted themselves well, and three hours later Smith had at his disposal two seal skins, which he intended to use just as they were, without tanning.

The colonists, waiting until low water, re-crossed the channel and returned to the Chimneys.

It was no easy matter to stretch the skins upon the wooden frames and to sew them so as to make them sufficiently air-tight. Smith had nothing but the two knives to work with, yet he was so ingenious and his companions aided him so intelligently, that, three days later, the number of implements of the little colony was increased by a bellows intended to inject air into the midst of the ore during its treatment by heat—a requisite to the success of the operation.

It was on the morning of the 20th of April that what the reporter called in his notes the "iron age" began. The engineer had decided to work near the deposits of coal and iron, which were situated at the base of the northeasterly spurs of Mount Franklin, six miles from the Chimneys. And as it would not be possible to go back and forth each day, it was decided to camp upon the ground in a temporary hut, so that they could attend to the important work night and day.

This settled, they left in the morning, Neb and Pencroff carrying the bellows and a stock of provisions, which latter they would add to on the way.

The road led through the thickest part of Jacamar Wood, in a northwesterly direction. It was as well to break a path which would henceforth be the most direct route between Prospect Plateau and Mount Franklin. The trees belonging to the species already recognized were magnificent, and Herbert discovered another, the dragon tree, which Pencroff designated as an "overgrown onion," which, notwithstanding its height, belongs to the same family of liliaceous plants as the onion, the civet, the shallot, or the asparagus. These dragon trees have ligneous roots which, cooked, are excellent, and which, fermented, yield a very agreeable liquor. They therefore gathered some.

It took the entire day to traverse the wood, but the party were thus able to observe its fauna and flora. Top, specially charged to look after the fauna, ran about in the grass and bushes, flushing all kinds of game. Herbert and Spilett shot two kangaroos and an animal which was like a hedge-hog, in that it rolled itself into a ball and erected its quills, and like an ant-eater, in that it was provided with claws for digging, a long and thin snout terminating in a beak, and an extensile tongue furnished with little points, which enabled it to hold insects.

"And what does it look like boiling in the pot?" asked Pencroff, naturally.

"Like an excellent piece of beef," answered Herbert.

"We don't want to know any more than that," said the sailor.

During the march they saw some wild boars, but they did not attempt to attack the little troupe, and it seemed that they were not going to have any encounter with savage beasts, when the reporter saw in a dense thicket, among the lower branches of a tree, an animal which he took to be a bear, and which he began tranquilly to sketch. Fortunately for Spilett, the animal in question did not belong to that redoubtable family of plantigrades. It was an ai, better known as a sloth, which has a body like that of a large dog, a rough and dirty-colored skin, the feet armed with strong claws which enable it to grasp the branches of trees and feed upon the leaves. Having identified the animal without disturbing it, Spilett struck out "bear" and wrote "ai" under his drawing and the route was resumed.

At 5 o'clock Smith called a halt. They were past the forest and at the beginning of the massive spurs which buttressed Mount Franklin towards the east. A few hundred paces distant was Red Creek; so drinking water was not wanting.

The camp was made. In less than an hour a hut, constructed from the branches of the tropical bindweed, and stopped with loam, was erected under the trees on the edge of the forest. They deferred the geological work until the next day. Supper was prepared, a good fire blazed before the hut, the spit turned, and at 8 o'clock, while one of the party kept the fire going, in case some dangerous beast should prowl around, the others slept soundly.

The next morning, Smith, accompanied by Herbert, went to look for the place where they had found the specimen of ore. They found the deposit on the surface, near the sources of the creek, close to the base of one of the northeast buttresses. This mineral, very rich in iron, enclosed in its fusible vein-stone, was perfectly suited to the method of reduction which the engineer intended to employ, which was the simplified Catalonian process practised in Corsica.

This method properly required the construction of ovens and crucibles in which the ore and the coal, placed in alternate layers, were transformed and reduced. But Smith proposed to simplify matters by simply making a huge cube

564

of coal and ore, into the centre of which the air from the bellows would be introduced. This was, probably, what Tubal Cain did. And a process which gave such good results to Adam's grandson would doubtless succeed with the colonists of Lincoln Island.

The coal was collected with the same facility as the ore, and the latter was broken into little pieces and the impurities picked from it. Then the coal and ore were heaped together in successive layers—just as a charcoal-burner arranges his wood. Thus arranged, under the influence of the air from the bellows, the coal would change into carbonic acid, then into oxide of carbon, which would release the oxygen from the oxide of iron.

The engineer proceeded in this manner. The sealskin bellows, furnished with a pipe of refractory earth (an earth difficult of fusion), which had previously been prepared at the pottery, was set up close to the heap of ore. And, moved by a mechanism consisting of a frame, fibre-cords, and balance-weight, it injected into the mass a supply of air, which, by raising the temperature, assisted the chemical transformation which would give the pure metal.

The operation was difficult. It took all the patience and ingenuity of the colonists to conduct it properly; but finally it succeeded, and the result was a pig of iron in a spongy state, which must be cut and forged in order to expel the liquefied gangue. It was evident that these self-constituted smiths wanted a hammer, but they were no worse off than the first metallurgist, and they did as he must have done.

The first pig, fastened to a wooden handle, served as a hammer with which to forge the second upon an anvil of granite, and they thus obtained a coarse metal, but one which could be utilized.

At length, after much trouble and labor, on the 25th of April, many bars of iron had been forged and turned into crowbars, pincers, pickaxes, mattocks, etc., which Pencroff and Neb declared to be real jewels.

But in order to be in its most serviceable state, iron must be turned into steel. Now steel, which is a combination of iron and carbon, is made in two ways: first from cast iron, by decarburetting the molten metal, which gives natural or puddled steel; and, second, by the method of cementation, which consists in carburetting malleable iron. As the engineer had iron in a pure state, he chose the latter method, and heated the metal with powdered charcoal in a crucible made from refractory earth.

This steel, which was malleable hot and cold, he worked with the hammer. And Neb and Pencroff, skillfully directed, made axe-heads, which, heated red-hot and quickly plunged in cold water, took an excellent temper.

Other instruments, such as planes and hatchets, were rudely fashioned, and bands of steel were made into saws and chisels; and from the iron, mattocks, shovels, pickaxes, hammers, nails, etc., were manufactured.

By the 5th of May the first metallurgic period was ended, the smiths returned to the Chimneys, and new work would soon authorize their assumption of a new title.

CHAPTER XVI. THE QUESTION OF A DWELLING DISCUSSED AGAIN

PENCROFF'S IDEAS—AN EXPLORATION TO THE NORTH OF THE LAKE—THE WESTERN BOUNDARY OF THE PLATEAU—THE SERPENTS—THE OUTLET OF THE LAKE—TOP'S ALARM—TOP SWIMMING—A FIGHT UNDER WATER—THE DUGONG.

It was the 6th of May, corresponding to the 6th of November in the Northern Hemisphere. For some days the sky had been cloudy, and it was important to make provision against winter. However, the temperature had not lessened much, and a centigrade thermometer transported to Lincoln Island would have averaged 10° or 12° above zero. This would not be surprising, since Lincoln Island, from its probable situation in the Southern Hemisphere, was subject to the same climatic influences as Greece or Sicily in the Northern. But just as the intense cold in Greece and Sicily sometimes produces snow and ice, so, in the height of winter, this island would probably experience sudden changes in the temperature against which it would be well to provide.

At any rate, if the cold was not threatening, the rainy season was at hand, and upon this desolate island, in the wide Pacific, exposed to all the inclemency of the elements, the storms would be frequent, and, probably, terrible.

The question of a more comfortable habitation than the Chimneys ought, therefore, to be seriously considered, and promptly acted upon.

Pencroff having discovered the Chimneys, naturally had a predilection for them; but he understood very well that another place must be found. This refuge had already been visited by the sea, and it would not do to expose themselves to a like accident.

"Moreover," added Smith, who was discussing these things with his companions, "there are some precautions to take."

"Why? The island is not inhabited," said the reporter.

"Probably not," answered the engineer, "although we have not yet explored the whole of it; but if there are no human beings, I believe dangerous beasts are numerous. So it will be better to provide a shelter against a possible attack, than for one of us to be tending the fire every night. And then, my friends, we must foresee everything. We are here in a part of the Pacific often frequented by Malay pirates—"

"What, at this distance from land?" exclaimed Herbert.

"Yes, my boy, these pirates are hardy sailors as well as formidable villains, and we must provide for them accordingly."

"Well," said Pencroff, "we will fortify ourselves against two and four-footed savages. But, sir, wouldn't it be as well to explore the island thoroughly before doing anything else?"

"It would be better," added Spilett; "who knows but we may find on the opposite coast one or more of those caves which we have looked for here in vain."

"Very true," answered the engineer, "but you forget, my friends, that we must be somewhere near running water, and that from Mount Franklin we were unable to see either brook or river in that direction. Here, on the contrary, we are between the Mercy and Lake Grant, which is an advantage not to be neglected. And, moreover, as this coast faces the east, it is not as exposed to the trade winds, which blow from the northwest in this hemisphere."

"Well, then, Mr. Smith," replied the sailor, "let us build a house on the edge of the lake. We are no longer without bricks and tools. After having been brickmakers, potters, founders, and smiths, we ought to be masons easily enough."

"Yes, my friend; but before deciding it will be well to look about. A habitation all ready made would save us a great deal of work, and would, doubtless, offer a surer retreat, in which we would be safe from enemies, native as well as foreign?"

"But, Cyrus," answered the reporter, "have we not already examined the whole of this great granite wall without finding even a hole?"

"No, not one!" added Pencroff. "If we could only dig a place in it high out of reach, that would be the thing! I can see it now, on the part overlooking the sea, five or six chambers—"

"With windows!" said Herbert, laughing.

"And a staircase!" added Neb.

"Why do you laugh?" cried the sailor. "Haven't we picks and mattocks? Cannot Mr. Smith make powder to blow up the mine. You will be able, won't you, sir, to make powder when we want it?"

The engineer had listened to the enthusiastic sailor developing these imaginative projects. To attack this mass of granite, even by mining, was an Herculean task, and it was truly vexing that nature had not helped them in their necessity. But he answered Pencroff, by simply proposing to examine the wall more attentively, from the mouth of the river to the angle which ended it to the north. They therefore went out and examined it most carefully for about two miles. But everywhere it rose, uniform and upright, without any visible cavity. The rock-pigeons flying about its summit had their nests in holes drilled in the very crest, or upon the irregularly cut edge of the granite.

To attempt to make a sufficient excavation in such a massive wall even with pickaxe and powder was not to be thought of. It was vexatious enough. By chance, Pencroff had discovered in the Chimneys, which must now be abandoned, the only temporary, habitable shelter on this part of the coast.

When the survey was ended the colonists found themselves at the northern angle of the wall, where it sunk by long declivities to the shore. From this point to its western extremity it was nothing more than a sort of talus composed of stones, earth, and sand bound together by plants, shrubs, and grass, in a slope of about 45°. Here and there the granite thrust its sharp points out from the cliff. Groups of trees grew over these slopes and there was a thin carpet of grass.

But the vegetation extended but a short distance, and then the long stretch of sand, beginning at the foot of the talus, merged into the beach.

Smith naturally thought that the over flow of the lake fell in this direction, as the excess of water from Red Creek must be discharged somewhere, and this point had not been found less on the side already explored, that is to say from the mouth of the creek westward as far as Prospect Plateau.

The engineer proposed to his companions that they clamber up the talus and return to the Chimneys by the heights, exploring the eastern and western shores of the lake. The proposition was accepted, and, in a few minutes, Herbert and Neb had climbed to the plateau, the others following more leisurely.

Two hundred feet distant the beautiful sheet of water shone through the leaves in the sunlight. The landscape was charming. The trees in autumn tints, were harmoniously grouped. Some huge old weatherbeaten trunks stood out in sharp relief against the green turf which covered the ground, and brilliant cockatoos, like moving, prisms, glanced among the branches, uttering their shrill screams.

The colonists, instead of proceeding directly to the north bank of the lake, bore along the edge of the plateau, so as to come back to the mouth of the creek, on its left bank. It was a circuit of about a mile and a half. The walk was easy, as the trees, set wide apart, left free passage between them. They could see that the fertile zone stopped at this point, and that the vegetation here, was less vigorous than anywhere between the creek and the Mercy.

Smith and his companions moved cautiously over this unexplored neighborhood. Bows and arrows and iron-pointed sticks were their sole weapons. But no beast showed itself, and it was probable that the animals kept to the thicker forests in the south. The colonists, however, experienced a disagreeable sensation in seeing Top stop before a huge serpent 14 or 15 feet long. Neb killed it at a blow. Smith examined the reptile, and pronounced it to belong to the species of diamond-serpents eaten by the natives of New South Wales and not venomous, but it was possible others existed whose bite was mortal, such as the forked-tail deaf viper, which rise up under the foot, or the winged serpents, furnished with two ear-like appendages, which enable them to shoot forward with extreme rapidity. Top having gotten over his surprise, pursued these reptiles with reckless fierceness, and his master was constantly obliged to call him in.

The mouth of Red Creek, where it emptied into the lake, was soon reached. The party recognized on the opposite bank the point visited on their descent from Mount Franklin. Smith ascertained that the supply of water from the creek was considerable; there therefore must be an outlet for the overflow somewhere. It was this place which must be found, as, doubtless, it made a fall which could be utilized as a motive power.

The colonists, strolling along, without, however, straying too far from each other, began to follow round the bank of the lake, which was very abrupt. The water was full of fishes, and Pencroff promised himself soon to manufacture some apparatus with which to capture them.

It was necessary first to double the point at the northeast. They had thought that the discharge would be here, as the water flowed close to the edge of the plateau. But as it was not here, the colonists continued along the bank, which, after a slight curve, followed parallel with the sea-shore.

On this side the bank was less wooded, but clumps of trees, here and there, made a picturesque landscape. The whole extent of the lake, unmoved by a single ripple, was visible before, them. Top, beating the bush, flushed many coveys of birds, which Spilett and Herbert saluted with their arrows. One of these birds, cleverly hit by the lad, dropped in the rushes. Top rushing after it, brought back a beautiful slate-colored water fowl. It was a coot, as large as a big partridge, belonging to the group of machio-dactyls, which form the division between the waders and the palmipedes. Poor game and bad tasting, but as Top was not as difficult to please as his masters, it was agreed that the bird would answer for his supper.

Then the colonists, following the southern bank of the lake, soon came to the place they had previously visited. The engineer was very much surprised, as he had seen no indication of an outlet to the surplus water. In talking with the reporter and the sailor, he did not conceal his astonishment.

At this moment, Top, who had been behaving himself quietly, showed signs of alarm. The intelligent animal, running along the bank, suddenly stopped, with one foot raised, and looked into the water as if pointing some invisible game. Then he barked furiously, questioning it, as it were, and again was suddenly silent.

At first neither Smith nor his companions paid any attention to the dog's actions, but his barking became so incessant, that the engineer noticed it.

"What is it, Top?" he called.

The dog bounded towards his master, and, showing a real anxiety, rushed back to the bank. Then, suddenly, he threw himself into the lake.

"Come back here, Top," cried the engineer, not wishing his dog to venture in those suspicious waters.

"What's going on under there?" asked the sailor examining the surface of the lake.

"Top has smelt something amphibious," answered Herbert.

"It must be an alligator," said the reporter.

"I don't think so," answered Smith. "Alligators are not met with in this latitude."

Meantime, Top came ashore at the call of his master, but he could not be quiet; he rushed along the bank, through the tall grass, and, guided by instinct, seemed to be following some object, invisible under the water, which was hugging the shore. Nevertheless the surface was calm and undisturbed by a ripple. Often the colonists stood still on the bank and watched the water, but they could discover nothing. There certainly was some mystery here, and the engineer was much perplexed. "We will follow out this exploration," he said.

In half an hour all had arrived at the southeast angle of the lake, and were again upon Prospect Plateau. They had made the circle of the bank without the engineer having discovered either where or how the surplus water was discharged. "Nevertheless, this outlet exists," he repeated, "and, since it is not outside, it must penetrate the massive granite of the coast!"

"And why do you want to find that out?" asked Spilett.

"Because," answered the engineer, "if the outlet is through the solid rock it is possible that there is some cavity, which could be easily rendered habitable, after having turned the water in another direction."

"But may not the water flow into the sea, through a subterranean outlet at the bottom of the lake?" asked Herbert.

"Perhaps so," answered Smith, "and in that case, since Nature has not aided us, we must build our house ourselves."

As it was 5 o'clock, the colonists were thinking of returning to the Chimneys across the plateau, when Top again became excited, and, barking with rage, before his master could hold him, he sprang a second time into the lake. Every one ran to the bank. The dog was already twenty feet off, and Smith called to him to come back, when suddenly an enormous head emerged from the water.

Herbert instantly recognized it, the comical face, with huge eyes and long silky moustaches. "A manatee," he cried.

Although not a manatee, it was a dugong, which belongs to the same species. The huge monster threw himself upon the dog. His master could do nothing to save him, and, before Spilett or Herbert could draw their bows, Top, seized by the dugong, had disappeared under the water.

Neb, spear in hand, would have sprung to the rescue of the dog, and attacked the formidable monster in its own element, had he not been held back by his master.

Meanwhile a struggle was going on under the water—a struggle which, owing to the powerlessness of the dog, was inexplicable; a struggle which, they could see by the agitation of the surface, was becoming more terrible each moment; in short, a struggle which could only be terminated by the death of the dog. But suddenly, through the midst of a circle of foam, Top appeared, shot upward by some unknown force, rising ten feet in the air, and falling again into the tumultuous waters, from which he escaped to shore without any serious wounds, miraculously saved.

Cyrus Smith and his companions looked on amazed. Still more inexplicable, it seemed as if the struggle under water continued. Doubtless the dugong, after having seized the dog, had been attacked by some more formidable animal, and had been obliged to defend itself.

But this did not last much longer. The water grew red with blood, and the body of the dugong, emerging from the waves, floated on to a little shoal at the southern angle of the lake.

The colonists ran to where the animal lay, and found it dead. Its body was enormous, measuring between 15 and 16 feet long and weighing between 3,000 and 4,000 pounds. On its neck, yawned a wound, which seemed to have been made by some sharp instrument.

What was it that had been able, by this terrible cut, to kill the formidable dugong? None of them could imagine, and, preoccupied with these incidents, they returned to the Chimneys.

CHAPTER XVII. A VISIT TO THE LAKE

THE DIRECTION OF THE CURRENT—THE PROSPECTS OF CYRUS SMITH—
THE DUGONG FAT—THE USE OF THE SCHISTOUS LIMESTONE—THE
SULPHATE OF IRON—HOW GLYCERINE IS MADE—SOAP—SALTPETRE—
SULPHURIC ACID-NITRIC ACID-THE NEW OUTLET.

The next day, the 7th of May, Smith and Spilett, leaving Neb to prepare the breakfast, climbed the plateau, while Herbert and Pencroff went after a fresh supply of wood.

The engineer and the reporter soon arrived, at the little beach where the dugong lay stranded. Already flocks of birds had gathered about the carcass, and it was necessary to drive them off with stones, as the engineer wished to preserve the fat for the use of the colony. As to the flesh of the dugong, it would undoubtedly furnish excellent food, as in certain portions of the Malay archipelago it is reserved for the table of the native princes. But it was Neb's affair to look after that.

Just now, Cyrus Smith was thinking of other things. The incident of the day before was constantly presenting itself. He wanted to solve the mystery of that unseen combat, and to know what congener of the mastodons or other marine monster had given the dugong this strange wound.

He stood upon the border of the lake, looking upon its tranquil surface sparkling under the rays of the rising sun. From the little beach where the dugong lay, the waters deepened slowly towards the centre, and the lake might be likened to a large basin, filled by the supply from Red Creek.

"Well, Cyrus," questioned the reporter, "I don't see anything suspicious in this?"

"No, my dear fellow, and I am at a loss how to explain yesterday's affair."

"The wound on this beast is strange enough, and I can't understand how Top could have been thrown out of the water in that way. One would suppose that it had been done by a strong arm, and that that same arm, wielding a poignard, had given the dugong his death-wound."

"It would seem so," answered the engineer, who had become thoughtful. "There is something here which I cannot understand. But neither can we explain how I myself was saved; how I was snatched from the waves and borne to the downs. Therefore, I am sure there is some mystery which we will some day discover. In the meantime, let us take care not to discuss these singular incidents before our companions, but keep our thoughts for each other, and continue our work."

It will be remembered that Smith had not yet discovered what became of the surplus water of the lake, and as there was no indication of its ever overflowing, an outlet must exist somewhere. He was surprised, therefore, on noticing a slight current just at this place. Throwing in some leaves and bits of wood, and observing their drift, he followed this current, which brought him to the southern end of the lake. Here he detected a slight depression in the waters, as if they were suddenly lost in some opening below.

Smith listened, placing his ear to the surface of the lake, and distinctly heard the sound of a subterranean fall.

"It is there," said he, rising, "there that the water is discharged, there, doubtless, through a passage in the massive granite that it goes to join the sea, through cavities which we will be able to utilize to our profit! Well! I will find out!"

The engineer cut a long branch, stripped off its leaves, and, plunging it down at the angle of the two banks, he found that there was a large open hole a foot below the surface. This was the long-sought-for outlet, and such was the force of the current that the branch was snatched from his hands and disappeared.

"There can be no doubt of it now," repeated the engineer. "It is the mouth of the outlet, and I am going to work to uncover it.

"How?" inquired Spilett.

"By lowering the lake three feet."

"And how will you do that?"

"By opening another vent larger than this."

"Whereabouts, Cyrus?"

"Where the bank is nearest the coast."

"But it is a granite wall," exclaimed Spilett,

"Very well," replied Smith. "I will blow up the wall, and the waters, escaping, will subside so as to discover the orifice—"

"And will make a waterfall at the cliff," added the reporter.

"A fall that we will make use of!" answered Cyrus. "Come, come!"

The engineer hurried off his companion, whose confidence in Smith was such that he doubted not the success of the undertaking. And yet, this wall of granite, how would they begin: how, without powder, with but imperfect tools, could they blast the rock? Had not the engineer undertaken a work beyond his skill to accomplish?

When Smith and the reporter re-entered the Chimneys, they found Herbert and Pencroff occupied in unloading their raft.

"The wood-choppers have finished, sir," said the sailor, laughing, "and when you want masons—"

"Not masons, but chemists," interrupted the engineer.

"Yes," added Spilett, "we are going to blow up the island."

"Blow up the island?" cried the sailor.

"A part of it, at least," answered the reporter.

"Listen to me, my friends," said the engineer, who thereupon made known the result of his observations. His theory was, that a cavity, more or less considerable, existed in the mass of granite which upheld Prospect Plateau, and he undertook to penetrate to it. To do this, it was first necessary to free the present opening, in other words to lower the level of the lake by giving the water a larger issue. To do this they must manufacture an explosive with which to make a drain in another part of the bank. It was this Smith was going to attempt to do, with the minerals Nature had placed at his disposal.

All entered into the proposal with enthusiasm. Neb and Pencroff were at once detailed to extract the fat from the dugong and to preserve the flesh for food; and soon after their departure the others, carrying the hurdle, went up the shore to the vein of coal, where were to be found the schistous pyrites of which Smith had procured a specimen.

The whole day was employed in bringing a quantity of these pyrites to the Chimneys, and by evening they had several tons.

On the next day, the 8th of May, the engineer began his manipulations. The schistous pyrites were principally composed of carbon, of silica, of alumina, and sulphuret of iron,—these were in excess,—it was necessary to separate the sulphuret and change it into sulphate by the quickest means. The sulphate obtained, they would extract the Sulphuric acid, which was what they wanted.

Sulphuric acid is one of the agents in most general use, and the industrial importance of a nation can be measured by its consumption. In the future this acid would be of use to the colonists in making candles, tanning skins, etc., but at present the engineer reserved it for another purpose.

Smith chose, behind the Chimneys, a place upon which the earth was carefully levelled. On this he made a pile of branches and cut wood, on which were placed pieces of schistous pyrites leaning against each other, and then all was covered over with a thin layer of pyrites previously reduced to the size of nuts.

This done, they set the wood on, fire, which in turn inflamed the schist, as it contained carbon and sulphur. Then new layers of pyrites were arranged so as to form an immense heap, surrounded with earth, and grass, with air-holes left here and there, just as is done in reducing a pile of wood to charcoal.

Then they left the transformation to complete itself. It would take ten or twelve days for the sulphuret of iron and the alumina to change into sulphates, which substances were equally soluble; the others—silica, burnt carbon, and cinders—were not so.

While this chemical process was accomplishing itself, Smith employed his companions upon other branches of the work, which they undertook with the utmost zeal.

Neb and Pencroff had taken the fat from the dugong, which had been placed in large earthen jars. It was necessary to separate the glycerine from this fat by saponifying it. It was sufficient, in order to do this, to treat it with chalk or soda. Chalk was not wanting, but by this treatment the soap would be calcareous and useless, while by using soda, a soluble soap, which could be employed for domestic purposes, would be the result. Cyrus Smith, being a practical man, preferred to try to get the soda. Was this difficult? No, since many kinds of marine plants abounded on the shore, and all those fucaceæ which form wrack. They therefore gathered a great quantity of these seaweed, which were first dried, and, afterwards, burnt in trenches in the open air. The combustion of these plants was continued for many days, so that the heat penetrated throughout, and the result was the greyish compact mass, long known as "natural soda."

This accomplished, the engineer treated the fat with the soda, which gave both a soluble soap and the neutral substance, glycerine.

But this was not all. Smith wanted, in view of his future operations, another substance, nitrate of potash, better known as saltpetre.

He could make this by treating carbonate of potash, which is easily extracted from vegetable ashes, with nitric acid. But this acid, which was precisely what he wanted in order to complete his undertaking successfully, he did not have. Fortunately, in this emergency, Nature furnished him with saltpetre, without any labor other than picking it up. Herbert had found a vein of this mineral at the foot of Mount Franklin, and all they had to do was to purify the salt.

These different undertakings, which occupied eight days, were finished before the sulphate of iron was ready. During the interval the colonists made some refractory pottery in plastic clay, and constructed a brick furnace of a peculiar shape, in which to distil the sulphate of iron. All was finished on the 18th of May, the very day the chemical work was completed.

The result of this latter operation, consisting of sulphate of iron, sulphate of alumina, silica, and a residue of charcoal and cinders, was placed, in a basin full of water. Having stirred up the mixture, they let it settle, and at length poured off a clear liquid holding the sulphates of iron and alumina in solution. Finally, this liquid was partly evaporated, the sulphate of iron crystalized, and the mother-water was thrown away.

Smith had now a quantity of crystals, from which the sulphuric acid was to be extracted.

In commerce this acid is manufactured in large quantities and by elaborate processes. The engineer had no such means at his command, but he knew that in Bohemia an acid known as Nordhausen is made by simpler means, which has, moreover, the advantage of being non-concentrated. For obtaining the acid in this way, all the engineer had to do was to calcinize the crystals in a closed jar in such a manner that the sulphuric acid distilled in vapor, which would in turn produce the acid by condensation.

It was for this that the refractory jars and the furnace had been made. The operation was a success; and on the 20th of May, twelve days after having begun, Smith was the possessor of the agent which he expected to use later in different ways.

What did he want with it now? Simply to produce nitric acid, which was perfectly easy, since the saltpetre, attacked by the sulphuric acid, would give it by distillation.

But how would he use this acid? None of the others knew, as he had spoken no word on the subject.

The work approached completion, and one more operation would procure the substance which had required all this labor. The engineer mixed the nitric acid with the glycerine, which latter had been previously concentrated by evaporation in a water-bath, and without employing any freezing mixture, obtained many pints of an oily yellow liquid.

This last operation Smith had conducted alone, at some distance from the Chimneys, as he feared an explosion, and when he returned, with a flagon of this liquid, to his friends, he simply said:—"Here is some nitro-glycerine!"

It was, in truth, that terrible product, whose explosive power is, perhaps, ten times as great as that of gunpowder, and which has caused so many accidents! Although, since means have been found of transforming it into dynamite, that is, of mixing it with clay or sugar or some solid substance sufficiently porous to hold it, the dangerous liquid can be used with more safety. But dynamite was not known when the colonists were at work on Lincoln Island.

"And is that stuff going to blow up the rocks?" asked Pencroff, incredulously.

"Yes, my friend," answered the engineer, "and it will do all the better since the granite is very hard and will oppose more resistance to the explosion."

"And when will we see all this, sir?"

"To-morrow," when we have drilled a hole," answered the engineer.

Early the next morning, the 21st of May, the miners betook themselves to a point which formed the east bank of Lake Grant, not more than 500 feet from the coast. At this place the plateau was lower than the lake, which was upheld by the coping of granite. It was plain that could they break this the waters would escape by this vent, and, forming a stream, flow over the inclined surface of the plateau, and be precipitated in a waterfall over the cliff on to the shore. Consequently, there would be a general lowering of the lake, and the orifice of the water would be uncovered—this was to be the result.

The coping must be broken. Pencroff, directed by the engineer, attacked its outer facing vigorously. The hole which he made with his pick began under a horizontal edge of the bank, and penetrated obliquely so as to reach a level lower than the lake's surface. Thus the blowing up of the rocks would permit the water to escape freely and consequently lower the lake sufficiently.

The work was tedious, as the engineer, wishing to produce a violent shock, had determined to use not less than two gallons of nitro-glycerine in the operation. But Pencroff and Neb, taking turns at the work, did so well, that by 4 o'clock in the afternoon it was achieved.

Now came the question of igniting the explosive. Ordinarily, nitro-glycerine is ignited by the explosion of fulminated caps, as, if lighted without percussion, this substance burns and does not explode.

Smith could doubtless make a cap. Lacking fulminate, he could easily obtain a substance analogous to gun-cotton, since he had nitric acid at hand. This substance pressed in a cartridge, and introduced into the nitro-glycerine, could be lighted with a slow match, and produce the explosion.

But Smith knew that their liquid had the property of exploding under a blow. He determined, therefore, to make use of this property, reserving the other means in case this experiment failed.

The blow of a hammer upon some drops of the substance spread on a hard stone, suffices to provoke an explosion. But no one could give those blows without being a victim to the operation. Smith's idea was to suspend a heavy mass of iron by means of a vegetable fibre to an upright post, so as to have the iron hang directly over the hole. Another long fibre, previously soaked in sulphur, was to be fastened to the middle of the first and laid along the ground many feet from this excavation. The fire was to be applied to this second fibre, it would burn till it reached the first and set it on fire, then the latter would break and the iron be precipitated upon the nitro-glycerine.

The apparatus was fixed in place; then the engineer, after having made his companions go away, filled the hole so that the fluid overflowed the opening, and spread some drops underneath the mass of suspended iron.

This done, Smith lit the end of the sulfured fibre, and, leaving the place, returned with his companions to the Chimneys.

Twenty-five minutes after a tremendous explosion was heard. It seemed as if the whole island trembled to its base. A volley of stones rose into the air as if they had been vomited from a volcano. The concussion was such that it shook the Chimneys. The colonists, though two miles away, were thrown to the ground. Rising again, they clambered up to the plateau and hurried towards the place.

A large opening had been torn in the granite coping. A rapid stream of water escaped through it, leaping and foaming across the plateau, and, reaching the brink, fell a distance of 300 feet to the shore below.

CHAPTER XVIII. PENCROFF DOUBTS NO MORE

THE OLD OUTLET OF THE LAKE—A SUBTERRANEAN DESCENT—THE WAY THROUGH THE GRANITE—TOP HAS DISAPPEARED—THE CENTRAL CAVERN— THE LOWER WELL—MYSTERY—THE BLOWS WITH THE PICK—THE RETURN.

Smith's project had succeeded; but, as was his manner, he stood motionless, absorbed, his lips closed, giving no sign of satisfaction. Herbert was all enthusiasm; Neb jumped with joy; Pencroff, shaking his head, murmured:—

"Indeed, our engineer does wonders!"

The nitro-glycerine had worked powerfully. The opening was so great that at least a three times greater volume of water escaped by it than by the former outlet. In a little while, therefore, the level of the lake would be lowered two feet or more.

The colonists returned to the Chimneys, and collecting some picks, spears, ropes, a steel and tinder, returned to the plateau. Top went with them.

On the way the sailor could not resist saying to the engineer:— "But do you really think, Mr. Smith, that one could blow up the whole island with this beautiful liquid of yours?"

"Doubtless," replied the other, "island, continents, the world itself. It is only a question of quantity."

"Couldn't you use this nitro-glycerine to load firearms."

"No, Pencroff, because it is too shattering. But it would be easy to make gun-cotton, or even common powder, as we have the material. Unfortunately, the guns themselves are wanting."

"But with a little ingenuity!—"

Pencroff had erased "impossible" from his vocabulary.

The colonists having reached Prospect Plateau, hastened at once to the old outlet of the lake, which ought now to be uncovered. And when the water no longer poured through it, it would, doubtless, be easy to explore its interior arrangement.

In a few moments they reached the lower angle of the lake, and saw at a glance what the result was.

There, in the granite wall of the lake, above the water-level, appeared the long-looked for opening. A narrow ledge, left bare, by the subsidence of the water, gave them access to it. The opening was twenty feet wide, though only two feet high. It was like the gutter-mouth in a pavement. It was not open enough for the party to get in, but Neb and Pencroff, with their picks, in less than an hour had given it a sufficient height.

The engineer looked in and saw that the walls of the opening in its upper part showed a slope of from 30° to 35°. And, therefore, unless they became much steeper it would be easy to descend, perhaps, to the level of the sea. And if, as was probable, some vast cavern existed in the interior of the massive granite, it was possible that they could make use of it.

"What are we waiting for, Mr. Smith," cried the sailor, all impatience to begin the exploration, "Top, you see, has gone ahead!"

"We must have some light," said the engineer. "Go, Neb, and cut some resinous branches."

The black man and Herbert ran to some pine and evergreens growing upon the bank, and soon returned with branches which were made into torches. Having lit them, the colonists, with Smith leading, entered the dark passage, but recently filled with water.

Contrary to their expectation, the passage grew higher as they advanced, until soon they were able to walk upright. The granite walls, worn, by the water, were very slippery, and the party had to look out for falls. They, therefore, fastened themselves together with a cord, like mountain climbers. Fortunately, some granite steps made the descent less perilous. Drops of water, still clinging to the rocks, glistened like stalactites in the torchlight. The engineer looked carefully at this black granite. He could not see a stratum or a flaw. The mass was compact and of fine grain, and the passage must have been coeval with the island. It had not been worn little by little by the constant action of water. Pluto, and not Neptune, had shaped it; and the traces of igneous action were still visible upon its surface.

The colonists descended but slowly. They experienced some emotion in thus adventuring into the depths of the earth, in being its first human visitants. No one spoke, but each was busied with his own reflections and the thought occurred to more than one, that perhaps some pulp or other gigantic cephalopod might inhabit the interior cavities which communicated with the sea. It was, therefore, necessary to advance cautiously.

Top was ahead of the little troop and they could rely on the dog's sagacity to give the alarm on occasion. After having descended 100 feet, Smith halted, and the others came up with him. They were standing in a cavern of moderate size. Drops of water fell from the roof, but they did not ooze through the rocks, they were simply the last traces of the torrent which had so long roared through this place, and the air, though humid, emitted no mephitic vapor.

"Well, Cyrus," said Spilett, "here is a retreat sufficiently unknown and hidden in the depths, but it is uninhabitable."

"How, uninhabitable?" asked the sailor.

"Why, it is too small and too dark."

"Cannot we make it bigger, blast it out, and make openings for the light and air?" answered Pencroff, who now thought nothing impracticable.

"Let us push on," said Smith. "Perhaps lower down, nature will have spared us this work."

"We are only a third of the way down," observed Herbert.

"But 100 feet," responded Cyrus; "and it is possible that 100 feet lower—."

"Where is Top?" asked Neb, interrupting his master.

They looked about the cavern. The dog was not there.

"Let us overtake him," said Smith, resuming the march. The engineer noted carefully all the deviations of the route, and easily kept a general idea of their direction, which was towards the sea. The party had not descended more than fifty feet further, when their attention was arrested by distant sounds coming from the depths of the rock. They stopped and listened. These sounds, borne along the passage, as the voice through an acoustic tube, were distinctly heard.

"Its Top's barking!" cried Herbert.

"Yes, and the brave dog is barking furiously," added Pencroff.

"We have our spears," said Smith. "Come on, and be ready."

"It is becoming more and more interesting," whispered Spilett to the sailor, who nodded assent.

They hurried to the rescue of the dog. His barks grew more distinct. They could hear that he was in a strange rage. Had he been captured by some animal whom he had disturbed? Without thinking of the danger, the colonists felt themselves drawn on by an irresistible curiosity, and slipped rather than ran down the passage. Sixteen feet lower they came up with the dog.

There, the corridor opened out into a vast and magnificent cavern. Top, rushing about, was barking furiously. Pencroff and Neb, shaking their torches, lit up all the inequalities of the granite, and the others, with their spears ready, held themselves prepared for any emergency.

But the enormous cavern was empty. The colonists searched everywhere; they could find no living thing. Nevertheless, Top continued barking, and neither threats nor caresses could stop him.

"There must be some place where the water escaped to the sea," said the engineer.

"Yes, and look out for a hole," answered Pencroff.

"On, Top, on," cried Smith, and the dog, encouraged by his master, ran towards the end of the cavern, and redoubled his barking.

Following him, they saw by the light of the torches the opening of what looked like a well in the granite. Here, undoubtedly, was the place where the water had found its way out of the cavern, but this time, instead of being a corridor sloping and accessible, it was a perpendicular well, impossible to descend.

The torches were waved above the opening. They saw nothing. Smith broke off a burning branch and dropped it into the abyss. The resin, fanned by the wind of its fall, burned brightly and illuminated the interior of the pit, but showed nothing else. Then the flame was extinguished with a slight hiss, which indicated that it had reached the water, which must be the sea level.

The engineer calculated, from the time taken in the fall, that the depth was about ninety feet. The floor of the cavern was therefore that distance above the sea.

"Here is our house," said Smith.

"But it was preoccupied," said Spilett, whose curiosity was unsatisfied.

"Well, the thing that had it, whether amphibious or not, has fled by this outlet and vacated in our favor," replied the engineer.

"Any how, I should like to have been Top a quarter of an hour ago," said the sailor, "for he does not bark at nothing."

Smith looked at his dog, and those who were near him heard him murmur:—

"Yes, I am convinced that Top knows more than we do about many things!"

However, the wishes of the colonists had been in a great measure realized. Chance, aided by the marvelous acuteness of their chief, had done them good service. Here they had at their disposal a vast cavern, whose extent could not be estimated in the insufficient light of the torches, but which could certainly be easily partitioned off with bricks into chambers, and arranged, if not as a house, at least as a spacious suite of rooms. The water having left it, could not return. The place was free.

But two difficulties remained, the possibility of lighting the cavern and the necessity of rendering it easier of access. The first could not be done from above as the enormous mass of granite was over them; but, perhaps, they would be able to pierce the outer wall which faced the sea. Smith, who during the descent had kept account of the slope, and therefore of the length of the passage, believed that this part of the wall could not be very thick. If light could be thus obtained, so could entrance, as it was as easy to pierce a door as windows, and to fix a ladder on the outside.

Smith communicated his ideas to his companions.

"Then let us set to work!" answered Pencroff; "I have my pick and will I soon make daylight in the granite! Where shall I begin?"

"Here," answered the engineer, showing the strong sailor a considerable hollow in the wall, which greatly diminished its thickness.

Pencroff attacked the granite, and for half an hour, by the light of the torches, made the splinters fly about him. Then Neb took his place, and Spilett after Neb. The work continued, two hours longer, and, when it seemed as if the wall could not be thicker than the length of the pick, at the last stroke of Spilett the implement, passing through, fell on the outside.

"Hurrah forever!" cried Pencroff.

The wall was but three feet thick.

Smith looked through the opening, which was eighty feet above the ground. Before him extended the coast, the islet, and, beyond, the boundless sea.

Through the hole the light entered in floods, inundating the splendid cavern and producing a magical effect. While on the left hand it measured only thirty feet in height and one hundred in length, to the right it was enormous, and its vault rose to a height of more than eighty feet. In some places, granite pillars, irregularly disposed, supported the arches as in the nave of a cathedral. Resting upon a sort of lateral piers, here, sinking into elliptic arches, there, rising in ogive mouldings, losing itself in the dark bays, half seen in the shadow through the fantastic arches, ornamented by a profusion of projections which seemed like pendants, this vaulted roof afforded a picturesque blending of all the architectures—Byzantine, Roman, Gothic—that the hand of man has produced. And this was the work of nature! She alone had constructed this magic Alhambra in a granite rock!

The colonists were overcome with admiration. Expecting to find but a narrow cavern, they found themselves in a sort of marvellous palace, and Neb had taken off his hat as if he had been transported into a temple!

Exclamations of pleasure escaped from their lips, and the hurrahs echoed and reechoed from the depths of the dark nave.

"My friends," cried Smith, "when we shall have lighted the interior of this place, when we shall have arranged our chambers, our store-rooms, our offices in the left-hand portion, we will still have this splendid cavern, which shall be our study and our museum!

"And we will call it—" asked Herbert.

"Granite House," answered Smith; and his companions saluted the name with their cheers.

By this time the torches were nearly consumed, and as, in order to return, it was necessary to regain the summit of the plateau and to remount the corridor, it was decided to postpone until the morrow the work of arranging their new home.

Before leaving, Smith leaned over the dark pit once more and listened attentively. But there was no sound from these depths save that of the water agitated by the undulations of the surge. A resinous torch was again thrown in, lighting up anew for an instant the walls of the well, but nothing suspicions was revealed. If any marine monster had been inopportunely surprised by the retreat of the waters, he had already regained the open sea by the subterranean passage which extended under the shore.

Nevertheless the engineer stood motionless, listening attentively, his gaze plunged in the abyss, without speaking.

Then the sailor approached him. Touching his arm, he said: "Mr. Smith."

"What is it, my friend," responded the engineer, like one returning from the land of dreams.

"The torches are nearly out."

"Forward!" said Smith; and the little troop left the cavern and began the ascent through the dark weir. Top walked behind, still growling in an odd way. The ascension was sufficiently laborious, and the colonists stopped for a few minutes at the upper grotto, which formed a sort of landing half way up the long granite stairway. Then they began again to mount, and pretty soon they felt the fresh air. The drops, already evaporated, no longer shone on the walls. The light of the torches diminished; Neb's went out, and they had to hasten in order to avoid having to grope their way through, the profound darkness. A little before 4 o'clock, just as the torch of the sailor was burnt out, Smith and his companions emerged from the mouth of the passage.

CHAPTER XIX. SMITH'S PLAN

THE FRONT OF GRANITE HOUSE—THE ROPE LADDER—PENCROFF'S IDEAS—THE AROMATIC HERBS—A NATURAL WARREN—GETTING WATER—THE VIEW FROM THE WINDOWS OF GRANITE HOUSE.

On the next day, May 22, the colonists proceeded to take possession of their new abode. They longed to exchange their insufficient shelter for the vast retreat in the rock, impenetrable to wind and wave. Still they did not intend altogether to abandon the Chimneys, but to make a workshop of it. Smith's first care was to ascertain exactly over what point rose the face of Granite House.

He went down on the shore to the foot of the immense wall, and, as the pickaxe, which slipped from the reporter's hands, must have fallen perpendicularly, he could ascertain, by finding this pickaxe, the place where the granite had been pierced. And, in fact, when the implement was found, half buried in the sand, the hole in the rock could be seen eighty feet above it, in a straight line. Rock pigeons were already fluttering in and out by this narrow opening. They evidently thought Granite House had been discovered for their benefit.

The engineer intended to divide the right portion of the cavern into several chambers opening upon an entrance-corridor, and lighted by five windows and a door cut in the face of the rock. Pencroff agreed with him as to the window, but could not understand the use of the door, since the old weir furnished a natural staircase to Granite House.

"My friend," said Smith, "if we could get to our abode by the weir, so can others. I want to block up this passage at its month, to seal it hermetically, and even, if necessary, to conceal the entrance by damming up the lake."

"And how shall we get in?" said the sailor.

"By a rope ladder from the outside," answered Smith, "which we can pull up after us."

"But why take so many precautions?" said Pencroff. "So far, the animals we have found here have not been formidable; and there are certainly no natives."

"Are you so sure, Pencroff?" said the engineer, looking steadily at the sailor.

"Of course we shall not be perfectly sure till we have explored every part."

"Yes," said Smith, "for we know as yet only a small portion. But even if there are no enemies upon the island, they may come from the outside, for this part of the Pacific is a dangerous region. We must take every precaution."

So the facade of Granite House was lighted with five windows, and with a door opening upon the "apartments," and admitting plenty of light into that wonderful nave which was to serve as their principal hallroom. This facade, eighty feet above the ground, was turned to the east, and caught the first rays of the morning sun. It was protected by the slope of the rock from the piercing northeast wind. In the meantime, while the sashes of the windows were being made, the engineer meant to close the openings with thick shutters, which would keep out wind and rain, and which could be readily concealed. The first work was to hollow out these windows. But the pickaxe was at a disadvantage among these hard rocks, and Smith again had recourse to the nitro-glycerine, which, used in small quantities, had the desired effect. Then the work was finished by the pick and mattock—the five ogive windows, the bay, the bull's-eyes, and the door—and, some days after the work was begun, the sun shone in upon the innermost recesses of Granite House.

According to Smith's plan, the space had been divided into five compartments looking out upon the sea; upon the right was the hall, opposite to the door from which the ladder was to hang, then a kitchen thirty feet long, a dining-room forty feet long, a sleeping-room of the same size, and last a "guest chamber," claimed by Pencroff; and bordering on the great hall.

These rooms, or rather this suite of rooms, in which they were to live, did not occupy the full depth of the cave. They opened upon a corridor which ran between them and a long storehouse, where were kept their utensils and provisions. All the products of the island, animal and vegetable, could be kept there in good condition and free from damp. They had room enough, and there was a place for everything. Moreover, the colonists still had at their disposal the little grotto above the large cavern, which would serve them as a sort of attic. This plan agreed upon, they became brickmakers again, and brought their bricks to the foot of Granite House.

Until that time the colonists had had access to the cavern only by the old weir. This mode of communication compelled them first to climb up Prospect Plateau, going round by the river, to descend 200 feet through the passage, and then to ascend the same distance when they wanted to regain the plateau. This involved fatigue and loss of time. Smith resolved to begin at once the construction of a strong rope ladder, which, once drawn up after them, would render the entrance to Granite House absolutely inaccessible. This ladder was made with the greatest care, and its sides were twisted of fibres by means of a shuttle. Thus constructed, it had the strength of a cable. The rungs were made of a kind of red cedar, with light and durable branches; and the whole was put together by the practised hand of Pencroff.

Another kind of tackle was made of vegetable fibre, and a sort of derrick was setup at the door of Granite House. In this way the bricks could easily be carried to the level of Granite House; and when some thousands of them were on the spot, with abundance of lime, they began work on the interior. They easily set up the wood partitions, and in a short time the space was divided into chambers and a store-house, according to the plan agreed upon.

These labors went on quickly under the direction of the engineer, who himself wielded hammer and trowel. They worked confidently and gaily. Pencroff, whether carpenter, ropemaker, or mason, always had a joke ready, and all shared in his good humor. His confidence in the engineer was absolute. All their wants would be supplied in Smith's own time. He dreamed of canals, of quarries, of mines, of machinery, even of railroads, one day, to cover the island. The engineer let Pencroff talk. He knew how contagious is confidence; he smiled to hear him, and said nothing of his own inquietude. But in his heart he feared that no help could come from the outside. In that part of the Pacific, out of the track of ships, and at such a distance from other land that no boat could dare put out to sea, they had only themselves to rely upon.

But, as the sailor said, they were far ahead of the Swiss Family Robinson, for whom miracles were always being wrought. In truth they knew Nature; and he who knows Nature will succeed when others would lie down to die.

Herbert especially distinguished himself in the work. He understood at a word and was prompt in execution. Smith grew fonder of him every day and Herbert was devoted to the engineer. Pencroff saw the growing friendship, but the honest sailor was not jealous. Neb was courage, zeal, and self-denial in person. He relied on his master as absolutely as Pencroff, but his enthusiasm was not so noisy. The sailor and he were great friends. As to Spilett, his skill and efficiency were a daily wonder to Pencroff. He was the model of a newspaper man—quick alike to understand and to perform.

The ladder was put in place May 28. It was eighty feet high, and consisted of 100 rungs; and, profiting by a projection in the face of the cliff, about forty feet up, Smith had divided it into two parts. This projection served as a sort of landing-place for the head of the lower ladder, shortening it, and thus lessening its swing. They fastened it with a cord so that it could easily be raised to the level of Granite House. The upper ladder they fastened at top and bottom. In this way the ascent was much more easy. Besides, Smith counted upon putting up at some future time a hydraulic elevator, which would save his companions much fatigue and loss of time.

The colonists rapidly accustomed themselves to the use of this ladder. The sailor, who was used to shrouds and ratlines, was their teacher. The great trouble was with Top, whose four feet were not intended for ladders. But Pencroff was persevering, and Top at last learned to run up and down as nimbly as his brothers of the circus. We cannot say whether the sailor was proud of this pupil, but he sometimes carried Top up on his back, and Top made no complaints.

All this time, the question of provisions was not neglected. Every day Herbert and the reporter spent some hours in the chase. They hunted only through Jacamar Woods, on the left of the river, for, in the absence of boat or bridge, they had not yet crossed the Mercy. The immense woody tracts which they had named the Forests of the Far West were entirely unexplored. This important excursion was set apart for the first five days of the coming spring. But Jacamar Woods were not wanting in game; kangaroos and boars were plenty there, and the iron-tipped spears, the bows and arrows of the hunters did wonders. More than this, Herbert discovered, at the southwest corner of, the lagoon, a natural warren, a sort of moist meadow covered with willows and aromatic herbs, which perfumed the air, such as thyme, basil, and all sorts of mint, of which rabbits are so fond. The reporter said that when the feast was spread for them it would be strange if the rabbits did not come; and the hunters explored the warren carefully. At all events, it produced an abundance of useful plants, and would give a naturalist plenty of work. Herbert gathered a quantity of plants possessing different medicinal properties, pectoral, astringent, febrifuge, anti-rheumatic. When Pencroff asked of what good were all this collection of herbs:— "To cure us when we are sick," answered the boy.

"Why should we be sick, since there are no doctors on the island?" said Pencroff, quite seriously.

To this no reply could be made, but the lad went on gathering his bundle, which was warmly welcomed at Granite House; especially as he had found some Mountain Mint, known in North America as "Oswego Tea," which produces a pleasant beverage.

That day the hunters, in their search, reached the site of the warren. The ground was perforated with little holes like a colander.

"Burrows!" cried Herbert.

"But are they inhabited?"

"That is the question."

A question which was quickly resolved. Almost immediately, hundreds of little animals, like rabbits, took to flight in every direction, with such rapidity that Top himself was distanced. But the reporter was determined not to quit the place till he had captured half a dozen of the little beasts. He wanted them now for the kitchen: domestication would come later. With a few snares laid at the mouth of the burrows, the affair would be easy; but there were no snares, nor materials for snares; so they patiently rummaged every form with their sticks, until four rodents were taken.

They were rabbits, much like their European congeners, and commonly known as "American hares." They were brought back to Granite Home, and figured in that evening's meal. Delicious eating they were; and the warren bade fair to be a most valuable reserve for the colonists.

On May 31, the partitions were finished, and nothing remained but to furnish the rooms, which would occupy the long days of winter. A chimney was built in the room which served as a kitchen. The construction of the stove-pipe gave them a good deal of trouble. The simplest material was clay; and as they did not wish to have any outlet on the upper plateau, they pierced a hole above the kitchen window, and conducted the pipe obliquely to this hole. No doubt during an eastern gale the pipe would smoke, but the wind rarely blew from that quarter, and head-cook Neb was not particular

When these domestic arrangements had been made, the engineer proceeded to block up the mouth of the old weir by the lake, so as to prevent any approach from that quarter. Great square blocks were rolled to the opening, and strongly cemented together. Smith did not yet attempt to put in execution his project of damming up the waters of the lake so as to conceal this weir; he was satisfied with concealing the obstruction he had placed there by means of grass, shrubs, and thistles, which were planted in the interstices of the rocks, and which by the next spring would sprout up luxuriantly. Meanwhile he utilized the weir in conducting to their new abode a little stream of fresh water from the lake. A little drain, constructed just below its level, had the effect of supplying them with twenty-five or thirty gallons a day; so there was likely to be no want of water at Granite House.

At last, all was finished, just in time for the tempestuous season. They closed the windows with thick shutters till Smith should have time to make glass from the sand. In the rocky projections around the windows Spilett had arranged, very artistically, plants of various kinds and long floating grasses, and thus the windows were framed picturesquely in green. The denizens of this safe and solid dwelling could but be delighted with their work. The windows opened upon a limitless horizon, shut in only by the two Mandible Capes on the north and by Claw Cape at the south. Union Bay spread magnificently before them. They had reason enough to be satisfied, and Pencroff did not spare his praises of what he called "his suite on the fifth floor."

CHAPTER XX. THE RAINY SEASON

WHAT TO WEAR-A SEAL-HUNT—CANDLE-MAKING—-WORK IN THE
GRANITE HOUSE—THE TWO CAUSEWAYS—RETURN FROM A VISIT TO THE
OYSTER-BED—WHAT HERBERT FOUND IS HIS POCKET.

The winter season began in earnest with the month of June, which corresponded with December in our northern hemisphere. Showers and storms succeeded each other without an intermission, and the inmates of the Granite House could appreciate the advantages of a dwelling impervious to the weather. The Chimneys would indeed have proved a miserable shelter against the inclemency of the winter; they feared even lest the high tides driven by the sea-wind should pour in and destroy their furnaces and their foundry. All this month of June was occupied with various labors, which left plenty of time for hunting and fishing, so that the reserve stock of food was constantly kept up. Pencroff intended, as soon as he had time, to set traps, from which he expected great results. He had made snares of ligneous fibre, and not a day passed but some rodent was captured from the warren. Neb spent all his time in smoking and salting meat.

The question of clothes now came up for serious discussion. The colonists had no other garments than those which they wore when the balloon cast them on shore. These, fortunately, were warm and substantial; and by dint of extreme care, even their linen had been kept clean and whole; but everything would soon wear out, and moreover, during a vigorous winter, they would suffer severely from cold. Here Smith was fairly baffled. He had been occupied in providing for their most urgent wants, food and shelter, and the winter was upon them before the clothes problem could be solved. They must resign themselves to bear the cold with fortitude, and when the dry season returned would undertake a great hunt of the moufflons, which they had seen on Mount Franklin, and whose wool the engineer could surely make into warm thick cloth. He would think over the method.

"Well, we must toast ourselves before the fire!" said Pencroff." There's plenty of fire wood, no reason for sparing it."

"Besides," added Spilett, "Lincoln Island is not in very high latitude, and the winters are probably mild. Did you not say, Cyrus that the thirty-fifth parallel corresponded with that of Spain in the other hemisphere?"

"Yes," said the engineer, "but the winter in Spain is sometimes very cold, with snow and ice, and we may have a hard time of it. Still we are on an island, and have a good chance for more moderate weather."

"Why, Mr. Smith?" said Herbert.

"Because the sea, my boy, may be considered as an immense reservoir, in which the summer heat lies stored. At the coming of winter this heat is again given out, so that the neighboring regions have always a medium temperature, cooler in summer and warmer in winter."

"We shall see," said Pencroff. "I am not going to bother myself about the weather. One thing is certain, the days are getting short already and the evenings long. Suppose we talk a little about candles."

"Nothing is easier," said Smith.

"To talk about?" asked the sailor.

"To make."

"And when shall we begin?"

"To-morrow, by a seal-hunt."

"What! to make dips?"

"No, indeed, Pencroff, candles."

Such was the engineer's project, which was feasible enough, as he had lime and sulphuric acid, and as the amphibia of the island would furnish the necessary fat. It was now June 4, and Pentecost Sunday, which they kept as a day of rest and thanksgiving. They were no longer miserable castaways, they were colonists. On the next day, June 5, they started for the islet. They had to choose the time of low tide to ford the channel; and all determined that, somehow or other, they must build a boat which would give them easy communication with all parts of the island, and would enable them to go up the Mercy, when they should undertake that grand exploration of the southwestern district which they had reserved for the first good weather.

Seals were numerous, and the hunters, armed with their iron-spiked spears, easily killed half a dozen of them, which Neb and Pencroff skinned. Only the hides and fat were carried back to Granite House, the former to be made into shoes. The result of the hunt was about 300 pounds of fat, every pound of which could be used in making candles. The operation was simple enough, and the product, if not the best of its kind, was all they needed. Had Smith had at his disposition nothing but sulphuric acid, he could, by heating this acid with neutral fats, such as the fat of the seal, separate the glycerine, which again could be resolved, by means of boiling water, into oleine, margarine, and stearine. But, to simplify the operation, he preferred to saponify the fat by lime. He thus obtained a calcareous soap, easily decomposed by sulphuric acid, which precipitated the lime as a sulphate, and freed the fatty acids. The first of these three acids (oleine, margarine, and stearine) was a liquid which he expelled by pressure. The other two formed the raw material of the candles.

In twenty-four hours the work was done. Wicks were made, after some unsuccessful attempts, from vegetable fibre, and were steeped in the liquified compound. They were real stearine candles, made by hand, white and smooth.

During all this month work was going on inside their new abode. There was plenty of carpenter's work to do. They improved and completed their tools, which were very rudimentary. Scissors were made, among other things, so that they were able to cut their hair, and, if not actually to shave their beards, at least to trim them to their liking. Herbert had no beard, and Neb none to speak of, but the others found ample employment for the scissors.

They had infinite trouble in making a hand-saw; but at last succeeded in shaping an instrument which would cut wood by a rigorous application. Then they made tables, chairs and cupboards to furnish the principal rooms, and the frames of beds whose only bedding was mattrasses of wrack-grass. The kitchen, with its shelves, on which lay the terra-cotta utensils, its brick furnace, and its washing-stone, looked very comfortable, and Neb cooked with the gravity of a chemist in his laboratory.

But joiners work had to give place to carpentry. The new weir created by the explosion rendered necessary the construction of two causeways, one upon Prospect Plateau, the other on the shore itself. Now the plateau and the coast were transversely cut by a water-course which the colonists had to cross when ever they wished to reach the northern part of the island. To avoid this they had to make a considerable detour, and to walk westward as far as the sources of Red creek. Their best plan therefore was to build two causeways, one on the plateau and one on the shore, twenty to twenty-five feet long, simply constructed of trees squared by the axe. This was the work of some days. When these bridges had been built, Neb and Pencroff profited by them to go to the oyster-bed which had been discovered off the down. They dragged after them a sort of rough cart which had taken the place of the inconvenient hurdle; and they brought back several thousand oysters, which, were readily acclimated among the rocks, and formed a natural preserve at the mouth of the Mercy. They were excellent of their kind, and formed an almost daily article of diet. In fact, Lincoln Island, though the colonists had explored but a small portion of it, already supplied nearly all their wants, while it seemed likely that a minute exploration of the western forests would reveal a world of new treasures.

Only one privation still distressed the colonists. Azotic food they had in plenty, and the vegetables which corrected it; from the ligneous roots of the dragon-trees, submitted to fermentation, they obtained a sort of acidulated beer. They had even made sugar, without sugar-cane or beet-root, by collecting the juice which distills from the "acer saccharinum," a sort of maple which flourishes in all parts of the temperate zone, and which abounded on the island. They made a very pleasant tea from the plant brought from the warren; and, finally, they had plenty of salt, the only mineral component necessary to food—but bread was still to seek.

Perhaps, at some future time, they would have been able to replace this aliment by some equivalent, sago flour, or the breadfruit tree, which they might possibly have discovered in the woods of the southwest; but so far they had not met with them. Just at this time a little incident occurred which brought about what Smith, with all his ingenuity, could not have achieved.

One rainy day the colonists were together in the large hall of Granite House, when Herbert suddenly cried,

"See, Mr. Smith, a grain of corn."

And he showed his companions a single gram which had got into the lining of his waistcoat through a hole in his pocket. Pencroff had given him some ringdoves in Richmond, and in feeding them one of the grains had remained in his pocket.

"A grain of corn?" said the engineer, quickly.

"Yes, sir; but only one."

"That's a wonderful help," said Pencroff, laughing. "The bread that grain will make will never choke us."

Herbert was about to throw away the grain, when Cyrus Smith took it, examined it, found that it was in good condition, and said quietly to the sailor:—

"Pencroff, do you know how many ears of corn will spring from one grain?"

"One, I suppose," said the sailor, surprised at the question.

"Ten, Pencroff. And how many grains are there to an ear?"

"Faith, I don't know."

"Eighty on an average," said Smith. "So then, if we plant this grain, we shall get from it a harvest of 800 grains; from them in the second year 640,000; in the third, 512,000,000; in the fourth, more than 400,000,000,000. That is the proportion."

His companions listened in silence. The figures stupefied them.

"Yes, my friend," resumed the engineer. "Such is the increase of Nature. And what is even this multiplication of a grain of corn whose ears have only 800 grains, compared with the poppy plant, which has 32,000 seeds, or the tobacco plant, which has 360,000? In a few years, but for the numerous enemies which destroy them, these plants would cover the earth. And now, Pencroff," he resumed, "do you know how many bushels there are in 400,000,000,000 grains?"

"No," answered the sailor, "I only know that I am an idiot!"

"Well, there will be more than 3,000,000, at 130,000 the bushel!"

"Three millions!" cried Pencroff.

"Three millions."

"In four years?"

"Yes," said Smith, "and even in two, if, as I hope, we can get two harvests a year in this latitude."

Pencroff answered with a tremendous hurrah.

"So, Herbert," added the engineer, "your discovery is of immense importance. Remember, my friends, that everything may be of use to us in our present situation."

"Indeed, Mr. Smith, I will remember it," said Pencroff, "and if ever I find one of those grains of tobacco which increase 360,000 times, I'll take care not to throw it away. And now what must we do?"

"We must plant this grain," said Herbert.

"Yes," added Spilett, "and with the greatest care, for upon it depend our future harvests!"

"Provided that it grows," said the sailor.

"It will grow," answered Smith.

It was now the 20th of June, a good time for planting the precious grain. They thought at first of planting it in a pot; but upon consideration, they determined to trust it frankly to the soil. The same day it was planted, with the greatest precaution. The weather clearing a little, they walked up to the plateau above Granite House, and chose there a spot well sheltered from the wind, and exposed to the midday fervor of the sun. This spot was cleared, weeded, and even dug, so as to destroy insects and worms; it was covered with a layer of fresh earth, enriched with a little lime; a palissade was built around it, and then the grain was covered up in its moist bed.

They seemed to be laying the corner-stone of an edifice. Pencroff was reminded of the extreme care with which they had lighted their only match; but this was a more serious matter. The castaways could always have succeeded in obtaining fire by some means or other; but no earthly power could restore that grain of corn, if, by ill fortune, it should perish!

CHAPTER XXI. SEVERAL DEGREES BELOW ZERO

EXPLORATION OF THE SWAMP REGION TO THE SOUTHEAST—THE VIEW OF THE SEA—A CONVERSATION CONCERNING THE FUTURE OF THE PACIFIC OCEAN—THE INCESSANT LABOR OF THE INFUSORIA— WHAT WILL BECOME OF THIS GLOBE—THE CHASE—THE SWAMP OF THE TADORNS.

From this moment Pencroff did not let a day pass without visiting what he called with perfect gravity, his "corn field." And alas, for any insects that ventured there, no mercy would be shown them. Near the end of the month of June, after the interminable rains, the weather became decidedly cold, and on the 29th, a Fahrenheit thermometer would certainly have stood at only 20° above zero.

The next day, the 30th of June, the day which corresponds to the 31st of December in the Northern Hemisphere, was a Friday. Neb said the year ended on an unlucky day, but Pencroff answered that consequently the new year began on a lucky one, which was more important. At all events, it began with a very cold snap. Ice accumulated at the mouth of the Mercy, and the whole surface of the lake was soon frozen over.

Fresh firewood had continually to be procured. Pencroff had not waited for the river to freeze to convey enormous loads of wood to their destination. The current was a tireless motor, and conveyed the floating wood until the ice froze around it. To the fuel, which the forest so plentifully furnished, were added several cartloads of coal, which they found at the foot of the spurs of Mount Franklin. The powerful heat from the coal was thoroughly appreciated in a temperature which on the 4th of July fell to eight degrees above zero. A second chimney had been set up in the dining-room, where they all worked together.

During this cold spell Cyrus Smith could not be thankful enough that he had conducted to Granite House a small stream of water from Lake Grant. Taken below the frozen surface, then conducted through the old weir, it arrived unfrozen at the interior reservoir, which had been dug at the angle of the storehouse, and which, when too full, emptied itself into the sea. About this time the weather being very dry, the colonists, dressing as warmly as possible, determined to devote a day to the exploration of that part of the island situated to the southeast, between the Mercy and Claw Cape. It was a large swampy district and might offer good hunting, as aquatic birds must abound there. They would have eight or nine miles to go and as far to return, consequently the whole day must be given up. As it concerned the exploration of an unknown portion of the island, every one had to take part.

Therefore, on the 5th of July, at 6 o'clock in the morning, before the sun had fairly risen, the whole party, armed with spears, snares, bows and arrows, and furnished with enough provisions for the day, started from Granite House, preceded by Top, who gambolled before them. They took the shortest route, which was to cross the Mercy on the blocks of ice which then obstructed it.

"But," as the reporter very truly observed, "this cannot supply the place of a real bridge."

So the construction of a "real" bridge was set down as work for the future. This was the first time that the colonists had set foot on the right bank of the Mercy and had plunged into the forest of large and magnificent firs, then covered with snow. But they had not gone half a mile when the barking of Top frightened from a dense thicket where they had taken up their abode, a whole family of quadrupeds.

"Why they look like foxes," said Herbert, when he saw them scampering quickly away.

And they were foxes, but foxes of enormous size. They made a sort of bark which seemed to astonish Top, for he stopped in his chase and gave these swift animals time to escape. The dog had a right to be surprised, for he knew nothing of natural history; but by this barking, the greyish-red color of their hair, and their black tails, which ended in a white tuft, these foxes had betrayed their origin. So Herbert gave them without hesitation their true name of culpeux. These culpeux are often met with in Chili, in the Saint Malo group, and in all those parts of America lying between the 30th and 40th parallels.

Herbert was very sorry that Top had not caught one of these carnivora.

"Can we eat them?" asked Pencroff, who always considered the fauna of the island from that special point of view.

"No," said Herbert, "but zoologists have not yet ascertained whether the pupil of the eye of this fox is diurnal or nocturnal, or whether the animal would come under the genus "canine.""

Smith could not help smiling at this remark of the boy, which showed thoughtfulness beyond his years. As for the sailor, from the moment these foxes ceased to belong to the edible species, they ceased to interest him. Ever since the kitchen had been established at Granite House he had been saying that precautions ought to be taken against these four-footed plunderers. A fact which no one denied.

Having turned Jetsam Point the party came upon a long reach washed by the sea. It was then 8 o'clock in the morning. The sky was very clear, as is usual in prolonged cold weather; but, warmed by their work, Smith and his companions did not suffer from the sharpness of the atmosphere. Besides, there was no wind, the absence of which always renders a low temperature more endurable. The sun, bright but cold, rose from the ocean, and his enormous disc was poised in the horizon. The sea was a calm, blue sheet of water, like a land-locked sea under a clear sky. Claw Cape, bent in the shape of an ataghan, was clearly defined about four miles to the southeast. To the left, the border of the swamp was abruptly intercepted by a little point which shone brightly against the sun. Certainly in that part of Union Bay, which was not protected from the open sea, even by a sand bank, ships beaten by an east wind could not have found shelter.

By the perfect calm of the sea, with no shoals to disturb its waters, by its uniform color, with no tinge of yellow, and, finally, by the entire absence of reefs, they knew that this side was steep, and that here the ocean was fathoms deep. Behind them, in the west, at a distance of about four miles, they saw the beginning of the Forests of the Far West. They could almost have believed themselves upon some desolate island in the Antarctic regions surrounded by ice.

The party halted here for breakfast; a fire of brushwood and seaweed was lighted, and Neb prepared the meal of cold meat, to which he added some cups of Oswego tea. While eating they looked around them. This side of Lincoln island was indeed barren, and presented a strong contrast to the western part.

The reporter thought that if the castaways had been thrown upon this coast, they would have had a very melancholy impression of their future home.

"I do not believe we could even have reached it," said the engineer, "for the sea is very deep here, and there is not even a rock which would have served as a refuge; before Granite House there were shoals, at least, and a little island which multiplied our chances of safety; here is only the bottomless sea."

"It is curious enough," said Spilett, "that this island, relatively so small, presents so varied a soil. This diversity of appearance belongs, logically, only to continents of a considerable area. One would really think that the western side of Lincoln Island, so rich and fertile, was washed by the warm waters of the Gulf of Mexico, and that the northern and southern coasts extended into a sort of Arctic Sea."

"You are right, my dear Spilett," replied the engineer, "I have observed the same thing. I have found this island curious both in its shape and in its character. It has all the peculiarities of a continent, and I would not be surprised if it had been a continent formerly."

"What! a continent in the middle of the Pacific!" cried Pencroff.

"Why not?" answered Smith. "Why should not Australia, New Ireland, all that the English geographers call Australasia, joined to the Archipelagoes of the

Pacific Ocean, have formed in times past a sixth part of the world as important as Europe or Asia, Africa or the two Americas. My mind does not refuse to admit that all the islands rising from this vast ocean are the mountains of a continent now engulphed, but which formerly rose majestically from these waters."

"Like Atlantis?" asked Herbert. "Yes. my boy, if that ever existed." "And Lincoln Island may have been a part of this continent?" asked Pencroff. "It is probable," replied Smith. "And that would explain the diversity of products upon the surface, and the number of animals which still live here," added Herbert.

"Yes, my boy," answered the engineer, "and that gives me a new argument in support of my theory. It is certain after what we have seen that the animals in the island are numerous, and what is more curious, is that the species are extremely varied. There must be a reason for this, and mine is, that Lincoln Island was formerly a part of some vast continent, which has, little by little, sunk beneath the surface of the Pacific." "Then," said Pencroff, who did not seem entirely convinced, "what remains of this old continent may disappear in its turn and leave nothing between America and Asia." "Yes," said Smith, "there will be new continents which millions upon millions of animalculæ are building at this moment." "And who are these masons?" inquired Pencroff. "The coral insects," answered Smith. "It is these who have built by their constant labor the Island of Clermont Tonnerre, the Atolls and many other coral islands which abound in the Pacific. It takes 47,000,000 of these insects to deposit one particle; and yet with the marine salt which they absorb, and the solid elements of the water which they assimilate, these animalculæ produce limestone, and limestone forms those enormous submarine structures whose hardness and solidity is equal to that of granite.

Formerly, during the first epochs of creation, Nature employed heat to produce land by upheaval, but now she lets these microscopic insects replace this agent, whose dynamic power at the interior of this globe has evidently diminished. This fact is sufficiently proved by the great number of volcanoes actually extinct on the surface of the earth. I verily believe that century after century, and infusoria after infusoria will change the Pacific some day into a vast continent, which new generations will, in their turn, inhabit and civilize."

"It will take a long time," said Pencroff. "Nature has time on her side," replied the engineer. "But what is the good of new continents?" asked Herbert. "It seems to me that the present extent of habitable countries is enough for mankind. Now Nature does nothing in vain." "Nothing in vain, indeed," replied the engineer; "but let us see how we can explain the necessity of new continents in the future, and precisely in these tropical regions occupied by these coral islands. Here is an explanation, which seems to me at least plausible."

"We are listening, Mr. Smith," replied Herbert.

"This is my idea: Scientists generally admit that some day the globe must come to an end, or rather the animal and vegetable life will be no longer possible, on account of the intense cold which will prevail. What they cannot agree upon is the cause of this cold. Some think that it will be produced by the cooling of the sun in the course of millions of years; others by the gradual extinction of the internal fires of our own globe, which have a more decided influence than is generally supposed. I hold to this last hypothesis, based upon the fact that the moon is without doubt a refrigerated planet, which is no longer habitable, although the sun continues to pour upon its surface the same amount of heat. If then, the moon is refrigerated, it is because these internal fires, to which like all the stellar world it owes its origin, are entirely extinct. In short, whatever be the cause, our world will certainly some day cool; but this cooling will take place gradually. What will happen then? Why, the temperate zones, at a time more or less distant, will be no more habitable than are the Polar regions now. Then human, as well as animal life, will be driven to latitudes more directly under the influence of the solar rays. An immense emigration will take place. Europe, Central Asia, and North America will little by little be abandoned, as well as Australasia and the lower parts of South America. Vegetation will follow the human emigration. The flora will move towards the equator at the same time with the fauna, the central parts of South America and Africa will become the inhabited continent. The Laplanders and the Samoyedes will find the climate of the Polar Sea on the banks of the Mediterranean. Who can tell but that at this epoch, the equatorial regions will not be too small to contain and nourish the population of the globe. Now, why should not a provident nature, in order from this time, to provide a refuge for this animal and vegetable emigration, lay the foundation, under the equator, of a new continent, and charge these infusoria with the building of it? I have often thought of this, my friends, and I seriously believe that, some day, the aspect of our globe will be completely transformed, that after the upheaval of new continents the seas will cover the old ones, and that in future ages some Columbus will discover in the islands of Chimborazo or the Himalaya, or Mount Blanc, all that remains of an America, an Asia, and a Europe. Then at last, these new continents, in their turn, will become uninhabitable. The heat will die out as does the heat from a body whose soul has departed, and life will disappear from the globe, if not forever, at least for a time. Perhaps then our sphere will rest from its changes, and will prepare in death to live again under nobler conditions.

"But all this my friends, is with the Creator of all things. From the talking of the work of these infusoria I have been led into too deep a scrutiny of the secrets of the future."

"My dear Cyrus," said the reporter, "these theories are to me prophesies. Some day they will be accomplished."

"It is a secret with the Almighty," replied Smith.

"All this is well and good," said Pencroff, who had listened with all his ears, "but will you tell me, Mr. Smith, if Lincoln Island has been constructed by these infusoria."

"No," replied Smith, "it is of purely volcanic origin."

"Then it will probably disappear some day. I hope sincerely we won't be here."

"No, be easy, Pencroff, we will get away."

"In the meantime," said Spilett, "let us settle ourselves as if forever. It is never worth while to do anything by halves."

This ended the conversation. Breakfast was over, the exploration continued, and the party soon arrived at the beginning of the swampy district.

It was, indeed, a marsh which extended as far as the rounded side forming the southeastern termination of the island, and measuring twenty square miles. The soil was formed of a silicious clay mixed with decayed vegetation. It was covered by confervæ, rushes, sedges, and here and there by beds of herbage, thick as a velvet carpet. In many places frozen pools glistened under the sun's rays. Neither rains, nor any river swollen by a sudden increase could have produced this water. One would naturally conclude that this swamp was fed by the infiltration of water through the soil. And this was the fact. It was even to be feared that the air here during hot weather, was laden with that miasma which engenders the marsh fever. Above the aquatic herbs on the surface of the stagnant waters, a swarm of birds were flying. A hunter would not have lost a single shot. Wild ducks, teal, and snipe lived there in flocks, and it was easy to approach these fearless creatures. So thick were these birds that a charge of shot would certainly have brought down a dozen of them, but our friends had to content themselves with their bows and arrows. The slaughter was less, but the quiet arrow had the advantage of not frightening the birds, while the sound of fire-arms would have scattered them to every corner of the swamp. The hunters contented themselves this time with a dozen ducks, with white bodies, cinnamon-colored belts, green heads, wings black, white, and red, and feathered beaks. These Herbert recognized as the "Tadorns." Top did his share well in the capture of these birds, whose name was given this swampy district.

The colonists now had an abundant reserve of aquatic game. When the time should come the only question would be how to make a proper use of them, and it was probable that several species of these birds would be, if not domesticated, at least acclimated, upon the borders of the lake, which would bring them nearer to the place of consumption.

About 5 o'clock in the afternoon Smith and his companions turned their faces homewards. They crossed Tadorn's Fens, and re-crossed the Mercy upon the ice, arriving at Granite House at 8 o'clock in the evening.

CHAPTER XXII. THE TRAPS

THE FOXES—THE PECCARIES —THE WIND VEERS TO THE NORTHWEST —
THE SNOW-STORM—THE BASKET-MAKERS —THE COLDEST SNAP OF WINTER
—CRYSTALLIZATION OF THE SUGAR-MAPLE —THE MYSTERIOUS SHAFTS—
THE PROJECTED EXPLORATION—THE PELLET OF LEAD.

The intense cold lasted until the 15th of August, the thermometer never rising above the point hitherto observed. When the atmosphere was calm this low temperature could be easily borne; but when the wind blew, the poor fellows suffered much for want of warmer clothing. Pencroff regretted that Lincoln Island, instead of harboring so many foxes and seals, with no fur to speak of, did not shelter some families of bears.

"Bears," said he, "are generally well dressed; and I would ask nothing better for the winter than the loan of their warm cloaks.".

"But perhaps," said Neb, laughing "These bears would not consent to give you their cloak. Pencroff, these fellows are no Saint Martins."

"We would make them, Neb, we would make them," answered Pencroff in a tone of authority.

But these formidable carnivora did not dwell on the island, or if they did, had not yet shown themselves. Herbert, Pencroff, and the reporter were constantly at work getting traps on Prospect Plateau and on the borders of the forest. In the sailor's opinion any animal whatever would be a prize, and rodents or carnivora, whichever these new traps should entice, would be well received at Granite House. These traps were very simple. They were pits dug in the ground and covered with branches and grass, which hid the openings. At the bottom they placed some bait, whose odor would attract the animals. They used their discretion about the position of their traps, choosing places where numerous footprints indicated the frequent passage of quadrupeds. Every day they went to look at them, and at three different times during the first few days they found in them specimens of those foxes which had been already seen on the right bank of the Mercy.

"Pshaw! there are nothing but foxes in this part of the world," said Pencroff, as, for the third time, he drew one of these animals out of the pit. "Good-for-nothing beasts;"

"Stop," said Spilett; "they are good for something."

"For what?"

"To serve as bait to attract others!"

The reporter was right, and from this time the traps were baited with the dead bodies of foxes. The sailor had made snares out of the threads of curry-jonc, and these snares were more profitable than the traps. It was a rare thing for a day to pass without some rabbit from the warren being captured. It was always a rabbit, but Neb knew how to vary his sauces, and his companions did not complain. However, once or twice in the second week in August, the traps contained other and more useful animals than the foxes. There were some of those wild boars which had been already noticed at the north of the lake. Pencroff had no need to ask if these animals were edible, that was evident from their resemblance to the hog of America and Europe.

"But these are not hogs, let me tell you," said Herbert.

"My boy," replied the sailor, handing over the trap and drawing out one of these representatives of the swine family by the little appendage which served for a tail, "do let me believe them to be hogs."

"Why?"

"Because it pleases me."

"You are fond of hogs, then, Pencroff?"

"I am very fond of them," replied the sailor, "especially of their feet, and if any had eight instead of four I would like them twice as much."

These animals were peccaries, belonging to one of the four genera, which make up that family. This particular species were the "tajassans," known by there dark color and the absence of those long fangs which belong to the others of their race. Peccaries generally live in herds, and it was likely that these animals abounded in the woody parts of the island. At all events they were edible from head to foot, and Pencroff asked nothing more.

About the 15th of August the weather moderated suddenly by a change of wind to the northwest. The temperature rose several degrees higher, and the vapors accumulated in the air were soon resolved into snow. The whole island was covered with a white mantle, and presented a new aspect to its inhabitants. It snowed hard for several days and the ground was covered two feet deep. The wind soon rose with great violence and from the top of Granite House they could hear the sea roaring against the reefs.

At certain angles the wind made eddies in the air, and the snow, forming itself into high whirling columns, looked like those twisting waterspouts which vessels attack with cannon. The hurricane, coming steadily from the northwest, spent its force on the other side of the island, and the eastern lookout of Granite House preserved it from a direct attack.

During this snow-storm, as terrible as those of the polar regions, neither Smith nor his companions could venture outside. They were completely housed for five days, from the 20th to the 25th of August. They heard the tempest roar though Jacamar Woods, which must have suffered sadly. Doubtless numbers of trees were uprooted, but Pencroff comforted himself with the reflection that there would be fewer to cut down.

"The wind will be wood-cutter; let it alone," said he.

How fervently now the inhabitants of Granite House must have thanked Heaven for having given to them this solid and impenetrable shelter! Smith had his share of their gratitude, but after all, it was nature which had hollowed out this enormous cave, and he had only discovered it. Here all were in safety, the violence of the tempest could not reach them. If they had built a house of brick and wood on Prospect Plateau, it could not have resisted the fury of this hurricane. As for the Chimneys, they heard the billows strike them with such violence that they knew they must be uninhabitable, for the sea, having entirely covered their islet, beat upon them with all its force.

But here at Granite House, between these solid walls which neither wind nor water could effect, they had nothing to fear. During this confinement the colonists were not idle. There was plenty of wood in the storehouse cut into planks, and little by little they completed their stock of furniture. As far as tables and chairs went they were certainly solid enough, for the material was not spared. This furniture was a little too heavy to fulfil its essential purpose of being easily moved, but it was the pride of Neb and Pencroff, who would not have exchanged it for the handsomest Buhl.

Then the carpenters turned basket-makers, and succeeded remarkably well at this new occupation.

They had discovered at the northern part of the lake a thick growth of purple osiers. Before the rainy season, Pencroff and Herbert had gathered a good many of these useful shrubs; and their branches, being now well seasoned, could be used to advantage. Their first specimens were rough; but, thanks to the skill and intelligence of the workmen consulting together, recalling the models they had seen, and rivalling each other in their efforts, hampers and baskets of different sizes here soon added to the stock of the colony. The storehouse was filled with them, and Neb set away in special baskets his stock of pistachio nuts and roots of the dragon tree.

During the last week in August the weather changed again, the temperature fell a little, and the storm was over. The colonists at once started out. There must have been at least two feet of snow on the shore, but it was frozen over the top, which made it easy to walk over. Smith and his companions climbed up Prospect Plateau. What a change they beheld! The woods which they had left in bloom, especially the part nearest to them where the conifers were plenty, were now one uniform color.

Everything was white, from the top of Mount Franklin to the coast—forests, prairie, lake, river, beach. The waters of the Mercy ran under a vault of ice, which cracked and broke with a loud noise at every change of tide. Thousands of birds—ducks and wood-peckers—flew over the surface of the lake. The rocks between which the cascade plunged to the borders of the Plateau were blocked up with ice. One would have said that the water leaped out of a huge gargoyle, cut by some fantastic artist of the Renaissance. To calculate the damage done to the forest by this hurricane would be impossible until the snow had entirely disappeared.

Spilett, Pencroff, and Herbert took this opportunity to look after their traps and had hard work finding them under their bed of snow. There was danger of their falling in themselves; a humiliating thing to be caught in one's own trap! They were spared this annoyance, however, and found the traps had been untouched; not an animal had been caught, although there were a great many footprints in the neighborhood, among others, very clearly impressed marks of claws.

Herbert at once classified these carnivora among the cat tribe, a circumstance which justified the engineer's belief in the existence of dangerous beasts on Lincoln Island. Doubtless these beasts dwelt in the dense forests of the Far West; but driven by hunger, they had ventured as far as Prospect Plateau. Perhaps they scented the inhabitants of Granite House.

"What, exactly, are these carnivora?" asked Pencroff.

"They are tigers," replied Herbert.

"I thought those animals were only found in warm countries."

"In the New World," replied the lad, "they are to be found from Mexico to the pampas of Buenos Ayres. Now, as Lincoln Island is in almost the same latitude as La Plata, it is not surprising that tigers are found here."

"All right, we will be on our guard," replied Pencroff.

In the meantime, the temperature rising, the snow began to melt, it came on to rain, and gradually the white mantle disappeared. Notwithstanding the bad weather the colonists renewed their stock of provisions, both animal and vegetable.

This necessitated excursions into the forest, and thus they discovered how many trees had been beaten down by the hurricane. The sailor and Neb pushed forward with their wagon as far as the coal deposit in order to carry back some fuel. They saw on their way that the chimney of the pottery oven had been much damaged by the storm; at least six feet had been blown down.

They also renewed their stock of wood as well as that of coal, and the Mercy having become free once more, they employed the current to draw several loads to Granite House. It might be that the cold season was not yet over.

A visit had been made to the Chimneys also, and the colonists could not be sufficiently grateful that this had not been their home during the tempest. The sea had left undoubted signs of its ravages. Lashed by the fury of the wind from the offing, and rushing over Safety Island, it spent its full force upon these passages, leaving them half full of sand and the rocks thickly covered with seaweed.

While Neb, Herbert, and Pencroff spent their time in hunting and renewing their supply of fuel, Smith and Spilett set to work to clear out the Chimneys. They found the forge and furnaces almost unhurt, so carefully protected had they been by the banks of sand which the colonists had built around them.

It was a fortunate thing that they laid in a fresh supply of fuel, for the colonists had not yet seen the end of the intense cold. It is well known that in the Northern Hemisphere, the month of February is noted for its low temperature. The same rule held good in the Southern Hemisphere, and the end of August, which is the February of North America, did not escape from this climatic law.

About the 25th, after another snow and rain storm, the wind veered to the southeast, and suddenly the cold became intense. In the engineer's opinion, a Fahrenheit thermometer would have indicated about eight degrees below zero, and the cold was rendered more severe by a cutting wind which lasted for several days.

The colonists were completely housed again, and as they were obliged to block up all their windows, only leaving one narrow opening for ventilation, the consumption of candles was considerable. In order to economize them, the colonists often contented themselves with only the light from the fire; for fuel was plenty.

Once or twice some of them ventured to the beach, among the blocks of ice which were heaped up there by every fresh tide. But they soon climbed up to

Granite House again. This ascent was very painful, as their hands were frostbitten by holding on to the frozen sides of the ladder.

There were still many leisure hours to be filled up during this long confinement, so Smith undertook another indoor occupation.

The only sugar which they had had up to this time was a liquid substance which they had procured by making deep cuts in the bark of the maple tree. They collected this liquid in jars and used it in this condition for cooking purposes. It improved with age, becoming whiter and more like a syrup in consistency. But they could do better than this, and one day Cyrus Smith announced to his companions that he was going to turn them into refiners.

"Refiners! I believe that's a warm trade?" said Pencroff.

"Very warm!" replied the engineer.

"Then it will suit this season!" answered the sailor.

Refining did not necessitate a stock of complicated tools or skilled workmen; it was a very simple operation.

To crystallize this liquid they first clarified it, by putting it on the fire in earthenware jars, and submitting it to evaporation. Soon a scum rose to the surface, which, when it began to thicken, Neb removed carefully with a wooden ladle. This hastened the evaporation, and at the same time prevented it from scorching.

After several hours boiling over a good fire, which did as much good to the cooks as it did to the boiling liquid, it turned into a thick syrup. This syrup was poured into clay moulds which they had made beforehand, in various shapes in the same kitchen furnace.

The next day the syrup hardened, forming cakes and loaves. It was sugar of a reddish color, but almost transparent, and of a delicious taste.

The cold continued until the middle of September, and the inmates of Granite House began to find their captivity rather tedious. Almost every day they took a run out-doors, but they always soon returned. They were constantly at work over their household duties, and talked while they worked.

Smith instructed his companions in everything, and especially explained to them the practical applications of science. The colonists had no library at their disposal, but the engineer was a book, always ready, always open at the wished-for page. A book which answered their every question, and one which they often read. Thus the time passed, and these brave man had no fear for the future.

However, they were all anxious for the end of their captivity, and longed to see, if not fine weather, at least a cessation of the intense cold. If they had only had warmer clothing, they would have attempted excursions to the downs and to Tadorns' Fens, for game would have been easy to approach, and the hunt would assuredly have been fruitful. But Smith insisted that no one should compromise his health, as he had need of every hand; and his advice was taken.

The most impatient of the prisoners, after Pencroff, was Top. The poor dog found himself in close quarters in Granite House, and ran from room to room, showing plainly the uneasiness he felt at this confinement.

Smith often noticed that whenever he approached the dark well communicating with the sea, which had its opening in the rear of the storehouse, Top whined in a most curious manner, and ran around and around the opening, which had been covered over with planks of wood. Sometimes he even tried to slip his paws under the planks, as if trying to raise them up, and yelped in a way which indicated at the same time anger and uneasiness.

The engineer several times noticed this strange behavior, and wondered what there could be in the abyss to have such a peculiar effect upon this intelligent dog.

This well, of course, communicated with the sea. Did it then branch off into narrow passages through the rock-work of the island? Was it in communication with other caves? Did any sea-monsters come into it from time to time from the bottom of these pits?

The engineer did not know what to think, and strange thoughts passed through his mind. Accustomed to investigate scientific truths, he could not pardon himself for being drawn into the region of the mysterious and supernatural; but how explain why Top, the most sensible of dogs, who never lost his time in barking at the moon, should insist upon exploring this abyss with nose and ear, if there was nothing there to arouse his suspicions?

Top's conduct perplexed Smith more than he cared to own to himself. However, the engineer did not mention this to any one but Spilett, thinking it useless to worry his companions with what might be, after all, only a freak of the dog.

At last the cold spell was over. They had rain, snow-squalls, hail-storms, and gales of wind, but none of these lasted long. The ice thawed and the snow melted; the beach, plateau, banks of the Mercy, and the forest were again accessible. The return of spring rejoiced the inmates of Granite House, and they soon passed all their time in the open air, only returning to eat and sleep.

They hunted a good deal during the latter part of September, which led Pencroff to make fresh demands for those fire-arms which he declared Smith had promised him. Smith always put him off, knowing that without a special stock of tools it would be almost impossible to make a gun which would be of any use to them.

Besides, he noticed that Herbert and Spilett had become very clever archers, that all sorts of excellent game, both feathered and furred—agoutis, kangaroos, cabiais, pigeons, bustards, wild ducks, and snipe—fell under their arrows; consequently the firearms could wait. But the stubborn sailor did not see it in this light, and constantly reminded the engineer that he had not provided them with guns; and Gideon Spilett supported Pencroff.

"If," said he, "the island contains, as we suppose, wild beasts, we must consider how to encounter and exterminate them. The time may come when this will be our first duty."

But just now it was not the question of firearms which occupied Smith's mind, but that of clothes. Those which the colonists were wearing had lasted through the winter, but could not hold out till another. What they must have at any price was skins of the carnivora, or wool of the ruminants; and as moufflons (mountain goats), were plenty, they must consider how to collect a flock of them which they could keep for the benefit of the colony. They would also lay out a farm yard in a favorable part of the island, where they could have an enclosure for domestic animals and a poultry yard.

These important projects must be carried out during the good weather. Consequently, in view of these future arrangements, it was important to undertake a reconnoissance into the unexplored part of Lincoln Island, to wit:—the high forests which extended along the right bank of the Mercy, from its mouth to the end of Serpentine Peninsula. But they must be sure of their weather, and a month must yet elapse before it would be worth while to undertake this exploration. While they were waiting impatiently, an incident occurred which redoubled their anxiety to examine the whole island.

It was now the 24th of October. On this day Pencroff went to look after his traps which he always kept duly baited. In one of them, he found three animals, of a sort welcome to the kitchen. It was a female peccary with her two little ones. Pencroff returned to Granite House, delighted with his prize, and, as usual, made a great talk about it.

"Now, we'll have a good meal, Mr Smith," cried he, "and you too, Mr. Spilett, must have some."

"I shall be delighted," said the reporter, "but what is it you want me to eat?"

"Sucking pig," said Pencroff.

"Oh, a sucking-pig! To hear you talk one would think you had brought back a stuffed partridge!"

"Umph," said Pencroff, "so you turn up your nose at my sucking pig?"

"No," answered Spilett coolly, "provided one does not get too much of them—"

"Very well, Mr. Reporter!" returned the sailor, who did not like to hear his game disparaged. "You are getting fastidious! Seven months ago, when we were cast upon this island, you would have been only too glad to have come across such game."

"Well, well," said the reporter, "men are never satisfied."

"And now," continued Pencroff, "I hope Neb will distinguish himself. Let us see; these little peccaries are only three months old, they will be as tender as quail. Come, Neb, I will superintend the cooking of them myself."

The sailor, followed by Neb, hastened to the kitchen, and was soon absorbed over the oven. The two prepared a magnificent repast; the two little peccaries, kangaroo soup, smoked ham, pistachio nuts, dragon-tree wine, Oswego tea; in a word, everything of the best. But the favorite dish of all was the savory peccaries made into a stew. At 5 o'clock, dinner was served in the dining-room of Granite House. The kangaroo soup smoked upon the table. It was pronounced excellent.

After the soup came the peccaries, which Pencroff begged to be allowed to carve, and of which he gave huge pieces to every one. These sucking pigs were indeed delicious, and Pencroff plied his knife and fork with intense earnestness, when suddenly a cry and an oath escaped him.

"What's the matter?" said Smith.

"The matter is that I have just lost a tooth!" replied the sailor.

"Are there pebbles in your peccaries, then?" said Spilett.

"It seems so," said the sailor, taking out of his mouth the object which had cost him a grinder.

It was not a pebble, it was a leaden pellet.

PART II. THE ABANDONED

CHAPTER XXIII. CONCERNING THE LEADEN PELLET

MAKING A CANOE—HUNTING—IN THE TOP OF A KAURI—NOTHING TO INDICATE THE PRESENCE OF MAN—THE TURTLE ON ITS BACK—THE TURTLE DISAPPEARS—SMITH'S EXPLANATION.

It was exactly seven months since the passengers in the balloon had been thrown upon Lincoln Island. In all this time no human being had been seen. No smoke had betrayed the presence of man upon the island. No work of man's hands, either ancient or modern, had attested his passage. Not only did it seem uninhabited at present, but it appeared to have been so always. And now all the framework of deductions fell before a little bit of metal found in the body of a pig. It was certainly a bullet from a gun, and what but a human being would be so provided?

When Pencroff had placed it upon the table, his companions looked at it with profound astonishment. The possibilities suggested by this seemingly trivial incident flashed before them. The sudden appearance of a supernatural being could not have impressed them more.

Smith instantly began to reason upon the theories which this incident, as surprising as it was unexpected, suggested. Taking the bit of lead between his fingers he turned it round and about for some time before he spoke.

"You are sure, Pencroff," he asked, at length, "that the peccary was hardly three months old?"

"I'm sure, sir," answered the sailor. "It was sucking its mother when I found it in the ditch."

"Well, then, that proves that within three months a gun has been fired upon Lincoln Island."

"And that the bullet has wounded, though not mortally, this little animal," added Spilett.

"Undoubtedly," replied Smith; "and now let us see what conclusions are to be drawn from this incident. Either the island was inhabited before our arrival, or men have landed here within three months. How these men arrived, whether voluntarily or involuntarily, whether by landing or by shipwreck, cannot be settled at present. Neither have we any means of determining whether they are Europeans or Malays, friends or enemies; nor do we know whether they are living here at present or whether they have gone. But these questions are too important to be allowed to remain undecided."

"No!" cried the sailor springing from the table. "There can be no men besides ourselves on Lincoln Island. Why, the island is not large: and if it had been inhabited, we must have met some one of its people before this."

"It would, indeed, be astonishing if we had not," said Herbert.

"But it would be much more astonishing, I think," remarked the reporter, "if this little beast had been born with a bullet in his body!"

"Unless," suggested Neb, seriously, "Pencroff had had it—"

"How's that, Neb?" interrupted the sailor, "I, to have had a bullet in my jaw for five or six months, without knowing it? Where would it have been?" he added, opening his mouth and displaying the thirty-two splendid teeth that ornamented it. "Look, Neb, and if you can find one broken one in the whole set you may pull out half-a-dozen!"

"Neb's theory is inadmissible," said Smith, who, in spite of the gravity of his thoughts, could not restrain a smile. "It is certain that a gun has been discharged on the island within three months. But I am bound to believe that the persons on this island have been here but a short time, or else simply landed in passing; as, had the island had inhabitants when we made the ascent of Mount Franklin, we must have seen them or been seen. It is more probable, that within the past few weeks some people have been shipwrecked somewhere upon the coast; the thing, therefore, to do is to discover this point."

"I think we should act cautiously," said the reporter.

"I think so, too," replied Smith, "as I fear that they must be Malay pirates;"

"How would it do, Mr. Smith," said the sailor, "to build A canoe so that we could go up this river, or, if need be, round the coast? It won't do to be taken unawares."

"It's a good idea," answered the engineer; "but we have not the time now. It would take at least a month to build a canoe—"

"A regular one, yes," rejoined the sailor; "but we don't want it to stand the sea. I will guarantee to make one in less than five days that will do to use on the Mercy."

"Build a boat in five days," cried Neb.

"Yes, Neb, one of Indian fashion."

"Of wood?" demanded the black man, still incredulous.

"Of wood, or what is better, of bark," answered Pencroff. "Indeed, Mr. Smith, it could be done in five days!"

"Be it so, then," answered the engineer. "In five days."

"But we must look out for ourselves in the meantime!" said Herbert.

"With the utmost caution, my friends," answered Smith. "And be very careful to confine your hunting expeditions to the neighborhood of Granite House."

The dinner was finished in lower spirits than Pencroff had expected. The incident of the bullet proved beyond doubt that the island had been, or was now, inhabited by others, and such a discovery awakened the liveliest anxiety in the breasts of the colonists.

Smith and Spilett, before retiring, had a long talk about these things. They questioned, if by chance this incident had an connection with the unexplained rescue of the engineer, and other strange events which they had encountered in so many ways. Smith, after having discussed the pros and cons of the question, ended by saying:—

"In short, Spilett, do you want to know my opinion?"

"Yes, Cyrus."

"Well, this is it. No matter how minutely we examine the island, we will find nothing!"

Pencroff began his work the next day. He did not mean to build a boat with ribs and planks, but simply a flat bottomed float, which would do admirably in the Mercy, especially in the shallow water and its sources. Strips of bark fastened together would be sufficient for their purpose, and in places where a portage would be necessary the affair would be neither heavy nor cumbersome. The sailor's idea was to fasten the strips of bark together with clinched nails, and thus to make the craft staunch.

The first thing was to select trees furnishing a supple and tough bark. Now, it had happened that the last storm had blown down a number of Douglass pines, which were perfectly adapted to this purpose. Some of these lay prone upon the earth, and all the colonists had to do was to strip them of their bark, though this indeed was somewhat difficult, on account of the awkwardness of their tools.

While the sailor, assisted by the engineer was thus occupied, Herbert and Spilett, who had been made purveyors to the colony, were not idle. The reporter could not help admiring the young lad, who had acquired a remarkable proficiency in the use of the bow and arrows, and who exhibited, withal, considerable hardiness and coolness. The two hunters, remembering the caution of the engineer, never ventured more than two miles from Granite House, but the outskirts of the forest furnished a sufficient supply of agoutis, cabiais, kangaroos, peccaries, etc., and although the traps had not done so well since the cold had abated, the warren furnished a supply sufficient for the wants of the colonists.

Often, while on these excursions, Herbert conversed with Spilett about the incident of the bullet and of the engineer's conclusions, and one day—the 26th of October—he said:—

"Don't you think it strange, Mr. Spilett, that any people should have been wrecked on this island, and never have followed up the coast to Granite House?"

"Very strange if they are still here," answered the reporter, "but not at all astonishing if they are not."

"Then you think they have gone again?"

"It is likely, my boy, that, if they had staid any time, or were still here, something would have discovered their presence."

"But if they had been able to get off again they were not really shipwrecked."

"No, Herbert, they were what I should call shipwrecked temporarily. That is, it is possible that they were driven by stress of weather upon the island, without having to abandon their vessel, and when the wind moderated they set out again."

"One thing is certain," said Herbert, "and that is, that Mr. Smith has always seemed to dread, rather than to desire, the presence of human beings on our island."

"The reason is, that he knows that only Malays frequent these seas, and these gentlemen are a kind of rascals that had better be avoided."

"Is it not possible, sir, that some time we will discover traces of their landing and, perhaps, be able to settle this point?"

"It is not unlikely, my boy. An abandoned camp or the remains of a fire, we would certainly notice, and these are what we will look for on our exploration."

The hunters, talking in this way, found themselves in a portion of the forest near the Mercy, remarkable for its splendid trees. Among others, were those magnificent conifera, called by the New Zealanders "kauris," rising mere than 200 feet in height.

"I have an idea, Mr. Spilett," said Herbert, "supposing I climb to the top of one of these kauris, I could see, perhaps, for a good ways."

"It's a good idea," answered the other, "but can you climb one of these giants?"

"I am going to try, anyhow," exclaimed the boy, springing upon the lower branches of one, which grew in such a manner as to make the tree easy to mount. In a few minutes he was in its top, high above all the surrounding leafage of the forest.

From this height, the eye could take in all the southern portion of the island between Claw Cape on the southeast and Reptile Promontory on the southwest. To the northwest rose Mount Franklin, shutting out more than one-fourth of the horizon.

But Herbert, from his perch, could overlook the very portion of the island which was giving, or had given, refuge to the strangers whose presence they suspected. The lad looked about him with great attention, first towards the sea, where not a sail was visible, although it was possible that a ship, and especially one dismasted, lying close in to shore, would be concealed from view by the trees which hid the coast. In the woods of the Far West nothing could be seen.

The forest formed a vast impenetrable dome many miles in extent, without an opening or glade. Even the course of the Mercy could not be seen, and it might be that there were other streams flowing westward, which were equally invisible.

But, other signs failing, could not the lad catch in the air some smoke that would indicate the presence of man? The atmosphere was pure, and the slightest vapor was sharply outlined against the sky. For an instant Herbert thought he saw a thin film rising in the west, but a more careful observation convinced him that he was mistaken. He looked again, however, with all care, and his sight was excellent. No, certainly, it was nothing.

Herbert climbed down the tree, and he and the reporter returned to Granite House. There Smith listened to the lad's report without comment. It was plain he would not commit himself until after the island had been explored.

Two days later—the 28th of October—another unaccountable incident happened. In strolling along the beach, two miles from Granite House, Herbert and Neb had been lucky enough to capture a splendid specimen of the chelonia mydas (green turtle), whose carapace shone with emerald reflections. Herbert had caught sight of it moving among the rocks towards the sea.

"Stop him, Neb, stop him!" he cried.

Neb ran to it.

"It's a fine animal," said Neb, "but how are we going to keep it?"

"That's easy enough, Neb. All we have to do is to turn it on its back, and then it cannot get away. Take your spear and do as I do."

The reptile had shut itself in its shell, so that neither its head nor eyes were visible, and remained motionless as a rock. The lad and the black man placed their spears underneath it, and, after some difficulty, succeeded in turning it over. It measured three feet in length, and must have weighed at least 400 pounds.

"There, that will please Pencroff," cried Neb.

Indeed, the sailor could not fail to be pleased, as the flesh of these turtles, which feed upon eel-grass, is very savory.

"And now what can we do with our game?" asked Neb; "we can't carry it to Granite House."

"Leave it here, since it cannot turn back again," answered Herbert, "and we will come for it with the cart."

Neb agreed, and Herbert, as an extra precaution, which the black man thought useless, propped up the reptile with large stones. Then the two returned to Granite House, following the beach, on which the tide was down. Herbert, wishing to surprise Pencroff, did not tell him of the prize which was lying on its back upon the sand; but two hours later Neb and he returned with the cart to where they had left it, and—the "splendid specimen of chelonia mydas" was not there! The two looked about them. Certainly, this was where they had left it. Here were the stones he had used, and, therefore, the lad could not be mistaken.

"Did the beast turn over, after all?" asked Neb.

"It seems so," replied Herbert, puzzled, and examining the stones scattered over the sand.

"Pencroff will be disappointed."

"And Mr. Smith will be troubled to explain this!" thought Herbert.

"Well," said Neb, who wished to conceal their misadventure, "we won't say anything about it."

"Indeed, we will tell the whole story," answered Herbert.

And taking with them the useless cart, they returned to Granite House.

At the shipyard they found the engineer and the sailor working together. Herbert related all that happened.

"You foolish fellows," cried the sailor, "to let at least fifty pounds of soup, escape!"

"But, Pencroff," exclaimed Neb, "it was not our fault that the reptile got away; haven't I told you we turned it on its back?"

"Then you didn't turn it enough!" calmly asserted the stubborn sailor.

"Not enough!" cried Herbert; and he told how he had taken care to prop the turtle up with stones.

"Then it was a miracle!" exclaimed Pencroff.

"Mr. Smith," asked Herbert, "I thought that turtles once placed on their backs could not get over again, especially the very large ones?"

"That is the fact," answered Smith.

"Then how did it—"

"How far off from the sea did you leave this turtle," asked the engineer, who had stopped working and was turning this incident over in his mind.

"About fifteen feet," answered Herbert.

"And it was low water?"

"Yes, sir."

"Well," responded the engineer, "what the turtle could not do on land, he could do in water. When the tide rose over him he turned over, and—tranquilly paddled off."

"How foolish we are," cried Neb.

"That is just what I said you were," answered Pencroff.

Smith had given this explanation, which was doubtless admissible; but was he himself satisfied with it? He did not venture to say that.

CHAPTER XXIV. TRIAL OF THE CANOE

A WRECK ON THE SHORE—THE TOW—JETSAM POINT—INVENTORY OF
THE BOX—WHAT PENCROFF WANTED—A BIBLE—A VERSE FROM IT

On the 29th of October the canoe was finished. Pencroff had kept his word, and had built, in five days, a sort of bark shell, stiffened with flexible crejimba rods. A seat at either end, another midway to keep it open, a gunwale for the thole-pins of a pair of oars, and a paddle to steer with, completed this canoe, which was twelve feet in length, and did not weigh 200 pounds.

"Hurrah!" cried the sailor, quite ready to applaud his own success. "With this we can make the tour of—"

"Of the world?" suggested Spilett.

"No, but of the island. Some stones for ballast, a mast in the bow, with a sail which Mr. Smith will make some day, and away we'll go! But now let us try our new ship, for we must see if it will carry all of us."

The experiment was made. Pencroff, by a stroke of the paddle, brought the canoe close to the shore by a narrow passage between the rocks, and he was confident that they could at once make a trial trip of the craft by following the bank as far as the lower point where the rocks ended.

As they were stepping in, Neb cried:—

"But your boat leaks, Pencroff."

"Oh, that's nothing, Neb," answered the sailor. "The wood has to drink! But in two days it will not show, and there will be as little water in our canoe as in the stomach of a drunkard! Come, get in!"

They all embarked, and Pencroff pushed off. The weather was splendid, the sea was as calm as a lake, and the canoe could venture upon it with as much security as upon the tranquil current of the Mercy.

Neb and Herbert took the oars, and Pencroff sat in the stern with the paddle as steersman.

The sailor crossed the channel, and rounded the southern point of the islet. A gentle breeze was wafted from the south. There were no billows, but the canoe rose and fell with the long undulations of the sea, and they rowed out half a mile from the coast so as to get a view of the outline of Mount Franklin. Then, putting about, Pencroff returned towards the mouth of the river, and followed along the rounded shore which hid the low marshy ground of Tadorn's Fen. The point, made longer by the bend of the coast, was three miles from the Mercy, and the colonists resolved to go past it far enough to obtain a hasty glance at the coast as far as Claw Cape.

The canoe followed along the shore, keeping off some two cables length so as to avoid the line of rocks beginning to be covered by the tide. The cliff, beginning at the mouth of the river, lowered as it approached the promontory. It was a savage-looking, unevenly-arranged heap of granite blocks, very different from the curtain of Prospect Plateau. There was not a trace of vegetation on this sharp point, which projected two miles beyond the forest, like a giant's arm, thrust out from a green sleeve.

The canoe sped easily along. Spilett sketched the outline of the coast in his note-book, and Neb, Pencroff, and Herbert discussed the features of their new domain; and as they moved southward the two Mandible Capes seemed to shut together and enclose Union Bay. As to Smith, he regarded everything in silence, and from his distrustful expression it seemed as if he was observing some suspicious land.

The canoe had reached the end of the point and was about doubling it, when Herbert rose, and pointing out a black object, said:—

"What is that down there on the sand?"

Every one looked in the direction indicated.

"There is something there, indeed," said the reporter. "It looks like a wreck half buried in the sand."

"Oh, I see what it is!" cried Pencroff.

"What?" asked Neb.

"Barrels! they are barrels, and, may be, they are full!"

"To shore, Pencroff!" said Smith.

And with a few strokes the canoe was driven into a little cove, and the party went up the beach.

Pencroff was not mistaken. There were two barrels half buried in the sand; but firmly fastened to them was a large box, which, borne up by them, had been floated on to the shore.

"Has there been a shipwreck here?" asked Herbert.

"Evidently," answered Spilett.

"But what is in this box?" exclaimed Pencroff, with a natural impatience. "What is in this box? It is closed, and we have nothing with which to raise the lid. However, with a stone—"

And the sailor picked up a heavy rock, and was about to break one of the sides, when the engineer, stopping him, said:—

"Cannot you moderate your impatience for about an hour, Pencroff?"

"But, think, Mr. Smith! May be there is everything we want in it!"

"We will find out, Pencroff," answered the engineer, "but do not break the box, as it will be useful. Let us transport it to Granite House, where we can readily open it without injuring it. It is all prepared for the voyage, and since it has floated here, it can float again to the river month."

"You are right, sir, and I am wrong," answered the sailor, "but one is not always his own master!"

The engineer's advice was good. It was likely that the canoe could not carry the things probably enclosed in the box, since the latter was so heavy that it had to be buoyed up by two empty barrels. It was, therefore, better to tow it in this condition to the shore at the Granite House.

And now the important question was, from whence came this jetsam? Smith and his companions searched the beach for several hundred paces, but there was nothing else to be seen. They scanned the sea, Herbert and Neb climbing up a high rock, but not a sail was visible on the horizon.

Nevertheless, there must have been a shipwreck, and perhaps this incident was connected with the incident of the bullet. Perhaps the strangers had landed upon another part of the island. Perhaps they were still there. But the natural conclusion of the colonists was that these strangers could not be Malay pirates, since the jetsam was evidently of European or American production.

They all went back to the box, which measured five feet by three. It was made of oak, covered with thick leather, studded with copper nails. The two large barrels, hermetically sealed, but which sounded empty, were fastened to its sides by means of strong ropes, tied in what Pencroff recognized to be "sailor's knots." That it was uninjured seemed to be accounted for by the fact of its having been thrown upon the sand instead of the rocks. And it was evident that it had not been long either in the sea or upon the beach. It seemed probable, also, that the water had not penetrated, and that its contents would be found uninjured. It therefore looked as if this box must have been thrown overboard from a disabled ship making for the island. And, in the hope that it would reach the island, where they would find it later, the passengers had taken the precaution to buoy it up.

"We will tow this box to Granite House," said the engineer, "and take an inventory of its contents; then, if we discover any of the survivors of this supposed shipwreck, we will return them what is theirs. If we find no one—"

"We will keep the things ourselves!" cried the sailor. "But I wish I knew what is in it."

The sailor was already working at the prize, which would doubtless float at high water. One of the ropes which was fastened to the barrels was partly untwisted and served to fasten these latter to the canoe. Then, Neb and Pencroff dug out the sand with their oars, and soon the canoe, with the jetsam in tow, was rounding the promontory to which they gave the name of Jetsam Point. The box was so heavy that the barrels just sufficed to sustain it above the water; and Pencroff feared each moment that it would break loose and sink to the bottom. Fortunately his fears were groundless, and in an hour and a half the canoe touched the bank before Granite House.

The boat and the prize were drawn upon the shore, and as the tide was beginning to fall, both soon rested on dry ground. Neb brought some tools so as to open the box without injury, and the colonists forthwith proceeded to examine its contents.

Pencroff did not try to hide his anxiety. He began by unfastening the barrels, which would be useful in the future, then the fastenings were forced with pincers, and the cover taken off. A second envelope, of zinc, was enclosed within the case, in such a manner that its contents were impervious to moisture.

"Oh!" cried Pencroff, "they must be preserves which are inside."

"I hope for something better than that," answered the reporter.

"If it should turn out that there was—" muttered the sailor.

"What?" asked Neb.

"Nothing!"

The zinc cover was split, lengthwise and turned back, and, little by little, many different objects were lifted out on the sand. At each new discovery Pencroff cheered, Herbert clapped his hands, and Neb danced. There were books which made the lad crazy with pleasure, and cooking implements which Neb covered with kisses.

In truth the colonists had reason to be satisfied, as the following inventory, copied from Spilett's note-book, will show:—

TOOLS.—3 pocket-knives, with-several blades, 2 wood-chopper's hatchets, 2 carpenter's hatchets, 3 planes, I adzes, l axe, 6 cold chisels, 2 files, 3 hammers, 3 gimlets, 2 augers, 10 bags of nails and screws, 3 saws of different sizes, 2 boxes of needles.

ARMS.—2 flint-lock guns, 2 percussion guns, 2 central-fire carbines; 5 cutlasses, 4 boarding sabres, 2 barrels of powder, holding l5 pounds each, l2 boxes of caps.

INSTRUMENTS.—1 sextant, 1 opera-glass, 1 spyglass, 1 box compass, 1 pocket compass, 1 Fahrenheit thermometer, 1 aneroid barometer, 1 box containing a photographic apparatus, together with glasses, chemicals, etc.

CLOTHING.—2 dozen shirts of a peculiar material resembling wool, though evidently a vegetable substance; 3 dozen stockings of the same material.

UTENSILS.—1 Iron pot, 6 tinned copper stewpans, 3 iron plates, 10 aluminium knives and forks, 2 kettles, 1 small portable stove. 5 table knives.

BOOKS.-l Bible, 1 atlas, 1 dictionary of Polynesian languages, 1 dictionary of the Natural Sciences, 3 reams of blank paper, 2 blank books.

"Unquestionably," said the reporter, after the inventory had been taken, "the owner of this box was a practical man! Tools, arms, instruments, clothing, utensils, books, nothing is wanting. One would say that he had made ready for a shipwreck before-hand!"

"Nothing, Indeed, is wanting," murmured Smith, thoughtfully.

"And it is a sure thing," added Herbert, "that the ship that brought this box was not a Malay pirate!"

"Unless its owner had been taken prisoner," said Pencroff.

"That is not likely," answered the reporter. "It is more probable that an American or European ship has been driven to this neighborhood, and that the passengers, wishing to save what was, at least, necessary, have prepared this box and have thrown it overboard."

"And do you think so, Mr. Smith?" asked Herbert.

"Yes, my boy," answered the engineer, "that might have been the case. It is possible, that, anticipating a ship wreck, this chest has been prepared, so that it might be found again on the coast—"

"But the photographic apparatus!" observed the sailor incredulously.

"As to that," answered the engineer, "I do not see its use; what we, as well as any other ship wrecked person, would have valued more, would have been a greater assortment of clothing and more ammunition!"

"But have none of these things any mark by which we can tell where they came from," asked Spilett.

They looked to see. Each article was examined attentively, but, contrary to custom, neither books, instruments, nor arms had any name or mark; nevertheless, they were in perfect order, and seemed never to have been used. So also with the tools and utensils; everything was new, and this went to prove that the things had not been hastily thrown together in the box, but that their selection had been made thoughtfully and with care. This, also, was evident from the zinc case which had kept everything watertight, and which could not have been soldered in a moment.

The two dictionaries and the Bible were in English, and the latter showed that it had been often read. The Atlas was a splendid work, containing maps of every part of the world, and many charts laid out on Mercator's Projection. The nomenclature in this book was in French, but neither in it, nor in any of the others, did the name of the editor or publisher appear.

The colonists, therefore, were unable to even conjecture the nationality of the ship that had so recently passed near them. But no matter where it came from, this box enriched the party on Lincoln Island. Until now, in transforming the products of nature, they had created everything for themselves, and had succeeded by their own intelligence. Did it not now seem as if Providence had intended to reward them by placing these divers products of human industry in their hands? Therefore, with one accord, they all rendered thanks to Heaven.

Nevertheless, Pencroff was not entirely satisfied. It appeared that the box did not contain something to which he attached an immense importance, and as its contests lessened, his cheers had become less hearty, and when the inventory was closed, he murmured:—

"That's all very fine, but you see there is nothing for me here!"

"Why, what did you expect, Pencroff?" exclaimed Neb.

"A half pound of tobacco," answered the sailor, "and then I would have been perfectly happy!"

The discovery of this jetsam made the thorough exploration of the island more necessary than ever. It was, therefore, agreed that they should set out early the next morning, proceeding to the western coast via the Mercy. If anyone had been shipwrecked on that part of the island, they were doubtless without resources, and help must be given them at once.

During the day the contents of the box were carried to Granite House and arranged in order in the great hall. And that evening—the 29th of October—Herbert before retiring asked Mr. Smith to read some passages from the Bible.

"Gladly," answered the engineer, taking the sacred book in his hands; when Pencroff checking him, said: "Mr. Smith, I am superstitious. Open the book at random and read the first verse which you meet with. We will see if it applies to our situation."

Smith smiled at the words of the sailor, but yielding to his wishes he opened the Bible where the marker lay between the leaves. Instantly his eye fell upon a red cross made with a crayon, opposite the 8th verse of the seventh chapter of St. Matthew.

He read these words:— "For every one that asketh, receiveth; and he that seeketh, findeth."

CHAPTER XXV. THE DEPARTURE

THE RISING TIDE—ELMS AND OTHER TREES—DIFFERENT PLANTS—THE KINGFISHER—APPEARANCE OF THE FOREST—THE GIGANTIC EUCALYPTI— WHY THEY ARE CALLED FEVER-TREES—MONKEYS—THE WATERFALL— ENCAMPMENT FOR THE NIGHT.

The next day—the 30th of October—everything was prepared for the proposed exploration, which these last events had made so necessary. Indeed, as things had turned out, the colonists could well imagine themselves in a condition to give, rather than to receive, help.

It was agreed that they ascend the Mercy as far as practicable. They would thus be able to transport their arms and provisions a good part of the way without fatigue.

It was also necessary to think, not only of what they now carried, but of what they might perhaps bring back to Granite House. If, as all thought, there had been a shipwreck on the coast, they would find many things they wanted on the shore, and the cart would doubtless have proved more convenient than the canoe. But the cart was so heavy and unwieldy that it would have been too hard work to drag it, which fact made Pencroff regret that the box had not only held his half-pound of tobacco, but also a pair of stout New Jersey horses, which would have been so useful to the colony.

The provisions, already packed by Neb, consisted of enough dried meat, beer, and fermented liquor to last them for the three days which Smith expected they would be absent. Moreover, they counted on being able to replenish their stock at need along the route, and Neb had taken care not to forget the portable stove.

They took the two wood-choppers' hatchets to aid in making their way through the thick forest, and also the glass and the pocket compass.

Of the arms, they chose the two flint-lock guns in preference to the others, as the colonists could always renew the flints; whereas the caps could not be replaced. Nevertheless, they took one of the carbines and some cartridges. As for the powder, the barrels held fifty pounds, and it was necessary to take a certain amount of that; but the engineer expected to manufacture an explosive substance, by which it could be saved in the future. To the firearms they added the five cutlasses, in leather scabbards. And thus equipped, the party could venture into the forest with some chance of success.

Armed in this manner, Pencroff, Herbert, and Neb had all they could desire, although Smith made them promise not to fire a shot unnecessarily.

At 6 o'clock the party, accompanied by Top, started for the mouth of the Mercy. The tide had been rising half an hour, and there were therefore some hours yet of the flood which they could make use of. The current was strong, and they did not need to row to pass rapidly up between the high banks and the river. In a few minutes the explorers had reached the turn where, seven months before, Pencroff had made his first raft. Having passed this elbow, the river, flowing from the southwest, widened out under the shadow of the grand evergreen conifers; and Smith and his companions could not but admire the beautiful scenery. As they advanced the species of forest trees changed. On the right bank rose splendid specimens of ulmaceæ, those valuable elms so much sought after by builders, which have the property of remaining sound for a long time in water. There was, also, numerous groups belonging to the same family, among them the micocouliers, the root of which produces a useful oil. Herbert discovered some lardizabalaceæ, whose flexible branches, soaked in water, furnish excellent ropes, and two or three trunks of ebony of a beautiful black color, curiously veined.

From time to time, where a landing was easy, the canoe stopped, and Spilett, Herbert, and Pencroff, accompanied by Top, explored the bank. In addition to the game, Herbert thought that he might meet with some useful little plant which was not to be despised, and the young naturalist was rewarded by discovering a sort of wild spinach and numerous specimens of the genus cabbage, which would, doubtless, bear transplanting; they were cresses, horse-radishes, and a little, velvety, spreading plant, three-feet high, bearing brownish-colored seeds.

"Do you know what this is?" asked Herbert of the sailor.

"Tobacco!" cried Pencroff, who had evidently never seen the plant which he fancied so much.

"No, Pencroff," answered Herbert, "It is not tobacco, it is mustard."

"Only mustard!" exclaimed the other. "Well if you happen to come across a tobacco plant, my boy, do not pass it by."

"We will find it someday," said Spilett.

"All right," cried Pencroff, "and then I will be able to say that the island lacks nothing!"

These plants were taken up carefully and carried back to the canoe, where Cyrus Smith had remained absorbed in his own thoughts.

The reporter, Herbert, and Pencroff, made many of these excursions, sometimes on the right bank of the Mercy and sometimes upon the left. The latter was less abrupt, but more wooded. The engineer found, by reference to the pocket-compass, that the general direction of the river from its bend was southwest, and that it was nearly straight for about three miles. But it was probable that the direction would change further up, and that it would flow from the spurs of Mount Franklin, which fed its waters in the northwest.

During one of these excursions Spilett caught a couple of birds with long, slim beaks, slender necks, short wings, and no tails, which Herbert called tinamous, and which they resolved should be the first occupants of the future poultry-yard.

But the first report of a gun that echoed through the forests of the Far West, was provoked by the sight of a beautiful bird, resembling a kingfisher.

"I know it," cried Pencroff.

"What do you know?" asked the reporter.

"That bird! It is the bird which escaped on our first exploration, the one after which we named this part of the forest!"

"A jacamar!" exclaimed Herbert.

It was, indeed, one of those beautiful birds, whose harsh plumage is covered with a metallic lustre. Some small shot dropped it to the earth, and Top brought it, and also some touracolories, climbing birds, the size of pigeons, to the canoe. The honor of this first shot belonged to the lad, who was pleased enough with the result. The touracolories were better game than the jacamar, the flash of the latter being tough, but it would have been hard to persuade Pencroff that they had not killed the most delicious of birds.

It was 10 o'clock when the canoe reached the second bend of the river, some five miles from the mouth. Here they stopped half an hour, under the shadow of the trees, for breakfast.

The river measured from sixty to seventy feet in width, and was five or six feet deep. The engineer had remarked its several affluents, but they were simply unnavigable streams. The Forests of the Far West, or Jacamar Wood, extended farther than they could see, but no where could they detect the presence of man. If, therefore, any persons had been shipwrecked on the island, they had not yet quitted the shore, and it was not in those thick coverts that search must be made for the survivors.

The engineer began to manifest some anxiety to get to the western coast of the island, distant, as he calculated, about five miles or less. The journey was resumed, and, although the course of the Mercy, sometimes towards the shore, was oftener towards the mountain, it was thought better to follow it as long as possible, on account of the fatigue and loss of time incident to hewing a way through the wood. Soon, the tide having attained its height, Herbert and Neb took the oars, and Pencroff the paddle, wad they continued the ascent by rowing.

It seemed as if the forest of the Far West began to grow thinner. But, as the trees grew farther apart, they profited by the increased space, and attained a splendid growth.

"Eucalypti!" cried Herbert, descrying some of these superb plants, the loftiest giants of the extra-tropical zone, the congeners of the eucalypti of Australia and New Zealand, both of which countries were situated in the same latitude as Lincoln Island. Some rose 200 feet in height and measured twenty feet in circumference, and their bark, five fingers in thickness, exuded an aromatic resin. Equally wonderful were the enormous specimens of myrtle, their leaves extending edgewise to the sun, and permitting its rays to penetrate and fall upon the ground.

"What trees!" exclaimed Neb. "Are they good for anything?"

"Pshaw!" answered Pencroff. "They are like overgrown men, good for nothing but to show in fairs!"

"I think you're wrong, Pencroff," said Spilett, "the eucalyptus wood is beginning to be extensively used in cabinet work."

"And I am sure," added Herbert, "that it belongs to a most useful family," and thereupon the young naturalist enumerated many species of the plant and their uses.

Every one listened to the lad's lesson in botany, Smith smiling, Pencroff with an indescribable pride. "That's all very well, Herbert," answered the sailor, "but I dare swear that of all these useful specimens none are as large as these!"

"That is so."

"Then, that proves what I said," replied the sailor, "that giants are good for nothing."

"There's where you are wrong, Pencroff," said the engineer, "these very eucalypti are good for something."

"For what?"

"To render the country healthy about them. Do you know what they call them In Australia and New Zealand?"

"No sir."

"They call them 'fever' trees."

"Because they give it?"

"No; because they prevent it!"

"Good. I shall make a note of that," said the reporter.

"Note then, my dear Spilett, that it has been proved that the presence of these trees neutralizes marsh miasmas. They have tried this natural remedy in certain unhealthy parts of Europe, and northern Africa, with the best results. And there are no intermittent fevers in the region of these forests, which is a fortunate thing for us colonists of Lincoln Island."

"What a blessed island!" cried Pencroff. "It would lack nothing—if it was not—"

"That will come, Pencroff, we will find it," answered the reporter; "but now let us attend to our work and push on as far as we can get with the canoe."

They continued on through the woods two miles further, the river becoming more winding, shallow, and so narrow that Pencroff pushed along with a pole. The sun was setting, and, as it would be impossible to pass in the darkness through the five or six miles of unknown woods which the engineer estimated lay between them and the coast, it was determined to camp wherever the canoe was obliged to stop.

They now pushed on without delay through the forest, which grew more dense, and seemed more inhabited, because, if the sailor's eyes did not deceive him, he perceived troops of monkeys running among the underbrush. Sometimes, two or three of these animals would halt at a distance from the canoe and regard its occupants, as if, seeing men for the first time, they had not then learned to fear them. It would have been easy to have shot some of these quadrumanes, but Smith was opposed to the useless slaughter. Pencroff, however, looked upon the monkey from a gastronomic point of view, and, indeed, as these animals are entirely herberiferous, they make excellent game; but since provisions abounded, it was useless to waste the ammunition.

Towards 4 o'clock the navigation of the Mercy became very difficult, its course being obstructed by rocks and aquatic plants. The banks rose higher and higher, and, already, the bed of the stream was confined between the outer spurs of Mount Franklin. Its sources could not be far off, since the waters were fed by the southern watershed of that mountain.

"Before a quarter of an hour we will have to stop, sir," said Pencroff.

"Well, then, we will make a camp for the night."

"How far are we from Granite House?" asked Herbert.

"About seven miles, counting the bends of the river, which have taken us to the northwest."

"Shall we keep on?" asked the reporter.

"Yes, as far as we can get," answered the engineer. "To-morrow, at daylight, we will leave the canoe, and traverse, in two hours I hope, the distance which separates us from the coast, and then we will have nearly the whole day in which to explore the shore."

"Push on," cried Pencroff.

Very soon the canoe grated on the stones at the bottom of the river, which was not more than twenty feet wide. A thick mass of verdure overhung and descended the stream, and they heard the noise of a waterfall, which indicated that some little distance further on there existed a natural barrier.

And, indeed, at the last turn in the river, they saw the cascade shining through the trees. The canoe scraped over the bottom and then grounded on a rock near the right bank.

It was 5 o'clock, and the level rays of the setting sun illuminated the little fall. Above, the Mercy, supplied from a secret source, was hidden by the bushes. The various streams together had made it a river, but here it was but a shallow, limpid brook.

They made camp in this lovely spot. Having disembarked, a fire was lighted under a group of micocouliers, in whose branches Smith and his companions could, if need be, find a refuge for the night.

Supper was soon finished, as they were very hungry, and then there was nothing to do but to go to sleep. But some suspicious growling being heard at nightfall, the fire was so arranged as to protect the sleepers by its flames. Neb and Pencroff kept it lit, and perhaps they were not mistaken in believing to have seen some moving shadows among the trees and bushes; but the night passed without accident, and the next day—the 31st of October—by 5 o'clock all were on foot ready for the start.

CHAPTER XXVI. GOING TOWARD THE COAST

TROOPS OF MONKEYS—A NEW WATER-COURSE—WHY THE TIDE WAS NOT FELT—A FOREST ON THE SHORE—REPTILE PROMONTORY—SPILETT MAKES HERBERT ENVIOUS—THE BAMBOO FUSILADE.

It was 6 o'clock when the colonists, after an early breakfast, started with the intention of reaching the coast by the shortest route. Smith had estimated that it would take them two hours, but it must depend largely on the nature of the obstacles in the way. This part of the Far West was covered with trees, like an immense thicket composed of many different species. It was, therefore, probable that they would have to make a way with hatchets in hand—and guns also, if they were to judge from the cries heard over night.

The exact position of the camp had been determined by the situation of Mount Franklin, and since the volcano rose less than three miles to the north, it was only necessary to go directly toward the southwest to reach the west coast.

After having seen to the mooring of the canoe, the party started, Neb and Pencroff carrying sufficient provisions to last the little troop for two days at least. They were no longer hunting, and the engineer recommended his companions to refrain from unnecessary firing, so as not to give warning of their presence on the coast. The first blows of the hatchet were given in the bushes just above the cascade, while Smith, compass in hand, indicated the route. The forest was, for the most part, composed of such trees as had already been recognized about the lake and on Prospect Plateau. The colonists could advance but slowly, and the engineer believed that in time their route would join with that of Red Creek.

Since their departure, the party had descended the low declivities which constituted the orography of the island, over a very dry district, although the luxuriant vegetation suggested either a hydrographic network permeating the ground beneath, or the proximity to some stream. Nevertheless, Smith did not remember having seen, during the excursion to the crater, any other water courses than Bed Creek and the Mercy.

During the first few hours of the march, they saw troops of monkeys, who manifested the greatest astonishment at the sight of human beings. Spilett laughingly asked if these robust quadrumanes did not look upon their party as degenerate brethren; and, in truth, the simple pedestrians, impeded at each step by the bushes, entangled in the lianas, stopped by tree trunks, did not compare favorably with these nimble animals, which bounded from branch to branch, moving about without hindrance. These monkeys were very numerous, but, fortunately, they did not manifest any hostile disposition.

They saw, also, some wild-boars, some agoutis, kangaroos, and other rodents, and two or three koulas, which latter Pencroff would have been glad to shoot.

"But," said he, "the hunt has not begun. Play now, my friends, and we will talk to you when we come back."

At half-past 9, the route, which bore directly southwest, was suddenly interrupted by a rapid stream, rushing over rocks, and pent in between banks but thirty or forty feet apart. It was deep and clear, but absolutely unnavigable.

"We are stopped!" cried Neb.

"No," replied Herbert; "we can swim such a brook as this."

"Why should we do that?" answered Smith. "It is certain that this creek empties into the sea. Let us keep to this bank and I will be astonished if it does not soon bring us to the coast. Come on!"

"One minute," said the reporter. "The name of this creek, my friends? We must not leave our geography incomplete."

"True enough," said Pencroff.

"You name it, my boy," said the engineer, addressing Herbert.

"Will not it be better to wait till we have discovered its mouth?" asked Herbert.

"Right," replied Smith, "let us push on."

"Another minute," exclaimed Pencroff.

"What more?" demanded the reporter.

"If hunting is forbidden, fishing is allowed, I suppose," said the sailor.

"We haven't the time to waste," answered the engineer.

"But just five minutes," pleaded Pencroff; "I only want five minutes for the sake of breakfast!" And lying down on the bank he plunged his arms in the running waters and soon brought up several dozen of the fine crawfish which swarmed between the rocks.

"These will be good!" cried Neb, helping the sailor.

"Did not I tell you that the island had everything but tobacco?" sighed the sailor.

It took but five minutes to fill a sack with these little blue crustaceæ, and then the journey was resumed.

By following the bank the colonists moved more freely. Now and then they found traces of large animals which came to the stream for water, but they found no sign of human beings, and they were not yet in that part of the Far West where the peccary had received the leaden pellet which cost Pencroff a tooth.

Smith and his companions judged, from the fact that the current rushed towards the sea with such rapidity, that they must be much farther from, the coast than they imagined, because at this time the tide was rising, and its' effect would have been visible near the mouth of the creek. The engineer was greatly astonished, and often consulted his compass to be sure that the stream, was not returning towards the depths of the forest. Meantime, its waters, gradually widening, became less tumultuous. The growth of trees on the right bank was much denser than on the left, and it was impossible to see through this thicket; but these woods were certainly not inhabited, or Top would have discovered it.

At half-past 10, to the extreme surprise of Smith, Herbert, who was walking some paces ahead, suddenly stopped, exclaiming, "The sea!"

And a few minutes later the colonists, standing upon the border of the forest, saw the western coast of the island spread before them.

But what a contrast was this coast to the one on which chance had thrown them! No granite wall, no reef in the offing, not even a beach. The forest formed the shore, and its furthermost trees, washed by the waves, leaned over the waters. It was in no sense such a beach as is usually met with, composed of vast reaches of sand or heaps of rocks, but a fine border of beautiful trees. The bank was raised above the highest tides, and upon this rich soil, supported by a granite base, the splendid monarchs of the forest seemed to be as firmly set as were those which stood in the interior of the island.

The colonists stood in a hollow by a tiny rivulet, which served as a neck to the other stream; but, curiously enough, these waters, instead of emptying into the sea by a gently sloping opening, fell from a height of more than forty feet—which fact explained why the rising tide did not affect the current. And, on this account, they were unanimous in giving this water-course the name of Fall River.

Beyond, towards the north, the forest shore extended for two miles; then the trees became thinner, and, still further on, a line of picturesque heights extended from north to south. On the other hand, all that part of the coast comprised between Fall River and the promontory of Reptile End was bordered by masses of magnificent trees, some upright and others leaning over the sea, whose waves lapped their roots. It was evidently, therefore, on this part of the coast that the exploration must be continued, as this shore offered to the castaways, whoever they might be, a refuge, which the other, desert and savage, had refused.

The weather was beautiful, and from the cliff where the breakfast had been prepared, the view extended far and wide. The horizon was perfectly distinct, without a sail in sight, and upon the coast, as far as could be seen, there was neither boat nor wreck, but the engineer was not willing to be satisfied in this respect, until they had explored the whole distance as far as Serpentine Peninsula.

After a hurried breakfast he gave the signal to start. Instead of traversing a beach, the colonists followed along the coast, under the trees. The distance to Reptile End was about twelve miles, and, had the way been clear, they could have accomplished it in four hours, but the party were constantly obliged to turn out from the way, or to cut branches, or to break through thickets, and these hindrances multiplied as they proceeded. But they saw no signs of a recent shipwreck on the shore; although, as Spilett observed, as the tide was up, they could not say with certainty that there had not been one.

This reasoning was just, and, moreover, the incident of the bullet proved, indubitably, that within three months a gun had been fired on the island.

At 5 o'clock the extremity of the peninsula was still two miles distant, and it was evident that the colonists would have to camp for the night on the promontory of Reptile End. Happily, game was as plenty here as on the other coast, and birds of different kinds abounded. Two hours later, the party, tired out, reached the promontory. Here the forest border ended, and the shore assumed the usual aspect of a coast. It was possible that an abandoned vessel might be here, but, as the night was falling, it was necessary to postpone the exploration until the morrow.

Pencroff and Herbert hastened to find a suitable place for a camp. The outskirts of the forest died away here, and near them the lad found a bamboo thicket.

"Good," said he, "this is a valuable discovery."

"Valuable?" asked Pencroff.

"Yes, indeed, I need not tell you, Pencroff, all its uses, such as for making baskets, paper, and water-pipes; that the larger ones make excellent building material and strong jars. But—"

"But?"

"But perhaps you do not know that in India they eat bamboo as we do asparagus."

"Asparagus thirty feet high?" cried, Pencroff. "And is it good?"

"Excellent," answered the lad. "But they eat only the young sprouts."

"Delicious!" cried Pencroff.

"And I am sure that the pith of young plants preserved in vinegar makes an excellent condiment."

"Better and better."

"And, lastly, they exude a sweet liquor which makes a pleasant drink."

"Is that all?" demanded the sailor.

"That's all."

"Isn't it good to smoke?"

"No, my poor Pencroff, you cannot smoke it!"

They did not have to search far for a good place for the camp. The rocks, much worn by the action of the sea, had many hollows that would afford shelter from the wind. But just as they were about to enter one of these cavities they were arrested by formidable growlings.

"Get back!" cried Pencroff, "we have only small shot in our guns, and these beasts would mind it no more than salt!"

And the sailor, seizing Herbert, dragged him behind some rocks, just as a huge jaguar appeared at the mouth of the cavern. Its skin was yellow, striped with black, and softened off with white under its belly. The beast advanced, and looked about. Its hair was bristling, and its eyes sparkling as if it was not scenting man for the first time.

Just then Spilett appeared, coming round the high rocks, and Herbert, thinking he had not seen the jaguar, was about rushing towards him, when the reporter, motioning with his hand, continued his approach. It was not his first tiger.

Advancing within ten paces of the animal, he rested motionless, his gun at his shoulder, not a muscle quivering. The jaguar, crouching back, made a bound towards the hunter, but as it sprung a bullet struck it between the eyes, dropping it dead.

Herbert and Pencroff rushed to it, and Smith and Neb coming up at the moment, all stopped to look at the splendid animal lying at length upon the sand.

"Oh, Mr. Spilett, how I envy you!" cried Herbert, in an excess of natural enthusiasm.

"Well, my boy, you would have done as well," answered the reporter.

"I have been as cool as that!"

"Only imagine, Herbert, that a jaguar is a hare, and you will shoot him as unconcernedly as anything in the world! And now," continued the reporter, "since the jaguar has left his retreat I don't see, my friends, why we should not occupy the place during the night"

"But some others may return!" said Pencroff.

"We will only have to light a fire at the entrance of the cavern," said the reporter, "and they will not dare to cross the threshold."

"To the jaguar house, then," cried the sailor, dragging the body of the animal after him.

The colonists went to the abandoned cave, and, while Neb was occupied in skinning the carcass, the others busied themselves with piling a great quantity of dry wood around the threshold. This done they installed themselves in the cave, whose floor was strewn with bones; the arms were loaded for an emergency; and, having eaten supper, as soon as the time for sleep was come, the fire at the entrance was lit.

Immediately a tremendous fusilade ensued! It was the bamboo which, in burning, exploded like fire-works! The noise, in itself, would have been sufficient to frighten off the bravest beasts.

CHAPTER XXVII. PROPOSAL TO RETURN BY THE SOUTH COAST

ITS CONFIGURATION—SEARCH FOR THE SHIPWRECKED—A WAIF IN THE AIR—DISCOVERY OF A SMALL NATURAL HARBOR—MIDNIGHT ON THE MERCY—A DRIFTING CANOE.

Smith and his companions slept like mice in the cavern which the jaguar had so politely vacated, and, by sunrise, all were on the extremity of the promontory, and scrutinizing the horizon visible on either hand. No ship or wreck was to be seen, and not even with the spy-glass could any suspicious object be discerned. It was the same along the shore, at least on all that portion, three miles in length, which formed the south side of the promontory; as, beyond that, a slope of the land concealed the rest of the coast, and even from the extremity of Serpentine Peninsula, Claw Cape was hidden by high rocks.

The southern bank of the island remained to be explored. Had they not better attempt this at once, and give up this day to it? This procedure had not entered into their first calculations, as, when the canoe was left at the sources of the Mercy, the colonists thought that, having explored the west coast, they would return by the river; Smith having then believed that this coast sheltered either a wreck or a passing ship. But as soon as this shore disclosed no landing place, it became necessary to search the south side of the island for those whom they had failed to discover on the west.

It was Spilett who proposed continuing the exploration so as to settle definitely the question of the supposed shipwreck, and he inquired how far it would be to Claw Cape.

"About thirty miles," answered the engineer, "if we allow for the irregularity of the shore."

"Thirty miles!" exclaimed Spilett, "that would be a long walk. Nevertheless, I think we should return to Granite House by the south coast."

"But," observed Herbert, "from Claw Cape to Granite House is at least ten miles further."

"Call it forty miles altogether," answered the reporter, "and do not let us hesitate to do it. At least we will have seen this unknown shore, and will not have it to explore over again."

"That is so," said Pencroff. "But how about the canoe?"

"The canoe can stay where it is for a day or two," replied Spilett. "We can hardly say that the island is infested with thieves!" '

"Nevertheless, when I remember that affair of the turtle, I am not so confident."

"The turtle! the turtle!" cried the reporter, "don't you know that the sea turned it over?"

"Who can say?" murmured the engineer.

"But—," began Neb, who, it was evident, wished to say something.

"What is it, Neb?" questioned the engineer.

"If we do return by the shore to Claw Cape, after having gone round it, we will be stopped—"

"By the Mercy!" cried Herbert. "And we have no bridge or boat!"

"Oh!" answered Pencroff, "we can cross it readily enough with some logs."

"Nevertheless," said Spilett, "it would be well to build a bridge some time if we wish to have ready access to the Far West."

"A bridge!" cried Pencroff. "Well isn't Mr. Smith State Engineer? If we shall need a bridge we will have one. As to carrying you over the Mercy to-night without getting wet, I will look out for that. We still have a day's provision, which is all that is necessary, and, besides, the game may not give out to-day as It did yesterday. So let us go."

The proposal of the reporter, strongly seconded by the sailor, obtained general approval, as every one wished to end their doubts, and by returning by

624

Claw Cape the exploration would be complete. But no time was to be lost, for the tramp was long, and they counted on reaching Granite House that night. So by 6 o'clock the little party was on its way, the guns loaded with ball in case of an encounter, and Top, who went ahead, ordered to search the edge of the forest.

The first five miles of the distance was rapidly traversed, and not the slightest sign of any human being was seen. When the colonists arrived at the point where the curvature of the promontory ended, and Washington Bay began, they were able to take in at one view the whole extent of the southern coast. Twenty-five miles distant the shore was terminated by Claw Cape, which was faintly visible through the morning mists, and reproduced as a mirage in mid-air. Between the place occupied by the colonists and the upper end of the Great Bay the shore began with a flat and continuous beach, bordered in the background by tall trees; following this, it became very irregular, and thrust sharp points into the sea, and finally a heap of black rocks, thrown together in picturesque disorder, completed the distance to Claw Cape.

"A ship would surely be lost on these sands and shoals and reefs," said Pencroff.

"It is poor quarters!"

"But at least a portion of her would be left," observed the reporter.

"Some bits of wood would remain on the reefs, nothing on the sands," answered the sailor.

"How is that?"

"Because the sands are even more dangerous than the rocks, and swallow up everything that is thrown upon them; a few days suffice to bury out of sight the hull of a ship of many tons measurement."

"Then, Pencroff," questioned the engineer, "if a vessel had been lost on these banks, it would not be surprising if there was no trace left?"

"No, sir, that is after a time or after a tempest. Nevertheless, it would be surprising, as now, that no spars or timbers were thrown upon the shore beyond the reach of the sea."

"Let us continue our search," replied Smith.

By 1 o'clock the party had accomplished twenty miles, having reached the upper end of Washington Bay, and they stopped to lunch.

Here began an irregular shore, oddly cut into by a long line of rocks, succeeding the sand banks, and just beginning to show themselves by long streaks of foam, above the undulations of the receding waves. From this point to Claw Cape the beach was narrow and confined between the reef of rocks and the forest, and the march would therefore be more difficult. The granite wall sunk more and more, and above it the tops of the trees, undisturbed by a breath of air, appeared in the background.

After half an hour's rest the colonists took up the march again, on the lookout for any sign of a wreck, but without success. They found out, however, that edible mussels were plenty on this beach, although they would not gather them until means of transport between the two banks of the river should have been perfected.

Towards 3 o'clock, Smith and his companions reached a narrow inlet, unfed by any water-course. It formed a veritable little natural harbor, invisible from without, and approached by a narrow passage guarded by the reefs. At the upper end of this creek some violent convulsion had shattered the rock, and a narrow, sloping passage gave access to the upper plateau, which proved to be ten miles from Claw Cape, and therefore four miles in a direct line from Prospect Plateau.

Spilett proposed to his companions to halt here, and, as the march had sharpened their appetites, although it was not dinner time, no one objected to a bit of venison, and with this lunch they would be able to await supper at Granite House.

Soon the colonists, seated under a group of splendid pines, were eating heartily of the provisions which Neb had brought out from his haversack. The place was some fifty or sixty feet above the sea, and the view, extending beyond the furthest rock of the cape, was lost in Union Bay. But the islet and Prospect Plateau were invisible, as the high ground and the curtain of high trees shut out the horizon to the north. Neither over the extent of sea nor on that part of the coast which it was still necessary to explore could they discover even with the spyglass any suspicious object.

"Well" said Spilett, "we can console ourselves by thinking that no one is disputing the island with us."

"But how about the pellet?" said Herbert. "It was not a dream."

"Indeed it was not!" cried Pencroff, thinking of his missing tooth.

"Well, what are we to conclude?" asked the reporter.

"This," said Smith, "that within three months a ship, voluntarily or otherwise, has touched—"

"What! You will admit, Cyrus, that it has been swallowed up without leaving any trace?" cried the reporter.

"No, my dear Spilett; but you must remember that while it is certain that a human being has been here, it seems just as certain that he is not here now."

"Then, if I understand you sir," said Herbert, "the ship has gone again?"

"Evidently."

"And we have lost, beyond return, a chance to get home?" said Neb.

"I believe without return."

"Well then, since the chance is lost, let us push on," said Pencroff, already home-sick for Granite House.

"But, just as they were rising, Top's barking was heard, and the dog burst from the forest, holding in his mouth a soiled rag.

Neb took it from him. It was a bit of strong cloth. Top, still barking, seemed by his motions to invite his master to follow into the wood.

"Here is something which will explain my bullet," cried Pencroff.

"A shipwrecked person!" answered Herbert.

"Wounded, perhaps!" exclaimed Neb.

"Or dead!" responded the reporter.

And all holding their arms in readiness, hurried after the dog through the outskirts of the forests. They advanced some distance into the wood, but, to their disappointment, they saw no tracks. The underbrush and lianas were uninjured and had to be cut away with the hatchet, as in the depths of the forest. It was hard to imagine that any human creature had passed there, and yet Top's action showed no uncertainty, but was more like that of a human being having a fixed purpose.

In a few minutes the dog stopped. The colonists, who had arrived at a sort of glade surrounded by high trees, looked all about them, but neither in the underbrush or between the tree trunks could they discover a thing.

"What is it, Top?" said Smith.

Top, barking louder, ran to the foot of a gigantic pine.

Suddenly Pencroff exclaimed:—

"This is capital!"

"What's that," asked Spilett.

"We've been hunting for some waif on the sea or land—"

"Well?"

"And here it is in the air!"

And the sailor pointed out a mass of faded cloth caught on the summit of the pine, a piece of which Top had found on the ground.

"But that is no waif!" exclaimed Spilett.

"Indeed it is," answered Pencroff.

"How is it!"

"It is all that is left of our balloon, of our ship which is stranded on the top of this tree."

Pencroff was not mistaken, and he added, with a shout:—

"And there is good stuff in it which will keep us in linen for years. It will make us handkerchiefs and shirts. Aha, Mr. Spilett! what do you say of an island where shirts grow on the trees?"

It was, indeed, a fortunate thing for the colonists that the aerostat, after having made its last bound into the air, had fallen again on the island. They could, either keep the envelope in its present shape, in case they might desire to attempt a new flight through the air, or, after having taken off the varnish, they could make use of its hundreds of ells of good cotton cloth. At these thoughts all shared Pencroff's joy.

It was no easy task to take down this envelope from the tree top. But Neb, Herbert, and the sailor climbed up to it, and after two hours of hard work not only the envelope, with its valve, springs, and leather mountings, but the net, equivalent to a large quantity of cordage and ropes, together with the iron ring and the anchor, lay upon the ground. The envelope, excepting the rent, was in good order, and only its lower end had been torn away.

It was a gift from heaven.

"Nevertheless, Mr. Smith," said the sailor, "if we ever do decide to leave the island it won't be in a balloon, I hope. These air ships don't always go the way you want them to, as we have found out. If you will let me have my way, we will build a ship of twenty tons, and you will allow me to cut from this cloth a foresail and jib. The rest of it will do for clothes."

"We will see about it, Pencroff," answered Smith.

"And meanwhile it must all be put away carefully," said Neb.

In truth, they could not think of carrying all this weight of material to Granite House; and while waiting for a proper means of removing it, it was important not to leave it exposed to the weather. The colonists, uniting their efforts, succeeded in dragging it to the shore, where they discovered a cave so situated that neither wind, rain, nor sea could get at it.

"It is a wardrobe," said Pencroff; "but since it does not kick, it will be prudent to hide the opening, not, perhaps from two-footed, but from four-footed thieves!"

By 6 o'clock everything was stored away, and after having named the little inlet, Balloon, Harbor, they took the road for Claw Cape. Pencroff and the engineer discussed several projects, which it would be well to attend to at once. The first thing was to build a bridge across the Mercy, and, as the canoe was too small, to bring the balloon over in the cart. Then to build a decked launch, which Pencroff would make cutter-rigged, and in which they could make voyages of circumnavigation—around the island; then, etc.

In the meantime the night approached, and it was already dark, when the colonists reached Jetsam Point, where they had discovered the precious box. But here, as elsewhere, there was nothing to indicate a shipwreck, and it became necessary to adopt the opinions expressed by Smith.

The four miles from Jetsam Point to Granite House were quickly traversed, but it was midnight when the colonists arrived at the first bend above the mouth of the Mercy. There the river was eighty feet wide, and Pencroff, who had undertaken to overcome the difficulty of crossing it, set to work. It must be admitted that the colonists were fatigued. The tramp had been long, and the incident of the balloon had not rested their arms or legs. They were therefore anxious to get back to Granite House to supper and bed, and if they had only had the bridge, in a quarter of an hour they could have been at home.

The night was very dark. Pencroff and Neb, armed with the hatchets, chose two trees near the bank, and began cutting them down, in order to make a raft. Smith and Spilett, seated on the ground, waited to assist their companions, and Herbert sauntered about, doing nothing.

All at once the lad, who had gone up the stream, returned hurriedly, and, pointing back, exclaimed:—

"What is that drifting there?"

Pencroff stopped work and perceived an object resting motionless in the gloom.

"A canoe!" he exclaimed.

All came up and saw, to their astonishment, a boat following the current.

"Canoe, ahoy!" shouted Pencroff from force of habit, forgetting that it might be better to keep quiet.

There was no answer. The boat continued to drift, and it was not more than a dozen paces off, when the sailor exclaimed:—

"Why, it's our canoe! She has broken away and drifted down with the current. Well, we must admit that she comes in the nick of time!"

"Our canoe!" murmured the engineer.

Pencroff was right. It was indeed their canoe, which had doubtless broken loose and drifted all the way from the headwaters of the Mercy! It was important to seize it in passing before it should be drawn into the rapid current at the mouth of the river, and Pencroff and Neb, by the aid of a long pole, did this, and drew the canoe to the bank.

The engineer stepped in first, and, seizing the rope, assured himself that it had been really worn in two against the rocks.

"This," said the reporter in an undertone; "this is a coincidence—"

"It is very strange!" answered the engineer.

At least it was fortunate, and while no one could doubt that the rope had been broken by friction, the astonishing part of the affair was that the canoe had arrived at the moment when the colonists were there to seize it, for a quarter of an hour later, and it would have been carried out to sea. Had there been such things as genii, this incident would have been sufficient to make the colonists believe that the island was inhabited by a supernatural being, who placed his power at their disposal.

With a few strokes the party arrived at the mouth of the Mercy. The canoe was drawn on shore at the Chimneys, and all took their way to the ladder at Granite House.

But, just then, Top began barking furiously, and Neb, who was feeling for the lower rung, cried out:— "The ladder's gone!"

CHAPTER XXVIII. PENCROFF'S HALLOOS

A NIGHT IN THE CHIMNEYS—HERBERT'S ARROW—SMITH'S PLAN—AN UNEXPECTED SOLUTION—WHAT HAD HAPPENED IN GRANITE HOUSE—HOW THE COLONISTS OBTAINED A NEW DOMESTIC.

Smith stood silent. His companions searched in the obscurity along the wall, over the ground, for the broken part of the ladder, supposing it had been torn off by the wind. But the ladder had certainly disappeared, although it was impossible to tell in the darkness whether a gust of wind had not carried it up and lodged it on the first ledge.

"If this is a joke, it's a pretty poor one," cried Pencroff. "To get home and not be able to find the staircase, won't do for tired men."

Neb stood in open-mouthed amazement.

"It could not have been carried away by the wind!" said Herbert.

"I'm beginning to think that strange things happen in Lincoln Island!" said Pencroff.

"Strange?" rejoined Spilett. "Why no, Pencroff, nothing is more natural. Somebody has come while we have been absent, and has taken possession of the house and drawn up the ladder!".

"Some one!" cried the sailor. "Who could it be?"

"Why, the man who shot the bullet," answered the reporter "How else can you explain it?"

"Very well, if any one is up there," replied Pencroff, beginning to get angry, "I will hail him, and he had better answer."

And in a voice of thunder the sailor gave a prolonged "Ohe," which was loudly repeated by the echoes.

The colonists listened, and thought that they heard a sort of chuckling proceed from Granite House. But there was no answering voice to the sailor, who repeated his appeal in vain.

Here was an event that would have astonished people the most indifferent, and from their situation the colonists could not be that. To them, the slightest incident was of moment, and certainly during their seven months' residence nothing equal to this had happened.

They stood there at the foot of Granite House not knowing what to do or to say. Neb was disconsolate at not being able to get back to the kitchen, especially as the provisions taken for the journey had all been eaten, and they had no present means of renewing them.

"There is but one thing to do, my friends," said Smith, "to wait until daylight, and then to be governed by circumstances. Meanwhile let us go to the Chimneys, where we will be sheltered, and, even if we cannot eat, we can sleep."

"But who is the ill-mannered fellow that has played us this trick?" asked Pencroff again, who thought it no joke.

Whoever he was, there was nothing to do but to follow the engineer's advice. Top having been ordered to lie down under the windows of Granite House, took his place without complaint. The brave dog remained at the foot of the wall, while his master and his companions took shelter among the rocks.

The colonists, tired as they were, slept but little. Not only were their beds uncomfortable, but it was certain that their house was occupied at present, and they were unable to get into it. Now Granite House was not only their dwelling, it was their storehouse. Everything they possessed was stored there. It would be a serious thing if this should be pillaged and they should have again to begin at the beginning. In their anxiety, one or the other went out often to see if the dog remained on watch. Smith, alone, waited with his accustomed patience, although he was exasperated at finding himself confronted by something utterly inexplicable, and his reason shrank from the thought that around him, over him, perhaps, was exercising an influence to which he could give no name.

Spilett sharing his thoughts, they conversed together in an undertone of those unaccountable events which defied all their knowledge and experience. Certainly, there was a mystery about this island, but how discover it? Even Herbert did not know what to think, and often questioned Smith. As to Neb, he said that this was his master's business and not his; and if he had not feared offending his companions, the brave fellow would have slept this night as soundly as if he had been in his bed in Granite House.

Pencroff, however, was very much put out.

"It's a joke," he said. "It's a joke that is played on us. Well, I don't like such jokes, and the joker won't like it, if I catch him!"

At dawn the colonists, well armed, followed along the shore to the reefs. By 5 o'clock the closed windows of Granite House appeared through their leafy curtain. Everything, from this side, appeared to be in order, but an exclamation escaped from the colonists when they perceived that the door which they had left closed was wide open. There could be no more doubt that some one was in Granite House, The upper ladder was in its place; but the lower had been drawn up to the threshold. It was evident that the intruders wished to guard against a surprise. As to telling who or how many they were, that was still impossible, as none had yet shown themselves.

Pencroff shouted again, but without answer.

"The beggars!" he exclaimed, "to sleep as soundly as if they were at home! Halloo! pirates! bandits! corsairs! sons of John Bull!"

When Pencroff, as an American, called any one a "son of John Bull," he had reached the acme of insult.

Just then, the day broke and the facade of Granite House was illuminated by the rays of the rising sun. But inside as well as without all was still and calm. It was evident from the position of the ladder that whoever had been inside the house had not come out. But how could they get up to them?

Herbert conceived the idea of shooting an arrow attached to a cord between the lower rungs of the ladder which were hanging from the doorway: They would thus be able by means of the cord to pull this ladder down, and gain access to Granite House. There was evidently nothing else to do, and with a little skill this attempt might prove successful. Fortunately there were bows and arrows at the Chimneys, and they found there, also, some twenty fathoms of light hibiscus cord. Pencroff unrolled this, and fastened the end to a well-feathered arrow. Then Herbert having placed the arrow in his bow took careful aim at the hanging part of the ladder.

The others stationed themselves some distance in the background to observe what might happen, and the reporter covered the doorway with his carbine.

The bow bent, the arrow shot upward with the cord, and passed between the two lower rungs of the ladder. The operation had succeeded. But just as Herbert, having caught the end of the cord, was about giving it a pull to make the ladder fall, an arm thrust quickly between the door and the wall seized the ladder and drew it within Granite House.

"You little beggar!" cried Pencroff. "If a ball would settle you, you would not have to wait long!"

"But what is it?" demanded Neb.

"What! didn't you see?"

"No."

"Why, it's a monkey, a macauco, a sapajo, an orang, a baboon, a gorilla, a sagoin! Our house has been invaded by monkeys, which have climbed up the ladder while we were away."

And at the moment, as if to prove the truth of what the sailor said, three or four quadrumana threw open the window shutters and saluted the true proprietors of the place with a thousand contortions and grimaces.

"I knew all the time it was a joke," cried Pencroff, "But here's one of the jokers that will pay for the others!" he added, covering a monkey with his gun and firing. All disappeared but, this one, which, mortally wounded, fell to the ground.

This monkey was very large and evidently belonged to the first order of quadrumana. Whether a chimpanzee, an orang, a gorilla, or a gibbon, it ranked among these anthropomorphi, so called on account of their likeness to the human race. Herbert declared it was an orang-outang, and we all know that the lad understood zoology.

"What a fine beast!" cried Neb.

"As fine as you choose!" answered the reporter, "but I don't see yet how we are going to get in!"

"Herbert is a good shot," said the reporter, "and his bow is sure! We will try again—"

"But these monkeys are mischievous," cried Pencroff, "and if they don't come to the windows, we cannot shoot them; and when I think of the damage they can do in the rooms and, in the magazine—"

"Have patience," answered Smith. "These animals cannot hold us in check, very long."

"I will be sure of that when they are out of there, "rejoined Pencroff, "Can you say how many dozens of these fools there may be?"

It would have been hard to answer Pencroff, but it was harder to try again the experiment of the arrow, as the lower end of the ladder had been drawn within the doorway, and when they pulled on the cord again, it broke, and the ladder remained, as before.

It was, indeed, vexatious. Pencroff was in a fury, and, although the situation had a certain comic aspect, he did not think it funny at all. It was evident that the colonists would, eventually, get back into their house and drive out the monkeys, but when and how they could not say.

Two hours passed, during which the monkeys avoided showing themselves; but they were there, for all that, and, two or three times, a muzzle or paw slipped by the door or the windows, and was saluted by a shot.

"Let us conceal ourselves," said the engineer, at length. "And then the monkeys will think we have gone off, and will show themselves again. Let Herbert and Spilett remain hidden behind the rocks and fire on any that appear.

The directions of the engineer were followed, and while the reporter and the lad, who were the best shots in the party, took their positions, the others went over the plateau to the forest to shoot some game, as it was breakfast time and they had no food.

In half an hour the hunters returned with some wild pigeons, which would be pretty good roasted. Not a monkey had shown itself.

Spilett and Herbert went to their breakfast, while Top kept watch under the windows. Then they returned to their post. Two hours later the situation was unchanged. The quadrumana gave no sign of existence, and it seemed as if they must have disappeared; but it was more likely that, frightened by the death of one of their number and the detonations of the guns, they kept themselves hidden in the chambers or the store-room of Granite House. And, when the colonists thought of all that was stored in this latter room, the patience which the engineer had recommended turned into irritation, and indeed they could not be blamed for it.

"It is too bad!" exclaimed the reporter, at length; "and is there no way we can put an end to this?"

"We must make these beggars give up!" cried Pencroff. "We can readily do it, even if there are twenty of them, in a hand-to hand fight! Oh, is there no way we can get at them?"

"Yes," replied Smith, struck by an idea.

"Only one?" rejoined Pencroff. "Well, that's better than none at all. What is it?"

"Try to get into Granite House by the old weir," answered the engineer.

"Why in the mischief didn't I think of that!" cried the sailor.

This was, indeed, the only way to get into Granite House, in order to fight the band and drive them out. It is true that, if they tore down the cemented wall which closed the weir, the work would have all to be done over again; but, fortunately, Smith had not yet effected his design of hiding this opening by covering it again with the lake, as that operation necessitated a good deal of time.

It was already past noon when the colonists, well armed and furnished with picks and mattocks, left the Chimneys, passed under the windows of Granite House, and, having ordered Top to remain at his post, made ready to climb the left bank of the Mercy, so as to reach Prospect Plateau. But they had hardly gone fifty paces, when they heard the loud barkings of the dog, as if making a desperate appeal. All halted.

"Let us run back," cried Pencroff. And all did as proposed as fast as possible.

Arrived at the turn, the whole situation was changed. The monkeys, seized with a sudden fright, startled by some unknown cause, were trying to escape. Two or three were running and springing from window to window, with the agility of clowns. In their fright they seemed to have forgotten to replace the ladder, by which they could easily have descended. In a moment half a dozen were in such a position that they could be shot, and the colonists, taking aim, fired. Some fell, wounded or killed, within the chambers, uttering sharp cries. Others, falling to the ground without, were crushed by the fall, and a few moments afterwards it seemed as if there was not one living quadrumana in Granite House.

"Hurrah," said Pencroff, "hurrah, hurrah!"

"Don't cheer yet," said Spilett.

"Why not," asked Pencroff. "Ain't they all killed."

"Doubtless: but that does not give us the means of getting in."

"Let us go the weir!" exclaimed Pencroff.

"We will have to," said the engineer. "Nevertheless it would have been preferable—"

And at the instant, as if in answer to the observation of the engineer, they saw the ladder slide over the door-sill and roll over to the ground.

"By the thousand pipes, but that is lucky!" cried Pencroff, looking at Smith.

"Too lucky!" muttered Smith, springing up the ladder.

"Take care, Mr. Smith!" exclaimed Pencroff, "if there should be any sojourners—"

"We will soon see," responded the other.

All his companions followed him and in a moment were within the doorway.

They searched everywhere. No one was in the chambers or in the storeroom, which remained undisturbed by the quadrumana.

"And the ladder," said Pencroff; "where is the gentleman who pushed it down to us?"

But just then a cry was heard, and a huge monkey, that had taken refuge in the corridor, sprang into the great hall, followed by Neb.

"Ah, the thief!" cried Pencroff, about to spring with his hatchet at the head of the animal, when Smith stopped him.

"Spare it, Pencroff."

"What, spare this black ape?"

"Yes, it is he that has thrown us the ladder," said the engineer, in a voice so strange, that it was hard to say whether he was in earnest or not.

Nevertheless, all threw themselves on the monkey, which, after a brave resistance, was thrown down and tied.

"Ugh!" exclaimed Pencroff; "and now what will we do with it?"

"Make a servant of it," answered Herbert, half in earnest, as the lad knew how great was the intelligence of this race of quadrumana.

The colonists gathered round the monkey and examined it attentively. It appeared to belong to that species of anthropomorphi in which the facial angle is not visibly inferior to that of the Australians or Hottentots. He was an orang of the kind which has neither the ferocity of the baboon nor the macauco, nor the thoughtlessness of the sagoin, nor the impatience of the magot, nor the bad instincts of the cynocephalous. It was of a family of anthropomorphi which has traits indicating a half-human intelligence. Employed in houses, they can wait on the table, do chamber-work, brush clothes, black boots, clean the knives and forks, and—empty the bottles, as well as the best trained flunkey. Buffon possessed one of these monkeys, which served him a long time as a zealous and faithful servant.

The one at present tied in the hall of Granite House was a big fellow, six feet high, deep-chested, and finely built, a medium-sized head, with a sharp facial angle, a well-rounded skull, and a prominent nose, and a skin covered with smooth hair, soft and shining,—in short, a finished type of anthropomorphi. Its eyes, somewhat smaller than those of a human being, sparkled with intelligence; its teeth glistened beneath its moustache, and it wore a small nut-brown beard.

"He is a fine chap," said Pencroff. "If we only understood his language, one might talk with him!"

"Then," said Neb, "are they in earnest, my master? Will we take it as a domestic?"

"Yes, Neb," said the engineer, smiling. "But you need not be jealous."

"And I hope it will make an excellent servant. As it is young its education will be easy, and we will not have to use force to make it mind, nor to pull out its teeth as is sometimes done. It cannot fail to become attached to masters who only treat it well."

"And we will do that," said Pencroff, who having forgotten his recent wrath against the "jokers," approached the orang and accosted him with:—

"Hullo, my boy, how goes it?"

The orang responded with a little grunt, which seemed to denote a not bad temper.

"You want to join the colony, do you? Would you like to enter the service of Mr. Smith?"

The monkey gave another affirmative grunt.

"And you'll be satisfied with your board as wages?"

A third affirmative grunt.

"His conversation is a little monotonous," observed Spilett.

"Well," replied Pencroff, "the best domestics are those that speak least. And then, no wages! Do you hear, my boy? At first we give you no wages, but we will double them later, if you suit us!"

Thus the colonists added to their number one who had already done them a service. As to a name, the sailor asked that he should be called, in remembrance of another monkey, Jupiter, or by abbreviation, Jup. And thus, without more ado, Master Jup was installed in Granite House.

CHAPTER XXIX. PROJECTS TO BE CARRIED OUT

A BRIDGE OVER THE MERCY—TO MAKE AN ISLAND OF PROSPECT PLATEAU—THE DRAW-BRIDGE—THE CORN HARVEST—THE STREAM—THE CAUSEWAY—THE POULTRY YARD—THE PIGEON-HOUSE—THE TWO WILD ASSES—HARNESSED TO THE WAGON—EXCURSION TO BALLOON HARBOR.

The colonists had now reconquered their domicile without having been obliged to follow the weir. It was, indeed, fortunate, that at the moment they decided to destroy their masonry, the band of monkeys, struck by a terror not less sudden than inexplicable, had rushed from Granite House. Had these animals a presentiment that a dangerous attack was about to be made on them from another direction? This was the only way to account for their retreat.

The rest of the day was occupied in carrying the dead monkeys to the wood and burying them there, and in repairing the disorder made by the intruders,—disorder and not damage, as, though they had upset the furniture in the rooms, they had broken nothing. Neb rekindled the range, and the supply in the pantry furnished a substantial repast that was duly honored.

Jup was not forgotten, and he ate with avidity the pistachio nuts and the roots of the sumach, with which he saw himself abundantly provided. Pencroff had unfastened his arms, although he thought it best to keep the monkey's legs bound until they could be sure he had surrendered.

Seated at the table, before going to bed, Smith and his companions discussed three projects, the execution of which was urgent. The most important and the most pressing was the establishment of a bridge across the Mercy, then the building of a corral, designed for the accommodation of moufflons or other woolly animals which they had agreed to capture. These two plans tended to solve the question of clothing, which was then the most serious question.

It was Smith's intention to establish this corral at the sources of Red Creek, where there was abundant pasturage. Already the path between there and Prospect Plateau was partially cleared, and with a better constructed cart, carriage would be easy, especially if they should capture some animal that could draw it.

But while it would not be inconvenient to have the corral some distance from Granite House, it was different with the poultry-yard, to which Neb called attention. It was necessary that the "chickens" should be at the hand of the cook, and no place seemed more favorable for an establishment of this kind than that portion of the lake shore bordering on the former weir. The aquatic birds also would thrive there, and the pair of tinamons, taken in the last excursion, would serve as a beginning.

The next day—the 3d of November—work was begun on the bridge, and all hands were required on the important undertaking. Laden with tools the colonists descended to the shore.

Here Pencroff reflected as follows:—

"Supposing while we are away Master Jup takes the notion of hauling up the ladder, which he so gallantly unrolled for us yesterday."

"We would be dependent on his tail!" answered Spilett.

The ladder was therefore made fast to two stakes driven firmly into the ground. The colonists ascended the river, and soon arrived at its narrow bend, where they halted to examine whether the bridge could not be thrown across at this place. The situation was suitable, as from this point to Balloon Harbor the distance was three miles and a half, and a wagon road connecting Granite House with the southern part of the island, could easily be constructed.

Then Smith communicated to his companions a project which he had had in view for some time. This was to completely isolate Prospect Plateau, so as to protect it from all attacks of quadrupeds or quadrumana. By this means Granite House, the Chimneys, the poultry yard, and all the upper part of the plateau destined for sowing would be protected against the depredations of animals.

Nothing could be easier than to do this, and the engineer proposed to accomplish it as follows:—The plateau was already protected on three sides by either natural or artificial water courses. On the northwest, by the bank of Lake Grant, extending from the angle against the former weir to the cut made in the east bank to draw off the water. On the north, by this new water course which had worn itself a bed both above and below the fall, which could be dug out sufficiently to render the passage impracticable to animals. And upon the east, by the sea itself, from the mouth of this new creek to the mouth of the Mercy. Therefore the only part remaining open was the western part of the plateau included between the bend in the river and the southern angle of the lake, a distance of leas than a mile. But nothing could be easier than to dig a ditch, wide and deep, which would be filled from the lake, and flow into the Mercy. Doubtless the level of the lake would be lowered somewhat by this new drain on its resources, but Smith had assured himself that the flow of Red Creek was sufficient for his purpose.

"Thus," added the engineer, "Prospect Plateau will be a veritable island, unconnected with the rest of our domain, save by the bridge which we will throw over the Mercy, by the two causeways already built above and below the fall, and by the two others which are to be constructed, one over the proposed ditch, and the other over the left bank of the Mercy. Now if this bridge and the causeways can be raised at will, Prospect Plateau will be secured from surprise."

Smith, in order to make his companions comprehend clearly his plans, had made a plot of the plateau, and his project was rendered perfectly plain. It met with unanimous approval; and Pencroff, brandishing his hatchet, exclaimed:—

"And first, for the bridge!"

This work was the most urgent. Trees were selected, felled, lopped, and cut into beams, planks, and boards. The bridge was to be stationary on the right bank of the Mercy, but on the left it was to be so constructed as to raise by means of counterweights, as in some draw-bridges.

It will be seen that this work, even if it could be easily accomplished, would take considerable time, as the Mercy was eighty feet wide at this point. It was first necessary to drive piles in the bed of the river, to sustain the flooring of the bridge, and to set up a pile-driver to drive the piles, so as to form two arches capable of supporting heavy weights.

Fortunately they lacked neither the necessary tools for preparing the timber, nor the iron work, to bind it together, nor the ingenuity of a man who was an adept at this sort of work, nor, finally, the zeal of his companions who in these seven months had necessarily acquired considerable manual skill. And it should be added that Spilett began to do nearly as well as the sailor himself "who would never have expected so much from a newspaper man!"

It took three weeks of steady work to build this bridge. And as the weather was fine they lunched on the ground, and only returned to Granite House for supper.

During this period it was observed that Master Jup took kindly to and familiarized himself with his new masters, whom he watched with the greatest curiosity. Nevertheless, Pencroff was careful not to give him complete liberty until the limits of the plateau had been rendered impassible. Top and he were the best possible friends, and got on capitally together although Jup took everything gravely.

The bridge was finished on the 20th of November. The movable part balanced perfectly with the counterpoise, and needed but little effort to raise it; between the hinge and crossbeam on which the draw rested when closed, the distance was twenty feet, a gap sufficiently wide to prevent animals from getting across.

It was next proposed to go for the envelope of the balloon, which the colonists were anxious to place in safety; but in order to bring it, the cart would have to be dragged to Balloon Harbor, necessitating the breaking of a road through the dense underwood of the Far West, all of which would take time. Therefore Neb and Pencroff made an excursion to the harbor, and as they reported that the supply of cloth was well protected in the cave, it was decided that the works about the plateau should not be discontinued.

"This," said Pencroff, "will enable us to establish the poultry-yard under the most advantageous conditions, since we need have no fear of the visits of foxes or other noxious animals."

"And also," added Neb, "we can clear the plateau, and transplant wild plants"—

"And make ready our second corn-field," continued the sailor with a triumphant air.

Indeed the first corn-field, sowed with a single grain, had prospered admirably, thanks to the care of Pencroff. It had produced the ten ears foretold by the engineer, and as each ear had eighty grains, the colonists found themselves possessed of 800 grains—in six months—which promised them a double harvest each year. These 800 grains, excepting fifty which it was prudent to reserve, were now about to be sowed in a new field with as much care as the first solitary specimen.

The field was prepared, and inclosed with high, sharp-pointed palisades, which quadrupeds would have found very difficult to surmount. As to the birds, the noisy whirligigs and astonishing scarecrows, the product of Pencroff's genius, were enough to keep them at a distance. Then the 750 grains were buried in little hills, regularly disposed, and Nature was left to do the rest.

On the 21st of November, Smith began laying out the ditch which was to enclose the plateau on the west. There were two or three feet of vegetable earth, and beneath that the granite. It was, therefore, necessary to manufacture some more nitro-glycerine, and the nitro-glycerine had its accustomed effect. In less than a fortnight a ditch, twelve feet wide and six feet deep was excavated in the plateau. A new outlet was in like manner made in the rocky border of the lake, and the waters rushed into this new channel, forming a small stream, to which they gave the name of Glycerine Creek. As the engineer had foreseen the level of the lake was lowered but very slightly. Finally, for completing the enclosure, the bed of the stream across the beach was considerably enlarged, and the sand was kept up by a double palisade.

By the middle of December all these works were completed, and Prospect Plateau, shaped something like an irregular pentagon, having a perimeter of about four miles, was encircled with a liquid belt, making it absolutely safe from all aggression.

During this month the heat was very great. Nevertheless, the colonists, not wishing to cease work, proceeded to construct the poultry-yard. Jup, who since the enclosing of the plateau had been given his liberty, never quitted his masters nor manifested the least desire to escape. He was a gentle beast, though possessing immense strength and wonderful agility. No one could go up the ladder to Granite House as he could. Already he was given employment; he was instructed to fetch wood and carry off the stones which had been taken from the bed of Glycerine Creek.

"Although he's not yet a mason, he is already a 'monkey,'" said Herbert, making a joking allusion to the nickname masons give their apprentices. And if ever a name was well applied, it was so in this instance!

The poultry-yard occupied an area of 200 square yards on the southeast bank of the lake. It was enclosed with a palisade, and within were separate divisions for the proposed inhabitants, and huts of branches divided into compartments awaiting their occupants.

The first was the pair of tinamons, who were not long in breeding numerous little ones. They had for companions half-a-dozen ducks, who were always by the water-side. Some of these belonged to that Chinese variety whose wings open like a fan, and whose plumage rivals in brilliance that of the golden pheasant. Some days later, Herbert caught a pair of magnificent curassows, birds of the gallinaceæ family, with long rounding tails. These soon bred others, and as to the pellicans, the kingfishers, the moorhens, they came of themselves to the poultry-yard. And soon, all this little world, after some disputing, cooing, scolding, clucking, ended by agreeing and multiplying at a rate sufficient for the future wants of the colony.

Smith, in order to complete his work, established a pigeon-house in the corner of the poultry-yard, and placed therein a dozen wild pigeons. These birds readily habituated themselves to their new abode, and returned there each evening, showing a greater propensity to domestication than the wood pigeons, their congeners, which do not breed except in a savage state.

And now the time was come to make use of the envelope in the manufacture of clothing, for to keep it intact in order to attempt to leave the island by risking themselves in a balloon filled with heated air over a sea, which might be called limitless, was only to be thought of by men deprived of all other resources, and Smith, being eminently practical, did not dream of such a thing.

It was necessary to bring the envelope to Granite House, and the colonists busied themselves in making their heavy cart less unwieldly and lighter. But though the vehicle was provided, the motor was still to be found! Did not there exist in the island some ruminant of indigenous species which could replace the horse, ass, ox, or cow? That was the question.

"Indeed," said Pencroff, "a draught animal would be very useful to us, while we are waiting until Mr. Smith is ready to build a steam-wagon or a locomotive, though doubtless, some day we will have a railway to Balloon Harbor, with a branch road up Mount Franklin!"

And the honest sailor, in talking thus, believed what he said. Such is the power of imagination combined with faith!

But, in truth, an animal capable of being harnessed would have just suited Pencroff, and as Fortune favored him, she did not let him want.

One day, the 23d of December, the colonists, busy at the Chimneys, heard Neb crying and Top barking in such emulation, that dreading some terrible accident, they ran to them.

What did they see? Two large, beautiful animals, which had imprudently ventured upon the plateau, the causeways not having been closed. They seemed like two horses, or rather two asses, male and female, finely shaped, of a light bay color, striped with black on the head, neck, and body, and with white legs and tail. They advanced tranquilly, without showing any fear, and looked calmly on these men in whom they had not yet recognized their masters.

"They are onagers," cried Herbert. "Quadrupeds of a kind between the zebra and the quagga."

"Why aren't they asses?" asked Neb.

"Because they have not long ears, and their forms are more graceful."

"Asses or horses," added Pencroff—"they are what Mr. Smith would call "motors," and it will be well to capture them!"

The sailor, without startling the animals, slid through the grass to the causeway over Glycerine Creek, raised it, and the onagers were prisoners. Should they be taken by violence, and made to submit to a forced domestication? No. It was decided that for some days they would let these animals wander at will over the plateau where the grass was abundant, and a stable was at once constructed near to the poultry-yard in which the onagers would find a good bedding, and a refuge for the night.

The fine pair were thus left entirely at liberty, and the colonists avoided approaching them. In the meantime the onagers often tried to quit the plateau, which was too confined for them, accustomed to wide ranges and deep forests. The colonists saw them following around the belt of water impossible to cross, whinnying and galloping over the grass, and then resting quietly for hours regarding the deep woods from which they were shut off.

In the meantime, harness had been made from vegetable fibres, and some days after the capture of the onagers, not only was the cart ready, but a road, or rather a cut, had been made through the forest all the way from the bend in the Mercy to Balloon Harbor. They could therefore get to this latter place with the cart, and towards the end of the month the onagers were tried for the first time.

Pencroff had already coaxed these animals so that they ate from his hand, and he could approach them without difficulty, but, once harnessed, they reared and kicked, and were with difficulty kept from breaking loose, although it was not long before they submitted to this new service.

This day, every one except Pencroff, who walked beside his team, rode in the cart to Balloon Harbor. They were jolted about a little over this rough road, but the cart did not break down, and they were able to load it, the same day, with the envelope and the appurtenances to the balloon.

By 8 o'clock in the evening, the cart, having recrossed the bridge, followed down the bank of the Mercy and stopped on the beach. The onagers were unharnessed, placed in the stable, and Pencroff, before sleeping, gave a sigh of satisfaction that resounded throughout Granite House.

CHAPTER XXX. CLOTHING—SEAL-SKIN BOOTS

MAKING PYROXYLINE—PLANTING—THE FISH—TURTLES' EGGS—JUP'S EDUCATION—THE CORRAL-HUNTING MOUFFLONS—OTHER USEFUL ANIMALS AND VEGETABLES—HOME THOUGHTS.

The first week In January was devoted to making clothing. The needles found in the box were plied by strong, if not supple fingers, and what was sewed, was sewed strongly. Thread was plenty, as Smith had thought of using again that with which the strips of the balloon had been fastened together. These long bands had been carefully unripped by Spilett and Herbert with commendable patience, since Pencroff had thrown aside the work, which bothered him beyond measure; but when it came to sewing again the sailor was unequalled.

The varnish was then removed from the cloth by means of soda procured as before, and the cloth was afterwards bleached in the sun. Some dozens of shirts and socks—the latter, of course, not knitted, but made of sewed strips— were thus made. How happy it made the colonists to be clothed again in white linen—linen coarse enough, it is true, but they did not mind that—and to lie between sheets, which transformed the banks of Granite House into real beds! About this time they also made boots from seal leather, which were a timely substitute for those brought from America. They were long and wide enough, and never pinched the feet of the pedestrians.

In the beginning of the year (1866) the hot weather was incessant, but the hunting in the woods, which fairly swarmed with birds and beasts, continued; and Spilett and Herbert were too good shots to waste powder. Smith had recommended them to save their ammunition, and that they might keep it for future use the engineer took measures to replace it by substances easily renewable. How could he tell what the future might have in store for them in case they left the island? It behooved them, therefore, to prepare for all emergencies.

As Smith had not discovered any lead in the island he substituted iron shot, which were easily made. As they were not so heavy as leaden ones they had to be made larger, and the charges contained a less number, but the skill of the hunters counterbalanced this defect. Powder he could have made, since he had all the necessary materials but as its preparation requires extreme care, and as without special apparatus it is difficult to make it of good quality, Smith proposed to manufacture pyroxyline, a kind of gun-cotton, a substance in which cotton is not necessary, except as cellulose. Now cellulose is simply the elementary tissue of vegetables, and is found in almost a pure state not only in cotton, but also in the texile fibres of hemp and flax, in paper and old rags, the pith of the elder, etc. And it happened that elder trees abounded in the island towards the mouth of Red Creek:—the colonists had already used its shoots and berries in place of coffee.

Thus they had the cellulose at hand, and the only other substance necessary for the manufacture of pyroxyline was nitric acid, which Smith could easily produce as before. The engineer, therefore, resolved to make and use this combustible, although he was aware that it had certain serious inconveniences, such as inflaming at 170° instead of 240°, and a too instantaneous deflagration for firearms. On the other hand, pyroxyline had these advantages—it was not affected by dampness, it did not foul the gun-barrels, and its explosive force was four times greater than that of gunpowder.

In order to make the pyroxyline, Smith made a mixture of three parts of nitric acid with five of concentrated sulphuric acid, and steeped the cellulose in this mixture for a quarter of an hour; afterwards it was washed in fresh water and left to dry. The operation succeeded perfectly, and the hunters had at their disposal a substance perfectly prepared, and which, used with discretion, gave excellent results.

About this time the colonists cleared three acres of Prospect Plateau, leaving the rest as pasture for the onagers. Many excursions were made into Jacamar Wood and the Far West, and they brought back a perfect harvest of wild vegetables, spinach, cresses, charlocks, and radishes, which intelligent culture would greatly change, and which would serve to modify the flesh diet which the colonists had been obliged to put up with. They also hauled large quantities of wood and coal, and each excursion helped improve the roads by grinding down its inequalities under the wheels.

The warren always furnished its contingent of rabbits, and as it was situated without Glycerine creek, its occupants could not reach nor damage the new plantations. As to the oyster-bed among the coast rocks, it furnished a daily supply of excellent mollusks. Further, fish from the lake and river were abundant, as Pencroff had made set-lines on which they often caught trout and another very savory fish marked with small yellow spots on a silver-colored body. Thus Neb, who had charge of the culinary department, was able to make an agreeable change in the menu of each repast. Bread alone was wanting at the colonists' table, and they felt this privation exceedingly.

Sometimes the little party hunted the sea-turtles, which frequented the coast at Mandible Cape. At this season the beach was covered with little mounds enclosing the round eggs, which were left to the sun to hatch; and as each turtle produces two hundred and fifty eggs annually, their number was very great.

"It is a true egg-field," said Spilett, "and all we have to do is to gather them."

But they did not content themselves with these products; they hunted also the producers, and took back to Granite House a dozen of these reptiles, which were excellent eating. Turtle soup, seasoned with herbs, and a handful of shell-fish thrown in, gained high praise for its concoctor, Neb.

Another fortunate event, which permitted them to make new provision for winter, must be mentioned. Shoals of salmon ascended the Mercy for many miles, in order to spawn. The river was full of these fish, which measured upwards of two feet in length, and it was only necessary to place some barriers in the stream in order to capture a great many. Hundreds were caught in this way, and salted down for winter, when the ice would stop the fishing.

Jup, during this time, was elevated to the position of a domestic. He had been clothed in a jacket, and short trowsers, and an apron with pockets, which were his joy, as he kept his hands in them and allowed no one to search them. The adroit orang had been wonderfully trained by Neb, and one would have said they understood each other's conversation. Jup had, moreover, a real affection for the black man, which was reciprocated. When the monkey was not wanted to carry wood or to climb to the top of some tree, he was passing his time in the kitchen, seeking to imitate Neb in all that he was doing. The master also showed great patience and zeal in instructing his pupil, and the pupil showed remarkable intelligence in profiting by these lessons.

Great was the satisfaction one day when Master Jup, napkin on arm, came without having been called to wait on the table. Adroit and attentive, he acquitted himself perfectly, changing the plates, bringing the dishes, and pouring the drink, all with a gravity which greatly amused the colonists, and completely overcame Pencroff.

"Jup, some more soup! Jup, a bit more agouti! Jup, another plate! Jup, brave, honest Jup!"

Jup, not in the least disconcerted, responded to every call, looked out for everything, and nodded his head intelligently when the sailor, alluding to his former pleasantry said:—

"Decidedly, Jup, we must double your wages!"

The orang had become perfectly accustomed, to Granite House, and often accompanied his masters to the forest without manifesting the least desire to run off. It was laughable to see him march along with a stick of Pencroff's on his shoulder, like a gun. If any one wanted some fruit gathered from a treetop how quickly be was up there. If the wagon wheels stuck in the mire, with what strength he raised it onto the road again.

"What a Hercules!" exclaimed Pencroff. "If he was as mischievous as he is gentle we could not get along with him."

Towards the end of January the colonists undertook great work in the interior of the island. It had been decided that they would establish at the foot of Mount Franklin, near the sources of Red Creek, the corral destined to contain the animals whose presence would have been unpleasant near Granite House, and more particularly the moufflons, which were to furnish wool for winter clothing. Every morning all the colonists, or oftener Smith, Herbert, and Pencroff, went with the onagers to the site, five miles distant, over what they called Corral Road. There an extensive area had been chosen opposite the southern slope of the mountain. It was a level plain, having here and there groups of trees, situated at the base of one of the spurs, which closed it in on that side. A small stream, rising close by, crossed it diagonally, and emptied into Red Creek. The grass was lush, and the position of the trees allowed the air to circulate freely. All that was necessary was to build a palisade around to the mountain spur sufficiently high to keep in the animals. The enclosure would be large enough to contain one hundred cattle, moufflons or wild goats and their young.

The line of the corral was marked out by the engineer, and they all set to work to cut down the trees necessary for the palisade. The road which they had made furnished some hundred trees, which were drawn to the place and set firmly in the ground. At the back part of the palisade they made an entranceway, closed by a double gate made from thick plank, which could be firmly fastened on the outside.

The building of this corral took all of three weeks, as, besides the work on the palisades, Smith put up large sheds for the animals. These were made of planks, and, indeed, everything had to be made solidly and strong, as moufflons have great strength, and their first resistance was to be feared. The uprights, pointed at the end and charred, had been bolted together, and the strength of the whole had been augmented by placing braces at intervals.

The corral finished, the next thing was to inaugurate a grand hunt at the pasturages, near the foot of Mount Franklin, frequented by the animals. The time chosen was the 7th of February, a lovely summer day, and everybody took part in the affair. The two onagers, already pretty well trained, were mounted by Spilett and Herbert and did excellent service. The plan was to drive together the moufflons and goats by gradually narrowing the circle of the chase around them. Smith, Pencroff, Neb, and Jup posted themselves in different parts of the wood, while the two horsemen and Top scoured the country for half a mile around the corral. The moufflons were very numerous in this neighborhood. These handsome animals were as large as deer, with larger horns than those of rams, and a greyish-colored wool, mingled with long hair, like argali.

The hunt, with its going and coming, the racing backwards and forwards, the shouting and hallooing, was fatiguing enough. Out of a hundred animals that were driven together many escaped, but little by little some thirty moufflons and a dozen wild goats were driven within the corral, whose open gate seemed to offer a chance of escape. The result was, therefore, satisfactory; and as many of these moufflons were females with young, it was certain that the herd would prosper, and milk and skins be plenty in the future.

In the evening the hunters returned to Granite House nearly tired out. Nevertheless the next day they went back to look at the corral. The prisoners had tried hard to break down the palisade, but, not succeeding, they had soon become quiet.

Nothing of any importance happened during February. The routine of daily work continued, and while improving the condition of the existing roads, a third, starting from the enclosure, and directed towards the southern coast, was begun. This unknown portion of Lincoln Island was one mass of forest, such as covered Serpentine Peninsula, giving shelter to the beasts from whose presence Spilett proposed to rid their domain.

Before the winter returned careful attention was given to the cultivation of the wild plants which had been transplanted to the plateau, and Herbert seldom returned from an excursion without bringing back some useful vegetable. One day it was a kind of succory, from the seed of which an excellent oil can be pressed; another time, it was the common sorrel, whose anti-scorbutic properties were not to be neglected; and again, it was some of those valuable tubercles which have always been cultivated in South America, those potatoes, of which more than two hundred species are known at present. The kitchen garden, already well enclosed, well watered, and well defended against the birds, was divided into small beds of lettuce, sorrel, radish, charlock, and other crucifers; and as the soil upon the plateau was of wonderful richness, abundant crops might be anticipated.

Neither were various drinks wanting, and unless requiring wine, the most fastidious could not have complained. To the Oswego tea, made from the mountain mint, and the fermented liquor made from the roots of the dragon-tree, Smith added a genuine beer; this was made from the young shoots of the "abies nigra," which, after having been boiled and fermented, yielded that agreeable and particularly healthful drink, known to Americans as "spring beer," that is, spruce beer.

Toward the close of summer the poultry yard received a fine pair of bustards belonging to the species "houbara," remarkable for a sort of short cloak of feathers and a membranous pouch extending on either side of the upper mandible; also some fine cocks, with black skin, comb, and wattles, like those of Mozambique, which strutted about the lake shore.

Thus the zeal of these intelligent and brave men made every thing prosper. Providence, doubtless, assisted them; but, faithful to the precept, they first helped themselves, and Heaven helped them accordingly.

In the evenings, during this warm summer weather, after the day's work was ended, and when the sea breeze was springing up, the colonists loved to gather together on the edge of Prospect Plateau in an arbor of Neb's building, covered with climbing plants. There they conversed and instructed each other, and planned for the future; or the rough wit of the sailor amused this little world, in which the most perfect harmony had never ceased to reign.

They talked, too, of their country, dear and grand America. In what condition was the Rebellion? It certainly could not have continued. Richmond had, doubtless, soon fallen into General Grant's hands. The capture of the Confederate capital was necessarily the last act in that unhappy struggle. By this time the North must have triumphed. How a newspaper would have been welcomed by the colonists of Lincoln Island! It was eleven months since all communication between them and the rest of the world had been interrupted, and pretty soon, the 24th of March, the anniversary of the day when the balloon had thrown them on this unknown coast, would have arrived. Then they were castaways, struggling with the elements for life. Now thanks to the knowledge of their leader, thanks to their own intelligence, they were true colonists, furnished with arms, tools, instruments, who had turned to their use the animals, vegetables and minerals of the island, the three kingdoms of nature.

As to Smith, he listened to the conversation of his companions oftener than he spoke himself. Sometimes he smiled at some thought of Herbert's, or some sally of Pencroff's, but always and above all other things, he reflected upon those inexplicable events, upon that strange enigma whose secret still escaped him.

CHAPTER XXXI. BAD WEATHER

THE HYDRAULIC ELEVATOR—MAKING WINDOW GLASS AND TABLE WARE—THE BREAD TREE—FREQUENT VISITS TO THE CORRAL—THE INCREASE OF THE HERD—THE REPORTER'S QUESTION—THE EXACT POSITION OF LINCOLN ISLAND—PENCROFF'S PROPOSAL.

The weather changed during the first week in March. There was a full moon in the beginning of the month, and the heat was excessive. The electricity in the air could be felt, and the stormy weather was at hand. On the 2d the thunder was very violent, the wind came out east, and the hail beat against the front of Granite House, pattering like a volley of musketry. It was necessary to fasten the doors and shutters in order to keep the rooms from being inundated. Some of the hailstones were as large as pigeons' eggs, and made Pencroff think of his cornfield. He instantly ran there, and by covering the tiny young sprouts with a large cloth was able to protect them. The sailor was well pelted, but he did not mind that.

The stormy weather lasted for eight days, and the thunder was almost continuous. The heavens were full of lightning, and many trees in the forest were struck, and also a huge pine growing upon the border of the lake. Two or three times the electric fluid struck the beach, melting and vitrifying the sand. Finding these fulgurites, Smith conceived the idea that it would be possible to furnish the windows of Granite House with glass thick and solid enough to resist the wind and rain and hail.

The colonists, having no immediate out-of-doors work, profited by the bad weather to complete and perfect the interior arrangements of Granite House. The engineer built a lathe with which they were able to turn some toilette articles and cooking utensils, and also some buttons, the need of which had been pressing. They also made a rack for the arms, which were kept with the utmost care. Nor was Jup forgotten; he occupied a chamber apart, a sort of cabin with a frame always full of good bedding, which suited him exactly.

"There's no such thing as fault-finding with Jup," said Pencroff. "What a servant he is, Neb!"

"He is my pupil and almost my equal!"

"He's your superior," laughed the sailor, "as you can talk, Neb, and he cannot!"

Jup had by this time become perfectly familiar with all the details of his work. He brushed the clothes, turned the spit, swept the rooms, waited at table, and—what delighted Pencroff—never laid down at night before he had tucked the worthy sailor in his bed.

As to the health of the colony, bipeds and bimana, quadrupeds and quadrumana, it left nothing to be desired. With the out-of-doors work, on this salubrious soil, under this temperate zone, laboring with head and hand, they could not believe that they could ever be sick, and all were in splendid health. Herbert had grown a couple of inches during the year; his figure had developed and knitted together, and he promised to become a fine man physically and morally. He profited by the lessons which he learned practically and from the books in the chest, and he found in the engineer and the reporter masters pleased to teach him. It was the engineer's desire to teach the lad all he himself knew.

"If I die," thought Smith, "he will take my place."

The storm ended on the 9th of March, but the sky remained clouded during the remainder of the month, and, with the exception of two or three fine days, rainy or foggy.

About this time a little onager was born, and a number of moufflons, to the great joy of Neb and Herbert, who had each their favorites among these new comers.

The domestication of piccaries was also attempted—a pen being built near the poultry-yard, and a number of the young animals placed therein under Neb's care. Jup was charged with taking them their daily nourishment, the kitchen refuse, and he acquitted himself conscientiously of the task. He did, indeed, cut off their tails, but this was a prank and not naughtiness, because those little twisted appendages amused him like a toy, and his instinct was that of a child.

One day in March, Pencroff, talking with the engineer, recalled to his mind a promise made some time before.

"You have spoken of something to take the place of our long ladder, Mr. Smith. Will you make it some day?"

"You mean a kind of elevator?" answered Smith.

"Call it an elevator if you wish," responded the sailor. "The name does not matter, provided we can get to our house easily."

"Nothing is easier, Pencroff; but is it worth while?"

"Certainly, sir, it is. After we have the necessaries, let us think of the conveniences. For people this will be a luxury, if you choose; but for things, it is indispensable. It is not so easy to climb a long ladder when one is heavily loaded."

"Well, Pencroff, we will try to satisfy you," answered Smith.

"But you haven't the machine."

"We will make one."

"To go by steam?"

"No, to go by water."

Indeed, a natural force was at hand. All that was necessary was to enlarge the passage which furnished Granite House with water, and make a fall at the end of the corridor. Above this fall the engineer placed a paddle-wheel, and wrapped around its axle a strong rope attached to a basket. In this manner, by means of a long cord which reached to the ground, they could raise or lower the basket by means of the hydraulic motor.

On the 17th of March the elevator was used for the first time, and after that everything was hoisted into Granite House by its means. Top was particularly pleased by this improvement, as he could not climb like Jup, and he had often made the ascent on the back of Neb or of the orang.

Smith also attempted to make glass, which was difficult enough, but after numerous attempts he succeeded in establishing a glass-works at the old pottery, where Herbert and Spilett spent several days. The substances entering into the composition of glass—sand, chalk, and soda—the engineer had at hand; but the "cane" of the glassmaker, an iron tube five or six feet long, was wanting. This Pencroff, however, succeeded in making, and on the 28th of March the furnace was heated.

One hundred parts of sand, thirty-five of chalk, forty of sulphate of soda, mixed with two of three parts of powdered charcoal, composed the substance which was placed in earthen vessels and melted to a liquid, or rather to the consistency of paste. Smith "culled" a certain quantity of this paste with his cane, and turned it back and forth on a metal plate so placed that it could be blown on; then he passed the cane to Herbert, telling him to blow in it.

"As you do to make soap bubbles?"

"Exactly."

So Herbert, puffing out his cheeks, blew through the cane, which he kept constantly turning about, in such a manner as to inflate the vitreous mass. Other quantities of the substance in fusion were added to the first, and the result was a bubble, measuring a foot in diameter. Then Smith took the cane again, and swinging it like a pendulum, he made this bubble lengthen into the shape of cylinder.

This cylinder was terminated at either end by two hemispherical caps, which were easily cut off by means of a sharp iron dipped in cold water; in the same way the cylinder was cut lengthwise, and after having been heated a second time it was spread on the plate and smoothed with a wooden roller.

Thus the first glass was made, and by repeating the operation fifty times they had as many glasses, and the windows of Granite House were soon garnished with transparent panes, not very clear, perhaps, but clear enough.

As to the glassware, that was mere amusement. They took whatever shape happened to come at the end of the cane. Pencroff had asked to be allowed to blow in his turn and he enjoyed it, but he blew so hard that his products took the most diverting forms, which pleased him amazingly.

During one of the excursions undertaken about this time a new tree was discovered, whose products added much to the resources of the colony.

Smith and Herbert, being out hunting one day, went into the forests of the Far West, and as usual the lad asked the engineer a thousand questions, and as Smith was no sportsman, and Herbert was deep in physics and chemistry, the game did not suffer; and so it fell out that the day was nearly ended, and the two hunters were likely to have made a useless excursion, when Herbert, stopping suddenly, exclaimed joyfully:—

"Oh, Mr. Smith, do you see that tree?"

And he pointed out a shrub rather than a tree, as it was composed of a single stem with a scaly bark, and leaves striped with small parallel veins.

"It looks like a small palm. What is it?" asked Smith.

"It is a "cycas revoluta," about which I have read in our Dictionary of Natural History."

"But I see no fruit on this shrub?"

"No, sir, but its trunk contains a flour which Nature furnishes all ground."

"Is it a bread-tree?"

"That's it, exactly."

"Then, my boy, since we are waiting for our wheat crop, this is a valuable discovery. Examine it, and pray heaven you are not mistaken."

Herbert was not mistaken. He broke the stem of the cycas, which was composed of a glandular tissue containing a certain quantity of farinaceous flour, traversed by ligneous fibres and separated by concentric rings of the same substance. From the fecula oozed a sticky liquid of a disagreeable taste, but this could readily be removed by pressure. The substance itself formed a real flour of superior quality, extremely nourishing, and which used to be forbidden exportation by the laws of Japan.

Smith and Herbert, after baring carefully noted the location of the cycas, returned to Granite House and made known their discovery, and the next day all the colonists went to the place, and, Pencroff, jubilant, asked the engineer:—

"Mr Smith, do you believe there are such things as castaways' islands?"

"What do you mean, Pencroff?."

"Well, I mean islands made especially for people to be shipwrecked upon, where the poor devils could always get along!"

"Perhaps," said the engineer, smiling.

"Certainly!" answered the sailor, "and just as certainly Lincoln Island is one of them!"

They returned to Granite House with an ample supply of cycas stems, and the engineer made a press by which the liquid was expelled, and they obtained a goodly quantity of flour which Neb transformed into cakes and puddings. They had not yet real wheaten bread, but it was the next thing to do.

The onager, the goats, and the sheep in the corral furnished a daily supply of milk to the colony, and the cart, or rather a light wagon, which had taken its place, made frequent trips to the corral. And when Pencroff's turn came, he took Jup along, and made him drive, and Jup, cracking his whip, acquitted himself with his usual intelligence. Thus everything prospered, and the colonists, if they had not been so far from their country, would have had nothing to complain of. They liked the life and they were so accustomed to the island that they would have left it with regret. Nevertheless, such is man's love of country, that had a ship hove in sight the colonists would have signalled it, have gone aboard and departed. Meantime, they lived this happy life and they had rather to fear than to wish for any interruption of its course.

But who is able to flatter himself that he has attained his fortune and reached the summit of his desires?

The colonists often discussed the nature of their Island, which they had inhabited for more than a year, and one day a remark was made which, was destined, later, to bring about the most serious result.

It was the 1st of April, a Sunday, and the Pascal feast, which Smith and his companions had sanctified by rest and prayer. The day had been lovely, like a day in October in the Northern Hemisphere. Towards evening all were seated in the arbor on the edge of the plateau, watching the gradual approach of night, and drinking some of Neb's elderberry coffee. They had been talking of the island and its isolated position in the Pacific, when something made Spilett say:— "By the way, Cyrus, have you ever taken the position of the island again since you have had the sextant?"

"No," answered the engineer.

"Well, wouldn't it be well enough to do so?".

"What would be the use?" asked Pencroff. "The island is well enough where it is."

"Doubtless," answered Spilett, "but it is possible that the imperfections of the other instruments may have caused an error in that observation, and since, it is easy to verify it exactly—"

"You are right, Spilett," responded the engineer, "and I would have made this verification before, only that if I have made an error it cannot exceed five degrees in latitude or longitude."

"Who knows," replied the reporter, "who knows but that we are much nearer an inhabited land than we believe?"

"We will know to-morrow," responded the engineer," and had it not been for the other work, which has left us no leisure, we would have known already."

"Well," said Pencroff, "Mr. Smith is too good an observer to have been mistaken, and if the island has not moved, it is just where he put it!"

So the next day the engineer made the observations with the sextant with the following result:—Longitude 150° 30' west; latitude 34° 57' south. The previous observation had given the situation of the island as between longitude 150° and 155° west, and latitude 36° and 35° south, so that, notwithstanding the rudeness of his apparatus, Smith's error had not been more than five degrees.

"Now," said Spilett, "since, beside a sextant, we have an atlas, see, my dear Cyrus, the exact position of Lincoln Island in the Pacific."

Herbert brought the atlas, which it will be remembered gave the nomenclature in the French language, and the volume was opened at the map of the Pacific. The engineer, compass in hand, was about to determine their situation, when, suddenly he paused, exclaiming:—"Why, there is an island marked in this part of the Pacific!"

"An island?" cried Pencroff.

"Doubtless it is ours." added Spilett.

"No." replied Smith. "This island is situated in 153° of longitude and 37° 11' of latitude."

"And what's the name?" asked Herbert.

"Tabor Island."

"Is it important?"

"No, it is an island lost in the Pacific, and which has never, perhaps, been visited."

"Very well, we will visit it," said Pencroff.

"We?"

"Yes, sir; We will build a decked boat, and I will undertake to steer her. How far are we from this Tabor Island?"

"A hundred and fifty miles to the northeast."

"Is that all?" responded Pencroff.

"Why in forty-eight hours, with a good breeze, we will be there!"

"But what would be the use?" asked the reporter.

"We cannot tell till we see it!"

And upon this response it was decided that a boat should be built so that it might be launched by about the next October, on the return of good weather.

CHAPTER XXXII. SHIP BUILDING

THE SECOND HARVEST—AI HUNTING—A NEW PLANT—A WHALE—THE HARPOON FROM THE VINEYARD—CUTTING UP THIS CETACEA—USE OF THE WHALEBONE—THE END OF MAY—PENCROFF IS CONTENT.

When Pencroff was possessed of an idea, he would not rest till it was executed. Now, he wanted to visit Tabor Island, and as a boat of some size was necessary, therefore the boat must be built. He and the engineer accordingly determined upon the following model:—

The boat was to measure thirty-five feet on the keel by nine feet beam—with the lines of a racer—and to draw six feet of water, which would be sufficient to prevent her making leeway. She was to be flush-decked, with the two hatchways into two holds separated by a partition, and sloop-rigged with mainsail, topsail, jib, storm-jib and brigantine, a rig easily handled, manageable in a squall, and excellent for lying close in the wind. Her hull was to be constructed of planks, edge to edge, that is, not overlapping, and her timbers would be bent by steam after the planking had been adjusted to a false frame.

On the question of wood, whether to use elm or deal, they decided on the latter as being easier to work, and supporting immersion in water the better.

These details having been arranged, it was decided that, as the fine weather would not return before six months, Smith and Pencroff should do this work alone. Spilett and Herbert were to continue hunting, and Neb and his assistant, Master Jup, were to attend to the domestic cares as usual.

At once trees were selected and cut down and sawed into planks, and a week later a ship-yard was made in the hollow between Granite House and the Cliff, and a keel thirty-five feet long, with stern-post and stem lay upon the sand.

Smith had not entered blindly upon this undertaking. He understood marine construction as he did almost everything else, and he had first drawn the model on paper. Moreover, he was well aided by Pencroff, who had worked as a ship-carpenter. It was, therefore, only after deep thought and careful calculation that the false frame was raised on the keel.

Pencroff was very anxious to begin the new enterprise, and but one thing took him away, and then only for a day, from the work. This was the second harvest, which was made on the 15th of April. It resulted as before, and yielded the proportion of grains calculated.

"Five bushels, Mr. Smith," said Pencroff, after having scrupulously measured these riches.

"Five bushels," answered the engineer, "or 650,000 grains of corn."

"Well, we will sow them all this time, excepting a small reserve."

"Yes, and if the next harvest is proportional to this we will have 4,000 bushels."

"And we will eat bread."

"We will, indeed."

"But we must build a mill?"

"We will build one."

The third field of corn, though incomparably larger than the others, was prepared with great care and received the precious seed. Then Pencroff returned to his work.

In the meantime, Spilett and Herbert hunted in the neighborhood, or with their guns loaded with ball, adventured into the unexplored depths of the Far West. It was an inextricable tangle of great trees growing close together. The exploration of those thick masses was very difficult and the engineer never undertook it without taking with him the pocket compass, as the sun was rarely visible through the leaves. Naturally, game was not plenty in these thick undergrowths, but three ai were shot during the last fortnight in April, and their skins were taken to Granite House, where they received a sort of tanning with sulfuric acid.

On the 30th of April, a discovery, valuable for another reason, was made by Spilett. The two hunters were deep in the south-western part of the Far West when the reporter, walking some fifty paces ahead of his companion, came to a sort of glade, and was surprised to perceive an odor proceeding from certain straight stemmed plants, cylindrical and branching, and bearing bunches of flowers and tiny seeds. The reporter broke off some of these stems, and, returning to the lad, asked him if he knew what they were.

"Where did you find this plant?" asked Herbert.

"Over there in the glade; there is plenty of it."

"Well, this is a discovery that gives you Pencroff's everlasting gratitude."

"Is it tobacco?"

"Yes, and if it is not first quality it is all the same, tobacco."

"Good Pencroff, how happy he'll be. But he cannot smoke all. He'll have to leave some for us."

"I'll tell you what, sir. Let us say nothing to Pencroff until the tobacco has been prepared, and then some fine day we will hand him a pipe full."

"And you may be sure, Herbert, that on that day the good fellow will want nothing else in the world."

The two smuggled a good supply of the plant into Granite House with as much precaution as if Pencroff had been the strictest of custom house officers. Smith and Neb were let into the secret, but Pencroff never suspected any thing during the two months it took to prepare the leaves, as he was occupied all day at the ship-yard.

On the 1st of May the sailor was again interrupted at his favorite work by a fishing adventure, in which all the colonists took part.

For some days they had noticed an enormous animal swimming in the sea some two or three miles distant from the shore. It was a huge whale, apparently belonging to the species *australis*, called "cape whales."

"How lucky for us if we could capture it!" cried the sailor. "Oh, if we only had a suitable boat and a harpoon ready, so that I could say:—Let's go for him! For he's worth all the trouble he'll give us!"

"Well, Pencroff, I should like to see you manage a harpoon. It must be interesting."

"Interesting and somewhat dangerous," said the engineer, "but since we have not the means to attack this animal, it is useless to think about him."

"I am astonished to see a whale in such comparatively high latitude."

"Why, Mr. Spilett, we are in that very part of the Pacific which whalers call the 'whale-field,' and just here whales are found in the greatest number."

"That is so," said Pencroff, "and I wonder we have not seen one before, but it don't matter much since we cannot go to it."

And the sailor turned with a sigh to his work, as all sailors are fishermen; and if the sport is proportionate to the size of the game, one can imagine what a whaler must feel in the presence of a whale. But, aside from the sport, such spoil would have been very acceptable to the colony, as the oil, the fat, and the fins could be turned to various uses.

It appeared as if the animal did not wish to leave these waters. He kept swimming about in Union Bay for two days, now approaching the shore, when his black body could be seen perfectly, and again darting through the water or spouting vapor to a vast height in the air. Its presence continually engaged the thoughts of the colonists, and Pencroff was like a child longing for some forbidden object.

Fortune, however, did for the colonists what they could not have done for themselves, and on the 3d of May, Neb looking from his kitchen shouted that the whale was aground on the island.

Herbert and Spilett, who were about starting on a hunt, laid aside their guns, Pencroff dropped his hatchet, and Smith and Neb, joining their companions, hurried down to the shore. It had grounded on Jetsam Point at high water, and it was not likely that the monster would be able to get off easily; but they must hasten in order to cut off its retreat if necessary. So seizing some picks and spears they ran across the bridge, down the Mercy and along the shore, and in less than twenty minutes the party were beside the huge animal, above whom myriads of birds were already hovering.

"What a monster!" exclaimed Neb.

And the term was proper, as it was one of the largest of the southern whales, measuring forty-five feet in length and weighing not less than 150,000 pounds.

Meantime the animal, although the tide was still high, made no effort to get off the shore, and the reason for this was explained later when at low water the colonists walked around its body.

It was dead, and a harpoon protruded from its left flank.

"Are there whalers in our neighborhood?" asked Spilett.

"Why do you ask?"

"Since the harpoon is still there—"

"Oh that proves nothing, sir," said Pencroff. "Whales sometimes go thousands of miles with a harpoon in them, and I should not be surprised if this one which came to die here had been struck in the North Atlantic."

"Nevertheless"—began Spilett, not satisfied with Pencroff's affirmation.

"It is perfectly possible," responded the engineer, "but let us look at the harpoon. Probably it will have the name of the ship on it."

Pencroff drew out the harpoon, and read this inscription:—

Maria-Stella Vineyard.

"A ship from the Vineyard! A ship of my country!" be cried. "The Maria-Stella! a good whaler! and I know her well! Oh, my friends, a ship from the Vineyard! A whaler from the Vineyard!"

And the sailor, brandishing the harpoon, continued to repeat that name dear to his heart, the name of his birthplace.

But as they could not wait for the Maria-Stella to come and reclaim their prize, the colonists resolved to cut it up before decomposition set in. The birds of prey were already anxious to become possessors of the spoil, and it was necessary to drive them away with gunshots.

The whale was a female, and her udders furnished a great quantity of milk, which, according to Dieffenbach, resembles in taste, color, and density, the milk of cows.

As Pencroff had served on a whaler he was able to direct the disagreeable work of cutting up the animal—an operation which lasted during three days. The blubber, cut in strips two feet and a half thick and divided into pieces weighing a thousand pounds each, was melted down in large earthen vats, which had been brought on to the ground. And such was its abundance, that notwithstanding a third of its weight was lost by melting, the tongue alone yielded 6,000 pounds of oil. The colonists were therefore supplied with an abundant supply of stearine and glycerine, and there was, besides, the whalebone, which would find its use, although there were neither umbrellas nor corsets in Granite House.

The operation ended, to the great satisfaction of the colonists, the rest of the animal was left to the birds, who made away with it to the last vestiges, and the daily routine of work was resumed. Still, before going to the ship-yard,

Smith worked on certain affairs which excited the curiosity of his companions. He took a dozen of the plates of baleen (the solid whalebone), which he cut into six equal lengths, sharpened at the ends.

"And what is that for?" asked Herbert, when they were finished.

"To kill foxes, wolves, and jaguars," answered the engineer.

"Now?"

"No, but this winter, when we have the ice."

"I don't understand," answered Herbert.

"You shall understand, my lad," answered the engineer. "This is not my invention; it is frequently employed by the inhabitants of the Aleutian islands. These whalebones which you see, when the weather is freezing I will bend round and freeze in that position with a coating of ice; then having covered them with a bit of fat, I will place them in the snow. Supposing a hungry animal swallows one of these baits? The warmth will thaw the ice, and the whalebone, springing back, will pierce the stomach."

"That is ingenious!" said Pencroff.

"And it will save powder and ball," said Smith.

"It will be better than the traps."

"Just wait till winter comes."

The ship-building continued, and towards the end of the month the little vessel was half-finished. Pencroff worked almost too hard, but his companions were secretly preparing a recompense for all his toil, and the 31st of May was destined to be one of the happiest times in his life.

After dinner on that day, just as he was leaving table, Pencroff felt a hand on his shoulder and heard Spilett saying to him:—

"Don't go yet awhile, Pencroff. You forget the dessert."

"Thank you, Spilett, but I must get back to work."

"Oh, well, have a cup of coffee."

"Not any."

"Well, then, a pipe?"

Pencroff started up quickly, and when he saw the reporter holding him a pipe full of tobacco, and Herbert with a light, his honest, homely face grew pale, and he could not say a word; but taking the pipe, he placed it to his lips, lit it, and drew five or six long puffs, one after the other.

A fragrant, blueish-colored smoke filled the air, and from the depths of this cloud came a voice, delirious with joy, repeating, "Tobacco! real tobacco!"

"Yes, Pencroff," answered Smith, "and good tobacco at that."

"Heaven be praised!" ejaculated the sailor. "Nothing now is wanting in our island. And he puffed and puffed and puffed.

"Who found it?" he asked, at length. "It was you, Herbert, I suppose?"

"No, Pencroff, it was Mr. Spilett."

"Mr. Spilett!" cried the sailor, hugging the reporter, who had never been treated that way before.

"Yes, Pencroff,"—taking advantage of a cessation in the embrace to get his breath—"But include in your thanksgiving Herbert, who recognized the plant, Mr. Smith, who prepared it, and Neb, who has found it hard to keep the secret."

"Well, my friends, I will repay you for this some day! Meanwhile I am eternally grateful!"

CHAPTER XXXIII. WINTER—FULLING CLOTH

THE MILL —PENCROFF'S FIXED PURPOSE—THE WHALEBONES—THE USE OF AN ALBATROSS —TOP AND JUP—STORMS—DAMAGE TO THE POULTRY-YARD—AN EXCURSION TO THE MARSH—SMITH ALONE—EXPLORATION OF THE PITS.

Winter came with June, and the principal work was the making of strong warm clothing. The moufflons had been clipped, and the question was how to transform the wool into cloth.

Smith, not having any mill machinery, was obliged to proceed in the simplest manner, in order to economize the spinning and weaving. Therefore he proposed to make use of the property possessed by the filaments of wool of binding themselves together under pressure, and making by their mere entanglement the substance known as felt. This felt can be obtained by a simple fulling, an operation which, while it diminishes the suppleness of the stuff, greatly augments its heat-preserving qualities; and as the moufflons' wool was very short it was in good condition for felting.

The engineer, assisted by his companions, including Pencroff—who had to leave his ship again—cleansed the wool of the grease and oil by soaking it in warm water and washing it with soda, and, when it was partially dried by pressure it was in a condition to be milled, that is, to produce a solid stuff, too coarse to be of any value in the industrial centres of Europe, but valuable enough in the Lincoln Island market.

The engineer's professional knowledge was of great service in constructing the machine destined to mill the wool, as he knew how to make ready use of the power, unemployed up to this time, in the water-fall at the cliff, to move a fulling mill.

Its construction was most simple. A tree furnished with cams, which raised and dropped the vertical millers, troughs for the wool, into which the millers fell, a strong wooden building containing and sustaining the contrivance, such was the machine in question.

The work, superintended by Smith, resulted admirably. The wool, previously impregnated with a soapy solution, came from the mill in the shape of a thick felt cloth. The striæ and roughnesses of the material had caught and blended together so thoroughly that they formed a stuff equally suitable for cloths or coverings. It was not, indeed, one of the stuffs of commerce, but it was "Lincoln felt," and the island had one more industry.

The colonists, being thus provided with good clothes and warm bed-clothing, saw the winter of 1866-67 approach without any dread. The cold really began to be felt on the 20th of June, and, to his great regret, Pencroff was obliged to suspend work on his vessel, although it would certainly be finished by the next spring.

The fixed purpose of the sailor was to make a voyage of discovery to Tabor Island, although Smith did not approve of this voyage of simple curiosity, as there was evidently no succor to be obtained from that desert and half arid rock. A voyage of 150 miles in a boat, comparatively small, in the midst of unknown seas, was cause for considerable anxiety. If the frail craft, once at sea, should be unable to reach Tabor Island, or to return to Lincoln Island, what would become of her in the midst of this ocean so fertile in disasters?

Smith often talked of this project with Pencroff, and he found in the sailor a strange obstinacy to make the voyage, an obstinacy for which Pencroff himself could not account.

"Well," said the engineer one day, "you must see, Pencroff, after having said every good of Lincoln Island, and expressing the regret you would feel should you have to leave it, that you are the first to want to get away."

"Only for a day or two," answered Pencroff, "for a few days, Mr. Smith; just long enough to go and return, and see what this island is."

"But it cannot compare with ours."

"I know that.""

"Then why go?"

"To find out what's going on there!"

"But there is nothing; there can be nothing there."

"Who knows?"

"And supposing you are caught in a storm?"

"That is not likely in that season," replied Pencroff. "But, sir, as it is necessary to foresee everything, I want your permission to take Herbert with me."

"Pencroff," said the engineer, laying his hand on the shoulder of the sailor, "If anything should happen to you and this child, whom chance has made our son, do you think that we would ever forgive ourselves?"

"Mr. Smith," responded Pencroff with unshaken confidence, "we won't discuss such mishaps. But we will talk again of this voyage when the time comes. Then, I think, when you have seen our boat well rigged, when you have seen how well she behaves at sea, when you have made the tour of the island—as we will, together—I think, I say, that you will not hesitate to let me go. I do not conceal from you that this will be a fine work, your ship."

"Say rather, our ship, Pencroff," replied the engineer, momentarily disarmed. And the conversation, to be renewed later, ended without convincing either of the speakers.

The first snow fell towards the end of the month. The corral had been well provisioned, and there was no further necessity for daily visits, but it was decided to go there at least once a week. The traps were set again, and the contrivances of Smith were tried, and worked perfectly. The bent whalebones, frozen, and covered with fat, were placed near the edge of the forest, at a place frequented by animals, and some dozen foxes, some wild boars, and a jaguar were found killed by this means, their stomachs perforated by the straightened whalebones.

At this time, an experiment, thought of by the reporter, was made. It was the first attempt of the colonists to communicate with their kindred.

Spilett had already often thought of throwing a bottle containing a writing into the sea, to be carried by the currents, perhaps, to some inhabited coast, or to make use of the pigeons. But it was pure folly to seriously believe that pigeons or bottles could cross the 1,200 miles separating the island from all lands.—

But on the 30th of June they captured, not without difficulty, an albatross, which Herbert had slightly wounded in the foot. It was a splendid specimen of its kind, its wings measuring ten feet from tip to tip, and it could cross seas as vast as the Pacific.

Herbert would have liked to have kept the bird and tamed it, but Spilett made him understand that they could not afford to neglect this chance of corresponding by means of this courier with the Pacific coasts. So Herbert gave up the bird, as, if it had come from some inhabited region, it was likely to return there if at liberty.

Perhaps, in his heart, Spilett, to whom the journalistic spirit returned sometimes, did not regret giving to the winds an interesting article relating the adventures of the colonists of Lincoln Island. What a triumph for the reporters of the New York *Herald*, and for the issue containing the chronicle, if ever the latter should reach his director, the honorable John Bennett!

Spilett, therefore, wrote out a succinct article, which was enclosed in a waterproof-cloth bag, with the request to whoever found it to send it to one of the offices of the *Herald*. This little bag was fastened around the neck of the albatross and the bird given its freedom, and it was not without emotion that the colonists saw this rapid courier of the air disappear in the western clouds.

"Where does he go that way?" asked Pencroff.

"Towards New Zealand," answered Herbert.

"May he have a good voyage," said the sailor, who did not expect much from this method of communication.

With the winter, in-door work was resumed; old clothes were repaired, new garments made, and the sails of the sloop made from the inexhaustible envelope of the balloon. During July the cold was intense, but coal and wood were abundant, and Smith had built another chimney in the great hall, where they passed the long evenings. It was a great comfort to the colonists, when, seated in this well-lighted and warm hall, a good dinner finished, coffee steaming in the cups, the pipes emitting a fragrant smoke, they listened to the roar of the tempest without. They were perfectly comfortable, if that is possible where one is far from his kindred and without possible means of communicating with them. They talked about their country, of their friends at home, of the grandeur of the republic, whose influence must increase; and Smith, who had had much to do with the affairs of the Union, entertained his hearers with his stories, his perceptions and his prophecies.

One evening as they had been sitting talking in this way for some time, they were interrupted by Top, who began barking in that peculiar way which had previously attracted the attention of the engineer, and running around the mouth of the well which opened at the end of the inner corridor.

"Why is Top barking that way again?" asked Pencroff.

"And Jup growling so?" added Herbert.

Indeed, both the dog and the orang gave unequivocal signs of agitation, and curiously enough these two animals seemed to be more alarmed than irritated.

It is evident," said Spilett, "that this well communicates directly with the sea, and that some animal comes to breathe in its depths."

"It must be so, since there is no other explanation to give. Be quiet, Top! and you, Jup! go to your room."

The animals turned away, Jup went to his bed, but Top remained in the hall, and continued whining the remainder of the evening. It was not, however, the question of this incident that darkened the countenance of the engineer.

During the remainder of the month, rain and snow alternated, and though the temperature was not as low as during the preceding winter, there were more storms and gales. On more than one occasion the Chimneys had been threatened by the waves, and it seemed as if an upraising of the sea, caused by some submarine convulsion, raised the monstrous billows and hurled them against Granite House.

During these storms it was difficult, even dangerous, to attempt using the roads on the island, as the trees were falling constantly. Nevertheless, the colonists never let a week pass without visiting the corral, and happily this enclosure, protected by the spur of the mountain, did not suffer from the storms. But the poultry-yard, from its position, exposed to the blast, suffered considerable damage. Twice the pigeon-house was unroofed, and the fence also was demolished, making it necessary to rebuild it more solidly. It was evident that Lincoln Island was situated in the worst part of the Pacific. Indeed, it seemed as if the island formed the central point of vast cyclones which whipped it as if it were a top; only in this case the top was immovable and the whip spun about.

During the first week in August the storm abated, and the atmosphere recovered a calm which it seemed never to have lost. With the calm the temperature lowered, and the thermometer of the colonists indicated 8° below zero. On the 3d of August, an excursion, which had been planned for some time was made to Tadorn's Fen. The hunters were tempted by the great number of aquatic birds which made these marshes their home, and not only Spilett and Herbert, but Pencroff and Neb took part in the expedition. Smith alone pleaded some excuse for remaining behind at Granite House.

The hunters promised to return by evening. Top and Jup accompanied them. And when they had crossed the bridge over the Mercy the engineer left them, and returned with the idea of executing a project in which he wished to be alone. This was to explore minutely the well opening into the corridor.

Why did Top run round this place so often? Why did he whine in that strange way? Why did Jup share Top's anxiety? Had this well other branches beside the communication with the sea? Did it ramify towards other portions of the island? This is what Smith wanted to discover, and, moreover, to be alone in his discovery. He had resolved to make this exploration during the absence of his companions, and here was the opportunity.

It was easy to descend to the bottom of the well by means of the ladder, which had not been used since the elevator had taken its place. The engineer dragged this ladder to the opening of the well, and, having made fast one end, let it unroll itself into the abyss. Then, having lit a lantern, and placing a revolver and cutlass in his belt, he began to descend the rungs. The sides of the well were smooth, but some projections of rocks appeared at intervals, and by means of these projections an athlete could have raised himself to the mouth of the well. The engineer noticed this, but in throwing the light of the lantern on these points he could discover nothing to indicate that they had ever been used in that way.

Smith descended deeper, examining every part of the well, but he saw nothing suspicious. When he had reached the lowermost rung, he was at the surface of the water, which was perfectly calm. Neither there, nor in any other part of the well, was there any lateral opening. The wall, struck by the handle of Smith's cutlass, sounded solid. It was a compact mass, through which no human being could make his way. In order to reach the bottom of the well, and from thence climb to its mouth, it was necessary to traverse the submerged passage under the shore, which connected with the sea, and this was only possible for marine animals. As to knowing whereabouts on the shore, and at what depth under the waves, this passage came out, that was impossible to discover.

Smith, having ended his exploration, remounted the ladder, covered over again the mouth of the well, and returned thoughtfully to the great hall of Granite House, saying to himself:—

"I have seen nothing, and yet, there is something there."

CHAPTER XXXIV. RIGGING THE LAUNCH

ATTACKED BY FOXES—JUP WOUNDED—JUP NURSED—JUP CURED—
COMPLETION OF THE LAUNCH—PENCROFF'S TRIUMPH—THE GOOD LUCK—
TRIAL TRIP, TO THE SOUTH OF THE ISLAND—AN UNEXPECTED DOCUMENT.

The same evening the hunters returned, fairly loaded down with game, the four men having all they could carry. Top had a circlet of ducks round his neck, and Jup belts of woodcock round his body.

"See, my master," cried Neb, "see how we have used our time. Preserves, pies, we will have a good reserve! But some one must help me, and I count upon you, Pencroff."

"No, Neb," responded the sailor, "the rigging of the launch occupies my time, and you will have to do without me."

"And you, Master Herbert?"

"I, Neb, must go to-morrow to the corral."

"Then will you help me, Mr. Spilett?"

"To oblige you, I will, Neb," answered the reporter, "but I warn you that if you discover your recipes to me I will publish them."

"Whenever you choose, sir," responded Neb; "whenever you choose."

And so the next day the reporter was installed as Neb's aid in his culinary laboratory. But beforehand the engineer had given him the result of the previous day's exploration, and Spilett agreed with Smith in his opinion that, although he had found out nothing, still there was a secret to be discovered.

The cold continued a week longer, and the colonists did not leave Granite House excepting to look after the poultry-yard. The dwelling was perfumed by the good odors which the learned manipulations of Neb and the reporter emitted; but all the products of the hunt in the fen had not been made into preserves, and as the game kept perfectly in the intense cold, wild ducks and others, were eaten fresh, and declared better than any waterfowl in the world.

During the week, Pencroff, assisted by Herbert, who used the sailor's needle skilfully, worked with such diligence that the sails of the launch were finished. Thanks to the rigging which had been recovered with the envelope of the balloon, hemp cordage was not wanting. The sails were bordered by strong bolt-ropes, and there was enough left to make halliards, shrouds, and sheets. The pulleys were made by Smith on the lathe which he had set up, acting under Pencroff's instruction. The rigging was, therefore, completed before the launch was finished. Pencroff made a red, white, and blue flag, getting the dye from certain plants; but to the thirty-seven stars representing the thirty-seven States of the Union, the sailor added another star, the star of the "State of Lincoln:" as he considered his island as already annexed to the great republic.

"And," said he, "it is in spirit, if it is not in fact!"

For the present the flag was unfurled from the central window of Granite House and saluted with three cheers.

Meantime, they had reached the end of the cold season; and it seemed as if this second winter would pass without any serious event, when during the night of the 11th of August, Prospect Plateau was menaced by a complete devastation. After a busy day the colonists were sleeping soundly, when towards 4 o'clock in the morning, they were suddenly awakened by Top's barking. The dog did not bark this time at the mouth of the pit, but at the door, and he threw himself against it as if he wished to break it open. Jup, also, uttered sharp cries.

"Be quiet, Top!" cried Neb, who was the first awake.

But the dog only barked the louder.

"What's the matter?" cried Smith. And every one dressing in haste, hurried to the windows and opened them.

"Beneath them a fall of snow shone white through the darkness. The colonists could see nothing, but they heard curious barkings penetrating the night. It was evident that the shore had been invaded by a number of animals which they could not see."

"What can they be?" cried Pencroff.

"Wolves, jaguars, or monkeys!" replied Neb.

"The mischief! They can get on to the plateau!" exclaimed the reporter.

"And our poultry-yard, and our garden!" cried Herbert.

"How have they got in?" asked Pencroff.

"They have come through the causeway," answered the engineer, "which one of us must have forgotten to close!"

"In truth," said Spilett, "I remember that I left it open—"

"A nice mess you have made of it, sir!" cried the sailor.

"What is done, is done," replied Spilett. "Let us consider what it is necessary to do!"

These questions and answers passed rapidly between Smith and his companions. It was certain that the causeway had been passed, that the shore had been invaded by animals, and that, whatever they were, they could gain Prospect Plateau by going up the left bank of the Mercy. It was, therefore, necessary quickly to overtake them, and, if necessary, to fight them!

"But what are they?" somebody asked a second time, as the barking resounded more loudly.

Herbert started at the sound, and he remembered having heard it during his first visit to the sources of Red Creek.

"They are foxes! they are foxes!" he said.

"Come on!" cried the sailor. And all, armed with hatchets, carbines, and revolvers, hurried into the elevator, and were soon on the shore.

These foxes are dangerous animals, when numerous or irritated by hunger. Nevertheless, the colonists did not hesitate to throw themselves into the midst of the band, and their first shots, darting bright gleams through the darkness, drove back the foremost assailants.

It was most important to prevent these thieves from gaining Prospect Plateau, as the garden and the poultry-yard would have been at their mercy, and the result would have been immense, perhaps, irreparable damage, especially to the corn-field. But as the plateau could only be invaded by the left bank of the Mercy, it would suffice to oppose a barrier to the foxes on the narrow portion of the shore comprised between the river and the granite wall.

This was apparent to all, and under Smith's direction the party gained this position and disposed themselves so as to form an impassable line. Top, his formidable jaws open, preceded the colonists, and was followed by Jup, armed with a knotty cudgel, which he brandished like a cricket-bat.

The night was very dark, and it was only by the flash of the discharges that the colonists could perceive their assailants, who numbered at least 100, and whose eyes shone like embers.

"They must not pass!" cried Pencroff.

"They shall not pass!" answered the engineer.

But if they did not it was not because they did not try. Those behind kept pushing on those in front, and it was an incessant struggle; the colonists using their hatchets and revolvers. Already the dead bodies of the foxes were strewn over the ground, but the band did not seem to lessen; and it appeared as if reinforcements were constantly pouring in through the causeway on the shore. Meantime the colonists fought side by side, receiving some wounds, though happily but trifling. Herbert shot one fox, which had fastened itself on Neb like a tiger-cat. Top fought with fury, springing at the throats of the animals and strangling them at once. Jup, armed with his cudgel, laid about him like a good fellow, and it was useless to try to make him stay behind. Gifted, doubtless, with a sight able to pierce the darkness, he was always in the thick of the fight, uttering from time to time a sharp cry, which was with him a mark of extreme jollification. At one time he advanced so far, that by the flash of a revolver he was seen, surrounded by five or six huge foxes, defending himself with rare coolness.

At length the fight ended in a victory for the colonists, but only after two hours of resistance. Doubtless the dawn of day determined the retreat of the foxes, who scampered off toward the north across the drawbridge, which Neb ran at once to raise. When daylight lit the battlefield, the colonists counted fifty dead bodies upon the shore.

"And Jup! Where is Jup?" cried Neb.

Jup had disappeared. His friend Neb called him, and for the first time he did not answer the call. Every one began to search for the monkey, trembling lest they should find him among the dead. At length, under a veritable mound of carcasses, each one marked by the terrible cudgel of the brave animal, they found Jup. The poor fellow still held in his hand the handle of his broken weapon; but deprived of this arm, he had been overpowered by numbers, and deep wounds scored his breast.

"He's alive!" cried Neb, who knelt beside him.

"And we will save him," answered the sailor, "We will nurse him as one of ourselves!"

It seemed as if Jup understood what was said, for he laid his head on Pencroff's shoulder as if to thank him. The sailor himself was wounded, but his wounds, like those of his companions, were trifling, as thanks to their firearms, they had always been able to keep the assailants at a distance. Only the orang was seriously hurt.

Jup, borne by Neb and Pencroff, was carried to the elevator, and lifted gently to Granite House. There he was laid upon one of the beds, and his wounds carefully washed. No vital organ seemed to have been injured, but the orang was very feeble from loss of blood, and a strong fever had set in. His wounds having been dressed, a strict diet was imposed upon him, "just as for a real person," Neb said, and they gave him a refreshing draught made from herbs.

He slept at first but brokenly, but little by little, his breathing became more regular, and they left him in a heavy sleep. From time to time Top came "on tip-toe" to visit his friend, and seemed to approve of the attentions which had been bestowed upon it.

One of Jup's hands hung over the side of the bed, and Top licked it sympathetically.

The same morning they disposed of the dead foxes by dragging the bodies to the Far West and burying them there.

This attack, which might have been attended with very grave results, was a lesson to the colonists, and thenceforth they never slept before having ascertained that all the bridges were raised and that no invasion was possible.

Meantime Jup, after having given serious alarm for some days, began to grow better. The fever abated gradually, and Spilett, who was something of a physician, considered him out of danger. On the 16th of August Jup began to eat. Neb made him some nice, sweet dishes, which the invalid swallowed greedily, for if he had a fault, it was that he was a bit of a glutton, and Neb had never done anything to correct this habit.

"What would you have?" he said to Spilett, who sometimes rebuked the black man for indulging him. "Poor Jup has no other pleasure than to eat! and I am only too glad to be able to reward his services in this way!"

By the 21st of August he was about again. His wounds were healed, and the colonists saw that he would soon recover his accustomed suppleness and vigor. Like other convalescents he was seized with an excessive hunger, and the reporter let him eat what he wished, knowing that the monkey's instinct would preserve him from excess. Neb was overjoyed to see his pupil's appetite returned.

"Eat Jup," he said, "and you shall want for nothing. You have shed your blood for us, and it is right that I should help you to make it again!"

At length, on the 25th of August, the colonists seated in the great hall, were called by Neb to Jup's room.

"What is it?" asked the reporter.

"Look!" answered Neb, laughing, and what did they see but Jup, seated like a Turk within the doorway of Granite House, tranquilly and gravely smoking!

"My pipe!" cried Pencroff. "He has taken my pipe! Well, Jup, I give it to you. Smoke on my friend, smoke on!"

And Jup gravely puffed on, seeming to experience the utmost enjoyment.

Smith was not greatly astonished at this incident, and he cited numerous examples of tamed monkeys that had become accustomed to the use of tobacco.

And after this day master Jup had his own pipe hung in his room beside his tobacco-bag, and, lighting it himself with a live coal, he appeared to be the happiest of quadrumana. It seemed as if this community of taste drew closer together the bonds of friendship already existing between the worthy monkey and the honest sailor.

"Perhaps he is a man," Pencroff would sometimes say to Neb. "Would it astonish you if some day he was to speak?"

"Indeed it would not," replied Neb. "The wonder is that he don't do it, as that is all he lacks!"

"Nevertheless, it would be funny if some fine day he said to me:—Pencroff, suppose we change pipes!"

"Yes," responded Neb. "What a pity he was born mute!"

Winter ended with September, and the work was renewed with ardor. The construction of the boat advanced rapidly. The planking was completed, and as wood was plenty Pencroff proposed that they line the interior with a stout ceiling, which would insure the solidity of the craft. Smith, not knowing what might be in store for them, approved the sailor's idea of making his boat as strong as possible. The ceiling and the deck were finished towards the 13th of September. For caulking, they used some dry wrack, and the seams were then covered with boiling pitch, made from the pine trees of the forest.

The arrangement of the boat was simple. She had been ballasted with heavy pieces of granite, set in a bed of lime, and weighing 12,000 pounds. A deck was placed over this ballast, and the interior was divided into two compartments, the larger containing two bunks, which served as chests. The foot of the mast was at the partition separating the compartments, which were entered through hatchways.

Pencroff had no difficulty in finding a tree suitable for a mast. He chose a young straight fir, without knots, so that all he had to do was to square the foot and round it off at the head. All the iron work had been roughly but solidly made at the Chimneys; and in the first week of October yards, topmast, spars, oars, etc., everything, in short, was completed; and it was determined that they would first try the craft along the shores of the island, so as to see how she acted.

She was launched on the 10th of October. Pencroff was radiant with delight. Completely rigged, she had been pushed on rollers to the edge of the shore, and, as the tide rose, she was floated on the surface of the water, amid the applause of the colonists, and especially of Pencroff, who showed no modesty on this occasion. Moreover, his vanity looked beyond the completion of the craft, as, now that she was built, he was to be her commander. The title of captain was bestowed upon him unanimously.

In order to satisfy Captain Pencroff it was necessary at once to name his ship, and after considerable discussion they decided upon Good Luck—the name chosen by the honest sailor. Moreover, as the weather was fine, the breeze fresh, and the sea calm, the trial must be made at once in an excursion along the coast.

"Get aboard! Get aboard!" cried Captain Pencroff.

At half-past 10, after having eaten breakfast and put some provisions aboard, everybody, including Top and Jup, embarked, the sails were hoisted, the flag set at the masthead, and the Good Luck, with Pencroff at the helm, stood out to sea.

On going out from Union Bay they had a fair wind, and they were able to see that, sailing before it, their speed was excellent. After doubling Jetsam Point and Claw Cape, Pencroff had to lie close to the wind in order to skirt along the shore, and he observed the Good Luck would sail to within five points of the wind, and that she made but little lee-way. She sailed very well, also, before the wind, minding her helm perfectly, and gained even in going about.

The passengers were enchanted. They had a good boat, which, in case of need, could render them great service, and in this splendid weather, with the fair wind, the sail was delightful. Pencroff stood out to sea two or three miles, opposite Balloon Harbor, and then the whole varied panorama of the island from Claw Cape to Reptile Promontory was visible under a new aspect. In the foreground were the pine forests, contrasting with the foliage of the other trees, and over all rose Mt. Franklin, its head white with snow.

"How beautiful it is!" exclaimed Herbert.

"Yes, she is a pretty creature," responded Pencroff. "I love her as a mother. She received us poor and needy, and what has she denied to these five children who tumbled upon her out of the sky?"

"Nothing, captain, nothing," answered Neb. And the two honest fellows gave three hearty cheers in honor of their island.

Meantime, Spilett, seated by the mast, sketched the panorama before him, while Smith looked on in silence.

"What do you say of our boat, now, sir?" demanded Pencroff.

"It acts very well," replied the engineer.

"Good. And now don't you think it could undertake a voyage of some length?"

"Where, Pencroff?"

"To Tabor Island, for instance."

"My friend," replied the engineer, "I believe that in a case of necessity there need be no hesitancy in trusting to the Good Luck even for a longer journey;

but, you know, I would be sorry to see you leave for Tabor Island, because nothing obliges you to go."

"One likes to know one's neighbors," answered Pencroff, whose mind was made up. "Tabor Island is our neighbor, and is all alone. Politeness requires that at least we make her a visit."

"The mischief!" exclaimed Spilett, "our friend Pencroff is a stickler for propriety."

"I am not a stickler at all," retorted the sailor, who was a little vexed by the engineer's opposition.

"Remember, Pencroff," said Smith, "that you could not go the island alone."

"One other would be all I would want."

"Supposing so," replied the engineer, "would you risk depriving our colony of five, of two of its colonists?"

"There are six," rejoined Pencroff. "You forget Jup."

"There are seven," added Neb. "Top is as good as another."

"There is no risk in it, Mr. Smith," said Pencroff again.

"Possibly not, Pencroff; but, I repeat, that it is exposing oneself without necessity."

The obstinate sailor did not answer, but let the conversation drop for the present. He little thought that an incident was about to aid him, and change to a work of humanity what had been merely a caprice open to discussion.

The Good Luck, after having stood out to sea, was returning towards the coast and making for Balloon Harbor, as it was important to locate the channel-way between the shoals and reefs so as to buoy them, for this little inlet was to be resting place of the sloop.

They were half a mile off shore, beating up to windward and moving somewhat slowly, as the boat was under the lee of the land. The sea was as smooth as glass. Herbert was standing in the bows indicating the channel-way. Suddenly he cried:—

"Luff, Pencroff, luff."

"What is it?" cried the sailor, springing to his feet. "A rock?"

"No—hold on, I cannot see very well—luff again—steady—bear away a little—" and while thus speaking, the lad lay down along the deck, plunged his arm quickly into the water, and then rising up again with something in his hand, exclaimed:—

"It is a bottle!"

Smith took it, and without saying a word, withdrew the cork and took out a wet paper, on which was written these words:—

"A shipwrecked man—Tabor Island:—l53° W. lon.—37° 11' S. lat."

CHAPTER XXXV. DEPARTURE DECIDED UPON

PREPARATIONS—THE THREE PASSENGERS—THE FIRST NIGHT—THE SECOND NIGHT—TABOR ISLAND—SEARCH ON THE SHORE—SEARCH IN THE WOODS—NO ONE—ANIMALS—PLANTS—A HOUSE—

"Some one shipwrecked!" cried Pencroff, "abandoned some hundred miles from us upon Tabor Island! Oh! Mr. Smith, you will no longer oppose my project!"

"No, Pencroff, and you must leave as soon as possible.".

"To-morrow?"

"To-morrow."

The engineer held the paper which he had taken from the bottle in his hand. He considered for a few moments, and then spoke:—

"From this paper, my friends," said he, "and from the manner in which it is worded, we must conclude that, in the first place, the person cast away upon Tabor Island is a man well informed, since he gives the latitude and longitude of his island exactly; secondly, that he is English or American, since the paper is written in English."

"That is a logical conclusion," answered Spilett, "and the presence of this person explains the arrival of the box on our coast. There has been a shipwreck, since some one has been shipwrecked. And he is fortunate in that Pencroff had the idea of building this boat and even of trying it to-day, for in twenty-four hours the bottle would have been broken on the rocks."

"Indeed,!' said Herbert, "it is a happy chance that the Good Luck passed by the very spot where this bottle was floating."

"Don't it seem to you odd?" asked Smith of Pencroff.

"It seems fortunate, that's all," replied the sailor. "Do you see anything extraordinary in it, sir? This bottle must have gone somewhere, and why not here as well as anywhere else?"

"Perhaps you are right, Pencroff," responded the engineer, "and nevertheless—"

"But," interrupted Herbert, "nothing proves that this bottle has floated in the water for a long time."

"Nothing," responded Spilett, "and moreover the paper seems to have been recently written. What do you think, Cyrus?"

"It is hard to decide" answered Smith.

Meanwhile Pencroff had not been idle. He had gone about, and the Good Luck, with a free wind, all her sails drawing, was speeding toward Claw Cape. Each one thought of the castaway on Tabor Island. Was there still time to save him? This was a great event in the lives of the colonists. They too were but castaways, but it was not probable that another had been as favored as they had been, and it was their duty to hasten at once to this one's relief. By 2 o'clock

Claw Cape was doubled, and the Good Luck anchored at the mouth of the Mercy.

That evening all the details of the expedition were arranged. It was agreed that Herbert and Pencroff, who understood the management of a boat, were to undertake the voyage alone. By leaving the next day, the 11th of October, they would reach the island, supposing the wind continued, in forty-eight hours. Allowing for one day there, and three or four days to return in, they could calculate on being at Lincoln Island again on the 17th. The weather was good, the barometer rose steadily, the wind seemed as if it would continue, everything favored these brave men, who were going so far to do a humane act.

Thus, Smith, Neb, and Spilett was to remain at Granite House; but at the last moment, the latter, remembering his duty as reporter to the New York *Herald*, having declared that he would swim rather than lose such an opportunity, was allowed to take part in the voyage.

The evening was employed in putting bedding, arms, munitions, provisions, etc., on board, and the next morning, by 5 o'clock, the good-byes were spoken, and Pencroff, hoisting the sails, headed for Claw Cape, which had to be doubled before taking the route to the southeast. The Good Luck was already a quarter of a mile from shore when her passengers saw upon the heights of Granite House two men signalling farewells. They were Smith and Neb, from whom they were separating for the first time in fifteen months.

Pencroff, Herbert, and the reporter returned the signal, and soon Granite House disappeared behind the rocks of the Cape.

During the morning, the Good Luck remained in view of the southern coast of the island, which appeared like a green clump of trees, above which rose Mount Franklin. The heights, lessened by distance, gave it an appearance little calculated to attract ships on its coasts. At 1 o'clock Reptile Promontory was passed ten miles distant. It was therefore impossible to distinguish the western coast, which extended to the spurs of the mountain, and three hours later, Lincoln Island had disappeared behind the horizon.

The Good Luck behaved admirably. She rode lightly over the seas and sailed rapidly. Pencroff had set his topsail, and with a fair wind he followed a straight course by the compass. Occasionally Herbert took the tiller, and the hand of the young lad was so sure, that the sailor had nothing to correct.

Spilett chatted with one and the other, and lent a hand when necessary in manœuvring the sloop. Captain Pencroff was perfectly satisfied with his crew, and was constantly promising them an extra allowance of grog.

In the evening the slender crescent of the moon glimmered in the twilight. The night came on dark but starlit, with the promise of a fine day on the morrow. Pencroff thought it prudent to take in the topsail, which was perhaps an excess of caution in so still a night, but he was a careful sailor, and was not to be blamed.

The reporter slept during half the night, Herbert and Pencroff taking two-hour turns at the helm. The sailor had as much confidence in his pupil as he had in himself, and his trust was justified by the coolness and judgment of the lad. Pencroff set the course as a captain to his helmsman, and Herbert did not allow the Good Luck to deviate a point from her direction.

The night and the next day passed quietly and safely. The Good Luck held her southeast course, and, unless she was drawn aside by some unknown current, she would make Tabor Island exactly. The sea was completely deserted, save that sometimes an albatross or frigate-bird passed within gun-shot distance.

"And yet," said Herbert, "this is the season when the whalers usually come towards the southern part of the Pacific. I don't believe that there is a sea more deserted than this."

"It is not altogether deserted," responded Pencroff.

"What do you mean?"

"Why we are here. Do you take us for porpoises or our sloop for driftwood?" And Pencroff laughed at his pleasantry.

By evening they calculated the distance traversed at 130 miles, or three and a third miles an hour. The breeze was dying away, but they had reason to hope, supposing their course to have been correct, that they would sight Tabor Island at daylight.

No one of the three slept during this night. While waiting for morning they experienced the liveliest emotions. There was so much uncertainty in their enterprise. Were they near the island? Was the shipwrecked man still there? Who was he? Might not his presence disturb the unity of the colony? Would he, indeed, consent to exchange one prison for another? All these questions, which would doubtless be answered the next day, kept them alert, and at the earliest dawn they began to scan the western horizon.

What was the joy of the little crew when towards 6 o'clock Pencroff shouted— "Land!"

In a few hours they would be upon its shore.

The island was a low coast, raised but a little above the waves, not more than fifteen miles away. The sloop, which had been heading south of it, was put about, and, as the sun rose, a few elevations became visible here and there.

"It is not as large as Lincoln Island," said Herbert, "and probably owes its origin to like submarine convulsions."

By 11 o'clock the Good Luck was only two miles distant from shore, and Pencroff, while seeking some place to land, sailed with extreme caution through these unknown waters. They could see the whole extent of this island, on which were visible groups of gum and other large trees of the same species as those on Lincoln Island. But, it was astonishing, that no rising smoke indicated that the place was inhabited, nor was any signal visible upon the shore. Nevertheless the paper had been precise: it stated that there was a shipwrecked man here; and he should have been upon the watch.

Meanwhile the Good Luck went in through the tortuous passages between the reefs, Herbert steering, and the sailor stationed forward, keeping a sharp lookout, with the halliards in his hand, ready to run down the sail. Spilett, with the spy-glass, examined all the shore without perceiving anything. By noon the sloop touched the beach, the anchor was let go, the sails furled, and the crew stepped on shore.

There could be no doubt that that was Tabor Island, since the most recent maps gave no other land in all this part of the Pacific.

After having securely moored the sloop, Pencroff and his companion, well armed, ascended the coast towards a round hill, some 250 feet high, which was distant about half a mile, from the summit of which they expected to have a good view of the island.

The explorers followed the edge of grassy plain which ended at the foot of the hill. Rock-pigeons and sea-swallows circled about them, and in the woods bordering the plain to the left they heard rustlings in the bushes and saw movements in the grass indicating the presence of very timid animals, but nothing, so far, indicated that the island was inhabited.

Having reached the hill the party soon climbed to its summit, and their gaze traversed the whole horizon. They were certainly upon an island, not more than six miles in circumference, in shape a long oval, and but little broken by inlets or promontories. All around it, the sea, absolutely deserted, stretched away to the horizon.

This islet differed greatly from Lincoln Island in that it was covered over its entire surface with woods, and the uniform mass of verdure clothed two or three less elevated hills. Obliquely to the oval of the island a small stream crossed a large grassy plain and emptied into the sea on the western side by a narrowed mouth.

"The place is small," said Herbert.

"Yes," replied the sailor. "It would have been too small for us."

"And," added the reporter, "it seems uninhabited."

"Nevertheless," said Pencroff, "let us go down and search."

The party returned to the sloop, and they decided to walk round the entire island before venturing into its interior, so that no place could escape their investigation.

The shore was easily followed, and the explorers proceeded towards the south, starting up flocks of aquatic birds and numbers of seals, which latter threw themselves into the sea as soon as they caught sight of the party.

"Those beasts are not looking on man for the first time. They fear what they know," said the reporter.

An hour after their departure the three had reached the southern point of the islet, which terminated in a sharp cape, and they turned towards the north, following the western shore, which was sandy, like the other, and bounded by a thick wood. In four hours after they had set out the party had made the circuit of the island, without having seen any trace of a habitation, and not even a footprint. It was most extraordinary, to say the least, and it seemed necessary to believe that the place was not and had not been inhabited. Perhaps, after all, the paper had been in the water for many months, or even years, and it was possible, in that case, that the shipwrecked one had been rescued or that he had died from suffering. The little party, discussing all sorts of possibilities, made a hasty dinner on board the sloop, and at 5 o'clock started to explore the woods.

Numerous animals fled before their approach, principally, indeed solely, goats and pigs, which it was easy to see were of European origin. Doubtless some whaler had left them here, and they had rapidly multiplied. Herbert made up his mind to catch two or three pairs to take back to Lincoln Island.

There was no longer any doubt that the island had previously been visited. This was the more evident as in passing through the forest they saw the traces of pathways, and the trunks of trees felled by the hatchet, and all about, marks of human handiwork; but these trees had been felled years before; the hatchet marks were velvetted with moss, and the pathways were so overgrown with grass that it was difficult to discover them.

"But," observed Spilett, "this proves that men not only landed here, but that they lived here. Now who and how many were these men, and how many remain?"

"The paper speaks of but one," replied Herbert.

"Well," said Pencroff, "if he is still here we cannot help finding him."

The exploration was continued, following diagonally across the island, and by this means the sailor and his companions reached the little stream which flowed towards the sea.

If animals of European origin, if works of human hands proved conclusively that man had once been here, many specimens of the vegetable kingdom also evidenced the fact. In certain clear places it was plain that kitchen vegetables had formerly been planted. And Herbert was overjoyed when he discovered potatoes, succory, sorrel, carrots, cabbage, and turnips, the seeds of which would enrich the garden at Granite House.

"Indeed," exclaimed Pencroff, "this will rejoice Neb. Even if we don't find the man, our voyage will not have been useless, and Heaven will have rewarded us."

"Doubtless," replied Spilett, "but from the conditions of these fields, it looks as if the place had not been inhabited for a long time."

"An inhabitant, whoever he was, would not neglect anything so important as this."

"Yes, this man has gone. It must be—"

"That the paper had been written a long time ago?"

"Undoubtedly."

"And that the bottle had been floating in the sea a good while before it arrived at Lincoln Island?"

"Why not?" said Pencroff. "But, see, it is getting dark," he added, "and I think we had better give over the search."

"We will go aboard, and to-morrow we will begin again," replied the reporter.

They were about adopting this counsel, when Herbert, pointing to something dimly visible, through the trees, exclaimed:— "There's a house!"

All three directed their steps towards the place indicated, and they made out in the twilight that it was built of planks, covered with heavy tarpaulin. The door, half closed, was pushed back by Pencroff, who entered quickly.

The place was empty!

CHAPTER XXXVI. THE INVENTORY

THE NIGHT—SOME LETTERS—THE SEARCH CONTINUED—PLANTS AND ANIMALS—HERBERT IN DANGER—ABOARD—THE DEPARTURE—BAD WEATHER—A GLIMMER OF INTELLIGENCE —LOST AT SEA—A TIMELY LIGHT.

Pencroff, Spilett and Herbert stood silent in darkness. Then the former gave a loud call. There was no answer. He lit a twig, and the light illuminated for a moment a small room, seemingly deserted. At one end was a large chimney, containing some cold cinders and an armful of dry wood. Pencroff threw the lighted twig into it, and the wood caught fire and gave out a bright light.

The sailor and his companions thereupon discovered a bed in disorder, its damp and mildewed covers proving that it had been long unused; in the corner of the fireplace were two rusty kettles and an overturned pot; a clothes-press with some sailors' clothing, partially moulded; on the table a tin plate, and a Bible, injured by the dampness; in a corner some tools, a shovel, a mattock, a pick, two shot guns, one of which was broken; on a shelf was a barrel full of powder, a barrel of lead, and a number of boxes of caps. All were covered with a thick coating of dust.

"There is no one here," said the reporter.

"Not a soul."

"This room has not been occupied in a long time."

"Since a very long time."

"Mr. Spilett," said Pencroff, "I think that instead of going on board we had better stay here all night."

"You are right, Pencroff, and if the proprietor returns he will not be sorry, perhaps, to find the place occupied."

"He won't come back, though," said the sailor, shaking his head.

"Do you think he has left the island?"

"If he had left the island he would have taken these things with him. You know how much a shipwrecked person would be attached to these objects. No, no," repeated the sailor, in the tone of a man perfectly convinced; "no, he has not left the island. He is surely here."

"Alive?"

"Alive or dead. But if he is dead he could not have buried himself, I am sure, and we will at least find his remains."

It was therefore agreed to pass the night in this house, and a supply of wood in the corner gave them the means of heating it. The door having been closed, the three explorers, seated upon a bench, spoke little, but remained deep in thought. They were in the mood to accept anything that might happen, and they listened eagerly for any sound from without. If the door had suddenly opened and a man had stood before them, they would not have been much surprised, in spite of all the evidence of desolation throughout the house; and their hands were ready to clasp the hands of this man, of this shipwrecked one, of this unknown friend whose friends awaited him.

But no sound was heard, the door did not open, and the hours passed by.

The night seemed interminable to the sailor and his companions. Herbert, alone, slept for two hours, as at his age, sleep is a necessity. All were anxious to renew the search of the day before, and to explore the innermost recesses of the islet. Pencroff's conclusions were certainly just, since the house and its contents had been abandoned. They determined, therefore, to search for the remains of its inhabitant, and to give them Christian burial.

As soon as it was daylight they began to examine the house. It was prettily situated under a small hill, on which grew several fine gum trees. Before it a large space had been cleared, giving a view over the sea. A small lawn, surrounded by a dilapidated fence, extended to the bank of the little stream. The house had evidently been built from planks taken from a ship. It seemed likely that a ship had been thrown upon the island, that all or at least one of the crew had been saved, and that this house had been built from the wreck. This was the more probable, as Spilett, in going round the dwelling, saw on one of the planks these half-effaced letters:—

BR ... TAN ... A.

"Britannia," exclaimed Pencroff, who had been called by the reporter to look at it; "that is a common name among ships, and I cannot say whether it is English or American. However, it don't matter to what country the man belongs, we will save him, if he is alive. But before we begin our search let us go back to the Good Luck."

Pencroff had been seized with a sort of anxiety about his sloop. Supposing the island was inhabited, and some one had taken it—but he shrugged his shoulders at this unlikely thought. Nevertheless the sailor was not unwilling to go on board to breakfast. The route already marked was not more than a mile in length, and they started on their walk, looking carefully about them in the woods and underbrush, through which ran hundreds of pigs and goats.

In twenty minutes the party reached the place where the Good Luck rode quietly at anchor. Pencroff gave a sigh of satisfaction.

After all, this boat was his baby, and it is a father's right to be often anxious without reason.

All went on board and ate a hearty breakfast, so as not to want anything before a late dinner; then the exploration was renewed, and conducted with the utmost carefulness. As it was likely that the solitary inhabitant of this island was dead, the party sought rather to find his remains than any traces of him living. But during all the morning they were unable to find anything; if he was dead, some animal must have devoured his body.

"We will leave to-morrow at daylight," said Pencroff to his companions, who towards 2 o'clock were resting for a few moments under a group of trees.

"I think we need not hesitate to take those things which belonged to him?" queried Herbert.

"I think not," answered Spilett; "and these arms and tools will add materially to the stock at Granite House. If I am not mistaken, what is left of the lead and powder is worth a good deal."

"And we must not forget to capture a couple of these pigs," said Pencroff.

"Nor to gather some seed," added Herbert, "which will give us some of our own vegetables."

"Perhaps it would be better to spend another day here, in order to get together everything that we want," suggested the reporter.

"No, sir;" replied the sailor. "I want to get away to-morrow morning. The wind seems to be shifting to the west, and will be in our favor going back."

"Then don't let us lose any time," said Herbert, rising.

"We will not," replied Pencroff. "Herbert, you get the seed, and Spilett and I will chase the pigs, and although we haven't Top, I think we will catch some."

Herbert, therefore, followed the path which led to the cultivated part of the island, while the others plunged at once into the forest. Although the pigs were plenty they were singularly agile, and not in the humor to be captured. However, after half an hour's chasing the hunters had captured a couple in their lair, when cries mingled with horrible hoarse sounds, having nothing human in them, were heard. Pencroff and Spilett sprang to their feet, regardless of the pigs, which escaped.

"It is Herbert!" cried the reporter.

"Hurry!" cried the sailor, as the two ran with their utmost speed towards the place from whence the cries came.

They had need to hasten, for at a turn in the path they saw the lad prostrate beneath a savage, or perhaps a gigantic ape, who was throttling him.

To throw themselves on this monster and pinion him to the ground, dragging Herbert away, was the work of a moment. The sailor had herculean strength. Spilett, too, was muscular, and, in spite of the resistance of the monster, it was bound so that it could not move.

"You are not wounded, Herbert?"

"No, oh no."

"Ah! if it had hurt you, this ape-"

"But he is not an ape!" cried Herbert.

At these words Pencroff and Spilett looked again at the object lying on the ground. In fact, it was not an ape, but a human being—a man! But what a man! He was a savage, in all the horrible acceptation of the word; and, what was more frightful, he seemed to have fallen to the last degree of brutishness.

Matted hair, tangled beard descending to his waist, his body naked, save for a rag about his loins, wild eyes, long nails, mahogany-colored skin, feet as hard as if they had been made of horn; such was the miserable creature which it was, nevertheless, necessary to call a man. But one might well question whether this body still contained a soul, or whether the low, brutish instinct alone survived.

"Are you perfectly sure that this is what has been a man?" questioned Pencroff of the reporter.

"Alas! there can be no doubt of it," replied Spilett.

"Can he be the person shipwrecked?" asked Herbert

"Yes," responded the reporter, "but the poor creature is no longer human."

Spilett was right. Evidently, if the castaway had ever been civilized, isolation had made him a savage, a real creature of the woods. He gave utterance to hoarse sounds, from between teeth which were as sharp as those of animals living on raw flesh. Memory had doubtless long ago left him, and he had long since forgotten the use of arms and tools, and even how to make a fire. One could see that he was active and supple, but that his physical qualities had developed to the exclusion of his moral perception.

Spilett spoke to him, but he neither understood nor listened, and, looking him in the eye, the reporter could see that all intelligence had forsaken him. Nevertheless, the prisoner did not struggle or strive to break his bonds. Was he cowed by the presence of these men, whom he had once resembled? Was there in some corner of his brain a flitting remembrance which drew him towards humanity? Free, would he have fled or would he have remained? They did not know, and they did not put him to the proof. After having looked attentively at the miserable creature, Spilett said:—

"What he is, what he has been, and what he will be; it is still our duty to take him to Lincoln Island."

"Oh yes, yes," exclaimed Herbert, "and perhaps we can, with care, restore to him some degree of intelligence."

"The soul never dies," answered the reporter, "and it would be a great thing to bring back this creature of God's making from his brutishness."

Pencroff shook his head doubtfully.

"It is necessary to try at all events," said the reporter, "humanity requires it of us."

"It was, indeed, their duty as civilized and Christian beings, and they well knew that Smith would approve of their course.

"Shall we leave him bound?" inquired the sailor.

"Perhaps if we unfasten his feet he will walk," said Herbert.

"Well, let us try," replied the sailor.

And the cords binding the creature's legs were loosened, although his arms were kept firmly bound. He rose without manifesting any desire to escape. His tearless eyes darted sharp glances upon the three men who marched beside him, and nothing denoted that he remembered being or having been like them. A wheezing sound escaped from his lips, and his aspect was wild, but he made no resistance.

By the advice of the reporter, the poor wretch was taken to the house, where, perhaps, the sight of the objects in it might make some impression upon him. Perhaps a single gleam would awaken his sleeping consciousness, illuminate his darkened mind. The house was near by, and in a few minutes they were there; but the prisoner recognized nothing—he seemed to have lost consciousness of everything. Could it be that this brutish state was due to his long imprisonment on the island? That, having come here a reasoning being, his isolation had reduced him to this state?

The reporter thought that perhaps the sight of fire might affect him, and in a moment one of those lovely flames which attract even animals lit up the fireplace. The sight of this flame seemed at first to attract the attention of the unfortunate man, but very soon he ceased regarding it. Evidently, for the present at least, there was nothing to do but take him aboard the Good Luck, which was accordingly done. He was left in charge of Pencroff, while the two others returned to the island and brought over the arms and implements, a lot of seeds, some game, and two pairs of pigs which they had caught. Everything was put on board, and the sloop rode ready to hoist anchor as soon as the next morning's tide would permit.

The prisoner had been placed in the forward hold, where he lay calm, quiet, insensible, and mute. Pencroff offering him some cooked meat to eat, he pushed it away; but, on being shown one of the ducks which Herbert had killed, he pounced on it with bestial avidity and devoured it.

"You think he'll be himself again?" asked the sailor, shaking his head.

"Perhaps," replied the reporter. "It is not impossible that our attentions will react on him, since it is the isolation that has done this; and he will be alone no longer."

"The poor fellow has doubtless been this way for a long time."

"Perhaps so."

"How old do you think he is?" asked the lad.

"That is hard to say," replied the reporter, "as his matted beard obscures his face; but he is no longer young, and I should say he was at least fifty years old."

"Have you noticed how his eyes are set deep in his head?"

"Yes, but I think that they are more human than one would suspect from his general appearance."

"Well, we will see," said Pencroff; "and I am curious to have Mr. Smith's opinion of our savage. We went to find a human being, and we are bringing back a monster. Any how, one takes what he can get."

The night passed, and whether the prisoner slept or not he did not move, although he had been unbound. He was like one of those beasts that in the first moments of their capture submit, and to whom the rage returns later.

At daybreak the next day, the 17th, the change in the weather was as Pencroff had predicted. The wind hauled round to the northwest and favored the return of the Good Luck; but at the same time it had freshened, so as to make the sailing more difficult. At 5 o'clock the anchor was raised, Pencroff took a reef in the mainsail and headed directly towards home.

The first day passed without incident. The prisoner rested quietly in the forward cabin, and, as he had once been a sailor, the motion of the sloop produced upon him a sort of salutary reaction. Did it recall to him some remembrance of his former occupation? At least he rested tranquil, more astonished than frightened.

On the 16th the wind freshened considerably, coming round more to the north, and therefore in a direction less favorable to the course of the Good Luck, which bounded over the waves. Pencroff was soon obliged to hold her nearer to the wind, and without saying so, he began to be anxious at the lookout ahead. Certainly, unless the—wind moderated, it would take much longer to go back than it had taken to come.

On the 17th they had been forty-eight hours out, and yet nothing indicated they were in the neighborhood of Lincoln Island. It was, moreover, impossible to reckon their course, or even to estimate the distance traversed, as the direction and the speed had been too irregular. Twenty-four hours later there was still no land in view. The wind was dead ahead, and an ugly sea running. On the 18th a huge wave struck the sloop, and had not the crew been lashed to the deck, they would have been swept overboard.

On this occasion Pencroff and his companions, busy in clearing things away, received an unhoped-for assistance from the prisoner, who sprang from the hatchway as if his sailor instinct had returned to him, and breaking the rail by a, vigorous blow—with a spar, enabled the water on the deck to flow off more freely. Then, the boat cleared, without having said a word, he returned to his cabin.

Nevertheless, the situation was bad, and the sailor had cause to believe himself lost upon this vast sea, without the possibility of regaining his course. The night of the 18th was dark and cold. But about 11 o'clock the wind lulled, the sea fell, and the sloop, less tossed about, moved more rapidly. None of the crew thought of sleep. They kept an eager lookout, as either Lincoln Island must be near at hand and they would discover it at daybreak, or the sloop had been drifted from her course by the currents, and it would be next to impossible to rectify the direction.

Pencroff, anxious to the last degree, did not, however, despair; but, seated at the helm, he tried to see through the thick darkness around him. Towards 2 o'clock he suddenly started up, crying:—"A light! a light!" It was indeed a bright light appearing twenty miles to—the northeast. Lincoln Island was there, and this light, evidently lit by Smith, indicated the direction to be followed.

Pencroff, who had been heading much too far towards the north, changed his course, and steered directly towards the light, which gleamed above the horizon like a star of the first magnitude.

CHAPTER XXXVII. THE RETURN-DISCUSSION

At 7 o'clock the next morning the boat touched the shore at the mouth of the Mercy. Smith and Neb, who had become very anxious at the stormy weather and the prolonged absence of their companions, had climbed, at daylight, to Prospect Plateau, and had at length perceived the sloop in the distance.

"Thank Heaven! There they are," exclaimed Smith; while Neb, dancing with pleasure, turned towards his master, and, striking his hands together, cried, "Oh, my master!"-a more touching expression than, the first polished phrase.

The engineer's first thought, on counting the number of persons on the deck of the Good Luck, was that Pencroff had found no one on Tabor Island, or that the unfortunate man had refused to exchange one prison for another.

The engineer and Neb were on the beach at the moment the sloop arrived, and before the party had leaped ashore, Smith said:— "We have been very anxious about you, my friends. Did anything happen to you?"

"No, indeed; everything went finely," replied Spilett. "We will tell you all about it."

"Nevertheless, you have failed in your search, since you are all alone.", "But, sir, there are four of us," said the sailor.

"Have you found this person?". "Yes." "And brought him back?" "Yes."

"Living? Where is he, and what is he, then?"

"He is, or rather, he was a human being; and that is all, Cyrus, that we can say."

The engineer was thereupon, informed of everything that had happened; of the search, of the long-abandoned house, of the capture of the scarcely human inhabitant.

"And," added Pencroff," I don't know whether we have done right in bringing him here."

"Most certainly you have done right," replied the engineer.

"But the poor fellow has no sense at all." "Not now, perhaps; in a few months, he will be as much a man as any of us. "Who knows what might happen to the last one of us, after living for a long time alone on this island? It is terrible to be all alone, my friends, and it is probable that solitude quickly overthrows reason, since you have found this poor being in such a condition."

"But, Mr. Smith," asked Herbert, "what makes you think that the brutishness of this man has come on within a little while?"

"Because the paper we found had been recently written, and no one but this shipwrecked man could have written it."

"Unless," suggested Spilett, "it had been written by a companion of this man who has since died."

"That is impossible, Spilett."

"Why so?"

"Because, then, the paper would have mentioned two persons instead of one."

Herbert briefly related the incident of the sea striking the sloop, and insisted that the prisoner must then have had a glimmer of his sailor instinct.

"You are perfectly right, Herbert," said the engineer, "to attach great importance to this fact. This poor man will not be incurable; despair has made him what he is. But here he will find his kindred, and if he still has any reason, we will save it."

Then, to Smith's great pity and Neb's wonderment, the man was brought up from the cabin of the sloop, and as soon as he was on land, he manifested a desire to escape. But Smith, approaching him, laid his hand authoritatively upon his shoulder and looked at him with infinite tenderness. Thereupon the poor wretch, submitting to a sort of instantaneous power, became quiet, his eyes fell, his head dropped forward, and he made no further resistance.

"Poor shipwrecked sailor," murmured the reporter.

Smith regarded him attentively. To judge from his appearance, this miserable creature had little of the human left in him; but Smith caught in his glance, as the reporter had done, an almost imperceptible gleam of intelligence.

It was decided that the Unknown, as his new companions called him, should stay in one of the rooms of Granite House, from which he could not escape. He made no resistance to being conducted there, and with good care they might, perhaps, hope that some day he would prove a companion to them.

Neb hastened to prepare breakfast, for the voyagers were very hungry, and during the meal Smith made them relate in detail every incident of the cruise. He agreed with them in thinking that the name of the Britannia gave them reason to believe that the Unknown was either English or American; and, moreover, under all the growth of hair covering the man's face, the engineer thought he recognized the features characteristic of an Anglo-Saxon.

"But, by the way, Herbert," said the reporter, "you have never told us how you met this savage, and we know nothing, except that he would have strangled you, had we not arrived so opportunely."

"Indeed, I am not sure that I can tell just what happened," replied Herbert. "I was, I think, gathering seeds, when I heard a tremendous noise in a high tree near by. I had hardly time to turn, when this unhappy creature, who had, doubtless, been hidden crouching in the tree, threw himself upon me; and, unless Mr. Spilett and Pencroff—"

"You were in great danger, indeed, my boy," said Smith; "but perhaps, if this had not happened, this poor being would have escaped your search, and we would have been without another companion."

"You expect, then, to make him a man again?" asked the reporter.

"Yes," replied Smith.

Breakfast ended, all returned to the shore and began unloading the sloop; and the engineer examined the arms and tools, but found nothing to establish the identity of the Unknown.

The pigs were taken to the stables, to which they would soon become accustomed. The two barrels of powder and shot and the caps were a great acquisition, and it was determined to make a small powder magazine in the upper cavern of Granite House, where there would be no danger of an explosion. Meantime, since the pyroxyline answered very well, there was no present need to use this powder.

When the sloop was unloaded Pencroff said:—

"I think, Mr. Smith, that it would be better to put the Good Luck in a safe place."

"Is it not safe enough at the mouth of the Mercy?"

"No, sir," replied the sailor. "Most of the time she is aground on the sand, which strains her."

"Could not she be moored out in the stream?"

"She could, but the place is unsheltered, and in an easterly wind I am afraid she would suffer from the seas."

"Very well; where do you want to put her?"

"In Balloon Harbor," replied the sailor. "It seems to me that that little inlet, hidden by the rocks, is just the place for her."

"Isn't it too far off?"

"No, it is only three miles from Granite House, and we have a good straight road there."

"Have your way, Pencroff," replied the engineer. "Nevertheless, I should prefer to have the sloop under our sight. We must, when we have time, make a small harbor."

"Capital!" cried Pencroff. "A harbor with a light house, a breakwater, and a dry dock! Oh, indeed, sir, everything will be easy enough with you!"

"Always provided, my good man, that you assist me, as you do three fourths of the work."

Herbert and the sailor went aboard the Good Luck, and set sail, and in a couple of hours the sloop rode quietly at anchor in the tranquil water of Balloon Harbor.

During the first few days that the Unknown was at Granite House, had he given any indication of a change in his savage nature? Did not a brighter light illumine the depths of his intelligence? Was not, in short, his reason returning to him? Undoubtedly, yes; and Smith and Spilett questioned whether this reason had ever entirely forsaken him.

At first this man, accustomed to the air and liberty which he had had in Tabor Island, was seized with fits of passion, and there was danger of his throwing himself out of one of the windows of Granite House. But little by little he grew more quiet, and he was allowed to move about without restraint.

Already forgetting his carnivorous instincts, he accepted a less bestial nourishment, and cooked food did not produce in him the sentiment of disgust which he had shown on board the Good Luck.

Smith had taken advantage of a time when the man was asleep to cut the hair and beard which had grown like a mane about his face, and had given him such a savage aspect. He had also been clothed more decently, and the result was that the Unknown appeared more like a human being, and it seemed as if the expression of his eyes was softened. Certainly, sometimes, when intelligence was visible, the expression of this man had a sort of beauty.

Every day, Smith made a point of passing some hours in his company. He worked beside him, and occupied himself in various ways to attract his attention. It would suffice, if a single ray of light illuminated his reason, if a single remembrance crossed his mind. Neither did the engineer neglect to speak in a loud voice, so as to penetrate by both sound and sight to the depths of this torpid intelligence. Sometimes one or another of the party joined the engineer, and they usually talked of such matters pertaining to the sea as would be likely to interest the man. At times the Unknown gave a sort of vague attention to what was said, and soon the colonists began to think that he partly understood them. Again his expression would be dolorous, proving that he suffered inwardly. Nevertheless, he did not speak, although they thought, at times, from his actions, that words were about to pass his lips.

The poor creature was very calm and sad. But was not the calmness only on the surface, and the sadness the result of his confinement? They could not yet say. Seeing only certain objects and in a limited space, always with the colonists, to whom he had become accustomed, having no desire to satisfy, better clothed and better fed, it was natural that his physical nature should soften little by little; but was he imbued with the new life, or, to use an expression justly applicable to the case, was he only tamed, as an animal in the presence of its master? This was the important question Smith was anxious to determine, and meantime he did not wish to be too abrupt with his patient. For to him, the unknown was but a sick person. Would he ever be a convalescent?

Therefore, the engineer watched him unceasingly. How he laid in wait for his reason, so to speak, that he might lay hold of it.

The colonists followed with strong interest all the phases of this cure undertaken by Smith. All aided him in it, and all, save perhaps the incredulous Pencroff, came to share in his belief and hope.

The submission of the Unknown was entire, and it seemed as if he showed for the engineer, whose influence over him was apparent, a sort of attachment, and Smith resolved now to test it by transporting him to another scene, to that ocean which he had been accustomed to look upon, to the forest border, which would recall those woods where he had lived such a life!"

"But," said Spilett, "can we hope that once at liberty, he will not escape?"

"We must make the experiment," replied the engineer.

"All right," said Pencroff. "You will see, when this fellow snuffs the fresh air and sees the coast clear, if he don't make his legs spin!"

"I don't think it," replied the engineer.

"We will try, any how," said Spilett.

It was the 30th of October, and the Unknown had been a prisoner for nine days. It was a beautiful, warm, sunshiny day. Smith and Pencroff went to the room of the Unknown, whom they found at the window gazing out at the sky.

"Come, my friend," said the engineer to him.

The Unknown rose immediately. His eye was fixed on Smith, whom he followed; and the sailor, little confident in the results of the experiment, walked with him.

Having reached the door, they made him get into the elevator, at the foot of which the rest of the party were waiting. The basket descended, and in a few seconds all were standing together on the shore.

The colonists moved off a little distance from the Unknown, so as to leave him quite at liberty. He made some steps forward towards the sea, and his face lit up with pleasure, but he made no effort to escape. He looked curiously at the little waves, which, broken by the islet, died away on the shore.

"It is not, indeed, the ocean," remarked Spilett, "and it is possible that this does not give him the idea of escaping."

"Yes," replied Smith, "we must take him to the plateau on the edge of the forest. There the experiment will be more conclusive."

"There he cannot get away, since the bridges are all raised," said Neb.

"Oh, he is not the man to be troubled by such a brook as Glycerine Creek; he could leap it at a bound," returned Pencroff.

"We will see presently," said Smith, who kept his eye fixed on his patient.

And thereupon all proceeded towards Prospect Plateau. Having reached the place they encountered the outskirts of the forest, with its leaves trembling in the wind, The Unknown seemed to drink in with eagerness the perfume in the air, and a long sigh escaped from his breast.

The colonists stood some paces back, ready to seize him if he attempted to escape.

The poor creature was upon the point of plunging in the creek that separated him from the forest; he placed himself ready to spring—then all at once he turned about, dropping his arms beside him, and tears coursed down his cheeks.

"Ah!" cried Smith, "you will be a man again, since you weep!"

CHAPTER XXXVIII. A MYSTERY TO BE SOLVED

THE FIRST WORDS OF THE UNKNOWN—TWELVE YEARS ON THE ISLAND— CONFESSIONS—DISAPPEARANCE—SMITH'S CONFIDENCE —BUILDING A WIND-MILL—THE FIRST BREAD—AN ACT OF DEVOTION—HONEST HANDS.

Yes, the poor creature had wept. Some remembrance had flashed across his spirit, and, as Smith had said, he would be made a man through his tears. The colonists left him for some time, withdrawing themselves, so that he could feel perfectly at liberty; but he showed no inclination to avail himself of this freedom, and Smith soon decided to take him back to Granite House.

Two days after this occurrence, the Unknown showed a disposition to enter little by little into the common life. It was evident that he heard, that he understood, but it was equally evident that he manifested a strange disinclination to speak to them. Pencroff, listening at his room, heard these words escape him:—

"No! here! I! never!"

The sailor reported this to his companions, and Smith said:—

"There must be some sad mystery here."

The Unknown had begun to do some little chores, and to work in the garden. When he rested, which was frequent, he seemed entirely self-absorbed; but, on the advice of the engineer, the others respected the silence, which he seemed desirous of keeping. If one of the colonists approached him he recoiled, sobbing as if overcome. Could it be by remorse? or, was it, as Spilett once suggested:—

"If he does not speak I believe it is because he has something on his mind too terrible to mention."

Some days later the Unknown was working on the plantation, when, of a sudden, he stopped and let his spade fall, and Smith, who was watching him from a distance, saw that he was weeping again. An irresistible pity drew the engineer to the poor fellow's side; and, touching his arm lightly,

"My friend," said he.

The Unknown tried to look away, and when Smith sought to take his hand he drew back quickly.

"My friend," said Smith, with decision, "I wish you to look at me."

The Unknown obeyed, raising his eyes and regarding the other as one does who is under the influence of magnetism. At first he wished to break away, then his whole expression changed; his eyes flashed, and, unable longer to contain himself, he muttered some incoherent words. Suddenly he crossed his arms, and in a hollow voice:— "Who are you?" he demanded.

"Men shipwrecked as you have been," replied the engineer, greatly moved. "We have brought you here among your kindred."

"My kindred! I have none!

"You are among friends—,"

"Friends! I! Friends!" cried the Unknown, hiding his face in his hands. "Oh, no! never! Leave me! leave me!" and he rushed to the brink of the plateau overlooking the sea, and stood there, motionless, for a long time. Smith had rejoined his companions and had related to them what had happened.

"There certainly is a mystery in this man's life," said Spilett, "and it seems as if his first human sensation was remorse."

"I don't understand what kind of a man we have brought back," says the sailor. "He has secrets—"

"Which we will respect," answered the engineer, quickly. "If he has committed some fault he has cruelly expiated it, and in our sight it is absolved."

For two hours the Unknown remained upon the shore, evidently under the influence of remembrances which brought back to him all his past, a past which, doubtless, was hateful enough, and the colonists, though keeping watch upon him, respected his desire to be alone.

Suddenly he seemed to have taken a resolution, and he returned to the engineer. His eyes were red with the traces of tears, and his face wore an expression of deep humility. He seemed apprehensive, ashamed, humiliated, and his looks were fixed on the ground.

"Sir," said he, "are you and your companions English?"

"No," replied Smith, "we are Americans."

"Ah!" murmured the Unknown, "I am glad of that."

"And what are you, my friend?" asked the engineer.

"English," he responded, as if these few words had cost him a great effort. He rushed to the shore, and traversed its length to the mouth of the Mercy, in a state of extreme agitation.

Having, at one place, met Herbert, he stopped, and in a choking voice, accosted him:— "What month is it?"

"November," replied the lad.

"And what year?"

"1866."

"Twelve years! Twelve years!" he cried, and then turned quickly away.

Herbert related this incident to the others.

"The poor creature knew neither the month nor the year," remarked Spilett.

"And he had been twelve years on the island, when we found him."

"Twelve years," said Smith. "Twelve years of isolation, after a wicked life, perhaps; that would indeed affect a man's reason."

"I cannot help thinking," observed Pencroff, "that this man was not wrecked on that island, but that he has been left there for some crime."

"You may be right, Pencroff," replied the reporter, "and if that is the case, it is not impossible that whoever left him there may return for him some day."

"And they would not find him," said Herbert.

"But, then," exclaimed Pencroff, "he would want to go back, and—"

"My friends," interrupted Smith, "do not let us discuss this question till we know what we are talking about. I believe that this unhappy man has suffered, and that he has paid bitterly for his faults, whatever they may have been, and that he is struggling with the need of opening his heart to someone. Do not provoke him to speak; he will tell us of his own accord some day, and when we have learned all, we will see what course it will be necessary to follow. He alone can tell us if he has more than the hope, the certainty of some day being restored to his country, but I doubt it."

"Why?" asked the reporter.

"Because, had he been sure of being delivered after a fixed time, he would have awaited the hour of his deliverance, and not have thrown that paper in the sea. No, it is more likely that be was condemned to die upon this island, to never look upon his kind again."

"But there still is something which I cannot understand," said the sailor.

"What is that?"

"Why, if this man had been left on Tabor Island twelve years ago, it seems probable that he must have been in this savage condition for a long time."

"That is probable," replied the engineer.

"And, therefore, it is a long time since he wrote that paper."

"Doubtless—and yet that paper seemed to have been written recently—"

"Yes, and how account for the bottle taking so many years in coming from Tabor Island here?"

"It is not absolutely impossible," responded the reporter. "Could not it have been in the neighborhood of the island for a long time?"

"And have remained floating? No," answered the sailor, "for sooner or later it would have been dashed to pieces on the rocks."

"It would, indeed," said Smith, thoughtfully.

"And, moreover," continued the sailor, if the paper had been enclosed in the bottle for a long time, it would have been injured by the moisture, whereas, it was not damaged in the least."

The sailor's remark was just, and, moreover, this paper, recently written, gave the situation of the island with an exactness which implied a knowledge of hydrography, such as a simple sailor could not have.

"There is, as I said before, something inexplicable in all this," said the engineer, "but do not let us urge our new companion to speak, when he wishes it we will be ready to listen."

For several days after this the Unknown neither spoke nor left the plateau. He worked incessantly, digging in the garden apart from the colonists, and at meal times, although he was often asked to join them, he remained alone, eating but a few uncooked vegetables. At night, instead of returning to his room in Granite House, he slept under the trees, or hid himself, if the weather was bad, in some hollow of the rocks. Thus he returned again to that manner of life in which he had lived when he had no other shelter than the forests of Tabor Island, and all endeavor to make him modify this life having proved fruitless, the colonists waited patiently. But the moment came when, irresistibly and as if involuntarily forced from him by his conscience, the terrible avowals were made.

At dusk on the evening of the 10th of November, as the colonists were seated in the arbor, the Unknown stood suddenly before them. His eyes glowed, and his whole appearance wore again the savage aspect of former days. He stood there, swayed by some terrible emotion, his teeth chattering like those of a person in a fever. The colonists were astounded. "What was the matter with him? Was the sight of his fellow-creatures unendurable? Had he had enough of this honest life? Was he homesick for his brutish life? One would have thought so, hearing him give utterance to these incoherent phrases: "Why am I here? By what right did you drag me from my island? Is there any bond between you and me? Do you know who I am—what I have done—why I was there—alone? And who has told you that I was not abandoned—that I was not condemned to die there? Do you know my past? Do you know whether I have not robbed, murdered—if I am not a miserable—a wicked being—fit to live like a wild beast—far from all—say—do you know?"

The colonists listened silently to the unhappy creature, from whom these half avowals came in spite of himself. Smith, wishing to soothe him, would have gone to him, but the Unknown drew back quickly.

"No! no!" he cried. "One word only—am I free?".

"You are free," replied the engineer.

"Then, good-bye!" he cried, rushing off. Neb, Pencroff, and Herbert ran to the border of the wood, but they returned alone.

"We must let him have his own way," said the engineer.

"He will never come back," exclaimed Pencroff.

"He will return," replied the engineer.

And after that conversation many days passed, but Smith—was it a presentiment—persisted in the fixed idea that the unhappy man would return sooner or later.

"It is the last struggle of this rude nature, which is touched by remorse, and which would be terrified by a new isolation."

In the meantime, work of all kinds was continued, both on Prospect Plateau and at the corral, where Smith proposed to make a farm. It is needless to say that the seeds brought from Tabor Island had been carefully sown. The plateau was a great kitchen-garden, well laid out and enclosed, which kept the colonists always busy. As the plants multiplied, it was necessary to increase the size of the beds, which threatened to become fields, and to take the place of the grass land. But as forage abounded in other parts of the island, there was no fear of the onagers having to be placed on rations; and it was also better to make Prospect Plateau, defended by its belt of creeks, a garden of this kind, and to extend the fields, which required no protection, beyond the belt.

On the 15th of November they made their third harvest. Here was a field which had indeed increased in the eighteen months since the first grain of corn had been sown. The second crop of 600,000 grains produced this time 4,000 bushels or more than 500,000,000 grains. The colonists were, therefore, rich in corn; as it was only necessary to sow a dozen bushels each year in order to have a supply sufficient for the nourishment of man and beast.

After harvesting they, gave up the last fortnight in the month to bread-making. They had the grain but not the flour, and a mill was therefore necessary. Smith could have used the other waterfall which fell into the Mercy, but, after discussing the question, it was decided to build a simple wind-mill on the summit of the plateau. Its construction would be no more difficult than a water-mill, and they would be sure of always having a breeze on this open elevation.

"Without counting," said Pencroff, "the fine aspect a wind-mill will give to the landscape."

They began the work by selecting timber for the cage and machinery for the mill. Some large sand-stones, which the colonists found to the north of the lake, were readily made into mill-stones, and the inexhaustible envelope of the balloon furnished the cloth necessary for the sails.

Smith made his drawings, and the site for the mill was chosen a little to the right of the poultry-yard, and close to the lake shore. The whole cage rested upon a pivot, held in position by heavy timbers, in such a manner that it could turn, with all the mechanism within it, towards any quarter of the wind.

The work progressed rapidly. Neb and Herbert had become expert carpenters, and had only to follow the plans furnished by the engineer, so that in a very short time a sort of round watch-house, a regular pepper-box, surmounted by a sharp roof, rose upon the site selected. The four wings had been firmly fastened by iron tenons to the main shaft, in such a manner as to make a certain angle with it. As for the various parts of the interior mechanism—the two mill-stones, the runner and the feeder; the hopper, a sort of huge square trough, large above and small below, permitting the grains to fall upon the mill-stones; the oscillating bucket, designed to regulate the passage of the grain; and, finally, the bolter, which, by the operation of the sieve, separated the bran from the flour—all these were easily made. And as their tools were good, the work simple, and everybody took part in it, the mill was finished by the 1st of December.

As usual, Pencroff was overjoyed by his work, and he was sure that the machine was perfection.

"Now, with a good wind, we will merrily grind our corn."

"Let it be a good wind, Pencroff, but not too strong," said the engineer.

"Bah! our mill will turn the faster."

"It is not necessary to turn rapidly," replied the engineer. "Experience has demonstrated that the best results are obtained by a mill whose wings make six times the number of turns in a minute that the wind travels feet in a second. Thus, an ordinary wind, which travels twenty-four feet in a second, will turn the wings of the mill sixteen times in a minute, which is fast enough."

"Already!" exclaimed Herbert, "there is a fine breeze from the northeast, which will be just the thing!"

There was no reason to delay using the mill, and the colonists were anxious to taste the bread of Lincoln Island; so this very morning two or three bushels of corn were ground, and the next day, at breakfast, a splendid loaf, rather heavy perhaps, which had been raised with the barm of beer, was displayed upon the table of Granite House. Each munched his portion with a pleasure perfectly inexpressible.

Meantime the Unknown had not come back again. Often Spilett and Herbert had searched the forest in the neighborhood of Granite House without finding any trace of him, and all began to be seriously alarmed at his prolonged absence. Undoubtedly the former savage of Tabor Island would not find it difficult to live in the forests of the Far West, which were so rich in game; but was it not to be feared that he would resume his former habits, and that his independence would revive in him his brutish instincts? Smith alone, by a sort of presentiment, persisted in saying that the fugitive would return.

"Yes, he will come back," he repeated with a confidence in which his companions could not share. "When this poor creature was on Tabor Island, he knew he was alone, but here, he knows that his kindred await him. Since he half-spoke of his past life, he will return to tell us everything, and on that day he will be ours."

The event proved the correctness of Cyrus Smith's reasoning.

On the 3d of December, Herbert had gone to the southern shore of the lake, to fish, and, since the dangerous animals never showed themselves in this part of the island, he had gone unarmed.

Pencroff and Neb were working in the poultry-yard, while Smith and the reporter were occupied at the Chimneys making soda, the supply of soap being low.

Suddenly sharp cries of help were heard by Neb and Pencroff, who summoned the others, and all rushed towards the lake.

But before them, the Unknown, whose presence in the neighborhood had not been suspected, leapt over Glycerine Creek and bounded along the opposite bank.

There, Herbert stood facing a powerful jaguar, like the one which had been killed at Reptile End. Taken by surprise, he stood with his back against a tree, and the animal, crouching on his haunches, was about to spring upon him, when the Unknown, with no other arm than his knife, threw himself on the brute, which turned upon its new adversary.

The struggle was short. This man, whose strength and agility was prodigious, seized the jaguar by the throat in a vice-like grip, and, not heeding the claws of the beast tearing his flesh, he thrust his knife into its heart.

The jaguar fell, and the Unknown was about turning to go away, when the colonists came up, and Herbert, catching hold of him, exclaimed:— "No, no, you must not leave us!"

Smith walked towards the man, who frowned at his approach. The blood was flowing from a wound in his shoulder, but he did not heed it.

"My friend," said Smith, "we are in your debt. You have risked your life to save our boy."

"My life," murmured the Unknown; "what is it worth? less than nothing."

"You are wounded?"

"That does not matter."

"Will you not shake hands with me?" asked Herbert.

But on the lad's seeking to take his hand, the Unknown folded his arms, his chest heaved, and he looked about as if he wished to escape; but, making a violent effort at self-control, and in a gruff voice:— "Who are you?" he asked, "and what are you going to do with me?"

It was their history that he thus asked for, for the first time. Perhaps, if that was related, he would tell his own. So Smith, in a few words, recounted all that had happened since their departure from Richmond; how they had succeeded, and the resources now at their disposal.

The Unknown listened with the utmost attention.

Then Smith told him who they all were, Spilett, Herbert, Pencroff, Neb, himself, and he added that the greatest happiness that had come to them since their arrival on Lincoln Island was on their return from the islet, when they could count one more companion.

At these words the other colored up, and bowing his head, seemed greatly agitated.

"And now that you know us," asked Smith, "will you give us your hand?"

"No," answered the Unknown in a hoarse voice; "no! You are honest men. But I—"

CHAPTER XXXIX. ALWAYS APART

A BEQUEST OF THE UNKNOWN'S—THE FARM ESTABLISHED AT THE CORRAL—TWELVE YEARS—THE BOATSWAIN'S MATE OF THE BRITANNIA — LEFT ON TABOR ISLAND—THE HAND OF SMITH—THE MYSTERIOUS PAPER

These last events justified the presentiments of the colonists. There was some terrible past in the life of this man, expiated, perhaps, in the eyes of men, but which his conscience still held unabsolved. At any rate, he felt remorse; he had repented, and his new friends would have cordially grasped that hand, but he did not feel himself worthy to offer it to honest men. Nevertheless, after the struggle with the jaguar, he did not go back to the forest, but remained within the bounds of Granite House.

What was the mystery of this life? Would he speak of it some day? The colonists thought so, but they agreed that, under no circumstances, would they ask him for his secret; and, in the meantime, to associate with him as if they suspected nothing.

For some days everything went on as usual. Smith and Spilett worked together, sometimes as chemists, sometimes as physicists, the reporter never leaving the engineer, except to hunt with Herbert, as it was not prudent to allow the young lad to traverse the forest alone. As to Neb and Pencroff, the work in the stables and poultry-yard, or at the corral, besides the chores about Granite House, kept them busy.

The Unknown worked apart from the others. He had gone back to his former habit of taking no share in the meals, of sleeping under the trees, of having nothing to do with his companions. It seemed, indeed, as if the society of those who had saved him was intolerable.

"But why, then," asked Pencroff, "did he seek succor from his fellow-creatures; why did he throw this paper in the sea?"

"He will tell us everything," was Smith's invariable answer.

"But when?"

"Perhaps sooner than you think, Pencroff."

And, indeed, on the 10th of December, a week after his return to Granite House, the Unknown accosted the engineer and in a quiet humble voice said:—

"Sir, I have a request to make."

"Speak," replied the engineer, "but, first, let me ask you a question?"

At these words the Unknown colored and drew back. Smith saw what was passing in the mind of the culprit, who feared, doubtless, that the engineer would question him upon his past.

Smith took him by the hand. "Comrade," said he, "we are not only companions, we are friends. I wanted to say this to you first, now I will listen."

The Unknown covered his eyes with his hand; a sort of tremor seized him, and for some moments he was unable to articulate a word.

"Sir," said he, at length, "I came to implore a favor from you."

"What is it?"

"You have, four or five miles from here, at the foot of the mountain, a corral for your animals. These require looking after. Will you permit me to live over there with them?"

Smith regarded the unhappy man for some time, with deep commiseration. Then:— "My friend," said he, "the corral has nothing but sheds, only fit for the animals—"

"It will be good enough, for me, sir."

"My friend," replied Smith, "we will never thwart you in anything. If you wish to live in the corral, you may; nevertheless, you will always be welcome at Granite House. But since you desire to stay at the corral, we will do what is necessary to make you comfortable."

"Never mind about that, I will get along well enough."

"My friend," responded Smith, who persisted in the use of this cordial title, "you must let us be the judges in that matter."

The Unknown thanked the engineer and went away. And Smith, having told his companions of the proposition that had been made, they decided to build a log house at the corral, and to make it as comfortable as possible.

The same day the colonists went, with the necessary tools, to the place, and before the week was out the house was ready for its guest. It was built twenty feet from the sheds, at a place where the herd of moufflons, now numbering twenty-four animals, could be easily overlooked. Some furniture, including a bed, table, bench, clothes-press, and chest was made, and some arms, ammunition, and tools, were carried there.

The Unknown, meanwhile, had not seen his new home, letting the colonists work without him, while he remained at the plateau, wishing, doubtless, to finish up his work there. And, indeed, by his exertion the ground was completely tilled, and ready for the sowing when the time should arrive.

On the 20th everything was prepared at the corral, aid the engineer told the Unknown that his house was ready for him, to which the other replied that he would sleep there that night.

The same evening, the colonists were all together in the great hall of Granite House. It was 8 o'clock, the time of their companion's departure; and not wishing by their presence to impose on him the leave-taking, which would, perhaps, have cost him an effort, they had left him alone and gone up into Granite House.

They had been conversing together in the hall for some minutes, when there was a light knock on the door, the Unknown entered, and without further introduction:— "Before I leave you, sirs," said he, "it is well that you should know my history. This is it."

These simple words greatly affected Smith and companions. The engineer started up.

"We ask to hear nothing, my friend," he said. "It is your right to be silent—"

"It is my duty to speak."

"Then sit down."

"I will stand where I am."

"We are ready to hear what you have to say," said Smith.

The Unknown stood in a shadowed corner of the hall, bare-headed, his arms crossed on his breast. In this position, in a hoarse voice, speaking as one who forces himself to speak, he made the following recital, uninterrupted by any word from his auditors:— "On the 20th of December, 1854, a steam pleasure-yacht, the Duncan, belonging to a Scotch nobleman, Lord Glenarvan, cast anchor at Cape Bernoulli, on the western coast of Australia, near the thirty-seventh parallel. On board the yacht were Lord Glenarvan, his wife, a major in the English army, a French geographer, a little boy, and a little girl. These two last were the children of Captain Grant, of the ship Britannia, which, with its cargo, had been lost the year before. The Duncan was commanded by Captain John Mangles, and was manned by a crew of fifteen men.

"This is the reason why the yacht was on the Australian coast at that season:—

"Six months before, a bottle containing a paper written in English, German, and French, had been picked up by the Duncan in the Irish Sea. This paper said, in substance, that three persons still survived from the wreck of the

Britannia; that they were the captain and two of the men; that they had found refuge on a land of which the latitude and longitude was given, but the longitude, blotted by the sea water, was no longer legible.

"The latitude was 37° 11' south. Now, as the longitude was unknown, if they followed the latitude across continents and seas, they were certain to arrive at the land inhabited by Captain Grant and his companions.

"The English Admiralty, having hesitated to undertake the search, Lord Glenarvan had resolved to do everything in his power to recover the captain. Mary and Robert Grant had been in correspondence with him, and the yacht Duncan was made ready for a long voyage, in which the family of Lord Glenarvan and the children of the captain intended to participate. The Duncan, leaving Glasgow, crossed the Atlantic, passed the Straits of Magellan, and proceeded up the Pacific to Patagonia, where, according to the first theory suggested by the paper, they might believe that Captain Grant was a prisoner to the natives.

"The Duncan left its passengers on the western coast of Patagonia, and sailed for Cape Corrientes on the eastern coast, there to wait for them.

"Lord Glenarvan crossed Patagonia, following the 37th parallel, and, not having found any trace of the captain, he reembarked on the 13th of November, in order to continue his search across the ocean.

"After having visited without success the islands of Tristan d'Acunha and of Amsterdam, lying in the course, the Duncan, as I have stated, arrived at Cape Bernouilli on the 20th of December, 1854.

"It was Lord Glenarvan's intention to cross Australia, as he had crossed Patagonia, and he disembarked. Some miles from the coast was a farm belonging to an Irishman, who offered hospitality to the travellers. Lord Glenarvan told the Irishman the object which had brought him to that region, and asked if he had heard of an English three-master, the Britannia, having been lost, within two years, on the west coast of Australia.

"The Irishman had never heard of this disaster, but, to the great surprise of everybody, one of his servants, intervening, said:— "'Heaven be praised, my lord. If Captain Grant is still alive he is in Australia.'

"'Who are you?' demanded Lord Glenarvan.

"'A Scotchman, like yourself, my lord,' answered this man, 'and one of the companions of Captain Grant, one of the survivors of the Britannia.'

"This man called himself Ayrton. He had been, in short, boatswain's mate of the Britannia, as his papers proved. But, separated from Captain Grant at the moment when the ship went to pieces on the rocks, he had believed until this moment that every one had perished but himself.

"'Only,' he added, 'it was not on the western but on the eastern coast of Australia that the Britannia was lost; and if the Captain is still living he is a prisoner to the natives, and he must be searched for there.'

"This man said these things frankly and with a confident expression. No one would have doubted what he said. The Irishman, in whose service he had been for more than a year, spoke in his favor. Lord Glenarvan believed in his loyalty, and, following his advice, he resolved to cross Australia, following the 37th parallel. Lord Glenarvan, his wife, the children, the major, the Frenchman, Captain Mangles and some sailors formed the little party under the guidance of Ayrton, while the Duncan, under the command of the mate, Tom Austin, went to Melbourne, to await further instructions.

"They left on the 23d of December, 1861.

"It is time to say that this Ayrton was a traitor. He was, indeed, the boatswain's mate of the Britannia; but, after some dispute with his captain, he had tried to excite the crew to mutiny and seize the ship, and Captain Grant had put him ashore, the 8th of April, 1832, on the west coast of Australia, and had gone off, leaving him there, which was no more than right.

"Thus this wretch knew nothing of the shipwreck of the Britannia. He had just learned it from Lord Glenarvan's recital! Since his abandonment, he had become, under the name of Ben Joyce, the leader of some escaped convicts; and, if he impudently asserted the ship had been lost on the east coast, if he urged Lord Glenarvan to go in that direction, it was in the hope of separating him from his ship, of seizing the Duncan, and of making this yacht a pirate of the Pacific."

Here the Unknown stopped for a moment. His voice trembled, but he began again in these words:— "The expedition across Australia set out. It was naturally unfortunate, since Ayrton, or Ben Joyce, whichever you wish, led it, sometimes preceded, sometimes followed by the band of convicts, who had been informed of the plot.

"Meanwhile, the Duncan had been taken to Melbourne to await instructions. It was therefore necessary to persuade Lord Glenarvan to order her to leave Melbourne and to proceed to the east coast of Australia, where it would be easy to seize her. After having led the expedition sufficiently near this coast, into the midst of vast forests, where all resources were wanting, Ayrton obtained a letter which he was ordered to deliver to the mate of the Duncan; a letter which gave the order directing the yacht to proceed immediately to the east coast, to Twofold Bay, a place some days journey from the spot where the expedition had halted. It was at this place that Ayrton had given the rendezvous to his accomplices.

"At the moment when this letter was to have been sent, the traitor was unmasked and was obliged to flee. But this letter, giving him the Duncan, must be had at any cost. Ayrton succeeded in getting hold of it, and, in two days afterwards, he was in Melbourne.

"So far, the criminal had succeeded in his odious projects. He could take the Duncan to this Twofold Bay, where it would be easy for the convicts to seize her; and, her crew massacred, Ben Joyce would be master of the sea. Heaven stopped him in the consummation of these dark designs.

"Ayrton, having reached Melbourne, gave the letter to the mate, Tom Austin, who made ready to execute the order; but one can judge of the disappointment and the rage of Ayrton, when, the second day out, he learned that the mate was taking the ship, not to Twofold Bay on the east coast of Australia, but to the east coast of New Zealand. He wished to oppose this, but the mate showed him his order. And, in truth, by a providential error of the French geographer who had written this letter, the eastern coast of New Zealand had been named as their place of destination.

"All the plans of Ayrton had miscarried. He tried to mutiny. They put him in irons; and he was taken to the coast of New Zealand, unaware of what had become of his accomplices, or of Lord Glenarvan.

"The Duncan remained on this coast until the 3d of March. On that day, Ayrton heard firing. It was a salute from the Duncan, and, very soon, Lord Glenarvan and all his party came on board.

"This is what had happened:—

"After innumerable fatigues and dangers, Lord Glenarvan had been able to accomplish his journey and arrived at Twofold Bay. The Duncan was not there! He telegraphed to Melbourne, and received a reply:—'Duncan sailed on the 18th. Destination unknown.'

"Lord Glenarvan could think of but one explanation, that was that the good yacht had fallen into the hands of Ben Joyce, and had become a pirate ship.

"Nevertheless, Lord Glenarvan did not wish to give up his undertaking. He was an intrepid and a generous man. He embarked on a merchant vessel, which took him to the west coast of New Zealand, and he crossed the country, following the 37th parallel without finding any trace of Captain Grant; but on the other coast, to his great surprise, and by the bounty of Heaven, he found the Duncan, commanded by the mate, which had been waiting for him for five weeks!

"It was the 3d of March, 1855. Lord Glenarvan was again on the Duncan, but Ayrton was there also. He was brought before his lordship, who wished to get from this bandit all that he knew concerning Captain Grant. Ayrton refused to speak. Lord Glenarvan told him, then, that at the first port, he would be given over to the English authorities. Ayrton remained silent.

"The Duncan continued along the thirty-seventh parallel. Meanwhile, Lady Glenarvan undertook to overcome the obstinacy of the bandit, and, finally, her influence conquered him. Ayrton, in exchange for what he would tell, proposed to Lord Glenarvan to leave him upon one of the islands in the Pacific, instead of giving him up to the English authorities. Lord Glenarvan, ready to do anything to gain information concerning Captain Grant, consented.

"Then Ayrton told the history of his life, and declared that he knew nothing about Captain Grant since the day when the latter had left him on the Australian coast.

"Nevertheless, Lord Glenarvan kept the promise he had made. The Duncan, continuing her route, arrived at Tabor Island. It was there that Ayrton was to be left, and it was there, too, that, by a miracle, they found Captain Grant and his two companions. The convict was put upon the island in their stead, and when he left the yacht, Lord Glenarvan spoke to him in these words:—

"'Here, Ayrton, you will be far from any country, and without any possible means of communicating with your fellow-men. You will not be able to leave this island. You will be alone, under the eye of a God who looks into the depths of our hearts, but you will neither be lost nor neglected, like Captain Grant. Unworthy as you are of the remembrance of men, you will be remembered. I know where you are, Ayrton, and I know where to find you. I will never forget it.'

"And the Duncan, setting sail, soon disappeared.

"This was the 18th of March, 1855.

"Ayrton was alone; but he lacked neither ammunition nor arms nor seeds. He, the convict, had at his disposal the house built by the honest Captain Grant. He had only to live and to expiate in solitude the crimes which he had committed.

"Sirs, he repented; he was ashamed of his crimes, and he was very unhappy. He said to himself that, as some day men would come to seek him on this islet, he must make himself worthy to go back with them. How he suffered, the miserable man! How he labored to benefit himself by labor! How he prayed to regenerate himself by prayer!

"For two years, for three years, it was thus. Ayrton, crushed by this isolation, ever on the watch for a ship to appear upon the horizon of his island, asking himself if the time of expiation was nearly ended, suffered as one has rarely suffered. Oh! but solitude is hard, for a soul gnawed by remorse!

"But, doubtless, Heaven found this unhappy wretch insufficiently punished, for he fell, little by little, till he became a savage! He felt, little by little, the brute nature taking possession of him. He cannot say whether this was after two or four years of abandonment, but at last he became the miserable being whom you found.

"I need not tell you, sirs, that Ayrton and Ben Joyce and I are one!"

Smith and his companions rose as this recital was finished. It is hard to say how deeply they were affected! Such misery, such grief, and such despair, had been shown to them!

"Ayrton," said Smith, "you have been a great criminal, but Heaven has, doubtless, witnessed the expiation of your crimes. This is proved, in that you have been restored to your fellow-men. Ayrton, you are pardoned! And now, will you be our companion?"

The man drew back.

"Here is my hand," said the engineer.

Ayrton darted forward and seized it, great tears streaming from his eyes.

"Do you desire to live with us?" asked Smith.

"Oh, Mr. Smith, let me have yet a little time," he answered, "let me remain alone in the house at the corral!"

"Do as you wish, Ayrton," responded Smith.

The unhappy man was about retiring, when Smith asked him a last question.

"One word more, my friend. Since it is your wish to live in solitude, why did you throw that paper, which put us in the way of finding you, into the sea?"

"A paper?" answered Ayrton, who seemed not to understand what was said.

"Yes, that paper, which we found enclosed in a bottle, and which gave the exact situation of Tabor Island?"

The man put his hand to his forehead, and, after some reflection, said:— "I never threw any paper into the sea!"

"Never!" cried Pencroff.

"Never!"

And then, inclining his head, Ayrton left the room.

CHAPTER XL. A TALK—SMITH AND SPILETT

THE ENGINEER'S IDEA—THE ELECTRIC TELEGRAPH—THE WIRES—THE BATTER-THE ALPHABET—FINE WEATHER—THE PROSPERITY OF THE COLONY—PHOTOGRAPHY—A SNOW EFFECT—TWO YEARS ON LINCOLN ISLAND.

"The poor man!" said Herbert, returning from the door, after having watched Ayrton slide down the rope of the elevator and disappear in the darkness.

"He will come back," said Smith.

"What does it mean?" exclaimed Pencroff. "That he had not thrown this bottle into the sea? Then who did it?"

Certainly, if there was a reasonable question this was.

"He did it," replied Neb; "only the poor fellow was half out of his senses at the time."

"Yes," said Herbert, "and he had no knowledge of what he was doing."

"It can be explained in no other way, my friends," responded Smith, hurriedly, "and I understand, now, how Ayrton was able to give the exact situation of the island, since the events prior to his abandonment gave him that knowledge."

"Nevertheless," observed Pencroff, "he was not a brute when he wrote that paper, and if it is seven or eight years since it was thrown into the sea, how is it that the paper has not been injured by moisture?"

"It proves," said Smith, "that Ayrton retained possession of his faculties to a period much more recent than he imagines."

"That must be it," replied Pencroff, "for otherwise the thing would be inexplicable."

"Inexplicable, indeed," answered the engineer, who seemed not to wish to prolong this talk.

"Has Ayrton told the truth?" questioned the sailor.

"Yes," answered the reporter, "the history he has related is true in every particular. I remember, perfectly well, that the papers reported Lord Glenarvan's undertaking and its result."

"Ayrton has told the truth," added Smith, "without any doubt, Pencroff, since it was trying enough for him to do so. A man does not lie when he accuses himself in this way."

The next day—the 21st—the colonists went down to the beach, and then clambered up to the plateau, but they saw nothing of Ayrton. The man had gone to his house the night before, and they judged it best not to intrude upon him. Time would, doubtless, effect what sympathy would fail to accomplish.

Herbert, Pencroff, and Neb resumed their accustomed occupations; and it happened that their work brought Smith and Spilett together at the Chimneys.

"Do you know, Cyrus, that your explanation of yesterday about the bottle does not satisfy me at all? It is impossible to suppose that this unhappy creature could have written that paper, and thrown the bottle into the sea, without remembering anything about it!"

"Consequently, it is not he who threw it there, my dear Spilett!"

"Then you believe—"

"I believe nothing, I know nothing!" replied Smith, interrupting the reporter. "I place this incident with those others which I have not been able to explain!"

"In truth, Cyrus," said Spilett, "these things are incredible. Your rescue, the box thrown up on the beach, Top's adventures, and now this bottle. Will we never have an answer to these enigmas?"

"Yes," answered the engineer, earnestly, "yes, when I shall have penetrated the bowels of this island!"

"Chance will, perhaps, give us the key to this mystery."

"Chance, Spilett! I do not believe in chance any more than I believe in mystery in this world. There is a cause for everything, however inexplicable, which has happened here, and I will discover it. But, while waiting, let us watch and work."

January arrived, and the year 1867 began. The works had been pushed forward vigorously. One day Herbert and Spilett, passing the corral, ascertained that Ayrton had taken possession of his abode. He occupied himself with the large herd confided to his care, and thus saved his companions the necessity of visiting it two or three times a week. Nevertheless, in order not to leave Ayrton too much alone, they frequently went there.

It was just as well—owing to certain suspicions shared by Smith and Spilett—that this part of the island should be under a certain supervision, and Ayrton, if anything happened, would not fail to let the inhabitants of Granite House know of it.

Possibly, some sudden event might happen, which it would be important to communicate to the engineer without delay. And, aside from whatever might be connected with the mystery of the island, other things, requiring the prompt intervention of the colonists, might occur, as, for example, the discovering of a ship in the offing and in sight of the west coast, a wreck on that shore, the possible arrival of pirates, etc.

So Smith determined to place the corral in instant communication with Granite House. It was the 10th of January when he told his project to his companions.

"How are you going to do such a thing as that, Mr. Smith?" asked Pencroff. "Maybe you propose to erect a telegraph!"

"That is precisely what I propose to do."

"Electric?" exclaimed Herbert.

"Electric," responded Smith. "We have everything necessary for making a battery, and the most difficult part will be to make the wires, but I think we can succeed."

"Well, after this," replied the sailor, "I expect some day to see us riding along on a railway!"

They entered upon the work at once, beginning with the most difficult part, that is to say, the manufacture of the wires, since, if that failed, it would be useless to make the battery and other accessories.

The iron of Lincoln Island was, as we know, of excellent quality, and, therefore, well adapted to the purpose. Smith began by making a steel plate, pierced with conical holes of different sizes, which would bring the wire to the desired size. This piece of steel, after having been tempered "through and through," was fixed firmly to a solid frame-work sunk in the ground, only a few feet distant from the waterfall—the motive power which the engineer intended to use.

And, indeed, there was the fulling-mill, not then in use, the main shaft of which turned with great force, and would serve to draw out the wire and roll it around itself.

The operation was delicate and required great care. The iron, previously made into long and thin bars, with tapering ends, having been introduced into the largest hole of the drawing-plate, was drawn out by the main shaft of the mill, rolled out to a length of 25 or 30 feet, then unrolled, and pulled, in turn, through the smaller holes; and at length, the engineer obtained wires 30 or 40 feet long, which it was easy to join together and place along the five miles between the corral and Granite House.

It took but a little while to get this work under way, and then, Smith, making his companions the wire-drawers, busied himself in the construction of his battery.

It was necessary to make a battery with a constant circuit. We know that modern batteries are usually made of a certain kind of coke, zinc, and copper. Copper the engineer was without, since, in spite of all his efforts, he had been unable to find a trace of it on the island. The coke, which is that hard deposit obtained from gas retorts could be procured, but it would be necessary to arrange a special apparatus—a difficult thing to do. As to the zinc, it will be remembered that the box found on Jetsam Point, was lined with a sheet of that metal, which could not be better utilized than at present.

Smith, after deep reflection, resolved to make a very simple battery, something like that which Becquerel invented in 1820, in which zinc alone is used. The other substances, nitric-acid and potash, he had at hand.

The manner in which he made this battery, in which the current was produced by the action of the acid and the potash on each other, was as follows:— A certain number of glass vessels were made and filled with nitric-acid. They were corked with perforated corks, containing glass tubes reaching into the acid, and stopped: with clay plugs, connected with threads. Into these tubes the engineer poured a solution of potash—obtained from burnt plants— and thus the acid and the potash reacted on each other through the clay.

Then Smith plunged two plates of zinc, the one in the nitric acid, the other in the solution, and thus produced a circuit between the tube and jar, and as these plates had been connected by a bit of wire, the one in the tube became the positive and the other the negative pole of the apparatus. Each jar produced its currents, which, together, were sufficient to cause all the phenomena of the electric telegraph.

On the 6th of February they began to erect the poles, furnished with glass insulators, and some days later the wire was stretched, ready to produce the electric current, which travels with the speed of 100,000 kilometres a second.

Two batteries had been made, one for Granite House, and the other for the corral, as, if the corral had to communicate with Granite House, it might, also, be needful for Granite House to communicate with the corral.

As to the indicator and manipulator, they were very simple. At both stations the wire was wrapped around an electro-magnet of soft iron. Communication was established between the two poles; the current, leaving the positive pole, traversed the wire, passed into the electro-magnet, and returned under ground to the negative pole. The current closed, the attraction of the electro-magnet ceased. It was, therefore, sufficient to place a plate of soft iron before the electro-magnet which, attracted while the current is passing, falls, when it is interrupted. The movement of the plate thus obtained, Smith easily fastened to it a needle, pointing to a dial, which bore the letters of the alphabet upon its face.

Everything was finished by the 12th of February. On that day Smith, having turned on the current, asked if everything was all right at the corral, and received, in a few moments, a satisfactory reply from Ayrton.

Pencroff was beside himself with delight, and every morning and evening he sent a telegraph to the corral, which never remained unanswered.

This method of communication presented evident advantages, both in informing the colonists of Ayrton's presence at the corral, and in preventing his complete isolation. Moreover, Smith never allowed a week to pass without visiting him, and Ayrton came occasionally to Granite House, where he always found a kind reception.

Continuing their accustomed work, the fine weather passed away, and the resources of the colony, particularly in vegetables and cereals, increased from day to day, and the plants brought from Tabor Island had been perfectly acclimated. The plateau presented a most attractive appearance. The fourth crop of corn had been excellent, and no one undertook to count the 400,000,000,000 grains produced in the harvest; although Pencroff had had some such idea, until Smith informed him that, supposing he could count 300 grains a minute, or 18,000 an hour, it would take him 5,500 years to accomplish his undertaking.

The weather was superb, though somewhat warm during the day; but, in the evening, the sea-breeze sprung up, tempering the air and giving refreshing nights to the inhabitants of Granite House. Still there were some storms, which, although not long continued, fell upon Lincoln Island with extraordinary violence. For several hours at a time the lightning never ceased illuminating the heavens, and the thunder roared without cessation.

This was a season of great prosperity to the little colony. The denizens of the poultry-yard increased rapidly, and the colonists lived on this increase, as it was necessary to keep the population within certain limits. The pigs had littered, and Pencroff and Neb's attention to these animals absorbed a great part of their time. There were too young onagers, and their parents were often ridden by Spilett and Herbert, or hitched to the cart to drag wood or bring the minerals which the engineer made use of.

Many explorations were made about this time into the depths of the Far West. The explorers did not suffer from the heat, as the sun's rays could not penetrate the leafy roof above them. Thus, they visited all that part to the left of the Mercy, bordering on the route from the corral to the mouth of Fall River.

But during these excursions the colonists took care to be well armed, as they often encountered exceedingly savage and ferocious wild boars. They also waged war against the jaguars, for which animals Spilett had a special hatred, and his pupil, Herbert, seconded him well. Armed as they were, the hunters never shunned an encounter with these beasts, and the courage of Herbert was superb, while the coolness of the reporter was astonishing. Twenty magnificent skins already ornamented the hall at Granite House, and at this rate the jaguars would soon be exterminated.

Sometimes the engineer took part in explorations of the unknown portions of the island, which he observed with minute attention. There were other traces than those of animals which he sought for in the thickest places in the forests, but not once did anything suspicions appear. Top and Jup, who accompanied him, showed by their action that there was nothing there, and yet the dog had growled more than once again above that pit which the engineer had explored without result.

During this season Spilett, assisted by Herbert, took numerous views of the most picturesque portions of the island, by means of the photographic apparatus, which had not been used until now.

This apparatus, furnished with a powerful lens, was very complete. All the substances necessary in photographic work were there; the nitrate of silver, the hyposulphata of soda, the chloride of ammonium, the acetate of soda, and the chloride of gold. Even the paper was there, all prepared, so that all that was necessary, in order to use it, was to steep it for a few moments in diluted nitrate of silver.

The reporter and his assistant soon became expert operators, and they obtained fine views of the neighborhood, such as a comprehensive view of the island taken from Prospect Plateau, with Mount Franklin on the horizon, the mouth of the Mercy so picturesquely framed between its high rocks, the glade and the corral, with the lower spurs of the mountain in the background, the curious outline of Claw Cape, Jetsam Point, etc. Neither did the photographers forget to take portraits of all the inhabitants of the island, without exception.

"Its people," as Pencroff expressed it.

And the sailor was charmed to see his likeness, faithfully reproduced, ornamenting the walls of Granite House, and he stood before this display as pleased as if he had been gazing in one of the richest show-windows on Broadway.

It must be confessed, however, that the portrait, showing the finest execution, was that of master Jup. Master Jup has posed with a gravity impossible to describe, and his picture was a speaking likeness!

"One would say he was laughing!" exclaimed Pencroff.

And if Jup had not been satisfied, he must have been hard to please. But there it was, and he contemplated his image with such a sentimental air, that it was evident he was a little conceited.

The heat of the summer ended with March. The season was rainy, but the air was still warm, and the month was not as pleasant as they had expected. Perhaps it foreboded an early and a rigorous winter.

One morning, the 21st, Herbert had risen early, and, looking from the window, exclaimed:—

"Hullo, the islet is covered with snow!"

"Snow at this season!" cried the reporter, joining the lad.

Their companions were soon beside them, and every one saw that not only the islet, but that the entire beach below Granite House, was covered with the white mantle.

"It is, indeed, snow," said Pencroff.

"Or something very much like it," replied Neb.

"But the thermometer stands at 58°," said Spilett.

Smith looked at the white covering without speaking, for he was, indeed, at a loss how to explain such a phenomenon in this season and in this temperature.

"The deuce!" cried the sailor; "our crops will have been frost-bitten."

And he was about descending when Jup sprang before him and slid down the rope to the ground.

The orang had scarcely touched the earth before the immense body of snow rose and scattered itself through the air in such innumerable flocks as to darken all the heavens for a time.

"They are birds!" cried Herbert.

The effect had, indeed, been produced by myriads of sea-birds, with plumage of brilliant whiteness. They had come from hundreds of miles around on to the islet and the coast, and they now disappeared in the horizon, leaving the colonists as amazed as if they had witnessed a transformation scene, from winter to summer, in some fancy spectacle. Unfortunately, the change had been so sudden that neither the reporter nor the lad had had an opportunity of knocking over some of these birds, whose species they did not recognize.

A few days later, and it was the 26th of March. Two years had passed since the balloon had been thrown upon Lincoln Island.

CHAPTER XLI. THOUGHTS OF HOME

CHANCES OF RETURN —PLAN TO EXPLORE THE COAST—THE DEPARTURE OF THE 16TH OF APRIL—SERPENTINE PENINSULA SEEN FROM SEA—THE BASALTIC CLIFFS OF THE WESTERN COAST—BAD WEATHER—NIGHT—A NEW INCIDENT.

Two years already! For two years the colonists had had no communication with their fellows! They knew no more of what was happening in the world, lost upon this island, than if they had been upon the most distant asteroid of the solar system.

What was going on in their country? Their fatherland was always present to their eyes, that land which, when they left it, was torn by civil strife, which perhaps was still red with rebellious blood. It was a great grief to them, this war, and they often talked about it, never doubting, however, that the cause of the North would triumph for the honor of the American confederation.

During these two years not a ship had been seen. It was evident that Lincoln Island was out of the route of vessels; that it was unknown—the maps proved this—was evident, because, although it had no harbor, yet its streams would have drawn thither vessels desiring to renew their supply of water. But the surrounding sea was always desert, and the colonists could count on no outside help to bring them to their home.

Nevertheless, one chance of rescue existed, which was discussed one day in the first week of April, when the colonists were gathered in the hall of Granite House.

They had been talking of America and of the small hope of ever seeing it again.

"Undoubtedly, there is but one way of leaving the island," said Spilett, "which is, to build a vessel large enough to make a voyage of some hundreds of miles. It seems to me, that, when one can build a shallop, they can readily build a ship."

"And that they can as easily go to the Low Archipelago as to Tabor Island," added Herbert.

"I do not say we cannot," replied Pencroff, who always had the most to say on questions of a maritime nature; "I do not say we cannot, although it is very different whether one goes far or near! If our sloop had been threatened with bad weather when we went to Tabor Island, we knew that a shelter was not far off in either direction; but 1,200 miles to travel is a long bit of road, and the nearest land is at least that distance!"

"Do you mean, supposing the case to occur, Pencroff, that you would not risk it?" questioned the reporter.

"I would undertake whatever you wished, sir," replied the sailor, "and you know I am not the man to draw back."

"Remember, moreover, that we have another sailor with us, now," said Neb.

"Who do you mean," asked Pencroff.

"Ayrton."

"That is true," responded Herbert.

"If he would join us," remarked Pencroff.

"Why," said the reporter, "do you think that if Lord Glenarvan's yacht had arrived at Tabor Island while Ayrton was living there, that he would have refused to leave?"

"You forget, my friends," said Smith, "that Ayrton was not himself during the last few years there. But that is not the question. It is important to know whether we can count on the return of this Scotch vessel as among our chances for rescue. Now, Lord Glenarvan promised Ayrton that he would return to Tabor Island, when he judged his crimes sufficiently punished, and I believe that he will return."

"Yes," said the reporter, "and, moreover, I think he will return soon, as already Ayrton has been here twelve years!"

"I, also, think this lord will come back, and, probably, very soon. But where will he come to? Not here, but to Tabor Island."

"That is as sure as that Lincoln Island is not on the maps," said Herbert.

"Therefore, my friends," replied Smith, "we must take the necessary precautions to have Ayrton's and our presence on Lincoln Island advertised on Tabor Island."

"Evidently," said the reporter, "and nothing can be easier than to place in Captain Grant's cabin a notice, giving the situation of our island."

"It is, nevertheless, annoying," rejoined the sailor, "that we forgot to do that on our first voyage to the place."

"Why should we have done so?" replied Herbert. "We knew nothing about Ayrton at that time, and when we learned his history, the season was too far advanced to allow of our going back there."

"Yes," answered Smith, "it was too late then, and we had to postpone the voyage until spring."

"But supposing the yacht comes in the meantime?" asked Pencroff.

"It is not likely," replied the engineer, "as Lord Glenarvan would not choose the winter season to adventure into these distant seas. Either it has already been to the island, in the five months that Ayrton has been with us, or it will come later, and it will be time enough, in the first fine weather of October, to go to Tabor Island and leave a notice there."

"It would, indeed, be unfortunate," said Neb, "if the Duncan has been to and left these seas within a few months."

"I hope that it is not so," answered Smith, "and that Heaven has not deprived us of this last remaining chance."

"I think," observed the reporter, "that, at least, we will know what our chances are, when we have visited the island; for those Stockmen would, necessarily, leave some trace of their visit, had they been there."

"Doubtless," answered the engineer. "And, my friends, since we have this chance of rescue, let us wait patiently, and if we find it has been taken from us, we will see then what to do."

"At any rate," said Pencroff, "it is agreed that if we do leave the inland by some way or another, it will not be on account of ill-treatment!"

"No indeed, Pencroff," replied the reporter, "it will be because we are far from everything which a man loves in this world, his family, his friends, his country!"

Everything having been thus arranged there was no longer any question of building a ship, and the colonists occupied themselves in preparing for their third winter in Granite House.

But they determined, before the bad weather set in, to make a voyage in the sloop around the island. The exploration of the coast had never been completed, and the colonists had only an imperfect idea of its western and northern portions from the mouth of Fall River to the Mandible Capes, and of the narrow bay between them.

Pencroff had proposed this excursion, and Smith had gladly agreed to it, as he wished to see for himself all that part of his domain.

The weather was still unsettled, but the barometer made no rapid changes, and they might expect fair days. So, in the first week of April, after a very low barometer, its rise was followed by a strong west wind, which lasted for five or six weeks; then the needle of the instrument became stationary at a high figure, and everything seemed propitious for the exploration.

The day of departure was set for the 16th, and the Good Luck, moored in Balloon Harbor, was provisioned for a long cruise.

Smith told Ayrton of the excursion, and proposed to him to take part in it; but as Ayrton preferred to remain on shore, it was decided that he should come to Granite House while his companions were absent. Jup was left to keep him company, and made no objection.

On the morning of the 16th all the colonists, including Top, went on board the Good Luck. The breeze blew fresh from the south-west, so that from Balloon Harbor they had to beat up against the wind in order to make Reptile End. The distance between these two points, following the coast, was twenty miles. As the wind was dead ahead, and they had had on starting but two hours of the ebb, it took all day to reach the promontory, and it was night before the point was doubled.

Pencroff proposed to the engineer that they should keep on slowly, sailing under a double-reef, but Smith preferred mooring some cable lengths from shore, in order to survey this part of the coast by daylight.

And it was agreed that henceforth, as a minute exploration of the island was to be made, they would not sail at night, but cast anchor every evening at the most available point.

The wind fell as night approached, and the silence was unbroken. The little party, excepting Pencroff, slept less comfortably than in their beds at Granite House, but still they slept; and at daylight the next morning the sailor raised anchor, and, with a free wind, skirted the shore.

The colonists knew this magnificently wooded border, as they had traversed it formerly, on foot; but its appearance excited renewed admiration. They ran as close in as possible, and moderated their speed in order to observe it carefully. Often, they would cast anchor that Spilett might take photographic views of the superb scenery.

About noon the Good Luck arrived at the mouth of the Fall River. Above, upon the right bank, the trees were less numerous, and three miles further on they grew in mere isolated groups between the western spurs of the mountain, whose arid declivities extended to the very edge of the ocean.

How great was the contrast between the southern and the northern portions of this coast! The one wooded and verdant, the other harsh and savage! It was what they call in certain countries, an "iron-bound coast," and its tempestuous aspect seemed to indicate a sudden crystallization of the boiling basalt in the geologic epochs. How appalling would this hideous mass have been to the colonists if they had chanced to have been thrown on this part of the island! When they were on Mount Franklin, their position had been too elevated for them to recognize the awfully forbidding aspect of this shore; but, viewed from the sea, it presented an appearance, the like of which cannot be seen, perhaps, in any portion of the globe.

The sloop passed for half a mile before this coast. It was composed of blocks of all dimensions from twenty to thirty feet high, and of all sorts of shapes, towers, steeples, pyramids, obelisks, and cones. The ice-bergs of the polar seas could not have been thrown together in more frightful confusion! Here, the rocks formed bridges, there, nave-like arches, of indistinguishable depth; in one place, were excavations resembling monumental vaults, in another a crowd of points outnumbering the pinnacles of a Gothic cathedral. All the caprices of nature, more varied than those of the imagination, were here displayed over a distance of eight or nine miles.

Smith and companions gazed with a surprise approaching stupefaction. But, though they rested mute, Top kept up an incessant barking, which awoke a thousand echoes. The engineer noticed the same strangeness in the dog's action as he showed at the month of the well in Granite House.

"Go alongside," said Smith.

And the Good Luck ran in as close to the rocks as possible. Perhaps there was some cavern here which it would be well to explore. But Smith saw nothing, not even a hollow which could serve as a retreat for any living thing, and the base of the rocks was washed by the surf of the sea. After a time the dog stopped barking, and the sloop kept off again at some cable lengths from the shore.

In the northwest portion of the island the shore became flat and sandy. A few trees rose above the low and swampy ground, the home of myriads of aquatic birds.

In the evening the sloop moored in a slight hollow of the shore, to the north of the island. She was close into the bank, as the water here was of great depth. The breeze died away with nightfall, and the night passed without incident.

The next morning Spilett and Herbert went ashore for a couple of hours and brought back many bunches of ducks and snipe, and by 8 o'clock the Good Luck, with a fair, freshening breeze, was speeding on her way to North Mandible Cape.

"I should not be surprised," said Pencroff, "if we had a squall. Yesterday the sun set red, and, this morning, the cats-tails foreboded no good."

These "cats-tails"—were slender cyrrhi, scattered high above, in the zenith. These feathery messengers usually announce the near disturbance of the elements.

"Very well, then," said Smith, "crowd on all sail and make for Shark Gulf. There, I think the sloop will be safe."

"Perfectly," replied the sailor, "and, moreover, the north coast is nothing but uninteresting downs."

"I shall not regret," added the engineer, "passing, not only the night, but also tomorrow in that bay, which deserves to be explored with care."

"I guess we'll have to, whether we want to or no," replied Pencroff, "as it is beginning to be threatening in the west. See how dirty it looks!"

"Any how, we have a good wind to make Mandible Cape," observed the reporter.

"First rate; but, we will have to tack to get into the gulf, and I would rather have clear weather in those parts which I know nothing about."

"Parts which are sown with reefs," added Herbert, "if I may judge from what we have seen of the coast to the south of the gulf."

"Pencroff," said Smith, "do whatever you think best, we leave everything to you."

"Rest assured, sir," responded the sailor, "I will not run any unnecessary risk. I would rather have a knife in my vitals, than that my Good Luck should run on a rock!"

"What time is it?" asked Pencroff.

"10 o'clock."

"And how far is it to the cape?"

"About fifteen miles."

"That will take two hours and a half. Unfortunately, the tide then will be going down, and it will be a hard matter to enter the gulf with wind and tide against us."

"Moreover," said Herbert, "it is full moon to-day, and these April tides are very strong."

"But, Pencroff," asked Smith, "cannot you anchor at the cape?"

"Anchor close to land, with bad weather coming on!" cried the sailor. "That would be to run ourselves ashore."

"Then what will you do?"

"Keep off, if possible, until the tide turns, which will be about 1 o'clock, and if there is any daylight left try to enter the gulf; if not, we will beat on and off until daylight."

"I have said, Pencroff, that we will leave everything to your judgment."

"Ah," said Pencroff, "if only there was a light-house on this coast it would be easier for sailors."

"Yes," answered Herbert, "and this time we have no thoughtful engineer to light a fire to guide us into harbor."

"By the way, Cyrus," said Spilett, "we have never thanked you for that; but indeed, without that fire we would not have reached—"

"A fire?" demanded Smith, astounded by the words of the reporter.

"We wish to say, sir," said Pencroff, "that we would have been in a bad fix on board the Good Luck, when we were nearly back, and that we would have passed to windward of the island unless you had taken the precaution to light a fire, on the night of the 19th of October, upon the plateau above Granite House."

"Oh, yes, yes! It was a happy thought!" replied Smith.

"And now," added Pencroff, "unless Ayrton thinks of it, there is not a soul to do us this little service."

"No—no one!" replied Smith.

And a moment or two later, being alone with Spilett, the engineer whispered to him:—

"If there is anything sure in this world, Spilett, it is that I never lit a fire on that night, either on the plateau or anywhere else!"

CHAPTER XLII. NIGHT AT SEA—SHARK GULF

CONFIDENCES—PREPARATIONS FOR WINTER—EARLY ADVENT OF BAD WEATHER—COLD—IN-DOOR WORK—SIX MONTHS LATER—A SPECK ON THE PHOTOGRAPH—AN UNEXPECTED EVENT.

The sailor's predictions were well founded. The breeze changed to a strong blow such as would hare caused a ship in the open sea to have lowered her topmasts and sailed under close reefs. The sloop was opposite the gulf at 6 o'clock, but the tide was running out, so all that Pencroff could do was to bend the jib down to the mainmast as a stay-sail and lie to with the bows of the Good Luck pointing on shore.

Fortunately, although the wind was strong, the ocean, protected by the coast, was not very rough, and there was no danger from heavy seas, which would have tried the staunchness of the little craft. Pencroff, although he had every confidence in his boat, waited anxiously for daylight.

During the night Smith and Spilett had not another opportunity to talk alone, although the whispered words of the engineer made the reporter anxious to discuss with him again the mysterious influence which seemed to pervade Lincoln Island. Spilett could not rid himself of the thought of this new and inexplicable incident. He and his companions also had certainly seen this light, and yet Smith declared that he knew nothing about it.

He determined to return to this subject as soon as they returned home, and to urge Smith to inform their companions of these strange events. Perhaps, then, they would decide to make, altogether, a thorough search into every part of the island.

Whatever it was, no light appeared upon these unknown shores during this night, and at daylight the wind, which had moderated somewhat, shifted a couple of points, and permitted Pencroff to enter the gulf without difficulty. About 7 o'clock the Good Luck passed into these waters enclosed in a grotesque frame of lava.

"Here," said Pencroff, "is a fine roadstead, where fleets could ride at ease."

"It is curious," remarked Smith, "that this gulf has been formed by two successive streams of lava, completely enclosing its waters; and it is probable that, in the worst weather, the sea here is perfectly calm."

"It is a little too large for the Good Luck," remarked the reporter.

"I admit that," replied the sailor, "but if the navy of the United States needed a shelter in the Pacific, I don't think they could find a better roadstead than this!"

"We are in the shark's jaws," said Neb, alluding to the form of the gulf.

"We are, indeed," replied Herbert; "but, Neb, you are not afraid that they will close on us?"

"No, sir, not that; and yet I don't like the looks of the place. It has a wicked aspect."

"So Neb begins running down my roadstead just as I was thinking to offer it to the United States!" cried Pencroff.

"But are its waters deep enough?" asked the engineer.

"That is easily seen," answered the sailor, taking the sounding line, which measured fifty fathoms, and letting it down. It unrolled to the end without touching bottom.

"There," said Pencroff, "our iron-clads could come here without running aground!"

"In truth," said Smith, "this gulf is an abyss; but when we remember the plutonic origin of the island, that is not extraordinary."

"One might think," said Herbert, "that these walls had been cut with an instrument, and I believe that at their very base, even with a line six times as long, we could not reach the bottom."

"All this is very well," said the reporter, "but I would suggest that Pencroff's roadstead lacks one important element."

"What is that?"

"A cut, or pathway of some kind, by which one could go inland. I do not see a place where there is even a foothold."

And, indeed, these steep lava walls afforded no landing place on all their circumference. The Good Luck, skirting within touching distance of the lava, found no place where the passengers could disembark.

Pencroff consoled himself by saying that they could blow up the wall, if they wanted to, and then, as there was certainly nothing to be done here, he turned towards the narrow opening, which was passed at 2 o'clock.

Neb gave a long sigh of relief. It was evident that the brave man had not been comfortable in those enormous jaws!

The sloop was now headed for Granite House, eight miles distant, and, with a fair wind, coasted along within a mile of the shore. The enormous lava rocks were soon succeeded by the oddly-disposed downs, among which the engineer had been so singularly discovered, and the place was covered with sea-birds.

Towards 4 o'clock, Pencroff, leaving the islet to the left, entered the channel separating it from the island, and an hour later cast anchor in the Mercy.

The colonists had been absent three days. Ayrton was waiting for them on the shore, and Jup came joyously to welcome them, grinning with satisfaction.

The entire exploration of the coast had been made, and nothing suspicious had been seen. So that if any mysterious being resided on the island, it must be under cover of the impenetrable woods on Serpentine Peninsula, which the colonists had not, as yet, investigated.

Spilett talked the matter over with the engineer, and it was agreed that they should call their comrades' attention to these strange events, the last one of which was the most inexplicable of all.

"Are you sure you saw it, Spilett?" asked Smith, for the twentieth time. "Was it not a partial eruption of the volcano, or some meteor?"

"No, Cyrus, it was certainly a fire lit by the hand of man. For that matter, question Pencroff and Herbert. They saw it also, and they will confirm my words."

So, some evenings later, on the 26th of April, when all the colonists were gathered together on Prospect Plateau, Smith began:— "My friends, I want to call your attention to certain things which are happening in our island, and to a subject on which I am anxious to have your advice. These things are almost supernatural—"

"Supernatural!" exclaimed the sailor, puffing his pipe. "Can anything be supernatural?"

"No, Pencroff, but certainly mysterious; unless, indeed, you can explain what Spilett and I have been unable to account for up to this time."

"Let us hear it, Mr. Smith," replied the sailor.

"Very well. Have you understood, then, how, after being thrown into the sea, I was found a quarter of a mile inland, without my having been conscious of getting there?"

"Possibly, having fainted,"—began the sailor.

"That is not admissible," answered the engineer; "but, letting that go, have you understood how Top discovered your retreat five miles from the place where I lay?"

"The dog's instinct," replied Herbert.

"A singular instinct," remarked the reporter, "since, in spite of the storm that was raging, Top arrived at the Chimneys dry and clean!"

"Let that pass," continued the engineer; "have you understood how our dog was so strangely thrown up from the lake, after his struggle with the dugong?"

"No! that I avow," replied Pencroff, "and the wound in the dugong which seemed to have been made by some sharp instrument, I don't understand that at all."

"Let us pass on again," replied Smith. "Have you understood, my friends, how that leaden bullet was in the body of the peccary; how that box was so fortunately thrown ashore, without any trace of a shipwreck; how that bottle, enclosing the paper, was found so opportunely; how our canoe, having broken its rope, floated down the Mercy to us at the very moment when we needed it; how, after the invasion of the monkeys, the ladder was let down from Granite House; how, finally, the document, which Ayrton pretends not to have written, came into our hands?"

Smith had thus enumerated, without forgetting one, the strange events that had happened on the island. Herbert, Pencroff, and Neb looked at each other, not knowing what to say, as this succession of events, thus grouped together, gave them the greatest surprise.

"Upon my faith," said Pencroff, at length, "you are right, Mr. Smith, and it is hard to explain those things."

"Very well, my friends," continued the engineer, "one thing more is to be added, not less incomprehensible than the others!"

"What is that?" demanded Herbert, eagerly.

"When you returned from Tabor Island, Pencroff, you say that you saw a light on Lincoln Island?"

"Certainly I did."

"And you are perfectly sure that you saw it?"

"As sure as that I see you."

"And you, Herbert?"

"Why, Mr. Smith," cried Herbert, "it shone like a star of the first magnitude!"

"But was it not a star?" insisted the engineer.

"No," replied Pencroff, "because the sky was covered with heavy clouds, and, under any circumstances, a star would not have been so low on the horizon. But Mr. Spilett saw it, and he can confirm what we say."

"I would add," said the reporter, "that it was as bright as an electric light."

"Yes, and it was certainly placed above Granite House!" exclaimed Herbert.

"Very well, my friends," replied Smith, "during all that night neither Neb nor I lit any fire at all!"

"You did not!—" cried Pencroff, so overcome with astonishment that he could not finish the sentence.

"We did not leave Granite House, and if any fire appeared upon the coast, it was lit by another hand!"

The others were stupefied with amazement. Undoubtedly a mystery existed! Some inexplicable influence, evidently favorable to the colonists, but exciting their curiosity, made itself felt upon Lincoln Island. Was there then some being hidden in its innermost retreats? They wished to know this, cost what it might!

Smith also recalled to his companions the singular actions of Top and Jup, about the mouth of the well, and he told them that he had explored its depths without discovering anything. And the conversation ended by a determination, on the part of the colonists, to make a thorough search of the island as soon as the spring opened.

After this Pencroff became moody. This island, which he had looked upon as his own, did not belong to him alone, but was shared by another, to whom, whether he would or not, the sailor felt himself inferior. Neb and he often discussed these inexplicable circumstances, and readily concluded that Lincoln Island was subject to some supernatural influence.

The bad weather began early, coming in with May; and the winter occupations were undertaken without delay. The colonists were well protected from the rigor of the season. They had plenty of felt clothing, and the moufflons had furnished a quantity of wool for its further manufacture.

Ayrton had been comfortably clothed, and when the bad weather began, he had returned to Granite House; but he remained humble and sad, never joining in the amusements of his companions.

The most of this third winter was passed by the colonists indoors at Granite House. The storms were frequent and terrible, the sea broke over the islet, and any ship driven upon the coast would have been lost without any chance of rescue. Twice the Mercy rose to such a height that the bridge and causeways were in danger of destruction. Often the gusts of wind, mingled with snow and rain, damaged the fields and the poultry-yard, and made constant repairs necessary.

In the midst of this season, some jaguars and quadrumanes came to the very border of the plateau, and there was danger of the bolder of these beasts making a descent on the fields and domestic animals of the colonists. So that a constant watch had to be kept upon these dangerous visitors, and this, together with the work indoors, kept the little party in Granite House busy.

Thus the winter passed, with now and then a grand hunt in the frozen marshes of Tadorn's Fen. The damage done to the corral during the winter was unimportant, and was soon repaired by Ayrton, who, in the latter part of October, returned there to spend some days at work.

The winter had passed without any new incident. Top and Jup passed by the well without giving any sign of anxiety, and it seemed as if the series of supernatural events had been interrupted. Nevertheless, the colonists were fixed in their determination to make a thorough exploration of the most inaccessible parts of the island, when an event of the gravest moment, which set aside all the plans of Smith and his companions, happened.

It was the 28th of October. Spring was rapidly approaching, and the young leaves were appearing on the trees on the edge of the forest. Herbert, tempted by the beauty of the day, determined to take a photograph of Union Bay, as it lay facing Prospect Plateau, between Mandible and Claw Capes.

It was 3 o'clock, the horizon was perfectly clear, and the sea, just stirred by the breeze, scintillated with light. The instrument had been placed at one of the windows of Granite House, and the lad, having secured his negative, took the glass into the dark room, where the chemicals were kept, in order to fix it. Returning to the light, after this operation, he saw a speck on the plate, just at the horizon, which he was unable to wash out.

"It is a defect in the glass," he thought.

And then he was seized by a curiosity to examine this speck by means of a magnifying glass made from one of the lenses of the instrument.

Hardly had he given one look, when, uttering a cry of amazement, he ran with the plate and the glass to Smith. The latter examined the speck, and immediately seizing the spy-glass hurried to the window.

The engineer, sweeping the horizon with the glass, found the speck, and spoke one word. "A ship!"

In truth, a ship was in sight of Lincoln Island.

PART III. THE SECRET OF THE ISLAND

CHAPTER XLIII. LOST OR SAVED?

AYRTON RECALLED—IMPORTANT DISCUSSION—IT IS NOT THE DUNCAN—SUSPICION AND PRECAUTION—APPROACH OF THE SHIP—A CANNON SHOT—THE BRIG ANCHORS IN SIGHT OF THE ISLAND—NIGHT FALL.

Two years and a half ago, the castaways had been thrown on Lincoln Island; and up to this time they had been cut off from their kind. Once the reporter had attempted to establish communication with the civilized world, by a letter tied to the neck of a bird; but this was an expedient on whose success they could place no reliance. Ayrton, indeed, under the circumstances which have been related, had joined the little colony. And now, on the 17th of October, other men had appeared within sight of the island, on that desert sea! There could be no doubt of it; there was a ship, but would she sail away into the offing, or put in shore? The question would soon be decided. Smith and Herbert hastened to call the others into the great hall of Granite House, and inform them of what had been observed. Pencroff seized the spy-glass and swept the horizon till his gaze fell upon the point indicated.

"No doubt of it, she's a ship!" said he in a tone of no great pleasure.

"Is she coming towards us?" asked Spilett.

"Impossible to say yet," replied Pencroff, "for only her sails are visible; her hull is below the horizon.

"What must we do?" said the boy.

"We must wait," said Smith.

And for a time which seemed interminable, the colonists remained in silence, moved alternately by fear and hope. They were not in the situation of castaways upon a desert island, constantly struggling with niggardly Nature for the barest means of living, and always longing to got back to their fellow-men. Pencroff and Neb, especially, would have quitted the island with great regret. They were made, in truth, for the new life which they were living in a region civilized by their own exertions! Still, this ship would bring them news of the Continent; perhaps it was an American vessel; assuredly it carried men of their own race, and their hearts beat high at the thought!

From time to time, Pencroff went to the window with the glass. From thence he examined the ship carefully. She was still twenty miles to the east, and they had no means of communication with her. Neither flag nor fire would have been seen; nor would the report of a gun be heard. Yet the island, with Mount Franklin towering high above it, must be visible to the lookout men on the ship. But why should the vessel land there? Was it not mere chance which brought it into that part of the Pacific, out of the usual track, and when Tabor Island was the only land indicated on the maps? But here a suggestion came from Herbert.

"May it not be the Duncan?" cried he.

The Duncan, as our readers will remember, was Lord Glenarvan's yacht, which had abandoned Ayrton on the islet, and was one day to come back for him. Now the islet was not so far from Lincoln Island but that a ship steering for one might pass within sight of the other. They were only 150 miles distant in longitude, and 75 in latitude.

"We must warn Ayrton," said Spilett, "and tell him to come at once. Only he can tell us whether she is the Duncan."

This was every one's opinion, and the reporter, going to the telegraph apparatus, which communicated with the corral, telegraphed. "Come at once." Soon the wire clicked, "I am coming." Then the colonists turned again to watch the ship.

"If it is the Duncan," said Herbert, "Ayrton will readily recognize her, since he was aboard her so long."

"It will make him feel pretty queer!" said Pencroff.

"Yes," replied Smith, "but Ayrton is now worthy to go on board again, and may Heaven grant it to be indeed the Duncan! These are dangerous seas for Malay pirates."

"We will fight for our island," said Herbert.

"Yes, my boy," answered the engineer, smiling, "but it will be better not to have to fight for her."

"Let me say one thing," said Spilett. "Our island is unknown to navigators, and it is not down in the most recent maps. Now, is not that a good reason for a ship which unexpectedly sighted it to try to run in shore?"

"Certainly," answered Pencroff.

"Yes," said the engineer, "it would even be the duty of the captain to report the discovery of any island not on the maps, and to do this he must pay it a visit."

"Well," said Pencroff, "suppose this ship casts anchor within a few cables' length of our island, what shall we do?"

This downright question for a while remained unanswered. Then Smith, after reflection, said in his usual calm tone:—

"What we must do, my friends, is this. We will open communication with the ship, take passage on board of her, and leave our island, after having taken possession of it in the name of the United States of America.

Afterwards we will return with a band of permanent colonists, and endow our Republic with a useful station on the Pacific!"

"Good!" said Pencroff, "that will be a pretty big present to our country! We have really colonized it already. We have named every part of the island; there is a natural port, a supply of fresh water, roads, a line of telegraph, a wood yard, a foundry; we need only put the island on the maps!"

"But suppose some one else should occupy it while we are gone?" said Spilett.

"I would sooner stay here alone to guard it," cried the sailor, "and, believe me, they would not steal it from me, like a watch from a gaby's pocket!"

For the next hour, it was impossible to say whether or not the vessel was making for the island. She had drawn nearer, but Pencroff could not make out her course. Nevertheless, as the wind blew from the northeast, it seemed probable that she was on the starboard tack. Besides, the breeze blew straight for the landing, and the sea was so calm that she would not hesitate to steer for the island, though the soundings were not laid down in the charts.

About 4 o'clock, an hour after he had been telegraphed for, Ayrton arrived. He entered the great hall, saying, "Here I am, gentlemen."

Smith shook hands with him, and drawing him to the window, "Ayrton," said he, "we sent for you for a weighty reason. A ship is within sight of the island."

For a moment Ayrton looked pale, and his eyes were troubled. Then he stooped down and gazed around the horizon.

"Take this spy-glass," said Spilett, "and look well, Ayrton, for it may be the Duncan come to take you home."

"The Duncan!" murmured Ayrton. "Already!"

The last word escaped him involuntarily and he buried his face in his hands. Did not twelve years' abandonment on a desert island seem to him a sufficient expiation?

"No," said he, "no, it cannot be the Duncan."

"Look, Ayrton," said the engineer, "for we must know beforehand with whom we have to deal."

Ayrton took the glass and levelled it in the direction indicated. For some minutes he observed the horizon in silence. Then he said:—

"Yes, it is a ship, but I do not think it is the Duncan.

"Why not?" asked Spilett.

"Because the Duncan is a steam-yacht, and I see no trace of smoke about this vessel."

"Perhaps she is only under sail," observed Pencroff. "The wind is behind her, and she may want to save her coal, being go far from land."

"You may be right, Mr. Pencroff," said Ayrton. "But, let her come in shore, and we shall soon know what to make of her."

So saying, he sat down in a corner and remained silent, taking no part in the noisy discussion about the unknown ship. No more work was done. Spilett and Pencroff were extremely nervous; they walked up and down, changing place every minute. Herbert's feeling was one of curiosity. Neb alone remained calm; his master was his country. The engineer was absorbed in his thoughts, and was inclined to believe the ship rather an enemy than a friend. By the help of the glass they could make out that she was a brig, and not one of those Malay proas, used by the pirates of the Pacific. Pencroff, after a careful look, affirmed that the ship was square-rigged, and was running obliquely to the coast, on the starboard tack, under mainsail, topsail, and top-gallant sail set.

Just then the ship changed her tack, and drove straight towards the island. She was a good sailer, and rapidly neared the coast. Ayrton took the glass to try to ascertain whether or not she was the Duncan. The Scotch yacht, too, was square-rigged. The question therefore was whether a smokestack could be seen between the two masts of the approaching vessel. She was now only ten miles off, and the horizon was clear. Ayrton looked for a moment, and then dropped his glass.

"It is not the Duncan," said he.

Pencroff sighted the brig again, and made out that she was from 300 to 400 tons burden, and admirably built for sailing. To what nation she belonged no one could tell.

"And yet," added the sailor, "there's a flag floating at her peak, but I can't make out her colors."

"In half an hour we will know for certain," answered the reporter. "Besides, it is evident that their captain means to run in shore, and to-day, or to-morrow at latest, we shall make her acquaintance."

"No matter, "said Pencroff, "we ought to know with whom we have to deal, and I shall be glad to make out those colors."

And he kept the glass steadily at his eye. The daylight began to fail, and the sea-wind dropped with it. The brig's flag wrapped itself around the tackle, and could hardly be seen.

"It is not the American flag," said Pencroff, at intervals, "nor the English, whose red would be very conspicuous, nor the French, nor German colors, nor the white flag of Russia, nor the yellow flag of Spain. It seems to be of one solid color. Let us see; what would most likely be found in these waters? The Chilian—no, that flag is tri-colored; the Brazilian is green; the Japanese is black and yellow; while this—"

Just then a breeze struck the flag. Ayrton took the glass and raised it to his eyes.

"Black!" cried he, in a hollow voice.

They had suspected the vessel with good reason. The piratical ensign was fluttering at the peak!

A dozen ideas rushed across the minds of the colonists; but there was no doubt as to the meaning of the flag. It was the ensign of the spoilers of the sea; the ensign which the Duncan would have carried, if the convicts had succeeded in their criminal design. There was no time to be lost in discussion.

"My friends," said Smith, "this vessel, perhaps, is only taking observations of the coast of our island, and will send no boats on shore. We must do all we can to hide our presence here. The mill on Prospect Plateau is too conspicuous. Let Ayrton and Neb go at once and take down its fans. "We must cover, the windows of Granite House under thicker branches. Let the fires be put out, and nothing be left to betray the existence of man!"

"And our sloop?" said Herbert.

"Oh," said Pencroff, "she is safe in port in Balloon Harbor, and I defy the rascals to find her there!"

The engineer's orders were instantly carried out. Neb and Ayrton went up to the plateau and concealed every trace of human habitation. Meanwhile their companions went to Jacamar Woods and brought back a great quantity of branches and climbing plants, which could not, from a distance, be distinguished from a natural foliation, and would hide well enough the windows in the rock. At the same time their arms and munitions were piled ready at hand, in case of a sudden attack. When all these precautions had been taken Smith turned to his comrades—

"My friends," said he, in a voice full of emotion, "if these wretches try to get possession of the island we will defend it, will we not?"

"Yes, Cyrus," answered the reporter, "and, if need be, we will die in its defense."

And they shook hands upon it. Ayrton alone remained seated in his corner. Perhaps he who had been a convict himself once, still deemed himself unworthy! Smith understood what was passing in his mind, and, stepping towards him, asked

"And what will you do, Ayrton?"

"My duty," replied Ayrton. Then he went to the window, and his eager gaze sought to penetrate the foliage. It was then half-past 7 o'clock. The sun had set behind Granite House twenty minutes before, and the eastern horizon was darkening. The brig was nearing Union Bay. She was now about eight miles away, and just abreast of Prospect Plateau, for having tacked off Claw Cape, she had been carried in by the rising tide. In fact she was already in the bay, for a straight line drawn from Claw Cape to Mandible Cape would have passed to the other side of her.

Was the brig going to run into the bay? And if so, would she anchor there? Perhaps they would be satisfied with taking an observation. They could do nothing but wait. Smith was profoundly anxious. Had the pirates been on the island before, since they hoisted their colors on approaching it? Might they not have effected a descent once before, and might not some accomplice be now concealed in the unexplored part of the island. They were determined to resist to the last extremity. All depended on the arms and the number of the pirates.

Night had come. The new moon had set a few moments after the sun. Profound darkness enveloped land and sea. Thick masses of clouds were spread over the sky. The wind had entirely died away. Nothing could be seen of the vessel, for all her lights were hidden—they could tell nothing of her whereabouts.

"Who knows?" said Pencroff. "Perhaps the confounded ship will be off by morning."

His speech was answered by a brilliant flash from the offing, and the sound of a gun. The ship was there, and she had artillery. Six seconds had elapsed between the flash and the report; the brig, therefore, was about a mile and a-quarter from the shore. Just then, they heard the noise of chain-cables grinding across the hawse-holes. The vessel was coming to anchor in sight of Granite House!

CHAPTER XLIV. DISCUSSIONS

PRESENTIMENTS—AYRTON'S PROPOSAL—IT IS ACCEPTED—AYRTON AND PENCROFF ON SAFETY ISLET—NORFOLK CONVICTS—THEIR PROJECTS— HEROIC ATTEMPT OF AYRTON—HIS RETURN—SIX AGAINST FIFTY.

There was no longer room for doubt as to the pirate's intentions. They had cast anchor at a short distance from the island, and evidently intended to land on the morrow.

Brave as they were, the colonists felt the necessity of prudence. Perhaps their presence could yet be concealed in case the pirates were contented with landing on the coast without going up into the interior. The latter, in fact, might have nothing else in view than a supply of fresh water, and the bridge, a mile and a half up stream, might well escape their eye.

The colonists knew now that the pirate ship carried heavy artillery, against which they had nothing but a few shot-guns.

"Still," said Smith, "our situation is impregnable. The enemy cannot discover the opening in the weir, so thickly is it covered with reeds and grass, and consequently cannot penetrate into Granite House."

"But our plantations, our poultry-yard, our corral,—in short everything," cried Pencroff, stamping his foot. "They can destroy everything in a few hours."

"Everything, Pencroff!" answered Smith, "and we have no means of preventing them?"

"Are there many of them?" said the reporter. "That's the question. If there are only a dozen, we can stop them, but forty, or fifty, or more—"

"Mr. Smith," said Ayrton, coming up to the engineer, "will you grant me one request!"

"What, my friend?"

"To go to the ship, and ascertain how strongly she is manned."

"But, Ayrton," said the engineer, hesitating, "your life will be in danger."

"And why not, sir?"

"That is more than your duty."

"I must do more than my duty," replied Ayrton.

"You mean to go to the ship in the canoe?" asked Spilett.

"No, sir. I will swim to her. A man can slip in where a boat could not pass."

"Do you know that the brig is a mile and a half from the coast?" said Herbert.

"I am a good swimmer, sir."

"I repeat to you that you are risking your life," resumed the engineer.

"No matter," answered Ayrton—"Mr. Smith, I ask it as a favor. It may raise me in my own estimation."

"Go, Ayrton," said the engineer, who knew how deeply a refusal would affect the ex-convict, now become an honest man.

"I will go with you," said Pencroff.

"You distrust me!" said Ayrton, quickly. Then, he added, more humbly, "and it is just."

"No, no!" cried Smith, eagerly, "Pencroff has no such feeling. You have misunderstood him."

"Just so," answered the sailor; "I am proposing to Ayrton to accompany him only as far as the islet. One of these rascals may possibly have gone on shore there, and if so, it will take two men to prevent him from giving the alarm. I will wait for Ayrton on the islet."

Everything thus arranged, Ayrton got ready for departure. His project was bold but not impracticable, thanks to the dark night. Once having reached the ship, Ayrton, by clinging to the chains of the shrouds, might ascertain the number and perhaps the designs of the convicts. They walked down upon the beach. Ayrton stripped himself and rubbed himself with grease, the better to endure the chill of the water; for he might have to be in it several hours. Meanwhile Pencroff and Neb had gone after the canoe, fastened on the bank of the Mercy some hundreds of paces further up. When they came back, Ayrton was ready to start.

They threw a wrap over his shoulders, and shook hands with him all round. Then he got into the boat with Pencroff, and pushed off into the darkness. It was now half-past 10, and their companions went back to wait for them at the Chimneys.

The channel was crossed without difficulty, and the canoe reached the opposite bank of the islet. They moved cautiously, lest pirates should have landed there. But the island was deserted. The two walked rapidly over it, frightening the birds from their nests in the rocks. Having reached the further side, Ayrton cast himself unhesitatingly into the sea, and swam noiselessly towards the ship's lights, which now were streaming across the water. Pencroff hid himself among the rocks, to await his companion's return.

Meanwhile, Ayrton swam strongly towards the ship, slipping through the water. His head only appeared above the surface; his eyes were fixed on the dark hull of the brig, whose lights were reflected in the water. He thought only of his errand, and nothing of the danger he encountered, not only from the pirates but from the sharks which infested these waters. The current was in his favor, and the shore was soon far behind.

Half an hour afterwards, Ayrton, without having been perceived by any one, dived under the ship, and clung with one hand to the bowsprit. Then he drew breath, and, raising himself by the chains, climbed to the end of the cut-water. There some sailors' clothes hung drying. He found an easy position, and listened.

They were not asleep on board of the brig. They were talking, singing, and laughing. These words, intermingled with oaths, came to Ayrton's ears;—

"What a famous find our brig was!"

"The Speedy is a fast sailor. She deserves her name."

"All the Norfolk shipping may do their best to take her."

"Hurrah for her commander. Hurrah for Bob Harvey!"

Our readers will understand what emotion was excited in Ayrton by this name, when they learn that Bob Harvey was one of his old companions in Australia, who had followed out his criminal projects by getting possession, off Norfolk Island, of this brig, charged with arms, ammunition, utensils, and tools of all kinds, destined for one of the Sandwich Islands. All his band had gotten on board, and, adding piracy to their other crimes, the wretches scoured the Pacific, destroying ships and massacring their crews. They were drinking deep and talking loudly over their exploits, and Ayrton gathered the following facts:—

The crew were composed entirely of English convicts, escaped from Norfolk Island. In 29° 2' south latitude, and 165° 42' east longitude, to the east of Australia, is a little island about six leagues in circumference, with Mount Pitt rising in the midst, 1,100 feet above the level of the sea. It is Norfolk Island, the seat of an establishment where are crowded together the most dangerous of the transported English convicts. There are 500 of them; they undergo a rigid discipline, with severe punishment for disobedience, and are guarded by 150 soldiers and 150 civil servants, under the authority of a Governor. A worse set of villains cannot be imagined. Sometimes, though rarely, in spite of the extreme precautions of their jailors, some of them contrive to escape by seizing a ship, and become the pest of the Polynesian archipelagos. Thus had done Harvey and his companions. Thus had Ayrton formerly wished to do. Harvey had seized the Speedy, which was anchored within sight of Norfolk Island, had massacred the crew, and for a year had made the brig the terror of the Pacific.

The convicts were most of them gathered on the poop, in the after part of the ship; but a few were lying on deck, talking in loud voices. The conversation went on amid noise and drunkenness. Ayrton gathered that chance only had brought them within sight of Lincoln Island. Harvey had never set foot there; but, as Smith had foreseen, coming upon an island not in the maps, he had determined to go on shore, and, if the land suited him, to make it the Speedy's headquarters. The black flag and the cannon-shot were a mere freak of the pirates, to imitate a ship-of-war running up her colors.

The colonists were in very serious danger. The island, with its easy water supply, its little harbor, its varied resources so well turned to account by the colonists, its secret recesses of Granite House—all these would be just what the convicts wanted. In their hands the island would become an excellent place of refuge, and the fact of its being unknown would add to their security. Of course the colonists would instantly be put to death. They could not even escape to the interior, for the convicts would make the island their headquarters, and if they went on an expedition would leave some of the crew behind. It would be a struggle for life and death with these wretches, every one of whom must be destroyed before the colonists would be safe. Those were Ayrton's thoughts, and he knew that Smith would agree with him. But was a successful resistance possible? Everything depended on the calibre of the brig's guns and the number of her men. These were facts which Ayrton must know at any cost.

An hour after he had reached the brig the noise began to subside, and most of the convicts lay plunged in a drunken sleep. Ayrton determined to risk himself on the ship's deck, which the extinguished lanterns left in profound darkness. He got in the chains by the cut-water, and by means of the bowsprit climbed to the brig's forecastle. Creeping quietly through the sleeping crew, who lay stretched here and there on the deck, he walked completely around the vessel and ascertained that the Speedy carried four guns, from eight to ten-pounders. He discovered also that the guns were breech-loading, of modern make, easily worked, and capable of doing great damage.

There were about ten men lying on deck, but it might be that others were asleep in the hold. Moreover, Ayrton had gathered from the conversation that there were some fifty on board; rather an overmatch for the six colonists. But, at least, the latter would not be surprised; thanks to Ayrton's devotion, they would know their adversaries force, and would make their dispositions accordingly. Nothing remained for Ayrton but to go back to his comrades with the information he had gathered, and he began walking towards the forecastle to let himself down into the sea.

And now to this man, who wished to do more than his duty, there came a heroic thought, the thought of sacrificing his life for the safety of his comrades. Smith could not of course resist fifty well-armed marauders, who would either overcome him or starve him out. Ayrton pictured to himself his preservers who had made a man of him, and an honest man, to whom he owed everything, pitilessly murdered, their labors brought to nothing, their island changed to a den of pirates. He said to himself that he, Ayrton, was the first cause of these disasters, since his old companion, Harvey, had only carried out Ayrton's projects; and a feeling of horror came over him. Then came the irresistible desire to blow up the brig, with all on board. He would perish in the explosion, but he would have done his duty.

He did not hesitate! It was easy to reach the powder magazine, which is always in the after part of the ship. Powder must be plenty on board such a vessel, and a spark would bring destruction.

Ayrton lowered himself carefully between-decks, where he found many of the pirates lying about, overcome rather by drunkenness than sleep. A ship's lantern, was lighted at the foot of the mainmast, from which hung a rack full of all sorts of firearms. Ayrton took from the rack a revolver, and made sure that it was loaded and capped. It was all that he needed to accomplish the work of destruction. Then he glided back to the poop, where the powder magazine would be. Between decks it was dark, and he could hardly step without knocking against some half-asleep convict, and meeting with an oath or a blow. More than once he had to stop short, but at length he reached the partition separating the after-compartment, and found the door of the magazine. This he had to force, and it was a difficult matter to accomplish without noise, as he had to break a padlock. But at last, under his vigorous hand, the padlock fell apart and the door opened. Just then a hand was laid upon his shoulder.

"What are you doing there?" said a harsh voice, and a tall form rose from the shadow and turned the light of a lantern fall on Ayrton's face.

Ayrton turned around sharply. By a quick flash from the lantern, he saw his old accomplice, Harvey; but the latter, believing Ayrton, as he did, to be dead, failed to recognize him.

"What are you doing there?" said Harvey, seizing Ayrton by the strap of his trousers. Ayrton made no answer but a vigorous push, and sprang forward to the magazine. One shot into those tons of powder, and all would have been over!

"Help, lads!" cried Harvey.

Two or three pirates, roused by his voice, threw themselves upon Ayrton, and strove to drag him to the ground. He rid himself of them with two shots from his revolver; but received in so doing, a wound from a knife in the fleshy part of the shoulder. He saw in a moment that his project was no longer feasible. Harvey had shut the door of the magazine, and a dozen pirates were half-awake. He most save himself for the sake of his comrades.

Four barrels were left. He discharged two of them right and left, one at Harvey, though without effect; and then, profiting by his enemies' momentary recoil, rushed towards the ladder which led to the deck of the brig. As he passed the lantern he knocked it down with a blow from the butt-end of his pistol, and left everything in darkness.

Two or three pirates, awakened by the noise, were coming down the ladder at that moment. A fifth shot stretched one at the foot of the steps, and the others got out of the way, not understanding what was going on. In two bounds Ayrton was on the brig's deck, and three seconds afterwards, after discharging his last shot at a pirate who tried to seize him by the neck, he made his way down the netting and leaped into the sea. He had not swam six fathoms before the bullets began to whistle around him like hail.

What were the feelings of Pencroff, hidden behind a rock on the islet, and of his comrades in the Chimneys, when they heard these shots from the brig! They rushed out upon the shore, and, with their guns at their shoulders, stood ready to meet any attack. For them no doubt remained. They believed that Ayrton had been killed, and the pirates were about to make a descent on the island. Thus half an hour passed away. They suffered torments of anxiety. They could not go to the assistance of Ayrton or Pencroff, for the boat had been taken, and the high tide forbade them crossing the channel.

Finally, at half-past 12, a boat with two men came along shore. It was Ayrton, with a slight wound in his shoulder, and Pencroff. Their friends received them with open arms.

Then all took refuge at the Chimneys. There Ayrton told them all that happened, including his plan to blow up the brig.

Every one grasped the man's hand, but the situation was desperate. The pirates knew that Lincoln Island was inhabited, and would come down upon it in force. They would respect nothing. If the colonists fell into their hands they had no mercy to hope for!

"We can die like men," said the reporter.

"Let us go in and keep watch," said the engineer.

"Do you think there is any chance, Mr. Smith?" said the sailor.

"Yes, Pencroff."

"How! Six against fifty!"

"Yes, six—and one other—"

"Who?" asked Pencroff.

Smith did not answer, but he looked upwards

CHAPTER XLV. THE MIST RISES

THE ENGINEER'S DISPOSITION OF FORCES—THREE POSTS—AYRTON AND PENCROFF—THE FIRST ATTACK —TWO OTHER BOAT LOADS—ON THE ISLET— SIX CONVICTS ON SHORE—THE BRIG WEIGHS ANCHOR—THE SPEEDY'S PROJECTILES—DESPERATE SITUATION—UNEXPECTED DENOUEMENT.

The night passed without incident. The colonists were still at the Chimneys, keeping a constant lookout. The pirates made no attempt at landing. Since the last shots fired at Ayrton, not a sound betrayed the presence of the brig in the bay. They might have supposed she had weighed anchor and gone off in the night.

But it was not so, and when daylight began to appear the colonists could see her dark hulk dim through the morning mists.

"Listen, my friends," then said the engineer. "These are the dispositions it seems to me best to make before the mist dispels, which conceals us from view. We must make these convicts believe that the inhabitants of the island are numerous and well able to resist them. Let us divide ourselves into three groups, one posted at the Chimneys, one at the mouth of the Mercy, and the third upon the islet, to hinder, or at least, retard, every attempt to land. We have two carbines and four guns, so that each of us will be armed; and as we have plenty of powder and ball, we will not spare our shots. We have nothing to fear from the guns, nor even from the cannon of the brig. What can they effect against these rocks? And as we shall not shoot from the windows of Granite House, the pirates will never think of turning their guns upon it. What we have to fear is a hand-to-hand fight with an enemy greatly superior in numbers. We must try to prevent their landing without showing ourselves. So don't spare your ammunition. Shoot fast, and shoot straight. Each of us has eight or ten enemies to kill, and must kill them."

Smith had precisely defined the situation, in a voice as quiet as if he were directing some ordinary work. His companions acted upon his proposal without a word. Each hastened to take his place before the mist should be entirely dissipated.

Neb and Pencroff went back to Granite House and brought back thence abundance of ammunition. Spilett and Ayrton, both excellent shots, were armed with the two carbines, which would carry nearly a mile. The four shot-guns were divided between Smith, Neb, Pencroff, and Herbert. The posts were thus filled:—Smith and Herbert remained in ambush at the Chimneys, commanding a large radius of the shore in front of Granite House. Spilett and Neb hid themselves among the rocks at the mouth of the Mercy (the bridge and causeways over which had been removed), so as to oppose the passage of any boat or even any landing on the opposite side. As to Ayrton and Pencroff, they pushed the canoe into the water, and got ready to push across the channel, to occupy two different points on the islet, so that the firing, coming from four different points, might convince the pirates that the island was both well manned and vigorously defended.

In case a landing should be effected in spite of their opposition, or should they be in danger of being cut off by a boat from the brig, Pencroff and Ayrton could return with the canoe to the shore of the island, and hasten to the threatened point.

Before going to their posts, the colonists shook hands all round. Pencroff concealed his emotion as he embraced "his boy" Herbert, and they parted. A few minutes afterwards each was at his post. None of them could have been seen, for the brig itself was barely visible through the mist. It was half-past 6 in the morning. Soon the mist rose gradually; the ocean was covered with ripples, and, a breeze rising, the sky was soon clear. The Speedy appeared, anchored by two cables, her head to the north, and her larboard quarter to the island. As Smith had calculated, she was not more than a mile and a quarter from the shore. The ominous black flag floated at the peak. The engineer could see with his glass that the four guns of the ship had been trained on the island, ready to be fired at the first signal; but so far there was no sound. Full thirty pirates could be seen coming and going on the deck. Some were on the poop; two on the transoms of the main topmast were examining the island with spy-glasses. In fact, Harvey and his crew must have been exceedingly puzzled by the adventure of the night, and especially by Ayrton's attempt upon the powder magazine. But they could not doubt that the island before them was inhabited by a colony ready to defend it. Yet no one could be seen either on the shore or the high ground.

For an hour and a half there was no sign of attack from the brig. Evidently Harvey was hesitating. But about 8 o'clock there was a movement on board. They were hauling at the tackle, and a boat was being let down into the sea. Seven men jumped into it, their guns in their hands. One was at the tiller, four at the oars, and the two others squatting in the bow, ready to shoot, examined the island. No doubt their intention was to make a reconnoissance, and not to land, or they would have come in greater number.

The pirates, perched on the rigging of the topmast, had evidently perceived that an islet concealed the shore, lying about half a mile away. The boat was apparently not running for the channel, but was making for the islet, as the most prudent beginning of the reconnoissance. Pencroff and Ayrton, lying hidden among the rocks, saw it coming down upon them, and even waiting for it to get within good reach.

It came on with extreme caution. The oars fell at considerable intervals. One of the convicts seated in front had a sounding-line in his hand, with which he was feeling for the increased depth of water caused by the current of the Mercy. This indicated Harvey's intention of bringing his brig as near shore as possible. About thirty pirates were scattered among the shrouds watching the boat and noting certain sea-marks which would enable them to land without danger. The boat was but two cables' length from the islet when it stopped. The helmsman, standing erect, was trying to find the best place to land. In a moment burst forth a double flash and report. The helmsman and the man with the line fell over into the boat. Ayrton and Pencroff had done their work. Almost at once came a puff of smoke from the brig, and a cannon ball struck the rock, at whose foot the two lay sheltered, making it fly into shivers; but the marksmen remained unhurt.

With horrible imprecations the boat resumed its course. The helmsman was replaced by one of his comrades, and the crew bent to their oars, eager to get beyond reach of bullets. Instead of turning back, they pulled for the southern extremity of the islet, evidently with the intention of coming up on the other side and putting Pencroff and Ayrton between two fires. A quarter of an hour passed thus without a sound. The defenders of the islet, though they understood the object of the flanking movement, did not leave their post. They feared the cannon of the Speedy, and counted upon their comrades in ambush.

Twenty minutes after the first shots, the boat was less than two cables' length off the Mercy. The tide was running up stream with its customary swiftness, due to the narrowness of the river, and the convicts had to row hard to keep themselves in the middle of the channel. But as they were passing within easy range of the river's mouth, two reports were heard, and two of the crew fell back into the boat. Neb and Spilett had not missed their shot. The brig opened fire upon their hiding place, which was indicated by the puff of smoke; but with no result beyond shivering a few rocks.

The boat now contained only three men fit for action. Getting into the current, it shot up the channel like an arrow, passed Smith and Herbert, who feared to waste a shot upon it, and turned the northern point of the islet, whence the two remaining oarsmen pulled across to the brig.

So far the colonists could not complain. Their adversaries had lost the first point in the game. Four pirates had been grievously wounded, perhaps killed, while they were without a scratch. Moreover, from the skilful disposition of their little force, it had no doubt given the impression of a much greater number.

A half hour elapsed before the boat, which was rowing against the current, could reach the Speedy. The wounded were lifted on deck, amid howls of rage. A dozen furious convicts manned the boat; another was lowered into the sea, and eight more jumped into it; and while the former rowed straight for the islet, the latter steered around its southern point, heading for the Mercy.

Pencroff and Ayrton were in a perilous situation. They waited till the first boat was within easy range, sent two balls into her, to the great discomfort of the crew; then they took to their heels, running the gauntlet of a dozen shots, reached their canoe on the other side of the islet, crossed the channel just as the second boat load of pirates rounded the southern point, and hastened to hide themselves at the Chimneys. They had hardly rejoined Smith and Herbert, when the islet was surrounded and thoroughly searched by the pirates.

Almost at the same moment shots were heard from the mouth of the Mercy. As the second boat approached them, Spilett and Neb disposed of two of the crew; and the boat itself was irresistibly hurried upon the rocks at the mouth of the river. The six survivors, holding their guns above their heads to keep them from contact with the water, succeeded in getting on shore on the right bank of the river; and, finding themselves exposed to the fire of a hidden enemy, made off towards Jetsam Point, and were soon out of range.

On the islet, therefore, there were twelve convicts, of whom some no doubt were wounded, but who had a boat at their service. Six more had landed on the island itself, but Granite House was safe from them, for they could not get across the river, the bridges over which were raised.

"What do you think of the situation, Mr. Smith?" said Pencroff.

"I think," said the engineer, "that unless these rascals are very stupid, the battle will soon take a new form."

"They will never get across the channel," said Pencroff. "Ayrton and Mr. Spilett have guns that will carry a mile!"

"No doubt," said Herbert, "but of what avail are two carbines against the brig's cannon?"

"The brig is not in the channel yet," replied Pencroff.

"And suppose she comes there?" said Smith.

"She will risk foundering and utter destruction."

"Still it is possible," said Ayrton. "The convicts may profit by the high tide to run into the channel, taking the risk of running aground; and then, under their heavy guns, our position will become untenable."

"By Jove!" said the sailor, "the beggars are weighing anchor."

It was but too true. The Speedy began to heave her anchor, and showed her intention of approaching the islet.

Meanwhile, the pirates on the islet had collected on the brink of the channel. They knew that the colonists were out of reach of their shot-guns, but forgot that their enemies, might carry weapons of longer range. Suddenly, the carbines of Ayrton and Spilett rang out together, carrying news to the convicts, which must have been very disagreeable, for two of them fell flat on their faces.

There was a general scamper. The other ten, leaving their wounded or dying comrades, rushed to the other side of the islet, sprang into the boat which had brought them over, and rowed rapidly off.

"Eight off!" cried Pencroff, exultingly.

But a more serious danger was at hand. The Speedy had raised her anchor, and was steadily nearing the shore. From their two posts at the Mercy and the Chimneys, the colonists watched her movements without stirring a finger, but not without lively apprehension. Their situation would be most critical, exposed as they would be at short range to the brig's cannon, without power to reply by an effective fire. How then could they prevent the pirates from landing?

Smith felt that in a few minutes he must make up his mind what to do. Should they shut themselves up in Granite House, and stand a siege there? But their enemies would thus become masters of the island, and starve them out at leisure. One chance was still left; perhaps Harvey would not risk his ship in the channel. If he kept outside his shots would be fired from a distance of half a mile, and would do little execution.

"Bob Harvey is too good a sailor," repeated Pencroff, "to risk his ship in the channel. He knows that he would certainly lose her if the sea turned rough! And what would become of him without his ship?"

But the brig came nearer and nearer, and was evidently heading for the lower extremity of the islet. The breeze was faint, the current slack, and Harvey could manœuvre in safety. The route followed by the boats had enabled him to ascertain where the mouth of the river was, and he was making for it with the greatest audacity. He intended to bring his broadside to bear on the Chimneys, and to riddle them with shell and cannon balls. The Speedy soon reached the extremity of the islet, easily turning it, and, with a favoring wind, was soon off the Mercy.

"The villains are here!" cried Pencroff. As he spoke, Neb and Spilett rejoined their comrades. They could do nothing against the ship, and it was better that the colonists should be together when the decisive action was about to take place. Neither of the two were injured, though a shower of balls had been poured upon them as they ran from rock to rock.

"You are not wounded, lad?" said the engineer.

"No, only a few contusions from the ricochet of a ball. But that cursed brig is in the channel!"

"We must take refuge in Granite House," said Smith, "while we have time, and before the convicts can see us. Once inside, we can act as the occasion demands."

"Let us start at once, then," said the reporter.

There was not a moment to lose. Two or three detonations, and the thud of balls on the rocks apprised them that the Speedy was near at hand.

To jump into the elevator, to hoist themselves to the door of Granite House, where Top and Jup had been shut up since the day before, and to rush into the great hall, was the work of a moment. Through the leaves they saw the Speedy, environed with smoke, moving up the channel. They had not left a moment too soon, for balls were crashing everywhere through the hiding places they had quitted. The rocks were splintered to pieces.

Still they hoped that Granite House would escape notice behind its leafy covering, when suddenly a ball passed through the doorway and penetrated into the corridor.

"The devil! we are discovered!" cried Pencroff.

But perhaps the colonists had not been seen, and Harvey had only suspected that something lay behind the leafy screen of the rock. And soon another ball, tearing apart the foliage, exposed the opening in the granite.

The situation of the colonists was now desperate. They could make no answer to the fire, under which the rock was crashing around them. Nothing remained but to take refuge in the upper corridor of Granite House, giving up their abode to devastation, when a hollow sound was heard, followed by dreadful shrieks!

Smith and his comrades rushed to the window.

The brig, lifted on the summit of a sort of waterspout, had just split in half; and in less than ten seconds she went to the bottom with her wicked crew!!

CHAPTER XLVI. THE COLONISTS ON THE BEACH

AYRTON AND PENCROFF AS SALVORS—TALK AT BREAKFAST— PENCROFF'S REASONING—EXPLORATION OF THE BRIG'S HULL IN DETAIL— THE MAGAZINE UNINJURED—NEW RICHES—A DISCOVERY—A PIECE OF A BROKEN CYLINDER.

"They have blown up!" cried Herbert.

"Yes, blown up as if Ayrton had fired the magazine," answered Pencroff, jumping into the elevator with Neb and the boy,

"But what has happened?" said Spilett, still stupefied at the unexpected issue.

"Ah, this time we shall find out—" said the engineer,

"What shall we find out?"

"All in time; the chief thing is that the pirates have been disposed of."

And they rejoined the rest of the party on beach. Not a sign of the brig could be seen, not even the masts. After having been upheaved by the water-spout, it had fallen back upon its side, and had sunk in this position, doubtless owing to some enormous leak.' As the channel here was only twenty feet deep, the masts of the brig would certainly reappear at low tide.

Some waifs were floating on the surface of the sea. There was a whole float, made up of masts and spare yards, chicken coops with the fowls still living, casks and barrels, which little by little rose to the surface, having escaped by the traps; but no debris was adrift, no flooring of the deck, no plankage of the hull; and the sudden sinking of the Speedy seemed still more inexplicable.

However, the two masts, which had been broken some feet above the "partner," after having snapped their stays and shrouds, soon rose to the surface of the channel, with their sails attached, some of them furled and some unfurled. But they could not wait for low tide to carry away all their riches, and Ayrton and Pencroff jumped into the canoe, for the purpose of lashing these waifs either to the shore of the island or of the islet. But just as they were about to start, they were stopped by a word from Spilett.

"And the six convicts who landed on the right bank of the Mercy," said he.

In fact, it was as well to remember the six men who had landed at Jetsam Point, when their boat was wrecked off the rocks. They looked in that direction, but the fugitives were not to be seen. Very likely, when they saw the brig go down, they had taken flight into the interior of the island.

"We will see after them later," said Smith. "They may still be dangerous, for they are armed; but with six to six, we have an even chance. Now we have more urgent work on hand."

Ayrton and Pencroff jumped into the canoe and pulled vigorously out to the wreck. The sea was quiet now and very high, for the moon was only two days old. It would be a full hour before the hull of the brig would appear above the water of the channel.

Ayrton and Pencroff had time enough to lash together the masts and spars by means of ropes, whose other end was carried along the shore to Granite House, where the united efforts of the colonists succeeded in hauling them in. Then the canoe picked up the chicken coops, barrels, and casks which were floating in the water, and brought them to the Chimneys.

A few dead bodies were also floating on the surface. Among them Ayrton recognized that of Bob Harvey, and pointed it out to his companion, saying with emotion:— "That's what I was, Pencroff."

"But what you are no longer, my worthy fellow," replied the sailor.

It was a curious thing that so few bodies could be seen floating on the surface. They could count only five or six, which the current was already carrying out to sea. Very likely the convicts, taken by surprise, had not had time to escape, and the ship having sunk on its side, the greater part of the crew were left entangled under the nettings. So the ebb which was carrying the bodies of these wretches out to sea would spare the colonists the unpleasant task of burying them on the island.

For two hours Smith and his companions were wholly occupied with hauling the spars up on the sands, and in unfurling the sails, which were entirely uninjured, and spreading them out to dry. The work was so absorbing that they talked but little; but they had time for thought. What a fortune was the possession of the brig, or rather of the brig's contents! A ship is a miniature world, and the colonists could add to their stock a host of useful articles. It was a repetition, on a large scale, of the chest found on Jetsam Point.

"Moreover," thought Pencroff, "why should it be impossible to get this brig afloat? If she has only one leak, a leak can be stopped up, and a ship of 300 or 400 tons is a real ship compared to our Good Luck! We would go where we pleased in her. We must look into this matter. It is well worth the trouble."

In fact, if the brig could be repaired, their chance of getting home again would be very much greater. But in order to decide this important question, they must wait until the tide was at its lowest, so that the brig's hull could be examined in every part.

After their prizes had been secured upon the beach, Smith and his companions, who were nearly famished, allowed themselves a few minutes for breakfast. Fortunately the kitchen was not far off, and Neb could cook them a good breakfast in a jiffy. They took this meal at the Chimneys, and one can well suppose that they talked of nothing during the repast but the miraculous deliverance of the colony.

"Miraculous is the word," repeated Pencroff, "for we must own that these blackguards were blown up just in time! Granite House was becoming rather uncomfortable."

"Can you imagine, Pencroff, how it happened that the brig blew up?" asked the reporter.

"Certainly, Mr. Spilett; nothing is more simple," replied Pencroff. "A pirate is not under the same discipline as a ship-of-war. Convicts don't make sailors. The brig's magazine must have been open, since she cannonaded us incessantly, and one awkward fellow might have blown up the ship."

"Mr. Smith," said Herbert, "what astonishes me is that this explosion did not produce more effect. The detonation was not loud, and the ship is very little broken up. She seems rather to have sunk than to have blown up."

"That astonishes you, does it, my boy?" asked the engineer.

"Yes, sir."

"And it astonishes me too, Herbert," replied the engineer; "but when we examine the hull of the brig, we shall find some explanation of this mystery."

"Why, Mr. Smith," said Pencroff, "you don't mean to say that the Speedy has just sunk like a ship which strikes upon a rock?"

"Why not," asked Neb, "if there are rocks in the channel?"

"Good, Neb," said Pencroff. "You did not look at the right minute. An instant before she went down I saw the brig rise on an enormous wave, and fall back over to larboard. Now, if she had struck a rock, she'd have gone straight to the bottom like an honest ship."

"And that's just what she is not," said Neb.

"Well, we'll soon find out, Pencroff," said the engineer.

"We will find out," added the sailor, "but I'll bet my head there are no rocks in the channel. But do you really think, Mr. Smith, that there is anything wonderful in this event?"

Smith did not answer.

"At all events," said Spilett, "whether shock or explosion, you must own, Pencroff, that it came in good time."

"Yes! yes!" replied the sailor, "but that is not the question. I ask Mr. Smith if he sees anything supernatural in this affair?"

"I give no opinion, Pencroff," said the engineer; a reply which was not satisfactory to Pencroff, who believed in the explosion theory, and was reluctant to give it up. He refused to believe that in the channel which he had crossed so often at low tide, and whose bottom was covered with sand as fine as that of the beach, there existed an unknown reef.

At about half-past 1, the colonists got into the canoe, and pulled out to the stranded brig. It was a pity that her two boats had not been saved; but one, they knew, had gone to pieces at the mouth of the Mercy, and was absolutely useless, and the other had gone down with the brig, and had never reappeared.

Just then the hull of the Speedy began to show itself above the water. The brig had turned almost upside down, for after having broken its masts under the weight of its ballast, displaced by the fall, it lay with its keel in the air. The colonists rowed all around the hull, and as the tide fell, they perceived, if not the cause of the catastrophe, at least the effect produced. In the fore part of the brig, on both sides of the hull, seven or eight feet before the beginning of the stem, the sides were fearfully shattered for at least twenty feet. There yawned two large leaks which it would have been impossible to stop. Not only had the copper sheathing and the planking disappeared, no doubt ground to powder, but there was not a trace of the timbers, the iron bolts, and the treenails which fastened them. The false-keel had been torn off with surprising violence, and the keel itself, torn from the carlines in several places, was broken its whole length.

"The deuce!" cried Pencroff, "here's a ship which will be hard to set afloat."

"Hard! It will be impossible," said Ayrton.

"At all events," said Spilett, "the explosion, if there has been an explosion, has produced the most remarkable effects. It has smashed the lower part of the hull, instead of blowing up the deck and the topsides. These great leaks seem rather to have been made by striking a reef than by the explosion of a magazine."

"There's not a reef in the channel," answered the sailor. "I will admit anything but striking a reef."

"Let us try to get into the hold," said the engineer. "Perhaps that will help us to discover the cause of the disaster."

This was the best course to take, and would moreover enable them to make an inventory of the treasures contained in the brig, and to get them ready for transportation to the island. Access to the hold was now easy; the tide continued to fall, and the lower deck, which, as the brig lay, was now uppermost, could easily be reached. The ballast, composed of heavy pigs of cast iron, had staved it in several places. They heard the roaring of the sea, as it rushed through the fissures of the hull.

Smith and his companions, axe in hand, walked along the shattered deck. All kinds of chests encumbered it, and as they had not been long under water, perhaps their contents had not been damaged.

They set to work at once to put this cargo in safety. The tide would not return for some hours, and these hours were utilized to the utmost at the opening into the hull. Ayrton and Pencroff had seized upon tackle which served to hoist the barrels and chests. The canoe received them, and took them ashore at once. They took everything indiscriminately, and left the sorting of their prizes to the future.

In any case, the colonists, to their extreme satisfaction, had made sure that the brig possessed a varied cargo, an assortment of all kinds of articles, utensils, manufactured products, and tools, such as ships are loaded with for the coasting trade of Polynesia. They would probably find there a little of everything, which was precisely what they needed on Lincoln Island.

Nevertheless, Smith noticed, in silent astonishment, that not only the hull of the brig had suffered frightfully from whatever shock it was which caused the catastrophe, but the machinery was destroyed, especially in the fore part. Partitions and stanchions were torn down as if some enormous shell had burst inside of the brig. The colonists, by piling on one side the boxes which littered their path, could easily go from stem to stern. They were not heavy bales which would have been difficult to handle, but mere packages thrown about in utter confusion.

The colonists soon reached that part of the stern where the poop formerly stood. It was here Ayrton told them they must search for the powder magazine. Smith, believing that this had not exploded, thought they might save some barrels, and that the powder, which is usually in metal cases, had not been damaged by the water. In fact, this was just what had happened. They found, among a quantity of projectiles, at least twenty barrels, which were lined with copper, and which they pulled out with great care. Pencroff was now convinced by his own eyes that the destruction of the Speedy could not have been caused by an explosion. The part of the hull in which the powder magazine was situated was precisely the part which had suffered the least.

"It may be so," replied the obstinate sailor, "but as to a rock, there is not one in the channel." Then he added:—"I know nothing about it, even Mr. Smith does not know. No one knows, or ever will."

Several hours passed in these researches, and the tide was beginning to rise. They had to stop their work of salvage, but there was no fear that the wreck would be washed out to sea, for it was as solidly imbedded as if it had been anchored to the bottom. They could wait with impunity for the turn of the tide to commence operations. As to the ship itself, it was of no use; but they must hasten to save the debris of the hull, which would not take long to disappear in the shifting sands of the channel.

It was 5 o'clock in the afternoon. The day had been a hard one, and they sat down to their dinner with great appetite; but afterwards, notwithstanding their fatigue, they could not resist the desire of examining some of the chests. Most of them contained ready-made clothes, which, as may be imagined, were very welcome. There was enough to clothe a whole colony, linen of every description, boots of all sizes.

"Now we are too rich," cried Pencroff. "What shall we do with all these things?"

Every moment the sailor uttered exclamations of joy, as he came upon barrels of molasses and rum, hogsheads of tobacco, muskets and side-arms, bales of cotton, agricultural implements, carpenters' and smiths' tools, and packages of seeds of every kind, uninjured by their short sojourn in the water. Two years before, how these things would have come in season! But even now that the industrious colonists were so well supplied, these riches would be put to use. There was plenty of storage room in Granite House, but time failed them now to put everything in safety. They must not forget that six survivors of the Speedy's crew were now on the island, scoundrels of the deepest dye, against whom they must be on their guard.

Although the bridge over the Mercy and the culverts had been raised, the convicts would make little account of a river or a brook; and, urged by despair, these rascals would be formidable. Later, the colonists could decide what course to take with regard to them; in the meantime, the chests and packages piled up near the Chimneys must be watched over, and to this they devoted themselves during the night.

The night passed, however, without any attack from the convicts. Master Jup and Top, of the Granite House guard, would have been quick to give notice.

The three days which followed, the 19th, 20th, and 21st of October, were employed in carrying on shore everything of value either in the cargo or in the rigging. At low tide they cleaned out the hold, and at high tide, stowed away their prizes. A great part of the copper sheathing could be wrenched from the hull, which every day sank deeper; but before the sands had swallowed up the heavy articles which had sunk to the bottom, Ayrton and Pencroff dived and brought up the chains and anchors of the brig, the iron ballast, and as many as four cannon, which could be eased along upon empty barrels and brought to land; so that the arsenal of the colony gained as much from the wreck as the kitchens and store-rooms. Pencroff, always enthusiastic in his projects, talked already about constructing a battery which should command the channel and the mouth of the river. With four cannon, he would guarantee to prevent any fleet, however powerful, from coming within gunshot of the island.

Meanwhile, after nothing of the brig had been left but a useless shell, the bad weather came to finish its destruction. Smith had intended to blow it up, so as to collect the debris on shore, but a strong northeast wind and a high sea saved his powder for him. On the night of the 23d, the hull was thoroughly broken up, and part of the wreck stranded on the beach. As to the ship's papers, it is needless to say, although they carefully rummaged the closet in the poop, Smith found no trace of them. The pirates had evidently destroyed all that concerned either the captain or the owner of the Speedy, and as the name of its port was not painted on the stern, there was nothing to betray its nationality.

However, from the shape of the bow, Ayrton and Pencroff believed the brig to be of English construction.

A week after the ship went down, not a trace of her was to be seen even at low tide. The wreck had gone to pieces, and Granite House had been enriched with almost all its contents. But the mystery of its strange destruction would never have been cleared up, if Neb, rambling along the beach, had not come upon a piece of a thick iron cylinder, which bore traces of an explosion. It was twisted and torn at the edge, as if it had been submitted to the action of an explosive substance. Neb took it to his master, who was busy with his companions in the workshop at the Chimneys. Smith examined it carefully, and then turned to Pencroff.

"Do you still maintain, my friend," said he, "that the Speedy did not perish by a collision?"

"Yes, Mr. Smith," replied the sailor, "you know as well as I that there are no rocks in the channel."

"But suppose it struck against this piece of iron?" said the engineer, showing the broken cylinder.

"What, that pipe stem!" said Pencroff, incredulously.

"Do you remember, my friends," continued Smith, "that before foundering the brig was lifted up by a sort of waterspout?"

"Yes, Mr. Smith," said Herbert.

"Well, this was the cause of the waterspout," said Smith, holding up the broken tube.

"That?" answered Pencroff.

"Yes; this cylinder is all that is left of a torpedo!"

"A torpedo!" cried they all.

"And who put a torpedo there?" asked Pencroff, unwilling to give up.

"That I cannot tell you," said Smith, "but there it was, and you witnessed its tremendous effects!"

CHAPTER XLVII. THE ENGINEER'S THEORY

PENCROFF'S MAGNIFICENT SUPPOSITIONS—A BATTERY IN THE AIR—
FOUR PROJECTILES—THE SURVIVING CONVICTS—AYRTON HESITATES—
SMITH'S GENEROSITY AND PENCROFF'S DISSATISFACTION.

Thus, then, everything was explained by the submarine action of this torpedo. Smith had had some experience during the civil war of these terrible engines of destruction, and was not likely to be mistaken. This cylinder, charged with nitro-glycerine, had been the cause of the column of water rising in the air, of the sinking of the brig, and of the shattered condition of her hull. Everything was accounted for, except the presence of this torpedo in the waters of the channel!

"My friends," resumed Smith, "we can no longer doubt the existence of some mysterious being, perhaps a castaway like ourselves, inhabiting our island. I say this that Ayrton may be informed of all the strange events which have happened for two years. Who our unknown benefactor may be, I cannot say, nor why he should hide himself after rendering us so many services; but his services are not the less real, and such as only a man could render who wielded some prodigious power. Ayrton is his debtor as well; as he saved me from drowning after the fall of the balloon, so he wrote the document, set the bottle afloat in the channel, and gave us information of our comrade's condition. He stranded on Jetsam Point that chest, full of all that we needed; he lighted that fire on the heights of the island which showed you where to land; he fired that ball which we found in the body of the peccary; he immersed in the channel that torpedo which destroyed the brig; in short, he has done all those inexplicable things of which we could find no explanation. Whatever he is, then, whether a castaway or an exile, we should be ungrateful not to feel how much we owe him. Some day, I hope, we shall discharge our debt."

"We may add," replied Spilett, "that this unknown friend has a way of doing things which seems supernatural. If he did all these wonderful things, he possesses a power which makes him master of the elements."

"Yes," said Smith, "there is a mystery here, but if we discover the man we shall discover the mystery also. The question is this:—Shall we respect the incognito of this generous being, or should we try to find him? What do you think?"

"Master," said Neb, "I have an idea that we may hunt for him as long as we please, but that we shall only find him when he chooses to make himself known."

"There's something in that, Neb," said Pencroff.

"I agree with you, Neb," said Spilett; "but that is no reason for not making the attempt. Whether we find this mysterious being or not, we shall have fulfilled our duty towards him."

"And what is your opinion, my boy?" said the engineer, turning to Herbert.

"Ah," cried Herbert, his eye brightening; "I want to thank him, the man who saved you first and now has saved us all."

"It wouldn't be unpleasant for any of us, my boy," returned Pencroff. "I am not curious, but I would give one of my eyes to see him face to face."

"And you, Ayrton?" asked the engineer.

"Mr. Smith," replied Ayrton, "I can give no advice. Whatever you do will be right, and whenever you want my help in your search, I am ready."

"Thanks, Ayrton," said Smith, "but I want a more direct answer. You are our comrade, who has offered his life more than once to save ours, and we will take no important step without consulting you."

"I think, Mr. Smith," replied Ayrton, "that we ought to do everything to discover our unknown benefactor. He may be sick or suffering. I owe him a debt of gratitude which I can never forget, for he brought you to save me. I will never forget him!"

"It is settled," said Smith. "We will begin our search as soon as possible. We will leave no part of the island unexplored. We will pry into its most secret recesses, and may our unknown friend pardon our zeal!"

For several days the colonists were actively at work haymaking and harvesting. Before starting upon their exploring tour, they wanted to finish all their important labors. Now, too, was the time for gathering the vegetable products of Tabor Island. Everything had to be stored; and, happily, there was plenty of room in Granite House for all the riches of the island. There all was ranged in order, safe from man or beast. No dampness was to be feared in the midst of this solid mass of granite. Many of the natural excavations in the upper corridor were enlarged by the pick, or blown out by mining, and Granite House thus became a receptacle for all the goods of the colony.

The brig's guns were pretty pieces of cast-steel, which, at Pencroff's instance, were hoisted, by means of tackle and cranes, to the very entrance of Granite House; embrasures were constructed between the windows, and soon they could be seen stretching their shining nozzles through the granite wall. From this height these fire-breathing gentry had the range of all Union Bay. It was a little Gibraltar, to whose fire every ship off the islet would inevitably be exposed.

"Mr. Smith," said Pencroff one day—it was the 8th of November—"now that we have mounted our guns, we ought to try their range."

"For what purpose?"

"Well, we ought to know how far we can send a ball."

"Try, then, Pencroff," answered the engineer; "but don't use our powder, whose stock I do not want to diminish; use pyroxyline, whose supply will never fail."

"Can these cannon support the explosive force of pyroxyline?" asked the reporter, who was as eager as Pencroff to try their new artillery.

"I think so. Besides," added the engineer, "we will be careful."

Smith had good reason to think that these cannon were well made. They were of cast steel, and breech-loaders, they could evidently bear a heavy charge, and consequently would have a long range, on account of the tremendous initial velocity.

"Now," said Smith, "the initial velocity being a question of the amount of powder in the charge, everything depends upon the resisting power of the metal; and steel is undeniably the best metal in this respect; so that I have great hope of our battery."

The four cannon were in perfect condition. Ever since they had been taken out of the water, Pencroff had made it his business to give them a polish. How many hours had been spent in rubbing them, oiling them, and cleaning the separate parts! By this time they shone as if they had been on board of a United States frigate.

That very day, in the presence of all the colony, including Jup and Top, the new guns were successively tried. They were charged with pyroxyline, which, as we have said, has an explosive force fourfold that of gunpowder; the projectile was cylindro-conical in shape. Pencroff, holding the fuse, stood ready to touch them off. Upon a word from Smith, the shot was fired. The ball, directed seaward, passed over the islet and was lost in the offing, at a distance which could not be computed.

The second cannon was trained upon the rocks terminating Jetsam Point, and the projectile, striking a sharp boulder nearly three miles from Granite House, made it fly into shivers. Herbert had aimed and fired the shot, and was quite proud of his success. But Pencroff was prouder of it even than he. Such a feather in his boy's cap!

The third projectile, aimed at the downs which formed the upper coast of Union Bay, struck the sand about four miles away, then ricocheted into the water. The fourth piece was charged heavily to test its extreme range, and every one got out of the way for fear it would burst; then the fuse was touched off by means of a long string. There was a deafening report, but the gun stood the charge, and the colonists, rushing to the windows, could see the projectile graze the rocks of Mandible Cape, nearly five miles from Granite House, and disappear in Shark Gulf.

"Well, Mr. Smith," said Pencroff, who had cheered at every shot, "what do you say to our battery? I should like to see a pirate land now!"

"Better have them stay away, Pencroff," answered the engineer.

"Speaking of that," said the sailor, "what are we going to do with the six rascals who are prowling about the island? Shall we let them roam about unmolested? They are wild beasts, and I think we should treat them as such. What do you think about it, Ayrton?" added Pencroff, turning towards his companion.

Ayrton hesitated for a moment, while Smith regretted the abrupt question, and was sincerely touched when Ayrton answered humbly: "I was one of these wild beasts once, Mr. Pencroff, and I am not worthy to give counsel."

And, with bent head, he walked slowly away. Pencroff understood him.

"Stupid ass that I am!" cried he. "Poor Ayrton! and yet he has as good a right to speak as any of us. I would rather have bitten off my tongue than have given him pain! But, to go back to the subject, I think these wretches have no claim to mercy, and that we should rid the island of them."

"And before we hunt them down, Pencroff, shall we not wait for some fresh act of hostility?"

"Haven't they done enough already?" said the sailor, who could not understand these refinements.

"They may repent," said Smith.

"They repent!" cried the sailor, shrugging his shoulders.

"Think of Ayrton, Pencroff!" said Herbert, taking his hand. "He has become an honest man."

Pencroff looked at his companions in stupefaction. He could not admit the possibility of making terms with the accomplices of Harvey, the murderers of the Speedy's crew.

"Be it so!" he said. "You want to be magnanimous to these rascals. May we never repent of it!"

"What danger do we run if we are on our guard?" said Herbert.

"H'm!" said the reporter, doubtfully. "There are six of them, well-armed. If each of them sighted one of us from behind a tree—"

"Why haven't they tried it already?" said Herbert. "Evidently it was not their cue."

"Very well, then," said the sailor, who was stubborn in his opinion, "we will let these worthy fellows attend to their innocent occupations without troubling our heads about them."

"Pencroff," said the engineer, "you have often shown respect for my opinions. Will you trust me once again?"

"I will do whatever you say, Mr. Smith," said the sailor, nowise convinced.

"Well, let us wait, and not be the first to attack."

This was the final decision, with Pencroff in the minority. They would give the pirates a chance, which their own interest might induce them to seize upon, to come to terms. So much, humanity required of them. But they would have to be constantly on their guard, and the situation was a very serious one. They had silenced Pencroff, but, perhaps, after all, his advice would prove sound.

CHAPTER XLVIII. THE PROJECTED EXPEDITION

AYRTON AT THE CORRAL—VISIT TO PORT BALLOON—PENCROFF'S REMARKS—DESPATCH SENT TO THE CORRAL—NO ANSWER FROM AYRTON—SETTING OUT NEXT DAY—WHY THE WIRE DID NOT ACT—A DETONATION.

Meanwhile the thing uppermost in the colonists' thought was to achieve the complete exploration of the island which had been decided upon, an exploration which now would have two objects: —First, to discover the mysterious being whose existence was no longer a matter of doubt; and, at the same time to find out what had become of the pirates, what hiding place they had chosen, what sort of life they were leading, and what was to be feared from them.

Smith would have set off at once, but as the expedition would take several days, it seemed better to load the wagon with all the necessaries for camping out. Now at this time one of the onagers, wounded in the leg, could not bear harness; it must have several days' rest, and they thought it would make little difference if they delayed the departure a week, that is, till November 20. November in this latitude corresponds to the May of the Northern Hemisphere, and the weather was fine. They were now at the longest days in the year, so that everything was favorable to the projected expedition, which, if it did not attain its principal object, might be fruitful in discoveries, especially of the products of the soil; for Smith intended to explore those thick forests of the Far West, which stretched to the end of Serpentine Peninsula.

During the nine days which would precede their setting out, it was agreed that they should finish work on Prospect Plateau. But Ayrton had to go back to the corral to take care of their domesticated animals. It was settled that he should stay there two days, and leave the beasts with plenty of fodder. Just as he was setting out, Smith asked him if he would like to have one of them with him, as the island was no longer secure. Ayrton replied that it would be useless, as he could do everything by himself, and that there was no danger to fear. If anything happened at or near the corral, he would instantly acquaint the colonists of it by a telegram sent to Granite House.

So Ayrton drove off in the twilight, about 9 o'clock, behind one onager, and two hours afterwards the electric wire gave notice that he had found everything in order at the corral.

During these two days Smith was busy at a project which would finally secure Granite House from a surprise. The point was to hide completely the upper orifice of the former weir, which had been already blocked up with stones, and half hidden under grass and plants, at the southern angle of Lake Grant. Nothing could be easier, since by raising the level of the lake two or three feet, the hole would be entirely under water.

Now to raise the level, they had only to make a dam across the two trenches by which Glycerine Creek and Waterfall Creek were fed. The colonists were incited to the task, and the two dams, which were only seven or eight feet long, by three feet high, were rapidly erected of closely cemented stones. When the work had been done, no one could have suspected the existence of the subterranean conduit. The little stream which served to feed the reservoir at Granite House, and to work the elevator, had been suffered to flow in its channel, so that water might never be wanting. The elevator once raised, they might defy attack.

This work had been quickly finished, and Pencroff, Spilett, and Herbert found time for an expedition to Port Balloon. The sailor was anxious to know whether the little inlet up which the Good Luck was moored had been visited by the convicts.

"These gentry got to land on the southern shore," he observed, "and if they followed the line of the coast they may have discovered the little harbor, in which case I wouldn't give half a dollar for our Good Luck."

So off the three went in the afternoon of November 10. They were well armed, and as Pencroff slipped two bullets into each barrel of his gun, he had a look which presaged no good to whoever came too near, "beast or man," as he said. Neb went with them to the elbow of the Mercy, and lifted the bridge after them. It was agreed that they should give notice of their return by firing a shot, when Neb would come back to put down the bridge.

The little band walked straight for the south coast. The distance was only three miles and a half, but they took two hours to walk it. They searched on both sides of the way, both the forest and Tadorn's Fens; but they found no trace of the fugitives. Arriving at Port Balloon, they saw with great satisfaction that the Good Luck was quietly moored in the narrow inlet, which was so well hidden by the rocks that it could be seen neither from sea nor shore, but only from directly above or below.

"After all," said Pencroff, "the rascals haven't been here. The vipers like tall grass better, and we shall find them in the Far-West."

"And it's a fortunate thing," added Herbert, "for if they had found the Good Luck, they would have made use of her in getting away, and we could never have gone back to Tabor Island."

"Yes," replied the reporter, "it will be important to put a paper there stating the situation of Lincoln Island, Ayrton's new residence, in case the Scotch yacht should come after him."

"Well, here is our Good Luck, Mr. Spilett," said the sailor, "ready to start with her crew at the first signal!"

Talking thus, they got on board and walked about the deck. On a sudden the sailor, after examining the bit around which the cable of the anchor was wound, cried, "Hallo! this is a bad business!"

"What's the matter, Pencroff?" asked the reporter.

"The matter is that that knot was never tied by me——"

And Pencroff pointed to a rope which made the cable fast to the bit, so as to prevent its tripping.

"How, never tied by you?" asked Spilett.

"No, I can swear to it. I never tie a knot like that."

"You are mistaken, Pencroff."

"No, I'm not mistaken," insisted the sailor. "That knot of mine is second nature with me."

"Then have the convicts been on board?" asked Herbert.

"I don't know," said Pencroff, "but somebody has certainly raised and dropped this anchor!"

The sailor was so positive that neither Spilett nor Herbert could contest his assertion. It was evident that the beat had shifted place more or less since Pencroff had brought it back to Balloon Harbor. As for the sailor, he had no doubt that the anchor had been pulled up and cast again. Now, why had these manœuvres taken place unless the boat had been used on some expedition?

"Then why did we not see the Good Luck pass the offing?" said the reporter, who wanted to raise every possible objection.

"But, Mr. Spilett," answered the sailor, "they could have set out in the night with a good wind, and in two hours have been out of sight of the island."

"Agreed," said Spilett, but I still ask with what object the convicts used the Good Luck, and why, after using her, they brought her back to port?"

"Well, Mr. Spilett," said the sailor, "we will have to include that among our mysterious incidents, and think no more of it. One thing is certain, the Good Luck was there, and is here! If the convicts take it a second time, it may never find its way back again."

"Then, Pencroff," said Herbert, "perhaps we had better take the Good Luck back and anchor her in front of Granite House."

"I can hardly say," answered the sailor, "but I think not. The mouth of the Mercy is a bad place for a ship; the sea is very heavy there."

"But by hauling it over the sand to the foot of the Chimneys——"

"Well, perhaps," answered Pencroff. "In any case, as we have to leave Granite House for a long expedition, I believe the Good Luck will be safer here during oar absence, and he will do well to leave her here until the island is rid of these rascals."

"That is my opinion, too," said the reporter. At least in case of bad weather, she will not be exposed as she would be at the mouth of the Mercy."

"But if the convicts should pay her another visit?" said Herbert.

"Well, my boy," said Pencroff, "if they do not find the boat here they will search until they do find her; and in our absence there is nothing to prevent their carrying her off from the front of Granite House. I agree with Mr. Spilett that we had better leave her at Balloon Harbor; but if we have not rid the island of these wretches by the time we come back it will be more prudent to take our ship back to Granite House, until we have nothing more to fear from our enemies."

"All right," said Spilett. "Let us go back now."

When they returned to Granite House, they told Smith what had happened, and the latter approved their present and future plans. He even promised Pencroff he would examine that part of the channel situated between the island and the coast, so as to see if it would be possible to make an artificial harbor by means of a dam. In this way the Good Luck would be always within reach, in sight of the colonists, and locked up if necessary.

On the same evening they sent a telegram to Ayrton, asking him to bring back from the corral a couple of goats, which Neb wished to acclimatize on the plateau. Strange to say, Ayrton did not acknowledge the receipt of this despatch, as was his custom to do. This surprised the engineer, but he concluded that Ayrton was not at the corral at the moment, and perhaps had started on his way back to Granite House. In fact, two days had elapsed since his departure; and it had been agreed that on the evening of the 10th or the morning of the 11th, at latest, he would return.

The colonists were now waiting to see Ayrton on Prospect Plateau. Neb and Herbert both looked after the approach by way of the bridge, so as to let it down when their companion should appear, but when 6 o'clock in the evening came, and there was no sign of Ayrton, they agreed to send another despatch, asking for an immediate answer.

The wire at Granite House remained silent.

The uneasiness of the colonists was now extreme. What had happened? "Was Ayrton not at the corral? or, if there, had he not power over his own movements? Ought they to go in search of him on this dark night?

They discussed the point. Some were for going, and others for waiting.

"But," said Herbert, "perhaps some accident has happened to the wires which prevents their working."

"That may be," said the reporter.

"Let us wait until to-morrow," said Smith. "It is just possible that either Ayrton has not received our despatch, or we have missed his."

They waited, as may be imagined, with much anxiety. At daylight on the 11th of November, Smith sent a message across the wires, but received no answer. Again, with the same result.

"Let us set off at once for the corral," said he.

"Aid will armed," added Pencroff.

It was agreed that Granite House must not be deserted, so Neb was left behind to take charge. After accompanying his companions to Glycerine Creek, he put up the bridge again, and hid behind a tree, to wait either for their return or for that of Ayrton. In case the pirates should appear, and should attempt to force the passage, he would try to defend it with his gun; and in the last resort he would take refuge in Granite House, where, the elevator once drawn up, he would be in perfect safety. The others were to go direct to the corral, and failing to find Ayrton there, were to scour the neighboring woods.

At 6 o'clock in the morning the engineer and his three companions had crossed Glycerine Creek, and Neb posted himself behind a low cliff, crowned by some large dragon trees on the left side of the brook. The colonists, after leaving Prospect Plateau, took the direct route to the corral. They carried their guns on their shoulders, ready to fire at the first sign of hostility. The two rifles and the two guns had been carefully loaded.

On either side of the path was a dense thicket, which might easily hide enemies, who, as they were armed, would be indeed formidable. The colonists walked on rapidly without a word. Top preceded them, sometimes keeping to the path, and sometimes making a detour into the wood, but not appearing to suspect anything unusual; and they might depend upon it that the faithful dog would not be taken by surprise, and would bark at the slightest appearance of danger.

Along this same path Smith and his companions followed the telegraphic wires which connected the corral with Granite House. For the first two miles they did not notice any solution of continuity. The posts were in good condition, the insulators uninjured, and the wire evenly stretched. From this point the engineer noticed that the tension was less complete, and at last, arriving at post No. 74, Herbert, who was ahead of the others, cried, "The wire is broken!"

His companions hastened forward and arrived at the spot where the boy had stopped. There the overturned post was lying across the path. They had discovered the break, and it was evident that the dispatches from Granite House could not have been received at the corral.

"It can't be the wind that has overturned this post," said Pencroff.

"No," answered the reporter, "there are marks of footsteps on the ground; it has been uprooted by the hand of man."

"Besides, the wire is broken," added Herbert, showing the two ends of the wire which had been violently torn asunder.

"Is the break a fresh one?" asked Smith.

"Yes," said Herbert, "it was certainly made a very short time ago."

"To the corral! to the corral!" cried the sailor.

The colonists were then midway between Granite House and the corral, and had still two miles and a half to go. They started on a run.

In fact, they might well fear that something had happened at the corral. Ayrton doubtless might have sent a telegram which had not arrived. It was not this which alarmed his companions, but a circumstance more remarkable. Ayrton, who had promised to come back the evening before, had not reappeared! The communication, between Granite House and the corral had been out with a sinister design.

They hurried on, their hearts beating quick with fear for their comrade, to whom they were sincerely attached; Were they to find him struck down by the hand of those he had formerly led?

Soon they reached the place where the road lay along by the little brook flowing from Red Creek, which watered the meadows of the corral. They had moderated their pace, so as not to be out of breath at the moment when a deadly struggle might occur. Their guns were uncocked, but loaded. Each of them watched one side of the woods. Top kept up an ill-omened growling.

At last the fenced enclosure appeared behind the trees. They saw no signs of devastation. The door was closed as usual; a profound silence reigned at the corral. Neither the accustomed bleatings of the sheep nor the voice of Ayrton was to be heard.

"Let us go in," said Smith, and the engineer advanced, while his companions, keeping guard twenty feet in the rear, stood ready to fire.

Smith raised the inner latch, and began to push back the door, when Top barked loudly. There was a report from behind the fence, followed by a cry of pain, and Herbert, pierced by a bullet, fell to the ground!

CHAPTER XLIX. THE REPORTER AND PENCROFF

IN THE CORRAL—MOVING HERBERT—DESPAIR OF THE SAILOR—CONSULTATION OF THE ENGINEER AND THE REPORTER—MODE OF TREATMENT—A GLIMMER OF HOPE—HOW TO WARN NEB—A FAITHFUL MESSENGER—NEB'S REPLY.

At Herbert's cry, Pencroff, dropping his gun, sprang towards him.

"They have killed him!" cried he. "My boy—they have killed him."

Smith and Spilett rushed forward. The reporter put his ear to the boy's heart to see if it were still beating. "He's alive, but he must be taken." said he.

"To Granite House? Impossible!" said the engineer.

"To the corral, then," cried Pencroff.

"One moment," said Smith, and he rushed to the left around the fence. There he found himself face to face with a convict, who fired at him and sent a ball through his cap. An instant later, before he had time to fire again, he fell, struck to the heart by Smith's poniard, a surer weapon even than his gun.

While this was going on, the reporter and Pencroff hoisted themselves up to the angle of the fence, strode over the top, jumped into the enclosure, made their way into the empty house, and laid Herbert gently down on Ayrton's bed.

A few minutes afterwards Smith was at his side. At the sight of Herbert, pale and unconscious, the grief of the sailor was intense. He sobbed and cried bitterly; neither the engineer nor the reporter could calm him. Themselves overwhelmed with emotion, they could hardly speak.

They did all in their power to save the poor boy's life. Spilett, in his life of varied experience, had acquired some knowledge of medicine. He knew a little of everything; and had had several opportunities of learning the surgery of gunshot wounds. With Smith's assistance, he hastened to apply the remedies which Herbert's condition demanded.

The boy lay in a complete stupor, caused either by the hemorrhage or by concussion of the brain. He was very pale, and his pulse beat only at long intervals, as if every moment about to stop. This, taken in conjunction with his utter loss of consciousness, was a grave symptom. They stripped his chest, and, staunching the blood by means of handkerchiefs, kept bathing the wounds in cold water.

The ball had entered between the third and fourth rib, and there they found the wound. Smith and Spilett turned the poor boy over. At this he uttered a moan so faint that they feared it was his last breath. There was another wound on his back, for the bullet had gone clean through.

"Thank Heaven!" said the reporter, "the ball is not in his body; we shall not have to extract it."

"But the heart?" asked Smith.

"The heart has not been touched, or he would be dead."

"Dead!" cried Pencroff, with a groan. He had only heard the reporter's last word.

"No, Pencroff," answered Smith. "No he is not dead; his pulse still beats; he has even uttered a groan. For his sake, now, you must be calm. We have need of all our self-possession; you must not be the means of our losing it, my friend."

Pencroff was silent, but large tears rolled down his cheeks.

Meanwhile, Spilett tried to recall to memory the proper treatment of the case before him. There seemed no doubt that the ball had entered in front and gone out by the back; but what injuries had it done by the way? Had it reached any vital spot? This was a question which even a professional surgeon could not have answered at once.

There was something, however, which Spilett knew must be done, and that was to keep down the inflammation, and to fight against the fever which ensues upon a wound. The wound must be dressed without delay. It was not necessary to bring on a fresh flow of blood by the use of tepid water and compresses, for Herbert was already too weak. The wounds, therefore, were bathed with cold water.

Herbert was placed upon his left side and held in that position.

"He must not be moved," said Spilett; "he is in the position most favorable to an easy suppuration, and absolute repose is necessary."

"Cannot we take him to Granite House?" asked Pencroff.

"No, Pencroff," said the reporter.

Spilett was examining the boy's wounds again with close attention. Herbert was so frightfully pale that he became alarmed.

"Cyrus," said he, "I am no doctor. I am in a terrible strait; you must help me with your advice and assistance."

"Calm yourself, my friend," answered the engineer, pressing his hand. "Try to judge coolly. Think only of saving Herbert."

Spilett's self-possession, which in a moment of discouragement his keen sense of responsibility had caused him to lose, returned again at these words. He seated himself upon the bed; Smith remained standing, Pencroff had torn up his shirt and began mechanically to make lint.

Spilett explained that the first thing to do was to check the hemorrhage, but not to close the wounds or bring on immediate cicatrization—for there had been internal perforation, and they must not let the suppurated matter collect within. It was decided therefore to dress the two wounds, but not to press them together. The colonists possessed a most powerful agent for quelling inflamation, and one which nature supplies in the greatest abundance; to-wit, cold water, which is now used by all doctors. It has, moreover, the advantage of allowing the wound perfect rest, and dispensing with the frequent dressing, which by exposing the wound to the air in the early stages, is so often attended with lamentable results.

Thus did Smith and Spilett reason, with clear, native good sense, and acted as the best surgeon would have done. The wounds were bandaged with linen and constantly soaked with fresh water. The sailor had lighted a fire in the chimney, and the house fortunately contained all the necessaries of life. They had maple-sugar and the medicinal plants which the boy had gathered on the shores of Lake Grant. From these they made a refreshing drink for the sick boy. His fever was very high, and he lay all that day and night without a sign of consciousness. His life was hanging on a thread.

On the next day, November 12, they began to have some hopes of his recovery. His consciousness returned, he opened his eyes and recognized them all. He even said two or three words, and wanted to know what had happened. Spilett told him, and begged him to keep perfectly quiet; that his life was not in danger, and his wounds would heal in a few days. Herbert suffered very little, for the inflammation was successfully kept down by the plentiful use of cold water. A regular suppuration had set in, the fever did not increase, and they began to hope that this terrible accident would not end in a worse catastrophe.

Pencroff took heart again; he was the best of nurses, like a Sister of Charity, or a tender mother watching over her child. Herbert had fallen into another stupor, but this time the sleep appeared more natural.

"Tell me again that you have hope, Mr. Spilett," said Pencroff; "tell me again that you will save my boy!"

"We shall save him," said the reporter. "The wound is a serious one, and perhaps the ball has touched the lung; but a wound in that organ is not mortal."

"May God grant it!" answered the sailor.

As may be imagined, the care of Herbert had occupied all their time and thoughts for the first twenty-four hours at the corral. They had not considered the urgent danger of a return of the convicts, nor taken any precautions for the future. But on this day while Pencroff was watching over the invalid, Smith and the reporter took counsel together as to their plans.

They first searched the corral. There was no trace of Ayrton, and it seemed probable that he had resisted his former companions, and fallen by their hands. The corral had not been pillaged, and as its gates had remained shut, the domestic animals had not been able to wander away into the woods. They could see no traces of the pirates either in the dwelling or the palisade. The only thing gone was the stock of ammunition.

"The poor fellow was taken by surprise," said Smith, "and as he was a man to show fight, no doubt they made an end of him."

"Yes," replied the reporter, "and then, no doubt, they took possession here, where they found everything in great plenty, and took to flight only when they saw us coming."

"We must beat the woods," said the engineer, and rid the island of these wretches. But we will have to wait some time in the corral, till the day comes when we can safely carry Herbert to Granite House."

"But Neb?" asked the reporter.

"Neb's safe enough."

"Suppose he becomes anxious and risks coming here?"

"He must not come," said Smith sharply. "He would be murdered on the way!"

"It's very likely he will try."

"Ah! if the telegraph was only in working order, we could warn him! But now it's impossible. We can't leave Pencroff and Herbert here alone. Well, I'll go by myself to Granite House!"

"No, no, Cyrus," said the reporter, "you must not expose yourself. These wretches are watching the corral from their ambush, and there would be two mishaps instead of one!"

"But Neb has been without news of us for twenty-four hours," repeated the engineer. "He will want to come."

While he reflected, his gaze fell upon Top, who, by running to and fro, seemed to say, "Have you forgotten me?"

"Top!" cried Smith.

The dog sprang up at this master's call.

"Yes, Top shall go!" cried the reporter, who understood in a flash. Top will make his way where we could not pass, will take our message and bring us back an answer."

"Quick!" said Smith, "quick!"

Spilett tore out a page of his note-book and wrote these lines:—

"Herbert wounded. We are at the corral. Be on your guard. Do not leave Granite House. Have the convicts shown themselves near you? Answer by Top!"

This laconic note was folded and tied in a conspicuous way to Top's collar.

"Top, my dog," said the engineer, caressing the animal, "Neb, Top, Neb! Away! away!"

Top sprang high at the words. He understood what was wanted, and the road was familiar to him. The engineer went to the door of the corral and opened one of the leaves.

"Neb, Top, Neb!" he cried again, pointing towards Granite House.

Top rushed out and disappeared almost instantly.

"He'll get there!" said the reporter.

"Yes, and come back, the faithful brute!"

"What time is it?" asked Spilett.

"Ten o'clock."

"In an hour he may be here. We will watch for him.

The door of the corral was closed again. The engineer and the reporter re-entered the house. Herbert lay in a profound sleep. Pencroff kept his compresses constantly wet with cold water. Spilett, seeing that just then there was nothing else to do, set to work to prepare some food, all the time keeping his eye on that part of the inclosure which backed up against the spur, from which an attack might be made.

The colonists awaited Top's return with much anxiety. A little before 11 o'clock Smith and Spilett stood with their carbines behind the door, ready to open it at the dog's first bark. They knew that if Top got safely to Granite House, Neb would send him back at once.

They had waited about ten minutes, when they heard a loud report, followed instantly by continuous barking. The engineer opened the door, and, seeing smoke still curling up among the trees a hundred paces off, he fired in that direction. Just then Top bounded into the corral, whose door was quickly shut.

"Top, Top!" cried the engineer, caressing the dog's large, noble head. A note was fastened to his collar, containing these words in Neb's sprawling handwriting:—— "No pirates near Granite House. I will not stir. Poor Mr. Herbert!"

CHAPTER L. THE CONVICTS IN THE NEIGHBORHOOD

OF THE CORRAL—PROVISIONAL OCCUPATION—CONTINUATION OF HERBERT'S TREATMENT—PENCROFF'S JUBILATION—REVIEW OF THE PAST—FUTURE PROSPECTS—SMITH'S IDEAS.

So, then, the convicts were close by, watching the corral, and waiting to kill the colonists one after another. They must be attacked like wild beasts, but with the greatest precaution, for the wretches had the advantage of position, seeing and not being seen, able to make a sudden attack, yet not themselves to be surprised.

So Smith made his arrangements to live at the corral, which was fully provisioned. Ayrton's house was furnished with all the necessaries of life, and the convicts, frightened away by the colonists' arrival, had not had time to pillage. It was most likely, as Spilett suggested, that the course of events had been this:—The convicts had followed the southern coast, and after getting over into Serpentine Peninsula, and being in no humor to risk themselves in the woods of the Far West, they had reached the month of Fall River. Then, walking up the right bank of the stream, they had come to the spur of Mount Franklin; here was their most natural place of refuge. And they had soon discovered the corral. They had probably installed themselves there, had been surprised by Ayrton, had overcome the unfortunate man, and—the rest was easily divined!

Meanwhile the convicts, reduced to five, but well armed, were prowling in the woods, and to pursue them was to be exposed to their fire without the power either of avoiding or of anticipating them.

"There is nothing else to do but wait," repeated Smith. "When Herbert is well again, we will beat the island, and have a shot at these rascals; while at the same time——"

"We search for our mysterious protector," added Spilett, finishing the sentence. "Ah! we must confess, dear Cyrus, that, for once, his protection has failed us."

"We don't know about that," answered the engineer.

"What do you mean?" asked the reporter.

"We are not at the end of our troubles, my dear Spilett, and his powerful interference may still be exercised. But now we must think of Herbert."

Several days passed, and the poor boy's condition was happily no worse; and to gain time was a great thing. The cold water, always kept at the proper temperature, had absolutely prevented the inflammation of the wounds. Nay, it seemed to the reporter that this water, which contained a little sulphur, due to the neighborhood of the volcano, had a direct tendency towards cicatrization. The suppuration was much less copious, and, thanks to excellent nursing, Herbert had returned to consciousness, and his fever had abated. He was, moreover, strictly dieted, and, of course, was very weak; but he had plenty of broths and gruels, and absolute rest was doing him great good.

Smith, Spilett, and Pencroff had become very skilful in tending him. All the linen in the house had been sacrificed. The wounded parts, covered with lint and compresses, were subjected to just enough pressure to cicatrize them without bringing on a reaction of inflammation. The reporter dressed the wounds with the greatest care, repeating to his companions the medical axiom that good dressing is as rare as a good operation.

At the end of ten days, by the 22d of November, Herbert was decidedly better. He had begun to take some nourishment. The color came back to his cheeks, and he smiled at his nurse. He talked a little, in spite of Pencroff, who chattered away all the time to keep the boy from saying a word, and told the most remarkable stories. Herbert inquired about Ayrton, and was surprised not to see him at the bedside; but the sailor, who would not distress his patient, answered merely that Ayrton had gone to be with Neb at Granite House in case the convicts attacked it. "Nice fellows they are," said he. "To think that Mr. Smith wanted to appeal to their feelings! I'll send them my compliments in a good heavy bullet!"

"And nobody has seen them?" asked Herbert.

"No, my boy," answered the sailor, "but we will find them, and when you are well we shall see whether these cowards, who strike from behind, will dare to meet us face to face."

"I am still very weak, dear Pencroff."

"Oh! your strength will come back little by little. What's a ball through the chest? Nothing to speak of. I have seen several of them, and feel no worse for it."

In fine, things were growing better, and it no unlucky complication occurred, Herbert's cure might be regarded as certain. But what would have been the colonists' situation if the ball had remained in his body, if his arm or leg had had to be amputated? They could not think of it without a shudder.

It seemed to Smith that he and his companions, until now so fortunate, had entered upon an ill-omened time. For the two and a half years which had elapsed since their escape from Richmond they had succeeded in everything. But now luck seemed to be turning against them. Ayrton, doubtless, was dead, and Herbert severely wounded; and that strange but powerful intervention, which had done them such mighty services, seemed now to be withdrawn. Had the mysterious being abandoned the island, or himself been overcome?

They could give no answer to these questions; but though they talked together about them, they were not men to despair. They looked the situation in the face; they analyzed the chances; they prepared themselves for every contingency; they stood firm and undaunted before the future; and if adversity should continue to oppress them, she would find them men prepared to do their utmost.

CHAPTER LI. NO NEWS OF NEB

A PROPOSAL FROM PENCROFF AND SPILETT—THE REPORTER'S
SORTIES—A FRAGMENT OF CLOTH—A MESSAGE—HURRIED DEPARTURE—
ARRIVAL AT PROSPECT PLATEAU.

Herbert's convalescence progressed steadily. Only one thing was left to wish for, to wit, that he would get well enough to be taken to Granite House. However well-arranged and provisioned might be the dwelling in the corral, there was nothing like the solid comfort of their abode in the rock. Besides, they were not safe here, and, in spite of their watchfulness, they were always in dread of a shot from the woods. Whereas there in the midst of that unassailable and inaccessible mass of rock there would be nothing to fear. They waited, therefore, with impatience for the moment when Herbert could be carried, without danger to his wound, across the difficult route through Jacamar Woods.

Though without news of Neb, they had no fear for him. The brave man, occupying a position of such strength, would not let himself be surprised. Top had not been sent back to him, for it seemed useless to expose the faithful dog to some shot which might deprive the colonists of their most useful helper. The engineer regretted to see his forces divided, and thus to play into the hands of the pirates. Since Ayrton's disappearance, they were only four against five, for Herbert could not be counted. The poor boy knew and lamented the danger of which he was the cause.

One day, November 29, when he was asleep, they discussed their plans of action against the convicts.

"My friends," said the reporter, after they had talked over the impossibility of communicating with Neb, "I agree with you that to risk ourselves on the path leading from the corral would be a useless exposure. But why should we not beat the woods for these wretches?"

"That's what I was thinking," replied Pencroff. "We're not afraid of a bullet, and for my part, if Mr. Smith approves, I am ready to take to the woods. Surely one man is as good as another!"

"But is he as good as five?" asked the engineer.

"I will go with Pencroff,' answered the reporter, "and the two of us, well armed, and Top with us—"

"My dear Spilett, and you, Pencroff, let us discuss the matter coolly. If the convicts were in hiding in some place known to us, from which we could drive them by an attack, it would be a different affair. But have we not every reason to fear that they will get the first shot?"

"Well, sir," cried Pencroff, "a bullet doesn't always hit its mark!"

"That which pierced Herbert did not go astray," answered the engineer. "Besides, remember that if you both leave the corral, I shall be left alone to defend it. Can you answer that the convicts will not see you go off, that they will not wait till you are deep in the woods, and then make their attack in your absence upon a man and a sick boy?"

There was nothing to say in answer to this reasoning, which went home to the minds of all.

"If only Ayrton was yet one of the party!" said Spilett. "Poor fellow! his return to a life with his kind was not for long!"

"If he is dead!" added Pencroff, in a peculiar tone.

"Have you any hope that those rascals have spared him, Pencroff?" asked Spilett.

"Yes, if their interest led them to do so."

"What! do you suppose that Ayrton, among his former companions in guilt, would forget all he owed to us—"

"Nobody can tell," answered the sailor, with some hesitation.

"Pencroff," said Smith, laying his hand on the sailor's arm, "that was an unworthy thought. I will guarantee Ayrton's fidelity!"

"And I too," added the reporter, decidedly.

"Yes, yes, Mr. Smith, I am wrong," answered Pencroff. "But really I am a little out of my mind. This imprisonment in the corral is driving me to distraction."

"Be patient, Pencroff," answered the engineer. "How soon, my dear Spilett, do you suppose Herbert can be carried to Granite House?"

"That is hard to say, Cyrus," answered the reporter, "for a little imprudence might be fatal. But if he goes on as well as he is doing now for another week, why then we will see."

At that season the spring was two months advanced. The weather was good, and the heat began to be oppressive. The woods were in fall leaf, and it was almost time to reap the accustomed harvest. It can easily be understood how this siege in the corral upset the plans of the colonists.

Once or twice the reporter risked himself outside, and walked around the palisade. Top was with him, and his carbine was loaded.

He met no one and saw nothing suspicious. Top would have warned him of any danger, and so long as the dog did not bark, there was nothing to fear.

But on his second sortie, on the 27th of November, Spilett, who had ventured into the woods for a quarter of a mile to the south of the mountain, noticed that Top smelt something. The dog's motions were no longer careless; he ran to and fro, ferreting about in the grass and thistles, as if his keen nose had put him on the track of an enemy.

Spilett followed the dog, encouraging and exciting him by his voice; his eye on the alert, his carbine on his shoulder, and availing himself of the shelter of the trees. It was not likely that Top had recognized the presence of a man, for in that case he would have announced it by a half-stifled but angry bark. Since not even a growl was to be heard, the danger was evidently neither near nor approaching.

About five minutes had passed in this way, Top ferreting about and the reporter cautiously following him, when the dog suddenly rushed towards a thicket and tore from it a strip of cloth. It was a piece from a garment, dirty and torn. Spilett went back with it to the corral. There the colonists examined it and recognized it as a piece of Ayrton's waistcoat, which was made of the felt prepared only in the workshop at Granite House.

"You see, Pencroff," observed Smith, "Ayrton resisted manfully, and the convicts dragged him off in spite of his efforts. Do you still doubt his good faith?"

"No, Mr. Smith," replied the sailor; "I have long ago given up that momentary suspicion. But I think we may draw one conclusion from this fact."

"What is that?"

"That Ayrton was not killed at the corral. They must have dragged him out alive, and perhaps he is still alive."

"It may be so," said the engineer, thoughtfully.

The most impatient of them all to get back to Granite House was Herbert. He knew how necessary it was for them all to be there, and felt that it was he who was keeping them at the corral. The one thought which had taken possession of his mind was to leave the corral, and to leave it as soon as possible. He believed that he could bear the journey to Granite House. He was sure that his strength would come back to him sooner in his own room, with the sight and the smell of the sea.

It was now November 29. The colonists were talking together in Herbert's room, about 7 o'clock in the morning, when they heard Top barking loudly. They seized their guns, always loaded and cocked, and went out of the house.

Top ran to the bottom of the palisade, jumping and barking with joy.

"Some one is coming!"

"Yes."

"And not an enemy."

"Neb, perhaps?"

"Or Ayrton?"

These words had scarcely been exchanged between the engineer and his comrade, when something leaped the palisade and fell on the ground inside. It was Jup. Master Jup himself, who was frantically welcomed by Top.

"Neb has sent him!" said the reporter.

"Then he must have some note on him," said the engineer.

Pencroff rushed to the orang. Neb could not have chosen a better messenger, who could get through obstacles which none of the others could have surmounted. Smith was right. Around Jup's neck was hung a little bag, and in it was a note in Neb's handwriting. The dismay of the colonists may be imagined when they read these words:—

"FRIDAY, 6 A. M."—The convicts are on the plateau. NEB."

They looked at each other without saying a word, then walked back to the house. What was there to do? The convicts on Prospect Plateau meant disaster, devastation and ruin! Herbert knew at once from their faces that the situation had become grave, and when he saw Jup, he had no more doubt that misfortune was threatening Granite House.

"Mr. Smith," said he, "I want to go. I can bear the journey. I want to start."

Spilett came up to Herbert and looked at him intently.

"Let us start then," said he.

The question of Herbert's transportation was quickly decided. A litter would be the most comfortable way of travelling, but it would necessitate two porters; that is, two guns would be subtracted from their means of defense. On the other hand, by placing the mattresses on which Herbert lay in the wagon, so as to deaden the motion, and by walking carefully they could escape jolting him, and would leave their arms free.

The wagon was brought out and the onagga harnessed to it; Smith and the reporter lifted the mattresses with Herbert on them, and laid them in the bottom of the wagon between the rails. The weather was fine, and the sun shone brightly between the trees.

"Are the arms ready?" asked Smith.

They were. The engineer and Pencroff, each armed with a double-barrelled gun, and Spilett with his carbine, stood ready to set out.

"How do you feel, Herbert?" asked the engineer.

"Don't be troubled, Mr. Smith," answered the boy, "I shall not die on the way."

They could see that the poor fellow was making a tremendous effort. The engineer felt a grievous pang. He hesitated to give the signal for departure. But to stay would have thrown Herbert into despair.

"Let us start," said Smith.

The corral door was opened. Jup and Top, who knew how to be quiet on emergency, rushed on ahead. The wagon went out, the gate was shut, and the onagga, under Pencroff's guidance, walked on with a slow pace.

It was necessary, on account of the wagon, to keep to the direct road from the corral to Granite House, although it was known to the convicts. Smith and Spilett walked on either side of the chariot, ready to meet any attack. Still it was not likely that the convicts had yet abandoned Prospect Plateau. Neb's note had evidently been sent as soon as they made their appearance. Now this note was dated at 6 o'clock in the morning, and the active orang, who was accustomed to the way, would have got over the five miles from Granite House in three-quarters of an hour. Probably they would have no danger to fear till they approached Granite House.

But they kept on the alert. Top and Jup, the latter armed with his stick, sometimes in front, and sometimes beating the woods on either side, gave no signal of approaching danger. The wagon moved on slowly, and an hour after leaving the corral, they had passed over four of the five miles without any incident.

They drew near the plateau another mile, and they saw the causeway over Glycerine Creek. At last, through an opening in the wood, they saw the horizon of the sea. But the wagon went on slowly, and none of its defenders could leave it for a moment. Just then Pencroff stopped the wagon and cried, fiercely,

"Ah, the wretches!"

And he pointed to a thick smoke which curled up from the mill, the stables, and the buildings of the poultry-yard. In the midst of this smoke a man was running about. It was Neb. His companions uttered a cry. He heard them and rushed to meet them. The convicts had abandoned the plateau half an hour before, after having done all the mischief they could.

"And Mr. Herbert?" cried Neb.

Spilett went back to the wagon. Herbert had fainted.

CHAPTER LII. HERBERT CARRIED TO GRANITE HOUSE

—NEB RELATES WHAT HAD HAPPENED—VISIT OF SMITH TO THE PLATEAU—RUIN AND DEVASTATION—THE COLONISTS HELPLESS—WILLOW BARK—A MORTAL FEVER—TOP BARKS AGAIN.

The convicts, the dangers threatening Granite House, the ruin on the plateau, none of these were thought of, in the present condition of Herbert. It was impossible to say whether the transportation had occasioned some internal rupture, but his companions were almost hopeless.

The wagon had been taken to the bend of the river, and there the mattress, on which lay the unconscious lad, was placed on a litter of branches, and within a few minutes Herbert was lying on his bed in Granite House. He smiled for a moment on finding himself again in his chamber, and a few words escaped feebly from his lips. Spilett looked at his wounds, fearing that they might have opened, but the cicatrices were unbroken. What, then, was the cause of this prostration, or why had his condition grown worse?

Soon the lad fell into a feverish sleep, and the reporter and Pencroff watched beside him.

Meantime, Smith told Neb of all that had happened at the corral, and Neb told his master of what had passed at the plateau.

It was not until the previous night that the convicts had shown themselves beyond the edge of the forest, near Glycerine Creek. Neb, keeping watch near the poultry-yard, had not hesitated to fire at one of them who was crossing the bridge; but he could not say with what result. At least, it did not disperse the band, and Neb had but just time to climb up into Granite House, where he, at least, would be safe.

But what was the next thing to do? How prevent the threatened devastation to the plateau? How could he inform his master? And, moreover, in what situation were the occupants of the corral?

Smith and his companions had gone away on the 11th inst., and here it was the 29th. In that time all the information that Neb had received was the disastrous news brought by Top. Ayrton gone, Herbert badly wounded, the engineer, the reporter, and the sailor imprisoned in the corral.

The poor black man asked himself what was to be done. Personally, he had nothing to fear, as the convicts could not get into Granite House. But the works, the fields, all the improvements, were at the mercy of the pirates. Was it not best to let Smith know of the threatened danger?

Then Neb thought of employing Jup on this errand. He knew the intelligence of the orang. Jup knew the word "corral." It was not yet daylight. The agile brute could slip through the woods unperceived. So the black man wrote a note, which he fastened round Jup's neck, and taking the monkey to the door and unrolling a long cord, he repeated the words:—

"Jup! Jup! To the corral! the corral!"

The animal understood him, and, seizing the cord, slid down to the ground, and disappeared in the darkness.

"You did well, Neb, although In not forewarning us perhaps you would have done better!" said Smith, thinking of Herbert, and how the carrying him back had been attended with such serious results.

Neb finished his recital. The convicts had not shown themselves upon the beach, doubtless fearing the inhabitants of Granite House, whose number they did not know. But the plateau was open and unprotected by Granite House. Here, therefore, they gave loose reins to their instinct of depredation and destruction, and they had left but half-an-hour before the colonists returned.

Neb had rushed from his retreat, and at the risk of being shot, he had climbed to the plateau and had tried to put out the fire which was destroying the inclosure to the poultry-yard. Ho was engaged in this work when the others returned.

Thus the presence of the convicts was a constant menace to the colonists, heretofore so happy, and they might expect the most disastrous results from them.

Smith, accompanied by Neb, went to see for himself, the extent of the injury done. He walked along by the Mercy and up the left bank without seeing any trace of the convicts. It was likely that the latter had either witnessed the return of the colonists, and had gone back to the corral, now undefended, or that they had gone back to their camp to await an occasion to renew the attack.

At present, however, all attempts to rid the island of these pests were subject to the condition of Herbert.

The engineer and Neb reached the place. It was a scene of desolation. Fields trampled; the harvest scattered; the stables and other buildings burned; the frightened animals roaming at large over the plateau. The fowls, which had sought refuge on the lake, were returning to their accustomed place on its banks. Everything here would have to be done over again.

The succeeding days were the saddest which the colonists had passed on the island. Herbert became more and more feeble. He was in a sort of stupor, and symptoms of delirium began to manifest themselves. Cooling draughts were all the remedies at the disposition of the colonists. Meantime, the fever became intermittent, and it was necessary to check, it before it developed greater strength.

"To do this," said Spilett, "we must have a febrifuge."

"And we have neither cinchonia nor quinine," answered the engineer.

"No, but we can make a substitute from the bark of the willow trees at the lake."

"Let us try it immediately," replied Smith.

Indeed, willow bark has been partly considered succedaneous to cinchonia, but since they had no means of extracting the salicin, the bark must be used in its natural state. Smith, therefore, cut some pieces of bark from a species of black willow, and, reducing them to powder, this powder was given to Herbert the same evening. The night passed without incident. Herbert was somewhat delirious, but the fever did not manifest itself. Pencroff became more hopeful, but Spilett, who knew that the fever was intermittent, looked forward to the next day with anxiety. They noticed that during the apyrexy, Herbert seemed completely prostrated, his head heavy, and subject to dizziness. Another alarming symptom was a congestion of the liver, and soon a more marked delirium manifested itself.

Spilett was overwhelmed by this new complication. He drew the engineer aside and said to him:—"It is a pernicious fever!"

"A pernicious fever!" cried Smith. "You must be mistaken, Spilett. A pernicious fever never declares itself spontaneously; it must have a germ."

"I am not mistaken," replied the reporter. "Herbert may have caught the germ in the marshes. He has already had one attack; if another follows, and we cannot prevent a third—he is lost!"

"But the willow bark?——"

"Is insufficient. And a third attack of pernicious fever, when one cannot break it by means of quinine, is always mortal!"

Happily Pencroff had not heard this conversation. It would have driven him wild.

Towards noon of the 7th, the second attack manifested itself. The crisis was terrible. Herbert felt that he was lost! He stretched out his arms towards Smith, towards Spilett, towards Pencroff! He did not want to die! The scene was heartrending, and it became necessary to take Pencroff away.

The attack lasted five hours. It was plain that the lad could not support a third. The night was full of torture. In his delirium, Herbert wrestled with the convicts; he called Ayrton; he supplicated that mysterious being, that protector, who had disappeared but whose image haunted him—then he fell into a profound prostration, and Spilett, more than once, thought the poor boy was dead!

The next day passed with only a continuation of the lad's feebleness. His emaciated hands clutched the bed clothing. They continued giving him doses of the willow powder, but the reporter anticipated no result from it.

"If," said he, "before to-morrow morning we cannot give him a more powerful febrifuge than this, Herbert will die!"

The night came—doubtless the last night for this brave lad, so good, so clever, whom all loved as their own child! The sole remedy against this pernicious fever, the sole specific which could vanquish it, was not to be found on Lincoln Island!

During the night Herbert became frightfully delirious. He recognized no one. It was not even probable that he would live till morning. His strength was exhausted. Towards 3 o'clock he uttered a frightful cry. He was seized by a terrible convulsion. Neb, who was beside him, rushed, frightened, into the adjoining chamber, where his companions were watching.

At the same moment Top gave one of his strange barks.

All returned to the chamber and gathered round the dying lad, who struggled to throw himself from the bed. Spilett, who held his arms, felt his pulse slowly rising.

Five o'clock came. The sun's rays shone into the chambers of Granite House. A beautiful day, the last on earth for poor Herbert, dawned over Lincoln Island.

A sunbeam crept on to the table beside the bed.

Suddenly Pencroff, uttering an exclamation, pointed to something on that table. It was a small oblong box, bearing these words:—*Sulphate of quinine.*

CHAPTER LIII. AN INEXPLICABLE MYSTERY

HERBERT'S CONVALESCENCE—THE UNEXPLORED PARTS OF THE ISLAND—PREPARATIONS FOR DEPARTURE—THE FIRST DAY—NIGHT— SECOND DAY—THE KAURIS—CASSOWARIES—FOOTPRINTS IN THE SAND— ARRIVAL AT REPTILE END.

Spilett took the box and opened it. It contained a white powder, which he tasted. Its extreme bitterness was unmistakable. It was indeed that precious alkaloid, the true anti-periodic.

It was necessary to administer it to Herbert without delay. How it came there could be discussed later.

Spilett called for some coffee, and Neb brought a lukewarm infusion, in which the reporter placed eighteen grains of quinine and gave the mixture to Herbert to drink.

There was still time, as the third attack of the fever had not yet manifested itself. And, indeed, it did not return. Moreover, every one became hopeful. The mysterious influence was again about them, and that too in a moment when they had despaired of its aid.

After a few hours, Herbert rested more quietly, and the colonists could talk of the incident. The intervention of this unknown being was more evident than ever, but how had he succeeded in getting in to Granite House during the night? It was perfectly inexplicable, and, indeed, the movements of this "genius of the island" were as mysterious as the genius himself.

The quinine was administered to Herbert every three hours, and the next day the lad was certainly better. It is true he was not out of danger, since these fevers are often followed by dangerous relapses; but, then, here was the specific, and, doubtless, not far off, the one who had brought it. In two days more Herbert became convalescent. He was still feeble, but there had been no relapse, and he cheerfully submitted to the rigorous diet imposed upon, him. He was so anxious to get well.

Pencroff was beside himself with joy. After the critical period had been safely passed he seized the reporter in his arms, and called him nothing but Doctor Spilett. But the true physician was still to be found.

"We will find him!" said the sailor.

The year 1867, during which the colonists had been so hardly beset, came to an end, and the new year began with superb weather. A fine warmth, a tropical temperature, moderated by the sea breeze. Herbert's bed was drawn close to the window, where he could inhale long draughts of the salt, salubrious air. His appetite began to return, and what tempting savory morsels Neb prepared for him!

"It made one wish to be ill," said Pencroff.

During this time the convicts had not shown themselves, neither was there any news of Ayrton. The engineer and Herbert still hoped to get him back, but the others thought that the unhappy man had succumbed. In a month's time, when the lad should have regained his strength, the important search would be undertaken, and all these questions set at rest.

During January the work on the plateau consisted simply in collecting the grain and vegetables undestroyed in the work of devastation, and planting some for a late crop during the next season. Smith preferred to wait till the island was rid of the convicts before he repaired the damage to the mill, poultry-yard, and stable.

In the latter part of the month Herbert began to take some exercise. He was eighteen years old, his constitution was splendid, and from this moment the improvement in his condition was visible daily.

By the end of the month he walked on the shore and over the plateau, and strengthened himself with sea-baths. Smith felt that the day for the exploration could be set, and the 15th of February was chosen. The nights at this season were very clear, and would, therefore, be advantageous to the search.

The necessary preparations were begun. These were important, as the colonists had determined not to return to Granite House until their double end had been obtained—to destroy the convicts and find Ayrton, if he was still alive; and to discover the being who presided so efficiently over the destinies of the colony.

The colonists were familiar with all the eastern coast of the island between Claw Cape and the Mandibles; with Tadorn's Fens; the neighborhood of Lake Grant; the portion of Jacamar Wood lying between the road to the corral and the Mercy; the courses of the Mercy and Red Creek, and those spurs of Mount Franklin where the corral was located.

They had partially explored the long sweep of Washington Bay from Claw Cape to Reptile End; the wooded and marshy shore of the west coast, and the interminable downs which extended to the half-open mouth of Shark Gulf.

But they were unacquainted with the vast woods of Serpentine Peninsula; all the right bank of the Mercy; the left bank of Fall River, and the confused mass of ravines and ridges which covered three-fourths of the base of Mount Franklin on the west, north, and east, and where, doubtless, there existed deep recesses. Therefore, many thousands of acres had not yet been explored.

It was decided that the expedition should cross the Forest of the Far West, in such a manner as to go over all that part situated on the right of the Mercy. Perhaps it would have been better to have gone at once to the corral, where it was probable the convicts had either pillaged the place or installed themselves there. But either the pillage was a work accomplished or the convicts had purposed to entrench themselves there, and it would always be time to dislodge them.

So the first plan was decided upon, and it was resolved to cut a road through these woods, placing Granite House in communication with the end of the peninsula, a distance of sixteen or seventeen miles.

The wagon was in perfect order. The onagers, well rested, were in excellent condition for a long pull. Victuals, camp utensils, and the portable stove, were loaded into the wagon, together with a careful selection of arms and ammunition.

No one was left in Granite House; even Top and Jup took part in the expedition. The inaccessible dwelling could take care of itself.

Sunday, the day before the departure, was observed as a day of rest and prayer, and on the morning of the 15th Smith took the measures necessary to defend Granite House from invasion. The ladders were carried to the Chimneys and buried there, the basket of the elevator was removed, and nothing left of the apparatus. Pencroff, who remained behind in Granite House, saw to this latter, and then slid down to the ground by means of a double cord which, dropped to the ground, severed the last connection between the entrance and the shore.

The weather was superb.

"It is going to be a warm day," said the reporter, joyfully.

"But, Doctor Spilett," said Pencroff, "our road is under the trees, and we will never see the sun!"

"Forward!" said the engineer.

The wagon was ready on the bank. The reporter insisted on Herbert taking a seat in it, at least for the first few hours. Neb walked by the onagers. Smith, the reporter, and the sailor went on ahead. Top bounded off into the grass; Jup took a seat beside Herbert, and the little party started.

The wagon went up the left bank of the Mercy, across the bridge, and there, leaving the route to Balloon Harbor to the left, the explorers began to make a way through the forest.

For the first two miles, the trees grew sufficiently apart to permit the wagon to proceed easily, without any other obstacle than here and there a stump or some bushes to arrest their progress. The thick foliage made a cool shadow over the ground. Birds and beasts were plenty, and reminded the colonists of their early excursions on the island.

"Nevertheless," remarked Smith, "I notice that the animals are more timid than formerly. These woods have been recently traversed by the convicts, and we shall certainly find their traces."

And, indeed, in many places, they saw where a party of men had passed, or built a fire, but in no one place was there a definite camp.

The engineer had charged his companions to abstain from hunting, so as not to make the convicts aware of their presence by the sound of firearms.

In the afternoon, some six miles from Granite House, the advance became very difficult, and they had to pass certain thickets, into which Top and Jup were sent as skirmishers.

The halt for the night was made, nine miles from Granite House, on the bank of a small affluent to the Mercy, of whose existence they had been unaware. They had good appetites, and all made a hearty supper, after which the camp was carefully organized, in order to guard against a surprise from the convicts. Two of the colonists kept guard together in watches of two hours, but Herbert, in spite of his wishes, was not allowed to do duty.

The night passed without incident. The silence was unbroken save by the growling of jaguars and the chattering of monkeys, which seemed particularly to annoy Jup.

The next day, they were unable to accomplish more than six miles. Like true "frontiersmen," the colonists avoided the large trees and cut down only the smaller ones, so that their road was a winding one.

During the day Herbert discovered some specimens of the tree ferns, with vase-shaped leaves, and the algarobabeau (St. John's bread), which the onagers eat greedily. Splendid kauris, disposed in groups, rose to a height of two hundred feet, their cylindrical trunks surmounted by a crown of verdure.

As to fauna, they discovered no new specimens, but they saw, without being able to approach them, a couple of large birds, such as are common in Australia, a sort of cassowary, called emus, which were five feet high, of brown plumage, and belonged to the order of runners. Top tried his best to catch them, but they outran him easily, so great was their speed.

The colonists again found traces of the convicts. Near a recently-extinguished fire they found footprints, which they examined with great attention. By measuring these tracks they were able to determine the presence of five men. The five convicts had evidently camped here; but—and they made minute search—they could not discover a sixth track, which would have been that of Ayrton.

"Ayrton is not with them!" said Herbert.

"No," replied Pencroff, "the wretches have shot him." But they must have a den, to which we can track them."

"No," replied the reporter. "It is more likely that they intend to camp about in places, after this manner, until they become masters of the island."

"Masters of the island!" cried the sailor. "Masters of the island, indeed" he repeated in a horrified voice. Then he added:— "The ball in my gun is the one which wounded Herbert and it will do its errand!"

But this just reprisal would not restore Ayrton to life, and the only conclusion to be drawn, from the footprints was that they would never see him again!

That evening the camp was made fourteen miles front Granite House, and Smith estimated that it was still five miles to Reptile End.

The next day this point was reached, and the full length of the forest had been traversed; but nothing indicated the retreat of the convicts, nor the asylum of the mysterious unknown.

CHAPTER LIV. EXPLORATION OF REPTILE END

CAMP AT THE MOUTH OF FALL RIVER—BY THE CORRAL—THE RECONNOISSANCE—THE RETURN—FORWARD—AN OPEN DOOR—A LIGHT IN THE WINDOW—BY MOONLIGHT.

The next day, the 18th, was devoted to an exploration of the wooded shore lying between Reptile End and Fall River. The colonists were searching through the heart of the forest, whose width, bounded by the shores of the promontory, was from three to four miles. The trees, by their size and foliage, bore witness to the richness of the soil, more productive here than in any other portion of the island. It seemed as if a portion of the virgin forests of America or Central Africa had been transported here. It seemed, also, as if these superb trees found beneath the soil, moist on its surface, but heated below by volcanic fires, a warmth not belonging to a temperate climate. The principal trees, both in number and size, were the kauris and eucalypti.

But the object of the colonists was not to admire these magnificent vegetables. They knew already that, in this respect, their island merited a first place in the Canaries, called, formerly, the Fortunate Isles. But, alas! their island no longer belonged to them alone; others had taken possession, wretches whom it was necessary to destroy to the last man.

On the west coast they found no further traces of any kind.

"This does not astonish me," said Smith. "The convicts landed near Jetsam Point, and, after having crossed Tadorn's Fens, they buried themselves in the forests of the Far West. They took nearly the same route which we have followed. That explains the traces we have seen in the woods. Arrived upon the shore, the convicts saw very clearly that it offered no convenient shelter, and it was then, on going towards the north, that they discovered the corral—"

"Where they may have returned," said Pencroff.

"I do not think so," answered the engineer, "as they would judge that our searches would be in that direction. The corral is only a provisional and not a permanent retreat for them."

"I think so, too," said the reporter, "and, further, that they have sought a hiding place among the spurs of Mount Franklin."

"Then let us push on to the corral!" cried Pencroff. "An end must be put to this thing, and we are only losing time here."

"No, my friend," replied the engineer.

"You forget that we are interested in determining whether the forests of the Far West do not shelter some habitation. Our exploration has a double end, Pencroff; to punish crime and to make a discovery."

"That is all very well, sir," replied the sailor, "but I have an idea that we will not discover our friend unless he chooses!"

Pencroff had expressed the opinion of the others as well as his own. It was, indeed, probable that the retreat of the unknown being was no less mysterious than his personality.

This evening the wagon halted at the mouth of Fall River. The encampment was made in the usual way, with the customary precautions. Herbert had recovered his former strength by this march in the fresh salt air, and his place was no longer on the wagon, but at the head of the line.

On the 19th, the colonists left the shore and followed up the left bank of Fall River. The route was already partially cleared, owing to the previous excursions made from the corral to the west coast. They reached a place six miles from Mount Franklin.

The engineer's project was to observe with great care all the valley through which flowed the river, and to work cautiously up to the corral. If they should find it occupied, they were to secure it by main force, but if it should be empty, it was to be used as the point from which the explorations of Mount Franklin would be made.

The road was through a narrow valley, separating two of the most prominent spurs of Mount Franklin. The trees grew closely together on the banks of the river, but were more scattered on the upper slopes. The ground was very much broken, affording excellent opportunities for an ambush, so that it was necessary to advance with great caution. Top and Jup went ahead, exploring the thickets on either hand, but nothing indicated either the presence or nearness of the convicts, or that these banks had been recently visited.

About 5 o'clock the wagon halted 600 paces from the enclosure, hidden by a curtain of tall trees.

It was necessary to reconnoitre the place, in order to find out whether it was occupied, but to do this in the day-time was to run the risk of being shot;

nevertheless Spilett wanted to make the experiment at once, and Pencroff, out of all patience, wanted to go with him. But Smith would not permit it.

"No, my friends," said he, "wait until nightfall. I will not allow one of you to expose yourselves in the daylight."

"But, sir,"—urged the sailor, but little disposed to obey.

"Pray do not go, Pencroff," said the engineer.

"All right," said the sailor. But he gave vent to his anger by calling the convicts everything bad that he could think of.

The colonists remained about the wagon, keeping a sharp lookout in the adjoining parts of the forest.

Three hours passed in this manner. The wind fell, and absolute silence reigned over everything. The slightest sound—the snapping of a twig, a step on the dry leaves—could easily have been heard. But all was quiet. Top rested with his head between his paws, giving no sign of inquietude.

By 8 o'clock the evening was far enough advanced for the reconnoissance to be undertaken, and Spilett and Pencroff set off alone. Top and Jup remained behind with the others, as it was necessary that no bark or cry should give the alarm.

"Do not do anything imprudently," urged Smith. "Remember, you are not to take possession of the corral, but only to find out whether it is occupied or not."

"All right," answered Pencroff.

The two set out, advancing with the greatest caution. Under the trees, the darkness was such as to render objects, thirty or forty paces distant, invisible. Five minutes after having left the wagon they reached the edge of the opening, at the end of which rose the fence of the enclosure. Here they halted. Some little light still illuminated the glade. Thirty paces distant was the gate of the corral, which seemed to be closed. These thirty paces which it was necessary to cross constituted, to use a ballistic expression, the dangerous zone, as a shot from the palisade would certainly have killed any one venturing himself within this space,

Spilett and the sailor were not men to shirk danger, but they knew that any imprudence of theirs would injure their companions as well as themselves. If they were killed what would become of the others?

Nevertheless, Pencroff was so excited in finding himself again close to the corral that he would have hurried forward had not the strong hand of Spilett detained him. "In a few minutes it will be dark," whispered the reporter.

Pencroff grasped his gun nervously, and waited unwillingly.

Very soon the last rays of light disappeared. Mount Franklin loomed darkly against the western sky, and the night fell with the rapidity peculiar to these low latitudes. Now was the time.

The reporter and Pencroff, ever since their arrival on the edge of the wood, had watched the corral. It seemed to be completely deserted. The upper edge of the palisade was in somewhat stronger relief than the surrounding shades, and nothing broke its outlines. Nevertheless, if the convicts were there, they must have posted one of their number as a guard.

Spilett took the hand of his companion, and crept cautiously forward to the gate of the corral. Pencroff tried to push it open, but it was, as they had supposed, fastened. But the sailor discovered that the outer bars were not in place. They, therefore, concluded that the convicts were within, and had fastened the gate so that it could only be broken open.

They listened. No sound broke the silence. The animals were doubtless sleeping in their sheds. Should they scale the fence? It was contrary to Smith's instructions. They might be successful or they might fail. And, if there was now a chance of surprising the convicts, should they risk that chance in this way?

The reporter thought not. He decided that it would be better to wait until they were all together before making the attempt. Two things were certain, that they could reach the fence unseen, and that the place seemed unguarded.

Pencroff, probably, agreed to this, for he returned with the reporter to the wood, and a few minutes later Smith was informed of the situation.

"Well," said he after reflecting for a moment, "I don't think that the convicts are here."

"We will find out when we have climbed in." cried Pencroff.

"To the corral, my friends."

"Shall we leave the wagon in the wood?" cried Neb.

"No," said Smith, "it may serve as a defense in case of need."

The wagon issued from the wood and rolled noiselessly over the ground. The darkness and the silence were profound. The colonists kept their guns in readiness to fire. Jup kept behind, at Pencroff's order, and Neb held Top.

Soon the dangerous zone was crossed, and the wagon was drawn up beside the fence. Neb stood at the head of the onagers to keep them quiet, and the others went to the gate to determine if it was barricaded on the inside.

One of its doors was open!

"What did you tell us?" exclaimed the engineer, turning to the sailor and Spilett.

They were stupefied with amazement.

"Upon my soul," cried the sailor, "It was shut a minute ago!"

The colonists hesitated. The convicts must have been in the corral when Pencroff and the reporter had made their reconnoissance; for the gate could only have been opened by them. Were they still there?

At this moment, Herbert, who had ventured some steps within the inclosure, rushed back and seized Smith's hand.

"What have you seen?" asked the engineer.

"A light!"

"In the house?"

"Yes, sir."

All went forward and saw a feeble ray of light trembling through the windows of the building. Smith determined what to do at once.

"It is a fortunate chance, finding the convicts shut up in this house not expecting anything! They are ours! Come on!"

The wagon was left under charge of Top and Jup, and the colonists glided into the enclosure. In a few moments they were before the closed door of the house.

Smith, making a sign to his companions not to move, approached the window. He looked into the one room which formed the lower story of the building. On the table was a lighted lantern, Near by was Ayrton's bed. On it was the body of a man.

Suddenly, Smith uttered a stiffled exclamation.

"Ayrton!" he cried.

And, at once, the door was rather forced than opened, and all rushed into the chamber.

Ayrton seemed to be sleeping. His face showed marks of long and cruel suffering. His wrists and ankles were much bruised. Smith leaned over him.

"Ayrton!" cried the engineer, seizing in his arms this man found so unexpectedly.

Ayrton opened his eyes, and looked first at Smith, then at the others.

"You! Is it you?" he cried.

"Ayrton! Ayrton!" repeated the engineer.

"Where am I?"

"In the corral."

"Am I alone?"

"Yes."

"Then they will come here!" cried Ayrton. "Look out for yourselves! Defend yourselves!" and he fell back, fainting.

"Spilett," said the engineer, "We may be attacked at any minute. Bring the wagon inside the enclosure, and bar the gate, and then come back here."

Pencroff, Neb, and the reporter hastened to execute the orders of the engineer. There was not an instant to be lost. Perhaps the wagon was already in the hands of the convicts!

In a moment the reporter and his companions had gained the gate of the enclosure, behind which they heard Top growling.

The engineer, leaving Ayrton for a moment, left the house, and held his gun in readiness to fire. Herbert was beside him. Both scrutinized the outline of the mountain spur overlooking the corral. If the convicts were hidden in that place they could pick off the colonists one after the other.

Just then the moon appeared in the east above the black curtain of the forest, throwing a flood of light over the interior of the corral, and bringing into relief the trees, the little water-course, and the grassy carpet. Towards the mountain, the house and a part of the palisade shone white; opposite it, towards the gate, the fence was in shadow.

A black mass soon showed itself. It was the wagon entering within the circle of light, and Smith could hear the sound of the gate closing and being solidly barricaded by his companions.

But at that moment Top, by a violent effort, broke his fastening, and, barking furiously, rushed to the extremity of the corral to the right of the house.

"Look out, my friends, be ready!" cried Smith.

The colonists waited, with their guns at the shoulder. Top continued to bark, and Jup, running towards the dog, uttered sharp cries.

The colonists, following him, came to the border of the little brook, overshadowed by large trees.

And there, in the full moonlight, what did they see?

Five corpses lay extended upon the bank!

They were the bodies of the convicts, who, four months before, had landed upon Lincoln Island.

CHAPTER LV. AYRTON'S RECITAL

PLANS OF HIS OLD COMRADES—TAKING POSSESSION OF THE CORRAL— THE RULES OF THE ISLAND—THE GOOD LUCK—RESEARCHES ABOUT MOUNT FRANKLIN—THE UPPER VALLEYS —SUBTERRANEAN RUMBLINGS— PENCROFF'S ANSWER—AT THE BOTTOM OF THE CRATER-THE RETURN

How had it happened? Who had killed the convicts? Ayrton? No, since the moment before he had feared their return!

But Ayrton was now in a slumber from which it was impossible to arouse him. After he had spoken these few words, he had fallen back upon his bed, seized by a sudden torpor.

The colonists, terribly excited, preyed upon by a thousand confused thoughts, remained all night in the house. The next morning Ayrton awoke from his sleep, and his companions demonstrated to him their joy at finding him safe and sound after all these months of separation.

Then Ayrton related in a few words all that had happened.

The day after his return to the corral, the 10th of November, just at nightfall, he had been surprised by the convicts, who had climbed over the fence. He was tied and gagged and taken to a dark cavern at the foot of Mount Franklin, where the convicts had a retreat.

His death had been resolved upon, and he was to be killed the following day, when one of the convicts recognized him and called him by the name he had borne in Australia. These wretches, who would have massacred Ayrton, respected Ben Joyce.

From this moment Ayrton was subjected to the importunities of his old comrades. They wished to gain him over to them, and they counted upon him to take Granite House, to enter that inaccessible dwelling, and to become masters of the island, after having killed the colonists.

Ayrton resisted. The former convict, repentant and pardoned, would rather die than betray his companions. For four months, fastened, gagged, watched, he had remained in this cavern. Meanwhile the convicts lived upon the stock in the corral, but did not inhabit the place.

On the 11th of November, two of these bandits, inopportunely surprised by the arrival of the colonists, fired on Herbert, and one of them returned boasting of having killed one of the inhabitants. His companion, as we know, had fallen at Smith's hand.

One can judge of Ayrton's despair, when he heard of Herbert's death! It left but four of the colonists, almost at the mercy of the convicts!

Following this event, and during all the time that the colonists, detained by Herbert's illness, remained at the corral, the pirates did not leave their cave; indeed, after having pillaged Prospect Plateau, they did not deem it prudent to leave it.

The bad treatment of Ayrton was redoubled. His hands and feet still bore the red marks of the lines with which he remained bound, day and night. Each moment he expected to be killed.

This was the third week in February. The convicts, awaiting a favorable opportunity, rarely left their retreat, and then only to a point in the interior or on the west coast. Ayrton had no news of his friends, and no hopes of seeing them again.

Finally, the poor unfortunate, enfeebled by bad treatment, fell in a profound prostration in which he neither saw nor heard anything. From this moment, he could not say what had happened.

"But, Mr. Smith," he added, "since I was imprisoned in this cavern, how is it that I am here?"

"How is that the convicts are lying there, dead, in the middle of the corral?" answered the engineer.

"Dead!" cried Ayrton, half rising, notwithstanding his feebleness. His companions assisted him to get up, and all went to the little brook.

It was broad daylight. There on the shore, in the position in which they had met their deaths, lay the five convicts.

Ayrton was astounded. The others looked on without speaking. Then, at a sign from Smith, Neb and Pencroff examined the bodies. Not a wound was visible upon them. Only after minute search, Pencroff perceived on the forehead of one, on the breast of another, on this one's back, and on the shoulder of a fourth, a small red mark, a hardly visible bruise, made by some unknown instrument.

"There is where they have been hit!" said Smith.

"But with what sort of a weapon?" cried the reporter.

"A destructive weapon enough, though unknown to us!"

"And who has destroyed them?" asked Pencroff.

"The ruler of the island," answered Smith, "he who has brought you here, Ayrton, whose influence is again manifesting itself, who does for us what we are unable to do for ourselves, and who then hides from us."

"Let us search for him!" cried Pencroff.

"Yes, we will search," replied Smith; "but the being who accomplishes such prodigies will not be found until it pleases him to call us to him!"

This invisible protection, which nullified their own actions, both annoyed and affected the engineer. The relative inferiority in which it placed him wounded his pride. A generosity which so studiously eluded all mark of recognition denoted a sort of disdain for those benefited, which, in a measure, detracted from the value of the gift.

"Let us search," he repeated, "and Heaven grant that some day we be permitted to prove to this haughty protector that he is not dealing with ingrates! What would I not give to be able, in our turn, to repay him, and to render him, even at the risk of our lives, some signal service!"

From this time, this search was the single endeavor of the inhabitants of Lincoln Island. All tried to discover the answer to this enigma, an answer which involved the name of a man endowed with an inexplicable, an almost superhuman power.

In a short time, the colonists entered the house again, and their efforts soon restored Ayrton to himself. Neb and Pencroff carried away the bodies of the convicts and buried them in the wood. Then, Ayrton was informed by the engineer of all that had happened during his imprisonment.

"And now," said Smith, finishing his recital, "we have one thing more to do. Half of our task is accomplished; but if the convicts are no longer to be feared, we did not restore ourselves to the mastership of the island!"

"Very well," replied Spilett, "let us search all the mazes of Mount Franklin. Let us leave no cavity, no hole unexplored! Ah! if ever a reporter found himself in the presence of an exciting mystery. I am in that position!"

"And we will not return to Granite House," said Herbert, "until we have found our benefactor."

"Yes," said Smith, "we will do everything that is possible for human beings to do—but, I repeat it, we will not find him till he wills it."

"Shall we stay here at the corral?" asked Pencroff.

"Yes," replied the engineer, "let us remain here. Provisions are abundant, and we are in the centre of our circle of investigation, and, moreover, if it is necessary, the wagon can go quickly to Granite House."

"All right," said Pencroff. "Only one thing."

"What is that?"

"Why, the fine weather is here, and we must not forget that we have a voyage to make."

"A voyage?" asked Spilett.

"Yes, to Tabor Island. We most put up a notice, indicating our island, in case the Scotch yacht returns. Who knows that it is not already too late?"

"But, Pencroff," asked Ayrton, "how do you propose to make this voyage?"

"Why, on the Good Luck!"

"The Good Luck!" cried Ayrton. "It's gone!"

"Gone!" shouted Pencroff, springing to his feet.

"Yes. The convicts discovered where the sloop lay, and, a week ago, they put out to sea in her, and—"

"And?" said Pencroff, his heart trembling.

"And, not having Harvey to manage her, they ran her upon the rocks, and she broke all to pieces!"

"Oh! the wretches! the pirates! the devils!" exclaimed the sailor.

"Pencroff," said Herbert, taking his hand, "we will build another, a larger Good Luck. We have all the iron, all the rigging of the brig at our disposal!"

"But, do you realize," answered Pencroff, "that it will take at least five or six months to build a vessel of thirty or forty tons."

"We will take our time," replied the reporter, "and we will give up our voyage to Tabor Island for this year."

"We must make the best of it, Pencroff," said the engineer, "and I hope that this delay will not be prejudicial to us."

"My poor Good Luck! my poor boat!" exclaimed the sailor, half broken-hearted at the loss of what was so dear to him.

The destruction of the sloop was a thing much to be regretted, and it was agreed that this loss must be repaired as soon as the search was ended.

This search was begun the same day, the 19th of February, and lasted throughout the week. The base of the mountain was composed of a perfect labyrinth of ravines and gorges, and it was here that the explorations must be made. No other part of the island was so well suited to hide an inhabitant who wished to remain concealed. But so great was the intricacy of these places that Smith explored them by a settled system.

In the first place, the colonists visited the valley opening to the south of the volcano, in which Fall River rose. Here was where Ayrton showed them the cavern of the convicts. This place was in exactly the same condition as Ayrton had left it. They found here a quantity of food and ammunition left there as a reserve by the convicts.

All this beautiful wooded valley was explored with great care, and then, the south-western spur having been turned, the colonists searched a narrow gorge where the trees were less numerous. Here the stones took the place of grass, and the wild goats and moufflons bounded among the rocks. The arid part of the island began at this part. They saw already that, of the numerous valleys ramifying from the base of Mount Franklin, three only, bounded on the west by Fall River and on the east by Red Creek, were as rich and fertile as the valley of the corral. These two brooks, which developed into rivers as they progressed, received the whole of the mountain's southern water-shed and fertilized that portion of it. As to the Mercy it was more directly fed by abundant springs, hidden in Jacamar Wood.

Now any one of these three valleys would have answered for the retreat of some recluse, who would have found there all the necessaries of life. But the colonists had explored each of them without detecting the presence of man. Was it then at the bottom of these arid gorges, in the midst of heaps of rocks, in the rugged ravines to the north, between the streams of lava, that they would find this retreat and its occupant?

The northern part of Mount Franklin had at its base two large, arid valleys strewn with lava, sown with huge rocks, sprinkled with pieces of obsidian and labradorite. This part required long and difficult exploration. Here were a thousand cavities, not very comfortable, perhaps, but completely hidden and difficult of access. The colonists visited sombre tunnels, made in the plutonic epoch, still blackened by the fires of other days, which plunged into the heart of the mountain. They searched these dark galleries by the light of torches, peering into their least excavations and sounding their lowest depths. But everywhere was silence, obscurity. It did not seem as if any human being had ever trodden these antique corridors or an arm displaced one of these stones.

Nevertheless, if these places were absolutely deserted, if the obscurity was complete, Smith was forced to notice that absolute silence did not reign there.

Having arrived at the bottom of one of those sombre cavities, which extended several hundred feet into the interior of the mountain, he was surprised to hear deep muttering sounds which were intensified by the sonority of the rocks.

Spilett, who was with him, also heard these distant murmurs, which indicated an awakening of the subterranean fires.

Several times they listened, and they came to the conclusion that some chemical reaction was going on in the bowels of the earth.

"The volcano is not entirely extinct," said the reporter.

"It is possible that, since our exploration of the crater, something has happened in its lower regions. All volcanoes, even those which are said to be extinct, can, evidently, become active again."

"But if Mount Franklin is preparing for another eruption, is not Lincoln Island in danger?"

"I don't think so," answered the engineer, "The crater, that is to say, the safety-valve, exists, and the overflow of vapors and lavas will escape, as heretofore, by its accustomed outlet."

"Unless the lavas make a new passage towards the fertile parts of the island."

"Why, my dear Spilett, should they not follow their natural course?"

"Well, volcanoes are capricious."

"Notice," said Smith, "that all the slope of the mountain favors the flow of eruptive matter towards the valleys which we are traversing at present. It would take an earthquake to so change the centre of gravity of the mountain as to modify this slope."

"But an earthquake is always possible under these conditions."

"True," replied the engineer, "especially when the subterranean forces are awakening, and the bowels of the earth, after a long repose, chance to be obstructed. You are right, my dear Spilett, an eruption would be a serious thing for us, and it would be better if this volcano has not the desire to wake up; but we can do nothing. Nevertheless, in any case, I do not think Prospect Plateau could be seriously menaced. Between it and the lake there is quite a depression in the land, and even if the lavas took the road to the lake, they would be distributed over the downs and the parts adjoining Shark Gulf."

"We have not yet seen any smoke from the summit, indicating a near eruption," said Spilett.

"No," answered the engineer, "not the least vapor has escaped from the crater. It was but yesterday that I observed its upper part. But it is possible that rocks, cinders, and hardened lavas have accumulated in the lower part of its chimney, and, for the moment, this safety-valve is overloaded. But, at the first serious effort, all obstacles will disappear, and you may be sure, my dear Spilett, that neither the island, which is the boiler, nor the volcano, which is the valve, will burst under the pressure. Nevertheless, I repeat, it is better to wish for no eruption."

"And yet we are not mistaken," replied the reporter. "We plainly hear ominous rumblings in the depths of the volcano!"

"No," replied the engineer, after listening again with the utmost attention, "that is not to be mistaken. Something is going on there the importance of which cannot be estimated nor what the result will be."

Smith and Spilett, on rejoining their companions, told them of these things.

"All right!" cried Pencroff. "This volcano wants to take care of us! But let it try! It will find its master!"

"Who's that?" asked the black man.

"Our genius, Neb, our good genius, who will put a gag in the mouth of the crater if it attempts to open it."

The confidence of the sailor in the guardian of the island was absolute, and, indeed, the occult power which had so far been manifested seemed limitless; but, thus far this being had escaped all the efforts the colonists had made to discover him.

From the 19th to the 25th of February, the investigations were conducted in the western portion of Lincoln Island, where the most secret recesses were searched. They even sounded each rocky wall, as one knocks against the walls of a suspected house. The engineer went so far as to take the exact measure of the mountain, and he pushed his search to the last strata sustaining it. It was explored to the summit of the truncated cone which rose above the first rocky level, and from there to the upper edge of the enormous cap at the bottom of which opened the crater.

They did more; they visited the gulf, still extinct, but in whose depths the rumblings were distinctly heard. Nevertheless, not a smoke, not a vapor, no heat in the wall, indicated a near eruption. But neither there, nor in any other part of Mount Franklin, did the colonists find the traces of him whom they sought.

Their investigations were then directed over all the tract of downs. They carefully examined the high lava walls of Shark Gulf from base to summit, although it was very difficult to reach the water level. No one! Nothing!

These two words summed up in brief the result of all the useless fatigues Smith and his companions had been at, and they were a trifle annoyed at their ill success.

But it was necessary now to think of returning, as these researches could not be pursued indefinitely. The colonists were convinced that this mysterious being did not reside upon the surface of the island, and strange thoughts floated through their over-excited imaginations; Neb and Pencroff, particularly, went beyond the strange into the region of the supernatural. The 25th of February, the colonists returned to Granite House, and by means of the double cord, shot by an arrow to the door-landing, communication was established with their domain.

One month later, they celebrated the third anniversary of their arrival on Lincoln Island.

CHAPTER LVI. AFTER THREE YEARS

THE QUESTION OF A NEW SHIP—ITS DETERMINATION—PROSPERITY OF THE COLONY—THE SHIPYARD—THE COLD WEATHER—PENCROFF RESIGNED—WASHING—MOUNT FRANKLIN.

Three years had passed since the prisoners had fled from Richmond, and in all that time their conversation and their thoughts had been of the fatherland.

They had no doubt that the war was ended, and that the North had triumphed. But how? At what cost? What friends had fallen in the struggle? They often talked of these things, although they had no knowledge when they would be able to see that country again. To return, if only for a few days; to renew their intercourse with civilization; to establish a communication between their island and the mother country, and then to spend the greater part of their lives in this colony which they had founded and which would then be raised to a metropolis, was this a dream which could not be realized?

There were but two ways of realizing it: either a ship would some day show itself in the neighborhood of Lincoln Island, or the colonists must themselves build a vessel staunch enough to carry them to the nearest land.

"Unless our genius furnishes us with the means of returning home," said Pencroff.

And, indeed, if Neb and Pencroff had been told that a 300-ton ship was waiting for them in Shark Gulf or Balloon Harbor, they would not have manifested any surprise. In their present condition they expected every thing.

But Smith, less confident, urged them to keep to realities, and to build the vessel, whose need was urgent, since a paper should be placed on Tabor Island as soon as possible, in order to indicate the new abode of Ayrton.

The Good Luck was gone. It would take at least six mouths to build another vessel, and, as winter was approaching, the voyage could not be made before the next spring.

"We have time to prepare ourself for the fine weather," said the engineer, talking of these things with Pencroff. "I think, therefore, since we have to build our own ship, it will be better to make her dimensions greater than before. The arrival of the

Scotch yacht is uncertain. It may even have happened that it has come and gone. What do you think? Would it not be better to build a vessel, that, in case of need, could carry us to the archipelagoes or New Zealand?"

"I think, sir, that you are as able to build a large vessel as a small one. Neither wood nor tools are wanting. It is only a question of time."

"And how long would it take to build a ship of 250 or 300 tons?"

"Seven or eight months at least. But we must not forget that winter is at hand, and that the timber will be difficult to work during the severe cold. So, allowing for some weeks' delay, you can be happy if you have your ship by next November."

"Very well, that will be just the season to undertake a voyage of some length, be it to Tabor Island of further."

"All right, Mr. Smith, make your plans. The workmen are ready, and I guess that Ayrton will lend a helping hand."

The engineer's project met the approval of the colonists, and indeed it was the best thing to do. It is true that it was a great undertaking, but they had that confidence in themselves, which is one of the elements of success.

While Smith was busy preparing the plans of the vessel, the others occupied themselves in felling the trees and preparing the timber. The forests of the Far West furnished the best oak and elm, which were carried over the new road through the forest to the Chimneys, where the ship-yard was established.

It was important that the timber should be cut soon, as it was necessary to have it seasoning for some time. Therefore the workmen worked vigorously during April, which was not an inclement month, save for some violent wind storms. Jup helped them by his adroitness, either in climbing to the top of a tree to fasten a rope, or by carrying loads on his strong shoulders.

The timber was piled under a huge shed to await its use; and, meanwhile, the work in the fields was pushed forward, so that soon all traces of the devastation caused by the pirates had disappeared. The mill was rebuilt, and a new inclosure for the poultry yard. This had to be much larger than the former, as the number of its occupants had increased largely. The stables contained five onagas, four of them well broken, and one little colt. A plough had been added to the stock of the colony, and the onagas were employed in tillage as if they were Yorkshire or Kentucky cattle. All the colonists did their share, and there were no idle hands. And thus, with good health and spirits, they formed a thousand projects for the future.

Ayrton, of course, partook of the common existence, and spoke no longer of returning to the corral. Nevertheless, he was always quiet and uncommunicative, and shared more in the work than the pleasure of his companions. He was a strong workman, vigorous, adroit, intelligent, and he could not fail to see that he was esteemed and loved by the others. But the corral was not abandoned. Every other day some one went there and brought back the supply of milk for the colony, and these occasions were also hunting excursions. So that, Herbert and Spilett, with Top in advance, oftenest made the journey, and all kinds of game abounded in the kitchen of Granite House. The products of the warren and the oyster-bed, some turtles, a haul of excellent salmon, the vegetables from the plateau, the natural fruits of the forest, were riches upon riches, and Neb, the chief cook, found it difficult to store them all away. The telegraph had been repaired, and was used whenever one of the party remained over night at the corral. But the island was secure now from any aggression—at least from men.

Nevertheless, what had happened once might happen again, and a descent of pirates was always to be feared. And it was possible that accomplices of Harvey, still in Norfolk, might be privy to his projects and seek to imitate them. Every day the colonists searched the horizon visible from Granite House with the glass, and whenever they were at the corral they examined the west coast. Nothing appeared, but they were always on the alert.

One evening the engineer told his companions of a project to fortify the corral. It seemed prudent to heighten the palisade, and to flank it with a sort of block house, in which the colonists could defend themselves against a host of enemies. Granite House, owing to its position, was impregnable, and the corral would always be the objective point of pirates.

About the 15th of May the keel of the new vessel was laid, and the stem and stern posts raised. This keel was of oak, 110 feet long, and the breadth of beam was 25 feet. But, with the exception of putting up a couple of the frame pieces, this was all that could be done before the bad weather and the cold set in.

During the latter part of the month the weather was very inclement. Pencroff and Ayrton worked as long as they were able, but severely cold weather following the rain made the wood impossible to handle, and by the 10th of June the work was given up entirely, and the colonists were often obliged to keep in-doors. This confinement was hard for all of them, but especially so for Spilett.

"I'll tell you what, Neb," he said, "I will give you everything I own if you will get me a newspaper! All that I want to make me happy is to know what is going on in the world!"

Neb laughed. "Faith!" said he, "I am busy enough with my daily work."

And, indeed, occupation was not wanting. The colony was at the summit of prosperity. The accident to the brig had been a new source of riches. Without counting a complete outfit of sails, which would answer for the new ship, utensils and tools of all sorts, ammunition, clothing, and instruments filled the store-rooms of Granite House. There was no longer a necessity to manufacture cloth in the felting mill. Linen, also, was plenty, and they took great care of it. From the chloride of sodium Smith had easily extracted soda and chlorine. The soda was easily transformed into carbonate of soda, and the chlorine was employed for various domestic purposes, but especially for cleaning the linen. Moreover, they made but four washings a year, as was the custom in old times, and Pencroff and Spilett, while waiting for the postman to bring the paper, made famous washermen!

Thus passed June, July, and August; very rigorous months, in which the thermometer measured but 8° Fahrenheit. But a good fire burned in the chimney of Granite House, and the superfluity of wood from the ship-yard enabled them to economize the coal, which required a longer carriage.

All, men and beasts, enjoyed good health. Jup, it is true, shivered a little with the cold, and they had to make him a good wadded wrapper. What servant he was! Adroit, zealous, indefatigable, not indiscreet, not talkative. He was, indeed, a model for his biped brethren in the New and the Old World!

"But, after all," said Pencroff "when one has four hands, they cannot help doing their work well!"

During the seven months that had passed since the exploration of the mountain nothing had been seen or heard of the genius of the island. Although, it is true, that nothing had happened to the colonists requiring his assistance.

Smith noticed, too, that the growling of the dog and the anxiety of the orang had ceased during this time. These two friends no longer ran to the orifice of the well nor acted in that strange way which had attracted the attention of the engineer. But did this prove that everything had happened that was going to happen? That they were never to find an answer to the enigma? Could it be affirmed that no new conjunction of circumstances would make this mysterious personage appear again? Who knows what the future may bring forth? On the 7th of September, Smith, looking towards Mount Franklin, saw a smoke rising and curling above the crater.

CHAPTER LVII. THE AWAKENING OF THE VOLCANO

THE FINE WEATHER—RESUMPTION OF WORK—THE EVENING OF THE 15TH OF OCTOBER—A TELEGRAPH—A DEMAND—AN ANSWER—DEPARTURE FOR THE CORRAL—THE NOTICE—THE EXTRA WIRE—THE BASALT WALL—AT HIGH TIDE—AT LOW TIDE—THE CAVERN—A DAZZLING LIGHT.

The colonists, called by Smith, had left their work, and gazed in silence at the summit of Mount Franklin.

The volcano had certainly awakened, and its vapors had penetrated the mineral matter of the crater, but no one could say whether the subterranean fires would bring on a violent eruption.

But, even supposing an eruption, it was not likely that Lincoln Island would suffer in every part. The discharges of volcanic matter are not always disastrous. That the island had already been subjected to an eruption was evident from the currents of lava spread over the western slope of the mountain. Moreover, the shape of the crater was such as to vomit matter in the direction away from the fertile parts of the island.

Nevertheless, what had been was no proof of what would be. Often the old craters of volcanoes close and new ones open. An earthquake phenomenon, often accompanying volcanic action, may do this by changing the interior arrangement of the mountain and opening new passages for the incandescent lavas.

Smith explained these things to his companions, and without exaggerating the situation, showed them just what might happen.

After all, they could do nothing. Granite House did not seem to be menaced, unless by a severe earthquake. But all feared for the corral, if any new crater opened in the mountain.

From this time the vapor poured from the cone without cessation, and, indeed, increased in density and volume, although no flame penetrated its thick folds. The phenomenon was confined, as yet, to the lower part of the central chimney.

Meanwhile, with good weather, the work out of doors had been resumed. They hastened the construction of the ship, and Smith established a saw-mill at the waterfall, which cut the timber much more rapidly. *The mechanism of this apparatus was as simple as those used in the rustic sawmills of Norway. A first horizontal movement to move the piece of wood, a second vertical movement to move the saw—this was all that was wanted; and the engineer succeeded by means of a wheel, two cylinders, and pulleys properly arranged.*

Towards the end of September the frame of the ship, which was to be schooner-rigged, was so far completed that its shape could be recognized. The schooner, sheer forward and wide aft, was well adapted for a long voyage, in case of necessity, but the planking, lining, and decking still demanded a long time before they could be finished. Fortunately, the iron-work of the brig had been saved after the explosion, and Pencroff and Ayrton had obtained a great quantity of copper nails from the broken timber, which economized the labor for the smiths; nevertheless the carpenters had much to accomplish.

Shipbuilding was interrupted for a week for the harvest, the haymaking, and the gathering in of the different crops on the plateau. This work finished, every moment was devoted to finishing the schooner. When night came the workmen were really quite exhausted. So as not to lose any time they had changed the hours for their meals; they dined at twelve o'clock, and only had their supper when daylight failed them. They then ascended to Granite House, when they were always ready to go to bed.

Often, however, after the day's work was ended, the colonists sat late into the night, conversing together of the future and what might happen in a voyage in the schooner to the nearest land. But in discussing these projects they always

778

planned to return to Lincoln Island. Never would they abandon this colony, established with so much difficulty, but so successfully, and which would receive a new development through communication with America.

Pencroff and Neb, indeed, hoped to end their days here.

"Herbert," asked the sailor, "you would never abandon Lincoln Island?"

"Never, Pencroff, especially if you made up your mind to remain."

"Then, it's agreed, my boy. I shall expect you! You will bring your wife and children here, and I will make a jolly playmate for the babies!"

"Agreed," answered Herbert, laughing and blushing at the same time.

"And you, Mr. Smith," continued the sailor, enthusiastically, "you will always remain governor of the island! And, by the way, how many inhabitants can the island support? Ten thousand, at the very least!"

They chatted in this way, letting Pencroff indulge in his whims, and one thing leading to another, the reporter finished by founding the *New Lincoln Herald*!

Thus it is with the spirit of man. The need of doing something permanent, something which will survive him, is the sign of his superiority over everything here below. It is that which has established and justifies his domination over the whole world. After all, who knows if Jup and Top had not their dream of the future?

Ayrton, silent, said to himself that he wanted to see Lord Glenarvan, and show him the change in himself.

One evening, the 15th of October, the conversation was prolonged longer than usual. It was 9 o'clock, and already, long, ill-concealed yawns showed that it was bed-time. Pencroff was about starting in that direction, when, suddenly, the electric bell in the hall rang.

Every one was present, so none of their party could be at the corral.

Smith rose. His companions looked as if they had not heard aright.

"What does he want?" cried Neb. "Is it the devil that's ringing?"

No one replied.

"It is stormy weather," said Herbert; "perhaps the electric influence——"

Herbert did not finish the sentence. The engineer, towards whom all were looking, shook his head.

"Wait a minute," said Spilett. "If it is a signal, it will be repeated."

"But what do you think it is?" asked Neb.

"Perhaps it——"

The sailor's words were interrupted by another ring.

Smith went to the apparatus, and, turning on the current, telegraphed to the corral:—— "What do you want?"

A few minutes later the needle, moving over the lettered card, gave this answer to the inmates of Granite House:— "Come to the corral as quickly as possible."

"At last!" cried Smith.

Yes! At last! The mystery was about to be solved! Before the strong interest in what was at the corral, all fatigue and need of repose vanished. Without saying a word, in a few minutes they were out of Granite House and following the shore. Only Top and Jup remained behind.

The night was dark. The moon, new this day, had set with the sun. Heavy clouds obscured the stars, but now and then heat-lightning, the reflection of a distant storm, illuminated the horizon.

But, great as the darkness was, it could not hinder persons as familiar with the route as were the colonists. All were very much excited, and walked rapidly. There could be no doubt that they were going to find the answer to the engineer, the name of that mysterious being, who was so generous in his influence, so powerful to accomplish! It could not be doubted that this unknown had been familiar with the least detail of their daily lives, that he overheard all that was said in Granite House.

Each one, lost in his reflections, hurried onward. The darkness under the trees was such that the route was invisible. There was no sound in the forest. Not a breath of wind moved the leaves.

This silence during the first quarter of an hour was uninterrupted, save by Pencroff, who said:—"We should have brought a lantern."

And by the engineer's answer:— "We will find one at the corral."

Smith and his companions had left Granite House at twelve minutes past 9. In thirty-five minutes they had traversed three of the five miles between the mouth of the Mercy and the corral.

Just then, brilliant flashes of lightning threw the foliage into strong relief. The storm was evidently about to burst upon them. The flashes became more frequent and intense. Heavy thunder rolled through the heavens. The air was stifling.

The colonists rushed on, as if impelled by some irresistible force.

At a quarter past 9, a sudden flash showed them the outline of the palisade; and scarcely had they passed the gateway when there came a terrible clap of thunder. In a moment the corral was crossed, and Smith stood before the house. It was possible that the unknown being was here, since it was from this place that the telegraph had come. Nevertheless, there was no light in the window.

The engineer knocked at the door, but without response.

He opened it, and the colonists entered the room, which was in utter darkness.

A light was struck by Neb, and in a moment the lantern was lit, and its light directed into every corner of the chamber.

No one was there, and everything remained undisturbed.

"Are we victims to a delusion?" murmured Smith.

No! that was impossible! The telegraph had certainly said:—"Come to the corral quickly as possible."

He went to the table on which the apparatus was arranged. Everything was in place and in order.

"Who was here last?" asked the engineer.

"I, sir," answered Ayrton.

"And that was——"

"Four days ago."

"Ah! here is something!" exclaimed Herbert, pointing to a paper lying on the table.

On the paper were these words, written in English:— "Follow the new wire."

"Come on!" cried Smith, who comprehended in a moment that the dispatch had not been sent from the corral, but from the mysterious abode which the new wire united directly with Granite House.

Neb took the lantern and all left the corral.

Then the storm broke forth with extreme violence. Flashes of lightning and peals of thunder followed in rapid succession. The island was the centre of the storm. By the flashes of lightning they could see the summit of Mount Franklin enshrouded in smoke.

There were no telegraph poles inside the corral, but the engineer, having passed the gate, ran to the nearest post, and saw there a new wire fastened to the insulator, and reaching to the ground.

"Here it is!" he cried.

The wire lay along the ground, and was covered with some insulating substance, like the submarine cables. By its direction it seemed as if it went towards the west, across the woods, and the southern spurs of the mountain.

"Let us follow it," said Smith.

And sometimes by the light of the lantern, sometimes by the illumination of the heavens, the colonists followed the way indicated by the thread.

They crossed in the first place, the spur of the mountain between the valley of the corral and that of Fall River, which stream was crossed in its narrowest part. The wire, sometimes hanging on the lower branches of the trees, sometimes trailing along the ground, was a sure guide.

The engineer had thought that, perhaps, the wire would end at the bottom of the valley, and that the unknown retreat was there.

But not so. It extended over the southwestern spur and descended to the arid plateau which ended that fantastic wall of basalt. Every now and then one or other of the party stooped and took the direction of the wire. There could be no doubt that it ran directly to the sea. There, doubtless, in some profound chasm in the igneous rocks, was the dwelling so vainly sought for until now.

At a few minutes before 10, the colonists arrived upon the high coast overhanging the ocean. Here the wire wound among the rocks, following a steep slope down a narrow ravine.

The colonists followed it, at the risk of bringing down upon themselves a shower of rocks or of being precipitated into the sea. The descent was extremely perilous, but they thought not of the danger; they were attracted to this mysterious place as the needle is drawn to the magnet.

At length, the wire making a sudden turn, touched the shore rocks, which were beaten by the sea. The colonists had reached the base of the granite wall.

Here there was a narrow projection running parallel and horizontal to the sea. The thread led along this point, and the colonists followed. They had not proceeded more than a hundred paces, when this projection, by a south inclination, sloped down into the water.

The engineer seized the wire and saw that it led down into the sea.

His companions stood, stupefied, beside him.

Then a cry of disappointment, almost of despair, escaped them! Must they throw themselves into the water and search some submarine cavern? In their present state of excitement, they would not have hesitated to have done it.

An observation made by the engineer stopped them. He led his companions to the shelter of a pile of rocks and said:—"Let as wait here. The tide is up. At low water the road will be open."

"But how do you think—" began Pencroff.

"He would not have called us, unless the means of reaching him had been provided."

Smith had spoken with an air of conviction, and, moreover, his observation was logical. It was, indeed, quite possible that an opening existed at low water which was covered at present.

It was necessary to wait some hours. The colonists rested in silence under their shelter. The rain began to fall in torrents. The echoes repeated the roaring of the thunder in sonorous reverberations.

At midnight the engineer took the lantern and went down to the water's edge. It was still two hours before low tide.

Smith had not been mistaken. The entrance to a vast excavation began to be visible, and the wire, turning at a right angle, entered this yawning mouth.

Smith returned to his companions and said: "In an hour the opening will be accessible."

"Then there is one," said Pencroff.

"Do you doubt it?" replied Smith.

"But it will be half full of water," said Herbert.

"Either it will be perfectly dry," answered the engineer, "in which case we will walk, or it will not be dry, and some means of transport will be furnished us."

An hour passed. All went down through the rain to the sea. In these hours the tide had fallen fifteen feet. The top of the mouth of the opening rose eight feet above the water, like the arch of a bridge.

Looking in, the engineer saw a black object floating on the surface. He drew it toward him. It was a canoe made of sheet-iron bolted together. It was tied to a projecting rock inside the cavern wall. A pair of oars were under the seats.

"Get in," said Smith.

The colonists entered the boat, Neb and Ayrton took the oars, Pencroff the tiller, and Smith, in the bows holding the lantern, lit the way.

The vault, at first very low, rose suddenly; but the darkness was too great for them to recognize the size of this cavern, its heighth and depth. An imposing silence reigned throughout this granite chamber. No sound, not even the pealing of the thunder penetrated its massive walls.

In certain parts of the world there are immense caves, a sort of natural crypts which date back to the geologic epoch. Some are invaded by the sea; others contain large lakes within their walls. Such is Fingal's Cave, in the Island of Staffa; such are the caves of Morgat on the Bay of Douarnenez in Brittany; the caves of Bonifacio, in Corsica; those of Lyse-Fjord, in Norway; such is that immense cavern, the Mammoth Cave of Kentucky, which is 500 feet high and more than twenty miles long!

As to this cavern which the colonists were exploring, did it not reach to the very centre of the island? For a quarter of an hour the canoe advanced under the directions of the engineer. At a certain moment he said:"Go over to the right"

The canoe, taking this direction, brought up beside the wall. The engineer wished to observe whether the wire continued along this side. It was there fastened to the rock.

"Forward!" said Smith.

The canoe kept on a quarter of an hour longer, and it must have been half a mile from the entrance, when Smith's voice was heard again.

"Halt!" he exclaimed.

The canoe stopped, and the colonists saw a brilliant light illuminating the enormous crypt, so profoundly hidden in the bowels of the earth.

They were now enabled to examine this cavern of whose existence they had had no suspicion.

A vault, supported on basaltic shafts, which might all have been cast in the same mould, rose to a height of 100 feet. Fantastic arches sprung at irregular intervals from these columns, which Nature had placed here by thousands. They rose to a height of forty or fifty feet, and the water, in despite of the tumult without, quietly lapped their base. The light noticed by the engineer seized upon each prismatic point and tipped it with fire; penetrated, so to speak, the walls as if they had been diaphanous, and changed into sparkling jewels the least projections of the cavern.

Following a phenomenon of reflection, the water reproduced these different lights upon its surface, so that the canoe seemed to float between two sparkling zones.

They had not yet thought of the nature of irradiation projected by the luminous centre whose rays, straight and clear, were broken on all the angles and mouldings of the crypt. The white color of this light betrayed its origin. It was electric. It was the sun of this cavern.

On a sign from Smith, the oars fell again into the water, and the canoe proceeded towards the luminous fire, which was half a cable's length distant.

In this place, the sheet of water measured some 300 feet across, and an enormous basaltic wall, closing all that side, was visible beyond the luminous centre. The cavern had become much enlarged, and the sea here formed a little lake. But the vault, the side walls, and those of the apsis, all the prisms, cylinders, cones, were bathed in the electric fluid.

In the centre of the lake a long fusiform object floated on the surface of the water, silent, motionless. The light escaped from its sides as from two ovens heated to a white heat. This machine, looking like the body of an enormous cetacea, was 250 feet long, and rose ten to twelve feet above the water.

The canoe approached softly. In the bows stood Smith. He was greatly excited. Suddenly he seized the arm of the reporter.

"It is he! It can be no other than he." he cried. "He!——"

Then he fell back upon the seat murmuring a name which Spilett alone heard.

Doubtless the reporter knew this name, for it affected him strangely, and he answered in a hoarse voice:— "He! a man outlawed!"

"The same!" said Smith.

Under the engineer's direction the canoe approached this singular floating machine, and came up to it on its left side, from which escaped a gleam of light through a thick glass.

Smith and his companions stepped on to the platform. An open hatchway was there, down which all descended.

At the bottom of the ladder appeared the waist of the vessel lit up by electric light. At the end of the waist was a door, which Smith pushed open.

A richly ornamented library, flooded with light, was rapidly crossed by the colonists. Beyond, a large door, also closed, was pushed open by the engineer.

A vast saloon, a sort of museum, in which were arranged all the treasures of the mineral world, works of art, marvels of industry, appeared before the eyes of the colonists, who seemed to be transported to the land of dreams.

Extended upon a rich divan they saw a man, who seemed unaware of their presence.

Then Smith raised his voice, and, to the extreme surprise of his companions, pronounced these words:—"Captain Nemo, you have called us. Here we are.'

CHAPTER LVIII. CAPTAIN NEMO

HIS FIRST WORDS—HISTORY OF A HERO OF LIBERTY—HATRED OF THE INVADERS—HIS COMPANIONS—THE LIFE UNDER WATER—ALONE—THE LAST REFUGE OF THE NAUTILUS—THE MYSTERIOUS GENIUS OF THE ISLAND.

At these words the man arose, and the light shone full upon his face: a magnificent head, with abundance of hair thrown back from a high forehead, a white beard, and an expression of haughtiness.

This man stood, resting one hand upon the divan, from which he had risen. One could see that a slow disease had broken him down, but his voice was still powerful, when he said in English, and in a tone of extreme surprise: "I have no name, sir!"

"I know you!" answered Smith.

Captain Nemo looked at the engineer as if he would have annihilated him. Then, falling back upon the cushions, he murmured:——

"After all, what does it matter; I am dying!"

Smith approached Captain Nemo, and Spilett took his hand, which was hot with fever. The others stood respectfully in a corner of the superb saloon, which was flooded with light.

Captain Nemo withdrew his hand, and signed to Smith and the reporter to be seated.

All looked at him with lively emotion. Here was the being whom they had called the "genius of the island," the being whose intervention had been so efficacious, the benefactor to whom they owed so much. Before their eyes, here where Pencroff and Neb had expected to find some godlike creature, was only a man-a dying man!

But how did Smith know Captain Nemo? Why had the latter sprung up on hearing that name pronounced?

The Captain had taken his seat upon the divan, and, leaning upon his arm, he regarded the engineer, who was seated near him.

"You know the name I bore?" he asked.

"I know it as well as I know the name of this admirable submarine apparatus."

"The Nautilus," said the Captain, with a half smile.

"The Nautilus."

"But do you know-do you know, who I am?"

"I do."

"For thirty years I have had no communication with the inhabited world, for thirty years have I lived in the depths of the sea, the only place where I have found freedom! Who, now, has betrayed my secret?"

"A man who never pledged you his word, Captain Nemo, one who, therefore, cannot be accused of betraying you."

"The Frenchman whom chance threw in my way?"

"The same."

"Then this man and his companions did not perish in the maelstrom into which the Nautilus had been drawn?"

"They did not, and there has appeared under the title of *Twenty Thousand Leagues Under the Sea*, a work which contains your history."

"The history of but a few months of my life, sir," answered the Captain, quickly.

"True," replied Smith, "but a few months of that strange life sufficed to make you known—"

"As a great criminal, doubtless," said Captain Nemo, smiling disdainfully. "Yes, a revolutionist, a scourge to humanity."

The engineer did not answer.

"Well, sir?"

"I am unable to judge Captain Nemo," said Smith, "at least in what concerns his past life. I, like the world at large, am ignorant of the motives for this strange existence, and I am unable to judge of the effects without knowing the causes, but what I do know is that a beneficent hand has been constantly extended to us since our arrival here, that we owe everything to a being good, generous, and powerful, and that this being, powerful, generous, and good, is you, Captain Nemo!"

"It is I," answered the captain, quietly.

The engineer and the reporter had risen, the others had drawn near, and the gratitude which swelled their hearts would have sought expression in words and gesture, when Captain Nemo signed to them to be silent, and in a voice more moved, doubtless, than he wished:—"When you have heard me," he said. And then, in a few short, clear sentences, he told them the history of his life.

The history was brief. Nevertheless, it took all his remaining strength to finish it. It was evident that he struggled against an extreme feebleness. Many times Smith urged him to take some rest, but he shook his head, like one who knew that for him there would be no to-morrow, and when the reporter offered his services—

"They are useless," he answered, "my hours are numbered."

Captain Nemo was an Indian prince, the Prince Dakkar, the son of the rajah of the then independent territory of Bundelkund, and nephew of the hero of India, Tippo Saib. His father sent him, when ten years old, to Europe, where he received a complete education; and it was the secret intention of the rajah to have his son able some day to engage in equal combat with those whom he considered as the oppressors of his country.

From ten years of age until he was thirty, the Prince Dakkar, with superior endowments, of high heart and courage, instructed himself in everything; pushing his investigations in science, literature, and art to the uttermost limits.

He travelled over all Europe. His birth and fortune made his company much sought after, but the seductions of the world possessed no charm for him. Young and handsome, he remained serious, gloomy, with an insatiable thirst for knowledge, with implacable anger fixed in his heart.

He hated. He hated the only country where he had never wished to set foot, the only nation whose advances he had refused: he hated England more and more as he admired her. This Indian summed up in his own person all the fierce hatred of the vanquished against the victor. The invader is always unable to find grace with the invaded. The son of one of those sovereigns whose submission to the United Kingdom was only nominal, the prince of the family of Tippo-Saib, educated in ideas of reclamation and vengeance, with a deep-seated love for his poetic country weighed down with the chains of England, wished never to place his foot on that land, to him accursed, that land to which India owed her subjection.

The Prince Dakkar became an artist, with a lively appreciation of the marvels of art; a savant familiar with the sciences; a statesman educated in European courts. In the eyes of a superficial observer, he passed, perhaps, for one of those cosmopolites, curious after knowledge, but disdaining to use it; for one of those opulent travellers, high-spirited and platonic, who go all over the world and are of no one country.

It was not so. This artist, this savant, this man was Indian to the heart, Indian in his desire for vengeance, Indian in the hope which he cherished of being able some day to re-establish the rights of his country, of driving on the stranger, of making it independent.

He returned to Bundelkund in the year 1849. He married a noble Indian woman whose heart bled as his did at the woes of their country. He had two children whom he loved. But domestic happiness could not make him forget the servitude of India. He waited for an opportunity. At length it came.

The English yoke was pressed, perhaps, too heavily upon the Indian people. The Prince Dakkar became the mouthpiece of the malcontents. He instilled into their spirits all the hatred he felt against the strangers. He went over not only the independent portions of the Indian peninsula, but into those regions directly submitted to the English control. He recalled to them the grand days of Tippo-Saib, who died heroically at Seringapatam for the defense of his country.

In 1857 the Sepoy mutiny broke forth. Prince Dakkar was its soul. He organized that immense uprising. He placed his talents and his wealth at the service of that cause. He gave himself; he fought in the first rank; he risked his life as the humblest of those heroes who had risen to free their country; he was wounded ten times in twenty battles, and was unable to find death when the last soldiers of independence fell before the English guns.

Never had British rule in India been in such danger; and, had the Sepoys received the assistance from without which they had hoped for, Asia would not to-day, perhaps, be under the dominion of the United Kingdom.

At that time the name of Prince Dakkar was there illustrious. He never hid himself, and he fought openly. A price was put upon his head, and although he was not delivered up by any traitor, his father, mother, wife, and children suffered for him before he knew of the dangers which they ran on his account.

Once again right fell before might. Civilization never goes backwards, and her laws are like those of necessity. The Sepoys were vanquished, and the country of the ancient rajahs fell again under the strict rule of England.

Prince Dakkar, unable to die, returned again to his mountains in Bundelkund. There, thenceforward alone, he conceived an immense disgust against all who bore the name of man—a hatred and a horror of the civilized world—and wishing to fly from it, he collected the wreck of his fortune, gathered together twenty of his most faithful companions, and one day disappeared.

Where did Prince Dakkar seek for that independence which was refused him upon the inhabited earth? Under the waters, in the depths of the seas, where no one could follow him.

From a man of war he became a man of science. On a desert island of the Pacific he established his workshops, and there he constructed a submarine ship after plans of his own. By means which will some day be known, he utilized electricity, that incommensurable force, for all the necessities of his apparatus as a motor, for lighting and for heat. The sea, with its infinite treasures, its myriads of fishes, its harvests of varech and sargassum, its enormous mammifers, and not only all that nature held, but all that man had lost, amply sufficed for the needs of the Prince and his equipage;—and thus he accomplished his heart's desire, to have no further communication with the earth. He named his submarine ship the Nautilus, he called himself Captain Nemo, and he disappeared under the seas.

During many years, the Captain visited all the oceans, from one pole to the other. Pariah of the earth, he reaped the treasures of the unknown worlds. The millions lost in Vigo Bay, in 1702, by the Spanish galleons, furnished him with an inexhaustible mine of wealth, which he gave, anonymously, to people fighting for their independence.

For years he had had no communication with his kindred, when, during the night of the 6th of November, 1866, three men were thrown upon his deck. They were a French professor, his servant, and a Canadian fisherman. These men had been thrown overboard by the shock of the collision between the Nautilus and the United States frigate Abraham Lincoln, which had given it chase.

Captain Nemo learned from the Professor that the Nautilus, sometimes taken for a gigantic mammifer of the cetacean family, sometimes for a submarine apparatus containing a gang of pirates, was hunted in every sea.

Captain Nemo could have thrown these three men, whom chance had thrown across his mysterious life, into the ocean. He did not do it, he kept them prisoners, and, during seven months, they were able to perceive all the marvels of a voyage of 20,000 leagues under the sea.

One day, the 22nd of June, 1867, these three men, who knew nothing of Captain Nemo's past life, seized the boat belonging to the Nautilus and attempted to escape. But just then the Nautilus was upon the coast of Norway in the eddy of the Maelstrom, and the Captain believed that the fugitives, caught in its terrible vortex, had been swallowed up in the gulf. He was unaware that the Frenchman and his companions had been miraculously thrown upon the coast, that the fishermen of the Loffodin Islands had rescued them, and that the Professor, on his return to France, had published a book in which seven months of this strange and adventurous navigation was narrated.

For a long time Captain Nemo continued this mode of life, traversing the sea. One by one his companions died and found their rest in the coral cemetery at the bottom of the Pacific, and in time Captain Nemo was the last survivor of those who had sought refuge in the depths of the oceans.

He was then sixty years old. As he was alone, it was necessary to take his Nautilus to one of those submarine ports which served him in former days as a harbor.

One of these ports was under Lincoln Island, and was the present asylum of the Nautilus. For six years the Captain had remained there awaiting that death which would reunite him with his companions, when chance made him witness to the fall of the balloon which carried the prisoners. Clothed in his impermeable jacket, he was walking under the water, some cables' lengths from the shore of the islet, when the engineer was thrown into the sea. A good impulse moved Captain Nemo—and he saved Cyrus Smith.

On the arrival of these five castaways he wished to go from them, but his port of refuge was closed. Some volcanic action had raised up the basalt so that the Nautilus could not cross the entrance to the crypt, although there was still sufficient water for a boat of light draught.

Captain Nemo, therefore, remained and watched these men, thrown without resources upon a desert island, but he did not wish to be seen. Little by little, as he saw their honest, energetic lives, how they were bound together in fraternal amity, he interested himself in their efforts. In spite of himself, he found out all the secrets of their existence. Clothed in his impermeable jacket, he could easily reach the bottom of the well in Granite House, and climbing by the projections of the rock to its mouth, he heard the colonists talk of their past and discuss their present and future. He learned from them of the struggle of America against itself, for the abolition of slavery. Yes! these men were worthy to reconcile Captain Nemo with that humanity which they represented so honestly on the island.

Captain Nemo had saved Smith. It was he who had led the dog to the Chimneys, who threw Top out of the water, who stranded the box of useful articles on Jetsam Point, who brought the canoe down the Mercy, who threw the cord from Granite House, when it was attacked by the monkeys, who made known the presence of Ayrton on Tabor Island by means of the paper inclosed in the bottle, who blew up the brig by means of a torpedo, who saved Herbert from certain death by bringing the quinine, who, finally, killed the convicts by those electric balls which he employed in his submarine hunting excursions. Thus was explained all those seemingly supernatural incidents, which, all of them, attested the generosity and the power of the Captain.

Nevertheless, this intense misanthrope thirsted to do good. He had some useful advice to give to his proteges, and moreover, feeling the approach of death, he had summoned, as we have seen, the colonists from Granite House, by means of the wire which reached from the corral to the Nautilus. Perhaps he would not have done it, had he thought that Smith knew enough of his history to call him by his name of Nemo.

The Captain finished the recital of his life, and then Smith spoke. He recalled all the instances of the salutary influences exercised over the colonists, and then, in the name of his companions, and in his own, he thanked this generous being for all that he had done.

But Captain Nemo had never dreamed of asking any return for his services. One last thought agitated his spirit, and, before taking the hand which the engineer held out to him, he said: "Now, sir, you know my life, judge of it!"

In speaking thus, the Captain evidently alluded to an incident of a serious nature which had been witnessed by the three strangers on the Nautilus—an incident which the French professor had necessarily recounted in his book, an incident whose very recital was terrible.

In brief, some days before the flight of the professor and his companions, the Nautilus, pursued by a frigate in the North Atlantic, had rushed upon her like a battering-ram, and sunk her without mercy.

Smith, understanding this allusion, made no answer.

"It was an English frigate, sir!" cried Captain Nemo, becoming for the moment Prince Dakkar, "an English frigate, you understand! She attacked me! I was shut in, in a narrow and shallow bay; I had to pass out, and—I passed!"

Then, speaking with more calmness: "I had right and justice on my side," he added. "I did good when I could, and evil when I must. All justice is not in forgiveness."

Some moments of silence followed this response, and Captain Nemo asked again: "What do you think of me?"

Smith took the hand of the Captain, and answered him in a grave voice:—

"Captain, your mistake has been in believing that you could bring back the old order of things, and you have struggled against necessary progress. It was one of those errors which some of us admire, others blame, but of which God alone can judge, and which the human mind exonerates. We can disagree with one who misleads himself in an intention which he believes laudable, and at the same time esteem him. Your error is of a kind which does not preclude admiration, and your name has nothing to fear from the judgment of history. She loves heroic follies, though she condemns the results which follow."

The breast of Captain Nemo heaved; he raised his hand towards heaven.

"Was I wrong, or was I right?" he murmured.

Smith continued:"All great actions return to God, from whom they came! Captain Nemo, the worthy men here, whom you have succored, will always weep for you!"

Herbert approached him. He knelt down and took the hand of the captain, and kissed it.

A tear glistened in the eye of the dying man.

"My child," he said, "bless you!"

CHAPTER LIX. THE LAST HOURS OF CAPTAIN NEMO

HIS DYING WISHES—A SOUVENIR FOR HIS FRIENDS—HIS TOMB—SOME COUNSEL TO THE COLONISTS—THE SUPREME MOMENT—AT THE BOTTOM OF THE SEA.

It was morning, though no ray of daylight penetrated the vault. The sea, at this moment high, covered the outlet. But the artificial light escaping in long rays from the sides of the Nautilus, had not diminished, and the sheet of water around the vessel glowed resplendent.

Captain Nemo, overcome by an extreme fatigue, fell back upon the divan. They did not dream of transporting him to Granite House, as he had shown a wish to remain among the priceless treasures of the Nautilus, awaiting that death which could not be long in coming.

Smith and Spilett observed with great attention his prostration. They saw that he was slowly sinking. His strength, formerly so great, was almost gone, and his body was but a frail envelope for the spirit about escaping. All life was concentrated at the heart and brain.

The engineer and the reporter consulted together in low tones. Could they do anything for the dying man? Could they, if not save him, at least prolong his life for a few days? He himself had said that there was no remedy, and he awaited death calmly and without fear.

"We can do nothing," said Spilett.

"What is he dying of?" asked Pencroff.

"Of exhaustion," answered the reporter.

"Supposing we take him out into the open air, into the sunlight, perhaps he would revive?"

"No, Pencroff," responded the engineer, "there is nothing to do. Moreover, Captain Nemo would not be willing to leave here. He has lived on the Nautilus for thirty years, and on the Nautilus he wishes to die."

Doubtless Captain Nemo heard Smith's words, for, raising himself up a little, and speaking in a feeble but intelligible voice, he said:—

"You are right. I wish to die here. And I have a request to make."

Smith and his companions had gathered round the divan, and they arranged the cushions so that the dying man was more comfortably placed.

They saw that his gaze was fixed upon the marvels of the saloon, lit up by the rays of electric light sifting through the arabesques of the luminous ceiling. He looked upon the pictures, those *chefs d'œuvre* of Italian, Flemish, French, and Spanish masters, which hung on the tapestried walls, upon the marbles and bronzes, upon the magnificent organ at the opposite end of the saloon, upon the glasses arranged around a central vase in which were disposed the rarest products of the seas, marine plants, zoophytes, chaplets of pearls of an inappreciable value, and at length his attention was fixed upon this device, the device of the Nautilus inscribed upon the front of this museum:—

MOBILIS IN MOBILI.

It seemed as if he wished to caress with his regard, one last time, those *chefs d'oeuvre* of art and nature which had been ever visible to him in the years of his sojourn in the depths of the sea!

Smith respected Captain Nemo's silence. He waited for him to speak.

After some moments, during which passed before him, doubtless, his whole life, Cap-Nemo turned to the colonists and said:—

"You wish to do me a favor?"

"Captain, we would give our lives to prolong yours!"

"Well, then, promise me that you will execute my last wishes, and I will be repaid for all that I have done for you."

"We promise," answered Smith, speaking for his companions and himself.

"To-morrow," said the Captain, "to-morrow I will be dead."

He made a sign to Herbert, who was about to protest.

"To-morrow I will be dead, and I wish for no other tomb than the Nautilus. It is my coffin! All my friends rest at the bottom of the sea, and I wish to rest there also."

A profound silence followed the words of Captain Nemo.

"Attend to what I say," he continued. "The Nautilus is imprisoned in this grotto. But if she cannot leave this prison, she can at least sink herself in the abyss, which will cover her and guard my mortal remains."

The colonists listened religiously to the words of the dying man.

"To-morrow, after I am dead, Mr. Smith," continued the Captain, "you and your companions will leave the Nautilus, all of whose riches are to disappear with me. One single remembrance of Prince Dakkar, whose history you now know, will remain to you. That coffer, there, encloses diamonds worth many millions, most of them souvenirs of the time when, a husband and father, I almost believed in happiness, and a collection of pearls gathered by my friends and myself from the bottom of the sea. With this treasure, you will be able, some time, to accomplish good. In your hands and those of your companions, Mr. Smith, wealth will not be dangerous. I shall be ever present with you in your works."

After some moments of rest, necessitated by his extreme feebleness, Captain Nemo continued as follows:— "To-morrow, you will take this coffer, you will leave this saloon, and close the door; then you will ascend to the platform of the Nautilus and you will bolt down the hatchway."

"We will do it, sir," replied Smith.

"Very well. You will then embark in the boat which brought you here. But, before abandoning the Nautilus, go to the stern, and there, open two large cocks which you will find at the water-line. The water will penetrate and the Nautilus will sink beneath the waves and rest upon the bottom of the abyss."

Then, upon a gesture from Smith, the Captain added:—

"Fear nothing! you will only be burying the dead!"

Neither Smith nor his companions could say a word to Captain Nemo. These were his last wishes, and they had nothing else to do but obey them.

"I have your promise?" asked Captain Nemo.

"You have it, sir," answered the engineer.

The Captain made a sign thanking them, and then motioned to be left alone for a few hours. Spilett insisted on remaining with him, in case of an emergency, but the other refused, saying:—

"I will live till morning, sir."

All left the salon, passing through the library, the dining-room, and reached the forward part of the vessel, where the electric apparatus, furnishing heat, light, and motive power to the Nautilus was placed.

The Nautilus was a *chef-d'oeuvre* containing *chefs-d'oeuvre*, which filled the engineer with amazement.

The colonists mounted the platform, which rose seven or eight feet above the water. Then they saw a thick lenticular glass closing up a sort of bull's-eye, through which penetrated a ray of light. Behind this bull's-eye was the wheel-house, where the steersman stood when directing the Nautilus under the sea, by means of the electric light.

Smith and his companions stood here in silence, impressed by what they saw, and what they had heard, and their hearts bled to think that he, their protector, whose arm had been so often raised to aid them, would soon be counted among the dead.

Whatever would be the judgment of posterity upon this, so to say, extra-human existence, Prince Dakkar would always remain one of those strange characters who cannot be forgotten.

"What a man!" said Pencroff. "Is it credible that he has lived so at the bottom of the ocean! And to think that he has not found rest even there!"

"The Nautilus," observed Ayrton, "would, perhaps, have served us to leave Lincoln Island and gain some inhabited country."

"A thousand devils!" cried Pencroff. "You couldn't get me to steer such a craft. To sail over the seas is all very well, but under the seas,—no, sir!"

"I think, Pencroff," said the reporter, "that it would be easy to manage a submarine apparatus like the Nautilus, and that we would soon get accustomed to it. No storms, no boarding to fear. At some little distance under the waves the waters are as calm as those of a lake."

"That's likely enough," answered the sailor, "but give me a stiff breeze and a well rigged ship. A ship is made to go on the water and not under it."

"My friends," said the engineer, "it is useless, at least as far as the Nautilus is concerned, to discuss this question of submarine vessels. The Nautilus is not ours, and we have no right to dispose of it. It could not, moreover, serve us under any circumstances. Aside from the fact that it cannot get out of this cavern, Captain Nemo wishes it to be engulfed with him after his death. His wish is law, and we will obey it."

Smith and his companions, after talking for a while longer, descended into the interior of the Nautilus. There they ate some food and returned to the salon.

Captain Nemo had recovered from his prostration, and his eyes had regained their brilliancy. They saw a smile upon his lips.

The colonists approached him. "Sirs," said the Captain, "you are brave men, and good and honest. You have given yourselves up to the common cause. I have often watched you. I have loved you. I do love you!—Give me your hand, Mr. Smith."

Smith gave his hand to the Captain, who pressed it affectionately.

"That is well!" he murmured. Then he added:—"But I have said enough about myself. I wish to speak of yourselves and of Lincoln Island, on which you have found refuge. You want to leave it?"

"To come back again!" said Pencroff eagerly.

"To return?—Oh! yes, Pencroff," answered the Captain, smiling, "I know how much you love this island. It has been improved by your care, and it is, indeed, yours."

"Our project, Captain," added Smith, "would be to make it over to the United States, and to establish a station, which would be well situated here in this part of the Pacific."

"You think of your country," replied the Captain. "You work for her prosperity, for her glory. You are right. The Fatherland! It is there we wish to return! It is there we wish to die! And I, I die far from everything that I have loved!"

"Have you no last wish to have executed," asked the engineer earnestly, "no souvenir to send to those friends you left in the mountains of India?"

"No, Mr. Smith, I have no friends! I am the last of my race—and I die long after those whom I have known.—But to return to yourselves. Solitude, isolation are sorrowful things, beyond human endurance. I die from having believed that man could live alone!—You wish to leave Lincoln Island and to return to your country. I know that these wretches have destroyed your boat-"

"We are building a ship," said Spilett, "a ship large enough to take us to the nearest country; but if sooner or later we leave the island, we will come back again. Too many associations attach us to the place, for us ever to forget it."

"Here we met Captain Nemo," said Smith.

"Here only will we find the perfect remembrance of you!" added Herbert."

"It is here that I will rest in an eternal sleep, if—" answered the Captain.

He hesitated, and, instead of finishing his sentence, said: "Mr. Smith, I wish to speak with you,—with you alone."

The companions of the engineer retired, and Smith remained for some time alone with Captain Nemo. He soon called back his friends, but said nothing to them of the secrets which the dying prince had confided to him.

Spilett observed the Captain with extreme attention. He was evidently living by the strength of his will, which could not long hold out against his physical weakness.

The day ended without any change manifesting itself. The colonists did not leave the Nautilus. Night came, although unseen in this crypt.

Captain Nemo did not suffer pain, but sunk slowly. His noble face, pale by the approach of death, was perfectly calm. Now and then he spoke, incoherently, of events in his strange existence.—All saw that life was retreating. His feet and hands were already cold.

Once or twice, he spoke a word to the colonists who were about him, and he looked upon them with that smile which remained when he was no more.

At last, just after midnight, Captain Nemo made a supreme effort, and crossed his arms upon his breast, as if he wished to die in that attitude.

Towards 1 o'clock all the life that was left was concentrated in his expression. One last spark burned in that eye which had formerly flashed fire! Then, murmuring these words, "God and Fatherland," he expired quietly.

Smith, stooping down, closed the eyes of him who had been Prince Dakkar, who was no more even Captain Nemo.

Herbert and Pencroff wept. Ayrton wiped away a furtive tear. Neb was on his knees near the reporter, who was immobile as a statue.

Smith raising his hand above the head of the dead man:—

"May God receive his soul!" he said, and then, turning towards his friends, he added:—"Let us pray for him whom we have lost!"

****

Some hours later, the colonists, in fulfillment of their promise, carried out the last wishes of the dead.

They left the Nautilus, taking with them the sole souvenir of their benefactor, the coffer containing a hundred fortunes.

The marvellous salon, still flooded with light, was carefully closed. The cover to the hatchway was bolted down in such a manner that not a drop of water could penetrate to the inner chambers of the Nautilus. Then the colonists entered the boat, which was moored beside the submarine ship.

The boat was taken to the stern. There, at the water-line, they opened the two large cocks which communicated with the reservoirs designed to immerse the apparatus.

The cocks were opened, the reservoirs filled, and the Nautilus, sinking slowly, disappeared beneath the sea.

But the colonists were able still to follow her coarse through the lower depths. Her strong light lit up the transparent waters, as the crypt became darkened. Then at length the vast effusion of electric effulgence was effaced, and the Nautilus, the tomb of Captain Nemo, rested upon the bottom of the sea.

CHAPTER LX. THE REFLECTIONS OF THE COLONISTS

RENEWAL OF WORK—THE 1ST OF JANUARY, 1869—A SMOKE FROM THE VOLCANO—SYMPTOMS OF AN ERUPTION AYRTON AND SMITH AT THE CORRAL—EXPLORATION OF THE CRYPT DAKKAR —WHAT CAPTAIN NEMO HAD SAID TO THE ENGINEER.

In the early morning the colonists reached the entrance of the cavern, which they called Crypt Dakkar, in remembrance of Captain Nemo. The tide was low, and they easily passed under the archway, whose piers were washed by the waves.

The iron boat could remain in this place without danger from the sea; but as additional precaution they drew it up on a little beach on one side of the crypt.

The storm had ceased during the night. The last mutterings of the thunder were dying away in the west. It was not raining, although the sky was still clouded. In short, this month of October, the beginning of the southern spring, did not come in good fashion, and the wind had a tendency to shift from one point of the compass to another, so that it was impossible to say what the weather would be.

Smith and his companions, on leaving Crypt Dakkar, went towards the corral. On the way Neb and Herbert took care to take up the wire which had been stretched by Captain Nemo, as it might be useful in the future.

While walking the colonists spoke but little. The incidents of this night had made a vivid impression upon them. This unknown, whose influence had protected them so well, this man whom they imagined a genii, Captain Nemo, was no more. His Nautilus and himself were buried in the depths of the abyss. It seemed to each one of them that they were more isolated than before. They were, so to speak, accustomed to count upon this powerful intervention which to-day was wanting, and Spilett, and even Smith, did not escape this feeling. So, without speaking, they followed the road to the corral.

By 9 o'clock the colonists were in Granite House again.

It had been agreed that the construction of the ship should be pushed forward as rapidly as possible, and Smith gave the work more of his time and care than ever before. They did not know what the future might bring forth, and it would be a guarantee of safety for them to have a strong vessel, able to stand rough weather, and large enough to carry them, if need be, a long distance. If, when it was finished, the colonists decided not to leave the island they could at least make the voyage to Tabor Island and leave a notice there. This was an indispensable precaution in case the Scotch yacht returned to these seas, and it must on no account be neglected.

The work was undertaken at once. All worked at it without ceasing, except to prosecute other necessary work. It was important to have the new ship finished in five months, if they wished to make the voyage to Tabor Island before the equinoxial storms would render it impracticable. All the sails of the Speedy had been saved, so that they need not trouble themselves about making rigging.

The year ended in the midst of this work. At the end of two months and a half the ribs had been put in place and the planking began, so that they were able to see that Smith's plans were excellent. Pencroff worked with ardor, and always grumbled when any of the others left off work to go hunting. It was, nevertheless, necessary to lay in a stock of provisions for the approaching winter. But that made no difference. The honest sailor was unhappy unless every one was at work in the ship-yard. At these times he grumbled and did— he was so put out—the work of half a dozen men.

All this summer season was bad. The heat was overpowering, and the atmosphere, charged with electricity, discharged itself in violent storms. It was seldom that the distant muttering of the thunder was unheard. It was like a dull, but permanent murmur, such as is produced in the equatorial regions of the globe.

On the 1st of January, 1869, a terrific storm burst over the island, and the lightning struck in many places. Tall trees were shattered, and among them was one of the enormous micocouliers which shaded the poultry-yard. Had this meteoric storm any relation to the phenomena which were occurring In the bowels of the earth? Was there a sort of connection between the disturbances in the air and those in the interior of the globe. Smith believed it to be so, since the development of these storms was marked by a recrudescence of the volcanic symptoms.

On the 3d of January, Herbert, who had gone at daybreak to Prospect Plateau to saddle one of the onagers, saw an immense black cloud rolling out from the summit of the volcano.

Herbert hastened to inform the others, who came at once to look at the mountain.

"Ah!" said Pencroff, "it is not vapor this time! It seems to me that the giant is not content to breathe, he must smoke!"

The image employed by the sailor expressed with exactness the change which had taken place at the mouth of the volcano. For three months the crater had been emitting vapors more or less intense, but there had been no ebullition of mineral matters. This time, instead of vapors, a thick column of smoke rose, like an immense mushroom, above the summit of the mountain.

"The chimney is on fire!" said Spilett.

"And we cannot put it out!" answered Herbert.

"It would be well to sweep the volcanoes," said Neb, in good earnest.

"All right, Neb," said Pencroff, laughing. "Will you undertake the job?"

Smith looked attentively at the thick smoke, and at the same time he listened as if he expected to detect some distant rumbling. Then, turning towards his companions, who were at some little distance, he said:—

"In truth, my friends, it cannot be denied that an important change has taken place. The volcanic matters are not only in a state of ebullition, they have taken fire, and, without doubt, we are threatened with an eruption!"

"Very well, sir; we will witness this eruption," cried Pencroff, "and we will applaud it if it is a success! I don't think that anything over there need worry us!"

"No, Pencroff," answered Smith, "for the old course of the lava is open, and, thanks to its position, the crater has heretofore discharged towards the north. Nevertheless—"

"Nevertheless, since there is nothing to be gained by an eruption, it would be better not to have it," said the reporter.

"Who knows?" replied the sailor. "There may be some useful and precious matter in the volcano, which it will be good enough to throw up, which will be advantageous for us!"

Smith shook his head, as a man who anticipated nothing good from this phenomenon. He did not think so lightly of the consequences of an eruption. If the lava, on account of the position of the crater, did not menace the wooded and cultivated portions of the island, other complications might arise. Eruptions are often accompanied by earthquakes, and an island formed, like Lincoln Island, of such different materials: basalt on one side, granite on another, lavas to the north, a mixed soil inland, material which, therefore, could not be solidly bound together, ran the risk of being torn asunder. If, therefore, the outpouring of volcanic substances did not threaten serious results, any movement in the framework upholding the island might be followed by the gravest consequences.

"It seems to me," said Ayrton, who was kneeling down, with his ear to the ground, "it seems to me that I hear a noise, like the rattling of a wagon, loaded with iron bars."

The colonists listened carefully, and were convinced that Ayrton was not mistaken. With the rumbling mingled subterranean roaring, making a sort of "rinfordzando," which died away slowly, as if from some violent cleavage in the interior of the globe. But no detonation was heard, and it was fair to conclude that the smoke and vapor found a free passage through the central chimney, and, if the escape-pipe was sufficiently large, no explosion need be feared.

"Come," said Pencroff at length, "shall we not go back to work? Let Mount Franklin smoke, brawl, moan, and vomit fire and flames as much as it chooses, but that is no excuse for us to quit work! Come, Ayrton, Neb, all of you, we want all hands to-day! I want our new Good Luck—we will keep the name, will we not?—to be moored in Balloon Harbor before two months are passed! So there is not an hour to be lost!"

All the colonists went down to the shipyard and worked steadily all day without giving too much thought to the volcano, which could not be seen from the beach before Granite House. But once or twice heavy shadows obscured the sunlight, and, as the day was perfectly clear, it was evident that thick clouds of smoke were passing between the sun's disc and the island. Smith and Spilett noticed these sombre voyagers, and talked of the progress that the volcanic phenomenon was making, but they did not cease work. It was, moreover, of great importance, in every sense, that the ship should be finished with as little delay as possible. In the presence of events which might happen, the security of the colonists would be better assured. Who could say but that this ship might not, some day, be their sole refuge?

That evening, after supper, Smith, Spilett, and Herbert climbed to the plateau. It was already dark, and they would be able to distinguish whether flames or incandescent matter was mingled with the smoke and vapor of the volcano.

"The crater is on fire!" cried Herbert, who, more active than his companions, had reached the plateau the first.

Mount Franklin, six miles distant, appeared like a gigantic torch, with fuliginous flames twisting about its summit. So much smoke, such quantities of scoriæ and cinders, perhaps, were mingled with the flames, that their light did not glare upon the shades of night. But a sort of dull yellow glow spread over the island, making dimly visible the higher masses of forest. Enormous clouds obscured the heavens, between which glittered a few stars.

"The progress is rapid," said the engineer.

"It is not astonishing," answered the reporter. "The volcano has been awake for some time already. You remember, Cyrus, that the first vapors appeared about the time we were searching the mountain for the retreat of Captain Nemo. That was, if I am not mistaken, about the 15th of October."

"Yes" replied Herbert, "two months and a half ago."

"The subterranean fires have been brooding for ten weeks," continued Spilett, "and it is not astonishing that they develop now with this violence."

"Do not you feel certain vibrations in the ground?" asked Smith.

"I think so," replied Spilett, "but an earthquake—"

"I did not say that we were menaced by an earthquake," said Smith, "and Heaven preserve us from one! No. These vibrations are due to the effervesence of the central fire. The crust of the earth is nothing more than the covering of a boiler, and you know how the covering of a boiler, under pressure, vibrates like a sonorous plate. That is what is happening at this moment."

"What magnificent flames!" cried Herbert, as a sheaf of fire shot up, unobscured by the vapors, from the crater. From its midst luminous fragments and bright scintillations were thrown in every direction. Some of them pierced the dome of smoke, leaving behind them a perfect cloud of incandescent dust.

This outpouring was accompanied by rapid detonations like the discharge of a battery of mitrailleuses.

Smith, the reporter, and the lad, after having passed an hour on Prospect Plateau, returned to Granite House. The engineer was pensive, and so much preoccupied that Spilett asked him if he anticipated any near danger.

"Yes and no," responded Smith.

"But the worst that could happen," said the reporter, "would be an earthquake, which would overthrow the island. And I don't think that is to be feared, since the vapors and lava have a free passage of escape."

"I do not fear an earthquake," answered Smith, "of the ordinary kind, such as are brought about by the expansion of subterranean vapors. But other causes may bring about great disaster."

"For example?"

"I do not know exactly—I must see—I must visit the mountain. In a few days I shall have made up my mind."

Spilett asked no further questions, and soon, notwithstanding the increased violence of the volcano, the inhabitants of Granite House slept soundly.

Three days passed, the 4th 5th, and 6th of January, during which they worked on the ship, and, without explaining himself further, the engineer hastened the work as much as possible. Mount Franklin was covered with a sinister cloud, and with the flames vomited forth incandescent rocks, some of which fell back into the crater. This made Pencroff, who wished to look upon the phenomenon from an amusing side, say—

"Look! The giant plays at cup and ball! He is a juggler."

And, indeed, the matters vomited forth fell back into the abyss, and it seemed as if the lavas, swollen by the interior pressure, had not yet risen to the mouth of the crater. At least, the fracture on the northeast, which was partly visible, did not pour forth any torrent on the western side of the mountain.

Meanwhile, however pressing the ship-building, other cares required the attention of the colonists in different parts of the island. First of all, they must go to the corral, where the moufflons and goats were enclosed, and renew the provisions for these animals. It was, therefore, agreed that Ayrton should go there the next day, and, as it was customary for but one to do this work, the others were surprised to hear the engineer say to Ayrton:——

"As you are going to the corral to-morrow, I will go with you."

"Oh! Mr. Smith!" cried the sailor, "our time is very limited, and, if you go off in this way, we lose just that much help!"

"We will return the next day," answered Smith, "but I must go to the corral—I wish to see about this eruption."

"Eruption! Eruption!" answered Pencroff, with a dissatisfied air. "What is there important about this eruption? It don't bother me!"

Notwithstanding the sailor's protest, the exploration was decided upon for the next day. Herbert wanted to go with Smith, but he did not wish to annoy Pencroff by absenting himself. So, early the next morning, Smith and Ayrton started off with the wagon and onagers.

Over the forest hung huge clouds constantly supplied from Mount Franklin with fuliginous matter. They were evidently composed of heterogeneous substances. It was not altogether the smoke from the volcano that made them so heavy and opaque. Scoriæ in a state of powder, pulverized puzzolan and grey cinder as fine as the finest fecula, were held in suspension in their thick folds. These cinders remain in air, sometimes, for months at a time. After the eruption of 1783, in Iceland, for more than a year the atmosphere was so charged with volcanic powder that the sun's rays were scarcely visible.

Usually, however, these pulverized matters fall to the earth at once, and it was so in this instance. Smith and Ayrton had hardly reached the corral, when a sort of black cloud, like fine gunpowder, fell, and instantly modified the whole aspect of the ground. Trees, fields, everything was covered with a coating several fingers deep. But, most fortunately, the wind was from the northeast, and the greater part of the cloud was carried off to sea.

"That is very curious," said Ayrton.

"It is very serious," answered Smith. This puzzolan, this pulverized pumice stone, all this mineral dust in short, shows how deep-seated is the commotion in the volcano.

"But there is nothing to be done."

"Nothing, but to observe the progress of the phenomenon. Employ yourself, Ayrton, at the corral, and meanwhile I will go up to the sources of Red Creek and examine the state of the mountain on its western side. Then——"

"Then, sir?"

"Then we will make a visit to Crypt Dakkar—I wish to see—Well, I will come back for you in a couple of hours."

Ayrton went into the corral, and while waiting for the return of the engineer occupied himself with the moufflons and goats, which showed a certain uneasiness before these first symptoms of an eruption.

Meantime Smith had ventured to climb the eastern spurs of the mountain, and he arrived at the place where his companions had discovered the sulphur spring on their first exploration.

How everything was changed! Instead of a single column of smoke, he counted thirteen escaping from the ground as if thrust upward by a piston. It was evident that the crust of earth was subjected in this place to a frightful pressure. The atmosphere was saturated with gases and aqueous vapors. Smith felt the volcanic tufa, the pulverulent cinders hardened by time, trembling beneath him, but he did not yet see any traces of fresh lava.

It was the same with the western slope of the mountain. Smoke and flames escaped from the crater; a hail of scoriæ fell upon the soil; but no lava flowed from the gullet of the crater, which was another proof that the volcanic matter had not attained the upper orifice of the central chimney.

"And I would be better satisfied if they had!" said Smith to himself. "At least I would be certain that the lavas had taken their accustomed route. Who knows if they may not burst forth from some new mouth? But that is not the danger! Captain Nemo has well foreseen it! No! the danger is not there!"

Smith went forward as far as the enormous causeway, whose prolongation enframed Shark Gulf. Here he was able to examine the ancient lava marks. There could be no doubt that the last eruption had been at a far distant epoch.

Then he returned, listening to the subterranean rumblings, which sounded like continuous thunder, and by 9 o'clock he was at the corral.

Ayrton was waiting for him.

"The animals are attended to, sir," said he.

"All right, Ayrton."

"They seem to be restless, Mr. Smith."

"Yes, it is their instinct, which does not mislead them."

"When you are ready—"

"Take a lantern and tinder, Ayrton, and let us go."

Ayrton did as he was told. The onagers had been unharnessed and placed in the corral, and Smith, leading, took the route to the coast.

They walked over a soil covered with the pulverulent matter which had fallen from the clouds. No animal appeared. Even the birds had flown away. Sometimes a breeze passed laden with cinders, and the two colonists, caught in the cloud, were unable to see. They had to place handkerchiefs over their eyes and nostrils or they would have been blinded and suffocated.

Under these circumstances they could not march rapidly. The air was heavy, as if all the oxygen had been burned out of it, making it unfit to breathe. Every now and then they had to stop, and it was after 10 o'clock when the engineer and his companion reached the summit of the enormous heap of basaltic and porphyrytic rocks which formed the northwest coast of the island.

They began to go down this abrupt descent, following the detestable road, which, during that stormy night had led them to Crypt Dakkar. By daylight this descent was less perilous, and, moreover, the covering of cinders gave a firmer foothold to the slippery rocks.

The projection was soon attained, and, as the tide was low, Smith and Ayrton found the opening to the crypt without any difficulty.

"Is the boat there?" asked the engineer.

"Yes, sir," answered Ayrton, drawing the boat towards him.

"Let us get in, then, Ayrton," said the engineer.

The two embarked in the boat. Ayrton lit the lantern, and, placing it in the bow of the boat, took the oars, and Smith, taking the tiller, steered into the darkness. The Nautilus was no longer here to illuminate this sombre cavern.

Perhaps the electric irradiation still shone under the waters, but no light came from the abyss where Captain Nemo reposed.

The light of the lantern was barely sufficient to permit the engineer to advance, following the right hand wall of the crypt. A sepulchral silence reigned in this portion of the vault, but soon Smith heard distinctly the mutterings which came from the interior of the earth. "It is the volcano," he said.

Soon, with this noise, the chemical combinations betrayed themselves by a strong odor, and sulphurous vapors choked the engineer and his companion.

"It is as Captain Nemo feared," murmured Smith, growing pale. "We must go on to the end."

Twenty-five minutes after having left the opening the two reached the terminal wall and stopped.

Smith standing on the seat, moved the lantern about over this wall, which separated the crypt from the central chimney of the volcano. How thick was it? Whether 100 feet or but 10 could not be determined. But the subterranean noises were too plainly heard for it to be very thick.

The engineer, after having explored the wall along a horizontal line, fixed the lantern to the end of an oar and went over it again at a greater height.

There, through scarcely visible cracks, came a pungent smoke, which infected the air of the cavern. The wall was striped with these fractures, and some of the larger ones came to within a few feet of the water.

At first, Smith rested thoughtful. Then he murmured these words:—

"Yes! Captain Nemo was right! There is the danger, and it is terrible!"

Ayrton said nothing, but, on a sign from the engineer, he took up the oars, and, a half hour later, he and Smith came out of Crypt Dakkar.

CHAPTER LXI. SMITH'S RECITAL

HASTENING THE WORK—A LAST VISIT TO THE CORRAL—THE COMBAT BETWEEN THE FIRE AND THE WATER—THE ASPECT OF THE ISLAND—THEY DECIDE TO LAUNCH THE SHIP—THE NIGHT OF THE 8TH OF MARCH.

The next morning, the 8th of January, after a day and night passed at the corral, Smith and Ayrton returned to Granite House.

Then the engineer assembled his companions, and told them that Lincoln Island was in fearful danger—a danger which no human power could prevent.

"My friends," said he,—and his voice betrayed great emotion,—"Lincoln Island is doomed to destruction sooner or later; the cause is in itself and there is no means of removing it!"

The colonists looked at each other. They did not understand him.

"Explain yourself, Cyrus," said Spilett.

"I will, or rather I will give you the explanation which Captain Nemo gave me, when I was alone with him."

"Captain Nemo!" cried the colonists.

"Yes; it was the last service he rendered us before he died."

"The last service!" cried Pencroff. "The last service! You think, because he is dead, that he will help us no more!"

"What did he say?" asked the reporter.

"This, my friends," answered the engineer. "Lincoln Island is not like the other islands of the Pacific, and a particular event, made known to me by Captain Nemo, will cause, sooner or later, the destruction of its submarine framework."

"Destruction of Lincoln Island! What an idea!" cried Pencroff, who, in spite of his respect for Smith, could not help shrugging his shoulders.

"Listen to me, Pencroff," continued the engineer. "This is what Captain Nemo ascertained and what I verified yesterday In Crypt Dakkar. The crypt extends under the island as far as the volcano, and is only separated from the central chimney by the wall. Now this wall is seamed with fractures and cracks, through which the sulphurous gas is already escaping."

"Well?" asked Pencroff, wrinkling his forehead.

"Well, I have ascertained that these fractures are widening under the pressure from within, that the basalt wall la gradually bursting open, and that, sooner or later, it will give a passage to the waters of the sea."

"That's all right!" exclaimed Pencroff, trying still to make light of the subject. "That's all right! The sea will put out the volcano, and that will be the end of it."

"Yes, that will be the end of it!" answered Smith. "On the day that the sea rushes through the wall and penetrates by the central chimney to the bowels of the island, where the eruptive matter is boiling, on that day, Pencroff, Lincoln Island will go up, as Sicily would go up, if the Mediterranean was emptied into Aetna!"

The colonists made no reply. They understood the threatened danger.

It was no longer doubtful that the island was menaced by a frightful explosion. That it would last only as long as the wall to Crypt Dakkar remained intact. This was not a question of months, nor of weeks, bat of days, of hours, perhaps!

The first sensation the colonists experienced was one of profound sorrow. They did not think of the peril which menaced them directly, but of the destruction of that land which had given them asylum, of that island which they had cultivated, which they loved, which they wished to render so prosperous some day! All their labor uselessly employed, all their work lost!

Pencroff did not attempt to hide the tears which rolled down his cheeks.

They talked for some little time longer. The chances which they might count upon were discussed; but, in conclusion, they realized that not an hour was to be lost; that the ship must be completed as soon as possible, as, now, it was the only chance of safety left, to the inhabitants of Lincoln Island!

All hands were required. Where was the use, now, of sowing, or harvesting, of hunting or increasing the reserve at Granite House? The present contents of the magazine were sufficient to provision the ship for as long a voyage as she could make! What was necessary was that these should be at the disposal of the colonists before the accomplishment of the inevitable catastrophe.

The work was undertaken with feverish eagerness. By the 23d of January the ship was half planked. Up to this time there had been no change in the volcano. It was always the vapors, the smoke mixed with flames and pierced by incandescent stones, which escaped from the crater. But during the night of the 23d the upper cone, which formed the cap of the volcano, was lifted off by the pressure of the lava, which had reached the level of the lower cone. A terrible noise was heard. The colonists, believing that the island was going to pieces, rushed out of Granite House.

It was 2 o'clock in the morning. The heavens were on fire. The upper cone— a mass a thousand feet high, and weighing thousands of millions of pounds— had been thrown upon the island, making the earth tremble. Happily, this cone leaned to the north, and it fell upon the plain of sand and tufa which lay between the volcano and the sea. The crater, by this means greatly widened, threw towards the sky a light so intense, that, by the simple effect of reverberation, the atmosphere seemed to be incandescent. At the same time a torrent of lava swelled up over this new summit, falling in long streams, like water escaping from an overflowing vase, and a thousand fiery serpents writhed upon the talus of the volcano.

"The corral! The corral!" cried Ayrton.

It was, indeed, towards the corral that the lava took their way, following the slope of the new crater, and, consequently, the fertile parts of the island. The sources of Red Creek, and Jacamar Wood were threatened with immediate destruction.

At the cry of Ayrton, the colonists had rushed towards the stable of the onagers, and harnessed the animals. All had but one thought. To fly to the corral and let loose the beasts confined there.

Before 3 o'clock they were there. Frightful cries indicated the terror of the moufflons and goats. Already a torrent of incandescent matter, of liquified minerals, fell over the mountain spur upon the plain, destroying that side of the palisade. The gate was hastily opened by Ayrton, and the animals, wild with terror, escaped in every direction.

An hour later the boiling lava filled the corral, volatilizing the water of the little brook which traversed it, firing the house, which burned like a bit of stubble, devouring to the last stake the surrounding palisade. Nothing was left of the corral.

The colonists wanted to struggle against this invasion; they had tried it, but foolishly and uselessly: man is helpless before these grand cataclysms.

The morning of the 24th arrived. Smith and his companions, before returning to Granite House, wished to observe the definite direction which this inundation of lava would take. The general slope of the ground from Mount Franklin was towards the east coast, and it was to be feared that, notwithstanding the thick Jacamar Woods, the torrent would extend to Prospect Plateau.

"The lake will protect us," said Spilett.

"I hope so," answered Smith. But that was all he said.

The colonists would have liked to have advanced as far as the place on which the upper cone of Mount Franklin abutted, but their passage was barred by the lavas, which followed, on the one hand, the valley of Red Creek, and, on the other, the course of Fall River, vaporizing these two streams in their passage. There was no possible way of crossing this stream; it was necessary, on the contrary, to fly before it. The flattened volcano was no longer recognizable. A sort of smooth slab terminated it, replacing the old crater. Two outlets, broken in the south and east sides, poured forth unceasing streams of lava, which formed two distinct currents. Above the new crater, a cloud of smoke and cinders mixed with the vapors of the sky, and hung over the island. Peals of thunder mingled with the rumbling of the mountain. Burning rocks were thrown up thousands of feet, bursting in the sky and scattering like grape-shot. The heavens answered with lightning-flashes the eruption of the volcano.

By 7 o'clock the colonists were no longer able to keep their position on the edge of Jacamar Wood. Not only did the projectiles begin to fall about them, but the lavas, overflowing the bed of Red Creek, threatened to cut off the road from the corral. The first ranks of trees took fire, and their sap, vaporized, made them explode like fire-crackers; while others, less humid, remained intact in the midst of the inundation.

The colonists started back. The torrent, owing to the slope of the land, gained eastward rapidly, and as the lower layers of lava hardened, others, boiling, covered them.

Meantime the principal current in the Red Creek Valley became more and more threatening. All that part of the forest was surrounded, and enormous clouds of smoke rolled above the trees, whose roots were already in the lava.

The colonists stopped at the lake shore, half a mile from the mouth of Red Creek. A question of life or death was about to be decided for them. Smith, accustomed to think and reason in the presence of danger, and aware that he was speaking to men who could face the truth, whatever it might be, said to them:—"Either the lake will arrest this current, and a part of the island will be preserved from complete devastation, or the current will invade the forests of the Far West, and not a tree, not a plant will be left upon the face of the ground. We will have, upon these rocks stripped of life, the prospect of a death which the explosion of the island may anticipate!

"Then," cried Pencroff, crossing his arms and stamping his foot on the ground, "it is useless to work on the ship! Isn't that so?"

"Pencroff," answered Smith, "it is necessary to do one's duty to the end."

At this moment, the flood of lava, after having eaten its way through the splendid trees of the forest, neared the lake. There was a certain depression in the ground, which, if it had been larger, might, perhaps, suffice to hold the torrent.

"Let us try!" cried Smith.

The idea of the engineer was instantly understood by all. It was necessary to dam, so to speak, this torrent and force it into the lake.

The colonists ran to the shipyard and brought back from there shovels, picks, and hatchets, and by means of earthworks and hewn trees they succeeded, in a few hours, in raising a barrier three feet high and some hundreds of feet long. It seemed to them, when they had finished, that they had not worked more than a few minutes!

It was time. The liquified matter already reached the extremity of the barrier. The flood spread like a swollen river seeking to overflow its banks and threatening to break down the only obstacle which could prevent its devastating all the Far West. But the barrier was sufficient to withstand it, and, after one terrible moment of hesitation, it precipitated itself into Lake Grant by a fall twenty feet high.

The colonists, breathless, without a word, without a gesture, looked upon this struggle of the elements.

What a sight was this, the combat between fire and water! What pen can describe this scene of marvellous horror; what pencil can portray it? The water hissed and steamed at the contact of the boiling lavas. The steam was thrown, whirling, to an immeasurable height in the air, as if the valves of an immense boiler had been suddenly opened. But, great as was the mass of water contained in the lake, it must, finally, be absorbed, since it was not renewed, while the torrent, fed from an inexhaustible source, was ceaselessly pouring in fresh floods of incandescent matter.

The first lavas which fell into the lake solidified at once, and accumulated in such a manner as soon to emerge above the surface. Over these slid other lavas, which in their turn became stone, forming a breakwater, which threatened to fill up the lake, which could not overflow, as its surplus water was carried off in steam. Hissings and shrivellings filled the air with a stunning noise, and the steam, carried off by the wind, fell to the ground in rain. The jetty spread, and where formerly had been peaceable waters appeared an enormous heap of smoking rocks, as if some upheaval of the ground had raised these thousands of reefs. If one can imagine these waters tossed about by a storm, and then suddenly solidified by cold, he will have the appearance of the lake three hours after the irresistible torrent had poured into it.

This time the water had been overcome by the fire.

Nevertheless, it was a fortunate thing for the colonists that the lavas had been turned into the lake. It gave them some days' respite. Prospect Plateau, Granite House, and the ship-yard were safe for the moment. In these few days they must plank and caulk the vessel, launch it, and take refuge upon it, rigging it after it was on the sea. With the fear of the explosion menacing the destruction of the island, it was no longer safe to remain on land. Granite House, so safe a retreat up to this time, might, at any moment, fall!

During the next six days, the colonists worked on the ship with all their might. Sleeping but little, the light of the flames from the volcano permitted them to work by night as well as by day. The eruption continued without cessation, but, perhaps, less abundantly. A fortunate circumstance, since Lake Grant was nearly full; and if fresh lavas had slid over the surface of the former layers, they would inevitably have spread over Prospect Plateau and from there to the shore.

But while this part of the island was partially protected it was otherwise with the west coast.

The second current of lava, following the valley of Fall River, met with no obstacle. The ground on either side of the bank was low, and the incandescent liquid was spread through the forest of the Far West. At this season of the year the trees were dried by the warmth of the summer and took fire instantly, and the high interlacing branches hastened the progress of the conflagration. It seemed as if the current of flame traversed the surface of the forest more swiftly than the current of lavas its depths.

The beasts and birds of the woods sought refuge on the shore of the Mercy and in the marshes of Tadorn's Fens. But the colonists were too busy to pay any attention to these animals. They had, moreover, abandoned Granite House; they had not even sought refuge in the Chimneys, but they camped in a tent near the mouth of the Mercy.

Every day Smith and Spilett climbed up to Prospect Plateau. Sometimes Herbert went with them, but Pencroff never. The sailor did not wish to look upon the island in its present condition of devastation.

It was, indeed, a desolate spectacle. All its wooded part was now denuded. One single group of green trees remained on the extremity of Serpentine Peninsula. Here and there appeared some blackened stumps. The site of the forests was more desolate than Tadorn's Fens. The invasion of the lavas had been complete. Where formerly had been a pleasant verdure, was now nothing but a waste covered with volcanic tufa. The valleys of Fall River and Red Creek contained no water, and if Lake Grant had been completely filled up, the colonists would have had no means to slack their thirst. But fortunately its southern extremity had been spared, and formed a sort of pool, which held all the fresh water remaining on the island. To the northwest the spurs of the mountain, in jagged outline, looked like a gigantic claw grasping the ground. What a doleful spectacle! What a frightful aspect! How grievous for the colonists, who, from a domain, fertile, wooded, traversed by water-courses, enriched by harvests, found themselves, in an instant, reduced to a devastated rock, upon which, without their stores, they would not have had the means of living.

"It is heart-breaking!" said the reporter.

"Yes, Spilett," answered the engineer. And pray heaven that we are given time to finish the ship, which is now our sole refuge!"

"Does it not seem to you, Cyrus, that the volcano is subsiding? It still vomits lava, but, I think, less freely!"

"It matters little," answered Smith. "The fire is still fierce in the bowels of the mountain, and the sea may rush in there at any moment. We are like persons on a ship devoured by a fire which they cannot control, who know that sooner or later the flames will reach the powder magazine. Come, Spilett, come, we have not an hour to lose!"

For eight days longer, that is to say until the 8th of February, the lavas continued to flow, but the eruption confined itself to the limits described. Smith feared more than anything else an overflow of the lavas on to the beach, in which case the ship-yard would be destroyed. But about this time the colonists felt vibrations in the ground which gave them the greatest uneasiness.

The 20th of February arrived. A month longer was necessary to fit the ship for sea. Would the island last that long? It was Smith's intention to launch her as soon as her hull should be sufficiently caulked. The deck, lining, arranging the interior, and the rigging could be done afterwards, but the important thing was to secure a refuge off the island. Perhaps it would be better to take the vessel round to Balloon Harbor, the point farthest from the eruptive centre, as, at the mouth of the Mercy, between the islet and the granite wall, she ran the risk of being crushed, in case of a breaking up of the island. Therefore, all the efforts of the workmen were directed to completing the hull.

On the 3d of March they were able to calculate that the ship could be launched in twelve days.

Hope returned to the hearts of these colonists, who had been so sorely tried during this fourth year of their sojourn on Lincoln Island! Even Pencroff was roused from the taciturnity into which he had been plunged by the ruin and devastation of his domain. He thought of nothing else but the ship, on which he concentrated all his hopes.

"We will finish her!" he said to the engineer, "we will finish her, Mr. Smith, and it is high time, for you see how far advanced the season is, and it will soon be the equinox. Well, if it is necessary, we will winter at Tabor Island! But Tabor Island after Lincoln Island! Alas! how unlucky I am! To think that I should live to see such a thing as this!"

"Let us make haste!" was the invariable answer of the engineer.

And every one worked unceasingly.

"Master," asked Neb, some days later, "if Captain Nemo had been alive, do you think this would have happened?"

"Yes, Neb," answered the engineer.

"I don't think so!" whispered Pencroff to the black man.

"Nor I!" replied Neb.

During the first week in March Mount Franklin became again threatening. Thousands of threads of glass, made by the fluid lavas, fell like rain to the ground. The crater gave forth fresh torrents of lava that flowed down every side of the volcano. These torrents flowed over the surface of hardened lava, and destroyed the last vestiges of the trees which had survived the first eruption. The current, this time following the southwest shore of Lake Grant, flowed along Glycerine Creek and invaded Prospect Plateau. This last calamity was a terrible blow to the colonists; of the mill, the poultry-yard, the stables, nothing remained. The frightened inhabitants of these places fled in every direction.

Top and Jup gave signs of the utmost terror, and their instinct warned them of an impending disaster. A large number of animals had perished in the first eruption, and those which survived had found their only refuge in Tadorn's Fens, and on Prospect Plateau. But this last retreat was now closed from them, and the torrent of lava having reached the edge of the granite wall, began to fall over on to the shore in cataracts of fire. The sublime horror of this spectacle passes all description. At night it looked like a Niagara of molten matter, with its incandescent spray rising on high and its boiling masses below!

The colonists were driven to their last refuge, and, although the upper seams were uncaulked, they resolved to launch their ship into the sea!

Pencroff and Ayrton made the preparations for this event, which was to take place on the morning of the next day, the 9th of March.

But, during that night, an enormous column of steam escaped from the crater, rising in the midst of terrific detonations to a height of more than 3,000 feet. The wall of Crypt Dakkar had given way under the pressure of the gas, and the sea, pouring through the central chimney into the burning gulf, was turned into steam! The crater was not a sufficient vent for this vapor!

An explosion, which could have been heard a hundred miles away, shook the very heavens! Fragments of the mountain fell into the Pacific, and, in a few minutes, the ocean covered the place where Lincoln Island had been!

CHAPTER LXII. AN ISOLATED ROCK IN THE PACIFIC

THE LAST REFUGE OF THE COLONISTS—THE PROSPECT OF DEATH—
UNEXPECTED SUCCOR—HOW AND WHY IT CAME—THE LAST GOOD ACTION—
AN ISLAND ON TERRA FIRMA-THE TOMB OF CAPTAIN NEMO.

An isolated rock, thirty feet long, fifteen feet wide, rising ten feet above the surface of the water, this was the sole solid point which had not vanished beneath the waves of the Pacific.

It was all that remained of Granite House! The wall had been thrown over, then broken to pieces, and some of the rocks of the great hall had been so heaped together as to form this culminating point. All else had disappeared in the surrounding abyss: the lower cone of Mount Franklin, torn to pieces by the explosion; the lava jaws of Shark Gulf; Prospect Plateau, Safety Islet, the granite of Balloon Harbor; the basalt of Crypt Dakkar; Serpentine Peninsula— had been precipitated into the eruptive centre! All that remained of Lincoln Island was this rock, the refuge of the six colonists and their dog Top.

All the animals had perished in the catastrophe. The birds as well as the beasts, all were crashed or drowned, and poor Jup, alas! had been swallowed up in some crevasse in the ground!

Smith, Spilett, Herbert, Pencroff, Neb, and Ayrton had survived, because, being gathered together in their tent, they had been thrown into the sea, at the moment when the debris of the island rained down upon the water.

When they came again to the surface they saw nothing but this rock, half a cable length away, to which they swam.

They had been here nine days! Some provisions, brought from the magazine of Granite House before the catastrophe, a little soft water left by the rain in the crevice of the rock—this was all that the unfortunates possessed. Their last hope, their ship, had been broken to pieces. They had no means of leaving this reef. No fire, nor anything with which to make it. They were doomed to perish!

This day, the 18th of March, there remained a supply of food, which, with the strictest care, could last but forty-eight hours longer. All their knowledge, all their skill, could avail them nothing now. They were entirely at God's mercy.

Smith was calm, Spilett somewhat nervous, and Pencroff, ready to throw himself into the sea. Herbert never left the engineer; and gazed upon him, as if demanding the succor which he could not give. Neb and Ayrton were resigned after their manner.

"Oh, misery! misery!" repeated Pencroff. "If we had but a walnut-shell to take us to Tabor Island! But nothing; not a thing!"

"And Captain Nemo is dead!" said Neb.

During the five days which followed, Smith and his companions ate just enough of the supply of food to keep them from famishing. Their feebleness was extreme. Herbert and Neb began to show signs of delirium.

In this situation had they a shadow of hope? No! What was their sole chance? That a ship would pass in sight of the rock? They knew, by experience, that ships never visited this part of the Pacific. Could they count, then, by a coincidence which would be truly providential, upon the Scotch yacht coming just at this time to search for Ayrton at Tabor Island? It was not probable. And, moreover, supposing that it came, since the colonists had placed no notice there indicating the place where Ayrton was to be found, the captain of the yacht, after a fruitless search of the island, would proceed at once to regain the lower latitudes.

No! they could entertain no hope of being saved, and a horrible death, a death by hunger and thirst, awaited them upon this rock!

Already they lay stretched out, inanimate, unconscious of what was going on around them. Only, Ayrton, by a supreme effort, raised his head, and cast a despairing look over this desert sea!

But, behold! on this morning of the 24th of March, Ayrton extended his arms towards some point in space; he rose up, first to his knees, then stood upright; he waved his hand—

A ship was in sight of the island! This ship did not sail these seas at haphazard. The reef was the point towards which she directed her course, crowding on all steam, and the unfortunates would have seen her many hours before, had they had the strength to scan the horizon!

"The Duncan!" murmured Ayrton, and then he fell senseless upon the rock.

****

When Smith and his companions regained consciousness, thanks to the care lavished upon them, they found themselves in the cabin of a steamer, unaware of the manner in which they had escaped death.

A word from Ayrton was sufficient to enlighten them.

"It is the Duncan," he murmured.

"The Duncan!" answered Smith. And then, raising his arms to heaven, he exclaimed: "Oh, all powerful Providence! thou hast wished that we should be saved!"

It was, indeed, the Duncan, Lord Glenarvan's yacht, at this time commanded by Robert, the son of Captain Grant, who had been sent to Tabor Island to search for Ayrton and bring him home after twelve years of expatriation!

The colonists were saved, they were already on the homeward route!

"Captain Robert," asked Smith, "what suggested to you the idea, after leaving Tabor Island, where you were unable to find Ayrton, to come in this direction?"

"It was to search, not only for Ayrton, Mr. Smith, but for you and your companions!"

"My companions and myself?"

"Doubtless! On Lincoln Island!"

"Lincoln Island!" cried the others, greatly astonished.

"How did you know of Lincoln Island?" asked Smith. "It is not on the maps."

"I knew of it by the notice which you left on Tabor Island," answered Grant.

"The notice?" cried Spilett.

"Certainly, and here it is," replied the other, handing him a paper indicating the exact position of the Lincoln Island, "the actual residence of Ayrton and of five American colonists."

"Captain Nemo!" said Smith, after having read the notice, and recognized that it was in the same handwriting as the paper found at the corral.

"Ah!" said Pencroff, "it was he who took our Good Luck, he who ventured alone to Tabor Island!"

"To place this notice there!" answered Herbert.

"Then I was right when I said," cried the sailor, "that he would do us a last service even after his death!"

"My friends," said Smith, in a voice moved by emotion, "may the God of sinners receive the soul of Captain Nemo; he was our savior!"

The colonists, uncovering as Smith spake thus, murmured the name of the captain.

Then Ayrton, approaching the engineer, said to him, simply:—

"What shall be done with the coffer?"

Ayrton had saved this coffer at the risk of his life, at the moment when the island was engulfed. He now faithfully returned it to the engineer.

"Ayrton! Ayrton!" exclaimed Smith, greatly affected.

Then addressing Grant: "Captain," he said, "where you left a criminal, you have found a man whom expiation has made honest, and to whom I am proud to give my hand!"

Thereupon Grant was informed of all the strange history of Captain Nemo and the colonists of Lincoln Island. And then, the bearings of this remaining reef having been taken, Captain Grant gave the order to go about.

Fifteen days later the colonists landed in America, which they found at peace after the terrible war which had ended in the triumph of justice and right. Of the wealth contained in the coffer, the greater part was employed in the purchase of a vast tract of land in Iowa. One single pearl, the most beautiful of all, was taken from the treasure and sent to Lady Glenarvan in the name of the castaways, who had been rescued by the Duncan.

To this domain the colonists invited to labor—that is, to fortune and to happiness—all those whom they had counted on receiving at Lincoln Island. Here they founded a great colony, to which they gave the name of the island which had disappeared in the depths of the Pacific. They found here a river which they called the Mercy, a mountain to which they gave the name of Franklin, a little lake which they called Lake Grant, and forests which became the forests of the Far West. It was like an island on terra-firma.

Here, under the skillful hand of the engineer and his companions, everything prospered. Not one of the former colonists was missing, for they had agreed always to live together, Neb wherever his master was, Ayrton always ready to sacrifice himself, Pencroff a better farmer than he had been a sailor, Herbert who finished his studies under Smith's direction, Spilett who founded the New Lincoln *Herald*, which was the best edited journal in the whole world.

Here Smith and his companions often received visits from Lord and Lady Glenarvan, from Captain John Mangles and his wife, sister to Robert Grant, from Robert Grant himself, from Major MacNabbs, from all those who had been mixed up in the double history of Captain Grant and Captain Nemo.

Here, finally, all were happy, united in the present as they had been in the past; but never did they forget that island upon which they had arrived poor and naked, that island which, for four years, had sufficed for all their needs, and of which all that remained was a morsel of granite, beaten by the waves of the Pacific, the tomb of him who was Captain Nemo!

THE END.

Manufactured by Amazon.ca
Bolton, ON

20170247R00450